James Fenimore Cooper

THE LEATHERSTOCKING SAGA

Being those parts of
THE DEERSLAYER, THE LAST OF THE MOHICANS, THE PATHFINDER, THE PIONEERS, *and* THE PRAIRIE
which specially pertain to
NATTY BUMPPO
otherwise known as Pathfinder, Deerslayer, *or* Hawkeye;
the whole arranged in chronological order from Hawkeye's youth on the New York frontier in King George's War until his death on the Western prairies in Jefferson's Administration.

Edited by
ALLAN NEVINS

Illustrated by
REGINALD MARSH

PANTHEON BOOKS · NEW YORK

333 SIXTH AVENUE, NEW YORK 14, N. Y.

LIBRARY OF CONGRESS CATALOGUE CARD NUMBER: 54-9502

MANUFACTURED IN THE U. S. A.
BY KINGSPORT PRESS, INC., KINGSPORT, TENNESSEE
Designed by Andor Braun

"The most memorable character American fiction has given to the world."

CAMBRIDGE HISTORY OF AMERICAN LITERATURE

CONTENTS

Preface ix

Introduction 1

I. Cooper and the Leatherstocking Tales 1

II. Cooper and the Frontier 20

III. Cooper and the Indians 25

Chronology of Cooper's Life 35

The Leatherstocking Tales: A Chronological Table 36

THE LEATHERSTOCKING SAGA

I. THE DEERSLAYER 39

II. THE LAST OF THE MOHICANS 275

III. THE PATHFINDER 463

IV. THE PIONEERS 615

V. THE PRAIRIE 763

Bibliography 831

PREFACE

SLANTING sunlight falls through deep woods of tamarack, birch, elm, beech, and spruce. Along the rocky watercourse grows a thick cover of juniper, alder, and sassafras. In the distance suddenly gleams the bright expanse of Lake Ontario, its waves tipped with foam by the stiff breeze. As a dry stick cracks, a deer, startled by the noise, leaps swiftly away through the trees.

(Actually this is Garrett's Woods, mostly soft maple, with some hickory, ash, and white oak. The sedgy little creek winds through earth banks—for no rock could be found anywhere in this flat Illinois country—widening occasionally into a cat-tail pool. In the distance appears the tawny expanse of the C. B. & Q. Railroad reservoir, a muddy-bottomed pond of thirty acres, with a pumping station at the foot. As a dry stick cracks, a grazing cow lifts an inquiring head beside a mullein stalk.)

Chingachgook, slipping with stealthy tread from tree to tree, suddenly stiffens with alarm. Hawkeye, Hutter, Uncas, and Hurry Harry, following in single file, freeze in their tracks. A mute gesture suffices. Uncas, crouched double, slips to the left to scout the Mingo position. Hawkeye covers his movement with lifted barrel. Hurry Harry looks for the wilted leaf that will betray an enemy in cover.

(Five urchins this late Saturday afternoon, released from farm tasks, have been allowed to roam down to the only bit of forest and water for miles around. They have hooks and lines for the bullheads, sunfish, and perch in the reservoir; but the walk would be duller if they could not act out their recent reading. Among these farm boys, Pierces, Cateses, Becketts, Nevinses, Reads, thumbworn books are constantly current. G. A. Henty, Captain Mayne Reid, Oliver Optic, and John T. Trowbridge compete with more famous authors; but for an afternoon's expedition Cooper best stirs the imagination.)

It is largely out of a boyhood affection for Fenimore Cooper that this volume has grown. To meddle with a classic is a serious affair, and the editor would never have touched Cooper but for three considerations. To begin with, he believes that our first great American novelist is less read than he should be, that appreciation of his genius flags, and that any book which will help redirect attention to him is defensible.

In the second place, he thinks that while a good many people doubtless read *one* Leatherstocking tale, usually *The Last of the Mohicans,* or even two, few indeed read all five; and that they therefore miss the interest and value of that full-length depiction of Leatherstocking from youth to death which the whole series gives. In the third place, he conceives that for many readers the five novels will become more interesting if love-passages or supposedly humorous passages, not related to the career and character of Leatherstocking and not today very convincing, are shorn away.

In this presentation of the story of Hawkeye, or Deerslayer, or Leatherstocking, the procedure is based upon one determining rule. All those parts of the five books which deal with him, his perils, vicissitudes, and exploits, his character, ideas, and philosophy, have been retained. No internal cuts have been made in any section here printed; the text is intact. Where matter irrelevant under the rule has been excised, the gap is bridged over by a brief narrative written by the editor and printed in italics. It is hoped that the resulting narrative, bringing Leatherstocking more fully into the foreground, and making the five romances more of a continuous tale than they are in the original, will appeal to many busy readers. For those who disagree with the presentation, the five novels are always available. The editor does not for a moment deny that most Americans ought to read them complete; he merely doubts whether many, faced by nearly 2,500 pages of print, will do so.

Special thanks are due to Mrs. Helen Wolff and Miss Amy Loveman for their insistence that a book of this kind was feasible and desirable; indeed, they may be called prime movers in the enterprise. The editor also thanks Mr. Van Wyck Brooks for some words of encouragement, and Mr. Henry Seidel Canby, an expert student of Cooper, for both approbation and advice.

April 15, 1954

Columbia University

INTRODUCTION

I. *Cooper and the Leatherstocking Tales*

EVERYONE loves a good story well told. Some books have the faculty not only of themselves remaining ever fresh and young, but of keeping their readers ever youthful. For these many centuries the tales of *The Arabian Nights,* of old Malory's *Court of King Arthur,* and of Froissart's great *Chronicle* have not only beguiled adolescents from their sports, but have seduced elderly people into thinking themselves young again. Nothing recreates the sentiments and associations of boyhood and girlhood like a rereading of some stirring narrative that helped gild the morning of life. The sea of literature is vast, and tastes vary. Some youthful readers may miss *The Pilgrim's Progress,* or *Redgauntlet,* or even *Huckleberry Finn.* But assuredly those who did discover them in early years never tire of coming back to them, nor fail to find in them some drops of Ponce de Leon's fountain.

Ever since Fenimore Cooper's death in 1851 most of his readers have unquestionably been found among young people—and among older folk who wish to keep young in heart. His best books remain in the golden category of great stories greatly narrated. We may well pity those who have never hung with bated breath over the clash of Richard-the-Lion-Hearted and Saladin in *The Talisman;* who have not thrilled to the escape of Edmond Dantès disguised as a corpse from the Château d'If in *The Count of Monte Cristo;* who have not relived the Robinson Crusoe story in *Masterman Ready;* whose blood has not run faster as the eruption of Vesuvius halts the designs of the villainous Arbaces upon the beautiful Nydia in *The Last Days of Pompeii.* Men do not easily forget an early devotion to Scott, Dumas, Marryat, and Bulwer Lytton. Particularly do Scott and Dumas always retain their spell: writers who tempt us to forget ourselves and our cares in scenes, as Robert Louis Stevenson said, "busy as a city, bright as a theatre, thronged with memorable faces, and sounding with delightful speech."

And alongside these great romancers we must range Fenimore Cooper; those who have not sat absorbed over John Paul Jones's escape through shoal waters from British cruisers in *The Pilot,* or Leatherstocking's rescue from Indian torture in *The Deerslayer,* have missed some of the brightest pages of the storyteller's art. Both novels, one with the expert sailor as hero, the other with the expert scout, have the same magic. Their power lies in the triumph of civilized man, through reason and knowledge, over romantic peril: over the terrors of tempest, rocky waters, and enemy warships in *The Pilot*, the terrors of the forest and the painted savage in *The Deerslayer*.

It was a mighty literary movement which brought in the masters of modern romance. That impulse swept away the creaky melodramas of the Gothic school in England, the sentimentalities of Chateaubriand's *Atala* and Saint-Pierre's *Paul and Virginia* in France, and the misty allegories of Tieck and Richter in Germany. The rich dawn of the new age began when, as the Napoleonic era ended, Scott in rapid succession brought out *Waverley, Guy Mannering,* and other Scottish stories, to be followed by the world's first great historical novels, *Ivanhoe* and *Quentin Durward*.

Some of the authors who made the next thirty years so fertile in novels of adventure and character are now half forgotten. Who reads Eugene Sue? How many turn the pages of G. P. R. James, who liked to begin his tales with a solitary horseman, or of Harrison Ainsworth, who made the most of scoundrels like Jack Sheppard and Guy Fawkes? How many Americans possess any direct acquaintance with their own John P. Kennedy, whose *Horseshoe Robinson* once had wide currency, or with the Revolutionary romances of William Gilmore Simms, or with the excursions of William Ware into the Palmyra of Zenobia, and the Rome of Aurelian? But Scott, Cooper, and Dumas survive changing fashions; they may age, their faults may become more evident, their old spell may diminish—yet still they have multitudes of followers.

Few storytellers in all history have enjoyed so wide a popularity as Fenimore Cooper. He is easily translatable, and his best work was soon rendered into nearly all the important languages of the globe. The historian Parkman, visiting Italy, found his Leatherstocking Tales well thumbed in a remote mountain village of Sicily, and his *L'Ultimo de Mohecanni* a favorite book from Milan to Naples. He and Irving were the first Americans who established a high and permanent literary reputation in Britain; Cooper's feat being the more remarkable because he was a cantankerous, prickly man, and his kindly reception owed little to his personality. Thackeray, reading voraciously during his voyage to Cairo, thought that *The Prairie* was better than any of Scott's novels he had on shipboard; and he enshrined Cooper in his burlesque series of "Novels by Eminent Hands." Balzac and Victor Hugo admired the American, Hugo indulging in lavish praise. One French imitator, Gustave Aimard, the author of a long list of tales, *The Trappers of the Arkansas, The Virgin Forest,* and so on, openly donned Cooper's mantle. When the United States entered the World

War in 1917, a French leader could think of no better characterization of the nation's fervent determination than to say: "The spirit of Leatherstocking is awake."

In the field of the novel, the influence of Cooper can be traced in many a title of Erastus Beadle's dime thrillers, and in many a piece of Wild Western fiction. In the domain of poetry, more than one touch in Walt Whitman (a professed admirer) and Joaquin Miller bears Cooper's coloring. In that of history, his influence upon Francis Parkman is plainly evident. Reading Cooper, the historian of the struggle between the British and French for North America learned lessons of vigor, vividness, and narrative power; lessons so important that Parkman's best biographer credits part of his special technique to the Leatherstocking Tales. A subtle emanation of Cooper's spirit is doubtless diffused through nearly all modern writing on the North American forest, the frontiersman, and the Indian. He impressed on the national mind so memorable an image of the noble savage in Chingachgook and Uncas, of Indian deviltry in Magua and Mahtoree, of the best type of pioneer in Leatherstocking and the more disreputable type in Hurry Harry and Ishmael Bush; he painted so strongly the wild majesty of untouched forests, mountains, and lakes; and he described so skilfully the conditions of frontier garrison life and settlement, that no subsequent author can shake off the subconscious authority of his books.

The question arises, however, whether it is not time that Cooper were read in a different spirit; with more attention to those qualities which appeal to adult tastes, and less to those which touch the adolescent heart. We may even ask whether he will continue certain of a large audience unless such a change in attitude takes place. After all, the roster of able storytellers grows steadily longer. Cooper has to compete not merely with his early rivals, but with all the tale-spinners of Stevenson's time, of Joseph Conrad's era, and of our own busy period. But if we fasten attention upon those qualities which bear a stamp peculiar to his own genius and to the temper of youthful America; if we analyze his art, for art he had; if we do justice to his skilful and largely veracious depiction of the frontier and of pioneer types; if we study his treatment of the virgin landscape of the West—if, in short, we take a mature attitude toward his works, we shall be well rewarded. Cooper's faults are easy to deride, as Mark Twain in one of his least felicitous essays derided them; his merits do not lie so clearly on the surface.

In his own day he *was* read by adults for a mature instruction and enjoyment. Scott and Thackeray, Balzac and Hugo, so read him. William Cullen Bryant has recorded with what delighted astonishment, in the late 1820's, he scanned *The Pioneers*. Here, he said to himself, is the poet of rural life in America, our Hesiod, our Theocritus, unfettered by the restraints of verse, and even more poetical than they. Here is an animated picture of the hardy pursuits and jovial amusements of a prosperous little settlement belted by leagues of primeval woods. The changing aspects of the seasons; the conquest of the forest by the ax; the turkey-shooting at Christmastide, with Indian pitted against white man for the prize; swift sleigh rides under the January sun; the chase of the deer, and a combat with a panther; the exodus of the merry population, in early spring, to tap the sugar maples; the spring run of bass, and the flight of the multitudinous passenger pigeons—all this is drawn from nature by a hand familiar with its materials. No wonder it enchanted Bryant; and no wonder that he was enchanted also by *The Prairie*. That book the poet read "with a certain awe, an undefined sense of sublimity," justly appertaining to the vast unpeopled plains of the West. And Bryant was equally impressed by the lawless frontier family of Ishmael Bush: "that brawny old man and his large-limbed sons, living in a sort of primitive and patriarchal barbarism, sluggish on ordinary occasions, but terrible when roused, like the hurricane that sweeps the grand but monotonous wilderness in which they dwell."

If we read Cooper with an adult purpose, we may well center our attention upon the Leatherstocking Tales. These five romances constitute his acknowledged masterwork. He himself so regarded them. "As a creator of aught but romantic incident, indeed," wrote William E. Henley, giving the general foreign verdict, "Cooper's claims to renown must rest on the fine figure of the Leatherstocking, and, in a less degree, on that of his friend and companion, the Big Serpent." Though this statement does less than full justice to Cooper, it is essentially true.

No doubt *The Spy*, that absorbing tale of the Revolution, introducing George Washington as well as the sharply individualized figure of the peddler-secret-agent, Harvey Birch, and giving a veracious picture of Westchester when it was hotly debated by Whig and Tory, will always have readers. The sea stories, and their hero the devoted Nantucket seaman Long Tom Coffin, brought into American fiction its fullest ocean breath, and an oakenhearted Yankee shaped by his seafaring occupation. The inland frontier, however, has been far more important to the United States than the sea frontier; woods, lake, river, and prairie offer much more variety than the waves, while they are distinctively American; and Leatherstocking himself is the most striking and memorable single creation in all our letters.

In looking for the more adult qualities of the Leatherstocking Tales, we may brush aside most of the detailed criticism with which he has been assailed. It is mainly true, but it is of no great consequence. What are the charges? That Cooper's women were sometimes weak and inane, and his characterizations of them affected and simpering; that his graver personages, including Leatherstocking, indulged in tiresome moralizing; that he racked his limited vocabulary to write stilted, pretentious descriptions; that he sometimes made his tales the vehicle of prejudice and propaganda; that some of his situations were as stagy as his feebler characters were unnatural—all this has often been argued. Mark Twain, himself no purist in English, could make game of Cooper's literary solecisms, as Stevenson made game of Scott's hasty writing. (Of one sentence of Scott's R. L. S. remarks: "A man who gave in such copy would be discharged from the staff of a daily paper.") Cooper's dialogue could be as artificial as some of Dickens's; he could bore us with local minutiae almost as much as Balzac. All this is true —but in the large view it matters little.

The proper course in reading Cooper (as with Scott, Hugo, and many another) is to cast aside all his inferior works; to fasten on the best books; to practice judicious skipping; and to dwell judiciously on elements of strength. When this is done, Cooper stands forth as a great writer. Some of his heroines are women as staunch, true, and fearless as any American life ever produced. His descriptions, harder to detach from the structure of his novels than careless readers suppose, sometimes rank with our best word paintings; for they are filled, as Bryant noted, with a true poetry. Many of the quaint utterances of Leatherstocking and Tom Coffin go as straight to the heart of knotty human problems as their balls went to their targets. Most of the dialogue is simplicity and naturalness itself. And the cumulative effect of the Leatherstocking Tales, like that of Scott's stories of his native land, is tremendous. Those who take the pains to read the five novels attentively, taking them in proper succession from Deerslayer's awkward youth to the trapper's mellow old age, will find that they have read nothing less than the nearest approach yet made to an American epic.

What counts in Cooper, in short, is the general impression, to which all the main elements of his work—headlong plot, wild nature, the frontiersmen, the Indians, and pioneer society advancing on the wilderness—contribute. We cannot disentangle these elements from each other. Cooper has mingled them to create an undying record of our rude heroic age, our Homeric period of national life.

The plots, as numerous critics have noted, tend to follow a pattern: the pattern of wilderness journey, conflict, capture, pursuit, and rescue, sometimes culminating in a romantic union of hero and heroine. This pattern requires a somewhat similar stageful of characters in each novel. Leatherstocking, always the most prominent of the rescuers (though in *The Pioneers* it is only a panther that he thwarts), must have one or two young women to befriend and help snatch from dire peril. Murderous Indians, abetted sometimes by hostile or treacherous white men, must play the roles of assailants and captors, offering a threat of death or torture to those who intervene. In the background, in the first three novels, pass some figures borrowed from history; the history of the wars of the British against the French and Indians. Suspense hangs upon hairbreadth escapes, upon breathless pursuits (either the villains pursuing the heroes and heroines, as in *The Deerslayer*, or the heroes pursuing the villains, as in *The Last of the Mohicans*), and upon armed clashes. These tense scenes alternate with intervals of peace and contemplation, which enable Cooper to describe his wild settings, to introduce the awkward bits of humor supplied by David Gamut in *The Last of the Mohicans* and by Dr. Obed Battius in *The Prairie*, and to let Leatherstocking offer his peculiar personal interpretations of current happenings.

To this general pattern, however, Cooper manages to impart due variety, and each novel draws much that is fresh and original from its special setting: *The Deerslayer* from wild Lake Otsego, *The Pathfinder* from Ontario, *The Last of the Mohicans* from the Lake George country, *The Pioneers* from infant Cooperstown, and *The Prairie* from the trans-Mississippi plains. The swiftest of the books are the first three, as is proper for romances of Leatherstocking's dynamic youth; the richest in human interest is the fourth; the most wildly sublime is the fifth. No reader has any sense of repetition. It is evidence of the highly individual character of each book that good critics have differed widely in their choice of favorite. Henley termed *The Prairie* clearly the best. Bryant evidently gave his preference to *The Pioneers*. Cooper himself, like Parkman, regarded *The Deerslayer* as his finest performance, though he must have had a special fondness for *The Pathfinder* as uniting nautical and woodland adventure. The general favorite, by the test of international currency and use in schools, is *The Last of the Mohicans*. A more variegated group of books in one series it would be difficult to find.

In *The Deerslayer* we have the best of Cooper's plots, an exciting scheme of action with no major element of the improbable from beginning to end. Its mainspring is the bold conception of a refugee from law-abiding society, Old Tom Hutter, his lake castle in the deep forest, and his two motherless daughters; just the group about whom a struggle of Indians and whites would rage. When the kidnapping of the beautiful Wah-ta-Wah by hostile savages brings Leatherstocking and Chingachgook on the scene, we are prepared for thrilling events. The conflict on the lake shore, the battle inside the castle, the capture of Leatherstocking himself, the peril of Judith, all follow naturally. It is a little too bad that the plot has to be given its denouement by the arrival of a British detachment—but that, too, is logical.

Nor is the plot of *The Pathfinder* much inferior. Leatherstocking in love seems out of his proper element; his true devotion is to the wilderness. Every part of the action, however, has verisimilitude. It was natural that the British garrison at Oswego should send a force to the

Thousand Islands to capture French supply boats venturing down the St. Lawrence to Lake Ontario; natural even that the commander of the little force involved should take his daughter along. Once more the stage has been well set for battle, siege, peril, and rescue. It was a feat to combine plausibly in one novel two such diverse scenes of danger as the storm on the lake, and the French and Indian attack on the blockhouse in the Thousand Islands—scenes each of which Cooper made stirring by his special magic of nautical lore and woodcraft.

By contrast, the plot of *The Last of the Mohicans* abounds in improbabilities. Why should so shrewd and farsighted a soldier as Colonel Munro, passionately devoted to his daughters, wish them to leave the safety of Fort Edward for the dangers of Fort William Henry, about to be captured by Montcalm's army? Why should so sensible an officer as Major Heyward, the maidens' escort, leave the protection of a column of troops marching to William Henry, and take a devious path through woods besprinkled with war parties of Indians? The unscathed emergence of Cora and Alice from their headlong journey as captives of the Hurons is also difficult to credit. The two heroines had no handbag or toilet case on that long arduous trip through woods, swamps, and thickets; they dropped gloves, veil, and other fragments of clothing to mark their route; and as Parkman commented, they must have looked more like scarecrows when rescued than Cooper's "lovely beings." But Parkman also noted that Longfellow did even worse than Cooper, carrying Evangeline through two thousand miles of forest pilgrimage, in the course of which she eluded a half dozen tribes of warring savages!

Cooper is not a realist; he is a romancer. The fable on which the canvas of *The Pioneers* is stretched—the story of the lost Colonel Effingham, loyalist, and his estate—is too creakily unconvincing to detain the reader's attention. *The Prairie* fortunately has almost no plot at all, being merely a string of episodes; but the long arm of coincidence was never stretched further than in Leatherstocking's meeting, on the boundless plains swept by Sioux and Pawnee, with the grandson of the Major Duncan Heyward of *The Last of the Mohicans.* These flaws, singly and collectively, matter almost as little as Shakespeare's gift of a seacoast to Bohemia. Nor does it greatly matter that Mark Twain could throw just ridicule upon Cooper's management of the episode in which the hostile Indians of *The Deerslayer* tried to waylay Hutter's ark as it emerged from the Susquehanna upon Lake Otsego; or that Stewart Edward White could call into just question some of Leatherstocking's alleged feats of marksmanship. What does matter is the grand imaginative sweep which Cooper imparts to all the Leatherstocking series, and the skill with which he knits thrilling episodes into a large panoramic drama.

It is, after all, the succession of episodes, not the plot, which rivets us to each book, and which we remember when the last pages are closed. Some of these episodes rank among the most vivid and original in fiction. How wonderful, in *The Deerslayer,* is the scene in which the dying Mingo, the first man Leatherstocking has killed, christens his slayer with the new name of Hawkeye, and in which the young man then agonizes aloud over the necessity of taking life in war! The scene in that book in which Hutter's chest (and with it the secret of his earlier life) is opened; the two long parleys between Leatherstocking and the chief Rivenoak; and the frantic denunciation of Hurry Harry by Wah-ta-Wah for wantonly taking the life of an Indian girl, are all admirably wrought. In *The Last of the Mohicans* the massacre at Fort William Henry and some of the armed clashes are spiritedly related; but many readers will remember longest the Hurons' execution of the young warrior Reed-that-bends for cowardice, and the delight of the venerable Tamenund when Uncas reveals his identity before one of the scattered branches of the Mohican tribe. The speech of Tamenund over Uncas's grave, too, is worthy of its poignant occasion.

In *The Last of the Mohicans* the scenes of Indian life and warfare are best, but *The Pioneers* gives us a long panorama of bright pictures of the life of the thriving frontier settlement. The episodes before mentioned—the fish-spearing on the lake by torchlight, the maple-tapping, the dispute over the deer, the turkey-shooting match, the militia muster to shoot down the sky-darkening flocks of pigeons—are delightful. Cooper, who had himself participated in such episodes or heard Cooperstown elders describe them, clearly wrote of them *con amore.* The most striking episodes in *The Prairie,* studied from books and not nature, lack this naturalness of touch. They have rather the quality of set pieces. They are executed with almost inimitable energy, however: the prairie fire, the thunderous sweep of the buffalo herd, the intertribal feuds of the Western Indians, and the death of Abiram White at the hands of his enraged brother-in-law. If *The Prairie* has less plot and less graphic verisimilitude than its predecessors, perhaps for that reason it possesses a grander poetic sweep.

The importance of the part played in Cooper's romances by nature is remarkable; in English literature we must come down to Joseph Conrad's stories of sea and jungle to find it matched. Obviously, in most respects Cooper stood at a disadvantage beside Walter Scott, with whom he was often compared. American life and legend were thin and barren compared with the European life and lore on which Scott levied. His creative powers were far below Scott's; he could not touch the emotions with the power of *The Heart of Midlothian* and *The Bride of Lammermoor,* or conjure up a wealth of such characters as Meg Merrilies, Dandie Dinmont, Dugald Dalgetty, Diana Vernon, Dirk Hatteraick, Jeanie Deans, and Nicol Jarvie, or paint such powerful historical portraits as those of Leicester in *Kenilworth,* Louis XI in *Quentin Durward,* and James I in *The Fortunes of Nigel.* But Cooper did have the broad American wilderness, far grander than the Highlands and Trossachs, to lend depth and dignity to his novels; and most successfully did he make use of this one advantage over Scott. It was fortunate for the country that he threw its shaggy woods and blue waters on his canvases, for even as he wrote they were yielding to ax, saw, and steamboat smoke.

We cannot correctly speak of landscape in Cooper as a mere background for his action; it is a participant—just as it was a participant in the events of our national history. Take the opening situation in *The Pathfinder,* when Leatherstocking, old Cap the ocean mariner, his niece Mabel, her suitor Jasper Western, and Chingachgook, journeying through the woods of northern New York, approach their goal, Fort Oswego. Leatherstocking finds in front of them a direful Mingo trail, as fresh as unsalted venison. How can they descend the Oswego River, past the Indians lying in ambush, to the lake fort? The party light a fire of damp wood back of them in the hope that it will draw the red devils up the river. They then hide themselves in two canoes behind an overhanging canopy of bushes which affords a complete screen. The hostile Indians, however, are shrewd; half of them remain in ambush below while the other half search out the campfire and discover the artifice. Efforts to flush the whites from cover are redoubled. Suddenly a single savage discovers the party; Chingachgook fells him; but at once the whole swarm descend on their prey—and the group take to their canoes as the only means of escape. As Cap, Mabel, and Jasper whirl rapidly down toward the fort, Leatherstocking, alone in one canoe, deliberately exposes himself to draw the Indians' fire; and before long the fusillade forces him to abandon his craft and take refuge behind a rock in midstream. From that point, rock, river, waterfall, and forested margin are as much sharers in the drama as the human beings, and it is through apt management of them that Leatherstocking and Chingachgook triumph.

Many an incident of this sort could be extracted from the five volumes. Parkman was particularly struck by one in *The Last of the Mohicans* showing the role of nature in the combat of red men and white. "Of this species of description," he writes, "the conflict at Glens Falls is an admirable example, unsurpassed, we think, even by the combat of Balfour and Bothwell, or by any other passage of the kind in the novels of Scott. The scenery of the fight, the foaming cataract, the little islet with its stouthearted defenders, the precipices and dark pine-woods, add greatly to the effect. The scene is conjured before the reader's eye not as a vision or a picture, but like the tangible presence of rock, river, and forest. His very senses seem conspiring to deceive him. He seems to feel against his cheek the wind and spray of the cataract, and hear its sullen roar, amid the yells of the assailants and the sharp crack of the answering rifle." That others were equally impressed is evidenced by the fame which Glens Falls long enjoyed as a tourist attraction. Factories and houses took the place of the wilderness setting; a bridge spanned the river; yet still, where wet black sheets of rock and foaming waters recalled a little of the atmosphere of Cooper's tale, guides pointed out the caves where the two sisters sought refuge, and the rocky point whence the Huron brave was flung to his death.

Cooper, feeling the mystical appeal of the wild North American scene, tended to idealize it just as he idealized his best frontiersmen and his two Mohican chiefs. The forest in actuality was full of hardship, toil, insect pests, and plain dirt, as well as the finer aspects noted by the novelist. Travel across its noble landscapes was slow and exhausting. The "ocean of leaves," the "lively verdure of a generous vegetation," in which Cooper glories, could be dreary indeed when drenched with rain, and impassable when choked with snow. The fierce heat of August and the bitter cold of January were often more than unpleasant; they were murderous. Little of this appears in the romancer's pages. His characters never get bemired in bogs, their clothing is never torn to pieces by thorns and snags, they never find life made miserable by wood ticks, mosquitoes, midges, and deer flies; nobody ever treads on a rattlesnake, or breaks a leg slipping down a ravine. Heyward, Chingachgook, and Leatherstocking follow the trail of captive Cora and Alice for days, scaling rocks, pushing through brush, crawling on the ground when in peril, and are still fresh and well panoplied at the end. Those who wish to know what a grueling forest march was really like must turn to the Jesuit Relations, or among modern books to Kenneth Roberts's *Northwest Passage*.

Various critics have marvelled that Cooper, who never saw the West, should have rendered the character of the plains so successfully in *The Prairie*. "Nowhere else," says Carl Van Doren, "has Cooper shown such sheer imaginative power as in the handling of this mighty landscape"; a landscape which the novelist regarded as an ocean of grass, and described partly by analogy. But his is a limited kind of success. True, Cooper does convey the sublimity of vast distances, and does enable us to see the waving greenery, tossed by the wind, melting into a sealike horizon. His treatment, however, is singularly wanting in concrete detail—and indeed, this is true of all the Leatherstocking Tales but one.

He identifies hardly a single tree, plant, or animal by name. His bee hunter would have no vocation if bees did not feed on flowers; but Cooper never mentions the puccoon, the Spanish needle, the wild rose, the buttercup, goldenrod, paintbrush, yucca, or other prairie flowers.

He says nothing of the cottonwood, the wild plum, the pecan, the papaw, or other indigenous trees. Leatherstocking as a trapper must seek out the beaver; but he would get very few beaver in the "dreary fields" (to use his phrase) where we find him, and had better join the mountain men. Cooper simply lacked the knowledge to insert graphic detail; in this book (and at most points in others) he is purely the impressionist.

Impressionism, we must add, is enough. Not only would a mass of botanic and zoological detail bore the reader; it would stifle the imagination. Cooper says just enough of lake, glen, waterfall, copse, and knoll to stimulate us to form our own vivid images. His paintings are all the better for having the broad hazy outlines of George Inness rather the intimate metallic accuracy of A. H. Wyant and Albert Bierstadt. Most of his scenes possess a breadth, a freshness, and an untamed wildness that can never be recaptured in North America. This is the quality, for example, of his picture in *The Pathfinder* of the voyage of the *Scud* along the southern shore of Ontario:

> All that day the wind hung to the southward, and the cutter continued her course about a league from the land, running six or eight knots an hour in perfectly smooth water. Although the scene had one feature of monotony, the outline of unbroken forest, it was not without its interest and pleasures. Various headlands presented themselves, and the cutter, in running from one to another, stretched across bays so deep as almost to deserve the name of gulfs, but nowhere did the eye meet with the evidences of civilization. Rivers occasionally poured their tribute into the great reservoir of the lake, but their banks could be traced inland for miles by the same outline of trees; and even large bays that lay enbosomed in woods, communicating with Ontario only by narrow outlets, appeared and disappeared without bringing with them a single trace of human habitation.

The same untamed largeness appertains to a typical bit of woodland description in *The Last of the Mohicans:*

> The eye could range, in every direction, through the long and shadowed vista of the trees; but nowhere was any object to be seen that did not properly belong to the peaceful and slumbering scenery. Here and there a bird was heard fluttering among the branches of the beeches, and occasionally a squirrel dropped a nut, drawing thc startled looks of the company, for a moment, to the place; but the instant the casual interruption ceased, the passing air was heard murmuring above their heads, along that verdant and undulating surface of forest which spread itself unbroken, unless by stream oı

> lake, over such a vast region of country. Across the tract of wilderness which lay between the Delwares and the village of their enemies, it seemed as if the foot of man had never trodden, so breathing and deep was the silence in which it lay.

To one of the Leatherstocking series, however, Cooper did bring the talents of a Dutch painter of genre pictures. Versed from early boyhood in all the sights and activities of Cooperstown, delighting in the primitive ways and picturesque social contrasts of that frontier village, he depicts nature (as well as manners) in *The Pioneers* with a wealth of concrete fact. He knows well enough, for example, that when eagles hover near frozen Otsego, migrating birds will avoid crossing the icy plain, keeping instead close to the woods; that winter is the time when the pioneer farmer takes his sacked wheat and barreled potash by sled to market; that only frantic anxiety for its cub will lead a panther to attack a human being; that a walnut sapling makes a good bow, and a birch canoe looks light-colored on green water. His depiction of the valley as spring comes in April contains just the concrete detail that is so conspicuously absent in the other romances:

> The snow . . . finally disappeared, and the green wheatfields were seen in every direction, spotted with the dark and charred stumps that had, the preceding season, supported some of the proudest trees of the forest. Ploughs were in motion, wherever these useful implements could be used, and the smokes of the sugar-camps were no longer seen issuing from the woods of maple. The lake had lost the beauty of a field of ice, but still a dark and gloomy covering concealed its waters, for the absence of currents left them yet hidden under a porous crust, which, saturated with the fluid, barely retained enough strength to preserve the contiguity of its parts. Large flocks of wild geese were seen passing over the country, which hovered, for a time, around the hidden sheet of water, apparently searching for a resting place; and then, on finding themselves excluded by the chill covering, would soar away to the north, filling the air with discordant screams, as if venting their complaints at the tardy operations of nature.

The personages of the Leatherstocking Tales fall into two distinct groups: on the one hand Leatherstocking, Chingachgook, and Uncas, prime favorites of the author, and recipients of his best pains; on the other the minor characters—soldiers, random hunters, young women to furnish objects of rescue, young men to furnish suitors for the girls, and figures of comic relief—who obviously sometimes get Cooper's second-best efforts. The humorous characters are particularly horrible. It is possible that when the itinerant psalm-singer of *The Last of the Mohicans,* David Gamut, was first presented, he seemed funny. Today he is as tiresome as he is unconvincing. In part he seems a weak copy of the lank, awkward, courting schoolmaster in "The Legend of Sleepy Hollow," in part an invention to enable Cooper to display the historic prejudice of Yorkers against Yankees; altogether he is about as real and amusing as a clotheshorse.

Dr. Obed Battius, the pedantic naturalist in *The Prairie,* is even worse. Probably the most labored attempt at humor in American fiction is the sketch of this learned fool trying to identify a roast buffalo-hump as a new species of animal. As for the soldiers, they are mainly made of lath and canvas, hastily painted. Major Heyward in *The Last of the Mohicans,* Sergeant Dunham in *The Pathfinder,* and Captain Middleton in *The Prairie* have stock parts to play, and do it in stock fashion. With mellow old Major Duncan of Lundie, worrying because his Oswego garrison have complained of being over-venisoned and over-pigeoned, Cooper—relying here partly on history—is more successful.

An emphatic word must be said in defense of Cooper's depiction of feminine character; it has been said before, by W. C. Brownell in his *American Prose Masters* and by Lucy Lockwood Hazard in *The Frontier in American Literature,* but it may well be said again. The charge that Cooper's heroines tend toward the insipid, made by Lowell and others, can be sustained if we confine our gaze to Cora and Alice in *The Last of the Mohicans,* and to the fair Inez of Spanish blood in *The Prairie;* but it has no validity whatever as respects various other women of the Leatherstocking series. "You will find Mabel," said Sergeant Dunham of his daughter to Leatherstocking, "like her mother, no screamer or a fainthearted girl to trouble a man in his need, but one who would encourage her mate, and help to keep his heart up when sorest pressed by danger."

That he was right Mabel abundantly proved. She comes through the Indian ambuscade on the road to Fort Oswego with nerve unshaken. The fearful storm on the lake, threatening to overwhelm the tiny cutter *Scud,* daunts her so little that as soon as it subsides she demands that Dunham and Leatherstocking take her ashore in a canoe, through the rolling surf, on a pleasure jaunt. When her companions on the island are slain, she is ready to hold the blockhouse alone against an Indian siege. One of the tensest of all Cooper's episodes is that in which she suddenly realizes that she is *not* alone in the little fort; that as she stands on the second floor, some stranger is moving about on the first; that she must keep still as the unknown occupant climbs the ladder, alert to strike if a savage Huron comes into view. Later, as quick in action as she is heroic in temper, she rushes forth to drag her mortally wounded father into shelter. She shows a remarkable combination of coolness and tact in dismissing the scout's suit, and a true pioneer's aplomb in embarking on her new life with the stout sailor Jasper.

The variety of Cooper's feminine figures is unusual, and the complexity of several would do credit to the best latter-day novelists. Even Cora Munro, stronger than her half-sister Alice, is given unusual interest by her infusion of Negro blood, and her unrequited love for Heyward. As for Judith and Hetty Hutter in *The Deerslayer*, both are masterly creations. Judith is a full-blown European beauty, fit for state drawing rooms and gay social circles, whose worldly tastes have led her too near the flame that burns in the nearest British garrisons, with the result that her wings have been a little singed. She is disillusioned and repentant; she realizes that she has nothing in common with the sordid, brutish Hutter who has been accepted as her father, and no future in her lake home, while she equally comprehends that her fate in any garrison town would be unhappy. Deeply attracted by the vigor, innocence, and integrity of young Leatherstocking, she seeks a way out through marriage with him. The scenes in which, with dignity yet pathetic humility, she discloses her love to the young man, and with inner agony but outer submission accepts his rebuff, could not have been written with more fidelity to human nature by Thackeray or Balzac.

Her sister Hetty, touching in her weakness of mind and lovely in her gentle purity, is portrayed with equal fineness of touch. The story demands a young woman who can pass through the worst trials and hardships of frontier life without soil, and who can face Indian peril with utter fearlessness. Hetty, gifted with a strength of character that contrasts strangely with her feebleness of intellect, is always interesting and often moving. Cooper evidently found her portrayal sympathetic, as he found that of Judith fascinating. Judith has her counterparts, to some degree, in Scott's Di Vernon, and in the spoilt young woman of fashion shown in Miss Ferrier's novel *Marriage;* but Hetty is a purely American creation. Particularly delightful are the passages in which she cultivates Hist, and tries to employ the Indian girl in coaxing the Mingoes to better ways. Hist herself, so far as we see her, is a sharply individualized young woman, intense in her emotions. We have spoken of her swift response to Hurry Harry's murder of an Indian woman:

> Rushing through the hut, or cabin, the girl stood at the side of Harry, almost as soon as his rifle touched the bottom of the scow; and with a fearlessness that did credit to her heart, she poured out her reproaches with the generous warmth of a woman.
>
> "What for you shoot?" she said. "What Huron gal do, dat you kill him? What you t'ink Manitou *say?* What you t'ink Manitou *feel?* What Iroquois *do?* No get honor—no get camp—no get prisoner—no get battle—no get scalp—no get not'ing at all. Blood come after blood! How you feel you wife killed? Who pity you when tear come for moder or sister? You big as great pine—Huron

gal little slender birch—why you fall on her and crush her? You t'ink Huron forget it? No; redskin never forget. Never forget friend; never forget enemy. Redman Manitou in *dat.* Why you so wicked, paleface?"

Ellen Wade in *The Prairie* is as vigorous, independent, and intrepid as Mabel Dunham. The greatest achievement of Cooper in that romance, however, and one of the greatest of all his feats of characterization, is the portrait of the fierce termagant mother of the squatter's brood, Hester Bush. Uneducated, fearless, violent, ready to slave at household tasks and to scold her family with equal energy, "old Eester" gains heroic stature when she mourns her murdered son Asa. She had been willing to abuse him for his errant ways and unfailing hunger—"His stomach is as true as the best clock in Kentucky, and seldom wants winding up to tell the time." When he is lost she is beside herself with grief, and the scene in which she plucks at his hair and garments, too stunned for words, is as powerful as any that Cooper ever wrote.

It is Chingachgook, Uncas, and Leatherstocking, however, who give the novels their oaken strength, and Leatherstocking above all who lifts them to high distinction. In the preface to *The Deerslayer,* Cooper remarks that the physical Leatherstocking was a composite of several frontiersmen he had known in early life; but that in mind and spirit he was purely a creation. The novelist intimates also that Leatherstocking represented the pioneer seen from a poetical point of view. To some extent the portrait was affected by Daniel Boone, the most famous of pioneers and Indian-fighters, whose well-attested talents—unfailing courage, iron endurance, sure marksmanship, integrity, truthfulness, and modesty—were done more than justice in contemporaneous chronicles, and who was even celebrated by Byron in *Don Juan* at the very time Cooper began his Leatherstocking series. It seems clear, however, that the character of Leatherstocking was not at first *planned,* but was found by a happy accident, and grew upon the author. A lucky inspiration brought him, very imperfectly conceived, into Cooper's pages; the romancer fell in love with him and rapidly perfected the image, making him so real and lively a figure that he had to be shown from youth to age.

The evidence that Leatherstocking was thus *ben trovato* lies plain in the first-written novel of the series. Cooper had seen in boyhood an old hunter named Shipman about Cooperstown; in pursuits, rude accoutrements, and speech a typical pioneer unhappy at being overtaken by civilization. He introduced the man into *The Pioneers.* We find him in the early chapters a mere rough sketch: surly, discontented, illiterate, ignorant, and despite his sententious moralizing, rather dull and unimpressive. As thus first drawn, Leatherstocking represents only the querulous uneasiness of those countless frontiersmen who, after a lifetime of rude forest freedom, had to accustom themselves to houses, streets, busy crowds, and worst of all, the restrictions of law. Angular, irritable, a hater of civilization, he mourns his youth and deplores the advance of society upon the wilderness.

But Cooper quickly perceived that this figure did an injustice to the true pioneer type; what was more, that it had rich possibilities, so that the portrait must be enlarged and improved. In the later chapters of *The Pioneers* Cooper makes the old scout a central, not a peripheral figure; gives him energy, serenity, and poise; and carries him halfway toward the wise, philosophical, and largehearted Leatherstocking whom we meet in *The Prairie.* His courtroom defense of himself when arraigned for illegal deer-killing is one of the most spirited pages in the whole series. Already, it is plain, Cooper has a well-rounded vision of the manly hero whom he is to present in the series as a whole.

That hero is idealized as a philosopher of the wilderness, yet he is convincing. Indeed, Leatherstocking is as natural as he is noble. Once we get away from the false start, Cooper makes him perfectly consistent from young manhood to death.

The boyish Deerslayer, full of awkward naïveté in social relationships, is nevertheless shrewd, self-reliant, and prudent. He grows naturally into the full-blooded Pathfinder, as candid, honest, and generous as before, but more mature in judgment, more resourceful, more confident—and, we must add, more talkative. In *The Last of the Mohicans,* still simple-minded, faithful, and unspoilt, he has made an equal advance. Now at the height of his powers, he is as swift, cool, and energetic as Chingachgook, and much more sagacious. One of his traits is not wholly agreeable: far from being an aggressive type of frontiersman, he has more than a touch of humbleness. He is as deferential to Major Duncan Heyward and to the commander at Fort Oswego as if he had a marked sense of social rank. Cooper, proud of his own family and of the aristocratic DeLancey clan into which he had married, thought that in Colonial and early National days an unlettered hunter would thus acknowledge caste lines; and it is probable that some pioneers *did* make speeches like Leatherstocking's—"Now, I come of a humble stock, though we have white gifts and a white natur'." The last novel again shows a natural development of the scout's character. Now escaped to the broad free plains beyond the Mississippi, he is serene, well-adjusted to his new environment, and reconciled to his approaching end; as just, wise, and freshhearted as ever, but more prejudiced, and still more inveterately talkative.

The nature of the scout is a curious combination of combativeness and pacifism, enterprise and fatalism, fearlessness and caution, insistence on personal dignity and modesty. Sometimes he expresses a number of these traits in one speech, as when after slaying his first foe he moralizes to Judith Hutter: "These things must be, and they bring with 'em a mixed feelin' of sorrow and triumph. Human natur' is a fightin' natur', I suppose." By preference he is a man of peace, some speeches suggesting a Quaker philosophy. Love of peace is one reason why he prefers the forest: "All is contradiction in the settlements, while all is concord in the woods," he says. In the woods, too, he can indulge his naturally contemplative turn of mind. He has been in the churches of Albany and other towns, but like a good Quaker he does not think churches necessary. "They call 'em the temples of the Lord; but the whole 'arth is the temple of the Lord to such as have the right mind." When hunting and scouting, he takes time to cultivate the gifts of the spirit. "Many's the hour I've passed," he remarks to Chingachgook, "pleasantly enough, too, in what is termed contemplation by my people. On such occasions the mind is actyve, though the body seems lazy and listless. An open spot on a mountain side, where a wide look can be had at the heavens and the 'arth, is a most judicious place for a man to get a just idee of the power of the Manitou, and of his own littleness." Any crisis, however, found him all action; and when he views the rotting corpses of the Americans and British whom the French allowed to be slain in the massacre at Fort William Henry, he is fierceness itself:

> "I have been on many a shocking field, and have followed a trail of blood for weary miles," he said, "but never have I found the hand of the devil so plain as is here to be seen! Revenge is an Indian feeling, and all who know me know that there is no cross in my veins; but this much will I say,—here, in the face of heaven, and with the power of the Lord so manifest in this howling wilderness,—that should these Frenchers ever trust themselves again within the range of a ragged bullet, there is one rifle shall play its part, so long as flint will fire or powder burn! I leave the tomahawk and knife to such as have a natural gift to use them. What say you, Chingachgook," he added in Delaware; "shall the Hurons boast of this to their women when the deep snows come?"

Leatherstocking, like many a frontiersman in real life, expresses a strong love of nature. It is this, in part, which makes him an ardent conservationist, lamenting the spoliation of the wilderness. In *The Pioneers* he repeatedly expresses his horror at the devastation of natural wealth and beauty; in *The Prairie* he bitterly declares that when the Yankee choppers have cut their path from the Atlantic to the Pacific, they will "turn on their tracks like a fox that doubles, and then the rank smell of their own footsteps will show them the madness of their waste." In mastery of wilderness lore, however, Cooper very properly makes Chingachgook and Uncas superior to the scout. Capable as Leatherstocking is in reading weather, stalking game, or matching wits against a Mingo, he always defers to the past master of forest pursuits, Chingachgook. This is specially evident in *The Last of the Mohicans*, which far more than the others is a novel of Indian life. One striking scene in *The Pioneers* illustrates the superior powers of observation possessed by the Delaware; a scene which almost anticipates Sherlock Holmes. Leatherstocking suspects that his hounds have been cut loose by his enemy the carpenter, so that they might chase deer and justify an arrest. But it is the sharp-eyed Chingachgook who supplies the proof:

> In the meantime, Mohegan had been examining, with an Indian's sagacity, the place where the leather thong had been separated. After scrutinizing it closely, he said, in Delaware,—
>
> "It was cut with a knife—a sharp blade and a long handle; the man was afraid of the dogs."
>
> "How is this, Mohegan?" exclaimed Edwards: "You saw it not. How can you know these facts?"
>
> "Listen, son," said the warrior. "The knife was sharp, for the cut is smooth; the handle was long, for a man's arm would not reach from this gash to the cut that did not go through the skin: he was a coward, or he would have cut the thongs around the necks of the hounds."
>
> "On my life," cried Natty, "John is on the scent! It was the carpenter; and he has got on the rock back of the kennel, and let the dogs loose by fastening his knife to a stick."

Chingachgook, Uncas, and Leatherstocking are Cooper's supreme achievement, and one of the principal glories of American literature. Leatherstocking in particular is, as Thackeray wrote, one of the great prize men of world fiction. "He ranks with your Uncle Toby, Sir Roger de Coverley, Falstaff—heroic figures all, American or British—and the artist has deserved well of his country who devised them." Cooper wrote, apropos of *The Spy*, that Americans differed from Europeans: "Man is not the same creature here as he is in other countries." This was what Crevecoeur had written previously, and what Tocqueville was to state with emphasis a few years later. Cooper also put some pithy words on the subject into Leatherstocking's mouth. Different environments, said the scout, produce special traits. "Now gifts come of sarcumstances. Thus, if you put a man in a town, he gets town gifts; in a settlement, settlement gifts; in a forest, gifts of the woods." New types and a new society were being created in America; and no type was more essentially American than the frontiersman represented by Leatherstocking.

Viewing the five romances as a whole, we are struck by their breadth and grandeur. Their faults, which are many, are faults of detail; their virtues are large and enduring virtues. It was Cooper's felicity to unroll a canvas whose panoramic width matched the shaggy continent; to paint on it the pageant of the primeval Atlantic forests, the Great Lakes, the smaller canoe-threaded waterways, and the rolling prairies; and to fill the foreground with the clangorous action of the era when Indian, Briton, Frenchman, and Spaniard disputed the destiny of the continent. We can go to him in youth for entertainment, and come back to him in maturity for our fullest presentation of the color and magnitude of the American scene in its primitive epoch.

II. *Cooper and the Frontier*

WE READ of Leatherstocking today in the light of the studies made of a varied array of frontier figures: Daniel Boone, Davy Crockett, and Kit Carson foremost, with Simon Kenton, Jim Bridger, William L. Sublette, Thomas Fitzpatrick, and Jedediah S. Smith behind them. We are influenced still more, as we read, by F. J. Turner's essay on the frontier. Turner placed the hunter and fur trader foremost in the column of white men advancing into the wilderness. The advance of civilization, as he graphically showed, was a complex process of destruction and reconstruction. It ruined the world of the Indian, trapper, and hunter, who fled ever westward. It created the world of the pioneer log cabin farmer, nomadic in habit, and a varied body of adventurers. As their era ended, that of the settled farmer, land speculator, railroad builder, and town planner began. Not a line but a process, the frontier in its passage across the United States had its good and bad sides, its heroic and disreputable figures.

In some ways Cooper's study of the pioneer age usefully supplements and modifies Turner. The Wisconsin historian emphasizes the set of kinetic and individualistic traits which the frontier cultivated among Americans. They drew from pioneer life their coarse strength, inquisitive curiosity, practical inventiveness, nervous restlessness, and much of their materialism. They took from it also an aversion to discipline. "Complex society," wrote Turner, "is precipitated by the wilderness into a kind of primitive organization based on the family. The tendency is antisocial. It promotes antipathy to control, and particularly to any direct control." Yet while Leatherstocking is certainly an individualist, Cooper does not endow him with aggressive, restless, materialistic traits. One of the most prominent characteristics of the scout, from youth to age, is a quiet, ruminative, philosophical cast of mind—a natural creation, we are told, of wilderness solitude. As for materialism, Leatherstocking is utterly devoid of it. He cares naught for money; land to him, as to the Indians, is merely space to be hunted over; he prizes his freedom from material cares just as Thoreau did.

History bears evidence that Cooper's depiction of the quiet contemplative type of frontiersman is just as valid as Turner's emphasis on the combative, uncontrolled, and grasping type. Everything depended on the man and the special environment. Daniel Boone united an adventurous spirit with a placid temperament and an indifference to most material considerations. He was a man of greater force and more varied occupations than Leatherstocking, being hunter, trader, cattle grower, farmer, surveyor, and explorer. (Had Pathfinder married Mabel Dunham he would of necessity have turned to such gainful pursuits.) Boone, stalwart and rugged, fought hard at need. Yet at heart he was much the patient, unaggressive, reflective man that Cooper drew in Leatherstocking. So was Kit Carson, a knightly figure of almost perfect truth and integrity, modest, restrained, and in his later years prone to moralizing. Both Boone and Carson united patient self-command with daring; both were quite free from bluster and harshness; both had endless fortitude, and perfect confidence in their own power to meet danger.

A still sturdier exemplar than Boone of Leatherstocking's qualities is Jedediah S. Smith, the buckskin hero who when Cooper wrote *The Prairie* (1826) was already familiar with the Great Salt Lake region and Columbia River Basin, and who in the next few years made his famous journeys by the central route to California, and northward to Oregon. He was a rugged frontiersman, daunted by nothing. Like Leatherstocking, he was "foremost in all warrantable enterprises." He was also a gentleman, of simple honesty, strong moral sense, and peaceable temper; he was ready to sacrifice himself for others, as when he braved imprisonment by the Mexicans to obtain supplies for his party stranded on the American River; a devout Methodist, he could preach as loquaciously as Cooper's hero. Such men should be remembered when we hear the frontier described as a seedbed of aggressive materialism.

Cooper fully realized that the frontier had its lawless fringe and disintegrating moral influences. It gave American history the desperado, the rustler, the bandit, the horse thief, the train robber, and the white Indian like Simon Girty. It carried criminals and riffraff across the continent as a wind carries chaff and leaves. The frontier offered a natural haven for outlaws like the retired buccaneer, Tom Hutter. It encouraged casual, indolent, ungirt habits. Hurry Harry in *The Deerslayer* is not positively vicious; but he is lazy, insincere, irresponsible, and thoughtlessly brutal. He represents the happy-go-lucky frontier hunter who endured hardships bravely, fought Indians recklessly, and when he got a few dollars spent them at the nearest settlement on drink, gambling, and women.

A further stage in the corrupting aspect of the frontier is shown in the squatter Ishmael Bush, his passionate wife, and his undisciplined sons, all so well drawn in *The Prairie*. These roving Kentuckians are akin to the dirty, unstable "Pikes" long prominent in Western annals and well presented in Clarence King's *Mountaineering in the Sierra Nevada*. Bush and his sons are by no means degenerate or unprincipled; if rough, hard, and ignorant, they are also virile and energetic; but they are hostile to orderly society. Far worse is Ishmael's brother-in-law Abiram White, the kidnapper and murderer. He is the kind of outlaw that associated with the La Harpes on the Natchez Trace, and that Henry Plummer brought into his murderous gang in Montana. While Ishmael is no paragon of virtue, he does have his scruples. When reproached by Abiram for being a posted lawbreaker, he turns hotly on the scoundrel:

> "If the hounds of the law can put their bills on the trees and stumps of the clearings, it was for no act of dishonesty, as you know, but because we maintain the rule that 'arth is common property. No, Abiram; could I wash my hands of things done by your advice, as easily as I can of the things done by the whisperings of the devil, my sleep would be quieter at night, and none who hear my name need blush to hear it mentioned."

At the end, Ishmael Bush assumes the role of a dispenser of justice. His dull mind emancipates itself from the spell long exercised by Abiram; he coolly but determinedly pays the murderer for his crime. Here we have the very portrait of the vigilante, or volunteer leader of a frontier posse. "Grave in exterior, saturnine by temperament, formidable by physical means, and dangerous from his lawless obstinacy, his self-constituted tribunal excited a degree of awe to which even the intelligent Middleton could not bring himself to be entirely insensible." Leatherstocking sympathizes with Bush's belief that where the public law is weak, private law must be strong. At the same time, Leatherstocking delivers a statement of the frontier's antagonism toward excessive use of law and police that could hardly be bettered. It has the modern ring of American denunciation of the totalitarian state. To Middleton, speaking of the nation's long arm, he rejoins:

> "A busy and a troublesome arm it often proves to be here in this land of America; where, as they say, man is left greatly to the following of his own wishes, compared to other countries; and happier, aye, and more manly and more honest too, is he for the privilege! Why, do you know, my men, that there are regions where the law is so busy as to say, In this fashion shall you live, in that fashion shall you die, and in such another fashion shall you take leave of the world, to be sent before the judgment seat of the Lord! A wicked and a troublesome meddling is that, with the business of One who has not made his creatures to be herded like oxen. . . . A miserable land must that be where they fetter the mind as well as the body, and where the creatures of God, being born children, are kept so by the wicked inventions of men who would take upon themselves the office of the great Governor of them all!"

In still another respect Cooper supplements the famous hypothesis of Turner. His account of early Cooperstown in *The Pioneers* shows how secure a hold Eastern and European civilization kept upon some elements of frontier society, and how quickly this civilization followed on the heels of the Indian-fighter and trailmaker. The book fits perfectly the argument of those who hold that Turner failed adequately to grasp the quick transit of culture to the West. Hard on the trail of the Hutters and Leatherstockings came the men who cleared the farms and planted the villages; and their social organization soon took on complexity and polish.

Historic Cooperstown did in fact illustrate the rapidity and potency with which civilization infiltrated the wilderness. Turner writes of "isolated frontier settlements," and of the decisive way in which West and East "began to get out of touch with each other." To be sure, he is speaking mainly of the trans-Allegheny frontier; but a reading of Cooper's *Chronicles of Cooperstown* in combination with *The Pioneers* suggests that Turner overstressed the detachment and the loss of touch. Settlement of the Cooperstown area did not really begin until 1787, the year the novelist's father, William Cooper, took possession of his wide tract of land there; the spot was remote (as distances then went) from Albany or New York City; the firstcomers were poor. Yet how promptly Eastern culture gripped the community! In depicting its hold, *The Pioneers* is a faithful picture of what happened, with differences, in Lexington, Kentucky, in Galesburg, Illinois, and in Grinnell, Iowa, as well as on Otsego Lake.

The novel (its action dated in 1793) describes the polite society and good conversation found at the home of Marmaduke Temple; just such society and talk as were really met in William Cooper's mansion. It takes note of the cosmopolitan figures in or about the village, British, Spanish, French, and German; Cooperstown actually had such men, including M. Le Quoi de Mersereau, who had been civil governor of Martinique until the French Revolution. The novel gives a chapter to the impressive Christmas Eve service conducted by the Episcopal clergyman, half of the congregation being horny-handed pioneers who listened "with great decency and attention." This conforms to fact. The first Episcopal services were held in Cooperstown in 1797 by Dr. Thomas Ellison, a graduate of Oxford; and within a few years the first permanent rector, the Rev. Daniel Nash, and the first Presbyterian clergyman, were men of wide influence. One of the best scenes of *The Pioneers* is that of the courtroom, Judge Marmaduke Temple administering justice in careful and fairly formal fashion. In the same manner did William Cooper, who was judge of the Otsego County Court of Common Pleas from 1791 to 1800, preside over his courtroom.

In short, just as *The Deerslayer* and *The Prairie* throw broad shafts of light upon the transit of the raw frontier zone across the continent, so *The Pioneers* illuminates the transit of civilization close in its wake. The more carefully we study Cooper's Leatherstocking series, the more we see that he had a realistic understanding of many facets of pioneer life: the romance, the heroism, the lawlessness, the crudity, the simplicity, the provincialism, the honesty, the corruption. The conquest of the wilderness could be a spiritual adventure, as it was with Hawkeye in fiction and Jedediah S. Smith in fact; it could be a degrading experience, as with the Bush family and the border ruffians of Kansas. Cooper also understood something of the complex interaction between the frontier and the old civilization of Europe and the seaboard. Though he did not attempt formal history, much good frontier history can be found in suspension in his novels. Above all, he caught the grandeur of the frontier, as reflected in the minds of all who, like Leatherstocking, felt a profound sense of unity between man and nature. Disturbed by any conflict between the two, and keenly distrustful of much that he saw in civilization, Natty Bumppo satisfied a restless thirst for the ideal in moving from the virgin forest to the virgin prairie. Cooper knew that Leatherstocking's career did not falter at the end. Instead, like that of many another pioneer, it rose to a climax; until, serenely independent, his rifle on his knee, his friends about him, the aged hunter died sitting erect and still facing the West.

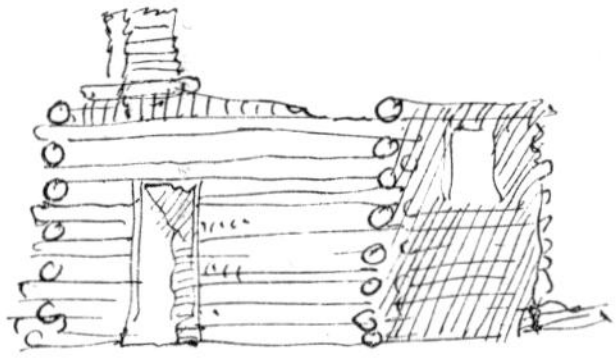

III. *Cooper and the Indians*

IN COOPER'S boyhood not many Indians were left in New York State; they had migrated to the deeper woods of the West, and as Susan Fenimore Cooper writes, only a few came occasionally to Otsego Lake to catch bass or make maple sugar. The Cherry Valley massacre had become a dim memory. As a youth Cooper had no opportunity to become acquainted with the savages at first hand. To him the tribesman was as romantic a stranger as to most Americans today; nor is it likely that he ever talked with men who had traded with the Iroquois, or fought against the Huron remnants, in the time of the old French wars. When he met Charles Augustus Murray, the Englishman who published his interesting account of the Western Indians (*Travels in North America*) in 1839, he remarked: "You have had the advantage of me, for I was never among the Indians. All that I know of them is from reading and from hearing my father speak of them."

According to his daughter, he did have one other source of knowledge. Before he went to Europe to complete *The Last of the Mohicans* and write *The Prairie* (1826–27), he had sought out Indians visiting the East. She writes, without giving any specific date:

> Delegations from the Western tribes were frequently seen at that period on their way to Washington. Since his interest in the race had become specially wakened, he lost no opportunity of visiting these parties, which often lingered for several months in the great eastern cities. He followed them from New York to Philadelphia, to Baltimore, to Washington; he studied the different individuals who composed these embassies of warriors; he admired their physical appearance, he was impressed with the vein of poetry and laconic eloquence, if the expression may be used, marking their brief speeches; and their natural dignity of manner and grace of gesture, blended with their strongly marked savage mien and accoutrements, struck him forcibly. He made the personal acquaintance of the prominent chiefs. He questioned the interpreters closely. The army officers who accompanied these delegations were often old friends. He listened with the deepest interest and with vivid sympathy to their accounts of great buffalo hunts, of wild battles between mounted tribes, of the fires sweeping over those vast plains. Full of life and spirit himself, he was always keenly interested in narratives of adventure.

But Cooper never visited any Indian village, much less dwelt therein; he never consorted with Indians on the trail or the hunt; his knowledge of the Eastern tribes was derived almost wholly from print. By the time he wrote *The Pathfinder* and *The Deerslayer* (1840–41) the amount of material in print was large. Nevertheless, he was too early for the really scientific studies of the ethnologists, which were ushered in the year that Cooper died by Lewis Henry Morgan's book *League of the Ho-dé-no-sau-nee, or Iroquois.* The novelist's main ideas about the Indian, given at some length in his preface to *The Last of the Mohicans,* point plainly to a rather elementary kind of literary information. He tells us that in war the Indian is "daring, boastful, cunning, ruthless, self-denying, and self-devoted"; in peace, "just, generous, hospitable, revengeful, superstitious, modest, and commonly chaste." A much more discriminating characterization than this is needed. It is not strange that Parkman, who really had lived among the red men, was a little scornful of Cooper's depiction. Uncas, says the historian, is utterly unlike any real Indian; the villainous Magua is "a less untruthful portrait." In short, Parkman thinks Cooper tended to idealize his figures.

The published sources upon which Cooper levied were various. He knew well Jonathan Carver's *Travels in the Interior Parts of North America* (1778), the second part of which specially deals with Indian life, warfare, customs, and religion; indeed, his description of the burial of Cora by Indian maidens in *The Last of the Mohicans* is largely derived from Carver. The novelist of course knew Cadwallader Colden's *History of the Five Indian Nations Depending on the Province of New York,* first brought out in 1727 and enlarged in later editions; a work not the worse for embodying much French observation. It is plain that Cooper was strongly influenced by the writings of the brave Moravian missionary J. G. E. Heckewelder, who lived much with the converted Indians in Pennsylvania and elsewhere before, during, and after the Revolution, and did much work among the tribes for the American Government. His *History, Manners, and Customs of the Indian Nations Who Once Inhabited Pennsylvania and the Neighboring States,* brought out in 1819, had a large circulation not only in English but in French and German translations. James Adair's *History of the American Indians* (1775) certainly reached Cooper's attention, though Adair was preoccupied with the Southern tribes.

It was doubtless from Heckewelder that Cooper drew the inspiration for his grandly venerable Tamenund, or Tammany, for the missionary gives a rather vague chapter to this renowned Delaware leader and to the only less famous Tadeuskund. "All we know of Tamaned is," writes Heckewelder, "that he was an ancient Delaware chief, who never had his equal." Samuel G. Drake, in his *Biography and History of the Indians of North America,* a 700-page work brought out the same year as *The Deerslayer,* furnishes more information about him. On Indian psychology and ways Cooper may have learned a good deal from the books of the artist-author George Catlin, who decided about 1830 that he would devote the remainder of his life to depicting "the vanishing races of native man," and launched on that undertaking two years later. His notes of travel among the Indians began appearing in the New York *Commercial Advertiser* in 1830, and his valuable two-volume work on the Western tribes, with four hundred illustrations, appeared in 1841. Like Longfellow, Cooper was also well acquainted with the writings of Henry R. Schoolcraft, who travelled widely among the aborigines, and developed a special affection for those Algonquin peoples who were also the novelist's favorites. Schoolcraft, who married a Chippewa girl and was just the robust type of man Cooper liked, brought out his books on the lead mine country of Missouri and on the upper reaches of the Mississippi, both full of Indian lore, in 1819 and 1821, before the first Leatherstocking romance was conceived; and his two volumes of *Algic Researches* were ready before the first words of *The Pathfinder* and *The Deerslayer* were written.

What is most striking about Cooper's Indians is that, except for the chapters which close *The Last of the Mohicans,* they appear as individuals, not as tribes or communities. We are told much of their personal traits, little of their social organization. Cooper knew nothing about their tribal structure; he had none of the modern ethnologist's expert knowledge of their economy, ceremonials, and polity; and he so devised his plots as to keep off dangerous ground. The final chapters in *The Last of the Mohicans* which treat of the villages of Hurons and Delawares are actually a little incongruous in their setting. Cooper tells us that the Huron lodges were permanent, and that the Delawares had spent the whole summer at their own camp, raising corn; women and children were living in both villages. Yet he also tells us that both the Hurons and this particular group of Delawares were war parties in French service. It is obvious that war parties would not have taken along women and children, nor have paused to grow corn. We may rejoice, however, that he has given us these chapters. His pictures of the Indian councils, speeches, and rites, his presentation of their attitude toward the ill, the feeble-minded, and the old, his account of the significance of the totem, and his sketch of their religious beliefs, are generally accurate and quite enthralling.

Since Cooper nowhere offers a systematic statement of the Indian history that comes into his five Leatherstocking books, a brief exposition of the facts as now known will be useful to readers. He deals with two great peoples, the Algonkians and the Iroquoians. The village-dwelling Iroquois are justly rated among the most famous Indians of the continent, for the government of the Five Nations which they ultimately established was the strongest and most orderly north of the Rio Grande. The Algonkians, living in a wide belt along the Atlantic Coast from the Kennebec to the James, were the savages whom the English colonists first encountered. They included the Mahicans (Mohicans), a confederacy in the upper Hudson Valley, and the Delawares or Lenape, a larger confederacy spread over Delaware, eastern Pennsylvania, and New Jersey. Much of the background of Cooper is furnished by the conflict between Iroquois and Algonkian.

This conflict reached back into prehistory. The Iroquois were invaders. During the fourteenth and fifteenth centuries they had thrust inexorably forward from the West. One strong branch, the Hurons, passed north of Lake Ontario. Another group of tribes rolled into upper New York, slowly pushing back the Algonkians and entrenching themselves on hills, crags, and river islands. Two Nations, the Senecas and Eries, seem to have acted as spearhead, establishing stockaded forts and palisaded villages in the Finger Lakes area and on the upper Mohawk; and with or just behind them came the Mohawks and Onondagas. As they crumpled the front of the Algonkian tribes, conflict grew intense. The Mahicans in the lower Mohawk and upper Hudson valleys fought with particular vigor and address. Sometimes they were victorious, sometimes defeated; the tide of battle swayed back and forth.

But the Iroquois gradually gained ground. They had the greater weight of numbers, a genius for organization, a fervent belief that they were the Chosen People destined to hold the earth, and a set of traditions which granted high eminence to the warrior and developed fighting leaders. The brave who gave special evidence of courage, endurance, and resourcefulness was made a captain by his admiring fellows. The opposing Mahicans, whose country extended from Lake Champlain in the north to Westchester, and who had "castles" at Cohoes and Schodack, seem to have been a people of many admirable traits. They had a democratic form of government with an hereditary sachem at its head, and a body of councillors, whose duty was to look to the public safety and maintain order. Their chief warrior or hero made war; their sachem and councillors made peace. Among the Iroquois also civil chiefs and military chiefs were rigidly separated, and if a civil chief wished to be a warrior he had to give up his council seat. The Mahicans, however, were less fierce and bloodthirsty than the Iroquois. Little by little, they were pushed down the Hudson Valley.

The Iroquois of necessity developed fierceness in battle; and of necessity they also developed their organizing talents. Not only did they have to fight the Mahicans, but in time they became involved in equally desperate warfare with their old family allies, the Hurons. As the Hurons migrated north of Ontario and the St. Lawrence, they resented the independence which the southern tribes developed. They regarded their New York kinsmen as rebels, trying to escape from a just control. Thus battling on two fronts, the southern Iroquois were forced

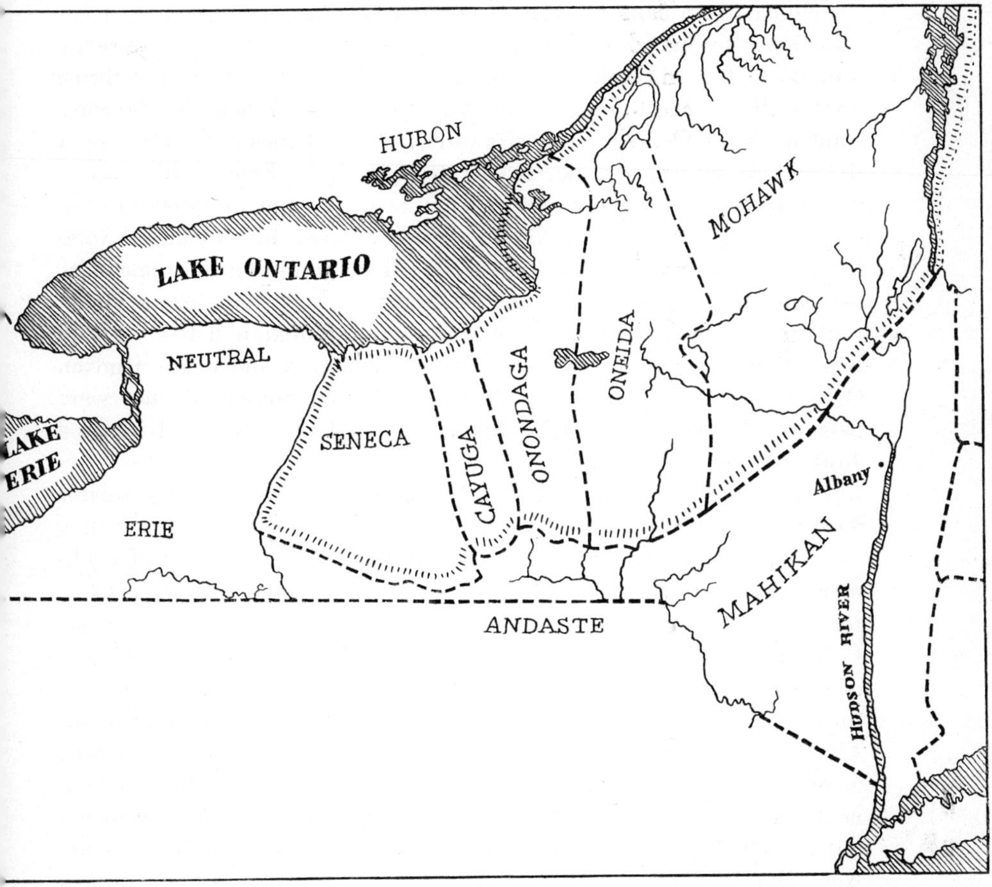

THE IROQUOIS AND OTHER TRIBES ABOUT 1650
(Data by Arthur C. Parker; from A. C. Flick, editor, *History of the State of New York,* New York State Historical Association.)

to give up their old intertribal feuds. The warriors were waging one bloody war after another to maintain their hold on central New York; the women and children were suffering cruelly; their outlook was dark indeed unless they united.

Hence two idealists, lovers of peace and concord, gradually gained a hearing for the idea of a federation of Iroquois tribes. One was a thoughtful Indian dwelling among the Mohawks, named Dekanwidah; a man who wished to devise a code of laws to lessen the misery of constant warfare. The other was Hiawatha, an Onondaga Indian who had suffered heavy personal bereavements in the loss of his children. The two joined hands, made a long journey to the Niagara country to gain the support of the Neutral Nation (which tried to keep aloof from the battles of Hurons with the New York tribes), and enlisted the aid of the powerful "peace woman" of the Neutrals. Then they besought the southern Iroquois to adopt a common code of laws and form a confederation. They finally converted to their plan the Mohawks, Senecas, Onondagas, Cayugas, and Oneidas; "the five brother Nations sat down beneath the tree of peace." This Iroquois confederacy had perhaps 4,000 good fighting men. It could now hold what it had taken, and before long it had established a secure domination over most of New York west of Schenectady.

World history was affected by these events. Every reader of Parkman knows how Samuel de Champlain was induced by the Hurons to join one of their expeditions against the Five Nations; and how his rash participation made the resentful Iroquois long the staunch allies of the English. Well this was for the British colonies! The Iroquois fought and defeated the Hurons, who sued for peace and received it (1634). Then, when some intransigent young Hurons committed atrocities, in 1648 the Five Nations renewed the war, and during the next two years, by systematic campaigning, they almost utterly wiped out the Huron nation. This accomplished, the Iroquois destroyed the Neutral Nation as a separate tribe, incorporating its remnants into their own people; and soon afterward, in 1654, they meted out the same fate to the Eries. The Five Nations (which after the adhesion of the Tuscaroras became the Six Nations) thereafter controlled practically all of New York State except a southeastern corner still occupied by the weakened Mahicans.

This powerful confederacy was at first united with the British by a military alliance, reinforced by economic ties; for they sold their furs to British and colonial traders from Albany. Sometimes they concluded peace engagements with the French, as in 1666–67, but in general they fought both the French and the Indian allies of the Bourbons. The stand they took was one of the factors which eventually gave the British a dominant position in America; indeed, it was of the greatest historic importance, for during the seventeenth century the French and British were not unevenly matched, and Gallic supremacy was a possibility.

By the time of Queen Anne's War, however, many Iroquois became convinced that they could play the two white Powers against each other, and thus maintain a balanced position between them. The colonists in New York labored amain to hold the confederacy to its old alliance. But many Iroquois were lukewarm, and some even fought on the French side. The surviving Hurons who had been taken into the Iroquois ranks were very likely to be found, with other Great Lakes Indians, under the Bourbon banner. When the Abbé François Picquet planted a mission at Ogdensburgh, New York, he persuaded a number of the Onondagas and Cayugas to accept his teachings, and some of them enlisted with the French. So did various Andastes, Susquehannocks, and other mixed-blood savages whom the Iroquois had conquered, and whom Leatherstocking contemptuously calls Mingoes. In short, the situation as respected the New York tribes became confused. In the main the Iroquois remained loyal to the English, but some took the other side; and we can well understand why Chingachgook and Uncas had a double hatred of these renegades—as foes both of their own tribe and of the British cause.

The Mahicans were finally pushed east of the Hudson by the Mohawks. Here the tribe gradually broke up. It sold off its lands, and the members removed to various places—some to western New York, some to Pennsylvania, some to Ohio, and a few to the shelter of a mission at Stockbridge, Massachusetts, where they lost their old identity and became known as Stockbridge Indians. Their kinsmen the Delawares met an equally sad fate. Weakened by white encroachments, early in the eighteenth century this "grandfather nation" was defeated and completely broken up by the all-conquering Iroquois. Once the Delawares had been the most influential of all the Algonkian stock. The Mahicans had been proud to claim descent from them—which explains why Chingachgook and Uncas are given both tribal names. When their conquest was completed in 1720, the Iroquois forbade them to hold land or wage war. An Ishmaelite people, the foes of every other tribe, they migrated westward. As the only wilderness tribe to master the lore of the prairies, they became accomplished scouts, accompanying Frémont, Kit Carson, and other explorers on their Western journeys, and gaining the esteem of the United States Army. Eventually, a remnant of the Delawares received from the government a reservation in Kansas.

The last of the Mohicans—that is, last of the line of Mahican chiefs—Uncas held that mournful place, and so fits into a grand and tragic pattern of history. When we first meet Chingachgook in *The*

Deerslayer, Leatherstocking identifies him as an hereditary chief, his father having been the greatest warrior and councillor of his people. But, adds the scout sadly, "the nation is so dispersed and diminished, that chieftainship among 'em has got to be little more than a name." In the last novel of the series, Leatherstocking finds that the very existence of the Mahicans and Delawares is likely to be forgotten. "Tell me," he says to the Pawnee chief, Hard-Heart, "have you ever in your traditions heard of a mighty people who once lived on the shore of the salt lake, hard by the rising sun? . . . . Do not your traditions tell you of the greatest, the bravest, and the wisest nation of redskins that the Wahcondah has ever breathed upon?" The Pawnee knows them not, and the aged scout moralizes: "Such is mortal vanity and pride!"

The young Chingachgook and still more the youthful Uncas are clearly idealized portraits. They are men of nearly every virtue, few limitations, and no vices. The main charge to be brought against Cooper's treatment of the Indian, however, is not that he idealizes the red men, but that he fails to do them sober realistic justice. They usually appear in the guise of enemies and villains. "A band of beings, who resembled demons rather than men"—such is Cooper's characterization of a squad of Sioux. "Devils," "miscreants," "thieves," are the terms Leatherstocking applies to all hostile savages. He speaks again and again of even the better Indians as being divided by an impassable gulf from "men of white blood and Christian feelin's." Apparently Cooper shared the scout's belief. When a white man uses artifice or surprise, according to Cooper, he shows his superior wisdom; when an Indian does so, he betrays his treachery. "The accursed Mingoes!" Leatherstocking bursts out at one point, and when Chingachgook corrects him, saying the Indians in question are Iroquois, he proceeds: "No matter—no matter—Iroquois—devil—Mingo—Mengwes or furies—all are pretty much the same. I call all rascals Mingoes." Delawares and Pawnees taking the side of the whites are tolerably good Indians; all the others are "knaves" at best, "riptyles" at worst.

Had Cooper known a few Indian tribes at first hand, he would have understood that these primitive men who first populated North America, who discovered its most useful plants and animals, and who developed methods of agriculture, hunting, finding shelter and clothing, and preparing food that were well adapted to the land, possessed much the same human qualities as white people. They loved, hated, feared, warred, and even worshipped in much the same way. From some of their collective institutions the white man could have learned a good deal. Cooper's oversimplified study of them could have been made both richer and more sympathetic. A closer acquaintance would have enabled him to bring more of the tribal life into his stories, to analyze Indian psychology more shrewdly, and to give us some scenes like Longfellow's happy picture of the cornhusking:

On the border of the forest,
Underneath the fragrant pine-trees,
Sat the old men and the warriors
Smoking in the pleasant shadow. . . .
Looked they at the gamesome labor
Of the young men and the women;
Listened to their noisy talking,
To their laughter and their singing,
Heard them chattering like the magpies,
Heard them laughing like the bluejays,
Heard them singing like the robins.
And whene'er some lucky maiden
Found a red ear in the husking,
Found a maize-ear red as blood is,
"Nushka!" cried they all together,
"Nushka, you shall have a sweetheart,
You shall have a handsome husband!"
"Ugh!" the old men all responded.

Such writers as Henry R. Schoolcraft and George Catlin must have regretted that the novelist dealt so unscientifically with the Indian. Theirs was a deeper sympathy with the aborigine. It was white contact which corrupted the red man, declared Catlin. In "the proud and chivalrous pale of savage society" he had often found "the noblest traits of honor and magnanimity," and he believed that in some respects "their lives were much more happy than ours." Certainly Cooper, relying only on literary materials and random impressions, missed much that was most interesting in Indian life; certainly he was wrong when he declared that Indian nature possessed little variety. Had his knowledge been fuller he would have been more sparing of such phrases as "fiendish coolness" and "heathen craftiness"; he would better have equated Indian and white psychology; he would have done greater justice to Indian arts, ceremonials, legendry, and religion. He must then have lent heavier weight to the Indian chief's stern demand of the whites: "Why hath the Manitou made thy race like hungry wolves?"

But it should be remembered that all Cooper's art is romantic, not realistic, and that as he took a romantic view of nature and the pioneer, so he naturally romanticized the Indian as either hero or villain. He was concerned with the large impression. For the favorable pictures he does give us—for Chingachgook, Uncas, and the wonderful final chapters of *The Last of the Mohicans*—we must be grateful. In one book outside the Leatherstocking series, *The Wept of Wish-Ton-Wish,* he makes the Wampanoag chieftain King Philip a heroic figure, and in his account of King Philip's War holds the scales fairly even between red and white. A spokesman of the warring Pequots bursts out to a white girl: "You see all around you land that is covered with hill and valley, and which once bore wood without the fear of the ax, and over which game was spread with a bountiful hand. There are hunters and runners in our tribe, who have been on a straight path toward the setting sun, until their legs were weary and their eyes could not see the clouds that hang over the salt lake, and yet they say, 'tis everywhere beautiful as yonder green mountain. Tall trees and shady woods, rivers and lakes filled with fish, and deer and beaver plentiful as the sands on the seashore. All this land and water the Great Spirit gave to men of red skins, for them he loved. . . . Then the Great Spirit grew angry; he hid his face from his children, because they quarrelled among themselves. Big canoes came out of the rising sun, and brought a hungry and wicked people into the land." In this utterance Cooper does justice both to Indian eloquence and to the grievance of the first Americans against their invaders.

To wish that Cooper had been more realistic and scientific in his portrayal of the forest, and frontiersman, and the savage, is to wish that he had been a different kind of writer, and to miss his true achievement. The answer to that wish is Leatherstocking's sage remark: "A natur' is the creature itself, the wishes, wants, idees, and feelins, as all are born in him." Cooper was a born romancer. He once lamented, as did Hawthorne and Melville, that America was bare of events, people, and atmosphere suited to fiction. But he proved that it was not. Taking elements neglected until his eye fell on them, the forest, the scout, and the Indian, he wrought them into a richly variegated tapestry, an enduring triumph of the romancer's art. In all romance, creation counts for more than exact observation, and the conflict between reality and credibility has to be resolved with emphasis on what is readily credible; for his own purposes, Cooper's Indian was just right.

CHRONOLOGY

of James Fenimore Cooper

1789. Born, Burlington, New Jersey, September 15.
1790. Taken to Cooperstown, Otsego Lake, New York.
1803–05. In Yale College.
1806–07. Sailor before the mast on the ship *Sterling*.
1808–11. In the United States Navy.
1811–21. Lives in Mamaroneck, Cooperstown, and Scarsdale, New York.
1820. Publishes first novel, *Precaution*.
1821. Publishes *The Spy: A Tale of the Neutral Ground*.
1823. *The Pioneers; or the Sources of the Susquehanna*.
1823. *The Pilot: A Tale of the Sea*.
1826. *The Last of the Mohicans: A Tale of 1757*. Sails for Europe.
1827. *The Prairie: A Tale*.
1828. *The Red Rover: A Tale*.
1828. *Notions of the Americans; Picked up by a Travelling Bachelor*.
1830. *The Water Witch; or the Skimmer of the Seas*.
1833. Returns to New York.
1834. Acquires his father's place in Cooperstown.
1839. *The History of the Navy of the United States of America*.
1840. *The Pathfinder; or the Inland Sea*.
1841. *The Deerslayer; or the First War Path*.
1842. *The Two Admirals: A Tale*.
1844. *Afloat and Ashore; or The Adventures of Miles Wallingford*.
1848. *The Oak Openings; or the Bee Hunter*.
1851. Dies at Cooperstown, September 14.

THE LEATHERSTOCKING TALES

A Chronological Table

Age of Leatherstocking	*Historical Background*	*Date of Publication*
	THE DEERSLAYER	
Stating that Hurry Harry is 26 or 28, Cooper remarks that Deerslayer is "several years his junior." We may guess he is 23 or 24.	Cooper dates the action between the years 1740 and 1745. He accounts for the hostility of the Indian party on the shores of Lake Otsego by the fact that they had heard of war between Britain and France. News of this conflict ("King George's War") reached America in the spring of 1744.	1841
	THE LAST OF THE MOHICANS	
If Leatherstocking was 23 or 24 in 1744, he would now be 36 or 37 years old.	"A Narrative of 1757" is Cooper's subtitle. The central event is Montcalm's capture of Fort William Henry on August 9, 1757, and the ensuing massacre of British and colonials. The Seven Years' War had begun in America in 1754; it was ended by the surrender of New France to the British in 1760.	1826
	THE PATHFINDER	
If 23 in 1744, Leatherstocking would have been 38 in 1759. He is not too old, as Cooper says, to fall in love. But	Cooper says merely that the action took place in "the same war of '56." Actually it is hard to offer a plausible date. The story centers about Fort Oswego. That British post on the south shore of Ontario	1840

Mabel Dunham wants only a fatherly affection from him.

was captured and levelled by Montcalm in 1756 and the British did not begin rebuilding it until 1759. The novel shows Fort Niagara in French hands. That post was captured by the British in July, 1759. If we hold Cooper to rigid historical dates (which we must not do) the story can be put in the spring of 1759.

THE PIONEERS

1823

When put in the stocks, Leatherstocking says he is in his 71st year. By our previous chronology, he would be 72 or 73.

Cooper explicitly dates the story in 1793, "about seven years" after settlement in the Otsego area commenced.

THE PRAIRIE

1827

Cooper at one point says Leatherstocking is 80; at another that he is some years past 80. If 23 in 1744, he would now be 83.

The author gives the date 1804. Historically, this is absurd; for the country indicated—the Kansas plains disputed by Sioux and Pawnee—had no American squatters, trappers, naturalists, and others then wandering about in it. Lewis and Clark set forth in the spring of 1804. Cooper is really writing about the West of 1820–1825, but has to date the action earlier.

THE DEERSLAYER

Being the FIRST SERIES OF ADVENTURES *of*

LEATHERSTOCKING

THIS is the story of Leatherstocking in the naïve ardor of his youth, the tale set amid the fresh forest scenes of the New York frontier in the period when only the boldest hunters and trappers ventured to intrude upon the domain of the panther and Indian. The time is just before the opening of King George's War (in Europe called the War of the Austrian Succession), in the year 1744. The place is Glimmerglass, or Otsego Lake, lying about seventy miles west of Albany, and nearly as far northwest of the heart of the Catskill Mountains. As the background of the action, we have the mighty struggle of the British and French for the mastery of North America, each side mobilizing in time of war its Indian allies.

Of the four valleys so important to the settlement of the Middle Colonies, the Hudson, Delaware, Mohawk, and Susquehanna, the fourth was the last to be peopled. In various parts of its winding course, the Susquehanna had become known during the seventeenth century to the French, Dutch, and English. Governor Burnet of the Province of New York had established a

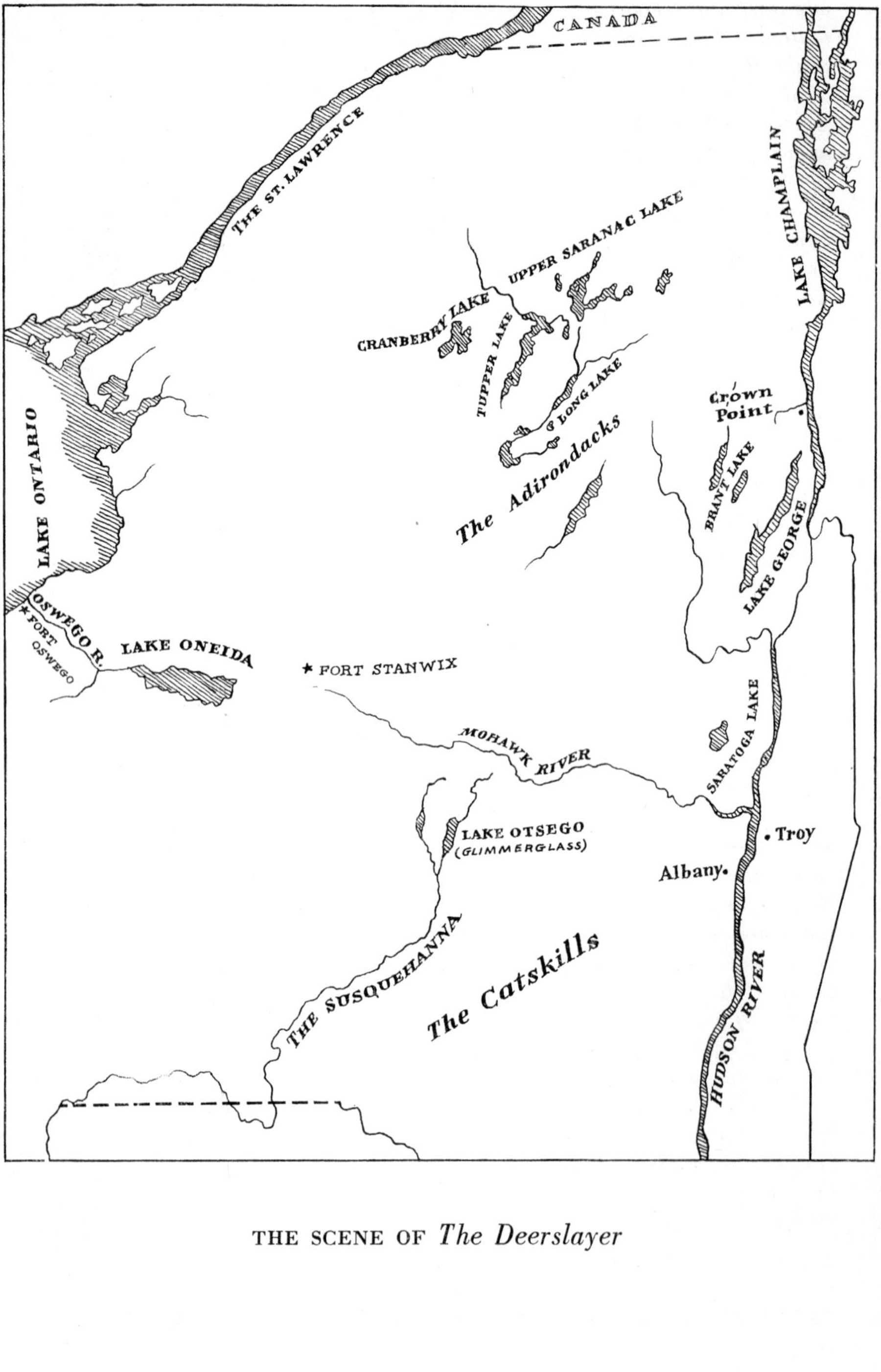

THE SCENE OF *The Deerslayer*

fur-trading post at Oghwaga on the river, well to the southwest of Lake Otsego, in 1722, and fifteen years later Cadwallader Colden, another British administrator, reported that goods could be carried from the lake in flat-bottomed boats through southern New York and Pennsylvania to Chesapeake Bay. But the district about Otsego remained a wild, trackless area until after the Seven Years' War had ended French dominion in North America and the British had negotiated the epochal Treaty of Fort Stanwix with the Indians. Then settlers at last came in and rapidly pushed the frontier farther west.

When this story opens we must think of Glimmerglass, or Lake Otsego, lying in the primeval wilderness, visited only by a rare hunter or trader. Far to the east, as distance was measured in those days, lay the Hudson River belt of settlement; somewhat nearer on the north and northeast was the thin, broken thread of Mohawk River colonization. We must remember that even in 1770 the whole Province had only about 150,000 people, nearly all of them in the coastal and Hudson River areas. At the date when this novel opens, the French had established a chain of forts to command the Great Lakes: Fort Frontenac at what is now Kingston, Ontario, to hold the entrance to the St. Lawrence; Fort Niagara frowning over the passage between Lakes Ontario and Erie; a fort at Detroit to guard the transit between Erie and Huron; and another at Michilimackinac to watch over the area where Lakes Michigan, Superior, and Huron meet. The French had even planted a fort at Crown Point on the western bank of Lake Champlain to threaten New England and New York. The British had a fort at Oswego on the southern shore of Ontario, and military establishments on the Hudson and the Mohawk. The tribe of Hurons, who play the part of the savage foe in this story, were the historic allies of the French.

Here Leatherstocking, at 23 or 24, in the morning of his career, appears already as a hunter of renown, and a young man of clearly marked character. Under the name of Deerslayer, he has to kill his first foe, to solve in his relations with Judith Hutter his first difficult human problems, and to show, under threat of torture and death, the stern fortitude and unbending integrity which remained cardinal traits throughout his life. He is capable of playing an heroic role. Though he reveals great anguish of soul when he has to take human life, he never flinches in battle. He is willing to make any sacrifice for the beautiful Judith Hutter, but not—stained as she is by too free association with garrison officers—to marry her. A master of woodcraft, a devoted comrade of the young Delaware brave Chingachgook, a devout believer in the ethics taught him by the Moravians, a youngster as sincere as he is awkward and uncouth, he is thoroughly attractive. He already has his own philosophy of life, founded on a passionate love of nature and an unshakable faith in the elementary human virtues. But Cooper does not let him stand alone as a pioneer type; for the crime-stained Tom Hutter and the rough, impetuous, unprincipled Harry March are presented as representing another and important side of frontier life.

1

THE INCIDENTS of this tale occurred between the years 1740 and 1745, when the settled portions of the colony of New York were confined to the four Atlantic counties, a narrow belt of country on each side of the Hudson, extending from its mouth to the falls near its head, and to a few advanced "neighborhoods" on the Mohawk and the Scoharie. Broad belts of the virgin wilderness not only reached the shores of the first river, but they even crossed it, stretching away into New England, and affording forest covers to the noiseless moccasin of the native warrior, as he trod the secret and bloody warpath. A bird's-eye view of the whole region east of the Mississippi must then have offered one vast expanse of woods, relieved by a comparatively narrow fringe of cultivation along the sea, dotted by the glittering surfaces of lakes, and intersected by the waving lines of river. In such a vast picture of solemn solitude, the district of country we design to paint sinks into insignificance, though we feel encouraged to proceed by the conviction that, with slight and immaterial distinctions, he who succeeds in giving an accurate idea of any portion of this wild region must necessarily convey a tolerably correct notion of the whole.

Whatever may be the changes produced by man, the eternal round of the seasons is unbroken. Summer and winter, seedtime and harvest, return in their stated order with a sublime precision, affording to man one of the noblest of all the occasions he enjoys of proving the high powers of his far-reaching mind, in compassing the laws that control their exact uniformity, and in calculating their never-ending revolutions. Centuries of summer suns had warmed the tops of the same noble oaks and pines, sending their heats even to the tenacious roots, when voices were heard calling to each other, in the depths of a forest, of which the leafy surface lay bathed in the brilliant light of a cloudless day in June, while the trunks of the trees rose in gloomy grandeur in the shades beneath. The calls were in different tones, evidently proceeding from two men who had lost their way, and were searching in different directions for their path. At length a shout proclaimed success, and presently a man of gigantic mould broke out of the tangled labyrinth of a small swamp, emerging into an opening that appeared to have been formed partly by the ravages of the wind, and partly by those of fire. This little area, which afforded a good view of the sky, although it was pretty well filled with dead trees, lay on the side of one of the high hills, or low mountains, into which nearly the whole surface of the adjacent country was broken.

"Here is room to breathe in!" exclaimed the liberated forester, as soon as he found himself under a clear sky, shaking his huge frame like a mastiff that has just escaped from a snowbank. "Hurrah! Deerslayer; here is daylight, at last, and yonder is the lake."

These words were scarcely uttered when the second forester dashed aside the bushes of the swamp, and appeared in the area. After making a hurried adjustment of his arms and disordered dress, he joined his companion, who had already begun his disposition for a halt.

"Do you know this spot?" demanded the one called Deerslayer, "or do you shout at the sight of the sun?"

"Both, lad, both; I know the spot, and am not sorry to see so useful a fri'nd as the sun. Now we have got the p'ints of the compass in our minds once more, and 'twill be our own faults if we let anything turn them topsy-turvy ag'in, as has just happened. My name is not Hurry Harry, if this be not the very spot where the land hunters 'camped the last summer, and passed a week. See! yonder are the dead bushes of their bower, and here is the spring. Much as I like the sun, boy, I've no occasion for it to tell me it is noon; this stomach of mine is as good a timepiece as is to be found in the colony, and it already p'ints to half-past twelve. So open the wallet, and let us wind up for another six hours' run."

At this suggestion, both set themselves about making the preparations necessary for their usual frugal but hearty meal. We will profit by this pause in the discourse to give the reader some idea of the appearance of the men, each of whom is destined to enact no insignificant part in our legend. It would not have been easy to find a more noble specimen of vigorous manhood than was offered in the person of him who called himself Hurry Harry. His real name was Henry March; but the frontiersmen having caught the practice of giving *sobriquets* from the Indians, the appellation of Hurry was far oftener applied to him than his proper designation, and not unfrequently he was termed Hurry Skurry, a nickname he had obtained from a dashing, reckless, offhand manner, and a physical restlessness that kept him so constantly on the move, as to cause him to be known along the whole line of scattered habitations that lay between the province and the Canadas. The stature of Hurry Harry exceeded six feet four, and being unusually well proportioned, his strength fully realized the idea created by his gigantic frame. The face did not discredit to the rest of the man, for it was both good-humored and handsome. His air was free, and though his manner necessarily partook of the rudeness of a border life, the grandeur that pervaded so noble a physique prevented it from becoming altogether vulgar.

Deerslayer, as Hurry called his companion, was a very different person in appearance, as well as in character. In stature he stood about six feet in his moccasins, but his frame was comparatively light and slender, showing muscles, however, that promised unusual agility, if not unusual strength. His face would have had little to recommend it except youth, were it not for an expression that seldom failed to win upon those who had leisure to examine it, and to yield to the feeling of confidence it created. This expression was simply that of guileless truth, sustained by an earnestness of purpose, and a sincerity of feeling, that rendered it remarkable. At times this air of integrity seemed to be so simple as to awaken the suspicion of a want of the usual means to discriminate between artifice and truth; but few came in serious contact with the man, without losing this distrust in respect for his opinions and motives.

Both these frontiersmen were still young, Hurry having reached the age of six or eight and twenty, while Deerslayer was several years his junior. Their attire needs no particular description, though it may be well to add that it was composed in no small degree of dressed deerskins, and had the usual signs of belonging to those who pass their time between the skirts of civilized society and the boundless forests. There was, notwithstanding, some attention to smartness and the picturesque in the arrangements of Deerslayer's dress, more particularly in the part connected with his arms and accoutrements. His rifle was in perfect condition, the handle of his hunting knife was neatly carved, his powder horn was ornamented with suitable devices lightly cut into the material, and his shot pouch was decorated with wampum. On the other hand, Hurry Harry, either from constitutional recklessness, or from a secret consciousness how little his appearance required artificial aids, wore everything in a careless, slovenly manner, as if he felt a noble scorn for the trifling accessories of dress and ornaments. Perhaps the peculiar effect of his fine form and great stature was increased rather than lessened, by this unstudied and disdainful air of indifference.

"Come, Deerslayer, fall to, and prove that you have a Delaware stomach, as you say you have had a Delaware edication," cried Hurry, setting the example by opening his mouth to receive a slice of cold venison steak that would have made an entire meal for a European peasant; "fall to, lad, and prove your manhood on this poor devil of a doe with your teeth, as you've already done with your rifle."

"Nay, nay, Hurry, there's little manhood in killing a doe, and that, too, out of season; though there might be some in bringing down a painter or a catamount," returned the other, disposing himself to comply. "The Delawares have given me my name, not so much on account of a bold heart, as on account of a quick eye, and an actyve foot. There may not be any cowardyce in overcoming a deer, but sartain it is, there's no great valor."

"The Delawares themselves are no heroes," muttered Hurry through his teeth, the mouth being too full to permit it to be fairly opened, "or they would never have allowed them loping vagabonds, the Mingoes, to make them women."

"That matter is not rightly understood—has never been rightly explained," said Deerslayer earnestly, for he was as zealous a friend as his companion was dangerous as an enemy; "the Mengwe fill the woods with their lies, and misconstruct words and treaties. I have now lived ten years with the Delawares, and know them to be as manful as any other nation, when the proper time to strike comes."

"Harkee, Master Deerslayer, since we are on the subject, we may as well open our minds to each other in a man-to-man way; answer me one question; you have had so much luck among the game as to have gotten a title, it would seem, but did you ever hit anything human or intelligible: did you ever pull trigger on an inimy that was capable of pulling one upon you?"

This question produced a singular collision between mortification and correct feeling, in the bosom of the youth, that was easily to be traced in the workings of his ingenuous countenance. The struggle was short, however; uprightness of heart soon getting the better of false pride and frontier boastfulness.

"To own the truth, I never did," answered Deerslayer; "seeing that a fitting occasion never offered. The Delawares have been peaceable since my sojourn with 'em, and I hold it to be onlawful to take the life of man, except in open and generous warfare."

"What! did you never find a fellow thieving among your traps and skins, and do the law on him with your own hands, by way of saving the magistrates trouble in the settlements, and the rogue himself the cost of the suit?"

"I am no trapper, Hurry," returned the young man proudly: "I live by the rifle, a we'pon at which I will not turn my back on any man of my years, atween the Hudson and the St. Lawrence. I never offer a skin that has not a hole in its head besides them which natur' made to see with or to breathe through."

"Ay, ay, this is all very well, in the animal way, though it makes but a poor figure alongside of scalps and ambushes. Shooting an Indian from an ambush is acting up to his own principles, and now we have what you call a lawful war on our hands, the sooner you wipe that disgrace off your character, the sounder will be your sleep; if it only come from knowing there is one inimy the less prowling in the woods. I shall not frequent your society long, friend Natty, unless you look higher than four-footed beasts to practyse your rifle on."

"Our journey is nearly ended, you say, Master March, and we can part tonight, if you see occasion. I have a fri'nd waiting for me, who will think it no disgrace to consort with a fellow-creatur' that has never yet slain his kind."

"I wish I knew what has brought that skulking Delaware into this part of the country so early in the season," muttered Hurry to himself, in a way to show equally distrust and a recklessness of its betrayal. "Where did you say the young chief was to give you the meeting?"

"At a small round rock, near the foot of the lake, where, they tell me, the tribes are given to resorting to make their treaties, and to bury their hatchets. This rock have I often heard the Delawares mention, though lake and rock are equally strangers to me. The country is claimed by both Mingoes and Mohicans, and is a sort of common territory to fish and hunt through, in time of peace, though what it may become in wartime, the Lord only knows!"

"Common territory!" exclaimed Hurry, laughing aloud. "I should like to know what Floating Tom Hutter would say to that? He claims the lake as his own property, in vartue of fifteen years' possession, and will not be likely to give it up to either Mingo or Delaware without a battle for it."

"And what will the colony say to such a quarrel? All this country must have some owner, the gentry pushing their cravings into the wilderness, even where they never dare to ventur', in their own persons, to look at the land they own."

"That may do in other quarters of the colony, Deerslayer, but it will not do here. Not a human being, the Lord excepted, owns a foot of sile in this part of the country. Pen was never put to paper consarning either hill or valley here-a-way, as I've heard old Tom say time and ag'in, and so he claims the best right to it of any man breathing; and what Tom claims, he'll be very likely to maintain."

"By what I've heard you say, Hurry, this Floating Tom must be an oncommon mortal; neither Mingo, Delaware, nor paleface. His possession, too, has been long, by your tell, and altogether beyond frontier endurance. What's the man's history and natur'?"

"Why, as to old Tom's human natur', it is not much like other men's human natur', but more like a muskrat's human natur', seeing that he takes more to the ways of that animal than to the ways of any other fellow-creatur'. Some think he was a free liver on the salt water, in his youth, and a companion of a sartain Kidd, who was hanged for piracy, long afore you and I were born or acquainted, and that he came up into these regions, thinking that the King's cruisers could never cross the mountains, and that he might enjoy the plunder peaceably in the woods."

"Then he was wrong, Hurry; very wrong. A man can enjoy plunder *peaceably* nowhere."

"That's much as his turn of mind may happen to be. I've known them that never could enjoy it at all, unless it was in the midst of a jollification, and them ag'in that enjoyed it best in a corner. Some men have no peace if they don't find plunder, and some if they do. Human natur' is crooked in these matters. Old Tom seems to belong to neither set, as he enjoys his, if plunder he has really got, with his darters, in a very quiet and comfortable way, and wishes for no more."

"Ay, he has darters, too; I've heard the Delawares, who've hunted this a way, tell their histories of these young women. Is there no mother, Hurry?"

"There was *once,* as in reason; but she has now been dead and sunk these two good years."

"Anan?" said Deerslayer, looking up at his companion in a little surprise.

"Dead and sunk, I say, and I hope that's good English. The old fellow lowered his wife into the lake, by way of seeing the last of her, as I can testify, being an eyewitness of the ceremony; but whether Tom did it to save digging, which is no easy job among roots, or out of a consait that water washes away sin sooner than 'arth, is more than I can say."

"Was the poor woman oncommon wicked, that her husband should take so much pains with her body?"

"Not onreasonable; though she had her faults. I consider Judith Hutter to have been as graceful, and about as likely to make a good ind as any woman who had lived so long beyond the sound of church bells; and I conclude old Tom sunk her as much by way of *saving* pains, as by way of *taking* it. There was a little steel in her temper, it's true, and, as old Hutter is pretty much flint, they struck out sparks once-and-a-while; but, on the whole, they might be said to live amicable like. When they did kindle, the listeners got some such insights into their past lives, as one gets into the darker parts of the woods, when a stray gleam of sunshine finds its way down to the roots of the trees. But Judith I shall always esteem, as it's recommend enough to one woman to be the mother of such a creatur' as her darter, Judith Hutter!"

"Ay, Judith was the name the Delawares mentioned, though it was pronounced after a fashion of their own. From their discourse, I do not think the girl would much please my fancy."

"Thy fancy!" exclaimed March, taking fire equally at the indifference and at the presumption of his companion, "what the devil have you to do with a fancy, and that, too, consarning one like Judith? You are but a boy—a sapling, that has scarce got root. Judith has had *men* among her suitors, ever since she was fifteen; which is now near five years; and will not be apt even to cast a look upon a half-grown creatur' like you!"

"It is June, and there is not a cloud atween us and the sun, Hurry, so all this heat is not wanted," answered the other, altogether undisturbed; "anyone may have a fancy, and a squirrel has a right to make up his mind touching a catamount."

"Ay, but it might not be wise, always, to let the catamount know it," growled March. "But you're young and thoughtless, and I'll overlook your ignorance. Come, Deerslayer," he added, with a good-natured laugh, after pausing a moment to reflect, "come, Deerslayer, we are sworn fri'nds, and will not quarrel about a light-minded, jilting jade, just because she happens to be handsome; more especially as you have never seen her. Judith is only for a man whose teeth show the full marks, and it's foolish to be afeard of a boy. What *did* the Delawares say of the hussy? for an Indian, after all, has his notions of womankind, as well as a white man."

"They said she was fair to look on, and pleasant of speech; but overgiven to admirers, and light-minded."

"They are devils incarnate! After all, what schoolmaster is a match for an Indian, in looking into natur'? Some people think they are only good on a trail or the warpath, but I say that they are philosophers, and understand a man as well as they understand a beaver, and a woman as well as they understand either. Now that's Judith's character to a ribbon! To own the truth to you, Deerslayer, I should have married the gal two years since, if it had not been for two particular things, one of which was this very light-mindedness."

"And what may have been the other?" demanded the hunter, who continued to eat like one that took very little interest in the subject.

"T'other was an insartainty about her having *me*. The hussy is handsome, and she knows it. Boy, not a tree that is growing in these hills is straighter, or waves in the wind with an easier bend, nor did you ever see the doe that bounded with a more nat'ral motion. If that was all, every tongue would sound her praises; but she has such failings that I find it hard to overlook them, and sometimes I swear I'll never visit the lake ag'in."

"Which is the reason that you always come back? Nothing is ever made more sure by swearing about it."

"Ah, Deerslayer, you are a novelty in these partic'lars; keeping as true to edication as if you had never left the settlements. With me the case is different, and I never want to clinch an idee, that I do not feel a wish to swear about it. If you know'd all that I know consarning Judith, you'd find a justification for a little cussing. Now, the officers sometimes stray over to the lake, from the forts on the Mohawk, to fish and hunt, and then the creatur' seems beside herself! You can see in the manner which she wears her finery, and the airs she gives herself with the gallants."

"That is unseemly in a poor man's darter," returned Deerslayer gravely, "the officers are all gentry, and can only look on such as Judith with evil intentions."

"There's the unsartainty, and the damper! I have my misgivings about a particular captain, and Jude has no one to blame but her own folly, if I'm right. On the whole, I wish to look upon her as modest and becoming, and yet the clouds that drive among these hills are not more unsartain. Not a dozen white men have ever laid eyes upon her since she was a child, and yet her airs, with two or three of these officers, are extinguishers!"

"I would think no more of such a woman, but turn my mind altogether to the forest; *that* will not deceive you, being ordered and ruled by a hand that never wavers."

"If you know'd Judith, you would see how much easier it is to say this than it would be to do it. Could I bring my mind to be easy about the officers, I would carry the gal off to the Mohawk by force, make her marry me in spite of her whiffling, and leave old Tom to the care of Hetty, his other child, who, if she be not as handsome or as quick-witted as her sister, is much the most dutiful."

"Is there another bird in the same nest?" asked Deerslayer, raising his eyes with a species of half-awakened curiosity,—"the Delawares spoke to me only of one."

"That's nat'ral enough, when Judith Hutter and Hetty Hutter are in question. Hetty is only comely, while her sister, I tell thee, boy, is such another as is not to be found atween this and the sea: Judith is as full of wit, and talk, and cunning, as an old Indian orator, while poor Hetty is at the best but 'compass meant us.' "

"Anan?" inquired, again, the Deerslayer.

"Why, what the officers call 'compass meant us,' which I understand to signify that she means always to go in the right direction, but sometimes doesn't know how. 'Compass' for the p'int, and 'meant us' for the intention. No, poor Hetty is what I call on the varge of ignorance, and sometimes she stumbles on one side of the line, and sometimes on t'other."

"Them are beings that the Lord has in his 'special care," said Deerslayer, solemnly; "for he looks carefully to all who fall short of their proper share of reason. The redskins honor and respect them who are so gifted, knowing that the Evil Spirit delights more to dwell in an artful body, than in one that has no cunning to work upon."

"I'll answer for it, then, that he will not remain long with poor Hetty; for the child is just 'compass meant us,' as I have told you. Old Tom has a feeling for the gal, and so has Judith, quick-witted and glorious as she is herself; else would I not answer for her being altogether safe among the sort of men that sometimes meet on the lake shore."

"I thought this water an onknown and little-frequented sheet," observed the Deerslayer, evidently uneasy at the idea of being too near the world.

"It's all that, lad, the eyes of twenty white men never having been laid on it; still, twenty true-bred frontiersmen—hunters and trappers, and scouts, and the like,—can do a deal of mischief if they try. 'Twould be an awful thing to me, Deerslayer, did I find Judith married, after an absence of six months!"

"Have you the gal's faith, to encourage you to hope otherwise?"

"Not at all. I know not how it is: I'm good-looking, boy,—that much I can see in any spring on which the sun shines,—and yet I could not get the hussy to a promise, or even a cordial willing smile, though she will laugh by the hour. If she *has* dared to marry in my absence, she'll be like to know the pleasures of widowhood afore she is twenty!"

"You would not harm the man she has chosen, Hurry, simply because she found him more to her liking than yourself?"

"Why not? If an inimy crosses my path, will I not beat him out of it! Look at me! am I a man like to let any sneaking, crawling, skin trader get the better of me in a matter that touches me as near as the kindness of Judith Hutter? Besides, when we live beyond law, we must be our own judges and executioners. And if a man *should* be found dead in the woods, who is there to say who slew him, even admitting that the colony took the matter in hand and made a stir about it?"

"If that man should be Judith Hutter's husband, after what has passed, I might tell enough, at least, to put the colony on the trail."

"You!—half-grown, venison-hunting bantling! You dare to think of informing against Hurry Harry in so much as a matter touching a mink or a woodchuck!"

"I would dare to speak truth, Hurry, consarning you or any man that ever lived."

March looked at his companion, for a moment, in silent amazement; then seizing him by the throat with both hands, he shook his comparatively slight frame with a violence that menaced the dislocation of some of the bones. Nor was this done jocularly, for anger flashed from the giant's eyes, and there were certain signs that seemed to threaten much more earnestness than the occasion would appear to call for. Whatever might be the real intention of March, and it is probable there was none settled in his mind, it is certain that he was unusually aroused; and most men who found themselves throttled by one of a mould so gigantic, in such a mood, and in a solitude so deep and helpless, would have felt intimidated, and tempted to yield even the right. Not so, however, with Deerslayer. His countenance remained unmoved; his hand did not shake, and his answer was given in a voice that did not resort to the artifice of louder tones, even by way of proving its owner's resolution.

"You may shake, Hurry, until you bring down the mountain," he said quietly, "but nothing beside truth will you shake from me. It is probable that Judith Hutter has no husband to slay, and you may never have a chance to waylay one, else would I tell her of your threat, in the first conversation I held with the gal."

March released his grip, and sat regarding the other in silent astonishment.

"I thought we had been friends," he at length added; "but you've got the last secret of mine that will ever enter your ears."

"I want none, if they are to be like this. I know we live in the woods, Hurry, and are thought to be beyond human laws,—and perhaps we are so, in fact, whatever it may be in right,—but there is a law and a lawmaker, that rule across the whole continent. He that flies in the face of either need not call me a friend."

"Damme, Deerslayer, if I do not believe you are at heart a Moravian, and no fair-minded, plain-dealing hunter, as you've pretended to be!"

"Fair-minded or not, Hurry, you will find me as plain-dealing in deeds as I am in words. But this giving way to sudden anger is foolish, and proves how little you have sojourned with the red man. Judith

Hutter no doubt is still single, and you spoke but as the tongue ran, and not as the heart felt. There's my hand, and we will say and think no more about it."

Hurry seemed more surprised than ever; then he burst forth in a loud, good-natured laugh, which brought tears to his eyes. After this he accepted the offered hand, and the parties became friends.

" 'Twould have been foolish to quarrel about an idee," March cried, as he resumed his meal, "and more like lawyers in the towns than like sensible men in the woods. They tell me, Deerslayer, much ill blood grows out of idees among the people in the lower counties, and that they sometimes get to extremities upon them."

"That do they,—that do they; and about other matters that might better be left to take care of themselves. I have heard the Moravians say that there are lands in which men quarrel even consarning their religion; and if they can get their tempers up on such a subject, Hurry, the Lord have marcy on 'em. Howsever, there is no occasion for our following their example, and more especially about a husband that this Judith Hutter may never see, or never wish to see. For my part, I feel more cur'osity about the feeble-witted sister than about your beauty. There's something that comes close to a man's feelin's, when he meets with a fellow-creatur' that has all the outward show of an accountable mortal, and who fails of being what he seems, only through a lack of reason. This is bad enough in a man, but when it comes to a woman, and she a young, and maybe a winning creatur' it touches all the pitiful thoughts his natur' has. God knows, Hurry, that such poor things be defenceless enough with all their wits about 'em; but it's a cruel fortun' when that great protector and guide fails 'em."

"Harkee, Deerslayer,—you know what the hunters, and trappers, and peltry-men in general be; and their best friends will not deny that they are headstrong and given to having their own way, without much bethinking 'em of other people's rights or feelin's,—and yet I don't think the man is to be found, in all this region, who would harm Hetty Hutter, if he could; no, not even a redskin."

"Therein, fri'nd Hurry, you do the Delawares, at least, and all their allied tribes, only justice, for a redskin looks upon a being thus struck by God's power as especially under his care. I rejoice to hear what you say, however, I rejoice to hear it; but as the sun is beginning to turn towards the a'ternoon's sky, had we not better strike the trail ag'in, and make forward, that we may get an opportunity of seeing these wonderful sisters?"

Harry March giving a cheerful assent, the remnants of the meal were soon collected; then the travellers shouldered their packs, resumed their arms, and, quitting the little area of light, they again plunged into the deep shadows of the forest.

2

PUSHING forward into the forest that bordered Lake Otsego, Hurry Harry and Deerslayer soon came to the spot where Hurry had concealed his canoe. It lay under the trunk of a huge prostrate linden or basswood, and neither it nor its contents—seats, paddles, fishing rods—had been disturbed. "Everything is as snug as if it had been left in an old woman's cupboard," exclaimed Hurry. He shouldered the craft; Deerslayer led the way, opening a path through the bushes. After ten minutes, they broke suddenly into brilliant sunlight on a low gravelly point, the lake lying before them.

Its length was about three leagues, while its breadth was irregular, expanding to half a league, or even more, opposite to the point, and contracting to less than half that distance, more to the southward. Of course, its margin was irregular, being indented by bays, and broken by many projecting, low points. At its northern, or nearest end, it was bounded by an isolated mountain, lower land falling off east and west, gracefully relieving the sweep of the outline. Still the character of the country was mountainous; high hills, or low mountains, rising abruptly from the water, on quite nine tenths of its circuit. The exceptions, indeed, only served a little to vary the scene; and even beyond the parts of the shore that were comparatively low, the background was high, though more distant.

But the most striking peculiarities of this scene were its solemn solitude and sweet repose. On all sides, wherever the eye turned, nothing met it but the mirror-like surface of the lake, the placid view of heaven, and the dense setting of woods. So rich and fleecy were the outlines of the forest, that scarce an opening could be seen, the whole visible earth, from the rounded mountaintop to the water's edge, presenting one unvaried hue of unbroken verdure. As if vegetation were not satisfied with a triumph so complete, the trees overhung the lake itself, shooting out toward the light; and there were miles along its eastern shore, where a boat might have pulled beneath the branches of dark Rembrandt-looking hemlocks, "quivering aspens," and melancholy pines. In a word, the hand of man had never yet defaced or deformed any part of this native scene, which lay bathed in the sunlight, a glorious picture of affluent forest grandeur, softened by the balminess of June, and relieved by the beautiful variety afforded by the presence of so broad an expanse of water.

"This is grand!—'tis solemn!—'tis an edication of itself, to look upon!" exclaimed Deerslayer, as he stood leaning on his rifle, and gazing to the right and left, north and south, above and beneath, in whichever direction his eye could wander; "not a tree disturbed even by redskin hand, as I can discover, but everything left in the ordering of the Lord, to live and die according to his own designs and laws! Hurry, your Judith ought to be a moral and well-disposed young woman, if she has passed half the time you mention in the center of a spot so favored."

"That's naked truth; and yet the gal has the vagaries. *All* her time has not been passed here, howsever, old Tom having the custom, afore I know'd him, of going to spend the winters in the neighborhood of the settlers, or under the guns of the forts.[1] No, no, Jude has caught more than is for her good from the settlers, and especially from the gallantifying officers."

"If she has—if she has, Hurry, this is a school to set her mind right ag'in. But what is this I see off here, abreast of us, that seems too small for an island, and too large for a boat, though it stands in the midst of the water?"

"Why, that is what these gallanting gentry from the forts call Muskrat Castle; and old Tom himself will grin at the name, though it bears so hard on his own natur' and character. 'Tis the stationary house, there being two; this, which never moves, and the other, that floats, being sometimes in one part of the lake and sometimes in another.

[1] Nearly twenty years before this period, Fort Bull and Fort Williams had been built by the British on the site of present-day Rome, New York, to protect the portage between the Mohawk River and Wood Creek, a tributary of Oneida Lake. Still earlier, Fort Hunter, just west of Schenectady, had been built by direction of Queen Anne herself.—Ed.

The last goes by the name of the ark, though what may be the meaning of the word is more than I can tell you."

"It must come from the missionaries, Hurry, whom I have heard speak and read of such a thing. They say that the 'arth was once covered with water, and that Noah, with his children, was saved from drowning by building a vessel called an ark, in which he embarked in season. Some of the Delawares believe this tradition, and some deny it; but it behooves you and me, as white men born, to put our faith in its truth. Do you see anything of this ark?"

" 'Tis down south, no doubt, or anchored in some of the bays. But the canoe is ready, and fifteen minutes will carry two such paddles as your'n and mine to the castle."

At this suggestion, Deerslayer helped his companion to place the different articles in the canoe, which was already afloat. This was no sooner done than the two frontiersmen embarked, and by a vigorous push sent the light bark some eight or ten rods from the shore. Hurry now took the seat in the stern, while Deerslayer placed himself forward, and by leisurely but steady strokes of the paddles, the canoe glided across the placid sheet, toward the extraordinary-looking structure that the former had styled Muskrat Castle. Several times the men ceased paddling, and looked about them at the scene, as new glimpses opened from behind points, enabling them to see farther down the lake, or to get broader views of the wooded mountains. The only changes, however, were in the new forms of the hills, the varying curvature of the bays, and the wider reaches of the valley south; the whole earth apparently being clothed in a gala dress of leaves.

"This *is* a sight to warm the heart!" exclaimed Deerslayer, when they had thus stopped for the fourth or fifth time; "the lake seems made to let us get an insight into the noble forests; and land and water alike stand in the beauty of God's providence! Do you say, Hurry, that there is no man who calls himself lawful owner of all these glories?"

"None but the King, lad. He may pretend to some right of that natur', but he is so far away that his claim will never trouble old Tom Hutter, who has got possession, and is like to keep it as long as his life lasts. Tom is no squatter, not being on land; I call him a floater."

"I invy that man! I know it's wrong, and I strive ag'in the feelin', but I invy that man! Don't think, Hurry, that I'm consarting any plan to put myself in his moccasins, for such a thought doesn't harbor in my mind; but I can't help a little invy? 'Tis a nat'ral feeling', and the best of us are but nat'ral, a'ter all, and give way to such feelin's at times."

"You've only to marry Hetty to inherit half the estate," cried Hurry, laughing; "the gal is comely; nay, if it wasn't for her sister's beauty she would be even handsome; and then her wits are so small that you may easily convart her into one of your own way of thinking, in all things. Do *you* take Hetty off the old fellow's hands, and *I*'ll engage he'll give you an interest in every deer you can knock over within five miles of his lake."

"Does game abound?" suddenly demanded the other, who paid but little attention to March's raillery.

"It has the country to itself. Scarce a trigger is pulled on it; and as for the trappers, this is not a region they greatly frequent. I ought not to be so much here myself, but Jude pulls one way, while the beaver pulls another. More than a hundred Spanish dollars has that creatur' cost me the last two seasons, and yet I could not forego the wish to look upon her face once more."

"Do the red men often visit this lake, Hurry?" continued Deerslayer, pursuing his own train of thought.

"Why, they come and go; sometimes in parties, and sometimes singly. The country seems to belong to no native tribe in particular; and so it has fallen into the hands of the Hutter tribe. The old man tells me that some sharp ones have been wheedling the Mohawks for an Indian deed, in order to get a title out of the colony; but nothing has come of it, seeing that no one heavy enough for such a trade has yet meddled with the matter. The hunters have a good life lease still of this wilderness."

"So much the better, so much the better, Hurry. If I was King of England, the man that felled one of these trees without good occasion for the timber, should be banished to a desarted and forlorn region, in which no four-footed animal ever trod. Right glad am I that Chingachgook app'inted our meeting on this lake, for hitherto eye of mine never looked on such a glorious spectacle."

"That's because you've kept so much among the Delawares, in whose country there are no lakes. Now, farther north and farther west these bits of water abound; and you're young, and may yet live to see 'em. But though there be other lakes, Deerslayer, there's no other Judith Hutter!"

At this remark his companion smiled, and then he dropped his paddle into the water, as if in consideration of a lover's haste. Both now pulled vigorously until they got within a hundred yards of the castle, as Hurry familiarly called the house of Hutter, when they again ceased paddling; the admirer of Judith restraining his impatience the more readily, as he perceived that the building was untenanted, at the moment. This new pause was to enable Deerslayer to survey the singular edifice, which was of a construction so novel as to merit a particular description.

Muskrat Castle, as the house had been facetiously named by some waggish officer, stood in the open lake, at a distance of fully a quarter of a mile from the nearest shore. On every other side the water extended much farther, the precise position being distant about two miles from the northern end of the sheet, and near, if not quite, a mile from its eastern shore. As there was not the smallest appearance of any island, but the house stood on piles, with the water flowing beneath it, and Deerslayer had already discovered that the lake was of a great depth, he was fain to ask an explanation of this singular circumstance. Hurry solved the difficulty by telling him that on this spot alone, a long, narrow shoal, which extended for a few hundred yards in a north and south direction, rose within six or eight feet of the surface of the lake, and that Hutter had driven piles into it, and placed his habitation on them, for the purpose of security.

"The old fellow was burnt out three times, atween the Indians and the hunters; and in one affray with the redskins he lost his only son, since which time he has taken to the water for safety. No one can attack him here, without coming in a boat, and the plunder and scalps would scarce be worth the trouble of digging out canoes. Then it's by no means sartain which would whip in such a scrimmage, for old Tom is well supplied with arms and ammunition, and the castle, as you may see, is a tight breastwork ag'in light shot."

Deerslayer had some theoretical knowledge of frontier warfare, though he had never yet been called on to raise his hand in anger against a fellow-creature. He saw that Hurry did not overrate the strength of this position in a military point of view, since it would not be easy to attack it without exposing the assailants to the fire of the besieged. A good deal of art had also been manifested in the disposition of the timber of which the building was constructed and which afforded a protection much greater than was usual to the ordinary log cabins of the frontier. The sides and ends were composed of the trunks of large pines, cut about nine feet long, and placed upright, instead of being laid horizontally, as was the practice of the country. These logs were squared on three sides, and had large tenons on each end. Massive sills were secured on the heads of the piles, with suitable grooves dug out of their upper surfaces, which had been squared for the purpose, and the lower tenons of the upright pieces were placed in these grooves, giving them a secure fastening below. Plates had been laid on the upper ends of the upright logs, and were kept in their places by a similar contrivance; the several corners of the structure being well fastened by scarfing and pinning the sills and plates. The floors were made of smaller logs, similarly squared, and the roof was composed of light poles, firmly united, and well covered with bark. The effect of this ingenious arrangement was to give its owner a house that could be approached only by water, the sides of which were composed of logs closely wedged together, which were two feet thick in their thinnest parts, and which could be separated only by a deliberate and laborious use of human hands, or by the slow operation of time. The outer surface of the building was rude and uneven, the logs being of unequal sizes; but the squared surfaces within gave both the sides and floor as uniform an appearance as was desired, either for use or show. The chimney was not the least singular portion of the castle, as Hurry made his companion observe, while he explained the process by which it had been made. The material was a stiff clay, properly worked, which had been put together in a mould of sticks, and suffered to harden, a foot or two at a time, commencing at the bottom. When the entire chimney had thus been raised, and had been properly bound in with outward props, a brisk fire was kindled, and kept going until it was burned to something like a brick red. This had not been an easy operation, nor had it succeeded entirely; but by dint of filling the cracks with fresh clay, a safe fireplace and chimney had been obtained in the end. This part of the work stood on the log floor, secured beneath by an extra pile. There were a few other peculiarities about this dwelling, which will better appear in the course of the narrative.

"Old Tom is full of contrivances," added Hurry, "and he set his heart on the success of his chimney, which threatened more than once to give out altogether; but parseverance will even overcome smoke; and now he has a comfortable cabin of it, though it did promise, at one time, to be a chinky sort of a flue to carry flames and fire."

"You seem to know the whole history of the castle, Hurry, chimney and sides," said Deerslayer, smiling; "is love so overcoming that it causes a man to study the story of his sweetheart's habitation?"

"Partly that, lad, and partly eyesight," returned the good-natured giant, laughing; "there was a large gang of us in the lake, the summer the old fellow built, and we helped him along with the job. I raised no small part of the weight of them uprights with my own shoulders, and the axes flew, I can inform you, Master Natty, while we were bee-ing it among the trees ashore. The old devil is no way stingy about food, and as we had often eat at his hearth, we thought we would just house him comfortably, afore we went to Albany with our skins. Yes, many is the meal I've swallowed in Tom Hutter's cabins; and Hetty, though so weak in the way of wits, has a wonderful particular way about a frying pan or a gridiron!"

While the parties were thus discoursing, the canoe had been gradually drawing nearer to the castle, and was now so close as to require but a single stroke of a paddle to reach the landing. This was at a floored platform in front of the entrance, that might have been some twenty feet square.

"Old Tom calls this sort of a wharf his dooryard," observed Hurry, as he fastened the canoe, after he and his companion had left it; "and the gallants from the forts have named it the castle court, though what a court can have to do here is more than I can tell you, seeing that there is no law. 'Tis as I supposed; not a soul within, but the whole family is off on a v'y'ge of discovery!"

While Hurry was bustling about the dooryard, examining the fishing spears, rods, nets, and other similar appliances of a frontier cabin, Deerslayer, whose manner was altogether more rebuked and quiet, entered the building with a curiosity that was not usually exhibited by one so long trained in Indian habits. The interior of the castle was as faultlessly neat as its exterior was novel. The entire space, some twenty feet by forty, was subdivided into several, small sleeping rooms; the apartment into which he first entered, serving equally for the ordinary uses of its inmates, and for a kitchen. The furniture was of the strange mixture that it is not uncommon to find in the remotely situated log tenements of the interior. Most of it was rude, and to the last degree rustic; but there was a clock, with a handsome case of dark wood, in a corner, and two or three chairs, with a table and bureau, that had evidently come from some dwelling of more than usual pretension. The clock was industriously ticking, but its leaden-looking hands did no discredit to their dull aspect, for they pointed to the hour of eleven, though the sun plainly showed it was some time past the turn of the day. There was also a dark, massive chest. The kitchen utensils were of the simplest kind, and far from numerous, but every article was in its place, and showed the nicest care in its condition.

After Deerslayer had cast a look about him in the outer room, he raised a wooden latch, and entered a narrow passage that divided the inner end of the house into two equal parts. Frontier usages being no way scrupulous, and his curiosity being strongly excited, the young man now opened a door, and found himself in a bedroom. A single glance sufficed to show that the apartment belonged to females. The bed was of the feathers of wild geese, and filled nearly to overflowing; but it lay in a rude bunk, raised only a foot from the floor. On one side of it were arranged, on pegs, various dresses, of a quality much superior to what one would expect to meet in such a place, with ribbons and other similar articles to correspond. Pretty shoes, with handsome silver buckles, such as were then worn by females in easy circumstances, were not wanting; and no less than six fans, of gay colors, were placed half open, in a way to catch the eye by their conceits and hues. Even the pillow, on this side of the bed, was covered with finer linen than its companion, and it was ornamented with a small ruffle. A cap, coquettishly decorated with ribbons, hung above it, and a pair of long gloves, such as were rarely used in those days by persons of the laboring classes, were pinned ostentatiously to it, as if with an intention to exhibit them there, if they could not be shown on the owner's arms.

All this Deerslayer saw, and noted with a degree of minuteness that would have done credit to the habitual observation of his friends, the Delawares. Nor did he fail to perceive the distinction that existed between the appearances on the different sides of the bed, the head of which stood against the wall. On that opposite to the one just described, everything was homely and uninviting, except through its perfect neatness. The few garments that were hanging from the pegs were of the coarsest materials and of the commonest forms, while nothing seemed made for show. Of ribbons there was not one; nor was there either cap or kerchief beyond those which Hutter's daughters might be fairly entitled to wear.

It was now several years since Deerslayer had been in a spot especially devoted to the uses of females of his own color and race. The sight brought back to his mind a rush of childish recollections; and he lingered in the room with a tenderness of feeling to which he had long been a stranger. He bethought him of his mother, whose homely vestments he remembered to have seen hanging on pegs like those which he felt must belong to Hetty Hutter; and he bethought himself of a sister, whose incipient and native taste for finery had exhibited itself somewhat in the manner of that of Judith, though necessarily in a less degree. These little resemblances opened a long-hidden vein of sensations; and as he quitted the room, it was with a saddened mien. He looked no further, but returned slowly and thoughtfully toward the dooryard.

"Old Tom has taken to a new calling, and has been trying his hand at the traps," cried Hurry, who had been coolly examining the borderer's implements; "if that is his humor, and you're disposed to remain in these parts, we can make an oncommon comfortable season of it; for, while the old man and I out-knowledge the beaver, you can fish, and knock down the deer, to keep body and soul together. We always give the poorest hunters half a share, but one as actyve and sartain as yourself might expect a full one."

"Thank'ee, Hurry; thank'ee, with all my heart—but I do a little beavering for myself as occasions offer. 'Tis true, the Delawares call me Deerslayer, but it's not so much because I'm pretty fatal with the venison as because that while I kill so many bucks and does, I've never yet taken the life of a fellow-creatur'. They say their traditions do not tell of another who had shed so much blood of animals that had not shed the blood of man."

"I hope they don't account you chickenhearted, lad? A faint-hearted man is like a no-tailed beaver."

"I don't believe, Hurry, that they account me as out-of-the-way timorsome, even though they may not account me as out-of-the-way brave. But I'm not quarrelsome; and that goes a great way toward keeping blood off the hands, among the hunters and redskins; and then, Harry March, it keeps blood off the conscience, too."

"Well, for my part I account game, a redskin, and a Frenchman as pretty much the same thing; though I'm as onquarrelsome a man, too, as there is in all the colonies. I despise a quarreller as I do a cur dog; but one has no need to be overscrupulsome when it's the right time to show the flint."

"I look upon him as the most of a man who acts nearest the right, Hurry. But this is a glorious spot, and my eyes never a-weary looking at it!"

" 'Tis your first acquaintance with a lake; and these idees come over us all at such times. Lakes have a general character, as I say, being pretty much water and land, and points and bays."

As this definition by no means met the feelings that were uppermost in the mind of the young hunter, he made no immediate answer, but stood gazing at the dark hills and the glassy water in silent enjoyment.

"Have the Governor's or the King's people given this lake a name?" he suddenly asked, as if struck with a new idea. "If they've not begun to blaze their trees, and set up their compasses, and line off their maps, it's likely they've not bethought them to disturb natur' with a name."

"They've not got to that, yet; and the last time I went in with skins, one of the King's surveyors was questioning me consarning all the region hereabouts. He had heard that there was a lake in this quarter, and had got some general notions about it, such as that there was water and hills; but how much of either, he know'd no more than you know of the Mohawk tongue.[1] I didn't open the trap any wider than was necessary, giving him but poor encouragement in the way of farms and clearings. In short, I left on his mind some such opinion of this country as a man gets of a spring of dirty water, with a path to it that is so muddy that one mires afore he sets out. He told me they hadn't got the spot down yet, on their maps; though I conclude that is a mistake, for he showed me his parchment, and there is a lake down on it where there is no lake in fact, and which is about fifty miles from the place where it ought to be, if they meant it for this. I don't think my account will encourage him to mark down another, by way of improvement."

Here Hurry laughed heartily, such tricks being particularly grateful to a set of men who dreaded the approaches of civilization as a curtailment of their own lawless empire. The egregious errors that existed

[1] Actually, two Dutchmen interested in this region had reached Otsego in 1614 or 1615; the upper Susquehanna area had been ceded by the Indians to the British in 1684; and the Province granted a patent for a tract at the north end of the lake to one J. J. Petrie in 1740.—Ed.

in the maps of the day, all of which were made in Europe, were, moreover, a standing topic of ridicule among them; for, if they had not science enough to make any better themselves, they had sufficient local information to detect the gross blunders contained in those that existed. Any one who will take the trouble to compare these unanswerable evidences of the topographical skill of our fathers a century since, with the more accurate sketches of our own time, will at once perceive that the men of the woods had a sufficient justification for all their criticism on this branch of the skill of the Colonial governments, which did not at all hesitate to place a river or a lake a degree or two out of the way, even though they lay within a day's march of the inhabited parts of the country.

"I'm glad it has no name," resumed Deerslayer, "or, at least, no paleface name; for their christenings always foretell waste and destruction. No doubt, howsever, the redskins have their modes of knowing it, and the hunters and trappers, too; they are likely to call the place by something reasonable and resembling."

"As for the tribes, each has its own tongue, and its own way of calling things; and they treat this part of the world just as they treat all others. Among ourselves, we've got to calling the place the Glimmerglass, seeing that its whole basin is so often fringed with pines, cast upward from its face; as if it would throw back the hills that hang over it."

"There is an outlet, I know, for all lakes have outlets, and the rock at which I am to meet Chingachgook stands near an outlet. Has *that* no colony name yet?"

"In that particular they've got the advantage of us, having one end, and that the biggest, in their own keeping: they've given it a name which has found its way up to its source; names nat'rally working up stream. No doubt, Deerslayer, you've seen the Susquehanna, down in the Delaware country?"

"That have I, and hunted along its banks a hundred times."

"That and this are the same in fact, and, I suppose, the same in sound. I am glad they've been compelled to keep the red men's name, for it would be too hard to rob them of both land and name!"

Deerslayer made no answer; but he stood leaning on his rifle, gazing at the view which so much delighted him. The reader is not to suppose, however, that it was the picturesque alone which so strongly attracted his attention. The spot was very lovely, of a truth, and it was then seen in one of its most favorable moments, the surface of the lake being as smooth as glass and as limpid as pure air, throwing back the mountains, clothed in dark pines, along the whole of its eastern boundary, the points thrusting forward their trees even to nearly horizontal lines, while the bays were seen glittering through an occasional arch beneath, left by a vault fretted with branches and leaves. It was the air of deep repose—the solitudes, that spoke of scenes and forests untouched by the hands of man—the reign of nature, in a word, that gave so much pure delight to one of his habits and turn of mind. Still, he felt, though it was unconsciously, like a poet also. If he found a pleasure in studying this large, and to him unusual opening into the mysteries and forms of the woods, as one is gratified in getting broader views of any subject that has long occupied his thoughts, he was not insensible to the innate loveliness of such a landscape neither, but felt a portion of that soothing of the spirit which is a common attendant of a scene so thoroughly pervaded by the holy calm of nature.

Hurry Harry thought more of the beauties of Judith Hutter than of those of the Glimmerglass and its accompanying scenery. As soon as he had taken a sufficiently intimate survey of Floating Tom's implements, therefore, he summoned his companion to the canoe, that they might go down the lake in quest of the family. Previously to embarking, however, Hurry carefully examined the whole of the northern end of the water with an indifferent ship's glass, that formed a part of Hutter's effects. In this scrutiny, no part of the shore was overlooked; the bays and points in particular being subjected to a closer inquiry than the rest of the wooded boundary.

" 'Tis as I thought," said Hurry, laying aside the glass, "the old fellow is drifting about the south end this fine weather, and has left the castle to defend itself. Well, now we know that he is not up this-a-way, 'twill be but a small matter to paddle down and hunt him up in his hiding place."

"Does Master Hutter think it necessary to burrow on this lake?" inquired Deerslayer, as he followed his companion into the canoe; "to my eye it is such a solitude as one might open his whole soul in, and fear no one to disarrange his thoughts or his worship."

"You forget your friends, the Mingoes, and all the French savages. Is there a spot on 'arth, Deerslayer, to which them disquiet rogues don't go? Where is the lake, or even the deer lick, that the blackguards don't find out; and, having found out, don't sooner or later discolor its water with blood?"

"I hear no good character of them, sartainly, friend Hurry, though I've never been called on, as yet, to meet them, or any other mortal, on the warpath. I dare to say that such a lovely spot as this would not be likely to be overlooked by such plunderers; for, though I've not been in the way of quarrelling with them tribes myself, the Delawares give me such an account of 'em that I've pretty much set 'em down, in my own mind, as thorough miscreants."

"You may do that with a safe conscience, or, for that matter, any other savage you may happen to meet."

Here Deerslayer protested, and as they went paddling down the lake a hot discussion was maintained concerning the respective merits of the palefaces and the redskins. Hurry had all the prejudices and antipathies of a white hunter, who generally regards the Indian as a sort of natural competitor, and not unfrequently as a natural enemy. As a matter of course, he was loud, clamorous, dogmatical, and not very argumentative. Deerslayer, on the other hand, manifested a very different temper; proving, by the moderation of his language, the fairness of his views, and the simplicity of his distinctions, that he possessed every disposition to hear reason, a strong, innate desire to do justice, and an ingenuousness that was singularly indisposed to have recourse to sophisms to maintain an argument, or to defend a prejudice. Still, he was not altogether free from the influence of the latter feeling. This tyrant of the human mind, which rushes on its prey through a thousand avenues, almost as soon as men begin to think and feel, and which seldom relinquishes its iron sway until they cease to do either, had made some impression on even the just propensities of this individual, who probably offered in these particulars a fair specimen of what absence from bad example, the want of temptation to go wrong, and native good feeling, can render youth.

"You will allow, Deerslayer, that a Mingo is more than half devil," cried Hurry, following up the discussion with an animation that touched closely on ferocity, "though you want to overpersuade me that the Delaware tribe is pretty much made up of angels. Now, I gainsay that proposal, consarning white men, even. All white men are not faultless, and therefore all Indians *can't* be faultless. And so your argument is out at the elbow in the start. But this is what I call reason. Here's three colors on 'arth: white, black, and red. White is the highest color, and therefore the best man; black comes next, and is put to live in the neighborhood of the white man, as tolerable, and fit to be made use of; and red comes last, which shows that those that made 'em never expected an Indian to be accounted as more than half human."

"God made all three alike, Hurry."

"Alike! Do you call a nigger like a white man, or me like an Indian?"

"You go off at half-cock, and don't hear me out. God made us all, white, black, and red; and, no doubt, had his own wise intentions in coloring us differently. Still, he made us, in the main, much the same in feelin's; though I'll not deny that he gave each race its gifts. A white man's gifts are Christianized, while a redskin's are more for the wilderness. Thus, it would be a great offence for a white man to scalp the dead; whereas it's a signal vartue in an Indian. Then ag'in, a white man cannot amboosh women and children in war, while a redskin may.

'Tis *cruel* work, I'll allow; but for them it's *lawful* work; while for *us*, it would be grievous work."

"That depends on your inimy. As for scalping, or even skinning a savage, I look upon them pretty much the same as cutting off the ears of wolves for the bounty, or stripping a bear of its hide. And then you're out significantly, as to taking the poll of a redskin in hand, seeing that the very colony has offered a bounty for the job; all the same as it pays for wolves' ears and crows' heads."

"Ay, and a bad business it is, Hurry. Even the Indians themselves cry shame on it, seeing it's ag'in a white man's gifts. I do not pretend that all that white men do, is properly Christianized, and according to the lights given them, for then they would be what they *ought* to be; which we know they are not; but I will maintain that tradition, and use, and color, and laws, make such a difference in races as to amount to gifts. I do not deny that there are tribes among the Indians that are nat'rally pervarse and wicked, as there are nations among the whites. Now, I account the Mingoes as belonging to the first, and the Frenchers, in the Canadas, to the last. In a state of lawful warfare, such as we have lately got into, it is a duty to keep down all compassionate feelin's, so far as life goes, ag'in either; but when it comes to scalps, it's a very different matter."

"Just hearken to reason, if you please, Deerslayer, and tell me if the colony can make an onlawful law? Isn't an onlawful law more ag'in natur' than scalpin' a savage? A law can no more be onlawful, than truth can be a lie."

"That *sounds* reasonable; but it has a most onreasonable bearing, Hurry. Laws don't all come from the same quarter. God has given us his'n, and some come from the colony, and others come from the King and Parliament. When the colony's laws, or even the King's laws, run ag'in the laws of God, they get to be onlawful, and ought not to be obeyed. I hold to a white man's respecting white laws, so long as they do not cross the track of a law comin' from a higher authority; and for a red man to obey his own redskin usages, under the same privilege. But, 'tis useless talking, as each man will think for himself, and have his say agreeable to his thoughts. Let us keep a good lookout for your friend Floating Tom, lest we pass him, as he lies hidden under this bushy shore."

Deerslayer had not named the borders of the lake amiss. Along their whole length, the smaller trees overhung the water, with their branches often dipping in the transparent element. The banks were steep, even from the narrow strand; and, as vegetation invariably struggles toward the light, the effect was precisely that at which the lover of the picturesque would have aimed, had the ordering of this glorious setting of forest been submitted to his control. The points and bays, too, were sufficiently numerous to render the outline broken and diversified. As the canoe kept close along the western side of the lake, with a view, as Hurry had explained to his companion, of reconnoitering for enemies, before he trusted himself too openly in sight, the expectations of the two adventurers were kept constantly on the stretch, as neither could foretell what the next turning of a point might reveal. Their progress was swift, the gigantic strength of Hurry enabling him to play with the light bark as if it had been a feather, while the skill of his companion almost equalized their usefulness, notwithstanding the disparity in natural means.

Each time the canoe passed a point, Hurry turned a look behind him, expecting to see the ark anchored, or beached in the bay. He was fated to be disappointed, however; and they had got within a mile of the southern end of the lake, or a distance of quite two leagues from the castle, which was now hidden from view by half a dozen intervening projections of the land, when he suddenly ceased paddling, as if uncertain in what direction next to steer.

"It is possible that the old chap has dropped into the river," said Hurry, after looking carefully along the whole of the eastern shore, which was about a mile distant, and open to his scrutiny for more than half its length; "for he has taken to trapping considerable, of late, and, barring flood-wood, he might drop down it a mile or so; though he would have a most scratching time in getting back again!"

"Where is this outlet?" asked Deerslayer; "I see no opening in the banks or the trees, that looks as if it would let a river like the Susquehanna run through it."

"Ay, Deerslayer, rivers are like human mortals; having small beginnings, and ending with broad shoulders and wide mouths. You don't see the outlet, because it passes atween high, steep banks; and the pines, and hemlocks, and basswoods hang over it, as a roof hangs over a house. If old Tom is not in the Rat's Cove, he must have burrowed in the river; we'll look for him first in the cove, and then we'll cross to the outlet."

As they proceeded, Hurry explained that there was a shallow bay, formed by a long, low point, that had got the name of the Rat's Cove, from the circumstance of its being a favorite haunt of the muskrat; and which offered so complete a cover for the ark, that its owner was fond of lying in it, whenever he found it convenient.

"As a man never knows who may be his visitors, in this part of the country," continued Hurry, "it's a great advantage to get a good look at 'em afore they come too near. Now it's war, such caution is more than commonly useful, since a Canada man or a Mingo might get into his hut afore he invited 'em. But Hutter is a first-rate lookouter, and can pretty much scent danger, as a hound scents the deer."

"I should think the castle so open, that it would be sartain to draw inimies, if any happened to find the lake; a thing onlikely enough, I will allow, as it's off the trail of the forts and settlements."

"Why, Deerslayer, I've got to believe that a man meets with inimies easier than he meets with fri'nds. It's skearful to think for how many causes one gets to be your inimy, and for how few your fri'nd. Some take up the hatchet because you don't think just as they think; other some because you run ahead of 'em in the same idees; and I once know'd a vagabond that quarrelled with a fri'nd because he didn't think him handsome. Now, you're no monument in the way of beauty, yourself, Deerslayer, and yet you wouldn't be so onreasonable as to become my inimy for just saying so."

"I'm as the Lord made me; and I wish to be accounted no better, nor any worse. Good looks I may not have; that is to say, to a degree that the light-minded and vain crave; but I hope I'm not altogether without some ricommend in the way of good conduct. There's few nobler looking men to be seen than yourself, Hurry; and I know that I am not to expect any to turn their eyes on me, when such a one as you can be gazed on; but I do not know that a hunter is less expart with the rifle, or less to be relied on for food, because he doesn't wish to stop at every shining spring he may meet, to study his own countenance in the water."

Here Hurry burst into a fit of loud laughter; for while he was too reckless to care much about his own manifest physical superiority, he was well aware of it, and, like most men who derive an advantage from the accidents of birth or nature, he was apt to think complacently on the subject, whenever it happened to cross his mind.

"No, no, Deerslayer, you're no beauty, as you will own yourself, if you'll look over the side of the canoe," he cried; "Jude will say *that* to your face, if you start her, for a parter tongue isn't to be found in any gal's head, in or out of the settlements, if you provoke her to use it. My advice to you is, never to aggravate Judith; though you may tell anything to Hetty, and she'll take it as meek as a lamb. No, Jude will be just as like as not to tell you her opinion consarning your looks."

"And if she does, Hurry, she will tell me no more than you have said already—"

"You're not thick'ning up about a small remark, I hope, Deerslayer, when no harm is meant. You are *not* a beauty, as you must know, and why shouldn't fri'nds tell each other these little trifles? If you *was* handsome, or ever like to be, I'd be one of the first to tell you of it; and that ought to content you. Now, if Jude was to tell me that I'm as ugly as a sinner, I'd take it as a sort of obligation, and try not to believe her."

"It's easy for them that natur' has favored, to jest about such matters, Hurry, though it is sometimes hard for others. I'll not deny but I've had my cravings toward good looks; yes, I have; but then I've always been able to get them down by considering how many I've known with fair outsides, who have had nothing to boast of inwardly. I'll not deny, Hurry, that I often wish I'd been created more comely to the eye, and more like such a one as yourself, in them particulars; but then I get the feelin' under by remembering how much better off I am, in a great many respects, than some fellow-mortals. I might have been born lame, and onfit even for a squirrel hunt, or blind, which would have made me a burden on myself as well as on my fri'nds; or without hearing, which would have totally onqualified me for ever campaigning or scouting; which I look forward to as part of a man's duty in troublesome times. Yes, yes; it's not pleasant, I will allow, to see them that's more comely, and more sought a'ter, and honored than yourself; but it may all be borne, if a man looks the evil in the face, and don't mistake his gifts and his obligations."

Hurry, in the main, was a goodhearted as well as good-natured fellow; and the self-abasement of his companion completely got the better of the passing feeling of personal vanity. He regretted the allusion he had made to the other's appearance, and endeavored to express as much, though it was done in the uncouth manner that belonged to the habits and opinions of the frontier.

"I meant no harm, Deerslayer," he answered, in a deprecating manner, "and hope you'll forget what I've said. If you're not downright handsome, you've a sartain look that says, plainer than any words, that all's right within. Then you set no valie by looks, and will the sooner forgive any little slight to your appearance. I will not say that Jude will greatly admire you, for that might raise hopes that would only breed disapp'intment; but there's Hetty, now, would be just as likely to find satisfaction in looking at *you,* as in looking at any other man. Then you're altogether too grave and considerate-like, to care much about Judith; for, though the gal *is* oncommon, she is so general in her admiration, that a man need not be exalted because she happens to smile. I sometimes think the hussy loves herself better than she does anything else breathin'!"

"If she did, Hurry, she'd do no more, I'm afeard, than most queens on their thrones, and ladies in the towns," answered Deerslayer, smiling, and turning back toward his companion with every trace of feeling banished from his honest-looking and frank countenance. "I never yet know'd even a Delaware of whom you might not say that much. But here is the end of the long p'int you mentioned, and the Rat's Cove can't be far off."

This point, instead of thrusting itself forward, like all the others, ran in a line with the main shore of the lake, which here swept within it, in a deep and retired bay, circling round south again, at the distance of a quarter of a mile, and crossed the valley, forming the southern termination of the water. In this bay Hurry felt almost certain of finding the ark, since, anchored behind the trees that covered the narrow strip of the point, it might have lain concealed from prying eyes an entire summer. So complete, indeed, was the cover, in this spot, that a boat hauled close to the beach, within the point, and near the bottom of the bay, could by any possibility be seen from only one direction; and that was from a densely wooded shore within the sweep of the water, where strangers would be little apt to go.

"We shall soon see the ark," said Hurry, as the canoe glided round the extremity of the point, where the water was so deep as actually to appear black; "he loves to burrow up among the rushes, and we shall be in his nest in five minutes, although the old fellow may be off among the traps himself."

March proved a false prophet. The canoe completely doubled the point, so as to enable the two travellers to command a view of the whole cove or bay, for it was more properly the last, and no object, but those that nature had placed there, became visible. The placid water swept round in a graceful curve, the rushes bent gently toward its surface, and the trees overhung it as usual; but all lay in the soothing and sublime solitude of a wilderness. The scene was such as a poet or an artist would have delighted in, but it had no charm for Hurry Harry, who was burning with impatience to get a sight of his light-minded beauty.

The motion of the canoe had been attended with little or no noise, the frontiersmen habitually getting accustomed to caution in most of their movements, and it now lay on the glassy water appearing to float in air, partaking of the breathing stillness that seemed to pervade the entire scene. At this instant a dry stick was heard cracking on the narrow strip of land that concealed the bay from the open lake. Both the adventurers started, and each extended a hand towards his rifle, the weapon never being out of reach of the arm.

" 'Twas too heavy for any light creatur'," whispered Hurry, "and it sounded like the tread of a man!"

"Not so—not so," returned Deerslayer;; " 'twas, as you say, too heavy for one, but it was too light for the other. Put your paddle in the water, and send the canoe in, to that log; I'll land and cut off the creatur's retreat up the p'int, be it a Mingo, or be it a muskrat."

As Hurry complied, Deerslayer was soon on the shore, advancing into the thicket with a moccasined foot, and a caution that prevented the least noise. In a minute he was in the center of the narrow strip of land, and moving slowly down toward its end, the bushes rendering extreme watchfulness necessary. Just as he reached the center of the thicket the dried twigs cracked again, and the noise was repeated at short intervals, as if some creature having life walked slowly toward the point. Hurry heard these sounds also, and pushing the canoe off into the bay, he seized his rifle to watch the result. A breathless minute succeeded, after which a noble buck walked out of the thicket, proceeded with a stately step to the sandy extremity of the point, and began to slake his thirst from the water of the lake.

Hurry hesitated an instant; then raising his rifle hastily to his shoulder, he took sight and fired. The effect of this sudden interruption of the solemn stillness of such a scene was not its least striking peculiarity. The report of the weapon had the usual sharp, short sound of the rifle: but when a few moments of silence had succeeded the sudden crack, during which the noise was floating in air across the water, it reached the rocks of the opposite mountain, where the vibrations accumulated, and were rolled from cavity to cavity for miles along the hills, seeming to awaken the sleeping thunders of the woods. The buck merely shook his head at the report of the rifle and the whistling of the bullet, for never before had he come in contact with man; but the echoes of the hills awakened his distrust, and leaping forward, with his four legs drawn under his body, he fell at once into deep water, and began to swim toward the foot of the lake. Hurry shouted and dashed forward in chase, and for one or two minutes the water foamed around the pursuer and the pursued. The former was dashing past the point, when Deerslayer appeared on the sand, and signed to him to return.

" 'Twas inconsiderate to pull a trigger afore we had reconnitered the shore, and made sartain that no inimies harbored near it," said the latter, as his companion slowly and reluctantly complied. "This much I have l'arned from the Delawares, in the way of schooling and traditions, even though I've never yet been on a warpath. And, moreover, venison can hardly be called in season now, and we do not want for food. They call me Deerslayer, I'll own; and perhaps I desarve the name, in the way of understanding the creatur's habits, as well as for sartainty in the aim; but they can't accuse me of killing an animal when there is no occasion for the meat or the skin. I may be a slayer, it's true, but I'm no slaughterer."

" 'Twas an awful mistake to miss that buck!" exclaimed Hurry, doffing his cap, and running his fingers through his handsome but matted curls, as if he would loosen his tangled ideas by the process; "I've not done so onhandy a thing since I was fifteen."

"Never lament it; the creatur's death could have done neither of us any good, and might have done us harm. Them echoes are more awful in my ears than your mistake, Hurry; for they sound like the voice of natur' calling out ag'in a wasteful and onthinking action."

"You'll hear plenty of such calls, if you tarry long in this quarter of the world, lad," returned the other, laughing. "The echoes repeat pretty much all that is said or done on the Glimmerglass, in this calm summer weather. If a paddle falls, you hear of it sometimes ag'in and ag'in, as if the hills were mocking your clumsiness; and a laugh or a whistle comes out of them pines, when they're in the humor to speak, in a way to make you believe they can r'ally convarse."

"So much the more reason for being prudent and silent. I do not think the inimy can have found their way into these hills yet, for I don't know what they are to gain by it; but all the Delawares tell me, that as courage is a warrior's first vartue, so is prudence his second. One such call, from the mountains, is enough to let a whole tribe into the secret of our arrival."

"If it does no other good, it will warn old Tom to put the pot over, and let him know visitors are at hand. Come, lad; get into the canoe, and we will hunt the ark up while there is yet day."

Deerslayer complied, and the canoe left the spot. Its head was turned diagonally across the lake, pointing toward the southeastern curvature of the sheet. In that direction, the distance to the shore, or to the termination of the lake, on the course the two were now steering, was not quite a mile, and their progress being always swift, it was fast lessening, under the skilful but easy sweeps of the paddles. When about halfway across, a slight noise drew the eyes of the men toward the nearest land, and they saw that the buck was just emerging from the lake, and wading toward the beach. In a minute the noble animal shook the water from his flanks, gazed upward at the covering of trees, and, bounding against the bank, plunged into the forest.

"That creatur' goes off with gratitude in his heart," said Deerslayer, "for natur' tells him he has escaped a great danger. You ought to have some of the same feelin's, Hurry, to think your eye wasn't truer—that your hand was onsteady, when no good could come of a shot that was intended onmeaningly, rather than in reason."

"I deny the eye and the hand," cried March, with some heat. "You've got a little character, down among the Delawares, there, for quickness and sartainty, at a deer; but I should like to see you behind one of them pines, and a full-painted Mingo behind another, each with a cocked rifle, and a-striving for the chance! Them's the situations, Nathaniel, to try the sight and the hand, for they begin with trying the narves. I never look upon killing a creatur' as an explite; but killing a savage is. The time will come to try your hand, now we've got to blows ag'in, and we shall soon know what a ven'son reputation can do in the field. I deny that either hand or eye was onsteady; it was all a miscalculation of the buck, which stood still when he ought to have kept in motion, and so I shot ahead of him."

"Have it your own way, Hurry; all I contend for is, that it's lucky.

I dare say I shall not pull upon a human mortal as steadily or with as light a heart, as I pull upon a deer."

"Who's talking of mortals, or of human beings at all, Deerslayer? I put the matter to you on the supposition of an Injin. I dare say any man would have his feelin's when it got to be life or death, ag'in another human mortal; but there would be no such scruples in regard to an Injin; nothing but the chance of his hitting you, or the chance of your hitting him."

"I look upon the red men to be quite as human as we are ourselves, Hurry. They have their gifts, and their religion, it's true; but that makes no difference in the end, when each will be judged according to his deeds, and not according to his skin."

"That's downright missionary, and will find little favor up in this part of the country, where the Moravians don't congregate.[1] Now, skin makes the man. This is reason; else how are people to judge of each other. The skin is put on, over all, in order when a creatur', or a mortal, is fairly seen, you may know at once what to make of him. You know a bear from a hog, by his skin, and a gray squirrel from a black."

"True, Hurry," said the other looking back and smiling, "nevertheless, they are both squirrels."

"Who denies it? But you'll not say that a red man and a white man are both Injins?"

"No; but I *do* say they are both men. Men of different races and colors, and having different gifts and traditions, but, in the main, with the same natur'. Both have souls; and both will be held accountable for their deeds in this life."

Hurry was one of those theorists who believed in the inferiority of all the human race who were not white. His notions on the subject were not very clear, nor were his definitions at all well settled; but his opinions were none the less dogmatical or fierce. His conscience accused him of sundry lawless acts against the Indians, and he had found it an exceedingly easy mode of quieting it, by putting the whole family of red men, incontinently, without the category of human rights. Nothing angered him sooner than to deny his proposition, more especially if the denial were accompanied by a show of plausible argument; and he did not listen to his companion's remarks with much composure of either manner or feeling.

"You're a boy, Deerslayer, misled and misconsaited by Delaware arts, and missionary ignorance," he exclaimed, with his usual indif-

[1] The persecuted Protestants from Moravia and Bohemia, descendants of the followers of John Huss, began migrating to America in numbers in the 1720's. Some went to Georgia, more to the Middle Colonies. The Moravian or United Brethren missionaries became ubiquitous. Some taught the Indians in the Susquehanna Valley, notably at the village of Shamokin. Leatherstocking would have had many opportunities of hearing them, and it is clear that they greatly influenced him. The names of Comenius and Count Zinzendorf, the great Moravian leaders, became widely known in America.—Ed.

ference to the forms of speech, when excited. "*You* may account yourself as a redskin's brother, but *I* hold 'em all to be animals; with nothing human about 'em but cunning. *That* they have, I'll allow; but so has a fox, or even a bear. I'm older than you, and have lived longer in the woods—or, for that matter, have lived always there, and am not to be told what an Injin is or what he is not. If you wish to be considered a savage, you've only to say so, and I'll name you as such to Judith and the old man, and then we'll see how you'll like your welcome."

Here Hurry's imagination did his temper some service, since, by conjuring up the reception his semi-aquatic acquaintance would be likely to bestow on one thus introduced, he burst into a hearty fit of laughter. Deerslayer too well knew the uselessness of attempting to convince such a being of anything against his prejudices, to feel a desire to undertake the task; and he was not sorry that the approach of the canoe to the southeastern curve of the lake gave a new direction to his ideas. They were now, indeed, quite near the place that March had pointed out for the position of the outlet, and both began to look for it with a curiosity that was increased by the expectation of finding the ark.

It may strike the reader as a little singular, that the place where a stream of any size passed through banks that had an elevation of some twenty feet, should be a matter of doubt with men who could not now have been more than two hundred yards distant from the precise spot. It will be recollected, however, that the trees and bushes here, as elsewhere, fairly overhung the water, making such a fringe to the lake, as to conceal any little variations from its general outline.

"I've not been down at this end of the lake these two summers," said Hurry, standing up in the canoe, the better to look about him. "Ay, there's the rock, showing its chin above the water, and I know that the river begins in its neighborhood."

The men now plied the paddles again, and they were presently within a few yards of the rock, floating toward it, though their efforts were suspended. This rock was not large, being merely some five or six feet high, only half of which elevation rose above the lake. The incessant washing of the water for centuries had so rounded its summit, that it resembled a large beehive in shape, its form being more than usually regular and even. Hurry remarked, as they floated slowly past, that this rock was well known to all the Indians in that part of the country, and that they were in the practice of using it as a mark to designate the place of meeting, when separated by their hunts and marches.[1]

---

[1] Otsego Rock or Council Rock is still visible, though the damming of the Susquehanna to furnish water power to Cooperstown has diminished its surface. The Susquehanna flows out from the lake at this point, a rapid, narrow stream.—Ed.

"And here is the river, Deerslayer," he continued, "though so shut in by trees and bushes as to look more like an and-bush, than the outlet of such a sheet as the Glimmerglass."

Hurry had not badly described the place, which did truly seem to be a stream lying in ambush. The high banks might have been a hundred feet asunder; but, on the western side, a small bit of lowland extended so far forward as to diminish the breadth of the stream to half that width. As the bushes hung in the water beneath, and pines that had the stature of church steeples, rose in tall columns above, all inclining toward the light, until their branches intermingled, the eye, at a little distance, could not easily detect any opening in the shore, to mark the egress of the water. In the forest above, no traces of this outlet were to be seen from the lake, the whole presenting the same connected and seemingly interminable carpet of leaves. As the canoe slowly advanced, sucked in by the current, it entered beneath an arch of trees, through which the light from the heavens struggled by casual openings, faintly relieving the gloom beneath.

"This is a nat'ral and-bush," half whispered Hurry, as if he felt that the place was devoted to secrecy and watchfulness; "depend on it, old Tom has burrowed with the ark somewhere in this quarter. We will drop down with the current a short distance, and ferret him out."

"This seems no place for a vessel of any size," returned the other; "it appears to me that we shall have hardly room enough for the canoe."

Hurry laughed at the suggestion, and, as it soon appeared, with reason; for the fringe of bushes immediately on the shore of the lake was no sooner passed, than the adventurers found themselves in a narrow stream, of a sufficient depth of limpid water, with a strong current, and a canopy of leaves upheld by arches composed of the limbs of hoary trees. Bushes lined the shores, as usual, but they left sufficient space between them to admit the passage of anything that did not exceed twenty feet in width, and to allow of a perspective ahead of eight or ten times that distance.

Neither of our two adventurers used his paddle, except to keep the light bark in the center of the current, but both watched each turning of the stream, of which there were two or three within the first hundred yards, with jealous vigilance. Turn after turn, however, was passed, and the canoe had dropped down with the current some little distance, when Hurry caught a bush, and arrested its movement so suddenly and silently as to denote some unusual motive for the act. Deerslayer laid his hand on the stock of his rifle as soon as he noted this proceeding, but it was quite as much with a hunter's habit as from any feeling of alarm.

"There the old fellow is!" whispered Hurry, pointing with a finger, and laughing heartily, though he carefully avoided making a noise, "ratting it away, just as I supposed; up to his knees in the mud and water, looking to the traps and the bait. But for the life of me I can see nothing of the ark; though I'll bet every skin I take this season, Jude isn't trusting her pretty little feet in the neighborhood of that black mud. The gal's more likely to be braiding her hair by the side of some spring, where she can see her own good looks, and collect scornful feelings ag'in us men."

"You overjudge young women—yes, you do, Hurry—who as often bethink them of their failings as they do of their perfections. I dare to say this Judith, now, is no such admirer of herself, and no such scorner of our sex as you seem to think; and that she is quite as likely to be sarving her father in the house, wherever that may be, as he is to be sarving her among the traps."

"It's a pleasure to hear truth from a man's tongue, if it be only once in a girl's life," cried a pleasant, rich, and yet soft female voice, so near the canoe as to make both the listeners start. "As for you, Master Hurry, fair words are so apt to choke you, that I no longer expect to hear them from your mouth; the last you uttered sticking in your throat, and coming near to death. But I'm glad to see you keep better society than formerly, and that they who know how to esteem and treat women are not ashamed to journey in your company."

As this was said, a singularly handsome and youthful female face was thrust through an opening in the leaves, within reach of Deerslayer's paddle. Its owner smiled graciously on the young man; and the frown that she cast on Hurry, though simulated and pettish, had the effect to render her beauty more striking, by exhibiting the play of an expressive but capricious countenance; one that seemed to change from the soft to the severe, the mirthful to the reproving, with facility and indifference.

A second look explained the nature of the surprise. Unwittingly, the men had dropped alongside of the ark, which had been purposely concealed in bushes cut and arranged for the purpose; and Judith Hutter had merely pushed aside the leaves that lay before a window, in order to show her face, and speak to them.

3

THE ARK, as the floating habitation of the Hutters was generally called, was a very simple contrivance. A large flat, or scow, composed the buoyant part of the vessel; and in its center, occupying the whole of its breadth, and about two-thirds of its length, stood a low fabric, resembling the castle in construction, though made of materials so light as barely to be bulletproof. As the sides of the scow were a little higher than usual, and the interior of the cabin had no more elevation than was necessary for comfort, this unusual addition had neither a very clumsy nor a very obtrusive appearance. It was, in short, little more than a modern canalboat, though more rudely constructed, of greater breadth than common, and bearing about it the signs of the wilderness, in its bark-covered posts and roof. The scow, however, had been put together with some skill, being comparatively light, for its strength, and sufficiently manageable. The cabin was divided into two apartments, one of which served for a parlor, and the sleeping room of the father, and the other was appropriated to the uses of the daughters. A very simple arrangement sufficed for the kitchen, which was in one end of the scow, and removed from the cabin, standing in the open air; the ark being altogether a summer habitation.

The "and-bush," as Hurry in his ignorance of English termed it, is quite as easily explained. In many parts of the lake and river, where the banks were steep and high, the smaller trees and larger bushes, as has been already mentioned, fairly overhung the stream, their branches not unfrequently dipping into the water. In some instances they grew out in nearly horizontal lines, for thirty or forty feet. The water being uniformly deepest near the shores, where the banks were highest and the nearest to a perpendicular, Hutter had found no difficulty in letting the ark drop under one of these covers, where it had been anchored with a view to conceal its position; security requiring some such precautions, in his view of the case. Once beneath the trees and bushes, a few stones fastened to the ends of the branches had caused them to bend sufficiently to dip into the river; and a few severed bushes, properly disposed, did the rest. The reader has seen that this cover was so complete as to deceive two men accustomed to the woods, and who were actually in search of those it concealed; a circumstance that will be easily understood by those who are familiar with the matted and wild luxuriance of a virgin American forest, more especially in a rich soil.

The discovery of the ark produced very different effects on our two adventurers. As soon as the canoe could be got round to the proper opening, Hurry leaped on board, and in a minute was closely engaged in a gay, and a sort of recriminating discourse with Judith, apparently forgetful of the existence of all the rest of the world. Not so with Deerslayer. He entered the ark with a slow, cautious step, examining every arrangement of the cover with curious and scrutinizing eyes. It is true, he cast one admiring glance at Judith, which was extorted by her brilliant and singular beauty; but even this could detain him but a single instant from the indulgence of his interest in Hutter's contrivances. Step by step did he look into the construction of the singular abode, investigate its fastenings and strength, ascertain its means of defence, and make every inquiry that would be likely to occur to one whose thoughts dwelt principally on such expedients. Nor was the cover neglected. Of this he examined the whole minutely, his commendation escaping him more than once, in audible comments. Frontier usages admitting of this familiarity, he passed through the rooms as he had previously done at the castle; and, opening a door, issued into the end of the scow opposite to that where he had left Hurry and Judith. Here he found the other sister, employed on some coarse needlework, seated beneath the leafy canopy of the cover.

As Deerslayer's examination was by this time ended, he dropped the butt of his rifle, and, leaning on the barrel with both hands, he turned toward the girl with an interest the singular beauty of her sister had not awakened. He had gathered from Hurry's remarks that Hetty was considered to have less intellect than ordinarily falls to the share of human beings; and his education among Indians had taught him to treat those who were thus afflicted by Providence, with more than common tenderness. Nor was there anything in Hetty Hutter's appearance, as so often happens, to weaken the interest her situation excited. An idiot she could not properly be termed, her mind being just enough enfeebled to lose most of those traits that are connected with the more artful qualities, and to retain its ingenuousness and love of truth. It had often been remarked of this girl, by the few who had seen her, and who possessed sufficient knowledge to discriminate, that her perception of the right seemed almost intuitive, while her aversion to the wrong formed so distinctive a feature of her mind, as to surround her with an atmosphere of pure morality; peculiarities that are not unfrequent with persons who are termed feeble-minded; as if God had forbidden the evil spirits to invade a precinct so defenceless, with the benign purpose of extending a direct protection to those who have been left without the usual aids of humanity. Her person, too, was agreeable, having a strong resemblance to that of her sister, of which it was a subdued and humble copy. If it had none of the brilliancy of Judith's, the calm, quiet, almost holy expression of her meek countenance, seldom failed to win on the observer; and few noted it long, that did not begin to feel a deep and lasting interest in the girl. She had no color, in common, nor was her simple mind apt to present images that caused her cheek to brighten; though she retained a modesty so innate, that it almost raised her to the unsuspecting purity of a being superior to human infirmities. Guileless, innocent, and without distrust, equally by nature and from her mode of life, Providence had, nevertheless, shielded her from harm by a halo of moral light, as it is said "to temper the wind to the shorn lamb."

"You are Hetty Hutter," said Deerslayer, in the way one puts a question unconsciously to himself, assuming a kindness of tone and manner that were singularly adapted to win the confidence of her he addressed. "Hurry Harry has told me of you, and I know you must be the child?"

"Yes, I'm Hetty Hutter," returned the girl, in a low, sweet voice, which nature, aided by some education, had preserved from vulgarity of tone and utterance: "I'm Hetty; Judith Hutter's sister, and Thomas Hutter's youngest daughter."

"I know your history, then, for Hurry Harry talks considerable, and he is free of speech, when he can find other people's consarns to dwell on. You pass most of your life on the lake, Hetty."

"Certainly. Mother is dead; father is gone a-trapping, and Judith and I stay at home. What's *your* name?"

"That's a question more easily asked than it is answered, young woman; seeing that I'm so young, and yet have borne more names than some of the greatest chiefs in all America."

"But you've *got* a name—you don't throw away one name before you come honestly by another?"

"I hope not, gal—I hope not. My names have come nat'rally; and

I suppose the one I bear now will be of no great lasting, since the Delawares seldom settle on a man's r'al title, until such time as he has opportunity of showing his true natur', in the council or on the warpath; which has never behappened me; seeing, firstly, because I'm not born a redskin, and have no right to sit in *their* councillings, and am much too humble to be called on for opinions from the great of my own color; and, secondly, because this is the first war that has befallen in my time, and no inimy has yet inroaded far enough into the colony to be reached by an arm even longer than mine."

"Tell me your names," added Hetty, looking up at him artlessly, "and, maybe, I'll tell you your character."

"There is some truth in that, I'll not deny, though it often fails. Men are deceived in other men's characters, and frequently give 'em names they by no means desarve. You can see the truth of this in the Mingo names, which, in their own tongue, signify the same things as the Delaware names,—at least, so they tell me, for I know little of that tribe, unless it be by report,—and no one can say they are as honest or as upright a nation. I put no great dependence, therefore, on names."

"Tell me *all* your names," repeated the girl, earnestly, for her mind was too simple to separate things from professions, and she *did* attach importance to a name; "I want to know what to think of you."

"Well, sartain; I've no objections, and you shall hear them all. In the first place, then, I'm Christian, and white-born, like yourself, and my parents had a name that came down from father to son, as is a part of their gifts. My father was called Bumppo; and I was named after him, of course, the given name being Nathaniel, or Natty, as most people saw fit to tarm it."

"Yes, yes—Natty—and Hetty"—interrupted the girl quickly, and looking up from her work again, with a smile: "you are Natty, and I'm Hetty—though you are Bumppo, and I'm Hutter. Bumppo isn't as pretty as Hutter, is it?"

"Why, that's as people fancy. Bumppo has no lofty sound, I admit; and yet men have bumped through the world with it. I did not go by this name, howsever, very long; for the Delawares soon found out, or thought they found out, that I was not given to lying, and they called me, firstly, Straight-Tongue."

"That's a *good* name," interrupted Hetty, earnestly, and in a positive manner; "don't tell me there's no virtue in names!"

"I do not say *that*, for perhaps I desarved to be so called, lies being no favorites with me, as they are with some. After a while they found out that I was quick of foot, and then they called me the Pigeon; which, you know, has a swift wing, and flies in a direct line."

"*That* was a *pretty* name!" exclaimed Hetty; "pigeons are pretty birds!"

"Most things that God has created are pretty in their way, my good gal, though they get to be deformed by mankind, so as to change their natur's, as well as their appearance. From carrying messages, and striking blind trails, I got at last to following the hunters, when it was thought I was quicker and surer at finding the game than most lads, and then they called me the Lap-Ear; as, they said, I partook of the sagacity of a hound."

"That's not so pretty," answered Hetty; "I hope you didn't keep *that* name long."

"Not after I was rich enough to buy a rifle," returned the other, betraying a little pride through his usually quiet and subdued manner; "*then* it was seen I could keep a wigwam in ven'son; and in time I got the name of Deerslayer, which is that I now bear; homely as some will think it, who set more valie on the scalp of a fellow-mortal than on the horns of a buck."

"Well, Deerslayer, I'm not one of them," answered Hetty, simply; "Judith likes soldiers, and flary coats, and fine feathers; but they're all naught to me. *She* says the officers are great, and gay, and of soft speech; but they make me shudder, for their business is to kill their fellow-creatures. I like your calling better; and your last name is a very good one—better than Natty Bumppo."

"This is nat'ral in one of your turn of mind, Hetty, and much as I should have expected. They tell me your sister is handsome—oncommon, for a mortal; and beauty is apt to seek admiration."

"Did you never see Judith?" demanded the girl, with quick earnestness; "if you never have, go at once and look at her. Even Hurry Harry isn't more pleasant to look at; though *she* is a woman, and *he* is a man."

Deerslayer regarded the girl for a moment with concern. Her pale face had flushed a little, and her eye, usually so mild and serene, brightened as she spoke, in the way to betray the inward impulses.

"Ay, Hurry Harry," he muttered to himself, as he walked through the cabin toward the other end of the boat; "this comes of good looks, if a light tongue has had no consarn in it. It's easy to see which way that poor creatur's feelin's are leanin', whatever may be the case with your Jude's."

But an interruption was put to the gallantry of Hurry, the coquetry of his mistress, the thoughts of Deerslayer, and the gentle feelings of Hetty, by the sudden appearance of the canoe of the ark's owner, in the narrow opening among the bushes that served as a sort of moat to his position. It would seem that Hutter, or Floating Tom, as he was familiarly called by all the hunters who knew his habits, recognized the canoe of Hurry, for he expressed no surprise at finding him in the scow. On the contrary, his reception was such as to denote not only gratification, but a pleasure, mingled with a little disappointment at his not having made his appearance some days sooner.

"I looked for you last week," he said, in a half-grumbling, half-welcoming manner; "and was disappointed uncommonly that you didn't arrive. There came a runner through, to warn all the trappers and hunters that the colony and the Canadas were again in trouble; [1] and I felt lonesome, up in these mountains, with three scalps to see to, and only one pair of hands to protect them."

"That's reasonable," returned March; "and 'twas feeling like a parent. No doubt, if I had two such darters as Judith and Hetty, my exper'ence would tell the same story, though in gin'ral I am just as well satisfied with having the nearest neighbor fifty miles off, as when he is within call."

"Notwithstanding, you didn't choose to come into the wilderness alone, now you knew that the Canada savages are likely to be stirring," returned Hutter, giving a sort of distrustful, and at the same time inquiring glance at Deerslayer.

"Why should I? They say a bad companion, on a journey, helps to shorten the path; and this young man I account to be a reasonably good one. This is Deerslayer, old Tom, a noted hunter among the Delawares, and Christian-born, and Christian-edicated, too, like you and me. The lad is not parfect, perhaps, but there's worse men in the country that he came from, and it's likely he'll find some that's no better, in this part of the world. Should we have occasion to defend our traps, and the territory, he'll be useful in feeding us all; for he's a reg'lar dealer in ven'son."

"Young man, you are welcome," growled Tom, thrusting a hard, bony hand toward the youth, as a pledge of his sincerity; "in such times, a white face is a friend's, and I count on you as a support. Children sometimes make a stout heart feeble, and these two daughters of mine give me more concern than all my traps, and skins, and rights in the country."

"That's nat'ral!" cried Hurry. "Yes, Deerslayer, you and I don't know it yet by experience; but, on the whole, I consider that as nat'ral. If we *had* darters, it's more than probable we should have some such feelin's; and I honor the man that owns 'em. As for Judith, old man, I enlist, at once, as her soldier, and here is Deerslayer to help you to take care of Hetty."

"Many thanks to you, Master March," returned the beauty, in a full, rich voice, and with an accuracy of intonation and utterance that she shared in common with her sister, and which showed that she had

[1] When Frederick the Great seized Silesia in the War of the Austrian Succession, the French and British colonies were soon in arms. News of the impending conflict reached Boston and New York by the summer of 1744, and warnings were soon sent to exposed settlements.—Ed.

been better taught than her father's life and appearance would give reason to expect; "many thanks to you; but Judith Hutter has the spirit and the experience that will make her depend more on herself than on good-looking rovers like you. Should there be need to face the savages, do you land with my father, instead of burrowing in the huts, under the show of defending us females, and—"

"Girl—girl," interrupted the father, "quiet that glib tongue of thine, and hear the truth. There are savages on the lake shore already, and no man can say how near to us they may be at this very moment, or when we may hear more from them!"

"If this be true, Master Hutter," said Hurry, whose change of countenance denoted how serious he deemed the information, though it did not denote any unmanly alarm, "if this be true, your ark is in a most misfortunate position, for, though the cover did deceive Deerslayer and myself, it would hardly be overlooked by a full-blooded Injin, who was out seriously in s'arch of scalps!"

"I think as you do, Hurry, and wish, with all my heart, we lay anywhere else, at this moment, than in this narrow, crooked stream, which has many advantages to hide in, but which is almost fatal to them that are discovered. The savages are near us, moreover, and the difficulty is, to get out of the river without being shot down like deer standing at a lick!"

"Are you sartain, Master Hutter, that the redskins you dread are ra'al Canadas?" asked Deerslayer, in a modest but earnest manner. "Have you seen any, and can you describe their paint?"

"I have fallen in with the signs of their being in the neighborhood, but have seen none of 'em. I was downstream a mile or so, looking to my traps, when I struck a fresh trail, crossing the corner of a swamp, and moving northward. The man had not passed an hour; and I know'd it for an Indian footstep, by the size of the foot, and the intoe, even before I found a worn moccasin, which its owner had dropped as useless. For that matter, I found the spot where he halted to make a new one, which was only a few yards from the place where he had dropped the old one."

"That doesn't look much like a redskin on the warpath!" returned the other, shaking his head. "An exper'enced warrior, at least, would have burned, or buried, or sunk in the river such signs of his passage; and your trail is, quite likely, a peaceable trail. But the moccasin may greatly relieve my mind, if you bethought you of bringing it off. I've come here to meet a young chief myself; and his course would be much in the direction you've mentioned. The trail may have been his'n."

"Hurry Harry, you're well acquainted with this young man, I hope, who has meetings with savages in a part of the country where he has never been before?" demanded Hutter, in a tone and in a manner that sufficiently indicated the motive of the question; these rude beings seldom hesitating, on the score of delicacy, to betray their feelings. "Treachery is an Indian virtue; and the whites, that live much in their tribes, soon catch their ways and practices."

"True—true as the Gospel, old Tom; but not personable to Deerslayer, who's a young man of truth, if he has no other ricommend. I'll answer for his *honesty*, whatever I may do for his valor in battle."

"I should like to know his errand in this strange quarter of the country."

"That is soon told, Master Hutter," said the young man, with the composure of one who kept a clean conscience. "I think, moreover, you've a *right* to ask it. The father of two such darters, who occupies a lake, after your fashion, has just the same right to inquire into a stranger's business in his neighborhood, as the colony would have to demand the reason why the Frenchers put more rijiments than common along the lines. No, no, I'll not deny your right to know why a stranger comes into your habitation or country, in times as serious as these."

"If such is your way of thinking, friend, let me hear your story without more words."

" 'Tis soon told, as I said afore; and shall be honestly told. I'm a young man, and, as yet, have never been on a warpath; but no sooner did the news come among the Delawares, that wampum and a hatchet were about to be sent in to the tribe, than they wished me to go out among the people of my own color, and get the exact state of things for 'em. This I did, and, after delivering my talk to the chiefs, on my return, I met an officer of the Crown on the Schoharie, who had moneys to send to some of the friendly tribes, that live farther west. This was thought a good occasion for Chingachgook, a young chief who had never struck a foe, and myself, to go on our first warpath in company; and an app'intment was made for us, by an old Delaware, to meet at the rock near the foot of this lake. I'll not deny that Chingachgook has *another* object in view, but it has no consarn with any here, and is his secret, and not mine; therefore I'll say no more about it."

" 'Tis something about a young woman," interrupted Judith, hastily; then laughing at her own impetuosity, and even having the grace to color a little at the manner in which she had betrayed her readiness to impute such a motive. "If 'tis neither war nor a hunt, it must be love."

"Ay, it comes easy for the young and handsome, who hear so much of them feelin's, to suppose that they lie at the bottom of most proceedin's; but, on that head, I say nothin'. Chingachgook is to meet me at the rock an hour afore sunset tomorrow evening, after which we shall go our way together, molesting none but the King's inimies, who are lawfully our own. Knowing Hurry of old, who once trapped in our hunting grounds, and falling in with him on the Schoharie, just as he was on the p'int of starting for his summer ha'nts, we agreed to journey in company; not so much from fear of the Mingoes as from good fellowship, and, as he says, to shorten a long road."

"And you think the trail I saw may have been that of your friend, ahead of his time?" said Hutter.

"That's my idee; which may be wrong, but which may be right. If I saw the moccasin, however, I could tell in a minute whether it is made in the Delaware fashion or not."

"Here it is, then," said the quick-witted Judith, who had already gone to the canoe in quest of it; "tell us what it says; friend or enemy. You look honest; and *I* believe all you say, whatever father may think."

"That's the way with you, Jude; forever finding out friends, where I distrust foes," grumbled Tom; "but, speak out, young man, and tell us what you think of the moccasin."

"That's not Delaware-made," returned Deerslayer, examining the worn and rejected covering for the foot with a cautious eye; "I'm too young on a warpath to be positive, but I should say that moccasin has a northern look, and comes from beyond the Great Lakes."

"If such is the case, we ought not to lie here a minute longer than is necessary," said Hutter, glancing through the leaves of his cover, as if he already distrusted the presence of an enemy on the opposite shore of the narrow and sinuous stream. "It wants but an hour or so of night, and to move in the dark will be impossible, without making a noise that would betray us. Did you hear the echo of a piece in the mountains, half an hour since?"

"Yes, old man, and heard the piece itself," answered Hurry, who now felt the indiscretion of which he had been guilty, "for the last was fired from my own shoulder."

"I feared it came from the French Indians; still it may put them on the lookout, and be a means of discovering us. You did wrong to fire in wartime, unless there was good occasion."

"So I begin to think myself, Uncle Tom; and yet, if a man can't trust himself to let off his rifle in a wilderness that is a thousand miles square, lest some inimy should hear it, where's the use in carrying one?"

Hutter now held a long consultation with his two guests, in which the parties came to a true understanding of their situation. He explained the difficulty that would exist in attempting to get the ark out of so swift and narrow a stream, in the dark, without making a noise that could not fail to attract Indian ears. Any strollers in their vicinity would keep near the river or the lake; but the former had swampy shores in many places, and was both so crooked and so fringed with bushes, that it was quite possible to move by daylight without incurring much danger of being seen. More was to be apprehended, perhaps, from the ear than from the eye, especially as long as they were in the short, straitened, and canopied reaches of the stream.

"I never drop down into this cover, which is handy to my traps, and safer than the lake, from curious eyes, without providing the means of getting out ag'in," continued this singular being; "and that is easier done by a pull than a push. My anchor is now lying above the suction, in the open lake; and here is a line, you see, to haul us up to it. Without some such help, a single pair of hands would make heavy work in forcing a scow like this upstream. I have a sort of a crab, too, that lightens the pull, on occasion. Jude can use the oar astarn as well as myself; and when we fear no enemy, to get out of the river gives us but little trouble."

"What should we gain, Master Hutter, by changing the position?" asked Deerslayer, with a good deal of earnestness; "this is a safe cover, and a stout defence might be made from the inside of this cabin. I've never fou't unless in the way of tradition; but it seems to me we might beat off twenty Mingoes, with palisades like them afore us."

"Ay, ay; you've never fought except in traditions, that's plain enough, young man! Did you ever see as broad a sheet of water as this above us, before you came in upon it with Hurry?"

"I can't say that I ever did," Deerslayer answered, modestly. "Youth is the time to l'arn; and I'm far from wishing to raise my voice in counsel, afore it is justified by exper'ence."

"Well, then, I'll teach you the disadvantage of fighting in this position, and the advantage of taking to the open lake. Here, you may see, the savages will know where to aim every shot; and it would be too much to hope that *some* would not find their way through the crevices of the logs. Now, on the other hand, *we* should have nothing but a forest to aim at. Then we are not safe from fire, here, the bark of this roof being little better than so much kindling wood. The castle, too, might be entered and ransacked in my absence, and all my possessions overrun and destroyed. Once in the lake, we can be attacked only in boats or on rafts—shall have a fair chance with the enemy—and can protect the castle with the ark. Do you understand this reasoning, youngster?"

"It sounds well—yes, it has a rational sound; and I'll not gainsay it."

"Well, old Tom," cried Hurry, "If we are to move, the sooner we make a beginning, the sooner we shall know whether we are to have our scalps for nightcaps, or not."

As this proposition was self-evident, no one denied its justice. The three men, after a short preliminary explanation, now set about their preparations to move the ark in earnest. The slight fastenings were quickly loosened; and, by hauling on the line, the heavy craft slowly emerged from the cover. It was no sooner free from the incumbrance of the branches, than it swung into the stream, sheering quite close to the western shore, by the force of the current. Not a soul on board heard the rustling of the branches, as the cabin came against the bushes and trees of the western bank, without a feeling of uneasiness; for no one knew at what moment, or in what place, a secret and murderous enemy might unmask himself. Perhaps the gloomy light that still struggled through the impending canopy of leaves, or found its way through the narrow, ribbon-like opening, which seemed to mark, in the air above, the course of the river that flowed beneath, aided in augmenting the appearance of the danger; for it was little more than sufficient to render objects visible, without giving up all their outlines at a glance. Although the sun had not absolutely set, it had withdrawn its direct rays from the valley; and the hues of evening were beginning to gather around objects that stood uncovered, rendering those within the shadows of the woods still more somber and gloomy.

No interruption followed the movement, however, and, as the men continued to haul on the line, the ark passed steadily ahead, the great breadth of the scow preventing its sinking into the water, and from offering much resistance to the progress of the swift element beneath its bottom. Hutter, too, had adopted a precaution suggested by experience, which might have done credit to a seaman, and which completely prevented any of the annoyances and obstacles which otherwise would have attended the short turns of the river. As the ark descended, heavy stones, attached to the line, were dropped in the center of the stream, forming local anchors, each of which was kept from dragging by the assistance of those above it, until the uppermost of all was reached, which got its "backing" from the anchor, or grapnel, that lay well out in the lake. In consequence of this expedient, the ark floated clear of the incumbrances of the shore, against which it would otherwise have been unavoidably hauled at every turn, producing embarrassments that Hutter, singlehanded, would have found it very difficult to overcome.

Favored by this foresight, and stimulated by the apprehension of discovery, Floating Tom and his two athletic companions hauled the ark ahead with quite as much rapidity as comported with the strength of the line. At every turn in the stream, a stone was raised from the bottom, when the direction of the scow changed to one that pointed toward the stone that lay above. In this manner, with the channel buoyed out for him, as a sailor might term it, did Hutter move forward, occasionally urging his friends, in a low and guarded voice, to increase their exertions, and then, as occasions offered, warning them against efforts that might, at particular moments, endanger all by too much zeal. In spite of their long familiarity with the woods, the gloomy character of the shaded river added to the uneasiness that each felt; and when the ark reached the first bend in the Susquehanna, and the eye caught a glimpse of the broader expanse of the lake, all felt a relief, that perhaps none would have been willing to confess. Here the last stone was raised from the bottom, and the line led directly toward the grapnel, which, as Hutter had explained, was dropped above the suction of the current.

"Thank God!" ejaculated Hurry, "*there* is daylight, and we shall soon have a chance of *seeing* our inimies, if we are to *feel* 'em."

"That is more than you or any man can say," growled Hutter. "There is no spot so likely to harbor a party as the shore around the outlet, and the moment we clear these trees and get into open water, will be the most trying time, since it will leave the enemy a cover, while it puts us out of one. Judith, girl, do you and Hetty leave the oar to take care of itself, and go within the cabin; and be mindful not to show your faces at a window; for they who will look at them won't stop to praise their beauty. And now, Hurry, we'll step into this outer room ourselves, and haul through the door, where we shall all be safe, from a surprise, at least. Friend Deerslayer, as the current is lighter, and the line has all the strain on it that is prudent, do you keep moving from window to window, taking care not to let your head be seen, if you set any value on life. No one knows when or where we shall hear from our neighbors."

Deerslayer complied, with a sensation that had nothing in common with fear, but which had all the interest of a perfectly novel and a most exciting situation. For the first time in his life he was in the vicinity of enemies, or had good reason to think so; and that, too, under all the thrilling circumstances of Indian surprises and Indian artifices. As he took his stand at the window, the ark was just passing through the narrowest part of the stream, a point where the water first entered what was properly termed the river, and where the trees fairly interlocked overhead, causing the current to rush into an arch of verdure; a feature as appropriate and peculiar to the country, perhaps, as that of Switzerland, where the rivers come rushing literally from chambers of ice.

The ark was in the act of passing the last curve of this leafy entrance, as Deerslayer, having examined all that could be seen of the eastern bank of the river, crossed the room to look from the opposite window, at the western. His arrival at this aperture was most opportune, for he had no sooner placed his eye at a crack, than a sight met his gaze that might well have alarmed a sentinel so young and inexperienced. A sapling overhung the water, in nearly half a circle, having first grown toward the light, and then been pressed down into this form by the weight of the snows; a circumstance of common occurrence in the American woods. On this no less than six Indians had already appeared, others standing ready to follow them, as they left room; each evidently bent on running out on the trunk, and dropping on the roof of the ark as it passed beneath. This would have been an exploit of no great difficulty, the inclination of the tree admitting of an easy passage, the adjoining branches offering ample support for the hands, and the fall being too trifling to be apprehended. When Deerslayer first saw this party, it was just unmasking itself, by ascending the part of the tree nearest to the earth, or that which was much the most difficult to overcome; and his knowledge of Indian habits told him at once that they were all in their war paint, and belonged to a hostile tribe.

"Pull, Hurry," he cried; "pull for your life, and as you love Judith Hutter! Pull, man, pull!"

This call was made to one that the young man knew had the strength of a giant. It was so earnest and solemn, that both Hutter and March felt it was not idly given, and they applied all their force to the line simultaneously, and at a most critical moment. The scow redoubled its motion, and seemed to glide from under the tree as if conscious of the danger that was impending overhead. Perceiving that they were discovered, the Indians uttered the fearful war whoop, and running forward on the tree, leaped desperately towards their fancied prize. There were six on the tree, and each made the effort. All but their leader fell into the river more or less distant from the ark, as they came, sooner or later, to the leaping place. The chief, who had taken the dangerous post in advance, having an earlier opportunity than the others, struck the scow just within the stern. The fall proving so much greater than he had anticipated, he was slightly stunned, and for a moment he remained half bent and unconscious of his situation. At this instant Judith rushed from the cabin, her beauty heightened by the excitement that produced the bold act, which flushed her cheek to crimson, and, throwing all her strength into the effort, she pushed the intruder over the edge of the scow, headlong into the river. This decided feat was no sooner accomplished than the woman resumed her sway; Judith looked over the stern to ascertain what had become of the man, and the expression of her eyes softened to concern, next, her cheek crimsoned between shame and surprise, at her own temerity, and then she laughed in her own merry and sweet manner. All this occupied less than a minute, when the arm of Deerslayer was thrown around her waist, and she was dragged swiftly within the protection of the cabin. This retreat was not effected too soon. Scarcely were the two in safety, when the forest was filled with yells, and bullets began to patter against the logs.

The ark being in swift motion all this while, it was beyond the danger of pursuit by the time these little events had occurred; and the savages, as soon as the first burst of their anger had subsided, ceased firing, with the consciousness that they were expending their ammunition in vain. When the scow came up over her grapnel, Hutter tripped the latter, in a way not to impede the motion; and being now beyond the influence of the current, the vessel continued to drift ahead, until fairly in the open lake, though still near enough to the land to render exposure to a rifle bullet dangerous. Hutter and March got out two small sweeps, and, covered by the cabin, they soon urged the ark far enough from the shore to leave no inducement to their enemies to make any further attempt to injure them.

Another consultation took place in the forward part of the scow, at which both Judith and Hetty were present. As no danger could now approach unseen, immediate uneasiness had given place to the concern which attended the conviction that enemies were in considerable force on the shores of the lake, and that they might be sure no practicable means of accomplishing their own destruction would be neglected. As a matter of course Hutter felt these truths the deepest, his daughters having an habitual reliance on his resources, and knowing too little to appreciate fully all the risks they ran; while his male companions were at liberty to quit him at any moment they saw fit. His first remark showed that he had an eye to the latter circumstance, and might have betrayed, to a keen observer, the apprehension that was just then uppermost.

"We've a great advantage over the Iroquois, or the enemy, whoever they are, in being afloat," he said. "There's not a canoe on the lake that I don't know where it's hid; and now yours is here, Hurry, there are but three more on the land, and they's so snug in hollow logs that I don't believe the Indians could find them, let them try ever so long."

"There's no telling that—no one can say that," put in Deerslayer; "a hound is not more sartain on the scent than a redskin, when he expects to get anything by it. Let this party see scalps afore 'em, or plunder, or honor accordin' to their idees of what honor is, and 'twill be a tight log that hides a canoe from their eyes."

"You're right, Deerslayer," cried Harry March; "you're downright Gospel in this matter, and I rej'ice that my bunch of bark is safe enough here, within reach of my arm. I calcilate they'll be at all the rest of the canoes afore tomorrow night, if they are in ra'al 'arnest to smoke you out, old Tom, and we may as well overhaul our paddles for a pull."

Hutter made no immediate reply. He looked about him in silence for quite a minute, examining the sky, the lake, and the belt of forest which inclosed it, as it might be hermetically, like one consulting their signs. Nor did he find any alarming symptoms. The boundless woods were sleeping in the deep repose of nature, the heavens were placid, but still luminous with the light of the retreating sun, while the lake looked more lovely and calm than it had before done that day. It was a scene altogether soothing, and of a character to lull the passions into a species of holy calm. How far this effect was produced, however, on the party in the ark, must appear in the progress of our narrative.

"Judith," called out the father, when he had taken this close but short survey of the omens, "night is at hand; find our friends food; a long march gives a sharp appetite."

"We're not starving, Master Hutter," March observed, "for we filled up just as we reached the lake, and for one, I prefar the company of Jude even to her supper. This quiet evening is very agreeable to sit by her side."

"Natur' is natur'," objected Hutter, "and must be fed. Judith, see to the meal, and take your sister to help you. I've a little discourse to hold with you, friends," he continued, as soon as his daughters were out of hearing, "and wish the girls away. You see my situation, and I should like to hear your opinions concerning what is best to be done. Three times have I been burnt out already, but that was on the shore; and I've considered myself as pretty safe ever since I got the castle built, and the ark afloat. My other accidents, however, happened in peaceable times, being nothing more than such flurries as a man must meet with, in the woods; but this matter looks series, and your ideas would greatly relieve my mind."

"It's my notion, old Tom, that you, and your huts, and your traps, and your whole possessions, here-a-way, are in desperate jippardy," returned the matter-of-fact Hurry, who saw no use in concealment. "Accordin' to my idees of valie, they're altogether not worth half as much today as they was yesterday, nor would I give more for 'em, taking the pay in skins."

"Then I've children!" continued the father, making the allusion in a way that it might have puzzled even an indifferent observer to say was intended as a bait, or as an exclamation of paternal concern, "daughters, as you know, Hurry, and good girls too, I may say, though I *am* their father."

"A man may say anything, Master Hutter, particularly when pressed by time and circumstances. You've darters, as you say, and one of them hasn't her equal on the frontiers for good looks, whatever she may have for good behavior. As for poor Hetty, she's Hetty Hutter, and that's as much as one can say about the poor thing. Give me Jude, if her conduct was only equal to her looks!"

"I see, Harry March, I can only count on you as a fair-weather friend; and I suppose that your companion will be of the same way of thinking," returned the other, with a slight show of pride, that was not altogether without dignity; "well, I must depend on Providence, which will not turn a deaf ear, perhaps, to a father's prayers."

"If you've understood Hurry, here, to mean that he intends to desart you," said Deerslayer, with an earnest simplicity that gave double assurance of its truth, "I *think* you do him injustice, as I *know* you do me, in supposing I would follow him, was he so ontrue-hearted as to leave a family of his own color in such a strait as this. I've come on this lake, Master Hutter, to rende'vous a fri'nd, and I only wish he was here himself, as I make no doubt he will be at sunset tomorrow, when you'd have another rifle to aid you; an inexper'enced one, I'll allow, like my own, but one that has proved true so often ag'in the game, big and little, that I'll answer for its sarvice ag'in mortals."

"May I depend on *you* to stand by me and my daughters, then, Deerslayer?" demanded the old man, with a father's anxiety in his countenance.

"That may you, Floating Tom, if that's your name; and as a brother would stand by a sister, a husband his wife, or a suitor his sweetheart. In this strait you may count on me, through all advarsities; and I think Hurry does discredit to his natur' and wishes, if you can't count on him."

"Not he," cried Judith, thrusting her handsome face out of the door; "his nature is hurry, as well as his name, and he'll hurry off, as soon as he thinks his fine figure in danger. Neither old Tom, nor his gals, will depend much on Master March, now they know him, but *you* they will rely on, Deerslayer; for your honest face and honest heart tell us that what you promise you will perform."

This was said, as much, perhaps, in affected scorn for Hurry, as in sincerity. Still, it was not said without feeling. The fine face of Judith sufficiently proved the latter circumstance; and if the conscious March fancied that he had never seen in it a stronger display of contempt—a feeling in which the beauty was apt to indulge—than while she was looking at him, it certainly seldom exhibited more of womanly softness and sensibility, than when her speaking blue eyes were turned on his travelling companion.

"Leave us, Judith," Hutter ordered sternly, before either of the young men could reply; "leave us; and do not return until you come with the venison and fish. The girl has been spoilt by the flattery of the officers, who sometimes find their way up here, Master March, and you'll not think any harm of her silly words."

"You never said truer syllable, old Tom," retorted Hurry, who smarted under Judith's observations; "the devil-tongued youngsters of the garrison have proved her undoing! I scarce know Jude any longer, and shall soon take to admiring her sister, who is getting to be much more to my fancy."

"I'm glad to hear this, Harry, and look upon it as a sign that you're coming to your right senses. Hetty would make a much safer and more rational companion than Jude, and would be much the most likely to listen to your suit, as the officers have, I greatly fear, unsettled her sister's mind."

"No man needs a safer wife than Hetty," said Hurry, laughing, "though I'll not answer for her being of the most rational. But no matter; Deerslayer has not misconceived me, when he told you I should be found at my post. I'll not quit *you,* Uncle Tom, just now, whatever may be my feelin's and intentions respecting your eldest darter."

Hurry had a respectable reputation for prowess among his associates, and Hutter heard this pledge with a satisfaction that was not concealed. Even the great personal strength of such an aid became of moment, in moving the ark, as well as in the species of hand-to-hand conflicts, that were not unfrequent in the woods; and no commander who was hard-pressed could feel more joy at hearing of the arrival of reinforcements, than the borderer experienced at being told this important auxiliary was not about to quit him. A minute before, Hutter would have been well content to compromise his danger, by entering into a compact to act only on the defensive; but no sooner did he feel some security on this point, than the restlessness of man induced him to think of the means of carrying the war into the enemy's country.

"High prices are offered for scalps on both sides," he observed, with a grim smile, as if he felt the force of the inducement, at the very time he wished to affect a superiority to earning money by means that the ordinary feelings of those who aspire to be civilized men repudiated, even while they were adopted. "It isn't right, perhaps, to take gold for human blood; and yet, when mankind is busy in killing one another, there can be no great harm in adding a little bit of skin to the plunder. What's your sentiments, Hurry, touching these p'ints?"

"That you've made a vast mistake, old man, in calling savage blood human blood, at all. I think no more of a redskin's scalp than I do of a pair of wolf's ears; and would just as lief finger money for the one as for the other. With *white* people 'tis different, for they've a nat'ral avarsion to being scalped; whereas your Indian shaves his head in readiness for the knife, and leaves a lock of hair by way of braggadocio, that one can lay hold of in the bargain." [1]

"That's manly, however, and I felt from the first that we had only

[1] When Indians in the pay of the French burned farmhouses and slew settlers all along the frontier, the New York Assembly hastened to offer bounties for the scalps of the red assailants.—Ed.

to get you on our side, to have your heart and hand," returned Tom, losing all his reserve, as he gained a renewed confidence in the disposition of his companions. "Something more may turn up from this inroad of the redskins than they bargained for. Deerslayer, I conclude you're of Hurry's way of thinking, and look upon money 'arned in this way as being as likely to pass as money 'arned in trapping or hunting."

"I've no such feelin', nor any wish to harbor it, not I," returned the other. "My gifts are not scalpers' gifts, but such as belong to my religion and color. I'll stand by you, old man, in the ark or in the castle, the canoe or the woods, but I'll not unhumanize my natur' by falling into ways that God intended for another race. If you and Hurry have got any thoughts that lean toward the colony's gold, go by yourselves in s'arch of it, and leave the females to my care. Much as I must differ from you both on all gifts that do not properly belong to a white man, we shall agree that it is the duty of the strong to take care of the weak, especially when the last belong to them that natur' intended man to protect and console by his gentleness and strength."

"Hurry Harry, that is a lesson you might learn and practice on to some advantage," said the sweet, but spirited voice of Judith, from the cabin; a proof that she had overheard all that had hitherto been said.

"No more of this, Jude," called out the father angrily. "Move farther off; we are about to talk of matters unfit for a woman to listen to."

Hutter did not take any steps, however, to ascertain whether he was obeyed or not; but dropping his voice a little, he pursued the discourse.

"The young man is right, Hurry," he said; "and we can leave the children in his care. Now, my idea is just this; and I think you'll agree that it is rational and correct. There's a large party of these savages on shore and, though I didn't tell it before the girls, for they're womanish, and apt to be troublesome when anything like real work is to be done, there's women among 'em. This I know from moccasin prints; and 'tis likely they are hunters, after all, who have been out so long that they know nothing of the war, or of the bounties."

"In which case, old Tom, why was their first salute an attempt to cut our throats?"

"We don't know that their design was so bloody. It's natural and easy for an Indian to fall into ambushes and surprises; and, no doubt they wished to get on board the ark first, and to make their conditions afterwards. That a disapp'inted savage should fire at us, is in rule; and I think nothing of that. Besides, how often they burned me out, and robbed my traps—ay, and pulled trigger on me, in the most peaceful times?"

"The blackguards will do such things, I must allow; and we pay 'em off pretty much in their own c'ine. Women would not be on the warpath, sartainly; and, so far, there's reason in your idee."

"Nor would a hunter be in his war paint," returned Deerslayer. "I saw the Mingoes, and *know* that they are out on the trail of mortal men; and not for beaver or deer."

"There you have it ag'in, old fellow," said Hurry. "In the way of an eye, now, I'd as soon trust this young man, as trust the oldest settler in the colony; if he says paint, why paint it was."

"Then a hunting party and a war party have met, for women must have been with 'em. It's only a few days since the runner went through with the tidings of the troubles; and it may be that warriors have come out to call in their women and children, to get an early blow."

"That would stand the courts, and is just the truth," cried Hurry; "you've got it now, old Tom, and I should like to hear what you mean to make out of it."

"The bounty," returned the other, looking up at his attentive companion, in a cool, sullen manner, in which, however, heartless cupidity and indifference to the means were far more conspicuous than any feelings of animosity or revenge. "If there's women, there's children; and big and little have scalps; the colony pays for all alike."

"More shame to it, that it should do so," interrupted Deerslayer; "more shame to it, that it don't understand its gifts, and pay greater attention to the will of God."

"Hearken to reason, lad, and don't cry out afore you understand a case," returned the unmoved Hurry; "the savages scalp your fri'nds, the Delawares, or Mohicans, whichever they may be, among the rest; and why shouldn't we scalp? I will own, it would be ag'in right for you and me, now, to go into the settlements and bring out scalps, but it's a very different matter as concerns Indians. A man shouldn't take scalps, if he isn't ready to be scalped, himself, on fitting occasions. One good turn desarves another, all the world over. That's reason, and I believe it to be good religion."

"Ay, Master Hurry," again interrupted the rich voice of Judith, "is it religion to say that one *bad* turn deserves another?"

"I'll never reason ag'in you, Judy, for you beat me with beauty, if you can't with sense. Here's the Canadas paying their Injins for scalps, and why not we pay—"

"*Our* Indians!" exclaimed the girl, laughing with a sort of melancholy merriment. "Father, father! think no more of this, and listen to the advice of Deerslayer, who *has* a conscience; which is more than I can say or think of Harry March."

Hutter now rose, and, entering the cabin, he compelled his daughters to go into the adjoining room, when he secured both the doors, and returned. Then he and Hurry pursued the subject; but, as the purport of all that was material in this discourse will appear in the narrative, it need not be related here in detail.

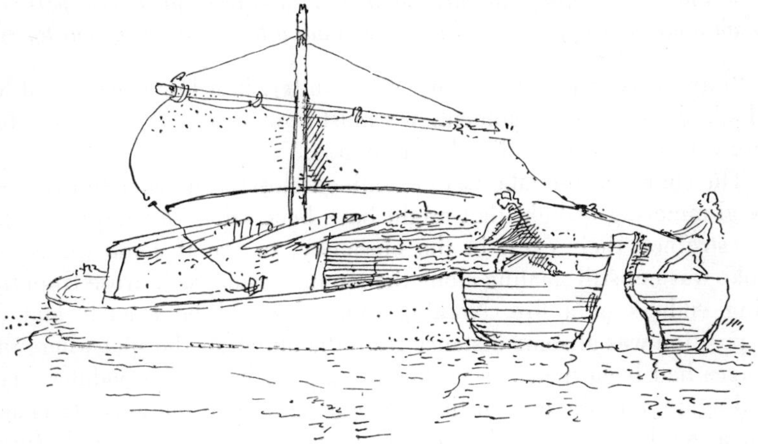

4

OLD TOM HUTTER in a short after-dinner chat with his simple-minded daughter Hetty revealed his hope that Hurry Harry might prevail upon Judith to accept him in marriage. "Harry March is the handsomest, and the strongest, and the boldest young man that ever visits the lake; and, as Jude is the greatest beauty, I don't see why they shouldn't come together." Hetty, however, was certain that Judith disliked Hurry and would have none of him. In a brief conversation with Deerslayer, Judith confirmed this. She accused Hurry Harry of slandering her; of repeating malicious gossip about herself and some of the officers at the British garrisons on the Mohawk. She also confessed that she had taken an instant liking to Deerslayer. "I know not how it is—but you are the first man I ever met, who did not seem to wish to flatter—to wish my ruin—to be an enemy in disguise."

When a breeze arose during the evening, Hutter set a large square sail on his ark, and brought the vessel up to his castle in the middle of the lake. This, he explained, was his refuge from hostile savages. "I built this dwelling in order to have 'em at arm's length, in case we should ever get to blows again." He added that the great object for a party posted like themselves was to command the water. "So long as there is no other craft on the lake, a bark canoe is as good as a man-of-war, since the castle will not be easily taken by swimming." He was uneasy, however, over two canoes that had been hidden on the shore in hollow logs. The venomous Hurons or Mingoes, he feared, might find them. Deerslayer and Hurry Harry agreed that it would be wise to land and secure these boats. At midnight, therefore, the three men embarked in a canoe, and half an hour later approached the shore about a league from the castle.

"Lay on your paddles, men," said Hutter, in a low voice, "and let us look about us for a moment. We must now be all eyes and ears, for these vermin have noses like bloodhounds."

The shores of the lake were examined closely, in order to discover any glimmering of light that might have been left in a camp; and the men strained their eyes, in the obscurity, to see if some thread of smoke was not still stealing along the mountainside, as it arose from the dying embers of a fire. Nothing unusual could be traced; and as the position was at some distance from the outlet, or the spot where the savages had been met, it was thought safe to land. The paddles were plied again, and the bow of the canoe ground upon the gravelly beach with a gentle motion, and a sound barely audible. Hutter and Hurry immediately landed, the former carrying his own and his friend's rifle, leaving Deerslayer in charge of the canoe. The hollow log lay a little distance up the side of the mountain, and the old man led the way toward it, using so much caution as to stop at every third or fourth step, to listen if any tread betrayed the presence of a foe. The same deathlike stillness, however, reigned on the midnight scene, and the desired place was reached without an occurrence to induce alarm.

"This is it," whispered Hutter, laying a foot on the trunk of a fallen linden; "hand me the paddles first, and draw the boat out with care, for the wretches may have left it for a bait, after all."

"Keep my rifle handy, butt toward me, old fellow," answered March. "If they attack me loaded, I shall want to unload the piece at 'em, at least. And feel if the pan is full."

"All's right," muttered the other; "move slow, when you get your load, and let me lead the way."

The canoe was drawn out of the log with the utmost care, raised by Hurry to his shoulder, and the two began to return to the shore, moving but a step at a time, lest they should tumble down the steep declivity. The distance was not great, but the descent was extremely difficult; and, toward the end of their little journey, Deerslayer was obliged to land and meet them, in order to aid in lifting the canoe through the bushes. With his assistance the task was successfully accomplished, and the light craft soon floated by the side of the other canoe. This was no sooner done, than all three turned anxiously toward the forest and the mountain, expecting an enemy to break out of the one, or to come rushing down the other. Still the silence was unbroken, and they all embarked with the caution that had been used in coming ashore.

Hutter now steered broad off toward the center of the lake. Having got a sufficient distance from the shore, he cast his prize loose, knowing that it would drift slowly up the lake before the light southerly air, and intending to find it on his return. Thus relieved of his tow, the old man held his way down the lake, steering toward the very point where Hurry had made his fruitless attempt on the life of the deer. As the distance from this point to the outlet was less than a mile, it was like entering an enemy's country; and redoubled caution became necessary. They reached the extremity of the point, however, and landed in safety on the little gravelly beach already mentioned. Unlike the last place at which they had gone ashore, here was no acclivity to ascend, the mountains looming up in the darkness quite a quarter of a mile farther west, leaving a margin of level ground between them and the strand. The point itself, though long, and covered with tall trees, was nearly flat, and for some distance only a few yards in width. Hutter and Hurry landed as before, leaving their companion in charge of the boat.

In this instance, the dead tree that contained the canoe of which they had come in quest lay about halfway between the extremity of the narrow slip of land and the place where it joined the main shore; and knowing that there was water so near him on his left, the old man led the way along the eastern side of the belt with some confidence, walking boldly, though still with caution. He had landed at the point expressly to get a glimpse into the bay, and to make certain that the coast was clear; otherwise he would have come ashore directly abreast of the hollow tree. There was no difficulty in finding the latter, from which the canoe was drawn as before, and instead of carrying it down to the place where Deerslayer lay, it was launched at the nearest favorable spot. As soon as it was in the water, Hurry entered it, and paddled round to the point, whither Hutter also proceeded, following the beach. As the three men had now in their possession all the boats on the lake, their confidence was greatly increased, and there was no longer the same feverish desire to quit the shore, or the same necessity for extreme caution. Their position on the extremity of the long, narrow bit of land, added to the feeling of security, as it permitted an enemy to approach in only one direction, that in their front, and under circumstances that would render discovery, with their habitual vigilance, almost certain. The three now landed together, and stood grouped in consultation on the gravelly point.

"We've fairly tree'd the scamps," said Hurry, chuckling at their success; "if they wish to visit the castle, let 'em wade or swim! Old Tom, that idee of your'n, in burrowing out in the lake, was high proof, and carries a fine bead. There be men who would think the land safer than the water; but, after all, reason shows it isn't; the beaver, and rats, and other l'arned creatur's taking to the last when hard-pressed. I call our position now, entrenched, and set the Canadas at defiance."

"Let us paddle along this south shore," said Hutter, "and see if there's no sign of an encampment; but, first, let me have a better look into the bay, for no one has been far enough round the inner shore of the point to make sure of that quarter yet."

As Hutter ceased speaking, all three moved in the direction he had named. Scarce had they fairly opened the bottom of the bay, when a general start proved that their eyes had lighted on a common object at the same instant. It was no more than a dying brand, giving out its flickering and failing light; but at that hour, and in that place, it was at once as conspicuous as "a good deed in a naughty world." There was not a shadow of doubt that this fire had been kindled at an encampment of the Indians. The situation, sheltered from observation on all sides but one, and even on that except for a very short distance, proved that more care had been taken to conceal the spot than would be used for ordinary purposes, and Hutter, who knew that a spring was near at hand, as well as one of the best fishing stations on the lake, immediately inferred that this encampment contained the women and children of the party.

"That's not a warrior's encampment," he growled to Hurry; "and there's bounty enough sleeping round that fire to make a heavy division of head money. Send the lad to the canoes, for there'll come no good of him in such an onset, and let us take the matter in hand at once, like men."

"There's judgment in your notion, old Tom, and I like it to the backbone. Deerslayer, do you get into the canoe, lad, and paddle off into the lake with the spare one, and set it adrift, as we did with the other; after which you can float along shore, as near as you can get to the head of the bay, keeping outside the point, however, and outside the rushes, too. You can hear us when we want you; and if there's any delay, I'll call like a loon—yes, that'll do it—the call of a loon shall be the signal. If you hear rifles, and feel like sogering, why, you may close in, and see if you can make the same hand with the savages that you do with the deer."

"If my wishes could be followed, this matter would not be undertaken, Hurry—"

"Quite true—nobody denies it, boy; but your wishes *can't* be followed; and that inds the matter. So just canoe yourself off into the middle of the lake, and by the time you get back there'll be movements in that camp!"

The young man set about complying with great reluctance and a heavy heart. He knew the prejudices of the frontiersmen too well, however, to attempt a remonstrance. The latter, indeed, under the circumstances, might prove dangerous, as it would certainly prove useless. He paddled the canoe, therefore, silently, and with the former caution, to a spot near the center of the placid sheet of water, and set the boat just recovered adrift, to float toward the castle, before the light southerly air. This expedient had been adopted, in both cases, under the certainty that the drift could not carry the light barks more than a league or two, before the return of light, when they might easily be overtaken. In order to prevent any wandering savage from using them, by swimming off and getting possession, a possible, but scarcely a probable event, all the paddles were retained.

No sooner had he set the recovered canoe adrift, than Deerslayer turned the bow of his own toward the point on the shore that had been indicated by Hurry. So light was the movement of the little craft, and so steady the sweep of its master's arm, that ten minutes had not elapsed ere it was again approaching the land, having, in that brief time, passed over fully half a mile of distance. As soon as Deerslayer's eye caught a glimpse of the rushes, of which there were many growing in the water a hundred feet from the shore, he arrested the motion of the canoe, and anchored his boat by holding fast to the delicate but tenacious stem of one of the drooping plants. Here he remained, awaiting, with an intensity of suspense that can be easily imagined, the result of the hazardous enterprise.

It would be difficult to convey to the minds of those who have never witnessed it, the sublimity that characterizes the silence of a solitude as deep as that which now reigned over the Glimmerglass. In the present instance, this sublimity was increased by the gloom of night, which threw its shadowy and fantastic forms around the lake, the forest, and the hills. It is not easy, indeed, to conceive of any place more favorable to heighten these natural impressions, than that Deerslayer now occupied. The size of the lake brought all within the reach of human senses, while it displayed so much of the imposing scene at a single view, giving up, as it might be, at a glance, a sufficiency to produce the deepest impressions. As has been said, this was the first lake Deerslayer had ever seen. Hitherto, his experience had been limited to the courses of rivers and smaller streams, and never before had he seen so much of that wilderness, which he so well loved, spread before his gaze. Accustomed to the forest, however, his mind was capable of portraying all its hidden mysteries, as he looked upon its leafy surface. This was also the first time he had been on a trail where human lives depended on the issue. His ears had often drunk in the traditions of frontier warfare, but he had never yet been confronted with an enemy.

The reader will readily understand, therefore, how intense must have been the expectation of the young man, as he sat in his solitary canoe, endeavoring to catch the smallest sound that might denote the course of things on shore. His training had been perfect, so far as theory could go, and his self-possession, notwithstanding the high excitement, that was the fruit of novelty, would have done credit to a veteran. The visible evidences of the existence of the camp, or of the fire, could not be detected from the spot where the canoe lay, and he was compelled to depend on the sense of hearing alone. He did not feel impatient, for the lessons he had heard taught him the virtue of patience, and, most of all, inculcated the necessity of wariness in conducting any covert assault on the Indians. Once he thought he heard the cracking of a dried twig, but expectation was so intense it might mislead him. In this manner minute after minute passed, until the whole time since he left his companions was extended to quite an hour. Deerslayer knew not whether to rejoice in or to mourn over this cautious delay, for, if it augured security to his associates, it foretold destruction to the feeble and innocent.

It might have been an hour and a half after his companions and he had parted, when Deerslayer was aroused by a sound that filled him equally with concern and surprise. The quavering call of a loon arose from the opposite side of the lake, evidently at no great distance from its outlet. There was no mistaking the note of this bird, which is so familiar to all who know the sounds of the American lakes. Shrill, tremulous, loud, and sufficiently prolonged, it seems the very cry of warning. It is often raised, also, at night—an exception to the habits of most of the other feathered inmates of the wilderness; a circumstance which had induced Hurry to select it as his own signal. There had been sufficient time, certainly, for the two adventurers to make their way by land from the point where they had been left to that whence the call had come, but it was not probable that they would adopt such a course. Had the camp been deserted they would have summoned Deerslayer to the shore, and, did it prove to be peopled, there could be no sufficient motive for circling it, in order to re-embark at so great a distance. Should he obey the signal, and be drawn away from the landing, the lives of those who depended on him might be the forfeit—and, should he neglect the call, on the supposition that it had been really made, the consequences might be equally disastrous, though from a different cause. In this indecision he waited, trusting that the call, whether feigned or natural, would be speedily renewed. Nor was he mistaken. A very few minutes elapsed before the same shrill warning cry was repeated, and from the same part of the lake. This time, being on the alert, his senses were not deceived. Although he had often heard admirable imitations of this bird, and was no mean adept himself in raising its notes, he felt satisfied that Hurry, to whose efforts in that way he had attended, could never so completely and closely follow nature. He determined, therefore, to disregard that cry, and to wait for one less perfect and nearer at hand.

Deerslayer had hardly come to this determination, when the profound stillness of night and solitude was broken by a cry so startling, as to drive all recollection of the more melancholy call of the loon from the listener's mind. It was a shriek of agony, that came either from one of the female sex, or from a boy so young as not yet to have attained a manly voice. This appeal could not be mistaken. Heart-rending terror—if not writhing agony—was in the sounds, and the anguish that had awakened them was as sudden as it was fearful. The young man released his hold of the rush, and dashed his paddle into the water; to do, he knew not what—to steer, he knew not whither. A very few moments, however, removed his indecision. The breaking of branches, the cracking of dried sticks, and the fall of feet were distinctly audible; the sounds appearing to approach the water, though in a direction that led diagonally toward the shore, and a little farther north than the spot that Deerslayer had been ordered to keep near. Following this clue, the young man urged the canoe ahead, paying but little attention to the manner in which he might betray its presence. He had reached a part of the shore, where its immediate bank was tolerably high and quite steep. Men were evidently threshing through the bushes and trees on the summit of this bank, following the line of the shore, as if those who fled sought a favorable place for descending. Just at this instant five or six rifles flashed, and the opposite hills gave back, as usual, the sharp reports in prolonged rolling echoes. One or two shrieks, like those which escape the bravest when suddenly overcome by unexpected anguish and alarm, followed; and then the threshing among the bushes was renewed, in a way to show that man was grappling with man.

"Slippery devil!" shouted Hurry with the fury of disappointment—"his skin's greased! I sha'n't grapple!—Take *that* for your cunning!"

The words were followed by the fall of some heavy object among the smaller trees that fringed the bank, appearing to Deerslayer as if his gigantic associate had hurled an enemy from him in this unceremonious manner. Again the flight and pursuit were renewed, and then the young man saw a human form break down the hill, and rush several yards into the water. At this critical moment the canoe was just near enough to the spot to allow this movement, which was accompanied by no little noise, to be seen, and feeling that there he must take in his companion, if anywhere, Deerslayer urged the canoe forward to the rescue. His paddle had not been raised twice, when the voice of Hurry was heard filling the air with imprecations, and he rolled on the narrow beach, literally loaded down with enemies. While prostrate, and almost smothered with his foes, the athletic frontiersman gave his loon call, in a manner that would have excited laughter under circumstances less terrific. The figure in the water seemed suddenly to repent his own flight, and rushed to the shore to aid his companion, but was met and immediately overpowered by half a dozen fresh pursuers, who, just then, came leaping down the bank.

"Let up, you painted riptyles—let up!" cried Hurry, too hard-pressed to be particular about the terms he used; "isn't it enough that I am withed like a saw log that ye must choke too!"

This speech satisfied Deerslayer that his friends were prisoners, and that to land would be to share their fate. He was already within a hundred feet of the shore, when a few timely strokes of the paddle not only arrested his advance, but forced him off to six or eight times that distance from his enemies. Luckily for him, all of the Indians had dropped their rifles in the pursuit, or this retreat might not have been effected with impunity; though no one had noted the canoe in the first confusion of the *mêlée*.

"Keep off the land, lad," called out Hutter; "the girls depend only on you, now; you will want all your caution to escape these savages. Keep off, and God prosper you, as you aid my children!"

There was little sympathy in general between Hutter and the young man, but the bodily and mental anguish with which this appeal was made served at the moment to conceal from the latter the former's faults. He saw only the father in his sufferings, and resolved at once to give a pledge of fidelity to its interests, and to be faithful to his word.

"Put your heart at ease, Master Hutter," he called out; "the gals shall be looked to, as well as the castle. The inimy has got the shore, 'tis no use to deny, but he hasn't got the water. Providence has the charge of all, and no one can say what will come of it; but, if good will can sarve you and your'n, depend on that much. My exper'ence is small, but my will is good."

"Ay, ay, Deerslayer," returned Hurry, in this stentorian voice, which was losing some of its heartiness, notwithstanding,—"Ay, ay, Deerslayer, you *mean* well enough, but what can you *do?* You're no great matter in the best of times, and such a person is not likely to turn out a miracle in the worst. If there's one savage on this lake shore, there's forty, and that's an army you ar'n't the man to overcome. The best way, in my judgment, will be to make a straight course to the castle; get the gals into the canoe, with a few eatables; then strike off for the corner of the lake where we came in, and take the best trail for the Mohawk. These devils won't know where to look for you for some hours, and if they did, and went off hot in the pursuit, they must turn either the foot or the head of the lake to get at you. That's my judgment in the matter; and if old Tom here wishes to make his last will and testament in a manner favorable to his darters, he'll say the same."

" 'Twill never do, young man," rejoined Hutter. "The enemy has scouts out at this moment, looking for canoes, and you'll be seen and taken. Trust to the castle; and above all things, keep clear of the land. Hold out a week, and parties from the garrisons will drive the savages off."

" 'Twon't be four-and-twenty hours, old fellow, afore these foxes will be rafting off to storm your castle," interrupted Hurry, with more of the heat of argument than might be expected from a man who was bound and a captive, and about whom nothing could be called free but his opinions and his tongue. "Your advice has a stout sound, but it will have a fatal tarmination. If you or I was in the house, we might hold out a few days, but remember that this lad has never seen an inimy afore tonight, and is what you yourself called settlement-conscienced; though for my part, I think the consciences in the settlements pretty much the same as they are out here in the woods. These savages are making signs, Deerslayer, for me to encourage you to come ashore with the canoe; but that I'll never do, as its ag'in reason and natur'. As for old Tom and myself, whether they'll scalp us tonight, keep us for the torture by fire, or carry us to Canada, is more than any one knows but the devil that advises them how to act. I've such a big and bushy head that it's quite likely they'll indivor to get two scalps off it, for the bounty is a tempting thing, or old Tom and I wouldn't be in this scrape. Ay—there they go with their signs ag'in, but if I advise you to land, may they eat me as well as roast me. No, no, Deerslayer—do you keep off where you are, and after daylight, on no account come within two hundred yards—"

This injunction of Hurry's was stopped by a hand being rudely slapped against his mouth, the certain sign that someone in the party sufficiently understood English to have at length detected the drift of his discourse. Immediately after, the whole group entered the forest, Hutter and Hurry apparently making no resistance to the movement. Just as the sounds of the cracking bushes were ceasing, however, the voice of the father was again heard.

"As you're true to my children, God prosper you, young man!" were the words that reached Deerslayer's ears; after which he found himself left to follow the dictates of his own discretion.

Several minutes elapsed, in deathlike stillness, when the party on the shore had disappeared in the woods. Owing to the distance—rather more than two hundred yards—and the obscurity, Deerslayer had been able barely to distinguish the group, and to see it retiring; but even this dim connection with human forms gave an animation to the scene that was strongly in contrast to the absolute solitude that remained. Although the young man leaned forward to listen, holding his breath and condensing every faculty in the single sense of hearing, not another sound reached his ears to denote the vicinity of human beings. It seemed as if a silence that had never broken reigned on the spot again; and, for an instant, even that piercing shriek, which had so lately broken the stillness of the forest, or the execrations of March, would have been a relief to the feeling of desertion to which it gave rise.

This paralysis of mind and body, however, could not last long in one constituted mentally and physically like Deerslayer. Dropping his paddle into the water, he turned the head of the canoe, and proceeded slowly, as one walks who thinks intently, towards the center of the lake. When he believed himself to have reached a point in a line with that where he had set the last canoe adrift, he changed his direction northward, keeping the light air as nearly on his back as possible. After paddling a quarter of a mile in this direction, a dark object became visible on the lake, a little to the right; and turning on one side for the purpose, he had soon secured his lost prize to his own boat. Deerslayer now examined the heavens, the course of the air, and the position of the two canoes. Finding nothing in either to induce a change of plan, he lay down, and prepared to catch a few hours' sleep, that the morrow might find him equal to its exigencies.

Although the hardy and the tired sleep profoundly, even in scenes of danger, it was some time before Deerslayer lost his recollection. His mind dwelt on what had passed, and his half-conscious faculties kept figuring the events of the night, in a sort of waking dream. Suddenly he was up and alert, for he fancied he heard the preconcerted signal of Hurry summoning him to the shore. But all was still as the grave again. The canoes were slowly drifting northward, the thoughtful stars were glimmering in their mild glory over his head, and the forest-bound sheet of water lay embedded between its mountains, as calm and melancholy as if never troubled by the winds, or brightened by a noonday sun. Once more the loon raised his tremulous cry, near the foot of the lake, and the mystery of the alarm was explained. Deerslayer adjusted his hard pillow, stretched his form in the bottom of the canoe, and slept.

5

DAY HAD fairly dawned before the young man, whom we have left in the situation described in the last chapter, again opened his eyes. This was no sooner done, than he started up, and looked about him with the eagerness of one who suddenly felt the importance of accurately ascertaining his precise position. His rest had been deep and undisturbed; and when he awoke, it was with a clearness of intellect and a readiness of resources that were very much needed at that particular moment. The sun had not risen, it is true, but the vault of heaven was rich with the winning softness that "brings and shuts the day," while the whole air was filled with the carols of birds, the hymns of the feathered tribe. These sounds first told Deerslayer the risks he ran. The air, for wind it could scarce be called, was still light, it is true, but it had increased a little in the course of the night, and as the canoes were mere feathers on the water, they had drifted twice the expected distance; and, what was still more dangerous, had approached so near the base of the mountain that here rose precipitously from the eastern shore, as to render the carols of the birds plainly audible. This was not the worst. The third canoe had taken the same direction, and was slowly drifting toward a point where it must inevitably touch, unless turned aside by a shift of wind, or human hands. In other respects, nothing presented itself to attract attention, or to awaken alarm. The castle stood on its shoal, nearly abreast of the canoes, for the drift had amounted to miles in the course of the night, and the ark lay fastened to its piles, as both had been left so many hours before.

As a matter of course, Deerslayer's attention was first given to the canoe ahead. It was already quite near the point, and a very few strokes of the paddle sufficed to tell him that it must touch before he could possibly overtake it. Just at this moment, too, the wind inopportunely freshened, rendering the drift of the light craft much more rapid than certain. Feeling the impossibility of preventing a contact with the land, the young man wisely determined not to heat himself with unnecessary exertions; but first looking to the priming of his piece, he proceeded slowly and warily toward the point, taking care to make a little circuit, that he might be exposed on only one side, as he approached.

The canoe adrift being directed by no such intelligence, pursued its proper way, and grounded on a small sunken rock, at the distance of three or four yards from the shore. Just at that moment, Deerslayer had got abreast of the point, and turned the bow of his own boat to the land; first casting loose his tow, that his movements might be unencumbered. The canoe hung an instant on the rock; then it rose a hairs-breadth on an almost imperceptible swell of the water, swung round, floated clear, and reached the strand. All this the young man noted, but it neither quickened his pulses, nor hastened his hand. If anyone had been lying in wait for the arrival of the waif, he must be seen, and the utmost caution in approaching the shore became indispensable; if no one was in ambush, hurry was unnecessary. The point being nearly diagonally opposite to the Indian encampment, he hoped the last, though the former was not only possible, but probable; for the savages were prompt in adopting all the expedients of their particular modes of warfare, and quite likely had many scouts searching the shores for craft to carry them off to the castle. As a glance at the lake from any height or projection would expose the smallest object on its surface, there was little hope that either of the canoes would pass unseen; and Indian sagacity needed no instruction to tell which way a boat or a log would drift, when the direction of the wind was known. As Deerslayer drew nearer and nearer to the land, the stroke of his paddle grew slower, his eye became more watchful, and his ears and nostrils almost dilated with the effort to detect any lurking danger. 'Twas a trying moment for a novice, nor was there the encouragement which even the timid sometimes feel, when conscious of being observed and commended. He was entirely alone, thrown on his own resources, and was cheered by no friendly eye, emboldened by no encouraging voice. Notwithstanding all these circumstances, the most experienced veteran in forest warfare could not have behaved better. Equally free from recklessness and hesitation, his advance was marked by a sort of philosophical prudence, that appeared to render him superior to all motives but those which were best calculated to effect his purpose. Such was the commencement of a career in forest exploits, that afterwards rendered this man, in his way, and under the limits of his habits and opportunities, as renowned as many a hero whose name has adorned the pages of works more celebrated than legends simple as ours can ever become.

When about a hundred yards from the shore, Deerslayer rose in the canoe, gave three or four vigorous strokes with the paddle, sufficient of themselves to impel the bark to land, and then quickly laying aside the instrument of labor, he seized that of war. He was in the very act of raising the rifle, when a sharp report was followed by the buzz of a bullet that passed so near his body as to cause him involuntarily to start. The next instant Deerslayer staggered, and fell his whole length in the bottom of the canoe. A yell—it came from a single voice—followed, and an Indian leaped from the bushes upon the open area of the point, bounding toward the canoe. This was the moment the young man desired. He rose on the instant, and levelled his own rifle at his uncovered foe; but his finger hesitated about pulling the trigger on one whom he held at such a disadvantage. This little delay, probably, saved the life of the Indian, who bounded back into the cover as swiftly as he had broken out of it. In the meantime, Deerslayer had been swiftly approaching the land, and his own canoe reached the point just as his enemy disappeared. As its movements had not been directed, it touched the shore a few yards from the other boat; and though the rifle of his foe had to be loaded, there was not time to secure his prize, and carry it beyond danger, before he would be exposed to another shot. Under the circumstances, therefore, he did not pause an instant, but dashed into the woods and sought a cover.

On the immediate point there was a small open area, partly in native grass, and partly beach, but a dense fringe of bushes lined its upper side. This narrow belt of dwarf vegetation passed, one issued immediately into the high and gloomy vaults of the forest. The land was tolerably level for a few hundred feet, and then it rose precipitously in a mountainside. The trees were tall, large, and so free from underbrush, that they resembled vast columns, irregularly scattered, upholding a dome of leaves. Although they stood tolerably close together, for their ages and size, the eye could penetrate to considerable distances; and bodies of men, even, might have engaged beneath their cover, with concert and intelligence.

Deerslayer knew that his adversary must be employed in reloading, unless he had fled. The former proved to be the case, for the young man had no sooner placed himself behind a tree, than he caught a glimpse of the arm of the Indian, his body being concealed by an oak, in the very act of forcing the leathered bullet home. Nothing would have been easier than to spring forward, and decide the affair by a close assault on his unprepared foe; but every feeling of Deerslayer revolted at such a step, although his own life had just been attempted from a cover. He was yet unpracticed in the ruthless expedients of savage warfare, of which he knew nothing except by tradition and theory, and it struck him as an unfair advantage to assail an unarmed foe. His color had heightened, his eye frowned, his lips were compressed, and all his energies were collected and ready; but, instead of advancing to fire, he dropped his rifle to the usual position of a sportsman in readiness to catch his aim, and muttered to himself, unconscious that he was speaking—

"No, no—that may be redskin warfare, but it's not a Christian's gifts. Let the miscreant charge, and then we'll take it out like men; for the canoe he *must* not, and *shall* not have. No, no; let him have time to load, and God will take care of the right!"

All this time the Indian had been so intent on his own movements, that he was even ignorant that his enemy was in the woods. His only apprehension was, that the canoe would be recovered and carried away before he might be in readiness to prevent it. He had sought the cover from habit, but was within a few feet of the fringe of bushes, and could be at the margin of the forest in readiness to fire in a moment. The distance between him and his enemy was about fifty yards, and the trees were so arranged by nature that the line of sight was not interrupted, except by the particular trees behind which each party stood.

His rifle was no sooner loaded, than the savage glanced around him, and advanced incautiously as regarded the real, but stealthily as respected the fancied position of his enemy, until he was fairly exposed. Then Deerslayer stepped from behind his own cover, and hailed him.

"This-a-way, redskin; this-a-way, if you're looking for me," he called out. "I'm young in war, but not so young as to stand on an open beach to be shot down like an owl, by daylight. It rests on yourself whether it's peace or war atween us; for my gifts are white gifts, and I'm not one of them that thinks it valiant to slay human mortals, singly, in the woods."

The savage was a good deal startled by this sudden discovery of the danger he ran. He had a little knowledge of English, however, and caught the drift of the other's meaning. He was also too well schooled to betray alarm, but, dropping the butt of his rifle to the earth, with an air of confidence, he made a gesture of lofty courtesy. All this was done with the ease and self-possession of one accustomed to consider no man his superior. In the midst of this consummate acting, however, the volcano that raged within caused his eyes to glare, and his nostrils to dilate, like those of some wild beast that is suddenly prevented from taking the fatal leap.

"Two canoes," he said, in the deep guttural tones of his race, holding up the number of fingers he mentioned, by way of preventing mistakes; "one for you—one for me."

"No, no, Mingo, that will never do. You own neither; and neither shall you have, as long as I can prevent it. I know it's war atween your people and mine, but that's no reason why human mortals should slay each other, like savage creatur's that meet in the woods; go your way, then, and leave me to go mine. The world is large enough for us both; and when we meet fairly in battle, why, the Lord will order the fate of each of us."

"Good!" exclaimed the Indian; "my brother missionary—great talk; all about Manitou."

"Not so—not so, warrior. I'm not good enough for the Moravians, and am too good for most of the other vagabonds that preach about in the woods. No, no; I'm only a hunter, as yet, though afore the peace is made, 'tis like enough there'll be occasion to strike a blow at some of your people. Still, I wish it to be done in fair fight, and not in a quarrel about the ownership of a miserable canoe."

"Good! My brother very young—but he is very wise. Little warrior—great talker. Chief, sometimes, in council."

"I don't know this, nor do I say it, Injin," returned Deerslayer, coloring a little at the ill-concealed sarcasm of the other's manner; "I look forward to a life in the woods, and I only hope it may be a peaceable one. All young men must go on the warpath, when there's occasion, but war isn't needfully massacre. I've seen enough of the last, this very night, to know that Providence frowns on it; and I now invite you to go your own way, while I go mine; and hope that we may part fri'nds."

"Good! My brother has two scalp—gray hair under t'other. Old wisdom—young tongue."

Here the savage advanced with confidence, his hand extended, his face smiling, and his whole bearing denoting amity and respect. Deerslayer met his offered friendship in a proper spirit, and they shook hands cordially, each endeavoring to assure the other of his sincerity and desire to be at peace.

"All have his own," said the Indian; "my canoe, mine; your canoe, your'n. Go look; if your'n, you keep; if mine, I keep."

"That's just, redskin, though you must be wrong in thinking the canoe your property. Howsever, seein' is believin', and we'll go down to the shore, where you may look with your own eyes; for it's likely you'll object to trustin' altogether to mine."

The Indian uttered his favorite exclamation of "Good!" and then they walked side by side, toward the shore. There was no apparent distrust in the manner of either, the Indian moving in advance, as if he wished to show his companion that he did not fear turning his back to him. As they reached the open ground, the former pointed toward Deerslayer's boat, and said emphatically—

"No mine—paleface canoe. *This* redman's. No want other man's canoe—want his own."

"You're wrong, redskin, you're altogether wrong. This canoe was left in old Hutter's keeping, and is his'n according to law, red or white, till its owner comes to claim it. Here's the seats and the stitching of the bark to speak for themselves. No man ever know'd an Injin to turn off such work."

"Good! My brother little old—big wisdom. Injin no make him. White man's work."

"I'm glad you think so, for holding out to the contrary might have made ill blood atween us, everyone having a right to take possession of his own. I'll just shove the canoe out of reach of dispute at once, as the quickest way of settling difficulties."

While Deerslayer was speaking, he put a foot against the end of the light boat, and giving a vigorous shove, he sent it out into the lake a hundred feet or more, where, taking the true current, it would necessarily float past the point, and be in no further danger of coming ashore. The savage started at this ready and decided expedient, and his companion saw that he cast a hurried and fierce glance at his own canoe, or that which contained the paddles. The change of manner, however, was but momentary, and then the Iroquois resumed his air of friendliness, and a smile of satisfaction.

"Good!" he repeated, with stronger emphasis than ever. "Young head, old mind. Know how to settle quarrel. Farewell, brother. He go to house in water—muskrat house—Injin go to camp; tell chiefs no find canoe."

Deerslayer was not sorry to hear this proposal, for he felt anxious to join the females, and he took the offered hand of the Indian very willingly. The parting words were friendly, and while the red man walked calmly toward the wood, with the rifle in the hollow of his arm, without once looking back in uneasiness or distrust, the white man moved toward the remaining canoe, carrying his piece in the same pacific manner, it is true, but keeping his eye fastened on the movements of the other. This distrust, however, seemed to be altogether uncalled-for, and as if ashamed to have entertained it, the young man averted his look, and stepped carelessly up to his boat. Here he began to push the canoe from the shore, and to make his other preparations for departing. He might have been thus employed a minute, when, happening to turn his face toward the land, his quick and certain eye told him, at a glance, the imminent jeopardy in which his life was placed. The black, ferocious eyes of the savage were glancing on him, like those of the crouching tiger, through a small opening in the bushes, and the muzzle of his rifle seemed already to be opening in a line with his own body.

Then, indeed, the long practice of Deerslayer, as a hunter, did him good service. Accustomed to fire with the deer on the bound, and often when the precise position of the animal's body had in a manner to be guessed at, he used the same expedients here. To cock and poise his rifle were the acts of a single moment and a single motion; then aiming almost without sighting, he fired into the bushes where he knew a body ought to be, in order to sustain the appalling countenance which alone was visible. There was not time to raise the piece any higher, or to take a more deliberate aim. So rapid were his movements that both parties discharged their pieces at the same instant, the concussions mingling in one report. The mountains, indeed, gave back but a single echo. Deerslayer dropped his piece, and stood with head erect, steady as one of the pines in the calm of a June morning, watching the result; while the savage gave the yell that has become historical for its appalling influence, leaped through the bushes, and came bounding across the open ground, flourishing a tomahawk. Still Deerslayer moved not, but stood with his unloaded rifle fallen against his shoulders, while, with a hunter's habits, his hands were mechanically feeling for the powder horn and charger. When about forty feet from his enemy, the savage hurled his keen weapon; but it was with an eye so vacant, and a hand so unsteady and feeble, that the young man caught it by the handle as it was flying past him. At that instant the Indian staggered and fell his whole length on the ground.

"I know'd it—I know'd it!" exclaimed Deerslayer, who was already preparing to force a fresh bullet into his rifle; "I know'd it must come to this, as soon as I had got the range from the creatur's eyes. A man sights suddenly, and fires quick when his own life's in danger; yes, I know'd it would come to this. I was about the hundredth part of a second too quick for him, or it might have been bad for me! The riptyle's bullet has just grazed my side—but say what you will for or ag'in 'em, a redskin is by no means as sartain with powder and ball as a white man. Their gifts don't seem to lie that-a-way. Even Chingachgook, great as he is in other matters, isn't downright deadly with the rifle."

By this time the piece was reloaded, and Deerslayer, after tossing the tomahawk into the canoe, advanced to his victim, and stood over him, leaning on his rifle, in melancholy attention. It was the first instance in which he had seen a man fall in battle—it was the first fellow-creature against whom he had ever seriously raised his own hand. The sensations were novel; and regret, with the freshness of our better feelings, mingled with his triumph. The Indian was not dead, though shot directly through the body. He lay on his back motionless, but his eyes, now full of consciousness, watched each action of his victor—as the fallen bird regards the fowler—jealous of every movement. The man probably expected the fatal blow which was to precede the loss of his scalp; or perhaps he anticipated that this latter act of cruelty would precede his death. Deerslayer read his thoughts; and he found a melancholy satisfaction in relieving the apprehensions of the helpless savage.

"No, no, redskin," he said; "you've nothing more to fear from me. I am of a Christian stock, and scalping is not of my gifts. I'll just make sartain of your rifle, and then come back and do you what sarvice I can. Though here I can't stay much longer, as the crack of three rifles will be apt to bring some of your devils down upon me."

The close of this was said in a sort of a soliloquy, as the young man went in quest of the fallen rifle. The piece was found where its owner had dropped it, and was immediately put into the canoe. Laying his own rifle at its side, Deerslayer then returned and stood over the Indian again.

"All inmity atween you and me's at an ind, redskin," he said; "and you may set your heart at rest on the score of the scalp, or any further injury. My gifts are white, as I've told you; and I hope my conduct will be white also!"

Could looks have conveyed all they meant, it is probable Deerslayer's innocent vanity on the subject of color would have been rebuked a little; but he comprehended the gratitude that was expressed in the eyes of the dying savage, without in the least detecting the bitter sarcasm that struggled with the better feeling.

"Water!" ejaculated the thirsty and unfortunate creature; "give poor Injin water."

"Ay, water you shall have, if you drink the lake dry. I'll just carry you down to it, that you may take your fill. This is the way, they tell me, with all wounded people—water is their greatest comfort and delight."

So saying, Deerslayer raised the Indian in his arms, and carried him to the lake. Here he first helped him to take an attitude in which he could appease his burning thirst; after which he seated himself on a stone, and took the head of his wounded adversary in his own lap, and endeavored to soothe his anguish in the best manner he could.

"It would be sinful in me to tell you your time hadn't come, warrior," he commenced, "and therefore I'll not say it. You've passed the middle age already, and, considerin' the sort of lives ye lead, your days have been pretty well filled. The principal thing now, is to look forward to what comes next. Neither redskin nor paleface, on the whole, calculates much on sleepin' forever; but both expect to live in another world. Each has his gifts, and will be judged by 'em, and I suppose you've thought these matters over enough not to stand in need of sarmons when the trial comes. You'll find your happy hunting grounds, if you've been a just Injin; if an onjust, you'll meet your desarts in another way. I've my own idees about these things; but you're too old and exper'enced to need any explanations from one as young as I."

"Good!" ejaculated the Indian, whose voice retained its depth even as life ebbed away; "young head—old wisdom!"

"It's sometimes a consolation, when the ind comes, to know that them we've harmed, or *tried* to harm, forgive us. I suppose natur' seeks this relief, by way of getting a pardon on 'arth; as we never can know whether He pardons, who is all in all, till judgment itself comes. It's soothing to know that *any* pardon at such times; and that, I conclude, is the secret. Now, as for myself, I overlook altogether your designs ag'in my life; first, because no harm came of 'em; next, because it's your gifts, and natur', and trainin', and I ought not to have trusted you at all; and, finally and chiefly, because I can bear no ill will to a dying man, whether heathen or Christian. So put your heart at ease, so far as I'm consarned; you know best what other matters ought to trouble you, or what ought to give you satisfaction in so trying a moment."

It is probable that the Indian had some of the fearful glimpses of the unknown state of being which God, in mercy, seems at times to afford to all the human race; but they were necessarily in conformity with his habits and prejudices. Like most of his people, and like too many of our own, he thought more of dying in a way to gain applause among those he left than to secure a better state of existence hereafter. While Deerslayer was speaking, his mind was a little bewildered, though he felt that the intention was good; and when he had done, a regret passed over his spirit that none of his own tribe were present to witness his stoicism, under extreme bodily suffering, and the firmness with which he met his end. With the high innate courtesy that so often distinguishes the Indian warrior before he becomes corrupted by too much intercourse with the worst class of the white men, he endeavored to express his thankfulness for the other's good intentions, and to let him understand that they were appreciated.

"Good!" he repeated, for this was an English word much used by the savages, "good! young head; young *heart,* too. *Old* heart tough; no shed tear. Hear Indian when he die, and no want to lie—what he call him?"

"Deerslayer is the name I bear now, though the Delawares have said that when I get back from this warpath, I shall have a more manly title, provided I can 'arn one."

"That good name for boy—poor name for warrior. He get better quick. No fear *there*,"—the savage had strength sufficient, under the strong excitement he felt, to raise a hand and tap the young man on his breast,—"eye sartain—finger lightning—aim, death—great warrior soon. No Deerslayer—Hawkeye—Hawkeye—Hawkeye. Shake hand."

Deerslayer—or Hawkeye, as the youth was then first named, for in after years he bore the appellation throughout all that region—Deerslayer took the hand of the savage, whose last breath was drawn in that attitude, gazing in admiration at the countenance of a stranger, who had shown so much readiness, skill, and firmness, in a scene that was equally trying and novel. When the reader remembers it is the highest gratification an Indian can receive to see his enemy betray weakness, he will be better able to appreciate the conduct which had extorted so great a concession at such a moment.

"His spirit has fled!" said Deerslayer, in a suppressed, melancholy voice. "Ah's me! Well, to this we must all come, sooner or later; and he is happiest, let his skin be what color it may, who is best fitted to meet it. Here lies the body of no doubt a brave warrior, and the soul is already flying toward its heaven or hell, whether that be a happy hunting ground, a place scant of game, regions of glory, according to Moravian doctrine, or flames of fire! So it happens, too, as regards other matters! Here have old Hutter and Hurry Harry got themselves into difficulty, if they haven't got themselves into torment and death, and all for a bounty that luck offers to me in what many would think a lawful and suitable manner. But not a farthing of such money shall cross my hand. White I was born, and white will I die; clinging to color to the last, even though the King's majesty, his governors, and all his councils, both at home and in the colonies, forget from what they come, and where they hope to go, and all for a little advantage in warfare. No, no, warrior, hand of mine shall never molest your scalp, and so your soul may rest in peace on the p'int of making a decent appearance when the body comes to join it, in your own land of spirits."

Deerslayer arose as soon as he had spoken. Then he placed the body of the dead man in a sitting posture, with its back against the little rock, taking the necessary care to prevent it from falling or in any way settling into an attitude that might be thought unseemly by the sensitive, though wild notions of a savage. When this duty was performed, the young man stood gazing at the grim countenance of his fallen foe, in a sort of melancholy abstraction. As was his practice, however, a habit gained by living so much alone in the forest, he then began again to give utterance to his thoughts and feelings aloud.

"I didn't wish your life, redskin," he said, "but you left me no choice atween killing or being killed. Each party acted according to his gifts, I suppose, and blame can light on neither. You were treacherous, according to your natur' in war, and I was a little oversightful, as I'm apt to be in trusting others. Well, this is my first battle with a human mortal, though it's not likely to be the last. I have fou't most of the creatur's of the forest, such as bears, wolves, painters, and catamounts, but this is the beginning with the redskins. If I was Injin born, now, I might tell of this, or carry in the scalp, and boast of the expl'ite afore the whole tribe; or, if my inimy had only been even a bear, 'twould have been nat'ral and proper to let everybody know what had happened; but I don't well see how I'm to let even Chingachgook into this secret, so long as it can be done only by boasting with a white tongue. And why should I wish to boast of it a'ter all? It's slaying a human, although he was a savage; and how do I know that he was a just Injin; and that he has not been taken away suddenly to anything but happy hunting grounds. When it's onsartain whether good or evil has been done, the wisest way is not to be boastful—still, I *should* like Chingachgook to know that I haven't discredited the Delawares, or my training!"

Part of this was uttered aloud, while part was merely muttered between the speaker's teeth; his more confident opinions enjoying the first advantage, while his doubts were expressed in the latter mode. Soliloquy and reflection received a startling interruption, however, by the sudden appearance of a second Indian on the lake shore, a few hundred yards from the point. This man, evidently another scout, who had probably been drawn to the place by the reports of the rifles, broke out of the forest with so little caution that Deerslayer caught a view of his person before he was himself discovered. When the latter event did occur, as was the case a moment later, the savage gave a loud yell, which was answered by a dozen voices from different parts of the mountainside. There was no longer any time for delay; in another minute the boat was quitting the shore under long and steady sweeps of the paddle.

As soon as Deerslayer believed himself to be at a safe distance, he ceased his efforts, permitting the little bark to drift, while he leisurely took a survey of the state of things. The canoe first sent adrift was floating before the air, quite a quarter of a mile above him, and a little nearer to the shore than he wished, now that he knew more of the savages were so near at hand. The canoe shoved from the point was within a few yards of him, he having directed his own course toward it on quitting the land. The dead Indian lay in grim quiet where he had left him, the warrior who had shown himself from the forest had already vanished, and the woods themselves were as silent and seemingly deserted as the day they came fresh from the hands of their great Creator. This profound stillness, however, lasted but a moment. When time had been given to the scouts of the enemy to reconnoiter, they burst out of the thicket upon the naked point, filling the air with yells of fury at discovering the death of their companion. These cries were immediately succeeded by shouts of delight when they reached the body and clustered eagerly around it. Deerslayer was a sufficient adept in the usages of the natives to understand the reason of the change. The yell was the customary lamentation at the loss of a warrior, the shout a sign of rejoicing that the conqueror had not been able to secure the scalp; the trophy, without which a victory is never considered complete. The distance at which the canoes lay probably prevented any attempts to injure the conqueror, the American Indian, like the panther of his own woods, seldom making any effort against his foe unless tolerably certain it is under circumstances that may be expected to prove effective.

As the young man had no longer any motive to remain near the point, he prepared to collect his canoes, in order to tow them off to the castle. That nearest was soon in tow, when he proceeded in quest of the other, which was all this time floating up the lake. The eye of Deerslayer was no sooner fastened on this last boat, than it struck him that it was nearer to the shore than it would have been had it merely followed the course of the gentle current of air. He began to suspect the influence of some unseen current in the water, and he quickened his exertions, in order to regain possession of it before it could drift into a dangerous proximity to the woods. On getting nearer, he thought that the canoe had a perceptible motion through the water, and, as it lay broadside to the air, that this motion was taking it toward the land. A few vigorous strokes of the paddle carried him still nearer, when the mystery was explained. Something was evidently in motion on the off side of the canoe, or that which was farthest from himself, and closer scrutiny showed that it was a naked human arm. An Indian was lying in the bottom of the canoe, and was propelling it slowly but certainly to the shore, using his hand as a paddle. Deerslayer understood the whole artifice at a glance. A savage had swum off to the boat while he was occupied with his enemy on the point, got possession, and was using these means to urge it to the shore.

Satisfied that the man in the canoe could have no arms, Deerslayer did not hesitate to dash close alongside of the retiring boat, without deeming it necessary to raise his own rifle. As soon as the wash of the water, which he made in approaching, became audible to the prostrate savage, the latter sprang to his feet, and uttered an exclamation that proved how completely he was taken by surprise.

"If you've enj'yed yourself enough in that canoe, redskin," Deerslayer coolly observed, stopping his own career in sufficient time to prevent an absolute collision between the two boats,—"if you've enj'yed yourself enough in that canoe, you'll do a prudent act by taking to the lake ag'in. I'm reasonable in these matters, and don't crave your blood, though there's them about that would look upon you more as a due bill for the bounty than a human mortal. Take to the lake this minute, afore we get to hot words."

The savage was one of those who did not understand a word of English, and he was indebted to the gestures of Deerslayer, and to the expression of an eye that did not often deceive, for an imperfect comprehension of his meaning. Perhaps, too, the sight of the rifle that lay so near the hand of the white man quickened his decision. At all events, he crouched like a tiger about to take his leap, uttered a yell, and the next instant his naked body disappeared in the water. When he rose to take breath, it was at the distance of several yards from the canoe, and the hasty glance he threw behind him denoted how much he feared the arrival of a fatal messenger from the rifle of his foe. But the young man made no indication of any hostile intention. Deliberately securing the canoe to the others, he began to paddle from the shore; and by the time the Indian reached the land, and had shaken himself, like a spaniel, on quitting the water, his dreaded enemy was already beyond rifleshot on his way to the castle. As was so much his practice, Deerslayer did not fail to soliloquize on what had just occurred, while steadily pursuing his course toward the point of destination.

"Well, well,"—he commenced,—" 'twould have been wrong to kill a human mortal without an object. Scalps are of no account with me, and life is sweet, and ought not to be taken marcilessly by them that have white gifts. The savage was a Mingo, it's true; and I make no doubt he is, and will be as long as he lives, a ra'al riptyle and vagabond; but that's no reason I should forget my gifts and color. No, no, —let him go; if ever we meet ag'in, rifle in hand, why then 'twill be seen which has the stoutest heart and the quickest eye. Hawkeye! That's not a bad name for a warrior, sounding much more manful and valiant than Deerslayer! 'Twouldn't be a bad title to begin with, and it has been fairly 'arned. If 'twas Chingachgook, now, he might go home and boast of his deeds, and the chiefs would name him Hawkeye in a minute; but it don't become white blood to brag, and 'tisn't easy to see how the matter can be known unless I do. Well, well,—everything is in the hands of Providence; this affair as well as another; I'll trust to that for getting my desarts in all things."

Having thus betrayed what might be termed his weak spot, the young man continued to paddle in silence, making his way diligently, and as fast as his tows would allow him, toward the castle. By this time the sun had not only risen, but it had appeared over the eastern mountains, and was shedding a flood of glorious light on this as yet unchristened sheet of water. The whole scene was radiant with beauty; and no one unaccustomed to the ordinary history of the woods would fancy it had so lately witnessed incidents so ruthless and barbarous. As he approached the building of old Hutter, Deerslayer thought, or rather *felt,* that its appearance was in singular harmony with all the rest of the scene. Although nothing had been consulted but strength and security, the rude, massive logs, covered with their rough bark, the projecting roof, and the form, would contribute to render the building picturesque in almost any situation, while its actual position added novelty and piquancy to its other points of interest.

When Deerslayer drew nearer the castle, however, objects of interest presented themselves that at once eclipsed any beauties that might have distinguished the scenery of the lake, and the site of the singular edifice. Judith and Hetty stood on the platform before the door, Hurry's dooryard, awaiting his approach with manifest anxiety; the former, from time to time, taking a survey of his person and of the canoes through the old ship's spyglass that has been already mentioned. Never probably did this girl seem more brilliantly beautiful than at that moment; the flush of anxiety and alarm increasing her color to its richest tints, while the softness of her eyes, a charm that even poor Hetty shared with her, was deepened by intense concern. Such, at least, without pausing or pretending to analyze motives, or to draw any other very nice distinction between cause and effect, were the opinions of the young man, as his canoes reached the side of the ark, where he carefully fastened all three before he put his foot on the platform.

Neither of the girls spoke as Deerslayer stood before them alone, his countenance betraying all the apprehension he felt on account of the two absent members of their party.

"Father!" Judith at length exclaimed, succeeding in uttering the word, as it might be by a desperate effort.

"He's met with misfortune, and there's no use in concealing it," answered Deerslayer, in his direct and simple-minded manner. "He and Hurry are in Mingo hands, and Heaven only knows what's to be the tarmination. I've got the canoes safe, and that's a consolation, since the vagabonds will have to swim for it, or raft off, to come near this place. At sunset we'll be reinforced by Chingachgook, if I can manage to get him into a canoe; and then, I think, we two can answer for the ark and the castle, till some of the officers in the garrisons hear of this warpath, which sooner or later must be the case, when we may look for succor from that quarter, if from no other."

"The officers!" exclaimed Judith, impatiently, her color deepening, and her eye expressing a lively but passing emotion. "Who thinks or speaks of the heartless gallants now? We are sufficient of ourselves to defend the castle. But what of my father, and of poor Hurry Harry?"

" 'Tis natural you should feel this consarn for your own parent,

Judith, and I suppose it's equally so that you should feel it for Hurry Harry, too."

Deerslayer then commenced a succinct but clear narrative of all that occurred during the night, in no manner concealing what had befallen his two companions, or his own opinion of what might prove to be the consequences. The girls listened with profound attention, but neither betrayed that feminine apprehension and concern which would have followed such a communication when made to those who were less accustomed to the hazards and accidents of a frontier life. To the surprise of Deerslayer, Judith seemed the most distressed, Hetty listening eagerly, but appearing to brood over the facts in melancholy silence, rather than betraying any outward signs of feeling. The former's agitation, the young man did not fail to attribute to the interest she felt in Hurry, quite as much as to her filial love, while Hetty's apparent indifference was ascribed to that mental darkness which, in a measure, obscured her intellect, and which possibly prevented her from foreseeing all the consequences. Little was said, however, by either, Judith and her sister busying themselves in making the preparations for the morning meal, as they who habitually attend to such matters toil on mechanically even in the midst of suffering and sorrow. The plain but nutritious breakfast was taken by all three in somber silence. The girls ate little, but Deerslayer gave proof of possessing one material requisite of a good soldier, that of preserving his appetite in the midst of the most alarming and embarrassing circumstances. The meal was nearly ended before a syllable was uttered; then, however, Judith spoke in the convulsive and hurried manner in which feeling breaks through restraint, after the latter has become more painful than even the betrayal of emotion.

"Father would have relished this fish!" she exclaimed; "he says the salmon of the lakes is almost as good as the salmon of the sea."

"Your father has been acquainted with the sea, they tell me, Judith," returned the young man, who could not forbear throwing a glance of inquiry at the girl; for, in common with all who knew Hutter, he had some curiosity on the subject of his early history. "Hurry Harry tells me he was once a sailor."

Judith first looked perplexed; then, influenced by feelings that were novel to her, in more ways than one, she became suddenly communicative, and seemingly much interested in the discourse.

"If Hurry knows anything of father's history, I would he had told it to me!" she cried. "Sometimes I think, too, he was once a sailor, and then again I think he was not. If that chest were open, or if it could speak, it might let us into his whole history. But its fastenings are too strong to be broken like packthread."

Deerslayer turned to the chest in question, and for the first time examined it closely. Although discolored, and bearing proofs of having received much ill-treatment, he saw that it was of materials and workmanship altogether superior to anything of the same sort he had ever before beheld. The wood was dark, rich, and had once been highly polished, though the treatment it had received left little gloss on its surface, and various scratches and indentations proved the rough collisions that it had encountered with substances still harder than itself. The corners were firmly bound with steel, elaborately and richly wrought, while the locks, of which it had no less than three, and the hinges, were of a fashion and workmanship that would have attracted attention even in a warehouse of curious furniture. This chest was quite large; and when Deerslayer arose, and endeavored to raise an end by its massive handle, he found that the weight fully corresponded with the external appearance.

"Did you never see that chest opened, Judith?" the young man demanded with frontier freedom, for delicacy on such subjects was little felt among the people on the verge of civilization, in that age, even if it be today.

"Never. Father has never opened it in my presence, if he ever opens it at all. No one here has ever seen its lid raised, unless it be father; nor do I even know that he has ever seen it."

"Now, you're wrong, Judith," Hetty quietly answered. "Father *has* raised the lid, and *I've* seen him do it."

A feeling of manliness kept the mouth of Deerslayer shut; for, while he would not have hesitated about going far beyond what would be thought the bounds of propriety, in questioning the elder sister, he had just scruples about taking what might be thought an advantage of the feeble intellect of the younger. Judith, being under no such restraint, however, turned quickly to the last speaker and continued the discourse.

"When and where did you ever see that chest opened, Hetty?"

"Here, and again and again. Father often opens it when *you* are away, though he don't in the least mind my being by, and seeing all he does, as well as hearing all he says."

"And what is it that he does, and what does he say?"

"That I cannot tell *you*, Judith," returned the other in a low but resolute voice. "*Father's* secrets are not *my* secrets."

"Secrets! This is stranger still, Deerslayer, that father should tell them to Hetty, and not tell them to me!"

"There's good reason for that, Judith, though you're not to know it. Father's not here to answer for himself, and I'll say no more about it."

Judith and Deerslayer looked surprised, and for a minute the first seemed pained. But, suddenly recollecting herself, she turned away from her sister, as if in pity for her weakness, and addressed the young man.

"You've told but half your story," she said, "breaking off at the place where you went to sleep in the canoe—or rather where you rose to listen to the cry of the loon. We heard the call of the loons, too, and thought their cries might bring a storm, though we are little used to tempests on this lake at this season of the year."

"The winds blow and the tempests howl as God pleases; sometimes at one season, and sometimes at another," answered Deerslayer; "and the loons speak accordin' to their natur'. Better would it be if men were as honest and frank. After I rose to listen to the birds, finding it could not be Hurry's signal, I lay down and slept. When the day dawned I was up and stirring, as usual, and then I went in chase of the two canoes, lest the Mingoes should lay hands on 'em."

"You have not told us all, Deerslayer," said Judith earnestly. "We heard rifles under the eastern mountain; the echoes were full and long, and came so soon after the reports, that the pieces must have been fired on or quite near to the shore. Our ears are used to these signs, and are not to be deceived."

"They've done their duty, gal, this time; yes, they've done their duty. Rifles have been sighted this morning, ay, and triggers pulled, too, though not as often as they might have been. One warrior has gone to his happy hunting grounds, and that's the whole of it. A man of white blood and white gifts is not to be expected to boast of his expl'ites, and to flourish scalps."

Judith listened almost breathlessly; and when Deerslayer, in his quiet, modest manner, seemed disposed to quit the subject, she rose, and crossing the room, took a seat by his side. The manner of the girl had nothing forward about it, though it betrayed the quick instinct of a female's affection, and the sympathizing kindness of a woman's heart. She even took the hard hand of the hunter, and pressed it in both her own, unconsciously to herself, perhaps, while she looked earnestly and even reproachfully into his sunburnt face.

"You have been fighting the savages, Deerslayer, singly and by yourself!" she said. "In your wish to take care of us—of Hetty—of me, perhaps, you've fought the enemy bravely, with no eye to encourage your deeds, or to witness your fall, had it pleased Providence to suffer so great a calamity!"

"I've fou't, Judith; yes, I *have* fou't the inimy, and that too, for the first time in my life. These things must be, and they bring with 'em a mixed feelin' of sorrow and triumph. Human natur' is a fightin' natur', I suppose, as all nations kill in battle, and we must be true to our rights and gifts. What has yet been done is no great matter, but should Chingachgook come to the rock this evening, as is agreed atween us, and I get him off it onbeknown to the savages or, if known to them, ag'in their wishes and designs, then may we all look to something like warfare, afore the Mingoes shall get possession of either the castle, or the ark, or yourselves."

"Who is this Chingachgook; from what place does he come, and *why* does he come *here?*"

"The questions are nat'ral and right, I suppose, though the youth has a great name, already, in his own part of the country. Chingachgook is a Mohican by blood, consorting with the Delawares by usage, as is the case with most of his tribe, which has long been broken up by the increase of our color. He is of the family of the great chiefs; Uncas, his father, having been the considerablest warrior and counsellor of his people. Even old Tamenund honors Chingachgook, though he is thought to be yet too young to lead in war; and then the nation is so dispersed and diminished, that chieftainship among 'em has got to be little more than a name.

"Well, this war having commenced in 'arnest, the Delaware and I rendezvous'd an app'intment, to meet this evening at sunset on the rendezvous rock at the foot of this very lake, intending to come out on our first hostile expedition ag'in the Mingoes. *Why* we come exactly this-a-way is our own secret; but thoughtful young men on the war-path, as you may suppose, do nothing without a calculation and a design."

"A Delaware can have no unfriendly intentions toward us," said Judith, after a moment's hesitation, "and we know you to be friendly."

"Treachery is the last crime I hope to be accused of," returned Deerslayer, hurt at the gleam of distrust that had shot through Judith's mind; "and least of all, treachery to my own color."

"No one suspects *you,* Deerslayer," the girl impetuously cried. "No—no—your honest countenance would be sufficient surety for the truth of a thousand hearts! If all men had as honest tongues, and no more promised what they did not mean to perform, there would be less wrong done in the world, and fine feathers and scarlet cloaks would not be excuses for baseness and deception."

The girl spoke with strong, nay, even with convulsed feeling, and her fine eyes, usually so soft and alluring, flashed fire as she concluded. Deerslayer could not but observe this extraordinary emotion; but with the tact of a courtier, he avoided not only any allusion to the circumstance, but succeeded in concealing the effect of his discovery on himself. Judith gradually grew calm again, and as she was obviously anxious to appear to advantage in the eyes of the young man, she was soon able to renew the conversation as composedly as if nothing had occurred to disturb her.

"I have no right to look into your secrets, or the secrets of your friend, Deerslayer," she continued, "and am ready to take all you say on trust. If we can really get another male ally to join us at this trying moment, it will aid us much; and I am not without hope that when the savages find that we are able to keep the lake, they will offer to give up their prisoners in exchange for skins, or at least for the keg of powder that we have in the house."

The young man had the words "scalps," and "bounty," on his lips, but a reluctance to alarm the feelings of the daughters prevented him from making the allusion he had intended to the probable fate of their father. Still, so little was he practiced in the arts of deception, that his expressive countenance was, of itself, understood by the quickwitted Judith, whose intelligence had been sharpened by the risks and habits of her life.

"I understand what you mean," she continued, hurriedly, "and what you would say, but for the fear of hurting me—*us,* I mean; for Hetty loves her father quite as well as I do. But this is not as we think of Indians. They never scalp an unhurt prisoner, but would rather take him away alive, unless, indeed, the fierce wish for torturing should get the mastery of them. I fear nothing for my father's scalp, and little for his life. Could they steal on us in the night, we should all probably suffer in this way; but men taken in open strife are seldom injured; not, at least, until the time of torture comes."

"That's tradition, I'll allow, and it's accordin' to practice—but, Judith, do you know the arr'nd on which your father and Hurry went ag'in the savages?"

"I do; and a cruel errand it was! But what will you have? Men will be men, and some even that flaunt in their gold and silver, and carry the King's commission in their pockets, are not guiltless of equal cruelty." Judith's eye again flashed, but by a desperate struggle she resumed her composure. "I get warm when I think of all the wrong that men do," she added, affecting to smile, an effort in which she only succeeded indifferently well. "All this is silly. What is done is done, and it cannot be mended by complaints. But the Indians think so little of the shedding of blood, and value men so much for the boldness of their undertakings, that, did they know the business on which their prisoners came, they would be more likely to honor than to injure them for it."

"For a time, Judith; yes, I allow *that,* for a time. But when that feelin' dies away, then will come the love of revenge. We must indivor,

—Chingachgook and I,—we must indivor to see what we can do to get Hurry and your father free; for the Mingoes will no doubt hover about this lake some days, in order to make the most of their success."

"You think this Delaware can be depended on, Deerslayer?" demanded the girl, thoughtfully.

"As much as I can myself. You say you do not suspect *me,* Judith?"

"*You!*" taking his hand again, and pressing it between her own, with a warmth that might have awakened the vanity of one less simple-minded, and more disposed to dwell on his own good qualities, "I would as soon suspect a brother! I have known you but a day, Deerslayer, but it has awakened the confidence of a year. Your name, however, is not unknown to me; for the gallants of the garrisons frequently speak of the lessons you have given them in hunting, and all proclaim your honesty."

"Do they ever talk of the shooting, gal?" inquired the other eagerly, after, however, laughing in a silent but heartfelt manner. "Do they ever talk of the shooting? I want to hear nothing about my own, for if that isn't sartified to by this time, in all these parts, there's little use in being skilful and sure; but what do the officers say of their own—yes, what do they say of their own? Arms, as they call it, is their trade, and yet there's some among 'em that know very little how to use 'em!"

"Such I hope will not be the case with your friend Chingachgook, as you call him—what is the English of his Indian name?"

"Big Sarpent—so called for his wisdom and cunning, Uncas is his ra'al name—all his family being called Uncas, until they get a title that has been 'arned by deeds."

"If he has all this wisdom, we may expect a useful friend in him, unless his own business in this part of the country should prevent him from serving us."

"I see no great harm in telling you his arr'nd, a'ter all, and, as you may find means to help us, I will let you and Hetty into the whole matter, trusting that you'll keep the secret as if it was your own. You must know that Chingachgook is a comely Injin, and is much looked upon and admired by the young women of his tribe, both on account of his family, and on account of himself. Now, there is a chief that has a daughter called Wah-ta-Wah, which is intarpreted into Hist-oh-Hist, in the English tongue, the rarest gal among the Delawares, and the one most sought a'ter and craved for a wife by all the young warriors of the nation. Well, Chingachgook, among others, took a fancy to Wah-ta-Wah, and Wah-ta-Wah took a fancy to him." Here Deerslayer paused an instant; for, as he got thus far in his tale, Hetty Hutter arose, approached, and stood attentive at his knee, as a child draws near to listen to the legends of its mother. "Yes, he fancied *her,* and she fancied *him,*" resumed Deerslayer, casting a friendly and approving glance at the innocent and interested girl; "and when that is the case, and all the elders are agreed, it does not often happen that the young couple keep apart. Chingachgook couldn't well carry off such a prize without making inimies among them that wanted her as much as he did himself. A sartain Briarthorn, as we call him in English, or Yocommon, as he is tarmed in Injin, took it most to heart, and we mistrust him of having a hand in all that followed. Wah-ta-Wah went with her father and mother, two moons ago, to fish for salmon on the western streams, where it is agreed by all in these parts that fish most abounds, and while thus empl'yed the gal vanished. For several weeks we could get no tidings of her; but here, ten days since, a runner, that came through the Delaware country, brought us a message, by which we l'arn that Wah-ta-Wah was stolen from her people,—we think, but do not know it, by Briarthorn's sarcumventions,—and that she was now with the inimy, who had adopted her, and wanted her to marry a young Mingo. The message said that the party intended to hunt and forage through this region for a month or two, afore it went back into the Canadas, and that if we could contrive to get on a scent in this quarter, something might turn up that would lead to our getting the maiden off."

"And how does that concern *you,* Deerslayer?" demanded Judith, a little anxiously.

"It consarns me, as all things that touches a fri'nd consarns a fri'nd. I'm here as Chingachgook's aid and helper, and if we can get the young maiden he likes back ag'in, it will give me almost as much pleasure as if I had got back my own sweetheart."

"And where, then, is *your* sweetheart, Deerslayer?"

"She's in the forest, Judith—hanging from the boughs of the trees, in a soft rain—in the dew on the open grass—the clouds that float about in the blue heavens—the birds that sing in the woods—the sweet springs where I slake my thirst—and in all the other glorious gifts that come from God's Providence!"

"You mean that, as yet, you've never loved one of my sex, but love best your haunts, and your own manner of life."

"That's it—that's just it. I am white—have a white heart and can't, in reason, love a red-skinned maiden, who must have a redskin heart and feelin's. No, no, I'm sound enough in them partic'lars, and hope to remain so, at least till this war is over. I find my time too much taken up with Chingachgook's affair, to wish to have one of my own on my hands afore that is settled."

"The girl that finally wins you, Deerslayer, will at least win an *honest* heart,—one without treachery or guile; and that will be a victory that most of her sex ought to envy."

As Judith uttered this, her beautiful face had a resentful frown on it; while a bitter smile lingered around a mouth that no derangement of the muscles could render anything but handsome. Her companion observed the change, and though little skilled in the workings of the female heart, he had sufficient native delicacy to understand that it might be well to drop the subject.

As the hour when Chingachgook was expected still remained distant, Deerslayer had time enough to examine into the state of the defences, and to make such additional arrangements as were in his power, and the exigency of the moment seemed to require. The experience and foresight of Hutter had left little to be done in these particulars; still, several precautions suggested themselves to the young man, who may be said to have studied the art of frontier warfare, through the traditions and legends of the people among whom he had so long lived. The distance between the castle and the nearest point on the shore, prevented any apprehension on the subject of rifle bullets thrown from the land. The house was within musketshot in one sense, it was true, but aim was entirely out of the question, and even Judith professed a perfect disregard of any danger from that source. So long, then, as the party remained in possession of the fortress, they were safe, unless their assailants could find the means to come off and carry it by fire or storm, or by some of the devices of Indian cunning and Indian treachery. Against the first source of danger Hutter had made ample provision, and the building itself, the bark roof excepted, was not very combustible. The floor was scuttled in several places, and buckets provided with ropes were in daily use, in readiness for any such emergency. One of the girls could easily extinguish any fire that might be lighted, provided it had not time to make much headway. Judith, who appeared to understand all her father's schemes of defence, and who had the spirit to take no unimportant share in the execution of them, explained all these details to the young man, who was thus saved much time and labor in making his investigations.

Little was to be apprehended during the day. In possession of the canoes and of the ark, no other vessel was to be found on the lake. Nevertheless, Deerslayer well knew that a raft was soon made, and, as dead trees were to be found in abundance near the water, did the savages seriously contemplate the risks of an assault, it would not be a very difficult matter to find the necessary means. The celebrated American ax, a tool that is quite unrivalled in its way, was then not very extensively known, and the savages were far from expert in the use of its hatchet-like substitute; still, they had sufficient practice in crossing streams by this mode to render it certain they would construct a raft, should they deem it expedient to expose themselves to the risks of an assault. The death of their warrior might prove a sufficient incentive, or it might act as a caution; but Deerslayer thought it more than possible that the succeeding night would bring matters to a crisis, and in this precise way. This impression caused him to wish ardently for the presence and succor of his Mohican friend, and to look forward to the approach of sunset with an increasing anxiety.

As the day advanced, the party in the castle matured their plans, and made their preparations. Judith was active, and seemed to find a pleasure in consulting and advising with her new acquaintance, whose indifference to danger, manly devotion to herself and sister, guilelessness of manner, and truth of feeling, had won rapidly on both her imagination and her affections. Although the hours appeared long in some respects to Deerslayer, Judith did not find them so, and when the sun began to descend towards the pine-clad summits of the western hills, she felt and expressed her surprise that the day should so soon be drawing to a close. On the other hand, Hetty was moody and silent. She was never loquacious, or if she occasionally became communicative, it was under the influence of some temporary excitement that served to arouse her unsophisticated mind; but, for hours at a time, in the course of this all-important day, she seemed to have absolutely lost the use of her tongue. Nor did apprehension on account of her father materially affect the manner of either sister. Neither appeared seriously to dread any evil greater than captivity, and once or twice, when Hetty did speak, she intimated the expectation that Hutter would find the means to liberate himself. Although Judith was less sanguine on this head, she, too, betrayed the hope that propositions for a ransom would come, when the Indians discovered that the castle set their expedients and artifices at defiance. Deerslayer, however, treated these passing suggestions as the ill-digested fancies of girls, making his own arrangements as steadily, and brooding over the future as seriously, as if they had never fallen from their lips.

At length the hour arrived when it became necessary to proceed to the place of rendezvous appointed with the Mohican, or Delaware, as Chingachgook was more commonly called. As the plan had been matured by Deerslayer, and fully communicated to his companions, all three set about its execution, in concert, and intelligently. Hetty passed into the ark, and fastening two of the canoes together, she entered one, and paddled up to a sort of gateway in the palisades that surrounded the building, through which she carried both; securing them beneath the house by chains that were fastened within the building. These palisades were trunks of trees driven firmly into the mud, and served the double purpose of a small inclosure that was intended to be used in this very manner, and to keep any enemy that might approach in boats at arm's-length. Canoes thus *docked* were, in a measure, hid from sight, and as the gate was properly barred and fastened, it would not be an easy task to remove them, even in the event of their being seen. Previously, however, to closing the gate, Judith also entered within the inclosure with the third canoe, leaving Deerslayer busy in securing the door and windows inside the building, over her head. As everything was massive and strong, and small saplings were used as bars, it would have been the work of an hour or two to break into the building, when Deerslayer had ended his task, even allowing the assailants the use of any tools but the ax, and to be unresisted. This attention to security arose from Hutter's having been robbed once or twice by the lawless whites of the frontiers, during some of his many absences from home.

As soon as all was fast in the inside of the dwelling, Deerslayer appeared at a trap, from which he descended into the canoe of Judith. When this was done, he fastened the door with a massive staple and stout padlock. Hetty was then received in the canoe, which was shoved outside of the palisades. The next precaution was to fasten the gate, and the keys were carried into the ark. The three were now fastened out of the dwelling, which could only be entered by violence, or by following the course taken by the young man in quitting it.

The glass had been brought outside as a preliminary step, and Deerslayer next took a careful survey of the entire shore of the lake, as far as his own position would allow. Not a living thing was visible, a few birds excepted, and even the last fluttered about in the shades of the trees, as if unwilling to encounter the heat of a sultry afternoon. All the nearest points, in particular, were subjected to severe scrutiny, in order to make certain that no raft was in preparation; the result everywhere giving the same picture of calm solitude. A few words will explain the greatest embarrassment belonging to the situation of our party. Exposed themselves to the observation of any watchful eyes, the movements of their enemies were concealed by the drapery of a dense forest. While the imagination would be very apt to people the latter with more warriors than it really contained, their own weakness must be too apparent to all who might chance to cast a glance in their direction.

"Nothing is stirring, howsever," exclaimed Deerslayer, as he finally lowered the glass, and prepared to enter the ark. "If the vagabonds do harbor mischief in their minds, they are too cunning to let it be seen; it's true, a raft may be in preparation in the woods, but it has not yet been brought down to the lake. They can't guess that we are about to quit the castle, and, if they did, they've no means of knowing where we intend to go."

6

DEERSLAYER gradually brought the ark down the lake to a point near the council rock which rose from the water about fifty feet from the southern outlet. Here he halted a minute or two before sunset.

"Is the rock empty, Judith?" inquired Deerslayer, as soon as he had checked the drift of the ark, deeming it imprudent to venture unnecessarily near the shore. "Is anything to be seen of the Delaware chief?"

"Nothing, Deerslayer. Neither rock, shore, tree, nor lake seems to have ever held a human form."

"Keep close, Judith—keep close, Hetty—a rifle has a prying eye, a nimble foot, and a desperate fatal tongue. Keep close, then, but keep up actyve looks, and be on the alart. 'Twould grieve me to the very heart did any harm befall either of you."

"And *you*, Deerslayer!" exclaimed Judith, turning her handsome face from the loop, to bestow a gracious and grateful look on the young man; "do *you* 'keep close,' and have a proper care that the savages do not catch a glimpse of you! A bullet might be as fatal to *you* as to one of us; and the blow that you felt would be felt by all."

"No fear of me, Judith—no fear of me, my good gal. Do not look this-a-way, although you look so pleasant and comely, but keep your eyes on the rock, and the shore, and the—"

Deerslayer was interrupted by a slight exclamation from the girl, who, in obedience, to his hurried gestures, as much as in obedience to his words, had immediately bent her looks again in the opposite direction.

"What is 't?—what is 't, Judith?" he hastily demanded. "Is anything to be seen?"

"There is a man on the rock!—an Indian warrior in his paint, and armed!"

"Where does he wear his hawk's feather?" eagerly added Deerslayer, relaxing his hold of the line, in readiness to drift nearer the place of rendezvous. "Is it fast to the warlock, or does he carry it above the left ear?"

" 'Tis as you say, above the left ear; he smiles, too, and mutters the word 'Mohican.' "

"God be praised, 'tis the Sarpent at last!" exclaimed the young man, suffering the line to slip through his hands, until hearing a light bound, in the other end of the craft, he instantly checked the rope, and began to haul it in again, under the assurance that his object was effected.

At that moment the door of the cabin was opened hastily, and a warrior, darting through the little room, stood at Deerslayer's side, simply uttering the exclamation "Hugh!" At the next instant Judith and Hetty shrieked, and the air was filled with the yell of twenty savages, who came leaping through the branches down the bank, some actually falling headlong into the water in their haste.

"Pull, Deerslayer!" cried Judith, hastily barring the door, in order to prevent an inroad by the passage through which the Delaware had just entered; "pull for life and death—the lake is full of savages wading after us!"

The young men—for Chingachgook immediately came to his friend's assistance—needed no second bidding; but they applied themselves to their task in a way that showed how urgent they deemed the occasion. The great difficulty was in suddenly overcoming the *vis inertiæ* of so large a mass; for once in motion, it was easy to cause the scow to skim the water with all the necessary speed.

"Pull, Deerslayer, for Heaven's sake!" cried Judith again at the loop. "These wretches rush into the water like hounds following their prey! Ah!—the scow moves! and now the water deepens to the armpits of the foremost; still they rush forward, and will seize the ark!"

A slight scream, and then a joyous laugh followed from the girl; the first produced by a desperate effort of their pursuers, and the last by its failure; the scow, which had now got fairly in motion, gliding ahead into deep water with a velocity that set the designs of their enemies at naught. As the two men were prevented by the position of the cabin from seeing what passed astern, they were compelled to inquire of the girls into the state of the chase.

"What now, Judith?—what next? Do the Mingoes still follow, or are we quit of 'em for the present?" demanded Deerslayer, when he felt the rope yielding, as if the scow was going fast ahead, and heard the scream and the laugh of the girl almost in the same breath.

"They have vanished!—one, the last, is just burying himself in the bushes of the bank—there, he has disappeared in the shadows of the trees! You have got your friend, and we are all safe!"

The two men now made another great effort, pulled the ark up swiftly to the grapnel, tripped it, and when the scow had shot some distance, and lost its way, they let the anchor drop again; then, for the first time since their meeting, they ceased their efforts. As the floating house now lay several hundred feet from the shore, and offered a complete protection against bullets, there was no longer any danger, or any motive for immediate exertion.

The manner in which the two friends now recognized each other was highly characteristic. Chingachgook, a noble, tall, handsome, and athletic young Indian warrior, first examined his rifle with care, opening the pan to make sure the priming was not wet; and assured of this important fact, he next cast furtive but observant glances around him at the strange habitation and at the two girls; still he spoke not, and most of all did he avoid the betrayal of a womanish curiosity by asking questions.

"Judith and Hetty," said Deerslayer, with an untaught, natural courtesy, "this is the Mohican chief of whom you've heard me speak; Chingachgook, as he is called, which signifies the Big Sarpent; so named for his wisdom, and prudence, and cunning; my 'arliest and latest friend. I know'd it must be he, by the hawk's feather over the left ear, most other warriors wearing 'em on the warlock."

As Deerslayer ceased speaking, he laughed heartily, excited more perhaps by the delight of having got his friend safe at his side, under circumstances so trying, than by any conceit that happened to cross his fancy, and exhibiting this outbreaking of feeling in a manner that was a little remarkable, since his merriment was not accompanied by any noise. Although Chingachgook both understood and spoke English, he was unwilling to communicate his thoughts in it, like most Indians; and when he had met Judith's cordial shake of the hand, and Hetty's milder salute, in the courteous manner that became a chief, he turned away, apparently to await the moment when it might suit his friend to enter into an explanation of his future intentions, and to give a narrative of what had passed since their separation. The other understood his meaning, and discovered his own mode of reasoning in the matter by addressing the girls.

"This wind will soon die away altogether, now the sun is down," he said, "and there is no need of rowing ag'in it. In half an hour or so, it will either be a flat calm or the air will come off from the south shore, when we will begin our journey back ag'in to the castle; in the meanwhile, the Delaware and I will talk over matters, and get correct ideas of each other's notions consarning the course we ought to take."

No one opposed this proposition, and the girls withdrew into the cabin to prepare the evening meal, while the two young men took their seats on the head of the scow, and began to converse. The dialogue was in the language of the Delawares. As that dialect, however, is but little understood, even by the learned, we shall, not only on this but on all subsequent occasions, render such parts as it may be necessary to give closely into liberal English; preserving, as far as possible, the idioms and peculiarities of the respective speakers, by way of presenting the pictures in the most graphic forms to the minds of the readers.

It is unnecessary to enter into the details first related by Deerslayer, who gave a brief narrative of the facts that are already familiar to those who have read our pages. In relating these events, however, it may be well to say that the speaker touched only on the outlines, more particularly abstaining from saying anything about his encounter with, and victory over the Iroquois, as well as to his own exertions in behalf of the deserted young women. When Deerslayer ended, the Delaware took up the narrative in turn, speaking sententiously, and with great dignity. His account was both clear and short, nor was it embellished by any incidents that did not directly concern the history of his departure from the villages of his people, and his arrival in the valley of the Susquehanna. On reaching the latter, which was at a point only half a mile south of the outlet, he had soon struck a trail, which gave him notice of the probable vicinity of enemies. Being prepared for such an occurrence, the object of the expedition calling him directly into the neighborhood of the party of Iroquois that was known to be out, he considered the discovery as fortunate, rather than the reverse, and took the usual precautions to turn it to account. First following the river to its source, and ascertaining the position of the rock, he met another trail, and had actually been hovering for hours on the flanks of his enemies, watching equally for an opportunity to meet his mistress and to take a scalp; and it may be questioned which he most ardently desired. He kept near the lake, and occasionally he ventured to some spot where he could get a view of what was passing on its surface. The ark had been seen and watched from the moment it hove in sight, though the young chief was necessarily ignorant that it was to be the instrument of effecting the desired junction with his friend. The uncertainty of its movements, and the fact that it was unquestionably managed by white men, led him to conjecture the truth, however, and he held himself in readiness to get on board whenever a suitable occasion might offer. As the sun drew near the horizon, he repaired to the rock, where, on emerging from the forest, he was gratified in finding the ark lying apparently in readiness to receive him. The manner of his appearance, and of his entrance into the craft, is known.

Although Chingachgook had been closely watching his enemies for hours, their sudden and close pursuit, as he reached the scow, was as much a matter of surprise to himself as it had been to his friend. He could only account for it by the fact of their being more numerous than he had at first supposed, and by their having out parties, of the existence of which he was ignorant. Their regular and permanent encampment, if the word permanent can be applied to the residence of a party that intended to remain out, in all probability, but a few weeks, was not far from the spot where Hutter and Harry had fallen into their hands, and, as a matter of course, near a spring.

"Well, Sarpent,"—asked Deerslayer, when the other had ended his brief but spirited narrative, speaking always in the Delaware tongue, which, for the reader's convenience only, we render into the peculiar vernacular of the speaker,—"Well, Sarpent, as you've been scouting around these Mingoes, have you anything to tell us of their captyves; the father of these young women and another, who, I somewhat conclude, is the lovyer of one of 'em?"

"Chingachgook has seen them. An old man and a young warrior,—the falling hemlock and the tall pine."

"You're not so much out, Delaware; you're not so much out. Old Hutter is decaying, of a sartainty, though many solid blocks might be hewn out of his trunk yet; and, as for Hurry Harry, so far as height, and strength, and comeliness go, he may be called the pride of the human forest. Were the men bound, or in any manner suffering torture? I ask on account of the young women; who, I dare say, would be glad to know."

"It is not so, Deerslayer. The Mingoes are too many to cage their game. Some watch, some sleep, some scout, some hunt. The palefaces are treated like brothers today; tomorrow they will lose their scalps."

"Yes, that's red natur', and must be submitted to! Judith and Hetty, here's comfortable tidings for you, the Delaware telling me that neither your father nor Hurry Harry is in suffering; but, bating the loss of liberty, as well off as we are ourselves. Of course they are kept in the camp; otherwise they do much as they please."

"I rejoice to hear this, Deerslayer," returned Judith, "and now we are joined by your friend, I make no manner of question that we shall find an opportunity to ransom the prisoners. If there are any women in the camp, I have articles of dress that will catch their eyes; and, should the worst come to the worst, we can open the good chest, which, I think, will be found to hold things that may tempt the chiefs."

"Judith," said the young man, looking up at her with a smile, and an expression of earnest curiosity, that, in spite of the growing obscurity, did not escape the watchful looks of the girl, "can you find it in your heart to part with your own finery to release prisoners; even though one be your own father, and the other is your sworn suitor and lovyer?"

The flush on the face of the girl arose in part from resentment, but more perhaps from a gentler and novel feeling, that, with the capricious waywardness of taste, had been rapidly rendering her more sensitive to the good opinion of the youth who questioned her, than to that of any other person. Suppressing the angry sensation with instinctive quickness, she answered with a readiness and truth that caused her sister to draw near to listen, though the obtuse intellect of the latter was far from comprehending the workings of a heart as treacherous, as uncertain, and as impetuous in its feelings as that of the spoiled and flattered beauty.

"Deerslayer," answered Judith, after a moment's pause, "I shall be honest with *you*. I confess that the time *has* been when what you call finery was to me the dearest thing on earth; but I begin to feel differently. Though Hurry Harry is naught to me, nor ever can be, I would give all I own to set him free. If I would do this for blustering, bullying, talking Hurry, who has nothing but good looks to recommend him, you may judge what I would do for my own father."

"This sounds well, and is according to woman's gifts. Ah's me! The same feelin's is to be found among the young women of the Delawares. I've known 'em, often and often, sacrifice their vanity to their hearts. 'Tis as it should be—'tis as as it should be, I suppose, in both colors. Woman was created for the feelin's, and is pretty much ruled by feelin'!"

"Would the savages let father go, if Judith and I gave them all our best things?" demanded Hetty, in her innocent, mild manner.

"Their women might interfere, good Hetty; yes, their women might interfere with such an ind in view. But, tell me, Sarpent, how it is as to squaws among the knaves; have they many of their own women in the camp?"

The Delaware heard and understood all that passed; though with Indian gravity and finesse he had sat, with averted face, seemingly inattentive to a discourse in which he had no direct concern. Thus appealed to, however, he answered his friend in his ordinary sententious manner.

"Six," he said, holding up all the fingers of one hand, and the thumb of the other; "besides *this*." The last number denoted his betrothed; whom, with the poetry and truth of nature, he described by laying his hand on his own heart.

"Did you see her, chief—did you get a glimpse of her pleasant countenance, or come close enough to her ear to sing in it the song she loves to hear?"

"No, Deerslayer,—the trees were too many, and leaves covered their boughs, like clouds hiding the heavens in a storm. But,"—and the young warrior turned his dark face toward his friend, with a smile on it that illuminated its fierce-looking paint and naturally stern lineaments with a bright gleam of human feeling,—"Chingachgook heard the laugh of Wah-ta-Wah; he knew it from the laugh of the women of the Iroquois. It sounded in his ears like the chirp of the wren."

"Ay, trust a lovyer's ear for that; and a Delaware's ear for all sounds that are ever heard in the woods. I know not why it is so, Judith, but when young men—and I dare to say it may be all the same with young women too—but when they get to have kind feelin's towards each other, it's wonderful how pleasant the laugh or the speech becomes to the other person. I've seen grim warriors listening to the chattering and the laughing of young gals as if it was church music; such as is heard in the old Dutch church that stands in the great street of Albany, where I've been more than once, with peltry and game."

"And *you*, Deerslayer," said Judith quickly, and with more sensibility than marked her usually light and thoughtless manner; "have *you* never felt how pleasant it is to listen to the laugh of the girl you love?"

"Lord bless you, gal!—why I've never lived enough among my own color to drop into them sort of feelin's,—no, never! I dare to say, they are nat'ral and right; but to me there's no music so sweet as the sighing of the wind in the treetops, and the rippling of a stream from a full, sparkling, natyve fountain of pure fresh water; unless, indeed," he continued, dropping his head for an instant in a thoughtful manner, "unless, indeed, it be the open mouth of a sartain hound, when I'm on the track of a fat buck. As for unsartain dogs, I care little for their cries, seein' they are as likely to speak when the deer is not in sight as when it is."

Judith walked slowly and pensively away, nor was there any of her ordinary calculating coquetry in the light tremulous sigh that, unconsciously to herself, arose to her lips. On the other hand, Hetty listened with guileless attention; though it struck her simple mind as singular that the young man should prefer the melody of the woods to the songs of girls, or even to the laugh of innocence and joy. Accustomed, however, to defer in most things to her sister, she soon followed

Judith into the cabin, where she took a seat, and remained pondering intensely over some occurrence, or resolution, or opinion, which was a secret to all but herself. Left alone, Deerslayer and his friend resumed their discourse.

"Has the young paleface hunter been long on this lake?" demanded the Delaware, after courteously waiting for the other to speak first.

"Only since yesterday noon, Sarpent; though that has been long enough to see and do much."

The gaze that the Indian fastened on his companion was so keen that it seemed to mock the gathering darkness of the night. As the other furtively returned his look, he saw the two black eyes glistening on him, like the balls of the panther, or those of the penned wolf. He understood the meaning of this glowing gaze, and answered evasively, as he fancied would best become the modesty of a white man's gifts.

" 'Tis as you suspect, Sarpent; yes, 'tis somewhat that-a-way. I *have* fell in with the inimy, and I suppose it may be said I've fou't them, too."

An exclamation of delight and exultation escaped the Indian; and then, laying his hand eagerly on the arm of his friend, he asked if there were any scalps taken.

"That I *will* maintain, in the face of all the Delaware tribe, old Tamenund, and your father, the great Uncas, as well as the rest, is ag'in white gifts! *My* scalp is on my head, as you can see, Sarpent, and that was the only scalp that was in danger, when one side was altogether Christian and white."

"Did no warrior fall?—Deerslayer did not get his name by being slow of sight, or clumsy with the rifle!"

"In that particular, chief, you're nearer reason, and therefore nearer being right. I may say one Mingo fell."

"A chief!" demanded the other, with startling vehemence.

"Nay, that's more than I know or can say. He was artful, and treacherous, and stouthearted, and may well have gained popularity enough with his people to be named to that rank. The man fou't well, though his eye wasn't quick enough for one who had had his schooling in your company, Delaware."

"My brother and friend struck the body?"

"That was uncalled for, seeing that the Mingo died in my arms. The truth may as well be said at once; he fou't like a man of red gifts, and I fou't like a man with gifts of my own color. God gave me the victory; I couldn't fly in the face of his providence by forgetting my birth and natur'. White he made me, and white I shall live and die."

"Good! Deerslayer is a paleface, and has paleface hands. A Delaware will look for the scalp, and hang it on a pole, and sing a song in his honor, when we go back to our people. The honor belongs to the tribe; it must not be lost."

"This is easy talking, but 'twill not be as easy doing. The Mingo's body is in the hands of his fri'nds, and, no doubt, is hid in some hole, where Delaware cunning will never be able to get at his scalp."

The young man then gave his friend a succinct, but clear account of the event of the morning, concealing nothing of any moment, and yet touching on everything modestly and with a careful attention to avoid the Indian habit of boasting. Chingachgook again expressed his satisfaction at the honor won by his friend, and then both arose, the hour having arrived when it became prudent to move the ark farther from the land.

It was now quite dark; the heavens having become clouded, and the stars hid. The north wind had ceased, as was usual, with the setting of the sun, and a light air arose from the south. This change favoring the design of Deerslayer, he lifted his grapnel, and the scow immediately and quite perceptibly began to drift more into the lake. The sail was set, when the motion of the craft increased to a rate not much less than two miles in the hour. As this superseded the necessity of rowing —an occupation that an Indian would not be likely to desire—Deerslayer, Chingachgook, and Judith seated themselves in the stern of the scow, where the first governed its movements by holding the oar. Here they discoursed on their future movements, and on the means that ought to be used in order to effect the liberation of their friends.

In this dialogue Judith held a material part; the Delaware readily understanding all she said, while his own replies and remarks, both of which were few and pithy, were occasionally rendered into English by his friend. Judith rose greatly in the estimation of her companions, in the half hour that followed. Prompt of resolution and firm of purpose, her suggestions and expedients partook of her spirit and sagacity, both of which were of a character to find favor with men of the frontier. The events that had occurred since their meeting, as well as her isolated and dependent situation, induced the girl to feel toward Deerslayer like the friend of a year, instead of an acquaintance of a day; and so completely had she been won by his guileless truth of character and of feeling—pure novelties in our sex, as respected her own experience—that his peculiarities excited her curiosity, and created a confidence that had never been awakened by any other man. Hitherto she had been compelled to stand on the defensive, in her intercourse with men,—with what success was best known to herself; but here had she been suddenly thrown into the society, and under the protection of a youth, who evidently as little contemplated evil toward herself as if he had been her brother. The freshness of his integrity, the poetry and truth of his feelings, and even the quaintness of his forms of speech, all had their influence, and aided in awakening an interest that she found as pure as it was sudden and deep. Hurry's fine face and manly form had never compensated for his boisterous and vulgar turn; and her intercourse with the officers had prepared her to make comparisons under which even his great natural advantages suffered. But this very intercourse with the officers who occasionally came upon the lake to fish and hunt, had an effect in producing her present sentiments toward the young stranger. With them, while her vanity had been gratified, and her self-love strongly awakened, she had many causes deeply to regret the acquaintance,—if not to mourn over it in secret sorrow,—for it was impossible for one of her quick intellect not to perceive how hollow was the association between superior and inferior, and that she was regarded as the plaything of an idle hour, rather than as an equal and a friend, by even the best intentioned and least designing of her scarlet-clad admirers. Deerslayer, on the other hand, had a window in his breast, through which the light of his honesty was ever shining; and even his indifference to charms that so rarely failed to produce a sensation piqued the pride of the girl, and gave him an interest that another, seemingly more favored by nature, might have failed to excite.

In this manner half an hour passed, during which time the ark had been slowly stealing over the water, the darkness thickening around it; though it was easy to see that the gloom of the forest at the southern end of the lake was getting to be distant, while the mountains that lined the sides of the beautiful basin were overshadowing it, nearly from side to side. There was, indeed, a narrow stripe of water, in the center of the lake, where the dim light that was still shed from the heavens fell upon its surface, in a line extending north and south; and along this faint tract—a sort of inverted Milky Way, in which the obscurity was not quite as dense as in other places—the scow held her course, he who steered well knowing that it led in the direction he wished to go. The reader is not to suppose, however, that any difficulty could exist as to the course. This would have been determined by that of the air, had it not been possible to distinguish the mountains, as well as by the dim opening to the south, which marked the position of the valley in that quarter, above the plain of tall trees, by a sort of lessened obscurity; the difference between the darkness of the forest, and that of the night, as seen only in the air. The peculiarities at length caught the attention of Judith and the Deerslayer, and the conversation ceased, to allow each to gaze at the solemn stillness and deep repose of nature.

" 'Tis a gloomy night," observed the girl, after a pause of several minutes. "I hope we may be able to find the castle."

"Little fear of our missing *that*, if we keep this path, in the middle of the lake," returned the young man. "Natur' has made us a road here, and, dim as it is, there'll be little difficulty in following it."

"Do you hear nothing, Deerslayer? It seemed as if the water was stirring quite near us!"

"Sartainly something *did* move the water, oncommon like; it must have been a fish. Them creatur's prey upon each other like men and animals on the land; one has leaped into the air, and fallen back hard into his own element. 'Tis of little use, Judith, for any to strive to get out of their elements, since it's natur' to stay in 'em; and natur' will have its way. Ha! *that* sounds like a paddle, used with more than common caution!"

At this moment the Delaware bent forward and pointed significantly into the boundary of gloom, as if some object had suddenly caught his eye. Both Deerslayer and Judith followed the direction of his gesture, and each got a view of a canoe at the same instant. The glimpse of this startling neighbor was dim, and, to eyes less practiced, it might have been uncertain; though to those in the ark, the object was evidently a canoe, with a single individual in it; the latter standing erect and paddling. How many lay concealed in its bottom, of course could not be known. Flight, by means of oars, from a bark canoe impelled by vigorous and skilful hands, was utterly impracticable, and each of the men seized his rifle in expectation of a conflict.

"I can easily bring down the paddler," whispered Deerslayer, "but we'll first hail him and ask his arr'nd." Then raising his voice, he continued in a solemn manner, "Hold! If you come nearer I must fire, though contrary to my wishes, and then sartain death will follow. Stop paddling, and answer!"

"Fire, and slay a poor defenceless girl," returned a soft, tremulous female voice, "and God will never forgive you! Go your way, Deerslayer, and let me go mine."

"Hetty!" exclaimed the young man and Judith in a breath; and the former sprang instantly to the spot where he had left the canoe they had been towing. It was gone, and he understood the whole affair. As for the fugitive, frightened at the menace, she ceased paddling, and remained dimly visible, resembling a spectral outline of a human form, standing on the water. At the next moment the sail was lowered to prevent the ark from passing the spot where the canoe lay. This last expedient, however, was not taken in time; for the momentum of so heavy a craft and the impulsion of the air soon set her by, bringing Hetty directly to windward, though still visible, as the change in the positions of the two boats now placed her in that species of Milky Way which has been mentioned.

"What can this mean, Judith?" demanded Deerslayer. "Why has your sister taken the canoe, and left us?"

"You know she is feeble-minded, poor girl! and she has her own ideas of what ought to be done. She loves her father more than most children love their parents—and then—"

"Then what, girl? This is a trying moment; one in which truth must be spoken!"

Judith felt a generous and womanly regret at betraying her sister, and she hesitated ere she spoke again. But once more urged by Deerslayer, and conscious herself of all the risks the whole party was running by the indiscretion of Hetty, she could refrain no longer.

"Then I fear, poor, weak-minded Hetty has not been altogether able to see the vanity, and madness, and folly, that lie behind the handsome face and fine form of Hurry Harry."

7

SIMPLE-MINDED HETTY, landing on the forested shore of the lake, slept there until dawn. Then, approaching the Indian encampment, she encountered Chingachgook's betrothed, the beautiful Delaware maiden Wah-ta-Wah or Hist-oh-Hist, who warned her to furnish the hostile savages no useful information. Hetty's intention was to rescue her father by converting the Indians to Christianity; and being admitted to the circle of the chiefs, she opened a small English Bible and began exhorting them to love their neighbors as themselves. It transpired that the Indians were a small party of Hurons (as such allied with the French) who had been hunting near

Lake Oneida when they heard that the British and French were at war, and who had taken an indirect line in returning to Canada. They paid little attention to Hetty, though the chiefs hoped to use her as a tool. Meanwhile, it was clear that old Hutter and Hurry Harry were in a serious predicament, for the chiefs questioned them, and elicited a confession that they had entered the encampment hoping to take scalps.

After losing Hetty on the lake, Deerslayer, Judith, and Chingachgook returned to the castle to gain what rest they could.

Once or twice, in the course of the night, Deerslayer or the Delaware arose and looked out upon the tranquil lake, when, finding all safe, each returned to his pallet, and slept like a man who was not easily deprived of his natural rest. At the first signs of the dawn, the former arose, however, and made his personal arrangements for the day; though his companion, whose nights had not been tranquil or without disturbance of late, continued on his blanket until the sun had fairly risen. Judith, too, was later than common that morning, for the earlier hours of the night had brought her little of either refreshment or sleep. But ere the sun had shown himself over the eastern hills, these too were up and afoot; even the tardy, in that region, seldom remaining on their pallets after the appearance of the great luminary.

Chingachgook was in the act of arranging his forest toilet, when Deerslayer entered the cabin of the ark, and threw him a few coarse, but light summer vestments, that belonged to Hutter.

"Judith hath given me them for your use, chief," said the latter, as he cast the jacket and trousers at the feet of the Indian; "for it's ag'in all prudence and caution to be seen in your war dress and paint. Wash off all them fiery streaks from your cheeks, put on these garments, and here is a hat, such as it is, that will give you an awful oncivilized sort of civilization, as the missionaries call it. Remember that Hist is at hand, and what we do for the maiden must be done while we are doing for others. I know it's ag'in your gifts and your natur' to wear clothes, unless they are cut and carried in a red man's fashion, but make a vartue of necessity, and put these on at once, even if they do rise a little in your throat."

Chingachgook, or the Serpent, eyed the vestments with strong disgust; but he saw the usefulness of the disguise, if not its absolute necessity. Should the Iroquois discover a red man in or about the castle, it might, indeed, place them more on their guard, and give their suspicions a direction toward their female captive. Anything was better than a failure, as it regarded his betrothed, and, after turning the different garments round and round, examining them with a species of grave irony, affecting to draw them on in a way that defeated itself, and otherwise manifesting the reluctance of a young savage to confine his limbs in the usual appliances of civilized life, the chief submitted to the directions of his companion, and finally stood forth, so far as the eye could detect, a red man in color alone. Little was to be apprehended from this last peculiarity, however, the distance from the shore, and the want of glasses, preventing any very close scrutiny, and Deerslayer himself, though of a brighter and fresher tint, had a countenance that was burned by the sun to a hue scarcely less red than that of his Mohican companion. The awkwardness of the Delaware, in his new attire, caused his friend to smile more than once that day, but he carefully abstained from the use of any of those jokes which would have been bandied among white men on such an occasion; the habits of a chief, the dignity of a warrior on his first path, and the gravity of the circumstances in which they were placed, uniting to render so much levity out of season.

The meeting at the morning meal of the three islanders, if we may use the term, was silent, grave, and thoughtful. Judith showed by her looks that she had passed an unquiet night, while the two men had the future before them, with its unseen and unknown events. A few words of courtesy passed between Deerslayer and the girl in the course of the breakfast, but no allusion was made to their situation. At length, Judith, whose heart was full, and whose novel feelings disposed her to entertain sentiments more gentle and tender than common, introduced the subject, and this in a way to show how much of her thoughts it had occupied in the course of the last sleepless night.

"It would be dreadful, Deerslayer," the girl abruptly exclaimed, "should anything serious befall my father and Hetty! We cannot remain quietly here and leave them in the hands of the Iroquois, without bethinking us of some means of serving them."

"I'm ready, Judith, to sarve them, and all others who are in trouble, could the way to do it be pointed out. It's no trifling matter to fall into redskin hands, when men set out on an arr'nd like that which took Hutter and Hurry ashore; that I know as well as another; and I wouldn't wish my worst inimy in such a strait, much less them with whom I've journeyed, and eat, and slept. Have you any scheme that you would like to have the Sarpent and me indivor to carry out?"

"I know of no other means to release the prisoners, than by bribing the Iroquois. They are not proof against presents; and we might offer enough, perhaps, to make them think it better to carry away what to them will be rich gifts than to carry away poor prisoners; if, indeed, they should carry them away at all!"

"This is well enough, Judith; yes, it's well enough, if the inimy is to be bought, and we can find articles to make the purchase with. Your father has a convenient lodge, and it is most cunningly placed; though it doesn't seem overstocked with riches that will be likely to buy his ransom. There's the piece he calls Killdeer might count for something, and I understand there's a keg of powder about, which might be a makeweight, sartain; and yet two able-bodied men are not to be bought off for a trifle—besides—"

"Besides what?" demanded Judith, impatiently, observing that the other hesitated to proceed, probably from a reluctance to distress her.

"Why, Judith, the Frenchers offer bounties as well as our own side; and the price of two scalps would purchase a keg of powder and a rifle; though I'll not say one of the latter altogether as good as Killdeer there, which your father va'nts as oncommon, and onequalled, like. But fair powder, and a pretty sartain rifle; then the red men are not the expartest in firearms, and don't always know the difference atwixt that which is ra'al and that which is seeming."

"This is horrible!" muttered the girl, struck by the homely manner in which her companion was accustomed to state his facts. "But you overlook my own clothes, Deerslayer; and they, I think, might go far with the women of the Iroquois."

"No doubt they would; no doubt they would, Judith," returned the other, looking at her keenly, as if he would ascertain whether she were really capable of making such a sacrifice. "But are you sartain, gal, you could find it in your heart to part with your own finery for such a purpose? Many is the man who has thought he was valiant till danger stared him in the face; I've known them, too, that consaited they were kind and ready to give away all they had to the poor, when they've been listening to other people's hardheartedness, but whose fists have clenched as tight as the riven hickory, when it came to downright offerings of their own. Besides, Judith, you're handsome—oncommon in that way, one might obsarve, and do no harm to the truth; and they that have beauty like to have that which will adorn it. Are you sartain you could find it in your heart to part with your own finery?"

The soothing allusion to the personal charms of the girl was well timed, to counteract the effect produced by the distrust that the young man expressed of Judith's devotion to her filial duties. Had another said as much as Deerslayer, the compliment would most probably have been overlooked, in the indignation awakened by the doubts; but even the unpolished sincerity, that so often made this simple-minded hunter bare his thoughts, had a charm for the girl; and, while she colored, and for an instant her eyes flashed fire, she could not find it in her heart to be really angry with one whose very soul seemed truth and manly kindness. Look her reproaches she did; but conquering the desire to retort, she succeeded in answering in a mild and friendly manner.

"You must keep all your favorable opinions for the Delaware girls, Deerslayer, if you seriously think thus of those of your own color," she said, affecting to laugh. "But, *try* me; if you find that I regret either ribbon or feather, silk or muslin, then you may think what you please of my heart, and say what you think."

"That's justice! The rarest thing to find on 'arth is a truly just man. So says Tamenund, the wisest prophet of the Delawares; and so all must think that have occasion to see, and talk, and act among mankind. I love a just man,—Sarpent; his eyes are never covered with darkness toward his inimies, while they are all sunshine and brightness toward his fri'nds. He uses the reason that God has given him, and he uses it with a feelin' of his being ordered to look at, and to consider things as they *are*, and not as he *wants* them to be. It's easy enough to find men who *call* themselves just; but it's wonderfully oncommon to find them that are the very thing, in fact. How often have I seen Indians, gal, who believed they were lookin' into a matter agreeable to the will of the Great Spirit, when, in truth, they were only striving to act up to their own will and pleasure, and this, half of the time, with a temptation to go wrong, that could no more be seen by themselves, than the stream that runs in the next valley can be seen by us through yonder mountain; though any looker-on might have discovered it as plainly as we can discover the parch that are swimming around this hut."

"Very true, Deerslayer," rejoined Judith, losing every trace of displeasure in a bright smile; "very true; and I hope to see you act on this love of justice, in all matters in which I am concerned. Above all, I hope you will judge for yourself, and not believe every evil story that a prating idler, like Hurry Harry, may have to tell, that goes to touch the good name of any young woman who may not happen to have the same opinions of his face and person that the blustering gallant has of himself."

"Hurry Harry's idees do not pass for gospel with me, Judith; but even worse than he may have eyes and ears," returned the other gravely.

"Enough of this!" exclaimed Judith, with flashing eye, and a flush that mounted to her temples; "and more of my father and his ransom. 'Tis as you say, Deerslayer; the Indians will not be likely to give up their prisoners without a heavier bribe than my clothes can offer, and father's rifle and powder. There is the chest."

"Ay, there is the chist, as you say, Judith; and when the question gets to be between a secret and a scalp, I should think most men would prefar keeping the last. Did your father ever give you any downright command consarning that chist?"

"Never. He has always appeared to think its locks, and its steel bands, and its strength, its best protection."

" 'Tis a rare chist, and altogether of curious build," returned Deerslayer, rising and approaching the thing in question, on which he seated himself, with a view to examine it with greater ease. "Chingachgook, this is no wood that comes of any forest that you or I have ever trailed through! 'Tisn't the black walnut; and yet it's quite as comely, if not more so, did the smoke and the treatment give it fair play."

The Delaware drew near, felt of the wood, examined its grain, endeavored to indent the surface with a nail, and passed his hand curiously over the steel bands, the heavy padlocks, and the other novel peculiarities of the massive box.

"No—nothing like this grows in these regions," resumed Deerslayer; "I've seen all the oaks, both the maples, the elms, the basswood, all the walnuts, the butternuts, and every tree that has a substance and color, wrought into some form or other; but never have I before seen such a wood as this! Judith, the chist itself would buy your father's freedom, or Iroquois cur'osity isn't as strong as redskin cur'osity, in general; especially in the matter of woods."

"The purchase might be cheaper made, perhaps, Deerslayer. The chest is full, and it would be better to part with half than to part with the whole. Besides, father—I know not why—but father values that chest highly."

"He would seem to prize what it holds more than the chist itself, judging by the manner in which he treats the outside and secures the inside. Here are three locks, Judith; is there no key?"

"I've never seen one; and yet key there must be, since Hetty told us *she* had often seen the chest opened."

"Keys no more lie in the air, or float on the water, than humans, gal; if there is a key, there must be a place in which it is kept."

"That is true, and it might not be difficult to find it, did we dare to search!"

"This is for you, Judith; it is altogether for you. The chist is your'n, or your father's; and Hutter is your father, not mine. Cur'osity is a woman's and not a man's failing; and there you have got all the reasons before you. If the chist has articles for ransom, it seems to me they would be wisely used in redeeming their owner's life, or even in saving his scalp; but that is a matter for your judgment, and not for our'n. When the lawful owner of a trap, or a buck, or a canoe, isn't present, his next of kin becomes his riprisentatyve, by all the laws of the woods. We therefore leave you to say whether the chist shall or shall not be opened."

"I hope you do not believe I can hesitate, when my father's life's in danger, Deerslayer!"

"Why, it's pretty much putting a scolding ag'in tears and mourning. It's not onreasonable to foretell that old Tom may find fault with what you've done, when he sees himself once more in his hut, here; but there's nothing unusual in men's falling out with what has been done for their own good; I dare to say that even the moon would seem a different thing from what it now does, could we look at it from the other side."

"Deerslayer, if we can find the key, I will authorize you to open the chest, and to take such things from it as you may think will buy father's ransom."

"First find the key, gal; we'll talk of the rest a'terwards. Sarpent, you've eyes like a fly, and a judgment that's seldom out; can you help us in calculating where Floating Tom would be apt to keep the key of a chist that he holds to be as private as this?"

The Delaware had taken no part in the discourse, until he was thus directly appealed to, when he quitted the chest, which had continued to attract his attention, and cast about him for the place in which a key would be likely to be concealed under such circumstances. As Judith and Deerslayer were not idle the while, the whole three were soon engaged in an anxious and spirited search. As it was certain that the desired key was not to be found in any of the common drawers or closets, of which there were several in the building, none looked there, but all turned their inquiries to those places that struck them as ingenious hiding places, and more likely to be used for such a purpose. In this manner the outer room was thoroughly but fruitlessly examined, when they entered the sleeping apartment of Hutter. This part of the rude building was better furnished than the rest of the structure, containing several articles that had been especially devoted to the service of the deceased wife of its owner; but as Judith had all the rest of the keys, it was soon rummaged, without bringing to light the particular key desired.

They now entered the bedroom of the daughters. Chingachgook was immediately struck with the contrast between the articles, and the arrangement of that side of the room that might be called Judith's, and that which more properly belonged to Hetty. A slight exclamation escaped him, and pointing in each direction, he alluded to the fact in a low voice, speaking to his friend in the Delaware tongue.

"As you think, Sarpent," answered Deerslayer, whose remarks we always translate into English, preserving as much as possible of the peculiar phraseology and manner of the man. " 'Tis just so, as any one may see; and 'tis all founded in natur'. One sister loves finery, some say, overmuch; while t'other is as meek and lowly as God ever created goodness and truth. Yet, after all, I dare say that Judith has her vartues, and Hetty has her failin's."

"And the Feeble Mind has seen the chest opened?" inquired Chingachgook, with curiosity in his glance.

"Sartain; that much I've heard from her own lips; and, for that matter, so have you. It seems her father doesn't misgive *her* discretion, though he does that of his eldest darter."

"Then the key is hid only from the Wild Rose?" for so Chingachgook had begun gallantly to term Judith, in his private discourse with his friend.

"That's it! That's just it! One he trusts, and the other he doesn't. There's red and white in that, Sarpent; all tribes and nations agreeing in trusting some, and refusing to trust other some. It depends on character and judgment."

"Where could a key be put, so little likely to be found by the Wild Rose, as among coarse clothes?"

Deerslayer started, and turning to his friend with admiration expressed in every lineament of his face, he fairly laughed, in his silent but hearty manner, at the ingenuity and readiness of the conjecture.

"Your name's well bestowed, Sarpent—yes, 'tis well bestowed! Sure enough, where would a lover of finery be so little likely to s'arch, as among garments as coarse and unseemly as these of poor Hetty? I dare to say Judith's delicate fingers haven't touched a bit of cloth as rough and oncomely as that petticoat, now, since she first made acquaintance with the officers! Yet, who knows? the key may be as likely to be on the same peg as in any other place. Take down the garment, Delaware, and let us see if you are ra'ally a prophet."

Chingachgook did as desired, but no key was found. A coarse pocket, apparently empty, hung on the adjoining peg, and this was next examined. By this time, the attention of Judith was called in that direction, and she spoke hurriedly, and like one who wished to save unnecessary trouble.

"These are only the clothes of poor Hetty, dear simple girl!" she said; "nothing we seek would be likely to be there."

The words were hardly out of the handsome mouth of the speaker, when Chingachgook drew the desired key from the pocket. Judith was too quick of apprehension not to understand the reason a hiding place so simple and exposed had been used. The blood rushed to her face, as much with resentment, perhaps, as with shame; and she bit her lip, though she continued silent. Deerslayer and his friend now discovered the delicacy of men of native refinement, neither smiling, nor even by a glance betraying how completely he understood the motives and ingenuity of this clever artifice. The former, who had taken the key from the Indian, led the way into the adjoining room, and applying it to a lock, ascertained that the right instrument had actually been found. There were three padlocks, each of which, however, was easily opened by this single key. Deerslayer removed them all, loosened the hasps, raised the lid a little to make certain it was loose, and then he drew back from the chest several feet, signing to his friend to follow.

"This is a family chist, Judith," he said, "and 'tis like to hold family secrets. The Sarpent and I will go into the ark, and look to the canoes, and paddles, and oars; while you can examine it by yourself, and find out whether anything that will be a makeweight in a ransom is or is not among the articles. When you've got through, give us a call, and we'll all sit in council together, touching the valie of the articles."

"Stop, Deerslayer," exclaimed the girl, as he was about to withdraw; "not a single thing will I touch—I will not even raise the lid—unless you are present. Father and Hetty have seen fit to keep the inside of this chest a secret from me, and I am much too proud to pry into their hidden treasures, unless it were for their own good. But on no account will I open the chest alone. Stay with me, then; I want witnesses of what I do."

"I rather think, Sarpent, that the gal is right! Confidence and reliance beget security, but suspicion is like to make us all wary. Judith has a right to ask us to be present; and should the chist hold any of Master Hutter's secrets, they will fall into the keeping of two as close-mouthed young men as are to be found. We *will* stay with you, Judith—but first let us take a look at the lake and the shore, for this chist will not be emptied in a minute."

The two men now went out on the platform, and Deerslayer swept the shore with the glass, while the Indian gravely turned his eye on the water and the woods in quest of any sign that might betray the machinations of their enemies. Nothing was visible, and assured of their temporary security, the three collected around the chest again.

Judith had held this chest, and its unknown contents, in a species of reverence as long as she could remember. Neither her father nor her mother ever mentioned it in her presence, and there appeared to be a silent convention, that in naming the different objects that occasionally stood near it, or even lay on its lid, care should be had to avoid any allusion to the chest itself. Habit rendered this so easy, and so much a matter of course, that it was only quite recently the girl had begun even to muse on the singularity of the circumstance. But there had never been sufficient intimacy between Hutter and his eldest daughter to invite confidence. At times he was kind, but in general, with her more especially, he was stern and morose. Least of all had his authority been exercised in a way to embolden his child to venture on the liberty she was about to take, without many misgivings of the consequences, although the liberty proceeded from a desire to serve himself. Then Judith was not altogether free from a little superstition on the subject of this chest, which had stood a sort of tabooed relic before her eyes from childhood to the present hour. Nevertheless, the time had come when it would seem that this mystery was to be explained, and that under circumstances, too, which left her very little choice in the matter.

Finding that both her companions were watching her movements in grave silence, Judith placed a hand on the lid, and endeavored to raise it. Her strength, however, was insufficient, and it appeared to the girl, who was fully aware that all the fastenings were removed, that she was resisted in an unhallowed attempt by some supernatural power.

"I cannot raise the lid, Deerslayer," she said; "had we not better give up the attempt, and find some other means of releasing the prisoners?"

"Not so, Judith; not so, gal. No means are as sartain and easy as a good bribe," answered the other. "As for the lid, 'tis held by nothing but its own weight, which is prodigious for so small a piece of wood, loaded with iron as it is."

As Deerslayer spoke, he applied his own strength to the effort, and succeeded in raising the lid against the timbers of the house, where he took care to secure it by a sufficient prop. Judith fairly trembled, as she cast her first glance at the interior; and she felt a temporary relief in discovering that a piece of canvas that was carefully tucked in around the edges effectually concealed all beneath it. The chest was apparently well stored, however, the canvas lying within an inch of the lid.

"Here's a full cargo," said Deerslayer, eying the arrangement; "and we had needs go to work leisurely, and at our ease. Sarpent, bring some stools, while I spread this blanket on the floor, and then we'll begin work orderly and in comfort."

The Delaware complied; Deerslayer civilly placed a stool for Judith, took one himself, and commenced the removal of the canvas covering. This was done deliberately, and in as cautious a manner as if it were believed that fabrics of a delicate construction lay hidden beneath. When the canvas was removed, the first articles that came in view were some of the habiliments of the male sex. These were of fine materials, and, according to the fashions of the age, were gay in colors and rich in ornaments. One coat, in particular, was of scarlet, and had buttonholes worked in gold thread. Still it was not military, but was part of the attire of a civilian of condition, at a period when social rank was rigidly respected in dress. Chingachgook could not refrain from an exclamation of pleasure, as soon as Deerslayer opened this coat, and held it up to view; for, notwithstanding all his trained self-command, the splendor of the vestment was too much for the philosophy of an Indian. Deerslayer turned quickly, and he regarded his friend with a momentary displeasure, as this burst of weakness escaped him; and then he soliloquized, as was his practice whenever any strong feeling suddenly got the ascendency.

" 'Tis his gift!—yes, 'tis the gift of a redskin to love finery, and he is not to be blamed. This is an extr'ornary garment, too; and extr'ornary things get up extr'ornary feelin's. I think this will do, Judith, for the Indian heart is hardly to be found in all America that can withstand colors like these and glitter like that. If this coat was ever made for your father, you've come honestly by the taste for finery, you have."

"That coat was never made for father," answered the girl, quickly; "it is much too long; while father is short and square."

"Cloth was plenty, if it was, and glitter cheap," answered Deerslayer, with his silent, joyous laugh. "Sarpent, this garment was made for a man of your size, and I should like to see it on your shoulders."

Chingachgook, nothing loath, submitted to the trial; throwing aside the coarse and threadbare jacket of Hutter, to deck his person in a coat that was originally intended for a gentleman. The transformation was ludicrous; but as men are seldom struck with incongruities in their own appearance any more than in their own conduct, the Delaware studied this change in a common glass, by which Hutter was in the habit of shaving, with grave interest. At that moment he thought of Hist, and we owe it to truth to say, though it may militate a little against the stern character of a warrior to own it, that he wished he could be seen by her in his present improved aspect.

"Off with it, Sarpent—off with it," resumed the inflexible Deerslayer; "such garments as little become you as they would become me. Your gifts are for paint, and hawk's feathers, and blankets, and wampum; and mine are for doublets of skins, tough leggings, and sarviceable moccasins. I say moccasins, Judith, for though white, living as I do in the woods, it's necessary to take to some of the practyces of the woods, for comfort's sake and cheapness."

"I see no reason, Deerslayer, why one man may not wear a scarlet coat as well as another," returned the girl. "I wish I could see *you* in this handsome garment."

"See me in a coat fit for a lord! Well, Judith, if you wait till that day, you'll wait until you see me beyond reason and memory. No—no—gal, my gifts are my gifts, and I'll live and die in 'em, though I never bring down another deer or spear another salmon. What have I done that you should wish to see *me* in such a flaunting coat, Judith?"

"Because I think, Deerslayer, that the falsetongued and false-hearted young gallants of the garrison ought not alone to appear in fine feathers; but that truth and honesty have *their* claims to be honored and exalted."

"And what exaltification"—the reader will have remarked that Deerslayer had not very critically studied his dictionary—"And what exaltification would it be to me, Judith, to be bedizened and bescarleted like a Mingo chief that has just got his presents up from Quebec? No—

no—I'm well as I am; and if not, I can be no better. Lay the coat down on the blanket, Sarpent, and let us look further into the chist."

The tempting garment, one surely that was never intended for Hutter, was laid aside, and the examination proceeded. The male attire, all of which corresponded with the coat in quality, was soon exhausted, and then succeeded female. A beautiful dress of brocade, a little the worse from negligent treatment, followed; and this time open exclamations of delight escaped the lips of Judith. Much as the girl had been addicted to dress, and favorable as had been her opportunities of seeing some little pretension in that way, among the wives of the different commandants, and other ladies of the forts, never before had she beheld a tissue, or tints to equal those that were now so unexpectedly placed before her eyes. Her rapture was almost childish; nor would she allow the inquiry to proceed until she had attired her person in a robe so unsuited to her habits and her abode. With this end, she withdrew into her own room, where, with hands practiced in such offices, she soon got rid of her own neat gown of linen, and stood forth in the gay tints of the brocade. The dress happened to fit the fine, full person of Judith, and certainly it never adorned a being better qualified by natural gifts to do credit to its really rich hues and fine texture. When she returned, both Deerslayer and Chingachgook, who had passed the brief time of her absence in taking a second look at the male garments arose in surprise, each permitting exclamations of wonder and pleasure to escape him, in a way so unequivocal as to add new luster to the eyes of Judith, by flushing her cheeks with a glow of triumph. Affecting, however, not to notice the impression she had made, the girl seated herself with the stateliness of a queen, desiring that the chest might be looked into further.

"I don't know a better way to treat with the Mingoes, gal," cried Deerslayer, "than to send you ashore as you be, and to tell 'em that a queen has arrived among 'em! They'll give up old Hutter and Harry, and Hetty too, at such a spectacle!"

"I thought your tongue too honest to flatter, Deerslayer," returned the girl, gratified at this admiration more than she would have cared to own. "One of the chief reasons of my respect for you was your love for truth."

"And 'tis truth and solemn truth, Judith, and nothing else. Never did eyes of mine gaze on as glorious a lookin' creatur' as you be yourself, at this very moment. I've seen beauties in my time, too, both white and red; and them that was renowned and talked of far and near; but never have I beheld one that could hold any comparison with what you are at this blessed instant, Judith,—never."

The glance of delight which the girl bestowed on the frank-speaking hunter in no degree lessened the effect of her charms; and as the humid eyes blended with it a look of sensibility, perhaps Judith never appeared more truly lovely than at what the young man had called that "blessed instant." He shook his head, held it suspended a moment over the open chest like one in doubt, and then proceeded with the examination.

Several of the minor articles of female dress came next, all of a quality to correspond with the gown. These were laid at Judith's feet, in silence, as if she had a natural claim to their possession. One or two, such as gloves and laces, the girl caught up and appended to her already rich attire, in affected playfulness, but with the real design of decorating her person as far as circumstances would allow. When these two remarkable suits, male and female they might be termed, were removed, another canvas covering separated the remainder of the articles from the part of the chest which they had occupied. As soon as Deerslayer perceived this arrangement, he paused, doubtful of the propriety of proceeding any further.

"Every man has his secrets, I suppose," he said, "and all men have a right to their enj'yment; we've got low enough in this chist, in my judgment, to answer our wants, and it seems to me we should do well by going no further; and by letting Master Hutter have to himself and his own feelin's all that's beneath this cover."

"Do you mean, Deerslayer, to offer these clothes to the Iroquois as ransom?" demanded Judith, quickly.

"Sartain. What are we prying into another man's chist for, but to sarve its owner in the best way we can? This coat, alone, would be very apt to gain over the head-chief of the riptyles; and if his wife or darter should happen to be out with him, that there gownd would soften the heart of any woman that is to be found atween Albany and Montreal. I do not see that we want a larger stock in trade than them two articles."

"To you it may seem so, Deerslayer," returned the disappointed girl; "but of what use could a dress like this be to any Indian woman? She could not wear it among the branches of the trees; the dirt and smoke of the wigwam would soon soil it; and how would a pair of red arms appear thrust through these short, laced sleeves!"

"All very true, gal; and you might go on and say, it is altogether out of time, and place, and season, in this region at all. What is it to us how the finery is treated, so long as it answers our wishes? I do not see that your father can make any use of such clothes; and it's lucky he has things that are of no valie to himself, that will bear a high price with others. We can make no better trade for him than to offer these duds for his liberty. We'll throw in the light frivol'ties, and get Hurry off in the bargain!"

"Then you think, Deerslayer, that Thomas Hutter has no one in his family—no child—no daughter, to whom this dress may be thought becoming, and whom you could wish to see in it once and a while, even though it should be at long intervals, and only in playfulness?"

"I understand you, Judith—yes, I now understand your meaning; and I think I can say, your wishes. That you are as glorious in that dress as the sun when it rises or sets in a soft October day, I'm ready to allow; and that you greatly become it is a good deal more sartain than that it becomes you. There's gifts in clothes as well as in other things. Now I do not think that a warrior on his first path ought to lay on the same awful paints as a chief that has had his vartue tried, and knows from exper'ence he will not disgrace his pretensions. So it is with all of us, red or white. You are Thomas Hutter's darter, and that gownd was made for the child of some governor, or a lady of high station; and it was intended to be worn among fine furniture and in rich company. In my eyes, Judith, a modest maiden never looks more becoming than when becomingly clad, and nothing is suitable that is out of character. Besides, gal, if there's a creatur' in the colony that can afford to do without finery, and to trust to her own good looks and sweet countenance, it's yourself."

"I'll take off the rubbish this instant, Deerslayer," cried the girl, springing up to leave the room; "and never do I wish to see it on any human being again."

"So it is with 'em all, Sarpent," said the other, turning to his friend and laughing, as soon as the beauty had disappeared. "They like finery, but they like their natyve charms most of all. I'm glad the gal has consented to lay aside her furbelows, howsever, for it's ag'in reason for one of her class to wear 'em; and then she *is* handsome enough, as I call it, to go alone. Hist would show oncommon likely, too, in such a gownd, Delaware!"

"Wah-ta-Wah is a redskin girl, Deerslayer," returned the Indian; "like the young of the pigeon she is to be known by her own feathers. I should pass by without knowing her, were she dressed in such a skin. It's wisest always to be so clad that our friends need not ask us for our name. The Wild Rose is very pleasant, but she is no sweeter for so many colors."

"That's it!—that's natur', and the true foundation for love and protection. When a man stops to pick a wild strawberry, he does not expect to find a melon; and when he wishes to gather a melon, he's disapp'inted if it proves to be a squash; though squashes *be* often brighter to the eye than melons. That's it, and it means, stick to your gifts and your gifts will stick to you."

The two men had now a little discussion together, touching the propriety of penetrating any further into the chest of Hutter, when Judith reappeared, divested of her robes, and in her own simple linen frock again.

"Thank you, Judith," said Deerslayer, taking her kindly by the hand; "for I know it went a little ag'in the nat'ral cravings of woman to lay aside so much finery as it might be in a lump. But you're more pleasing to the eye as you stand, you be, than if you had a crown on your head, and jewels dangling from your hair. The question now is, whether to lift this covering to see what will be ra'ally the best bargain we can make for Master Hutter; for we must do as we think *he* would be willing to do, did he stand here in our places."

Judith looked very happy. Accustomed as she was to adulation, the humble homage of Deerslayer had given her more true satisfaction than she had ever yet received from the tongue of man. It was not the terms in which this admiration had been expressed, for *they* were simple enough, that produced so strong an impression; nor yet their novelty, or their warmth of manner, nor any of those peculiarities that usually give value to praise; but the unflinching truth of the speaker, that carried his words so directly to the heart of the listener. This is one of the great advantages of plain dealing and frankness. The habitual and wily flatterer may succeed until his practices recoil on himself, and, like other sweets, his ailment cloys by its excess; but he who deals honestly, though he often necessarily offend, possesses a power of praising that no quality but sincerity can bestow; since his words go directly to the heart, finding their support in the understanding. Thus it was with Deerslayer and Judith; so soon and so deeply did this simple hunter impress those who knew him with a conviction of his unbending honesty, that all he uttered in commendation was as certain to please, as all he uttered in the way of rebuke was as certain to rankle and excite enmity where his character had not awakened a respect and affection, that in another sense rendered it painful. In after life, when the career of this untutored being brought him in contact with officers of rank, and others intrusted with the care of the interests of the state, this same influence was exerted on a wider field; even generals listening to his commendations with a glow of pleasure that it was not always in the power of their official superiors to awaken. Perhaps Judith was the first individual of his own color who fairly submitted to this natural consequence of truth and fair-dealing, on the part of Deerslayer. She had actually pined for his praise, and she had now received it; and that in the form which was most agreeable to her weaknesses and habits of thought. The result will appear in the course of the narrative.

"If we knew all that chest holds, Deerslayer," returned the girl, when she had a little recovered from the immediate effect produced by his commendations of her personal appearance, "we could better determine on the course we ought to take."

"That's not onreasonable, gal, though it's more a paleface than a redskin gift, to be prying into other people's secrets."

"Curiosity is natural, and it is expected that all human beings should have human failings. Whenever I've been at the garrisons, I've found that most, in and about them, had a longing to learn their neighbor's secrets."

"Yes, and sometimes to fancy them, when they couldn't find 'em out! That's the difference atween an Indian gentleman and a white gentleman. The Sarpent, here, would turn his head aside, if he found himself onknowingly lookin' into another chief's wigwam; whereas, in the settlements, while all pretend to be great people, most prove they've got betters, by the manner in which they talk of their consarns. I'll be bound, Judith, you wouldn't get the Sarpent, there, to confess there was another in the tribe so much greater than himself, as to become the subject of his idees, and to empl'y his tongue in conversations about his movements, and ways, and food, and all the other little matters that occupy a man when he's not empl'yed in his greater duties. He who does this is but little better than a blackguard in the grain, and them that encourages him is pretty much of the same kidney, let them wear coats as fine as they may, or of what dye they please."

"But this is not another man's wigwam; it belongs to my father; these are his things, and they are wanted in his service."

"That's true, gal, that's true; and it carries weight with it. Well, when all is before us, we may, indeed, best judge which to offer for the ransom, and which to withhold."

Judith was not altogether as disinterested in her feelings as she affected to be. She remembered that the curiosity of Hetty had been indulged, in connection with this chest, while her own had been disregarded; and she was not sorry to possess an opportunity of being placed on a level with her less gifted sister, in this one particular. It appearing to be admitted all round that the inquiry into the contents of the chest ought to be renewed, Deerslayer proceeded to remove the second covering of canvas.

The articles that lay uppermost, when the curtain was again raised on the secrets of the chest, were a pair of pistols, curiously inlaid with silver. Their value would have been considerable in one of the towns, though as weapons, in the woods, they were a species of arms seldom employed, never indeed, unless it might be by some officer from Europe, who visited the colonies, as many were then wont to do, so much impressed with the superiority of the usages of London, as to fancy they were not to be laid aside on the frontiers of America.

No sooner did Deerslayer raise the pistols, than he turned to the Delaware, and held them up for his admiration.

"Child gun," said the Serpent, smiling, while he handled one of the instruments as if it had been a toy.

"Not it, Sarpent; not it. 'Tis made for a man, and would satisfy a giant if rightly used. But stop; white men are remarkable for their carelessness in putting away firearms in chists and corners. Let me look if care has been given to these."

As Deerslayer spoke, he took the weapon from the hand of his friend and opened the pan. The last was filled with priming, caked like a bit of cinder, by time, moisture, and compression. An application of the ramrod showed that both the pistols were charged, although Judith could testify that they had probably lain for years in the chest. It is not easy to portray the surprise of the Indian at this discovery, for he was in the practice of renewing his priming daily, and of looking to the contents of his piece at other short intervals.

"This is white neglect," said Deerslayer, shaking his head, "and scarce a season goes by that someone in the settlements doesn't suffer from it. It's extr'ornary too, Judith—yes, it's downright extr'ornary that the owner shall fire his piece at a deer, or some other game, or perhaps at an inimy, and twice out of three times he'll miss; but let him catch an accident with one of these forgotten charges, and he makes it sartain death to a child, or a brother, or a fri'nd! Well, we shall do a good turn to the owner if we fire these pistols for him; and as they're novelties to you and me, Sarpent, we'll try our hand at a mark. Freshen that priming, and I'll do the same with this, and then we'll see who is the best man with a pistol; as for the rifle, that's long been settled atween us."

Deerslayer laughed heartily at his own conceit, and, in a minute or two, they were both standing on the platform, selecting some object in the ark for their target. Judith was led by curiosity to their side.

"Stand back, gal, stand a little back; these we'pons have been long loaded," said Deerslayer, "and some accident may happen in the discharge."

"Then *you* shall not fire them! Give them both to the Delaware; or it would be better to unload them without firing."

"That's ag'in usage—and some people say ag'in manhood; though I hold no such silly doctrine. We must fire 'em, Judith; yes, we must fire 'em; though I foresee that neither will have any great reason to boast of his skill."

Judith, in the main, was a girl of great personal spirit, and her habits prevented her from feeling any of the terror that is apt to come over her sex at the report of firearms. She had discharged many a rifle, and had even been known to kill a deer, under circumstances that were favorable to the effort. She submitted, therefore, falling a little back by the side of Deerslayer, giving the Indian the front of the platform to himself. Chingachgook raised the weapon several times, endeavored to steady it by using both hands, changed his attitude, from one that was awkward to another still more so, and finally drew the trigger with a sort of desperate indifference, without having, in reality, secured any aim at all. The consequence was, that instead of hitting the knot, which had been selected for the mark, he missed the ark altogether; the bullet skipping along the water like a stone that was thrown by hand.

"Well done! Sarpent; well done!" cried Deerslayer, laughing with his noiseless glee, "you've hit the lake, and that's an expl'ite, for some men! I know'd it, and as much as said it here, to Judith; for your short we'pons don't belong to redskin gifts. You've hit the lake, and that's better than only hitting the air! Now, stand back, and let us see what white gifts can do with a white we'pon. A pistol isn't a rifle; but color is color."

The aim of Deerslayer was both quick and steady, and the report followed almost as soon as the weapon rose. Still the pistol hung fire, as it is termed, and fragments of it flew in a dozen directions, some falling on the roof of the castle, others in the ark, and one in the water. Judith screamed, and when the two men turned anxiously toward the girl, she was as pale as death, trembling in every limb.

"She's wounded—yes, the poor gal's wounded, Sarpent, though one couldn't foresee it, standing where she did. We'll lead her in to a seat, and we must do the best for her that our knowledge and skill can afford."

Judith allowed herself to be supported to a seat, swallowed a mouthful of the water that the Delaware offered to her in a gourd, and after a violent fit of trembling, that seemed ready to shake her fine frame to dissolution, she burst into tears.

"The pain must be borne, poor Judith—yes, it must be borne," said Deerslayer, soothingly; "though I am far from wishing you not to weep; for weeping often lightens galish feelin's. Where can she be hurt, Sarpent? I see no signs of blood, nor any rent of skin or garments."

"I am uninjured, Deerslayer," stammered the girl through her tears. "It's fright—nothing more, I do assure you; and, God be praised! no one, I find, has been harmed by the accident."

"This is extr'ornary!" exclaimed the unsuspecting and simple-minded hunter. "I thought, Judith, you'd been above settlement weaknesses, and that you was a gal not to be frightened by the sound of a bursting we'pon. No, I didn't think you so skeary! *Hetty* might well have been startled; but you've too much judgment and reason to be frightened when the danger's all over. They're pleasant to the eye, chief, and changeful, but very unsartain in their feelin's!"

Shame kept Judith silent. There had been no acting in her agitation, but all had fairly proceeded from sudden and uncontrollable alarm—an alarm that she found almost as inexplicable to herself, as it proved to be to her companions. Wiping away the traces of tears, however, she smiled again, and was soon able to join in the laugh at her own folly.

"And you, Deerslayer," she at length succeeded in saying, "are you, indeed, altogether unhurt? It seems almost miraculous that a pistol should have burst in your hand, and you escape without the loss of a limb, if not of life!"

"Such wonders aren't oncommon, at all, among worn-out arms. The first rifle they gave me played the same trick, and yet I lived through it, though not as onharmless as I've got out of this affair. Thomas Hutter is master of one pistol less than he was this morning; but as it happened in trying to sarve him, there's no ground of complaint. Now, draw near, and let us look further into the inside of the chist."

Judith, by this time, had so far got the better of her agitation as to resume her seat, and the examination went on. The next article that offered was enveloped in cloth, and, on opening it, it proved to be one of the mathematical instruments that were then in use among seamen, possessing the usual ornaments and fastenings in brass. Deerslayer and Chingachgook expressed their admiration and surprise at the appearance of the unknown instrument, which was bright and glittering, having apparently been well cared for.

"This goes beyond the surveyors, Judith!" Deerslayer exclaimed, after turning the instrument several times in his hands. "I've seen all their tools often, and wicked and heartless enough are they, for they never come into the forest but to lead the way to waste and destruction; but none of them has as designing a look as this! I fear me, after all, that Thomas Hutter has journeyed into the wilderness with no fair intentions toward its happiness. Did you ever see any of the cravings of a surveyor about your father, gal?"

"He is no surveyor, Deerslayer, nor does he know the use of that instrument, though he seems to own it. Do you suppose that Thomas Hutter ever wore that coat? It is as much too large for him as this instrument is beyond his learning."

"That's it—that must be it, Sarpent; and the old fellow, by some onknown means, has fallen heir to another man's goods! They say he has been a mariner, and no doubt this chist and all it holds—Ha! what have we here? This far outdoes the brass and black wood of the tool!"

Deerslayer had opened a small bag, from which he was taking, one by one, the pieces of a set of chessmen. They were of ivory, much larger than common, and exquisitely wrought. Each piece represented the character or thing after which it is named; the knights being mounted, the castles stood on elephants, and even the pawns possessed the heads and busts of men. The set was not complete, and a few fractures betrayed bad usage; but all that was left had been carefully put away and preserved. Even Judith expressed wonder as these novel objects were placed before her eyes, and Chingachgook fairly forgot his Indian dignity in admiration and delight. The latter took up each piece and examined it with never-tiring satisfaction, pointing out to the girl the more ingenious and striking portions of the workmanship. But the elephants gave him the greatest pleasure. The "Hughs!" that he uttered as he passed his fingers over their trunks and ears and tails were very distinct; nor did he fail to note the pawns, which were armed as archers. This exhibition lasted several minutes, during which time Judith and the Indian had all the rapture to themselves. Deerslayer sat silent, thoughtful, and even gloomy, though his eyes followed each movement of the two principal actors, noting every new peculiarity about the pieces as they were held up to view. Not an exclamation of pleasure nor a word of condemnation passed his lips. At length his companions observed his silence, and then, for the first time since the chessmen had been discovered, did he speak.

"Judith," he asked earnestly, but with a concern that amounted almost to tenderness of manner, "did your parents ever talk to you of religion?"

The girl colored, and the flashes of crimson that passed over her beautiful countenance were like the wayward tints of a Neapolitan sky in November. Deerslayer had given her so strong a taste for truth, however, that she did not waver in her answer, replying simply and with sincerity,—

"My *mother* did, often," she said; "my father, *never*. I thought it made my mother sorrowful to speak of our prayers and duties, but my father has never opened his mouth on such matters before or since her death."

"That I can believe—that I can believe. He has no God—no such God as it becomes a man of white skin to worship, or even a redskin. Them things are idols!"

Judith started, and for a moment she seemed seriously hurt. Then she reflected, and in the end she laughed.

"And you think, Deerslayer, that these ivory toys are my father's gods? I have heard of idols, and know what they are."

"Them are idols!" repeated the other positively. "Why should your father keep 'em if he doesn't worship 'em?"

"Would he keep his gods in a bag, and locked up in a chest? No, no, Deerslayer; my poor father carries his god with him wherever he goes, and that is in his own cravings. These things may really be idols—I think they are, myself from what I have heard and read of idolatry, but they have come from some distant country, like all the other articles, and have fallen into Thomas Hutter's hands when he was a sailor."

"I'm glad of it—I am downright glad to hear it, Judith, for I do not think I could have mustered the resolution to strive to help a white idolater out of his difficulties. The old man is of my color and nation, and I wish to sarve him; but as one who denied all his gifts in the way of religion, it would have come hard to do so. That animal seems to give you great satisfaction, Sarpent, though it's an idolatrous head, at the best."

"It is an elephant," interrupted Judith, "I've often seen pictures of such animals at the garrisons; and mother had a book in which there was a printed account of the creature. Father burnt that, with all the other books, for he said mother loved reading too well. This was not long before mother died, and I've sometimes thought that the loss hastened her end."

This was said equally without levity and without any deep feeling. It was said without levity, for Judith was saddened by her recollections, and yet she had been too much accustomed to live for self, and for the indulgence of her own vanities, to feel her mother's wrongs very heavily. It required extraordinary circumstances to awaken a proper sense of her situation, and to stimulate the better feelings of this beautiful, but misguided girl; and these circumstances had not yet occurred in her brief existence.

"Elephant, or no elephant, 'tis an idol," returned the hunter, "and not fit to remain in Christian keeping."

"Good for Iroquois!" said Chingachgook, parting with one of the castles with reluctance, as his friend took it from him to replace it in the bag. "Elephon buy whole tribe—buy Delaware, almost!"

"Ay, that it would, as any one who comprehends redskin natur' must know," answered Deerslayer; "but the man that passes false money, Sarpent, is as bad as he who makes it. Did you ever know a just Injin that wouldn't scorn to sell a coonskin for the true marten, or to pass off a mink for a beaver. I know that a few of these idols, perhaps *one* of them elephants, would go far toward buying Thomas Hutter's liberty, but it goes ag'in conscience to pass such counterfeit money. Perhaps no Injin tribe, here-a-way, is downright idolaters, but there's some that come so near it, that white gifts ought to be particular about encouraging them in their mistake."

"If idolatry is a *gift*, Deerslayer, and *gifts* are what you seem to think them, idolatry in such people can hardly be a sin," said Judith, with more smartness than discrimination.

"God grants no such gifts to any of his creatur's, Judith," returned the hunter seriously. "*He* must be adored, under some name or other, and not creatur's of brass or ivory. It matters not whether the Father of all is called God or Manitou, Deity or Great Spirit, He is none the less our common Maker and Master; nor does it count for much whether the souls of the just go to Paradise or happy hunting grounds, since He may send each his own way, as suits his own pleasure and wisdom; but it curdles my blood, when I find human mortals so bound up in darkness and consait, as to fashion the 'arth, or wood, or bones—things made by their own hands—into motionless, senseless effigies, and then fall down before them, and worship 'em as a Deity!"

"After all, Deerslayer, these pieces of ivory may not be idols at all. I remember, now, to have seen one of the officers at the garrison, with a set of fox and geese made in some such a design as these; and here is something hard, wrapped in cloth, that may belong to your idols."

Deerslayer took the bundle the girl gave him, and, unrolling it, he found the board within. Like the pieces, it was large, rich, and inlaid with ebony and ivory. Putting the whole in conjunction, the hunter, though not without many misgivings, slowly came over to Judith's opinion, and finally admitted that the fancied idols must be merely the curiously carved men of some unknown game. Judith had the tact to use her victory with great moderation; nor did she once, even in the most indirect manner, allude to the ludicrous mistake of her companion.

This discovery of the uses of the extraordinary-looking little images settled the affair of the proposed ransom. It was agreed generally—and all understood the weaknesses and tastes of Indians—that nothing could be more likely to tempt the cupidity of the Iroquois, than the elephants, in particular. Luckily, the whole of the castles were among the pieces, and these four tower-bearing animals it was finally determined should be the ransom offered. The remainder of the men, and, indeed, all the rest of the articles in the chest, were to be kept out of view, and to be resorted to only as a last appeal. As soon as these preliminaries were settled, everything but those intended for the bribe was carefully replaced in the chest, and all the covers were "tucked in" as they had been found; and it was quite possible, could Hutter have been put in possession of the castle again, that he might have passed the remainder of his days in it, without even suspecting the invasion that had been made on the privacy of the chest. The rent pistol would have been the most likely to reveal the secret; but this was placed by the side of its fellow, and all were passed down as before—some half-a-dozen packages in the bottom of the chest not having been opened at all. When this was done, the lid was lowered, the padlocks replaced, and the key turned. The latter was then replaced in the pocket from which it had been taken.

More than an hour was consumed in settling the course proper to be pursued, and in returning everything to its place. The pauses to converse were frequent; and Judith, who experienced a lively pleasure in the open, undisguised admiration with which Deerslayer's honest eye gazed at her handsome face, found the means to prolong the interview, with a dexterity that seems to be innate in female coquetry. Deerslayer, indeed, appeared to be the first who was conscious of the time that had been thus wasted, and to call the attention of his companions to the necessity of doing something towards putting the plan of ransoming into execution. Chingachgook had remained in Hutter's bedroom, where the elephants were laid, to feast his eyes with the images of animals so wonderful and so novel. Perhaps an instinct told him that his presence would not be as acceptable to his companions as this holding himself aloof; for Judith had not much reserve in the manifestations of her preferences, and the Delaware had not got so far as one betrothed without acquiring some knowledge of the symptoms of the master passion.

"Well, Judith," said Deerslayer, rising, after the interview had lasted much longer than even he himself suspected, " 'tis pleasant convarsing with you, and settling all these matters, but duty calls us another way. All this time, Hurry and your father, not to say Hetty—"

The word was cut short in the speaker's mouth, for, at that critical moment, a light step was heard on the platform or courtyard, a human figure darkened the doorway, and the person last mentioned stood before him. The low exclamation that escaped Deerslayer, and the slight scream of Judith were hardly uttered, when an Indian youth, between the ages of fifteen and seventeen, stood beside her. These two entrances had been made with moccasined feet, and consequently almost without noise; but, unexpected and stealthy as they were, they had not the effect to disturb Deerslayer's self-possession. His first measure was to speak rapidly in Delaware to his friend, cautioning him to keep out of sight, while he stood on his guard; the second was to step to the door to ascertain the extent of the danger. No one else, however, had come; and a simple contrivance, in the shape of a raft, that lay floating at the side of the ark, at once explained the means that had been used in bringing Hetty off. Two dead and dry, and consequently buoyant logs of pine were bound together with pins and withes, and a little platform of riven chestnut had been rudely placed on their surfaces. Here Hetty had been seated on a billet of wood, while the young Iroquois had rowed the primitive and slow-moving, but perfectly safe craft from the shore. As soon as Deerslayer had taken a close survey of this raft, and satisfied himself nothing else was near, he shook his head, and muttered, in his soliloquizing way,—

"This comes of prying into another man's chist! Had we been watchful and keen-eyed, such a surprise could never have happened; and getting this much from a boy, teaches us what we may expect when the old warriors set themselves about their sarcumventions. It opens the way, however, to a treaty for the ransom, and I will hear what Hetty has to say."

Judith, as soon as her surprise and alarm had a little abated, discovered a proper share of affectionate joy at the return of her sister. She folded her to her bosom, and kissed her, as had been her wont in the days of their childhood and innocence. Hetty herself was less affected, for to her there was no surprise, and her nerves were sustained by the purity and holiness of her purpose. At her sister's request she took a seat, and entered into an account of her adventures since they had parted. Her tale commenced just as Deerslayer returned, and he also became an attentive listener, while the young Iroquois stood near the door, seemingly as indifferent to what was passing as one of its posts.

The narrative of the girl was sufficiently clear, until she reached the time where we left her in the camp, after the interview with the chiefs. The sequel of the story may be told in her own language.

"When I read the texts to the chiefs, Judith, you could not have seen that they made any changes on their minds," she said, "but if seed is planted, it *will* grow. God planted the seeds of all the trees—"

"Ay, that did he," muttered Deerslayer; "and a goodly harvest has followed."

"God planted the seeds of all the trees," continued Hetty, after a moment's pause, "and you see to what a height and shade they have grown! So it is with the Bible. You may read a verse this year, and forget it, and it will come back to you a year hence, when you least expect to remember it."

"And did you find anything of this, among the savages, poor Hetty?"

"Yes, Judith, and sooner, and more fully than I had even hoped. I did not stay long with father and Hurry, but went to get my breakfast with Hist. As soon as we had done, the chiefs came to us, and *then* we found the fruits of the seed that had been planted. They said what I had read from the Good Book was right—it *must* be right—it sounded *right;* like a sweet bird singing in their ears; and they told me to come back and say as much to the great warrior who had slain one of their braves; and to tell it to you, and to say how happy they should be to come to church here, in the castle, or to come out in the sun, and hear me read more of the sacred volume—and to tell you that they wish you would lend them some canoes, that they can bring father and Hurry, and their women, to the castle, that we might all sit on the platform there, and listen to the singing of the paleface Manitou. There, Judith; did you ever know of anything that so plainly shows the power of the Bible as *that?*"

"If it were true 'twould be a miracle, indeed, Hetty. But all this is no more than Indian cunning and Indian treachery, striving to get the better of us by management, when they find it is not to be done by force."

"Do you doubt the Bible, sister, that you judge the savages so harshly?"

"I do not doubt the Bible, poor Hetty, but I much doubt an Indian and an Iroquois. What do you say to this visit, Deerslayer?"

"First let me talk a little with Hetty," returned the party appealed to; "was this raft made a'ter you had got your breakfast, gal; and did you walk from the camp to the shore opposite to us, here?"

"O! no, Deerslayer. The raft was ready-made, and in the water—could that have been by a miracle, Judith?"

"Yes—yes—an Indian miracle," rejoined the hunter. "They're expart enough in them sort of miracles. And you found the raft ready-made to your hands, and in the water, and in waiting like for its cargo?"

"It was all as you say. The raft was near the camp, and the Indians put me on it, and had ropes of bark, and they dragged me to the place opposite to the castle, and then they told that young man to row me off, here."

"And the woods are full of the vagabonds, waiting to know what is to be the upshot of the miracle. We comprehend this affair, now, Judith—but I'll first get rid of this young Canadian bloodsucker, and then we'll settle our own course. Do you and Hetty leave us together, first bringing me the elephants, which the Sarpent is admiring; for 'twill never do to let this loping deer be alone a minute, or he'll borrow a canoe without asking."

Judith did as desired, first bringing the pieces, and retiring with her sister into their own room. Deerslayer had acquired some knowledge of most of the Indian dialects of that region, and he knew enough of the Iroquois to hold a dialogue in the language. Beckoning to the lad, therefore, he caused him to take a seat on the chest, when he placed two of the castles suddenly before him. Up to that moment, this youthful savage had not expressed a single intelligible emotion or fancy. There were many things in and about the place that were novelties to him, but he had maintained his self-command with philosophical composure. It is true, Deerslayer had detected his dark eye scanning the defences and the arms, but the scrutiny had been made with such an air of innocence, in such a gaping, indolent, boyish manner, that no one but a man who had himself been taught in a similar school, would have even suspected his object. The instant, however, the eyes of the savage fell upon the wrought ivory, and the images of the wonderful, unknown beasts, surprise and admiration got the mastery of him. The manner in which the natives of the South Sea Islands first beheld the toys of civilized life, has been often described; but the reader is not to confound it with the manner of an American Indian under similar circumstances. In this particular case, the young Iroquois, or Huron, permitted an exclamation of rapture to escape him, and then he checked himself, like one who had been guilty of an indecorum. After this, his eyes ceased to wander, but became riveted on the elephants, one of which, after a short hesitation he even presumed to handle. Deerslayer did not interrupt him for quite ten minutes; knowing that the lad was taking such note of the curiosities, as would enable him to give the most minute and accurate description of their appearance to his seniors, on his return. When he thought sufficient time had been allowed to produce the desired effect, the hunter laid a finger on the naked knee of the youth, and drew his attention to himself.

"Listen," he said; "I want to talk with my young friend from the Canadas. Let him forget that wonder for a minute."

"Where t'other pale brother?" demanded the boy, looking up, and letting the idea that had been most prominent in his mind, previously to the introduction of the chessmen, escape him involuntarily.

"He sleeps—or if he isn't fairly asleep, he is in the room where the men do sleep," returned Deerslayer. "How did my young friend know there was another?"

"See him from the shore. Iroquois have got long eyes—see beyond the clouds—see the bottom of the great spring!"

"Well, the Iroquois are welcome. Two palefaces are prisoners in the camp of your fathers, boy."

The lad nodded, treating the circumstance with great apparent indifference; though a moment after he laughed as if exulting in the superior address of his own tribe.

"Can you tell me, boy, what your chiefs intend to do with these captyves; or haven't they yet made up their minds?"

The lad looked a moment at the hunter with a little surprise; then he coolly put the end of his forefinger on his own head, just above the left ear, and passed it round his crown, with an accuracy and readiness that showed how well he had been drilled in the peculiar art of his race.

"When?" demanded Deerslayer, whose gorge rose at this cool

demonstration of indifference to human life. "And why not take them to your wigwams?"

"Road too long, and full of palefaces. Wigwam full, and scalps sell high. Small scalp, much gold."

"Well, that explains it—yes, that does explain it. There's no need of being any plainer. Now, you know, lad, that the oldest of your prisoners is the father of these two young women, and the other is the suitor of one of them. The gals nat'rally wish to save the scalps of such fri'nds, and they will give them two ivory creatur's as ransom; one for each scalp. Go back and tell this to your chiefs, and bring me the answer before the sun sets."

The boy entered zealously into this project, and with a sincerity that left no doubt of his executing his commission with intelligence and promptitude. For a moment he forgot his love of honor, and all his clannish hostility to the British and their Indians, in his wish to have such a treasure in his tribe, and Deerslayer was satisfied with the impression he had made. It is true, the lad proposed to carry one of the elephants with him, as a specimen of the other, but to this his brother negotiator was too sagacious to consent; well knowing that it might never reach its destination if confided to such hands. This little difficulty was soon arranged, and the boy prepared to depart. As he stood on the platform ready to step aboard of the raft, he hesitated, and turned short with a proposal to borrow a canoe, as the means most likely to shorten the negotiation. Deerslayer quietly refused the request, and, after lingering a little longer, the boy rowed slowly away from the castle, taking the direction of a thicket on the shore, that lay less than half a mile distant. Deerslayer seated himself on a stool, and watched the progress of the ambassador; sometimes scanning the whole line of the shore, as far as eye could reach, and then placing an elbow on a knee, he remained a long time with his chin resting on the hand.

During the interview between Deerslayer and the lad, a different scene took place in the adjoining room. Hetty had inquired for the Delaware, and being told why and where he remained concealed, she joined him. The reception which Chingachgook gave his visitor was respectful and gentle. He understood her character; and, no doubt, his disposition to be kind to such a being was increased by the hope of learning some tidings of his betrothed. As soon as the girl entered she took a seat, and invited the Indian to place himself near her; then she continued silent, as if she thought it decorous for him to question her, before she consented to speak on the subject she had on her mind. But, as Chingachgook did not understand this feeling, he remained respectfully attentive to anything she might be pleased to tell him.

"You are Chingachgook—the Great Serpent of the Delawares,

aren't you?" the girl at length commenced, in her own simple way, losing her self-command in the desire to proceed, but anxious first to make sure of the individual.

"Chingachgook," returned the Delaware, with grave dignity. "They say Great Serpent in Deerslayer tongue."

"Well, that is my tongue. Deerslayer, and father, and Judith, and I, and poor Hurry Harry—do you know Henry March, Great Serpent? I know you don't, however, or *he* would have spoken of *you*, too."

"Did any tongue name Chingachgook, Drooping Lily?" for so the chief had named poor Hetty. "Was his name sung by a little bird among the Iroquois?"

Hetty did not answer at first; but with that indescribable feeling that awakens sympathy and intelligence among the youthful and unpracticed of her sex, she hung her head, and the blood suffused her cheek ere she found her tongue. It would have exceeded her stock of intelligence to explain this embarrassment; but though poor Hetty could not reason on every emergency, she could always feel. The color slowly receded from her cheek, and the girl looked up archly at the Indian, smiling with the innocence of a child, mingled with the interest of a woman.

"My sister, the Drooping Lily, hear such bird!" Chingachgook added, and this with a gentleness of tone and manner that would have astonished those who sometimes heard the discordant cries that often came from the same throat; these transitions from the harsh and guttural to the soft and melodious not being infrequent in ordinary Indian dialogues. "My sister's ears were open—has she lost her tongue?"

"You *are* Chingachgook—you *must* be; for there is no other red man here, and she thought Chingachgook would come."

"Chin-gach-gook," pronouncing the name slowly, and dwelling on each syllable; "Great Serpent, Yengeese [1] tongue."

"Chin-gach-gook," repeated Hetty, in the same deliberate manner. "Yes, so Hist called it, and you *must* be the chief."

"Wah-ta-Wah," added the Delaware.

"Wah-ta-Wah, or Hist-oh-Hist. I think Hist prettier than Wah, and so I call her Hist."

"Wah very sweet in Delaware ears!"

---

[1] It is singular there should be any question concerning the origin of the well-known *sobriquet* of "Yankees." Nearly all the old writers who speak of the Indians first known to the colonists make them pronounce the word "English" as "Yengeese." Even at this day, it is a provincialism of New England to say "*En*glish" instead of "*In*glish," and there is a close conformity of sound between "*En*glish," and "Yengeese," more especially if the latter word, as was probably the case, be pronounced short. The transition from "Yengeese," thus pronounced, to "Yankees" is quite easy. If the former is pronounced "Yangis," it is almost identical with "Yankees," and Indian words have seldom been spelt as they are pronounced. Thus the scene of this tale is spelt "Ots*e*go," and is properly pronounced "Ots*a*go." The liquids of the Indians would easily convert "En" into "Yen." (*Cooper's note*)

"You make it sound differently from me. But never mind; I *did* hear the bird you speak of sing, Great Serpent."

"Will my sister say words of song? What she sing most—how she look—often she laugh?"

"She sang Chin-gach-gook oftener than anything else; and she laughed heartily when I told how the Iroquois waded into the water after us, and couldn't catch us. I hope these logs haven't ears, Serpent!"

"No fear logs; fear sister next room. No fear Iroquois; Deerslayer stuff his eyes and ears with strange beast."

"I understand you, Serpent, and I understood Hist. Sometimes I think I'm not half as feeble-minded as they say I am. Now, do you look up at the roof, and I'll tell you all. But you frighten me, you look so eager when I speak of Hist."

The Indian controlled his looks, and affected to comply with the simple request of the girl.

"Hist told me to say, in a very low voice, that you mustn't trust the Iroquois in anything. They are more artful than any Indians she knows. Then she says that there is a large bright star that comes over the hill, about an hour after dark,"—Hist had pointed out the planet Jupiter, without knowing it—"and just as that star comes in sight, she will be on the point where I landed last night, and that you must come for her, in a canoe."

"Good! Chingachgook understand well enough now, but he understand better if my sister sing to him ag'in."

Hetty repeated her words, more fully explaining what star was meant, and mentioning the part of the point where he was to venture ashore. She now proceeded in her own unsophisticated way to relate her intercourse with the Indian maid, and to repeat several of her expressions and opinions that gave great delight to the heart of her betrothed. She particularly renewed her injunctions to be on their guard against treachery; a warning that was scarcely needed, however, as addressed to men as wary as those to whom it was sent. She also explained, with sufficient clearness—for on all such subjects the mind of the girl seldom failed her—the present state of the enemy, and the movements they had made since morning. Hist had been on the raft with her, until it quitted the shore; and was now somewhere in the woods, opposite to the castle, and did not intend to return to the camp until night approached; when she hoped to be able to slip away from her companions, as they followed the shore on their way home, and conceal herself on the point. No one appeared to suspect the presence of Chingachgook, though it was necessarily known that an Indian had entered the ark the previous night, and it was suspected that he had since appeared in and about the castle, in the dress of a paleface. Still, some little doubt existed on the latter point, for as this was the season when white men might be expected to arrive, there was some fear that the garrison of the castle was increasing by these ordinary means. All this had Hist communicated to Hetty while the Indians were dragging them alongshore; the distance, which exceeded six miles, affording abundance of time.

"Hist don't know, herself, whether they suspect her or not, or whether they suspect *you*, but she hopes neither is the case. And now, Serpent, since I have told you so much from your betrothed," continued Hetty, unconsciously taking one of the Indian's hands, and playing with the fingers, as a child is often seen to play with those of a parent, "you must let me tell you something from myself. When you marry Hist, you must be kind to her, and smile on her, as you do now on me; and not look cross, as some of the chiefs do at their squaws. Will you promise this?"

"Always good to Wah!—too tender to twist hard; else she break."

"Yes, and smile, too; you don't know how much a girl craves smiles from them she loves. Father scarce smiled on me once, while I was with him—and, Hurry—yes—Hurry talked loud, and laughed; but I don't think *he* smiled once either. You know the difference between a smile and a laugh?"

"Laugh, best. Hear Wah laugh, think bird sing!"

"I know that; her laugh *is* pleasant, but *you* must smile. And then, Serpent, you mustn't make her carry burdens and hoe corn, as so many Indians do; but treat her more as the palefaces treat their wives."

"Wah-ta-Wah no paleface—got red skin; red heart, red feelin's. All red; no paleface. *Must* carry papoose."

"Every woman is willing to carry her child," said Hetty, smiling; "and there is no harm in *that*. But you must love Hist, and be gentle and good to her; for she is gentle and good herself."

Chingachgook gravely bowed, and then he seemed to think this part of the subject might be dismissed. Before there was time for Hetty to resume her communications, the voice of Deerslayer was heard calling on his friend, in the outer room. At this summons the Serpent arose to obey, and Hetty joined her sister.

The first act of the Delaware, on rejoining his friend, was to proceed gravely to disencumber himself of his civilized attire, and to stand forth an Indian warrior again. The protest of Deerslayer was met by his communicating the fact that the presence of an Indian in the hut was known to the Iroquois, and that his maintaining the disguise would be more likely to direct suspicions to his real object, than if he came out openly as a member of a hostile tribe. When the latter understood the truth, and was told that he had been deceived in supposing the chief had succeeded in entering the ark undiscovered, he cheerfully consented to the change, since further attempt at concealment was useless. A gentler feeling than the one avowed, however, lay at the bottom of the Indian's desire to appear as a son of the forest. He had been told that Hist was on the opposite shore; and nature so far triumphed over all distinctions of habit, and tribes, and people, as to reduce this young savage warrior to the level of a feeling which would have been found in the most refined inhabitant of a town, under similar circumstances. There was a mild satisfaction in believing that she he loved could see him; and as he walked out on the platform in his scanty native attire, an Apollo of the wilderness, a hundred of the tender fancies that fleet through lovers' brains beset his imagination and softened his heart.

All this was lost on Deerslayer, who was no great adept in the mysteries of Cupid, but whose mind was far more occupied with the concerns that forced themselves on his attention, than with any of the truant fancies of love. He soon recalled his companion, therefore, to a sense of their actual condition, by summoning him to a sort of council of war, in which they were to settle their future course. In the dialogue that followed, the parties mutually made each other acquainted with what had passed in their several interviews. Chingachgook was told the history of the treaty about the ransom; and Deerslayer heard the whole of Hetty's communications. The latter listened with generous interest to his friend's hopes, and promised cheerfully all the assistance he could lend.

" 'Tis our main arr'nd, Sarpent, as you know; this battling for the castle and old Hutter's darters, coming in as a sort of accident. Yes—yes—I'll be actyve in helping little Hist, who's not only one of the best and handsomest maidens of the tribe, but the *very* best and handsomest. I've always encouraged you, chief, in that liking; and it's proper, too, that a great and ancient race like your'n shouldn't come to an end. If a woman of red skin and red gifts could get to be near enough to me to wish her for a wife, I'd s'arch for just such another, but that can *never* be; no, that can *never* be. I'm glad Hetty has met with Hist, howsever, for though the first is a little short of wit and understanding, the last has enough for both. Yes, Sarpent," laughing heartily, "put 'em together, and two smarter gals isn't to be found in all York colony!"

"I will go to the Iroquois camp," returned the Delaware, gravely. "No one knows Chingachgook but Wah, and a treaty for lives and scalps should be made by a chief! Give me the strange beasts, and let me take a canoe."

Deerslayer dropped his head, and played with the end of a fish pole in the water, as he sat, dangling his legs over the edge of the platform, like a man who was lost in thought by the sudden occurrence of a novel idea. Instead of directly answering the proposal of his friend, he began to soliloquize; a circumstance, however, that in no manner rendered his words more true, as he was remarkable for saying what he thought, whether the remarks were addressed to himself or to anyone else.

"Yes—yes," he said, "this must be what they call love! I've heard say that it sometimes upsets reason altogether, leaving a young man as helpless, as to calculation and caution, as a brute beast. To think that the Sarpent should be so lost to reason, and cunning, and wisdom! We must sartainly manage to get Hist off, and have 'em married as soon as we get back to the tribe, or this war will be of no more use to the chief than a hunt a little oncommon and extr'ornary. Yes—yes—he'll never be the man he was till this matter is off his mind, and he comes to his senses, like all the rest of mankind. Sarpent, you can't be in airnest, and therefore I shall say but little to your offer. But you're a chief, and will soon be sent out on the warpath at the head of parties, and I'll just ask if you'd think of putting your forces into the inimy's hands, afore the battle is fou't?"

"Wah!" ejaculated the Indian.

"Ay—Wah!—I know well enough it's Wah! and altogether Wah! Ra'ally, Sarpent, I'm consarned and mortified about you! I never heard so weak an idea come from a chief, and he, too, one that's already got a name for being wise, young and inexper'enced as he is. Canoe you shan't have, so long as the v'ice of fri'ndship and warning can count for anything."

"My paleface friend is right. A cloud came over the face of Chingachgook, and weakness got into his mind, while his eyes were dim. My brother has a good memory for good deeds, and a weak memory for bad. He will forget."

"Yes, that's easy enough. Say no more about it, chief; but if another of them clouds blow near you, do your endivor to get out of its way. Clouds are bad enough in the weather; but when they come to the reason it gets to be serious. Now, sit down by me here, and let us calculate our movements a little, for we shall soon either have a truce and a peace, or we shall come to an actyve and bloody war. You see the vagabonds can make logs sarve their turn, as well as the best raftsmen on the rivers, and it would be no great expl'ite for them to invade us in a body. I've been thinking of the wisdom of putting all old Tom's stores into the ark, of barring and locking up the castle, and of taking to the ark altogether. That is movable, and by keeping the sail up, and shifting places, we might worry through a great many nights, without them Canada wolves finding a way into our sheepfold."

Chingachgook listened to this plan with approbation. Did the negotiation fail, there was now little hope that the night would pass without an assault; and the enemy had sagacity enough to understand, that, in carrying the castle, they would probably become masters of all it contained, the offered ransom included, and still retain the advantages they had hitherto gained. Some precaution of the sort appeared to be absolutely necessary; for now the numbers of the Iroquois were known, a night attack could scarcely be successfully met. It would be impossible to prevent the enemy from getting possession of the canoes and the ark, and the latter itself would be a hold in which the assailants would be as effectually protected against bullets as were those in the building. For a few minutes both men thought of sinking the ark in the shallow water, of bringing the canoes into the house, and of depending altogether on the castle for protection. But reflection satisfied them that, in the end, this expedient would fail. It was so easy to collect logs on the shore, and to construct a raft of almost any size, that it was certain the Iroquois, now they had turned their attention to such means, would resort to them seriously, so long as there was the certainty of success by perseverance. After deliberating maturely, and placing all the considerations fairly before them, the two young beginners in the art of forest warfare settled down into the opinion that the ark offered the only available means of security. This decision was no sooner come to, than it was communicated to Judith. The girl had no serious objection to make, and all four set about the measures necessary to carrying the plan into execution.

The reader will readily understand that Floating Tom's worldly goods were of no great amount. A couple of beds, some wearing apparel, the arms and ammunition, a few cooking utensils, with the mysterious but half-examined chest, formed the principal items. These were all soon removed, the ark having been hauled on the eastern side of the building, so that the transfer could be made without being seen from the shore. It was thought unnecessary to disturb the heavier and coarser articles of furniture, as they were not required in the ark, and were of but little value in themselves. As great caution was necessary in removing the different objects, most of which were passed out of a window with a view to conceal what was going on, it required two or three hours before all could be effected. By the expiration of that time the raft made its appearance, moving from the shore. Deerslayer immediately had recourse to the glass, by the aid of which he perceived that two warriors were on it, though they appeared to be unarmed. The progress of the raft was slow, a circumstance that formed one of the great advantages that would be possessed by the scow in any future collision between them, the movements of the latter being comparatively swift and light. As there was time to make the dispositions for the reception of the two dangerous visitors, everything was prepared for them, long before they had got near enough to be hailed. The Serpent and the girls retired into the building, where the former stood near the door, well provided with rifles; while Judith watched the proceedings without through a loop. As for Deerslayer, he had brought a stool to the edge of the platform, at the point toward which the raft was advancing, and taken his seat, with his rifle leaning carelessly between his legs.

As the raft drew nearer, every means possessed by the party in the castle was resorted to, in order to ascertain if their visitors had any firearms. Neither Deerslayer nor Chingachgook could discover any; but Judith, unwilling to trust to simple eyesight, thrust the glass through the loop, and directed it toward the hemlock boughs that lay between the two logs of the raft, forming a sort of flooring, as well as a seat for the use of the rowers. When the heavy-moving craft was within fifty feet of him, Deerslayer hailed the Hurons, directing them to cease rowing, it not being his intention to permit them to land. Compliance, of course, was necessary, and the two grim-looking warriors instantly quitted their seats, though the raft continued slowly to approach, until it had driven in much nearer to the platform.

"Are ye chiefs?" demanded Deerslayer, with dignity. "Are ye chiefs?—or have the Mingoes sent me warriors without names, on such an arr'nd? If so, the sooner ye go back, the sooner the one will be likely to come that a warrior can talk with."

"Hugh!" exclaimed the elder of the two on the raft, rolling his glowing eyes over the different objects that were visible in and about the castle, with a keenness that showed how little escaped him. "My brother is very proud, but Rivenoak (we use the literal translation of the term, writing as we do in English) is a name to make a Delaware turn pale."

"That's true, or it's a lie, Rivenoak, as it may be; but I am not likely to turn pale, seeing that I was born pale. What's your arr'nd, and why do you come among light bark canoes on logs that are not even dug out?"

"The Iroquois are not ducks, to walk on water! Let the palefaces give them a canoe, and they'll come in a canoe."

"That's more rational, than likely to come to pass. We have but four canoes, and being four persons, that's only one for each of us. We thank you for the offer, howsever, though we ask leave not to accept it. You are welcome, Iroquois, on your logs!"

"Thanks—my young paleface warrior—he has got a name—how do the chiefs call him?"

Deerslayer hesitated a moment, and a gleam of pride and human weakness came over him. He smiled, muttered between his teeth, and then looking up proudly, he said,—

"Mingo, like all who are young and actyve, I've been known by different names, at different times. One of your warriors whose spirit started for the happy grounds of your people as lately as yesterday morning, thought I desarved to be known by the name of Hawkeye; and this because my sight happened to be quicker than his own, when it got to be life or death atween us."

Chingachgook, who was attentively listening to all that passed, heard and understood this proof of passing weakness in his friend, and on a future occasion he questioned him more closely concerning the transaction on the point where Deerslayer had first taken human life. When he had got the whole truth, he did not fail to communicate it to the tribe, from which time the young hunter was universally known among the Delawares by an appellation so honorably earned. As this, however, was a period posterior to all the incidents of this tale, we shall continue to call the young hunter by the name under which he has been first introduced to the reader. Nor was the Iroquois less struck with the vaunt of the white man. He knew of the death of his comrade, and had no difficulty in understanding the allusion; the intercourse between the conqueror and his victim on that occasion having been seen by several savages on the shore of the lake, who had been stationed at different points just within the margin of the bushes, to watch the drifting canoes, and who had not time to reach the scene of action ere the victor had retired. The effect on this rude being of the forest was an exclamation of surprise; then such a smile of courtesy and wave of the hand succeeded, as would have done credit to Asiatic diplomacy. The two Iroquois spoke to each other in low terms, and both drew near the end of the raft that was closest to the platform.

"My brother, Hawkeye, has sent a message to the Hurons," resumed Rivenoak, "and it has made their hearts very glad. They hear he has images of beasts with two tails! Will he show them to his friends?"

"Inimies would be truer," returned Deerslayer; "but sound isn't sense, and does little harm. Here is one of the images; I toss it to you under faith of treaties. If it's not returned, the rifle will settle the p'int atween us."

The Iroquois seemed to acquiesce in the conditions, and Deerslayer arose and prepared to toss one of the elephants to the raft, both parties using all the precaution that was necessary to prevent its loss. As practice renders men expert in such things, the little piece of ivory was soon successfully transferred from one hand to the other; and then followed another scene on the raft, in which astonishment and delight got the mastery of Indian stoicism. These two grim old warriors manifested even more feeling, as they examined the curiously wrought chessman, than had been betrayed by the boy; for, in the case of the latter, recent schooling had interposed its influence; while the men, like all who are sustained by well-established characters, were not ashamed to let some of their emotions be discovered. For a few minutes they apparently lost the consciousness of their situation in the intense scrutiny they bestowed on a material so fine, work so highly wrought, and an animal so extraordinary. The lip of the moose is, perhaps, the nearest approach to the trunk of the elephant that is to be found in the American forest; but this resemblance was far from being sufficiently striking to bring the new creature within the range of their habits and ideas, and the more they studied the image, the greater was their astonishment. Nor did these children of the forest mistake the structure on the back of the elephant for a part of the animal. They were familiar with horses and oxen, and had seen towers in the Canadas, and found nothing surprising in creatures of burden. Still, by a very natural association, they supposed the carving meant to represent that the animal they saw was of a strength sufficient to carry a fort on its back; a circumstance that in no degree lessened their wonder.

"Has my paleface brother any more such beasts?" at last the senior of the Iroquois asked, in a sort of petitioning manner.

"There's more where them came from, Mingo," was the answer; "one is enough, however, to buy off fifty scalps."

"One of my prisoners is a great warrior—tall as a pine—strong as the moose—active as a deer—fierce as the panther. Some day he'll be a great chief, and lead the army of King George!"

"Tut—tut—Mingo; Harry Hurry is Harry Hurry, and you'll never make more than a corporal of him, if you do that. He's tall enough, of a sartainty; but that's of no use, as he only hits his head ag'in the branches as he goes through the forest. He's strong, too; but a strong body isn't a strong head, and the King's generals are not chosen for their sinews. He's swift, if you will, but a rifle bullet is swifter; and as for f'erceness, it's no great ricommend to a soldier; they that think they feel the stoutest, often givin' out at the pinch. No—no—you'll never make Hurry's scalp pass for more than a good head of curly hair, and a rattlepate beneath it!"

"My old prisoner very wise—king of the lake—great warrior, wise counsellor!"

"Well, there's them that might gainsay all this, too, Mingo. A very wise man wouldn't be apt to be taken in so foolish a manner as befell Master Hutter; and if he gives good counsel, he must have listened to very bad in that affair. There's only one king of this lake, and he's a long way off, and isn't likely ever to see it. Floating Tom is some such king of this region, as the wolf that prowls through the woods is king of the forest. A beast with two tails is well worth two such scalps!"

"But my brother has another beast. He will give two," holding up as many fingers, "for old father."

"Floating Tom is no father of mine, but he'll fare none the worse for that. As for giving two beasts for his scalp, and each beast with two tails, it is quite beyond reason. Think yourself well off, Mingo, if you make a much worse trade."

By this time the self-command of Rivenoak had got the better of his wonder, and he began to fall back on his usual habits of cunning, in order to drive the best bargain he could. It would be useless to relate more than the substance of the desultory dialogue that followed, in which the Indian manifested no little management, in endeavoring to recover the ground lost under the influence of surprise. He even affected to doubt whether any original for the image of the beast existed, and asserted that the oldest Indian had never heard a tradition of any such animal. Little did either of them imagine at the time that long ere a century elapsed, the progress of civilization would bring even much more extraordinary and rare animals into that region, as curiosities to be gazed at by the curious, and that the particular beast about which the disputants contended would be seen laving its sides and swimming in the very sheet of water on which they had met.[1] As is not uncommon on such occasions, one of the parties got a little warm in the course of the discussion; for Deerslayer met all the arguments and prevarications of this subtle opponent with his own cool directness of manner and unmoved love of truth. What an elephant was he knew little better than the savage; but he perfectly understood that the carved pieces of ivory must have some such value in the eyes of an Iroquois as a bag of gold, or a package of beaver-skins, would in those of a trader. Under the circumstances, therefore, he felt it to be prudent not to concede too much at first, since there existed a nearly unconquerable obstacle to making the transfers, even after the contracting parties had actually agreed upon the terms. Keeping this difficulty in view, he held the extra chessmen in reserve as a means of smoothing any difficulty in the moment of need.

At length the savage pretended that further negotiation was useless, since he could not be so unjust to his tribe as to part with the honor and emoluments of two excellent, full-grown male scalps, for a consideration so trifling as a toy like that he had seen—and he prepared to take his departure. Both parties now felt as men are wont to feel, when a bargain that each is anxious to conclude, is on the eve of being broken off in consequence of too much pertinacity in the way of management. The effect of the disappointment was very different, however, on the respective individuals. Deerslayer was mortified, and filled with regret; for he not only felt for the prisoners, but he also felt

[1] The Otsego is a favorite place for the caravan keepers to let their elephants bathe. The writer has seen two at a time, since the publication of this book, swimming about in company. (*Cooper's note*)

deeply for the two girls. The conclusion of the treaty, therefore, left him melancholy and full of regret. With the savage, his defeat produced the desire of revenge. In a moment of excitement, he loudly announced his intention to say no more; and he felt equally enraged with himself and with his cool opponent, that he had permitted a paleface to manifest more indifference and self-command than an Indian chief. When he began to urge his raft away from the platform, his countenance lowered, and his eye glowed even while he affected a smile of amity and a gesture of courtesy, at parting.

It took some little time to overcome the *vis inertiæ* of the logs, and while this was doing by the silent Indian, Rivenoak stalked over the hemlock boughs that lay between the logs, in sullen ferocity, eying keenly, the while, the hut, the platform, and the person of his late disputant. Once he spoke in low, quick terms to his companion, and he stirred the boughs with his feet, like an animal that is restive. At that moment the watchfulness of Deerslayer had a little abated, for he sat musing on the means of renewing the negotiation without giving too much advantage to the other side. It was, perhaps, fortunate for him that the keen and bright eyes of Judith were as vigilant as ever. At the instant when the young man was least on his guard, and his enemy was the most on the alert, she called out in a warning voice to the former, most opportunely giving the alarm.

"Be on your guard, Deerslayer!" the girl cried; "I see rifles, with the glass, beneath the hemlock brush, and the Iroquois is loosening them with his feet!"

It would seem that the enemy had carried the artifices so far as to employ an agent who understood English. The previous dialogue had taken place in his own language, but it was evident, by the sudden manner in which his feet ceased their treacherous occupation, and in which the countenance of Rivenoak changed from sullen ferocity to a smile of courtesy, that the call of the girl was understood. Signing to his companion to cease his efforts to set the logs in motion, he advanced to the end of the raft which was nearest to the platform, and spoke.

"Why should Rivenoak and his brother leave any cloud between them?" he said. "They are both wise, both brave, and both generous; they ought to part friends. One beast shall be the price of one prisoner."

"And, Mingo," answered the other, delighted to renew the negotiation on almost any terms, and determined to clench the bargain if possible by a little extra liberality, "you'll see that a paleface knows how to pay a full price, when he trades with an open heart and an open hand. Keep the beast that you had forgotten to give back to me, as you was about to start, and which I forgot to ask for, on account of consarn at parting in anger. Show it to your chiefs. When you bring us our fri'nds two more shall be added to it—and"—hesitating a moment in distrust of the expediency of so great a concession, then deciding in its favor—"and, if we see them afore the sun sets, we may find a fourth to make up an even number."

This settled the matter. Every gleam of discontent vanished from the dark countenance of the Iroquois, and he smiled as graciously, if not as sweetly, as Judith Hutter herself. The piece already in his possession was again examined, and an ejaculation of pleasure showed how much he was pleased with this unexpected termination of the affair. In point of fact, both he and Deerslayer had momentarily forgotten what had become of the subject of their discussion, in the warmth of their feelings; but such had not been the case with Rivenoak's companion. This man retained the piece, and had fully made up his mind, were it claimed under such circumstances as to render its return necessary, to drop it in the lake, trusting to his being able to find it again at some future day. This desperate expedient, however, was no longer necessary; and, after repeating the terms of agreement, and professing to understand them, the two Indians finally took their departure, moving slowly toward the shore.

"Can any faith be put in such wretches?" asked Judith, when she and Hetty had come out on the platform, and were standing at the side of Deerslayer watching the dull movement of the logs. "Will they not rather keep the toy they have, and send us off some bloody proofs of their getting the better of us in cunning, by way of boasting? I've heard of acts as bad as this."

"No doubt, Judith; no manner of doubt, if it wasn't for Indian natur'. But I'm no judge of a redskin, if that two-tailed beast doesn't set the whole tribe in some such stir as a stick raises in a beehive! Now, there's the Sarpent; a man with narves like flint, and no more cur'osity in everyday consarns than is befitting prudence. Why, he was so overcome with the sight of the creatur', carved as it is in bone, that I felt ashamed for him! That's just their gifts, however, and one can't well quarrel with a man for his gifts, when they are lawful. Chingachgook will soon get over his weakness, and remember that he's a chief, and that he comes of a great stock, and has a renowned name to support and uphold; but, as for yonder scamps, there'll be no peace among 'em until they think they've got possession of everything of the natur' of that bit of carved bone that's to be found among Thomas Hutter's stores!"

"They only know of the elephants, and can have no hopes about the other things."

"That's true, Judith; still, covetousness is a craving feelin'. They'll say if the palefaces have these curious beasts with two tails, who knows but they've got some with three, or, for that matter, with four! That's what the schoolmasters call nat'ral arithmetic, and 'twill be sartain to beset the feelin's of savages. They'll never be easy till the truth is known."

"Do you think, Deerslayer," inquired Hetty, in her simple and innocent manner, "that the Iroquois won't let father and Hurry go? I read to them several of the very best verses in the whole Bible, and you see what they have done already."

The hunter, as he always did, listened kindly and even affectionately to Hetty's remarks; then he mused a moment in silence. There was something like a flush on his cheek, as he answered after quite a minute had passed,—

"I don't know whether a white man ought to be ashamed, or not, to own he can't read; but such is my case, Judith. You are skilful, I find, in all such matters, while I have only studied the hand of God, as it is seen in the hills and the valleys, the mountaintops, the streams, the forest, and the springs. Much l'arning may be got in this way, as well as out of books; and yet, I sometimes think it is a white man's gift to read! When I hear from the mouths of the Moravians the words of which Hetty speaks, they raise a longing in my mind, and I think I *will* know how to read 'em myself; but the game in summer, and the traditions, and lessons in war, and other matters, have always kept me behindhand."

"Shall I teach you, Deerslayer?" asked Hetty, earnestly. "I'm weak-minded, they say, but I can read as well as Judith. It might save your life, to know how to read the Bible to the savages, and it will certainly save your soul; for mother told me *that*, again and again!"

"Thankee, Hetty—yes, thankee, with all my heart. There are like to be too stirring times for much idleness; but, after it's peace, and I come to see you ag'in on this lake, then I'll give myself up to it, as if 'twas pleasure and profit, in a single business. Perhaps I ought to be ashamed, Judith, that 'tis so; but truth is truth. As for these Iroquois, 'tisn't very likely they'll forget a beast with two tails, on account of a varse or two from the Bible. I rather expect they'll give up the prisoners, and trust to some sarcumvention or other to get 'em back ag'in, with us and all in the castle, and the ark in the bargain. Howsever, we must humor the vagabonds first, to get your father and Hurry out of their hands, and next, to keep the peace atween us until such times as the Sarpent there can make out to get off his betrothed wife. If there's any sudden outbreakin' of anger and ferocity, the Indians will send off all their women and children to the camp, at once; whereas, by keeping 'em calm and trustful, we may manage to meet Hist at the spot she has mentioned. Rather than have the bargain fall through now, I'd throw in half a dozen of them effigy bow-and-arrow men, such as we've in plenty in the chist."

Judith cheerfully assented, for she would have resigned even the flowered brocade, rather than not redeem her father and please Deerslayer.

The prospects of success were now so encouraging as to raise the spirits of all in the castle, though a due watchfulness on the movements of the enemy was maintained. Hour passed after hour, notwithstanding, and the sun had once more begun to fall toward the summits of the western hills, and yet no signs were seen of the return of the raft. By dint of sweeping the shore with the glass, Deerslayer at length discovered a place in the dense and dark woods, where, he entertained no doubt, the Iroquois were assembled in considerable numbers. It was near the thicket whence the raft had issued, and a little rill that trickled into the lake announced the vicinity of a spring. Here, then, the savages were probably holding their consultation, and the decision was to be made that went to settle the question of life or death for the prisoners. There was one ground for hope in spite of the delay, however, that Deerslayer did not fail to place before his anxious companions. It was far more probable that the Indians had left their prisoners in the camp, than that they had encumbered themselves, by causing them to follow through the woods, a party that was out on a merely temporary excursion. If such was the fact, it required considerable time to send a messenger the necessary distance, and to bring the two white men to the spot where they were to embark. Encouraged by these reflections, a new stock of patience was gathered, and the declension of the sun was viewed with less alarm.

The result justified Deerslayer's conjecture. Not long before the sun had finally disappeared, the two logs were seen coming out of the thicket again; and, as the raft drew near, Judith announced that her father and Hurry, both of them pinioned, lay on the bushes in the center. As before, the Indians were rowing. The latter seemed to be conscious that the lateness of the hour demanded unusual exertions, and contrary to the habits of their people, who are ever averse to toil, they labored hard at the rude substitutes for oars. In consequence of this diligence, the raft occupied its old station in about half the time that had been taken in the previous visits.

Even after the conditions were so well understood, and matters had proceeded so far, the actual transfer of the prisoners was not a duty to be executed without difficulty. The Iroquois were compelled to place great reliance on the good faith of their foes, though it was reluctantly given, and was yielded to necessity rather than to confidence. As soon as Hutter and Hurry should be released, the party in the castle numbered two to one, as opposed to those on the raft, and escape by flight was out of the question, as the former had three bark canoes, to say nothing of the defences of the house and the ark. All this was understood by both parties, and it is probable the arrangement never could have been completed, had not the honest countenance and manner of Deerslayer wrought their usual effect on Rivenoak.

"My brother knows I put faith in *him*," said the latter as he advanced with Hutter, whose legs had been released to enable the old man to ascend to the platform. "One scalp—one more beast."

"Stop, Mingo," interrupted the hunter, "keep your prisoner a moment. I have to go and seek the means of payment."

This excuse, however, though true in part, was principally a fetch. Deerslayer left the platform, and entering the house, he directed Judith to collect all the arms, and to conceal them in her own room. He then spoke earnestly to the Delaware who stood on guard as before, near the entrance of the building, put the three remaining castles in his pocket, and returned.

"You are welcome back to your old abode, Master Hutter," said Deerslayer, as he helped the other up on the platform, slyly passing into the hand of Rivenoak, at the same time, another of the castles. "You'll find your darters right glad to see you; and here's Hetty come herself to say as much in her own behalf."

Here the hunter stopped speaking and broke out into a hearty fit of his silent and peculiar laughter. Hurry's legs were just released, and he had been placed on his feet. So tightly had the ligatures been drawn, that the use of his limbs was not immediately recovered, and the young giant presented, in good sooth, a very helpless and a somewhat ludicrous picture. It was this unusual spectacle, particularly the bewildered countenance, that excited the merriment of Deerslayer.

"You look like a girdled pine in a clearin', Harry Hurry, that is rocking in a gale," said Deerslayer, checking his unseasonable mirth, more from delicacy to the others than from any respect to the liberated captive. "I'm glad, howsever, to see that you haven't had your hair dressed by any of the Iroquois barbers, in your late visit to their camp."

"Harkee, Deerslayer," returned the other, a little fiercely; "it will be prudent for you to deal less in mirth and more in friendship on this occasion. Act like a Christian, for once, and not like a laughing gal in a country school when the master's back is turned, and just tell me whether there's any feet or not at the end of these legs of mine. I think I can see them, but as for feelin', they might as well be down on the banks of the Mohawk, as where they seem to be."

"You've come off whole, Hurry, and that's not a little," answered the other, secretly passing to the Indian the remainder of the stipulated ransom, and making an earnest sign, at the same moment, for him to commence his retreat. "You've come off whole, feet and all, and are only a little numb, from a tight fit of the withes. Natur'll soon set the blood in motion, and then you may begin to dance, to celebrate what I call a most wonderful and onexpected deliverance from a den of wolves."

Deerslayer released the arms of his friends, as each landed, and the two were now stamping and limping about on the platform, growling, and uttering denunciations, as they endeavored to help the returning circulation. They had been tethered too long, however, to regain the use of their limbs in a moment; and the Indians being quite as diligent on their return as on their advance, the raft was fully a hundred yards from the castle when Hurry, turning accidentally in that direction, discovered how fast it was getting beyond the reach of his vengeance.

8

HUTTER and Hurry Harry had hardly regained the castle when its inmates received a flat declaration of war from the Hurons: a bundle of fagots, the ends dipped in blood, was thrown close to their refuge. The whole party took counsel, and agreed to follow Deerslayer's plan of abandoning the castle during the night, and taking refuge in the ark. The Hurons would have no difficulty in using rafts to storm the castle, and the moving fortress would be much safer. Under cover of darkness, all therefore embarked. Steering the craft along the shore, they found that the savages had moved their encampment to the very point where Hist had agreed to meet Chingachgook. Nevertheless, Deerslayer and the noble Delaware slipped into their canoe and landed on the dangerous shore. Reconnoitering, they found the Hurons all alert, and observed Hist walking in the company of a young Indian. She was well guarded by an old hag with a watchful, soured aspect. Determined to rescue Hist, they finally succeeded in seizing both the maiden and the old woman as they went to a spring for water. Pursued fiercely by the warriors, they reached their canoe; Chingachgook and Hist threw themselves into it; but Deerslayer was seized by a powerful Indian. He thrust the canoe far out into deep water and safety, but was himself carried back to the campfires by the exultant Hurons.

Among those who eyed the captive most grimly was Deerslayer's new acquaintance Rivenoak. All the Indians knew that Leatherstocking had but recently killed one of their number in single combat, and they regarded him with mingled ferocity and admiration.

The arms of Deerslayer were not pinioned, and he was left the free use of his hands, his knife having been first removed. The only precaution that was taken to secure his person was untiring watchfulness, and a strong rope of bark that passed from ankle to ankle, not so much to prevent his walking as to place an obstacle in the way of his attempting to escape by any sudden leap. Even this extra provision against flight was not made until the captive had been brought to the light and his character ascertained. It was, in fact, a compliment to his prowess, and he felt proud of the distinction. That he might be bound when the warriors slept he thought probable, but to be bound in the moment of capture showed that he was already, and thus early, attaining a name. While the young Indians were fastening the rope, he wondered if Chingachgook would have been treated in the same manner, had he too fallen into the hands of the enemy. Nor did the reputation of the young paleface rest altogether on his success in the previous combat, or in his discriminating and cool manner of managing the late negotiation; for it had received a great accession by the occurrences of the night. Ignorant of the movements of the ark, and of the accident that had brought their fire into view, the Iroquois attributed the discovery of their new camp to the vigilance of so shrewd a foe. The manner in which he ventured upon the point, the abstraction or escape of Hist, and most of all the self-devotion of the prisoner, united to the readiness with which he had sent the canoe adrift, were so many important links in the chain of facts on which his growing fame was founded. Many of these circumstances had been seen, some had been explained, and all were understood.

While this admiration and these honors were so unreservedly bestowed on Deerslayer, he did not escape some of the penalties of his situation. He was permitted to seat himself on the end of a log, near the fire, in order to dry his clothes, his late adversary standing opposite, now holding articles of his own scanty vestments to the heat, and now feeling his throat, on which the marks of his enemy's fingers were still quite visible. The rest of the warriors consulted together, near at hand, all those who had been out having returned to report that no signs of any other prowlers near the camp were to be found. In this state of things, the old woman, whose name was Shebear, in plain English, approached Deerslayer, with her fists clenched and her eyes flashing fire. Hitherto she had been occupied with screaming, an employment at which she had played her part with no small degree of success, but having succeeded in effectually alarming all within reach of a pair of lungs that had been strengthened by long practice, she next turned her attention to the injuries her own person had sustained in the struggle. These were in no manner material, though they were of a nature to arouse all the fury of a woman who had long ceased to attract by means of the gentler qualities, and who was much disposed to revenge the hardships she had so long endured, as the neglected wife and mother of savages, on all who came within her power. If Deerslayer had not permanently injured her, he had temporarily caused her to suffer, and she was not a person to overlook a wrong of this nature on account of its motive.

"Skunk of the palefaces," commenced this exasperated and semipoetic fury, shaking her fist under the nose of the impassible hunter, "you are not even a woman. Your friends, the Delawares, are only women, and you are their sheep. Your own people will not own you, and no tribe of red *men* would have you in their wigwams; you skulk among petticoated warriors. *You* slay our brave friend who has left us?—no—his great soul scorned to fight you, and left his body rather than have the shame of slaying *you!* But the blood that you spilt when the spirit was not looking on has not sunk into the ground. It must be buried in your groans! What music do I hear? Those are not the wailings of a red man!—no red warrior groans so much like a hog. They come from a paleface throat—a Yengeese bosom, and sound as pleasant as girls singing. Dog—skunk—woodchuck—mink—hedgehog—pig—toad—spider—Yengee"—

Here the old woman, having expended her breath, and exhausted her epithets, was fain to pause a moment, though both her fists were shaken in the prisoner's face, and the whole of her wrinkled countenance was filled with fierce resentment. Deerslayer looked upon these impotent attempts to arouse him, as indifferently as a gentleman in our own state of society regards the vituperative terms of a blackguard: the one party feeling that the tongue of an old woman could never injure a warrior, and the other knowing that mendacity and vulgarity can only permanently affect those who resort to their use; but he was spared any further attack at present, by the interposition of Rivenoak, who shoved aside the hag, bidding her quit the spot, and prepared to take his seat at the side of his prisoner. The old woman withdrew, but the hunter well understood that he was to be the subject of all her means of annoyance, if not of positive injury, so long as he remained in the power of his enemies; for nothing rankles so deeply as the consciousness that an attempt to irritate has been met by contempt, a feeling that is usually the most passive of any that is harbored in the human breast. Rivenoak quietly took the seat we have mentioned, and after a short pause, he commenced a dialogue, which we translate as usual.

"My paleface friend is very welcome," said the Indian, with a familiar nod, and a smile so covert that it required all Deerslayer's vigilance to detect, and not a little of his philosophy to detect unmoved; "he is welcome. The Hurons keep a hot fire to dry the white man's clothes."

"I thank you, Huron, or Mingo, as I most like to call you," returned the other; "I thank you for the welcome, and I thank you for the fire. Each is good in its way, and the last is very good, when one has been in a spring as cold as the Glimmerglass. Even Huron warmth may be pleasant, at such a time, to a man with a Delaware heart."

"The paleface—but my brother has a name? So great a warrior would not have lived without a name?"

"Mingo," said the hunter, a little of the weakness of human nature exhibiting itself in the glance of his eye, and the color on his cheek, "Mingo, *your* brave called me Hawkeye, I suppose on account of a quick and sartain aim, when he was lying with his head in my lap, afore his spirit started for the happy hunting grounds."

" 'Tis a good name! The hawk is sure of his blow. Hawkeye is not a woman; why does he live with the Delawares?"

"I understand you, Mingo, but we look on all that as a sarcumvention of some of your subtle devils, and deny the charge. Providence placed me among the Delawares young; and, 'bating what Christian usages demand of my color and gifts, I hope to live and die in their tribe. Still, I do not mean to throw away altogether my natyve rights, and shall strive to do a paleface's duty in redskin society."

"Good! a Huron is a redskin, as well as a Delaware. Hawkeye is more of a Huron than of a woman."

"I suppose you know, Mingo, your own meaning; if you don't, I make no question 'tis well known to Satan. But if you wish to get anything out of me, speak plainer, for bargains cannot be made blindfolded or tongue-tied."

"Good! Hawkeye has not a forked tongue, and he likes to say what he thinks. He is an acquaintance of the Muskrat,"—this was a name by which all the Indians designated Hutter,—"and he has lived in his wigwam; but he is not a friend. He wants no scalps, like a miserable Indian, but fights like a stouthearted paleface. The Muskrat is neither white nor red; neither a beast nor a fish. He is a water snake, sometimes in the spring and sometimes on the land. He looks for scalps like an outcast. Hawkeye can go back and tell him how he has outwitted the Hurons, how he has escaped; and when his eyes are in a fog, when he can't see as far as from his cabin to the woods, then Hawkeye can open the door for the Hurons. And how will the plunder be divided? Why, Hawkeye will carry away the most, and the Hurons will take what he may choose to leave behind him. The scalps can go to Canada, for a paleface has no satisfaction in *them.*"

"Well, well, Rivenoak,—for so I hear 'em tarm you,—this is plain English enough, though spoken in Iroquois. I understand all you mean, now, and must say it outdevils even Mingo deviltry! No doubt, 'twould be easy enough to go back and tell the Muskrat that I had got away from you, and gain some credit, too, by the expl'ite."

"Good! that is what I want the paleface to do."

"Yes—yes—that's plain enough. I know what you want me to do, without more words. When inside the house, and eating the Muskrat's bread, and laughing and talking with his pretty darters, I might put his eyes into so thick a fog, that he couldn't even see the door, much less the land."

"Good! Hawkeye should have been born a Huron! His blood is not more than half white!"

"There you're out, Huron; yes there you're as much out, as if you mistook a wolf for a catamount. I'm white in blood, heart, natur', and gifts, though a little redskin in feelin's and habits. But when old Hutter's eyes are well befogged, and his pretty darters, perhaps, in a deep sleep, and Hurry Harry, the Great Pine, as you Indians tarm him, is dreaming of anything but mischief, and all suppose Hawkeye is acting as a faithful sentinel, all I have to do is, to set a torch somewhere in sight for a signal, open the door, and let in the Hurons to knock 'em all on the head."

"Surely my brother is mistaken; he *cannot* be white! He is worthy to be a great chief among the Hurons!"

"That is true enough, I dare to say, if he could do all this. Now, harkee, Huron, and for once hear a few honest words from the mouth of a plain man. I am a Christian born, and them that come of such a stock, and that listen to the words that were spoken to their fathers, and will be spoken to their children, until 'arth and all it holds perishes, can never lend themselves to such wickedness. Sarcumventions in war may be, and *are* lawful; but sarcumventions, and deceit, and treachery, among fri'nds, are fit only for the paleface devils. I know that there are white men enough to give you this wrong idee of our natur', but such are ontrue to their blood and gifts, and ought to be, if they are not, outcasts and vagabonds. No upright paleface could do what you wish, and to be as plain with you as I wish to be, in my judgment no upright Delaware either; with a Mingo it may be different."

The Huron listened to his rebuke with obvious disgust; but he had his ends in view, and was too wily to lose all chance of effecting them by a precipitate avowal of resentment. Affecting to smile, he seemed to listen eagerly, and he then pondered on what he had heard.

"Does Hawkeye love the Muskrat?" he abruptly demanded; "or does he love his daughters?"

"Neither, Mingo. Old Tom is not a man to gain my love; and as for the darters, they are comely enough to gain the liking of any young man; but there's reason ag'in any very great love for either. Hetty is a good soul, but natur' has laid a heavy hand on her mind, poor thing!"

"And the Wild Rose!" exclaimed the Huron—for the fame of Judith's beauty had spread among those who could travel the wilderness as well as the highway, by means of old eagles' nests, rocks, and riven trees, known to them by report and tradition, as well as among the white borderers—"And the Wild Rose; is she not sweet enough to be put in the bosom of my brother?"

Deerslayer had far too much of the innate gentleman to insinuate aught against the fair fame of one who, by nature and position, was so helpless; and as he did not choose to utter an untruth, he preferred being silent. The Huron mistook the motive, and supposed that disappointed affection lay at the bottom of his reserve. Still bent on corrupting or bribing his captive, in order to obtain possession of the treasures with which his imagination filled the castle, he persevered in his attack.

"Hawkeye is talking with a friend," he continued. "He knows that Rivenoak is a man of his word, for they have traded together, and trade opens the soul. My friend has come here on account of a little string held by a girl, that can pull the whole body of the stoutest warrior?"

"You are nearer the truth now, Huron, than you've been afore, since we began to talk. This is true. But one end of that string was not fast to my heart, nor did the Wild Rose hold the other."

"This is wonderful! Does my brother love in his head, and not in his heart? And can the Feeble Mind pull so hard against so stout a warrior?"

"There it is ag'in; sometimes right and sometimes wrong! The string you mean is fast to the heart of a great Delaware; one of the Mohican stock in fact, living among the Delawares since the dispersion of his own people, and of the family of Uncas—Chingachgook by name, or Great Sarpent. He has come here, led by the string, and I've followed, or rather come afore, for I got here first, pulled by nothing stronger than fri'ndship; which is strong enough for such as are not niggardly of their feelin's, and are willing to live a little for their fellow-creatur's, as well as for themselves."

"But a string has two ends—one is fast to the mind of a Mohican, and the other—?"

"Why the other was here close to the fire, half an hour since. Wah-ta-Wah held it in her hand, if she didn't hold it to her heart."

"I understand what you mean, my brother," returned the Indian gravely, for the first time catching a direct clue to the adventures of the evening. "The Great Serpent being strongest, pulled the hardest, and Hist was forced to leave us."

"I don't think there was much pulling about it," answered the other, laughing, always in his silent manner, with as much heartiness as if he were not a captive, and in danger of torture or death. "I don't think there was much pulling about it; no, I don't. Lord help you, Huron! he likes the gal, and the gal likes him, and it surpassed Huron sarcumventions to keep two young people apart when there was so strong a feelin' to bring 'em together."

"And Hawkeye and Chingachgook came into our camp on this errand only?"

"That's a question that'll answer itself, Mingo! Yes, if a question could talk, it would answer itself to your perfect satisfaction. For what else should we come? And yet, it isn't exactly so, neither; for we didn't come into your camp at all, but only as far as that pine, there, that you see on the other side of the ridge, where we stood watching your movements and conduct as long as we liked. When we were ready the Sarpent gave his signal, and then all went just as it should, down to the moment when yonder vagabond leaped upon my back. Sartain; we came for that and no other purpose, and we got what we came for, there's no use in pretending otherwise. Hist is off with a man who's the next thing to her husband, and come what will to me, *that's* one good thing detarmined."

"What sign or signal told the young maiden that her lover was nigh?" asked the old Huron, with more curiosity than it was usual for him to betray.

Deerslayer laughed again, and seemed to enjoy the success of the exploit with as much glee as if he had not been its victim.

"Your squirrels are great gadabouts, Mingo!" he cried, still laughing—"yes, they're sartainly great gadabouts! When other folks' squirrels are at home and asleep, your'n keep in motion among the trees, and chirrup and sing in a way that even a Delaware girl can understand their music! Well, there's four-legged squirrels, and there's two-legged squirrels, and give me the last, when there's a good tight string atween two hearts. If one brings 'em together, t'other tells when to pull the hardest."

The Huron looked vexed, though he succeeded in suppressing any violent exhibition of resentment. He soon quitted his prisoner, and joining the rest of his warriors, he communicated the substance of what he had learned. As in his own case admiration was mingled with anger at the boldness and success of their enemies. Three or four of them ascended the little acclivity and gazed at the tree where it was understood the adventurers had posted themselves, and one even descended and examined for footprints around its roots, in order to make sure that the statement was true. The result confirmed the story of the captive, and they all returned to the fire with increased wonder and respect. The messenger, who had arrived with some communication from the party above while the two adventurers were watching the camp, was now dispatched with some answer, and doubtless bore with him the intelligence of all that had happened.

Down to this moment, the young Indian who had been seen walking in company with Hist and another female, had made no advances to any communication with Deerslayer. He had held himself aloof from his friends even, passing near the bevy of younger women who were clustering together, apart as usual, and conversed in low tones on the subject of the escape of their late companion. Perhaps it would be true to say, that these last were pleased as well as vexed at what had just occurred. Their female sympathies were with the lovers, while their pride was bound up in the success of their own tribe. It is possible, too, that the superior personal advantages of Hist rendered her dangerous to some of the younger part of the group, and they were not sorry to find she was no longer in the way of their own ascendency. On the whole, however, the better feeling was most prevalent; for neither the wild condition in which they lived, the clannish prejudices of tribes, nor their hard fortunes as Indian women, could entirely conquer the inextinguishable leaning of their sex to the affections. One of the girls even laughed at the disconsolate look of the swain who might fancy himself deserted, a circumstance that seemed suddenly to arouse his energies, and induced him to move toward the log on which the prisoner was still seated, drying his clothes.

"This is Catamount!" said the Indian, striking his hand boastfully on his naked breast as he uttered the words, in a manner to show how much weight he expected them to carry.

"This is Hawkeye," quietly returned Deerslayer, adopting the name by which he knew he would be known in future among all the tribes of the Iroquois. "My sight is keen; is my brother's leap long?"

"From here to the Delaware villages. Hawkeye has stolen my wife; he must bring her back, or his scalp will hang on a pole and dry in my wigwam."

"Hawkeye has stolen nothing, Huron. He doesn't come of a thieving breed, nor has he thieving gifts. Your wife, as you call Wah-ta-Wah, will never be the wife of any redskin of the Canadas; her mind is in the cabin of a Delaware, and her body has gone to find it. The catamount is actyve, I know; but it's legs can't keep pace with a woman's wishes."

"The Serpent of the Delawares is a dog; he is a poor bullpout that keeps in the water; he is afraid to stand on the hard earth like a brave Indian!"

"Well, well, Huron, that's pretty impudent, considering it's not an hour since the Sarpent stood within a hundred feet of you, and would have tried the toughness of your skin with a rifle bullet, when I pointed you out to him, hadn't I laid the weight of a little judgment on his hand. You may take in timersome gals in the settlements with your catamount whine; but the ears of a man can tell truth from ontruth."

"Hist laughs at him! She sees he is lame, and a poor hunter, and he has never been on a warpath. She will take a man for a husband, and not a fool."

"How do you know that, Catamount? how do you know that?" returned Deerslayer, laughing. "She has gone into the lake, you see, and maybe she prefers a trout to a mongrel cat. As for warpaths, neither the Sarpent nor I have much exper'ence, we are ready to own; but if you don't call this one, you must tarm it what the gals in the settlements tarm it, the high road to matrimony. Take my advice, Catamount, and s'arch for a wife among the Huron women; you'll never get one with a willing mind from among the Delawares."

Catamount's hand felt for his tomahawk, and when the fingers reached the handle they worked convulsively, as if their owner hesitated between policy and resentment. At this critical moment Rivenoak approached, and, by a gesture of authority, induced the young man to retire, assuming his former position, himself on the log at the side of Deerslayer. Here he continued silent for a little time, maintaining the grave reserve of an Indian chief.

"Hawkeye is right," the Iroquois at length began; "his sight is so strong that he can see truth in a dark night, and our eyes have been blinded. He is an owl, darkness hiding nothing from him. He ought not to strike his friends. He is right."

"I'm glad you think so, Mingo," returned the other, "for a traitor, in my judgment, is worse than a coward. I care as little for the Muskrat as one paleface ought to care for another; but I care too much for him to ambush him in the way you wished. In short, according to my idees, any sarcumvention, except open-war sarcumventions, are ag'in both law, and what we whites call 'gospel,' too."

"My paleface brother is right; he is no Indian to forget his Manitou and his color. The Hurons know that they have a great warrior for their prisoner, and they will treat him as one. If he is to be tortured, his torments shall be such as no common man can bear; if he is to be treated as a friend, it will be the friendship of chiefs."

As the Huron uttered this extraordinary assurance of consideration his eye furtively glanced at the countenance of his listener, in order to discover how he stood the compliment; though his gravity and apparent sincerity would have prevented any man but one practiced in artifices, from detecting his motives. Deerslayer belonged to the class of the unsuspicious; and acquainted with the Indian notions of what constituted respect, in matters connected with the treatment of captives, he felt his blood chill at the announcement, even while he maintained an aspect so steeled that his quick-sighted enemy could discover in it no sign of weakness.

"God has put me in your hands, Huron," the captive at length answered, "and I suppose you will act your will on me. I shall not boast of what I can do, under torment, for I've never been tried, and no man can say till he has been; but I'll do my endivors not to disgrace the people among whom I got my training. Howsever, I wish you now to bear witness, that I'm altogether of white blood, and, in a nat'ral way, of white gifts, too; so, should I be overcome and forget myself, I hope you'll lay the fault where it properly belongs; and in no manner put it on the Delawares, or their allies and friends the Mohicans. We're all created with more or less weakness, and I'm afeard it's a paleface's to give in under great bodily torment, when a redskin will sing his songs, and boast of his deeds in the very teeth of his foes!"

"We shall see. Hawkeye has a good countenance, and he is tough—but why should he be tormented when the Hurons love him? He is not born their enemy; and the death of one warrior will not cast a cloud between them forever."

"So much the better, Huron; so much the better. Still, I don't wish to owe anything to a mistake about each other's meaning. It is so much the better that you bear no malice for the loss of a warrior who fell in war; and yet it is ontrue that there is no inmity—lawful inmity, I mean, atween us. So far as I have redskin feelin's at all, I've Delaware feelin's; and I leave you to judge for yourself, how far they are likely to be fri'ndly to the Mingoes—"

Deerslayer ceased, for a sort of specter stood before him that put a stop to his words, and, indeed, caused him for a moment to doubt the fidelity of his boasted vision. Hetty Hutter was standing at the side of the fire, as quietly as if she belonged to the tribe.

As the hunter and the Indian sat watching the emotions that were betrayed in each other's countenance, the girl had approached unnoticed, doubtless ascending the beach on the southern side of the point, or that next to the spot where the ark had anchored, and had advanced to the fire with the fearlessness that belonged to her simplicity, and which was certainly justified by the treatment formerly received from the Indians. As soon as Rivenoak perceived the girl, she was recognized, and calling to two or three of the young warriors, the chief sent them out to reconnoiter, lest her appearance should be the forerunner of another attack. He then motioned to Hetty to draw near.

"I hope your visit is a sign that the Sarpent and Hist are in safety, Hetty," said Deerslayer, as soon as the girl had complied with the Huron's request. "I don't think you'd come ashore ag'in on the arr'nd that brought you here afore."

"Judith told me to come this time, Deerslayer," Hetty replied; "she paddled me ashore herself, in a canoe, as soon as the Serpent had shown her Hist, and told his story. How handsome Hist is tonight, Deerslayer, and how much happier she looks than when she was with the Hurons!"

"That's natur', gal; yes, that may be set down as human natur'. She's with her betrothed, and no longer fears a Mingo husband. In my judgment, Judith herself would lose most of her beauty if she thought she was to bestow it all on a Mingo! Content is a great fortifier of good looks; and I'll warrant you, Hist is contented enough now she is out of the hands of these miscreants and with her chosen warrior! Did you say that your sister told you to come ashore—why should Judith do that?"

"She bid me come to see you, and to try and persuade the savages to take more elephants to let you off; but I've brought the Bible with me—*that* will do more than all the elephants in father's chest!"

"And your father, good little Hetty—and Hurry; did they know of your arr'nd?"

"Nothing. Both are asleep; and Judith and the Serpent thought it best they should not be woke, lest they might want to come again after scalps, when Hist had told them how few warriors, and how many women and children there were in the camp, Judith would give me no peace till I had come ashore, to see what had happened to *you*."

"Well, that's remarkable as consarns Judith! Why should she feel so much unsartainty about me? Ah, I see how it is now; yes, I see into the whole matter now. You must understand, Hetty, that your sister is oneasy lest Harry March should wake, and come blundering here into the hands of the inimy ag'in, under some idee that, being a travelling comrade, he ought to help me in this matter! Hurry is a blunderer, I will allow; but I don't think he'd risk as much for my sake as he would for his own."

"Judith don't care for Hurry, though Hurry cares for her," replied Hetty innocently, but quite positively.

"I've heard you say as much as that afore; yes, I've heard that from you afore, gal, and yet it isn't true. One don't live in a tribe, not to see something of the way in which liking works in a woman's heart. Though no way given to marrying myself, I've been a looker-on among the Delawares, and this is a matter in which paleface and redskin gifts are all as one the same. When the feelin' begins, the young woman is thoughtful, and has no eyes or ears onless for the warrior that has taken her fancy; then follows melancholy and sighing, and such sort of actions; after which, especially if matters don't come to a plain discourse, she often flies round to backbiting and faultfinding, blaming the youth for the very things she likes best in him. Some young creatur's are forward in this way of showing their love, and I'm of opinion Judith is one of 'em. Now I've heard her as much as deny that Hurry was good-looking; and the young woman who could do *that*, must be far gone indeed."

"The young woman who liked Hurry would own that he is handsome. *I* think Hurry *very* handsome, Deerslayer, and I'm sure everybody must think so that has eyes. Judith don't like Harry March, and that's the reason she finds fault with him."

"Well—well—my good little Hetty, have it your own way. If we should talk from now till winter, each would think as at present; and there's no use in words. I must believe that Judith is much wrapped up in Hurry, and that sooner or later she'll have him; and this, too, all the more from the manner in which she abuses him; and I dare to say, you think just the contrary. But mind what I now tell you, gal, and pretend not to know it," continued this being, who was so obtuse on a point on which men are usually quick enough to make discoveries, and so acute in matters that would baffle the observation of much the greater portion of mankind; "I see how it is with them vagabonds. Rivenoak has left us, you see, and is talking yonder with his young men; and though too far to be *heard*, I can *see* what he is telling them. Their orders is to watch your movements, and to find where the canoe is to meet you, to take you back to the ark, and then to seize all and what they can. I'm sorry Judith sent you, for I suppose she wants you to go back ag'in."

"All that's settled, Deerslayer," returned the girl in a low, confidential, and meaning manner; "and you may trust me to outwit the best Indian of them all. I know I am feeble-minded, but I've got *some* sense, and you'll see how I'll use it in getting back, when my errand is done!"

"Ah's me! poor girl; I'm afeard all that's easier said than done. They're a venomous set of riptyles, and their pi'son's none the milder for the loss of Hist. Well, I'm glad the Sarpent was the one to get off with the gal; for now they'll be two happy, at least; whereas had *he* fallen into the hands of the Mingoes, there'd be two miserable, and another far from feelin' as a man likes to feel."

"Now you put me in mind of a part of my errand, that I had almost forgotten, Deerslayer. Judith told me to ask you what you thought the Hurons would do with you if you couldn't be bought off, and what *she* had best do to serve you. Yes, this was the most important part of the errand—what she had best do in order to serve you."

"That's as *you* think, Hetty; but it's no matter. Young women are apt to lay most stress on what most touches their feelin's; but no matter; have it your own way, so you be but careful not to let the vagabonds get the mastery of a canoe. When you get back to the ark, tell 'em to keep close, and to keep moving too, most especially at night. Many hours can't go by without the troops on the river hearing of this party, and then your fri'nds may look for relief. 'Tis but a day's march from the nearest garrison, and true soldiers will never lie idle with the foe in their neighborhood. This is my advice, and you must say to your father and Hurry that scalp-hunting will be a poor business now, as the Mingoes are up and awake, and nothing can save 'em 'till the troops come, except keeping a good belt of water atween 'em and the savages."

"What shall I tell Judith about you, Deerslayer? I know she will send me back again, if I don't bring her the truth about *you*."

"Then tell her the *truth*. I see no reason Judith Hutter shouldn't hear the *truth* about me as well as a *lie*. I'm a captyve in Indian hands, and Providence only knows what will come of it! Harkee, Hetty," dropping his voice and speaking still more confidentially, "you *are* a little weak-minded, it must be allowed, but you know something of Injins. Here I am in their hands, after having slain one of their stoutest warriors, and they've been endivoring to work upon me, through fear of consequences, to betray your father and all in the ark. I understand the blackguards as well as if they told it all out plainly with their tongues. They hold up avarice afore me on one side, and fear on t'other, and think honesty will give way atween 'em both. But let your father and Hurry know 'tis all useless; as for the Sarpent, *he* knows it already."

"But what shall I tell *Judith?* She will certainly send me back if I don't satisfy her mind."

"Well, tell Judith the same. No doubt the savages will try the torments to make me give in, and to revenge the loss of their warrior, but I must hold out ag'in nat'ral weakness in the best manner I can. You may tell Judith to feel no consarn on my account—it will come hard, I know, seeing that a white man's gifts don't run to boasting and singing under torment, for he generally feels smallest when he suffers most—but you may tell her not to have any consarn. I think I shall make out to stand it; and she may rely on this, let me give in as much as I may, and prove completely that I am white, by wailings, and howlings, and even tears, yet I'll never fall so far as to betray my fri'nds. When it gets to burning holes in the flesh with heated ramrods, and to hacking the body, and tearing the hair out by the roots, natur' may get the upper hand, so far as groans and complaints are consarned, but there the triumph of the vagabonds will ind; nothing short of God's abandoning him to the devils, can make an honest man ontrue to his color and duty."

Hetty listened with great attention, and her mild but speaking countenance manifested a strong sympathy in the anticipated agony of the supposititious sufferer. At first she seemed at a loss how to act; then, taking a hand of Deerslayer's, she affectionately recommended to him to borrow her Bible, and to read it while the savages were inflicting their torments. When the other honestly admitted that it exceeded his power to read, she even volunteered to remain with him and to perform this holy office in person. The offer was gently declined. . . .

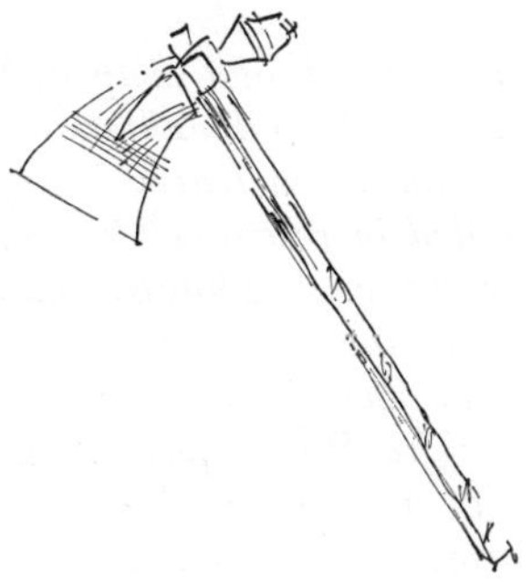

9

WHILE DEERSLAYER was held a prisoner by the Hurons, and thus stopped from playing any active part in the drama, a confused and terrible struggle raged on the lake. The savages were quick to place themselves in the abandoned castle. They installed eight of their best warriors in a room inside, there to lie concealed and await the return of the whites. With characteristic recklessness, Hurry Harry and old Hutter soon walked into the trap. Next day they brought the ark up to the castle, and finding the place apparently still and deserted, entered it with exultant comments. The Hurons sprang from their hiding place, and a tremendous battle ensued. Hurry Harry was finally taken prisoner and bound; Hutter was knocked senseless, stabbed, and scalped. Meanwhile, however, Chingachgook, Hist, and the two daughters of Hutter drew the ark off to a safe distance; and when Hurry Harry rolled himself into the water, they succeeded in rescuing him. Shortly thereafter, the Indians evacuated the castle. As soon as this happened Chingachgook, Hurry Harry, and the two daughters returned. They were stricken with horror to find the old trapper, his head all gore, dying in a corner. Before Hutter passed away, however, he revealed the fact that he was not really the father of Hetty and Judith. The party buried him in the lake, Hurry Harry pronouncing his eulogy: "He was a brave companion on a scout, and a notable hand with traps." Then they brought the ark up to the castle and moored it there.

Hardly had this been accomplished when Deerslayer was seen returning, alone and quite free, in a canoe. He had been released by the Hurons, but on stern conditions. He was to take word to the ark that he would be freed, and peace would return to the lake, if Hist came back to the Hurons, and if Judith consented to become the wife of a Huron brave who had lost his squaw. Unless this was done, Deerslayer or Hawkeye, as he was now termed, would have to return to torture and death. "I'm out on furlough!" Deerslayer exclaimed to Judith. He had until noon of the next day as his last hours of freedom. Judith, who had been the first to greet him, conducted him into the ark to talk with the others.

The meeting between Deerslayer and his friends in the ark was grave and anxious. The two Indians, in particular, read in his manner that he was not a successful fugitive, and a few sententious words sufficed to let them comprehend the nature of what their friend had termed his "furlough." Chingachgook immediately became thoughtful; while Hist, as usual, had no better mode of expressing her sympathy than by those little attentions which mark the affectionate manner of woman.

In a few minutes, however, something like a general plan for the proceedings of the night was adopted, and, to the eye of an uninstructed observer, things would be thought to move in their ordinary train. It was now getting to be dark, and it was decided to sweep the ark up to the castle, and secure it in its ordinary berth. The decision was come to, in some measure, on account of the fact that all the canoes were again in the possession of their proper owners, but principally from the security that was created by the representations of Deerslayer. He had examined the state of things among the Hurons, and felt satisfied that they meditated no further hostilities during the night, the loss they had met having indisposed them to further exertions for the moment. Then he had a proposition to make,—the object of his visit; and, if this were accepted, the war would at once terminate between the parties; and it was improbable that the Hurons would anticipate the failure of a project on which their chiefs had apparently set their hearts by having recourse to violence previously to the return of their messenger.

As soon as the ark was properly secured, the different members of the party occupied themselves in their several peculiar manners; haste in council, or in decision, no more characterizing the proceedings of the border whites, than it did those of their red neighbors. The women busied themselves in preparations for the evening meal, sad and silent, but ever attentive to the first wants of nature.

Hurry set about repairing his moccasins by the light of a blazing knot; Chingachgook seated himself in gloomy thought; while Deerslayer proceeded, in a manner equally free from affectation and concern, to examine Killdeer, the rifle of Hutter, that has been already mentioned, and which subsequently became so celebrated in the hands of the individual who was now making a survey of its merits. The piece was a little longer than usual, and had evidently been turned out from the workshop of some manufacturer of a superior order. It had a few silver ornaments; though, on the whole, it would have been deemed a plain piece by most frontiersmen; its great merit consisting in the accuracy of its bore, the perfection of the details, and the excellence of the metal. Again and again did the hunter apply the breech to his shoulder, and glance his eye along the sights, and as often did he poise his body, and raise the weapon slowly, as if about to catch an aim at a deer, in order to try the weight, and to ascertain its fitness for quick and accurate firing. All this was done by the aid of Hurry's torch, simply, but with an earnestness and abstraction that would have been found touching by any spectator who happened to know the real situation of the man.

" 'Tis a glorious we'pon, Hurry!" Deerslayer at length exclaimed, "and it may be thought a pity that it has fallen into the hands of women. The hunters have told me of its expl'ites, and by all I have heard, I should set it down as sartain death in exper'enced hands. Hearken to the tick of this lock—a wolf trap hasn't a livelier spring; pan and cock speak together, like two singing masters undertaking a psalm in meetin'. I never *did* see so true a bore, Hurry, that's sartain."

"Ay, old Tom used to give the piece a character, though he wasn't the man to particularize the ra'al natur' of any sort of firearms, in practice," returned March, passing the deer's thongs through the moccasin with the coolness of a cobbler. "He was no marksman, that we must all allow; but he had his good p'ints as well as his bad ones. I have had hopes that Judith might consait the idee of giving Killdeer to me."

"There's no saying what young women may do, that's a truth, Hurry; and I suppose you're as likely to own the rifle as another. Still, when things are so very near perfection, it's a pity not to reach it entirely."

"What do you mean by that? Would not that piece look as well on my shoulder as on any man's?"

"As for looks, I say nothing. You are both good-looking, and might make what is called a good-looking couple. But the true p'int is as to conduct. More deer would fall in one day, by that piece, in some men's hands, than would fall in a week in your'n, Hurry! I've seen you try; you remember the buck, t'other day?"

"That buck was out of season; and who wishes to kill venison out of season? I was merely trying to frighten the creatur', and I think you will own that he was pretty well skeared at any rate."

"Well, well, have it as you say. But this is a lordly piece, and would make a steady hand and quick eye the king of the woods."

"Then keep it, Deerslayer, and become king of the woods," said Judith, earnestly, who had heard the conversation, and whose eye was never long averted from the honest countenance of the hunter. "It can never be in better hands than it is at this moment; there I hope it will remain these fifty years."

"Judith, you can't be in 'arnest!" exclaimed Deerslayer, taken so much by surprise as to betray more emotion than it was usual for him to manifest on ordinary occasions. "Such a gift would be fit for a ra'al king to make; yes, and for a ra'al king to receive."

"I never was more in earnest in my life, Deerslayer, and I am as much in earnest in the wish as in the gift."

"Well, gal, well; we'll find time to talk of this ag'in. You mustn't be downhearted, Hurry, for Judith is a sprightly young woman, and she has a quick reason; she knows that the credit of her father's rifle is safer in my hands than it can possibly be in your'n; and, therefore, you mustn't be downhearted. In other matters, more to your liking, too, you'll find she'll give you the preference."

Hurry growled out his dissatisfaction; but he was too intent on quitting the lake, and in making his preparations, to waste his breath on a subject of this nature. Shortly after, the supper was ready; it was eaten in silence, as is so much the habit of those who consider the table as merely a place of animal refreshment. On this occasion, however, sadness and thought contributed their share to the general desire not to converse; for Deerslayer was so far an exception to the usages of men of his cast, as not only to wish to hold discourse on such occasions, but as often to create a similar desire in his companions.

The meal ended, and the humble preparations removed, the whole party assembled on the platform to hear the expected intelligence from Deerslayer on the subject of his visit. It had been evident he was in no haste to make his communications; but the feelings of Judith would no longer admit of delay. Stools were brought from the ark and the hut, and the whole six placed themselves in a circle near the door, watching each other's countenances, as best they could, by the scanty means that were furnished by a lovely starlight night. Along the shore, beneath the mountains, lay the usual body of gloom; but in the broad lake no shadow was cast, and a thousand mimic stars were dancing in the limpid element, that was just stirred enough by the evening air to set them all in motion.

"Now, Deerslayer," commenced Judith, whose impatience resisted further restraint; "now, Deerslayer, tell us all the Hurons have to say, and the reason why they have sent you on parole, to make us some offer."

"Furlough, Judith; furlough is the word; and it carries the same meaning with a captyve at large as it does with a soldier who has leave to quit his colors. In both cases the word is passed to come back: and now I remember to have heard that's the ra'al signification, 'furlough,' meaning a 'word' passed for the doing of anything, or the like. Parole, I rather think, is Dutch, and has something to do with the tattoos of the garrisons. But this makes no great difference, since the vartue of a pledge lies in the idee, and not in the word. Well, then, if the message must be given, it must; and perhaps there is no use in putting it off. Hurry will soon be wanting to set out on his journey to the river, and the stars rise and set, just as if they cared for neither Injin nor message. Ah's me! 'tisn't a pleasant, and I know it's a useless arr'nd; but it must be told."

"Harkee, Deerslayer," put in Hurry, a little authoritatively; "you're a sensible man in a hunt, and as good a fellow on a march as a sixty-miler-a-day could wish to meet with; but you're oncommon slow about messages, especially them that you think won't be likely to be well received. When a thing is to be told, why, tell it, and don't hang back like a Yankee lawyer pretending he can't understand a Dutchman's English, just to get a double fee out of him."

"I understand you, Hurry, and well are you named tonight, seeing you've no time to lose. But let us come at once to the p'int, seeing that's the object of this council; for council it may be called, though women have seats among us. The simple fact is this. When the party came back from the castle, the Mingoes held a council, and bitter thoughts were uppermost, as was plainly to be seen by their gloomy faces. No one likes to be beaten, and a redskin as little as a paleface. Well, when they had smoked upon it, and made their speeches, and their council fire had burnt low, the matter came out. It seems the elders among 'em consaited I was a man to be trusted on a furlough. They're wonderful obsarvant, them Mingoes; *that* their worst inimies must allow; but they consaited I was such a man; and it isn't often"—added the hunter, with a pleasing consciousness that his previous life justified this implicit reliance on his good faith—"it isn't often they consait anything so good of a paleface; but so they did with me, and therefore they didn't hesitate to speak their minds, which is just this: You see the state of things. The lake and all on it, they fancy, lie at their marcy. Thomas Hutter is deceased, and as for Hurry, they've got the idee he has been near enough to death today not to wish to take another look at him this summer. Therefore, they account all your forces as reduced to Chingachgook and the two young women, and, while they know the Delaware to be of a high race, and a born warrior, they know he's now on his first warpath. As for the gals, of course they set them down much as they do women in gin'ral."

"You mean that they despise us!" interrupted Judith, with eyes that flashed so brightly as to be observed by all present.

"That will be seen in the ind. They hold that all on the lake lies at their marcy, and, therefore, they send by me this belt of wampum," showing the article in question to the Delaware, as he spoke, "with these words: Tell the Sarpent, they say, that he has done well for a beginner; he may now strike across the mountains, for his own villages, and no one shall look for his trail. If he has found a scalp, let him take it with him; the Huron braves have hearts, and can feel for a young warrior who doesn't wish to go home empty-handed. If he is nimble, he is welcome to lead out a party in pursuit. Hist, howsever, must go back to the Hurons; when she left them in the night, she carried away, by mistake, that which doesn't belong to her."

"That *can't* be true!" said Hetty, earnestly. "Hist is no such girl; but one that gives everybody his due—"

How much more she would have said, in remonstrance, cannot be known, inasmuch as Hist, partly laughing, and partly hiding her face in shame, put her own hand across the speaker's mouth, in a way to check the words.

"You don't understand Mingo messages, poor Hetty," resumed Deerslayer, "which seldom mean what lies exactly uppermost. Hist has brought away with her the inclinations of a young Huron, and they want her back again, that the poor young man may find them where he last saw them! The Sarpent, they say, is too promising a young warrior not to find as many wives as he wants, but this one he cannot have. That's their meaning, and nothing else, as I understand it."

"They were very obliging and thoughtful, in supposing a young woman can forget all her own inclinations in order to let this unhappy youth find his!" said Judith ironically, though her manner became more bitter as she proceeded. "I suppose a woman is a woman, let her color be white or red: and your chiefs know little of a woman's heart, Deerslayer, if they think it can ever forgive when wronged, or ever forget when it fairly loves."

"I suppose that's pretty much the truth, with some women, Judith, though I've known them that could do both. The next message is to you. They say the Muskrat, as they call your father, has dove to the bottom of the lake; that he will never come up again, and that his young will soon be in want of wigwams, if not of food. The Huron huts, they think, are better than the huts of York; they wish you to come and try them. Your color is white, they own, but they think young women who've lived so long in the woods, would lose their way in the clearin's. A great warrior among them has lately lost his wife, and he would be glad to put the Wild Rose on her bench at his fireside. As for the Feeble Mind, she will always be honored and taken care of by red warriors. Your father's goods, they think, ought to go to enrich the tribe; but your own property, which is to include everything of a female natur', will go, like that of all wives, into the wigwam of the husband. Moreover, they've lost a young maiden by violence, lately, and 'twill take two palefaces to fill her seat."

"And do *you* bring such a message to *me?*" exclaimed Judith, though the tone in which the words were uttered had more in it of sorrow than of anger. "Am I a girl to be an Indian's slave?"

"If you wish my honest thoughts on this p'int, Judith, I shall answer that I don't think you'll willingly ever become any man's slave, redskin or white. You're not to think hard, howsever, of my bringing the message, as near as I could, in the very words in which it was given to me. Them was the conditions on which I got my furlough, and a bargain is a bargain, though it is made with a vagabond. I've told you what *they've* said, but I've not yet told you what I think you ought, one and all, to answer."

"Ay; let's hear that, Deerslayer," put in Hurry. "My cur'osity is up on that consideration, and I should like right well to hear your idees of the reasonableness of the reply. For my part, though, my own mind is pretty much settled on the p'int of my own answer, which shall be made known as soon as necessary."

"And so is mine, Hurry, on all the different heads, and on no one is it more sartainly settled than on your'n. If I was you, I should say—'Deerslayer, tell them scamps they don't know Harry March! He is human; and having a white skin he has also a white natur', which natur' won't let him desart females of his own race and gifts, in their greatest need. So set me down as one that will refuse to come into your treaty, though you should smoke a hogshead of tobacco over it.' "

March was a little embarrassed at this rebuke, which was uttered with sufficient warmth of manner, and with a point that left no doubt of the meaning. Had Judith encouraged him, he would not have hesitated about remaining to defend her and her sister, but under the circumstances, a feeling of resentment rather urged him to abandon them. At all events, there was not a sufficiency of chivalry in Hurry Harry to induce him to hazard the safety of his own person, unless he could see a direct connection between the probable consequences and his own interests. It is no wonder, therefore, that his answer partook equally of his intention, and of the reliance he so boastingly placed on his gigantic strength, which, if it did not always make him courageous, usually made him impudent as respects those with whom he conversed.

"Fair words make long friendships, Master Deerslayer," he said, a little menacingly. "You're but a stripling, and you know, by exper'ence, what you are in the hands of a man. As you're not me, but only a go-between, sent by the savages to us Christians, you may tell your empl'yers that they do know Harry March, which is a proof of their sense as well as his. He's human enough to follow human natur', and that tells him to see the folly of one man's fighting a whole tribe. If females desart him, they must expect to be desarted *by* him, whether they're of his own gifts or another man's gifts. Should Judith see fit to change her mind, she's welcome to my company to the river, and Hetty with her; but shouldn't she come to this conclusion, I start as soon as I think the enemy's scouts are beginning to nestle themselves in among the brush and leaves for the night."

"Judith will *not* change her mind, and she does not ask your company, Master March," returned the girl, with spirit.

"That p'int's settled, then," resumed Deerslayer, unmoved by the other's warmth. "Hurry Harry must act for himself, and do that which will be most likely to suit his own fancy. The course he means to take will give him an easy race, if it don't give him an easy conscience. Next comes the question with Hist—what say you, gal?—will you desart your duty, too, and go back to the Mingoes and take a Huron husband; and all, not for the love of the man you're to marry, but for the love of your own scalp?"

"Why you talk so to Hist?" demanded the girl, half offended. "You t'ink a redskin girl make like captain's lady, to laugh and joke with any officer that come."

"What I think, Hist, is neither here nor there, in this matter. I must carry back your answer, and in order to do so, it is necessary that you should send it. A faithful messenger gives his arr'nd word for word."

Hist no longer hesitated to speak her mind fully. In the excitement she rose from her bench, and naturally recurring to that language in which she expressed herself the most readily, she delivered her thoughts and intentions, beautifully and with dignity, in the tongue of her own people.

"Tell the Hurons, Deerslayer," she said, "that they are as ignorant as moles; they don't know the wolf from the dog. Among my people, the rose dies on the stem where it budded; the tears of the child fall on the graves of its parents; the corn grows where the seed has been planted. The Delaware girls are not messengers, to be sent, like belts of wampum, from tribe to tribe. They are honeysuckles, that are sweetest in their own woods; their own young men carry them away in their bosoms, because they are fragrant; they are sweetest when plucked from their native stems. Even the robin and the martin come back, year after year, to their old nests; shall a woman be less true-hearted than a bird? Set the pine in the clay, and it will turn yellow; the willow will not flourish on the hill; the tamarack is healthiest in the swamp; the tribes of the sea love best to hear the winds that blow over the salt water. As for a Huron youth, what is he to a maiden of the Lenni Lenape? He may be fleet, but her eyes do not follow him in the race; they look back toward the lodges of the Delawares. He may sing a sweet song for the girls of Canada, but there is no music for Wah, but in the tongue she has listened to from childhood. Were the Huron born of the people that once roamed the shores of the salt lake, it would be in vain, unless he were of the family of Uncas. The young pine will rise to be as high as any of its fathers. Wah-ta-Wah has but one heart, and it can love but one husband."

Deerslayer listened to this characteristic message, which was given with an earnestness suited to the feelings from which it sprang, with undisguised delight; meeting the ardent eloquence of the girl, as she concluded, with one of his own heartfelt, silent, and peculiar fits of laughter.

"That's worth all the wampum in the woods!" he exclaimed. "You don't understand it, I suppose, Judith; but if you'll look into your feelin's, and fancy that an inimy had sent to tell you to give up the man of your ch'ice, and to take up with another that wasn't the man of your ch'ice, you'll get the substance of it, I'll warrant! Give me a woman for ra'al eloquence, if they'll only make up their minds to speak what they *feel.* By speakin', I don't mean, chatterin', howsever; for most of them will do *that* by the hour; but comin' out with their honest, deepest feelin's, in proper words. And now, Judith, having got the answer of a redskin girl, it is fit I should get that of a paleface, if indeed, a countenance that is as blooming as your'n can in any wise so be tarmed. You are well named the Wild Rose, and so far as color goes, Hetty ought to be called the Honeysuckle."

"Did this language come from one of the garrison gallants, I should deride it, Deerslayer; but coming from *you,* I know it can be depended on," returned Judith, deeply gratified by his unmeditated and characteristic compliments. "It is too soon, however, to ask my answer; the Great Serpent has not yet spoken."

"The Sarpent? Lord; I could carry back his speech without hearing a word of it! I didn't think of putting the question to him at all, I will allow; though 'twould be hardly right either, seeing that truth is truth, and I'm bound to tell these Mingoes the fact, and nothing else. So, Chingachgook, let us hear *your* mind on this matter: are you inclined to strike across the hills toward your village, to give up Hist to a Huron, and to tell the chiefs at home, that if they're actyve and successful they may possibly get *on* the end of the Iroquois trail some two or three days a'ter the inimy has got *off* of it?"

Like his betrothed, the young chief arose, that his answer might be given with due distinctness and dignity. Hist had spoken with her hands crossed upon her bosom, as if to suppress the emotions within; but the warrior stretched an arm before him, with a calm energy that aided in giving emphasis to his expressions.

"Wampum should be sent for wampum," he said; "a message must be answered by a message. Hear what the Great Serpent of the Delawares has to say to the pretended wolves from the Great Lakes, that are howling through our woods. They are no wolves; they are dogs that have come to get their tails and ears cropped by the hands of the Delawares. They are good at stealing young women: bad at keeping them. Chingachgook takes his own where he finds it; he asks leave of no cur from the Canadas. If he has a tender feeling in his heart, it is no business of the Hurons. He tells it to her who most likes to know it; he will not bellow it in the forest for the ears of those that only understand yells of terror. What passes in his lodge is not for the chiefs of his own people to know; still less for Mingo rogues—"

"Call 'em vagabonds, Sarpent," interrupted Deerslayer, unable to restrain his delight,—"yes, just call 'em up-and-down vagabonds, which is a word easily intarpreted, and the most hateful to all their ears, it's so true. Never fear me; I'll give 'em your message, syllable for syllable, sneer for sneer, idee for idee, scorn for scorn, and they desarve no better at your hands. Only call 'em vagabonds, once or twice, and that will set the sap mounting in 'em, from their lowest roots to the uppermost branches."

"Still less for Mingo vagabonds!" resumed Chingachgook, quite willingly complying with his friend's request. "Tell the Huron dogs to howl louder, if they wish a Delaware to find them in the woods, where they burrow like foxes, instead of hunting like warriors. When they had a Delaware maiden in their camp, there was a reason for hunting them up; now they will be forgotten, unless they make a noise. Chingachgook don't like the trouble of going to his villages for more warriors; he can strike their runaway trail; unless they hide it underground, he will follow it to Canada, alone. He will keep Wah-ta-Wah with him to cook his game; they two will be Delawares enough to scare all the Hurons back to their own country."

"That's a grand despatch, as the officers call them things!" cried Deerslayer; " 'twill set all the Huron blood in motion; most particularly that part where he tells 'em Hist, too, will keep on their heels, till they're fairly driven out of the country. Ah's me! big words aren't always big deeds, notwithstanding. The Lord send that we be able to be only one half as good as we promise to be. And now, Judith, it's your turn to speak, for them miscreants will expect an answer from each person, poor Hetty, perhaps, excepted."

"And why not, Hetty, Deerslayer? She often speaks to the purpose; the Indians may respect her words, for they feel for people in her condition."

"That is true, Judith, and quick thoughted in you. The redskins *do* respect misfortunes of all kinds, and Hetty's in particular. So, Hetty, if you have anything to say, I'll carry it to the Hurons as faithfully as if it was spoken by a schoolmaster or a missionary."

The girl hesitated a moment, and then she answered in her own gentle, soft tones, as earnestly as any who had preceded her.

"The Hurons can't understand the difference between white people and themselves," she said, "or they wouldn't ask Judith and me to go and live in their villages. God has given one country to the red men and another to us. He means us to live apart. Then mother always said that we should never dwell with any but Christians, if possible, and *that* is a reason why we can't go. This lake is ours, and we won't leave it. Father's and mother's graves are in it, and even the worst Indians love to stay near the graves of their fathers. I will come and see them again, if they wish me to, and read more out of the Bible to them, but I can't quit father's and mother's graves."

"That will do—that will do, Hetty, just as well as if you sent them a message twice as long," interrupted the hunter. "I'll tell 'em all you've said, and all you mean, and I'll answer for it, that they'll be easily satisfied. Now, Judith, your turn comes next, and then this part of my arr'nd will be tarminated for the night."

Judith manifested a reluctance to give her reply, that had awakened a little curiosity in the messenger. Judging from her known spirit, he had never supposed the girl would be less true to her feelings and principles than Hist or Hetty; and yet there was a visible wavering of purpose that rendered him slightly uneasy. Even now, when directly required to speak, she seemed to hesitate; nor did she open her lips until the profound silence told her how anxiously her words were expected. Then, indeed, she spoke, but it was doubtingly and with reluctance.

"Tell me, first—tell *us*, first, Deerslayer," she commenced, repeating the words merely to change the emphasis, "what effect will our answers have on *your* fate? If you are to be the sacrifice of our spirit, it would have been better had we all been more wary as to the language we use. What, then, are likely to be the consequences to yourself?"

"Lord, Judith, you might as well ask me the way the wind will blow next week, or what will be the age of the next deer that will be shot! I can only say that their faces look a little dark upon me, but it doesn't thunder every time a black cloud rises, nor does every puff of wind blow up rain. That's a question, therefore, much more easily put than answered."

"So is this message of the Iroquois to me," answered Judith, rising, as if she had determined on her own course for the present. "My answer shall be given, Deerslayer, after you and I have talked together alone, when the others have laid themselves down for the night."

There was a decision in the manner of the girl that disposed Deerslayer to comply, and this he did the more readily as the delay could produce no material consequences, one way or the other. The meeting now broke up, Hurry announcing his resolution to leave them speedily. During the hour that was suffered to intervene, in order that the darkness might deepen before the frontiersman took his departure, the different individuals occupied themselves in their customary modes, the hunter, in particular, passing most of the time in making further inquiries into the perfection of the rifle already mentioned.

The hour of nine soon arrived, however, and then it had been determined that Hurry should commence his journey. Instead of making his adieus frankly, and in a generous spirit, the little he thought it necessary to say was uttered sullenly and in coldness. Resentment at what he considered Judith's obstinacy was blended with mortification at the career he had run since reaching the lake; and, as is usual with the vulgar and narrow-minded, he was more disposed to reproach others with his failures than to censure himself. Judith gave him her hand, but it was quite as much in gladness as with regret, while the two Delawares were not sorry to find he was leaving them. Of the whole party, Hetty alone betrayed any real feeling. Bashfulness, and the timidity of her sex and character, kept even her aloof, so that Hurry entered the canoe, where Deerslayer was already waiting for him, before she ventured near enough to be observed. Then, indeed, the girl came into the ark, and approached its end just as the little bark was turning from it, with a movement so light and steady as to be almost imperceptible. An impulse of feeling now overcame her timidity, and Hetty spoke.

"Good-by, Hurry,"—she called out in her sweet voice,—"good-by, dear Hurry. Take care of yourself in the woods, and don't stop once till you reach the garrison. The leaves on the trees are scarcely plentier than the Hurons round the lake, and they'd not treat a strong man like you as kindly as they treat me."

The ascendency which March had obtained over this feeble-minded, but right-thinking and right-feeling girl, arose from a law of nature. Her senses had been captivated by his personal advantages; and her moral communications with him had never been sufficiently intimate to counteract an effect that must have been otherwise lessened, even with one whose mind was as obtuse as her own. Hetty's instinct of right, if such a term can be applied to one who seemed taught by some kind spirit how to steer her course with unerring accuracy between good and evil, would have revolted at Hurry's character, on a thousand points, had there been opportunities to enlighten her; but while he conversed and trifled with her sister, at a distance from herself, his perfection of form and feature had been left to produce their influence on her simple imagination and naturally tender feelings, without suffering by the alloy of his opinions and coarseness. It is true, she found him rough and rude; but her father was that, and most of the other men she had seen; and that which she believed to belong to all of the sex, struck her less unfavorably in Hurry's character than it might otherwise have done. Still, it was not absolutely love that Hetty felt for Hurry, nor do we wish so to portray it, but merely that awakening sensibility and admiration which, under more propitious circumstances, and always supposing no untoward revelations of character on the part of the young man had supervened to prevent it, might soon have ripened into that engrossing feeling. She felt for him an incipient tenderness, but scarcely any passion. Perhaps the nearest approach to the latter that Hetty had manifested, was to be seen in the sensitiveness which had caused her to detect March's predilection for her sister; for, among Judith's many admirers, this was the only instance in which the dull mind of the girl had been quickened into an observation of the circumstance.

Hurry received so little sympathy at his departure, that the gentle tones of Hetty, as she thus called after him, sounded soothingly. He checked the canoe, and with one sweep of his powerful arm brought it back to the side of the ark. This was more than Hetty, whose courage had risen with the departure of her hero, expected, and she now shrank timidly back at his unexpected return.

"You're a good gal, Hetty, and I can't quit you without shaking hands," said March, kindly. "Judith, a'ter all, isn't worth as much as you, though she may be a trifle better looking. As to wits, if honesty and fair dealing with a young man is a sign of sense in a young woman, you're worth a dozen Judiths; ay, and for that matter, most young women of my acquaintance."

"Don't say anything against Judith, Harry," returned Hetty, imploringly. "Father's gone, and mother's gone, and nobody's left but Judith and me, and it isn't right for sisters to speak evil, or to hear evil, of each other. Father's in the lake, and so is mother, and we should all fear God, for we don't know when we may be in the lake, too."

"That sounds reasonable, child, as does most you say. Well, if we ever meet again, Hetty, you'd find a fri'nd in me, let your sister do what she may. I was no great fri'nd of your mother, I'll allow, for we didn't think alike on most p'ints; but then your father, old Tom, and I fitted each other as remarkably as a buckskin garment will fit any reasonable-built man. I've always been unanimous of opinion that old Floating Tom Hutter, at the bottom, was a good fellow, and will maintain that ag'in all inimies for his sake, as well as for your'n."

"Good-by, Hurry," said Hetty, who now wanted to hasten the young man off, as ardently as she had wished to keep him only the moment before, though she could give no clearer account of the latter than of the former feeling; "good-by, Hurry; take care of yourself in the woods; don't halt till you reach the garrison. I'll read a chapter in the Bible for you, before I go to bed, and I'll think of you in my prayers."

This was touching a point on which March had no sympathies, and without more words he shook the girl cordially by the hand and re-entered the canoe. In another minute the two adventurers were a hundred feet from the ark, and half a dozen had not elapsed before they were completely lost to view. Hetty sighed deeply, and rejoined her sister and Hist.

For some time Deerslayer and his companion paddled ahead in silence. It had been determined to land Hurry at the precise point where he is represented, in the commencement of our tale, as having embarked; not only as a place little likely to be watched by the Hurons, but because he was sufficiently familiar with the signs of the woods, at that spot, to thread his way through them in the dark. Thither, then, the light craft proceeded, being urged as diligently, and as swiftly as two vigorous and skilful canoemen could force their little vessel through, or rather *over*, the water. Less than a quarter of an hour sufficed for the object; and, at the end of that time, being within the shadows of the shore, and quite near the point they sought, each ceased his efforts in order to make their parting communications out of earshot of any straggler who might happen to be in the neighborhood.

"You will do well to persuade the officers at the garrison to lead out a party ag'in these vagabonds, as soon as you get in, Hurry," Deerslayer commenced; "and you'll do better if you volunteer to guide it up yourself. You know the paths, and the shape of the lake, and the natur' of the land, and can do it better than a common, gin'ralizing scout. Strike at the Huron camp first, and follow the signs that will then show themselves. A few looks at the hut and the ark will satisfy you as to the state of the Delaware and the women; and, at any rate, there'll be a fine opportunity to fall on the Mingo trail, and to make a mark on the memories of the blackguards that they'll be apt to carry with 'em for a long time. It won't be likely to make much difference with me, since *that* matter will be detarmined afore tomorrow's sun has set; but it may make a great change in Judith and Hetty's hopes and prospects!"

"And as for yourself, Nathaniel," Hurry inquired with more interest than he was accustomed to betray in the welfare of others,—"and as for yourself, what do you think is likely to turn up?"

"The Lord in his wisdom only can tell, Henry March! The clouds look black and threatening, and I keep my mind in a state to meet the worst. Vengeful feelin's are uppermost in the hearts of the Mingoes, and any little disapp'intment about the plunder, or the prisoners, or Hist, may make the torments sartain. The Lord, in his wisdom, can only detarmine my fate, or your'n!"

"This is a black business, and ought to be put a stop to, in some way or other," answered Hurry, confounding the distinctions between right and wrong, as is usual with selfish and vulgar men. "I heartily wish old Hutter and I had scalped every creatur' in their camp, the night we first landed with that capital object! Had you not held back, Deerslayer, it might have been done; then you wouldn't have found yourself, at the last moment, in the desperate condition you mention."

" 'Twould have been better had you said you wished you had never attempted to do what it little becomes any white man's gifts to undertake; in which case, not only might we have kept from coming to blows, but Thomas Hutter would now have been living, and the hearts of the savages would be less given to vengeance."

This was so apparent, and it seemed so obvious to Hurry himself, at the moment, that he dashed his paddle into the water, and began to urge the canoe toward the shore, as if bent only on running away from his own lively remorse. His companion humored this feverish desire for change, and in a minute or two the bow of the boat grated lightly on the shingle of the beach. To land, shoulder his pack and rifle, and to get ready for his march, occupied Hurry but an instant, and with a growling adieu, he had already commenced his march, when a sudden twinge of feeling brought him to a dead stop, and immediately after to the other's side.

"You cannot mean to give yourself up ag'in to them murdering savages, Deerslayer!" he said, quite as much in angry remonstrance as with generous feeling. " 'Twould be the act of a madman or a fool!"

"There's them that thinks it madness to keep their words, and there's them that don't, Hurry Harry. You may be one of the first, but I'm one of the last. No redskin breathing shall have it in his power to say that a Mingo minds his word more than a man of white blood and white gifts, in anything that consarns me. I'm out on a furlough, and if I've strength and reason, I'll go in on a furlough afore noon tomorrow!"

"What's an Injin, or a word passed, or a furlough taken from creatur's like them, that have neither souls nor names?"

"If they've got neither souls nor names, you and I have both, Harry March, and one is accountable for the other. This furlough is not, as you seem to think, a matter altogether atween me and the Mingoes, seeing it is a solemn bargain made atween me and God. He who thinks that he can say what he pleases, in his distress, and that 'twill all pass for nothing, because 'tis uttered in the forest, and into red men's ears, knows little of his situation, and hopes, and wants. The words are said to the ears of the Almighty. The air is his breath, and the light of the sun is little more than a glance of his eye. Farewell, Harry; we may not meet ag'in; but I would never wish you to treat a furlough, or any other solemn thing that your Christian God has been called on to witness, as a duty so light that it may be forgotten according to the wants of the body, or even according to the cravings of the spirit."

March was now glad again to escape. It was quite impossible that he could enter into the sentiments that ennobled his companion, and he broke away from both with an impatience that caused him secretly to curse the folly that could induce a man to rush, as it were, on his own destruction. Deerslayer, on the contrary, manifested no such excitement. Sustained by his principles, inflexible in the purpose of acting up to them, and superior to any unmanly apprehension, he regarded all before him as a matter of course, and no more thought of making any unworthy attempt to avoid it, than a Mussulman thinks of counteracting the decrees of Providence. He stood calmly on the shore, listening to the reckless tread with which Hurry betrayed his progress through the bushes, shook his head in dissatisfaction at the want of caution, and then stepped quietly into his canoe. Before he dropped the paddle again into the water, the young man gazed about him at the scene presented by the starlit night. This was the spot where he had first laid his eyes on the beautiful sheet of water on which he floated. If it was then glorious in the bright light of summer's noontide, it was now sad and melancholy under the shadows of night. The mountains rose around it, like black barriers to exclude the outer world; and the gleams of pale light that rested on the broader parts of the basin, were no bad symbols of the faintness of the hopes that were so dimly visible in his own future. Sighing heavily, he pushed the canoe from the land, and took his way back with steady diligence toward the ark and the castle.

Judith was waiting the return of Deerslayer, on the platform, with stifled impatience, when the latter reached the hut. Hist and Hetty were both in a deep sleep, on the bed usually occupied by the two daughters of the house, and the Delaware was stretched on the floor of the adjoining room, his rifle at his side, and a blanket over him, already dreaming of the events of the last few days. There was a lamp burning in the ark, for the family was accustomed to indulge in this luxury on extraordinary occasions, and possessed the means, the vessel being of a form and material to render it probable it had once been an occupant of the chest.

As soon as the girl got a glimpse of the canoe, she ceased her hurried walk up and down the platform, and stood ready to receive the young man, whose return she had now been anxiously expecting for some time. She helped him to fasten the canoe, and by aiding in the other little similar employments, manifested her desire to reach a moment of liberty as soon as possible. When this was done, in answer to an inquiry of his she informed him of the manner in which their companions had disposed of themselves. He listened attentively, for the manner of the girl was so earnest and impressive as to apprise him that she had something on her mind of more than common concern.

"And now, Deerslayer," Judith continued, "you see I have lighted the lamp, and put it in the cabin of the ark. That is never done with us, unless on great occasions, and I consider this night as the most important of my life. Will you follow me and see what I have to show you—hear what I have to say?"

The hunter was a little surprised; but making no objections, both were soon in the scow, and in the room that contained the light. Here two stools were placed at the side of the chest, with the lamp on another, and a table near by to receive the different articles, as they might be brought to view. This arrangement had its rise in the feverish impatience of the girl, which could brook no delay that it was in her power to obviate. Even all the padlocks were removed, and it only remained to raise the heavy lid, and to expose the treasures of this long-secreted hoard.

"I see, in part, what all this means," observed Deerslayer, "yes, I see through it, in part. But why is not Hetty present? Now Thomas Hutter is gone, she is one of the owners of these cur'osities, and ought to see them opened and handled."

"Hetty sleeps," answered Judith, hastily. "Happily for her, fine clothes and riches have no charms. Besides, she has this night given her share of all that the chest may hold to me, that I may do with it as I please."

"Is poor Hetty composs enough for that, Judith?" demanded the just-minded young man. "It's a good rule, and a righteous one, never to take when those that give don't know the valie of their gifts; and such as God has visited heavily in their wits, ought to be dealt with as carefully as children that haven't yet come to their understandings."

Judith was hurt at this rebuke, coming from the person it did; but she would have felt it far more keenly had not her conscience fully acquitted her of any unjust intentions toward her feeble-minded but confiding sister. It was not a moment, however, to betray any of her usual mountings of the spirit, and she smothered the passing sensation in the desire to come to the great object she had in view.

"Hetty will not be wronged," she mildly answered; "she even knows not only what I am about to do, Deerslayer, but *why* I do it. So take your seat, raise the lid of the chest, and this time we will go to the bottom. I shall be disappointed if something is not found to tell us more of the history of Thomas Hutter and my mother."

"Why Thomas Hutter, Judith, and not your father? The dead ought to meet with as much reverence as the living!"

"I have long suspected that Thomas Hutter was not *my* father, though I did think he might have been Hetty's; but now we know he was father of neither. He acknowledged that much in his dying moments. I am old enough to remember better things than we have seen on this lake, though they are so faintly impressed on my memory that the earlier part of my life seems like a dream."

"Dreams are but miserable guides when one has to detarmine about realities, Judith," returned the other admonishingly. "Fancy nothing and hope nothing on their account; though I've known chiefs that thought 'em useful."

"I expect nothing for the future from them, my good friend, but cannot help remembering what has been. This is idle, however, when half an hour of examination may tell us all, or even more than I want to know."

Deerslayer, who comprehended the girl's impatience, now took his seat, and proceeded once more to bring to light the different articles that the chest contained. As a matter of course, all that had been previously examined were found where they had been last deposited; and they excited much less interest or comment than when formerly exposed to view. Even Judith laid aside the rich brocade with an air of indifference, for she had a far higher aim before her than the indulgence of vanity, and was impatient to come at the still hidden, or rather unknown, treasures.

"All these we have seen before," she said, "and will not stop to open. The bundle under your hand, Deerslayer, is a fresh one; that we will look into. God send it may contain something to tell poor Hetty and myself who we really are."

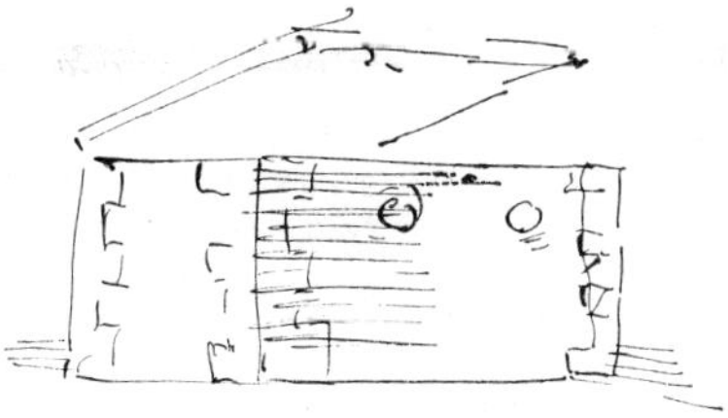

10

JUDITH, while Deerslayer watched her, spent more than an hour reading the various packets of letters. It was a dark story which they unfolded. They showed that her mother, as a young girl, had formed a connection with a European officer sojourning in America; that she had borne him two children, Judith and Hetty; that he had gradually become tired of the alliance, and after a period of coldness had deserted the family; and that the mother had then fallen into a morbid frame of mind bordering on insanity. In this sad condition of mental disorder, she had cast about for protection, and had willingly entered into marriage with one Thomas Hovey—this evidently being Tom Hutter. She was anxious to escape from civilization into the wilderness, where her unhappy history would not be known. She was also anxious to injure some of her relatives, even if in doing so she injured herself. Hovey or Hutter, as the letters showed, was quite prepared to conceal himself in the woods. He had been a pirate, and a reward had been offered by the Crown for his capture. Hence it was that the pair had established themselves in the castle and ark on Otsego Lake. But Judith was still left in the dark as to the precise identity of her parents, for all dates, signatures, and addresses had been cut from the letters.

When Judith finished reading this correspondence, she turned back to Deerslayer, who had greatly attracted her, and in whose frank nature she felt she could confide. They talked at some length about her future. With great candor, Judith made it plain that she would be glad to marry a man like Deerslayer; she wanted a husband of truth and constancy, she said, and had no desire for social rank. But Deerslayer, who regarded her statements as hypothetical, not personal, took a different view. He could conceive of no such union being happy. "Judith," he said, "you come of people altogether above mine, in the world, and onequal matches, like onequal fr'indships, can't often terminate kindly." That ended Judith's approaches—for the time being.

The two closed the chest and parted silently. Judith lay down with Hist and Hetty for a sleepless night; but Deerslayer, although he knew that he must return to the Hurons next day and would certainly meet torture and death, was asleep within five minutes. Next morning, before leaving to keep his word with his Huron captors, he paused to say a solemn farewell to Judith, Hist, and Chingachgook.

The Delaware got the canoe ready for his friend as soon as apprised of his intention, while Hist busied herself in making the few arrangements that were thought necessary to his comfort. All this was done without ostentation, but in a way that left Deerslayer fully acquainted with, and equally disposed to appreciate the motive. When all was ready, both returned to the side of Judith and Hetty—neither of whom had moved from the spot where the young hunter sat.

"The best fri'nds must often part," the last began, when he saw the whole party grouped around him. "Yes, fri'ndship can't alter the ways of Providence; and let our feelin's be as they may, we must part. I've often thought there's moments when our words dwell longer on the mind than common, and when advice is remembered, just because the mouth that gives it isn't likely to give it ag'in. No one knows what will happen in the world; and therefore it may be well, when fri'nds separate under a likelihood that the parting may be long, to say a few words in kindness, as a sort of keepsakes. If all but one will go into the ark, I'll talk to each in turn, and what is more, I'll listen to what you may have to say back ag'in; for it's a poor counsellor that won't take as well as give."

As the meaning of the speaker was understood, the two Indians immediately withdrew as desired, leaving the sisters, however, still standing at the young man's side. A look of Deerslayer's induced Judith to explain.

"You can advise Hetty as you land," she said, hastily; "I intend that she shall accompany you to the shore."

"Is this wise, Judith? It's true that, under common sarcumstances, a feeble mind is a great protection among redskins; but when their feelin's are up, and they're bent on revenge, it's hard to say what may come to pass. Besides——"

"What were you about to say, Deerslayer?" asked Judith, whose gentleness of voice and manner amounted nearly to tenderness, though she struggled hard to keep her emotions and apprehensions in subjection.

"Why, simply that there are sights and doin's that one even as little gifted with reason and memory as Hetty, here, might better not witness. So, Judith, you would do well to let me land alone, and to keep your sister back."

"Never fear for me, Deerslayer," put in Hetty, who comprehended enough of the discourse to know its general drift; "I'm feeble-minded, and that, they say, is an excuse for going anywhere; and what that won't excuse will be overlooked on account of the Bible I always carry. It is wonderful, Judith, how all sorts of men, the trappers as well as the hunters, red men as well as white, Mingoes as well as Delawares, do reverence and fear the Bible!"

"I think you have not the least ground to fear any injury, Hetty," answered the sister, "and therefore I shall insist on your going to the Huron camp with our friend. Your being there can do no harm, not even to yourself, and may do great good to Deerslayer."

"This is not a moment, Judith, to dispute; and so have the matter your own way," returned the young man. "Get yourself ready, Hetty, and go into the canoe, for I've a few parting words to say to your sister, which can do you no good."

Judith and her companion continued silent, until Hetty had so far complied as to leave them alone, when Deerslayer took up the subject as if it had been interrupted by some ordinary occurrence, and in a very matter-of-fact way.

"Words spoken at parting, and which may be the last we ever hear from a fri'nd, are not soon forgotten," he repeated, "and so, Judith, I intend to speak to you like a brother, seein' I'm not old enough to be your father. In the first place, I wish to caution you ag'in your inimies, of which two may be said to ha'nt your very footsteps, and to beset your ways. The first is oncommon good looks, which is as dangerous a foe to some young women as a whole tribe of Mingoes could prove, and which calls for great watchfulness; not to admire and praise; but to distrust and sarcumvent. Yes, good looks may be sarcumvented, and fairly outwitted, too. In order to do this, you've only to remember that they melt like the snows; and, when once gone, they never come back ag'in. The seasons come and go, Judith; and if we have winter, with storms and frosts, and spring, with chills and leafless trees, we have summer, with its sun and glorious skies, and fall, with its fruits, and a garment thrown over the forest that no beauty of the town could rummage out of all the shops in America. 'Arth is an eternal round, the goodness of God bringing back the pleasant when we've had enough of the onpleasant. But it's not so with good looks. *They* are lent for a short time in youth, to be used and not abused; and as I never met with a young woman to whom Providence has been as bountiful as it has to you, Judith, in this partic'lar, I warn you, as it might be with my dyin' breath, to beware of the inimy; fri'nd or inimy, as we deal with the gift."

It was so grateful to Judith to hear these unequivocal admissions of her personal charms, that much would have been forgiven to the man who made them, let him be who he might. But, at that moment, and from a far better feeling, it would not have been easy for Deerslayer seriously to offend her; and she listened with a patience which, had it been foretold only a week earlier, would have excited her indignation to hear.

"I understand your meaning, Deerslayer," returned the girl, with a meekness and humility that a little surprised her listener, "and hope to be able to profit by it. But you have mentioned only one of the enemies I have to fear; who, or what, is the other?"

"The other is givin' way afore your own good sense and judgment, I find, Judith; yes, he's not as dangerous as I supposed. Howsever, havin' opened the subject, it will be as well to end it honestly. The first inimy you have to be watchful of, as I've already told you, Judith, is oncommon good looks, and the next is an oncommon knowledge of the sarcumstance. If the first is bad, the last doesn't in any way mend the matter, so far as safety and peace of mind are consarned."

How much longer the young man would have gone on in his simple and unsuspecting, but well-intentioned manner, it might not be easy to say, had he not been interrupted by his listener's bursting into tears, and giving way to an outbreak of feeling, which was so much the more violent from the fact that it had been with so much difficulty suppressed. At first her sobs were so violent and uncontrollable that Deerslayer was a little appalled, and he was abundantly repentant from the instant that he discovered how much greater was the effect produced by his words than he had anticipated. Even the austere and exacting are usually appeased by the signs of contrition, but the nature of Deerslayer did not require proofs of intense feeling so strong, in order to bring him down to a level with the regrets felt by the girl herself. He arose as if an adder had stung him, and the accents of the mother that soothes her child were scarcely more gentle and winning than the tones of his voice, as he now expressed his contrition at having gone so far.

"It was well meant, Judith," he said, "but it was not intended to hurt your feelin's so much. I have overdone the advice, I see; yes, I've overdone it, and I crave your pardon for the same. Fri'ndship's an awful thing! Sometimes it chides us for not having done enough; and then ag'in it speaks in strong words for havin' done too much. Howsever, I acknowledge I've overdone the matter, and as I've a ra'al and strong regard for you, I rej'ice to say it, inasmuch as it proves how much better you are than my own vanity and consaits had made you out to be."

Judith now moved her hands from her face, her tears had ceased, and she unveiled a countenance so winning, with the smile which rendered it even radiant, that the young man gazed at her for a moment with speechless delight.

"Say no more, Deerslayer," she hastily interposed, "it pains me to hear you find fault with yourself. I know my own weakness all the better, now I see that you have discovered it; the lesson, bitter as I have found it for a moment, shall not be forgotten. We will not talk any longer of these things, I do not feel myself brave enough for the undertaking, and I should not like the Delawares, or Hist, or even Hetty, to notice my weakness. Farewell, Deerslayer; may God bless and protect you as your honest heart deserves blessing and protection, and as I must think he will."

Judith had so far regained the superiority that properly belonged to her better education, high spirit, and surpassing personal advantages, as to preserve the ascendency she had thus accidentally obtained, and effectually prevented any return to the subject that was as singularly interrupted as it had been singularly introduced. The young man permitted her to have everything her own way, and when she pressed his hard hand in both her own, he made no resistance, but submitted to the homage as quietly, and with quite as matter of course a manner, as a sovereign would have received a similar tribute from a subject, or the mistress from her suitor. Feeling had flushed the face and illuminated the whole countenance of the girl, and her beauty was never more resplendent than when she cast a parting glance at the youth. That glance was filled with anxiety, interest, and gentle pity. At the next instant she darted into the hut and was seen no more; though she spoke to Hist from a window, to inform her that their friend expected her appearance.

"You know enough of redskin natur' and redskin usages, Wah-ta-Wah, to see the condition I am in on account of this furlough," commenced the hunter, in Delaware, as soon as the patient and submissive girl of that people had moved quietly to his side; "you will therefore best understand how onlikely I am ever to talk with you ag'in. I've but little to say; but that little comes from long livin' among your people, and from havin' observed and noted their usages. The life of a woman is hard at the best, but, I must own, though I'm not opinionated in favor of my own color, that it is harder among the red men than it is among the palefaces. This is a point on which Christians may well boast, if boasting can be set down for Christianity in any manner or form, which I rather think it cannot. Howsever, all women have their trials. Red women have their'n in what I should call the nat'ral way, while white women take 'em inoculated like. Bear your burden, Hist, becomingly, and remember, if it be a little toilsome, how much lighter it is than that of most Indian women. I know the Sarpent well—what I call cordially—and he will never be a tyrant to anything he loves, though he will expect to be treated himself like a Mohican chief. There will be cloudy days in your lodge, I suppose, for they happen under all usages, and among all people; but, by keepin' the windows of the heart open, there will always be room for the sunshine to enter. You come of a great stock yourself, and so does Chingachgook. It's not very likely that either will ever forget the sarcumstance, and do anything to disgrace your forefathers. Nevertheless, likin' is a tender plant, and never thrives long when watered with tears. Let the 'arth around your married happiness be moistened by the dews of kindness."

"My pale brother is very wise; Wah will keep in her mind all that his wisdom tells her."

"That's judicious and womanly, Hist. Care in listening, and stoutheartedness in holding to good counsel, is a wife's great protection. And, now, ask the Sarpent to come and speak with me, for a moment, and carry away with you all my best wishes and prayers. I shall think of you, Hist, and of your intended husband, let what may come to pass, and always wish you well, here and hereafter, whether the last is to be according to Indian idees or Christian doctrines."

Hist shed no tears at parting. She was sustained by the high resolution of one who had decided on her course; but her dark eyes were luminous with the feelings that glowed within, and her pretty countenance beamed with an expression of determination that was in marked and singular contrast to its ordinary gentleness. It was but a minute ere the Delaware advanced to the side of his friend with the light, noiseless tread of an Indian.

"Come this-a-way, Sarpent, here more out of sight of the women," commenced the Deerslayer, "for I've several things to say that mustn't so much as be suspected, much less overheard. *You* know too well the natur' of furloughs and Mingoes to have any doubts or misgivin's consarnin' what is likely to happen, when I get back to the camp. On them two p'ints, therefore, a few words will go a great way. In the first place, chief, I wish to say a little about Hist, and the manner in which you red men treat your wives. I suppose it's accordin' to the gifts of your people that the women should work, and the men hunt; but there's such a thing as moderation in all matters. As for huntin', I see no good reason why any limits need be set to *that*, but Hist comes of too good a stock to toil like a common drudge. One of your means and standin' need never want for corn, or potatoes, or anything that the fields yield; therefore, I hope the hoe will never be put into the hands of any wife of your'n. You know I am not quite a beggar, and all I own, whether in ammunition, skins, arms, or calicoes, I give to Hist, should I not come back to claim them by the end of the season. This will set the maiden up, and will buy labor for her, for a long time to come. I suppose I needn't tell you to love the young woman, for that you do already, and whosever the man ra'ally loves, he'll be likely enough to cherish. Nevertheless, it can do no harm to say that kind words never rankle, while bitter words do. I know you're a man, Sarpent, that is less apt to talk in his own lodge than to speak at the council fire; but forgetful moments may overtake us all, and the practyce of kind doin', and kind talkin', is a wonderful advantage in keepin' peace in a cabin, as well as on a hunt."

"My ears are open," returned the Delaware, gravely; "the words of my brother have entered so far that they never can fall out again. They are like rings that have no end, and cannot drop. Let him speak on; the song of the wren and the voice of a friend never tire."

"I will speak a little longer, chief, but you will excuse it for the sake of old companionship, should I now talk about myself. If the worst comes to the worst, it's not likely there'll be much left of me but ashes; so a grave would be useless, and a sort of vanity. On that score I'm no way partic'lar, though it might be well enough to take a look at the remains of the pile, and should any bones or pieces be found, 'twould be more decent to gather them together and bury them than to let them lie for the wolves to gnaw at and howl over. These matters can make no great difference in the ind, but men of white blood and Christian feelin's have rather a gift for graves."

"It shall be done as my brother says," returned the Indian, gravely. "If his mind is full let him empty it in the bosom of a friend."

"Thank you, Sarpent; my mind's easy enough; yes, it's tolerable easy. Idees will come uppermost that I'm not apt to think about in common, it's true; but by striving ag'in some, and lettin' others come out, all will be right in the long run. There's one thing, howsever, chief, that *does* seem to be *on*reasonable, and ag'in natur', though the missionaries say it's true; and bein' of my religion and color, I feel bound to believe them. They say an Injin may torment and tortur' the body to the heart's content, and scalp, and cut, and tear, and burn, and consume all his inventions and diviltries, until nothin' is left but ashes, and they shall be scattered to the four winds of heaven, yet, when the trumpet of God shall sound, all will come together ag'in, and the man will stand forth in his flesh the same creatur' as to looks, if not as to feelin's, that he was afore he was harmed!"

"The missionaries are good men; they mean well," returned the Delaware, courteously; "they are not great medicines. They think all they say, Deerslayer; that is no reason why warriors and orators should be all ears. When Chingachgook shall see the father of Tamenund standing in his scalp, and paint, and warlock, then will he believe the missionaries."

"Seein' *is* believin', of a sartainty—ah's me! and some of us may see these things sooner than we thought. I comprehend your meanin' about Tamenund's father, Sarpent, and the idee's a close idee. Tamenund is now an elderly man, say eighty, every day of it; and his father was scalped, and tormented, and burnt when the present prophet was a youngster. Yes, if one could see *that* come to pass, there wouldn't be much difficulty in yieldin' faith to all that the missionaries say. Howsever, I'm not ag'in the opinion now; for you must know, Sarpent, that the great principle of Christianity is to believe *without* seeing; and a man should always act up to his religion and principles, let them be what they may."

"That is strange for a wise nation," said the Delaware, with emphasis. "The red man looks hard, that he may *see* and understand."

"Yes, that's plauserble and is agreeable to mortal pride; but it's not as deep as it seems. If we could understand *all* we see, Sarpent, there might be not only sense, but safety, in refusin' to give faith to any *one* thing that we might find oncomprehensible; but when there's so many things about which it may be said we know nothing at all, why, there's little use and no reason in bein' difficult touchin' any one in partic'lar. For my part, Delaware, all my thoughts haven't been on the game, when outlyin' in the hunts and scoutin's of our youth. Many's the hour I've passed, pleasantly enough too, in what is tarmed conterplation by my people. On such occasions the mind is actyve, though the body seems lazy and listless. An open spot on a mountainside, where a wide look can be had at the heavens and the 'arth, is a most judicious place for a man to get a just idee of the power of the Manitou, and of his own littleness. At such times there isn't any great disposition to find fault with little difficulties in the way of comprehension, as there are so many big ones to hide them. Believin' comes easy enough to me, at such times; and if the Lord made man first, out of 'arth, as they tell me it is written in the Bible, then turns him into dust at death, I see no great difficulty in the way to bringin' him back in the body, though ashes be the only substance left. These things lie beyond our understandin', though they may and do lie so close to our feelin's. But of all the doctrines, Sarpent, that which disturbs me, and disconsarts my mind the most, is the one which teaches us to think that a paleface goes to one heaven and a redskin to another; it may separate in death them which lived much together, and loved each other well in life!"

"Do the missionaries teach their white brethren to think it is so?" demanded the Indian, with serious earnestness. "The Delawares believe that good men and brave warriors will hunt together in the same pleasant woods, let them belong to whatever tribe they may; that all the unjust Indians, and cowards, will have to sneak in with the dogs and the wolves, to get venison for their lodges."

" 'Tis wonderful how many consaits mankind have consarnin' happiness and misery, hereafter!" exclaimed the hunter, borne away by the power of his own thoughts. "Some believe in burnin's and flames, and some think punishment is to eat with the wolves and dogs. Then, ag'in, some fancy heaven to be only the carryin' out of their own 'arthly longin's; while others fancy it all gold and shinin' lights! Well, I've an idee of my own, in that matter, which is just this, Sarpent. Whenever I've done wrong, I've gin'rally found 'twas owin' to some blindness of the mind, which hid the right from view, and when sight has returned, then has come sorrow and repentance. Now, I consait that, after death, when the body is laid aside, or, if used at all, is purified and without its longin's, the spirit sees all things in their ra'al light, and never becomes blind to truth and justice. Such bein' the case, all that has been done in life, is beheld as plainly as the sun is seen at noon; the good brings joy, while the evil brings sorrow. There's nothin' onreasonable in that, but it's agreeable to every man's experience."

"I thought the palefaces believed *all* men were wicked; who then could ever find the white man's heaven?"

"That's ingen'ous, but it falls short of the missionary teachin's. You'll be Christianized one day, I make no doubt, and then 'twill all come plain enough. You must know, Sarpent, that there's been a great deed of salvation done, that, by God's help, enables all men to find a pardon for their wickedness, and *that* is the essence of the white man's religion. I can't stop to talk this matter over with you any longer, for Hetty's in the canoe, and the furlough takes me away; but the time will come, I hope, when you'll *feel* these things; for, after all, they must be *felt*, rather than reasoned about. Ah's me! well, Delaware, there's my hand, you know it's that of a fri'nd, and will shake it as such, though it never has done you one half the good its owner wishes it had."

The Indian took the offered hand, and returned its pressure warmly. Then falling back on his acquired stoicism of manner, which so many mistake for constitutional indifference, he drew up in reserve, and prepared to part from his friend with dignity. Deerslayer, however, was more natural; nor would he have at all cared about giving way to his feelings, had not the recent conduct and language of Judith given him some secret, though ill-defined apprehensions of a scene. He was too humble to imagine the truth concerning the actual feelings of that beautiful girl, while he was too observant not to have noted the struggle she had maintained with herself, and which had so often led her to the very verge of discovery. That something extraordinary was concealed in her breast, he thought obvious enough; and, through a sentiment of manly delicacy that would have done credit to the highest human refinement, he shrank from any exposure of her secret that might subsequently cause regret to the girl herself. He therefore determined to depart now, and that without any further manifestations of feeling, either from himself or from others.

"God bless you! Sarpent—God bless you!" cried the hunter, as the canoe left the side of the platform. "Your Manitou and my God only knows when and where we shall meet ag'in; I shall count it a great blessing, and a full reward for any little good I may have done on 'arth, if we shall be permitted to know each other, and to consort together, hereafter, as we have so long done in these pleasant woods afore us!"

Chingachgook waved his hand. Drawing the light blanket he wore over his head, as a Roman would conceal his grief in his robes, he slowly withdrew into the ark, in order to indulge his sorrow and his musings alone.

11

WHILE DEERSLAYER and Hetty slowly paddled to the shore, they kept up an earnest conversation. The frontiersman warned the girl that the Hurons would put him to death, for "the tribe would reproach them if they failed to send the spirit of a paleface to keep the company of the spirit of their red brother," so lately slain by his hand. He urged Hetty to leave the scene when his torture began. Then, as a final word, he warned Hetty against Hurry Harry, saying that the man was insincere and untrustworthy. "A young woman without parents, in your state of mind, and who is not without beauty, must always be in danger in such a lawless region as this."

As high noon approached, Deerslayer paddled faster to keep his appointment with the vengeful Hurons.

One experienced in the signs of the heavens would have seen that the sun wanted but two or three minutes of the zenith, when Deerslayer landed on the point where the Hurons were now encamped, nearly abreast of the castle. This spot was similar to the one already described, with the exception that the surface of the land was less broken and less crowded with trees. Owing to these two circumstances, it was all the better suited to the purpose for which it had been selected, the space beneath the branches bearing some resemblance to a densely wooded lawn. Favored by its position and its spring, it had been much resorted to by savages and hunters, and the natural grasses had succeeded their fires, leaving an appearance of sward in places, a very unusual accompaniment of the virgin forest. Nor was the margin of water fringed with bushes as on so much of its shore, but the eye penetrated the woods immediately on reaching the strand, commanding nearly the whole area of the projection.

If it was a point of honor with the Indian warrior to redeem his word, when pledged to return and meet his death at a given hour, so was it a point of characteristic pride to show no womanish impatience, but to reappear as nearly as possible at the appointed moment. It was well not to exceed the grace accorded by the generosity of the enemy, but it was better to meet it to a minute. Something of this dramatic effect mingles with most of the graver usages of the American aborigines, and no doubt, like the prevalence of a similar feeling among people more sophisticated and refined, may be referred to a principle of nature. We all love the wonderful, and when it comes attended by chivalrous self-devotion and a rigid regard to honor, it presents itself to our admiration in a shape doubly attractive. As respects Deerslayer, though he took a pride in showing his white blood, by often deviating from the usages of the red men, he frequently dropped into their customs, and oftener into their feelings, unconsciously to himself, in consequence of having no other arbiters to appeal to, than their judgments and tastes. On the present occasion, he would have abstained from betraying a feverish haste by a too speedy return, since it would have contained a tacit admission that the time asked for was more than had been wanted; but, on the other hand, had the idea occurred to him, he would have quickened his movements a little in order to avoid the dramatic appearance of returning at the precise instant set as the utmost limit of his absence. Still, accident had interfered to defeat the last intention, for when the young man put his foot on the point, and advanced with a steady tread toward the group of chiefs that was seated in grave array on a fallen tree, the oldest of their number cast his eye upward at an opening in the trees, and pointed out to his companions the startling fact that the sun was just entering a space that was known to mark the zenith. A common, but low exclamation of surprise and admiration escaped every mouth, and the grim warriors looked at each other; some with envy and disappointment, some with astonishment, at the precise accuracy of their victim, and others with a more generous and liberal feeling. The American Indian always deemed his moral victories the noblest, prizing the groans and yielding of his victim under torture more than the trophy of his scalp; and the trophy itself more than his life. To slay, and not to bring off the proof of victory, indeed, was scarcely deemed honorable; even these rude and fierce tenants of the forest, like their more nurtured brethren of the court and the camp, having set up for themselves imaginary and arbitrary points of honor, to supplant the conclusions of the right, and the decisions of reason.

The Hurons had been divided in their opinions concerning the probability of their captive's return. Most among them, indeed, had not expected it possible for a paleface to come back voluntarily, and meet the known penalties of an Indian torture; but a few of the seniors expected better things from one who had already shown himself so singularly cool, brave, and upright. The party had come to its decision, however, less in the expectation of finding the pledge redeemed, than in the hope of disgracing the Delawares by casting into their teeth the delinquency of one bred in their villages. They would have greatly preferred that Chingachgook should be their prisoner, and prove the traitor; but the paleface scion of the hated stock was no bad substitute for their purposes, failing in their designs against the ancient stem. With a view to render the triumph as signal as possible, in the event of the hour's passing without the reappearance of the hunter, all the warriors and scouts of the party had been called in; and the whole band, men, women, and children, was now assembled at this single point, to be a witness of the expected scene. As the castle was in plain view, and by no means distant, it was easily watched by daylight; and it being thought that its inmates were now limited to Hurry, the Delaware, and the two girls, no apprehensions were felt of their being able to escape unseen. A large raft, having a breastwork of logs, had been prepared, and was in actual readiness to be used against either ark or castle, as occasion might require, as soon as the fate of Deerslayer was determined; the seniors of the party having come to the opinion that it was getting to be hazardous to delay their departure for Canada beyond the coming night. In short, the band awaited merely to dispose of this single affair, ere it brought matters to a crisis, and prepared to commence its retreat toward the distant waters of Ontario.

It was an imposing scene, into which Deerslayer now found himself advancing. All the older warriors were seated on the trunk of the fallen tree, waiting his approach with grave decorum. On the right stood the young men, armed, while the left was occupied by the women and children. In the center was an open space of considerable extent, always canopied by leaves, but from which the underbrush, dead wood, and other obstacles had been carefully removed. The more open area had probably been much used by former parties, for this was the place where the appearance of a sward was the most decided. The arches of the woods, even at high noon, cast their somber shadows on the spot, which the brilliant rays of the sun that struggled through the leaves contributed to mellow, and, if such an expression can be used, to illuminate. It was probably from a similar scene that the mind of man first got its idea of the effects of Gothic tracery and churchly hues; this temple of nature producing some such effect, so far as light and shadows were concerned, as the well-known offspring of human invention.

As was not unusual among the tribes and wandering bands of the aborigines, two chiefs shared, in nearly equal degrees, the principal and primitive authority that was wielded over these children of the forest. There were several who might claim the distinction of being chief men, but the two in question were so much superior to all the rest in influence, that when they agreed, no one disputed their mandates; and when they were divided, the band hesitated, like men who had lost their governing principle of action. It was also in conformity with practice—perhaps we might add, in conformity with nature, that one of the chiefs was indebted to his mind for his influence, whereas the other owed his distinction altogether to qualities that were physical. One was a senior, well known for eloquence in debate, wisdom in council, and prudence in measures; while his competitor, if not his rival, was a brave, distinguished in war, notorious for ferocity, and remarkable, in the way of intellect, for nothing but the cunning and expedients of the warpath. The first was Rivenoak, who has already been introduced to the reader, while the last was called Le Panthère, in the language of the Canadas; or the Panther, to resort to the vernacular of the English colonies. The appellation of the fighting chief was supposed to indicate the qualities of the warrior, agreeably to a practice of the red man's nomenclature; ferocity, cunning, and treachery being, perhaps, the distinctive features of his character. The title had been received from the French, and was prized so much the more from that circumstance, the Indian submitting profoundly to the greater intelligence of his paleface allies, in most things of this nature. How well the *sobriquet* was merited, will be seen in the sequel.

Rivenoak and the Panther sat side by side, awaiting the approach of their prisoner, as Deerslayer put his moccasined foot on the strand; nor did either move or utter a syllable until the young man had advanced into the center of the area, and proclaimed his presence with his voice. This was done firmly, though in a simple manner that marked the character of the individual.

"Here I am, Mingoes," he said, in the dialect of the Delawares, a language that most present understood; "here I am, and there is the sun. One is not more true to the laws of natur', than the other has proved true to his word. I am your prisoner; do with me what you please. My business with man and 'arth is settled; nothing remains now but to meet the white man's God, accordin' to a white man's duties and gifts."

A murmur of approbation escaped even the women at this address, and, for an instant, there was a strong and pretty general desire to adopt into the tribe one who owned so brave a spirit. Still there were dissenters from this wish, among the principal of whom might be classed the Panther, and his sister, Le Sumach, so called from the number of her children, who was the widow of Le Loup Cervier, now known to have fallen by the hand of the captive. Native ferocity held one in subjection, while the corroding passion of revenge prevented the other from admitting any gentler feeling at the moment. Not so with Rivenoak. This chief arose, stretched his arm before him, in a gesture of courtesy, and paid his compliments with an ease and dignity that a prince might have envied. As, in that band, his wisdom and eloquence were confessedly without rivals, he knew that on himself would properly fall the duty of first replying to the speech of the paleface.

"Paleface, you are honest," said the Huron orator. "My people are happy in having captured a man, and not a skulking fox. We now know you; we shall treat you like a brave. If you have slain one of our warriors, and helped to kill others, you have a life of your own ready to give away in return. Some of my young men thought that the blood of a paleface was too thin; that it would refuse to run under the Huron knife. You will show them it is not so; your heart is stout as well as your body. It is a pleasure to make such a prisoner; should my warriors say that the death of Le Loup Cervier ought not to be forgotten, and that he cannot travel toward the land of spirits alone, that his enemy must be sent to overtake him, they will remember that he fell by the hand of a brave, and send you after him with such signs of our friendship as shall not make him ashamed to keep your company. I have spoken; you know what I have said."

"True enough, Mingo, all true as the Gospel," returned the simple-minded hunter; "you *have* spoken, and I *do* know not only what you have *said*, but, what is still more important, what you *mean*. I dare say your warrior, the Lynx, was a stouthearted brave, and worthy of your fri'ndship and respect, but I do not feel unworthy to keep his company, without any passport from your hands. Nevertheless, I am ready to receive judgment from your council, if, indeed, the matter was not determined among you, afore I got back."

"My old men would not sit in council over a paleface until they saw him among them," answered Rivenoak, looking around him a little ironically; "they said it would be like sitting in council over the winds; they go where they will, and come back as they see fit, and not otherwise. There was one voice that spoke in your favor, Deerslayer, but it was alone, like the wren whose mate has been struck by the hawk."

"I thank that voice, whosever it may have been, Mingo, and will say it was as true a voice, as the rest were lying voices. A furlough is as binding on a paleface, if he be honest, as it is on a redskin; and was it not so, I would never bring disgrace on the Delawares, among whom I may be said to have received my edication. But words are useless, and lead to braggin' feelin's; here I am; act your will on me."

Rivenoak made a sign of acquiescence, and then a short conference was privately held among the chiefs. As soon as the latter ended, three or four young men fell back from among the armed group, and disappeared. Then it was signified to the prisoner that he was at liberty to go at large on the point, until a council was held concerning his fate. There was more of seeming, than of real confidence, however, in this apparent liberality, inasmuch as the young men mentioned already formed a line of sentinels across the breadth of the point, inland, and escape from any other part was out of the question. Even the canoe was removed beyond this line of sentinels, to a spot where it was considered safe from any sudden attempt. These precautions did not proceed from a failure of confidence, but from the circumstance that the prisoner had now complied with all the required conditions of his parole, and it would have been considered a commendable and honorable exploit to escape from his foes. So nice, indeed, were the distinctions drawn by the savages, in cases of this nature, that they often gave their victims a chance to evade the torture, deeming it as creditable to the captors to overtake, or to outwit a fugitive, when his exertions were supposed to be quickened by the extreme jeopardy of his situation, as it was for him to get clear from so much extraordinary vigilance.

Nor was Deerslayer unconscious of, or forgetful of, his rights, and of his opportunities. Could he now have seen any probable opening for an escape, the attempt would not have been delayed a minute. But the case seemed desperate. He was aware of the line of sentinels, and felt the difficulty of breaking through it, unharmed. The lake offered no advantages, as the canoe would have given his foes the greatest facilities for overtaking him; else would he have found it no difficult task to swim as far as the castle. As he walked about the point, he even examined the spot to ascertain if it offered no place of concealment; but its openness, its size, and the hundred watchful glances that were turned toward him, even while those who made them affected not to see him, prevented any such expedient from succeeding. The dread and disgrace of failure had no influence on Deerslayer, who deemed it ever a point of honor to reason and feel like white men, rather than as an Indian, and who felt it as a sort of duty to do all he could, that did not involve a dereliction from principle, in order to save his life. Still he hesitated about making the effort, for he also felt that he ought to see the chance of success before he committed himself.

In the meantime the business of the camp appeared to proceed in its regular train. The chiefs consulted apart, admitting no one but the Sumach to their councils; for she, the widow of the fallen warrior, had an exclusive right to be heard on such an occasion. The young men strolled about in indolent listlessness, awaiting the result with Indian impatience, while the females prepared the feast that was to celebrate the termination of the affair, whether it proved fortunate or otherwise for our hero. No one betrayed feeling; and an indifferent observer, beyond the extreme watchfulness of the sentinels, would have detected no extraordinary movement or sensation to denote the real state of things. Two or three old women put their heads together, and it appeared unfavorably to the prospect of Deerslayer, by their scowling looks and angry gestures; but a group of Indian girls were evidently animated by a different impulse, as was apparent by stolen glances that expressed pity and regret. In this condition of the camp, an hour soon glided away.

Suspense is, perhaps, the feeling of all others, that is most difficult to be supported. When Deerslayer landed, he fully expected in the course of a few minutes to undergo the tortures of an Indian revenge, and he was prepared to meet his fate manfully; but the delay proved far more trying than the nearer approach of suffering, and the intended victim began seriously to meditate some desperate effort at escape, as it might be from sheer anxiety to terminate the scene, when he was suddenly summoned to appear, once more, in front of his judges, who had already arranged the band in its former order, in readiness to receive him.

"Killer of the Deer," commenced Rivenoak, as soon as his captive stood before him, "my aged men have listened to wise words; they are ready to speak. You are a man whose fathers came from beyond the rising sun; we are children of the setting sun; we turn our faces toward the Great Sweet Lakes when we look toward our villages. It may be a wise country and full of riches toward the morning, but it is very pleasant toward the evening. We love most to look in that direction. When we gaze at the east we feel afraid, canoe after canoe bringing more and more of your people in the track of the sun, as if their land was so full as to run over. The red men are few already; they have need of help. One of our best lodges has lately been emptied by the death of its master; it will be a long time before his son can grow big enough to sit in his place. There is his widow! she will want venison to feed her and her children, for her sons are yet like the young of the robin before they quit the nest. By your hand has this great calamity befallen her. She has two duties; one to Le Loup Cervier, and one to his children. Scalp for scalp, life for life, blood for blood, is one law; to feed her young another. We know you, Killer of the Deer. You are honest; when you say a thing, it is so. You have but one tongue, and that is not forked like a snake's. Your head is never hid in the grass; all can see it. What you say, that will you do. You are just. When you have done wrong, it is your wish to do right again as soon as you can. Here is the Sumach; she is alone in her wigwam, with children crying around her for food; yonder is a rifle, it is loaded and ready to be fired. Take the gun; go forth and shoot a deer; bring the venison and lay it before the widow of Le Loup Cervier; feed her children; call yourself her husband. After which, your heart will no longer be Delaware but Huron; Le Sumach's ears will not hear the cries of her children; my people will count the proper number of warriors."

"I feared this, Rivenoak," answered Deerslayer, when the other had ceased speaking; "yes, I did dread that it would come to this. Howsever, the truth is soon told, and that will put an end to all expectations on this head. Mingo, I'm white, and Christian-born; 'twould ill become me to take a wife, under redskin forms, from among heathen. That which I wouldn't do in peaceable times, and under a bright sun, still less would I do behind clouds, in order to save my life. I may never marry; most likely Providence, in putting me up here in the woods, has intended I should live single, and without a lodge of my own; but should such a thing come to pass, none but a woman of my own color and gifts shall darken the door of my wigwam. As for feeding the young of your dead warrior, I would do that cheerfully, could it be done without discredit; but it cannot, seeing that I can never live in a Huron village. Your own young men must find the Sumach in venison, and the next time she marries, let her take a husband whose legs are not long enough to overrun territory that don't belong to him. We fou't a fair battle, and he fell; in this there is nothin' but what a brave expects, and should be ready to meet. As for getting a Mingo heart, as well might you expect to see gray hairs on a boy, or the blackberry growing on the pine. No, no, Huron; my gifts are white, so far as wives are consarned; it is Delaware in all things touchin' Injins."

These words were scarcely out of the mouth of Deerslayer, before a common murmur betrayed the dissatisfaction with which they had been heard. The aged women, in particular, were loud in their expressions of disgust; and the gentle Sumach herself, a woman quite old enough to be our hero's mother, was not the least pacific in her denunciations. But all the other manifestations of disappointment and discontent were thrown into the background, by the fierce resentment of the Panther. This grim chief had thought it a degradation to permit his sister to become the wife of a paleface of the Yengeese, at all, and had only given a reluctant consent to the arrangement—one by no means unusual among the Indians, however—at the earnest solicitations of the bereaved widow; and it goaded him to the quick to find his condescension slighted, the honor he had with so much regret been persuaded to accord, contemned. The animal from which he got his name does not glare on his intended prey with more frightful ferocity, than his eyes gleamed on the captive; nor was his arm backward in seconding the fierce resentment that almost consumed his breast.

"Dog of the palefaces!" he exclaimed, in Iroquois, "go yell among the curs of your own evil hunting grounds!"

The denunciation was accompanied by an appropriate action. Even while speaking, his arm was lifted and the tomahawk hurled. Luckily the loud tones of the speaker had drawn the eye of Deerslayer toward him, else would that moment have probably closed his career. So great was the dexterity with which this dangerous weapon was thrown, and so deadly the intent, that it would have riven the skull of the prisoner, had he not stretched forth an arm, and caught the handle in one of its turns, with a readiness quite as remarkable as the skill with which the missile had been hurled. The projectile force was so great, notwithstanding, that when Deerslayer's arm was arrested, his hand was raised above and behind his own head, and in the very attitude necessary to return the attack. It is not certain whether the circumstance of finding himself unexpectedly in this menacing posture and armed, tempted the young man to retaliate, or whether sudden resentment overcame his forbearance and prudence. His eye kindled, however, and a small red spot appeared on each cheek, while he cast all his energy into the effort of his arm, and threw back the weapon at his assailant. The unexpectedness of this blow contributed to its success; the Panther neither raising an arm nor bending his head to avoid it. The keen little ax struck the victim in a perpendicular line with the nose, directly between the eyes, literally braining him on the spot. Sallying forward, as the serpent darts at its enemy even while receiving its own death wound, this man of powerful frame fell his length into the open area formed by the circle, quivering in death. A common rush to his relief left the captive, for a single instant, quite without the crowd; and, willing to make one desperate effort for life, be bounded off with the activity of a deer. There was but a breathless instant, when the whole band, old and young, women and children, abandoning the lifeless body of the Panther where it lay, raised the yell of alarm, and followed in pursuit.

Sudden as had been the event which induced Deerslayer to make this desperate trial of speed, his mind was not wholly unprepared for the fearful emergency. In the course of the past hour, he had pondered well on the chances of such an experiment, and had shrewdly calculated all the details of success and failure. At the first leap, therefore, his body was completely under the direction of an intelligence that turned all its efforts to the best account, and prevented everything like hesitation or indecision, at the important instant of the start. To this alone was he indebted for the first great advantage, that of getting through the line of sentinels unharmed. The manner in which this was done, though sufficiently simple, merits a description.

Although the shores of the point were not fringed with bushes, as was the case with most of the others on the lake, it was owing altogether to the circumstance that the spot had been so much used by hunters and fishermen. This fringe commenced on what might be termed the mainland, and was as dense as usual, extending in long lines both north and south. In the latter direction, then, Deerslayer held his way; and, as the sentinels were a little without the commencement of this thicket before the alarm was clearly communicated to them, the fugitive had gained its cover. To run among the bushes, however, was out of the question, and Deerslayer held his way for some forty or fifty yards in the water, which was barely knee-deep, offering as great an obstacle to the speed of his pursuers as it did to his own. As soon as a favorable spot presented, he darted through the line of bushes, and issued into the open woods.

Several rifles were discharged at Deerslayer while in the water, and more followed as he came out into the comparative exposure of the clear forest. But the direction of his line of flight which partially crossed that of the fire, the haste with which the weapons had been aimed, and the general confusion that prevailed in the camp, prevented any harm from being done. Bullets whistled past him, and many cut twigs from the branches at his side, but not one touched even his dress. The delay caused by these fruitless attempts was of great service to the fugitive, who had gained more than a hundred yards on even the leading men of the Hurons, ere something like concert and order had entered into the chase. To think of following with rifle in hand was out of the question; and after emptying their pieces in vague hope of wounding their captive, the best runners of the Indians threw them aside, calling out to the women and boys to recover and load them again, as soon as possible.

Deerslayer knew too well the desperate nature of the struggle in which he was engaged, to lose one of the precious moments. He also knew that his only hope was to run in a straight line, for as soon as he began to turn, or double, the greater number of his pursuers would put escape out of the question. He held his way, therefore, in a diagonal direction up the acclivity, which was neither very high nor very steep, in this part of the mountain, but which was sufficiently toilsome for one contending for life, to render it painfully oppressive. There, however, he slackened his speed, to recover breath, proceeding even at a quick walk, or a slow trot, along the more difficult parts of the way. The Hurons were whooping and leaping behind him; but this he disregarded, well knowing they must overcome the difficulties he had surmounted, ere they could reach the elevation to which he had attained. The summit of the first hill was now quite near him, and he saw, by the formation of the land, that a deep glen intervened, before the base of a second hill could be reached. Walking deliberately to the summit, he glanced eagerly about him, in every direction, in quest of a cover. None offered in the ground; but a fallen tree lay near him, and desperate circumstances required desperate remedies. This tree lay in a line parallel to the glen, at the brow of the hill; to leap on it, and then to force his person as close as possible under its lower side, took but a moment. Previously to disappearing from his pursuers, however, Deerslayer stood on the height, and gave a cry of triumph, as if exulting at the sight of the descent that lay before him. In the next instant he was stretched beneath the tree.

No sooner was this expedient adopted, than the young man ascertained how desperate had been his own efforts, by the violence of the pulsation in his frame. He could hear his heart beat, and his breathing was like the action of a bellows in quick motion. Breath was gained, however, and the heart soon ceased to throb as if about to break through its confinement. The footsteps of those who toiled up the opposite side of the acclivity were now audible, and presently voices and treads announced the arrival of the pursuers. The foremost shouted as they reached the height; then, fearful that their enemy would escape under favor of the descent, each leaped upon the fallen tree, and plunged into the ravine, trusting to get a sight of the pursued, ere he reached the bottom. In this manner, Huron followed Huron, until Natty began to hope the whole had passed. Others succeeded, however, until quite forty had leaped over the tree; and then he counted them, as the surest mode of ascertaining how many could be behind. Presently all were in the bottom of the glen, quite a hundred feet below him, and some had even ascended part of the opposite hill, when it became evident an inquiry was making, as to the direction he had taken. This was the critical moment; and one of nerves less steady, or of a training that had been neglected, would have seized it to rise and fly. Not so with Deerslayer. He still lay quiet, watching with jealous vigilance every movement below, and fast regaining his breath.

The Hurons now resembled a pack of hounds at fault. Little was said, but each man ran about, examining the dead leaves, as the hound hunts for the lost scent. The great number of moccasins that had passed made the examination difficult, though the in-toe of an Indian was easily to be distinguished from the freer and wider step of a white man. Believing that no more pursuers remained behind, and hoping to steal away unseen, Deerslayer suddenly threw himself over the tree, and fell on the upper side. This achievement appeared to be effected successfully, and hope beat high in the bosom of the fugitive. Rising to his hands and feet, after a moment lost in listening to the sounds in the glen, in order to ascertain if he had been seen, the young man next scrambled to the top of the hill, a distance of only ten yards, in the expectation of getting its brow between him and his pursuers, and himself so far under cover. Even this was effected, and he rose to his feet, walking swiftly but steadily along the summit, in a direction opposite to that in which he had first fled. The nature of the calls in the glen, however, soon made him uneasy, and he sprang upon the summit, again, in order to reconnoiter. No sooner did he reach the height than he was seen, and the chase renewed. As it was better footing on the level ground, Deerslayer now avoided the sidehill, holding his flight along the ridge; while the Hurons, judging from the general formation of the land, saw that the ridge would soon melt into the hollow, and kept to the latter, as the easiest mode of heading the fugitive. A few, at the same time, turned south, with a view to prevent his escaping in that direction; while some crossed his trail toward the water, in order to prevent his retreat by the lake, running southerly.

The situation of Deerslayer was now more critical than it ever had been. He was virtually surrounded on three sides, having the lake on the fourth. But he had pondered well on all the chances, and took his measures with coolness, even while at the top of his speed. As is generally the case with the vigorous border-men, he could outrun any single Indian among his pursuers, who were principally formidable to him on account of their numbers, and the advantages they possessed in position; and he would not have hesitated to break off, in a straight line, at any spot, could he have got the whole band again fairly behind him. But no such chance did, or indeed could now offer; and when he found that he was descending toward the glen, by the melting away of the ridge, he turned short, at right angles to his previous course, and went down the declivity with tremendous velocity, holding his way toward the shore. Some of his pursuers came panting up the hill, in direct chase, while most still kept on, in the ravine, intending to head him at its termination. Deerslayer had now a different, though a desperate project in view. Abandoning all thoughts of escape by the woods, he made the best of his way toward the canoe. He knew where it lay: could it be reached, he had only to run the gauntlet of a few rifles, and success would be certain. None of the warriors had kept their weapons, which would have retarded their speed, and the risk would come either from the uncertain hands of the women, or from those of some well-grown boy; though most of the latter were already out in hot pursuit. Everything seemed propitious to the execution of this plan, and the course being a continued descent, the young man went over the ground at a rate that promised a speedy termination to his toil.

As Deerslayer approached the point, several women and children were passed, but, though the former endeavored to cast dried branches between his legs, the terror inspired by his bold retaliation on the redoubted Panther was so great, that none dared come near enough seriously to molest him. He went by all triumphantly, and reached the fringe of bushes. Plunging through these, our hero found himself once more in the lake and within fifty feet of the canoe. Here he ceased to run, for he well understood that his breath was now all-important to him. He even stooped, as he advanced, and cooled his parched mouth, by scooping up water in his hand to drink. Still the moments pressed, and he soon stood at the side of the canoe. The first glance told him that the paddles had been removed! This was a sore disappointment after all his efforts, and, for a single moment, he thought of turning and of facing his foes by walking with dignity into the center of the camp again. But an infernal yell, such as the American savage alone can raise, proclaimed the quick approach of the nearest of his pursuers, and the instinct of life triumphed. Preparing himself duly, and giving a right direction to its bow, he ran off into the water bearing the canoe before him, threw all his strength and skill into a last effort, and cast himself forward so as to fall into the bottom of the light craft, without materially impeding its way. Here he remained on his back, both to regain his breath and to cover his person from the deadly rifle. The lightness, which was such an advantage in paddling the canoe, now operated unfavorably. The material was so like a feather that the boat had no momentum; else would the impulse in that smooth and placid sheet have impelled it to a distance from the shore, that would have rendered paddling with the hands safe. Could such a point once be reached, Deerslayer thought he might get far enough out to attract the attention of Chingachgook and Judith, who would not fail to come to his relief with other canoes, a circumstance that promised everything. As the young man lay in the bottom of the canoe he watched its movements, by studying the tops of the trees on the mountainside, and judged of his distance by the time and the motion. Voices on the shore were now numerous, and he heard something said about manning the raft, which fortunately for the fugitive lay at a considerable distance on the other side of the point.

Perhaps the situation of Deerslayer had not been more critical that day than it was at this moment. It certainly had not been one half as tantalizing. He lay perfectly quiet for two or three minutes, trusting to the single sense of hearing, confident that the noise on the lake would reach his ears, did any one approach by swimming. Once or twice he fancied that the element was stirred by the cautious movement of an arm, and then he perceived it was the wash of the water on the pebbles of the strand; for in mimicry of the ocean, it is seldom that those little lakes are so totally tranquil, as not to possess a slight heaving and setting on their shores. Suddenly all the voices ceased, and a deathlike stillness pervaded the spot; a quietness as profound as if all lay in the repose of inanimate life. By this time the canoe had drifted so far as to render nothing visible to Deerslayer, as he lay on his back, except the blue void of space, and a few of those brighter rays that proceed from the effulgence of the sun, marking his proximity. It was not possible to endure this uncertainty long. The young man well knew that the profound stillness foreboded evil, the savages never being so silent as when about to strike a blow; resembling the stealthy foot of the panther ere he takes his leap. He took out a knife, and was about to cut a hole through the bark in order to get a view of the shore, when he paused from a dread of being seen in the operation, which would direct the enemy where to aim their bullets. At this instant a rifle *was* fired, and the ball pierced both sides of the canoe, within eighteen inches of the spot where his head lay. This was close work, but our hero had too lately gone through that which was closer, to be appalled. He lay still half a minute longer, and then he saw the summit of an oak coming slowly within his narrow horizon.

Unable to account for this change, Deerslayer could restrain his impatience no longer. Hitching his body along, with the utmost caution, he got his eye at the bullet hole, and fortunately commanded a very tolerable view of the point. The canoe, by one of those imperceptible impulses that so often decide the fate of men, as well as the course of things, had inclined southerly, and was slowly drifting down the lake. It was lucky that Deerslayer had given it a shove sufficiently vigorous to send it past the end of the point ere it took this inclination, or it must have gone ashore again. As it was, it drifted so near it as to bring the tops of two or three of the trees within the range of the young man's view, as has been mentioned, and, indeed, to come in quite as close proximity with the extremity of the point as was at all safe. The distance could not much have exceeded a hundred feet, though fortunately a light current of air from the southwest began to set it slowly off shore.

Deerslayer now felt the urgent necessity of resorting to some expedient to get farther from his foes, and, if possible, to apprise his friends of his situation. The distance rendered the last difficult, while the proximity to the point rendered the first indispensable. As was usual in such craft, a large, round, smooth stone was in each end of the canoe, for the double purpose of seats and ballast; one of these was within reach of his feet. The stone he contrived to get so far between his legs as to reach it with his hands, and then he managed to roll it to the side of its fellow in the bow, where the two served to keep the trim of the light boat, while he worked his own body as far aft as possible. Before quitting the shore, and as soon as he perceived that the paddles were gone, Deerslayer had thrown a bit of dead branch into the canoe, and this was within reach of his arm. Removing the cap he wore, he put it on the end of this stick, and just let it appear over the edge of the canoe, as far as possible from his own person. This *ruse* was scarcely adopted, before the young man had proof how much he had underrated the intelligence of his enemies. In contempt of an artifice so shallow and commonplace, a bullet was fired directly through another part of the canoe, which actually razed his skin. He dropped the cap, and instantly raised it immediately over his head, as a safeguard. It would seem that this second artifice was unseen, or what was more probable, the Hurons, feeling certain of recovering their captive, wished to take him alive.

Deerslayer lay passive a few minutes longer, his eye at the bullet hole, however, and much did he rejoice at seeing that he was drifting gradually farther and farther from the shore. When he looked upward, the treetops had disappeared, but he soon found that the canoe was slowly turning, so as to prevent his getting a view of anything at his peephole, but of the two extremities of the lake. He now bethought him of the stick, which was crooked, and offered some facilities for rowing, without the necessity of rising. The experiment succeeded, on trial, better even than he had hoped, though his great embarrassment was to keep the canoe straight. That his present maneuver was seen soon became apparent by the clamor on the shore, and a bullet entering the stern of the canoe, traversed its length, whistling between the arms of our hero, and passed out at the head. This satisfied the fugitive that he was getting away with tolerable speed, and induced him to increase his efforts. He was making a stronger push than common, when another messenger from the point broke the stick outboard, and at once deprived him of his oar. As the sound of voices seemed to grow more and more distant, however, Deerslayer determined to leave all to the drift, until he believed himself beyond the reach of bullets. This was nervous work, but it was the wisest of all the expedients that offered; and the young man was encouraged to persevere in it, by the circumstance that he felt his face fanned by the air, a proof that there was a little more wind.

By this time, Deerslayer had been twenty minutes in the canoe, and he began to grow a little impatient for some signs of relief from his friends. The position of the boat still prevented his seeing in any direction, unless it were up or down the lake; and, though he knew that this line of sight must pass within a hundred yards of the castle, it, in fact, passed that distance to the westward of the buildings. The profound stillness troubled him also, for he knew not whether to ascribe it to the increasing space between him and the Indians, or to some new artifice. At length, wearied with fruitless watchfulness, the young man turned himself on his back, closed his eyes, and awaited the result in determined acquiescence. If the savages could so completely control their thirst for revenge, he was resolved to be as calm as themselves, and to trust his fate to the interposition of the currents and air.

Some additional ten minutes may have passed in this quiescent manner, on both sides, when Deerslayer thought he heard a slight noise, like a low rubbing against the bottom of his canoe. He opened his eyes, of course, in expectation of seeing the face or arm of an Indian rising from the water, and found that a canopy of leaves was impending directly over his head. Starting to his feet, the first object that met his eyes was Rivenoak, who had so far aided the slow progress of the boat, as to draw it on the point, the grating on the strand being the sound that had first given our hero the alarm. The change in the drift of the canoe had been altogether owing to the baffling nature of the light currents of air, aided by some eddies in the water.

"Come," said the Huron, with a quiet gesture of authority to order his prisoner to land; "my young friend has sailed about till he is tired; he will forget how to run again, unless he uses his legs."

"You've the best of it, Huron," returned Deerslayer, stepping steadily from the canoe, and passively following his leader to the open area of the point; "Providence has helped you in an onexpected manner. I'm your prisoner ag'in, and I hope you'll allow that I'm as good at breaking jail as I am at keeping furlough."

"My young friend is a moose!" exclaimed the Huron. "His legs are very long; they have given my young men trouble. But he is not a fish; he cannot find his way in the lake. We did not shoot him; fish are taken in nets, and not killed by bullets. When he turns moose again he will be treated like a moose."

"Ay, have your talk, Rivenoak; make the most of your advantage. 'Tis your right, I suppose, and I know it is your gift. On that p'int there'll be no words atween us; for all men must and ought to follow their gifts. Howsever, when your women begin to ta'nt and abuse me, as I suppose will soon happen, let 'em remember that if a paleface struggles for life so long as it's lawful and manful, he knows how to loosen his hold on it, decently, when he feels that the time has come. I'm your captyve; work your will on me."

"My brother has had a long run on the hills, and a pleasant sail on the water," returned Rivenoak, more mildly, smiling, at the same time, in a way that his listener knew denoted pacific intentions. "He has seen the woods; he has seen the water; which does he like best? Perhaps he has seen enough to change his mind and make him hear reason."

"Speak out, Huron. Something is in your thoughts, and the sooner it is said, the sooner you'll get my answer."

"That is straight! There is no turning in the talk of my paleface friend, though he is a fox in running. I will speak to him; his ears are now open wider than before, and his eyes are not shut. The Sumach is poorer than ever. Once she had a brother and a husband. She had children too. The time came, and the husband started for the happy hunting grounds, without saying farewell; he left her alone with his children. This he could not help, or he would not have done it; Le Loup Cervier was a good husband. It was pleasant to see the venison, and wild ducks, and geese, and bear's meat, that hung in his lodge, in winter. It is now gone; it will not keep in warm weather. Who shall bring it back again? Some thought the brother would not forget his sister, and that, next winter, he would see that the lodge should not be empty. We thought this; but the Panther yelled, and followed the husband on the path of death. They are now trying which shall first reach the happy hunting grounds. Some think the Lynx can run fastest, and some think the Panther can jump the farthest. The Sumach thinks both will travel so fast and so far, that neither will ever come back. Who shall feed her and her young? The man who told her husband and her brother to quit her lodge, that there might be room for him to come into it. He is a great hunter, and we know that the woman will never want."

"Ay, Huron, this is soon settled, accordin' to your notions; but it goes sorely ag'in the grain of a white man's feelin's. I've heard of men's saving their lives this-a-way, and I've know'd them that would prefer death to such a sort of captivity. For my part, I do not seek my ind; nor do I seek matrimony."

"The paleface will think of this while my people get ready for the council. He will be told what will happen. Let him remember how hard it is to lose a husband and a brother. Go: when we want him, the name of Deerslayer will be called."

This conversation had been held with no one near but the speakers. Of all the band that had so lately thronged the place, Rivenoak alone was visible. The rest seemed to have totally abandoned the spot. Even the furniture, clothes, arms, and other property of the camp had entirely disappeared, and the place bore no other proofs of the crowd that had so lately occupied it, than the traces of their fires and resting places, and the trodden earth that still showed the marks of their feet. So sudden and unexpected a change caused Deerslayer a good deal of surprise and some uneasiness, for he had never known it to occur in the course of his experience among the Delawares. He suspected, however, and rightly, that a change of encampment was intended, and that the mystery of the movement was resorted to in order to work on his apprehensions.

Rivenoak walked up the vista of trees, as soon as he ceased speaking, leaving Deerslayer by himself. The chief disappeared behind the covers of the forest, and one unpracticed in such scenes might have believed the prisoner left to the dictates of his own judgment. But the young man, while he felt a little amazement at the dramatic aspect of things, knew his enemies too well to fancy himself at liberty, or a free agent. Still, he was ignorant how far the Hurons meant to carry their artifices, and he determined to bring the question, as soon as practicable, to the proof. Affecting an indifference he was far from feeling, he strolled about the area, gradually getting nearer and nearer to the spot where he had landed, when he suddenly quickened his pace, though carefully avoiding all appearance of flight, and, pushing aside the bushes, he stepped upon the beach. The canoe was gone, nor could he see any traces of it, after walking to the northern and southern verges of the point, and examining the shores in both directions. It was evidently removed beyond his reach and knowledge, and under circumstances to show that such had been the intention of the savages.

Deerslayer now better understood his actual situation. He was a prisoner on the narrow tongue of land, vigilantly watched beyond a question, and with no other means of escape than that of swimming. He again thought of this last expedient, but the certainty that the canoe would be sent in chase, and the desperate nature of the chances of success, deterred him from the undertaking. While on the strand, he came to a spot where the bushes had been cut, and thrown into a small pile. Removing a few of the upper branches, he found beneath them the dead body of the Panther. He knew that it was kept until the savages might find a place to inter it, when it would be beyond the reach of the scalping knife. He gazed wistfully toward the castle, but there all seemed to be silent and desolate; and a feeling of loneliness and desertion came over him to increase the gloom of the moment.

"God's will be done!" murmured the young man, as he walked sorrowfully away from the beach, entering again beneath the arches of the wood; "God's will be done on 'arth as it is in heaven! I did hope that my days would not be numbered so soon! but it matters little, a'ter all. A few more winters, and a few more summers, and 'twould have been over accordin' to natur'. Ah's me! the young and actyve seldom think death possible, till he grins in their faces and tells 'em the hour is come!"

While this soliloquy was being pronounced, the hunter advanced into the area, where, to his surprise, he saw Hetty alone, evidently awaiting his return. The girl carried the Bible under her arm, and her face, over which a shadow of gentle melancholy was usually thrown, now seemed sad and downcast.

Deerslayer and Hetty held a rapid colloquy, in the course of which the young man declared that he would never consider a union with the squaw Sumach, for a marriage of paleface with redskin, Christian with heathen, was "ag'in reason and natur'."

Here the stirring of leaves and the cracking of dried twigs interrupted the discourse, and apprised Deerslayer of the approach of his enemies. The Hurons closed around the spot that had been prepared for the coming scene, in a circle—the armed men being so distributed among the feebler members of the band, that there was no safe opening through which the prisoner could break. But the latter no longer contemplated flight; the recent trial having satisfied him of his inability to escape, when pursued so closely by numbers. On the contrary, all his energies were aroused, in order to meet his expected fate with a calmness that should do credit to his color and his manhood; one equally removed from recreant alarm and savage boasting.

When Rivenoak reappeared in the circle, he occupied his old place at the head of the area. Several of the elder warriors stood near him; but, now that the brother of Sumach had fallen, there was no longer any recognized chief present, whose influence and authority offered a dangerous rivalry to his own. Nevertheless, it is well known that little which could be called monarchical or despotic entered into the politics of the North American tribes, although the first colonists, bringing with them to this hemisphere the notions and opinions of their own countries, often dignified the chief men of those primitive nations with the titles of kings and princes. Hereditary influence did certainly exist; but there is much reason to believe it existed rather as a consequence of hereditary merit and acquired qualifications, than as a birthright.

Rivenoak, however, had not even this claim—having risen to consideration purely by the force of talents, sagacity, and, as Bacon expresses it, in relation to all distinguished statesmen, "by a union of great and mean qualities"; a truth of which the career of the profound Englishman himself furnishes so apt an illustration.

Next to arms, eloquence offers the great avenue to popular favor, whether it be in civilized or savage life; and Rivenoak had succeeded, as so many have succeeded before him, quite as much by rendering fallacies acceptable to his listeners, as by any profound or learned expositions of truth, or the accuracy of his logic. Nevertheless, he had influence; and was far from being altogether without just claims to its possession. Like most men who reason more than they feel, the Huron was not addicted to the indulgence of the mere ferocious passions of his people; he had been commonly found on the side of mercy, in all the scenes of vindictive torture and revenge that had occurred in his tribe, since his own attainment to power. On the present occasion, he was reluctant to proceed to extremities, although the provocation was so great; still it exceeded his ingenuity to see how that alternative could well be avoided. Sumach resented her rejection more than she did the deaths of her husband and brother, and there was little probability that the woman would pardon a man who had so unequivocally preferred death to her embraces. Without her forgiveness, there was scarce a hope that the tribe could be induced to overlook its loss; and even to Rivenoak himself, much as he was disposed to pardon, the fate of our hero now appeared to be almost hopelessly sealed.

When the whole band was arrayed around the captive, a grave silence, so much the more threatening from its profound quiet, pervaded the place. Deerslayer perceived that the women and boys had been preparing splinters of the fat pine roots, which he well knew were to be stuck into his flesh and set in flames, while two or three of the young men held the thongs of bark with which he was to be bound. The smoke of a distant fire announced that the burning brands were in preparation, and several of the elder warriors passed their fingers over the edges of their tomahawks, as if to prove their keenness and temper. Even the knives seemed loosened in their sheaths, impatient for the bloody and merciless work to begin.

"Killer of the Deer," recommenced Rivenoak, certainly without any signs of sympathy or pity in his manner, though with calmness and dignity, "Killer of the Deer, it is time that my people knew their minds. The sun is no longer over our heads; tired of waiting on the Hurons, he has begun to fall near the pines on this side of the valley. He is travelling fast toward the country of our French fathers; it is to warn his children that their lodges are empty, and that they ought to be at home. The roaming wolf has his den, and he goes to it when he wishes to see his young. The Iroquois are not poorer than the wolves. They have villages, and wigwams, and fields of corn; the good spirits will be tired of watching them alone. My people must go back and see to their own business. There will be joy in the lodges when they hear our whoop from the forest! It will be a sorrowful whoop; when it is understood, grief will come after it. There will be one scalp whoop, but there will be only one. We have the fur of the Muskrat; his body is among the fishes. Deerslayer must say whether another scalp shall be on our pole. Two lodges are empty; a scalp, living or dead, is wanted on each door."

"Then take 'em dead, Huron," firmly, but altogether without dramatic boasting, returned the captive. "My hour is come, I do suppose; and what must be, must. If you are bent on the tortur', I'll do my indivors to bear up ag'in it, though no man can say how far his natur' will stand pain, until he's been tried."

"The paleface cur begins to put his tail between his legs!" cried a young and garrulous savage, who bore the appropriate title of the Corbeau Rouge; a *sobriquet* he had gained from the French, by his facility in making unseasonable noises, and an undue tendency to hear his own voice; "he is no warrior; he has killed Le Loup Cervier when looking behind him not to see the flash of his own rifle. He grunts like a hog, already; when the Huron women begin to torment him, he will cry like the young of the catamount. He is a Delaware woman, dressed in the skin of a Yengeese!"

"Have your say, young man; have your say," returned Deerslayer, unmoved; "you know no better, and I can overlook it. Talking may aggravate women but can hardly make knives sharper, fire hotter, or rifles more sartain."

Rivenoak now interfered, reproving the Red Crow for his premature interference, and then directing the proper persons to bind the captive. This expedient was adopted, not from any apprehensions that he would escape, or from any necessity that was yet apparent, of his being unable to endure the torture with his limbs free, but from an ingenious design of making him feel his helplessness, and of gradually sapping his resolution, by undermining it; as it might be, little by little. Deerslayer offered no resistance. He submitted his arms and legs, freely if not cheerfully, to the ligaments of bark, which were bound around them, by order of the chief, in a way to produce as little pain as possible. These directions were secret, and given in a hope that the captive would finally save himself from any serious bodily suffering, by consenting to take the Sumach for a wife. As soon as the body of Deerslayer was withed in bark sufficiently to create a lively sense of helplessness, he was literally carried to a young tree, and bound against it, in a way that effectually prevented him from moving, as well as from falling. The hands were laid flat against the legs, and thongs were passed over all, in a way nearly to incorporate the prisoner with the tree. His cap was then removed, and he was left half-standing, half-sustained by his bonds, to face the coming scene in the best manner he could.

Previously to proceeding to anything like extremities, it was the wish of Rivenoak to put his captive's resolution to the proof, by renewing the attempt at a compromise. This could be effected only in one manner, the acquiescence of the Sumach being indispensably necessary to a compromise of her right to be revenged. With this view, then, the woman was next desired to advance, and to look to her own interest; no agent being considered as efficient as the principal herself in this negotiation. The Indian females, when girls, are usually mild and submissive, with musical tones, pleasant voices, and merry laughs; but toil and suffering generally deprive them of most of these advantages by the time they have reached an age which the Sumach had long before passed. To render their voices harsh, it would seem to require active, malignant passions, though, when excited, their screams can rise to a sufficiently conspicuous degree of discordancy to assert their claim to possess this distinctive peculiarity of the sex. The Sumach was not altogether without feminine attraction, however, and had so recently been deemed handsome in her tribe, as not to have yet learned the full influence that time and exposure produce on man as well as on woman. By an arrangement of Rivenoak's, some of the women around her had been employing the time in endeavoring to persuade the bereaved widow that there was still a hope Deerslayer might be prevailed on to enter her wigwam, in preference to entering the world of spirits, and this, too, with a success that previous symptoms scarcely justified. All this was the result of a resolution on the part of the chief to leave no proper means unemployed, in order to get the greatest hunter that was then thought to exist in all that region, transferred to his own nation, as well as a husband for a woman who he felt would be likely to be troublesome, were any of her claims to the attention and care of the tribe overlooked.

In conformity with this scheme the Sumach had been secretly advised to advance into the circle, and to make her appeal to the prisoner's sense of justice before the band had recourse to the last experiment. The woman, nothing loath, consented; for there was some such attraction in becoming the wife of a noted hunter, among the females of the tribes, as is experienced by the sex in more refined life when they bestow their hands on the affluent. As the duties of a mother were thought to be paramount to all other considerations, the widow felt none of that embarrassment in preferring her claims, to which even a female fortune hunter among ourselves might be liable. When she stood forth before the whole party, therefore, the children that she led by the hand fully justified all she did.

"You see me before you, cruel paleface," the woman commenced; "your spirit must tell you my errand. I have found *you;* I cannot find Le Loup Cervier, nor the Panther; I have looked for them in the lake, in the woods, in the clouds. I cannot say where they have gone."

"No man knows, good Sumach, no man knows," interposed the captive. "When the spirit leaves the body it passes into a world beyond our knowledge, and the wisest way for them that are left behind is to hope for the best. No doubt both your warriors have gone to the happy hunting grounds, and at the proper time you will see 'em ag'in in their improved state. The wife and sister of braves must have looked forward to some such tarmination of their 'arthly careers."

"Cruel paleface, what had my warriors done that you should slay them? They were the best hunters and the boldest young men of their tribe; the Great Spirit intended that they should live until they withered like the branches of the hemlock, and fell of their own weight."

"Nay, nay, good Sumach," interrupted the Deerslayer, whose love of truth was too indomitable to listen to such hyperbole with patience, even though it came from the torn breast of a widow; "Nay, nay, good Sumach, this is a little outdoing redskin privileges. Young man was neither, any more than you can be called a young woman; and as to the Great Spirit's intending that they should fall otherwise than they did, that's a grievous mistake, inasmuch as what the Great Spirit intends is sartain to come to pass. Then, ag'in, it's plain enough neither of your fri'nds did me any harm. I raised my hand ag'in 'em on account of what they were *striving* to do, rather than what they did. This is nat'ral law, 'to do, lest you should be done by.' "

"It is so. Sumach has but one tongue; she can tell but one story. The paleface struck the Hurons, lest the Hurons should strike him. The Hurons are a just nation; they will forget it. The chiefs will shut their eyes, and pretend not to have seen it. The young men will believe the Panther and the Lynx have gone to far-off hunts; and the Sumach will take her children by the hand, and go into the lodge of the paleface, and say, 'See! these are *your* children—they are also mine; feed us, and we will live with you.' "

"The tarms are onadmissible, woman; and though I feel for your losses, which must be hard to bear, the tarms cannot be accepted. As to givin' you ven'son, in case we lived near enough together, that would be no great expl'ite; but as for becomin' your husband, and the father of your children, to be honest with you, I feel no callin' that-a-way."

"Look at this boy, cruel paleface; he has no father to teach him to kill the deer, or to take scalps. See this girl; what young man will come to look for a wife in a lodge that has no head? There are more among my people in the Canadas, and the Killer of Deer will find as many mouths to feed as his heart can wish for."

"I tell you, woman," exclaimed Deerslayer, whose imagination was far from seconding the appeal of the widow, and who began to grow restive under the vivid pictures she was drawing, "all this is nothing to me. People and kindred must take care of their own fatherless, leaving them that have no children to their own loneliness. As for me, I have no offspring, and I want no wife. Now, go away, Sumach; leave me in the hands of your chiefs; for my color, and gifts, and natur' itself, cry out ag'in the idee of taking you for a wife."

It is unnecessary to expatiate on the effect of this downright refusal of the woman's proposals. If there was anything like tenderness in her bosom,—and no woman was probably ever entirely without that feminine quality,—it all disappeared at this plain announcement. Fury, rage, mortified pride, and a volcano of wrath, burst out at one explosion, converting her into a sort of maniac, as it might be at the touch of a magician's wand. Without deigning a reply in words, she made the arches of the forest ring with screams, and then flew forward at her victim, seizing him by the hair, which she appeared resolute to draw out by the roots. It was some time before her grasp could be loosened. Fortunately for the prisoner, her rage was blind, since his total helplessness left him entirely at her mercy; had it been better directed, it might have proved fatal before any relief could have been offered. As it was, she did succeed in wrenching out two or three handfuls of hair, before the young men could tear her away from her victim.

The insult that had been offered to the Sumach was deemed an insult to the whole tribe; not so much, however, on account of any respect that was felt for the woman, as on account of the honor of the Huron nation. Sumach, herself, was generally considered to be as acid as the berry from which she derived her name; and now that her great supporters, her husband and brother, were both gone, few cared about concealing their aversion. Nevertheless, it had become a point of honor to punish the paleface who disdained a Huron woman, and more particularly, one who coolly preferred death to relieving the tribe from the support of a widow and her children. The young men showed an impatience to begin to torture, that Rivenoak understood; and as his elder associates manifested no disposition to permit any longer delay, he was compelled to give the signal for the infernal work to proceed.

It was one of the common expedients of the savages, on such occasions, to put the nerves of their victims to the severest proofs. On the other hand, it was a matter of Indian pride to betray no yielding to terror or pain; but for the prisoner to provoke his enemies to such acts of violence as would soonest produce death. Many a warrior had been known to bring his own sufferings to a more speedy termination, by taunting reproaches and reviling language, when he found that his physical system was giving way under the agony of sufferings, produced by a hellish ingenuity, that might well eclipse all that has been said of the infernal devices of religious persecution. This happy expedient of taking refuge from the ferocity of his foes in their passions, was denied Deerslayer, however, by his peculiar notions of the duty of a white man; and he had stoutly made up his mind to endure everything, in preference to disgracing his color.

No sooner did the young men understand that they were at liberty to commence, than some of the boldest and most forward among them sprang into the arena, tomahawk in hand. Here they prepared to throw that dangerous weapon, the object being to strike the tree as near as possible to the victim's head, without absolutely hitting him. This was so hazardous an experiment, that none but those who were known to be exceedingly expert with the weapon were allowed to enter the lists at all, lest an early death might interfere with the expected entertainment. In the truest hands, it was seldom that the captive escaped injury in these trials; and it often happened that death followed even when the blow was not premeditated. In the particular case of our hero, Rivenoak and the older warriors were apprehensive that the example of the Panther's fate might prove a motive with some fiery spirit, suddenly to sacrifice his conqueror, when the temptation of effecting it in precisely the same manner, and possibly with the identical weapon with which the warrior had fallen, offered. This circumstance, of itself, rendered the ordeal of the tomahawk doubly critical for the Deerslayer.

It would seem, however, that all who now entered what we shall call the lists, were more disposed to exhibit their own dexterity than to resent the deaths of their comrades. Each prepared himself for the trial, with the feelings of rivalry, rather than with the desire for vengeance; and for the first few minutes, the prisoner had little more connection with the result, than grew out of the interest that necessarily attached itself to a living target. The young men were eager, instead of being fierce, and Rivenoak thought he still saw signs of being able to save the life of the captive, when the vanity of the young men had been gratified; always admitting that it was not sacrificed to the delicate experiments that were about to be made.

The first youth who presented himself for the trial, was called the Raven, having as yet had no opportunity of obtaining a more warlike *sobriquet*. He was remarkable for high pretension rather than for skill or exploits; and those who knew his character, thought the captive in imminent danger, when he took his stand, and poised the tomahawk. Nevertheless, the young man was good-natured, and no thought was uppermost in his mind, other than the desire to make a better cast than any of his fellows. Deerslayer got an inkling of this warrior's want of reputation, by the injunctions that he had received from the seniors; who, indeed, would have objected to his appearing in the arena at all, but for an influence derived from his father, an aged warrior of great merit, who was then in the lodges of the tribe. Still, our hero maintained an appearance of self-possession. He had made up his mind that his hour was come, and it would have been a mercy, instead of a calamity, to fall by the unsteadiness of the first hand that was raised against him. After a suitable number of flourishes and gesticulations, that promised much more than he could perform, the Raven let the tomahawk quit his hand. The weapon whirled through the air, with the usual evolutions, cut a chip from the sapling to which the prisoner was bound, within a few inches of his cheek, and stuck in a large oak that grew several yards behind him. This was decidedly a bad effort, and a common sneer proclaimed as much, to the great mortification of the young man. On the other hand, there was a general, but suppressed murmur of admiration, at the steadiness with which the captive stood the trial. The head was the only part he could move, and this had been purposely left free, that the tormentors might have the amusement, and the tormented endure the shame, of dodging, and otherwise attempting to avoid the blows. Deerslayer disappointed these hopes, by a command of nerve that rendered his whole body as immovable as the tree to which he was bound. Nor did he even adopt the natural and usual expedient of shutting his eyes: the firmest and oldest warrior of the red men never having more disdainfully denied himself this advantage, under similar circumstances.

The Raven had no sooner made his unsuccessful and puerile effort than he was succeeded by Le Daim-Mose, or the Moose; a middle-aged warrior, who was particularly skilful in the use of the tomahawk, and from whose attempt the spectators confidently looked for gratification. This man had none of the good nature of the Raven, but he would gladly have sacrificed the captive to his hatred of the palefaces generally, were it not for the greater interest he felt in his own success as one particularly skilful in the use of this weapon. He took his stand quietly, but with an air of confidence, poised his little ax but a single instant, advanced a foot with a quick motion, and threw. Deerslayer saw the keen instrument whirling toward him, and believed all was over; still he was not touched. The tomahawk had actually bound the head of the captive to the tree, by carrying before it some of his hair; having buried itself deep beneath the soft bark. A general yell expressed the delight of the spectators, and the Moose felt his heart soften a little toward the prisoner, whose steadiness of nerve alone enabled him to give this evidence of his consummate skill.

Le Daim-Mose was succeeded by the Bounding Boy, or Le Garçon qui Bondi, who came leaping into the circle, like a hound or a goat at play. This was one of those elastic youths, whose muscles seemed always in motion, and who either affected, or who from habit was actually unable to move in any other manner, than by showing the antics just mentioned. Nevertheless, he was both brave and skilful, and had gained the respect of his people by deeds in war as well as success in the hunts. A far nobler name would long since have fallen to his share, had not a Frenchman of rank inadvertently given him this *sobriquet*, which he religiously preserved as coming from his great father, who lived beyond the wide salt lake. The Bounding Boy skipped about in front of the captive, menacing him with his tomahawk, now on one side and now on another, and then again in front, in the vain hope of being able to extort some sign of fear, by this parade of danger. At length Deerslayer's patience became exhausted by all this mummery, and he spoke for the first time since the trial had actually commenced.

"Throw away, Huron!" he cried, "or your tomahawk will forget its arr'nd. Why do you keep loping about like a fa'an that's showing its dam how well it can skip, when you're a warrior grown, yourself, and a warrior grown defies you and all your silly antics? Throw, or the Huron gals will laugh in your face."

Although not intended to produce such an effect, the last words aroused the "Bounding" warrior to fury. The same nervous excitability which rendered him so active in his person, made it difficult to repress his feelings, and the words were scarcely past the lips of the speaker, than the tomahawk left the hand of the Indian. Nor was it cast without good will, and a fierce determination to slay. Had the intention been less deadly, the danger might have been greater. The aim was uncertain, and the weapon glanced near the cheek of the captive, slightly cutting the shoulder in its evolutions. This was the first instance in which any other object than that of terrifying the prisoner, and of displaying skill, had been manifested; and the Bounding Boy was immediately led from the arena, and was warmly rebuked for his intemperate haste, which had come so near defeating all the hopes of the band.

To this irritable person succeeded several other young warriors, who not only hurled the tomahawk but who cast the knife, a far more dangerous experiment, with reckless indifference; yet they always manifested a skill that prevented any injury to the captive. Several times Deerslayer was grazed, but in no instance did he receive what might be termed a wound. The unflinching firmness with which he faced his assailants, more especially in the sort of rally with which this trial terminated, excited a profound respect in the spectators; and when the chiefs announced that the prisoner had well withstood the trials of the knife and the tomahawk, there was not a single individual in the band who really felt any hostility towards him, with the exception of Sumach and the Bounding Boy. These two discontented spirits got together, it is true, feeding each other's ire; but, as yet, their malignant feelings were confined very much to themselves, though there existed the danger that the others, ere long, could not fail to be excited by their own efforts into that demoniacal state which usually accompanied all similar scenes among the red men.

Rivenoak now told his people that the paleface had proved himself to be a man. He might live with the Delawares, but he had not been made woman with that tribe. He wished to know whether it was the desire of the Hurons to proceed any further. Even the gentlest of the females, however, had received too much satisfaction in the late trials to forego their expectations of a gratifying exhibition; and there was but one voice in the request to proceed. The politic chief, who had some such desire to receive so celebrated a hunter into his tribe as a European minister has to devise a new and available means of taxation, sought every plausible means of arresting the trial in season; for he well knew, if permitted to go far enough to arouse the more ferocious passions of the tormentors, it would be as easy to dam the waters of the Great Lakes of his own region, as to attempt to arrest them in their bloody career. He therefore called four or five of the best marksmen to him, and bid them put the captive to the proof of the rifle, while, at the same time, he cautioned them touching the necessity of their maintaining their own credit, by the closest attention to the manner of exhibiting their skill.

When Deerslayer saw the chosen warriors step into the circle, with their arms prepared for service, he felt some such relief as the miserable sufferer, who had long endured the agonies of disease, feels at the certain approach of death. Any trifling variance in the aim of this formidable weapon would prove fatal; since, the head being the target, or rather the point it was desired to graze without injury, an inch or two of difference in the line of projection must at once determine the question of life or death.

In the torture by the rifle there was none of the latitude permitted that appeared in the case of even Gesler's apple, a hairsbreadth being, in fact, the utmost limits that an expert marksman would allow himself on an occasion like this. Victims were frequently shot through the head by too eager or unskilful hands; and it often occurred that, exasperated by the fortitude and taunts of the prisoner, death was dealt intentionally in a moment of ungovernable irritation. All this Deerslayer well knew, for it was in relating the traditions of such scenes, as well as of the battles and victories of their people, that the old men beguiled the long winter evenings in their cabins. He now fully expected the end of his career, and experienced a sort of melancholy pleasure in the idea that he was to fall by a weapon as much beloved as the rifle. A slight interruption, however, took place before the business was allowed to proceed.

Hetty Hutter witnessed all that passed, and the scene at first had pressed upon her feeble mind in a way to paralyze it entirely; but by this time she had rallied, and was growing indignant at the unmerited suffering the Indians were inflicting on her friend. Though timid, and shy as the young of the deer, on so many occasions, this right-feeling girl was always intrepid in the cause of humanity; the lessons of her mother, and the impulses of her own heart—perhaps we might say the promptings of that unseen and pure spirit that seemed ever to watch over and direct her actions—uniting to keep down the apprehensions of woman, and to impel her to be bold and resolute. She now appeared in the circle, gentle, feminine, even bashful in mien, as usual, but earnest in her words and countenance, speaking like one who knew herself to be sustained by the high authority of God.

"Why do you torment Deerslayer, red men?" she asked. "What has he done that you trifle with his life; who has given you the right to be his judges? Suppose one of your knives or tomahawks had hit him; what Indian among you all could cure the wound you would make? Besides, in harming Deerslayer, you injure your own friend; when father and Hurry Harry came after your scalps, he refused to be of the party, and stayed in the canoe by himself. You are tormenting your friend, in tormenting this young man!"

The Hurons listened with grave attention, and one among them, who understood English, translated what had been said into their native tongue. As soon as Rivenoak was made acquainted with the purport of her address, he answered it in his own dialect; the interpreter conveying it to the girl in English.

"My daughter is very welcome to speak," said the stern old orator, using gentle intonations, and smiling as kindly as if addressing a child; "the Hurons are glad to hear her voice; they listen to what she says. The Great Spirit often speaks to men with such tongues. This time her eyes have not been open wide enough, to see all that has happened. Deerslayer did not come for our scalps, that is true; why did he not come? Here they are, on our heads, the warlocks are ready to be taken hold of; a bold enemy ought to stretch out his hand to seize them. The Iroquois are too great a nation to punish men that take scalps. What they do themselves, they like to see others do. Let my daughter look around her, and count my warriors. Had I as many hands as four warriors, their fingers would be fewer than my people, when they came into your hunting grounds. Now, a whole hand is missing. Where are the fingers? Two have been cut off by this paleface; my Hurons wish to see if he did this by means of a stout heart, or by treachery; like a skulking fox, or like a leaping panther."

"You know yourself, Huron, how one of them fell. I saw it, and you all saw it, too. 'Twas too bloody to look at; but it was not Deerslayer's fault. Your warrior sought his life, and he defended himself. I don't know whether the good book says that it was right, but all men will do that. Come, if you want to know which of you can shoot best, give Deerslayer a rifle, and then you will find how much more expert he is than any of your warriors; yes, than *all* of them together!"

Could one have looked upon such a scene with indifference, he would have been amused at the gravity with which the savages listened to the translation of this unusual request. No taunt, no smile, mingled with their surprise; for Hetty had a character and a manner too saintly to subject her infirmity to the mockings of the rude and ferocious. On the contrary, she was answered with respectful attention.

"My daughter does not always talk like a chief at a council fire," returned Rivenoak, "or she would not have said this. Two of my warriors have fallen by the blows of our prisoner; their grave is too small to hold a third. The Hurons do not like to crowd their dead. If there is another spirit about to set out for the far-off world, it must not be the spirit of a Huron; it must be the spirit of a paleface. Go, daughter, and sit by Sumach, who is in grief; let the Huron warriors show how well they can shoot; let the paleface show how little he cares for their bullets."

Hetty's mind was unequal to a sustained discussion, and, accustomed to defer to the directions of her seniors, she did as told, seating herself passively on a log by the side of the Sumach, and averting her face from the painful scene that was occurring within the circle.

The warriors, as soon as this interruption had ceased, resumed their places, and again prepared to exhibit their skill, as there was a double object in view, that of putting the constancy of the captive to the proof, and that of showing how steady were the hands of the marksmen under circumstances of excitement. The distance was small, and, in one sense, safe. But in diminishing the distance taken by the tormentors, the trial to the nerves of the captive was essentially increased. The face of Deerslayer, indeed, was just removed sufficiently from the ends of the guns to escape the effects of the flash, and his steady eye was enabled to look directly into their muzzles, as it might be, in anticipation of the fatal messenger that was to issue from each. The cunning Hurons well knew this fact; and scarce one levelled his piece without first causing it to point as near as possible at the forehead of the prisoner, in the hope that his fortitude would fail him, and that the band would enjoy the triumph of seeing a victim quail under their ingenious cruelty. Nevertheless, each of the competitors was still careful not to injure; the disgrace of striking prematurely being second only to that of failing altogether in attaining the object. Shot after shot was made; all the bullets coming in close proximity to the Deerslayer's head, without touching it. Still, no one could detect even the twitching of a muscle on the part of the captive, or the slightest winking of an eye. This indomitable resolution, which so much exceeded everything of its kind that any present had before witnessed, might be referred to three distinct causes. The first was resignation to his fate, blended with natural steadiness of deportment; for our hero had calmly made up his mind that he must die, and preferred this mode to any other; the second was his great familiarity with this particular weapon, which deprived it of all the terror that is usually connected with the mere form of the danger; and the third was this familiarity carried out in practice, to a degree so nice as to enable the intended victim to tell, within an inch, the precise spot where each bullet must strike, for he calculated its range by looking in at the bore of the piece. So exact was Deerslayer's estimation of the line of fire, that his pride of feeling finally got the better of his resignation, and, when five or six had discharged their bullets into the trees, he could not refrain from expressing his contempt at their want of hand and eye.

"You may call this shooting, Mingoes," he exclaimed, "but we've squaws among the Delawares, and I have known Dutch gals on the Mohawk, that could outdo your greatest indivors. Ondo these arms of mine, put a rifle into my hands, and I'll pin the thinnest warlock in your party to any tree you can show me; and this at a hundred yards: ay, or at two hundred, if the object can be seen, nineteen shots in twenty: or, for that matter, twenty in twenty, if the piece is creditable and trusty!"

A low, menacing murmur followed this cool taunt; the ire of the warriors kindled at listening to such a reproach from one who so far disdained their efforts as to refuse even to wink, when a rifle was discharged as near his face as could be done without burning it. Rivenoak perceived that the moment was critical, and, still retaining his hope of adopting so noted a hunter into his tribe, the politic old chief interposed in time, probably, to prevent an immediate resort to that portion of the torture which must necessarily have produced death, through extreme bodily suffering, if in no other manner. Moving into the center of the irritated group, he addressed them with his usual wily logic and plausible manner, at once suppressing the fierce movement that had commenced.

"I see how it is," he said. "We have been like the palefaces when they fasten their doors at night, out of fear of the red man. They use so many bars, that the fire comes and burns them before they can get out. We have bound the Deerslayer too tight; the thongs keep his limbs from shaking, and his eyes from shutting. Loosen him; let us see what his own body is really made of."

It is often the case when we are thwarted in a cherished scheme, that any expedient, however unlikely to succeed, is gladly resorted to, in preference to a total abandonment of the project. So it was with the Hurons. The proposal of the chief found instant favor; and several hands were immediately at work cutting and tearing the ropes of bark from the body of our hero. In half a minute, Deerslayer stood as free from bonds, as when, an hour before, he had commenced his flight on the side of the mountain. Some little time was necessary that he should recover the use of his limbs, the circulation of the blood having been checked by the tightness of the ligatures; and this was accorded to him by the politic Rivenoak, under the pretence that his body would be more likely to submit to apprehension, if his true tone were restored; though really with a view to give time to the fierce passions which had been awakened in the bosoms of his young men, to subside. This *ruse* succeeded; and Deerslayer, by rubbing his limbs, stamping his feet, and moving about, soon regained the circulation; recovering all his physical powers as effectually as if nothing had occurred to disturb them.

It is seldom men think of death in the pride of their health and strength. So it was with Deerslayer. Having been helplessly bound, and, as he had every reason to suppose, so lately on the very verge of the other world, to find himself so unexpectedly liberated, in possession of his strength, and with a full command of limb, acted on him like a sudden restoration to life, reanimating hopes that he had once absolutely abandoned. From that instant all his plans changed. In this he simply obeyed a law of nature; for while we have wished to represent our hero as being resigned to his fate, it has been far from our intention to represent him as anxious to die. From the instant that his buoyancy of feeling revived, his thoughts were keenly bent on the various projects that presented themselves as modes of evading the designs of his enemies; and he again became the quick-witted, ingenious, and determined woodsman, alive to all his own powers and resources. The change was so great, that his mind resumed its elasticity; and, no longer thinking of submission, it dwelt only on the devices of the sort of warfare in which he was engaged.

As soon as Deerslayer was released, the band divided itself in a circle around him, in order to hedge him in; and the desire to break down his spirit grew in them, precisely as they saw proofs of the difficulty there would be in subduing it. The honor of the band was now involved in the issue; and even the sex lost all its sympathy with suffering, in the desire to save the reputation of the tribe. The voices of the girls, soft and melodious as nature had made them, were heard mingling with the menaces of the men; and the wrongs of Sumach suddenly assumed the character of injuries inflicted on every Huron female. Yielding to this rising tumult, the men drew back a little, signifying to the females that they left the captive, for a time, in their hands; it being a common practice, on such occasions, for the women to endeavor to throw the victim into a rage, by their taunts and revilings, and then to turn him suddenly over to the men, in a state of mind that was little favorable to resisting the agony of bodily suffering. Nor was this party without the proper instruments for effecting such a purpose. Sumach had a notoriety as a scold; and one or two crones, like the Shebear, had come out with the party, most probably as the conservators of its decency and moral discipline; such things occurring in savage as well as civilized life. It is unnecessary to repeat all that ferocity and ignorance could invent for such a purpose; the only difference between this outbreaking of feminine anger, and a similar scene among ourselves, consisting in the figures of speech and the epithets; the Huron women calling their prisoner by the names of the lower and least respected animals that were known to themselves.

But Deerslayer's mind was too much occupied to permit him to be disturbed by the abuse of excited hags; and their rage necessarily increasing with his indifference, as his indifference increased with their rage, the furies soon rendered themselves impotent by their own excesses. Perceiving that the attempt was a complete failure, the warriors interfered to put a stop to this scene; and this so much the more so, because preparations were now seriously making for the real tortures, or that which would put the fortitude of the sufferer to the test of severe pain. A sudden and unlooked-for announcement that proceeded from one of the lookouts, however, a boy ten or twelve years old, put a momentary check to the whole proceedings.

12

AT THIS MOMENT of suspense, as the worst part of Deerslayer's ordeal was about to begin, Judith Hutter suddenly stepped out of the forest aisles and into the circle of excited savages. She had dressed herself in a magnificent brocade gown taken from Hutter's chest, and had added to it many ornaments of harmonizing finery. Bearing herself majestically, she gave her garb a queenly aspect. "Had it been displayed in a capital, a thousand might have worn it before one could have been found to do more credit to its gay colors, glossy satins, and rich laces, than the beautiful creature whose person it now aided to adorn." The Hurons were thunderstruck, for the lustrous brocade surpassed the gayest uniforms of either the French or the British, and the handsome young woman shone with a splendor novel to savage eyes. The grim old warriors exclaimed "Hugh!"; the young men were still more strongly impressed; and even the women could not restrain murmurs of admiration. "Which of these warriors is the principal chief?" demanded Judith of Deerslayer; and he at once indicated old Rivenoak.

Judith had wagered everything upon a daring stroke. She introduced herself to Rivenoak as a noblewoman of high degree, close in rank to the Queen of England herself. Her intention was to overawe the Hurons, and compel them to release Deerslayer. The wily Rivenoak, however, was more than her match. Summoning simple-minded Hetty, he asked her to identify the lady of gorgeous brocade and lace. "That's my sister Judith," readily responded Hetty, "Thomas Hutter's daughter—Thomas Hutter, whom you called the Muskrat." Judith saw that all was lost—her bold expedient had failed. "I wish you hadn't come, my good Judith," exclaimed Deerslayer in deep chagrin. "It can do no good to me, while it may do great harm to yourself." He was certain that she would be held captive, to become the wife of one of the chiefs.

The heroic girl, however, still retained hope. She had been about to say something when Deerslayer interrupted her with his reproachful words. He remembered this. What statement, he asked (presumably in a low voice, for Rivenoak understood English), had she been about to make?

"It might not be safe to mention it here, Deerslayer," the girl hurriedly answered, moving past him carelessly that she might speak in a low tone; "half an hour is all in all to us. None of your friends are idle."

The hunter replied merely by a grateful look. Then he turned toward his enemies, as if ready again to face the torments. A short consultation had passed among the elders of the band, and by this time they also were prepared with their decision. The merciful purpose of Rivenoak had been much weakened by the artifice of Judith, which, failing of its real object, was likely to produce results the very opposite of those she had anticipated. This was natural; the feeling being aided by the resentment of an Indian, who found how near he had been to becoming the dupe of an inexperienced girl. By this time Judith's real character was fully understood—the widespread reputation of her beauty contributed to the exposure. As for the unusual attire, it was confounded with the profound mystery of the animals with two tails, and, for the moment, lost its influence.

When Rivenoak, therefore, faced the captive again, it was with an altered countenance. He had abandoned the wish of saving him, and was no longer disposed to retard the more serious part of the torture. This change of sentiment was, in effect, communicated to the young men, who were already eagerly engaged in making their preparations for the contemplated scene. Fragments of dried wood were rapidly collected near the sapling, the splinters which it was intended to thrust into the flesh of the victim, previously to lighting, were all collected, and the thongs were already produced that were again to bind him to the tree. All this was done in profound silence, Judith watching every movement with breathless expectation, while Deerslayer himself stood seemingly as unmoved as one of the pines of the hills. When the warriors advanced to bind him, however, the young man glanced at Judith, as if to inquire whether resistance or submission were most advisable. By a significant gesture she counselled the last; and, in a minute, he was once more fastened to the tree, a helpless object of any insult or wrong that might be offered. So eagerly did everyone now act, that nothing was said. The fire was immediately lighted in the pile, and the end of all was anxiously expected.

It was not the intention of the Hurons absolutely to destroy the life of their victim by means of fire. They designed merely to put his physical fortitude to the severest proofs it could endure, short of that extremity. In the end, they fully intended to carry his scalp with them into their village, but it was their wish first to break down his resolution, and to reduce him to the level of a complaining sufferer. With this view, the pile of brush and branches had been placed at a proper distance, or one at which it was thought the heat would soon become intolerable, though it might not be immediately dangerous. As often happened, however, on these occasions, this distance had been miscalculated, and the flames began to wave their forked tongues in a proximity to the face of the victim that would have proved fatal in another instant, had not Hetty rushed through the crowd, armed with a stick, and scattered the blazing pile in a dozen directions. More than one hand was raised to strike the presumptuous intruder to the earth; but the chiefs prevented the blows, by reminding their irritated followers of the state of her mind. Hetty, herself, was insensible to the risk she ran; but, as soon as she had performed this bold act, she stood looking about her in frowning resentment, as if to rebuke the crowd of attentive savages for their cruelty.

"God bless you, dearest sister, for that brave and ready act," murmured Judith, herself unnerved so much as to be incapable of exertion; "Heaven itself has sent you on its holy errand."

" 'Twas well meant, Judith," rejoined the victim; " 'twas excellently meant, and 'twas timely, though it may prove ontimely in the ind! What is to come to pass must come to pass soon, or 'twill quickly be too late. Had I drawn in one mouthful of that flame in breathing, the power of man couldn't save my life; and you see that this time they've so bound my forehead as not to leave my head the smallest chance. 'Twas well meant; but it might have been more marciful to let the flames act their part."

"Cruel, heartless Hurons!" exclaimed the still indignant Hetty; "would you burn a man and a Christian as you would burn a log of wood! Do you never read your Bibles? or do you think God will forget such things?"

A gesture from Rivenoak caused the scattered brands to be collected; fresh wood was brought, even the women and children busying themselves eagerly in the gathering of dried sticks. The flame was just kindling a second time, when an Indian female pushed through the circle, advanced to the heap, and with her foot dashed aside the lighted twigs in time to prevent the conflagration. A yell followed this second disappointment; but when the offender turned toward the circle, and presented the countenance of Hist, it was succeeded by a common exclamation of pleasure and surprise. For a minute, all thought of pursuing the business in hand was forgotten, and young and old crowded around the girl, in haste to demand an explanation of her sudden and unlooked-for return. It was at this critical instant that Hist spoke to Judith in a low voice, placed some small object, unseen, in her hand, and then turned to meet the salutations of the Huron girls, with whom she was personally a great favorite. Judith recovered her self-possession and acted promptly. The small, keen-edged knife, that Hist had given to the other, was passed by the latter into the hands of Hetty, as the safest and least-suspected medium of transferring it to Deerslayer. But the feeble intellect of the last defeated the well-grounded hopes of all three. Instead of first cutting loose the hands of the victim, and then concealing the knife in his clothes, in readiness for action at the most available instant, she went to work herself, with earnestness and simplicity, to cut the thongs that bound his head, that he might not again be in danger of inhaling flames. Of course this deliberate procedure was seen, and the hands of Hetty were arrested ere she had more than liberated the upper portion of the captive's body, not including his arms, below the elbows. This discovery at once pointed distrust toward Hist; and, to Judith's surprise, when questioned on the subject, that spirited girl was not disposed to deny her agency in what had passed.

"Why should I not help the Deerslayer?" the girl demanded, in the tones of a firm-minded woman. "He is the brother of a Delaware chief; my heart is all Delaware. Come forth, miserable Briarthorn, and wash the Iroquois paint from your face; stand before the Hurons, the crow that you are; you would eat the carrion of your own dead rather than starve. Put him face to face with Deerslayer, chiefs and warriors; I will show you how great a knave you have been keeping in your tribe."

This bold language, uttered in their own dialect, and with a manner full of confidence, produced a deep sensation among the Hurons. Treachery is always liable to distrust; and though the recreant Briarthorn had endeavored to serve the enemy well, his exertions and assiduities had gained for him little more than toleration. His wish to obtain Hist for a wife had first induced him to betray her and his own people; but serious rivals to his first project had risen up among his new friends, weakening still more their sympathies with treason. In a word, Briarthorn had been barely permitted to remain in the Huron encampment, where he was as closely and as jealously watched as Hist herself; seldom appearing before the chiefs, and sedulously keeping out of view of Deerslayer, who, until this moment, was ignorant even of his presence. Thus summoned, however, it was impossible to remain in the background. "Wash the Iroquois paint from his face," he did not; for when he stood in the center of the circle, he was so disguised in these new colors, that, at first, the hunter did not recognize him. He assumed an air of defiance, notwithstanding, and haughtily demanded what any could say against Briarthorn.

"Ask yourself that," continued Hist, with spirit, though her manner grew less concentrated; and there was a slight air of abstraction that became observable to Deerslayer and Judith, if to no others. "Ask that of your own heart, sneaking woodchuck of the Delawares; come not here with the face of an innocent man. Go look in the spring; see the colors of your enemies on your lying skin; and then come back and boast how you ran from your tribe, and took the blanket of the French for your covering. Paint yourself as bright as a hummingbird, you will still be black as the crow."

Hist had been so uniformly gentle while living with the Hurons, that they now listened to her language with surprise. As for the delinquent, his blood boiled in his veins; and it was well for the pretty speaker that it was not in his power to execute the revenge he burned to inflict on her, in spite of his pretended love.

"Who wishes Briarthorn?" he sternly asked. "If this paleface is tired of life; if afraid of Indian torments, speak, Rivenoak; I will send him after the warriors we have lost."

"No, chief,—no, Rivenoak," eagerly interrupted Hist. "The Deerslayer fears nothing; least of all a crow! Unbind him—cut his withes—place him face to face with this cawing bird; then let us see which is tired of life."

Hist made a forward movement, as if to take a knife from a young man, and perform the office she had mentioned in person; but an aged warrior interposed, at a sign from Rivenoak. The chief watched all the girl did, with distrust; for, even while speaking in her most boastful language and in the steadiest manner, there was an air of uncertainty and expectation about her, that could not escape so close an observer. She acted well; but two or three of the old men were equally satisfied that it was merely acting. Her proposal to release Deerslayer, therefore, was rejected; and the disappointed Hist found herself driven back from the sapling at the very moment she fancied herself about to be successful. At the same time the circle, which had got to be crowded and confused, was enlarged, and brought once more into order. Rivenoak now announced the intention of the old men again to proceed; the delay having been continued long enough, and leading to no result.

"Stop, Huron; stay, chiefs!" exclaimed Judith, scarce knowing what she said, or why she interposed, unless to obtain time; "for God's sake, a single minute longer—"

The words were cut short by another and a still more extraordinary interruption. A young Indian came bounding through the Huron ranks, leaping into the very center of the circle, in a way to denote the utmost confidence, or a temerity bordering on foolhardiness. Five or six sentinels were still watching the lake at different and distant points; and it was the first impression of Rivenoak that one of these had come in with tidings of import. Still, the movements of the stranger were so rapid, and his war dress, which scarcely left him more drapery than an antique statue, had so little distinguishing about it, that, at the first moment, it was impossible to ascertain whether he were friend or foe. Three leaps carried this warrior to the side of Deerslayer, whose withes were cut in the twinkling of an eye, with a quickness and precision that left the prisoner perfect master of his limbs. Not till this was effected did the stranger bestow a glance on any other object; then he turned and showed the astonished Hurons the noble brow, fine person, and eagle eye of a young warrior, in the paint and panoply of a Delaware. He held a rifle in each hand, the butts of both resting on the earth, while from one dangled its proper pouch and horn. This was Killdeer, which even as he looked boldly and in defiance on the crowd around him, he suffered to fall back into the hands of the proper owner. The presence of two armed men, though it was in their midst, startled the Hurons. Their rifles were scattered about against the different trees, and their only weapons were their knives and tomahawks. Still, they had too much self-possession to betray fear. It was little likely that so small a force would assail so strong a band; and each man expected some extraordinary proposition to succeed so decisive a step. The stranger did not seem disposed to disappoint them; he prepared to speak.

"Hurons," he said, "this earth is very big. The Great Lakes are big, too; there is room beyond them for the Iroquois; there is room for the Delawares on this side. I am Chingachgook, the son of Uncas; the kinsman of Tamenund. This is my betrothed; that paleface is my friend. My heart was heavy when I missed him. All the Delaware girls are waiting for Wah; they wonder that she stays away so long. Come, let us say farewell, and go on our path."

"Hurons, this is your mortal enemy, the Great Serpent of them you hate!" cried Briarthorn. "If he escape, blood will be in your moccasin prints from this spot to the Canadas. *I* am *all* Huron."

As the last words were uttered, the traitor cast his knife at the naked breast of the Delaware. A quick movement of the arm, on the part of Hist, who stood near, turned aside the blow, the dangerous weapon burying its point in a pine. At the next instant, a similar weapon glanced from the hand of the Serpent, and quivered in the recreant's heart. A minute had scarcely elapsed from the moment in which Chingachgook bounded into the circle, and that in which Briarthorn fell, like a dog, dead in his tracks. The rapidity of events prevented the Hurons from acting; but this catastrophe permitted no further delay. A common exclamation followed, and the whole party was in motion. At this instant, a sound unusual to the woods was heard, and every Huron, male and female, paused to listen, with ears erect and faces filled with expectation. The sound was regular and heavy, as if the earth were struck with beetles. Objects became visible among the trees of the background, and a body of troops was seen advancing with measured tread. They came upon the charge, the scarlet of the King's livery shining among the bright green foliage of the forest.

The scene that followed is not easily described. It was one in which wild confusion, despair, and frenzied efforts were so blended as to destroy the unity and distinctness of the action. A general yell burst from the inclosed Hurons; it was succeeded by the hearty cheers of England. Still, not a musket or rifle was fired, though that steady, measured tramp continued, and the bayonet was seen gleaming in advance of a line that counted nearly sixty men. The Hurons were taken at a fearful disadvantage. On three sides was the water, while their formidable and trained foes cut them off from flight on the fourth. Each warrior rushed for his arms, and then all on the point, man, woman, and child, eagerly sought the covers. In this scene of confusion and dismay, however, nothing could surpass the discretion and coolness of Deerslayer. His first care was to place Judith and Hist behind trees, and he looked for Hetty; but she had been hurried away in the crowd of Huron women. This effected, he threw himself on a flank of the retiring Hurons, who were inclining off toward the southern margin of the point, in the hope of escaping through the water. Deerslayer watched his opportunity, and finding two of his recent tormentors in a range, his rifle first broke the silence of the terrific scene. The bullet brought down both at one discharge. This drew a general fire from the Hurons, and the rifle and war cry of the Serpent were heard in the clamor. Still, the trained men returned no answering volley, the whoop and piece of Hurry alone being heard on their side, if we except the short, prompt word of authority, and that heavy, measured, and menacing tread. Presently, however, the shrieks, groans, and denunciations that usually accompany the use of the bayonet, followed. That terrible and deadly weapon was glutted in vengeance. The scene that succeeded was one of those, of which so many have occurred in our own times, in which neither age nor sex forms an exemption to the lot of a savage warfare.

The picture next presented by the point of land that the unfortunate Hurons had selected for their last place of encampment, need scarcely be laid before the eyes of the reader. Happily for the more tender-minded and the more timid, the trunks of the trees, the leaves, and the smoke, had concealed much of that which passed; and night shortly after drew its veil over the lake, and the whole of that seemingly interminable wilderness, which may be said to have then stretched, with few and immaterial interruptions, from the banks of the Hudson to the shores of the Pacific Ocean. Our business carries us into the following day, when light returned upon the earth, as sunny and as smiling as if nothing extraordinary had occurred.

When the sun rose on the following morning, every sign of hostility and alarm had vanished from the basin of the Glimmerglass. The frightful event of the preceding evening had left no impression on the placid sheet, and the untiring hours pursued their course in the placid order prescribed by the powerful Hand that set them in motion. The birds were again skimming the water, or were seen poised on the wing high above the tops of the tallest pines of the mountains, ready to make their swoops in obedience to the irresistible laws of their nature. In a word, nothing was changed but the air of movement and life that prevailed in and around the castle. Here, indeed, was an alteration that must have struck the least observant eye. A sentinel, who wore the light infantry uniform of a royal regiment, paced the platform with measured tread, and some twenty men of the same corps lounged about the place, or were seated in the ark. Their arms were stacked under the eye of their comrade on post. Two officers stood examining the shore with the ship's glass so often mentioned. Their looks were directed to that fatal point, where scarlet coats were still to be seen gliding among the trees, and where the magnifying power of the instrument also showed spades at work, and the sad duty of interment going on. Several of the common men bore proof on their persons that their enemies had not been overcome entirely without resistance; and the youngest of the two officers on the platform wore an arm in a sling. His companion, who commanded the party, had been more fortunate. He it was that used the glass, in making the reconnaissances in which the two were engaged.

A sergeant approached to make a report. He addressed the senior of these officers as Captain Warley, while the other was alluded to as Mr. ——, which was equivalent to Ensign —— Thornton. The former was, in truth, the very individual with whom the scandal of the garrisons had most freely connected the name of this beautiful but indiscreet girl. He was a hard-featured, red-faced man, of about five-and-thirty, but of a military carriage, and with an air of fashion that might easily impose on the imagination of one as ignorant of the world as Judith.

"Craig is covering us with benedictions," observed this person to his young ensign, with an air of indifference, as he shut the glass and handed it to his servant; "to say the truth, not without reason; it is certainly more agreeable to be here in attendance on Miss Judith Hutter, than to be burying Indians on a point of the lake, however romantic the position or brilliant the victory. By the way, Wright, is Davis still living?"

"He died about ten minutes since, your honor," returned the sergeant, to whom this question was addressed. "I knew how it would be, as soon as I found the bullet had touched the stomach. I never knew a man who could hold out long, if he had a hole in his stomach."

"No; it is rather inconvenient for carrying away anything very nourishing," observed Warley, gaping. "This being up two nights *de suite,* Arthur, plays the devil with a man's faculties! I'm as stupid as one of those Dutch parsons on the Mohawk—I hope your arm is not painful, my dear boy?"

"It draws a few grimaces from me, sir, as I suppose you see," answered the youth, laughing at the very moment his countenance was a little awry with pain. "But it may be borne. I suppose Graham can spare a few minutes, soon, to look at my hurt."

"She is a lovely creature, this Judith Hutter, after all, Thornton; and it shall not be my fault, if she is not seen and admired in the parks!" resumed Warley, who thought little of his companion's wound. "Your arm, eh! Quite true. Go into the ark, sergeant, and tell Dr. Graham I desire he would look at Mr. Thornton's injury as soon as he has done with the poor fellow with the broken leg. A lovely creature! and she looked like a queen in that brocade dress in which we met her. I find all changed here; father and mother both gone, the sister dying, if not dead, and none of the family left but the beauty! This has been a lucky expedition all round, and promises to terminate better than Indian skirmishes in general."

"Am I to suppose, sir, that you are about to desert your colors, in the great corps of bachelors, and close the campaign with matrimony?"

"I, Tom Warley, turn Benedict! Faith, my dear boy, you little know the corps you speak of, if you fancy any such thing. I do suppose there *are* women in the colonies that a captain of light-infantry need not disdain; but they are not to be found up here on a mountain lake; or even down on the Dutch river where we are posted. It is true my uncle, the general, once did me the favor to choose a wife for me, in Yorkshire; but she had no beauty—and I would not marry a princess unless she were handsome."

"If handsome, you would marry a beggar?"

"Ay, these are the notions of an ensign! Love in a cottage—doors

—and windows—the old story, for the hundredth time. The 20th—— don't *marry*. We are not a marrying corps, my dear boy. There's the colonel, old Sir Edwin——, now; though a full general, he has never thought of a wife; and when a man gets as high as a lieutenant-general, without matrimony, he is pretty safe. Then the lieutenant-colonel is *confirmed*, as I tell my cousin, the bishop. The major is a widower, having tried matrimony for twelve months in his youth; and we look upon him, now, as one of our most certain men. Out of ten captains, but one is in the dilemma; and he, poor devil, is always kept at regimental headquarters, as a sort of *memento mori* to the young men as they join. As for the subalterns, not one has ever yet had the audacity to speak of introducing a wife into the regiment. But your arm is troublesome, and we'll go ourselves and see what has become of Graham."

The surgeon who had accompanied the party was employed very differently from what the captain supposed. When the assault was over, and the dead and wounded were collected, poor Hetty had been found among the latter. A rifle bullet had passed through her body, inflicting an injury that was known at a glance to be mortal. How this wound was received, no one knew; it was probably one of those casualties that ever accompany scenes like that related in the previous chapter. The Sumach, all the elderly women, and some of the Huron girls, had fallen by the bayonet; either in the confusion of the *mêleé*, or from the difficulty of distinguishing the sexes, where the dress was so simple. Much the greater portion of the warriors suffered on the spot. A few had escaped, however, and two or three had been taken unharmed. As for the wounded, the bayonet saved the surgeon much trouble. Rivenoak had escaped with life and limb; but was injured and a prisoner. As Captain Warley and his ensign went into the ark, they passed him, seated in dignified silence, in one end of the scow, his head and leg bound, but betraying no visible signs of despondency or despair. That he mourned the loss of his tribe, is certain; still, he did it in a manner that best became a warrior and a chief.

The two soldiers found their surgeon in the principal room of the ark. He was just quitting the pallet of Hetty, with an expression of sorrowful regret on his hard, pock-marked, Scottish features, that it was not usual to see there. All his assiduity had been useless, and he was compelled reluctantly to abandon the expectation of seeing the girl survive many hours. Dr. Graham was accustomed to deathbed scenes, and ordinarily they produced but little impression on him. In all that relates to religion, his was one of those minds which, in consequence of reasoning much on material things, logically and consecutively, and overlooking the total want of premises which such a theory must ever possess, through its want of a primary agent, had become skeptical; leaving a vague opinion concerning the origin of things, that with high pretensions to philosophy, failed in the first of all philosophical principles, a cause. To him religious dependence appeared a weakness; but when he found one gentle and young like Hetty, with a mind beneath the level of her race, sustained at such a moment by these pious sentiments, and that, too, in a way that many a sturdy warrior and reputed hero might have looked upon with envy, he found himself affected by the sight, to a degree that he would have been ashamed to confess. Edinburgh and Aberdeen, then as now, supplied no small portion of the medical men of the British service; and Dr. Graham, as indeed his name and countenance equally indicated, was, by birth, a North Briton.

"Here is an extraordinary exhibition for a forest, and one but half-gifted with reason," he observed, with a decided Scotch accent, as Warley and the ensign entered; "I just hope, gentlemen, that when we three shall be called on to quit the 20th—we may be found as resigned to go on the half-pay of another existence as this poor demented chiel!"

13

HETTY DIED, and Deerslayer and others buried her in the lake beside her mother. That day, and the next, the British troops left Glimmerglass, or Otsego Lake, in two detachments, carrying the wounded, the prisoners, and the trophies back to their fort on the Mohawk. All of Hutter's effects, even his chest, were transported northward by the soldiers. On the second day, Deerslayer, Chingachgook, Hist, and Judith forsook the lake in company with the last of the King's men. Hutter's castle was left empty, its door and windows barred. Some of the soldiers used the ark to help them cover the length of the lake, intending then to abandon it. Chingachgook and Hist-oh-Hist took a canoe, and paddled away in the same direction as the troops. This left Deerslayer and Judith —"the beautiful and still weeping mourner"—to occupy another canoe.

The direction taken by Deerslayer and the young woman carried them past the graves in the lake. Judith expressed a hope that the innocence of Hetty might answer, in the eyes of God, for the salvation of her mother as well as herself; but honest Deerslayer thought this poor theology—"Each spirit answers for its own backslidings; though a hearty repentance will satisfy God's laws." As Judith gazed through the clear water at the graves, her feelings carried her away, and she spoke to Deerslayer with the most complete frankness.

"This lake will soon be entirely deserted," she said, "and this, too, at a moment when it will be a more secure dwelling place than ever. What has so lately happened will prevent the Iroquois from venturing again to visit it, for a long time to come."

"That it will!—yes, that may be set down as settled. I do not mean to pass this-a-way, ag'in, so long as the war lasts; for, to my mind, no Huron moccasin will leave its print on the leaves of this forest, until their traditions have forgotten to tell their young men of their disgrace and rout."

"And do you so delight in violence and bloodshed? I had thought better of *you*, Deerslayer—believed you one who could find his happiness in a quiet domestic home, with an attached and loving wife, ready to study your wishes, and healthy and dutiful children, anxious to follow in your footsteps, and to become as honest and just as yourself."

"Lord, Judith, what a tongue you're mistress of! Speech and looks go hand in hand, like; and what one can't do, the other is pretty sartain to perform! Such a gal, in a month, might spoil the stoutest warrior in the colony."

"And am I then so mistaken? Do you really love war, Deerslayer, better than the hearth and the affections?"

"I understand your meaning, gal; yes, I do understand what you mean, I believe, though I don't think you altogether understand *me*. Warrior I may now call myself, I suppose, for I've both fou't and conquered, which is sufficient for the name; neither will I deny that I've feelin's for the callin', which is both manful and honorable, when carried on accordin' to nat'ral gifts—but I've no relish for blood. Youth is youth, howsever, and a Mingo is a Mingo. If the young men of this region stood by, and suffered the vagabonds to overrun the land, why, we might as well all turn Frenchers at once, and give up country and kin. I'm no fire-eater, Judith, or one that likes fightin' for fightin's sake; but I can see no great difference atween *givin' up territory afore a war, out of a dread of war, and givin' it up a'ter a war, because we can't help it—onless it be that the last is the most manful and honorable.*"

"No woman would ever wish to see her husband or brother stand by, and submit to insult and wrong, Deerslayer, however she might mourn the necessity of his running into the dangers of battle. But you've done enough already, in clearing this region of the Hurons; since to you is principally owing the credit of our late victory. Now listen to me patiently, and answer me with that native honesty, which it is as pleasant to regard in one of your sex as it is unusual to meet with."

Judith paused; for now that she was on the very point of explaining herself, native modesty asserted its power, notwithstanding the encouragement and confidence she derived from the great simplicity of her companion's character. Her cheeks, which had so lately been pale, flushed, and her eyes lighted with some of their former brilliancy. Feeling gave expression to her countenance, and softness to her voice, rendering her who was always beautiful, trebly seductive and winning.

"Deerslayer," she said, after a considerable pause, "this is not a moment for affectation, deception, or a want of frankness of any sort. Here, over my mother's grave, and over the grave of truth-loving, truth-telling Hetty, everything like unfair dealing seems to be out of place. I will therefore speak to you without any reserve, and without any dread of being misunderstood. You are not an acquaintance of a week, but it appears to me as if I had known you for years. So much, and so much that is important, has taken place within that short time, that the sorrows, and dangers, and escapes of a whole life have been crowded into a few days; and they who have suffered and acted together in such scenes, ought not to feel like strangers. I know that what I am about to say might be misunderstood by most men, but I hope for a generous construction of my course from you. We are not here dwelling among the arts and deceptions of the settlements, but young people who have no occasion to deceive each other, in any manner or form. I hope I make myself understood?"

"Sartain, Judith; few convarse better than yourself, and none more agreeable, like. Your words are as pleasant as your looks."

"It is the manner in which you have so often praised those looks, that gives me courage to proceed. Still, Deerslayer, it is not easy for one of my sex and years to forget all her lessons of infancy, all her habits, and her natural diffidence, and say openly what her heart feels!"

"Why not, Judith? Why shouldn't women as well as men deal fairly and honestly by their fellow-creatur's? I see no reason why you should not speak as plainly as myself, when there is anything ra'ally important to be said."

This indomitable diffidence, which still prevented the young man from suspecting the truth, would have completely discouraged the girl, had not her whole soul, as well as her whole heart, been set upon making a desperate effort to rescue herself from a future that she dreaded with a horror as vivid as the distinctness with which she fancied she foresaw it. This motive, however, raised her above all common considerations, and she persevered even to her own surprise, if not to her great confusion.

"I will—I *must* deal as plainly with you, as I would with poor, dear Hetty, were that sweet child living!" she continued, turning pale, instead of blushing, the high resolution by which she was prompted reversing the effect that such a procedure would ordinarily produce on one of her sex; "yes, I will smother all other feelings, in the one that is now uppermost! You love the woods and the life that we pass, here, in the wilderness, away from the dwellings and towns of the whites."

"As I loved my parents, Judith, when they was living! This very spot would be all creation to me, could this war be fairly over, once; and the settlers kept at a distance."

"Why quit it, then? It has no owner—at least none who can claim a better right than mine, and *that* I freely give to you. Were it a kingdom, Deerslayer, I think I should delight to say the same. Let us then return to it, after we have seen the priest at the fort, and never quit it again, until God calls us away to that world where we shall find the spirits of my poor mother and sister."

A long, thoughtful pause succeeded; Judith having covered her face with both hands, after forcing herself to utter so plain a proposal, and Deerslayer musing equally in sorrow and surprise, on the meaning of the language he had just heard. At length the hunter broke the silence, speaking in a tone that was softened to gentleness by his desire not to offend.

"You haven't thought well of this, Judith," he said; "no, your feelin's are awakened by all that has lately happened, and believin' yourself to be without kindred in the world, you are in too great a haste to find some to fill the places of them that's lost."

"Were I living in a crowd of friends, Deerslayer, I should still think as I now think,—say as I now say," returned Judith, speaking with her hands still shading her lovely face.

"Thank you, gal—thank you, from the bottom of my heart. Howsever, I am not one to take advantage of a weak moment, when you're forgetful of your own great advantages, and fancy 'arth and all it holds is in this little canoe. No—no—Judith, 'twould be ongin'rous in me; what you've offered can never come to pass!"

"It all may be, and that without leaving cause of repentance to any," answered Judith, with an impetuosity of feeling and manner, that at once unveiled her eyes. "We can cause the soldiers to leave our goods on the road, till we return, when they can easily be brought back to the house; the lake will be no more visited by the enemy, this war at least; all your skins may be readily sold at the garrison; there *you* can buy the few necessaries we shall want, for I wish never to see the spot again; and Deerslayer," added the girl, smiling with a sweetness and nature that the young man found it hard to resist, "as a proof how wholly I am and wish to be yours—how completely I desire to be nothing but your wife, the very first fire that we kindle, after our return, shall be lighted with the brocade dress, and fed by every article I have that you may think unfit for the woman you wish to live with!"

"Ah's me!—you're a winning and a lovely creatur', Judith; yes, you *are* all that, and no one can deny it, and speak truth. These pictur's are pleasant to the thoughts, but they mightn't prove so happy as you now think 'em. Forget it all, therefore, and let us paddle after the Sarpent and Hist, as if nothing had been said on the subject."

Judith was deeply mortified, and what is more, she was profoundly grieved. Still there was a steadiness and quiet in the manner of Deerslayer, that completely smothered her hopes, and told her that for once, her exceeding beauty had failed to excite the admiration and homage it was wont to receive. Women are said seldom to forgive those who slight their advances; but this high-spirited and impetuous girl entertained no shadow of resentment, then or ever, against the fair-dealing and ingenuous hunter. At the moment, the prevailing feeling was the wish to be certain that there was no misunderstanding. After another painful pause, therefore, she brought the matter to an issue, by a question too direct to admit of equivocation.

"God forbid that we lay up regrets in after-life, through any want of sincerity now," she said. "I hope we understand each other at least. You will not accept me for a wife, Deerslayer?"

" 'Tis better for both that I shouldn't take advantage of your own forgetfulness, Judith. We can never marry."

"You do not love me,—cannot find it in your heart, perhaps, to esteem me, Deerslayer!"

"Everything in the way of fri'ndship, Judith—everything, even to sarvices and life itself. Yes, I'd risk as much for you, at this moment, as I would risk in behalf of Hist; and that is sayin' as much as I can say of any darter of woman. I do not think I feel toward either—mind I say *either,* Judith—as if I wished to quit father and mother—if father and mother was livin'; which, however, neither is—but if both was livin', I do not feel toward any woman as if I wish'd to quit 'em in order to cleave unto *her.*"

"This is enough!" answered Judith, in a rebuked and smothered voice; "I understand all that you mean. Marry you cannot, without loving; and that love you do not feel for me. Make no answer if I am right, for I shall understand your silence. *That* will be painful enough of itself."

Deerslayer obeyed her, and he made no reply. For more than a minute the girl riveted her bright eyes on him as if to read his soul; while he sat playing with the water, like a corrected schoolboy. Then Judith herself dropped the end of her paddle, and urged the canoe away from the spot, with a movement as reluctant as the feelings which controlled it. Deerslayer quietly aided the effort, however, and they were soon on the trackless line taken by the Delaware.

In their way to the point, not another syllable was exchanged between Deerslayer and his fair companion. As Judith sat in the bow of the canoe, her back was turned toward him, else it is probable the expression of her countenance might have induced him to venture some soothing terms of friendship and regard. Contrary to what would have been expected, resentment was still absent, though the color frequently changed from the deep flush of mortification to the paleness of disappointment. Sorrow, deep, heartfelt sorrow, however, was the predominant emotion, and this was betrayed in a manner not to be mistaken.

As neither labored hard at the paddle, the ark had already arrived, and the soldiers had disembarked before the canoe of the two loiterers reached the point. Chingachgook had preceded it, and was already some distance in the wood, at a spot where the two trails, that to the garrison, and that to the villages of the Delawares, separated. The soldiers, too, had taken up their line of march; first setting the ark adrift again, with a reckless disregard of its fate. All this Judith saw, but she heeded it not. The Glimmerglass had no longer any charms for her; and when she put her foot on the strand, she immediately proceeded on the trail of the soldiers, without casting a single glance behind her. Even Hist was passed unnoticed; that modest young creature shrinking from the averted face of Judith, as if guilty herself of some wrongdoing.

"Wait you here, Sarpent," said Deerslayer, as he followed in the footsteps of the dejected beauty, while passing his friend. "I will just see Judith among her party, and come and j'ine you."

A hundred yards had hid the couple from those in front, as well as those in the rear, when Judith turned and spoke.

"This will do, Deerslayer," she said, sadly. "I understand your kindness, but shall not need it. In a few minutes I shall reach the soldiers. As you cannot go with me on the journey of life, I do not wish you to go farther on this. But stop; before we part I would ask you a single question. And I require of you as you fear God, and reverence the truth, not to deceive me in your answer. I know you do not love another; and I can see but one reason why you cannot, *will* not love me. Tell me, then, Deerslayer"—The girl paused, the words she was about to utter, seeming to choke her. Then rallying all her resolution, with a face that flushed and paled at every breath she drew, she continued: "Tell me, then, Deerslayer, if anything light of me, that Henry March has said, may not have influenced your feelings?"

Truth was the Deerslayer's polar star. He ever kept it in view; and it was nearly impossible for him to avoid uttering it, even when prudence demanded silence. Judith read his answer in his countenance; and with a heart nearly broken by the consciousness of undeserving, she signed to him an adieu, and buried herself in the woods. For some time Deerslayer was irresolute as to his course; but in the end, he retraced his steps and joined the Delaware. That night, the three "camped" on the headwaters of their own river, and the succeeding evening they entered the village of the tribe; Chingachgook and his betrothed, in triumph; their companion honored and admired, but in a sorrow that it required months of activity to remove.

The war that then had its rise was stirring and bloody. The Delaware chief rose among his people, until his name was never mentioned without eulogiums; while another Uncas, the last of his race, was added to the long line of warriors who bore that distinguished appellation. As for the Deerslayer, under the *sobriquet* of Hawkeye, he made his fame spread far and near, until the crack of his rifle became as terrible to the ears of the Mingoes, as the thunders of the Manitou. His services were soon required by the officers of the Crown, and he especially attached himself, in the field, to one in particular, with whose after-life he had a close and important connection.

Fifteen years had passed away, ere it was in the power of the Deerslayer to revisit the Glimmerglass. A peace had intervened, and it was on the eve of another, and still more important war, when he and his constant friend, Chingachgook, were hastening to the forts to join their allies. A stripling accompanied them, for Hist already slumbered beneath the pines of the Delawares, and the three survivors had now become inseparable. They reached the lake just as the sun was setting. Here all was unchanged; the river still rushed through its bower of trees; the little rock was wasting away by the slow action of the waves in the course of centuries; the mountains stood in their native dress, dark, rich, and mysterious; while the sheet glistened in its solitude, a beautiful gem of the forest.

The following morning the youth discovered one of the canoes drifted on the shore, in a state of decay. A little labor put it in a state for service, and they all embarked, with a desire to examine the place. All the points were passed, and Chingachgook pointed out to his son the spot where the Hurons had first encamped, and the point whence he had succeeded in stealing his bride. Here they even landed; but all trace of the former visit had disappeared. Next they proceeded to the scene of the battle, and there they found a few of the signs that linger around such localities. Wild beasts had disinterred many of the bodies, and human bones were bleaching in the rains of summer. Uncas regarded all with reverence and pity, though traditions were already rousing his young mind to the ambition and sternness of a warrior.

From the point, the canoe took its way toward the shoal, where the remains of the castle were still visible, a picturesque ruin. The storms of winter had long since unroofed the house, and decay had eaten into the logs. All the fastenings were untouched, but the seasons rioted in the place, as if in mockery at the attempt to exclude them. The palisades were rotting, as were the piles; and it was evident that a few more recurrences of winter, a few more gales and tempests, would sweep all into the lake, and blot the building from the face of that magnificent solitude. The graves could not be found. Either the elements had obliterated their traces, or time had caused those who looked for them to forget their position.

The ark was discovered stranded on the eastern shore, where it had long before been driven, with the prevalent northwest winds. It lay on the sandy extremity of a long, low point, that is situated about two miles from the outlet, and which is itself fast disappearing before the action of the elements. The scow was filled with water, the cabin unroofed, and the logs were decaying. Some of its coarser furniture still remained, and the heart of Deerslayer beat quick as he found a ribbon of Judith's fluttering from a log. It recalled all her beauty, and we may add, all her failings. Although the girl had never touched his heart, the Hawkeye, for so we ought now to call him, still retained a kind and sincere interest in her welfare. He tore away the ribbon and knotted it to the stock of Killdeer, which had been the gift of the girl herself.

A few miles farther up the lake another of the canoes was discovered; and on the point where the party finally landed, were found those which had been left there upon the shore. That in which the present navigation was made, and the one discovered on the eastern shore, had dropped through the decayed floor of the castle, drifted past the falling palisades, and had been thrown as waifs upon the beach.

From all these signs, it was probable the lake had not been visited since the occurrence of the final scene of our tale. Accident or tradition had rendered it again a spot sacred to nature; the frequent wars, and the feeble population of the colonies, still confining the settlements within narrow boundaries. Chingachgook and his friend left the spot with melancholy feelings. It had been the region of their first warpath, and it carried back the minds of both to scenes of tenderness as well as to hours of triumph. They held their way toward the Mohawk in silence, however, to rush into new adventures, as stirring and as remarkable as those which had attended their opening career on this lovely lake. At a later day they returned to the place, where the Indian found a grave.

Time and circumstances have drawn an impenetrable mystery around all else connected with the Hutters. They lived, erred, died, and are forgotten. None connected have felt sufficient interest in the disgraced and disgracing, to withdraw the veil; and a century is about to erase even the recollection of their names. The history of crime is ever revolting, and it is fortunate that few love to dwell on its incidents. The sins of the family have long since been arraigned at the judgment seat of God, or are registered for the terrible settlement of the last great day.

The same fate attended Judith. When Hawkeye reached the garrison on the Mohawk, he inquired anxiously after that lovely, but misguided creature. None knew her—even her person was no longer remembered. Other officers had again and again succeeded the Warleys and Craigs and Grahams; though an old sergeant of the garrison, who had lately come from England, was enabled to tell our hero that Sir Robert Warley lived on his paternal estates, and that there was a lady of rare beauty in the lodge, who had great influence over him, though she did not bear his name. Whether this was Judith, relapsed into her early failing, or some other victim of the soldier's, Hawkeye never knew, nor would it be pleasant or profitable to inquire. We live in a world of transgressions and selfishness, and no pictures that represent us otherwise can be true; though happily for human nature, gleamings of that pure spirit in whose likeness man has been fashioned, are to be seen, relieving its deformities, and mitigating, if not excusing its crimes.

THE LAST OF THE MOHICANS

Being the SECOND SERIES OF ADVENTURES *of*

LEATHERSTOCKING

LEATHERSTOCKING reappears some fifteen years after the events of The Deerslayer, *now a well-matured man of thirty-eight, his mind and character enriched by a long array of wilderness experiences. A new war with the French and Indians has commenced; the Seven Years' War, begun when George Washington, dispatched by Governor Robert Dinwiddie of Virginia to warn the French from the forks of the Ohio, killed Ensign Jumonville and*

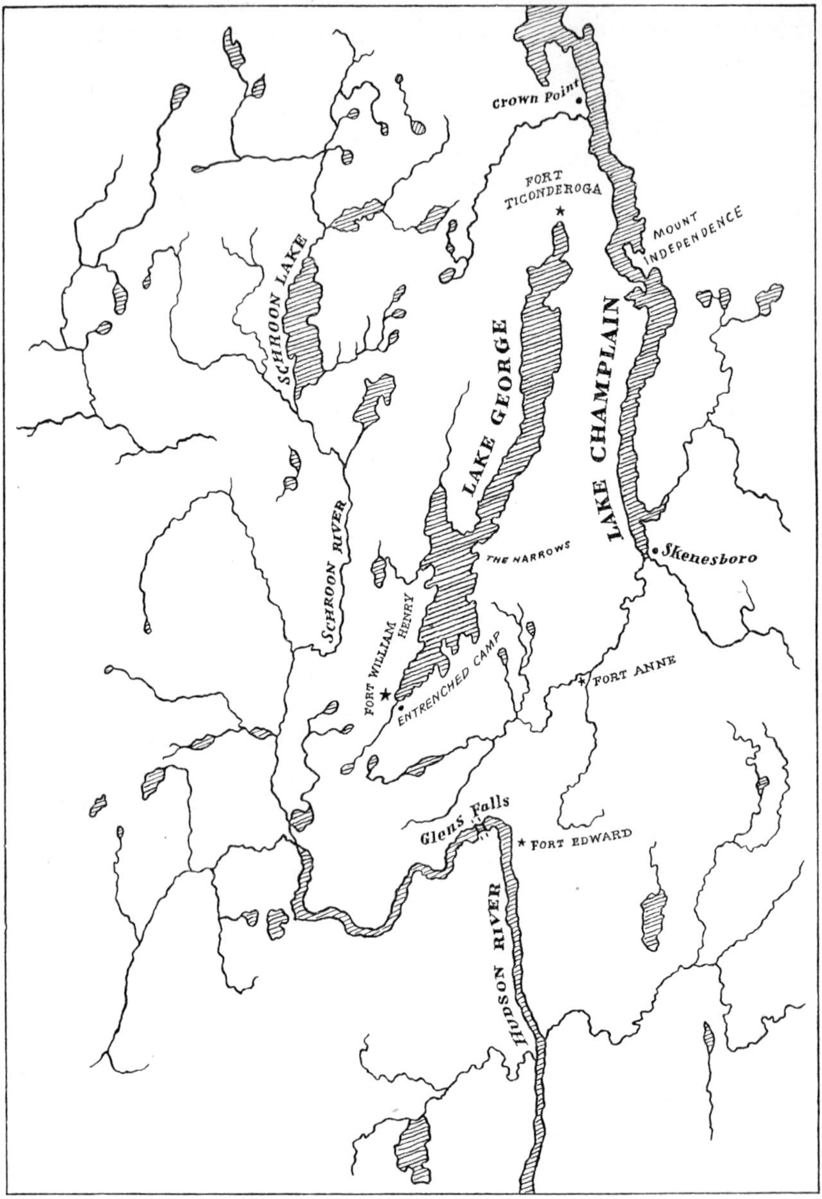

THE SCENE OF *The Last of the Mohicans*

(Fort St. Frédéric, which the French built in 1731, was replaced by Crown Point after its capture by the British in 1759; Fort Carillon, which the French built in 1755, was renamed Ticonderoga after the British captured it in 1759.)

nine of his men. Those shots in the Pennsylvania woods set the world ablaze. For the first three years the conflict has raged with varying fortunes. Braddock was routed in his march to the upper Ohio; the British and colonials defeated Dieskau on Lake George; the French captured Fort Oswego; Robert Rogers and his partisans harried the French in the area of Ticonderoga. Then, in the summer of 1757, came news that Montcalm, with nearly eight thousand French and Indians at his back, was marching southward from Lake Champlain to lay siege to Fort William Henry on Lake George.

As Montcalm approaches the fort, Leatherstocking (now called Hawkeye) finds a new and broader stage on which to display his intrepidity and resourcefulness. A brave and skilful Scotch veteran, Lieutenant-Colonel Munro, commands at William Henry, a rough fort of heavy logs and gravel, with ditches and chevaux-de-frise *in front. The British are suffering from a division of forces. At Fort Edward, but fourteen miles away, lies General Webb with two thousand six hundred men. Had he united with Munro, they would have had nearly four thousand in all, and could have summoned at least a thousand more from neighboring points. But Webb failed to move. Early in August Montcalm's host swept southward by water, the French and Canadians in two hundred and fifty bateaux, the painted savages in a swarm of canoes. Among these Indians were not merely familiar French allies like the Hurons and Abenakis, but Canadian Iroquois, Acadian Micmacs, and tribesmen from the West—Ottawas, Ojibways, Pottawatomies, Winnebagoes, and Miamis. No wonder that the brave Colonel Munro trembled for his daughters' safety.*

Leatherstocking, or Hawkeye, no longer has the callowness which blemished his fine qualities in The Deerslayer. *He is in his very prime: alert, swift, coolheaded, well-balanced, and sagacious. He is even nobler of spirit than before, wiser and more philosophically tolerant. A loyal son of the forest, he has learned the patience and the religious sensitiveness taught by nature. Chingachgook also, proud, cunning, relentless, and yet magnanimous, is in the full glory of his manhood. A special element of romance and even of poetry is supplied by Chingachgook's son, the youthful Uncas. The portrait of this flashing youth, as gallant as he is brave, as truthful and courteous as he is expert in war and woodcraft, is perhaps the most engaging study of an Indian ever made. In the impressive figures of Chingachgook and Uncas, Cooper admittedly idealized the red man. But to the charge that he idealized them too much we can reply that some Indians have actually measured up to ideal standards, as the famous figures of Black Hawk and Chief Joseph prove. It can also be said that the cruel, treacherous, greedy, and childish side of the Indian character are fully emphasized in Cooper's pages, and that the wily scoundrel Magua in this very book embodies all that is base in Indian nature.*

From the opening page, the movement of the story is swift and its suspense never slackens. One or two historic scenes, notably the massacre of the helpless prisoners at Fort William Henry, are unforgettable. In the main, however, it is simply an adventure story: a story of pursuit, escape, capture, and (the tables being turned) the pursuit of the captors. The plot affords ample room for swift clashes, hairbreadth evasions, ruses, sudden reversals of fortune, and displays of almost superhuman nerve and courage. Something more than a suffusing sense of peril supports the suspense. The action becomes a competition between Hawkeye and Magua in nerve, energy, foresight and endurance, and this rivalry of white man and red gives it a deeper interest. The most important part of the book, however, is not the adventure; it is the full and careful study of Leatherstocking's character.

1

IT WAS a feature peculiar to the Colonial wars of North America, that the toils and dangers of the wilderness were to be encountered before the adverse hosts could meet. A wide and apparently an impervious boundary of forests severed the possessions of the hostile provinces of France and England. The hardy colonist, and the trained European who fought at his side, frequently expended months in struggling against the rapids of the streams, or in effecting the rugged passes of the mountains, in quest of an opportunity to exhibit their courage in a more martial conflict. But, emulating the patience and self-denial of the practiced native warriors, they learned to overcome every difficulty; and it would seem that, in time, there was no recess of the woods so dark, nor any secret place so lovely, that it might claim exemption from the inroads of those who had pledged their blood to satiate their vengeance, or to uphold the cold and selfish policy of the distant monarchs of Europe.

Perhaps no district throughout the wide extent of the intermediate frontiers can furnish a livelier picture of the cruelty and fierceness of the savage warfare of those periods than the country which lies between the headwaters of the Hudson and the adjacent lakes.

The facilities which nature had there offered to the march of the combatants were too obvious to be neglected. The lengthened sheet of the Champlain stretched from the frontiers of Canada, deep within the borders of the neighboring province of New York, forming a natural passage across half the distance that the French were compelled to master in order to strike their enemies. Near its southern termination, it received the contributions of another lake, whose waters were so limpid as to have been exclusively selected by the Jesuit missionaries to perform the typical purification of baptism, and to obtain for it the title of lake "du Saint Sacrement." The less zealous English thought they conferred a sufficient honor on its unsullied fountains, when they bestowed the name of their reigning prince, the second of the house of Hanover.[1] The two united to rob the untutored possessors of its wooded scenery of their native right to perpetuate its original appellation of "Horican."[2]

Winding its way among countless islands, and imbedded in mountains, the "holy lake" extended a dozen leagues still further to the south. With the high plain that there interposed itself to the further passage of the water, commenced a portage of as many miles, which conducted the adventurer to the banks of the Hudson, at a point where, with the usual obstructions of the rapids, or rifts, as they were then termed in the language of the country, the river became navigable to the tide.

While, in the pursuit of their daring plans of annoyance, the restless enterprise of the French even attempted the distant and difficult gorges of the Alleghany, it may easily be imagined that their proverbial acuteness would not overlook the natural advantages of the district we have just described. It became, emphatically, the bloody arena, in which most of the battles for the mastery of the colonies were contested. Forts were erected at the different points that commanded the facilities of the route, and were taken and retaken, razed and rebuilt, as victory alighted on the hostile banners. While the husbandman shrank back from the dangerous passes, within the safer boundaries of the more ancient settlements, armies larger than those that had often disposed of the scepters of the mother countries, were seen to bury themselves in these forests, whence they rarely returned but in skeleton bands, that were haggard with care, or dejected by defeat. Though the arts of peace were unknown to this fatal region, its forests were alive with men; its shades and glens rang with the sounds of martial music, and the echoes of its mountains threw back the laugh, or repeated the

---

[1] It was the Jesuit missionary, Father Jogues, who first saw the lake, on Corpus Christi Day in 1646, and so gave it the pious appellation. General William Johnson, leading his troops against Dieskau in 1755, changed the name to Lake George.—Ed.

[2] As each nation of the Indians had either its language or its dialect, they usually gave different names to the same places, though nearly all of their appellations were descriptive of the object. Thus, a literal translation of the name of this beautiful sheet of water, used by the tribe that dwelt on its banks, would be "The Tail of the Lake." Lake George, as it is vulgarly, and now indeed legally, called, forms a sort of tail to Lake Champlain, when viewed on the map. Hence the name. (*Cooper's note*)

wanton cry, of many a gallant and reckless youth, as he hurried by them, in the noontide of his spirits, to slumber in a long night of forgetfulness.

It was in this scene of strife and bloodshed that the incidents we shall attempt to relate occurred, during the third year of the war which England and France last waged for the possession of a country that neither was destined to retain.

The imbecility of her military leaders abroad, and the fatal want of energy in her councils at home, had lowered the character of Great Britain from the proud elevation on which it had been placed, by the talents and enterprise of her former warriors and statesmen.[1] No longer dreaded by her enemies, her servants were fast losing the confidence of self-respect. In this mortifying abasement, the colonists, though innocent of her imbecility, and too humble to be the agents of her blunders, were but the natural participators. They had recently seen a chosen army from that country, which, reverencing as a mother, they had blindly believed invincible—an army led by a chief who had been selected from a crowd of trained warriors, for his rare military endowments, disgracefully routed by a handful of French and Indians, and only saved from annihilation by the coolness and spirit of a Virginian boy, whose riper fame has since diffused itself, with the steady influence of moral truth, to the uttermost confines of Christendom.[2] A wide frontier had been laid naked by this unexpected disaster, and more substantial evils were preceded by a thousand fanciful and imaginary dangers. The alarmed colonists believed that the yells of the savages mingled with every fitful gust of wind that issued from the interminable forest of the West. The terrific character of their merciless enemies increased immeasurably the natural horrors of warfare. Numberless recent massacres were still vivid in their recollections; nor was there any ear in the provinces so deaf as not to have drunk in with avidity the narrative of some fearful tale of midnight murder, in which the natives of the forests were the principal and barbarous actors. As the credulous and excited traveller related the hazardous chances of the wilderness, the blood of the timid curdled with terror, and mothers cast anxious glances even at those children which slum-

---

[1] The defeat of Braddock's expedition to the Ohio in 1755, the failure of Governor Shirley's attempt against Fort Niagara in the same year, and the lack of any real fruits from General Johnson's victory over Dieskau were all disheartening. But under William Pitt the tide was about to turn.—Ed.

[2] Washington: who, after uselessly admonishing the European general of the danger into which he was heedlessly running, saved the remnants of the British army, on this occasion, by his decision and courage. The reputation earned by Washington in this battle was the principal cause of his being selected to command the American armies at a later day. It is a circumstance worthy of observation, that, while all America rang with his well-merited reputation, his name does not occur in any European account of the battle; at least, the author has searched for it without success. In this manner does the mother country absorb even the fame, under that system of rule. (*Cooper's note*)

bered within the security of the largest towns. In short, the magnifying influence of fear began to set at naught the calculations of reason, and to render those who should have remembered their manhood, the slaves of the basest of passions. Even the most confident and the stoutest hearts began to think the issue of the contest was becoming doubtful; and that abject class was hourly increasing in numbers, who thought they foresaw all the possessions of the English crown in America subdued by their Christian foes, or laid waste by the inroads of their relentless allies.

When, therefore, intelligence was received at the fort which covered the southern termination of the portage between the Hudson and the lakes, that Montcalm had been seen moving up the Champlain, with an army "numerous as the leaves on the trees," its truth was admitted with more of the craven reluctance of fear than with the stern joy that a warrior should feel, in finding an enemy within reach of his blow. The news had been brought, toward the decline of a day in midsummer, by an Indian runner, who also bore an urgent request from Munro, the commander of a work on the shore of the "holy lake," for a speedy and powerful reinforcement. It has already been mentioned that the distance between these two posts was less than five leagues. The rude path, which originally formed their line of communication, had been widened for the passage of wagons; so that the distance which had been travelled by the son of the forest in two hours, might easily be effected by a detachment of troops, with their necessary baggage, between the rising and setting of a summer sun. The loyal servants of the British crown had given to one of these forest fastnesses the name of William Henry, and to the other that of Fort Edward; calling each after a favorite prince of the reigning family. The veteran Scotchman just named held the first, with a regiment of regulars and a few provincials; a force really by far too small to make head against the formidable power that Montcalm was leading to the foot of his earthen mounds. At the latter, however, lay General Webb, who commanded the armies of the King in the northern provinces, with a body of more than five thousand men. By uniting the several detachments of his command, this officer might have arrayed nearly double that number of combatants against the enterprising Frenchman, who had ventured so far from his reinforcements, with an army but little superior in numbers.

But under the influence of their degraded fortunes, both officers and men appeared better disposed to await the approach of their formidable antagonists, within their works, than to resist the progress of their march, by emulating the successful example of the French at Fort du Quesne, and striking a blow on their advance.

After the first surprise of the intelligence had a little abated, a rumor was spread through the entrenched camp, which stretched along the margin of the Hudson, forming a chain of outworks to the body of the fort itself, that a chosen detachment of fifteen hundred men was to depart, with the dawn, for William Henry, the post at the northern extremity of the portage. That which at first was only rumor, soon became certainty, as orders passed from the quarters of the commander-in-chief to the several corps he had selected for this service, to prepare for their speedy departure. All doubt as to the intention of Webb now vanished, and an hour or two of hurried footsteps and anxious faces succeeded. The novice in the military art flew from point to point, retarding his own preparations by the excess of his violent and somewhat distempered zeal; while the more practiced veteran made his arrangements with a deliberation that scorned every appearance of haste; though his sober lineaments and anxious eye sufficiently betrayed that he had no very strong professional relish for the, as yet, untried and dreaded warfare of the wilderness. At length the sun set in a flood of glory, behind the distant western hills, and as darkness drew its veil around the secluded spot the sounds of preparation diminished; the last light finally disappeared from the log cabin of some officer; the trees cast their deeper shadows over the mounds and the rippling stream, and a silence soon pervaded the camp, as deep as that which reigned in the vast forest by which it was environed.

According to the orders of the preceding night, the heavy sleep of the army was broken by the rolling of the warning drums, whose rattling echoes were heard issuing, on the damp morning air, out of every vista of the woods, just as day began to draw the shaggy outlines of some tall pines of the vicinity, on the opening brightness of a soft and cloudless eastern sky. In an instant the whole camp was in motion; the meanest soldier arousing from his lair to witness the departure of his comrades, and to share in the excitement and incidents of the hour. The simple array of the chosen band was soon completed. While the regular and trained hirelings of the King marched with haughtiness to the right of the line, the less pretending colonists took their humbler position on its left, with a docility that long practice had rendered easy. The scouts departed; strong guards preceded and followed the lumbering vehicles that bore the baggage; and before the gray light of the morning was mellowed by the rays of the sun, the main body of the combatants wheeled into column, and left the encampment with a show of high military bearing, that served to drown the slumbering apprehensions of many a novice, who was now about to make his first essay in arms. While in view of their admiring comrades, the same proud front and ordered array was observed, until the notes of their fifes growing fainter in distance, the forest at length appeared to swallow up the living mass which had slowly entered its bosom.

The deepest sounds of the retiring and invisible column had ceased to be borne on the breeze to the listeners, and the latest straggler had already disappeared in pursuit; but there still remained the signs of another departure, before a log cabin of unusual size and accommodations, in front of which those sentinels paced their rounds, who were known to guard the person of the English general. At this spot were gathered some half dozen horses, caparisoned in a manner which showed that two, at least, were destined to bear the persons of females, of a rank that it was not usual to meet so far in the wilds of the country. A third wore the trappings and arms of an officer of the staff; while the rest, from the plainness of the housings, and the travelling mails with which they were encumbered, were evidently fitted for the reception of as many menials, who were, seemingly, already awaiting the pleasure of those they served. At a respectful distance from this unusual show, were gathered divers groups of curious idlers; some admiring the blood and bone of the high-mettled military charger, and others gazing at the preparations, with the dull wonder of vulgar curiosity. There was one man, however, who, by his countenance and actions, formed a marked exception to those who composed the latter class of spectators, being neither idle, nor seemingly very ignorant.

The person of this individual was to the last degree ungainly, without being in any particular manner deformed. He had all the bones and joints of other men, without any of their proportions. Erect, his stature surpassed that of his fellows; though, seated, he appeared reduced within the ordinary limits of the race. The same contrariety in his members seemed to exist throughout the whole man. His head was large; his shoulders narrow; his arms long and dangling; while his hands were small, if not delicate. His legs and thighs were thin, nearly to emaciation, but of extraordinary length; and his knees would have been considered tremendous, had they not been outdone by the broader foundations on which this false superstructure of blended human orders was so profanely reared. The ill-assorted and judicious attire of the individual only served to render his awkwardness more conspicuous. A sky-blue coat, with short and broad skirts and low cape, exposed a long thin neck, and longer and thinner legs, to the worst animadversions of the evil disposed. His nether garment was of yellow nankeen, closely fitted to the shape, and tied at his bunches of knees by large knots of white riband, a good deal sullied by use. Clouded cotton stockings, and shoes, on one of the latter of which was a plated spur, completed the costume of the lower extremity of this figure, no curve or angle of which was concealed, but, on the other hand, studiously exhibited, through the vanity or simplicity of its owner. From beneath the flap of an enormous pocket of a soiled vest of embossed silk, heavily ornamented with tarnished silver lace, projected an instrument, which, from being seen in such martial company, might have been easily mistaken for some mischievous and unknown implement of war. Small as it was, this uncommon engine had excited the curiosity of most of the Europeans in the camp, though several of the provincials were seen to handle it, not only without fear, but with the utmost familiarity. A large, civil cocked hat, like those worn by clergymen within the last thirty years, surmounted the whole, furnishing dignity to a good-natured and somewhat vacant countenance, that apparently needed such artificial aid, to support the gravity of some high and extraordinary trust.

While the common herd stood aloof, in deference to the quarters of Webb, the figure we have described stalked into the center of the domestics, freely expressing his censures or commendations on the merits of the horses, as by chance they displeased or satisfied his judgment.

"This beast I rather conclude, friend, is not of home raising, but is from foreign lands, or perhaps from the little island itself, over the blue water?" he said, in a voice as remarkable for the softness and sweetness of its tones, as was his person for its rare proportions: "I may speak of these things, and be no braggart; for I have been down at both havens; that which is situate at the mouth of Thames, and is named after the capital of Old England, and that which is called 'Haven,' with the addition of the word 'New'; and have seen the scows and brigantines collecting their droves, like the gathering to the ark, being outward bound to the Island of Jamaica, for the purpose of barter and traffic in four-footed animals; but never before have I beheld a beast which verified the true scripture war horse like this; 'He paweth in the valley, and rejoiceth in his strength: he goeth on to meet the armed men. He saith among the trumpets, Ha, ha; and he smelleth the battle afar off, the thunder of the captains, and the shouting.'—It would seem that the stock of the horse of Israel has descended to our own time; would it not, friend?"

Receiving no reply to this extraordinary appeal, which, in truth, as it was delivered with the vigor of full and sonorous tones, merited some sort of notice, he who had thus sung forth the language of the Holy Book turned to the silent figure to whom he had unwittingly addressed himself, and found a new and more powerful subject of admiration in the object that encountered his gaze. His eyes fell on the still, upright, and rigid form of the "Indian runner," who had borne to the camp the unwelcome tidings of the preceding evening. Although in a state of perfect repose, and apparently disregarding, with characteristic stoicism, the excitement and bustle around him, there was a sullen fierceness mingled with the quiet of the savage, that was likely to arrest the attention of much more experienced eyes than those which now scanned him, in unconcealed amazement. The native bore both the tomahawk and knife of his tribe; and yet his appearance was not altogether that of a warrior. On the contrary, there was an air of neglect about his person, like that which might have proceeded from great and recent exertion, which he had not yet found leisure to repair. The colors of the war paint had blended in dark confusion about his fierce countenance, and rendered his swarthy lineaments still more savage and repulsive, than if art had attempted an effect, which had been thus produced by chance. His eye, alone, which glistened like a fiery star amid lowering clouds, was to be seen in its state of native wildness. For a single instant, his searching and yet wary glance met the wondering look of the other, and then changing its direction, partly in cunning, and partly in disdain, it remained fixed, as if penetrating the distant air.

It is impossible to say what unlooked for remark this short and silent communication, between two such singular men, might have elicited from the white man, had not his active curiosity been again drawn to other objects. A general movement amongst the domestics, and a low sound of gentle voices, announced the approach of those whose presence alone was wanted to enable the cavalcade to move. The simple admirer of the war horse instantly fell back to a low, gaunt, switch-tailed mare, that was unconsciously gleaning the faded herbage of the camp nigh by; where, leaning with one elbow on the blanket that concealed an apology for a saddle, he became a spectator of the departure, while a foal was quietly making its morning repast, on the opposite side of the same animal.

A young man, in the dress of an officer, conducted to their steeds two females, who, as it was apparent by their dresses, were prepared to encounter the fatigues of a journey in the woods. One, and she was the most juvenile in her appearance, though both were young, permitted glimpses of her dazzling complexion, fair golden hair, and bright blue eyes, to be caught, as she artlessly suffered the morning air to blow aside the green veil which descended low from her beaver. The flush which still lingered above the pines in the western sky was not more bright nor delicate than the bloom on her cheek; nor was the opening day more cheering than the animated smile which she bestowed on the youth, as he assisted her into the saddle. The other, who appeared to share equally in the attentions of the young officer, concealed her charms from the gaze of the soldiery with a care that seemed better fitted to the experience of four or five additional years. It could be seen, however, that her person, though moulded with the same exquisite proportions, of which none of the graces were lost by the travelling dress she wore, was rather fuller and more mature than that of her companion.

No sooner were these females seated, than their attendant sprang lightly into the saddle of the war horse, when the whole three bowed to Webb, who, in courtesy, awaited their parting on the threshold of his cabin, and turning their horses' heads, they proceeded at a slow amble, followed by their train, toward the northern entrance of the encampment. As they traversed that short distance, not a voice was heard amongst them; but a slight exclamation proceeded from the younger of the females, as the Indian runner glided by her, unexpectedly, and led the way along the military road in her front. Though this sudden and startling movement of the Indian produced no sound from the other, in the surprise, her veil also was allowed to open its folds, and betrayed an indescribable look of pity, admiration, and horror, as her dark eye followed the easy motions of the savage. The tresses of this lady were shining and black, like the plumage of the raven. Her complexion was not brown, but it rather appeared charged with the color of the rich blood, that seemed ready to burst its bounds. And yet there was neither coarseness nor want of shadowing in a countenance that was exquisitely regular and dignified, and surpassingly beautiful. She smiled, as if in pity at her own momentary forgetfulness, discovering by the act a row of teeth that would have shamed the purest ivory; when, replacing the veil, she bowed her face, and rode in silence, like one whose thoughts were abstracted from the scene around her.

While one of the lovely beings we have so cursorily presented to the reader was thus lost in thought, the other quickly recovered from the alarm which induced the exclamation, and, laughing at her own weakness, she inquired of the youth who rode by her side—

"Are such specters frequent in the woods, Heyward; or is this sight an especial entertainment ordered on our behalf? If the latter, gratitude must close our mouths; but if the former, both Cora and I shall have need to draw largely on that stock of hereditary courage which we boast, even before we are made to encounter the redoubtable Montcalm."

"Yon Indian is a 'runner' of the army; and, after the fashion of his people, he may be accounted a hero," returned the officer. "He has volunteered to guide us to the lake, by a path but little known, sooner than if we followed the tardy movements of the column; and, by consequence, more agreeably."

"I like him not," said the lady, shuddering, partly in assumed, yet more in real, terror. "You know him, Duncan, or you would not trust yourself so freely to his keeping?"

"Say, rather, Alice, that I would not trust you. I do know him, or he would not have my confidence, and least of all at this moment. He is said to be a Canadian too; and yet he served with our friends the Mohawks, who, as you know, are one of the six allied Nations.[1] He was brought amongst us, as I have heard, by some strange accident in which your father was interested, and in which the savage was rigidly dealt by—but I forget the idle tale; it is enough, that he is now our friend."

"If he has been my father's enemy, I like him still less!" exclaimed the now really anxious girl. "Will you not speak to him, Major Heyward, that I may hear his tones? Foolish though it may be, you have often heard me avow my faith in the tones of the human voice!"

"It would be in vain; and answered, most probably, by an ejaculation. Though he may understand it, he affects, like most of his people, to be ignorant of the English; and least of all will he condescend to speak it now, that war demands the utmost exercise of his dignity. But he stops; the private path by which we are to journey is, doubtless, at hand."

The conjecture of Major Heyward was true. When they reached the spot where the Indian stood, pointing into the thicket that fringed the military road, a narrow and blind path, which might, with some little inconvenience, receive one person at a time, became visible.

"Here, then, lies our way," said the young man, in a low voice. "Manifest no distrust, or you may invite the danger you appear to apprehend."

"Cora, what think you?" asked the reluctant fair one. "If we journey with the troops, though we may find their presence irksome, shall we not feel better assurance of our safety?"

"Being little accustomed to the practices of the savages, Alice, you mistake the place of real danger," said Heyward. "If enemies have reached the portage at all, a thing by no means probable, as our scouts are abroad, they will surely be found skirting the column, where scalps abound the most. The route of the detachment is known, while ours, having been determined within the hour, must still be secret."

"Should we distrust the man because his manners are not our manners, and that his skin is dark!" coldly asked Cora.

---

[1] There existed for a long time a confederation among the Indian tribes which occupied the northwestern part of the colony of New York, which was at first known as the "Five Nations." At a later day it admitted another tribe, when the appellation was changed to that of the "Six Nations." The original confederation consisted of the Mohawks, the Oneidas, the Senecas, the Cayugas, and the Onondagoes. The sixth tribe was the Tuscaroras. There are remnants of all these people still living on lands secured to them by the state; but they are daily disappearing, either by deaths or by removals, to scenes more congenial to their habits. In a short time there will be no remains of these extraordinary people, in those regions in which they dwelt for centuries, but their names. The state of New York has counties named after all of them but the Mohawks and the Tuscaroras. The second river of that state is called the Mohawk. (*Cooper's note*)

Alice hesitated no longer; but giving her Narragansett[1] a smart cut of the whip, she was the first to dash aside the slight branches of the bushes, and to follow the runner along the dark and tangled pathway. The young man regarded the last speaker in open admiration, and even permitted her fairer though certainly not more beautiful companion to proceed unattended, while he sedulously opened the way himself for the passage of her who has been called Cora. It would seem that the domestics had been previously instructed; for, instead of penetrating the thicket, they followed the route of the column; a measure which Heyward stated had been dictated by the sagacity of their guide, in order to diminish the marks of their trail, if, haply, the Canadian savages should be lurking so far in advance of their army. For many minutes the intricacy of the route admitted of no further dialogue; after which they emerged from the broad border of underbrush which grew along the line of the highway, and entered under the high but dark arches of the forest. Here their progress was less interrupted; and the instant the guide perceived that the females could command their steeds, he moved on, at a pace between a trot and a walk, and at a rate which kept the sure-footed and peculiar animals they rode, at a fast yet easy amble. The youth had turned to speak to the dark-eyed Cora, when the distant sounds of horses' hoofs, clattering over the roots of the broken way in his rear, caused him to check his charger; and, as his companions drew their reins at the same instant, the whole party came to a halt, in order to obtain an explanation of the unlooked for interruption.

In a few moments a colt was seen gliding, like a fallow deer, amongst the straight trunks of the pines; and, in another instant, the person of the ungainly man, described in the preceding chapter, came into view, with as much rapidity as he could excite his meager beast to endure without coming to an open rupture. Until now this personage had escaped the observation of the travellers. If he possessed the power to arrest any wandering eye when exhibiting the glories of his altitude on foot, his equestrian graces were still more likely to attract attention. Nothwithstanding a constant application of his one armed heel to the flanks of the mare, the most confirmed gait that he could establish was a Canterbury gallop with the hind legs, in which those more forward

[1] In the state of Rhode Island there is a bay called Narragansett, so named after a powerful tribe of Indians, which formerly dwelt on its banks. Accident, or one of those unaccountable freaks which nature sometimes plays in the animal world, gave rise to a breed of horses which were once well known in America by the name of the Narragansetts. They were small, commonly of the color called sorrel in America, and distinguished by their habit of pacing. Horses of this race were, and are still, in much request as saddle horses, on account of their hardiness and the ease of their movements. As they were also sure of foot, the Narragansetts were greatly sought for by females who were obliged to travel over the roots and holes in the "new countries." (*Cooper's note*)

assisted for doubtful moments, though generally content to maintain a loping trot. Perhaps the rapidity of the changes from one of these paces to the other created an optical illusion, which might thus magnify the powers of the beast; for it is certain that Heyward, who possessed a true eye for the merits of a horse, was unable, with his utmost ingenuity, to decide by what sort of movement his pursuer worked his sinuous way on his footsteps with such persevering hardihood.

2

WITH SOME RELUCTANCE, Major Duncan Heyward permitted the Yankee psalm singer, David Gamut, to accompany himself and the two daughters of Colonel Munro on their perilous journey from Fort Edward northward to Fort William Henry. Alice Munro pleaded for the picturesque stranger; she liked singing, she said, and (with a distrustful glance at their sullen guide Magua) "it may be a friend added to our strength, in time of need." She even suggested that the two might sing duets on the journey; but after David had favored the party with an air from a Boston version (1744) of "The Psalms, Hymns, and Spiritual Songs of the Old and New Testaments," Heyward vetoed any further chants, on the ground that they should all move as quietly as possible. He acted wisely. "The cavalcade had not long passed, before the branches of the bushes that formed the thicket were cautiously moved asunder, and a human visage, as fiercely wild as savage art and unbridled passions could make it, peered out on the retiring footsteps of the travellers. A gleam of exultation shot across the darkly painted lineaments of the inhabitant of the forest, as he traced the route of his intended victims. . . ." But the partly rode inattentively onward into the gloomy recesses of the woods.

On that day, two men were lingering on the banks of a small but rapid stream, within an hour's journey of the encampment of Webb, like those who awaited the appearance of an absent person, or the approach of some expected event. The vast canopy of woods spread itself to the margin of the river, overhanging the water, and shadowing its dark current with a deeper hue. The rays of the sun were beginning to grow less fierce, and the intense heat of the day was lessened, as the cooler vapors of the springs and fountains rose above their leafy beds, and rested in the atmosphere. Still that breathing silence, which marks the drowsy sultriness of an American landscape in July, pervaded the secluded spot, interrupted only by the low voices of the men, the occasional and lazy tap of a woodpecker, the discordant cry of some gaudy jay, or a swelling on the ear, from the dull roar of a distant waterfall.

These feeble and broken sounds were, however, too familiar to the foresters, to draw their attention from the more interesting matter of their dialogue. While one of these loiterers showed the red skin and wild accoutrements of a native of the woods, the other exhibited, through the mask of his rude and nearly savage equipments, the brighter, though sunburnt and long-faded complexion of one who might claim descent from a European parentage. The former was seated on the end of a mossy log, in a posture that permitted him to heighten the effect of his earnest language, by the calm but expressive gestures of an Indian engaged in debate. His body, which was nearly naked, presented a terrific emblem of death, drawn in intermingled colors of white and black.[1] His closely shaved head, on which no other hair than the well-known and chivalrous scalping tuft [2] was preserved, was without ornament of any kind, with the exception of a solitary eagle's plume, that crossed his crown, and depended over the left shoulder. A tomahawk and scalping knife, of English manufacture, were in his girdle; while a short military rifle, of that sort with which

---

1 That is, a painted design to signify that the brave was on the warpath, and would either take the life of a foe or lose his own.—Ed.

2 The North American warrior caused the hair to be plucked from his whole body; a small tuft, only, was left on the crown of his head, in order that his enemy might avail himself of it, in wrenching off the scalp in the event of his fall. The scalp was the only admissible trophy of victory. Thus, it was deemed more important to obtain the scalp than to kill the man. Some tribes lay great stress on the honor of striking a dead body. These practices have nearly disappeared among the Indians of the Atlantic states. (*Cooper's note*)

the policy of the whites armed their savage allies, lay carelessly across his bare and sinewy knee. The expanded chest, full formed limbs, and grave countenance of this warrior, would denote that he had reached the vigor of his days, though no symptoms of decay appeared to have yet weakened his manhood.

The frame of the white man, judging by such parts as were not concealed by his clothes, was like that of one who had known hardships and exertion from his earliest youth. His person, though muscular, was rather attenuated than full; but every nerve and muscle appeared strung and indurated by unremitted exposure and toil. He wore a hunting shirt of forest-green, fringed with faded yellow,[1] and a summer cap of skins which had been shorn of their fur. He also bore a knife in a girdle of wampum, like that which confined the scanty garments of the Indian, but no tomahawk. His moccasins were ornamented after the gay fashion of the natives, while the only part of his under dress which appeared below the hunting frock, was a pair of buckskin leggings, that laced at the sides, and which were gartered above the knees, with the sinews of a deer. A pouch and horn completed his personal accoutrements, though a rifle of great length,[2] which the theory of the more ingenious whites had taught them was the most dangerous of all firearms, leaned against a neighboring sapling. The eye of the hunter, or scout, whichever he might be, was small, quick, keen, and restless, roving while he spoke, on every side of him, as if in quest of game, or distrusting the sudden approach of some lurking enemy. Notwithstanding these symptoms of habitual suspicion, his countenance was not only without guile, but at the moment at which he is introduced, it was charged with an expression of sturdy honesty.

"Even your traditions make the case in my favor, Chingachgook," he said, speaking in the tongue which was known to all the natives who formerly inhabited the country between the Hudson and the Potomac, and of which we shall give a free translation for the benefit of the reader; endeavoring, at the same time, to preserve some of the peculiarities, both of the individual and of the language. "Your fathers came from the setting sun, crossed the Big River,[3] fought the people of the country, and took the land; and mine came from the red sky of the morning, over the Salt Lake, and did their work much after the

[1] The hunting shirt is a picturesque smock frock, being shorter, and ornamented with fringes and tassels. The colors are intended to imitate the hues of the wood, with a view to concealment. Many corps of American riflemen have been thus attired; and the dress is one of the most striking of modern times. The hunting shirt is frequently white. (*Cooper's note*)

[2] The rifle of the army is short; that of the hunter is always long. (*Cooper's note*)

[3] The Mississippi. The scout alludes to a tradition which is very popular among the tribes of the Atlantic states. Evidence of their Asiatic origin is deduced from the circumstances, though great uncertainty hangs over the whole history of the Indians. (*Cooper's note*)

fashion that had been set them by yours; then let God judge the matter between us, and friends spare their words!"

"My fathers fought with the naked red man!" returned the Indian, sternly, in the same language. "Is there no difference, Hawkeye, between the stone-headed arrow of the warrior, and the leaden bullet with which you kill?"

"There is reason in an Indian, though nature has made him with a red skin!" said the white man, shaking his head like one on whom such an appeal to his justice was not thrown away. For a moment he appeared to be conscious of having the worst of the argument, then rallying again, he answered the objection of his antagonist in the best manner his limited information would allow: "I am no scholar, and I care not who knows it; but judging from what I have seen, at deer chases and squirrel hunts, of the sparks below, I should think a rifle in the hands of their grandfathers was not so dangerous as a hickory bow and a good flint-head might be, if drawn with Indian judgment, and sent by an Indian eye."

"You have the story told by your fathers," returned the other, coldly waving his hand. "What say your old men? do they tell the young warriors, that the palefaces met the red men, painted for war and armed with the stone hatchet and wooden gun?"

"I am not a prejudiced man, nor one who vaunts himself on his natural privileges, though the worst enemy I have on earth, and he is an Iroquois, daren't deny that I am genuine white," the scout replied, surveying, with secret satisfaction, the faded color of his bony and sinewy hand; "and I am willing to own that my people have many ways, of which, as an honest man, I can't approve. It is one of their customs to write in books what they have done and seen, instead of telling them in their villages, where the lie can be given to the face of a cowardly boaster, and the brave soldier can call on his comrades to witness for the truth of his words. In consequence of this bad fashion, a man who is too conscientious to misspend his days among the women, in learning the names of black marks, may never hear of the deeds of his fathers, nor feel a pride in striving to outdo them. For myself, I conclude all the Bumppos could shoot; for I have a natural turn with a rifle, which must have been handed down from generation to generation, as, our holy commandments tell us, all good and evil gifts are bestowed; though I should be loath to answer for other people in such a matter. But every story has its two sides; so I ask you, Chingachgook, what passed, according to the traditions of the red men, when our fathers first met?"

A silence of a minute succeeded, during which the Indian sat mute; then, full of the dignity of his office, he commenced his brief tale, with a solemnity that served to heighten its appearance of truth.

"Listen, Hawkeye, and your ear shall drink no lie. 'Tis what my fathers have said, and what the Mohicans have done." He hesitated a single instant, and bending a cautious glance toward his companion, he continued, in a manner that was divided between interrogation and assertion—"Does not this stream at our feet run toward the summer, until its waters grow salt, and the current flows upward?"

"It can't be denied that your traditions tell you true in both these matters," said the white man; "for I have been there, and have seen them; though, why water, which is so sweet in the shade, should become bitter in the sun, is an alteration for which I have never been able to account."

"And the current!" demanded the Indian, who expected his reply with that sort of interest that a man feels in the confirmation of testimony, at which he marvels even while he respects it; "the fathers of Chingachgook have not lied!"

"The Holy Bible is not more true, and that is the truest thing in nature. They call this upstream current the tide, which is a thing soon explained, and clear enough. Six hours the waters run in, and six hours they run out, and the reason is this: when there is higher water in the sea than in the river, they run in until the river gets to be highest, and then it runs out again."

"The waters in the woods, and on the Great Lakes, run downward until they lie like my hand," said the Indian, stretching the limb horizontally before him, "and then they run no more."

"No honest man will deny it," said the scout, a little nettled at the implied distrust of his explanation of the mystery of the tides; "and I grant that it is true on the small scale, and where the land is level. But everything depends on what scale you look at things. Now, on the small scale, the 'arth is level; but on the large scale it is round. In this manner, pools and ponds, and even the great fresh-water lakes, may be stagnant, as you and I both know they are, having seen them; but when you come to spread water over a great tract, like the sea, where the earth is round, how in reason can the water be quiet? You might as well expect the river to lie still on the brink of those black rocks a mile above us, though your own ears tell you that it is tumbling over them at this very moment!"

If unsatisfied by the philosophy of his companion, the Indian was far too dignified to betray his unbelief. He listened like one who was convinced, and resumed his narrative in his former solemn manner.

"We came from the place where the sun is hid at night, over great plains where the buffaloes live, until we reached the Big River. There we fought the Alligewi, till the ground was red with their blood. From the banks of the Big River to the shores of the Salt Lake, there was none to meet us. The Maquas [1] followed at a distance. We said the country should be ours from the place where the water runs up no longer on this stream to a river twenty suns' journey toward the summer. The land we had taken like warriors we kept like men. We drove the Maquas into the woods with the bears. They only tasted salt at the licks; they drew no fish from the Great Lake; we threw them the bones."

"All this I have heard and believe," said the white man, observing that the Indian paused: "but it was long before the English came into the country."

"A pine grew then where this chestnut now stands. The first palefaces who came among us spoke no English. They came in a large canoe, when my fathers had buried the tomahawk with the red men around them. Then, Hawkeye," he continued, betraying his deep emotion only by permitting his voice to fall to those low, guttural tones, which render his language, as spoken at times, so very musical; "then, Hawkeye, we were one people, and we were happy. The Salt Lake gave us its fish, the wood its deer, and the air its birds. We took wives who bore us children; we worshipped the Great Spirit; and we kept the Maquas beyond the sound of our songs of triumph!"

"Know you anything of your own family at that time?" demanded the white. "But you are a just man, for an Indian! and, as I suppose you hold their gifts, your fathers must have been brave warriors, and wise men at the council fire."

"My tribe is the grandfather of nations, but I am an unmixed man. The blood of chiefs is in my veins, where it must stay forever. The Dutch landed, and gave my people the firewater; they drank until the heavens and the earth seemed to meet, and they foolishly thought they had found the Great Spirit. Then they parted with their land. Foot by foot, they were driven back from the shores, until I, that am a chief and a Sagamore, have never seen the sun shine but through the trees, and have never visited the graves of my fathers!"

"Graves bring solemn feelings over the mind," returned the scout, a good deal touched at the calm suffering of his companion; "and they often aid a man in his good intentions; though, for myself, I expect to leave my own bones unburied, to bleach in the woods, or to be torn asunder by the wolves. But where are to be found those of your race who came to their kin in the Delaware country, so many summers since?"

"Where are the blossoms of those summers!—fallen, one by one: so all of my family departed, each in his turn, to the land of spirits. I

[1] That is, the Mohawks, one of the Five Nations. Maqua was the name given them by the Dutch.—Ed.

am on the hilltop, and must go down into the valley; and when Uncas follows in my footsteps, there will no longer be any of the blood of the Sagamores, for my boy is the last of the Mohicans."

"Uncas is here!" said another voice, in the same, soft, guttural tones, near his elbow; "who speaks to Uncas?"

The white man loosened his knife in his leathern sheath, and made an involuntary movement of the hand toward his rifle, at this sudden interruption; but the Indian sat composed, and without turning his head at the unexpected sounds.

At the next instant, a youthful warrior passed between them, with a noiseless step, and seated himself on the bank of the rapid stream. No exclamation of surprise escaped the father, nor was any question asked, or reply given, for several minutes; each appearing to await the moment when he might speak, without betraying womanish curiosity or childish impatience. The white man seemed to take counsel from their customs, and, relinquishing his grasp of the rifle, he also remained silent and reserved. At length Chingachgook turned his eyes slowly toward his son, and demanded—

"Do the Maquas dare to leave the print of their moccasins in these woods?"

"I have been on their trail," replied the young Indian, "and know that they number as many as the fingers of my two hands; but they lie hid like cowards."

"The thieves are outlying for scalps and plunder!" said the white man, whom we shall call Hawkeye, after the manner of his companions. "That busy Frenchman, Montcalm, will send his spies into our very camp, but he will know what road we travel!"

" 'Tis enough!" returned the father, glancing his eye toward the setting sun; "they shall be driven like deer from their bushes. Hawkeye, let us eat tonight, and show the Maquas that we are men tomorrow."

"I am as ready to do the one as the other: but to fight the Iroquois 'tis necessary to find the skulkers; and to eat, 'tis necessary to get the game—talk of the devil and he will come; there is a pair of the biggest antlers I have seen this season, moving the bushes below the hill! Now, Uncas," he continued in a half whisper, and laughing with a kind of inward sound, like one who had learnt to be watchful, "I will bet my charger three times full of powder, against a foot of wampum that I take him atwix the eyes, and nearer to the right than to the left."

"It cannot be!" said the young Indian, springing to his feet with youthful eagerness; "all but the tips of his horns are hid!"

"He's a boy!" said the white man, shaking his head while he spoke, and addressing the father. "Does he think when a hunter sees a part of the creatur', he can't tell where the rest of him should be!"

Adjusting his rifle, he was about to make an exhibition of that skill, on which he so much valued himself, when the warrior struck up the piece with his hand, saying,

"Hawkeye! will you fight the Maquas?"

"These Indians know the nature of the woods, as it might be by instinct!" returned the scout, dropping his rifle, and turning away like a man who was convinced of his error. "I must leave the buck to your arrow, Uncas, or we may kill a deer for them thieves, the Iroquois, to eat."

The instant the father seconded this intimation by an expressive gesture of the hand, Uncas threw himself on the ground, and approached the animal with wary movements. When within a few yards of the cover, he fitted an arrow to his bow with the utmost care, while the antlers moved, as if their owner snuffed an enemy in the tainted air. In another moment the twang of the cord was heard, a white streak was seen glancing into the bushes, and the wounded buck plunged from the cover, to the very feet of his hidden enemy. Avoiding the horns of the infuriated animal, Uncas darted to his side, and passed his knife across the throat, when bounding to the edge of the river it fell, dyeing the waters with its blood.

" 'Twas done with Indian skill," said the scout, laughing inwardly, but with vast satisfaction; "and 'twas a pretty sight to behold! Though an arrow is a near shot, and needs a knife to finish the work."

"Hugh!" ejaculated his companion, turning quickly, like a hound who scented game.

"By the Lord, there is a drove of them!" exclaimed the scout, whose eyes began to glisten with the ardor of his usual occupation; "if they come within range of a bullet I will drop one, though the whole Six Nations should be lurking within sound! What do you hear, Chingachgook? for to my ears the woods are dumb."

"There is but one deer, and he is dead," said the Indian, bending his body till his ear nearly touched the earth. "I hear the sounds of feet!"

"Perhaps the wolves have driven the buck to shelter, and are following on his trail."

"No. The horses of white men are coming!" returned the other, raising himself with dignity, and resuming his seat on the log with his former composure. "Hawkeye, they are your brothers; speak to them."

"That will I, and in English that the King needn't be ashamed to answer," returned the hunter, speaking in the language of which he boasted; "but I see nothing, nor do I hear the sounds of man or beast; 'tis strange that an Indian should understand white sounds better than a man who, his very enemies will own, has no cross in his blood, although he may have lived with the redskins long enough to be suspected! Ha! there goes something like the cracking of a dry stick, too—now I hear the bushes move—yes, yes, there is a trampling that I mistook for the falls—and—but here they come themselves; God keep them from the Iroquois!"

The words were still in the mouth of the scout, when the leader of the party, whose approaching footsteps had caught the vigilant ear of the Indian, came openly into view. A beaten path, such as those made by the periodical passage of the deer, wound through a little glen at no great distance, and struck the river at the point where the white man and his red companions had posted themselves. Along this track the travellers, who had produced a surprise so unusual in the depths of the forest, advanced slowly towards the hunter, who was in front of his associates, in readiness to receive them.

"Who comes?" demanded the scout, throwing his rifle carelessly across his left arm, and keeping the forefinger of his right hand on the trigger, though he avoided all appearance of menace in the act—"Who comes hither, among the beasts and dangers of the wilderness?"

"Believers in religion, and friends to the law and to the King," returned he who rode foremost. "Men who have journeyed since the rising sun, in the shades of this forest, without nourishment, and are sadly tired of their wayfaring."

"You are, then, lost," interrupted the hunter, "and have found how helpless 'tis not to know whether to take the right hand or the left?"

"Even so; sucking babes are not more dependent on those who guide them than we who are of larger growth, and who may now be said to possess the stature without the knowledge of men. Know you the distance to a post of the Crown called William Henry?"

"Hoot!" shouted the scout, who did not spare his open laughter, though, instantly checking the dangerous sounds, he indulged his merriment at less risk of being overheard by any lurking enemies. "You are as much off the scent as a hound would be, with Horican atwixt him and the deer! William Henry, man! if you are friends to the King, and have business with the army, your better way would be to follow the river down to Edward, and lay the matter before Webb; who tarries there, instead of pushing into the defiles, and driving this saucy Frenchman back across Champlain, into his den again."

Before the stranger could make any reply to this unexpected proposition, another horseman dashed the bushes aside, and leaped his charger into the pathway, in front of his companion.

"What, then, may be our distance from Fort Edward?" demanded a new speaker; "the place you advise us to seek we left this morning, and our destination is the head of the lake."

"Then you must have lost your eyesight afore losing your way, for the road across the portage is cut to a good two rods, and is as grand a path, I calculate, as any that runs into London, or even before the palace of the King himself."

"We will not dispute concerning the excellence of the passage," returned Heyward, smiling; for, as the reader has anticipated, it was he. "It is enough, for the present, that we trusted to an Indian guide to take us by a nearer, though blinder path, and that we are deceived in his knowledge. In plain words, we know not where we are."

"An Indian lost in the woods!" said the scout, shaking his head doubtingly; "when the sun is scorching the tree tops, and the water-courses are full; when the moss on every beech he sees, will tell him in which quarter the North Star will shine at night! The woods are full of deer paths which run to the streams and licks, places well known to everybody; nor have the geese done their flight to the Canada waters altogether! 'Tis strange that an Indian should be lost atwixt Horican and the bend in the river! Is he a Mohawk?"

"Not by birth, though adopted in that tribe; I think his birthplace was farther north, and he is one of those you call a Huron."

"Hugh!" exclaimed the two companions of the scout, who had continued until this part of the dialogue, seated immovable, and apparently indifferent to what passed, but who now sprang to their feet with an activity and interest that had evidently got the better of their reserve, by surprise.

"A Huron!" repeated the sturdy scout, once more shaking his head in open distrust; "they are a thievish race, nor do I care by whom they are adopted; you can never make anything of them but skulks and vagabonds. Since you trusted yourself to the care of one of that nation, I only wonder that you have not fallen in with more."

"Of that there is little danger, since William Henry is so many miles in our front. You forget that I have told you our guide is now a Mohawk, and that he serves with our forces as a friend."

"And I tell you that he who is born a Mingo will die a Mingo," returned the other, positively. "A Mohawk! No, give me a Delaware or a Mohican for honesty; and when they will fight, which they won't all do, having suffered their cunning enemies the Maquas, to make them women—but when they will fight at all, look to a Delaware, or a Mohican, for a warrior!"

"Enough of this," said Heyward, impatiently; "I wish not to inquire into the character of a man that I know, and to whom you must be a stranger. You have not yet answered my question; what is our distance from the main army at Edward?"

"It seems that may depend on who is your guide. One would think such a horse as that might get over a good deal of ground atwixt sunup and sundown."

"I wish no contention of idle words with you, friend," said Heyward, curbing his dissatisfied manner, and speaking in a more gentle voice; "if you will tell me the distance to Fort Edward, and conduct me thither, your labor shall not go without its reward."

"And in so doing, how know I that I don't guide an enemy, and a spy of Montcalm, to the works of the army? It is not every man who can speak the English tongue that is an honest subject."

"If you serve with the troops, of whom I judge you to be a scout, you should know of such a regiment of the King as the 60th."

"The 60th! you can tell me little of the Royal Americans that I don't know, though I do wear a hunting shirt instead of a scarlet jacket."

"Well, then, among other things, you may know the name of its major?"

"Its major!" interrupted the hunter, elevating his body like one who is proud of his trust. "If there is a man in the country who knows Major Effingham, he stands before you."

"It is a corps which has many majors; the gentleman you name is the senior, but I speak of the junior of them all; he who commands the companies in garrison at William Henry."

"Yes, yes, I have heard that a young gentleman of vast riches, from one of the provinces far south, has got the place. He is over young, too, to hold such rank, and to be put above men whose heads are beginning to bleach; and yet they say he is a soldier in his knowledge, and a gallant gentleman!"

"Whatever he may be, or however he may be qualified for his rank, he now speaks to you, and of course can be no enemy to dread."

The scout regarded Heyward in surprise, and then lifting his cap, he answered, in a tone less confident than before—though still expressing doubt—

"I have heard a party was to leave the encampment this morning, for the lake shore?"

"You have heard the truth; but I preferred a nearer route, trusting to the knowledge of the Indian I mentioned."

"And he deceived you, and then deserted?"

"Neither, as I believe; certainly not the latter, for he is to be found in the rear."

"I should like to look at the creatur'; if it is a true Iroquois, I can tell him by his knavish look, and by his paint," said the scout, stepping past the charger of Heyward, and entering the path behind the mare of the singing master, whose foal had taken advantage of the halt to exact the maternal contribution. After shoving aside the bushes, and proceeding a few paces, he encountered the females, who awaited the result of the conference with anxiety, and not entirely without apprehension. Behind these, the runner leaned against a tree, where he stood the close examination of the scout with an air unmoved, though with a look so dark and savage, that it might itself excite fear. Satisfied with his scrutiny, the hunter soon left him. As he repassed the females, he paused a moment to gaze upon their beauty, answering to the smile and nod of Alice with a look of open pleasure. Thence he went to the side of the motherly animal, and spending a minute in a fruitless inquiry into the character of her rider, he shook his head and returned to Heyward.

"A Mingo is a Mingo, and God having made him so, neither the Mohawks nor any other tribe can alter him," he said, when he had regained his former position. "If we were alone, and you would leave that noble horse at the mercy of the wolves tonight, I could show you the way to Edward, myself, within an hour, for it lies only about an hour's journey hence; but with such ladies in your company 'tis impossible!"

"And why? they are fatigued, but they are quite equal to a ride of a few more miles."

" 'Tis a natural impossibility!" repeated the scout; "I wouldn't walk a mile in these woods after night gets into them, in company with that runner, for the best rifle in the colonies. They are full of outlying Iroquois, and your mongrel Mohawk knows where to find them too well, to be my companion."

"Think you so?" said Heyward, leaning forward in the saddle, and dropping his voice nearly to a whisper; "I confess I have not been without my own suspicions, though I have endeavored to conceal them, and affected a confidence I have not always felt, on account of my companions. It was because I suspected him that I would follow no longer; making him, as you see, follow me."

"I knew he was one of the cheats as soon as I laid eyes on him!" returned the scout, placing a finger on his nose, in sign of caution. "This thief is leaning against the foot of the sugar sapling, that you can see over them bushes; his right leg is in a line with the bark of the tree, and," tapping his rifle, "I can take him from where I stand, between the ankle and the knee, with a single shot, putting an end to his tramping through the woods, for at least a month to come. If I should go back to him, the cunning varmint would suspect something, and be dodging through the trees like a frightened deer."

"It will not do. He may be innocent, and I dislike the act. Though, if I felt confident of his treachery—"

" 'Tis a safe thing to calculate on the knavery of an Iroquois," said the scout, throwing his rifle forward, by a sort of instinctive movement.

"Hold!" interrupted Heyward, "it will not do—we must think of some other scheme;—and yet, I have much reason to believe the rascal has deceived me."

The hunter, who had already abandoned his intention of maiming the runner, mused a moment and then made a gesture, which instantly brought his two red companions to his side. They spoke together earnestly in the Delaware language, though in an undertone; and by the gestures of the white man, which were frequently directed toward the top of the sapling, it was evident he pointed out the situation of their hidden enemy. His companions were not long in comprehending his wishes, and laying aside their firearms, they parted, taking opposite sides of the path, and burying themselves in the thicket, with such cautious movements, that their steps were inaudible.

"Now, go you back," said the hunter, speaking again to Heyward, "and hold the imp in talk; these Mohicans here will take him without breaking his paint."

"Nay," said Heyward, proudly, "I will seize him myself."

"Hist! what could you do, mounted, against an Indian in the bushes?"

"I will dismount."

"And, think you, when he saw one of your feet out of the stirrup, he would wait for the other to be free? Whoever comes into the woods to deal with the natives, must use Indian fashions, if he would wish to prosper in his undertakings. Go, then; talk openly to the miscreant, and seem to believe him the truest friend you have on 'arth."

Heyward prepared to comply, though with strong disgust at the nature of the office he was compelled to execute. Each moment, however, pressed upon him a conviction of the critical situation in which he had suffered his invaluable trust to be involved through his own confidence. The sun had already disappeared, and the woods, suddenly deprived of his light,[1] were assuming a dusky hue, which keenly reminded him that the hour the savage usually chose for his most barbarous and remorseless acts of vengeance or hostility, was speedily drawing near. Stimulated by apprehension, he left the scout, who immediately entered into a loud conversation with the stranger that had so unceremoniously enlisted himself in the party of travellers that morning. In passing his gentler companions Heyward uttered a few words of encouragement, and was pleased to find that, though fatigued with the exercise of the day, they appeared to entertain no suspicion that their present embarrassment was other than the result of accident. Giving them reason to believe he was merely employed in consultation concerning the future route, he spurred his charger, and drew the

---

[1] The scene of this tale was in the 42d degree of latitude, where the twilight is never of long continuance. (*Cooper's note*)

reins again, when the animal had carried him within a few yards of the place where the sullen runner still stood, leaning against the tree.

"You may see, Magua," he said, endeavoring to assume an air of freedom and confidence, "that the night is closing around us, and yet we are no nearer to William Henry than when we left the encampment of Webb with the rising sun. You have missed the way, nor have I been more fortunate. But, happily, we have fallen in with a hunter, he whom you hear talking to the singer, that is acquainted with the deer-paths and byways of the woods, and who promises to lead us to a place where we may rest securely till the morning."

The Indian riveted his glowing eyes on Heyward as he asked, in his imperfect English, "Is he alone?"

"Alone!" hesitatingly answered Heyward, to whom deception was too new to be assumed without embarrassment. "Oh! not alone, surely, Magua, for you know that we are with him."

"Then Le Renard Subtil will go," returned the runner, coolly raising his little wallet from the place where it had lain at his feet; "and the palefaces will see none but their own color."

"Go! Whom call you Le Renard?"

" 'Tis the name his Canada fathers have given to Magua," returned the runner, with an air that manifested his pride at the distinction. "Night is the same as day to Le Subtil, when Munro waits for him."

"And what account will Le Renard give the chief of William Henry concerning his daughters? Will he dare to tell the hot-blooded Scotsman that his children are left without a guide, though Magua promised to be one?"

"Though the gray-head has a loud voice, and a long arm, Le Renard will not hear him, or feel him, in the woods."

"But what will the Mohawks say? They will make him petticoats, and bid him stay in the wigwam with the women, for he is no longer to be trusted with the business of a man."

"Le Subtil knows the path to the Great Lakes, and he can find the bones of his fathers," was the answer of the unmoved runner.

"Enough, Magua," said Heyward; "are we not friends? Why should there be bitter words between us? Munro has promised you a gift for your services when performed, and I shall be your debtor for another. Rest your weary limbs, then, and open your wallet to eat. We have a few moments to spare; let us not waste them in talk like wrangling women. When the ladies are refreshed we will proceed."

"The palefaces make themselves dogs to their women," muttered the Indian, in his native language, "and when they want to eat, their warriors must lay aside the tomahawk to feed their laziness."

"What say you, Renard?"

"Le Subtil says it is good."

The Indian then fastened his eyes keenly on the open countenance of Heyward, but meeting his glance, he turned them quickly away, and seating himself deliberately on the ground, he drew forth the remnant of some former repast, and began to eat, though not without first bending his looks slowly and cautiously around him.

"This is well," continued Heyward; "and Le Renard will have strength and sight to find the path in the morning"—he paused, for sounds like the snapping of a dried stick, and the rustling of leaves, rose from the adjacent bushes, but recollecting himself instantly, he continued—"we must be moving before the sun is seen, or Montcalm may lie in our path, and shut us out from the fortress."

The hand of Magua dropped from his mouth to his side, and though his eyes were fastened on the ground, his head was turned aside, his nostrils expanded, and his ears seemed even to stand more erect than usual, giving to him the appearance of a statue that was made to represent intense attention.

Heyward, who watched his movements with a vigilant eye, carelessly extricated one of his feet from the stirrup, while he passed a hand toward the bearskin covering of his holsters. Every effort to detect the point most regarded by the runner, was completely frustrated by the tremulous glances of his organs, which seemed not to rest a single instant on any particular object, and which, at the same time, could be hardly said to move. While he hesitated how to proceed, Le Subtil cautiously raised himself to his feet, though with a motion so slow and guarded, that not the slightest noise was produced by the change. Heyward felt it had now become incumbent on him to act. Throwing his leg over the saddle, he dismounted, with a determination to advance and seize his treacherous companion, trusting the result to his own manhood. In order, however, to prevent unnecessary alarm, he still preserved an air of calmness and friendship.

"Le Renard Subtil does not eat," he said, using the appellation he had found most flattering to the vanity of the Indian. "His corn is not well parched, and it seems dry. Let me examine; perhaps something may be found among my own provisions that will help his appetite."

Magua held out the wallet to the proffer of the other. He even suffered their hands to meet, without betraying the least emotion, or varying his riveted attitude of attention. But when he felt the fingers of Heyward moving gently along his own naked arm, he struck up the limb of the young man, and uttering a piercing cry as he darted beneath it, plunged, at a single bound, into the opposite thicket. At the next instant the form of Chingachgook appeared from the bushes, looking like a specter in its paint, and glided across the path in swift pursuit. Next followed the shout of Uncas, when the woods were lighted by a sudden flash, that was accompanied by the sharp report of the hunter's rifle.

The suddenness of the flight of his guide, and the wild cries of the pursuers, caused Heyward to remain fixed, for a few moments, in inactive surprise. Then recollecting the importance of securing the fugitive, he dashed aside the surrounding bushes, and pressed eagerly forward to lend his aid in the chase. Before he had, however, proceeded a hundred yards, he met the three foresters already returning from their unsuccessful pursuit.

"Why so soon disheartened!" he exclaimed; "the scoundrel must be concealed behind some of these trees, and may yet be secured. We are not safe while he goes at large."

"Would you set a cloud to chase the wind?" returned the disappointed scout; "I heard the imp, brushing over the dry leaves, like the black snake, and blinking a glimpse of him, just over ag'in yon big pine, I pulled as it might be on the scent; but 'twouldn't do! and yet for a reasoning aim, if anybody but myself had touched the trigger, I should call it a quick sight; and I may be accounted to have experience in these matters, and one who ought to know. Look at this sumach; its leaves are red, though everybody knows the fruit is in the yellow blossom, in the month of July!"

" 'Tis the blood of Le Subtil! he is hurt, and may yet fall!"

"No, no," returned the scout, in decided disapprobation of this opinion, "I rubbed the bark off a limb, perhaps, but the creature leaped the longer for it. A rifle bullet acts on a running animal, when it barks him, much the same as one of your spurs on a horse, that is, it quickens motion, and puts life into the flesh, instead of taking it away. But when it cuts the ragged hole, after a bound or two, there is, commonly, a stagnation of further leaping, be it Indian or be it deer!"

"We are four able bodies, to one wounded man!"

"Is life grievous to you?" interrupted the scout. "Yonder red devil would draw you within swing of the tomahawks of his comrades, before you were heated in the chase. It was an unthoughtful act in a man who has so often slept with the war whoop ringing in the air, to let off his piece within sound of an ambushment! But then it was a natural temptation! 'twas very natural! Come, friends, let us move our station, and in such a fashion, too, as will throw the cunning of a Mingo on a wrong scent, or our scalps will be drying in the wind in front of Montcalm's marquee, ag'in this hour tomorrow."

This appalling declaration, which the scout uttered with the cool assurance of a man who fully comprehended, while he did not fear to face, the danger, served to remind Heyward of the importance of the charge with which he himself had been intrusted. Glancing his eyes around, with a vain effort to pierce the gloom that was thickening beneath the leafy arches of the forest, he felt as if, cut off from human aid, his unresisting companions would soon lie at the entire mercy of those barbarous enemies, who, like beasts of prey, only waited till the gathering darkness might render their blows more fatally certain. His awakened imagination, deluded by the deceptive light, converted each waving bush, or the fragment of some fallen tree, into human forms, and twenty times he fancied he could distinguish the horrid visages of his lurking foes, peering from their hiding places, in never-ceasing watchfulness of the movements of his party. Looking upward, he found that the thin fleecy clouds, which evening had painted on the blue sky, were already losing their faintest tints of rose color, while the imbedded stream, which glided past the spot where he stood, was to be traced only by the dark boundary of its wooded banks.

"What is to be done?" he said, feeling the utter helplessness of doubt in such a pressing strait; "desert me not, for God's sake! remain to defend those I escort, and freely name your own record."

His companions, who conversed apart in the language of their tribe, heeded not this sudden and earnest appeal. Though their dialogue was maintained in low and cautious sounds, but little above a whisper, Heyward, who now approached, could easily distinguish the earnest tones of the young warrior from the more deliberate speeches of his seniors. It was evident, that they debated on the propriety of some measure, that nearly concerned the welfare of the travellers. Yielding to his powerful interest in the subject, and impatient of a delay that seemed fraught with so much additional danger, Heyward drew still nigher to the dusky group, with an intention of making his offers of compensation more definite, when the white man, motioning with his hand, as if he conceded the disputed point, turned away, saying in a sort of soliloquy, and in the English tongue:—

"Uncas is right! it would not be the act of men to leave such harmless things to their fate, even though it breaks up the harboring place forever. If you would save these tender blossoms from the fangs of the worst of sarpents, gentleman, you have neither time to lose nor resolution to throw away!"

"How can such a wish be doubted! have I not already offered—"

"Offer your prayers to Him, who can give us wisdom to circumvent the cunning of the devils who fill these woods," calmly interrupted the scout, "but spare your offers of money, which neither you may live to realize, nor I to profit by. These Mohicans and I will do what man's thoughts can invent, to keep such flowers, which, though so sweet, were never made for the wilderness, from harm, and that without hope of any other recompense but such as God always gives to upright dealings. First, you must promise two things, both in your own name and for your friends, or without serving you, we shall only injure ourselves!"

"Name them."

"The one is, to be still as these sleeping woods, let what will happen; and the other is, to keep the place where we shall take you forever a secret from all mortal men."

"I will do my utmost to see both these conditions fulfilled."

"Then follow, for we are losing moments that are as precious as the heart's blood to a stricken deer!"

Heyward could distinguish the impatient gesture of the scout, through the increasing shadows of the evening, and he moved in his footsteps, swiftly, toward the place where he had left the remainder of his party. When they rejoined the expecting and anxious females, he briefly acquainted them with the conditions of their new guide, and with the necessity that existed for their hushing every apprehension, in instant and serious exertions. Although his alarming communication was not received without much secret terror by the listeners, his earnest and impressive manner, aided perhaps by the nature of the danger, succeeded in bracing their nerves to undergo some unlooked for and unusual trial. Silently, and without a moment's delay, they permitted him to assist them from their saddles, when they descended quickly to the water's edge where the scout had collected the rest of the party, more by the agency of expressive gestures than by any use of words.

"What to do with these dumb creatures!" muttered the white man, on whom the sole control of their future movements appeared to devolve; "it would be time lost to cut their throats, and cast them into the river; and to leave them here, would be to tell the Mingoes that they have not far to seek to find their owners!"

"Then give them their bridles, and let them range the woods," Heyward ventured to suggest.

"No; it would be better to mislead the imps, and make them believe they must equal a horse's speed to run down their chase. Aye, aye, that will blind their fireballs of eyes! Chingach— Hist! what stirs the bush?"

"The colt."

"That colt, at least, must die," muttered the scout, grasping at the mane of the nimble beast, which easily eluded his hand; "Uncas, your arrows!"

"Hold!" exclaimed the proprietor of the condemned animal, aloud, without regard to the whispering tones used by the others; "spare the foal of Miriam! it is the comely offspring of a faithful dam, and would willingly injure naught."

"When men struggle for the single life God has given them," said the scout sternly, "even their own kind seem no more than the beasts of the wood. If you speak again, I shall leave you to the mercy of the Maquas! Draw to your arrow's head, Uncas; we have no time for second blows."

The low, muttering sounds of his threatening voice were still audible, when the wounded foal, first rearing on its hinder legs, plunged forward to its knees. It was met by Chingachgook, whose knife passed across its throat quicker than thought, and then precipitating the motions of the struggling victim, he dashed it into the river, down whose stream it glided away, gasping audibly for breath with its ebbing life. This deed of apparent cruelty, but of real necessity, fell upon the spirits of the travellers like a terrific warning of the peril in which they stood, heightened as it was by the calm though steady resolution of the actors in the scene. The sisters shuddered and clung closer to each other, while Heyward instinctively laid his hand on one of the pistols he had just drawn from their holsters, as he placed himself between his charge and those dense shadows that seemed to draw an impenetrable veil before the bosom of the forest.

The Indians, however, hesitated not a moment, but taking the bridles, they led the frightened and reluctant horses into the bed of the river.

At a short distance from the shore, they turned, and were soon concealed by the projection of the bank, under the brow of which they moved, in a direction opposite to the course of the waters. In the meantime, the scout drew a canoe of bark from its place of concealment beneath some low bushes whose branches were waving with the eddies of the current, into which he silently motioned for the females to enter. They complied without hesitation, though many a fearful and anxious glance was thrown behind them, toward the thickening gloom, which now lay like a dark barrier along the margin of the stream.

So soon as Cora and Alice were seated, the scout, without regarding the element, directed Heyward to support one side of the frail vessel, and posting himself at the other, they bore it up against the stream, followed by the dejected owner of the dead foal. In this manner they proceeded, for many rods, in a silence that was only interrupted by the rippling of the water, as its eddies played around them, or the low dash made by their own cautious footsteps. Heyward yielded the guidance of the canoe implicitly to the scout, who approached or receded from the shore, to avoid the fragments of rocks, or deeper parts of the river, with a readiness that showed his knowledge of the route they held. Occasionally he would stop; and in the midst of a breathing stillness, that the dull but increasing roar of the waterfall only served to render more impressive, he would listen with painful intenseness, to catch any sounds that might arise from the slumbering forest. When assured that all was still, and unable to detect, even by the aid of his practiced senses, any sign of his approaching foes, he would deliberately assume his slow and guarded progress. At length they reached a point in the river, where the roving eye of Heyward became riveted on a cluster of black objects, collected at a spot where the high bank threw a deeper shadow than usual on the dark waters. Hesitating to advance, he pointed out the place to the attention of his companion.

"Aye," returned the composed scout, "the Indians have hid the beasts with the judgment of natives! Water leaves no trail, and an owl's eyes would be blinded by the darkness of such a hole."

The whole party was soon reunited, and another consultation was held between the scout and his new comrades, during which they, whose fates depended on the faith and ingenuity of these unknown foresters, had a little leisure to observe their situation more minutely.

The river was confined between high and cragged rocks, one of which impended above the spot where the canoe rested. As these, again, were surmounted by tall trees, which appeared to totter on the brows of the precipice, it gave the stream the appearance of running through a deep and narrow dell. All beneath the fantastic limbs and ragged tree tops, which were, here and there, dimly painted against the starry zenith, lay alike in shadowed obscurity. Behind them, the curvature of the banks soon bounded the view, by the same dark and wooded outline; but in front, and apparently at no great distance, the water seemed piled against the heavens, whence it tumbled into caverns, out of which issued those sullen sounds that had loaded the evening atmosphere.[1] It seemed, in truth, to be a spot devoted to seclusion, and the sisters imbibed a soothing impression of security, as they gazed upon its romantic, though not unappalling beauties. A general movement among their conductors, however, soon recalled them from a contemplation of the wild charms that night had assisted to lend the place, to a painful sense of their real peril.

The horses had been secured to some scattering shrubs that grew in the fissures of the rocks, where, standing in the water, they were left to pass the night. The scout directed Heyward and his disconsolate fellow-travellers to seat themselves in the forward end of the canoe, and took possession of the other himself, as erect and steady as if he floated in a vessel of much firmer materials. The Indians warily retraced their steps toward the place they had left, when the scout, placing his pole against a rock, by a powerful shove, sent his frail bark directly into the center of the turbulent stream. For many minutes the

[1] The cataract at Glens Falls, some fifty-two miles up the Hudson from Albany, marks the entrance to two deep caves, still shown to tourists.—Ed.

struggle between the light bubble in which they floated, and the swift current, was severe and doubtful. Forbidden to stir even a hand, and almost afraid to breathe, lest they should expose the frail fabric to the fury of the stream, the passengers watched the glancing waters in feverish suspense. Twenty times they thought the whirling eddies were sweeping them to destruction, when the master hand of their pilot would bring the bow of the canoe to stem the rapid. A long, a vigorous, and, as it appeared to the females, a desperate effort, closed the struggle. Just as Alice veiled her eyes in horror, under the impression that they were about to be swept within the vortex at the foot of the cataract, the canoe floated, stationary, at the side of a flat rock, that lay on a level with the water.

"Where are we? and what is next to be done?" demanded Heyward, perceiving that the exertions of the scout had ceased.

"You are at the foot of Glens," returned the other, speaking aloud, without fear of consequences, within the roar of the cataract; "and the next thing is to make a steady landing, lest the canoe upset, and you should go down again the hard road we have travelled, faster than you came up; 'tis a hard rift to stem, when the river is a little swelled; and five is an unnatural number to keep dry, in the hurry-skurry, with a little birchen bark and gum. There, go you all on the rock, and I will bring up the Mohicans with the venison. A man had better sleep without his scalp, than famish in the midst of plenty."

His passengers gladly complied with these directions. As the last foot touched the rock, the canoe whirled from its station, when the tall form of the scout was seen, for an instant, gliding above the waters, before it disappeared in the impenetrable darkness that rested on the bed of the river. Left by their guide, the travellers remained a few minutes in helpless ignorance, afraid even to move along the broken rocks, lest a false step should precipitate them down some one of the many deep and roaring caverns, into which the water seemed to tumble, on every side of them. Their suspense, however, was soon relieved; for, aided by the skill of the natives, the canoe shot back into the eddy, and floated again at the side of the low rock, before they thought the scout had even time to rejoin his companions.

"We are now fortified, garrisoned, and provisioned," cried Heyward, cheerfully, "and may set Montcalm and his allies at defiance. How, now, my vigilant sentinel, can you see anything of those you call the Iroquois, on the mainland?"

"I call them Iroquois, because to me every native, who speaks a foreign tongue, is accounted an enemy, though he may pretend to serve the King! If Webb wants faith and honesty in an Indian, let him bring out the tribes of the Delaware, and send these greedy and lying Mohawks and Oneidas, with their Six Nations of varlets, where in nature they belong, among the French!"

"We should then exchange a warlike for a useless friend! I have heard that the Delawares have laid aside the hatchet, and are content to be called women!"

"Aye, shame on the Hollanders [1] and Iroquois, who circumvented them by their deviltries, into such a treaty! But I have known them for twenty years, and I call him liar, that says cowardly blood runs in the veins of a Delaware. You have driven their tribes from the seashore, and would now believe what their enemies say, that you may sleep at night upon an easy pillow. No, no; to me, every Indian who speaks a foreign tongue is an Iroquois, whether the castle [2] of his tribe be in Canada, or be in York."

Heyward, perceiving that the stubborn adherence of the scout to the cause of his friends the Delawares or Mohicans, for they were branches of the same numerous people, was likely to prolong a useless discussion, changed the subject.

"Treaty or no treaty, I know full well, that your two companions are brave and cautious warriors! have they heard or seen anything of our enemies?"

"An Indian is a mortal to be felt afore he is seen," returned the scout, ascending the rock, and throwing the deer carelessly down. "I trust to other signs than such as come in at the eye, when I am outlying on the trail of the Mingoes."

"Do your ears tell you that they have traced our retreat?"

"I should be sorry to think they had, though this is a spot that stout courage might hold for a smart scrimmage. I will not deny, however, but the horses cowered when I passed, as though they scented the wolves; and a wolf is a beast that is apt to hover about an Indian ambushment, craving the offals of the deer the savages kill."

"You forget the buck at your feet! or, may we not owe their visit to the dead colt? Ha! what noise is that?"

"Poor Miriam!" murmured the stranger; "thy foal was foreordained to become a prey to ravenous beasts!" Then, suddenly lifting up his voice, amid the eternal din of the waters, he sang aloud—

"First born of Egypt, smite did he,
Of mankind, and of beast also;
O, Egypt! wonders sent 'midst thee,
On Pharaoh and his servants too!"

"The death of the colt sits heavy on the heart of its owner," said the scout; "but it's a good sign to see a man account upon his dumb friends. He has the religion of the matter, in believing what is to hap-

[1] The reader will remember that New York was originally a colony of the Dutch. (*Cooper's note*)

[2] The principal villages of the Indians are still called "castles" by the whites of New York. "Oneida Castle" is no more than a scattered hamlet; but the name is in general use. (*Cooper's note*)

pen will happen; and with such a consolation, it won't be long afore he submits to the rationality of killing a four-footed beast, to save the lives of human men. It may be as you say," he continued, reverting to the purport of Heyward's last remark; "and the greater the reason why we should cut our steaks, and let the carcase drive down the stream, or we shall have the pack howling along the cliffs, begrudging every mouthful we swallow. Besides, though the Delaware tongue is the same as a book to the Iroquois, the cunning varlets are quick enough at understanding the reason of a wolf's howl."

The scout, whilst making his remarks, was busied in collecting certain necessary implements; as he concluded, he moved silently by the group of travellers, accompanied by the Mohicans, who seemed to comprehend his intentions with instinctive readiness, when the whole three disappeared in succession, seeming to vanish against the dark face of a perpendicular rock, that rose to the height of a few yards, within as many feet of the water's edge.

3

THE SUDDEN DISAPPEARANCE of Hawkeye, Chingachgook, and Uncas was soon explained. They had vanished inside a deep, narrow cavern in the rock, where they at once kindled a fire, and began preparing supper. The entrance to the cave was concealed by a blanket hung over it, lest, said Hawkeye, the fire "might light the Mingoes to our undoing." The cataract of Glens Falls poured down on two sides of them, for the cavern occupied a rocky little island in the middle of the Hudson. When Duncan Heyward objected that a single armed enemy, gaining the entrance, would hold them at his mercy, Chingachgook showed them that the cavern had a rear outlet—and also, that it communicated, by a deep, narrow transverse passage in the rock, with another cave. "Such old foxes as Chiangachgook and myself are not often caught in a burrow with one hole," commented Hawkeye.

The little company ate a supper of roast venison and drank spruce beer in the cave. The young woman accompanied David Gamut in singing a psalm—the rushing waterfall outside making this safe—when their sense of security was broken by an unearthly cry deep in the forest outside, which Hawkeye identified as an Indian war whoop. But Hawkeye assured them that their hiding place was still undiscovered by the savages. The two young women, on his advice, were just retiring to rest in the side-cave when the same strong, horrid cry again gave everyone pause. Even Hawkeye was clearly shaken by a mystery which seemed to threaten some peril against which even his cunning and experience might prove unavailing.

" 'Twould be neglecting a warning that is given for our good, to lie hid any longer," said Hawkeye, "when such sounds are raised in the forest! These gentle ones may keep close, but the Mohicans and I will watch upon the rock, where I suppose a major of the 60th would wish to keep us company."

"Is then our danger so pressing?" asked Cora.

"He who makes strange sounds, and gives them out for man's information, alone knows our danger. I should think myself wicked, unto rebellion against his will, was I to burrow with such warnings in the air! Even the weak soul who passes his days in singing, is stirred by the cry, and, as he says, is 'ready to go forth to the battle.' If 'twere only a battle, it would be a thing understood by us all, and easily managed; but I have heard that when such shrieks are atween heaven and 'arth, it betokens another sort of warfare!"

"If all our reasons for fear, my friend, are confined to such as proceed from supernatural causes, we have but little occasion to be alarmed," continued the undisturbed Cora; "are you certain that our enemies have not invented some new and ingenious method to strike us with terror, that their conquest may become more easy?"

"Lady," returned the scout, solemnly, "I have listened to all the sounds of the woods for thirty years, as a man will listen, whose life and death depend on the quickness of his ears. There is no whine of the panther; no whistle of the catbird; nor any invention of the devilish Mingoes, that can cheat me! I have heard the forest moan like mortal men in their affliction; often, and again, have I listened to the wind playing its music in the branches of the girdled trees; and I have heard the lightning cracking in the air, like the snapping of blazing brush, as it spitted forth sparks and forked flames; but never have I thought that I heard more than the pleasure of Him who sported with the things of his hand. But neither the Mohicans, nor I, who am a white man without a cross, can explain the cry just heard. We, therefore, believe it a sign given for our good."

"It is extraordinary!" said Heyward, taking his pistols from the place where he had laid them on entering; "be it a sign of peace or a signal of war, it must be looked to. Lead the way, my friend; I follow."

On issuing from their place of confinement, the whole party instantly experienced a grateful renovation of spirits, by exchanging the pent air of the hiding place for the cool and invigorating atmosphere, which played around the whirlpools and pitches of the cataract. A heavy evening breeze swept along the surface of the river, and seemed to drive the roar of the falls into the recesses of their own caverns, whence it issued heavily and constant, like thunder rumbling beyond the distant hills. The moon had risen, and its light was already glancing here and there on the waters above them; but the extremity of the rock where they stood still lay in shadow. With the exception of the sounds produced by the rushing waters, and an occasional breathing of the air, as it murmured past them in fitful currents, the scene was as still as night and solitude could make it. In vain were the eyes of each individual bent along the opposite shores, in quest of some signs of life, that might explain the nature of the interruption they had heard. Their anxious and eager looks were baffled by the deceptive light, or rested only on naked rocks, and straight and immovable trees.

"Here is nothing to be seen but the gloom and quiet of a lovely evening," whispered Duncan; "how much should we prize such a scene, and all this breathing solitude, at any other moment, Cora! Fancy yourselves in security, and what now, perhaps, increases your terror, may be made conducive to enjoyment—"

"Listen!" interrupted Alice.

The caution was unnecessary. Once more the same sound arose, as if from the bed of the river, and having broken out of the narrow bounds of the cliffs, was heard undulating through the forest, in distant and dying cadences.

"Can any here give the name to such a cry?" demanded Hawkeye, when the last echo was lost in the woods; "if so, let him speak; for myself, I judge it not to belong to 'arth!"

"Here, then, is one who can undeceive you," said Duncan; "I know the sound full well, for often have I heard it on the field of battle, and in situations which are frequent in a soldier's life. 'Tis the horrid shriek that a horse will give in his agony; oftener drawn from him in pain, though sometimes in terror. My charger is either a prey to the beasts of the forest, or he sees his danger, without the power to avoid it. The sound might deceive me in the cavern, but in the open air I know it too well to be wrong."

The scout and his companions listened to this simple explanation with the interest of men who imbibe new ideas, at the same time that they get rid of old ones, which had proved disagreeable inmates. The two latter uttered their usual and expressive exclamation, "hugh!" as the truth first glanced upon their minds, while the former, after a short musing pause, took upon himself to reply.

"I cannot deny your words," he said; "for I am little skilled in horses, though born where they abound. The wolves must be hovering above their heads on the bank, and the timorsome creatures are calling on man for help, in the best manner they are able. Uncas"—he spoke in Delaware—"Uncas, drop down in the canoe, and whirl a brand among the pack; or fear may do what the wolves can't get at to perform, and leave us without horses in the morning, when we shall have so much need to journey swiftly!"

The young native had already descended to the water, to comply, when a long howl was raised on the edge of the river, and was borne swiftly off into the depths of the forest, as though the beasts of their own accord, were abandoning their prey in sudden terror. Uncas, with instinctive quickness, receded, and the three foresters held another of their low, earnest conferences.

"We have been like hunters who have lost the points of the heavens, and from whom the sun has been hid for days," said Hawkeye, turning away from his companions; "now we begin again to know the signs of our course, and the paths are cleared from briers! Seat yourselves in the shade which the moon throws from yonder beech—'tis thicker than that of the pines—and let us wait for that which the Lord may choose to send next. Let all your conversation be in whispers; though it would be better, and perhaps, in the end, wiser, if each one held discourse with his own thoughts, for a time."

The manner of the scout was seriously impressive, though no longer distinguished by any signs of unmanly apprehension. It was evident that his momentary weakness had vanished with the explanation of a mystery which his own experience had not served to fathom; and though he now felt all the realities of their actual condition, that he was prepared to meet them with the energy of his hardy nature. This feeling seemed also common to the natives, who placed themselves in positions which commanded a full view of both shores, while their own persons were effectually concealed from observation. In such circumstances, common prudence dictated that Heyward and his companions should imitate a caution that proceeded from so intelligent a source. The young man drew a pile of the sassafras from the cave, and placing it in the chasm which separated the two caverns, it was occupied by the sisters; who were thus protected by the rocks from any missiles, while their anxiety was relieved by the assurance that no danger could approach without a warning. Heyward himself was posted at hand, so near that he might communicate with his companions without raising his voice to a dangerous elevation; while David, in imitation of the woodsmen, bestowed his person in such a manner among the fissures of the rocks, that his ungainly limbs were no longer offensive to the eye.

In this manner, hours passed by without further interruption. The moon reached the zenith, and shed its mild light perpendicularly on the lovely sight of the sisters slumbering peacefully in each other's arms. Duncan cast the wide shawl of Cora before a spectacle he so much loved to contemplate, and then suffered his own head to seek a pillow on the rock. David began to utter sounds that would have shocked his delicate organs in more wakeful moments; in short, all but Hawkeye and the Mohicans lost every idea of consciousness, in uncontrollable drowsiness. But the watchfulness of these vigilant protectors neither tired nor slumbered. Immovable as that rock, of which each appeared to form a part, they lay, with their eyes roving, without intermission, along the dark margin of trees that bounded the adjacent shores of the narrow stream. Not a sound escaped them; the most subtle examination could not have told they breathed. It was evident that this excess of caution proceeded from an experience that no subtlety on the part of their enemies could deceive. It was, however, continued without any apparent consequences, until the moon had set, and a pale streak above the treetops, at the bend of the river a little below, announced the approach of day.

Then, for the first time, Hawkeye was seen to stir. He crawled along the rock, and shook Duncan from his heavy slumbers.

"Now is the time to journey," he whispered; "awake the gentle ones, and be ready to get into the canoe when I bring it to the landing place."

"Have you had a quiet night?" said Heyward; "for myself, I believe sleep has got the better of my vigilance."

"All is yet still as midnight. Be silent, but be quick."

By this time Duncan was thoroughly awake, and he immediately lifted the shawl from the sleeping females. The motion caused Cora to raise her hand as if to repulse him, while Alice murmured, in her soft gentle voice, "No, no, dear father, we were not deserted; Duncan was with us!"

"Yes, sweet innocence," whispered the youth; "Duncan is here, and while life continues or danger remains, he will never quit thee. Cora! Alice! awake! The hour has come to move!"

A loud shriek from the younger of the sisters, and the form of the other standing upright before him, in bewildered horror, was the unexpected answer he received. While the words were still on the lips of Heyward, there had arisen such a tumult of yells and cries as served to drive the swift currents of his own blood back from its bounding course into the fountains of his heart. It seemed, for near a minute, as if the demons of hell had possessed themselves of the air about them, and were venting their savage humors in barbarous sounds. The cries came from no particular direction, though it was evident they filled the woods, and as the appalled listeners easily imagined, the caverns of the falls, the rocks, the bed of the river, and the upper air. David raised his tall person in the midst of the infernal din, with a hand on either ear, exclaiming—

"Whence comes this discord! Has hell broke loose, that man should utter sounds like these!"

The bright flashes and the quick report of a dozen rifles, from the opposite banks of the stream, followed this incautious exposure of his person, and left the unfortunate singing master senseless on that rock where he had been so long slumbering. The Mohicans boldly sent back the intimidating yell of their enemies, who raised a shout of savage triumph at the fall of Gamut. The flash of rifles was then quick and close between them, but either party was too well skilled to leave even a limb exposed to the hostile aim. Duncan listened with intense anxiety for the strokes of the paddle, believing that flight was now their only refuge. The river glanced by with its ordinary velocity, but the canoe was nowhere to be seen on its dark waters. He had just fancied they were cruelly deserted by the scout, as a stream of flame issued from the rock beneath him, and a fierce yell, blended with a shriek of agony, announced that the messenger of death, sent from the fatal weapon of Hawkeye, had found a victim. At this slight repulse the assailants instantly withdrew, and gradually the place became as still as before the sudden tumult.

Duncan seized the favorable moment to spring to the body of Gamut, which he bore within the shelter of the narrow chasm that protected the sisters. In another minute the whole party was collected in this spot of comparative safety.

"The poor fellow has saved his scalp," said Hawkeye, coolly passing his hand over the head of David; "but he is a proof that a man may be born with too long a tongue! 'Twas downright madness to show six feet of flesh and blood, on a naked rock, to the raging savages. I only wonder he has escaped with life."

"Is he not dead!" demanded Cora, in a voice whose husky tones showed how powerfully natural horror struggled with her assumed firmness. "Can we do aught to assist the wretched man?"

"No, no! the life is in his heart yet, and after he has slept awhile he will come to himself, and be a wiser man for it, till the hour of his real time shall come," returned Hawkeye, casting another oblique glance at the insensible body, while he filled his charger with admirable nicety. "Carry him in, Uncas, and lay him on the sassafras. The longer his nap lasts the better it will be for him, as I doubt whether he can find a proper cover for such a shape on these rocks; and singing won't do any good with the Iroquois."

"You believe, then, the attack will be renewed?" asked Heyward.

"Do I expect a hungry wolf will satisfy his craving with a mouthful! They have lost a man, and 'tis their fashion, when they meet a loss, and fail in the surprise, to fall back; but we shall have them on again, with new expedients to circumvent us, and master our scalps. Our main hope," he continued, raising his rugged countenance, across which a shade of anxiety just then passed like a darkening cloud, "will be to keep the rock until Munro can send a party to our help! God send it may be soon, and under a leader that knows the Indian customs!"

"You hear our probable fortunes, Cora," said Duncan; "and you know we have everything to hope from the anxiety and experience of your father. Come, then, with Alice, into this cavern, where you, at least, will be safe from the murderous rifles of our enemies, and where you may bestow a care suited to your gentle natures on our unfortunate comrade."

The sisters followed him into the outer cave, where David was beginning, by his sighs, to give symptoms of returning consciousness; and then commending the wounded man to their attention, he immediately prepared to leave them.

"Duncan!" said the tremulous voice of Cora, when he had reached the mouth of the cavern. He turned, and beheld the speaker, whose color had changed to a deadly paleness, and whose lip quivered, gazing after him, with an expression of interest which immediately recalled him to her side. "Remember, Duncan, how necessary your safety is to our own—how you bear a father's sacred trust—how much depends on your discretion and care—in short," she added, while the telltale blood stole over her features, crimsoning her very temples, "how very deservedly dear you are to all of the name of Munro."

"If anything could add to my own base love of life," said Heyward, suffering his unconscious eyes to wander to the youthful form of the silent Alice, "it would be so kind an assurance. As major of the 60th, our honest host will tell you I must take my share of the fray; but our task will be easy; it is merely to keep these bloodhounds at bay for a few hours."

Without waiting for reply, he tore himself from the presence of the sisters, and joined the scout and his companions, who still lay within the protection of the little chasm between the two caves.

"I tell you, Uncas," said the former, as Heyward joined them, "you are wasteful of your powder, and the kick of the rifle disconcerts your aim! Little powder, light lead, and a long arm, seldom fail of bringing the death screech from a Mingo! At least, such has been my experience with the creatur's. Come, friends; let us to our covers, for no man can tell when or where a Maqua [1] will strike his blow."

The Indians silently repaired to their appointed stations, which were fissures in the rocks, whence they could command the approaches to the foot of the falls. In the center of the little island, a few short and stunted pines had found root, forming a thicket, into which Hawkeye darted with the swiftness of a deer, followed by the active Duncan. Here they secured themselves, as well as circumstances would permit, among the shrubs and fragments of stone that were scattered about the place. Above them was a bare, rounded rock, on each side of which the water played its gambols, and plunged into the abysses beneath, in the manner already described. As the day had now dawned, the opposite shores no longer presented a confused outline, but they were able to look into the woods, and distinguish objects beneath the canopy of gloomy pines.

A long and anxious watch succeeded, but without any further evidences of a renewed attack; and Duncan began to hope that their fire had proved more fatal than was supposed, and that their enemies had been effectually repulsed. When he ventured to utter this impression to his companion, it was met by Hawkeye with an incredulous shake of the head.

"You know not the nature of a Maqua, if you think he is so easily beaten back without a scalp!" he answered. "If there was one of the imps yelling this morning, there were forty! and they know our number and quality too well to give up the chase so soon. Hist! look into the water above, just where it breaks over the rocks. I am no mortal, if the risky devils haven't swam down upon the very pitch, and, as bad luck would have it, they have hit the head of the island. Hist! man, keep close! or the hair will be off your crown in the turning of a knife!"

Heyward lifted his head from the cover, and beheld what he justly

[1] It will be observed that Hawkeye applies different names to his enemies. Mingo and Maqua are terms of contempt, and Iroquois is a name given by the French. The Indians rarely use the same name when different tribes speak of each other. (*Cooper's note*)

considered a prodigy of rashness and skill. The river had worn away the edge of the soft rock in such a manner, as to render its first pitch less abrupt and perpendicular than is usual at waterfalls. With no other guide than the ripple of the stream where it met the head of the island, a party of their insatiable foes had ventured into the current, and swam down upon this point, knowing the ready access it would give, if successful, to their intended victims. As Hawkeye ceased speaking, four human heads could be seen peering above a few logs of driftwood that had lodged on these naked rocks, and which had probably suggested the idea of the practicability of the hazardous undertaking. At the next moment, a fifth form was seen floating over the green edge of the fall, a little from the line of the island. The savage struggled powerfully to gain the point of safety, and, favored by the glancing water, he was already stretching forth an arm to meet the grasp of his companions, when he shot away again with the whirling current, appeared to rise into the air, with uplifted arms and starting eyeballs, and fell, with a sullen plunge, into that deep and yawning abyss over which he hovered. A single, wild, despairing shriek rose from the cavern, and all was hushed again, as the grave.

The first generous impulse of Duncan was to rush to the rescue of the hapless wretch: but he felt himself bound to the spot by the iron grasp of the immovable scout.

"Would ye bring certain death upon us, by telling the Mingoes where we lie?" demanded Hawkeye, sternly; " 'tis a charge of powder saved, and ammunition is as precious now as breath to a worried deer! Freshen the priming of your pistols—the mist of the falls is apt to dampen the brimstone—and stand firm for a close struggle, while I fire on their rush."

He placed a finger in his mouth, and drew a long, shrill whistle, which was answered from the rocks that were guarded by the Mohicans. Duncan caught glimpses of heads above the scattered driftwood, as this signal rose on the air, but they disappeared again as suddenly as they had glanced upon his sight. A low, rustling sound, next drew his attention behind him, and turning his head, he beheld Uncas within a few feet, creeping to his side. Hawkeye spoke to him in Delaware, when the young chief took his position with singular caution and undisturbed coolness. To Heyward this was a moment of feverish and impatient suspense; though the scout saw fit to select it as a fit occasion to read a lecture to his more youthful associates on the art of using firearms with discretion.

"Of all we'pons," he commenced, "the long-barrelled, true-grooved, soft-metalled rifle, is the most dangerous in skilful hands, though it wants a strong arm, a quick eye, and great judgment in charging, to put forth all its beauties. The gunsmiths can have but little insight into their trade, when they make their fowling pieces and short horsemen's—"

He was interrupted by the low but expressive "hugh" of Uncas.

"I see them, boy, I see them!" continued Hawkeye. "They are gathering for the rush, or they would keep their dingy backs below the logs. Well, let them," he added, examining his flint; "the leading man certainly comes on to his death, though it should be Montcalm himself!"

At that moment the woods were filled with another burst of cries, and at the signal four savages sprang from the cover of the driftwood. Heyward felt a burning desire to rush forward to meet them, so intense was the delirious anxiety of the moment; but he was restrained by the deliberate examples of the scout and Uncas. When their foes, who leaped over the black rocks that divided them, with long bounds, uttering the wildest yells, were within a few rods, the rifle of Hawkeye slowly rose among the shrubs, and poured out its fatal contents. The foremost Indian bounded like a stricken deer, and fell headlong among the clefts of the island.

"Now, Uncas!" cried the scout, drawing his long knife, while his quick eyes began to flash with ardor, "take the last of the screeching imps; of the other two we are sartain!"

He was obeyed; and but two enemies remained to be overcome. Heyward had given one of his pistols to Hawkeye, and together they rushed down a little declivity towards their foes; they discharged their weapons at the same instant, and equally without success.

"I know'd it! and I said it!" muttered the scout, whirling the despised little implement over the falls with bitter disdain. "Come on, ye bloody minded hell-hounds! ye meet a man without a cross!"

The words were barely uttered, when he encountered a savage of gigantic stature, and of the fiercest mien. At the same moment, Duncan found himself engaged with the other, in a similar contest of hand to hand. With ready skill, Hawkeye and his antagonist each grasped that uplifted arm of the other which held the dangerous knife. For near a minute they stood looking one another in the eye, and gradually exerting the power of their muscles for the mastery. At length, the toughened sinews of the white man prevailed over the less practiced limbs of the native. The arms of the latter slowly gave way before the increasing force of the scout, who suddenly wresting his armed hand from the grasp of his foe, drove the sharp weapon through his naked bosom to the heart. In the meantime, Heyward had been pressed in a more deadly struggle. His slight sword was snapped in the first encounter. As he was destitute of any other means of defence, his safety now depended entirely on bodily strength and resolution. Though deficient in neither of these qualities, he had met an enemy every way his equal. Happily, he soon succeeded in disarming his adversary, whose knife fell on the rock at their feet; and from this moment it became a fierce struggle who should cast the other over the dizzy height into a neighboring cavern of the falls. Every successive struggle brought them nearer to the verge, where Duncan perceived the final and conquering effort must be made. Each of the combatants threw all his energies into that effort, and the result was, that both tottered on the brink of the precipice. Heyward felt the grasp of the other at his throat, and saw the grim smile the savage gave, under the revengeful hope that he hurried his enemy to a fate similar to his own, as he felt his body slowly yielding to a resistless power, and the young man experienced the passing agony of such a moment in all its horrors. At that instant of extreme danger, a dark hand and glancing knife appeared before him; the Indian released his hold, as the blood flowed freely from around the severed tendons of his wrist; and while Duncan was drawn backward by the saving arm of Uncas, his charmed eyes were still riveted on the fierce and disappointed countenance of his foe, who fell sullenly and disappointed down the irrecoverable precipice.

"To cover! to cover!" cried Hawkeye, who just then had despatched his enemy; "to cover, for your lives! the work is but half ended!"

The young Mohican gave a shout of triumph, and, followed by Duncan, he glided up the acclivity they had descended to the combat, and sought the friendly shelter of the rocks and shrubs.

The warning call of the scout was not uttered without occasion. During the occurrence of the deadly encounter just related, the roar of the falls was unbroken by any human sound whatever. It would seem that interest in the result had kept the natives on the opposite shores in breathless suspense, while the quick evolutions and swift changes in the positions of the combatants, effectually prevented a fire that might prove dangerous alike to friend and enemy. But the moment the struggle was decided, a yell arose as fierce and savage as wild and revengeful passions could throw into the air. It was followed by the swift flashes of the rifles, which sent their leaden messengers across the rock in volleys, as though the assailants would pour out their impotent fury on the insensible scene of the fatal contest.

A steady, though deliberate return was made from the rifle of Chingachgook, who had maintained his post throughout the fray with unmoved resolution. When the triumphant shout of Uncas was borne to his ears, the gratified father raised his voice in a single responsive cry, after which his busy piece alone proved that he still guarded his pass with unwearied diligence. In this manner many minutes flew by with the swiftness of thought: the rifles of the assailants speaking, at times, in rattling volleys, and at others, in occasional, scattering shots. Though the rock, the trees, and the shrubs, were cut and torn in a hundred places around the besieged, their cover was so close, and so rigidly maintained, that, as yet, David had been the only sufferer in their little band.

"Let them burn their powder," said the deliberate scout, while bullet after bullet whizzed by the place where he securely lay; "there will be a fine gathering of lead when it is over, and I fancy the imps will tire of the sport, afore these old stones cry out for mercy! Uncas, boy, you waste the kernels by overcharging: and a kicking rifle never carries a true bullet. I told you to take that loping miscreant under the line of white paint; now, if your bullet went a hairsbreadth, it went two inches above it. The life lies low in a Mingo, and humanity teaches us to make a quick end of the sarpents."

A quiet smile lighted the haughty features of the young Mohican, betraying his knowledge of the English language, as well as of the other's meaning; but he suffered it to pass away without vindication or reply.

"I cannot permit you to accuse Uncas of want of judgment or of skill," said Duncan; "he saved my life in the coolest and readiest manner, and he has made a friend who never will require to be reminded of the debt he owes."

Uncas partly raised his body, and offered his hand to the grasp of Heyward. During this act of friendship, the two young men exchanged looks of intelligence which caused Duncan to forget the character and condition of his wild associate. In the meanwhile, Hawkeye, who looked on this burst of youthful feeling with a cool but kind regard, made the following reply:—

"Life is an obligation which friends often owe to each other in the wilderness. I dare say I may have served Uncas some such turn myself before now; and I very well remember that he has stood between me and death five different times: three times from the Mingoes, once in crossing Horican, and—"

"That bullet was better aimed than common!" exclaimed Duncan, involuntarily shrinking from a shot which struck the rock at his side with a smart rebound.

Hawkeye laid his hand on the shapeless metal, and shook his head, as he examined it, saying, "Falling lead is never flattened! had it come from the clouds this might have happened!"

But the rifle of Uncas was deliberately raised toward the heavens, directing the eyes of his companions to a point, where the mystery was immediately explained. A ragged oak grew on the right bank of the river, nearly opposite to their position, which, seeking the freedom of the open space, had inclined so far forward, that its upper branches overhung that arm of the stream which flowed nearest to its own shore. Among the topmost leaves, which scantily concealed the gnarled and stunted limbs, a savage was nestled, partly concealed by the trunk of the tree, and partly exposed, as though looking down upon them to ascertain the effect produced by his treacherous aim.

"These devils will scale heaven to circumvent us to our ruin," said Hawkeye; "keep him in play, boy, until I can bring Killdeer to bear, when we will try his metal on each side of the tree at once."

Uncas delayed his fire until the scout uttered the word. The rifles flashed, the leaves and bark of the oak flew into the air, and were scattered by the wind, but the Indian answered their assault by a taunting laugh, sending down upon them another bullet in return, that struck the cap of Hawkeye from his head. Once more the savage yells burst out of the woods, and the leaden hail whistled above the heads of the besieged, as if to confine them to a place where they might become easy victims to the enterprise of the warrior who had mounted the tree.

"This must be looked to!" said the scout, glancing about him with an anxious eye. "Uncas, call up your father; we have need of all our we'pons to bring the cunning varment from his roost."

The signal was instantly given; and, before Hawkeye had reloaded his rifle, they were joined by Chingachgook. When his son pointed out to the experienced warrior the situation of their dangerous enemy, the usual exclamatory "hugh" burst from his lips; after which, no further expression of surprise or alarm was suffered to escape him. Hawkeye and the Mohicans conversed earnestly together in Delaware for a few moments, when each quietly took his post, in order to execute the plan they had speedily devised.

The warrior in the oak had maintained a quick though ineffectual fire, from the moment of his discovery. But his aim was interrupted by the viligance of his enemies, whose rifles instantaneously bore on any part of his person that was left exposed. Still his bullets fell in the center of the crouching party. The clothes of Heyward, which rendered him peculiarly conspicuous, were repeatedly cut, and once blood was drawn from a slight wound in his arm.

At length, emboldened by the long and patient watchfulness of his enemies, the Huron attempted a better and more fatal aim. The quick eyes of the Mohicans caught the dark line of his lower limbs incautiously exposed through the thin foliage, a few inches from the trunk of the tree. Their rifles made a common report, when, sinking on his wounded limb, part of the body of the savage came into view. Swift as thought, Hawkeye seized the advantage, and discharged his fatal weapon into the top of the oak. The leaves were unusually agitated; the dangerous rifle fell from its commanding elevation, and after a few moments of vain struggling, the form of the savage was seen swinging in the wind, while he still grasped a ragged and naked branch of the tree, with hands clenched in desperation.

"Give him, in pity give him, the contents of another rifle!" cried Duncan, turning away his eyes in horror from the spectacle of a fellow creature in such awful jeopardy.

"Not a karnel!" exclaimed the obdurate Hawkeye; "his death is certain, and we have no powder to spare, for Indian fights sometimes last for days; 'tis their scalps or ours!—and God, who made us, has put into our natures the craving to keep the skin on the head!"

Against this stern and unyielding morality, supported as it was by such visible policy, there was no appeal. From that moment the yells in the forest once more ceased, the fire was suffered to decline, and all eyes, those of friends as well as enemies, became fixed on the hopeless condition of the wretch who was dangling between heaven and earth. The body yielded to the currents of air, and though no murmur or groan escaped the victim, there were instants when he grimly faced his foes, and the anguish of cold despair might be traced, through the intervening distance, in possession of his swarthy lineaments. There several times the scout raised his piece in mercy, and as often prudence getting the better of his intention, it was again silently lowered. At length one hand of the Huron lost its hold, and dropped exhausted to his side. A desperate and fruitless struggle to recover the branch succeeded, and then the savage was seen for a fleeting instant, grasping wildly at the empty air. The lightning is not quicker than was the flame from the rifle of Hawkeye; the limbs of the victim trembled and contracted, the head fell to the bosom, and the body parted the foaming waters like lead, when the element closed above it, in its ceaseless velocity, and every vestige of the unhappy Huron was lost forever.

No shout of triumph succeeded this important advantage, but even the Mohicans gazed at each other in silent horror. A single yell burst from the woods, and all was again still. Hawkeye, who alone appeared to reason on the occasion, shook his head at his own momentary weakness, even uttering his self-disapprobation aloud.

" 'Twas the last charge in my horn, and the last bullet in my pouch, and 'twas the act of a boy!" he said; "what mattered it whether he struck the rock living or dead! feeling would soon be over. Uncas, lad, go down to the canoe, and bring up the big horn; it is all the powder we have left, and we shall need it to the last grain, or I am ignorant of the Mingo nature."

The young Mohican complied, leaving the scout turning over the useless contents of his pouch, and shaking the empty horn with renewed discontent. From this unsatisfactory examination, however, he was soon called by a loud and piercing exclamation from Uncas, that sounded, even to the unpracticed ears of Duncan, as the signal of some new and unexpected calamity. Every thought filled with apprehension for the precious treasure he had concealed in the cavern, the young man started to his feet, totally regardless of the hazard he incurred by such an exposure. As if actuated by a common impulse, his movement was imitated by his companions, and, together, they rushed down the pass to the friendly chasm, with a rapidity that rendered the scattering fire of their enemies perfectly harmless. The unwonted cry had brought the sisters, together with the wounded David, from their place of refuge; and the whole party, at a single glance, was made acquainted with the nature of the disaster that had disturbed even the practised stoicism of their youthful Indian protector.

At a short distance from the rock, their little bark was to be seen floating across the eddy, toward the swift current of the river, in a manner which proved that its course was directed by some hidden agent. The instant this unwelcome sight caught the eye of the scout, his rifle was levelled, as by instinct, but the barrel gave no answer to the bright sparks of the flint.

" 'Tis too late, 'tis too late!" Hawkeye exclaimed, dropping the useless piece in bitter disappointment, "the miscreant has struck the rapid; and had we powder, it could hardly send the lead swifter than he now goes!"

The adventurous Huron raised his head above the shelter of the canoe, and while it glided swiftly down the stream, he waved his hand, and gave forth the shout, which was the known signal of success. His cry was answered by a yell and a laugh from the woods, as tauntingly exulting as if fifty demons were uttering their blasphemies at the fall of some Christian soul.

"Well may you laugh, ye children of the Devil!" said the scout, seating himself on a projection of the rock, and suffering his gun to fall neglected at his feet, "for the three quickest and truest rifles in these woods are no better than so many stalks of mullen, or the last year's horns of a buck!"

"What is to be done?" demanded Duncan, losing the first feeling of disappointment in a more manly desire for exertion; "what will become of us?"

Hawkeye made no other reply than by passing his finger around the crown of his head, in a manner so significant, that none who witnessed the action could mistake its meaning.

"Surely, surely, our case is not so desperate!" exclaimed the youth; "the Hurons are not here; we may make good the caverns; we may oppose their landing."

"With what?" coolly demanded the scout. "The arrows of Uncas, or such tears as women shed! No, no; we are young, and rich, and have friends, and at such an age I know it is hard to die! But," glancing his eyes at the Mohicans, "let us remember we are men without a cross, and let us teach these natives of the forest that white blood can run as freely as red, when the appointed hour is come."

Duncan turned quickly in the direction indicated by the other's eyes, and read a confirmation of his worst apprehensions in the conduct of the Indians. Chingachgook, placing himself in a dignified posture on another fragment of the rock, had already placed aside his knife and tomahawk, and was in the act of taking the eagle's plume from his head, and smoothing the solitary tuft of hair in readiness to perform its last and revolting office. His countenance was composed, though thoughtful, while his dark gleaming eyes were gradually loosing the fierceness of the combat in an expression better suited to the change he expected momentarily to undergo.

"Our case is not, cannot be so hopeless!" said Duncan; "even at this very moment succor may be at hand. I see no enemies! they have sickened of a struggle in which they risk so much with so little prospect of gain!"

"It may be a minute, or it may be an hour, afore the wily sarpents steal upon us, and it is quite in natur' for them to be lying within hearing at this very moment," said Hawkeye; "but come they will, and in such a fashion as will leave us nothing to hope! Chingachgook"—he spoke in Delaware—"my brother, we have fought our last battle together, and the Maquas will triumph in the death of the sage man of the Mohicans, and of the paleface, whose eyes can make night as day, and level the clouds to the mists of the springs!"

"Let the Mingo women go weep over their slain!" returned the Indian, with characteristic pride and unmoved firmness; "the Great Snake of the Mohicans has coiled himself in their wigwams, and has poisoned their triumph with the wailings of children, whose fathers have not returned! Eleven warriors lie hid from the graves of their tribes since the snows have melted, and none will tell where to find them when the tongue of Chingachgook shall be silent! Let them draw the sharpest knife, and whirl the swiftest tomahawk, for their bitterest enemy is in their hands. Uncas, topmost branch of a noble trunk, call on the cowards to hasten or their hearts will soften, and they will change to women!"

"They look among the fishes for their dead!" returned the low, soft voice of the youthful chieftain; "the Hurons float with the slimy eels! They drop from the oaks like fruit that is ready to be eaten! and the Delawares laugh!"

"Ay, ay," muttered the scout, who had listened to this peculiar burst of the natives with deep attention; "they have warmed their Indian feelings, and they'll soon provoke the Maquas to give them a speedy end. As for me, who am of the whole blood of the whites, it is befitting that I should die as becomes my color, with no words of scoffing in my mouth, and without bitterness at the heart!"

"Why die at all!" said Cora, advancing from the place where natural horror had, until this moment, held her riveted to the rock; "the path is open on every side; fly, then, to the woods, and call on God for succor! Go, brave men, we owe you too much already; let us no longer involve you in our hapless fortunes!"

"You but little know the craft of the Iroquois, lady, if you judge they have left the path open to the woods!" returned Hawkeye, who, however, immediately added in his simplicity: "the downstream current, it is certain, might soon sweep us beyond the reach of their rifles or the sounds of their voices."

"Then try the river. Why linger, to add to the number of the victims of our merciless enemies?"

"Why," repeated the scout, looking about him proudly, "because it is better for a man to die at peace with himself than to live haunted by an evil conscience! What answer could we give Munro, when he asked us where and how we left his children?"

"Go to him, and say, that you left them with a message to hasten to their aid," returned Cora, advancing nigher to the scout, in her generous ardor; "that the Hurons bear them into the northern wilds, but that by vigilance and speed they may yet be rescued; and if, after all, it should please heaven that his assistance come too late, bear to him," she continued, her voice gradually lowering, until it seemed nearly choked, "the love, the blessings, the final prayers of his daughters, and bid him not mourn their early fate, but to look forward with humble confidence to the Christian's goal to meet his children."

The hard, weather-beaten features of the scout began to work, and when she had ended, he dropped his chin to his hand, like a man musing profoundly on the nature of the proposal.

"There is reason in her words!" at length broke from his compressed and trembling lips; "ay, and they bear the spirit of Christianity; what might be right and proper in a redskin, may be sinful in a man who has not even a cross in blood to plead for his ignorance. Chingachgook! Uncas! hear you the talk of the dark-eyed woman?"

He now spoke in Delaware to his companions, and his address, though calm and deliberate, seemed very decided. The elder Mohican heard him with deep gravity, and appeared to ponder on his words, as though he felt the importance of their import. After a moment of hesitation, he waved his hand in assent, and uttered the English word "good," with the peculiar emphasis of his people. Then, replacing his knife and tomahawk in his girdle, the warrior moved silently to the edge of the rock which was most concealed from the banks of the river. Here he paused a moment, pointed significantly to the woods below, and saying a few words in his own language, as if indicating his intended route, he dropped into the water, and sank from before the eyes of the witnesses of his movements.

The scout delayed his departure to speak to the generous girl, whose breathing became lighter as she saw the success of her remonstrance.

"Wisdom is sometimes given to the young, as well as to the old," he said; "and what you have spoken is wise, not to call it by a better word. If you are led into the woods, that is such of you as may be spared for a while, break the twigs on the bushes as you pass, and make the marks of your trail as broad as you can, when, if mortal eyes can see them, depend on having a friend who will follow to the ends of 'arth afore he desarts you."

He gave Cora an affectionate shake of the hand, lifted his rifle, and after regarding it a moment with melancholy solicitude, laid it carefully aside, and descended to the place where Chingachgook had just disappeared. For an instant he hung suspended by the rock; and looking about him, with a countenance of peculiar care, he added, bitterly, "Had the powder held out, this disgrace could never have befallen!" then, loosening his hold, the water closed above his head, and he also became lost to view.

All eyes were now turned on Uncas, who stood leaning against the ragged rock, in immovable composure. After waiting a short time, Cora pointed down the river, and said:—

"Your friends have not been seen, and are now, most probably, in safety; is it not time for you to follow?"

"Uncas will stay," the young Mohican calmly answered in English.

"To increase the horror of our capture, and to diminish the chances of our release! Go, generous young man," Cora continued, lowering her eyes under the gaze of the Mohican, and, perhaps, with an intuitive consciousness of her power; "go to my father, as I have said, and be the most confidential of my messengers. Tell him to trust you with the means to buy the freedom of his daughters. Go! 'tis my wish, 'tis my prayer, that you will go!"

The settled, calm look of the young chief changed to an expression of gloom, but he no longer hesitated. With a noiseless step he crossed the rock, and dropped into the troubled stream. Hardly a breath was drawn by those he left behind, until they caught a glimpse of his head emerging for air, far down the current, when he again sank, and was seen no more.

These sudden and apparently successful experiments had all taken place in a few minutes of that time which had now become so precious. After the last look at Uncas, Cora turned, and, with a quivering lip, addressed herself to Heyward:—

"I have heard of your boasted skill in the water, too, Duncan," she said; "follow, then, the wise example set you by these simple and faithful beings."

"Is such the faith that Cora Munro would exact from her protector?" said the young man, smiling mournfully, but with bitterness.

"This is not a time for idle subtleties and false opinions," she answered; "but a moment when every duty should be equally considered. To us you can be of no further service here, but your precious life may be saved for other and nearer friends."

He made no reply, though his eyes fell wistfully on the beautiful form of Alice, who was clinging to his arm with the dependency of an infant.

"Consider," continued Cora, after a pause during which she seemed to struggle with a pang even more acute than any that her fears had excited, "that the worst to us can be but death; a tribute that all must pay at the good time of God's appointment."

"There are evils worse than death," said Duncan, speaking hoarsely, and as if fretful at her importunity, "but which the presence of one who would die in your behalf may avert."

Cora ceased her entreaties; and, veiling her face in her shawl, drew the nearly insensible Alice after her into the deepest recess of the inner cavern.

4

THE INDIANS soon discovered the hiding place of Major Heyward's party, and with loud and triumphant yells seized him, the two daughters of Colonel Munro, and the wounded psalm singer. Magua, or Le Renard Subtil, contemplated the prisoners with special exultation. He and the other Hurons were bitterly disappointed to learn that Hawkeye (or La longue Carabine) and Chingachgook had made good their escape; they prepared, therefore, to visit a cruel vengeance upon the four others. In vain did Heyward beg Magua to forget the hurts received in war. "Was it war when the tired Indian rested at the sugar tree to taste his corn?" demanded the embittered chief. "Who filled the bushes with creeeping enemies? Who drew the knife? Whose tongue was peace, while his heart was colored with blood? Did Magua say that the hatchet was out of the ground, and that his hand had dug it up?" In vain, too, did Heyward assure Magua that Colonel Munro would pay a very heavy ransom for the safe return of his two daughters. "Enough," was the reply; "Le Renard is a wise chief and what he does will be seen. Go, and keep the mouth shut. When Magua speaks, it will be time to answer." The Indians hurried the four whites away through the forest, stopping for the night at a steep hill where they gorged themselves upon the raw meat of a fawn they had killed.

Here Magua delivered his ultimatum to Heyward and the two girls. If the beautiful Cora would become his wife, he would restore Alice, the major, and the psalm singer to safety. He wanted

Cora, he stated, not because he found her attractive, but because he could thus glut a lifelong sentiment of revenge. "When the blows scorched the back of the Huron, he would know where to find a woman to feel the smart. The daughter of Munro would draw his water, hoe his corn, and cook his vension. The body of the gray-head would sleep among his cannon, but his heart would lie within reach of the knife of Le Subtil." To this Cora's reply was: "Monster!"

Preparations at once began to torture the four captives to death. They were bound to trees; fuel was collected to burn them at the stake. Magua, in a sudden access of passion, hurled his tomahawk at Alice Munro, but missed. At this Heyward burst his bonds of green twigs, and flung himself upon the nearest savage. As he did so, the sharp crack of a rifle broke upon the air, and the Indian whom he had grappled sank down dead.

The Hurons stood aghast at this sudden visitation of death on one of their band. But, as they regarded the fatal accuracy of an aim which had dared to immolate an enemy at so much hazard to a friend, the name of La longue Carabine burst simultaneously from every lip, and was succeeded by a wild and a sort of plaintive howl. The cry was answered by a loud shout from a little thicket, where the incautious party had piled their arms; and, at the next moment, Hawkeye, too eager to load the rifle he had regained, was seen advancing upon them, brandishing the clubbed weapon, and cutting the air with wide and powerful sweeps. Bold and rapid as was the progress of the scout, it was exceeded by that of a light and vigorous form which, bounding past him, leaped, with incredible activity and daring, into the very center of the Hurons, where it stood, whirling a tomahawk, and flourishing a glittering knife, with fearful menaces, in front of Cora. Quicker than the thoughts could follow these unexpected and audacious movements, an image, armed in the emblematic panoply of death, glided before their eyes, and assumed a threatening attitude at the other's side. The savage tormentors recoiled before these warlike intruders, and uttered as they appeared in such quick succession, the often repeated and peculiar exclamation of surprise, followed by the well known and dreaded appellations of—

"Le Cerf Agile! Le gros Serpent!"

But the wary and vigilant leader of the Hurons was not so easily disconcerted. Casting his keen eyes around the little plain, he comprehended the nature of the assault at a glance, and encouraging his followers by his voice as well as by his example, he unsheathed his long and dangerous knife, and rushed with a loud whoop upon the expecting Chingachgook. It was the signal for a general combat. Neither party had firearms, and the contest was to be decided in the deadliest manner; hand to hand, with weapons of offence, and none of defence.

Uncas answered the whoop, and leaping on an enemy, with a single, well-directed blow of his tomahawk, cleft him to the brain. Heyward tore the weapon of Magua from the sapling, and rushed eagerly toward the fray. As the combatants were now equal in number, each singled an opponent from the adverse band. The rush and blows passed with the fury of a whirlwind, and the swiftness of lightning. Hawkeye soon got another enemy within reach of his arm, and with one sweep of his formidable weapon he beat down the slight and inartificial defences of his antagonist, crushing him to the earth with the blow. Heyward ventured to hurl the tomahawk he had seized, too ardent to await the moment of closing. It struck the Indian he had selected on the forehead, and checked for an instant his onward rush. Encouraged by this slight advantage, the impetuous young man continued his onset, and sprang upon his enemy with naked hands. A single instant was sufficient to assure him of the rashness of the measure, for he immediately found himself fully engaged, with all his activity and courage, in endeavoring to ward the desperate thrusts made with the knife of the Huron. Unable longer to foil an enemy so alert and vigilant, he threw his arms about him, and succeeded in pinning the limbs of the other to his side, with an iron grasp, but one that was far too exhausting to himself to continue long. In this extremity he heard a voice near him, shouting—

"Extarminate the varlets! no quarter to an accursed Mingo!"

At the next moment, the breech of Hawkeye's rifle fell on the naked head of his adversary, whose muscles appeared to wither under the shock, as he sank from the arms of Duncan, flexible and motionless.

When Uncas had brained his first antagonist, he turned, like a hungry lion, to seek another. The fifth and only Huron disengaged at the first onset had paused a moment, and then seeing that all around him were employed in the deadly strife, he had sought, with hellish vengeance, to complete the baffled work of revenge. Raising a shout of triumph, he sprang towards the defenceless Cora, sending his keen ax, as the dreadful precursor of his approach. The tomahawk grazed her shoulder, and cutting the withes which bound her to the tree, left the maiden at liberty to fly. She eluded the grasp of the savage, and reckless of her own safety, threw herself on the bosom of Alice, striving, with convulsed and ill-directed fingers, to tear asunder the twigs which confined the person of her sister. Any other than a monster would have relented at such an act of generous devotion to the best and purest affection; but the breast of the Huron was a stranger to sympathy. Seizing Cora by the rich tresses which fell in confusion about her form, he tore her from her frantic hold, and bowed her down with brutal violence to her knees. The savage drew the flowing curls through his hand, and raising them on high with an outstretched arm, he passed the knife around the exquisitely moulded head of his victim, with a taunting and exulting laugh. But he purchased this moment of fierce gratification with the loss of the fatal opportunity. It was just then the sight caught the eye of Uncas. Bounding from his footsteps he appeared for an instant darting through the air, and descending in a ball he fell on the chest of his enemy, driving him many yards from the spot, headlong and prostrate. The violence of the exertion cast the young Mohican at his side. They arose together, fought, and bled, each in his turn. But the conflict was soon decided; the tomahawk of Heyward and the rifle of Hawkeye descended on the skull of the Huron, at the same moment that the knife of Uncas reached his heart.

The battle was now entirely terminated, with the exception of the protracted struggle between Le Renard Subtil and Le gros Serpent. Well did these barbarous warriors prove that they deserved those significant names which had been bestowed for deeds in former wars. When they engaged, some little time was lost in eluding the quick and vigorous thrusts which had been aimed at their lives. Suddenly darting on each other, they closed, and came to the earth, twisted together like twining serpents, in pliant and subtle folds. At the moment when the victors found themselves unoccupied, the spot where these experienced and desperate combatants lay, could only be distinguished by a cloud of dust and leaves which moved from the center of the little plain toward its boundary, as if raised by the passage of a whirlwind. Urged by the different motives of filial affection, friendship, and gratitude, Heyward and his companions rushed with one accord to the place, encircling the little canopy of dust which hung above the warriors. In vain did Uncas dart around the cloud, with a wish to strike his knife into the heart of his father's foe; the threatening rifle of Hawkeye was raised and suspended in vain, while Duncan endeavored to seize the limbs of the Huron with hands that appeared to have lost their power. Covered, as they were, with dust and blood, the swift evolutions of the combatants seemed to incorporate their bodies into one. The deathlike looking figure of the Mohican, and the dark form of the Huron, gleamed before their eyes in such quick and confused succession, that the friends of the former knew not where nor when to plant the succoring blow. It is true there were short and fleeting moments, when the fiery eyes of Magua were seen glittering, like the fabled organs of the basilisk, through the dusty wreath by which he was enveloped, and he read by those short and deadly glances the fate of the combat in the presence of his enemies; ere, however, any hostile hand could descend on his devoted head, its place was filled by the scowling visage of Chingachgook. In this manner the scene of the combat was removed from the center of the little plain to its verge. The Mohican now found an opportunity to make a powerful thrust with his knife; Magua suddenly relinquished his grasp, and fell backward without motion, and seemingly without life. His adversary leaped on his feet, making the arches of the forest ring with the sounds of triumph.

"Well done for the Delawares! victory to the Mohican!" cried Hawkeye, once more elevating the butt of the long and fatal rifle; "a finishing blow from a man without a cross will never tell against his honor, nor rob him of his right to the scalp."

But, at the very moment when the dangerous weapon was in the act of descending, the subtle Huron rolled swiftly from beneath the danger, over the edge of the precipice, and falling on his feet, was seen leaping, with a single bound, into the center of a thicket of low bushes, which clung along its sides. The Delawares, who had believed their enemy dead, uttered their exclamation of surprise, and were following with speed and clamor, like hounds in open view of the deer, when a shrill and peculiar cry from the scout instantly changed their purpose, and recalled them to the summit of the hill.

" 'Twas like himself," cried the inveterate forester, whose prejudices contributed so largely to veil his natural sense of justice in all matters which concerned the Mingoes; "a lying and deceitful varlet as he is. An honest Delaware now, being fairly vanquished, would have lain still, and been knocked on the head, but these knavish Maquas cling to life like so many cats-o'-the-mountain. Let him go—let him go; 'tis but one man, and he without rifle or bow, many a long mile from his French commerades; and, like a rattler that has lost his fangs, he can do no farther mischief, until such time as he, and we too, may leave the prints of our moccasins over a long reach of sandy plain. See, Uncas," he added, in Delaware, "your father is flaying the scalps already. It may be well to go round and feel the vagabonds that are left, or we may have another of them loping through the woods, and screeching like a jay that has been winged."

So saying, the honest, but implacable scout, made the circuit of the dead, into whose senseless bosoms he thrust his long knife, with as much coolness as though they had been so many brute carcasses. He had, however, been anticipated by the elder Mohican, who had already torn the emblems of victory from the unresisting heads of the slain.

But Uncas, denying his habits, we had almost said his nature, flew with instinctive delicacy, accompanied by Heyward, to the assistance of the females, and quickly releasing Alice, placed her in the arms of Cora. We shall not attempt to describe the gratitude to the Almighty Disposer of events which glowed in the bosoms of the sisters, who were thus unexpectedly restored to life and to each other. Their thanksgivings were deep and silent; the offerings of their gentle spirits, burning brightest and purest on the secret altars of their hearts; and their renovated and more earthly feelings exhibited themselves in long and fervent, though speechless caresses. As Alice rose from her knees, where she had sunk by the side of Cora, she threw herself on the bosom of the latter, and sobbed aloud the name of their aged father, while her soft, dovelike eyes sparkled with the rays of hope.

"We are saved! we are saved!" she murmured; "to return to the arms of our dear, dear father, and his heart will not be broken with grief. And you too, Cora, my sister; my more than sister, my mother; you too are spared. And Duncan," she added, looking round upon the youth with a smile of ineffable innocence, "even our own brave and noble Duncan has escaped without a hurt."

To these ardent and nearly incoherent words, Cora made no other answer than by straining the youthful speaker to her heart, as she bent over her, in melting tenderness. The manhood of Heyward felt no shame in dropping tears over this spectacle of affectionate rapture; and Uncas stood, fresh and bloodstained from the combat, a calm, and, apparently, an unmoved looker-on, it is true, but with eyes that had already lost their fierceness, and were beaming with a sympathy that elevated him far above the intelligence, and advanced him probably centuries before the practices, of his nation.

During this display of emotions so natural in their situation, Hawkeye, whose vigilant distrust had satisfied itself that the Hurons, who disfigured the heavenly scene, no longer possessed the power to interrupt its harmony, approached David, and liberated him from the bonds he had, until that moment, endured with the most exemplary patience.

"There," exclaimed the scout, casting the last withe behind him, "you are once more master of your own limbs, though you seem not to use them with much greater judgment than that in which they were first fashioned. If advice from one who is not older than yourself, but who, having lived most of his time in the wilderness, may be said to have experienced beyond his years, will give no offence, you are welcome to my thoughts; and these are, to part with the little tooting instrument in your jacket to the first fool you meet with, and buy some useful we'pon with the money, if it be only the barrel of a horseman's pistol. By industry and care, you might thus come to some prefarment; for by this time, I should think, your eyes would plainly tell you that a carrion crow is a better bird than a mocking thresher. The one will, at least, remove foul sights from before the face of man, while the other is only good to brew disturbances in the woods, by cheating the ears of all that hear them."

"Arms and the clarion for the battle, but the song of thanksgiving to the victory!" answered the liberated David. "Friend," he added, thrusting forth his lean, delicate hand toward Hawkeye, in kindness, while his eyes twinkled and grew moist, "I thank thee that the hairs of my head still grow where they were first rooted by Providence; for, though those of other men may be more glossy and curling, I have ere found mine own well suited to the brain they shelter. That I did not join myself to the battle, was less owing to disinclination, than to the bonds of the heather. Valiant and skilful hast thou proved thyself in conflict, and I hereby thank thee, before proceeding to discharge other and more important duties, because thou hast proved thyself well worthy of a Christian's praise."

"The thing is but a trifle, and what you may often see, if you tarry long among us," returned the scout, a good deal softened toward the man of song, by this unequivocal expression of gratitude. "I have got back my old companion, Killdeer," he added, striking his hand on the breech of his rifle; "and that in itself is a victory. These Iroquois are cunning, but they outwitted themselves when they placed their firearms out of reach; and had Uncas or his father been gifted with only their common Indian patience, we should have come in upon the knaves with three bullets instead of one, and that would have made a finish of the whole pack; yon loping varlet, as well as his commerades. But 'twas all fore-ordered, and for the best."

"Thou sayest well," returned David, "and hast caught the true spirit of Christianity. He that is to be saved will be saved, and he that is predestined to be damned will be damned. This is the doctrine of truth, and most consoling and refreshing it is to the true believer."

The scout, who by this time was seated, examining into the state of his rifle with a species of parental assiduity, now looked up at the other in a displeasure that he did not affect to conceal, roughly interrupting further speech.

"Doctrine or no doctrine," said the sturdy woodsman, " 'tis the belief of knaves, and the curse of an honest man. I can credit that yonder Huron was to fall by my hand, for with my own eyes I have seen it; but nothing short of being a witness will cause me to think he has met with any reward, or that Chingachgook, there, will be condemned at the final day."

"You have no warranty for such an audacious doctrine, nor any covenant to support it," cried David, who was deeply tinctured with the subtle distinctions which, in his time, and more especially in his province, had been drawn around the beautiful simplicity of revelation, by endeavoring to penetrate the awful mystery of the divine nature, supplying faith by self-sufficiency, and by consequence, involving those who reasoned from such human dogmas in absurdities and doubt;

"your temple is reared on the sands, and the first tempest will wash away its foundation. I demand your authorities for such an uncharitable assertion (like other advocates of a system, David was not always accurate in his use of terms). Name chapter and verse; in which of the holy books do you find language to support you?"

"Book!" repeated Hawkeye, with singular and ill-concealed disdain; "do you take me for a whimpering boy at the apron-string of one of your old gals; and this good rifle on my knee for the feather of a goose's wing, my ox's horn for a bottle of ink, and my leathern pouch for a crossbarred handkercher to carry my dinner? Book! what have such as I, who am a warrior of the wilderness, though a man without a cross, to do with books? I never read but in one, and the words that are written there are too simple and too plain to need much schooling; though I may boast that of nigh on forty long and hard-working years."

"What call you the volume?" said David, misconceiving the other's meaning.

" 'Tis open before your eyes," returned the scout; "and he who owns it is not a niggard of its use. I have heard it said that there are men who read in books to convince themselves there is a God. I know not but man may so deform his works in the settlements, as to leave that which is so clear in the wilderness a matter of doubt among traders and priests. If any such there be, and he will follow me from sun to sun, through the windings of the forest, he shall see enough to teach him that he is a fool, and that the greatest of his folly lies in striving to rise to the level of one he can never equal, be it in goodness, or be it in power."

The instant David discovered that he battled with a disputant who imbibed his faith from the lights of nature, eschewing all subtleties of doctrine, he willingly abandoned a controversy, from which he believed neither profit nor credit was to be derived. While the scout was speaking, he had also seated himself, and producing the ready little volume and the iron-rimmed spectacles, he prepared to discharge a duty, which nothing but the unexpected assault he had received in his orthodoxy could have so long suspended. He was, in truth, a minstrel of the Western continent—of a much later day, certainly, than those gifted bards, who formerly sang the profane renown of baron and prince, but after the spirit of his own age and country; and he was now prepared to exercise the cunning of his craft, in celebration of, or rather in thanksgiving for, the recent victory. He waited patiently for Hawkeye to cease, then lifting his eyes, together with his voice, he said, aloud—

"I invite you, friends, to join in praise for this signal deliverance from the hands of barbarians and infidels, to the comfortable and solemn tones of the tune, called 'Northampton.' "

He next named the page and verse where the rhymes selected were to be found, and applied the pitch pipe to his lips, with the decent gravity that he had been wont to use in the temple. This time he was, however, without any accompaniment, for the sisters were just then pouring out those tender effusions of affection which have been already alluded to. Nothing deterred by the smallness of his audience, which, in truth, consisted only of the discontented scout, he raised his voice, commencing and ending the sacred song without accident or interruption of any kind.

Hawkeye listened, while he coolly adjusted his flint and reloaded his rifle; but the sounds, wanting the extraneous assistance of scene and sympathy, failed to awaken his slumbering emotions. Never minstrel, or by whatever more suitable name David should be known, drew upon his talents in the presence of more insensible auditors; though considering the singleness and sincerity of his motive, it is probable that no bard of profane song ever uttered notes that ascended so near to that throne where all homage and praise is due. The scout shook his head, and muttering some unintelligible words, among which "throat" and "Iroquois" were alone audible, he walked away, to collect, and to examine into, the state of the captured arsenal of the Hurons. In this office he was now joined by Chingachgook, who found his own, as well as the rifle of his son, among the arms. Even Heyward and David were furnished with weapons; nor was ammunition wanting to render them all effectual.

When the foresters had made their selection, and distributed their prizes, the scout announced that the hour had arrived when it was necessary to move. By this time the song of Gamut had ceased, and the sisters had learned to still the exhibition of their emotions. Aided by Duncan and the younger Mohican, the two latter descended the precipitous sides of that hill which they had so lately ascended under so very different auspices, and whose summit had so nearly proved the scene of their massacre. At the foot, they found the Narragansetts browsing the herbage of the bushes; and having mounted, they followed the movements of a guide, who, in the most deadly straits, had so often proved himself their friend. The journey was, however, short. Hawkeye, leaving the blind path that the Hurons had followed, turned short to his right, and entering the thicket, he crossed a babbling brook, and halted in a narrow dell, under the shade of a few water elms. Their distance from the base of the fatal hill was but a few rods, and the steeds had been serviceable only in crossing the shallow stream.

The scout and the Indians appeared to be familiar with the sequestered place where they now were; for, leaning their rifles against the trees, they commenced throwing aside the dried leaves, and opening the blue clay, out of which a clear and sparkling spring of bright, glancing water quickly bubbled. The white man then looked about him, as though seeking for some object, which was not to be found as readily as he expected—

"Them careless imps, the Mohawks, with their Tuscarora and Onondaga brethren, have been here slaking their thirst," he muttered, "and the vagabonds have thrown away the gourd! This is the way with benefits, when they are bestowed on such disremembering hounds! Here has the Lord laid his hand, in the midst of the howling wilderness, for their good, and raised a fountain of water from the bowels of the 'arth, that might laugh at the richest shop of apothecary's ware in all the colonies; and see! the knaves have trodden in the clay, and deformed the cleanliness of the place, as though they were brute beasts, instead of human men."

Uncas silently extended toward him the desired gourd, which the spleen of Hawkeye had hitherto prevented from observing, on a branch of an elm. Filling it with water, he retired a short distance, to a place where the ground was more firm and dry; here he coolly seated himself, and after taking a long, and, apparently, a grateful draught, he commenced a very strict examination of the fragments of food left by the Hurons, which had hung in a wallet on his arm.

"Thank you, lad!" he continued, returning the empty gourd to Uncas; "now we will see how these rampaging Hurons lived, when outlying in ambushments. Look at this! The varlets know the better pieces of the deer; and one would think they might carve and roast a saddle, equal to the best cook in the land! But everything is raw, for the Iroquois are thorough savages. Uncas, take my steel, and kindle a fire; a mouthful of a tender broil will give natur' a helping hand, after so long a trail."

Heyward, perceiving that their guides now set about their repast in sober earnest, assisted the ladies to alight, and placed himself at their side, not unwilling to enjoy a few moments of grateful rest, after the bloody scene he had just gone through. While the culinary process was in hand, curiosity induced him to inquire into the circumstances which had led to their timely and unexpected rescue—

"How is it that we see you so soon, my generous friend," he asked, "and without aid from the garrison of Edward?"

"Had we gone to the bend in the river, we might have been in time to rake the leaves over your bodies, but too late to have saved your scalps," coolly answered the scout. "No, no; instead of throwing away strength and opportunity by crossing to the fort, we lay by, under the bank of the Hudson, waiting to watch the movements of the Hurons."

"You were, then, witnesses of all that passed?"

"Not of all; for Indian sight is too keen to be easily cheated, and we kept close. A difficult matter it was, too, to keep this Mohican boy snug in the ambushment. Ah! Uncas, Uncas, your behavior was more like that of a curious woman than of a warrior on his scent."

Uncas permitted his eyes to turn for an instant on the sturdy countenance of the speaker, but he neither spoke nor gave any indication of repentance. On the contrary, Heyward thought the manner of the young Mohican was disdainful, if not a little fierce, and that he suppressed passions that were ready to explode, as much in compliment to the listeners, as from the deference he usually paid to his white associate.

"You saw our capture?" Heyward next demanded.

"We heard it," was the significant answer. "An Indian yell is plain language to men who have passed their days in the woods. But when you landed, we were driven to crawl, like sarpents, beneath the leaves; and then we lost sight of you entirely, until we placed eyes on you again, trussed to the trees, and ready bound for an Indian massacre."

"Our rescue was the deed of Providence. It was nearly a miracle that you did not mistake the path, for the Hurons divided, and each band had its horses."

"Ay! there we were thrown off the scent, and might, indeed, have lost the trail, had it not been for Uncas; we took the path, however, that led into the wilderness; for we judged, and judged rightly, that the savages would hold that course with their prisoners. But when we had followed it for many miles, without finding a single twig broken, as I had advised, my mind misgave me; especially as all the footsteps had the prints of moccasins."

"Our captors had the precaution to see us shod like themselves," said Duncan, raising a foot, and exhibiting the buckskin he wore.

"Ay! 'twas judgmatical, and like themselves: though we were too expart to be thrown from a trail by so common an invention."

"To what, then, are we indebted for our safety?"

"To what, as a white man who has no taint of Indian blood, I should be ashamed to own; to the judgment of the young Mohican, in matters which I should know better than he, but which I can now hardly believe to be true, though my own eyes tell me it is so."

" 'Tis extraordinary! will you not name the reason?"

"Uncas was bold enough to say, that the beasts ridden by the gentle ones," continued Hawkeye, glancing his eyes, not without curious interest, on the fillies of the ladies, "planted the legs of one side on the ground at the same time, which is contrary to the movements of all trotting four-footed animals of my knowledge, except the bear. And yet here are horses that always journey in this manner, as my own eyes have seen, and as their trail has shown for twenty long miles."

" 'Tis the merit of the animal! They come from the shores of

Narragansett Bay, in the small province of Providence Plantations, and are celebrated for their hardihood, and the ease of this peculiar movement; though other horses are not unfrequently trained to the same."

"It may be—it may be," said Hawkeye, who had listened with singular attention to this explanation; "though I am a man who has the full blood of the whites, my judgment in deer and beaver is greater than in beasts of burden. Major Effingham has many noble chargers, but I have never seen one travel after such a sideling gait."

"True; for he would value the animals for very different properties. Still is this a breed highly esteemed, and as you witness, much honored with the burdens it is often destined to bear."

The Mohicans had suspended their operations about the glimmering fire, to listen; and when Duncan had done, they looked at each other significantly, the father uttering the never-failing exclamation of surprise. The scout ruminated, like a man digesting his newly acquired knowledge, and once more stole a curious glance at the horses.

"I dare to say there are even stranger sights to be seen in the settlements!" he said, at length; "natur' is sadly abused by man, when he once gets the mastery. But, go sideling or go straight, Uncas had seen the movement, and their trail led us on to the broken bush. The outer branch, near the prints of one of the horses, was bent upward, as a lady breaks a flower from its stem, but all the rest were ragged and broken down, as if the strong hand of a man had been tearing them! So I concluded, that the cunning varments had seen the twig bent, and had torn the rest, to make us believe a buck had been feeling the boughs with his antlers."

"I do believe your sagacity did not deceive you; for some such thing occurred!"

"That was easy to see," added the scout, in no degree conscious of having exhibited any extraordinary sagacity; "and a very different matter it was from a waddling horse! It then struck me the Mingoes would push for this spring, for the knaves well know the vartue of its waters!"

"Is it, then, so famous?" demanded Heyward, examining, with a more curious eye, the secluded dell, with its bubbling fountain, surrounded, as it was, by earth of a deep dingy brown.

"Few redskins, who travel south and east of the Great Lakes, but have heard of its qualities. Will you taste for yourself?"

Heyward took the gourd, and after swallowing a little of the water, threw it aside with grimaces of discontent. The scout laughed in his silent, but heartfelt manner, and shook his head with vast satisfaction.

"Ah! you want the flavor that one gets by habit; the time was when I liked it as little as yourself; but I have come to my taste, and I now crave it, as a deer does the licks.[1] Your high-spiced wines are not better liked than a redskin relishes this water; especially when his natur' is ailing. But Uncas has made his fire, and it is time we think of eating, for our journey is long, and all before us."

Interrupting the dialogue by this abrupt transition, the scout had instant recourse to the fragments of food which had escaped the voracity of the Hurons. A very summary process completed the simple cookery, when he and the Mohicans commenced their humble meal, with the silence and characteristic diligence of men, who ate in order to enable themselves to endure great and unremitting toil.

When this necessary, and, happily, grateful duty had been performed, each of the foresters stooped and took a long and parting draught, at that solitary and silent spring,[2] around which and its sister fountains, within fifty years, the wealth, beauty, and talents, of a hemisphere, were to assemble in throngs, in pursuit of health and pleasure. Then Hawkeye announced his determination to proceed. The sisters resumed their saddles; Duncan and David grasped their rifles, and followed on their footsteps; the scout leading the advance, and the Mohicans bringing up the rear. The whole party moved swiftly through the narrow path, toward the north, leaving the healing waters to mingle unheeded with the adjacent brook, and the bodies of the dead to fester on the neighboring mount, without the rites of sepulture; a fate but too common to the warriors of the woods, to excite either commiseration or comment.

The route taken by Hawkeye lay across those sandy plains, relieved by occasional valleys and swells of land, which had been traversed by their party on the morning of the same day, with the baffled Magua for their guide. The sun had now fallen low toward the distant mountains; and as their journey lay through the interminable forest, the heat was no longer oppressive. Their progress, in consequence, was proportionate; and long before the twilight gathered about them, they had made good many toilsome miles on their return.

The hunter, like the savage whose place he filled, seemed to select among the blind signs of their wild route, with a species of instinct, seldom abating his speed, and never pausing to deliberate. A rapid and oblique glance at the moss on the trees, with an occasional upward gaze toward the setting sun, or a steady but passing look at the direction of the numerous watercourses, through which he waded, were sufficient to determine his path, and remove his greatest difficulties. In

---

[1] Many of the animals of the American forests resort to those spots where salt springs are found. These are called "licks" or "salt licks," in the language of the country, from the circumstance that the quadruped is often obliged to lick the earth, in order to obtain the saline particles. These licks are great places of resort with the hunters, who waylay their game near the paths that lead to them. (*Cooper's note*)

[2] The scene of the foregoing incidents is on the spot where the village of Ballston now stands; one of the two principal watering places of America. (*Cooper's note*)

the meantime, the forest began to change its hues, losing that lively green which had embellished its arches, in the graver light which is the usual precursor of the close of day.

While the eyes of the sisters were endeavoring to catch glimpses through the trees, of the flood of golden glory which formed a glittering halo around the sun, tingeing here and there with ruby streaks, or bordering with narrow edgings of shining yellow, a mass of clouds that lay piled at no great distance above the western hills, Hawkeye turned suddenly, and, pointing upwards toward the gorgeous heavens, he spoke—

"Yonder is the signal given to man to seek his food and natural rest," he said; "better and wiser would it be, if he could understand the signs of nature, and take a lesson from the fowls of the air, and the beasts of the fields! Our night, however, will soon be over; for, with the moon, we must be up and moving again. I remember to have fou't the Maquas, hereaways, in the first war in which I ever drew blood from man; and we threw up a work of blocks, to keep the ravenous varments from handling our scalps. If my marks do not fail me, we shall find the place a few rods further to our left."

Without waiting for an assent, or, indeed, for any reply, the sturdy hunter moved boldly into a dense thicket of young chestnuts, shoving aside the branches of the exuberant shoots which nearly covered the ground, like a man who expected, at each step, to discover some object he had formerly known. The recollection of the scout did not deceive him. After penetrating through the brush, matted as it was with briers, for a few hundred feet, he entered an open space, that surrounded a low, green hillock, which was crowned by the decayed blockhouse in question. This rude and neglected building was one of those deserted works, which, having been thrown up on an emergency, had been abandoned with the disappearance of danger, and was now quietly crumbling in the solitude of the forest, neglected, and nearly forgotten, like the circumstances which had caused it to be reared. Such memorials of the passage and struggles of man are yet frequent throughout the broad barrier of wilderness which once separated the hostile provinces, and form a species of ruins that are intimately associated with the recollections of Colonial history, and which are in appropriate keeping with the gloomy character of the surrounding scenery.[1] The roof of bark had long since fallen, and mingled with the

[1] Some years since, the writer was shooting in the vicinity of the ruins of Fort Oswego, which stands on the shores of Lake Ontario. His game was deer, and his chase a forest that stretched, with little interruption, fifty miles inland. Unexpectedly he came upon six or eight ladders lying in the woods within a short distance of each other. They were rudely made and much decayed. Wondering what could have assembled so many of these instruments in such a place, he sought an old man who resided near for the explanation.

During the war of 1776 Fort Oswego was held by the British. An expedition had

soil; but the huge logs of pine, which had been hastily thrown together, still preserved their relative positions, though one angle of the work had given way under the pressure, and threatened a speedy downfall to the remainder of the rustic edifice. While Heyward and his companions hesitated to approach a building so decayed, Hawkeye and the Indians entered within the low walls, not only without fear, but with obvious interest. While the former surveyed the ruins, both internally and externally, with the curiosity of one whose recollections were reviving at each moment, Chingachgook related to his son, in the language of the Delawares, and with the pride of a conqueror, the brief history of the skirmish which had been fought, in his youth, in that secluded spot. A strain of melancholy, however, blended with his triumph, rendering his voice, as usual, soft and musical.

In the meantime, the sisters gladly dismounted, and prepared to enjoy their halt in the coolness of the evening, and in a security which they believed nothing but the beasts of the forest could invade.

"Would not our resting place have been more retired, my worthy friend," demanded the more vigilant Duncan, perceiving that the scout had already finished his short survey, "had we chosen a spot less known, and one more rarely visited than this?"

"Few live who know the blockhouse was ever raised," was the slow and musing answer; " 'tis not often that books are made, and narratives written, of such a scrimmage as was here fou't atween the Mohicans and the Mohawks, in a war of their own waging. I was then a younker, and went out with the Delawares, because I know'd they were a scandalized and wronged race. Forty days and forty nights did the imps crave our blood around this pile of logs, which I designed and partly reared, being, as you'll remember, no Indian myself, but a man without a cross. The Delawares lent themselves to the work, and we made it good, ten to twenty, until our numbers were nearly equal, and then we sallied out upon the hounds, and not a man of them ever got back to tell the fate of his party. Yes, yes; I was then young, and new to the sight of blood; and not relishing the thought that creatures who had spirits like myself should lay on the naked ground, to be torn asunder by beasts, or to bleach in the rains, I buried the dead with my own hands, under that very little hillock where you have placed yourselves; and no bad seat does it make neither, though it be raised by the bones of mortal men."

Heyward and the sisters arose, on the instant, from the grassy sepulcher; nor could the two latter, notwithstanding the terrific scenes

---

been sent two hundred miles through the wilderness to surprise the fort. It appears that the Americans, on reaching the spot named, which was within a mile or two of the fort, first learned that they were expected, and in great danger of being cut off. They threw away their scaling ladders, and made a rapid retreat. These ladders had lain unmolested thirty years in the spot where they had thus been cast. (*Cooper's note*)

they had so recently passed through, entirely suppress an emotion of natural horror, when they found themselves in such familiar contact with the grave of the dead Mohawks. The gray light, the gloomy little area of dark grass, surrounded by its border of brush, beyond which the pines rose, in breathing silence, apparently, into the very clouds, and the deathlike stillness of the vast forest, were all in unison to deepen such a sensation.

"They are gone, and they are harmless," continued Hawkeye, waving his hand, with a melancholy smile, at their manifest alarm: "they'll never shout the war whoop nor strike a blow with the tomahawk again! And of all those who aided in placing them where they lie, Chingachgook and I only are living! The brothers and family of the Mohican formed our war party; and you see before you all that are now left of his race."

The eyes of the listeners involuntarily sought the forms of the Indians, with a compassionate interest in their desolate fortune. Their dark persons were still to be seen within the shadows of the blockhouse, the son listening to the relation of his father with that sort of intenseness which would be created by a narrative that redounded so much to the honor of those whose names he had long revered for their courage and savage virtues.

"I had thought the Delawares a pacific people," said Duncan, "and that they never waged war in person; trusting the defence of their lands to those very Mohawks that you slew!"

" 'Tis true in part," returned the scout, "and yet, at the bottom, 'tis a wicked lie. Such a treaty was made in ages gone by, through the deviltries of the Dutchers, who wished to disarm the natives that had the best right to the country, where they had settled themselves. The Mohicans, though a part of the same nation, having to deal with the English, never entered into the silly bargain, but kept to their manhood; as in truth did the Delawares, when their eyes were opened to their folly. You see before you a chief of the great Mohican Sagamores! Once his family could chase their deer over tracts of country wider than that which belongs to the Albany Patteroon,[1] without crossing brook or hill that was not their own; but what is left to their decendant! He may find his six feet of earth when God chooses, and keep it in peace, perhaps, if he has a friend who will take the pains to sink his head so low, that the ploughshares cannot reach it!"

"Enough!" said Heyward, apprehensive that the subject might lead to a discussion that would interrupt the harmony so necessary to the preservation of his fair companions: "we have journeyed far, and

[1] By the Albany Patroon, Leatherstocking means the head of the great Van Rensselaer Manor, who controlled a huge tract of land on both banks of the Hudson above and below Albany. The first grant to the Van Rensselaers had been made by the Dutch East India Company in 1630.—Ed.

few among us are blessed with forms like that of yours, which seems to know neither fatigue nor weakness."

"The sinews and bones of a man carry me through it all," said the hunter, surveying his muscular limbs with a simplicity that betrayed the honest pleasure the compliment afforded him: "there are larger and heavier men to be found in the settlements, but you might travel many days in a city before you could meet one able to walk fifty miles without stopping to take breath, or who has kept the hounds within hearing during a chase of hours. However, as flesh and blood are not always the same, it is quite reasonable to suppose that the gentle ones are willing to rest, after all they have seen and done this day. Uncas, clear out the spring, while your father and I make a cover for their tender heads of these chestnut shoots, and a bed of grass and leaves."

The dialogue ceased, while the hunter and his companions busied themselves in preparations for the comfort and protection of those they guided. A spring, which many long years before had induced the natives to select the place for their temporary fortification, was soon cleared of leaves, and a fountain of crystal gushed from the bed, diffusing its waters over the verdant hillock. A corner of the building was then roofed in such a manner as to exclude the heavy dew of the climate, and piles of sweet shrubs and dried leaves were laid beneath it for the sisters to repose on.

While the diligent woodsmen were employed in this manner, Cora and Alice partook of that refreshment which duty required much more than inclination prompted them to accept. They then retired within the walls, and first offering up their thanksgiving for past mercies, and petitioning for a continuance of the Divine favor throughout the coming night, they laid their tender forms on the fragrant couch, and in spite of recollections and forebodings, soon sank into those slumbers which nature so imperiously demanded, and which were sweetened by hopes for the morrow. Duncan had prepared himself to pass the night in watchfulness near them, just without the ruin, but the scout, perceiving his intention, pointed toward Chingachgook, as he coolly disposed his own person on the grass, and said—

"The eyes of a white man are too heavy and too blind for such a watch as this! The Mohican will be our sentinel, therefore let us sleep."

"I proved myself a sluggard on my post during the past night," said Heyward, "and have less need of repose than you, who did more credit to the character of a soldier. Let all the party seek their rest, then, while I hold the guard."

"If we lay among the white tents of the 60th, and in front of an enemy like the French, I could not ask for a better watchman," returned the scout; "but in the darkness and among the signs of the wilderness your judgment would be like the folly of a child, and your vigilance thrown away. Do then, like Uncas and myself, sleep, and sleep in safety."

Heyward perceived, in truth, that the younger Indian had thrown his form on the side of the hillock while they were talking, like one who sought to make the most of the time allotted to rest, and that his example had been followed by David, whose voice literally "clove to his jaws" with the fever of his wound, heightened, as it was, by their toilsome march. Unwilling to prolong a useless discussion, the young man affected to comply, by posting his back against the logs of the blockhouse, in a half-recumbent posture, though resolutely determined, in his own mind, not to close an eye until he had delivered his precious charge into the arms of Munro himself. Hawkeye, believing he had prevailed, soon fell asleep, and a silence as deep as the solitude in which they had found it, pervaded the retired spot.

For many minutes Duncan succeeded in keeping his senses on the alert, and alive to every moaning sound that arose from the forest. His vision became more acute as the shades of evening settled on the place; and even after the stars were glimmering above his head, he was able to distinguish the recumbent forms of his companions, as they lay stretched on the grass, and to note the person of Chingachgook, who sat upright and motionless as one of the trees which formed the dark barrier on every side of them. He still heard the gentle breathings of the sisters, who lay within a few feet of him, and not a leaf was ruffled by the passing air, of which his ear did not detect the whispering sound. At length, however, the mournful notes of a whippoorwill became blended with the moanings of an owl; his heavy eyes occasionally sought the bright rays of the stars, and then he fancied he saw them through the fallen lids. At instants of momentary wakefulness he mistook a bush for his associate sentinel; his head next sank upon his shoulder, which, in its turn, sought the support of the ground; and, finally, his whole person became relaxed and pliant, and the young man sank into a deep sleep, dreaming that he was a knight of ancient chivalry, holding his midnight vigils before the tent of a recaptured princess, whose favor he did not despair of gaining, by such a proof of devotion and watchfulness.

How long the tired Duncan lay in this insensible state he never knew himself, but his slumbering visions had been long lost in total forgetfulness, when he was awakened by a light tap on the shoulder. Aroused by this signal, slight as it was, he sprang upon his feet with a confused recollection of the self-imposed duty he had assumed with the commencement of the night—

"Who comes?" he demanded, feeling for his sword, at the place where it was usually suspended. "Speak! friend or enemy?"

"Friend," replied the low voice of Chingachgook; who, pointing upward at the luminary which was shedding its mild light through the opening in the trees, directly on their bivouac, immediately added, in his rude English, "moon comes, and white man's fort far—far off; time to move, when sleep shuts both eyes of the Frenchman!"

"You say true! call up your friends, and bridle the horses, while I prepare my own companions for the march!"

"We are awake, Duncan," said the soft, silvery tones of Alice within the building, "and ready to travel very fast, after so refreshing a sleep; but you have watched through the tedious night in our behalf, after having endured so much fatigue the livelong day!"

"Say, rather, I would have watched, but my treacherous eyes betrayed me; twice have I proved myself unfit for the trust I bear."

"Nay, Duncan, deny it not," interrupted the smiling Alice, issuing from the shadows of the building into the light of the moon, in all the loveliness of her freshened beauty; "I know you to be a heedless one, when self is the object of your care, and but too vigilant in favor of others. Can we not tarry here a little longer, while you find the rest you need? Cheerfully, most cheerfully, will Cora and I keep the vigils, while you, and all these brave men, endeavor to snatch a little sleep!"

"If shame could cure me of my drowsiness, I should never close an eye again," said the uneasy youth, gazing at the ingenuous countenance of Alice, where, however, in its sweet solicitude, he read nothing to confirm his half-awakened suspicion. "It is but too true, that after leading you into danger by my heedlessness, I have not even the merit of guarding your pillows as should become a soldier."

"No one but Duncan himself should accuse Duncan of such a weakness. Go, then, and sleep; believe me, neither of us, weak girls as we are, will betray our watch."

The young man was relieved from the awkwardness of making any further protestations of his own demerits by an exclamation from Chingachgook, and the attitude of riveted attention assumed by his son.

"The Mohicans hear an enemy!" whispered Hawkeye, who, by this time, in common with the whole party, was awake and stirring. "They scent danger in the wind!"

"God forbid!" exclaimed Heyward. "Surely we have had enough of bloodshed!"

While he spoke, however, the young soldier seized his rifle, and advancing toward the front, prepared to atone for his venial remissness by freely exposing his life in defence of those he attended.

" 'Tis some creature of the forest prowling around us in quest of food," he said, in a whisper, as soon as the low, and apparently distant sounds, which had startled the Mohicans, reached his own ears.

"Hist!" returned the attentive scout; " 'tis man; even I can now tell his tread, poor as my senses are when compared to an Indian's! That scampering Huron has fallen in with one of Montcalm's outlying parties, and they have struck upon our trail. I shouldn't like, myself, to spill more human blood in this spot," he added, looking around with anxiety in his features, at the dim objects by which he was surrounded; "but what must be, must! Lead the horses into the blockhouse, Uncas; and, friends, do you follow to the same shelter. Poor and old as it is, it offers a cover, and has rung with the crack of a rifle afore tonight!"

He was instantly obeyed, the Mohicans leading the Narragansetts within the ruin, whither the whole party repaired, with the most guarded silence.

The sounds of approaching footsteps were now too distinctly audible to leave any doubts as to the nature of the interruption. They were soon mingled with voices calling to each other in an Indian dialect, which the hunter, in a whisper, affirmed to Heyward, was the language of the Hurons. When the party reached the point where the horses had entered the thicket which surrounded the blockhouse, they were evidently at fault, having lost those marks which, until that moment, had directed their pursuit.

It would seem by the voices that twenty men were soon collected at that one spot, mingling their different opinions and advice in noisy clamor.

"The knaves know our weakness," whispered Hawkeye, who stood by the side of Heyward, in deep shade, looking through an opening in the logs, "or they wouldn't indulge their idleness in such a squaw's march. Listen to the reptiles! each man among them seems to have two tongues, and but a single leg."

Duncan, brave as he was in the combat, could not, in such a moment of painful suspense, make any reply to the cool and characteristic remark of the scout. He only grasped his rifle more firmly, and fastened his eyes upon the narrow opening, through which he gazed upon the moonlight view with increasing anxiety. The deeper tones of one who spoke as having authority were next heard, amid a silence that denoted the respect with which his orders, or rather advice, was received. After which, by the rustling of leaves, and cracking of dried twigs, it was apparent the savages were separating in pursuit of the lost trail. Fortunately for the pursued, the light of the moon, while it shed a flood of mild luster upon the little area around the ruin, was not sufficiently strong to penetrate the deep arches of the forest, where the objects still lay in deceptive shadow. The search proved fruitless; for so short and sudden had been the passage from the faint path the travellers had journeyed into the thicket, that every trace of their footsteps was lost in the obscurity of the woods.

It was not long, however, before the restless savages were heard beating the brush, and gradually approaching the inner edge of that dense border of young chestnuts which encircled the little area.

"They are coming," muttered Heyward, endeavoring to thrust his rifle through the chink in the logs; "let us fire on their approach."

"Keep everything in the shade," returned the scout; "the snapping of a flint, or even the smell of a single karnel of the brimstone, would bring the hungry varlets upon us in a body. Should it please God that we must give battle for the scalps, trust to the experience of men who know the ways of the savages, and who are not often backward when the war whoop is howled."

Duncan cast his eyes behind him, and saw that the trembling sisters were cowering in the far corner of the building, while the Mohicans stood in the shadow, like two upright posts, ready, and apparently willing, to strike, when the blow should be needed. Curbing his impatience, he again looked out upon the area, and awaited the result in silence. At that instant the thicket opened, and a tall and armed Huron advanced a few paces into the open space. As he gazed upon the silent blockhouse, the moon fell upon his swarthy countenance, and betrayed its surprise and curiosity. He made the exclamation which usually accompanies the former emotion in an Indian, and, calling in a low voice, soon drew a companion to his side.

These children of the woods stood together for several moments pointing at the crumbling edifice, and conversing in the unintelligible language of their tribe. They then approached, though with slow and cautious steps, pausing every instant to look at the building, like startled deer, whose curiosity struggled powerfully with their awakened apprehensions for the mastery. The foot of one of them suddenly rested on the mound, and he stooped to examine its nature. At this moment, Heyward observed that the scout loosened his knife in its sheath, and lowered the muzzle of his rifle. Imitating these movements, the young man prepared himself for the struggle, which now seemed inevitable.

The savages were so near, that the least motion in one of the horses, or even a breath louder than common, would have betrayed the fugitives. But, in discovering the character of the mound, the attention of the Hurons appeared directed to a different object. They spoke together, and the sounds of their voices were low and solemn, as if influenced by a reverence that was deeply blended with awe. Then they drew warily back, keeping their eyes riveted on the ruin, as if they expected to see the apparitions of the dead issue from its silent walls, until having reached the boundary of the area, they moved slowly into the thicket, and disappeared.

Hawkeye dropped the breech of his rifle to the earth, and drawing a long, free breath, exclaimed in an audible whisper—

"Ay! they respect the dead, and it has this time saved their own lives, and it may be, the lives of better men too."

Heyward lent his attention, for a single moment, to his companion, but without replying, he again turned toward those who just then interested him more. He heard the two Hurons leave the bushes, and it was soon plain that all the pursuers were gathered about them, in deep attention to their report. After a few minutes of earnest and solemn dialogue, altogether different from the noisy clamor with which they had first collected about the spot, the sounds grew fainter and more distant, and finally were lost in the depths of the forest.

Hawkeye waited until a signal from the listening Chingachgook assured him that every sound from the retiring party was completely swallowed by the distance, when he motioned to Heyward to lead forth the horses, and to assist the sisters into their saddles. The instant this was done, they issued through the broken gateway, and stealing out by a direction opposite to the one by which they had entered, they quitted the spot, the sisters casting furtive glances at the silent grave and crumbling ruin, as they left the soft light of the moon, to bury themselves in the gloom of the woods.

During the rapid movement from the blockhouse, and until the party was deeply buried in the forest, each individual was too much interested in the escape to hazard a word, even in whispers. The scout resumed his post in the advance, though his steps, after he had thrown a safe distance between himself and his enemies, were more deliberate than in their previous march, in consequence of his utter ignorance of the localities of the surrounding woods. More than once he halted to consult with his confederates, the Mohicans, pointing upward at the moon, and examining the barks of the trees with care. In these brief pauses, Heyward and the sisters listened, with senses rendered doubly acute by the danger, to detect any symptoms which might announce the proximity of their foes. At such moments, it seemed as if a vast range of country lay buried in eternal sleep; not the least sound arising from the forest, unless it was the distant and scarcely audible rippling of a watercourse. Birds, beasts, and man appeared to slumber alike, if, indeed, any of the latter were to be found in that wide tract of wilderness. But the sounds of the rivulet, feeble and murmuring as they were, relieved the guides at once from no trifling embarrassment, and toward it they immediately held their way.

When the banks of the little stream were gained, Hawkeye made another halt; and, taking the moccasins from his feet, he invited Heyward and Gamut to follow his example. He then entered the water, and for near an hour they travelled in the bed of the brook, leaving no trail. The moon had already sunk into an immense pile of black clouds, which lay impending above the western horizon, when they issued from the low and devious watercourse to rise again to the light and level of the sandy but wooded plain. Here the scout seemed to be once more at home, for he held on his way with the certainty and diligence of a man who moved in the security of his own knowledge. The path soon became more uneven, and the travellers could plainly perceive that the mountains drew nigher to them on each hand, and that they were, in truth, about entering one of their gorges. Suddenly, Hawkeye made a pause, and waiting until he was joined by the whole party, he spoke, though in tones so low and cautious, that they added to the solemnity of his words, in the quiet and darkness of the place.

"It is easy to know the pathways, and to find the licks and watercourses of the wilderness," he said; "but who that saw this spot could venture to say that a mighty army was at rest among yonder silent trees and barren mountains?"

"We are then at no great distance from William Henry?" said Heyward, advancing nigher to the scout.

"It is yet a long and weary path, and when and where to strike it, is now our greatest difficulty. See," he said, pointing through the trees toward a spot where a little basin of water reflected the stars from its placid bosom, "here is the 'bloody pond'; and I am on ground that I have not only often travelled, but over which I have fou't the enemy, from the rising to the setting sun."

"Ha! that sheet of dull and dreary water, then, is the sepulcher of the brave men who fell in the contest. I have heard it named, but never have I stood on its banks before."

"Three battles did we make with the Dutch-Frenchman [1] in a day," continued Hawkeye, pursuing the train of his own thoughts, rather than replying to the remark of Duncan. "He met us hard by, in our outward march to ambush his advance, and scattered us, like driven deer, through the defile, to the shores of Horican. Then we rallied behind our fallen trees, and made head against him, under Sir William—who was made Sir William for that very deed; and well did we pay him for the disgrace of the morning. Hundreds of Frenchmen saw the sun that day for the last time; and even their leader, Dieskau himself, fell into our hands, so cut and torn with the lead, that he has gone back to his own country, unfit for further acts in war."

" 'Twas a noble repulse!" exclaimed Heyward, in the heat of his youthful ardor; "the fame of it reached us early, in our southern army."

"Ay! but it did not end there. I was sent by Major Effingham, at Sir William's own bidding, to outflank the French, and carry the tid-

---

[1] Baron Dieskau, a German, in the service of France. A few years previously to the period of this tale this officer was defeated by Sir William Johnson, of Johnstown, New York, on the shores of Lake George. (*Cooper's note*)

ings of their disaster across the portage, to the fort on the Hudson. Just here-a-way, where you see the trees rise into a mountain swell, I met a party coming down to our aid, and I led them where the enemy were taking their meal, little dreaming that they had not finished the bloody work of the day."

"And you surprised them?"

"If death can be a surprise to men who are thinking only of the cravings of their appetites. We gave them but little breathing time, for they had borne hard upon us in the fight of the morning, and there were few in our party who had not lost friend or relative by their hands. When all was over, the dead, and some say the dying, were cast into that little pond. These eyes have seen its waters colored with blood, as natural water never yet flowed from the bowels of the 'arth."

"It was a convenient, and, I trust, will prove a peaceful grave for a soldier. You have, then, seen much service on this frontier?"

"I!" said the scout, erecting his tall person with an air of military pride; "there are not many echoes among these hills that haven't rung with the crack of my rifle, nor is there the space of a square mile atwixt Horican and the river that Killdeer hasn't dropped a living body on, be it an enemy or be it a brute beast. As for the grave there being as quiet as you mention, it is another matter. There are them in the camp who say and think, man, to lie still, should not be buried while the breath is in the body; and certain it is that in the hurry of that evening the doctors had but little time to say who was living and who was dead. Hist! see you nothing walking on the shore of the pond?"

" 'Tis not probable that any are as houseless as ourselves, in this dreary forest."

"Such as he may care but little for house or shelter, and night dew can never wet a body that passes its days in the water," returned the scout, grasping the shoulder of Heyward with such convulsive strength as to make the young soldier painfully sensible how much superstitious terror had got the mastery of a man usually so dauntless.

"By heaven! there is a human form, and it approaches! Stand to your arms, my friends; for we know not whom we encounter."

"Qui vive?" demanded a stern, quick voice, which sounded like a challenge from another world, issuing out of that solitary and solemn place.

"What says it?" whispered the scout; "it speaks neither Indian nor English!"

"Qui vive?" repeated the same voice, which was quickly followed by the rattling of arms, and a menacing attitude.

"France!" cried Heyward, advancing from the shadow of the trees to the shore of the pond, within a few yards of the sentinel.

"D'où venez-vous—où allez-vous, d'aussi bonne heure?" demanded the grenadier, in the language and with the accent of a man from old France.

"Je viens de la découverte, et je vais me coucher."

"Etes-vous officier du roi?"

"Sans doute, mon camarade; me prends-tu pour un provincial! Je suis capitaine de chasseurs (Heyward well knew that the other was of a regiment in the line)—j'ai ici, avec moi, les filles du commandant de la fortification. Aha! tu en as entendu parler! je les ai fait prisonnières près de l'autre fort, et je les conduis au général."

"Ma foi! mesdames; j'en suis fâché pour vous," exclaimed the young soldier, touching his cap with grace; "mais—fortune de guerre! vous trouverez notre général un brave homme, et bien poli avec les dames."

"C'est le caractère des gens de guerre," said Cora, with admirable self-possession. "Adieu, mon ami; je vous souhaiterais un devoir plus agréable à remplir."

The soldier made a low and humble acknowledgment for her civility; and Heyward adding a "bonne nuit, mon camarade," they moved deliberately forward, leaving the sentinel pacing the banks of the silent pond, little suspecting an enemy of so much effrontery, and humming to himself those words, which were recalled to his mind by the sight of women, and perhaps by recollections of his own distant and beautiful France—

"Vive le vin, vive l'amour," etc., etc.

" 'Tis well you understood the knave!" whispered the scout when they had gained a little distance from the place, and letting his rifle fall into the hollow of his arm again; "I soon saw that he was one of them uneasy Frenchers; and well for him it was that his speech was friendly and his wishes kind, or a place might have been found for his bones amongst those of his countrymen."

He was interrupted by a long and heavy groan which arose from the little basin, as though, in truth, the spirits of the departed lingered about their watery sepulcher.

"Surely it was of flesh!" continued the scout; "no spirit could handle its arms so steadily."

"It *was* of flesh; but whether the poor fellow still belongs to this world may well be doubted," said Heyward, glancing his eyes around him, and missing Chingachgook from their little band. Another groan more faint than the former, was succeeded by a heavy and sullen plunge into the water, and all was as still again as if the borders of the dreary pool had never been awakened from the silence of creation. While they yet hesitated in uncertainty, the form of the Indian was seen gliding out of the thicket. As the chief rejoined them, with one hand he attached the reeking scalp of the unfortunate young Frenchman to his girdle, and with the other he replaced the knife and tomahawk that had drunk his blood. He then took his wonted station, with the air of a man who believed he had done a deed of merit.

The scout dropped one end of his rifle to the earth, and leaning his hands on the other, he stood musing in profound silence. Then, shaking his head in a mournful manner, he muttered—

" 'Twould have been a cruel and an unhuman act for a white-skin; but 'tis the gift and natur' of an Indian, and I suppose it should not be denied. I could wish, though, it had befallen an accursed Mingo, rather than that gay young boy from the old countries."

"Enough!" said Heyward, apprehensive the unconscious sisters might comprehend the nature of the detention, and conquering his disgust by a train of reflections very much like that of the hunter; " 'tis done; and though better it were left undone, cannot be amended. You see we are, too obviously, within the sentinels of the enemy; what course do you propose to follow?"

"Yes," said Hawkeye, rousing himself again, " 'tis as you say, too late to harbor further thoughts about it. Ay, the French have gathered around the fort in good earnest, and we have a delicate needle to thread in passing them."

"And but little time to do it in," added Heyward, glancing his eyes upward, toward the bank of vapor that concealed the setting moon.

"And little time to do it in!" repeated the scout. "The thing may be done in two fashions, by the help of Providence, without which it may not be done at all."

"Name them quickly, for time presses."

"One would be to dismount the gentle ones, and let their beasts range the plain; by sending the Mohicans in front, we might then cut a lane through their sentries, and enter the fort over the dead bodies."

"It will not do—it will not do!" interrupted the generous Heyward; "a soldier might force his way in this manner, but never with such a convoy."

" 'Twould be, indeed, a bloody path for such tender feet to wade in," returned the equally reluctant scout; "but I thought it befitting my manhood to name it. We must then turn on our trail, and get without the line of their lookouts, when we will bend short to the west, and enter the mountains; where I can hide you, so that all the devil's hounds in Montcalm's pay would be thrown off the scent for months to come."

"Let it be done, and that instantly."

Further words were unnecessary; for Hawkeye, merely uttering the mandate to "follow," moved along the route by which they had just entered their present critical and even dangerous situation. Their progress, like their late dialogue, was guarded, and without noise; for none knew at what moment a passing patrol, or a crouching picket, of the enemy, might rise upon their path. As they held their silent way along the margin of the pond, again Heyward and the scout stole furtive glances at its appalling dreariness. They looked in vain for the form they had so recently seen stalking along its silent shores, while a low and regular wash of the little waves, by announcing that the waters were not yet subsided, furnished a frightful memorial of the deed of blood they had just witnessed. Like all that passing and gloomy scene, the low basin, however, quickly melted in the darkness, and became blended with the mass of black objects, in the rear of the travellers.

Hawkeye soon deviated from the line of their retreat, and striking off toward the mountains which form the western boundary of the narrow plain, he led his followers, with swift steps, deep within the shadows that were cast from their high and broken summits. The route was now painful; lying over ground ragged with rocks, and intersected with ravines, and their progress proportionately slow. Bleak and black hills lay on every side of them, compensating in some degree for the additional toil of the march, by the sense of security they imparted. At length the party began slowly to rise a steep and rugged ascent, by a path that curiously wound among rocks and trees, avoiding the one, and supported by the other, in a manner that showed it had been devised by men long practiced in the arts of the wilderness. As they gradually rose from the level of the valleys, the thick darkness which usually precedes the approach of day began to disperse, and objects were seen in the plain and palpable colors with which they had been gifted by nature. When they issued from the stunted woods which clung to the barren sides of the mountain, upon a flat and mossy rock that formed its summit, they met the morning, as it came blushing above the green pines of a hill that lay on the opposite side of the valley of the Horican.

The scout now told the sisters to dismount; and taking the bridles from the mouths, and the saddles off the backs of the jaded beasts, he turned them loose, to glean a scanty subsistence among the shrubs and meager herbage of that elevated region.

"Go," he said, "and seek your food where natur' gives it you; and beware that you become not food to ravenous wolves yourselves, among these hills."

"Have we no further need of them?" demanded Heyward.

"See, and judge with your own eyes," said the scout, advancing toward the eastern brow of the mountain, whither he beckoned for the whole party to follow: "if it was as easy to look into the heart of man as it is to spy out the nakedness of Montcalm's camp from this spot, hypocrites would grow scarce, and the cunning of a Mingo might prove a losing game, compared to the honesty of a Delaware."

When the travellers reached the verge of the precipice, they saw, at a glance, the truth of the scout's declaration, and the admirable foresight with which he had led them to their commanding station.

The mountain on which they stood, elevated, perhaps, a thousand feet in the air, was a high cone that rose a little in advance of that range which stretches for miles along the western shores of the lake, until meeting its sister piles, beyond the water, it ran off toward the Canadas, in confused and broken masses of rock thinly sprinkled with evergreens. Immediately at the feet of the party, the southern shore of the Horican swept in a broad semicircle, from mountain to mountain, marking a wide strand, that soon rose into an uneven and somewhat elevated plain. To the north stretched the limpid, and, as it appeared from that dizzy height, the narrow sheet of the "holy lake," indented with numberless bays, embellished by fantastic headlands, and dotted with countless islands. At the distance of a few leagues, the bed of the waters became lost among mountains, or was wrapped in the masses of vapor that came slowly rolling along their bosom, before a light morning air. But a narrow opening between the crest of the hills pointed out the passage by which they found their way still further north, to spread their pure and ample sheets again, before pouring out their tribute into the distant Champlain. To the south stretched the defile or, rather, broken plain, so often mentioned. For several miles in this direction, the mountains appeared reluctant to yield their dominion, but within reach of the eye they diverged, and finally melted into the level and sandy lands, across which we have accompanied our adventurers in their double journey. Along both ranges of hills, which bounded the opposite sides of the lake and valley, clouds of light vapor were rising in spiral wreaths from the uninhabited woods, looking like the smokes of hidden cottages; or rolled lazily down the declivities, to mingle with the fogs of the lower land. A single, solitary, snow-white cloud floated above the valley, and marked the spot beneath which lay the silent pool of the "bloody pond."

Directly on the shore of the lake, and nearer to its western than to its eastern margin, lay the extensive earthen ramparts and low buildings of William Henry. Two of the sweeping bastions appeared to rest on the water which washed their bases, while a deep ditch and extensive morasses guarded its other sides and angles. The land had been cleared of wood for a reasonable distance around the work, but every other part of the scene lay in the green livery of nature, except where the limpid water mellowed the view, or the bold rocks thrust their black and naked heads above the undulating outline of the mountain ranges. In its front might be seen the scattered sentinels, who held a weary watch against their numerous foes; and within the walls themselves, the travellers looked down upon men still drowsy with a night of vigilance. Toward the southeast, but in immediate contact with the fort, was an entrenched camp, posted on a rocky eminence, that would have been far more eligible for the work itself, in which Hawkeye pointed out the presence of those auxiliary regiments that had so recently left the Hudson in their company. From the woods, a little further to the south, rose numerous dark and lurid smokes, that were easily to be distinguished from the purer exhalations of the springs, and which the scout also showed to Heyward, as evidences that the enemy lay in force in that direction.

But the spectacle which most concerned the young soldier was on the western bank of the lake, though quite near to its southern termination. On a strip of land, which appeared, from his stand, too narrow to contain such an army, but which, in truth, extended many hundreds of yards from the shores of the Horican to the base of the mountain, were to be seen the white tents and military engines of an encampment of ten thousand men. Batteries were already thrown up in their front, and even while the spectators above them were looking down, with such different emotions, on a scene which lay like a map beneath their feet, the roar of artillery rose from the valley, and passed off in thundering echoes, along the eastern hills.

"Morning is just touching them below," said the deliberate and musing scout, "and the watchers have a mind to wake up the sleepers by the sound of cannon. We are a few hours too late! Montcalm has already filled the woods with his accursed Iroquois."

"The place is, indeed, invested," returned Duncan, "but is there no expedient by which we may enter? Capture in the works would be far preferable to falling again into the hands of roving Indians."

"See!" exclaimed the scout, unconsciously directing the attention of Cora to the quarters of her own father, "how that shot has made the stones fly from the side of the commandant's house! Ay! these Frenchers will pull it to pieces faster than it was put together, solid and thick though it be."

"Heyward, I sicken at the sight of danger that I cannot share," said the undaunted, but anxious daughter. "Let us go to Montcalm, and demand admission: he dare not deny a child the boon."

"You would scarce find the tent of the Frenchman with the hair on your head," said the blunt scout. "If I had but one of the thousand boats which lie empty along that shore, it might be done. Ha! here will soon be an end of the firing, for yonder comes a fog that will turn day to night, and make an Indian arrow more dangerous than a moulded cannon. Now, if you are equal to the work, and will follow, I will make a push; for I long to get down into that camp, if it be only to scatter some Mingo dogs that I see lurking in the skirts of yonder thicket of birch."

"We are equal," said Cora, firmly: "on such an errand we will follow to any danger."

The scout turned to her with a smile of honest and cordial approbation, as he answered—

"I would I had a thousand men, of brawny limbs and quick eyes, that feared death as little as you! I'd send them jabbering Frenchers back into their den again, afore the week was ended, howling like so many fettered hounds or hungry wolves. But stir," he added, turning from her to the rest of the party, "the fog comes rolling down so fast, we shall have but just the time to meet it on the plain, and use it as a cover. Remember, if any accident should befall me, to keep the air blowing on your left cheeks—or, rather, follow the Mohicans; they'd scent their way, be it in day or be it at night."

5

HAWKEYE, HEYWARD, and the girls reached Fort William Henry at a time when it was closely invested by Montcalm's superior army, well supplied with artillery to batter down its walls. Colonel Munro sent repeated notes to General Webb at

Fort Edward, fourteen miles distant, imploring aid. Webb, however, had only 2600 men himself, for the British high command in North America had concentrated a heavy force against the French fortress of Louisbourg on Cape Breton Island; and Webb lacked sufficient energy and courage to use these 2600 effectively. Some 2000 New York militia were coming, but they came tardily, and were raw, ill-trained troops at best. Webb finally sent the hard-pressed Munro a letter stating that the French occupied the road between the two forts, that they were too strong to be dislodged, and that unless the provincial militia arrived soon in large force, Munro would do well to make what terms he could with Montcalm. The bearer of this letter was killed by the Indians, and the document was taken to French headquarters. Montcalm kept it until such time as he could use it to hasten Munro's surrender.

Meanwhile, Munro, knowing that the dispatch had been lost, sent Major Heyward to the French camp in an effort to learn its contents. Montcalm sent back word that he would have to see Munro himself. When Heyward returned to the colonel, they fell into a conversation on personal affairs. Munro revealed the fact that his dead wife, the mother of Cora and Alice, had been a West Indian lady with Negro blood in her veins; Heyward was nonetheless anxious to marry Alice. Then Munro turned from memories of his past to the distressing military situation.

There was something so commanding in the distress of the old man, that Heyward did not dare to venture a syllable of consolation. Munro sat utterly unconscious of the other's presence, his features exposed and working with the anguish of his regrets, while heavy tears fell from his eyes, and rolled unheeded from his cheeks to the floor. At length he moved, as if suddenly recovering his recollection; when he arose, and taking a single turn across the room, he approached his companion with an air of military grandeur, and demanded—

"Have you not, Major Heyward, some communication that I should hear from the Marquis de Montcalm?"

Duncan started, in his turn, and immediately commenced, in an embarrassed voice, the half-forgotten message. It is unnecessary to dwell upon the evasive, though polite manner, with which the French general had eluded every attempt of Heyward to worm from him the purport of the communication he had proposed making, or on the decided, though still polished message, by which he now gave his enemy to understand, that unless he chose to receive it in person, he should not receive it at all. As Munro listened to the detail of Duncan, the excited feelings of the father gradually gave way before the obligations of his station, and when the other was done, he saw before him nothing but the veteran, swelling with the wounded feelings of a soldier.

"You have said enough, Major Heyward!" exclaimed the angry

old man; "enough to make a volume of commentary on French civility. Here has this gentleman invited me to a conference, and when I send him a capable substitute, for ye're all that, Duncan, though your years are but few, he answers me with a riddle."

"He may have thought less favorably of the substitute, my dear sir; and you will remember that the invitation, which he now repeats, was to the commandant of the works, and not to his second."

"Well, sir, is not a substitute clothed with all the power and dignity of him who grants the commission? He wishes to confer with Munro! Faith, sir, I have much inclination to indulge the man, if it should only be to let him behold the firm countenance we maintain in spite of his numbers and his summons. There might be no bad policy in such a stroke, young man."

Duncan, who believed it of the last importance that they should speedily come at the contents of the letter borne by the scout, gladly encouraged this idea.

"Without doubt, he could gather no confidence by witnessing our indifference," he said.

"You never said truer word. I could wish, sir, that he would visit the works in open day, and in the form of a storming party: that is the least failing method of proving the countenance of an enemy, and would be far preferable to the battering system he has chosen. The beauty and manliness of warfare has much been deformed, Major Heyward, by the arts of your Monsieur Vauban. Our ancestors were far above such scientific cowardice!"

"It may be very true, sir; but we are now obliged to repel art by art. What is your pleasure in the matter of the interview?"

"I will meet the Frenchman, and that without fear or delay; promptly, sir, as becomes a servant of my royal master. Go, Major Heyward, and give them a flourish of the music; and send out a messenger to let them know who is coming. We will follow with a small guard, for such respect is due to one who holds the honor of his king in keeping; and hark'ee, Duncan," he added, in a half whisper, though they were alone, "it may be prudent to have some aid at hand, in case there should be treachery at the bottom of it all."

The young man availed himself of this order to quit the apartment; and, as the day was fast coming to a close, he hastened, without delay, to make the necessary arrangements. A very few minutes only were necessary to parade a few files, and to despatch an orderly with a flag to announce the approach of the commandant of the fort. When Duncan had done both these he led the guard to the sally port, near which he found his superior ready, waiting his appearance. As soon as the usual ceremonials of a military departure were observed, the veteran and his more youthful companion left the fortress, attended by the escort.

They had proceeded only a hundred yards from the works, when the little array which attended the French general to the conference, was seen issuing from the hollow way, which formed the bed of a brook that ran between the batteries of the besiegers and the fort. From the moment that Munro left his own works to appear in front of his enemies, his air had been grand, and his step and countenance highly military. The instant he caught a glimpse of the white plume that waved in the hat of Montcalm, his eye lighted, and age no longer appeared to possess any influence over his vast and still muscular person.

"Speak to the boys to be watchful, sir," he said, in an undertone, to Duncan; "and to look well to their flints and steel, for one is never safe with a servant of these Louis; at the same time, we will show them the front of men in deep security. Ye'll understand me, Major Heyward!"

He was interrupted by the clamor of a drum from the approaching Frenchmen, which was immediately answered, when each party pushed an orderly in advance, bearing a white flag, and the wary Scotsman halted, with his guard close at his back. As soon as this slight salutation had passed, Montcalm moved toward them with a quick but graceful step, baring his head to the veteran, and dropping his spotless plume nearly to the earth in courtesy.[1] If the air of Munro was more commanding and manly, it wanted both the ease and insinuating polish of that of the Frenchman. Neither spoke for a few moments, each regarding the other with curious and interested eyes. Then, as became his superior rank and the nature of the interview, Montcalm broke the silence. After uttering the usual words of greeting, he turned to Duncan, and continued, with a smile of recognition, speaking always in French—

"I am rejoiced, monsieur, that you have given us the pleasure of your company on this occasion. There will be no necessity to employ an ordinary interpreter; for, in your hands, I feel the same security as if I spoke your language myself."

Duncan acknowledged the compliment, when Montcalm, turning to his guard, which, in imitation of that of their enemies, pressed close upon him, continued—

"En arrière, mes enfans—il fait chaud; retirez-vous un peu."

[1] The Marquis de Montcalm, now fifty-five years old, had fought in Europe in the wars of the Polish Succession and the Austrian Succession, becoming a brigadier in 1747. He was sent out to Canada early in 1756, with the rank of major-general, to command the French regulars there. An efficient leader, he was much hampered by his jealous superior, the governor-general, the Marquis de Vaudreuil.—Ed.

Before Major Heyward would imitate this proof of confidence, he glanced his eyes around the plain, and beheld with uneasiness the numerous dusky groups of savages, who looked out from the margin of the surrounding woods, curious spectators of the interview.

"Monsieur de Montcalm will readily acknowledge the difference in our situation," he said, with some embarrassment, pointing at the same time toward those dangerous foes, who were to be seen in almost every direction. "Were we to dismiss our guard, we should stand here at the mercy of our enemies."

"Monsieur, you have the plighted faith of 'un gentilhomme Français,' for your safety," returned Montcalm, laying his hand impressively on his heart; "it should suffice."

"It shall. Fall back," Duncan added to the officer who led the escort; "fall back, sir, beyond hearing, and wait for orders."

Munro witnessed this movement with manifest uneasiness; nor did he fail to demand an instant explanation.

"Is it not our interest, sir, to betray no distrust?" retorted Duncan. "Monsieur de Montcalm pledges his word for our safety, and I have ordered the men to withdraw a little, in order to prove how much we depend on his assurance."

"It may be all right, sir, but I have no overweening reliance on the faith of these marquesses, or marquis, as they call themselves. Their patents of nobility are too common to be certain that they bear the seal of true honor."

"You forget, dear sir, that we confer with an officer, distinguished alike in Europe and America, for his deeds. From a soldier of his reputation we can have nothing to apprehend."

The old man made a gesture of resignation, though his rigid features still betrayed his obstinate adherence to a distrust, which he derived from a sort of hereditary contempt of his enemy, rather than from any present signs which might warrant so uncharitable a feeling. Montcalm waited patiently until this little dialogue in demi-voice was ended, when he drew nigher, and opened the subject of their conference.

"I have solicited this interview from your superior, monsieur," he said, "because I believe he will allow himself to be persuaded, that he has already done everything which is necessary for the honor of his prince, and will now listen to the admonitions of humanity. I will forever bear testimony that his resistance has been gallant, and was continued as long as there was hope."

When this opening was translated to Munro, he answered with dignity, but with sufficient courtesy.

"However I may prize such testimony from Monsieur Montcalm, it will be more valuable when it shall be better merited."

The French general smiled, as Duncan gave him the purport of this reply, and observed—

"What is now so freely accorded to approved courage, may be refused to useless obstinacy. Monsieur would wish to see my camp, and witness, for himself, our numbers, and the impossibility of his resisting them, with success?"

"I know that the King of France is well served," returned the unmoved Scotsman, as soon as Duncan ended his translation; "but my own royal master has as many and as faithful troops."

"Though not at hand, fortunately for us," said Montcalm, without waiting, in his ardor, for the interpreter. "There is a destiny in war to which a brave man knows how to submit with the same courage that he faces his foes."

"Had I been conscious that Monsieur Montcalm was master of the English, I should have spared myself the trouble of so awkward a translation," said the vexed Duncan, dryly; remembering instantly his recent byplay with Munro.

"Your pardon, monsieur," rejoined the Frenchman, suffering a slight color to appear on his dark cheek. "There is a vast difference between understanding and speaking a foreign tongue; you will, therefore, please to assist me still." Then, after a short pause, he added, "These hills afford us every opportunity of reconnoitering your works, messieurs, and I am possibly as well acquainted with their weak condition as you can be yourselves."

"Ask the French general if his glasses can reach to the Hudson," said Munro, proudly; "and if he knows when and where to expect the army of Webb."

"Let General Webb be his own interpreter," returned the politic Montcalm, suddenly extending an open letter towards Munro, as he spoke; "you will there learn, monsieur, that his movements are not likely to prove embarrassing to my army."

The veteran seized the offered paper, without waiting for Duncan to translate the speech, and with an eagerness that betrayed how important he deemed its contents. As his eye passed hastily over the words, his countenance changed from its look of military pride to one of deep chagrin: his lip began to quiver; and, suffering the paper to fall from his hand, his head dropped upon his chest, like that of a man whose hopes were withered at a single blow. Duncan caught the letter from the ground, and without apology for the liberty he took, he read at a glance its cruel purport. Their common superior, so far from encouraging them to resist, advised a speedy surrender, urging in the plainest language as a reason, the utter impossibility of his sending a single man to their rescue.

"Here is no deception!" exclaimed Duncan, examining the billet both inside and out; "this is the signature of Webb, and must be the captured letter."

"The man has betrayed me!" Munro at length bitterly exclaimed: "he has brought dishonor to the door of one where disgrace was never before known to dwell, and shame has he heaped heavily on my gray hairs."

"Say not so," cried Duncan; "we are yet masters of the fort, and of our honor. Let us then sell our lives at such a rate as shall make our enemies believe the purchase too dear."

"Boy, I thank thee," exclaimed the old man, rousing himself from his stupor; "you have, for once, reminded Munro of his duty. We will go back, and dig our graves behind those ramparts."

"Messieurs," said Montcalm, advancing toward them a step, in generous interest, "you little know Louis de St. Véran, if you believe him capable of profiting by this letter to humble brave men, or to build up a dishonest reputation for himself. Listen to my terms before you leave me."

"What says the Frenchman?" demanded the veteran, sternly; "does he make a merit of having captured a scout, with a note from headquarters? Sir, he had better raise this siege, to go and sit down before Edward if he wishes to frighten his enemy with words."

Duncan explained the other's meaning.

"Monsieur de Montcalm, we will hear you," the veteran added, more calmly, as Duncan ended.

"To retain the fort is now impossible," said his liberal enemy: "it is necessary to the interests of my master that it should be destroyed; but, as for yourselves, and your brave comrades, there is no privilege dear to a soldier that shall be denied."

"Our colors?" demanded Heyward.

"Carry them to England, and show them to your King."

"Our arms?"

"Keep them; none can use them better."

"Our march; the surrender of the place?"

"Shall all be done in a way most honorable to yourselves."

Duncan now turned to explain these proposals to his commander, who heard him with amazement, and a sensibility that was deeply touched by so unusual and unexpected generosity.

"Go you, Duncan," he said; "go with this marquess, as indeed marquess he should be; go to his marquee, and arrange it all. I have lived to see two things in my old age, that never did I expect to behold. An Englishman afraid to support a friend, and a Frenchman too honest to profit by his advantage."

So saying, the veteran again dropped his head to his chest, and returned slowly toward the fort, exhibiting, by the dejection of his air, to the anxious garrison, a harbinger of evil tidings.

From the shock of this unexpected blow the haughty feelings of Munro never recovered; but from that moment there commenced a change in his determined character, which accompanied him to a speedy grave. Duncan remained to settle the terms of the capitulation. He was seen to re-enter the works during the first watches of the night, and immediately after a private conference with the commandant, to leave them again. It was then openly announced that hostilities must cease—Munro having signed a treaty, by which the place was to be yielded to the enemy, with the morning; the garrison to retain their arms, their colors, and their baggage, and consequently, according to military opinion, their honor.

6

COLONEL MUNRO was forced to surrender Fort William Henry to the French. Montcalm agreed that the English troops should march out with the honors of war; that they should keep one fieldpiece in recognition of their brave defence; that they would be protected from the Indians, and would be escorted to Fort Edward by a French detachment; and that after a parole period of eighteen months, they might resume service. On an August morning in 1757, therefore, the English garrison (some of them colonial troops, some soldiers from the mother country), relying on Montcalm's pledges, made ready to begin the march.

The signal of departure had been given, and the head of the English column was in motion. The sisters started at the sound, and glancing their eyes around, they saw the white uniforms of the French grenadiers, who had already taken possession of the gates of the fort. At that moment, an enormous cloud seemed to pass suddenly above their heads, and looking upward, they discovered that they stood beneath the wide folds of the standard of France.

"Let us go," said Cora; "this is no longer a fit place for the children of an English officer."

Alice clung to the arm of her sister, and together they left the parade, accompanied by the moving throng that surrounded them.

As they passed the gates, the French officers, who had learned their rank, bowed often and low, forbearing, however, to intrude those attentions, which they saw, with peculiar tact, might not be agreeable. As every vehicle and each beast of burden was occupied by the sick and wounded, Cora had decided to endure the fatigues of a foot march, rather than interfere with their comforts. Indeed, many a maimed and feeble soldier was compelled to drag his exhausted limbs in the rear of the columns, for the want of the necessary means of conveyance, in that wilderness. The whole, however, was in motion; the weak and wounded, groaning, and in suffering; their comrades, silent and sullen; and the women and children in terror, they knew not of what.

As the confused and timid throng left the protecting mounds of the fort, and issued on the open plain, the whole scene was at once presented to their eyes. At a little distance on the right, and somewhat in the rear, the French army stood to their arms, Montcalm having collected his parties, as soon as his guards had possession of the works. They were attentive but silent observers of the proceedings of the vanquished, failing in none of the stipulated military honors, and offering no taunt or insult, in their success, to their less fortunate foes. Living masses of the English, to the amount in the whole of near three thousand, were moving slowly across the plain, toward the common center, and gradually approached each other, as they converged to the point of their march, a vista cut through the lofty trees, where the road to the Hudson entered the forest. Along the sweeping borders of the woods hung a dark cloud of savages, eyeing the passage of their enemies, and hovering, at a distance, like vultures, who were only kept from stooping on their prey by the presence and restraint of a superior army. A few had straggled among the conquered columns, where they stalked in sullen discontent; attentive, though, as yet, passive observers of the moving multitude.

The advance, with Heyward at its head, had already reached the defile, and was slowly disappearing, when the attention of Cora was drawn to a collection of stragglers by the sounds of contention. A truant provincial was paying the forfeit of his disobedience by being plundered of those very effects which had caused him to desert his place in the ranks. The man was of powerful frame, and too avaricious to part with his goods without a struggle. Individuals from either party interfered; the one side to prevent, and the other to aid, in the robbery. Voices grew loud and angry, and a hundred savages appeared, as it were by magic, where a dozen only had been seen a minute before. It was then that Cora saw the form of Magua gliding among his countrymen, and speaking with his fatal and artful eloquence. The mass of women and children stopped, and hovered together like alarmed and fluttering birds. But the cupidity of the Indian was soon gratified, and the different bodies again moved slowly onward.

The savages now fell back, and seemed content to let their enemies advance without further molestation. But as the female crowd approached them, the gaudy colors of a shawl attracted the eyes of a wild and untutored Huron. He advanced to seize it, without the least hesitation. The woman, more in terror than through love of the ornament, wrapped her child in the coveted article, and folded both more closely to her bosom. Cora was in the act of speaking, with an intent to advise the woman to abandon the trifle, when the savage relinquished his hold of the shawl, and tore the screaming infant from her arms. Abandoning everything to the greedy grasp of those around her, the mother darted, with distraction in her mien, to reclaim her child. The Indian smiled grimly, and extended one hand, in sign of a willingness to exchange, while, with the other, he flourished the babe over his head, holding it by the feet as if to enhance the value of the ransom.

"Here—here—there—all—any—everything!" exclaimed the breathless woman; tearing the lighter articles of dress from her person, with ill-directed and trembling fingers:—"take all, but give me my babe!"

The savage spurned the worthless rags, and perceiving that the shawl had already become a prize to another, his bantering but sullen smile changing to a gleam of ferocity, he dashed the head of the infant against a rock, and cast its quivering remains to her very feet. For an instant, the mother stood, like a statue of despair, looking wildly down at the unseemly object, which had so lately nestled in her bosom and smiled in her face; and then she raised her eyes and countenance toward heaven, as if calling on God to curse the perpetrator of the foul deed. She was spared the sin of such a prayer; for, maddened at his disappointment, and excited at the sight of blood, the Huron mercifully drove his tomahawk into her own brain. The mother sank under the blow, and fell, grasping at her child, in death, with the same engrossing love that had caused her to cherish it when living.

At that dangerous moment Magua placed his hands to his mouth, and raised the fatal and appalling whoop. The scattered Indians started at the well-known cry, as coursers bound at the signal to quit the goal; and, directly, there arose such a yell along the plain, and through the arches of the wood, as seldom burst from human lips before. They who heard it, listened with a curdling horror at the heart, little inferior to that dread which may be expected to attend the blasts of the final summons.

More than two thousand raving savages broke from the forest at the signal, and threw themselves across the fatal plain with instinctive alacrity. We shall not dwell on the revolting horrors that succeeded. Death was everywhere, and in his most terrific and disgusting aspects. Resistance only served to inflame the murderers, who inflicted their furious blows long after their victims were beyond the power of their resentment. The flow of blood might be likened to the outbreaking of a torrent; and as the natives became heated and maddened by the sight, many among them even kneeled to the earth, and drank freely, exultingly, hellishly, of the crimson tide.

The trained bodies of the troops threw themselves quickly into solid masses, endeavoring to awe their assailants by the imposing appearance of a military front. The experiment in some measure succeeded, though far too many suffered their unloaded muskets to be torn from their hands, in the vain hope of appeasing the savages.

In such a scene none had leisure to note the fleeting moments. It might have been ten minutes (it seemed an age) that the sisters had stood riveted to one spot, horror-stricken, and nearly helpless. When the first blow was struck, their screaming companions had pressed upon them in a body, rendering flight impossible; and now that fear or death had scattered most, if not all, from around them, they saw no avenue open, but such as conducted to the tomahawks of their foes. On every side arose shrieks, groans, exhortations, and curses. At this moment, Alice caught a glimpse of the vast form of her father, moving rapidly across the plain, in the direction of the French army. He was, in truth, proceeding to Montcalm, fearless of every danger, to claim the tardy escort, for which he had before conditioned.[1] Fifty glittering axes and barbed spears were offered unheeded at his life, but the savages respected his rank and calmness, even in their fury. The danger-

[1] Although Montcalm was horrified by the massacre, and made earnest efforts to halt it, the best historical judgment is that he was much at fault in not taking a few simple precautions which would have prevented the butchery.—Ed.

ous weapons were brushed aside by the still nervous arm of the veteran, or fell of themselves, after menacing an act that it would seem no one had courage to perform. Fortunately, the vindictive Magua was searching for his victim in the very band the veteran had just quitted.

"Father—father—we are here!" shrieked Alice, as he passed, at no great distance, without appearing to heed them. "Come to us, father, or we die!"

The cry was repeated, and in terms and tones that might have melted a heart of stone, but it was unanswered. Once, indeed, the old man appeared to catch the sounds, for he paused and listened; but Alice had dropped senseless on the earth, and Cora had sunk at her side, hovering in untiring tenderness over her lifeless form. Munro shook his head in disappointment, and proceeded, bent on the high duty of his station.

"Lady," said Gamut, who, helpless and useless as he was, had not yet dreamed of deserting his trust, "it is the jubilee of the devils, and this is not a meet place for Christians to tarry in. Let us up and fly."

"Go," said Cora, still gazing at her unconscious sister; "save thyself. To me thou canst not be of further use."

David comprehended the unyielding character of her resolution by the simple but expressive gesture that accompanied her words. He gazed, for a moment, at the dusky forms that were acting their hellish rites on every side of him, and his tall person grew more erect, while his chest heaved, and every feature swelled, and seemed to speak with the power of the feelings by which he was governed.

"If the Jewish boy might tame the evil spirit of Saul by the sound of his harp, and the words of sacred song, it may not be amiss," he said, "to try the potency of music here."

Then raising his voice to its highest tones, he poured out a strain so powerful as to be heard even amid the din of that bloody field. More than one savage rushed toward them, thinking to rifle the unprotected sisters of their attire, and bear away their scalps; but when they found this strange and unmoved figure riveted to his post, they paused to listen. Astonishment soon changed to admiration, and they passed on to other, and less courageous, victims, openly expressing their satisfaction at the firmness with which the white warrior sang his death song. Encouraged and deluded by his success, David exerted all his powers to extend what he believed so holy an influence. The unwonted sounds caught the ears of a distant savage, who flew raging from group to group, like one who, scorning to touch the vulgar herd, hunted for some victim more worthy of his renown. It was Magua, who uttered a yell of pleasure when he beheld his ancient prisoners again at his mercy.

"Come," he said, laying his soiled hands on the dress of Cora, "the wigwam of the Huron is still open. Is it not better than this place?"

"Away," cried Cora, veiling her eyes from his revolting aspect.

The Indian laughed tauntingly, as he held up his reeking hand, and answered—"It is red, but it comes from white veins!"

"Monster! there is blood, oceans of blood, upon thy soul: thy spirit has moved this scene."

"Magua is a great chief!" returned the exulting savage:—"will the darkhair go to his tribe?"

"Never! strike, if thou wilt, and complete thy revenge."

He hesitated a moment; and then catching the light and senseless form of Alice in his arms, the subtle Indian moved swiftly across the plain toward the woods.

"Hold!" shrieked Cora, following wildly on his footsteps: "release the child! wretch! what is it you do?"

But Magua was deaf to her voice; or rather he knew his power, and was determined to maintain it.

"Stay—lady—stay," called Gamut, after the unconscious Cora. "The holy charm is beginning to be felt, and soon shalt thou see this horrid tumult stilled."

Perceiving that, in his turn, he was unheeded, the faithful David followed the distracted sister, raising his voice again in sacred song, and sweeping the air to the measure, with his long arm, in diligent accompaniment. In this manner they traversed the plain, through the flying, the wounded, and the dead. The fierce Huron was, at any time, sufficient for himself and the victim that he bore; though Cora would have fallen, more than once, under the blows of her savage enemies, but for the extraordinary being who stalked in her rear, and who now appeared to the astonished natives gifted with the protecting spirit of madness.

Magua, who knew how to avoid the more pressing dangers, and also to elude pursuit, entered the woods through a low ravine, where he quickly found the Narragansetts, which the travellers had abandoned so shortly before, awaiting his appearance, in custody of a savage as fierce and as malign in his expression as himself. Laying Alice on one of the horses, he made a sign to Cora to mount the other.

Notwithstanding the horror excited by the presence of her captor, there was a present relief in escaping from the bloody scene enacting on the plain, to which Cora could not be altogether insensible. She took her seat, and held forth her arms for her sister, with an air of entreaty and love that even the Huron could not deny. Placing Alice, then, on the same animal with Cora, he seized the bridle, and commenced his route by plunging deeper into the forest. David, perceiving that he was left alone, utterly disregarded as a subject too worthless even to destroy, threw his long limb across the saddle of the beast they had deserted, and made such progress in the pursuit as the difficulties of the path permitted.

They soon began to ascend; but as the motion had a tendency to revive the dormant faculties of her sister, the attention of Cora was too much divided between the tenderest solicitude in her behalf, and in listening to the cries which were still too audible on the plain, to note the direction in which they journeyed. When, however, they gained the flattened surface of the mountaintop, and approached the eastern precipice, she recognized the spot to which she had once before been led under the more friendly auspices of the scout. Here Magua suffered them to dismount; and, notwithstanding their own captivity, the curiosity which seems inseparable from horror, induced them to gaze at the sickening sight below.

The cruel work was still unchecked. On every side the captured were flying before their relentless persecutors, while the armed columns of the Christian king stood fast in an apathy which has never been explained, and which has left an immovable blot on the otherwise fair escutcheon of their leader. Nor was the sword of death stayed until cupidity got the mastery of revenge. Then, indeed, the shrieks of the wounded and the yells of their murderers grew less frequent, until finally the cries of horror were lost to their ear, or were drowned in the loud, long, and piercing whoops of the triumphant savages.[1]

[1] The accounts of the number who fell in this unhappy affair vary between five and fifteen hundred. (*Cooper's note*)

7

THREE DAYS after the massacre at Fort William Henry placed such a stain on the fame of Montcalm, five men emerged from the forest near the ruined and desserted post. A cold rain fell on the hundreds of mouldering corpses. Of the five men three were whites, Colonel Munro, Major Heyward, and Hawkeye; two were Indians, Chingachgook and Uncas. They hunted among the heaps of slain in an effort to identify someone. Munro was in search of his two daughters, and fearful that at any moment he would come upon their corpses. The three white men shuddered at the terrible sights they saw, but the Indians viewed the groups of dead with unwavering eye. Suddenly Uncas rose on tiptoe, peered intently before him, and exclaimed, "Hugh!"

"What is it, boy?" whispered the scout, lowering his tall form into a crouching attitude, like a panther about to take his leap; "God send it be a tardy Frencher, skulking for plunder. I do believe Killdeer would take an oncommon range today!"

Uncas, without making any reply, bounded away from the spot, and in the next instant he was seen tearing from a bush, and waving in triumph, a fragment of the green riding veil of Cora. The movement, the exhibition, and the cry, which again burst from the lips of the young Mohican, instantly drew the whole party about him.

"My child!" said Munro, speaking quick and wildly; "give me my child!"

"Uncas will try," was the short and touching answer.

The simple but meaning assurance was lost on the father, who seized the piece of gauze, and crushed it in his hand, while his eyes roamed fearfully among the bushes, as if he equally dreaded and hoped for the secrets they might reveal.

"Here are no dead," said Heyward; "the storm seems not to have passed this way."

"That's manifest; and clearer than the heavens above our heads," returned the undisturbed scout; "but either she, or they that have robbed her, have passed the bush; for I remember the rag she wore to hide a face that all did love to look upon. Uncas, you are right; the dark-hair has been here, and she has fled, like a frighted fawn, to the wood; none who could fly would remain to be murdered. Let us search for the marks she left; for to Indian eyes, I sometimes think even a hummingbird leaves his trail in the air."

The young Mohican darted away at the suggestion, and the scout had hardly done speaking, before the former raised a cry of success from the margin of the forest. On reaching the spot, the anxious party perceived another portion of the veil fluttering on the lower branch of a beech.

"Softly, softly," said the scout, extending his long rifle in front of the eager Heyward; "we now know our work, but the beauty of the trail must not be deformed. A step too soon may give us hours of trouble. We have them though; that much is beyond denial."

"Bless ye, bless ye, worthy man!" exclaimed Munro; "whither, then, have they fled, and where are my babes?"

"The path they have taken depends on many chances. If they have gone alone, they are quite as likely to move in a circle as straight, and they may be within a dozen miles of us; but if the Hurons, or any of the French Indians, have laid hands on them, 'tis probable they are now near the borders of the Canadas. But what matters that?" continued the deliberate scout, observing the powerful anxiety and disappointment the listeners exhibited; "here are the Mohicans and I on one end of the trail, and, rely on it, we find the other, though they should be a hundred leagues asunder! Gently, gently, Uncas, you are as impatient as a man in the settlements; you forget that light feet leave but faint marks!"

"Hugh!" exclaimed Chingachgook, who had been occupied in examining an opening that had been evidently made through the low underbrush, which skirted the forest; and who now stood erect, as he pointed downward, in the attitude and with the air of a man who beheld a disgusting serpent.

"Here is the palpable impression of the footstep of a man," cried Heyward, bending over the indicated spot: "he has trod in the margin of this pool, and the mark cannot be mistaken. They are captives."

"Better so than left to starve in the wilderness," returned the scout; "and they will leave a wider trail. I would wager fifty beaver skins against as many flints, that the Mohicans and I enter their wigwams within the month! Stoop to it, Uncas, and try what you can make of the moccasin; for moccasin it plainly is, and no shoe."

The young Mohican bent over the track, and removing the scattered leaves from around the place, he examined it with much of that sort of scrutiny, that a money-dealer, in these days of pecuniary doubts, would bestow on a suspected due bill. At length, he arose from his knees, satisfied with the result of the examination.

"Well, boy," demanded the attentive scout, "what does it say? can you make anything of the tell-tale?"

"Le Renard Subtil!"

"Ha! that rampaging devil again! there never will be an end of his loping till Killdeer has said a friendly word to him."

Heyward reluctantly admitted the truth of this intelligence, and now expressed rather his hopes than his doubts by saying—

"One moccasin is so much like another, it is probable there is some mistake."

"One moccasin like another! you may as well say that one foot is like another; though we all know that some are long, and others short; some broad, and others narrow; some with high, and some with low, insteps; some in-toed, and some out. One moccasin is no more like another than one book is like another; though they who can read in one are seldom able to tell the marks of the other. Which is all ordered for the best, giving to every man his natural advantages. Let me get down to it, Uncas; neither book nor moccasin is the worse for having two opinions, instead of one." The scout stooped to the task, and instantly added, "You are right, boy; here is the patch we saw so often in the other chase. And the fellow will drink when he can get an opportunity: your drinking Indian always learns to walk with a wider toe than the natural savage, it being the gift of a drunkard to straddle, whether of white or red skin. 'Tis just the length and breadth too! look at it, Sagamore: you measured the prints more than once, when we hunted the varments from Glens to the health springs." [1]

Chingachgook complied; and after finishing his short examination, he arose, and with a quiet demeanor, he merely pronounced the word—

"Magua."

"Ay, 'tis a settled thing; here then have passed the dark-hair and Magua."

"And not Alice?" demanded Heyward.

"Of her we have not yet seen the signs," returned the scout, look-

[1] That is, from Glens Falls to Ballston and the Saratoga springs.—Ed.

ing closely around at the trees, the bushes, and the ground. "What have we there? Uncas, bring hither the thing you see dangling from yonder thornbush."

When the Indian had complied, the scout received the prize, and holding it on high, he laughed in his silent but heartfelt manner.

" 'Tis the tooting we'pon of the singer! now we shall have a trail a priest might travel," he said. "Uncas, look for the marks of a shoe that is long enough to uphold six feet two of tottering human flesh. I begin to have some hopes of the fellow, since he has given up squalling to follow some better trade."

"At least, he has been faithful to his trust," said Heyward; "and Cora and Alice are not without a friend."

"Yes," said Hawkeye, dropping his rifle, and leaning on it with an air of visible contempt, "he will do their singing! Can he slay a buck for their dinner; journey by the moss on the beeches, or cut the throat of a Huron? If not, the first catbird [1] he meets is the cleverest of the two. Well, boy, any signs of such a foundation?"

"Here is something like the footstep of one who has worn a shoe; can it be that of our friend?"

"Touch the leaves lightly, or you'll disconsart the formation. That! that is the print of a foot, but 'tis the dark-hair's; and small it is, too, for one of such a noble height and grand appearance. The singer would cover it with his heel."

"Where! let me look on the footsteps of my child," said Munro, shoving the bushes aside, and bending fondly over the nearly obliterated impression. Though the tread, which had left the mark, had been light and rapid, it was still plainly visible. The aged soldier examined it with eyes that grew dim as he gazed; nor did he rise from his stooping posture until Heyward saw that he had watered the trace of his daughter's passage with a scalding tear. Willing to divert a distress which threatened each moment to break through the restraint of appearances, by giving the veteran something to do, the young man said to the scout—

"As we now possess these infallible signs, let us commence our march. A moment, at such a time, will appear an age to the captives."

"It is not the swiftest leaping deer that gives the longest chase," returned Hawkeye, without moving his eyes from the different marks that had come under his view; "we know that the rampaging Huron has passed—and the dark-hair—and the singer—but where is she of

---

[1] The powers of the American mockingbird are generally known. But the true mockingbird is not found so far north as the State of New York, where it has, however, two substitutes of inferior excellence: the catbird, so often named by the scout, and the bird vulgarly called ground thresher. Either of these two last birds is superior to the nightingale, or the lark, though, in general, the American birds are less musical than those of Europe. (*Cooper's note*)

the yellow locks and blue eyes? Though little, and far from being as bold as her sister, she is fair to the view, and pleasant in discourse. Has she no friend, that none care for her?"

"God forbid she should ever want hundreds! Are we not now in her pursuit? for one, I will never cease the search till she be found."

"In that case we may have to journey by different paths; for here she has not passed, light and little as her footstep would be."

Heyward drew back, all his ardor to proceed seeming to vanish on the instant. Without attending to this sudden change in the other's humor, the scout, after musing a moment, continued—

"There is no woman in this wilderness could leave such a print as that, but the dark-hair or her sister. We know that the first has been here, but where are the signs of the other? Let us push deeper on the trail, and if nothing offers, we must go back to the plain and strike another scent. Move on, Uncas, and keep your eyes on the dried leaves. I will watch the bushes, while your father shall run with a low nose to the ground. Move on, friends; the sun is getting behind the hills."

"Is there nothing that I can do?" demanded the anxious Heyward.

"You!" repeated the scout, who, with his red friends, was already advancing in the order he had prescribed; "yes, you can keep in our rear, and be careful not to cross the trail."

Before they had proceeded many rods the Indians stopped, and appeared to gaze at some signs on the earth with more than their usual keenness. Both father and son spoke quick and loud, now looking at the object of their mutual admiration, and now regarding each other with the most unequivocal pleasure.

"They have found the little foot!" exclaimed the scout, moving forward, without attending further to his own portion of the duty. "What have we here? An ambushment has been planted in the spot! No, by the truest rifle on the frontiers, here have been them one-sided horses again! Now the whole secret is out, and all is plain as the North Star at midnight. Yes, here they have mounted. There the beasts have been bound to a sapling, in waiting; and yonder runs the broad path away to the north, in full sweep for the Canadas."

"But still there are no signs of Alice—of the younger Miss Munro," —said Duncan.

"Unless the shining bauble Uncas has just lifted from the ground should prove one. Pass it this way, lad, that we may look at it."

Heyward instantly knew it for a trinket that Alice was fond of wearing, and which he recollected, with the tenacious memory of a lover, to have seen, on the fatal morning of the massacre, dangling from the fair neck of his mistress. He seized the highly prized jewel; and as he proclaimed the fact, it vanished from the eyes of the wondering scout, who in vain looked for it on the ground, long after it was warmly pressed against the beating heart of Duncan.

"Pshaw!" said the disappointed Hawkeye, ceasing to rake the leaves with the breech of his rifle; " 'tis a certain sign of age when the sight begins to weaken. Such a glittering gewgaw, and not to be seen! Well, well, I can squint along a clouded barrel yet, and that is enough to settle all disputes between me and the Mingoes. I should like to find the thing, too, if it were only to carry it to the right owner, and that would be bringing the two ends of what I call a long trail together —for by this time the broad St. Lawrence or, perhaps, the Great Lakes themselves are atwixt us."

"So much the more reason why we should not delay our march," returned Heyward; "let us proceed."

"Young blood and hot blood, they say, are much the same thing. We are not about to start on a squirrel hunt, or to drive a deer into the Horican, but to outlie for days and nights, and to stretch across a wilderness where the feet of men seldom go, and where no bookish knowledge would carry you through harmless. An Indian never starts on such an expedition without smoking over his council fire; and though a man of white blood, I honor their customs in this particular, seeing that they are deliberate and wise. We will, therefore, go back, and light our fire tonight in the ruins of the old fort, and in the morning we shall be fresh, and ready to undertake our work like men, and not like babbling women or eager boys."

Heyward saw, by the manner of the scout, that altercation would be useless. Munro had again sunk into that sort of apathy which had beset him since his late overwhelming misfortunes, and from which he was apparently to be roused only by some new and powerful excitement.[1] Making a merit of necessity, the young man took the veteran by the arm, and followed in the footsteps of the Indians and the scout, who had already begun to retrace the path which conducted them to the plain.

The shades of evening had come to increase the dreariness of the place, when the party entered the ruins of William Henry. The scout and his companions immediately made their preparations to pass the night there; but with an earnestness and sobriety of demeanor that betrayed how much the unusual horrors they had just witnessed worked on even their practiced feelings. A few fragments of rafters were reared against a blackened wall; and when Uncas had covered them slightly with brush, the temporary accommodations were deemed sufficient.

[1] Lieutenant-Colonel George Munro was indeed heartbroken after the surrender of Fort William Henry. Early in 1756 he was promoted to be colonel as a reward for his brave defense; but the next month he died.—Ed.

The young Indian pointed toward his rude hut, when his labor was ended; and Heyward, who understood the meaning of the silent gesture, gently urged Munro to enter. Leaving the bereaved old man alone with his sorrows, Duncan immediately returned into the open air, too much excited himself to seek the repose he had recommended to his veteran friend.

While Hawkeye and the Indians lighted their fire, and took their evening's repast, a frugal meal of dried bear's meat, the young man paid a visit to that curtain of the dilapidated fort which looked out on the sheet of the Horican. The wind had fallen, and the waves were already rolling on the sandy beach beneath him, in a more regular and tempered succession. The clouds, as if tired of their furious chase, were breaking asunder; the heavier volumes gathering in black masses about the horizon, while the lighter scud still hurried above the water, or eddied among the tops of the mountains, like broken flights of birds hovering around their roosts. Here and there a red and fiery star struggled through the drifting vapor, furnishing a lurid gleam of brightness to the dull aspect of the heavens. Within the bosom of the encircling hills an impenetrable darkness had already settled; and the plain lay like a vast and deserted charnel house, without omen or whisper to disturb the slumbers of its numerous and hapless tenants.

Of this scene, so chillingly in accordance with the past, Duncan stood for many minutes a rapt observer. His eyes wandered from the bosom of the mound, where the foresters were seated around their glimmering fire, to the fainter light which still lingered in the skies, and then rested long and anxiously on the embodied gloom, which lay like a dreary void on that side of him where the dead reposed. He soon fancied that inexplicable sounds arose from the place, though so indistinct and stolen as to render not only their nature but even their existence uncertain. Ashamed of his apprehensions, the young man turned toward the water, and strove to divert his attention to the mimic stars that dimly glimmered on its moving surface. Still, his too conscious ears performed their ungrateful duty, as if to warn him of some lurking danger. At length a swift trampling seemed, quite audibly, to rush athwart the darkness. Unable any longer to quiet his uneasiness, Duncan spoke in a low voice to the scout, requesting him to ascend the mound to the place where he stood. Hawkeye threw his rifle across an arm, and complied, but with an air so unmoved and calm as to prove how much he counted on the security of their position.

"Listen," said Duncan, when the other placed himself deliberately at his elbow; "there are suppressed noises on the plain which may show that Montcalm has not yet entirely deserted his conquest."

"Then ears are better than eyes," said the undisturbed scout, who having just deposited a portion of a bear between his grinders, spoke thick and slow, like one whose mouth was doubly occupied. "I, myself, saw him caged in Ty, with all his host; for your Frenchers, when they have done a clever thing, like to get back, and have a dance, or a merrymaking with the women over their success."

"I know not. An Indian seldom sleeps in war, and plunder may keep a Huron here, after his tribe has departed. It would be well to extinguish the fire, and have a watch—Listen! you hear the noise I mean!"

"An Indian more rarely lurks about the graves. Though ready to slay, and not over regardful of the means, he is commonly content with the scalp, unless when blood is hot, and temper up; but after the spirit is once fairly gone, he forgets his enmity, and is willing to let the dead find their natural rest. Speaking of spirits, Major, are you of opinion that the heaven of a redskin and of us whites will be one and the same?"

"No doubt—no doubt. I thought I heard it again! or was it the rustling of the leaves in the top of the beech?"

"For my own part," continued Hawkeye, turning his face, for a moment, in the direction indicated by Heyward, but with a vacant and careless manner, "I believe that paradise is ordained for happiness; and that men will be indulged in it according to their dispositions and gifts. I therefore judge that a redskin is not far from the truth when he believes he is to find them glorious hunting grounds of which his traditions tell; nor, for that matter, do I think it would be any disparagement to a man without a cross to pass his time—"

"You hear it again?" interrupted Duncan.

"Ay, ay; when food is scarce, and when food is plenty, a wolf grows bold," said the unmoved scout. "There would be picking, too, among the skins of the devils, if there was light and time for the sport. But, concerning the life that is to come, Major: I have heard preachers say, in the settlements, that Heaven was a place of rest. Now men's minds differ as to their ideas of enjoyment. For myself, and I say it with reverence to the ordering of Providence, it would be no great indulgence to be kept shut up in those mansions of which they preach, having a natural longing for motion and the chase."

Duncan, who was now made to understand the nature of the noises he had heard, answered, with more attention to the subject which the humor of the scout had chosen for discussion, by saying—

"It is difficult to account for the feelings that may attend the last great change."

"It would be a change, indeed, for a man who has passed his days in the open air," returned the single-minded scout; "and who has so often broken his fast on the headwaters of the Hudson, to sleep within sound of the roaring Mohawk. But it is a comfort to know we serve a merciful Master, though we do it each after his fashion, and with great tracts of wilderness atween us—What goes there?"

"Is it not the rushing of the wolves you have mentioned?"

Hawkeye slowly shook his head, and beckoned for Duncan to follow him to a spot to which the glare from the fire did not extend. When he had taken this precaution, the scout placed himself in an attitude of intense attention, and listened long and keenly for a repetition of the low sound that had so unexpectedly startled him. His vigilance, however, seemed exercised in vain; for, after a fruitless pause, he whispered to Duncan—

"We must give a call to Uncas. The boy has Indian senses, and may hear what is hid from us; for being a white-skin, I will not deny my nature."

The young Mohican, who was conversing in a low voice with his father, started as he heard the moaning of an owl, and springing on his feet, he looked toward the black mounds, as if seeking the place whence the sounds proceeded. The scout repeated the call, and in a few moments Duncan saw the figure of Uncas stealing cautiously along the rampart, to the spot where they stood.

Hawkeye explained his wishes in a very few words, which were spoken in the Delaware tongue. So soon as Uncas was in possession of the reason why he was summoned, he threw himself flat on the turf; where, to the eyes of Duncan, he appeared to lie quiet and motionless. Surprised at the immovable attitude of the young warrior, and curious to observe the manner in which he employed his faculties to obtain the desired information, Heyward advanced a few steps, and bent over the dark object, on which he had kept his eyes riveted. Then it was he discovered that the form of Uncas had vanished, and that he beheld only the dark outline of an inequality in the embankment.

"What has become of the Mohican?" he demanded of the scout, stepping back in amazement: "it was here that I saw him fall, and I could have sworn that here he yet remained."

"Hist! speak lower; for we know not what ears are open, and the Mingoes are a quick-witted breed. As for Uncas, he is out on the plain, and the Maquas, if any such are about us, will find their equal."

"You think that Montcalm has not called off all his Indians? Let us give the alarm to our companions, that we may stand to our arms. Here are five of us, who are not unused to meet an enemy."

"Not a word to either, as you value life. Look at the Sagamore, how like a grand Indian chief he sits by the fire. If there are any skulkers out in the darkness, they will never discover, by his countenance, that we suspect danger at hand."

"But they may discover him, and it will prove his death. His person can be too plainly seen by the light of that fire, and he will become the first and most certain victim."

"It is undeniable that now you speak the truth," returned the scout, betraying more anxiety than was usual; "yet what can be done? A single suspicious look might bring on an attack before we are ready to receive it. He knows, by the call I gave to Uncas, that we have struck a scent: I will tell him that we are on the trail of the Mingoes; his Indian nature will teach him how to act."

The scout applied his fingers to his mouth, and raised a low hissing sound, that caused Duncan, at first, to start aside, believing that he heard a serpent. The head of Chingachgook was resting on a hand, as he sat musing by himself; but the moment he heard the warning of the animal whose name he bore, it arose to an upright position, and his dark eyes glanced swiftly and keenly on every side of him. With this sudden and perhaps involuntary movement, every appearance of surprise or alarm ended. His rifle lay untouched, and apparently unnoticed, within reach of his hand. The tomahawk that he had loosened in his belt for the sake of ease, was even suffered to fall from its usual situation to the ground, and his form seemed to sink, like that of a man whose nerves and sinews were suffered to relax for the purpose of rest. Cunningly resuming his former position, though with a change of hands, as if the movement had been made merely to relieve the limb, the native awaited the result with a calmness and fortitude that none but an Indian warrior would have known how to exercise.

But Heyward saw, that while to a less instructed eye the Mohican chief appeared to slumber, his nostrils were expanded, his head was turned a little to one side, as if to assist the organs of hearing, and that his quick and rapid glances ran incessantly over every object within the power of his vision.

"See the noble fellow!" whispered Hawkeye, pressing the arm of Heyward; "he knows that a look or a motion might disconsart our schemes, and put us at the mercy of them imps—"

He was interrupted by the flash and report of a rifle. The air was filled with sparks of fire, around that spot where the eyes of Heyward were still fastened with admiration and wonder. A second look told him that Chingachgook had disappeared in the confusion. In the meantime the scout had thrown forward his rifle, like one prepared for service, and awaited impatiently the moment when an enemy might rise to view. But with the solitary and fruitless attempt made on the life of Chingachgook, the attack appeared to have terminated. Once or twice the listeners thought they could distinguish the distant rustling of bushes, as bodies of some unknown description rushed through them; nor was it long before Hawkeye pointed out the "scampering of the wolves," as they fled precipitately before the passage of some intruder on their proper domains. After an impatient and breathless pause, a plunge was heard in the water, and it was immediately followed by the report of another rifle.

"There goes Uncas!" said the scout: "the boy bears a smart piece! I know its crack as well as a father knows the language of his child, for I carried the gun myself until a better offered."

"What can this mean?" demanded Duncan: "we are watched, and, as it would seem, marked for destruction."

"Yonder scattered brand can witness that no good was intended, and this Indian will testify that no harm has been done," returned the scout, dropping his rifle across his arm again, and following Chingachgook, who just then reappeared within the circle of light, into the bosom of the works. "How is it, Sagamore? Are the Mingoes upon us in earnest, or is it only one of those reptiles who hang upon the skirts of a war party, to scalp the dead, go in, and make their boast among the squaws of the valiant deeds done on the palefaces?"

Chingachgook very quietly resumed his seat; nor did he make any reply, until after he had examined the firebrand which had been struck by the bullet that had nearly proved fatal to himself. After which, he was content to reply, holding a single finger up to view, with the English monosyllable—

"One."

"I thought as much," returned Hawkeye, seating himself; "and as he had got the cover of the lake afore Uncas pulled upon him, it is more than probable the knave will sing his lies about some great engagement, in which he was outlying on the trail of two Mohicans and a white hunter—for the officers can be considered as little better than idlers in such a scrimmage. Well, let him—let him. There are always some honest men in every nation, though heaven knows, too, that they are scarce among the Maquas, to look down an upstart when he brags ag'in the face of reason. The varlet sent his lead within whistle of your ears, Sagamore."

Chingachgook turned a calm and incurious eye toward the place where the ball had struck, and then resumed his former attitude, with a composure that could not be disturbed by so trifling an incident. Just then Uncas glided into the circle, and seated himself at the fire, with the same appearance of indifference as was maintained by his father.

Of these several movements Heyward was a deeply interested and wondering observer. It appeared to him as though the foresters had some secret means of intelligence which had escaped the vigilance of his own faculties. In place of that eager and garrulous narration with which a white youth would have endeavored to communicate, and perhaps exaggerate, that which had passed out in the darkness of the plain, the young warrior was seemingly content to let his deeds speak for themselves. It was, in fact, neither the moment nor the occasion for an Indian to boast of his exploits; and it is probable that, had Heyward neglected to inquire, not another syllable would, just then, have been uttered on the subject.

"What has become of our enemy, Uncas?" demanded Duncan: "we heard your rifle, and hoped you had not fired in vain."

The young chief removed a fold of his hunting shirt, and quietly exposed the fatal tuft of hair, which he bore as the symbol of victory. Chingachgook laid his hand on the scalp, and considered it for a moment with deep attention. Then dropping it, with disgust depicted in his strong features, he ejaculated—

"Oneida!"

"Oneida!" repeated the scout, who was fast losing his interest in the scene, in an apathy nearly assimilated to that of his red associates, but who now advanced with uncommon earnestness to regard the bloody badge. "By the Lord, if the Oneidas are outlying upon the trail, we shall be flanked by devils on every side of us! Now, to white eyes there is no difference between this bit of skin and that of any other Indian, and yet the Sagamore declares it came from the poll of a Mingo; nay, he even names the tribe of the poor devil with as much ease as if the scalp was the leaf of a book, and each hair a letter. What right have Christian whites to boast of their learning, when a savage can read a language that would prove too much for the wisest of them all! What say *you*, lad; of what people was the knave?"

Uncas raised his eyes to the face of the scout, and answered, in his soft voice—

"Oneida."

"Oneida, again! when one Indian makes a declaration it is commonly true; but when he is supported by his people, set it down as gospel!"

"The poor fellow has mistaken us for French," said Heyward; "or he would not have attempted the life of a friend."

"He mistake a Mohican in his paint for a Huron! You would be as likely to mistake the white-coated grenadiers of Montcalm for the scarlet jackets of the Royal Americans," returned the scout. "No, no, the sarpent knew his errand; nor was there any great mistake in the matter, for there is but little love atween a Delaware and a Mingo, let their tribes go out to fight for whom they may, in a white quarrel. For that matter, though the Oneidas do serve his sacred Majesty, who is my own sovereign lord and master, I should not have deliberated long about letting off Killdeer at the imp myself, had luck thrown him in my way."

"That would have been an abuse of our treaties, and unworthy of your character."

"When a man consorts much with a people," continued Hawkeye, "if they are honest and he no knave, love will grow up atwixt them. It is true that white cunning has managed to throw the tribes into great confusion, as respects friends and enemies; so that the Hurons and the Oneidas, who speak the same tongue, or what may be called the same, take each other's scalps, and the Delawares are divided among themselves; a few hanging about their great council fire on their own river, and fighting on the same side with the Mingoes, while the greater part are in the Canadas, out of natural enmity to the Maquas—thus throwing everything into disorder, and destroying all the harmony of warfare. Yet a red natur' is not likely to alter with every shift of policy; so that the love atwixt a Mohican and a Mingo is much like the regard between a white man and a sarpent."

"I regret to hear it; for I had believed those natives who dwelt within our boundaries had found us too just and liberal not to identify themselves fully with our quarrels."

"Why, I believe it is natur' to give a preference to one's own quarrels before those of strangers. Now, for myself, I do love justice; and therefore I will not say I hate a Mingo,—for that may be unsuitable to my color and my religion,—though I will just repeat, it may have been owing to the night that Killdeer had no hand in the death of this skulking Oneida."

Then, as if satisfied with the force of his own reasons, whatever might be their effect on the opinions of the other disputant, the honest but implacable woodsman turned from the fire, content to let the controversy slumber. Heyward withdrew to the rampart, too uneasy and too little accustomed to the warfare of the woods to remain at ease under the possibility of such insidious attacks. Not so, however, with the scout and the Mohicans. Those acute and long practiced senses, whose powers so often exceed the limits of all ordinary credulity, after having detected the danger, had enabled them to ascertain its magnitude and duration. Not one of the three appeared in the least to doubt their perfect security, as was indicated by the preparations that were soon made to sit in council over their future proceedings.

The confusion of nations, and even of tribes, to which Hawkeye alluded, existed at that period in the fullest force. The great tie of language, and, of course, of a common origin, was severed in many places; and it was one of its consequences that the Delaware and the Mingo (as the people of the Six Nations were called) were found fighting in the same ranks, while the latter sought the scalp of the Huron, though believed to be the root of his own stock. The Delawares were even divided among themselves. Though love for the soil which had belonged to his ancestors kept the Sagamore of the Mohicans, with a small band of followers who were serving at Edward, under the banners of the English king, by far the largest portion of his nation were known to be in the field as allies of Montcalm. The reader probably knows, if enough has not already been gleaned from this narrative, that the Delaware, or Lenape, claimed to be the progenitors of that numerous people, who once were masters of most of the eastern and northern states of America, of whom the community of the Mohicans was an ancient and highly honored member.

It was, of course, with a perfect understanding of the minute and intricate interests which had armed friend against friend, and brought natural enemies to combat by each other's side, that the scout and his companions now disposed themselves to deliberate on the measures that were to govern their future movements, amid so many jarring and savage races of men. Duncan knew enough of Indian customs to understand the reason that the fire was replenished, and why the warriors, not excepting Hawkeye, took their seats within the curl of its smoke with so much gravity and decorum. Placing himself at an angle of the works, where he might be a spectator of the scene within, while he kept a watchful eye against any danger from without, he awaited the result with as much patience as he could summon.

After a short and impressive pause, Chingachgook lighted a pipe whose bowl was curiously carved in one of the soft stones of the country, and whose stem was a tube of wood, and commenced smoking. When he had inhaled enough of the fragrance of the soothing weed, he passed the instrument into the hands of the scout. In this manner the pipe had made its rounds there several times, amid the most profound silence, before either of the party opened his lips. Then the Sagamore, as the oldest and highest in rank, in a few calm and dignified words proposed the subject for deliberation. He was answered by the scout; and Chingachgook rejoined, when the other objected to his opinions. But the youthful Uncas continued a silent and respectful listener, until Hawkeye, in complaisance, demanded his opinion. Heyward gathered from the manners of the different speakers, that the father and son espoused one side of a disputed question, while the white man maintained the other. The contest gradually grew warmer until it was quite evident the feelings of the speakers began to be somewhat enlisted in the debate.

Notwithstanding the increasing warmth of the amicable contest, the most decorous Christian assembly, not even excepting those in which its reverend ministers are collected, might have learned a wholesome lesson of moderation from the forbearance and courtesy of the disputants. The words of Uncas were received with the same deep attention as those which fell from the maturer wisdom of his father; and so far from manifesting any impatience, neither spoke in reply until a few moments of silent meditation were, seemingly, bestowed in deliberating on what had already been said.

The language of the Mohicans was accompanied by gestures so direct and natural that Heyward had but little difficulty in following the thread of their argument. On the other hand, the scout was obscure; because, from the lingering pride of color, he rather affected the cold and artificial manner which characterizes all classes of Anglo-Americans when unexcited. By the frequency with which the Indians described the marks of a forest trail, it was evident they urged a pursuit by land, while the repeated sweep of Hawkeye's arm toward the Horican denoted that he was for a passage across its waters.

The latter was, to every appearance, fast losing ground, and the point was about to be decided against him, when he arose to his feet, and shaking off his apathy, he suddenly assumed the manner of an Indian, and adopted all the arts of native eloquence. Elevating an arm, he pointed out the track of the sun, repeating the gesture for every day that was necessary to accomplish their object. Then he delineated a long and painful path, amid rocks and watercourses. The age and weakness of the slumbering and unconscious Munro were indicated by signs too palpable to be mistaken. Duncan perceived that even his own powers were spoken lightly of, as the scout extended his palm, and mentioned him by the appellation of the Open Hand—a name his liberality had purchased of all the friendly tribes. Then came a representation of the light and graceful movements of a canoe, set in forcible contrast to the tottering steps of one enfeebled and tired. He concluded by pointing to the scalp of the Oneida, and apparently urging the necessity of their departing speedily, and in a manner that should leave no trail.

The Mohicans listened gravely, and with countenances that reflected the sentiments of the speaker. Conviction gradually wrought its influence, and towards the close of Hawkeye's speech his sentences were accompanied by the customary exclamation of commendation. In short, Uncas and his father became converts to his way of thinking, abandoning their own previously expressed opinions with a liberality and candor that had they been the representatives of some great and civilized people, would have infallibly worked their political ruin, by destroying, forever, their reputation for consistency.

The instant the matter in discussion was decided, the debate, and everything connected with it, except the result, appeared to be forgotten. Hawkeye, without looking round to read his triumph in applauding eyes, very composedly stretched his tall frame before the dying embers, and closed his own organs in sleep.

Left now in a measure to themselves, the Mohicans, whose time had been so much devoted to the interests of others, seized the moments to devote some attention to themselves. Casting off, at once, the grave and austere demeanor of an Indian chief, Chingachgook commenced speaking to his son in the soft and playful tones of affection. Uncas gladly met the familiar air of his father; and before the hard breathing of the scout announced that he slept, a complete change was effected in the manner of his two associates.

It is impossible to describe the music of their language, while thus engaged in laughter and endearments, in such a way as to render it intelligible to those whose ears have never listened to its melody. The compass of their voices, particularly that of the youth, was wonderful,—extending from the deepest bass to tones that were even feminine in softness. The eyes of the father followed the plastic and ingenious movements of the son with open delight, and he never failed to smile in reply to the other's contagious, but low laughter. While under the influence of these gentle and natural feelings, no trace of ferocity was to be seen in the softened features of the Sagamore. His figured panoply of death looked more like a disguise assumed in mockery, than a fierce annunciation of a desire to carry destruction and desolation in his footsteps.

After an hour passed in the indulgence of their better feelings, Chingachgook abruptly announced his desire to sleep by wrapping his head in his blanket and stretching his form on the naked earth. The merriment of Uncas instantly ceased; and carefully raking the coals in such a manner that they should impart their warmth to his father's feet, the youth sought his own pillow among the ruins of the place.

Imbibing renewed confidence from the security of these experienced foresters, Heyward soon imitated their example; and long before the night had turned, they who lay in the bosom of the ruined work, seemed to slumber as heavily as the unconscious multitude whose bones were already beginning to bleach on the surrounding plain.

The heavens were still studded with stars when Hawkeye came to arouse the sleepers. Casting aside their cloaks, Munro and Heyward were on their feet, while the woodsman was still making his low calls, at the entrance of the rude shelter where they had passed the night. When they issued from beneath its concealment they found the scout awaiting their appearance nigh by, and the only salutation between them was the significant gesture for silence, made by their sagacious leader.

"Think over your prayers," he whispered, as they approached him; "for He, to whom you make them, knows all tongues; that of the heart, as well as those of the mouth. But speak not a syllable; it is rare for a white voice to pitch itself properly in the woods, as we have seen by the example of that miserable devil, the singer. Come," he continued, turning toward a curtain of the works; "let us get into the ditch on this side, and be regardful to step on the stones and fragments of wood as you go."

His companions complied, though to two of them the reasons of this extraordinary precaution were yet a mystery. When they were in the low cavity that surrounded the earthen fort on three of its sides, they found the passage nearly choked by the ruins. With care and patience, however, they succeeded in clambering after the scout, until they reached the sandy shore of the Horican.

"That's a trail that nothing but a nose can follow," said the satisfied scout, looking back along their difficult way; "grass is a treacherous carpet for a flying party to tread on, but wood and stone take no print from a moccasin. Had you worn your armed boots, there might, indeed, have been something to fear; but with the deerskin suitably prepared, a man may trust himself, generally, on rocks with safety. Shove in the canoe nigher to the land, Uncas; this sand will take a stamp as easily as the butter of the Jarmans on the Mohawk. Softly, lad, softly; it must not touch the beach, or the knaves will know by what road we have left the place."

The young man observed the precaution; and the scout, laying a board from the ruins to the canoe, made a sign for the two officers to enter. When this was done, everything was studiously restored to its former disorder; and then Hawkeye succeeded in reaching his little birchen vessel without leaving behind him any of those marks which he appeared so much to dread. Heyward was silent until the Indians had cautiously paddled the canoe some distance from the fort, and within the broad and dark shadow that fell from the eastern mountain, on the glassy surface of the lake; then he demanded—

"What need have we for this stolen and hurried departure?"

"If the blood of an Oneida could stain such a sheet of pure water as this we float on," returned the scout, "your two eyes would answer your own question. Have you forgotten the skulking reptyle that Uncas slew?"

"By no means. But he was said to be alone, and dead men give no cause for fear."

"Ay, he was alone in his deviltry! but an Indian, whose tribe counts so many warriors, need seldom fear his blood will run without the death shriek coming speedily from some of his enemies."

"But our presence—the authority of Colonel Munro would prove a sufficient protection against the anger of our allies, especially in a case where the wretch so well merited his fate. I trust in Heaven you have not deviated a single foot from the direct line of our course, with so slight a reason."

"Do you think the bullet of that varlet's rifle would have turned aside, though his sacred Majesty the King had stood in its path?" returned the stubborn scout. "Why did not the grand Frencher, he who is captain-general of the Canadas, bury the tomahawks of the Hurons, if a word from a white can work so strongly on the natur' of an Indian?"

The reply of Heyward was interrupted by a groan from Munro; but after he had paused a moment, in deference to the sorrow of his aged friend, he resumed the subject.

"The Marquis of Montcalm can only settle that error with his God," said the young man solemnly.

"Ay, ay, now there is reason in your words, for they are bottomed on religion and honesty. There is a vast difference between throwing a regiment of white coats atwixt the tribes and the prisoners, and coaxing an angry savage to forget he carries a knife and a rifle, with words that must begin with calling him your son. No, no," continued the scout, looking back at the dim shore of William Henry, which was now fast receding, and laughing in his own silent but heartfelt manner; "I have put a trail of water atween us; and unless the imps can make friends with the fishes, and hear who has paddled across their basin this fine morning, we shall throw the length of the Horican behind us before they have made up their minds which path to take."

"With foes in front, and foes in our rear, our journey is like to be one of danger."

"Danger!" repeated Hawkeye, calmly; "no, not absolutely of danger; for, with vigilant ears and quick eyes we can manage to keep a few hours ahead of the knaves; or, if we must try the rifle, there are three of us who understand its gifts as well as any you can name on the borders. No, not of danger; but that we shall have what you may call a brisk push of it, is probable; and it may happen, a brush, a scrimmage, or some such divarsion, but always where covers are good and ammunition abundant."

It is possible that Heyward's estimate of danger differed in some degree from that of the scout, for, instead of replying, he now sat in silence, while the canoe glided over several miles of water. Just as the day dawned, they entered the narrows of the lake,[1] and stole swiftly

[1] The beauties of Lake George are well known to every American tourist. In the height of the mountains which surround it, and in artificial accessories, it is inferior to the finest of the Swiss and Italian lakes, while in outline and purity of water it is fully their equal; and in the number and disposition of its isles and islets much superior to them altogether. There are said to be some hundreds of islands in a sheet of water less than thirty miles long. The narrows, which connect what may be called, in truth, two lakes, are crowded with islands to such a degree as to leave passages between them frequently of only a few feet in width. The lake, itself, varies in breadth from one to three miles.

The state of New York is remarkable for the number and beauty of its lakes. One of its frontiers lies on the vast sheet of Ontario, while Champlain stretches nearly a

and cautiously among their numberless little islands. It was by this road that Montcalm had retired with his army, and the adventurers knew not but he had left some of his Indians in ambush, to protect the rear of his forces, and collect the stragglers. They, therefore, approached the passage with the customary silence of their guarded habits.

Chingachgook laid aside his paddle; while Uncas and the scout urged the light vessel through crooked and intricate channels, where every foot that they advanced exposed them to the danger of some sudden rising on their progress. The eyes of the Sagamore moved warily from islet to islet, and copse to copse, as the canoe proceeded; and when a clearer sheet of water permitted, his keen vision was bent along the bald rocks and impending forests, that frowned upon the narrow strait.

Heyward, who was a doubly interested spectator, as well from the beauties of the place as from the apprehension natural to his situation, was just believing that he had permitted the latter to be excited without sufficient reason, when the paddles ceased moving, in obedience to a signal from Chingachgook.

"Hugh!" exclaimed Uncas, nearly at the moment that the light tap his father had made on the side of the canoe notified them of the vicinity of danger.

"What now?" asked the scout; "the lake is as smooth as if the winds had never blown, and I can see along its sheet for miles; there is not so much as the black head of a loon dotting the water."

The Indian gravely raised his paddle, and pointed in the direction in which his own steady look was riveted. Duncan's eyes followed the motion. A few rods in their front lay another of the low wooded islets, but it appeared as calm and peaceful as if its solitude had never been disturbed by the foot of man.

"I see nothing," he said, "but land and water; and a lovely scene it is."

"Hist!" interrupted the scout. "Ay, Sagamore, there is always a reason for what you do. 'Tis but a shade, and yet it is not natural. You see the mist, Major, that is rising above the island; you can't call it a fog, for it is more like a streak of thin cloud—"

"It is vapor from the water."

"That a child could tell. But what is the edging of blacker smoke that hangs along its lower side, and which you may trace down into the thicket of hazel? 'Tis from a fire; but one that, in my judgment, has been suffered to burn low."

"Let us then push for the place, and relieve our doubts," said the

---

hundred miles along another. Oneida, Cayuga, Canandaigua, Seneca, and George are all lakes of thirty miles in length, while those of a size smaller are without number. On most of these lakes there are now beautiful villages, and on many of them steamboats. (*Cooper's note*)

impatient Duncan; "the party must be small that can lie on such a bit of land."

"If you judge of Indian cunning by the rules you find in books, or by white sagacity, they will lead you astray, if not to your death," returned Hawkeye, examining the signs of the place with that acuteness which distinguished him. "If I may be permitted to speak in this matter, it will be to say, that we have but two things to choose between: the one is, to return, and give up all thoughts of following the Hurons—"

"Never!" exclaimed Heyward, in a voice far too loud for their circumstances.

"Well, well," continued Hawkeye, making a hasty sign to repress his impatience; "I am much of your mind myself; though I thought it becoming my experience to tell the whole. We must then make a push, and if the Indians or Frenchers are in the narrows, run the gauntlet through these toppling mountains. Is there reason in my words, Sagamore?"

The Indian made no other answer than by dropping his paddle into the water, and urging forward the canoe. As he held the office of directing its course, his resolution was sufficiently indicated by the movement. The whole party now plied their paddles vigorously, and in a very few moments they had reached a point whence they might command an entire view of the northern shore of the island, the side that had hitherto been concealed.

"There they are, by all the truth of signs," whispered the scout; "two canoes and a smoke. The knaves haven't yet got their eyes out of the mist, or we should hear the accursed whoop. Together, friends—we are leaving them, and are already nearly out of whistle of a bullet."

The well-known crack of a rifle, whose ball came skipping along the placid surface of the strait, and a shrill yell from the island, interrupted his speech, and announced that their passage was discovered. In another instant several savages were seen rushing into the canoes, which were soon dancing over the water, in pursuit. These fearful precursors of a coming struggle produced no change in the countenances and movements of his three guides, so far as Duncan could discover, except that the strokes of their paddles were longer and more in unison, and caused the little bark to spring forward like a creature possessing life and volition.

"Hold them there, Sagamore," said Hawkeye, looking coolly backward over his left shoulder, while he still plied his paddle; "keep them just there. Them Hurons have never a piece in their nation that will execute at this distance; but Killdeer has a barrel on which a man may calculate."

The scout having ascertained that the Mohicans were sufficient of themselves to maintain the requisite distance, deliberately laid aside his paddle, and raised the fatal rifle. Then several times he brought the piece to his shoulder, and when his companions were expecting its report, he as often lowered it to request the Indians would permit their enemies to approach a little nigher. At length his accurate and fastidious eye seemed satisfied, and throwing out his left arm on the barrel, he was slowly elevating the muzzle, when an exclamation from Uncas, who sat in the bow, once more caused him to suspend the shot.

"What now, lad?" demanded Hawkeye; "you saved a Huron from the death shriek by that word; have you reason for what you do?"

Uncas pointed toward the rocky shore a little in their front, whence another war canoe was darting directly across their course. It was too obvious now that their situation was imminently perilous to need the aid of language to confirm it. The scout laid aside his rifle, and resumed the paddle, while Chingachgook inclined the bow of the canoe a little toward the western shore, in order to increase the distance between them and this new enemy. In the meantime they were reminded of the presence of those who pressed upon their rear by wild and exulting shouts. The stirring scene awakened even Munro from his apathy.

"Let us make for the rocks on the main," he said, with the mien of a tried soldier, "and give battle to the savages. God forbid that I, or those attached to me and mine, should ever trust again to the faith of any servant of the Louises!"

"He who wishes to prosper in Indian warfare," returned the scout, "must not be too proud to learn from the wit of a native. Lay her more along the land, Sagamore; we are doubling on the varlets, and perhaps they may try to strike our trail on the long calculation."

Hawkeye was not mistaken; for when the Hurons found their course was likely to throw them behind their chase, they rendered it less direct, until, by gradually bearing more and more obliquely, the two canoes were, ere long, gliding on parallel lines, within two hundred yards of each other. It now became entirely a trial of speed. So rapid was the progress of the light vessels that the lake curled in their front, in miniature waves, and their motion became undulating by its own velocity. It was, perhaps, owing to this circumstance, in addition to the necessity of keeping every hand employed at the paddles, that the Hurons had not immediate recourse to their firearms. The exertions of the fugitives were too severe to continue long, and the pursuers had the advantage of numbers. Duncan observed, with uneasiness, that the scout began to look anxiously about him, as if searching for some further means of assisting their flight.

"Edge her a little more from the sun, Sagamore," said the stubborn woodsman; "I see the knaves are sparing a man to the rifle. A single broken bone might lose us our scalps. Edge more from the sun and we will put the island between us."

The expedient was not without its use. A long, low island lay at a little distance before them, and as they closed with it, the chasing canoe was compelled to take a side opposite to that on which the pursued passed. The scout and his companions did not neglect this advantage, but the instant they were hid from observation by the bushes, they redoubled efforts that before had seemed prodigious. The two canoes came round the last low point like two coursers at the top of their speed, the fugitives taking the lead. This change had brought them nigher to each other, however, while it altered their relative positions.

"You showed knowledge in the shaping of birchen bark, Uncas, when you chose this from among the Huron canoes," said the scout, smiling, apparently more in satisfaction at their superiority in the race than from that prospect of final escape which now began to open a little upon them. "The imps have put all their strength again at the paddles, and we are to struggle for our scalps with bits of flattened wood, instead of clouded barrels and true eyes. A long stroke, and together, friends."

"They are preparing for a shot," said Heyward; "and as we are in a line with them, it can scarcely fail."

"Get you then into the bottom of the canoe," returned the scout; "you and the colonel; it will be so much taken from the size of the mark."

Heyward smiled, as he answered—

"It would be but an ill example for the highest in rank to dodge, while the warriors were under fire!"

"Lord! Lord! that is now a white man's courage!" exclaimed the scout; "and like too many of his notions, not to be maintained by reason. Do you think the Sagamore, or Uncas, or even I, who am a man without a cross, would deliberate about finding a cover in the scrimmage, when an open body would do no good? For what have the Frenchers reared up their Quebec, if fighting is always to be done in the clearings?"

"All that you say is very true, my friend," replied Heyward; "still, our customs must prevent us from doing as you wish."

A volley from the Hurons interrupted the discourse, and as the bullets whistled about them, Duncan saw the head of Uncas turned, looking back at himself and Munro. Notwithstanding the nearness of the enemy, and his own great personal danger, the countenance of the young warrior expressed no other emotion, as the former was compelled to think, than amazement at finding men willing to encounter so useless an exposure. Chingachgook was probably better acquainted with the notions of white men, for he did not even cast a glance aside from the riveted look his eye maintained on the object by which he governed their course. A ball soon struck the light and polished paddle from the hands of the chief, and drove it through the air, far in the advance. A shout arose from the Hurons, who seized the opportunity to fire another volley. Uncas described an arc in the water with his own blade, and as the canoe passed swiftly on, Chingachgook recovered his paddle, and flourishing it on high, he gave the war whoop of the Mohicans, and then lent his strength and skill again to the important task.

The clamorous sounds of "Le gros Serpent! La longue Carabine! Le Cerf Agile!" burst at once from the canoes behind, and seemed to give new zeal to the pursuers. The scout seized Killdeer in his left hand, and elevating it above his head, he shook it in triumph at his enemies. The savages answered the insult with a yell, and immediately another volley succeeded. The bullets pattered along the lake, and one even pierced the bark of their little vessel. No perceptible emotion could be discovered in the Mohicans during this critical moment, their rigid features expressing neither hope nor alarm; but the scout again turned his head, and laughing in his own silent manner, he said to Heyward—

"The knaves love to hear the sounds of their pieces; but the eye is not to be found among the Mingoes that can calculate a true range in a dancing canoe! You see the dumb devils have taken off a man to charge, and by the smallest measurement that can be allowed, we move three feet to their two!"

Duncan, who was not altogether as easy under this nice estimate of distances as his companions, was glad to find, however, that owing to their superior dexterity, and the diversion among their enemies, they were very sensibly obtaining the advantage. The Hurons soon fired again, and a bullet struck the blade of Hawkeye's paddle without injury.

"That will do," said the scout, examining the slight indentation with a curious eye; "it would not have cut the skin of an infant, much less of men, who, like us, have been blown upon by the Heavens in their anger. Now, Major, if you will try to use this piece of flattened wood, I'll let Killdeer take a part in the conversation."

Heyward seized the paddle, and applied himself to the work with an eagerness that supplied the place of skill, while Hawkeye was engaged in inspecting the priming of his rifle. The latter then took a swift aim, and fired. The Huron in the bow of the leading canoe had risen with a similar object, and he now fell backward, suffering his gun to escape from his hands into the water. In an instant, however, he recovered his feet, though his gestures were wild and bewildered. At the same moment his companions suspended their efforts, and the chasing canoes clustered together, and became stationary. Chingachgook and Uncas profited by the interval to regain their wind, though Duncan continued to work with the most persevering industry. The father and son now cast calm but inquiring glances at each other, to learn if either had sustained any injury by the fire; for both well knew that no cry or exclamation would, in such a moment of necessity, have been permitted to betray the accident. A few large drops of blood were trickling down the shoulder of the Sagamore, who, when he perceived that the eyes of Uncas dwelt too long on the sight, raised some water in the hollow of his hand, and washing off the stain, was content to manifest, in this simple manner, the slightness of the injury.

"Softly, softly, Major," said the scout, who by this time had reloaded his rifle; "we are a little too far already for a rifle to put forth its beauties, and you see yonder imps are holding a council. Let them come up within striking distance—my eye may well be trusted in such a matter—and I will trail the varlets the length of the Horican, guaranteeing that not a shot of theirs shall, at the worst, more than break the skin, while Killdeer shall touch the life twice in three times."

"We forget our errand," returned the diligent Duncan. "For God's sake let us profit by this advantage, and increase our distance from the enemy."

"Give me my children," said Munro, hoarsely; "trifle no longer with a father's agony, but restore me my babes."

Long and habitual deference to the mandates of his superiors had taught the scout the virtue of obedience. Throwing a last and lingering glance at the distant canoes, he laid aside his rifle, and relieving the wearied Duncan, resumed the paddle, which he wielded with sinews that never tired. His efforts were seconded by those of the Mohicans, and a very few minutes served to place such a sheet of water between them and their enemies that Heyward once more breathed freely.

The lake now began to expand, and their route lay along a wide reach, that was lined, as before, by high and ragged mountains. But the islands were few, and easily avoided. The strokes of the paddles grew more measured and regular, while they who plied them continued their labor, after the close and deadly chase from which they had just relieved themselves, with as much coolness as though their speed had been tried in sport, rather than under such pressing, nay, almost desperate, circumstances.

Instead of following the western shore, whither their errand led them, the wary Mohican inclined his course more toward those hills behind which Montcalm was known to have led his army into the formidable fortress of Ticonderoga. As the Hurons, to every appearance, had abandoned the pursuit, there was no apparent reason for this excess of caution. It was, however, maintained for hours, until they had reached a bay, nigh the northern termination of the lake. Here the canoe was driven upon the beach, and the whole party landed. Hawkeye and Heyward ascended an adjacent bluff, where the former, after considering the expanse of water beneath him, pointed out to the latter a small black object, hovering under a headland, at the distance of several miles.

"Do you see it?" demanded the scout. "Now, what would you account that spot, were you left alone to white experience to find your way through this wilderness?"

"But for its distance and its magnitude, I should suppose it a bird. Can it be a living object?"

" 'Tis a canoe of good birchen bark, and paddled by fierce and crafty Mingoes. Though Providence has lent to those who inhabit the woods eyes that would be needless to men in the settlements, where there are inventions to assist the sight, yet no human organs can see all the dangers which at this moment circumvent us. These varlets pretend to be bent chiefly on their sundown meal, but the moment it is dark they will be on our trail, as true as hounds on the scent. We must throw them off, or our pursuit of Le Renard Subtil may be given up. These lakes are useful at times, especially when the game takes the water," continued the scout, gazing about him with a countenance of concern; "but they give no cover, except it be to the fishes. God knows what the country would be if the settlements should ever spread far from the two rivers. Both hunting and war would lose their beauty."

"Let us not delay a moment, without some good and obvious cause."

"I little like that smoke, which you may see worming up along the rock above the canoe," interrupted the abstracted scout. "My life on it, other eyes than ours see it, and know its meaning. Well, words will not mend the matter, and it is time that we were doing."

Hawkeye moved away from the lookout, and descended, musing profoundly, to the shore. He communicated the result of his observations to his companions, in Delaware, and a short and earnest consultation succeeded. When it terminated, the three instantly set about executing their new resolutions.

The canoe was lifted from the water and borne on the shoulders of the party. They proceeded into the wood, making as broad and obvious a trail as possible. They soon reached a watercourse, which they crossed, and continued onward, until they came to an extensive and naked rock. At this point, where their footsteps might be expected to be no longer visible, they retraced their route to the brook, walking backwards, with the utmost care. They now followed the bed of the little stream to the lake, into which they immediately launched their canoe again. A low point concealed them from the headland, and the margin of the lake was fringed for some distance with dense and overhanging bushes. Under the cover of these natural advantages they toiled their way, with patient industry, until the scout pronounced that he believed it would be safe once more to land.

The halt continued until evening rendered objects indistinct and uncertain to the eye. Then they resumed their route, and, favored by the darkness, pushed silently and vigorously toward the western shore. Although the rugged outline of mountain, to which they were steering, presented no distinctive marks to the eyes of Duncan, the Mohican entered the little haven he had selected with the confidence and accuracy of an experienced pilot.

The boat was again lifted and borne into the woods, where it was carefully concealed under a pile of brush. The adventurers assumed their arms and packs, and the scout announced to Munro and Heyward that he and the Indians were at last in readiness to proceed.

The party had landed on the border of a region that is, even to this day, less known to the inhabitants of the states than the deserts of Arabia, or the steppes of Tartary. It was the sterile and rugged district which separates the tributaries of Champlain from those of the Hudson, the Mohawk, and the St. Lawrence. Since the period of our tale the active spirit of the country has surrounded it with a belt of rich and thriving settlements, though none but the hunter or the savage is ever known, even now, to penetrate its wild recesses.

As Hawkeye and the Mohicans had, however, often traversed the mountains and valleys of this vast wilderness, they did not hesitate to plunge into its depths with the freedom of men accustomed to its privations and difficulties. For many hours the travellers toiled on their laborious way, guided by a star, or following the direction of some watercourse, until the scout called a halt, and holding a short consultation with the Indians, they lighted their fire, and made the usual preparations to pass the remainder of the night where they then were.

Imitating the example, and emulating the confidence, of their more experienced associates, Munro and Duncan slept without fear, if not without uneasiness. The dews were suffered to exhale, and the sun had dispersed the mists, and was shedding a strong and clear light in the forest, when the travellers resumed their journey.

After proceeding a few miles, the progress of Hawkeye, who led the advance, became more deliberate and watchful. He often stopped to examine the trees; nor did he cross a rivulet without attentively considering the quantity, the velocity, and the color of its waters. Distrusting his own judgment, his appeals to the opinion of Chingachgook were frequent and earnest. During one of these conferences Heyward observed that Uncas stood a patient and silent, though, as he imagined, an interested listener. He was strongly tempted to address the young chief, and demand his opinion of their progress; but the calm and dignified demeanor of the native induced him to believe that, like himself, the other was wholly dependent on the sagacity and intelligence of the seniors of the party. At last the scout spoke in English, and at once explained the embarrassment of their situation.

"When I found that the home path of the Hurons runs north," he said, "it did not need the judgment of many long years to tell that they would follow the valleys, and keep atween the waters of the Hudson and the Horican, until they might strike the springs of the Canada streams, which would lead them into the heart of the country of the Frenchers. Yet here are we, within a short range of the Scaroon,[1] and not a sign of a trail have we crossed! Human natur' is weak, and it is possible we may not have taken the proper scent."

"Heaven protect us from such an error!" exclaimed Duncan. "Let us retrace our steps, and examine as we go, with keener eyes. Has Uncas no counsel to offer in such a strait?"

The young Mohican cast a glance at his father, but maintaining his quiet and reserved mien, he continued silent. Chingachgook had caught the look, and motioning with his hand, he bade him speak. The moment this permission was accorded the countenance of Uncas changed from its grave composure to a gleam of intelligence and joy. Bounding forward like a deer, he sprang up the side of a little acclivity, a few rods in advance, and stood, exultingly, over a spot of fresh earth, that looked as though it had been recently upturned by the passage of some heavy animal. The eyes of the whole party followed the unexpected movement, and read their success in the air of triumph that the youth assumed.

" 'Tis the trail!" exclaimed the scout, advancing to the spot: "the lad is quick of sight and keen of wit for his years."

" 'Tis extraordinary that he should have withheld his knowledge so long," muttered Duncan, at his elbow.

"It would have been more wonderful had he spoken without a bidding. No, no; your young white, who gathers his learning from books and can measure what he knows by the page, may conceit that his knowledge, like his legs, outruns that of his father; but where experience is the master, the scholar is made to know the value of years, and respects them accordingly."

"See!" said Uncas, pointing north and south, at the evident marks of the broad trail on either side of him: "the dark-hair has gone towards the frost."

"Hound never ran on a more beautiful scent," responded the

[1] That is, the Schroon, a tributary of the Hudson, which rises in the Adirondacks and flows into and out of the beautiful sheet of water called Schroon Lake.— Ed.

scout, dashing forward, at once, on the indicated route; "we are favored, greatly favored, and can follow with high noses. Ay, here are both your waddling beasts: this Huron travels like a white general. The fellow is stricken with a judgment, and is mad! Look sharp for wheels, Sagamore," he continued, looking back, and laughing in his newly awakened satisfaction; "we shall soon have the fool journeying in a coach, and that with three of the best pair of eyes on the borders in his rear."

The spirits of the scout, and the astonishing success of the chase, in which a circuitous distance of more than forty miles had been passed, did not fail to impart a portion of hope to the whole party. Their advance was rapid; and made with as much confidence as a traveller would proceed along a wide highway. If a rock, or a rivulet, or a bit of earth harder than common severed the links of the clue they followed, the true eye of the scout recovered them at a distance, and seldom rendered the delay of a single moment necessary. Their progress was much facilitated by the certainty that Magua had found it necessary to journey through the valleys; a circumstance which rendered the general direction of the route sure. Nor had the Huron entirely neglected the arts uniformly practiced by the natives when retiring in front of an enemy. False trails, and sudden turnings, were frequent, wherever a brook, or the formation of the ground, rendered them feasible; but his pursuers were rarely deceived, and never failed to detect their error before they had lost either time or distance on the deceptive track.

By the middle of the afternoon they had passed the Scaroon, and were following the route of the declining sun. After descending an eminence to a low bottom, through which a swift stream glided, they suddenly came to a place where the party of Le Renard had made a halt. Extinguished brands were lying around a spring, the offals of a deer were scattered about the place, and the trees bore evident marks of having been browsed by the horses. At a little distance Heyward discovered, and contemplated with tender emotion, the small bower under which he was fain to believe that Cora and Alice had reposed. But while the earth was trodden, and the footsteps of both men and beasts were so plainly visible around the place, the trail appeared to have suddenly ended.

It was easy to follow the tracks of the Narragansetts, but they seemed only to have wandered without guides, or any other object than the pursuit of food. At length Uncas, who, with his father, had endeavored to trace the route of the horses, came upon a sign of their presence that was quite recent. Before following the clue he communicated his success to his companions; and while the latter were consulting on the circumstance the youth reappeared, leading the two fillies, with their saddles broken and the housings soiled, as though they had been permitted to run at will for several days.

"What should this prove?" said Duncan, turning pale, and glancing his eyes around him, as if he feared the brush and leaves were about to give up some horrid secret.

"That our march is come to a quick end, and that we are in an enemy's country," returned the scout. "Had the knave been pressed, and the gentle ones wanted horses to keep up with the party, he might have taken their scalps; but without an enemy at his heels, and with such rugged beasts as these he would not hurt a hair of their heads. I know your thoughts, and shame be it to our color that you have reason for them; but he who thinks that even a Mingo would ill-treat a woman, unless it be to tomahawk her, knows nothing of Indian natur', or the laws of the woods. No, no; I have heard that the French Indians had come into these hills to hunt the moose, and we are getting within scent of their camp. Why should they not? the morning and evening guns of Ty may be heard any day among these mountains; for the Frenchers are running a new line atween the provinces of the King and the Canadas. It is true that the horses are here, but the Hurons are gone; let us then hunt for the path by which they departed."

Hawkeye and the Mohicans now applied themselves to their task in good earnest. A circle of a few hundred feet in circumference was drawn, and each of the party took a segment for his portion. The examination, however, resulted in no discovery. The impressions of footsteps were numerous, but they all appeared like those of men who had wandered about the spot, without any design to quit it. Again the scout and his companions made the circuit of the halting place, each slowly following the other, until they assembled in the center once more, no wiser than when they started.

"Such cunning is not without its deviltry," exclaimed Hawkeye, when he met the disappointed looks of his assistants.

"We must get down to it, Sagamore, beginning at the spring, and going over the ground by inches. The Huron shall never brag in his tribe that he has a foot which leaves no print."

Setting the example himself, the scout engaged in the scrutiny with renewed zeal. Not a leaf was left unturned. The sticks were removed and the stones lifted—for Indian cunning was known frequently to adopt these objects as covers, laboring with the utmost patience and industry, to conceal each footstep as they proceeded. Still no discovery was made. At length Uncas, whose activity had enabled him to achieve his portion of the task the soonest, raked the earth across the turbid little rill which ran from the spring, and diverted its course into another channel. So soon as its narrow bed below the dam was dry, he stooped over it with keen and curious eyes. A cry of exultation immediately announced the success of the young warrior. The whole party crowded to the spot, where Uncas pointed out the impression of a moccasin in the moist alluvion.

"The lad will be an honor to his people," said Hawkeye, regarding the trail with as much admiration as a naturalist would expend on the tusk of a mammoth or the rib of a mastodon; "ay, and a thorn in the sides of the Hurons. Yet that is not the footstep of an Indian! the weight is too much on the heel, and the toes are squared, as though one of the French dancers had been in, pigeonwinging his tribe! Run back, Uncas, and bring me the size of the singer's foot. You will find a beautiful print of it just opposite yon rock, ag'in the hillside."

While the youth was engaged in this commission, the scout and Chingachgook were attentively considering the impressions. The measurements agreed, and the former unhesitatingly pronounced that the footstep was that of David, who had, once more, been made to exchange his shoes for moccasins.

"I can now read the whole of it as plainly as if I had seen the arts of Le Subtil," he added; "the singer, being a man whose gifts lay chiefly in his throat and feet, was made to go first, and the others have trod in his steps, imitating their formation."

"But," cried Duncan, "I see no signs of—"

"The gentle ones," interrupted the scout; "the varlet has found a way to carry them until he supposed he had thrown any followers off the scent. My life on it, we see their pretty little feet again before many rods go by."

The whole party now proceeded, following the course of the rill, keeping anxious eyes on the regular impressions. The water soon flowed into its bed again, but watching the ground on either side, the foresters pushed their way, content with knowing that the trail lay beneath. More than half a mile was passed before the rill rippled close around the base of an extensive and dry dock. Here they paused to make sure that the Hurons had not quitted the water.

It was fortunate they did so. For the quick and active Uncas soon found the impression of a foot on a bunch of moss, where it would seem an Indian had inadvertently trodden. Pursuing the direction given by this discovery, he entered the neighboring thicket, and struck the trail, as fresh and obvious as it had been before they reached the spring. Another shout announced the good fortune of the youth to his companions, and at once terminated the search.

"Ay, it has been planned with Indian judgment," said the scout, when the party was assembled around the place; "and would have blinded white eyes."

"Shall we proceed?" demanded Heyward.

"Softly, softly: we know our path; but it is good to examine the formation of things. This is my schooling, Major; and if one neglects the book, there is little chance of learning from the open hand of Providence. All is plain but one thing, which is the manner that the knave contrived to get the gentle ones along the blind trail. Even a Huron would be too proud to let their tender feet touch the water."

"Will this assist in explaining the difficulty?" said Heyward, pointing toward the fragments of a sort of handbarrow, that had been rudely constructed of boughs, and bound together with withes, and which now seemed carelessly cast aside as useless.

" 'Tis explained!" cried the delighted Hawkeye. "If them varlets have passed a minute, they have spent hours in striving to fabricate a lying end to their trail! Well, I've known them waste a day in the same manner, to as little purpose. Here we have three pair of moccasins, and two of little feet. It is amazing that any mortal beings can journey on limbs so small! Pass me the thong of buckskin, Uncas, and let me take the length of this foot. By the Lord, it is no longer than a child's, and yet the maidens are tall and comely. That Providence is partial in its gifts, for its own wise reasons, the best and most contented of us must allow."

"The tender limbs of my daughters are unequal to these hardships," said Munro, looking at the light footsteps of his children, with a parent's love: "we shall find their fainting forms in this desert."

"Of that there is little cause of fear," returned the scout, slowly shaking his head: "this is a firm and straight, though a light step, and not over long. See, the heel has hardly touched the ground; and there the dark-hair has made a little jump, from root to root. No, no; my knowledge for it, neither of them was nigh fainting, here-a-way. Now, the singer was beginning to be footsore and leg-weary, as is plain by his trail. There, you see, he slipped; here he has travelled wide, and tottered; and there, again, it looks as though he journeyed on snowshoes. Ay, ay, a man who uses his throat altogether, can hardly give his legs a proper training."

From such undeniable testimony, did the practiced woodsman arrive at the truth, with nearly as much certainty and precision as if he had been a witness of all those events, which his ingenuity so easily elucidated. Cheered by these assurances, and satisfied by a reasoning that was so obvious, while it was so simple, the party resumed its course, after making a short halt, to take a hurried repast.

When the meal was ended, the scout cast a glance upward at the setting sun, and pushed forward with a rapidity which compelled Heyward and the still vigorous Munro to exert all their muscles to equal. Their route, now, lay along the bottom which has already been mentioned. As the Hurons had made no further efforts to conceal their footsteps, the progress of the pursuers was no longer delayed by uncertainty. Before an hour had elapsed, however, the speed of Hawkeye sensibly abated, and his head, instead of maintaining its former direct and forward look, began to turn suspiciously from side to side, as if he were conscious of approaching danger. He soon stopped again and waited for the whole party to come up.

"I scent the Hurons," he said, speaking to the Mohicans; "yonder is open sky, through the treetops, and we are getting too nigh their encampment. Sagamore, you will take the hillside, to the right; Uncas will bend along the brook to the left, while I will try the trail. If anything should happen, the call will be three croaks of a crow. I saw one of the birds fanning himself in the air, just beyond the dead oak—another sign that we are touching an encampment."

The Indians departed their several ways without reply, while Hawkeye cautiously proceeded with the two gentlemen. Heyward soon pressed to the side of their guide, eager to catch an early glimpse of those enemies he had pursued with so much toil and anxiety. His companion told him to steal to the edge of the wood, which, as usual, was fringed with a thicket, and wait his coming, for he wished to examine certain suspicious signs a little on one side. Duncan obeyed, and soon found himself in a situation to command a view which he found as extraordinary as it was novel.

The trees of many acres had been felled, and the glow of a mild summer's evening had fallen on the clearing, in beautiful contrast to the grey light of the forest. A short distance from the place where Duncan stood, the stream had seemingly expanded into a little lake, covering most of the lowland, from mountain to mountain. The water fell out of this wide basin, in a cataract so regular and gentle, that it appeared rather to be the work of human hands, than fashioned by nature. A hundred earthen dwellings stood on the margin of the lake, and even in its water, as though the latter had overflowed its usual banks. Their rounded roofs, admirably moulded for defence against the weather, denoted more of industry and foresight than the natives were wont to bestow on their regular habitations, much less on those they occupied for the temporary purposes of hunting and war. In short, the whole village or town, whichever it might be termed, possessed more of method and neatness of execution, than the white man had been accustomed to believe belonged, ordinarily, to the Indian habits. It appeared, however, to be deserted. At least, so thought Duncan for many minutes; but, at length, he fancied he discovered several human forms advancing toward him on all fours, and apparently dragging in their train some heavy, and as he was quick to apprehend, some formidable engine. Just then a few dark looking heads gleamed out of the dwellings, and the place seemed suddenly alive with beings, which, however, glided from cover to cover so swiftly, as to allow no opportunity of examining their humors or pursuits. Alarmed at these suspicious and inexplicable movements, he was about to attempt the signal of the crows, when the rustling of leaves at hand drew his eyes in another direction.

The young man started, and recoiled a few paces instinctively, when he found himself within a hundred yards of a stranger Indian. Recovering his recollection on the instant, instead of sounding an alarm, which might prove fatal to himself, he remained stationary, an attentive observer of the other's motions.

An instant of calm observation served to assure Duncan that he was undiscovered. The native, like himself, seemed occupied in considering the low dwellings of the village, and the stolen movements of its inhabitants. It was impossible to discover the expression of his features, through the grotesque mask of paint under which they were concealed; though Duncan fancied it was rather melancholy than savage. His head was shaved, as usual, with the exception of the crown, from whose tuft three or four faded feathers from a hawk's wing were loosely dangling. A ragged calico mantle half encircled his body, while his nether garment was composed of an ordinary shirt, the sleeves of which were made to perform the office that is usually executed by a much more commodious arrangement. His legs were bare, and sadly cut and torn by briers. The feet were, however, covered with a pair of good deerskin moccasins. Altogether, the appearance of the individual was forlorn and miserable.

Duncan was still curiously observing the person of his neighbor, when the scout stole silently and cautiously to his side.

"You see we have reached their settlement or encampment," whispered the young man; "and here is one of the savages himself, in a very embarrassing position for our further movements."

Hawkeye started, and dropped his rifle, when, directed by the finger of his companion, the stranger came under his view. Then lowering the dangerous muzzle, he stretched forward his long neck, as if to assist a scrutiny that was already intensely keen.

"The imp is not a Huron," he said, "nor of any of the Canada tribes; and yet you see, by his clothes, the knave has been plundering a white. Ay, Montcalm has raked the woods for his inroad, and a whooping, murdering set of varlets has he gathered together. Can you see where he has put his rifle or his bow?"

"He appears to have no arms; nor does he seem to be viciously inclined. Unless he communicate the alarm to his fellows, who, as you see, are dodging about the water, we have but little to fear from him."

The scout turned to Heyward, and regarded him a moment with unconcealed amazement. Then opening wide his mouth, he indulged in unrestrained and heartfelt laughter, though in that silent and peculiar manner which danger had so long taught him to practice.

Repeating the words, "fellows who are dodging about the water!" he added, "so much for schooling and passing a boyhood in the settlements! The knave has long legs, though, and shall not be trusted. Do you keep him under your rifle while I creep in behind, through the bush, and take him alive. Fire on no account."

Heyward had already permitted his companion to bury part of his person in the thicket, when, stretching forth an arm, he arrested him, in order to ask—

"If I see you in danger, may I not risk a shot?"

Hawkeye regarded him a moment, like one who knew not how to take the question; then nodding his head, he answered, still laughing, though inaudibly—

"Fire a whole platoon, Major."

In the next moment he was concealed by the leaves. Duncan waited several minutes in feverish impatience, before he caught another glimpse of the scout. Then he reappeared, creeping along the earth, from which his dress was hardly distinguishable, directly in the rear of his intended captive. Having reached within a few yards of the latter, he arose to his feet, silently and slowly. At that instant, several loud blows were struck on the water, and Duncan turned his eyes just in time to perceive that a hundred dark forms were plunging, in a body, into the troubled little sheet. Grasping his rifle, his looks were again bent on the Indian near him. Instead of taking the alarm, the unconscious savage stretched forward his neck, as if he also watched the movements about the gloomy lake, with a sort of silly curiosity. In the meantime, the uplifted hand of Hawkeye was above him. But, without any apparent reason, it was withdrawn, and its owner indulged in another long, though still silent, fit of merriment. When the peculiar and hearty laughter of Hawkeye was ended, instead of grasping his victim by the throat, he tapped him lightly on the shoulder, and exclaimed aloud—

"How now, friend! have you a mind to teach the beavers to sing?"

"Even so," was the ready answer. "It would seem that the Being that gave them power to improve his gifts so well, would not deny them voices to proclaim his praise."

8

THE DISCOVERY of David Gamut, about to begin his psalm singing to a congregation of beavers, enabled Hawkeye, Heyward, and their companions to gain news of Cora and Alice Munro. After the massacre of Fort William Henry, the cunning Magua had carried the girls northward along the west bank of Lake George in the direction of Canada. David had been tolerated as a companion because of the special regard which the savages manifested for all who seemed mentally affected. On arriving at his destination, Magua had separated his prisoners. He had sent Cora to a tribe temporarily occupying an adjacent valley—a tribe, as Hawkeye's shrewd questioning developed, of neutral Delawares; Alice he had kept with the hostile Hurons. These Delawares had long before separated from the main body of their people, to which Chingachgook and Uncas belonged, and become partial allies of the Hurons or Mingoes; but they were not assisting Montcalm, whom they had told that their hatchets were dull. As they used the totem of the tortoise, which Chingachgook had tattooed on his breast, it was possible that Chingachgook and Uncas could influence them. The two chiefs resolved to begin a negotiation.

Alice, however, was in dire danger from the Hurons. Major Heywood gallantly volunteered to make an effort to rescue his beloved. Hawkeye disguised him as a buffoon or juggler from the French garrison at Ticonderoga; and the major and simple David

Gamut at once made their way to the hostile encampment. They arrived just in time to witness an extraordinary tumult. A war party, shouting the death halloo, brought in Uncas; the savages instantly formed in two lines, with clubs, axes, and knives; and the prisoner was forced to run the gauntlet. He did this successfully, taking refuge at a protecting post in front of the principal lodge. His fate would now be decided by the tribe in council. But Magua, who recognized him as Le Cerf Agile, anticipated their action. "Mohican," he said, "you die!" Uncas was tightly bound for the night.

Major Heyward, posing as a juggler and physician from the French fort, was meanwhile allowed to wander about the camp. Here he encountered what seemed to be a tame bear; but he was electrified when he found the supposed bear mimicking a psalm which David Gamut was singing. Before long, the chief of the tribe summoned Heyward to cure his sick daughter; and with much trepidation, the officer allowed himself to be led into a mountain cave with several chambers and passages. David Gamut and the strange bear followed in his footsteps.

There was a strange blending of the ridiculous with that which was solemn in this scene. The beast still continued its rolling, and apparently untiring movements, though its ludicrous attempt to imitate the melody of David ceased the instant the latter abandoned the field. The words of Gamut were, as has been seen, in his native tongue; and to Duncan they seemed pregnant with some hidden meaning, though nothing present assisted him in discovering the object of their allusion. A speedy end was, however, put to every conjecture on the subject, by the manner of the chief, who advanced to the bedside of the invalid, and beckoned away the whole group of female attendants that had clustered there to witness the skill of the stranger. He was implicitly, though reluctantly, obeyed; and when the low echo which rang along the hollow, natural gallery, from the distant closing door, had ceased, pointing towards his insensible daughter, he said—

"Now let my brother show his power."

Thus unequivocally called on to exercise the functions of his assumed character, Heyward was apprehensive that the smallest delay might prove dangerous. Endeavoring then to collect his ideas, he prepared to perform that species of incantation, and those uncouth rites under which the Indian conjurors are accustomed to conceal their ignorance and impotency. It is more than probable that, in the disordered state of his thoughts, he would soon have fallen into some suspicious, if not fatal error, had not his incipient attempts been interrupted by a fierce growl from the quadruped. Three several times did he renew his efforts to proceed, and as often was he met by the same unaccountable opposition, each interruption seeming more savage and threatening than the preceding.

"The cunning ones are jealous," said the Huron; "I go. Brother, the woman is the wife of one of my bravest young men; deal justly by her. Peace," he added, beckoning to the discontented beast to be quiet; "I go."

The chief was as good as his word, and Duncan now found himself alone in that wild and desolate abode, with the helpless invalid, and the fierce and dangerous brute. The latter listened to the movements of the Indian with that air of sagacity that a bear is known to possess, until another echo announced that he had also left the cavern, when it turned and came waddling up to Duncan, before whom it seated itself, in its natural attitude, erect like a man. The youth looked anxiously about him for some weapon, with which he might make a resistance against the attack he now seriously expected.

It seemed, however, as if the humor of the animal had suddenly changed. Instead of continuing its discontented growls, or manifesting any further signs of anger, the whole of its shaggy body shook violently, as if agitated by some strange internal convulsion. The huge and unwieldy talons pawed stupidly about the grinning muzzle, and while Heyward kept his eyes riveted on its movements with jealous watchfulness, the grim head fell on one side, and in its place appeared the honest, sturdy countenance of the scout, who was indulging, from the bottom of his soul, in his own peculiar expression of merriment.

"Hist!" said the wary woodsman, interrupting Heyward's exclamation of surprise; "the varlets are about the place, and any sounds that are not natural to witchcraft would bring them back upon us in a body."

"Tell me the meaning of this masquerade; and why you have attempted so desperate an adventure?"

"Ah! reason and calculation are often outdone by accident," returned the scout. "But as a story should always commence at the beginning, I will tell you the whole in order. After we parted I placed the commandant and the Sagamore in an old beaver lodge, where they are safer from the Hurons than they would be in the garrison of Edward; for your high northwest Indians, not having as yet got the traders among them, continue to venerate the beaver. After which Uncas and I pushed for the other encampment, as we agreed; have you seen the lad?"

"To my great grief!—he is captive, and condemned to die at the rising of the sun."

"I had misgivings that such would be his fate," resumed the scout, in a less confident and joyous tone. But soon regaining his naturally firm voice, he continued—"His bad fortune is the true reason of my being here, for it would never do to abandon such a boy to the Hurons. A rare time the knaves would have of it, could they tie the Bounding Elk and the Long Carabine, as they call me, to the same stake! Though why they have given me such a name I never knew, there being as little likeness between the gifts of Killdeer and the performance of one of your real Canada carabynes, as there is between the natur' of a pipe-stone and a flint!"

"Keep to your tale," said the impatient Heyward; "we know not at what moment the Hurons may return."

"No fear of them. A conjuror must have his time, like a straggling priest in the settlements. We are as safe from interruption as a missionary would be at the beginning of a two hours' discourse. Well, Uncas and I fell in with a return party of the varlets; the lad was much too forward for a scout; nay, for that matter, being of hot blood, he was not so much to blame; and, after all, one of the Hurons proved a coward, and in fleeing led him into an ambushment."

"And dearly has he paid for the weakness!"

The scout significantly passed his hand across his own throat, and nodded, as if he said, "I comprehend your meaning." After which he continued, in a more audible though scarcely more intelligible language—

"After the loss of the boy I turned upon the Hurons, as you may judge. There have been scrimmages atween one or two of their outlyers and myself; but that is neither here nor there. So, after I had shot the imps, I got in pretty nigh to the lodges without further commotion. Then what should luck do in my favor, but lead me to the very spot where one of the most famous conjurors of the tribe was dressing himself, as I well knew, for some great battle with Satan—though why should I call that luck, which it now seems was an especial ordering of Providence. So a judgmatical rap over the head stiffened the lying impostor for a time, and leaving him a bit of walnut for his supper, to prevent an uproar, and stringing him up atween two saplings, I made free with his finery, and took the part of the bear on myself, in order that the operations might proceed."

"And admirably did you enact the character; the animal itself might have been shamed by the representation."

"Lord, major," returned the flattered woodsman, "I should be but a poor scholar for one who has studied so long in the wilderness, did I not know how to set forth the movements and natur' of such a beast. Had it been now a catamount or even a full-sized panther, I would have embellished a performance for you worth regarding. But it is no such marvellous feat to exhibit the feats of so dull a beast; though, for that matter too, a bear may be overacted. Yes, yes; it is not every imitator that knows natur' may be outdone easier than she is equalled. But all our work is yet before us: where is the gentle one?"

"Heaven knows; I have examined every lodge in the village, without discovering the slightest trace of her presence in the tribe."

"You heard what the singer said, as he left us,—'She is at hand, and expects you.' "

"I have been compelled to believe he alluded to this unhappy woman."

"The simpleton was frightened, and blundered through his message; but he had a deeper meaning. Here are walls enough to separate the whole settlement. A bear ought to climb; therefore, will I take a look above them. There may be honeypots hid in these rocks, and I am a beast, you know, that has a hankering for the sweets."

The scout looked behind him, laughing at his own conceit, while he clambered up the partition, imitating, as he went, the clumsy motions of the beast he represented; but the instant the summit was gained he made a gesture for silence, and slid down with the utmost precipitation.

"She is here," he whispered, "and by that door you will find her. I would have spoken a word of comfort to the afflicted soul; but the sight of such a monster might upset her reason. Though for that matter, major, you are none of the most inviting yourself in your paint."

Duncan, who had already sprung eagerly forward, drew instantly back on hearing these discouraging words.

"Am I, then, so very revolting?" he demanded with an air of chagrin.

"You might not startle a wolf, or turn the Royal Americans from a charge; but I have seen the time when you had a better-favored look; your streaked countenances are not ill-judged of by the squaws, but young women of white blood give the preference to their own color. See," he added, pointing to a place where the water trickled from a rock, forming a little crystal spring before it found an issue through the adjacent crevices: "you may easily get rid of the Sagamore's daub, and when you come back I will try my hand at a new embellishment. It's as common for a conjuror to alter his paint as for a buck in the settlements to change his finery."

The deliberate woodsman had little occasion to hunt for arguments to enforce his advice. He was yet speaking when Duncan availed himself of the water. In a moment every frightful or offensive mark was obliterated, and the youth appeared again in the lineaments with which he had been gifted by nature. Thus prepared for an interview with his mistress, he took a hasty leave of his companion, and disappeared through the indicated passage. The scout witnessed his departure with complacency, nodding his head after him, and muttering his good wishes; after which he very coolly set about an examination of the state of the larder, among the Hurons—the cavern, among other purposes, being used as a receptacle for the fruits of their hunts.

Duncan had no other guide than a distant glimmering light, which served, however, the office of a polar star to the lover. By its aid he was enabled to enter the haven of his hopes, which was merely another apartment of the cavern, that had been solely appropriated to the safekeeping of so important a prisoner as a daughter of the commandant of William Henry. It was profusely strewed with the plunder of that unlucky fortress. In the midst of this confusion he found her he sought, pale, anxious, and terrified, but lovely. David had prepared her for such a visit.

"Duncan!" she exclaimed, in a voice that seemed to tremble at the sounds created by itself.

"Alice!" he answered, leaping carelessly among trunks, boxes, arms, and furniture, until he stood at her side.

"I knew that you would never desert me," she said, looking up with a momentary glow on her otherwise dejected countenance. "But you are alone! grateful as it is to be thus remembered, I could wish to think you are not entirely alone."

Duncan observing that she trembled in a manner which betrayed her inability to stand, gently induced her to be seated while he recounted those leading incidents which it has been our task to record. Alice listened with breathless interest; and though the young man touched lightly on the sorrows of the stricken father, taking care, however, not to wound the self-love of his auditor, the tears ran as freely down the cheeks of the daughter as though she had never wept before. The soothing tenderness of Duncan, however, soon quieted the first burst of her emotions, and she then heard him to the close with undivided attention, if not with composure.

"And now, Alice," he added, "you will see how much is still expected of you. By the assistance of our experienced and invaluable friend, the scout, we may find our way from this savage people, but you will have to exert your utmost fortitude. Remember that you fly to the arms of your venerable parent, and how much his happiness, as well as your own, depends on those exertions."

"Can I do otherwise for a father who has done so much for me?"

"And for me too," continued the youth, gently pressing the hand he held in both his own.

The look of innocence and surprise which he received in return convinced Duncan of the necessity of being more explicit.

"This is neither the place nor the occasion to detain you with selfish wishes," he added; "but what heart loaded like mine would not wish to cast its burden? They say misery is the closest of all ties; our common suffering in your behalf left but little to be explained between your father and myself."

"And dearest Cora, Duncan; surely Cora was not forgotten?"

"Not forgotten! no, regretted; as woman was seldom mourned before. Your venerable father knew no difference between his children; but I—Alice, you will not be offended when I say, that to me her worth was in a degree obscured—"

"Then you knew not the merit of my sister," said Alice, withdrawing her hand; "of you she ever speaks as of one who is her dearest friend."

"I would gladly believe her such," returned Duncan, hastily; "I could wish her to be even more; but with you, Alice, I have the permission of your father to aspire to a still nearer and dearer tie."

Alice trembled violently, and there was an instant during which she bent her face aside, yielding to the emotions common to her sex; but they quickly passed away, leaving her mistress of her deportment, if not of her affections.

"Heyward," she said, looking him full in the face with a touching expression of innocence and dependency, "give me the sacred presence and the holy sanction of that parent before you urge me further."

"Though more I should not, less I could not say," the youth was about to answer, when he was interrupted by a light tap on his shoulder. Starting to his feet, he turned, and, confronting the intruder, his looks fell on the dark form and malignant visage of Magua. The deep guttural laugh of the savage sounded, at such a moment, to Duncan like the hellish taunt of a demon. Had he pursued the sudden and fierce impulse of the instant, he would have cast himself on the Huron, and committed their fortunes to the issue of a deadly struggle. But, without arms of any description, ignorant of what succor his subtle enemy could command, and charged with the safety of one who was just then dearer than ever to his heart, he no sooner entertained than he abandoned the desperate intention.

"What is your purpose?" said Alice, meekly folding her arms on her bosom, and struggling to conceal an agony of apprehension in behalf of Heyward, in the usual cold and distant manner with which she received the visits of her captor.

The exulting Indian had resumed his austere countenance, though he drew warily back before the menacing glance of the young man's fiery eye. He regarded both his captives for a moment with a steady look, and then stepping aside, he dropped a log of wood across a door different from that by which Duncan had entered. The latter now comprehended the manner of his surprise, and believing himself irretrievably lost, he drew Alice to his bosom, and stood prepared to meet a fate which he hardly regretted, since it was to be suffered in such company. But Magua meditated no immediate violence. His first measures were very evidently taken to secure his new captive; nor did he even bestow a second glance at the motionless forms in the center of the cavern, until he had completely cut off every hope of retreat through the private outlet he had himself used. He was watched in all his movements by Heyward, who, however, remained firm, still folding the fragile form of Alice to his heart, at once too proud and too hopeless to ask favor of an enemy so often foiled. When Magua had effected his object he approached his prisoners, and said in English—

"The palefaces trap the cunning beavers; but the redskins know how to take the Yengeese."

"Huron, do your worst!" exclaimed the excited Heyward, forgetful that a double stake was involved in his life; "you and your vengeance are alike despised."

"Will the white man speak these words at the stake?" asked Magua; manifesting, at the same time, how little faith he had in the other's resolution by the sneer that accompanied his words.

"Here; singly to your face, or in the presence of your nation."

"Le Renard Subtil is a great chief!" returned the Indian; "he will go and bring his young men, to see how bravely a paleface can laugh at the tortures."

He turned away while speaking, and was about to leave the place through the avenue by which Duncan had approached, when a growl caught his ear, and caused him to hesitate. The figure of the bear appeared in the door, where it sat, rolling from side to side in its customary restlessness. Magua, like the father of the sick woman, eyed it keenly for a moment, as if to ascertain its character. He was far above the more vulgar superstitions of his tribe, and so soon as he recognized the well known attire of the conjuror, he prepared to pass it in cool contempt. But a louder and more threatening growl caused him again to pause. Then he seemed as if suddenly resolved to trifle no longer, and moved resolutely forward. The mimic animal, which had advanced a little, retired slowly in his front, until it arrived again at the pass, when rearing on its hinder legs it beat the air with its paws, in the manner practiced by its brutal prototype.

"Fool!" exclaimed the chief, in Huron, "go play with the children and squaws; leave men to their wisdom."

He once more endeavored to pass the supposed empiric, scorning even the parade of threatening to use the knife, or tomahawk, that was pendent from his belt. Suddenly the beast extended its arms, or rather legs, and inclosed him in a grasp that might have vied with the far-famed power of the "bear's hug" itself. Heyward had watched the whole procedure, on the part of Hawkeye, with breathless interest. At first he relinquished his hold of Alice; then he caught up a thong of buckskin, which had been used around some bundle, and when he beheld his enemy with his two arms pinned to his side by the iron muscles of the scout, he rushed upon him, and effectually secured them there. Arms, legs, and feet were encircled in twenty folds of the thong, in less time than we have taken to record the circumstance. When the formidable Huron was completely pinioned, the scout released his hold, and Duncan laid his enemy on his back, utterly helpless.

Throughout the whole of this sudden and extraordinary operation, Magua, though he had struggled violently, until assured he was in the hands of one whose nerves were far better strung than his own, had not uttered the slightest exclamation. But when Hawkeye, by way of making a summary explanation of his conduct, removed the shaggy jaws of the beast, and exposed his own rugged and earnest countenance to the gaze of the Huron, the philosophy of the latter was so far mastered as to permit him to utter the never-failing—

"Hugh!"

"Ay! you've found your tongue," said his undisturbed conqueror; "now, in order that you shall not use it to our ruin, I must make free to stop your mouth."

As there was no time to be lost, the scout immediately set about effecting so necessary a precaution; and when he had gagged the Indian, his enemy might safely have been considered as "hors de combat."

"By what place did the imp enter?" asked the industrious scout, when his work was ended. "Not a soul has passed my way since you left me."

Duncan pointed out the door by which Magua had come, and which now presented too many obstacles to a quick retreat.

"Bring on the gentle one then," continued his friend; "we must make a push for the woods by the other outlet."

" 'Tis impossible!" said Duncan; "fear has overcome her, and she is helpless. Alice! my sweet, my own Alice, arouse yourself; now is the moment to fly. 'Tis in vain! she hears, but is unable to follow. Go, noble and worthy friend; save yourself, and leave me to my fate!"

"Every trail has its end, and every calamity brings its lesson!" retreated the scout. "There, wrap her in them Indian cloths. Conceal all of her little form. Nay, that foot has no fellow in the wilderness; it will betray her. All, every part. Now take her in your arms, and follow. Leave the rest to me."

Duncan, as may be gathered from the words of his companion, was eagerly obeying; and as the other finished speaking, he took the light person of Alice in his arms, and followed on the footsteps of the scout. They found the sick woman as they had left her, still alone, and passed swiftly on, by the natural gallery, to the place of entrance. As they approached the little door of bark, a murmur of voices without announced that the friends and relatives of the invalid were gathered about the place, patiently awaiting a summons to re-enter.

"If I open my lips to speak," Hawkeye whispered, "my English, which is the genuine tongue of a white-skin, will tell the varlets that an enemy is among them. You must give 'em your jargon, major; and say that we have shut the evil spirit in the cave, and are taking the woman to the woods in order to find strengthening roots. Practyse all your cunning, for it is a lawful undertaking."

The door opened a little, as if one without was listening to the proceedings within, and compelled the scout to cease his directions. A fierce growl repelled the eavesdropper, and then the scout boldly threw open the covering of bark, and left the place, enacting the character of the bear as he proceeded. Duncan kept close at his heels, and soon found himself in the center of a cluster of twenty anxious relatives and friends.

The crowd fell back a little, and permitted the father, and one who appeared to be the husband of the woman, to approach.

"Has my brother driven away the evil spirit?" demanded the former. "What has he in his arms?"

"Thy child," returned Duncan, gravely; "the disease has gone out of her; it is shut up in the rocks. I take the woman to a distance, where I will strengthen her against any further attacks. She shall be in the wigwam of the young man when the sun comes again."

When the father had translated the meaning of the stranger's words into the Huron language, a suppressed murmur announced the satisfaction with which this intelligence was received. The chief himself waved his hand for Duncan to proceed, saying aloud, in a firm voice, and with a lofty manner—

"Go—I am a man, and I will enter the rock and fight the wicked one."

Heyward had gladly obeyed, and was already past the little group, when these startling words arrested him.

"Is my brother mad!" he exclaimed; "is he cruel! He will meet the disease, and it will enter him; or he will drive out the disease, and it will chase his daughter into the woods. No—let my children wait without, and if the spirit appears beat him down with clubs. He is cunning, and will bury himself in the mountain, when he sees how many are ready to fight him."

This singular warning had the desired effect. Instead of entering the cavern the father and husband drew their tomahawks, and posted themselves in readiness to deal their vengeance on the imaginary tormentor of their sick relative, while the women and children broke branches from the bushes, or seized fragments of the rock, with a similar intention. At this favorable moment the counterfeit conjurors disappeared.

Hawkeye, at the same time that he had presumed so far on the nature of the Indian superstitions, was not ignorant that they were rather tolerated than relied on by the wisest of the chiefs. He well knew the value of time in the present emergency. Whatever might be the extent of the self-delusion of his enemies, and however it had tended to assist his schemes, the slightest cause of suspicion, acting on the subtle nature of an Indian, would be likely to prove fatal. Taking the path, therefore, that was most likely to avoid observation, he rather skirted than entered the village. The warriors were still to be seen in the distance, by the fading light of the fires, stalking from lodge to lodge. But the children had abandoned their sports for their beds of skins, and the quiet of night was already beginning to prevail over the turbulence and excitement of so busy and important an evening.

Alice revived under the renovating influence of the open air, and as her physical rather than her mental powers had been the subject of weakness, she stood in no need of any explanation of that which had occurred.

"Now let me make an effort to walk," she said, when they had entered the forest, blushing, though unseen, that she had not been sooner able to quit the arms of Duncan; "I am indeed restored."

"Nay, Alice you are yet too weak."

The maiden struggled gently to release herself, and Heyward was compelled to part with his precious burden. The representative of the bear had certainly been an entire stranger to the delicious emotions of the lover while his arms encircled his mistress; and he was, perhaps, a stranger also to the nature of that feeling of ingenuous shame that oppressed the trembling Alice. But when he found himself at a suitable distance from the lodges he made a halt, and spoke on a subject of which he was thoroughly the master.

"This path will lead you to the brook," he said; "follow its northern bank until you come to a fall; mount the hill on your right, and you will see the fires of the other people. There you must go, and demand protection; if they are true Delawares, you will be safe. A distant flight with that gentle one, just now, is impossible. The Hurons would follow up our trail, and master our scalps, before we had got a dozen miles. Go, and Providence be with you."

"And you!" demanded Heyward, in surprise; "surely we part not here?"

"The Hurons hold the pride of the Delawares; the last of the high blood of the Mohicans is in their power," returned the scout; "I go to see what can be done in his favor. Had they mastered your scalp, major, a knave should have fallen for every hair it held, as I promised; but if the young Sagamore is to be led to the stake, the Indians shall see also how a man without a cross can die."

Not in the least offended with the decided preference that the sturdy woodsman gave to one who might, in some degree, be called the child of his adoption, Duncan still continued to urge such reasons against so desperate an effort as presented themselves. He was aided by Alice, who mingled her entreaties with those of Heyward that he would abandon a resolution that promised so much danger, with so little hope of success. Their eloquence and ingenuity were expended in vain. The scout heard them attentively, but impatiently, and finally closed the discussion, by answering, in a tone that instantly silenced Alice, while it told Heyward how fruitless any further remonstrances would be.

"I have heard," he said, "that there is a feeling in youth which binds man to woman closer than the father is tied to the son. It may be so. I have seldom been where women of my color dwell; but such may be the gifts of nature in the settlements. You have risked life, and all that is dear to you, to bring off this gentle one, and I suppose that some such disposition is at the bottom of it all. As for me, I taught the lad the real character of a rifle; and well has he paid me for it. I have fou't at his side in many a bloody scrimmage; and so long as I could hear the crack of his piece in one ear, and that of the Sagamore in the other, I knew no enemy was on my back. Winters and summers, nights and days, have we roved the wilderness in company, eating of the same dish, one sleeping while the other watched; and afore it shall be said that Uncas was taken to the torment, and I at hand—There is but a single ruler of us all, whatever may be the color of the skin; and him I call to witness—that before the Mohican boy shall perish for the want of a friend, good faith shall depart the 'arth, and Killdeer become as harmless as the tooting we'pon of the singer!"

Duncan released his hold on the arm of the scout, who turned, and steadily retraced his steps toward the lodges. After pausing a moment to gaze at his retiring form, the successful and yet sorrowful Heyward, and Alice, took their way together toward the distant village of the Delawares.

Notwithstanding the high resolution of Hawkeye, he fully comprehended all the difficulties and dangers he was about to incur. In his return to the camp, his acute and practiced intellects were intently engaged in devising means to counteract a watchfulness and suspicion on the part of his enemies, that he knew were, in no degree, inferior to his own. Nothing but the color of his skin had saved the lives of Magua and the conjuror, who would have been the first victims sacrificed to his own security, had not the scout believed such an act, however congenial it might be to the nature of an Indian, utterly unworthy of one who boasted a descent from men that knew no cross of blood. Accordingly, he trusted to the withes and ligaments with which he had bound his captives, and pursued his way directly toward the center of the lodges.

As he approached the buildings, his steps became more deliberate, and his vigilant eye suffered no sign, whether friendly or hostile, to escape him. A neglected hut was a little in advance of the others, and appeared as if it had been deserted when half completed—most probably on account of failing in some of the more important requisites; such as wood or water. A faint light glimmered through its cracks, however, and announced that, notwithstanding its imperfect structure, it was not without a tenant. Thither, then, the scout proceeded, like a prudent general, who was about to feel the advanced positions of his enemy, before he hazarded the main attack.

Throwing himself into a suitable posture for the beast he represented, Hawkeye crawled to a little opening, where he might command a view of the interior. It proved to be the abiding place of David Gamut. Hither the faithful singing master had now brought himself, together with all his sorrows, his apprehensions, and his meek dependence on the protection of Providence. At the precise moment when his ungainly person came under the observation of the scout, in the manner just mentioned, the woodsman himself, though in his assumed character, was the subject of the solitary being's profoundest reflections.

However implicit the faith of David was in the performance of ancient miracles, he eschewed the belief of any direct supernatural agency in the management of modern morality. In other words, while he had implicit faith in the ability of Balaam's ass to speak, he was somewhat skeptical on the subject of a bear's singing; and yet he had been assured of the latter, on the testimony of his own exquisite organs. There was something in his air and manner that betrayed to the scout the utter confusion of the state of his mind. He was seated on a pile of brush, a few twigs from which occasionally fed his low fire, with his head leaning on his arm, in a posture of melancholy musing. The costume of the votary of music had undergone no other alteration from that so lately described, except that he had covered his bald head with the triangular beaver, which had not proved sufficiently alluring to excite the cupidity of any of his captors.

The ingenious Hawkeye, who recalled the hasty manner in which the other had abandoned his post at the bedside of the sick woman, was not without his suspicions concerning the subject of so much solemn deliberation. First making the circuit of the hut, and ascertaining that it stood quite alone, and that the character of its inmate was likely to protect it from visitors, he ventured through its low door, into the very presence of Gamut. The position of the latter brought the fire between them; and when Hawkeye had seated himself on end, near a minute elapsed, during which the two remained regarding each other without speaking. The suddenness and the nature of the surprise had nearly proved too much for—we will not say the philosophy—but for the faith and resolution of David. He fumbled for his pitchpipe, and arose with a confused intention of attempting a musical exorcism.

"Dark and mysterious monster!" he exclaimed, while with trembling hands he disposed of his auxiliary eyes, and sought his never-failing resource in trouble, the gifted version of the Psalms; "I know not your nature nor intents; but if aught you meditate against the person and rights of one of the humblest servants of the temple, listen to the inspired language of the youth of Israel, and repent."

The bear shook his shaggy sides, and then a well known voice replied—

"Put up the tooting we'pon, and teach your throat modesty. Five words of plain and comprehendible English are worth, just now, an hour of squalling."

"What are thou?" demanded David, utterly disqualified to pursue his original intention, and nearly gasping for breath.

"A man like yourself; and one whose blood is as little tainted by the cross of a bear, or an Indian, as your own. Have you so soon forgotten from whom you received the foolish instrument you hold in your hand?"

"Can these things be?" returned David, breathing more freely, as the truth began to dawn upon him. "I have found many marvels during my sojourn with the heathen, but surely nothing to excel this!"

"Come, come," returned Hawkeye, uncasing his honest countenance, the better to assure the wavering confidence of his companion; "you may see a skin, which, if it be not as white as one of the gentle ones, has no tinge of red to it that the winds of the heaven and the sun have not bestowed. Now let us to business."

"First tell me of the maiden, and of the youth who so bravely sought her," interrupted David.

"Ay, they are happily freed from the tomahawks of these varlets. But can you put me on the scent of Uncas?"

"The young man is in bondage, and much I fear his death is decreed. I greatly mourn that one so well disposed should die in his ignorance, and I have sought a goodly hymn—"

"Can you lead me to him?"

"The task will not be difficult," returned David, hesitating;

"though I greatly fear your presence would rather increase than mitigate his unhappy fortunes."

"No more words, but lead on," returned Hawkeye, concealing his face again, and setting the example in his own person, by instantly quitting the lodge.

As they proceeded, the scout ascertained that his companion found access to Uncas, under privilege of his imaginary infirmity, aided by the favor he had acquired with one of the guards, who, in consequence of speaking a little English, had been selected by David as the subject of a religious conversion. How far the Huron comprehended the intentions of his new friend, may well be doubted; but as exclusive attention is as flattering to a savage as to a more civilized individual, it had produced the effect we have mentioned. It is unnecessary to repeat the shrewd manner with which the scout extracted these particulars from the simple David; neither shall we dwell in this place on the nature of the instructions he delivered, when completely master of all the necessary facts; as the whole will be sufficiently explained to the reader in the course of the narrative.

The lodge in which Uncas was confined was in the very center of the village, and in a situation, perhaps, more difficult than any other to approach, or leave, without observation. But it was not the policy of Hawkeye to affect the least concealment. Presuming on his disguise, and his ability to sustain the character he had assumed, he took the most plain and direct route to the place. The hour, however, afforded him some little of that protection which he appeared so much to despise. The boys were already buried in sleep, and all the women, and most of the warriors, had retired to their lodges for the night. Four or five of the latter only lingered about the door of the prison of Uncas, wary but close observers of the manner of their captive.

At the sight of Gamut, accompanied by one in the well-known masquerade of their most distinguished conjuror, they readily made way for them both. Still they betrayed no intention to depart. On the other hand, they were evidently disposed to remain bound to the place by an additional interest in the mysterious mummeries that they, of course, expected from such a visit.

From the total inability of the scout to address the Hurons in their own language, he was compelled to trust the conversation entirely to David. Notwithstanding the simplicity of the latter, he did ample justice to the instructions he had received, more than fulfilling the strongest hopes of his teacher.

"The Delawares are women!" he exclaimed, addressing himself to the savage who had a slight understanding of the language in which he spoke; "the Yengeese, my foolish countrymen, have told them to take up the tomahawk, and strike their fathers in the Canadas, and they have forgotten their sex. Does my brother wish to hear Le Cerf Agile ask for his petticoats, and see him weep before the Hurons, at the stake?"

The exclamation "hugh!" delivered in a strong tone of assent, announced the gratification the savage would receive in witnessing such an exhibition of weakness in an enemy so long hated and so much feared.

"Then let him step aside, and the cunning man will blow upon the dog! Tell it to my brothers."

The Huron explained the meaning of David to his fellows, who, in their turn, listened to the project with that sort of satisfaction that their untamed spirits might be expected to find in such a refinement in cruelty. They drew back a little from the entrance, and motioned to the supposed conjuror to enter. But the bear, instead of obeying, maintained the seat it had taken, and growled.

"The cunning man is afraid that his breath will blow upon his brothers, and take away their courage too," continued David, improving the hint he received; "they must stand further off."

The Hurons, who would have deemed such a misfortune the heaviest calamity that could befall them, fell back in a body, taking a position where they were out of earshot, though at the same time they could command a view of the entrance to the lodge. Then, as if satisfied of their safety, the scout left his position, and slowly entered the place. It was silent and gloomy, being tenanted solely by the captive, and lighted by the dying embers of a fire, which had been used for the purposes of cookery.

Uncas occupied a distant corner, in a reclining attitude, being rigidly bound, both hands and feet, by strong and painful withes. When the frightful object first presented itself to the young Mohican, he did not deign to bestow a single glance on the animal. The scout, who had left David at the door, to ascertain they were not observed, thought it prudent to preserve his disguise until assured of their privacy. Instead of speaking, therefore, he exerted himself to enact one of the antics of the animal he represented. The young Mohican, who at first believed his enemies had sent in a real beast to torment him, and try his nerves, detected, in those performances that to Heyward had appeared so accurate, certain blemishes, that at once betrayed the counterfeit. Had Hawkeye been aware of the low estimation in which the more skilful Uncas held his representations, he would probably have prolonged the entertainment a little in pique. But the scornful expression of the young man's eye admitted of so many constructions, that the worthy scout was spared the mortification of such a discovery. As soon, therefore, as David gave the preconcerted signal, a low hissing sound was heard in the lodge, in place of the fierce growlings of the bear.

Uncas had cast his body back against the wall of the hut, and closed his eyes, as if willing to exclude so contemptible and disagreeable an object from his sight. But the moment the noise of the serpent was heard, he arose, and cast his looks on each side of him, bending his head low, and turning it inquiringly in every direction, until his keen eye rested on the shaggy monster, where it remained riveted, as though fixed by the power of a charm. Again the same sounds were repeated, evidently proceeding from the mouth of the beast. Once more the eyes of the youth roamed over the interior of the lodge, and returning to their former resting place, he uttered, in a deep, suppressed voice—

"Hawkeye!"

"Cut his bands," said Hawkeye to David, who just then approached them.

The singer did as he was ordered, and Uncas found his limbs released. At the same moment the dried skin of the animal rattled, and presently the scout arose to his feet, in proper person. The Mohican appeared to comprehend the nature of the attempt his friend had made, intuitively; neither tongue nor feature betraying another symptom of surprise. When Hawkeye had cast his shaggy vestment, which was done by simply loosing certain thongs of skin, he drew a long glittering knife, and put it in the hands of Uncas.

"The red Hurons are without," he said; "let us be ready."

At the same time he laid his finger significantly on another similar weapon, both being the fruits of his prowess among their enemies during the evening.

"We will go," said Uncas.

"Whither?"

"To the Tortoises; they are the children of my grandfathers."

"Ay, lad," said the scout in English—a language he was apt to use when a little abstracted in mind; "the same blood runs in your veins, I believe; but time and distance has a little changed its color. What shall we do with the Mingoes at the door? They count six, and this singer is as good as nothing."

"The Hurons are boasters," said Uncas scornfully; "their 'totem' is a moose, and they run like snails. The Delawares are children of the tortoise, and they outstrip the deer."

"Ay, lad, there is truth in what you say; and I doubt not, on a rush, you would pass the whole nation; and, in a straight race of two miles, would be in, and get your breath again, afore a knave of them all was within hearing of the other village. But the gift of a white man lies more in his arms than in his legs. As for myself, I can brain a Huron as well as a better man; but when it comes to a race, the knaves would prove too much for me."

Uncas, who had already approached the door, in readiness to lead the way, now recoiled; and placed himself, once more, in the bottom of the lodge. But Hawkeye, who was too much occupied with his own thoughts to note the movement, continued speaking more to himself than to his companion.

"After all," he said, "it is unreasonable to keep one man in bondage to the gifts of another. So, Uncas, you had better take the leap, while I will put on the skin again, and trust to cunning for want of speed."

The young Mohican made no reply, but quietly folded his arms, and leaned his body against one of the upright posts that supported the wall of the hut.

"Well," said the scout, looking up at him, "why do you tarry? There will be time enough for me, as the knaves will give chase to you at first."

"Uncas will stay," was the calm reply.

"For what?"

"To fight with his father's brother, and die with the friend of the Delawares."

"Ay, lad," returned Hawkeye, squeezing the hand of Uncas between his own iron fingers; " 'twould have been more like a Mingo than a Mohican had you left me. But I thought I would make the offer, seeing that youth commonly loves life. Well, what can't be done by main courage, in war, must be done by circumvention. Put on the skin; I doubt not you can play the bear nearly as well as myself."

Whatever might have been the private opinion of Uncas of their respective abilities in this particular, his grave countenance manifested no opinion of his own superiority. He silently and expeditiously encased himself in the covering of the beast, and then awaited such other movements as his more aged companion saw fit to dictate.

"Now, friend," said Hawkeye, addressing David, "an exchange of garments will be a great convenience to you, inasmuch as you are but little accustomed to the makeshifts of the wilderness. Here, take my hunting shirt and cap, and give me your blanket and hat. You must trust me with the book and spectacles, as well as the tooter, too; if we ever meet again, in better times, you shall have all back again, with many thanks into the bargain."

David parted with the several articles named with a readiness that would have done great credit to his liberality, had he not certainly profited, in many particulars, by the exchange. Hawkeye was not long in assuming his borrowed garments; and when his restless eyes were hid behind the glasses, and his head was surmounted by the triangular beaver, as their statures were not dissimilar, he might readily have passed for the singer by starlight. As soon as these dispositions were made, the scout turned to David, and gave him his parting instructions.

"Are you much given to cowardice?" he bluntly asked, by way of obtaining a suitable understanding of the whole case before he ventured a prescription.

"My pursuits are peaceful, and my temper, I humbly trust, is greatly given to mercy and love," returned David, a little nettled at so direct an attack on his manhood; "but there are none who can say that I have ever forgotten my faith in the Lord, even in the greatest straits."

"Your chiefest danger will be at the moment when the savages find out that they have been deceived. If you are not then knocked in the head, your being a noncomposser will protect you; and you'll then have good reason to expect to die in your bed. If you stay, it must be to sit down here in the shadow, and take the part of Uncas, until such times as the cunning of the Indians discover the cheat, when, as I have already said, your time of trial will come. So choose for yourself,—to make a rush or tarry here."

"Even so," said David, firmly; "I will abide in the place of the Delaware. Bravely and generously has he battled in my behalf; and this, and more, will I dare in his service."

"You have spoken as a man, and like one who, under wiser schooling, would have been brought to better things. Hold your head down, and draw in your legs; their formation might tell the truth too early. Keep silent as long as may be; and it would be wise, when you do speak, to break out suddenly in one of your shoutings, which will serve to remind the Indians that you are not altogether as responsible as men should be. If, however, they take your scalp, as I trust and believe they will not, depend on it, Uncas and I will not forget the deed, but revenge it as becomes true warriors and trusty friends."

"Hold!" said David, perceiving that with this assurance they were about to leave him; "I am an unworthy and humble follower of One who taught not the damnable principle of revenge. Should I fall, therefore, seek no victims to my manes, but rather forgive my destroyers; and if you remember them at all, let it be in prayers for the enlightening of their minds, and for their eternal welfare."

The scout hesitated, and appeared to muse.

"There is a principle in that," he said, "different from the law of the woods; and yet it is fair and noble to reflect upon." Then, heaving a heavy sigh, probably among the last he ever drew in pining for a condition he had so long abandoned, he added—"It is what I would wish to practice myself, as one without a cross of blood, though it is not always easy to deal with an Indian as you would with a fellow Christian. God bless you, friend; I do believe your scent is not greatly wrong, when the matter is duly considered, and keeping eternity before the eyes, though much depends on the natural gifts, and the force of temptation."

So saying, the scout returned and shook David cordially by the hand; after which act of friendship he immediately left the lodge, attended by the new representative of the beast.

The instant Hawkeye found himself under the observation of the Hurons, he drew up his tall form in the rigid manner of David, threw out his arm in the act of keeping time, and commenced what he intended for an imitation of his psalmody. Happily for the success of this delicate adventure, he had to deal with ears but little practiced in the concord of sweet sounds, or the miserable effort would infallibly have been detected. It was necessary to pass within a dangerous proximity of the dark group of the savages, and the voice of the scout grew louder as they drew nigher. When at the nearest point, the Huron who spoke the English thrust out an arm, and stopped the supposed singing master.

"The Delaware dog!" he said, leaning forward, and peering through the dim light to catch the expression of the other's features; "is he afraid? will the Hurons hear his groans?"

A growl so exceedingly fierce and natural proceeded from the beast, that the young Indian released his hold and started aside, as if to assure himself that it was not a veritable bear, and no counterfeit, that was rolling before him. Hawkeye, who feared his voice would betray him to his subtle enemies, gladly profited by the interruption, to break out anew in such a burst of musical expression as would, probably, in a more refined state of society have been termed "a grand crash." Among his actual auditors, however, it merely gave him an additional claim to that respect which they never withhold from such as are believed to be the subjects of mental alienation. The little knot of Indians drew back in a body, and suffered, as they thought, the conjuror and his inspired assistant to proceed.

It required no common exercise of fortitude in Uncas and the scout, to continue the dignified and deliberate pace they had assumed in passing the lodges; especially as they immediately perceived that curiosity had so far mastered fear, as to induce the watchers to approach the hut, in order to witness the effect of the incantations. The least injudicious or impatient movement on the part of David might betray them, and time was absolutely necessary to insure the safety of the scout. The loud noise the latter conceived it politic to continue, drew many curious gazers to the doors of the different huts as they passed; and once or twice a dark-looking warrior stepped across their path, led to the act by superstition or watchfulness. They were not, however, interrupted; the darkness of the hour, and the boldness of the attempt, proving their principal friends.

The adventurers had got clear of the village, and were now swiftly approaching the shelter of the woods, when a loud and long cry arose from the lodge where Uncas had been confined. The Mohican started on his feet, and shook his shaggy covering, as though the animal he counterfeited was about to make some desperate effort.

"Hold!" said the scout, grasping his friend by the shoulder, "let them yell again! 'Twas nothing but wonderment."

He had no occasion to delay, for at the next instant a burst of cries filled the outer air, and ran along the whole extent of the village. Uncas cast his skin, and stepped forth in his own beautiful proportions. Hawk-eye tapped him lightly on the shoulder, and glided ahead.

"Now let the devils strike our scent!" said the scout, tearing two rifles, with all their attendant accoutrements, from beneath a bush, and flourishing Killdeer as he handed Uncas his weapon; "two, at least, will find it to their deaths."

Then throwing their pieces to a low trail, like sportsmen in readiness for their game, they dashed forward, and were soon buried in the somber darkness of the forest.

9

THE INDIANS naturally soon discovered that they had been deceived by Hawkeye and Major Heyward in their ingenious disguises, and that all four of their captives had made good their escape. The rage of Magua knew no bounds. He was too wise, however, to yield to the hotheaded tribesmen who wished to make an immediate assault on the Delaware encampment. Instead, he hurried runners in various directions to collect intelligence, ordered several spies to reconnoiter the Delaware village, sent his warriors to their lodges with a warning that they would soon be needed, and, escorted by twenty of the the best braves, each armed with a rifle, himself took the trail. Arrived at the camp of the Delawares, he distributed presents, conciliated the chiefs, and warning them that they had the dreaded Hawkeye or La longue Carabine in their midst, asked for a council. To this body he proffered his demand for a return of the prisoners. It was at once decided that so important a question must be submitted to the whole tribe, presided over by the venerable chief Tamenund.

With due ceremony, Tamenund appeared. The dress of the patriarch was a robe of the finest skins; his bosom was loaded with gold and silver medals, the gifts of various Christian potentates; his tomahawk was plated with silver, his knife handle seemed a horn of solid gold; his white locks were encircled by a plated diadem which bore three drooping ostrich feathers. With closed eyes, leaning on two aged supporters, he passed through the throng, and seated himself in the center of his nation "with the dignity of a monarch and the air of a father." After a decent pause, the principal chiefs approached the patriarch and placed his hands on their heads, as if they entreated a blessing; while the younger warriors were content to touch his robe. These acts performed, the prisoners were brought in.

Cora stood foremost among the prisoners, entwining her arms in those of Alice, in the tenderness of sisterly love. Nothwithstanding the fearful and menacing array of savages on every side of her, no apprehension on her own account could prevent the noble-minded maiden from keeping her eyes fastened on the pale and anxious features of the trembling Alice. Close at their side stood Heyward, with an interest in both, that, at such a moment of intense uncertainty, scarcely knew a preponderance in favor of her whom he most loved. Hawkeye had placed himself a little in the rear, with a deference to the superior rank of his companions, that no similarity in the state of their present fortunes could induce him to forget. Uncas was not there.

When perfect silence was again restored, and after the usual long, impressive pause, one of the two aged chiefs who sat at the side of the patriarch arose, and demanded aloud, in very intelligible English—

"Which of my prisoners is La longue Carabine?"

Neither Duncan nor the scout answered. The former, however, glanced his eyes around the dark and silent assembly, and recoiled a pace, when they fell on the malignant visage of Magua. He saw, at once, that this wily savage had some secret agency in their present arraignment before the nation, and determined to throw every possible impediment in the way of the execution of his sinister plans. He had witnessed one instance of the summary punishments of the Indians, and now dreaded that his companion was to be selected for a second. In this dilemma, with little or no time for reflection, he suddenly determined to cloak his invaluable friend, at any or every hazard to himself. Before he had time, however, to speak, the question was repeated in a louder voice, and with a clearer utterance.

"Give us arms," the young man haughtily replied, "and place us in yonder woods. Our deeds shall speak for us!"

"This is the warrior whose name has filled our ears!" returned the chief, regarding Heyward with that sort of curious interest which seems inseparable from man, when first beholding one of his fellows to whom merit or accident, virtue or crime, has given notoriety. "What has brought the white man into the camp of the Delawares?"

"My necessities. I come for food, shelter, and friends."

"It cannot be. The woods are full of game. The head of a warrior needs no other shelter than a sky without clouds; and the Delawares are the enemies, and not the friends, of the Yengeese. Go—the mouth has spoken, while the heart said nothing."

Duncan, a little at a loss in what manner to proceed, remained silent; but the scout, who had listened attentively to all that passed, now advanced steadily to the front.

"That I did not answer to the call for La longue Carabine, was not owing either to shame or fear," he said; "for neither one nor the other is the gift of an honest man. But I do not admit the right of the Mingoes to bestow a name on one whose friends have been mindful of his gifts, in this particular; especially as their title is a lie, Killdeer being a grooved barrel and no carabyne. I am the man, however, that got the name of Nathaniel from my kin; the compliment of Hawkeye from the Delawares, who live on their own river; and whom the Iroquois have presumed to style the Long Rifle, without any warranty from him who is most concerned in the matter."

The eyes of all present, which had hitherto been gravely scanning the person of Duncan, were now turned, on the instant, toward the upright iron frame of this new pretender to the distinguished appellation. It was in no degree remarkable that there should be found two who were willing to claim so great an honor, for impostors, though rare, were not unknown amongst the natives; but it was altogether material to the just and severe intentions of the Delawares, that there should be no mistake in the matter. Some of their old men consulted together in private, and then, as it would seem, they determined to interrogate their visitor on the subject.

"My brother has said that a snake crept into my camp," said the chief to Magua; "which is he?"

The Huron pointed to the scout.

"Will a wise Delaware believe the barking of a wolf?" exclaimed Duncan, still more confirmed in the evil intentions of his ancient enemy: "a dog never lies, but when was a wolf known to speak the truth?"

The eyes of Magua flashed fire; but, suddenly recollecting the necessity of maintaining his presence of mind, he turned away in silent disdain, well assured that the sagacity of the Indians would not fail to extract the real merits of the point in controversy. He was not deceived; for, after another short consultation, the wary Delaware turned to him again, and expressed the determination of the chiefs, though in the most considerate language.

"My brother has been called a liar," he said, "and his friends are angry. They will show that he has spoken the truth. Give my prisoners guns, and let them prove which is the man."

Magua affected to consider the expedient, which he well knew proceeded from distrust of himself, as a compliment, and made a gesture of acquiescence, well content that his veracity should be supported by so skilful a marksman as the scout. The weapons were instantly placed in the hands of the friendly opponents, and they were bid to fire, over the heads of the seated multitude, at an earthen vessel, which lay, by accident, on a stump, some fifty yards from the place where they stood.

Heyward smiled to himself at the idea of a competition with the scout, though he determined to persevere in the deception, until apprised of the real designs of Magua. Raising his rifle with the utmost care, and renewing his aim three several times, he fired. The bullet cut the wood within a few inches of the vessel; and a general exclamation of satisfaction announced that the shot was considered a proof of great skill in the use of the weapon. Even Hawkeye nodded his head, as if he would say, it was better than he had expected. But, instead of manifesting an intention to contend with the successful marksman, he stood leaning on his rifle for more than a minute, like a man who was completely buried in thought. From this reverie he was, however, awakened by one of the young Indians who had furnished the arms, and who now touched his shoulder, saying in exceedingly broken English—

"Can the paleface beat it?"

"Yes, Huron!" exclaimed the scout, raising the short rifle in his right hand, and shaking it at Magua, with as much apparent ease as if it were a reed; "yes, Huron, I could strike you now, and no power of 'arth could prevent the deed! The soaring hawk is not more certain of the dove than I am this moment of you, did I choose to send a bullet to your heart! Why should I not? Why!—because the gifts of my color forbid it, and I might draw down evil on tender and innocent heads! If you know such a being as God, thank him, therefore, in your inward soul—for you have reason!"

The flushed countenance, angry eye, and swelling figure of the scout, produced a sensation of secret awe in all that heard him. The Delawares held their breath in expectation; but Magua himself, even while he distrusted the forbearance of his enemy, remained inmovable and calm, where he stood wedged in by the crowd, as one who grew to the spot.

"Beat it," repeated the young Delaware at the elbow of the scout.

"Beat what; fool!—what!"—exclaimed Hawkeye, still flourishing the weapon angrily above his head, though his eye no longer sought the person of Magua.

"If the white man is the warrior he pretends," said the aged chief, "let him strike nigher to the mark."

The scout laughed aloud—a noise that produced the startling effect of an unnatural sound on Heyward—then dropping the piece, heavily, into his extended left hand, it was discharged, apparently by the shock, driving the fragments of the vessel into the air, and scattering them on every side. Almost at the same instant, the rattling sound of the rifle was heard, as he suffered it to fall, contemptuously, to the earth.

The first impression of so strange a scene was engrossing admiration. Then a low, but increasing murmur, ran through the multitude, and finally swelled into sounds that denoted a lively opposition in the sentiments of the spectators. While some openly testified their satisfaction at so unexampled dexterity, by far the larger portion of the tribe were inclined to believe the success of the shot was the result of accident. Heyward was not slow to confirm an opinion that was so favorable to his own pretensions.

"It was chance!" he exclaimed; "none can shoot without an aim!"

"Chance!" echoed the excited woodsman, who was now stubbornly bent on maintaining his identity at every hazard, and on whom the secret hints of Heyward to acquiesce in the deception were entirely lost. "Does yonder lying Huron, too, think it chance? Give him another gun, and place us face to face, without cover or dodge, and let Providence, and our own eyes, decide the matter atween us! I do not make the offer to you, major; for our blood is of a color, and we serve the same master."

"That the Huron is a liar, is very evident," returned Heyward, coolly; "you have yourself heard him assert you to be La longue Carabine."

It were impossible to say what violent assertion the stubborn Hawkeye would have next made, in his headlong wish to vindicate his identity, had not the aged Delaware once more interposed.

"The hawk which comes from the clouds can return when he will," he said; "give them the guns."

This time the scout seized the rifle with avidity; nor had Magua, though he watched the movement of the marksman with jealous eyes, any further cause for apprehension.

"Now let it be proved, in the face of this tribe of Delawares, which is the better man," cried the scout, tapping the butt of his piece with that finger which had pulled so many fatal triggers. "You see the gourd hanging against yonder tree, major; if you are a marksman fit for the borders, let me see you break its shell!"

Duncan noted the object, and prepared himself to renew the trial. The gourd was one of the usual little vessels used by the Indians, and it was suspended from a dead branch of a small pine, by a thong of deerskin, at the full distance of a hundred yards. So strangely compounded is the feeling of self-love, that the young soldier, while he knew the utter worthlessness of the suffrages of his savage umpires, forgot the sudden motives of the contest in a wish to excel. It has been seen, already, that his skill was far from being contemptible, and he now resolved to put forth its nicest qualities. Had his life depended on the issue, the aim of Duncan could not have been more deliberate or guarded. He fired; and three or four young Indians, who sprang forward at the report, announced with a shout, that the ball was in the tree, a very little on one side of the proper object. The warriors uttered a common ejaculation of pleasure, and then turned their eyes, inquiringly, on the movements of his rival.

"It may do for the Royal Americans!" said Hawkeye, laughing once more in his own silent, heartfelt manner; "but had my gun often turned so much from the true line, many a marten, whose skin is now in a lady's muff, would still be in the woods; ay, and many a bloody Mingo, who has departed to his final account, would be acting his deviltries at this very day, atween the provinces. I hope the squaw who owns the gourd has more of them in her wigwam, for this will never hold water again!"

The scout had shook his priming, and cocked his piece, while speaking; and, as he ended, he threw back a foot, and slowly raised the muzzle from the earth: the motion was steady, uniform, and in one direction. When on a perfect level, it remained for a single moment, without tremor or variation, as though both man and rifle were carved in stone. During that stationary instant, it poured forth its contents, in a bright, glancing sheet of flame. Again the young Indians bounded forward; but their hurried search and disappointed looks announced that no traces of the bullet were to be seen.

"Go," said the old chief to the scout, in a tone of strong disgust; "thou art a wolf in the skin of a dog. I will talk to the Long Rifle of the Yengeese."

"Ah! had I that piece which furnished the name you use, I would obligate myself to cut the thong, and drop the gourd without breaking it!" returned Hawkeye, perfectly undisturbed by the other's manner. "Fools, if you would find the bullet of a sharpshooter of these woods, you must look *in* the object and not around it!"

The Indian youths instantly comprehended his meaning—for this time he spoke in the Delaware tongue—and tearing the gourd from the tree, they held it on high with an exulting shout, displaying a hole in its bottom, which had been cut by the bullet, after passing through the usual orifice in the center of its upper side. At this unexpected exhibition, a loud and vehement expression of pleasure burst from the mouth of every warrior present. It decided the question, and effectually established Hawkeye in the possession of his dangerous reputation. Those curious and admiring eyes which had been turned again on Heyward, were finally directed to the weather-beaten form of the scout, who immediately became the principal object of attention to the simple and unsophisticated beings by whom he was surrounded. When the sudden and noisy commotion had a little subsided, the aged chief resumed his examination.

"Why did you wish to stop my ears?" he said, addressing Duncan; "are the Delawares fools, that they could not know the young panther from the cat?"

"They will yet find the Huron a singing bird," said Duncan, endeavoring to adopt the figurative language of the natives.

"It is good. We will know who can shut the ears of men. Brother," added the chief, turning his eyes on Magua, "the Delawares listen."

Thus singled, and directly called on to declare his object, the Huron arose; and advancing with great deliberation and dignity, into the very center of the circle, where he stood confronted to the prisoners, he placed himself in an attitude to speak. Before opening his mouth, however, he bent his eyes slowly along the whole living boundary of earnest faces, as if to temper his expressions to the capacities of his audience. On Hawkeye he cast a glance of respectful enmity; on Duncan, a look of inextinguishable hatred; the shrinking figure of Alice he scarcely deigned to notice; but when his glance met the firm, commanding, and yet lovely form of Cora, his eye lingered a moment, with an expression that it might have been difficult to define. Then, filled with his own dark intentions, he spoke in the language of the Canadas, a tongue that he well knew was comprehended by most of his auditors.

"The Spirit that made men colored them differently," commenced the subtle Huron. "Some are blacker than the sluggish bear. These he said should be slaves; and he ordered them to work forever, like the beaver. You may hear them groan, when the south wind blows, louder than the lowing buffaloes, along the shores of the Great Salt Lake, where the big canoes come and go with them in droves. Some he made with faces paler than the ermine of the forests: and these he ordered to be traders; dogs to their women, and wolves to their slaves. He gave this people the nature of the pigeon; wings that never tire: young, more plentiful than the leaves on the trees, and appetites to devour the earth. He gave them tongues like the false call of the wildcat; hearts like rabbits; the cunning of the hog (but none of the fox), and arms longer than the legs of the moose. With his tongue, he stops the ears of the Indians; his heart teaches him to pay warriors to fight his battles; his cunning tells him how to get together the goods of the earth; and his arms inclose the land from the shores of the salt water to the islands of the Great Lake. His gluttony makes him sick. God gave him enough, and yet he wants all. Such are the palefaces.

"Some the Great Spirit made with skins brighter and redder than yonder sun," continued Magua, pointing impressively upward to the lurid luminary, which was struggling through the misty atmosphere of the horizon; "and these did he fashion to his own mind. He gave them this island as he had made it, covered with trees, and filled with game. The wind made their clearings; the sun and rains ripened their fruits; and the snows came to tell them to be thankful. What need had they of roads to journey by! They saw through the hills! When the beavers worked, they lay in the shade, and looked on. The winds cooled them in summer; in winter, skins kept them warm. If they fought among themselves, it was to prove that they were men. They were brave; they were just; they were happy."

Here the speaker paused, and again looked around him, to discover if his legend had touched the sympathies of his listeners. He met everywhere with eyes riveted on his own, heads erect, and nostrils expanded, as if each individual present felt himself able and willing, singly, to redress the wrongs of his race.

"If the Great Spirit gave different tongues to his red children," he continued, in a low, still melancholy voice, "it was that all animals might understand them. Some he placed among the snows, with their cousin the bear. Some he placed near the setting sun, on the road to the happy hunting grounds; some, on the lands around the great fresh waters; but to his greatest, and most beloved, he gave the sands of the Salt Lake. Do my brothers know the name of this favored people?"

"It was the Lenape!" exclaimed twenty eager voices, in a breath.

"It was the Lenni Lenape," returned Magua, affecting to bend his head in reverence to their former greatness. "It was the tribes of the Lenape! The sun rose from water that was salt, and set in water that was sweet, and never hid himself from their eyes. But why should I, a Huron of the woods, tell a wise people their own traditions? Why remind them of their injuries; their ancient greatness; their deeds; their glory; their happiness:—their losses; their defeats; their misery? Is there not one among them who has seen it all, and who knows it to be true? I have done. My tongue is still, for my heart is of lead. I listen."

As the voice of the speaker suddenly ceased, every face and all eyes turned, by a common movement, toward the venerable Tamenund.[1] From the moment that he took his seat, until the present instant, the lips of the patriarch had not severed, and scarcely a sign of life had escaped him. He sat bent in feebleness, and apparently unconscious of the presence he was in, during the whole of that opening scene, in which the skill of the scout had been so clearly established. At the nicely graduated sounds of Magua's voice, however, he betrayed some evidence of consciousness, and once or twice he even raised his head,

[1] Little is known of the career of Tamenund, a mythical rather than a historical figure. In 1683 he offered his totem or mark to a deed conveying land in what is now Bucks County, Pennsylvania, to William Penn. His reputation for wisdom, integrity, and benevolence was great in his own lifetime, and later grew. Some of the legends that clustered about his name were collected by Samuel G. Drake.—Ed.

as if to listen. But when the crafty Huron spoke of his nation by name, the eyelids of the old man raised themselves, and he looked out upon the multitude with that sort of dull unmeaning expression which might be supposed to belong to the countenance of a specter. Then he made an effort to rise, and being upheld by his supporters, he gained his feet, in a posture commanding by its dignity, while he tottered with weakness.

"Who calls upon the children of the Lenape!" he said, in a deep, guttural voice, that was rendered awfully audible by the breathless silence of the multitude: "who speaks of things gone! Does not the egg become a worm—the worm a fly, and perish? Why tell the Delawares of good that is past? Better thank the Manitou for that which remains."

"It is a Wyandot," said Magua, stepping nigher to the rude platform on which the other stood; "a friend of Tamenund." [1]

"A friend!" repeated the sage, on whose brow a dark frown settled, imparting a portion of that severity which had rendered his eye so terrible in middle age—"Are the Mingoes rulers of the earth? What brings a Huron here?"

"Justice. His prisoners are with his brothers, and he comes for his own."

Tamenund turned his head toward one of his supporters, and listened to the short explanation the man gave. Then facing the applicant, he regarded him a moment with deep attention; after which he said, in a low and reluctant voice:—

"Justice is the law of the great Manitou. My children, give the stranger food. Then, Huron, take thine own and depart."

On the delivery of this solemn judgment, the patriarch seated himself, and closed his eyes again, as if better pleased with the images of his own ripened experience than with the visible objects of the world. Against such a decree there was no Delaware sufficiently hardy to murmur, much less oppose himself. The words were barely uttered when four or five of the younger warriors stepping behind Heyward and the scout, passed thongs so dexterously and rapidly around their arms, as to hold them both in instant bondage. The former was too much engrossed with his precious and nearly insensible burden, to be aware of their intentions before they were executed; and the latter, who considered even the hostile tribes of the Delawares a superior race of beings, submitted without resistance. Perhaps, however, the manner of the scout would not have been so passive, had he fully comprehended the language in which the preceding dialogue had been conducted.

Magua cast a look of triumph around the whole assembly before he proceeded to the execution of his purpose. Perceiving that the men

[1] The Wyandots were a remnant of the Hurons, so nearly wiped out by the Iroquois.—Ed.

were unable to offer any resistance, he turned his looks on her he valued most. Cora met his gaze with an eye so calm and firm, that his resolution wavered. Then recollecting his former artifice, he raised Alice from the arms of the warrior against whom she leaned, and beckoning Heyward to follow, he motioned for the encircling crowd to open. But Cora, instead of obeying the impulse he had expected, rushed to the feet of the patriarch, and raising her voice, exclaimed aloud:—

"Just and venerable Delaware, on thy wisdom and power we lean for mercy! Be deaf to yonder artful and remorseless monster, who poisons thy ears with falsehoods to feed his thirst for blood. Thou that hast lived long, and that hast seen the evil of the world, should know how to temper its calamities to the miserable."

The eyes of the old man opened heavily, and he once more looked upward at the multitude. As the piercing tones of the supplicant swelled on his ears, they moved slowly in the direction of her person, and finally settled there in a steady gaze. Cora had cast herself to her knees; and, with hands clenched in each other and pressed upon her bosom, she remained like a beauteous and breathing model of her sex, looking up in his faded, but majestic countenance, with a species of holy reverence. Gradually the expression of Tamenund's features changed, and losing their vacancy in admiration, they lighted with a portion of that intelligence which a century before had been wont to communicate his youthful fire to the extensive bands of the Delawares. Rising without assistance, and seemingly without an effort, he demanded, in a voice that startled its auditors by its firmness—

"What art thou?"

"A woman. One of a hated race, if thou wilt—a Yengee. But one who has never harmed thee, and who cannot harm thy people, if she would; who asks for succor."

"Tell me, my children," continued the patriarch, hoarsely, motioning to those around him, though his eyes still dwelt upon the kneeling form of Cora, "where have the Delawares 'camped?"

"In the mountains of the Iroquois, beyond the clear springs of the Horican."

"Many parching summers are come and gone," continued the sage, "since I drank of the waters of my own river. The children of Minquon [1] are the justest white men; but they were thirsty, and they took it to themselves. Do they follow us so far?"

---

[1] William Penn was termed Minquon by the Delawares, and, as he never used violence or injustice in his dealings with them, his reputation for probity passed into a proverb. The American is justly proud of the origin of his nation, which is perhaps unequalled in the history of the world; but the Pennsylvanian and Jerseyman have more reason to value themselves in their ancestors than the natives of any other state, since no wrong was done the original owners of the soil. (*Cooper's note*)

"We follow none; we covet nothing," answered Cora. "Captives against our wills, have we been brought amongst you; and we ask but permission to depart to our own in peace. Art thou not Tamenund—the father—the judge—I had almost said, the prophet—of this people?"

"I am Tamenund of many days."

" 'Tis now some seven years that one of thy people was at the mercy of a white chief on the borders of this province. He claimed to be of the blood of the good and just Tamenund. 'Go,' said the white man, 'for thy parent's sake thou art free.' Does thou remember the name of that English warrior?"

"I remember, that when a laughing boy," returned the patriarch, with the peculiar recollection of vast age, "I stood upon the sands of the seashore, and saw a big canoe with wings whiter than the swan's, and wider than many eagles, come from the rising sun—"

"Nay, nay; I speak not of a time so very distant, but of favor shown to thy kindred by one of mine, within the memory of thy youngest warrior."

"Was it when the Yengeese and the Dutchmanne fought for the hunting grounds of the Delawares? Then Tamenund was a chief, and first laid aside the bow for the lightning of the palefaces—" "Nor yet then," interrupted Cora, "by many ages; I speak of a thing of yesterday. Surely, surely, you forget it not."

"It was but yesterday," rejoined the aged man with touching pathos, "that the children of the Lenape were masters of the world. The fishes of the salt lake, the birds, the beasts, and the Mengwee of the woods, owned them for Sagamores."

Cora bowed her head in disappointment, and, for a bitter moment, struggled with her chagrin. Then elevating her rich features and beaming eyes, she continued, in tones scarcely less penetrating than the unearthly voice of the patriarch himself—

"Tell me, is Tamenund a father?"

The old man looked down upon her from his elevated stand with a benignant smile on his wasted countenance, and then casting his eyes slowly over the whole assemblage, he answered—

"Of a nation."

"For myself I ask nothing. Like thee and thine, venerable chief," she continued, pressing her hands convulsively on her heart, and suffering her head to droop until her burning cheeks were nearly concealed in the maze of dark glossy tresses that fell in disorder upon her shoulders, "the curse of my ancestors has fallen heavily on their child. But yonder is one who has never known the weight of Heaven's displeasure until now. She is the daughter of an old and failing man, whose days are near their close. She has many, very many, to love her, and delight in her; and she is too good, much too precious, to become the victim of that villain."

"I know that the palefaces are a proud and hungry race. I know that they claim not only to have the earth, but that the meanest of their color is better than the Sachems of the red man. The dogs and crows of their tribes," continued the earnest old chieftain, without heeding the wounded spirit of his listener, whose head was nearly crushed to the earth in shame, as he proceeded, "would bark and caw before they would take a woman to their wigwams whose blood was not of the color of snow. But let them not boast before the face of the Manitou too loud. They entered the land at the rising, and may yet go off at the setting sun. I have often seen the locusts strip the leaves from the trees, but the season of blossoms has always come again."

"It is so," said Cora, drawing a long breath, as if reviving from a trance, raising her face, and shaking back her shining veil, with a kindling eye, that contradicted the deathlike paleness of her countenance; "but why—it is not permitted us to inquire. There is yet one of thine own people who has not been brought before thee; before thou lettest the Huron depart in triumph, hear him speak."

Observing Tamenund to look about him doubtingly, one of his companions said—

"It is a snake—a redskin in the pay of the Yengeese. We keep him for the torture."

"Let him come," returned the sage.

Then Tamenund once more sank into his seat, and a silence so deep prevailed, while the young men prepared to obey his simple mandate, that the leaves, which fluttered in the draught of the light morning air, were distinctly heard rustling in the surrounding forest.

The silence continued unbroken by human sounds for many anxious minutes. Then the waving multitude opened and shut again, and Uncas stood in the living circle. All those eyes, which had been curiously studying the lineaments of the sage, as the source of their own intelligence, turned on the instant, and were now bent in secret admiration on the erect, agile, and faultless person of the captive. But neither the presence in which he found himself, nor the exclusive attention that he attracted, in any manner disturbed the self-possession of the young Mohican. He cast a deliberate and observing look on every side of him, meeting the settled expression of hostility that lowered in the visages of the chiefs, with the same calmness as the curious gaze of the attentive children. But when, last in his haughty scrutiny, the person of Tamenund came under his glance, his eye became fixed, as though all other objects were already forgotten. Then advancing with a slow and noiseless step up the area, he placed himself immediately before the footstool of the sage. Here he stood unnoted, though keenly observant himself, until one of the chiefs apprised the latter of his presence.

"With what tongue does the prisoner speak to the Manitou?" demanded the patriarch without unclosing his eyes.

"Like his fathers," Uncas replied; "with the tongue of a Delaware."

At this sudden and unexpected annunciation, a low, fierce yell ran through the multitude, that might not inaptly be compared to the growl of the lion, as his choler is first awakened—a fearful omen of the weight of his future anger. The effect was equally strong on the sage, though differently exhibited. He passed a hand before his eyes, as if to exclude the least evidence of so shameful a spectacle, while he repeated, in his low, guttural tones, the words he had just heard.

"A Delaware! I have lived to see the tribes of the Lenape driven from their council fires, and scattered, like broken herds of deer, among the hills of the Iroquois! I have seen the hatchets of a strange people sweep woods from the valleys that the winds of Heaven had spared! The beasts that run on the mountains, and the birds that fly above the trees, have I seen living in the wigwams of men; but never before have I found a Delaware so base as to creep, like a poisonous serpent, into the camps of his nation."

"The singing birds have opened their bills," returned Uncas, in the softest notes of his own musical voice; "and Tamenund has heard their song."

The sage started, and bent his head aside, as if to catch the fleeting sounds of some passing melody.

"Does Tamenund dream!" he exclaimed. "What voice is at his ear! Have the winters gone backward! Will summer come again to the children of the Lenape!"

A solemn and respectful silence succeeded this incoherent burst from the lips of the Delaware prophet. His people readily construed his unintelligible language into one of those mysterious conferences he was believed to hold so frequently with a superior intelligence, and they awaited the issue of the revelation in awe. After a patient pause, however, one of the aged men, perceiving that the sage had lost the recollection of the subject before them, ventured to remind him again of the presence of the prisoner.

"The false Delaware trembles lest he should hear the words of Tamenund," he said. " 'Tis a hound that howls, when the Yengeese show him a trail."

"And ye," returned Uncas, looking sternly around him, "are dogs that whine, when the Frenchman casts ye the offals of his deer!"

Twenty knives gleamed in the air, and as many warriors sprang to their feet, at this biting, and perhaps merited, retort; but a motion from one of the chiefs suppressed the outbreaking of their tempers, and restored the appearance of quiet. The task might probably have been more difficult had not a movement made by Tamenund indicated that he was again about to speak.

"Delaware!" resumed the sage, "little art thou worthy of thy name. My people have not seen a bright sun in many winters; and the warrior who deserts his tribe when hid in clouds is doubly a traitor. The law of the Manitou is just. It is so; while the rivers run and the mountains stand, while the blossoms come and go on the trees, it must be so. He is thine, my children; deal justly by him."

Not a limb was moved, nor was a breath drawn louder and longer than common, until the closing syllable of this final decree had passed the lips of Tamenund. Then a cry of vengeance burst at once, as it might be, from the united lips of the nation; a frightful augury of their ruthless intentions. In the midst of these prolonged and savage yells, a chief proclaimed, in a high voice, that the captive was condemned to endure the dreadful trial of torture by fire. The circle broke its order, and screams of delight mingled with the bustle and tumult of preparation. Heyward struggled madly with his captors; the anxious eyes of Hawkeye began to look around him with an expression of peculiar earnestness; and Cora again threw herself at the feet of the patriarch, once more a suppliant for mercy.

Throughout the whole of these trying moments Uncas had alone preserved his serenity. He looked on the preparations with a steady eye, and when the tormentors came to seize him, he met them with a firm and upright attitude. One among them, if possible, more fierce and savage than his fellows, seized the hunting shirt of the young warrior, and at a single effort tore it from his body. Then, with a yell of frantic pleasure, he leaped toward his unresisting victim, and prepared to lead him to the stake. But, at that moment, when he appeared most a stranger to the feelings of humanity, the purpose of the savage was arrested as suddenly as if a supernatural agency had interposed in the behalf of Uncas. The eyeballs of the Delaware seemed to start from their sockets; his mouth opened, and his whole form became frozen in an attitude of amazement. Raising his hand with a slow and regulated motion, he pointed with a finger to the bosom of the captive. His companions crowded about him in wonder, and every eye was, like his own, fastened intently on the figure of a small tortoise, beautifully tattooed on the breast of the prisoner, in a bright blue tint.[1]

For a single instant Uncas enjoyed his triumph, smiling calmly on

[1] Not only was the tortoise, as Uncas says, supposed to bear the earth on his back; inhabiting both land and water, he was an agent of communication between the upper world and the nether.—Ed.

the scene. Then motioning the crowd away with a high and haughty sweep of his arm, he advanced in front of the nation with the air of a king, and spoke in a voice louder than the murmur of admiration that ran through the multitude.

"Men of the Lenni Lenape!" he said, "my race upholds the earth! Your feeble tribe stands on my shell! What fire that a Delaware can light would burn the child of my fathers," he added, pointing proudly to the simple blazonry on his skin; "the blood that came from such a stock would smother your flames! My race is the grandfather of nations!"

"Who art thou?" demanded Tamenund, rising at the startling tones he heard, more than at any meaning conveyed by the language of the prisoner.

"Uncas, the son of Chingachgook," answered the captive modestly, turning from the nation, and bending his head in reverence to the other's character and years; "a son of the great Unamis."

"The hour of Tamenund is nigh!" exclaimed the sage; "the day is come, at last, to the night! I thank the Manitou, that one is here to fill my place at the council fire. Uncas, the child of Uncas, is found! Let the eyes of a dying eagle gaze on the rising sun."

The youth stepped lightly, but proudly, on the platform, where he became visible to the whole agitated and wondering multitude. Tamenund held him long at the length of his arm, and read every turn in the fine lineaments of his countenance, with the untiring gaze of one who recalled days of happiness.

"Is Tamenund a boy?" at length the bewildered prophet exclaimed. "Have I dreamt of so many snows—that my people were scattered like floating sands—of Yengeese, more plenty than the leaves on the trees! The arrow of Tamenund would not frighten the fawn; his arm is withered like the branch of a dead oak; the snail would be swifter in the race; yet is Uncas before him as they went to battle against the palefaces! Uncas, the panther of his tribe, the eldest son of the Lenape, the wisest Sagamore of the Mohicans! Tell me, ye Delawares, has Tamenund been a sleeper for a hundred winters?"

The calm and deep silence which succeeded these words sufficiently announced the awful reverence with which his people received the communication of the patriarch. None dared to answer, though all listened in breathless expectation of what might follow. Uncas, however, looking in his face with the fondness and veneration of a favored child, presumed on his own high and acknowledged rank, to reply.

"Four warriors of his race have lived, and died," he said, "since the friend of Tamenund led his people in battle. The blood of the Turtle has been in many chiefs, but all have gone back into the earth from whence they came except Chingachgook and his son."

"It is true—it is true," returned the sage—a flash of recollection destroying all his pleasing fancies, and restoring him at once to a consciousness of the true history of his nation. "Our wise men have often said that two warriors of the unchanged race were in the hills of the Yengeese; why have their seats at the council fires of the Delawares been so long empty?"

At these words the young man raised his head, which he had still kept bowed a little, in reverence; and lifting his voice so as to be heard by the multitude, as if to explain at once and forever the policy of his family, he said aloud—

"Once we slept where we could hear the salt lake speak in its anger. Then we were rulers and Sagamores over the land. But when a paleface was seen on every brook, we followed the deer back to the river of our nation. The Delawares were gone. Few warriors of them all stayed to drink of the stream they loved. Then said my fathers, 'Here will we hunt. The waters of the river go into the salt lake. If we go toward the setting sun, we shall find streams that run into the great lakes of sweet water; there would a Mohican die, like fishes of the sea, in the clear springs. When the Manitou is ready, and shall say "come," we will follow the river to the sea, and take our own again.' Such, Delawares, is the belief of the children of the Turtle. Our eyes are on the rising, and not toward the setting sun. We know whence he comes, but we know not whither he goes. It is enough."

The men of the Lenape listened to his words with all the respect that superstition could lend, finding a secret charm even in the figurative language with which the young Sagamore imparted his ideas. Uncas himself watched the effect of his brief explanation with intelligent eyes, and gradually dropped the air of authority he had assumed, as he perceived that his auditors were content. Then permitting his looks to wander over the silent throng that crowded around the elevated seat of Tamenund, he first perceived Hawkeye in his bonds. Stepping eagerly from his stand, he made way for himself to the side of his friend; and cutting his thongs with a quick and angry stroke of his own knife, he motioned to the crowd to divide. The Indians silently obeyed, and once more they stood ranged in their circle, as before his appearance among them. Uncas took the scout by the hand, and led him to the feet of the patriarch.

"Father," he said, "look at this paleface; a just man, and the friend of the Delawares."

"Is he a son of Miquon?"

"Not so; a warrior known to the Yengeese, and feared by the Maquas."

"What name has he gained by his deeds?"

"We call him Hawkeye," Uncas replied, using the Delaware

phrase; "for his sight never fails. The Mingoes know him better by the death he gives their warriors: with them he is the Long Rifle."

"La longue Carabine!" exclaimed Tamenund, opening his eyes, and regarding the scout sternly. "My son has not done well to call him friend."

"I call him so who proves himself such," returned the young chief, with great calmness, but with a steady mien. "If Uncas is welcome among the Delawares, then is Hawkeye with his friends."

"The paleface has slain my young men; his name is great for the blows he has struck the Lenape."

"If a Mingo has whispered that much in the ear of the Delaware, he has only shown that he is a singing bird," said the scout, who now believed that it was time to vindicate himself from such offensive charges, and who spoke in the tongue of the man he addressed, modifying his Indian figures, however, with his own peculiar notions. "That I have slain the Maquas I am not the man to deny, even at their own council fires; but that, knowingly, my hand has ever harmed a Delaware, is opposed to the reason of my gifts, which is friendly to them, and all that belongs to their nation."

A low exclamation of applause passed among the warriors, who exchanged looks with each other like men that first began to perceive their error.

"Where is the Huron?" demanded Tamenund. "Has he stopped my ears?"

Magua, whose feelings during that scene in which Uncas had triumphed may be much better imagined than described, answered to the call by stepping boldly in front of the patriarch.

"The just Tamenund," he said, "will not keep what a Huron has lent."

"Tell me, son of my brother," returned the sage, avoiding the dark countenance of Le Subtil, and turning gladly to the more ingenuous features of Uncas, "has the stranger a conqueror's right over you?"

"He has none. The panther may get into snares set by the women; but he is strong, and knows how to leap through them."

"La longue Carabine?"

"Laughs at the Mingoes. Go, Huron, ask your squaws the color of a bear."

"The stranger and the white maiden that came into my camp together?"

"Should journey on an open path."

"And the woman that the Huron left with my warriors?"

Uncas made no reply.

"And the woman that the Mingo has brought into my camp," repeated Tamenund, gravely.

"She is mine," cried Magua, shaking his hand in triumph at Uncas. "Mohican, you know that she is mine."

"My son is silent," said Tamenund, endeavoring to read the expression of the face that the youth turned from him in sorrow.

"It is so," was the low answer.

A short and impressive pause succeeded, during which it was very apparent with what reluctance the multitude admitted the justice of the Mingo's claim. At length the sage, on whom alone the decision depended, said, in a firm voice,—

"Huron, depart."

"As he came, just Tamenund," demanded the wily Magua; "or with hands filled with the faith of the Delawares? The wigwam of Le Renard Subtil is empty. Make him strong with his own."

The aged man mused with himself for a time; and then bending his head towards one of his venerable companions, he asked—

"Are my ears open?"

"It is true."

"Is this Mingo a chief?"

"The first in his nation."

"Girl, what wouldst thou? A great warrior takes thee to wife. Go; thy race will not end."

"Better, a thousand times, it should," exclaimed the horror-struck Cora, "than meet with such a degradation!"

"Huron, her mind is in the tents of her fathers. An unwilling maiden makes an unhappy wigwam."

"She speaks with the tongue of her people," returned Magua, regarding his victim with a look of bitter irony. "She is of a race of traders, and will bargain for a bright look. Let Tamenund speak the words."

"Take you the wampum, and our love."

"Nothing hence but what Magua brought hither."

"Then depart with thine own. The Great Manitou forbids that a Delaware should be unjust."

Magua advanced, and seized his captive strongly by the arm; the Delawares fell back, in silence; and Cora, as if conscious that remonstrance would be useless, prepared to submit to her fate without resistance.

"Hold, hold!" cried Duncan, springing forward; "Huron, have mercy! her ransom shall make thee richer than any of thy people were ever yet known to be."

"Magua is a redskin; he wants not the beads of the palefaces."

"Gold, silver, powder, lead—all that a warrior needs shall be in thy wigwam; all that becomes the greatest chief."

"Le Subtil is very strong," cried Magua, violently shaking the hand which grasped the unresisting arm of Cora; "he has his revenge!"

"Mighty ruler of Providence!" exclaimed Heyward, clasping his hands together in agony, "can this be suffered! To you, just Tamenund, I appeal for mercy."

"The words of the Delaware are said," returned the sage, closing his eyes, and dropping back into his seat, alike wearied with his mental and his bodily exertion. "Men speak not twice."

"That a chief should not misspend his time in unsaying what has once been spoken, is wise and reasonable," said Hawkeye, motioning to Duncan to be silent; "but it is also prudent in every warrior to consider well before he strikes his tomahawk into the head of his prisoner. Huron, I love you not; nor can I say that any Mingo has ever received much favor at my hands. It is fair to conclude, that, if this war does not soon end, many more of your warriors will meet me in the woods. Put it to your judgment, then, whether you would prefer taking such a prisoner as that into your encampment, or one like myself, who am a man that it would greatly rejoice your nation to see with naked hands."

"Will the Long Rifle give his life for the woman?" demanded Magua, hesitatingly; for he had already made a motion towards quitting the place with his victim.

"No, no; I have not said so much as that," returned Hawkeye, drawing back with suitable discretion, when he noted the eagerness with which Magua listened to his proposal. "It would be an unequal exchange, to give a warrior, in the prime of his age and usefulness, for the best woman on the frontiers. I might consent to go into winter quarters, now—at least six weeks afore the leaves will turn—on condition you will release the maiden."

Magua shook his head, and made an impatient sign for the crowd to open.

"Well, then," added the scout, with the musing air of a man who had not half made up his mind, "I will throw Killdeer into the bargain. Take the word of an experienced hunter, the piece has not its equal atween the provinces."

Magua still disdained to reply, continuing his efforts to disperse the crowd.

"Perhaps," added the scout, losing his dissembled coolness, exactly in proportion as the other manifested an indifference to the exchange, "if I should condition to teach your young men the real virtue of the we'pon, it would smooth the little differences in our judgments."

Le Renard fiercely ordered the Delawares, who still lingered in an impenetrable belt around him, in hopes he would listen to the amicable proposal, to open his path, threatening, by the glance of his eye, another appeal to the infallible justice of their "prophet."

"What is ordered must sooner or later arrive," continued Hawkeye, turning with a sad and humbled look to Uncas. "The varlet knows his advantage, and will keep it! God bless you, boy; you have found friends among your natural kin, and I hope they will prove as true as some you have met who had no Indian cross. As for me, sooner or later, I must die; it is therefore fortunate there are but few to make my death howl. After all, it is likely the imps would have managed to master my scalp, so a day or two will make no great difference in the everlasting reckoning of time. God bless you," added the rugged woodsman, bending his head aside, and then instantly changing its direction again, with a wistful look towards the youth; "I loved both you and your father, Uncas, though our skins are not altogether of a color, and our gifts are somewhat different. Tell the Sagamore I never lost sight of him in my greatest trouble; and, as for you, think of me sometimes when on a lucky trail; and depend on it, boy, whether there be one heaven or two, there is a path in the other world by which honest men may come together again. You'll find the rifle in the place we hid it; take it, and keep it for my sake; and harkee, lad, as your natural gifts don't deny you the use of vengeance, use it a little freely on the Mingoes; it may unburden grief at my loss, and ease your mind. Huron, I accept your offer; release the woman. I am your prisoner."

A suppressed, but still distinct murmur of approbation, ran through the crowd at this generous proposition; even the fiercest among the Delaware warriors manifesting pleasure at the manliness of the intended sacrifice. Magua paused, and for an anxious moment, it might be said, he doubted; then casting his eyes on Cora, with an expression in which ferocity and admiration were strangely mingled, his purpose became fixed forever.

He intimated his contempt of the offer with a backward motion of his head, and said, in a steady and settled voice—

"Le Renard Subtil is a great chief; he has but one mind. Come," he added, laying his hand too familiarly on the shoulder of his captive to urge her onward; "a Huron is no tattler; we will go."

10

CORA MUNRO thanked Hawkeye for his proffered sacrifice, and commended Alice to the care of Major Heyward. Then she suffered the malignant Magua to lead her into the forest. But as the Huron departed, Uncas hurled a threat at him: "Look at the sun. He is now in the upper branches of the hemlock. Your path is short and open. When he is seen above the trees, there will be men on your trail." An hour was allowed for meditation. At its end the Delaware encampment sprang into furious life. Uncas lifted the wild chant of his war song; a hundred young braves struck the war post; all the fighters of the tribe joined in the war dance. The women, the aged, and the infirm, with Tamenund at their head, retired into the forest for safety, and Heyward saw Alice properly disposed before returning to join the expedition.

Hawkeye, after sending a boy for his rifle Killdeer, took his place as Uncas's principal lieutenant, in charge of twenty warriors. As the sun reached the zenith the whole body of Delaware braves set forth. They had hardly begun their march when David Gamut broke from cover to meet them, with news that "the heathen are abroad in goodly numbers, and, I fear, with evil intent." Magua had hidden Cora in a cave, and with his whole force of Hurons lay waiting in the thickets in front. All turned to Hawkeye for a plan of battle, which he had ready for them. "Give me my twenty rifles, and I will turn to the right, along the stream," he said; "and passing by the huts of the beaver, will join the Sagamore and the Colonel. You shall then hear the whoop from that quarter, with this wind one may easily send it a mile. Then, Uncas, do you drive in their front; . . . after which we shall carry their village, and take the woman from the cave." Uncas and the warriors at once accepted this scheme.

During the time Uncas was making this disposition of his forces, the woods were as still, and, with the exception of those who had met in council, apparently as much untenanted, as when they came fresh from the hands of their Almighty Creator. The eye could range, in every direction, through the long and shadowed vistas of the trees; but nowhere was any object to be seen that did not properly belong to the peaceful and slumbering scenery. Here and there a bird was heard fluttering among the branches of the beeches, and occasionally a squirrel dropped a nut, drawing the startled looks of the party, for a moment, to the place; but the instant the casual interruption ceased, the passing air was heard murmuring above their heads, along that verdant and undulating surface of forest, which spread itself unbroken, unless by stream or lake, over such a vast region of country. Across the tract of wilderness, which lay between the Delawares and the village of their enemies, it seemed as if the foot of man had never trodden, so breathing and deep was the silence in which it lay. But Hawkeye, whose duty led him foremost in the adventure, knew the character of those with whom he was about to contend too well to trust the treacherous quiet.

When he saw his little band collected, the scout threw Killdeer into the hollow of his arm, and making a silent signal that he would be followed, he led them many rods toward the rear, into the bed of a little brook which they had crossed in advancing. Here he halted, and after waiting for the whole of his grave and attentive warriors to close about him, he spoke in Delaware, demanding—

"Do any of my young men know whither this run will lead us?"

A Delaware stretched forth a hand, with the two fingers separated, and indicating the manner in which they were joined at the root, he answered—

"Before the sun could go his own length, the little water will be in the big." Then he added, pointing in the direction of the place he mentioned, "the two make enough for the beavers."

"I thought as much," returned the scout, glancing his eye upward at the opening in the treetops, "from the course it takes, and the bearings of the mountains. Men, we will keep within the cover of its banks till we scent the Hurons."

His companions gave the usual brief exclamation of assent, but perceiving that their leader was about to lead the way in person, one or two made signs that all was not as it should be. Hawkeye, who comprehended their meaning glances, turned, and perceived that his party had been followed thus far by the singing master.

"Do you know, friend," asked the scout gravely, and perhaps with a little of the pride of conscious deserving in his manner, "that this is a band of rangers chosen for the most desperate service, and put under the command of one who, though another might say it with a better face, will not be apt to leave them idle? It may not be five, it cannot be thirty, minutes before we tread on the body of a Huron, living or dead."

"Though not admonished of your intentions in words," returned David, whose face was a little flushed, and whose ordinarily quiet and unmeaning eyes glimmered with an expression of unusual fire, "your men have reminded me of the children of Jacob going out to battle against the Shechemites, for wickedly aspiring to wedlock with a woman of a race that was favored of the Lord. Now, I have journeyed far, and sojourned much in good and evil with the maiden ye seek; and though not a man of war, with my loins girded and my sword sharpened, yet would I gladly strike a blow in her behalf."

The scout hesitated, as if weighing the chances of such a strange enlistment in his mind before he answered—

"You know not the use of any we'pon. You carry no rifle; and believe me, what the Mingoes take they will freely give again."

"Though not a vaunting and bloodily disposed Goliath," returned David, drawing a sling from beneath his parti-colored and uncouth attire, "I have not forgotten the example of the Jewish boy. With this ancient instrument of war have I practiced much in my youth, and peradventure the skill has not entirely departed from me."

"Ay!" said Hawkeye, considering the deerskin thong and apron, with a cold and discouraging eye; "the thing might do its work among arrows, or even knives; but these Mengwe have been furnished by the Frenchers with a good grooved barrel a man. However, it seems to be your gift to go unharmed amid fire; and as you have hitherto been favored—major, you have left your rifle at a cock; a single shot before the time would be just twenty scalps lost to no purpose—singer, you can follow; we may find use for you in the shoutings."

"I thank you, friend," returned David, supplying himself, like his royal namesake, from among the pebbles of the brook; "though not given to the desire to kill, had you sent me away my spirit would have been troubled."

"Remember," added the scout, tapping his own head significantly on that spot where Gamut was yet sore, "we come to fight, and not to musickate. Until the general whoop is given, nothing speaks but the rifle."

David nodded, as much as to signify his acquiescence with the terms; and then Hawkeye, casting another observant glance over his followers, made the signal to proceed.

Their route lay, for the distance of a mile, along the bed of the watercourse. Though protected from any great danger of observation by the precipitous banks, and the thick shrubbery which skirted the stream, no precaution known to an Indian attack was neglected. A warrior rather crawled than walked on each flank, so as to catch occasional glimpses into the forest; and every few minutes the band came to a halt, and listened for hostile sounds, with an acuteness of organs that would be scarcely conceivable to a man in a less natural state. Their march was, however, unmolested, and they reached the point where the lesser stream was lost in the greater, without the smallest evidence that their progress had been noted. Here the scout again halted, to consult the signs of the forest.

"We are likely to have a good day for a fight," he said, in English, addressing Heyward, and glancing his eye upward at the clouds, which began to move in broad sheets across the firmament; "a bright sun and a glittering barrel are no friends to true sight. Everything is favorable; they have the wind, which will bring down their noises and their smoke too, no little matter in itself; whereas, with us it will be first a shot, and then a clear view. But here is an end of our cover; the beavers have had the range of this stream for hundreds of years, and what atween their food and their dams, there is, as you see, many a girdled stub, but few living trees."

Hawkeye had, in truth, in these few words, given no bad description of the prospect that now lay in their front. The brook was irregular in its width, sometimes shooting through narrow fissures in the rocks, and at others spreading over acres of bottom land, forming little areas that might be termed ponds. Everywhere along its banks were the mouldering relics of dead trees, in all the stages of decay, from those that groaned on their tottering trunks to such as had recently been robbed of those rugged coats that so mysteriously contain their principle of life. A few long, low, and moss-covered piles were scattered among them, like the memorials of a former and long-departed generation.

All these minute particulars were noted by the scout, with a gravity and interest that they probably had never before attracted. He knew that the Huron encampment lay a short half mile up the brook; and, with the characteristic anxiety of one who dreaded a hidden danger, he was greatly troubled at not finding the smallest trace of the presence of his enemy. Once or twice he felt induced to give the order for a rush, and to attempt the village by surprise; but his experience quickly admonished him of the danger of so useless an experiment. Then he listened intently, and with painful uncertainty, for the sounds of hostility in the quarter where Uncas was left; but nothing was audible except the sighing of the wind, that began to sweep over the bosom of the forest in gusts which threatened a tempest. At length, yielding rather to his unusual impatience than taking counsel from his knowledge, he determined to bring matters to an issue, by unmasking his force, and proceeding cautiously, but steadily, up the stream.

The scout had stood, while making his observations, sheltered by a brake, and his companions still lay in the bed of the ravine, through which the smaller stream debouched; but on hearing his low, though intelligible signal, the whole party stole up the bank, like so many dark specters, and silently arranged themselves around him. Pointing in the direction he wished to proceed, Hawkeye advanced, the band breaking off in single files, and following so accurately in his footsteps, as to leave it, if we except Heyward and David, the trail of but a single man.

The party was, however, scarcely uncovered before a volley from a dozen rifles was heard in their rear; and a Delaware leaping high into the air, like a wounded deer, fell at his whole length, perfectly dead.

"Ah! I feared some devilry like this!" exclaimed the scout, in English; adding, with the quickness of thought, in his adopted tongue, "To cover, men, and charge!"

The band dispersed at the word, and before Heyward had well recovered from his surprise, he found himself standing alone with David. Luckily, the Hurons had already fallen back, and he was safe from their fire. But this state of things was evidently to be of short continuance; for the scout set the example of pressing on their retreat, by discharging his rifle, and darting from tree to tree, as his enemy slowly yielded ground.

It would seem that the assault had been made by a very small party of the Hurons, which, however, continued to increase in numbers, as it retired on its friends, until the return fire was very nearly, if not quite, equal to that maintained by the advancing Delawares. Heyward threw himself among the combatants, and imitating the necessary caution of his companions, he made quick discharges with his own rifle. The contest now grew warm and stationary. Few were injured, as both parties kept their bodies as much protected as possible by the trees; never, indeed, exposing any part of their persons except in the act of taking aim. But the chances were gradually growing unfavorable to Hawkeye and his band. The quick-sighted scout perceived his danger, without knowing how to remedy it. He saw it was more dangerous to retreat than to maintain his ground; while he found his enemy throwing out men on his flank, which rendered the task of keeping themselves covered so very difficult to the Delawares, as nearly to silence their fire. At this embarrassing moment, when they began to think the whole of the hostile tribe was gradually encircling them, they heard the yell of combatants, and the rattling of arms, echoing under the arches of the wood, at the place where Uncas was posted; a bottom which, in a manner, lay beneath the ground on which Hawkeye and his party were contending.

The effects of this attack were instantaneous, and to the scout and his friends greatly relieving. It would seem that, while his own surprise had been anticipated, and had consequently failed, the enemy, in their turn, having been deceived in its object and in his numbers, had left too small a force to resist the impetuous onset of the young Mohican. This fact was doubly apparent, by the rapid manner in which the battle in the forest rolled upwards towards the village, and by an instant falling off in the number of their assailants, who rushed to assist in maintaining the front, and, as it now proved to be, the principal point of defence.

Animating his followers by his voice, and his own example, Hawkeye then gave the word to bear down upon their foes. The charge, in that rude species of warfare, consisted merely in pushing from cover to cover, nigher to the enemy; and in this maneuver he was instantly and successfully obeyed. The Hurons were compelled to withdraw, and the scene of the contest rapidly changed from the more open ground on which it had commenced, to a spot where the assailed found a thicket to rest upon. Here the struggle was protracted, arduous, and, seemingly, of doubtful issue; the Delawares, though none of them fell, beginning to bleed freely, in consequence of the disadvantage at which they were held.

In this crisis, Hawkeye found means to get behind the same tree as that which served for a cover to Heyward; most of his own combatants being within call, a little on his right, where they maintained rapid, though fruitless, discharges on their sheltered enemies.

"You are a young man, major," said the scout, dropping the butt of Killdeer to the earth, and leaning on the barrel, a little fatigued with his previous industry; "and it may be your gift to lead armies, at some future day, ag'in these imps, the Mingoes. You may here see the philosophy of an Indian fight. It consists, mainly, in a ready hand, a quick eye, and a good cover. Now, if you had a company of the Royal Americans here, in what manner would you set them to work in this business?"

"The bayonet would make a road."

"Ay, there is white reason in what you say; but a man must ask himself, in this wilderness, how many lives he can spare. No—horse," [1]

[1] The American forest admits of the passage of horse, there being little underbrush, and few tangled brakes. The plan of Hawkeye is the one which has always proved the most successful in the battles between the whites and the Indians. Wayne,

continued the scout, shaking his head, like one who mused; "horse, I am ashamed to say, must, sooner or later, decide these scrimmages. The brutes are better than men, and to horse must we come at last. Put a shodden hoof on the moccasin of a redskin; and if his rifle be once emptied, he will never stop to load it again."

"This is a subject that might better be discussed another time," returned Heyward; "shall we charge?"

"I see no contradiction to the gifts of any man, in passing his breathing spells in useful reflections," the scout replied. "As to a rush I little relish such a measure; for a scalp or two must be thrown away in the attempt. And yet," he added, bending his head aside, to catch the sounds of the distant combat, "if we are to be of use to Uncas, these knaves in our front must be got rid of!"

Then turning, with a prompt and decided air, he called aloud to his Indians, in their own language. His words were answered by a shout; and, at a given signal, each warrior made a swift movement around his particular tree. The sight of so many dark bodies, glancing before their eyes at the same instant, drew a hasty, and consequently an ineffectual, fire from the Hurons. Without stopping to breathe, the Delawares leaped, in long bounds, toward the wood, like so many panthers springing upon their prey. Hawkeye was in front, brandishing his terrible rifle, and animating his followers by his example. A few of the older and more cunning Hurons, who had not been deceived by the artifice which had been practiced to draw their fire, now made a close and deadly discharge of their pieces, and justified the apprehensions of the scout, by felling three of his foremost warriors. But the shock was insufficient to repel the impetus of the charge. The Delawares broke into the cover with the ferocity of their natures, and swept away every trace of resistance by the fury of the onset.

The combat endured only for an instant, hand to hand, and then the assailed yielded ground rapidly, until they reached the opposite margin of the thicket, where they clung to the cover, with the sort of obstinacy that is so often witnessed in hunted brutes. At this critical moment, when the success of the struggle was again becoming doubtful, the crack of a rifle was heard behind the Hurons, and a bullet came whizzing from among some beaver lodges, which were situated in the clearing, in their rear, and was followed by the fierce and appalling yell of the war whoop.

"There speaks the Sagamore!" shouted Hawkeye, answering the

---

in his celebrated campaign on the Miami, received the fire of his enemies in line; and then causing his dragoons to wheel round his flanks, the Indians were driven from their covers before they had time to load. One of the most conspicuous of the chiefs who fought in the battle of Miami assured the writer that the red men could not fight the warriors with "long knives and leather-stockings"; meaning the dragoons with their sabers and boots. (*Cooper's note*)

cry with his own stentorian voice; "we have them now in face and back!"

The effect on the Hurons was instantaneous. Discouraged by an assault from a quarter that left them no opportunity for cover, their warriors uttered a common yell of disappointment, and breaking off in a body, they spread themselves across the opening, heedless of every consideration but flight. Many fell, in making the experiment, under the bullets and the blows of the pursuing Delawares.

We shall not pause to detail the meeting between the scout and Chingachgook, or the more touching interview that Duncan held with Munro. A few brief and hurried words served to explain the state of things to both parties; and then Hawkeye, pointing out the Sagamore to his band, resigned the chief authority into the hands of the Mohican chief. Chingachgook assumed the station to which his birth and experience gave him so distinguished a claim, with the grave dignity that always gives force to the mandates of a native warrior. Following the footsteps of the scout, he led the party back through the thicket, his men scalping the fallen Hurons, and secreting the bodies of their own dead as they proceeded, until they gained a point where the former was content to make a halt.

The warriors, who had breathed themselves freely in the preceding struggle, were now posted on a bit of level ground, sprinkled with trees in sufficient numbers to conceal them. The land fell away rather precipitately in front, and beneath their eyes stretched, for several miles, a narrow, dark, and wooded vale. It was through this dense and dark forest that Uncas was still contending with the main body of the Hurons.

The Mohican and his friends advanced to the brow of the hill, and listened, with practiced ears, to the sounds of the combat. A few birds hovered over the leafy bosom of the valley, frightened from their secluded nests; and here and there a light vapory cloud, which seemed already blending with the atmosphere, arose above the trees, and indicated some spot where the struggle had been fierce and stationary.

"The fight is coming up the ascent," said Duncan, pointing in the direction of a new explosion of firearms; "we are too much in the center of their line to be effective."

"They will incline into the hollow, where the cover is thicker," said the scout, "and that will leave us well on their flank. Go, Sagamore, you will hardly be in time to give the whoop, and lead on the young men. I will fight this scrimmage with warriors of my own color. You know me, Mohican; not a Huron of them all shall cross the swell, into your rear, without the notice of Killdeer."

The Indian chief paused another moment to consider the signs of the contest, which was now rolling rapidly up the ascent, a certain evidence that the Delawares triumphed; nor did he actually quit the place until admonished of the proximity of his friends, as well as enemies, by the bullets of the former, which began to patter among the dried leaves on the ground, like the bits of falling hail which precede the bursting of the tempest. Hawkeye and his three companions withdrew a few paces to a shelter, and awaited the issue with calmness, that nothing but great practice could impart in such a scene.

It was not long before the reports of the rifles began to lose the echoes of the woods, and to sound like weapons discharged in the open air. Then a warrior appeared, here and there, driven to the skirts of the forest, and rallying as he entered the clearing, as at the place where the final stand was to be made. These were soon joined by others, until a long line of swarthy figures was to be seen clinging to the cover with the obstinacy of desperation. Heyward began to grow impatient, and turned his eyes anxiously in the direction of Chingachgook. The chief was seated on a rock, with nothing visible but his calm visage, considering the spectacle with an eye as deliberate as if he were posted there merely to view the struggle.

"The time is come for the Delaware to strike!" said Duncan.

"Not so, not so," returned the scout; "when he scents his friends, he will let them know that he is here. See, see; the knaves are getting in that clump of pines, like bees settling after their flight. By the Lord, a squaw might put a bullet into the center of such a knot of dark-skins!"

At that instant the whoop was given, and a dozen Hurons fell by a discharge from Chingachgook and his band. The shout that followed was answered by a single war cry from the forest, and a yell passed through the air that sounded as if a thousand throats were united in a common effort. The Hurons staggered, deserting the center of their line, and Uncas issued from the forest through the opening they left, at the head of a hundred warriors.

Waving his hands right and left, the young chief pointed out the enemy to his followers, who separated in pursuit. The war now divided, both wings of the broken Hurons seeking protection in the woods again, hotly pressed by the victorious warriors of the Lenape. A minute might have passed, but the sounds were already receding in different directions, and gradually losing their distinctness beneath the echoing arches of the woods. One little knot of Hurons, however, had disdained to seek a cover, and were retiring, like lions at bay, slowly and sullenly up the acclivity, which Chingachgook and his band had just deserted, to mingle more closely in the fray. Magua was conspicuous in this party, both by his fierce and savage mien, and by the air of haughty authority he yet maintained.

In his eagerness to expedite the pursuit, Uncas had left himself nearly alone; but the moment his eye caught the figure of Le Subtil, every other consideration was forgotten. Raising his cry of battle, which recalled some six or seven warriors, and reckless of the disparity of their numbers, he rushed upon his enemy. Le Renard, who watched the movement, paused to receive him with secret joy. But at the moment when he thought the rashness of his impetuous young assailant had left him at his mercy, another shout was given, and La longue Carabine was seen rushing to the rescue, attended by all his white associates. The Huron instantly turned, and commenced a rapid retreat up the ascent.

There was no time for greetings or congratulations; for Uncas, though unconscious of the presence of his friends, continued the pursuit with the velocity of the wind. In vain Hawkeye called to him to respect the covers; the young Mohican braved the dangerous fire of his enemies, and soon compelled them to a flight as swift as his own headlong speed. It was fortunate that the race was of short continuance, and that the white men were much favored by their position, or the Delaware would soon have outstripped all his companions, and fallen a victim to his own temerity. But ere such a calamity could happen, the pursuers and pursued entered the Wyandot village, within striking distance of each other.

Excited by the presence of their dwellings, and tired of the chase, the Hurons now made a stand, and fought around their council lodge with the fury of despair. The onset and the issue were like the passage and destruction of a whirlwind. The tomahawk of Uncas, the blows of Hawkeye, and even the still nervous arm of Munro, were all busy for that passing moment, and the ground was quickly strewed with their enemies. Still Magua, though daring and much exposed, escaped from every effort against his life, with that sort of fabled protection that was made to overlook the fortunes of favored heroes in the legends of ancient poetry. Raising a yell that spoke volumes of anger and disappointment, the subtle chief, when he saw his comrades fallen, darted away from the place, attended by his two only surviving friends, leaving the Delawares engaged in stripping the dead of the bloody trophies of their victory.

But Uncas, who had vainly sought him in the mêlée, bounded forward in pursuit; Hawkeye, Heyward, and David still pressing on his footsteps. The utmost that the scout could effect, was to keep the muzzle of his rifle a little in advance of his friend, to whom, however, it answered every purpose of a charmed shield. Once Magua appeared disposed to make another and a final effort to revenge his losses; but, abandoning his intention as soon as demonstrated, he leaped into a thicket of bushes, through which he was followed by his enemies, and suddenly entered the mouth of the cave already known to the reader.

Hawkeye, who had only forborne to fire in tenderness to Uncas, raised a shout of success, and proclaimed aloud, that now they were certain of their game. The pursuers dashed into the long and narrow entrance, in time to catch a glimpse of the retreating forms of the Hurons. Their passage through the natural galleries and subterraneous apartments of the cavern was preceded by the shrieks and cries of hundreds of women and children. The place, seen by its dim and uncertain light, appeared like the shades of the infernal regions, across which unhappy ghosts and savage demons were flitting in multitudes.

Still Uncas kept his eye on Magua, as if life to him possessed but a single object. Heyward and the scout still pressed on his rear, actuated, though possibly in a less degree, by a common feeling. But their way was becoming intricate, in those dark and gloomy passages, and the glimpses of the retiring warriors less distinct and frequent; and for a moment the trace was believed to be lost, when a white robe was seen fluttering in the further extremity of a passage that seemed to lead up the mountain.

" 'Tis Cora!" exclaimed Heyward, in a voice in which horror and delight were wildly mingled.

"Cora! Cora!" echoed Uncas, bending forward like a deer.

" 'Tis the maiden!" shouted the scout. "Courage, lady; we come! —we come."

The chase was renewed with a diligence rendered tenfold encouraging by this glimpse of the captive. But the way was rugged, broken, and in spots nearly impassable. Uncas abandoned his rifle, and leaped forward with headlong precipitation. Heyward rashly imitated his example, though both were, a moment afterward, admonished of its madness, by hearing the bellowing of a piece, that the Hurons found time to discharge down the passage in the rocks, the bullet from which even gave the young Mohican a slight wound.

"We must close!" said the scout, passing his friends by a desperate leap; "the knaves will pick us all off at this distance; and see, they hold the maiden so as to shield themselves!"

Though his words were unheeded, or rather unheard, his example was followed by his companions, who, by incredible exertions, got near enough to the fugitives to perceive that Cora was borne along between the two warriors, while Magua prescribed the direction and manner of their flight. At this moment the forms of all four were strongly drawn against an opening in the sky, and they disappeared. Nearly frantic with disappointment, Uncas and Heyward increased efforts that already seemed superhuman, and they issued from the cavern on the side of the mountain, in time to note the route of the pursued. The course lay up the ascent, and still continued hazardous and laborious.

Encumbered by his rifle, and, perhaps, not sustained by so deep an interest in the captive as his companions, the scout suffered the latter to precede him a little, Uncas, in his turn, taking the lead of Heyward. In this manner, rocks, precipices, and difficulties were surmounted in an incredibly short space, that at another time, and under other circumstances, would have been deemed almost insuperable. But the impetuous young men were rewarded, by finding that, encumbered with Cora, the Hurons were losing ground in the race.

"Stay, dog of the Wyandots!" exclaimed Uncas, shaking his bright tomahawk at Magua; "a Delaware girl calls stay!"

"I will go no further," cried Cora, stopping unexpectedly on a ledge of rocks, that overhung a deep precipice, at no great distance from the summit of the mountain. "Kill me if thou wilt, detestable Huron; I will go no further."

The supporters of the maiden raised their ready tomahawks with the impious joy that fiends are thought to take in mischief, but Magua stayed the uplifted arms. The Huron chief, after casting the weapons he had wrested from his companions over the rock, drew his knife, and turned to his captive, with a look in which conflicting passions fiercely contended.

"Woman," he said, "choose; the wigwam or the knife of Le Subtil!"

Cora regarded him not, but dropping on her knees, she raised her eyes and stretched her arms toward heaven, saying, in a meek and yet confiding voice,—

"I am Thine! do with me as Thou seest best!"

"Woman," repeated Magua, hoarsely, and endeavoring in vain to catch a glance from her serene and beaming eye, "choose!"

But Cora neither heard nor heeded his demand. The form of the Huron trembled in every fiber, and he raised his arm on high, but dropped it again with a bewildered air, like one who doubted. Once more he struggled with himself and lifted the keen weapon again—but just then a piercing cry was heard above them, and Uncas appeared, leaping frantically, from a fearful height, upon the ledge. Magua recoiled a step; and one of his assailants, profiting by the chance, sheathed his own knife in the bosom of Cora.

The Huron sprang like a tiger on his offending and already retreating countryman, but the falling form of Uncas separated the unnatural combatants. Diverted from his object by this interruption, and maddened by the murder he had just witnessed, Magua buried his weapon in the back of the prostrate Delaware, uttering an unearthly shout as he committed the dastardly deed. But Uncas arose from the blow, as the wounded panther turns upon his foe, and struck the murderer of Cora to his feet, by an effort in which the last of his failing strength was expended. Then, with a stern and steady look, he turned to Le Subtil, and indicated, by the expression of his eye, all that he would do, had not the power deserted him. The latter seized the nerveless arm of the unresisting Delaware, and passed his knife into his bosom three several times, before his victim, still keeping his gaze riveted on his enemy with a look of inextinguishable scorn, fell dead at his feet.

"Mercy! mercy! Huron," cried Heyward, from above, in tones nearly choked by horror; "give mercy, and thou shalt receive it!"

Whirling the bloody knife up at the imploring youth, the victorious Magua uttered a cry so fierce, so wild, and yet so joyous, that it conveyed the sounds of savage triumph to the ears of those who fought in the valley, a thousand feet below. He was answered by a burst from the lips of the scout, whose tall person was just then seen moving swiftly toward him, along those dangerous crags, with steps as bold and reckless as if he possessed the power to move in air. But when the hunter reached the scene of the ruthless massacre, the ledge was tenanted only by the dead.

His keen eye took a single look at the victims, and then shot its glances over the difficulties of the ascent in his front. A form stood at the brow of the mountain, on the very edge of the giddy height, with uplifted arms, in an awful attitude of menace. Without stopping to consider his person, the rifle of Hawkeye was raised; but a rock, which fell on the head of one of the fugitives below, exposed the indignant and glowing countenance of the honest Gamut. Then Magua issued from a crevice, and stepping with calm indifference over the body of the last of his associates, he leaped a wide fissure, and ascended the rocks at a point where the arm of David could not reach him. A single bound would carry him to the brow of the precipice, and assure his safety. Before taking the leap, however, the Huron paused, and shaking his hand at the scout, he shouted—

"The palefaces are dogs! the Delawares women! Magua leaves them on the rocks, for the crows!"

Laughing hoarsely, he made a desperate leap, and fell short of his mark; though his hands grasped a shrub on the verge of the height. The form of Hawkeye had crouched like a beast about to take its spring, and his frame trembled so violently with eagerness, that the muzzle of the half-raised rifle played like a leaf fluttering in the wind. Without exhausting himself with fruitless efforts, the cunning Magua suffered his body to drop to the length of his arms, and found a fragment for his feet to rest on. Then summoning all his powers, he renewed the attempt, and so far succeeded, as to draw his knees on the edge of the mountain. It was now, when the body of his enemy was most collected together, that the agitated weapon of the scout was drawn to his shoulder. The surrounding rocks, themselves, were not steadier than the piece became, for the single instant that it poured out its contents. The arms of the Huron relaxed, and his body fell back a little, while his knees still kept their position. Turning a relentless look on his enemy, he shook a hand in grim defiance. But his hold loosened, and his dark person was seen cutting the air with its head downward, for a fleeting instant, until it glided past the fringe of shrubbery which clung to the mountain, in its rapid flight to destruction.

The Delaware tribe gave to Cora and Uncas the honors due their characters and their positions. An Indian maiden extolled Uncas as the panther of his people; a warrior whose moccasin left no trail on the dews; whose bound was like the leap of the young fawn; whose eye was brighter than a star in the dark night; whose voice in battle equalled the thunders of Manitou. Another maiden praised Cora for her matchless beauty and noble resolution. The burden of other discourses was the evident intention of the Great Spirit to unite the two in Heaven, for He had taken them away together. The speakers admonished Uncas to be kind to the young woman, and overlook her inexperience in ministering to his wants; they urged Cora to be attentive to the needs of the young chief, and never to forget the distinction which the Manitou had placed between them. At these words Hawkeye, the only white person present who understood the language, shook his head over the error of the savages' simple creed.

At the grave of Cora, David Gamut sang his best psalms, and the stricken Colonel Munro made a broken little speech. At the grave of Uncas, the sorrowing Chingachgook lifted his voice in a wild monody. "The strains rose just so loud as to become intelligible, and then grew fainter and more trembling, until they finally sank on the ear, as if borne away by a passing breath of wind." Colonel Munro still had one daughter, and her marriage to Major Heyward would soon give him a son-in-law and grandchildren. Chingachgook, however, was utterly bereft. "My race has gone from the salt lake, and the hills of the Delawares," he said. "I am alone." At this Hawkeye interrupted him. "No, no," he exclaimed, grasping Chingachgook's hand across the fresh earth. "The boy has left us for a time; but Sagamore, you are not alone."

It was left for the venerable Tamenund to speak the last words. "Go, children of the Lenape," he said to the multitude. "Why should Tamenund stay? The palefaces are masters of the earth, and the time of the red men has not yet come again. My day has been too long. In the morning I saw the sons of Unamis happy and strong; and yet, before the night has come, have I lived to see the last warrior of the wise race of the Mohicans."

THE PATHFINDER

Being the THIRD SERIES OF ADVENTURES *of*

LEATHERSTOCKING

ONLY one of the Great Lakes, the easternmost, Ontario, was debated between the French and British forces. At the opening of King George's War, the French had two strongholds at either extremity of the lake, Frontenac on the east and Niagara on the west; the British held the southern shore, with a fort at the mouth of the Oswego River. Fort Oswego had a specially checkered history. It served the British well in King George's War, when Hawkeye was the young man called Deerslayer. At the opening of the Seven Years' War, in 1755–56, it was enlarged and strengthened by a sister stronghold, Fort Ontario, on the opposite or western side of the river. This had no sooner been done, however, than Montcalm swooped down, captured it, and thoroughly dismantled the works. The British and provincials,

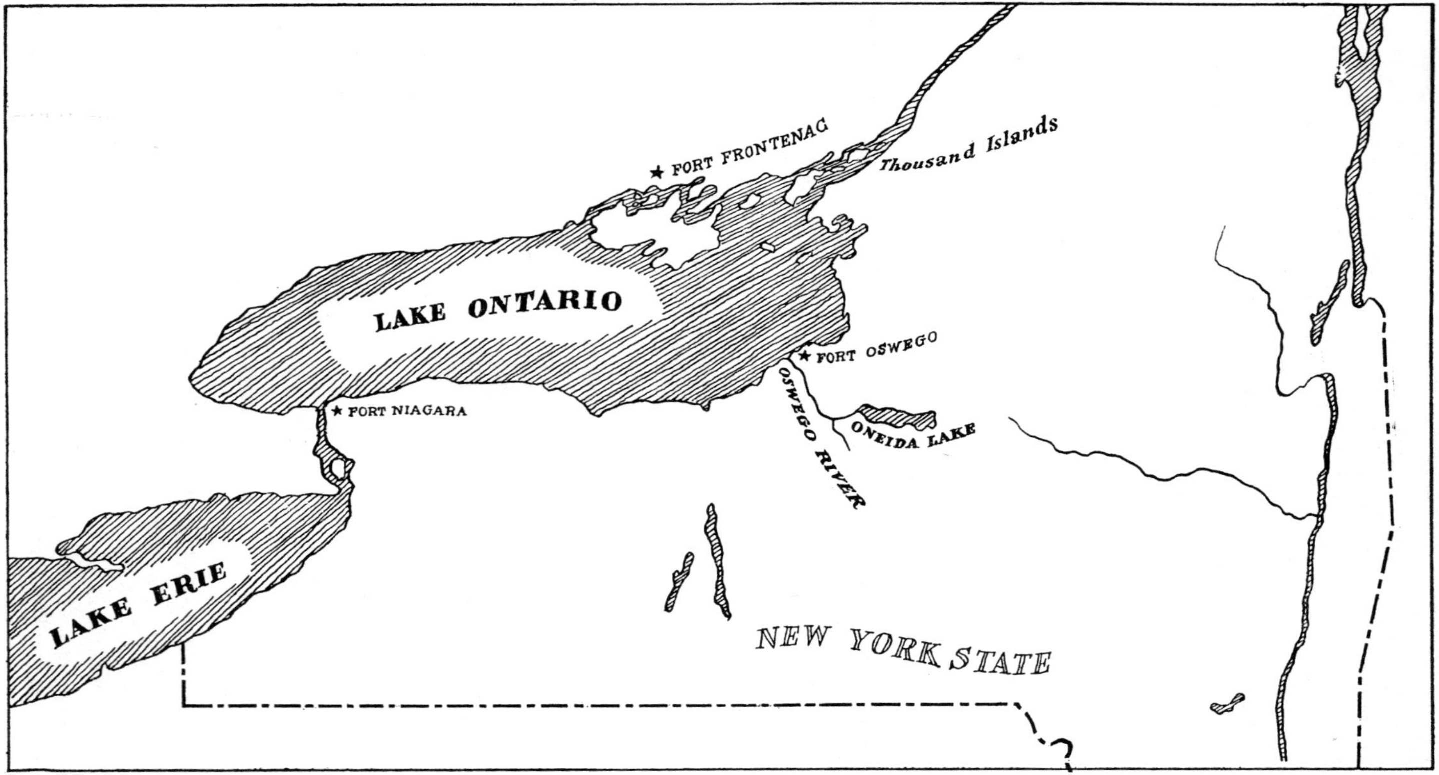

THE SCENE OF *The Pathfinder*

in a counterstroke of 1768, captured Fort Frontenac and gained control of the whole eastern end of Ontario. They then rebuilt Fort Oswego, garrisoned it strongly, and continued to hold it. Indeed, they kept possession long after the Revolution, not giving it up until 1796.

The time of this third Leatherstocking romance, though nowhere precisely indicated, was probably 1759; the only date, indeed, which even roughly fits the fact of British possession of rebuilt Fort Oswego, and French possession of Fort Niagara—both fundamental circumstances of the story. The British began reconstructing Oswego in the spring of the year named, and that summer they and the colonials triumphantly captured Fort Niagara and hauled down the French ensign. But it is well not to inquire too curiously into the dates of these tales. It is enough to know that The Pathfinder *is to be referred to the period when the great William Pitt had taken charge of the British Empire; when his plans had infused a new energy into British campaigning in all parts of the world; and when well-matured blows against the French at Fort Duquesne (the forks of the Ohio), at Niagara, at Ticonderoga, and at Canada were about to succeed. It was in 1759 that Wolfe, capturing Quebec, decided the destiny of the continent.*

Leatherstocking, or Pathfinder, was still at the height of his powers; still young enough to fall in love, for the first time, with a girl as lovely as she was vigorous and courageous. His honesty, shrewdness, frankness, self-reliance, and conscientiousness were as patent as ever. When he finds that his affection for Mabel is not reciprocated—that she respects and admires but does not love him—his sense of justice and generosity of spirit meet a new test. He surrenders Mabel, however, without any intolerable anguish of spirit; perhaps he realizes that the forest is his true mistress, and that he is better wedded to the wilderness than domesticated on a farm or in some town. As in the two previous novels, the wilderness is one of the most important actors in the story. The pathless woods north of the Mohawk; the falls of the Oswego; the placid beauty of Ontario's shore, and the tempestuous fury of its bosom when smitten by a storm; the unique attractions of the Thousand Islands, mirrored in the broad St. Lawrence—these are congenial themes for the novelist's pen. The simple plot offers just enough framework to carry the reader through shifting scenes of wilderness, river, and lake, and through varied adventures with plotting Frenchmen and treacherous Mingoes.

"It is beautiful, it is grand," said Balzac of The Pathfinder, *making plain that he liked above all the serenity and grandeur of its setting. "Never did the art of writing tread closer upon the art of the pencil. This is the school of study for literary landscape painters." The landscapes are indeed admirably wrought. It is the character study, however, which is the book's real title to the name of masterpiece (and Cooper himself thought it and* The Deerslayer *his best work). The homely sincerity, the earnestness, the combination of stern hardheaded sagacity with fineness of feeling, all so marked in Leatherstocking, are brought out in one vigorously written scene after another. The noble Chingachgook is again contrasted with a "riptyle," the dangerous Arrowhead. And in Mabel Dunham, who rides a lake storm and defends a blockhouse unterrified, we have a heroine of true pioneer endurance and energy.*

1

THE SUBLIMITY connected with vastness is familiar to every eye. The most abstruse, the most far-reaching, perhaps the most chastened of the poet's thoughts, crowd on the imagination as he gazes into the depths of the illimitable void. The expanse of the ocean is seldom seen by the novice with indifference; and the mind, even in the obscurity of night, finds a parallel to that grandeur which seems inseparable from images that the senses cannot compass. With feelings akin to this admiration and awe—the offspring of sublimity—were the different characters with which the action of this tale must open, gazing on the scene before them. Four persons in all,—two of each sex,—they had managed to ascend a pile of trees, that had been uptorn by a tempest, to catch a view of the objects that surrounded them. It is still the practice of the country to call these spots windrows. By letting in the light of heaven upon the dark and damp recesses of the wood, they form a sort of oasis in the solemn obscurity of the virgin forests of America. The particular windrow of which we are writing lay on the brow of a gentle acclivity, and it had opened the way for an extensive view to those who might occupy its upper margin, a rare occurrence to the traveller in the woods. As usual, the spot was small, but owing to the circumstances of its lying on the low acclivity mentioned, and that of the opening's extending downward, it offered more than common advantages to the eye. Philosophy has not yet determined the nature of the power that so often lays desolate spots of this description: some ascribing it to the whirlwinds that produce waterspouts on the ocean;

while others again impute it to sudden and violent passages of streams of the electric fluid; but the effects in the woods are familiar to all. On the upper margin of the opening to which there is allusion, the viewless influence had piled tree on tree, in such a manner as had not only enabled the two males of the party to ascend to an elevation of some thirty feet above the level of the earth, but, with a little care and encouragement, to induce their more timid companions to accompany them. The vast trunks that had been broken and driven by the force of the gust, lay blended like jackstraws; while their branches, still exhaling the fragrance of wilted leaves, were interlaced in a manner to afford sufficient support to the hands. One tree had been completely uprooted; and its lower end, filled with earth, had been cast uppermost, in a way to supply a sort of staging for the four adventurers, when they had gained the desired distance from the ground.

The reader is to anticipate none of the appliances of people of condition in the description of the personal appearances of the group in question. They were all wayfarers in the wilderness; and had they not been, neither their previous habits nor their actual social positions would have accustomed them to many of the luxuries of rank. Two of the party, indeed, a male and female, belonged to the native owners of the soil, being Indians of the well-known tribe of the Tuscaroras; while their companions were a man, who bore about him the peculiarities of one who had passed his days on the ocean, and this, too, in a station little, if any, above that of a common mariner; while his female associate was a maiden of a class in no great degree superior to his own; though her youth, sweetness of countenance, and a modest but spirited mien, lent that character of intellect and refinement which adds so much to the charm of beauty in the sex. On the present occasion her full blue eye reflected the feeling of sublimity that the scene excited, and her pleasant face was beaming with the pensive expression with which all deep emotions, even though they bring the most grateful pleasure, shadow the countenances of the ingenuous and thoughtful.

And, truly, the scene was of a nature deeply to impress the imagination of the beholder. Toward the west, in which direction the faces of the party were turned, and in which alone could much be seen, the eye ranged over an ocean of leaves, glorious and rich in the varied but lively verdure of a generous vegetation, and shaded by the luxuriant tints that belong to the forty-second degree of latitude. The elm, with its graceful and weeping top, the rich varieties of the maple, most of the noble oaks of the American forest, with the broad-leafed linden, known in the parlance of the country as the basswood, mingled their uppermost branches, forming one broad and seemingly interminable carpet of foliage, that stretched away toward the setting sun, until it bounded the horizon, by blending with the clouds, as the waves and the sky meet at the base of the vault of heaven. Here and there, by some accident of the tempests, or by a caprice of nature, a trifling opening among these giant members of the forest permitted an inferior tree to struggle upward toward the light, and to lift its modest head nearly to a level with the surrounding surface of verdure. Of this class were the birch, a tree of some account in regions less favored, the quivering aspen, various generous nut woods, and divers others that resembled the ignoble and vulgar, thrown by circumstances into the presence of the stately and great. Here and there, too, the tall, straight trunk of the pine pierced the vast field, rising high above it, like some grand monument reared by art on a plain of leaves.

It was the vastness of the view, the nearly unbroken surface of verdure, that contained the principle of grandeur. The beauty was to be traced in the delicate tints, relieved by gradations of light and shadow; while the solemn repose induced the feeling allied to awe.

"Uncle," said the wondering, but pleased girl, addressing her male companion, whose arm she rather touched than leaned on, to steady her own light but firm footing, "this is like a view of the ocean you so much love!"

"So much for ignorance, and a girl's fancy, Magnet,"—a term of affection the sailor often used in allusion to his niece's personal attractions; "no one but a child would think of likening this handful of leaves to a look at the real Atlantic. You might seize all these treetops to Neptune's jacket, and they would make no more than a nosegay for his bosom."

"More fanciful than true, I think, uncle. Look thither; it must be miles on miles, and yet we see nothing but leaves! what more could one behold, if looking at the ocean?"

"More!" returned the uncle, giving an impatient gesture with the elbow the other touched, for his arms were crossed, and the hands were thrust into the bosom of a vest of red cloth, a fashion of the times, "more, Magnet? say, rather, what less? Where are your combing seas, your blue water, your rollers, your breakers, your whales, or your waterspouts, and your endless motion, in this bit of a forest, child?"

"And where are your treetops, your solemn silence, your fragrant leaves, and your beautiful green, uncle, on the ocean?"

"Tut, Magnet; if you understood the thing, you would know that green water is a sailor's bane. He scarcely relishes a greenhorn less."

"But green trees are a different thing. Hist! that sound is the air breathing among the leaves!"

"You should hear a nor'wester breathe, girl, if you fancy wind aloft. Now, where are your gales, and hurricanes, and trades, and levanters, and suchlike incidents, in this bit of a forest, and what fishes have you swimming beneath yonder tame surface!"

"That there have been tempests here, these signs around us plainly show; and beasts, if not fishes, are beneath those leaves."

"I do not know that," returned the uncle, with a sailor's dogmatism. "They told us many stories at Albany, of the wild animals we should fall in with, and yet we have seen nothing to frighten a seal. I doubt if any of your inland animals will compare with a low latitude shark!"

"See!" exclaimed the niece, who was more occupied with the sublimity and beauty of the "boundless wood" than with her uncle's arguments, "yonder is a smoke curling over the tops of the trees; can it come from a house?"

"Ay, ay, there is a look of humanity in that smoke," returned the old seaman, "which is worth a thousand trees; I must show it to Arrowhead, who may be running past a port without knowing it. It is probable there is a caboose where there is a smoke."

As he concluded, the uncle drew a hand from his bosom, touched the male Indian who was standing near him lightly on the shoulder, and pointed out a thin line of vapor that was stealing slowly out of the wilderness of leaves, at a distance of about a mile, and was diffusing itself in almost imperceptible threads of humidity, in the quivering atmosphere. The Tuscarora was one of those noble-looking warriors that were oftener met with among the aborigines of this continent a century since, than today; and, while he had mingled sufficiently with the colonists to be familiar with their habits, and even with their language, he had lost little, if any, of the wild grandeur and simple dignity of a chief. Between him and the old seaman the intercourse had been friendly, but distant, for the Indian had been too much accustomed to mingle with the officers of the different military posts he had frequented, not to understand that his present companion was only a subordinate. So imposing, indeed, had been the quiet superiority of the Tuscarora's reserve, that Charles Cap, for so was the seaman named, in his most dogmatical or facetious moments had not ventured on familiarity, in an intercourse that had now lasted more than a week. The sight of the curling smoke, however, had struck the latter like the sudden appearance of a sail at sea, and, for the first time since they met, he ventured to touch the warrior, as has been related.

The quick eye of the Tuscarora instantly caught a sight of the smoke, and for quite a minute he stood, slightly raised on tiptoe, with distended nostrils, like the buck that scents a taint in the air, and a gaze as riveted as that of the trained pointer, while he waits his master's aim. Then falling back on his feet, a low exclamation, in the soft tones that form so singular a contrast to its harsher cries in the Indian warrior's voice, was barely audible; otherwise, he was undisturbed. His countenance was calm, and his quick, dark, eagle eye moved over the leafy panorama, as if to take in at a glance every circumstance that might enlighten his mind. That the long journey they had attempted to make through a broad belt of wilderness was necessarily attended with danger, both uncle and niece well knew; though neither could at once determine whether the sign that others were in the vicinity was the harbinger of good or evil.

"There must be Oneidas or Tuscaroras near us, Arrowhead," said Cap, addressing his Indian companion by his conventional English name; "will it not be well to join company with them, and get a comfortable berth for the night in their wigwam?"

"No wigwam there," Arrowhead answered, in his unmoved manner; "too much tree."

"But Indians must be there; perhaps some old messmates of your own, Master Arrowhead."

"No Tuscarora—no Oneida—no Mohawk; paleface fire."

"The devil it is! well, Magnet, this surpasses a seaman's philosophy; we old seadogs can tell a soldier's from a sailor's quid, or a lubber's nest from a mate's hammock; but I do not think the oldest admiral in His Majesty's fleet can tell a king's smoke from a collier's!"

The idea that human beings were in their vicinity in that ocean of wilderness, had deepened the flush on the blooming cheek and brightened the eye of the fair creature at his side, but she soon turned with a look of surprise to her relative, and said, hesitatingly, for both had often admired the Tuscarora's knowledge, or we might almost say, instinct,—

"A paleface's fire! Surely, uncle, he cannot know *that!*"

"Ten days since, child, I would have sworn to it; but now, I hardly know what to believe. May I take the liberty of asking, Arrowhead, why you fancy that smoke, now, a paleface's smoke, and not a redskin's?"

"Wet wood," returned the warrior, with the calmness with which the pedagogue might point out an arithmetical demonstration to his puzzled pupil. "Much wet—much smoke; much water—black smoke."

"But, begging your pardon, Master Arrowhead, the smoke is not black, nor is there much of it. To my eye, now, it is as light and fanciful a smoke as ever rose from a captain's teakettle, when nothing was left to make the fire but a few chips from the dunnage."

"Too much water," returned Arrowhead, with a slight nod of the head: "Tuscarora too cunning to make fire with water; paleface too much book, and burn anything; much book, little know."

"Well, that's reasonable, I allow," said Cap, who was no devotee of learning: "he means that as a hit at your reading, Magnet, for the chief has sensible notions of things in his own way. How far, now, Arrowhead, do you make us, by your calculation, from the bit of a pond that you call the Great Lake, and toward which we have been so many days shaping our course?"

The Tuscarora looked at the seaman with quiet superiority, as he answered,—

"Ontario, like heaven; one sun, and the great traveller will know it."

"Well, I have been a great traveller, I cannot deny, but of all my v'y'ges this has been the longest, the least profitable, and the farthest inland. If this body of fresh water is so high, Arrowhead, and at the same time so large, one might think a pair of good eyes would find it out, for, apparently, everything within thirty miles is to be seen from this lookout."

"Look," said Arrowhead, stretching an arm before him with quiet grace; "Ontario!"

"Uncle, you are accustomed to cry 'Land ho!' but not 'Water ho!' and you do not see it," cried the niece, laughing as girls will laugh at their own idle conceits.

"How now, Magnet! dost suppose that I shouldn't know my native element, if it were in sight?"

"But Ontario is not your native element, dear uncle, for you come from the salt water, while this is fresh."

"That might make some difference to your young mariner, but none in the world to the old one. I should know water, child, were I to see it in China."

"Ontario!" repeated Arrowhead, with emphasis, again stretching his hand toward the northwest.

Cap looked at the Tuscarora, for the first time since their acquaintance, with something like an air of contempt, though he did not fail to follow the direction of the chief's eye and arm, both of which were pointing, to all appearance, toward a vacant spot in the heavens, a short distance above the plain of leaves.

"Ay, ay; this is much as I expected, when I left the coast to come in search of a fresh-water pond," resumed Cap, shrugging his shoulders like one whose mind was made up, and who thought no more need be said. "Ontario may be there, or, for that matter, it may be in my pocket. Well, I suppose there will be room enough, when we reach it, to work our canoe. But, Arrowhead, if there be palefaces in our neighborhood, I confess I should like to get within hail of them."

The Tuscarora now gave a quiet inclination of his head, and the whole party descended from the roots of the uptorn tree, in silence. When they had reached the ground, Arrowhead intimated his intention to go toward the fire, and ascertain who had lighted it, while he advised his wife and the two others to proceed to a canoe, which they had left in the adjacent stream, and await his return.

"Why, chief, this might do on soundings, and in an offing where one knew the channel," returned old Cap, "but in an unknown region like this, I think it unsafe to trust the pilot alone too far from the ship; so, with your leave, we will not part company."

"What my brother want?" asked the Indian, gravely, though without taking offence at a distrust that was sufficiently plain.

"Your company, Master Arrowhead, and no more. I will go with you, and speak these strangers."

The Tuscarora assented without difficulty, and again he directed his patient and submissive little wife, who seldom turned her full, rich black eye on him, but to express equally her respect, her dread, and her love, to proceed to the boat. But here Magnet raised a difficulty. Although spirited, and of unusual energy under circumstances of trial, she was but woman, and the idea of being entirely deserted by her two male protectors, in the midst of a wilderness, that her senses had just told her was seemingly illimitable, became so keenly painful, that she expressed a wish to accompany her uncle.

"The exercise will be a relief, dear sir, after sitting so long in the canoe," she added, as the rich blood slowly returned to a cheek that had paled, in spite of her efforts to be calm, "and there may be females with the strangers."

"Come, then, child; it is but a cable's length, and we shall return an hour before the sun sets."

With this permission, the girl, whose real name was Mabel Dunham, prepared to be of the party, while the Dew-of-June, as the wife of Arrowhead was called, passively went her way toward the canoe, too much accustomed to obedience, solitude, and the gloom of the forest, to feel apprehension.

The three who remained in the windrow now picked their way around its tangled maze, and gained the margin of the woods, in the necessary direction. A few glances of the eye sufficed for Arrowhead, but old Cap deliberately set the smoke by a pocket compass, before he trusted himself within the shadows of the trees.

"This steering by the nose, Magnet, may do well enough for an Indian, but your thoroughbred knows the virtue of the needle," said the uncle, as he trudged at the heels of the light-stepping Tuscarora. "America would never have been discovered, take my word for it, if Columbus had been nothing but nostrils. Friend Arrowhead, didst ever see a machine like this?"

The Indian turned, cast a glance at the compass, which Cap held in a way to direct his course, and gravely answered,—

"A paleface eye. The Tuscarora see in his head. The Salt-water"—for so the Indian styled his companion—"all eye now; no tongue."

"He means, uncle, that we had needs be silent; perhaps he distrusts the persons we are about to meet."

"Ay—'tis an Indian's fashion of going to quarters. You perceive he has examined the priming of his rifle, and it may be as well if I look to that of my own pistols."

Without betraying alarm at these preparations, to which she had become accustomed by her long journey in the wilderness, Mabel followed with a step as light and elastic as that of the Indian, keeping close in the rear of her companions. For the first half mile no other caution beyond a rigid silence was observed, but as the party drew nearer to the spot where the fire was known to be, much greater care became necessary.

The forest, as usual, had little to intercept the view below the branches, but the tall straight trunks of trees. Everything belonging to vegetation had struggled toward the light, and beneath the leafy canopy one walked, as it might be, through a vast natural vault, that was upheld by myriads of rustic columns. These columns, or trees, however, often served to conceal the adventurer, the hunter, or the foe, and as Arrowhead swiftly approached the spot where his practiced and unerring senses told him the strangers ought to be, his footsteps gradually became lighter, his eye more vigilant, and his person was more carefully concealed.

"See, Salt-water," he said, exultingly, pointing at the same time through the vista of trees, "paleface fire!"

"By the Lord, the fellow is right!" muttered Cap; "there they are, sure enough, and eating their grub as quietly as if they were in the cabin of a three-decker."

"Arrowhead is but half right," whispered Mabel, "for there are two Indians and only one white man."

"Paleface," said the Tuscarora, holding up two fingers, "red man," holding up one.

"Well," rejoined Cap, "it is hard to say which is right and which is wrong. One is entirely white, and a fine comely lad he is, with an air of life and respectability about him; one is a redskin as plain as paint and nature can make him; but the third chap is half-rigged, being neither brig nor schooner."

"Paleface," repeated Arrowhead, again raising two fingers; "redman," showing but one.

"He must be right, uncle, for his eye seems never to fail. But it is now urgent to know whether we meet as friends or foes. They may be French."

"One hail will soon satisfy us on that head," returned Cap. "Stand you behind this tree, Magnet, lest the knaves take it into their heads to fire a broadside without a parley, and I will soon learn what colors they sail under."

The uncle had placed his two hands to his mouth to form a trumpet, and was about to give the promised hail, when a rapid movement from Arrowhead defeated the intention by deranging the instrument.

"Red man, Mohican," said the Tuscarora; "good; palefaces, Yengeese."

"These are heavenly tidings," murmured Mabel, who little relished the prospect of a deadly fray in that remote wilderness. "Let us approach at once, dear uncle, and proclaim ourselves friends."

"Good!" said the Tuscarora; "red man cool, and know; paleface hurried, and fire. Let squaw go."

"What!" said Cap, in astonishment, "send little Magnet ahead, as a lookout, while two lubbers, like you and me, lie to, to see what sort of a landfall she will make! If I do, I—"

"It is wisest, uncle," interrupted the generous girl, "and I have no fear. No Christian, seeing a woman approach alone, would fire upon her, and my presence will be a pledge of peace. Let me go forward, as Arrowhead wishes, and all will be well. We are as yet unseen, and the surprise of the strangers will not partake of alarm."

"Good!" returned Arrowhead, who did not conceal his approbation of Mabel's spirit.

"It has an unseaman-like look," answered Cap, "but being in the woods, no one will know it. If you think, Mabel—"

"Uncle, I know there is no cause to fear for me; and you are always nigh to protect me."

"Well, take one of the pistols, then—"

"Nay, I had better rely on my youth and feebleness," said the girl, smiling, while her color heightened under her feelings. "Among Christian men, a woman's best guard is her claim to their protection. I know nothing of arms, and wish to live in ignorance of them."

The uncle desisted; and, after receiving a few cautious instructions from the Tuscarora, Mabel rallied all her spirit, and advanced alone toward the group seated near the fire. Although the heart of the girl beat quick, her step was firm, and her movements, seemingly, were without reluctance. A deathlike silence reigned in the forest, for they toward whom she approached were too much occupied in appeasing that great natural appetite, hunger, to avert their looks for an instant from the important business in which they were all engaged. When Mabel, however, had got within a hundred feet of the fire, she trod upon a dried stick, and the trifling noise that was produced by her light footstep caused the Mohican, as Arrowhead had pronounced the Indian to be, and his companion whose character had been thought so equivocal, to rise to their feet, as quick as thought. Both glanced at the rifles that leaned against a tree, and then each stood without stretching out an arm, as his eyes fell on the form of the girl. The Indian uttered a few words to his companion, and resumed his seat and his meal as calmly as if no interruption had occurred. On the contrary, the white man left the fire, and came forward to meet Mabel.

The latter saw, as the stranger approached, that she was about to be addressed by one of her own color, though his dress was so strange a mixture of the habits of the two races, that it required a near look to be certain of the fact. He was of middle age, but there was an open honesty, a total absence of guile, in his face, which otherwise would not have been thought handsome, that at once assured Magnet she was in no danger. Still she paused, in obedience to a law of her habits if not of nature, which rendered her averse to the appearance of advancing too freely to meet one of the other sex, under the circumstances in which she was placed.

"Fear nothing, young woman," said the hunter, for such his attire would indicate him to be, "you have met Christian men in the wilderness, and such as know how to treat all kindly that are disposed to peace and justice. I'm a man well known in all these parts, and perhaps one of my names may have reached your ears. By the Frenchers, and the redskins on the other side of the Big Lakes, I am called La longue Carabine; by the Mohicans, a just-minded and upright tribe, what is left of them, Hawkeye; while the troops and rangers along this side of the water call me Pathfinder, inasmuch as I have never been know to miss one end of the trail, when there was a Mingo, or a friend who stood in need of me, at the other."

This was not uttered boastfully, but with the honest confidence of one who well knew that by whatever name others might have heard of him, he had no reason to blush at the reports. The effect on Mabel was instantaneous. The moment she heard the last *sobriquet*, she clasped her hands eagerly and repeated the word,—

"Pathfinder!"

"So they call me, young woman, and many a great lord has got a title that he did not half so well merit; though, if truth be said, I rather pride myself in finding my way where there is no path, than in finding it where there is. But the regular troops be by no means particular, and half the time they don't know the difference atween a trail and a path, though one is a matter for the eye, while the other is little more than scent."

"Then you are the friend my father promised to send to meet us!"

"If you are Sergeant Dunham's daughter, the great Prophet of the Delawares never uttered a plainer truth."

"I am Mabel, and yonder, hid by the trees, are my uncle, whose name is Cap, and a Tuscarora, called Arrowhead. We did not hope to meet you until we had nearly reached the shores of the lake."

"I wish a juster-minded Indian had been your guide," said Pathfinder, "for I am no lover of the Tuscaroras, who have travelled too far from the graves of their fathers always to remember the Great Spirit: and Arrowhead is an ambitious chief. Is Dew-of-June with him?"

"His wife accompanies us, and a humble and mild creature she is."

"Ay, and truehearted; which is more than any who knows him will say of Arrowhead. Well, we must take the fare that Providence bestows, while we follow the trail of life. I suppose worse guides might have been found than the Tuscarora; though he has too much Mingo blood for one who consorts altogether with the Delawares."

"It is then, perhaps, fortunate we have met," said Mabel.

"It is not misfortinate at any rate; for I promised the sergeant I would see his child safe to the garrison, though I died for it. We expected to meet you before you reached the falls, where we have left our own canoe; while we thought it might do no harm to come up a few miles, in order to be of sarvice if wanted. It's lucky we did, for I doubt if Arrowhead be the man to shoot the current."

"Here come my uncle and the Tuscarora, and our parties can now join."

As Mabel concluded, Cap and Arrowhead, who saw that the conference was amicable, drew nigh, and a few words sufficed to let them know as much as the girl herself had learned from the strangers. As soon as this was done, the party proceeded towards the two who still remained near the fire.

The Mohican continued to eat, though the second white man rose, and courteously took off his cap to Mabel Dunham. He was young, healthful, and manly in appearance; and he wore a dress, which, while it was less rigidly professional than that of the uncle, also denoted one accustomed to the water. In that age real seamen were a class entirely apart from the rest of mankind; their ideas, ordinary language, and attire, being as strongly indicative of their calling, as the opinions, speech, and dress of a Turk denote a Mussulman. Although the Pathfinder was scarcely in the prime of life, Mabel had met him with a steadiness that may have been the consequence of having braced her nerves for the interview; but, when her eyes encountered those of the young man at the fire, they fell before the gaze of admiration with which she saw, or fancied she saw, he greeted her. Each, in truth, felt that interest in the other, which similarity of age, condition, mutual comeliness, and their novel situation, would be likely to inspire in the young and ingenuous.

"Here," said Pathfinder, with an honest smile bestowed on Mabel, "are the friends your worthy father has sent to meet you. This is a great Delaware; and one that has had honors as well as troubles in his day. He has an Injin name fit for a chief, but as the language is not always easy for the inexperienced to pronounce, we nat'rally turn it into English, and call him the Big Sarpent. You are not to suppose, however, that by this name we wish to say that he is treacherous, beyond what is lawful in a redskin, but that he is wise, and has the cunning that becomes a warrior. Arrowhead, there, knows what I mean."

While the Pathfinder was delivering this address, the two Indians gazed on each other steadily, and the Tuscarora advanced and spoke to the other in an apparently friendly manner.

"I like to see this," continued Pathfinder; "the salutes of two redskins in the woods, Master Cap, are like the hailing of friendly vessels on the ocean. But, speaking of water, it reminds me of my young friend, Jasper Western, here, who can claim to know something of these matters, seeing that he has passed his days on Ontario."

"I am glad to see you, friend," said Cap, giving the young freshwater sailor a cordial grip; "though you must have something still to learn, considering the school to which you have been sent. This is my niece, Mabel; I call her Magnet, for a reason she never dreams of, though you may possibly have education enough to guess at it, having some pretensions to understand the compass, I suppose."

"The reason is easily comprehended," said the young man, involuntarily fastening his keen, dark eye, at the same time, on the suffused face of the girl; "and I feel sure that the sailor who steers by your Magnet, will never make a bad landfall."

"Ha! you do make use of some of the terms, I find, and that with propriety and understanding; though, on the whole, I fear you have seen more green than blue water!"

"It is not surprising that we should get some of the phrases that belong to the land, for we are seldom out of sight of it twenty-four hours at a time."

"More's the pity, boy; more's the pity. A very little land ought to go a great way with a seafaring man. Now, if the truth were known, Master Western, I suppose there is more or less land all round your lake."

"And, uncle, is there not more or less land all round the ocean?" said Magnet, quickly; for she dreaded a premature display of the old seaman's peculiar dogmatism, not to say pedantry.

"No, child, there is more or less ocean all round the land! that's what I tell the people ashore, youngster. They are living, as it might be, in the midst of the sea, without knowing it; by sufferance, as it were, the water being so much the more powerful, and the largest. But there is no end to conceit in this world, for a fellow who never saw salt water often fancies he knows more than one who has gone round the

Horn. No, no; this earth is pretty much an island, and all that can be truly said not to be so, is water."

Young Western had a profound deference for a mariner of the ocean, on which he had often pined to sail; but he had, also, a natural regard for the broad sheet on which he had passed his life, and which was not without its beauties in his eyes.

"What you say, sir," he answered, modestly, "may be true, as to the Atlantic; but we have a respect for the land up here, on Ontario."

"That is because you are always landlocked," returned Cap, laughing heartily. "But yonder is the Pathfinder, as they call him, with some smoking platters, inviting us to share in his mess; and I will confess that one gets no venison at sea. Master Western, civility to girls, at your time of life, comes as easy as taking in the slack of the ensign halyards; and if you will just keep an eye to her kid and can, while I join the mess of the Pathfinder and our Indian friends, I make no doubt she will remember it."

Master Cap uttered more than he was aware of at the time. Jasper Western did look to the wants of Mabel, and she long remembered the kind, manly attention of the young sailor, at this their first interview. He placed the end of a log for a seat, obtained for her a delicious morsel of the venison, gave her a draught of pure water from the spring, and, as he sat near and opposite to her, fast won his way to her esteem by his gentle but frank manner of manifesting his care; homage that woman always wishes to receive, but which is never so flattering, or so agreeable, as when it comes from the young to those of their own age; from the manly to the gentle. Like most of those who pass their time excluded from the society of the softer sex, young Western was earnest, sincere, and kind in his attentions, which though they wanted a conventional refinement that perhaps Mabel never missed, had those winning qualities that prove very sufficient as substitutes. Leaving these two inexperienced and unsophisticated young people to become acquainted through their feelings, rather than their expressed thoughts, we will turn to the group in which the uncle, with a facility for taking care of himself that never deserted him, had already become a principal actor.

The party had taken their places around a platter of venison steaks, which served for the common use, and the discourse naturally partook of the characters of the different individuals that composed it. The Indians were silent and industrious, the appetite of the aboriginal American for venison being seemingly unappeasable; while the two white men were communicative and discursive, each of the latter being garrulous and opinionated in his way. But, as the dialogue will serve to put the reader in possession of certain facts that may render the succeeding narrative more clear, it will be well to record it.

"There must be satisfaction in this life of yours, no doubt, Mr. Pathfinder," continued Cap, when the hunger of the travellers was so far appeased that they began to pick and choose among the savory morsels; "it has some of the chances and luck that we seamen like, and if ours is all water, yours is all land."

"Nay, we have water, too, in our journeyings and marches," returned his white companion: "we border-men handle the paddle and the spear almost as much as the rifle and the hunting knife."

"Ay; but do you handle the brace and the bow line; the wheel and the lead line; the reef point and the toprope? The paddle is a good thing, out of doubt, in a canoe, but of what use is it in the ship?"

"Nay, I respect all men in their callings, and I can believe the things you mention have their uses. One who has lived, like myself, in company with many tribes, understands differences in usages. The paint of a Mingo is not the paint of a Delaware; and he who should expect to see a warrior in the dress of a squaw, might be disapp'inted. I'm not very old, but I have lived in the woods, and have some acquaintance with human natur'. I never believed much in the larning of them that dwell in towns, for I never yet met with one that had an eye for a rifle or a trail."

"That's my manner of reasoning, Master Pathfinder, to a yarn. Walking about streets, going to church of Sundays, and hearing sermons, never yet made a man of a human being. Send the boy out upon the broad ocean, if you wish to open his eyes, and let him look upon foreign nations, or what I call the face of natur', if you wish him to understand his own character. Now, there is my brother-in-law, the sergeant; he is as good a fellow as ever broke a biscuit, in his own way; but what is he, after all? why, nothing but a soger. A sergeant, to be sure, but that is a sort of a soger, you know. When he wished to marry poor Bridget, my sister, I told the girl what he was, as in duty bound, and what she might expect from such a husband; but you know how it is with girls, when their minds are jammed by an inclination. It is true, the sergeant has risen in his calling, and they say he is an important man at the fort; but his poor wife has not lived to see it all, for she has now been dead these fourteen years."

"A soldier's calling is an honorable calling, provided he has fi't only on the side of right," returned the Pathfinder: "and as the Frenchers are always wrong, and His Sacred Majesty and these colonies are always right, I take it the sergeant has a quiet conscience, as well as a good character. I have never slept more sweetly than when I have fi't the Mingoes, though it is the law with me to fight always like a white man, and never like an Injin. The Sarpent, here, has his fashions, and I have mine; yet we have fou't side by side, these many years, without either's thinking a hard thought consarning the other's ways. I tell him there is but one heaven and one hell, notwithstanding his traditions, though there are many paths to both."

"That is rational, and he is bound to believe you, though I fancy most of the roads to the last are on dry land. The sea is what my poor sister, Bridget, used to call a 'purifying place,' and one is out of the way of temptation when out of sight of land. I doubt if as much can be said in favor of your lakes, up here-a-way."

"That towns and settlements lead to sin, I will allow; but our lakes are bordered by the forests, and one is every day called upon to worship God in such a temple. That men are not always the same, even in the wilderness, I must admit, for the difference atween a Mingo and a Delaware is as plain to be seen as the difference atween the sun and moon. I am glad, friend Cap, that we have met, however, if it be only that you may tell the Big Sarpent, here, that there be lakes in which the water is salt. We have been pretty much of one mind since our acquaintance began, and if the Mohican has only half the faith in me that I have in him, he believes all that I have told him, touching the white men's ways and natur's laws; but it has always seemed to me that none of the redskins have given as free a belief, as an honest man likes, to the accounts of the Big Salt Lakes, and to that of there being rivers that flow upstream."

"This comes of getting things wrong end foremost," answered Cap, with a condescending nod. "You have thought of your lakes and rifts, as the ship, and of the ocean and the tides, as the boat. Neither Arrowhead nor the Serpent need doubt what you have said concerning both, though I confess, myself, to some difficulty in swallowing the tale about there being inland seas at all, and still more that there is any sea of fresh water. I have come this long journey, as much to satisfy my own eyes and palate concerning these facts, as to oblige the sergeant and Magnet; though the first was my sister's husband, and I love the last like a child."

"You are wrong—you are wrong, friend Cap; very wrong, to distrust the power of God in anything," returned Pathfinder, earnestly. "Them that live in the settlements and the town get to have confined and unjust opinions consarning the might of His hand; but we who pass our time in His very presence, as it might be, see things differently. I mean such of us as have white natur's. A redskin has his notions, and it is right that it should be so; and if they are not exactly the same as a Christian white man's, there is no harm in it. Still, there are matters that belong altogether to the ordering of God's Providence, and these salt and fresh-water lakes are some of them. I do not pretend to account for these things, but I think it the duty of all to believe in them. For my part, I am one of them, who think that the same hand which made the sweet water, can make the salt."

"Hold on there, Master Pathfinder," interrupted Cap, not without some heat; "in the way of a proper and manly faith, I will turn my back on no one, when afloat. Although more accustomed to make all snug aloft, and to show the proper canvas, than to pray, when the hurricane comes, I know that we are but helpless mortals at times, and I hope I pay reverence where reverence is due. All I mean to say, and that is rather insiniated than said, is this, which is, as you all know, simply an intimation that, being accustomed to see water in large bodies *salt,* I should like to taste it, before I can believe it to be *fresh.*"

"God has given the salt lick to the deer, and He has given to man, redskin and white, the delicious spring at which to slake his thirst. It is onreasonable to think that He may not have given lakes of pure water to the west, and lakes of impure water to the east."

Cap was awed, in spite of his overweening dogmatism, by the earnest simplicity of the Pathfinder, though he did not relish the idea of believing a fact which, for many years, he had pertinaciously insisted could not be true. Unwilling to give up the point, and, at the same time, unable to maintain it against a reasoning to which he was unaccustomed, and which possessed equally the force of truth, faith, and probability, he was glad to get rid of the subject by evasion.

"Well, well, friend Pathfinder," he said, "we will nipper the argument where it is; and, as the sergeant has sent you to give us pilotage to this same lake, we can only try the water when we reach it. Only mark my words: I do not say that it may not be fresh on the surface; the Atlantic is sometimes fresh on the surface, near the mouths of great rivers; but rely on it, I shall show you a way of tasting the water many fathoms deep, of which you never dreamed; and then we shall know more about it."

The guide seemed content to let the matter rest, and the conversation changed.

"We are not overconsated consarning our gifts," observed the Pathfinder, after a short pause, "and well know that such as live in the towns, and near the sea—"

"On the sea," interrupted Cap.

"On the sea, if you wish it, friend—have opportunities that do not befall us of the wilderness. Still, we know our own callings, and they are what I consider nat'ral callings, and are not parvarted by vanity and wantonness. Now, my gifts are with the rifle, and on a trail, and in the way of game and scoutin'; for, though I can use the spear and the paddle, I pride not myself on either. The youth, Jasper, there, who is discoursing with the sergeant's daughter, is a different creatur', for he may be said to breathe the water, as it might be, like a fish. The Indians and Frenchers of the north shore call him Eau-douce, on account of his gifts in this particular. He is better at the oar, and the rope too, than in making fires on a trail."

"There must be something about these gifts of which you speak, after all," said Cap. "Now this fire, I will acknowledge, has overlaid all my seamanship. Arrowhead, there, said the smoke came from a paleface's fire, and that is a piece of philosophy that I hold to be equal to steering in a dark night by the edges of the scud."

"It's no great secret—it's no great secret," returned Pathfinder, laughing with great inward glee, though habitual caution prevented the emission of any noise. "Nothing is easier to us who pass our time in the great school of Providence, than to l'arn its lessons. We should be as useless on a trail, or in carrying tidings through the wilderness, as so many woodchucks, did we not soon come to a knowledge of these niceties. Eau-douce, as we call him, is so fond of the water, that he gathered a damp stick or two for our fire, and there be plenty of them, as well as those that are thoroughly dried, lying scattered about; and wet will bring dark smoke, as I suppose even you followers of the sea must know. It's no great secret—it's no great secret; though all is mystery to such as doesn't study the Lord and his mighty ways with humility and thankfulness."

"That must be a keen eye of Arrowhead's to see so slight a difference."

"He would be but a poor Injin if he didn't! No, no; it is wartime, and no redskin is outlying without using his senses. Every skin has its own natur', and every natur' has its own laws, as well as its own skin. It was many years afore I could master all them higher branches of a forest edication, for redskin knowledge doesn't come as easy to white-skin natur' as what I suppose is intended to be white-skin knowledge; though I have but little of the latter, having passed most of my time in the wilderness."

"You have been a ready scholar, Master Pathfinder, as is seen by your understanding these things so well. I suppose it would be no great matter, for a man regularly brought up to the sea, to catch these trifles, if he could only bring his mind fairly to bear upon them."

"I don't know that. The white man has his difficulties in getting redskin habits, quite as much as the Injin in getting white-skin ways. As for the raal natur', it is my opinion that neither can actually get that of the other."

"And yet we sailors, who run about the world so much, say there is but one nature, whether it be in the Chinaman or a Dutchman. For my own part, I am much of that way of thinking too; for I have generally found that all nations like gold and silver, and most men relish tobacco."

"Then you seafaring men know little of the redskins. Have you ever know any of your Chinamen who could sing their death songs, with their flesh torn with splinters and cut with knives, the fire raging around their naked bodies, and death staring them in the face? Until you can find me a Chinaman, or a Christian man, that can do all this, you cannot find a man with redskin natur', let him look ever so valiant, or know how to read all the books that was ever printed."

"It is the savages only that play each other such hellish tricks!" said Master Cap, glancing his eyes about him uneasily at the apparently endless arches of the forest. "No white man is ever condemned to undergo these trials."

"Nay, therein you are ag'in mistaken," returned the Pathfinder, coolly selecting a delicate morsel of the venison as his *bonne bouche;* "for though these torments belong only to the redskin natur', in the way of bearing them like braves, white-skin natur' may be, and often has been, agonized by them."

"Happily," said Cap, with an effort to clear his throat, "none of His Majesty's allies will be likely to attempt such damnable cruelties, on any of His Majesty's loyal subjects. I have not served much in the royal navy, it is true; but I have served—and that is something; and, in the way of privateering and worrying the enemy in his ships and cargoes, I've done my full share. But I trust there are no French savages on this side the lake, and I think you said that Ontario is a broad sheet of water?"

"Nay, it is broad in our eyes," returned Pathfinder, not caring to conceal the smile which lighted a face that had been burnt by exposure to a bright red, "though I mistrust that some may think it narrow; and narrow it is, if you wish it to keep off the foe. Ontario has two ends, and the enemy that is afraid to cross it will be sartain to come round it."

"Ah! that comes of your d——d fresh-water ponds!" growled Cap, hemming so loud as to cause him instantly to repent the indiscretion. "No man, now, ever heard of a pirate's or a ship's getting round one end of the Atlantic!"

"Mayhap the ocean has no ends?"

"That it hasn't; nor sides, nor bottom. The nation that is snugly moored on one of its coasts need fear nothing from the one anchored abeam, let it be ever so savage, unless it possesses the art of shipbuilding. No, no; the people who live on the shores of the Atlantic need fear but little for their skins or their scalps. A man may lie down at night, in those regions, in the hope of finding the hair on his head in the morning, unless he wears a wig."

"It isn't so here. I don't wish to flurry the young woman, and therefore I will be no way particular, though she seems pretty much listening to Eau-douce, as we call him; but without the edication I have received, I should think it, at this very moment, a risky journey to go over the very ground that lies atween us and the garrison, in the present state of this frontier. There are about as many Iroquois on this side of Ontario as there be on the other. It is for this very reason, friend Cap, that the sergeant has engaged us to come out and show you the path."

"What! do the knaves dare to cruise so near the guns of one of his majesty's works?"

"Do not the ravens resort near the carcass of the deer, though the fowler is at hand? They come this-a-way, as it might be, nat'rally. There are more or less whites passing atween the forts and the settlements, and they are sure to be on their trails. The Sarpent has come up on one side of the river, and I have come up the other, in order to scout for the outlying rascals, while Jasper brought up the canoe, like a bold-hearted sailor, as he is. The sergeant told him, with tears in his eyes, all about his child, and how his heart yearned for her, and how gentle and obedient she was, until I think the lad would have dashed into a Mingo camp, singlehanded, rather than not a-come."

"We thank him, we thank him; and shall think the better of him for his readiness; though I suppose the boy has run no great risk, after all."

"Only the risk of being shot from a cover, as he forced the canoe up a swift rift, or turned an elbow in the stream, with his eyes fastened on the eddies. Of all the risky journeys, that on an ambushed river is the most risky, in my judgment, and that risk has Jasper run."

"And why the devil has the sergeant sent for me to travel a hundred and fifty miles in this outlandish manner! Give me an offing, and the enemy in sight, and I'll play with him in his own fashion, as long as he pleases, long bowls or close quarters; but to be shot like a turtle asleep, is not to my humor. If it were not for little Magnet there, I would tack ship this instant, make the best of my way back to York, and let Ontario take care of itself, salt water or fresh water."

"That wouldn't mend the matter much, friend mariner, as the road to return is much longer, and almost as bad as the road to go on. Trust to us, and we will carry you through safe, or lose our scalps."

Cap wore a tight, solid queue, done up in eelskin, while the top of his head was nearly bald, and he mechanically passed his hand over both, as if to make certain that each was in its right place. He was at the bottom, however, a brave man, and had often faced death with coolness, though never in the frightful forms in which it presented itself under the brief but graphic pictures of his companion. It was too late to retreat; and he determined to put the best face on the matter, though he could not avoid muttering inwardly a few curses on the indifference and indiscretion with which his brother-in-law, the sergeant, had led him into his present dilemma.

"I make no doubt, Master Pathfinder," he answered, when these thoughts had found time to glance through his mind, "that we shall reach port in safety. What distance may we now be from the fort?"

"Little more than fifteen miles; and swift miles, too, as the river runs, if the Mingoes let us go clear."

"And I suppose the woods will stretch along, starboard and larboard, as heretofore?"

"Anan?"

"I mean that we shall have to pick our way through these damned trees!"

"Nay, nay; you will go in the canoe, and the Oswego has been cleared of its flood wood by the troops. It will be floating downstream, and that, too, with a swift current."

"And what the devil is to prevent these minks, of which you speak, from shooting us as we double a headland, or are busy in steering clear of the rocks?"

"The Lord! He who has so often helped others in greater difficulties. Many and many is the time that my head would have been stripped of hair, skin and all, hadn't the Lord fi't on my side. I never go into a scrimmage, friend mariner, without thinking of this great ally, who can do more in battle than all the battalions of the 60th, were they brought into a single line."

"Ay, ay; this may do well enough for a scouter; but we seamen like our offing, and to go into action with nothing in our minds but the business before us; plain broadside and broadside work, and no trees or rocks to thicken the water."

"And no Lord, too, I dare to say, if the truth was known. Take my word for it, Master Cap, that no battle is the worse fou't for having the Lord on your side. Look at the head of the Big Sarpent, there; you can see the mark of a knife all along by his left ear; now, nothing but a bullet from this long rifle of mine saved his scalp that day, for it had fairly started, and half a minute more would have left him without the warlock. When the Mohican squeezes my hand, and intermates that I befri'nded him in that matter, I tell him, no; it was the Lord, who led me to the only spot where execution could be done, or his necessity be made known, on account of the smoke. Sartain when I got the right position, I finished the affair of my own accord, for a friend under the tomahawk is apt to make a man think quick, and act at once, as was my case, or the Sarpent's spirit would be hunting in the happy land of his people at this very moment."

"Come, come, Pathfinder, this palaver is worse than being skinned from stem to stern; we have but a few hours of sun, and had better be drifting down this said current of yours, while we may. Magnet, dear, are you not ready to get under way?"

Magnet started, blushed brightly, and made her preparations for an immediate departure. Not a syllable of the discourse just related had she heard, for Eau-douce, as young Jasper was oftener called than anything else, had been filling her ears with a description of the yet distant forts toward which she was journeying, with accounts of her father, whom she had not seen since a child, and with the manner of life of those who lived in the frontier garrisons. Unconsciously, she had become deeply interested, and her thoughts had been too intently directed to these interesting matters, to allow any of the less agreeable subjects discussed by those so near to reach her ears. The bustle of departure put an end to the conversation entirely, and the baggage of the scouts, or guides, being trifling, in a few minutes the whole party was ready to proceed. As they were about to quit the spot, however, to the surprise of even his fellow guides, Pathfinder collected a quantity of branches, and threw them upon the embers of the fire, taking care even to see that some of the wood was damp, in order to raise as dark and dense a smoke as possible.

"When you can hide your trail, Jasper," he said, "a smoke at leaving an encampment may do good, instead of harm. If there are a dozen Mingoes within ten miles of us, some on 'em are on the heights, or in the trees, looking out for smokes; let them see this, and much good may it do them. They are welcome to our leavings."

"But may they not strike, and follow on our trail?" asked the youth, whose interest in the hazard of his situation had much increased since the meeting with Magnet. "We shall leave a broad path to the river."

"The broader the better; when there, it will surpass Mingo cunning even to say which way the canoe has gone; upstream or down. Water is the only thing in natur' that will thoroughly wash out a trail, and even water will not always do it, when the scent is strong. Do you not see, Eau-douce, that if any Mingoes have seen our path below the falls, they will strike off toward the smoke, and that they will nat'rally conclude that they who began by going upstream, will end by going upstream? If they know anything, they now know a party is out from the fort, and it will exceed even Mingo wit to fancy that we have come up here, just for the pleasure of going back again, and that, too, the same day, and at the risk of our scalps."

2

THE OSWEGO RIVER, fed by Lakes Oneida and Onondaga, flows northwest into Lake Ontario. Its course is at first gentle, but after dashing over a waterfall twelve or fifteen feet high, it moves more rapidly down to its destination. Pathfinder and his party placed themselves in a long bark canoe to descend the stream to Fort Oswego at its mouth. They intended to shoot the falls, letting Mabel Dunham walk around the portage. The scout ordered them to adopt a little artifice at the outset. "Should any of them infarnals, the Mingoes, strike our trail, or follow it to this point, they will not fail to look for the signs in the mud, and if they discover that we have left the shore with the nose of the canoe upstream, it is a natural belief to think we went that-a-way."

Pathfinder, standing upright, took his place in the bow of the canoe; the young sailor, Jasper Western, took a similar stand in the stern—each paddling steadily. The others seated themselves in the body of the craft. They moved steadily forward. The Oswego at that point was a deep, dark stream, rather narrow, so that where a tree had fallen into it some care was needed to avoid the limbs. It was one of the two great channels of communication between the settlements of New York and the Canadian frontier, the other being the Lake George–Lake Champlain route. No fort, however, existed between the head of the Mohawk River and the mouth of the Oswego. A hundred miles of wilderness between was open to the incursions of the savages. As they moved down their perilous course, Pathfinder began chatting.

"I sometimes wish for peace again," said the Pathfinder, "when one can range the forest without s'arching for any other enemy than the beasts and fishes. Ah's me! many is the day that the Sarpent, there, and I have passed happily among the streams, living on venison, salmon, and trout, without thought of a Mingo or a scalp! I sometimes wish that them blessed days might come back, for it is not my ra'al gift to slay my own kind. I'm sartain the sergeant's daughter don't think me a wretch that takes pleasure in preying on human natur'?"

At this remark, a sort of half interrogatory, Pathfinder looked behind him; and, though the most partial friend could scarcely term his sunburnt and hard features handsome, even Mabel thought his smile attractive, by its simple ingenuousness, and the uprightness that beamed in every lineament of his honest countenance.

"I do not think my father would have sent one like those you mention, to see his daughter through the wilderness," the young woman answered, returning the smile as frankly as it was given, and much more sweetly.

"That he wouldn't, that he wouldn't; the sergeant is a man of feelin', and many is the march and the fight that we have stood shoulder to shoulder in, as he would call it; though I always keep my limbs free, when near a Frencher or a Mingo."

"You are then the young friend of whom my father has spoken so often in his letters?"

"His *young* friend—the sergeant has the advantage of me by thirty years; yes, he is thirty years my senior, and as many my better."

"Not in the eyes of the daughter, perhaps, friend Pathfinder," put in Cap, whose spirits began to revive when he found the water once more flowing around him. "The thirty years that you mention are not often thought to be an advantage in the eyes of girls of nineteen."

Mabel colored, and in turning aside her face, to avoid the looks of those in the bow of the canoe, she encountered the admiring gaze of the young man in the stern. As a last resource her spirited, but soft blue eyes, sought refuge in the water. Just at this moment a dull heavy sound swept up the avenue formed by the trees, borne along by a light air that hardly produced a ripple on the water.

"That sounds pleasantly," said Cap, pricking up his ears like a dog that hears a distant baying; "it is the surf on the shores of your lake, I suppose?"

"Not so—not so," answered the Pathfinder; "it is merely this river tumbling over some rocks, half a mile below us."

"Is there a fall in the stream?" demanded Mabel, a still brighter flush glowing in her face.

"The devil! Master Pathfinder, or you, Mr. Oh-the-Deuce,"—for so Cap began to style Jasper, by way of entering cordially into the border usages,—"had you not better give the canoe a sheer, and get nearer to the shore? These waterfalls have generally rapids above them, and one might as well get into the Maelstrom at once as to run into their suction."

"Trust to us—trust to us, friend Cap," answered Pathfinder; "we are but fresh-water sailors, it is true, and I cannot boast of being much, even of that; but we understand rifts, and rapids, and cataracts; and in going down these, we shall do our endeavors not to disgrace our edication."

"In going down!" exclaimed Cap; "the devil, man! you do not dream of going down a waterfall in this eggshell of bark!"

"Sartain; the path lies over the falls, and it is much easier to shoot them than to unload the canoe, and to carry that, and all it contains, around a portage of a mile, by hand."

Mabel turned her pallid countenance toward the young man in the stern of the canoe, for just at that moment a fresh roar of the fall was borne to her ears, by a new current of the air, and it really sounded terrific, now that the cause was understood.

"We thought that by landing the females and the two Indians," Jasper quietly observed, "we three white men, all of whom are used to the water, might carry the canoe over in safety, for we often shoot these falls."

"And we counted on you, friend mariner, as a mainstay," said Pathfinder, winking at Jasper over his shoulder, "for you are accustomed to see waves tumbling about, and without some one to steady the cargo, all the finery of the sergeant's daughter might be washed into the river, and be lost."

Cap was puzzled. The idea of going over a waterfall was perhaps more serious, in his eyes, than it would have been in those of one totally ignorant of all that pertained to boats; for he understood the power of the element, and the total feebleness of man when exposed to its fury. Still, his pride revolted at the thought of deserting the boat, while others not only courageously, but coolly, proposed to continue in it. Notwithstanding the latter feeling, and his innate as well as acquired steadiness in danger, he would probably have deserted his post, had not the images of Indians tearing scalps from the human head taken so strong hold of his fancy, as to induce him to imagine the canoe a sort of sanctuary.

"What is to be done with Magnet?" he demanded, affection for his niece raising another qualm in his conscience. "We cannot allow Magnet to land, if there are enemy's Indians near?"

"Nay; no Mingo will be near the portage, for that is a spot too public for their deviltries," answered the Pathfinder, confidently.

"Natur' is natur', and it is an Injin's natur' to be found where he is least expected. No fear of him on a beaten path, for he wishes to come upon you when unprepared to meet him, and the fiery villains make it a point to deceive you, one way or another. Sheer in, Eau-douce; we will land the sergeant's daughter on the end of that log, where she can reach the shore with a dry foot."

The injunction was obeyed, and in a few minutes the whole party had left the canoe, with the exception of Pathfinder and the two sailors. Notwithstanding his professional pride, Cap would have gladly followed, but he did not like to exhibit so unequivocal a weakness in the presence of a fresh-water sailor.

"I call all hands to witness," he said, as those who had landed moved away, "that I do not look on this affair as anything more than canoeing in the woods. There is no seamanship in tumbling over a waterfall, which is a feat the greatest lubber can perform as well as the oldest mariner."

"Nay, nay; you needn't despise the Oswego Falls, neither," put in Pathfinder, "for though they may not be Niagara, nor the Genesee, nor the Cahoos, nor Glens, nor them on the Canada, they are narvous enough for a new beginner. Let the sergeant's daughter stand on yonder rock, and she will see the manner in which we ignorant backwoodsmen get over a difficulty that we can't get under. Now, Eau-douce, a steady hand and a true eye, for all rests on you, seeing that we can count Master Cap for no more than a passenger."

The canoe was leaving the shore, as he concluded, while Mabel went hurriedly and trembling to the rock that had been pointed out, talking to her companion of the danger her uncle so unnecessarily ran, while her eyes were riveted on the agile and vigorous form of Eau-douce, as he stood erect in the stern of the light boat, governing its movements. As soon, however, as she reached a point where she got a view of the fall, she gave an involuntary but suppressed scream, and covered her eyes. At the next instant, the latter were again free, and the entranced girl stood immovable as a statue, a scarcely breathing observer of all that passed. The two Indians seated themselves passively on a log, hardly looking toward the stream, while the wife of Arrowhead came near Mabel, and appeared to watch the motions of the canoe with some such interest as a child regards the leaps of a tumbler.

As soon as the boat was in the stream, Pathfinder sank on his knees, continuing to use the paddle, though it was slowly, and in a manner not to interfere with the efforts of his companion. The latter still stood erect, and, as he kept his eye on some object beyond the fall, it was evident that he was carefully looking for the spot proper for their passage.

"Farther west, boy; farther west," muttered Pathfinder; "there where you see the water foam. Bring the top of the dead oak in a line with the stem of the blasted hemlock."

Eau-douce made no answer, for the canoe was in the center of the stream, with its head pointed toward the fall, and it had already begun to quicken its motion, by the increased force of the current. At that moment Cap would cheerfully have renounced every claim to glory that could possibly be acquired by the feat, to have been safe again on shore. He heard the roar of the water, thundering as it might be, behind a screen, but becoming more and more distinct, louder and louder; and before him he saw its line cutting the forest below, along which the green and angry element seemed stretched and shining, as if the particles were about to lose their principle of cohesion.

"Down with your helm—down with your helm, man!" he exclaimed, unable any longer to suppress his anxiety, as the canoe glided towards the edge of the fall.

"Ay, ay; down it is, sure enough," answered Pathfinder, looking behind him for a single instant, with his silent, joyous laugh; "down we go, of a sartainty! Heave her starn up, boy; farther up with her starn!"

The rest was like the passage of the viewless wind. Eau-douce gave the required sweep with his paddle, the canoe glanced into the channel, and for a few seconds it seemed to Cap that he was tossing in a caldron. He felt the bow of the canoe tip, saw the raging, foaming water, careering madly by his side, was sensible that the light fabric in which he floated was tossed about like an eggshell, and then, not less to his great joy than to his surprise, he discovered that it was gliding across the basin of still water, below the fall, under the steady impulse of Jasper's paddle.

The Pathfinder continued to laugh, but he arose from his knees, and, searching for a tin pot and a horn spoon, he began deliberately to measure the water that had been taken in in the passage.

"Fourteen spoonfuls, Eau-douce; fourteen fairly measured spoonfuls. I have, you must acknowledge, known you to go down with only ten."

"Master Cap leaned so hard upstream," returned Jasper, seriously, "that I had difficulty in trimming the canoe."

"It may be so—it may be so; no doubt it *was* so, since you say it; but I have known you go over with only ten."

Cap now gave a tremendous hem, felt for his queue, as if to ascertain its safety, and then looked back, in order to examine the danger he had gone through. His impunity is easily explained. Most of the river fell perpendicularly ten or twelve feet; but near its center, the force of the current had so far worn away the rock, as to permit the water to shoot through a narrow passage, at an angle of about forty or forty-five degrees. Down this ticklish descent the canoe had glanced, amid fragments of broken rock, whirlpools, foam, and furious tossings of the element, which an uninstructed eye would believe menaced inevitable destruction to an object so fragile. But the very lightness of the canoe favored its descent; for, borne on the crests of the waves, and directed by a steady eye and an arm full of muscle, it had passed like a feather from one pile of foam to another, scarcely permitting its glossy side to be wetted. There were a few rocks to be avoided; the proper direction was to be rigidly observed, and the fierce current did the rest.[1]

To say that Cap was astonished, would not be expressing half his feelings. He felt awed, for the profound dread of rocks, which most seamen entertain, came in aid of his admiration of the boldness of the exploit. Still he was indisposed to express all he felt, lest it might be conceding too much in favor of fresh water, and inland navigation; and no sooner had he cleared his throat with the aforesaid hem, than he loosened his tongue in the usual strain of superiority.

"I do not gainsay your knowledge of the channel, Master Oh-the-Deuce,"—for such he religiously believed to be Jasper's *sobriquet,*—"and, after all, to know the channel in such a place is the main point. I have had coxswains with me who could come down that shoot too, if they only knew the channel."

"It isn't enough to know the channel, friend mariner," said Pathfinder; "it needs narves and skill to keep the canoe straight and to keep her clear of the rocks, too. There isn't another boatman in all this region that can shoot the Oswego, but Eau-douce, there, with any sartainty; though, now and then, one has blundered through. I can't do it myself, unless by means of Providence, and it needs Jasper's hand and Jasper's eye to make sure of a dry passage. Fourteen spoonfuls, after all, are no great matter, though I wish it had been but ten, seeing that the sergeant's daughter was a looker-on."

"And yet you conned the canoe; you told him how to head and how to sheer."

"Human frailty, master mariner; that was a little of white-skin natur'. Now, had the Sarpent, yonder, been in the boat, not a word would he have spoken, or thought would he have given to the public. An Injin knows how to hold his tongue; but we white folk fancy we are always wiser than our fellows. I'm curing myself fast of the weakness, but it needs time to root up the tree that has been growing more than thirty years."

---

[1] Lest the reader suppose we are dealing purely in fiction, the writer will add that he has known a long thirty-two pounder carried over these same falls in perfect safety. (*Cooper's note*)

"I think little of this affair, sir; nothing at all, to speak my mind freely. It's a mere wash of spray to shooting London Bridge, which is done every day by hundreds of persons, and often by the most delicate ladies in the land. The King's Majesty has shot the bridge in his royal person."

"Well, I want no delicate ladies or king's majesties (God bless 'em) in the canoe, in going over these falls; for a boat's breadth, either way, may make a drowning matter of it. Eau-douce, we shall have to carry the sergeant's brother over Niagara yet, to show him what may be done on a frontier!"

"The devil! Master Pathfinder, you must be joking, now! Surely it is not possible for a bark canoe to go over that mighty cataract!"

"You never were more mistaken, Master Cap, in your life. Nothing is easier, and many is the canoe I have seen go over it, with my own eyes, and, if we both live, I hope to satisfy you that the feat can be done. For my part, I think the largest ship that ever sailed on the ocean might be carried over, could she once get into the rapids."

Cap did not perceive the wink which Pathfinder exchanged with Eau-douce, and he remained silent for some time; for, sooth to say, he had never suspected the possibility of going down Niagara, feasible as the thing must appear to everyone, on a second thought, the real difficulty existing in going up it.

By this time, the party had reached the place where Jasper had left his own canoe concealed in the bushes, and they all re-embarked; Cap, Jasper, and his niece in one boat, and Pathfinder, Arrowhead, and the wife of the latter, in the other. The Mohican had already passed down the banks of the river by land, looking cautiously and with the skill of his people, for the signs of an enemy.

The cheek of Mabel did not recover all its bloom, until the canoe was again in the current, down which it floated swiftly, occasionally impelled by the paddle of Jasper. She witnessed the descent of the falls with a degree of terror that had rendered her mute, but her fright had not been so great as to prevent admiration of the steadiness of the youth who directed the movement, from blending with the passing terror. In truth, one much less quick and sensitive might have had her feelings awakened by the cool and gallant air with which Eau-douce had accomplished this clever exploit. He had stood firmly erect, notwithstanding the plunge; and to those who were on the shore, it was evident that by a timely application of his skill and strength, the canoe had received a sheer that alone carried it clear of a rock, over which the boiling water was leaping in *jets d'eau,*—now leaving the brown stone visible, and now covering it with a limpid sheet, as if machinery controlled the play of the element. The tongue cannot always express what the eyes view, but Mabel saw enough, even in that moment of fear, to blend forever in her mind, the pictures presented by the plunging canoe, and the unmoved steersman. She admitted that insidious sentiment, which binds woman so strongly to man, by feeling additional security in finding herself under his care; and for the first time since leaving Fort Stanwix, she was entirely at her ease in the frail bark in which she travelled. As the other canoe kept quite near her own, however, and the Pathfinder, by floating at her side, was most in view, the conversation was principally maintained with that person; Jasper seldom speaking unless addressed, and constantly exhibiting a wariness in the management of his own boat, that might have been remarked by one accustomed to his ordinary confident, careless manner, had such an observer been present to note what was passing.

"We know too well a woman's gifts, to think of carrying the sergeant's daughter over the falls," said Pathfinder, looking at Mabel, while he addressed her uncle; "though I've been acquainted with some of her sex, in them regions, that would think but little of doing the thing."

"Mabel is fainthearted, like her mother," returned Cap, "and you did well, friend, to humor her weakness. You will remember the child has never been at sea."

"No, no; it was easy to discover that, by your own fearlessness; any one might have seen how little you cared about the matter! I went over once with a raw hand, and he jumped out of the canoe, just as it tipped, and you may judge what a time he had of it!"

"What became of the poor fellow?" asked Cap, scarce knowing how to take the other's manner, which was so dry, while it was so simple, that a less obtuse subject than the old sailor might well have suspected its sincerity. "One who has passed the place knows how to feel for him."

"He was a *poor* fellow, as you say; and a poor frontiersman, too, though he came out to show his skill among us ignoranters. What became of him? Why, he went down the falls topsy-turvy-like, as would have happened to a courthouse or a fort."

"If it should jump out of a canoe," interrupted Jasper, smiling, though he was evidently more disposed than his friend to let the passage of the falls be forgotten.

"The boy is right," rejoined Pathfinder, laughing in Mabel's face, the canoes being now so near that they almost touched; "he is sartainly right. But you have not told us what you think of the leap we took?"

"It was perilous and bold," said Mabel; "while looking at it, I could have wished that it had not been attempted, though, now it is over, I can admire its boldness, and the steadiness with which it was made."

"Now, do not think that we did this thing, to set ourselves off in female eyes. It may be pleasant to the young to win each other's good opinions, by doing things that may seem praiseworthy and bold; but neither Eau-douce nor myself is of that race. My natur', though perhaps the Sarpent would be a better witness, has few turns in it, and is a straight natur'; nor would it be likely to lead me into a vanity of this sort, while out on duty. As for Jasper, he would sooner go over the Oswego Falls without a looker-on, than do it before a hundred pair of eyes. I know the lad well, from use and much consorting, and I am sure he is not boastful nor vainglorious."

Mabel rewarded the scout with a smile that served to keep the canoes together for some time longer, for the sight of youth and beauty was so rare on that remote frontier, that even the rebuked and self-mortified feelings of this wanderer of the forest were sensibly touched by the blooming loveliness of the girl.

"We did it for the best," Pathfinder continued; " 'twas all for the best. Had we waited to carry the canoe across the portage, time would have been lost, and nothing is so precious as time, when you are distrustful of Mingoes."

"But we can have little to fear, now! The canoes move swiftly, and two hours, you have said, will carry us down to the fort."

"It shall be a cunning Iroquois who hurts a hair of your head, pretty one, for all here are bound to the sergeant, and most, I think, to yourself, to see you safe from harm. Ha! Eau-douce; what is that in the river, at the lower turn, yonder, beneath the bushes,—I mean standing on the rock?"

" 'Tis the Big Serpent, Pathfinder; he is making signs to us, in a way I don't understand.

" 'Tis the Sarpent, as sure as I'm a white man, and he wishes us to drop in nearer to his shore. Mischief is brewin', or one of his deliberation and steadiness would never take this trouble. Courage, all! we are men, and must meet deviltry as becomes our color and our callings. Ah! I never knew good come of boastin'; and here, just as I was vauntin' of our safety, comes danger to give me the lie."

The Oswego, below the falls, is a more rapid, unequal stream than it is above them. There are places where the river flows in the quiet stillness of deep water, but many shoals and rapids occur; and, at that distant day, when everything was in its natural state, some of the passes were not altogether without hazard. Very little exertion was required on the part of those who managed the canoes, except in those places where the swiftness of the current and the presence of the rocks required care; when, indeed, not only vigilance, but great coolness, readiness and strength of arm became necessary, in order to avoid the dangers. Of all this the Mohican was aware, and he had judiciously selected a spot where the river flowed tranquilly, to intercept the canoes, in order to make his communication without hazard to those he wished to speak.

The Pathfinder had no sooner recognized the form of his red friend, than, with a strong sweep of his paddle, he threw the head of his own canoe toward the shore, motioning for Jasper to follow. In a minute both boats were silently drifting down the stream, within reach of the bushes that overhung the water, all observing a profound silence; some from alarm, and others from habitual caution. As the travellers drew nearer the Indian, he made a sign for them to stop; when he and Pathfinder had a short but earnest conference, in the language of the Delawares.

"The chief is not apt to see enemies in a dead log," observed the white man, to his red associate; "why does he tell us to stop?"

"Mingoes are in the woods."

"That we have believed these two days: does the chief know it?"

The Mohican quietly held up the head of a pipe, formed of stone.

"It lay on a fresh trail that led toward the garrison;" for so it was the usage of that frontier to term a military work, whether it was occupied or not.

"That may be the bowl of a pipe belonging to a soldier. Many use the redskin pipes."

"See," said the Big Serpent, again holding the thing he had found up to the view of his friend.

The bowl of the pipe was of soapstone, and it had been carved with great care, and with a very respectable degree of skill. In its center was a small Latin cross, made with an accuracy that permitted no doubt of its meaning.

"That does fortell deviltry and wickedness," said the Pathfinder, who had all the provincial horror of the holy symbol in question that then pervaded the country, and which became so incorporated with its prejudices, by confounding men with things, as to have left its traces strong enough on the moral feeling of the community, to be discovered even at the present hour; "no Injin who had not been parvarted by the cunning priests of the Canadas would dream of carving a thing like that on his pipe! I'll warrant ye, the knave prays to the image every time he wishes to sarcumvent the innocent, and work his fearful wickedness. It looks fresh, too, Chingachgook?"

"The tobacco was burning when I found it."

"That is close work, chief; where was the trail?"

The Mohican pointed to a spot not a hundred yards distant from that where they stood.

The matter now began to look very serious, and the two principal guides conferred apart for several minutes, when both ascended the bank, approached the indicated spot, and examined the trail with the utmost care. After this investigation had lasted a quarter of an hour, the white man returned alone, his red friend having disappeared in the forest.

The ordinary expression of the countenance of the Pathfinder was that of simplicity, integrity, and sincerity blended in an air of self-reliance, that usually gave great confidence to those who found themselves under his care; but now a look of concern cast a shade over his honest face, that struck the whole party.

"What cheer, Master Pathfinder?" demanded Cap, permitting a voice that was usually deep, loud, and confident, to sink into the cautious tones that better suited the dangers of the wilderness; "has the enemy got between us and our port?"

"Anan?"

"Have any of these painted scaramouches anchored off the harbor toward which we are running, with the hope of cutting us off in entering?"

"It may be all as you say, friend Cap, but I am none the wiser for your words; and, in ticklish times, the plainer a man makes his English, the easier he is understood. I know nothing of ports and anchors, but there is a direful Mingo trail within a hundred yards of this spot, and as fresh as venison without salt. If one of the fiery devils has passed, so have a dozen; and what is worse, they have gone down toward the garrison, and not a soul crosses the clearing around it that some of their piercing eyes will not discover, when sartain bullets will follow."

"Cannot this said fort deliver a broadside, and clear everything within the sweep of its hawse?"

"Nay, the forts this-a-way are not like forts in the settlements, and two or three light cannon are all they have down at the mouth of the river; and then, broadsides fired at a dozen outlying Mingoes, lying behind logs, and in a forest, would be powder spent in vain. We have but one course, and that is a very nice one. We are judgmatically placed here, both canoes being hid by the high bank and the bushes, from all eyes except them of any lurker directly opposite. Here, then, we may stay, without much present fear; but how to get the bloodthirsty devils up the stream again? Ha! I have it—I have it. If it does no good, it can do no harm. Do you see the wide-top chestnut, here, Jasper, at the last turn in the river? On our own side of the stream, I mean."

"That near the fallen pine?"

"The very same. Take the flint and tinderbox, creep along the bank, and light a fire at that spot; maybe the smoke will draw them above us. In the meanwhile, we will drop the canoes carefully down beyond the point below, and find another shelter. Bushes are plenty, and covers are easy to be had in this region, as witness the many ambushments."

"I will do it, Pathfinder," said Jasper, springing to the shore. "In ten minutes the fire shall be lighted."

"And, Eau-douce, use plenty of damp wood this time," half whispered the other, laughing heartily, in his own peculiar manner; "when smoke is wanted, water helps to thicken it."

The young man, who too well understood his duty to delay unnecessarily, was soon off, making his way rapidly toward the desired point. A slight attempt of Mabel to object to the risk was disregarded, and the party immediately prepared to change its position, as it could be seen from the place where Jasper intended to light his fire. The movement did not require haste, and it was made leisurely, and with care. The canoes were got clear of the bushes, then suffered to drop down with the stream, until they reached the spot where the chestnut, at the foot of which Jasper was to light the fire, was almost shut out from view, when they stopped, and every eye was turned in the direction of the adventurer.

"There goes the smoke!" exclaimed the Pathfinder, as a current of air whirled a little column of the vapor from the land, allowing it to rise spirally above the bed of the river. "A good flint, a small bit of steel, and plenty of dry leaves, make a quick fire! I hope Eau-douce will have the wit to bethink him of the damp wood, now, when it may sarve us all a good turn."

"Too much smoke—too much cunning," said Arrowhead, sententiously.

"That is gospel truth, Tuscarora, if the Mingoes didn't know that they are near soldiers; but soldiers commonly think more of their dinner, at a halt, than of their wisdom and danger. No, no; let the boy pile on his logs, and smoke them well, too; it will all be laid to the stupidity of some Scotch or Irish blunderer, who is thinking more of his oatmeal or his potatoes than of Injin sarcumventions or Injin rifles."

"And yet I should think, from all we have heard in the towns, that the soldiers on this frontier are used to the artifices of their enemies," said Mabel; "and have got to be almost as wily as the red men themselves."

"Not they—not they. Exper'ence makes them but little wiser; and they wheel, and platoon, and battalion it about, here in the forest, just as they did in their parks at home, of which they are all so fond of talking. One redskin has more cunning in his natur' than a whole rijiment from the other side of the water—that is, what I call cunning of the woods. But there is smoke enough, of all conscience, and we had better drop into another cover. This lad has thrown the river on his fire, and there is danger that the Mingoes will believe a whole rijiment is out."

While speaking, the Pathfinder permitted his canoe to drift away from the bush by which it had been retained, and in a couple of minutes the bend in the river concealed the smoke and the tree. Fortunately a small indentation in the shore presented itself within a few yards of the point they had just passed; and the two canoes glided into it, under the impulsion of the paddles.

A better spot could not have been found for the purpose of the travellers, than the one they now occupied. The bushes were thick, and overhung the water, forming a complete canopy of leaves. There was a small gravelly strand at the bottom of the little bay, where most of the party landed to be more at their ease, and the only position from which they could possibly be seen, was a point on the river directly opposite. There was little danger, however, of discovery from that quarter, as the thicket there was even denser than common, and the land beyond it was so wet and marshy, as to render it difficult to be trodden.

"This is a safe cover," said the Pathfinder, after he had taken a scrutinizing survey of his position; "but it may be necessary to make it safer. Master Cap, I ask nothing of you but silence, and a quieting of such gifts as you may have got at sea, while the Tuscarora and I make provision for the evil hour."

The guide then went a short distance into the bushes, accompanied by the Indian, where the two cut off the large stems of several alders and other bushes, using the utmost care not to make a noise. The ends of these little trees, for such in fact they were, were forced into the mud, outside of the canoes, the depth of water being very trifling; and in the course of ten minutes a very effectual screen was interposed between them and the principal point of danger. Much ingenuity and readiness were manifested in making this simple arrangement, in which the two workmen were essentially favored by the natural formation of the bank, the indentation in the shore, the shallowness of the water, and the manner in which the tangled bushes dipped into the stream. The Pathfinder had the address to look for bushes that had curved stems, things easily found in such a place; and by cutting them some distance beneath the bend, and permitting the latter to touch the water, the artificial little thicket had not the appearance of growing in the stream, which might have excited suspicion; but one passing it would have thought that the bushes shot out horizontally from the bank before they inclined upward toward the light. In short, the shelter was so cunningly devised, and so artfully prepared, that none but an unusually distrustful eye would have been turned for an instant towards the spot, in quest of a hiding place.

"This is the best cover I ever yet got into," said the Pathfinder, with his quiet laugh, after having been on the outside to reconnoiter; "the leaves of our new trees fairly touch the bushes over our heads, and even the painter who has been in the garrison of late, could not tell which belong to Providence and which are our'n. Hist! yonder comes Eau-douce, wading, like a sensible boy as he is, to leave his trail in the water; and we shall soon see whether our cover is good for anything or not."

Jasper had, indeed, returned from his duty above, and missing the canoes, he at once inferred that they had dropped round the next bend in the river, in order to get out of sight of the fire. His habits of caution immediately suggested the expediency of stepping into the water, in order that there might exist no visible communication between the marks left on the shore, by the party, and the place where he believed them to have taken refuge below. Should the Canadian Indians return on their own trail, and discover that made by the Pathfinder and the Serpent, in their ascent from, and descent to, the river, the clue to their movements would cease at the shore, water leaving no prints of footsteps. The young man had therefore waded, knee-deep, as far as the point, and was now seen making his way slowly down the margin of the stream, searching curiously for the spot in which the canoes were hid.

It was in the power of those behind the bushes, by placing their eyes near the leaves, to find many places to look through, while one at a little distance lost this advantage; or, even did his sight happen to fall on some small opening, the bank and the shadows beyond prevented him from detecting forms and outlines of sufficient dimensions to expose the fugitives. It was evident to those who watched his motions from behind their cover, and they were all in the canoes, that Jasper was totally at a loss to imagine where the Pathfinder had secreted himself. When fairly round the curvature in the shore, and out of sight of the fire he had lighted above, the young man stopped, and began examining the bank deliberately and with great care. Occasionally he advanced eight or ten paces, and then halted again, to renew the search. The water being much shoaler than common, he stepped aside, in order to walk with greater ease to himself, and came so near the artificial plantation, that he might have touched it with his hand. Still he detected nothing and was actually passing the spot, when Pathfinder made an opening beneath the branches, and called to him, in a low voice, to enter.

"This is pretty well," said the Pathfinder, laughing; "though pale-face eyes and redskin eyes are as different as human spyglasses. I would wager with the sergeant's daughter, here, a horn of powder ag'in a wampum belt for her girdle, that her father's rijiment should march by this ambushment of our'n, and never find out the fraud! But, if the Mingoes actilly get down into the bed of the river, where Jasper passed, I should tremble for the plantation. It will do for their eyes even, across the stream, howsever, and will not be without its use."

"Don't you think, Master Pathfinder, that it would be wisest after all," said Cap, "to get under way at once, and carry sail hard down-stream, as soon as we are satisfied these rascals are fairly astern of us? We seamen call a stern chase a long chase."

"I wouldn't move from this spot until we hear from the Sarpent, with the sergeant's pretty daughter, here, in our company, for all the powder in the magazine of the fort below! Sartain captivity or sartain death would follow. If a tender fa'n, such as the maiden we have in charge, could thread the forest like old deer, it might, indeed, do to quit the canoes, for by making a circuit we could reach the garrison before morning."

"Then let it be done," said Mabel, springing to her feet, under the sudden impulse of awakened energy. "I am young, active, used to exercise, and could easily outwalk my dear uncle. Let no one think me a hindrance. I cannot bear that all your lives should be exposed on my account."

"No, no, pretty one; we think you anything but a hindrance, or anything that is onbecoming, and would willingly run twice this risk to do you and the honest sergeant a service. Do I not speak your mind, Eau-douce?"

"To do *her* a service!" said Jasper, with emphasis. "Nothing shall tempt me to desert Mabel Dunham, until she is safe in her father's arms."

"Well said, lad; bravely and honestly said, too; and I join in it, heart and hand. No, no; you are not the first of your sex I have led through the wilderness, and never but once did any harm befall any of them; that was a sad day, sartainly; but its like may never come again!"

Mabel looked from one of her protectors to the other, and her fine eyes swam in tears. Frankly placing a hand in that of each, she answered them, though at first her voice was choked,—

"I have no right to expose you on my account. My dear father will thank you—I thank you—God will reward you; but let there be no unnecessary risk. I can walk far, and have often gone miles, on some girlish fancy; why not now exert myself for my life—nay, for your precious lives?"

"She is a true dove, Jasper," said the Pathfinder, neither relinquishing the hand he held until the girl herself, in native modesty, saw fit to withdraw it, "and wonderfully winning! We get to be rough, and sometimes even hardhearted, in the woods, Mabel; but the sight of one like you brings us back ag'in to our young feelin's, and does us good for the remainder of our days. I dare say Jasper, here, will tell you the same; for, like me in the forest, the lad sees but few such as yourself, on Ontario, to soften his heart, and remind him of love for his kind. Speak out, now, Jasper, and say if it is not so."

"I question if many like Mabel Dunham are to be found anywhere," returned the young man, gallantly, an honest sincerity glowing in his face, that spoke more eloquently than his tongue; "you need not mention woods and lakes to challenge her equals, but I would go into the settlements and towns."

"We had better leave the canoes," Mabel hurriedly rejoined; "for I feel it is no longer safe to be here."

"You can never do it—you can never do it. It would be a march of more than twenty miles, and that, too, of tramping over brush and roots, and through swamps, in the dark; the trail of such a party would be wide, and we might have to fight our way into the garrison, a'ter all. We will wait for the Mohican."

Such appearing to be the decision of him to whom all, in their present strait, looked up for counsel, no more was said on the subject. The whole party now broke up into groups; Arrowhead and his wife sitting apart under the bushes, conversing in a low tone, though the man spoke sternly, and the woman answered with the subdued mildness that marks the degraded condition of a savage's wife. Pathfinder and Cap occupied one canoe, chatting of their different adventures by sea and land, while Jasper and Mabel sat in the other, making greater progress in intimacy in a single hour, than might have been effected under other circumstances in a twelvemonth. Notwithstanding their situation as regards the enemy, the time flew by swiftly, and the young people in particular were astonished when Cap informed them how long they had been thus occupied.

"If one could smoke, Master Pathfinder," observed the old sailor, "this berth would be snug enough; for, to give the devil his due, you have got the canoes handsomely landlocked, and into moorings that would defy a monsoon. The only hardship is the denial of the pipe."

"The scent of the tobacco would betray us; and where is the use of taking all these precautions against the Mingoes' eyes if we are to tell them where the cover is to be found through the nose? No, no; deny your appetites, deny your appetites, and learn one virtue from a redskin, who will pass a week without eating even, to get a single scalp. Did you hear nothing, Jasper?"

"The Serpent is coming."

"Then let us see if Mohican eyes are better than them of the lad who follows the water."

The Mohican made his appearance in the same direction as that by which Jasper had rejoined his friends. Instead of coming directly on, however, no sooner did he pass the bend, where he was concealed from any who might be higher upstream, than he moved close under the bank, and, using the utmost caution, got a position where he could look back, with his person sufficiently concealed by the bushes to prevent its being seen by any in that quarter.

"The Sarpent sees the knaves!" whispered Pathfinder; "as I'm a Christian white man they have bit at the bait, and have ambushed the smoke!"

Here a hearty, but silent laugh, interrupted his words, and nudging Cap with his elbow, they all continued to watch the movements of Chingachgook in profound stillness. The Mohican remained stationary as the rock on which he stood, fully ten minutes; then it was apparent that something of interest had occurred within his view, for he drew back with a hurried manner, looked anxiously and keenly along the margin of the stream, and moved quickly down it, taking care to lose his trail in the shallow water. He was evidently in a hurry and concerned, now looking behind him, and then casting eager glances toward every spot on the shore where he thought a canoe might be concealed.

"Call him in," whispered Jasper, scarce able to restrain his impatience; "call him in, or it will be too late. See, he is actually passing us."

"Not so—not so, lad; nothing presses, depend on it," returned his companion, "or the Sarpent would begin to creep. The Lord help us, and teach us wisdom! I do believe even Chingachgook, whose sight is as faithful as the hound's scent, overlooks us, and will not find out the ambushment we have made!"

This exultation was untimely, for the words were no sooner spoken, than the Indian, who had actually got several feet lower down the stream than the artificial cover, suddenly stopped, fastened a keen riveted glance among the transplanted bushes, made a few hasty steps backward, and, bending his body and carefully separating the branches, he appeared among them.

"The accursed Mingoes!" said Pathfinder, as soon as his friend was near enough to be addressed with prudence.

"Iroquois," returned the sententious Indian.

"No matter, no matter; Iroquois, devil, Mingo, Mengwes, or furies, all are pretty much the same. I call all rascals Mingoes. Come hither, chief, and let us convarse rationally."

The two then stepped aside, and conversed earnestly in the dialect of the Delawares. When their private communication was over, Pathfinder rejoined the rest, and made them acquainted with all he had learned.

The Mohican had followed the trail of their enemies some distance towards the fort, until the latter caught a sight of the smoke of Jasper's fire, when they instantly retraced their steps. It now became necessary for Chingachgook, who ran the greatest risk of detection, to find a cover where he could secrete himself until the party might pass. It was, perhaps, fortunate for him that the savages were so intent on this recent discovery, that they did not bestow the ordinary attention on the signs of the forest. At all events, they passed him swiftly, fifteen in number, treading lightly in each other's footsteps; and he was enabled again to get into their rear. After proceeding to the place where the footsteps of Pathfinder and the Mohican joined the principal trail, the Iroquois had struck off to the river, which they reached just as Jasper disappeared behind the bend below. The smoke being now in plain view, the savages plunged into the woods, and endeavored to approach the fire unseen. Chingachgook profited by this occasion to descend to the water, and to gain the bend in the river also, which he thought had been effected undiscovered. Here he paused, as has been stated, until he saw his enemies at the fire, where their stay, however, was very short.

Of the motives of the Iroquois, the Mohican could judge only by their acts. He thought they had detected the artifice of the fire, and were aware that it had been kindled with a view to mislead them; for, after a hasty examination of the spot, they separated, some plunging again into the woods, while six or eight followed the footsteps of Jasper along the shore, and came down the stream toward the place where the canoes had landed. What course they might take on reaching that spot, was only to be conjectured, for the Serpent had felt the emergency to be too pressing to delay looking for his friends any longer. From some indications that were to be gathered from their gestures, however, he thought it probable that their enemies might follow down in the margin of the stream, but could not be certain.

As the Pathfinder related these facts to his companions, the professional feelings of the two other white men came uppermost, and both naturally reverted to their habits, in quest of the means of escape.

"Let us run out the canoes at once," said Jasper, eagerly, "the current is strong, and by using the paddles vigorously we shall soon be beyond the reach of these scoundrels!"

"And this poor flower, that first blossomed in the clearin's—shall it wither in the forest?" objected his friend, with a poetry that he had unconsciously imbibed by his long association with the Delawares.

"We must all die first," answered the youth, a generous color mounting to his temples; "Mabel and Arrowhead's wife may lie down in the canoes, while we do our duty, like men, on our feet."

"Ay, you are actyve at the paddle and the oar, Eau-douce, I will allow, but an accursed Mingo is more actyve at his mischief; the canoes are swift, but a rifle bullet is swifter."

"It is the business of men engaged as we have been, by a confiding father, to run this risk—"

"But it is not their business to overlook prudence."

"Prudence! a man may carry his prudence so far as to forget his courage."

The group was standing on the narrow strand, the Pathfinder leaning on his rifle, the butt of which rested on the gravelly beach, while both his hands clasped the barrel, at the height of his own shoulders. As Jasper threw out this severe and unmerited imputation, the deep red of his comrade's face maintained its hue unchanged, though the young man perceived that the fingers grasped the iron of the gun with the tenacity of a vice. Here all betrayal of emotion ceased.

"You are young and hotheaded," returned the Pathfinder, with a dignity that impressed his listener with a keen sense of his moral superiority; "but my life has been passed among dangers of this sort, and my exper'ence and gifts are not to be mastered by the impatience of a boy. As for courage, Jasper, I will not send back an angry and unmeaning word, to meet an angry and an unmeaning word, for I know that you are true, in your station and according to your knowledge; but take the advice of one who faced the Mingoes when you were a child, and know that their cunning is easier sarcumvented by prudence than outwitted by foolishness."

"I ask your pardon, Pathfinder," said the repentant Jasper, eagerly grasping the hand that the other permitted him to seize; "I ask your pardon, humbly and sincerely. 'Twas a foolish, as well as wicked thing to hint of a man whose heart, in a good cause, is as firm as the rocks on the lake shore."

For the first time the color deepened on the cheek of the Pathfinder, and the solemn dignity that he had assumed, under a purely natural impulse, disappeared in the expression of the earnest simplicity that was inherent in all his feelings. He met the grasp of his young friend with a squeeze as cordial as if no chord had jarred between them, and a slight sternness that had gathered about his eyes disappeared in a look of natural kindness.

" 'Tis well, Jasper, 'tis well," he answered, laughing. "I bear no ill will, nor shall anyone in my behalf. My natur' is that of a white man, and that is to bear no malice. It might have been ticklish work to have said half as much to the Sarpent here, though he is a Delaware, for color will have its way—"

A touch on his shoulder caused the speaker to cease. Mabel was standing erect in the canoe, her light but swelling form bent forward in an attitude of graceful earnestness, her finger on her lips, her head averted, the spirited eyes riveted on an opening in the bushes, and one arm extended with a fishing rod, the end of which had touched the Pathfinder. The latter bowed his head to a level with a lookout near which he had intentionally kept himself, and then whispered to Jasper,—

"The accursed Mingoes! Stand to your arms, my men, but lay quiet as the corpses of dead trees!"

Jasper advanced rapidly, but noiselessly, to the canoe, and with a gentle violence induced Mabel to place herself in such an attitude as concealed her entire body, though it would have probably exceeded his means to induce the girl so far to lower her head that she could not keep her gaze fastened on their enemies. He then took his own post near her, with his rifle cocked and poised, in readiness to fire. Arrowhead and Chingachgook crawled to the cover, and lay in wait like snakes, with their arms prepared for service, while the wife of the former bowed her head between her knees, covered it with her calico robe, and remained passive and immovable. Cap loosened both his pistols in their belt, but seemed quite at a loss what course to pursue. The Pathfinder did not stir. He had originally got a position where he might aim with deadly effect through the leaves, and where he could watch the movements of his enemies; and he was far too steady to be disconcerted at a moment so critical.

It was truly an alarming instant. Just as Mabel touched the shoulder of her guide, three of the Iroquois appeared in the water, at the bend of the river, within a hundred yards of the cover, and halted to examine the stream below. They were all naked to the waist, armed for an expedition against their foes, and in their war paint. It was apparent that they were undecided as to the course they ought to pursue, in order to find the fugitives. One pointed down the river, a second up the stream, and the third toward the opposite bank.

It was a breathless moment. The only clue the fugitives possessed to the intentions of their pursuers was in their gestures, and the indications that escaped them in the fury of disappointment. That a party had returned already on their own footsteps, by land, was pretty certain; and all the benefit expected from the artifices of the fire was necessarily lost. But that consideration became of little moment, just then, for the secreted were menaced with an immediate discovery by those who had kept on a level with the river. All the facts presented themselves clearly, and as it might be by intuition, to the mind of Pathfinder, who perceived the necessity of immediate decision, and of being in readiness to act in concert. Without making any noise, therefore, he managed to get the two Indians and Jasper near him, when he opened his communications in a whisper.

"We must be ready—we must be ready," he said. "There are but three of the scalping devils, and we are five, four of whom may be set down as manful warriors for such a scrimmage. Eau-douce, do you take the fellow that is painted like death; Chingachgook, I give you the chief; and Arrowhead must keep his eye on the young one. There must be no mistake; for two bullets in the same body would be sinful waste, with one like the sergeant's daughter in danger. I shall hold myself in resarve ag'in accidents, lest a fourth riptyle appear, for one of your hands may prove unsteady. By no means fire until I give the word; we must not let the crack of the rifle be heard except in the last resort, since all the rest of the miscreants are still within hearing. Jasper, boy, in case of any movement behind us, on the bank, I trust to you to run out the canoe, with the sergeant's daughter, and to pull for the garrison, by God's leave."

The Pathfinder had no sooner given these directions than the near approach of their enemies rendered profound silence necessary. The Iroquois in the river were slowly descending the stream, keeping of necessity near the bushes that overhung the water, whilst the rustling of leaves and the snapping of twigs soon gave fearful evidence that another party was moving along the bank at an equally graduated pace, and directly abreast of them. In consequence of the distance between the bushes planted by the fugitives and the true shore, the two parties became visible to each other, when opposite that precise point. Both stopped, and a conversation ensued, that may be said to have passed directly over the heads of those who were concealed. Indeed, nothing sheltered the travellers but the branches and leaves of plants so pliant, that they yielded to every current of air, and which a puff of wind, a little stronger than common, would have blown away. Fortunately the line of sight carried the eyes of the two parties of savages, whether they stood in the water or on the land, above the bushes; and the leaves appeared blended in a way to excite no suspicion. Perhaps the very boldness of the expedient prevented an exposure. The conversation that took place was conducted earnestly, but in guarded tones, as if those who spoke wished to defeat the intentions of any listeners. It was in a dialect that both the Indian warriors beneath, as well as the Pathfinder, understood. Even Jasper comprehended a portion of what was said.

"The trail is washed away by the water!" said one from below, who stood so near the artificial cover of the fugitives, that he might have been struck by the salmon spear that lay in the bottom of Jasper's canoe. "Water has washed it so clear, that a Yengeese hound could not follow."

"The palefaces have left the shore in their canoes," answered the speaker on the bank.

"It cannot be. The rifles of our warriors below are certain."

The Pathfinder gave a significant glance at Jasper, and he clenched his teeth in order to suppress the sound of his own breathing.

"Let my young men look as if their eyes were eagles'," said the eldest warrior among those who were wading in the river. "We have been a whole moon on the warpath, and have found but one scalp. There is a maiden among them, and some of our braves want wives."

Happily these words were lost on Mabel, but Jasper's frown became deeper, and his face fiercely flushed.

The savages now ceased speaking, and the party that was concealed heard the slow and guarded movements of those who were on the bank, as they pushed the bushes aside in their wary progress. It was soon evident that the latter had passed the cover; but the group in the water still remained, scanning the shore with eyes that glared through their war paint, like coals of living fire. After a pause of two or three minutes, these three began also to descend the stream, though it was step by step, as men move who look for an object that has been lost. In this manner they passed the artificial screen, and Pathfinder opened his mouth, in that hearty but noiseless laugh, that nature and habit had contributed to render a peculiarity of the man. His triumph, however, was premature; for the last of the retiring party, just at this moment casting a look behind him, suddenly stopped; and his fixed attitude and steady gaze at once betrayed the appalling fact that some neglected bush had awakened his suspicions.

It was, perhaps, fortunate for the concealed, that the warrior who manifested these fearful signs of distrust was young, and had still a reputation to acquire. He knew the importance of discretion and modesty in one of his years, and most of all did he dread the ridicule and contempt that would certainly follow a false alarm. Without recalling any of his companions, therefore, he turned on his own footsteps, and while the others continued to descend the river, he cautiously approached the bushes, on which his looks were still fastened, as by a charm. Some of the leaves which were exposed to the sun had drooped a little, and this slight departure from the usual natural laws had caught the quick eyes of the Indian; for so practiced and acute do the senses of the savage become, more especially when he is on the warpath, that trifles, apparently of the most insignificant sort, often prove to be clues to lead him to his object. The trifling nature of the change which had aroused the suspicion of this youth, was an additional motive for not acquainting his companions with his discovery. Should he really detect anything, his glory would be the greater for being unshared; should he not, he might hope to escape that derision which the young Indian so much dreads. Then there were the dangers of an ambush and a surprise, to which every warrior of the woods is keenly alive, to render his approach slow and cautious. In consequence of the delay that proceeded from these combined causes, the two parties had descended some fifty or sixty yards before the young savage was again near enough to the bushes of the Pathfinder to touch them with his hand.

Notwithstanding their critical situation, the whole party behind the cover had their eyes fastened on the working countenance of the young Iroquois, who was agitated by conflicting feelings. First came the eager hope of obtaining success, where some of the most experienced of his tribe had failed, and with it a degree of glory that had seldom fallen to the share of one of his years, or a brave on his first warpath; then followed doubts, as the drooping leaves seemed to rise again, and to revive in the currents of air; and distrust of hidden danger lent its exciting feeling to keep the eloquent features in play. So very slight, however, had been the alteration produced by the heat on bushes of which the stems were in the water, that when the Iroquois actually laid his hand on the leaves, he fancied that he had been deceived. As no man ever distrusts strongly, without using all convenient means of satisfying his doubts, however, the young warrior cautiously pushed aside the branches, and advanced a step within the hiding place, when the forms of the concealed party met his gaze, resembling so many breathless statues. The low exclamation, the slight start, and the glaring eye were hardly seen and heard, before the arm of Chingachgook was raised, and the tomahawk of the Delaware descended on the shaven head of his foe. The Iroquois raised his hands frantically, bounded backward, and fell into the water at a spot where the current swept the body away, the struggling limbs still tossing and writhing in the agony of death. The Delaware made a vigorous but unsuccessful attempt to seize an arm, with the hope of securing the scalp, but the bloodstained waters whirled down the current, carrying with them their quivering burden.

All this passed in less than a minute; and the events were so sudden and unexpected, that men less accustomed than the Pathfinder and his associates to forest warfare, would have been at a loss how to act.

"There is not a moment to lose!" said Jasper, tearing aside the bushes, as he spoke earnestly, but in a suppressed voice. "Do as I do, Master Cap, if you would save your niece; and you, Mabel, lie at your length in the canoe."

The words were scarcely uttered, when, seizing the bow of the light boat, he dragged it along the shore, wading himself while Cap aided behind, keeping so near the bank as to avoid being seen by the savages below, and striving to gain the turn in the river above him, which would effectually conceal the party from the enemy. The Pathfinder's canoe lay nearest to the bank, and it was necessarily the last to quit the shore. The Delaware leaped on the narrow strand, and plunged into the forest, it being his assigned duty to watch the foe in that quarter, while Arrowhead motioned to his white companion to seize the bow of the boat, and to follow Jasper. All this was the work of an instant. But when the Pathfinder reached the current that was sweeping round the turn, he felt a sudden change in the weight he was dragging, and looking back he found that both the Tuscarora and his wife had deserted him. The thought of treachery flashed upon his mind, but there was no time to pause; for the wailing shout that arose from the party below, proclaimed that the body of the young Iroquois had floated as low as the spot reached by his friends. The report of a rifle followed; and then the guide saw that Jasper, having doubled the bend in the river, was crossing the stream, standing erect in the stern of the canoe, while Cap was seated forward, both propelling the light boat with vigorous strokes of the paddles. A glance, a thought, and an expedient followed each other quickly, in one so trained in the vicissitudes of the frontier warfare. Springing into the stern of his own canoe, he urged it by a vigorous shove into the current, and commenced crossing the stream himself, at a point so much lower than that of his companions, as to offer his own person for a target to the enemy, well knowing that their keen desire to secure a scalp would control all other feelings.

"Keep well up the current, Jasper," shouted the gallant guide, as he swept the water with long, steady, vigorous strokes of the paddle; "keep well up the current, and pull for the alder bushes opposite. Presarve the sergeant's daughter before all things, and leave the Mingo knaves to the Sarpent and me."

Jasper flourished his paddle, as a signal of understanding, while shot succeeded shot in quick succession, all now being aimed at the solitary man in the nearest canoe.

"Ay, empty your rifles, like simpletons as you be," said the Pathfinder, who had acquired a habit of speaking when alone, from passing so much of his time in the solitude of the forest; "empty your rifles, with an onsteady aim, and give me time to put yard upon yard of river between us. I will not revile you, like a Delaware or a Mohican, for my gifts are a white man's gifts, and not an Injin's; and boasting in battle is no part of a Christian warrior; but I may say, here, all alone by myself, that you are little better than so many men from the town, shooting at robins in the orchards! That was well meant," throwing back his head, as a rifle bullet cut a lock of hair from his temple; "but the lead that misses by an inch is as useless as the lead that never quits the barrel."

3

AFTER a desperate and uncertain struggle, all the members of the party safely reached the shelter of Fort Oswego. To save the life of Chingachgook, the scout had to slay one of the Iroquois by a long shot from Killdeer. He was overjoyed when he found the Indian chief, who had been lost in the darkness, quite unscathed. "Often have we passed through blood and strife together," he said, "but I was afraid it was never to be so again." Chingachgook, however, was contemptuous. "Mingoes—squaws!" he remarked. "Three of their scalps hang at my girdle. They do not know how to strike the Great Serpent of the Delawares." Mabel Dunham was delightedly embraced by her father, the oldest sergeant at the post.

Fort Oswego was then garrisoned by a battalion composed partly of Scottish soldiers, partly of Americans. It had bastions of earth and logs, a dry ditch, a stockade, a parade ground, and log barracks. One or two heavy iron guns and a few light field-pieces comprised the main part of its armament. The morning after their arrival, Mabel came out on the solitary bastion to enjoy the view over lake and forest. At once Pathfinder came up and took his place beside her.

The Oswego threw its dark waters into the lake between banks of some height; that on its eastern side being bolder and projecting farther north than that on its western. The fort was on the latter, and immediately beneath it were a few huts of logs, which, as they could not interfere with the defense of the place, had been erected along the strand for the purpose of receiving and containing such stores as were landed or were intended to be embarked in the communications between the different ports on the shores of Ontario. There were two low, curved gravelly points that had been formed with surprising regularity by the counteracting forces of the northerly winds and the swift current, and which, inclining from the storms of the lake, formed two coves within the river. That on the western side was the most deeply indented, and as it also had the most water, it formed a sort of picturesque little port for the post. It was along the narrow strand that lay between the low height of the fort and the water of this cove, that the rude buildings just mentioned had been erected.[1]

Several skiffs, batteaux, and canoes were hauled up on the shore, and in the cove itself lay the little craft, from which Jasper obtained his claim to be considered a sailor. She was cutter-rigged, might have been of forty tons burden, was so neatly constructed and painted as to have something of the air of a vessel of war, though entirely without quarters, and rigged and sparred with so scrupulous a regard to proportions and beauty, as well as fitness and judgment, as to give her an appearance that even Mabel at once distinguished to be gallant and trim. Her mould was admirable, for a wright of great skill had sent her drafts from England at the express request of the officer who had caused her to be constructed; her paint dark, warlike, and neat; and the long coach-whip pennant that she wore at once proclaimed her to be the property of the King. Her name was the *Scud*.

"That, then, is the vessel of Jasper!" said Mabel, who associated the master of the little craft quite naturally with the cutter itself. "Are there many others on this lake?"

"The Frenchers have three; one of which they tell me is a real ship, such as are used on the ocean, another a brig, and a third is a cutter like the *Scud*, here, which they call the *Squirrel*, in their own tongue, however; and which seems to have a natural hatred of our own pretty boat, for Jasper seldom goes out that the *Squirrel* is not at his heels."

"And is Jasper one to run from a Frenchman, though he appears in the shape of a squirrel, and that, too, on the water!"

"Of what use would valor be without the means of turning it to account? Jasper is a brave boy, as all on this frontier know; but he has no gun except a little howitzer, and then his crew consists only of two

---

[1] The British and Dutch had begun to use the mouth of the Oswego River as a fur-trading post as early as 1722; and in 1726 Governor Burnet of New York began the erection of a fort on the west bank of the river. When the Seven Years War began, it seemed important to strengthen the place, and as we have seen, a sister post, Fort Ontario, was built, both being shortly lost and destroyed. Fort Oswego as now rebuilt by the British was not imposing but it served to protect Northern New York, threaten Canada, and serve as a British base for operations on Lake Ontario and the upper St. Lawrence.—Ed.

men besides himself, and a boy. I was with him in one of his trampooses, and the youngster was risky enough, for he brought us so near the enemy that rifles began to talk; but the Frenchers carry cannon, and ports, and never show their faces outside of Frontenac without having some twenty men, besides their *Squirrel,* in their cutter. No. no; this *Scud* was built for flying, and the major says he will not put her in a fighting humor by giving her men and arms, lest she should take him at his word and get her wings clipped. I know little of these things, for my gifts are not at all in that way; but I see the reason of the thing—I see its reason, though Jasper does not."

"Ah! here is my uncle, none the worse for his swim, coming to look at this inland sea."

Sure enough, Cap, who had announced his approach by a couple of lusty hems, now made his appearance on the bastion, where, after nodding to his niece and her companion, he made a deliberate survey of the expanse of water before him. In order to effect this at his ease, the mariner mounted on one of the old iron guns, folded his arms across his breast, and balanced his body, as if he felt the motion of a vessel. To complete the picture, he had a short pipe in his mouth.

"Well, Master Cap," asked the Pathfinder, innocently, for he did not detect the expression of contempt that was gradually settling on the features of the other, "is it not a beautiful sheet, and fit to be named a sea?"

"This, then, is what you call your lake?" demanded Cap, sweeping the northern horizon with his pipe. "I say, is this, really, your lake?"

"Sartain; and, if the judgment of one who has lived on the shores of many others can be taken, a very good lake it is."

"Just as I expected! A pond in dimensions, and a scuttle-butt in taste. It is all in vain to travel inland, in the hope of seeing anything either full-grown or useful. I knew it would turn out just in this way."

"What is the matter with Ontario, Master Cap? It is large, and fair to look at, and pleasant enough to drink, for those who can't get at the water of the springs."

"Do you call this large?" asked Cap, again sweeping the air with the pipe. "I will just ask you what there is large about it? Didn't Jasper himself confess that it was only some twenty leagues from shore to shore?"

"But uncle," interposed Mabel, "no land is to be seen, except here on our own coast. To me it looks exactly like the ocean."

"This bit of a pond look like the ocean! Well, Magnet, that from a girl who has had real seamen in her family is downright nonsense. What is there about it, pray, that has even the outline of a sea on it?"

"Why, there is water—water—water; nothing but water, for miles on miles, far as the eye can see."

"And isn't there water—water—water, nothing but water, for miles on miles, in your rivers, that you have been canoeing through, too? ay, and 'as far as the eye can see,' in the bargain?"

"Yes, uncle, but the rivers have their banks, and there are trees along them, and they are narrow."

"And isn't this a bank where we stand; don't these soldiers call this the bank of the lake, and aren't there trees in thousands, and aren't twenty leagues narrow enough of all conscience? Who the devil ever heard of the banks of the ocean, unless it might be the banks that are under the water?"

"But, uncle, we cannot see across this lake, as we can see across a river."

"There you are out, Magnet. Aren't the Amazon, and Oronoco, and La Plata rivers, and can you see across them? Harkee, Pathfinder, I very much doubt if this strip of water here be even a lake; for to me it appears to be only a river. You are by no means particular about your geography, I find, up here in the woods."

"There *you* are out, Master Cap. There is a river, and a noble one too, at each end of it; but this is old Ontario before you, and, though it is not my gift to live on a lake, to my judgment there are few better than this."

"And, uncle, if we stood on the beach at Rockaway, what more should we see, than we now behold? There is a shore on one side, or banks there, and trees, too, as well as those which are here."

"This is perverseness, Magnet, and young girls should steer clear of anything like obstinacy. In the first place, the ocean has coasts, but no banks, except the Grand Banks, as I tell you, which are out of sight of land; and you will not pretend that this bank is out of sight of land, or even under water!"

As Mabel could not very plausibly set up this extravagant opinion, Cap pursued the subject, his countenance beginning to discover the triumph of a successful disputant.

"And then them trees bear no comparison to these trees. The coasts of the ocean have farms, and cities, and countryseats, and, in some parts of the world, castles and monasteries, and lighthouses—ay, ay, lighthouses, in particular, on them; not one of all which things is to be seen here. No, no, Master Pathfinder, I never heard of an ocean that hadn't more or less light houses on it, whereas, here-a-way, there is not even a beacon."

"There is what is better—there's what is better: a forest and noble trees, a fit temple of God."

"Ay, your forest may do for a lake, but of what use would an ocean be, if the earth all around it were forest? Ships would be unnecessary, as timber might be floated in rafts, and there would be an end of trade, and what would a world be without trade! I am of that philosopher's opinion who says human nature was invented for the purposes of trade. Magnet, I am astonished that you should think this water even looks like sea water! Now, I dare say that there isn't such a thing as a whale in all your lake, Master Pathfinder!"

"I never heard of one, I will confess, but I am no judge of animals that live in the water, unless it be the fishes of the rivers and brooks."

"Nor a grampus, nor a porpoise even; not so much as a poor devil of a shark?"

"I will not take it on myself to say there is either. My gifts are not in that way, I tell you, Master Cap."

"Nor herring, nor albatross, nor flying fish?" continued Cap, who kept his eye fastened on the guide, in order to see how far he might venture. "No such thing as a fish that can fly, I dare say?"

"A fish that can fly! Master Cap—Master Cap, do not think because we are mere borderers, that we have no idees of natur', and what she has been pleased to do. I know there are squirrels that can fly—"

"A squirrel fly? the devil, Master Pathfinder! Do you suppose that you have got a boy on his first v'y'ge, up here among you?"

"I know nothing of your v'y'ges, Master Cap, though I suppose them to have been many; but, as for what belongs to natur' in the woods, what I have seen I may tell, and not fear the face of man."

"And do you wish me to understand that you have seen a squirrel fly?"

"If you wish to understand the power of God, Master Cap, you will do well to believe that, and many other things of a like natur', for you may be quite sartain it is true."

"And yet, Pathfinder," said Mabel, looking so pretty and sweet even while she played with the guide's infirmity, that he forgave her in his heart, "you, who speak so reverently of the power of the Deity, appear to doubt that a fish can fly?"

"I have not said it—I have not said it; and if Master Cap is ready to testify to the fact, onlikely as it seems, I am willing to try to think it true. I think it every man's duty to believe in the power of God, however difficult it may be."

"And why isn't my fish as likely to have wings as your squirrel?" demanded Cap, with more logic than was his wont. "That fishes do and can fly, is as true as it is reasonable—"

"Nay, that is the only difficulty in believing the story," rejoined the guide. "It seems onreasonable to give an animal that lives in the water wings, which seemingly can be of no use to them."

"And do you suppose that the fishes are such asses as to fly about under water, when they are once fairly fitted out with wings?"

"Nay, I know nothing of the matter, but that fish should fly in the air seems more contrary to natur' still, than that they should fly in their own quarters; that in which they were born and brought up, as one might say."

"So much for contracted ideas, Magnet. The fish fly out of water to run away from their enemies in the water; and there you see not only the fact but the reason for it."

"Then I suppose it must be true," said the guide, quietly. "How long are their flights?"

"Not quite as far as those of pigeons, perhaps, but far enough to make an offing. As for those squirrels of yours, we'll say no more about them, friend Pathfinder, as I suppose they were mentioned just as a makeweight to the fish in favor of the woods. But what is this thing, anchored here under the hill?"

"That is the cutter of Jasper, uncle," said Mabel, hurriedly; "and a very pretty vessel I think it is. Its name, too, is the *Scud*."

"Ay, it will do well enough for a lake, perhaps, but it's no great affair. The lad has got a standing bowsprit, and who ever saw a cutter with a standing bowsprit before!"

"But may there not be some good reason for it, on a lake like this, uncle?"

"Sure enough; I must remember this is not the ocean, though it does look so much like it."

"Ah! uncle, then Ontario *does* look like the ocean, after all!"

"In your eyes, I mean, and those of Pathfinder; not in the least in mine, Magnet. Now you might see me down out yonder, in the middle of this bit of a pond, and that too in the darkest night that ever fell from the heavens, and in the smallest canoe, and I could tell you it was only a lake. For that matter the *Dorothy*"—the name of his vessel—"would find it out as quick as I could myself. I do not believe that brig would make more than a couple of short stretches at the most, before she would perceive the difference between Ontario and the old Atlantic. I once took her down into one of the large South American bays, and she behaved herself as awkwardly as a booby would in a church, with the congregation in a hurry. And Jasper sails that boat? I must have a cruise with the lad, Magnet, before I quit you, just for the name of the thing. It would never do to say I got in sight of this pond, and went away without taking a trip on it."

"Well, well, you needn't wait long for that," returned Pathfinder; "for the sergeant is about to embark with a party, to relieve a post among the Thousand Islands; and, as I heard him say he intended that Mabel should go along, you can join company too."

"Is this true, Magnet?"

"I believe it is," returned the girl, a flush so imperceptible as to escape the observation of her companions, glowing on her cheeks, "though I have had so little opportunity to talk with my dear father, that I am not quite certain. Here he comes, however, and you can inquire of himself."

Notwithstanding his humble rank, there was something in the mien and character of Sergeant Dunham that commanded respect. Of a tall, imposing figure, grave and saturnine disposition, and accurate and precise in his acts and manner of thinking, even Cap, dogmatical and supercilious as he usually was with landsmen, did not presume to take the same liberties with the old soldier as he did with his other friends. It was often remarked that Sergeant Dunham received more true respect from Duncan of Lundie, the Scotch laird who commanded the post, than most of the subalterns; for experience and tried services were of quite as much value in the eyes of a veteran major, as birth and money. While the sergeant never even hoped to rise any higher, he so far respected himself and his present station, as always to act in a way to command attention; and the habit of mixing so much with inferiors, whose passions and dispositions he felt it necessary to restrain by distance and dignity, had so far colored his whole deportment that few were altogether free from its influence. While the captains treated him kindly, and as an old comrade, the lieutenants seldom ventured to dissent from his military opinions; and the ensigns, it was remarked, actually manifested a species of respect that amounted to something very like deference. It is no wonder then that the announcement of Mabel put a sudden termination to the singular dialogue we have just related, though it had been often observed that the Pathfinder was the only man on that frontier, beneath the condition of a gentleman, who presumed to treat the sergeant at all as an equal, or even with the cordial familiarity of a friend.

"Good morrow, brother Cap," said the sergeant, giving the military salute, as he walked in a grave, stately manner on the bastion. "My morning duty has made me seem forgetful of you and Mabel, but we have now an hour or two to spare, and to get acquainted. Do you not perceive, brother, a strong likeness in the girl to her we have so long lost?"

"Mabel is the image of her mother, sergeant, as I have always said, with a little of your firmer figure; though for that matter the Caps were never wanting in spring and activity."

Mabel cast a timid glance at the stern, rigid countenance of her father, of whom she had ever thought as the warmhearted dwell on the affection of their absent parents, and, as she saw that the muscles of his face were working, notwithstanding the stiffness and method of his manner, her very heart yearned to throw herself on his bosom, and to weep at will. But he was so much colder in externals, so much more formal and distant than she had expected to find him, that she would not have dared to hazard the freedom, even had they been alone.

"You have taken a long and troublesome journey, brother, on my account, and we will try to make you comfortable while you stay among us."

"I hear you are likely to receive orders to lift your anchor, sergeant, and to shift your berth into a part of the world where they say there are a thousand islands?"

"Pathfinder, this is some of your forgetfulness?"

"Nay, nay, sergeant; I forgot nothing, but it did not seem to me necessary to hide your intentions so very closely from your own flesh and blood."

"All military movements ought to be made with as little conversation as possible," returned the sergeant, tapping the guide's shoulder, in a friendly, but reproachful manner. "You have passed too much of your life in front of the French, not to know the value of silence. But, no matter; the thing must soon be known, and there is no great use in trying, now, to conceal it. We shall embark a relief party, shortly, for a post on the lake, though I do not say it is for the Thousand Islands, and I may have to go with it; in which case I intend to take Mabel to make my broth for me, and I hope, brother, you will not despise a soldier's fare, for a month or so."

"That will depend on the manner of marching. I have no love for woods and swamps."

"We shall sail in the *Scud;* and, indeed, the whole service, which is no stranger to us, is likely enough to please one accustomed to the water."

"Ay, to salt water, if you will, but not to lake water. If you have no person to handle that bit of a cutter for you, I have no objection to ship for the v'y'ge, notwithstanding, though I shall look on the whole affair as so much time thrown away; for I consider it an imposition to call sailing about this pond, going to sea."

"Jasper is every way able to manage the *Scud,* brother Cap, and in that light I cannot say that we have need of your services, though we shall be glad of your company. You cannot return to the settlements until a party is sent in, and that is not likely to happen until after my return. Well, Pathfinder, this is the first time I ever knew men on the trail of the Mingoes, and you not at their head!"

"To be honest with you, sergeant," returned the guide, not without a little awkwardness of manner, and a perceptible difference in the hue of a face that had become so uniformly red by exposure, "I have not felt that it was my gift, this morning. In the first place, I very well know that the soldiers of the 55th are not the lads to overtake Iroquois in the woods, and the knaves did not wait to be surrounded, when they knew that Jasper had reached the garrison. Then, a man may take a little rest, after a summer of hard work, and no impeachment of his good will. Besides, the Sarpent is out with them, and if the miscreants are to be found at all, you may trust to his inmity and sight: the first being stronger, and the last, nearly, if not quite, as good as my own. He loves the skulking vagabonds as little as myself; and, for that matter, I may say that my own feelin's toward a Mingo are not much more than the gifts of a Delaware grafted on a Christian stock. No, no; I thought I would leave the honor, this time, if honor there is to be, to the young ensign that commands, who, if he don't lose his scalp, may boast of his campaign in his letters to his mother, when he gets in. I thought I would play idler once in my life."

"And no one has a better right, if long and faithful service entitles a man to a furlough," returned the sergeant, kindly. "Mabel will think none the worse of you, for preferring her company to the trail of the savages; and, I dare say, will be happy to give you a part of her breakfast, if you are inclined to eat. You must not think, girl, however, that the Pathfinder is in the habit of letting prowlers around the fort beat a retreat, without hearing the crack of his rifle."

"If I thought she did, sergeant, though not much given to showy and parade evolutions, I would shoulder Killdeer and quit the garrison before her pretty eyes had time to frown. No, no; Mabel knows me better, though we are but new acquaintances, for there has been no want of Mingoes to enliven the short march we have already made in company."

"It would need a great deal of testimony, Pathfinder, to make me think ill of you in any way, and more than all in the way you mention," returned Mabel, coloring with the sincere earnestness with which she endeavored to remove any suspicion to the contrary from his mind. "Both father and daughter, I believe, owe you their lives, and believe me that neither will ever forget it."

"Thank you, Mabel, thank you with all my heart. But I will not take advantage of your ignorance neither, girl, and therefore shall say I do not think the Mingoes would have hurt a hair of your head, had they succeeded by their deviltries and contrivances in getting you into their hands. My scalp, and Jasper's, and Master Cap's, there, and the Sarpent's too, would sartainly have been smoked; but as for the sergeant's daughter, I do not think they would have hurt a hair of her head!"

"And why should I suppose that enemies known to spare neither women nor children, would have shown more mercy to me than to another? I feel, Pathfinder, that I owe you my life."

"I say nay, Mabel; they wouldn't have had the heart to hurt you. No, not even a fiery Mingo devil would have had the heart to hurt a hair of your head! Bad as I suspect the vampires to be, I do not suspect them of anything so wicked as that. They might have wished you—nay, forced you to become the wife of one of their chiefs, and that would be torment enough to a Christian young woman; but beyond that I do not think even the Mingoes themselves would have gone."

"Well, then, I shall owe my escape from this great misfortune to you," said Mabel, taking his hand into her own, frankly and cordially, and certainly in a way to delight the honest guide. "To me it would be a lighter evil to be killed, than to become the wife of an Indian."

"That is her gift, sergeant," exclaimed Pathfinder, turning to his old comrade, with gratification written on every lineament of his honest countenance, "and it will have its way. I tell the Sarpent, that no Christianizing will ever make even a Delaware a white man; nor any whooping and yelling convart a paleface into a redskin. That is the gift of a young woman born of Christian parents, and it ought to be maintained."

"You are right, Pathfinder; and so far as Mabel Dunham is concerned, it *shall* be maintained. But it is time to break your fasts, and if you will follow me, brother Cap, I will show you how we poor soldiers live, here on a distant frontier."

4

SERGEANT DUNHAM made no empty vaunt when he gave the promise conveyed in the closing words of the last chapter. Nothwithstanding the remote frontier position of the post, they who lived at it enjoyed a table that, in many respects, kings and princes might have envied. At the period of our tale, and indeed for half a century later, the whole of that vast region which has been called the West, or the new countries, since the war of the Revolution, lay a comparatively unpeopled desert, teeming with all the living productions of nature that properly belonged to the climate, man and the domestic animals excepted. The few Indians that roamed its forests then could produce no visible effects on the abundance of the game; and the scattered garrisons, or occasional hunters that here and there were to be met with on that vast surface, had no other influence than the bee on the buckwheat field, or the hummingbird on the flower.

The marvels that have descended to our own times, in the way of tradition, concerning the quantities of beasts, birds, and fishes, that were then to be met with, on the shores of the Great Lakes in particular, are known to be sustained by the experience of living men, else we might hesitate about relating them; but having been eyewitnesses of some of these prodigies, our office shall be discharged with the confidence that certainty can impart. Oswego was particularly well placed to keep the larder of an epicure amply supplied. Fish of various sorts abounded in its river, and the sportsman had only to cast his line to haul in a bass, or some other member of the finny tribe, which then peopled the waters, as the air above the swamps of this fruitful latitude is known to be filled with insects. Among others was the salmon of the lakes, a variety of that well-known species that is scarcely inferior to the delicious salmon of northern Europe. Of the different migratory birds that frequent forests and waters, there was the same affluence, hundreds of acres of geese and ducks being often seen at a time, in the great bays that indent the shores of the lake. Deer, bears, rabbits, and squirrels, with divers other quadrupeds, among which was sometimes included the elk or moose, helped to complete the sum of the natural supplies, on which all the posts depended, more or less, to relieve the unavoidable privations of their remote frontier positions.

In a place where viands that would elsewhere be deemed great luxuries were so abundant, no one was excluded from their enjoyment. The meanest individual at Oswego habitually feasted on game that would have formed the boast of a Parisian table; and it was no more than a healthful commentary on the caprices of taste and of the waywardness of human desires, that the very diet which in other scenes would have been deemed the subject of envy and repinings, got to pall on the appetite. The coarse and regular food of the army, which it became necessary to husband on account of the difficulty of transportation, rose in the estimation of the common soldier, and at any time he would cheerfully desert his venison, and ducks, and pigeons, and salmon, to banquet on the sweets of pickled pork, stringy turnips, and half-cooked cabbage.

The table of Sergeant Dunham, as a matter of course, partook of the abundance and luxuries of the frontier as well as of its privations. A delicious broiled salmon smoked on a homely platter, hot venison steaks sent up their appetizing odors, and several dishes of cold meats, all of which were composed of game, had been set before the guests in honor of the newly arrived visitors, and in vindication of the old soldier's hospitality.

"You do not seem to be on short allowance in this quarter of the world, sergeant," said Cap, after he had got fairly initiated into the mysteries of the different dishes; "your salmon might satisfy a Scotsman."

"It fails to do it, notwithstanding, brother Cap; for among two or three hundred of the fellows that we have in this garrison, there are not half a dozen who will not swear that the fish is unfit to be eaten. Even some of the lads who never tasted venison, except as poachers, at home, turn up their noses at the fattest haunches that we get here."

"Ay, that is Christian natur'," put in Pathfinder, "and I must say it is none to its credit. Now, a redskin never repines, but is always thankful for the food he gets, whether it be fat or lean, venison or bear, wild turkey's breast or wild goose's wing. To the shame of us white men be it said that we look upon blessings without satisfaction, and consider trifling evils matters of great account."

"It is so with the 55th, as I can answer, though I cannot say as much for their Christianity," returned the sergeant. "Even the major himself, old Duncan of Lundie, will sometimes swear an oatmeal cake is better fare than the Oswego bass, and sigh for a swallow of Highland water, when, if so minded, he has the whole of Ontario to quench his thirst in."

"Has Major Duncan a wife and children?" asked Mabel, whose thoughts naturally turned toward her own sex in her new situation.

"Not he, girl; though they do say that he has a betrothed at home. The lady, it seems, is willing to wait rather than suffer the hardships of service in this wild region, all of which, brother Cap, is not according to my notions of a woman's duties. Your sister thought differently, and had it pleased God to spare her would have been sitting at this moment on the very campstool that her daughter so well becomes."

"I hope, sergeant, you do not think of Mabel for a soldier's wife," returned Cap, gravely. "Our family has done its share in that way already, and it's high time that the sea was again remembered."

"I do not think of finding a husband for the girl in the 55th, or any other regiment, I can promise you, brother, though I do think it getting to be time that the child were respectably married."

"Father!"

" 'Tis not their gifts, sergeant, to talk of these matters in so open a manner," said the guide, "for I've seen it verified by exper'ence, that he who would follow the trail of a virgin's good will must not go shouting out his thoughts behind her. So, if you please, we will talk of something else."

"Well, then, brother Cap, I hope that bit of a cold roasted pig is to your mind; you seem to fancy the food."

"Ay, ay, give we civilized grub, if I must eat," returned the pertinacious seaman. "Venison is well enough for your inland sailors, but we of the ocean like a little of that which we understand."

Here Pathfinder laid down his knife and fork, and indulged in a hearty laugh, though always in his silent manner; then he asked, with a little curiosity in his manner,—

"Don't you miss the skin, Master Cap—don't you miss the skin?"

"It would have been better for its jacket, I think myself, Pathfinder; but I suppose it is a fashion of the woods to serve up shoats in this style."

"Well, well, a man may go round the 'arth and not know everything! If you had had the skinning of that pig, Master Cap, it would have left you sore hands. The creatur' is a hedgehog!"

"Blast me, if I thought it wholesome natural pork, either," returned Cap. "But then I believed even a pig might lose some of its good qualities, up here-a-way, in the woods. It seemed no more than reason that a fresh-water hog should not be altogether so good as a salt-water hog. I suppose, sergeant, by this time, it is all the same to you!"

"If the skinning of it, brother, does not fall to my duty. Pathfinder I hope you didn't find Mabel disobedient on the march?"

"Not she—not she. If Mabel is only half as well satisfied with Jasper and the Pathfinder, as the Pathfinder and Jasper are satisfied with her, sergeant, we shall be friends for the remainder of our days."

As the guide spoke, he turned his eyes toward the blushing girl, with a sort of innocent desire to know her opinion, and then, with an inborn delicacy that proved he was far superior to the vulgar desire to invade the sanctity of feminine feeling, he looked at his plate, and seemed to regret his own boldness.

"Well, well, we must remember that women are not men, my friend," resumed the sergeant, "and make proper allowances for nature and education. A recruit is not a veteran. Any man knows that it takes longer to make a good soldier than it takes to make anything else; and it ought to require unusual time to make a good soldier's daughter."

"This is new doctrine, sergeant," said Cap, with some spirit. "We old seamen are apt to think that six soldiers, ay, and capital soldiers too, might be made, while one sailor is getting his education."

"Ay, brother Cap, I've seen something of the opinions which seafaring men have of themselves," returned the brother-in-law, with a smile as bland as comported with his saturnine features; "for I was many years one of the garrison in a seaport. You and I have conversed on the subject before, and I'm afraid we shall never agree. But if you wish to know what the difference is, between a real soldier and man in what I should call a state of nature, you have only to look at a battalion of the 55th, on parade this afternoon, and then, when you get back to York, examine one of the militia regiments making its greatest efforts."

"Well, to my eye, sergeant, there is very little difference, not more than you'll find between a brig and a scow. To me they seem alike; all scarlet, and feathers, and powder, and pipe clay."

"So much, sir, for the judgment of a sailor," returned the sergeant with dignity; "but perhaps you are not aware that it requires a year to teach a true soldier how to eat."

"So much the worse for him! The militia know how to eat at

starting; for I have often heard that, on their marches, they commonly eat all before them, even if they do nothing else."

"They have their gifts, I suppose, like other men," observed Pathfinder, with a view to preserve the peace, which was evidently in some danger of being broken, by the obstinate predilection of each of the disputants in favor of his own calling; "and when a man has his gift from Providence, it is commonly idle to endeavor to bear up ag'in it. The 55th, sergeant, is a judicious rijiment, in the way of eating, as I know, from having been so long in its company, though I dare say militia corps could be found that would outdo them in feats of that natur' too."

"Uncle," said Mabel, "if you have breakfasted, I will thank you to go out upon the bastion with me again. We have neither of us seen the lake, and it would be hardly seemly for a young woman to be walking about the fort, the first day of her arrival, quite alone."

Cap understood the motive of Mabel, and having, at the bottom, a hearty friendship for his brother-in-law, he was willing enough to defer the argument until they had been longer together, for the idea of abandoning it altogether never crossed the mind of one so dogmatical and obstinate. He accordingly accompanied his niece, leaving Sergeant Dunham and his friend, the Pathfinder, alone together. As soon as his adversary had beaten a retreat, the sergeant, who did not quite so well understand the maneuver of his daughter, turned to his companion, and with a smile that was not without triumph, he remarked,—

"The army, Pathfinder, has never yet done itself justice; and, though modesty becomes a man whether he is in a red coat or a black one, or, for that matter, in his shirt sleeves, I don't like to let a good opportunity slip of saying a word in its behalf. Well, my friend," laying his own hand on one of the Pathfinder's, and giving it a hearty squeeze, "how do you like the girl?"

"You have reason to be proud of her, sergeant; you have reason to be proud at finding yourself the father of so handsome and well-mannered a young woman. I have seen many of her sex, and some that were great and beautiful, but never before did I meet with one, in whom I thought Providence had so well balanced the different gifts."

"And the good opinion, I can tell you, Pathfinder, is mutual. She told me last night all about your coolness, and spirit, and kindness, particularly the last; for kindness counts for more than half with females, my friend, and the first inspection seems to give satisfaction on both sides. Brush up the uniform, and pay a little more attention to the outside, Pathfinder, and you will have the girl heart and hand."

"Nay, nay, sergeant, I've forgotten nothing that you have told me, and grudge no reasonable pains to make myself as pleasant in the eyes of Mabel, as she is getting to be in mine. I cleaned and brightened up

Killdeer, this morning, as soon as the sun rose; and, in my judgment, the piece never looked better than it does at this very moment!"

"That is according to your hunting notions, Pathfinder; but fire-arms should sparkle and glitter in the sun, and I never yet could see any beauty in a clouded barrel."

"Lord Howe thought otherwise, sergeant; and he was accounted a good soldier!"

"Very true; his lordship had all the barrels of his regiment darkened, and what good came of it? You can see his scutcheon hanging in the English church at Albany! No, no, my worthy friend, a soldier should be a soldier, and at no time ought he to be ashamed or afraid to carry about him the signs and symbols of his honorable trade. Had you much discourse with Mabel, Pathfinder, as you came along in the canoe?"

"There was not much opportunity, sergeant, and then I found myself so much beneath her in idees, that I was afraid to speak of much beyond what belonged to my own gifts."

"Therein you are partly right and partly wrong, my friend. Women love trifling discourse, though they like to have most of it to themselves. Now, you know, I'm a man that do not loosen my tongue at every giddy thought, and yet there were days when I could see that Mabel's mother thought none the worse of me, because I descended a little from my manhood. It is true, I was twenty-two years younger then, than I am today; and, moreover, instead of being the oldest sergeant in the regiment, I was the youngest. Dignity is commanding and useful, and there is no getting on without it, as respects the men; but if you would be thoroughly esteemed by a woman, it is necessary to condescend a little, on occasions."

"Ah's me! sergeant; I sometimes fear it will never do!"

"Why do you think so discouragingly of a matter on which I thought both our minds were made up?"

"We did agree that if Mabel should prove what you told me she was, if the girl could fancy a rude hunter and guide, that I would quit some of my wandering ways, and try to humanize my mind down to a wife and children. But since I have seen the girl, I will own that many misgivin's have come over me!"

"How's this!" interrupted the sergeant, sternly; "did I not understand you to say that you were pleased? And is Mabel a young woman to disappoint expectation?"

"Ah! sergeant, it is not Mabel that I distrust, but myself. I am but a poor ignorant woodsman, after all, and perhaps I'm not, in truth, as good as even you and I may think me!"

"If you doubt your own judgment of yourself, Pathfinder, I beg you will not doubt mine. Am I not accustomed to judge men's characters? Is it not my especial duty, and am I often deceived? Ask Major Duncan, sir, if you desire any assurances in this particular."

"But, sergeant, we have long been friends; have fou't side by side a dozen times, and have done each other many sarvices. When this is the case, men are apt to think overkindly of each other, and I fear me that the daughter may not be so likely to view a plain, ignorant hunter as favorably as the father does."

"Tut, tut, Pathfinder! you don't know yourself, man, and may put all faith in my judgment. In the first place, you have experience, and as all girls must want that, no prudent young woman would overlook such a qualification. Then you are not one of the coxcombs that strut about when they first join a regiment, but a man who has seen service, and who carries the marks of it on his person and countenance. I dare say you have been under fire some thirty or forty times, counting all the skirmishes and ambushes that you've seen."

"All of that, sergeant, all of that; but what will it avail in gaining the good will of a tenderhearted young female?"

"It will gain the day. Experience in the field is as good in love as in war. But you are as honesthearted and as loyal a subject as the King can boast of—God bless him."

"That may be too—that may be too; but I'm afeard I'm too rude, and too old, and too wildlike, to suit the fancy of such a young and delicate girl as Mabel, who has been unused to our wilderness ways, and may think the settlements better suited to her gifts and inclinations."

"These are new misgivings for you, my friend, and I wonder they were never paraded before."

"Because I never knew my own worthlessness, perhaps, until I saw Mabel. I have travelled with some as fair, and have guided them through the forest, and seen them in their perils and in their gladness; but they were always too much above me to make me think of them as more than so many feeble ones I was bound to protect and defend. The case is now different. Mabel and I are so nearly alike, that I feel weighed down with a load that is hard to bear, at finding us so unlike. I do wish, sergeant, that I was ten years younger, more comely to look at, and better suited to please a handsome young woman's fancy!"

"Cheer up, my brave friend, and trust to a father's knowledge of womankind. Mabel half loves you already, and a fortnight's intercourse and kindness, down among the islands yonder, will close ranks with the other half. The girl as much as told me this herself, last night."

"Can this be so, sergeant?" said the guide, whose meek and modest nature shrank from viewing himself in colors so favorable. "Can this be truly so! I am but a poor hunter, and Mabel, I see, is fit to be an officer's lady. Do you think the gal will consent to quit all her beloved settlement usages, and her visitin's, and her church-goin's, to dwell with a plain guide and hunter, up here-a-way, in the woods? Will she not, in the end, crave her old ways, and a better man?"

"A better man, Pathfinder, would be hard to find," returned the father. "As for town usages, they are soon forgotten in the freedom of the forest, and Mabel has just spirit enough to dwell on a frontier. I've not planned this marriage, my friend, without thinking it over, as a general does his campaign. At first, I thought of bringing you into the regiment, that you might succeed me when I retire, which must be sooner or later; but on reflection, Pathfinder, I think you are scarcely fitted for the office. Still, if not a soldier in all the meanings of the word, you are a soldier in its best meaning, and I know that you have the good will of every officer in the corps. As long as I live, Mabel can dwell with me, and you will always have a home, when you return from your scoutings and marches."

"This is very pleasant to think of, sergeant, if the girl can only come into our wishes with good will. But, ah's me! it does not seem that one like myself can ever be agreeable in her handsome eyes! If I were younger, and more comely, now, as Jasper Western is, for instance, there might be a chance—yes, then, indeed, there might be some chance."

"That, for Jasper Eau-douce, and every younker of them in or about the fort!" returned the sergeant, snapping his fingers. "If not actually a younger, you are a younger looking, ay, and a better looking man than the *Scud's* master—"

"Anan!" said Pathfinder, looking up at his companion with an expression of doubt, as if he did not understand his meaning.

"I say, if not actually younger in days and years, you look more hardy and like whipcord, than Jasper, or any of them; and there will be more of you, thirty years hence, than of all of them put together. A good conscience will keep one like you a mere boy all his life."

"Jasper has as clear a conscience as any youth I know, sergeant!—and is as likely to wear, on that account, as any young man in the colony."

"Then you are my friend," squeezing the other's hand, "my tried, sworn, and constant friend."

"Yes, we have been friends, sergeant, near twenty years, before Mabel was born."

"True enough—before Mabel was born we were well-tried friends, and the hussy would never dream of refusing to marry a man who was her father's friend before she was born!"

"We don't know, sergeant, we don't know. Like loves like. The young prefar the young for companions, and the old the old."

"Not for wives, Pathfinder! I never knew an old man, now, who had an objection to a young wife. Then you are respected and esteemed by every officer in the fort, as I have said already, and it will please her fancy to like a man that everyone else likes."

"I hope I have no enemies but the Mingoes," returned the guide, stroking down his hair meekly, and speaking thoughtfully. "I've *tried* to do right, and that ought to make friends, though it sometimes fails."

"And you may be said to keep the best company, for even old Duncan of Lundie is glad to see you, and you pass hours in his society. Of all the guides, he confides most in you."

"Ay, even greater than he is have marched by my side for days, and have conversed with me as if I were their brother; but, sergeant, I have never been puffed up by their company, for I know that the woods often bring men to a level, who would not be so in the settlements."

"And you are known to be the greatest rifleshot that ever pulled a trigger in all this region."

"If Mabel could fancy a man for that, I might have no great reason to despair; and yet, sergeant, I sometimes think that it is all as much owing to Killdeer as to any skill of my own. It is sartainly a wonderful piece, and might do as much in the hands of another."

"That is your own humble opinion of yourself, Pathfinder; but we have seen too many fail with the same weapon, and you succeed too often with the rifles of other men, to allow me to agree with you. We will get up a shooting match in a day or two, when you can show your skill, and then Mabel will form some judgment concerning your true character."

"Will that be fair, sergeant? Everybody knows that Killdeer seldom misses, and ought we to make a trial of this sort, when we all know what must be the result?"

"Tut, tut, man! I foresee I must do half this courting for you. For one who is always inside of the smoke, in a skirmish, you are the faintest-hearted suitor I ever met with. Remember, Mabel comes of a bold stock; and the girl will be as likely to admire a man as her mother was before her."

Here the sergeant arose, and proceeded to attend to his never-ceasing duties, without apology; the terms on which the guide stood with all in the garrison, rendering this freedom quite a matter of course.

The reader will have gathered from the conversation just related, one of the plans that Sergeant Dunham had in view, in causing his daughter to be brought to the frontier. Although necessarily much weaned from the caresses and blandishments that had rendered his child so dear to him, during the first year or two of his widowhood, he had still a strong, but somewhat latent, love for her. Accustomed to command and to obey, without being questioned himself, questioning others concerning the reasonableness of the mandates, he was, perhaps, too much disposed to believe that his daughter would marry the man he might select, while he was far from being disposed to do violence to her wishes. The fact was, few knew the Pathfinder intimately, without secretly coming to believe him to be one of extraordinary qualities. Ever the same, simple-minded, faithful, utterly without fear, and yet prudent, foremost in all warrantable enterprises, or what the opinion of the day considered as such, and never engaged in anything to call a blush to his cheek, or censure on his acts; it was not possible to live much with this being, who, in his peculiar way, was a sort of type of what Adam might have been supposed to be before the fall, though certainly not without sin, and not feel a respect and admiration for him, that had no reference to his position in life. It was remarked that no officer passed him without saluting him as if he had been his equal; no common man, without addressing him with the confidence and freedom of a comrade. The most surprising peculiarity about the man himself, was the entire indifference with which he regarded all distinctions that did not depend on personal merit. He was respectful to his superiors from habit, but had often been known to correct their mistakes and to reprove their vices, with a fearlessness that proved how essentially he regarded the more material points, and with a natural discrimination that appeared to set education at defiance. In short, a disbeliever in the ability of man to distinguish between good and evil without the aid of instruction, would have been staggered by the character of this extraordinary inhabitant of the frontier. His feelings appeared to possess the freshness and nature of the forest in which he passed so much of his time, and no casuist could have made clearer decisions in matters relating to right and wrong; yet he was not without his prejudices, which, though few, and colored by the character and usages of the individual, were deep-rooted, and had almost got to form a part of his nature. But the most striking feature about the moral organization of Pathfinder, was his beautiful and unerring sense of justice. This noble trait (and without it no man can be truly great; with it, no man other than respectable) probably had its unseen influence on all who associated with him; for the common and unprincipled brawler of the camp had been known to return from an expedition made in his company, rebuked by his sentiments, softened by his language, and improved by his example. As might have been expected, with so elevated a quality, his fidelity was like the immovable rock. Treachery in him was classed among the things that are impossible, and as he seldom retired before his enemies, so was he never known, under any circumstances that admitted of an alternative, to abandon a friend. The affinities of such a character were, as a matter of course, those of like for like. His associates and intimates, though more or less determined by chance, were generally of the highest order, as to moral propensities; for he appeared to possess a species of instinctive discrimination that led him insensibly to himself, most probably, to cling closest to those whose characters would best reward his friendship. In short, it was said of the Pathfinder, by one accustomed to study his fellows, that he was a fair example of what a just-minded and pure man might be, while untempted by unruly or ambitious desires, and let to follow the bias of his feelings, amid the solitary grandeur and ennobling influences of a sublime nature; neither led aside by the inducements which influence all to do evil amid the incentives of civilization, nor forgetful of the Almighty Being, who spirit pervades the wilderness as well as the towns.

Such was the man whom Sergeant Dunham had selected as the husband of Mabel. In making this choice he had not been as much governed by a clear and judicious view of the merits of the individual, perhaps, as by his own likings; still, no one knew the Pathfinder as intimately as himself, without always conceding to the honest guide a high place in his esteem, on account of these very virtues. That his daughter could find any serious objection to the match, the old soldier did not apprehend; while, on the other hand, he saw many advantages to himself, in dim perspective, that were connected with the decline of his days, and an evening of life passing among descendants who were equally dear to him through both parents. He first made the proposition to his friend, who had listened to it kindly, but who, the sergeant was now pleased to find, already betrayed a willingness to come into his own views, that was proportioned to the doubts and misgivings proceeding from his humble distrust of himself.

5

TO HELP while away the summer routine of the fort at Oswego, the junior officers arranged a shooting match. All competitors were admitted, and three prizes were offered: a silver-mounted powder horn, a leather flask also silver-mounted, and a calash or bonnet of silk, which the winner might offer the lady of his preference. The spot selected for the contest was a parade ground west of the fort, on the shores of the lake. For the initial trial a bull's-eye target was set up at a distance of a hundred yards, to be shot at without a rest. A number of the men hit the mark, though Major Duncan took pains to miss it. Then Jasper Western or Eau-douce, the wily quartermaster, David Muir, and Hawkeye all came forward. As all aspired to the hand of Mabel Dunham, they were acutely aware of her presence among the spectators.

Jasper's handsome face flushed, he stepped upon the stand, cast a hasty glance at Mabel, whose pretty form he ascertained was bending eagerly forward, as if to note the result, dropped the barrel of his rifle, with but little apparent care, into the palm of his left hand, raised the muzzle for a single instant, with exceeding steadiness, and fired. The bullet passed directly through the center of the bull's-eye, much the best shot of the morning, since the others had merely touched the paint.

"Well performed, Master Jasper," said Muir, as soon as the result was declared; "and a shot that might have done credit to an older head and a more experienced eye. I'm thinking, notwithstanding, there was some of a youngster's luck in it, for ye were no partic'lar in the aim ye took. Ye may be quick, Eau-douce, in the movement, but ye'r not philosophic nor scientific in ye'r management of the weapon. Now, Sergeant Dunham, I'll thank you to request the ladies to give a closer attention than common, for I'm about to make that use of the rifle which may be called the intellectual. Jasper would have killed, I allow; but then there would not have been half the satisfaction in receiving such a shot, as in receiving one that is discharged scientifically."

All this time the quartermaster was preparing himself for the scientific trial; but he delayed his aim until he saw that the eye of Mabel, in common with those of her companions, was fastened on him in curiosity. As the others left him room, out of respect to his rank, no one stood near the competitor but his commanding officer, to whom he now said in his familiar manner,—

"You see, Lundie, that something is to be gained by exciting a female's curiosity. It's an active sentiment, is curiosity, and properly improved may lead to gentler inclinations in the end."

"Very true, Davy; but ye keep us all waiting while ye make your preparations; and here is Pathfinder drawing near to catch a lesson from your greater experience."

"Well, Pathfinder, and so *you* have come to get an idea too, concerning the philosophy of shooting! I do not wish to hide my light under a bushel, and ye're welcome to all ye'll learn. Do ye no mean to try a shot yersel', man?"

"Why should I, quartermaster—why should I? I want none of the prizes; and as for honor, I have had enough of that, if it's an honor to shoot better than yourself. I'm not a woman, to wear a calash."

"Very true; but ye might find a woman that is precious in your eyes to wear it for ye, as—"

"Come, Davy," interrupted the major, "your shot, or a retreat. The adjutant is getting to be impatient."

"The quartermaster's department, and the adjutant's department, are seldom compliable, Lundie; but I'm ready; stand a little aside, Pathfinder, and give the ladies an opportunity."

Lieutenant Muir now took his attitude with a good deal of studied elegance, raised his rifle slowly, lowered it, raised it again, repeated the maneuvers, and fired.

"Missed the target altogether!" shouted the man whose duty it was to mark the bullets, and who had little relish for the quartermaster's tedious science. "Missed the target!"

"It cannot be!" cried Muir, his face flushing equally with indignation and shame; "it cannot be, adjutant; for I never did so awkward a thing in my life. I appeal to the ladies for a juster judgment."

"The ladies shut their eyes when you fired," exclaimed the regimental wags. "Your preparations alarmed them."

"I will na believe such a calumny of the leddies, nor sic' a reproach on my own skill," returned the quartermaster, growing more and more Scotch, as he warmed with his feelings; "it's a conspiracy to rob a meritorious man of his dues."

"It's a dead miss, Muir," said the laughing Lundie, "and ye'll jist sit down quietly with the disgrace."

"No, no, major," Pathfinder at length observed, "the quartermaster *is* a good shot, for a slow one, and a measured distance; though nothing extr'ornary, for ra'al sarvice. He has covered Jasper's bullet, as will be seen, if any one will take the trouble to examine the target."

The respect for Pathfinder's skill, and for his quickness and accuracy of sight, was so profound and general, that the instant he made this declaration, the spectators began to distrust their own opinions, and a dozen rushed to the target, in order to ascertain the fact. There, sure enough, it was found that the quartermaster's bullet had gone through the hole made by Jasper's, and that, too, so accurately as to require a minute examination to be certain of the circumstance; which, however, was soon clearly established, by discovering one bullet over the other, in the stump against which the target was placed.

"I told ye, ladies, ye were about to witness the influence of science on gunnery," said the quartermaster, advancing towards the staging occupied by the females. "Major Duncan derides the idea of mathematics entering into target shooting; but I tell him philosophy colors, and enlarges, and improves, and dilates, and explains, everything that belongs to human life, whether it be a shooting match or a sermon. In a word, philosophy is philosophy, and that is saying all that the subject requires."

"I trust you exclude love from the catalogue," observed the wife of a captain, who knew the history of the quartermaster's marriages, and who had a woman's malice against the monopolizer of her sex; "it seems that philosophy has little in common with love."

"You wouldn't say that, madam, if your heart had experienced many trials. It's the man or the woman that has had many occasions to improve the affections that can best speak of such matters; and, believe me, of all love, philosophical is the most lasting, as it is the most rational."

"You would then recommend experience as an improvement on the passion?"

"Your quick mind has conceived the idea at a glance. The happiest marriages are those in which youth, and beauty, and confidence on one side, rely on the sagacity, moderation, and prudence of years—middle age, I mean, madam, for I'll no deny that there is such a thing as a husband's being too old for a wife. Here is Sergeant Dunham's charming daughter, now, to approve of such sentiments, I'm certain,—her character for discretion being already well established in the garrison, short as has been her residence among us."

"Sergeant Dunham's daughter is scarcely a fitting interlocutor in a discourse between you and me, Lieutenant Muir," rejoined the captain's lady, with careful respect for her own dignity; "and yonder is the Pathfinder about to take his chance, by way of changing the subject."

"I protest, Major Duncan, I protest"—cried Muir, hurrying back toward the stand, with both arms elevated by way of enforcing his words—"I protest, in the strongest terms, gentlemen, against Pathfinder's being admitted into these sports with Killdeer, which is a piece, to say nothing of long habit, that is altogether out of proportion, for a trial of skill against government rifles."

"Killdeer is taking its rest, quartermaster," returned Pathfinder, calmly, "and no one here thinks of disturbing it. I did not think myself of pulling a trigger today; but Sergeant Dunham has been persuading me that I shall not do proper honor to his handsome daughter, who came under my care, if I am backward on such an occasion. I'm using Jasper's rifle, quartermaster, as you may see, and that is no better than your own."

Lieutenant Muir was now obliged to acquiesce, and every eye turned toward the Pathfinder, as he took the required station. The air and attitude of this celebrated guide and hunter were extremely fine, as he raised his tall form and levelled the piece, showing perfect self-command, and a thorough knowledge of the power of the human frame, as well as of the weapon. Pathfinder was not what is usually termed a handsome man, though his appearance excited so much confidence, and commanded respect. Tall, and even muscular, his frame might have been esteemed nearly perfect, were it not for the total absence of everything like flesh. Whipcord was scarcely more rigid than his arms and legs, or, at need, more pliable; but the outlines of his person were rather too angular for the proportion that the eye most approves. Still, his motions being natural, were graceful; and being calm and regulated, they gave him an air of dignity that associated well with the idea that was so prevalent of his services and peculiar merits. His honest, open features were burnt to a bright red, that comported with the notion of exposure and hardships, while his sinewy hands denoted force, and a species of use that was removed from the stiffening and deforming effects of labor. Although no one perceived any of those gentler or more insinuating qualities which are apt to win upon a woman's affections, as he raised his rifle, not a female eye was fastened on him, without a silent approbation of the freedom of his movements, and the manliness of his air. Thought was scarcely quicker than his aim, and, as the smoke floated above his head, the breech of the rifle was seen on the ground, the hand of the Pathfinder was leaning on the barrel, and his honest countenance was illuminated by his usual silent, hearty laugh.

"If one dared to hint at such a thing," cried Major Duncan, "I should say that the Pathfinder had also missed the target!"

"No, no, major," returned the guide, confidently, "that *would* be a risky declaration. I didn't load the piece, and can't say what was in it; but if it was lead, you will find the bullet driving down those of the quartermaster's and Jasper's; else is not my name Pathfinder."

A shout from the target announced the truth of this assertion.

"That's not all—that's not all, boys," called out the guide, who was now slowly advancing toward the stage occupied by the females; "if you find the target touched at all, I'll own to a miss. The quartermaster cut the wood, but you'll find no wood cut by that last messenger."

"Very true, Pathfinder, very true," answered Muir, who was lingering near Mabel, though ashamed to address her particularly, in the presence of the officers' wives. "The quartermaster did cut the wood, and by that means he opened a passage for your bullet, which went through the hole he had made."

"Well, quartermaster, there goes the nail, and we'll see who can drive it closest, you or I; for, though I did not think of showing what a rifle can do today, now my hand is in, I'll turn my back to no man that carries King George's commission. Chingachgook is outlying, or he might force me into some of the niceties of the art; but as for you, quartermaster, if the nail don't stop you, the potato will."

"You're overboastful this morning, Pathfinder; but you'll find you've no green boy, fresh from the settlements and the towns, to deal with, I will assure ye!"

"I know that well, quartermaster; I know that well, and shall not deny your experience. You've lived many years on the frontiers, and I've heard of you in the colonies, and among the Injins, too, quite a human life ago."

"Na, na," interrupted Muir, in his broadest Scotch, "this is injustice, man. I've no lived so very long, either."

"I'll do you justice, lieutenant, even if you get the best in the potato trial. I say you've passed a good human life, for a soldier, in places where the rifle is daily used, and I know you are a creditable and ingenious marksman; but then you are not a true rifle shooter. As for boasting, I hope I'm not a vain talker about my own exploits; but a man's gifts are his gifts, and it's flying in the face of Providence to deny them. The sergeant's daughter, here, shall judge atween us, if you have the stomach to submit to so pretty a judge."

The Pathfinder had named Mabel as the arbiter, because he admired her, and because, in his eyes, rank had little or no value; but Lieutenant Muir shrank at such a reference in the presence of the wives of the officers. He would gladly keep himself constantly before the eyes and the imagination of the object of his wishes; but he was still too much under the influence of old prejudices, and perhaps too wary, to appear openly as her suitor, unless he saw something very like a certainty of success. On the discretion of Major Duncan he had a full reliance, and he apprehended no betrayal from that quarter; but he was quite aware, should it ever get abroad that he had been refused by the child of a noncommissioned officer, he would find great difficulty in making his approaches to any other woman of a condition to which he might reasonably aspire. Notwithstanding these doubts and misgivings, Mabel looked so prettily, blushed so charmingly, smiled so sweetly, and altogether presented so winning a picture of youth, spirit, modesty, and beauty, that he found it exceedingly tempting to be kept so prominently before her imagination, and to be able to address her freely.

"You shall have it your own way, Pathfinder," he answered, as soon as his doubts had settled down into determination; "let the sergeant's daughter—his charming daughter, I should have termed her—be the umpire then; and to her we will both dedicate the prize, that one or the other must certainly win. Pathfinder must be humored, ladies, as you perceive, else, no doubt, we should have had the honor to submit ourselves to one of your charming society."

A call for the competitors now drew the quartermaster and his adversary away; and in a few moments the second trial of skill commenced. A common wrought nail was driven lightly into the target, its head having been first touched with paint, and the marksman was required to hit it, or he lost his chances in the succeeding trials. No one was permitted to enter on this occasion who had already failed in the essay against the bull's-eye.

There might have been half a dozen aspirants for the honors of this trial; one or two who had barely succeeded in touching the spot of paint, in the previous strife, preferring to rest their reputations there; feeling certain that they could not succeed in the greater effort that was now exacted of them. The three first adventurers failed, all coming quite near the mark, but neither touching it. The fourth person who presented himself was the quartermaster, who, after going through his usual attitudes, so far succeeded as to carry away a small portion of the head of the nail, planting his bullet by the side of its point. This was not considered an extraordinary shot, though it brought the adventurer within the category.

"You've saved your bacon, quartermaster, as they say in the settlements of their creatur's," cried Pathfinder, laughing, "but it would take a long time to build a house with a hammer no better than your'n. Jasper, here, will show you how a nail is to be started, or the lad has lost some of his steadiness of hand and sartainty of eye. You would have done better yourself, lieutenant, had you not been so much bent on sogerizing your figure. Shooting is a nat'ral gift, and is to be exercised in a nat'ral way."

"We shall see, Pathfinder; I call that a pretty attempt at a nail; and I doubt if the 55th has another hammer, as you call it, that can do just that same thing over again."

"Jasper is not in the 55th—but there goes his rap!"

As the Pathfinder spoke, the bullet of Eau-douce hit the nail square, and drove it into the target, within an inch of the head.

"Be all ready to clench it, boys," cried out Pathfinder, stepping into his friend's tracks the instant they were vacant. "Never mind a new nail; I can see that, though the paint is gone, and what I can see, I can hit at a hundred yards, though it were only a mosquito's eye. Be ready to clench!"

The rifle cracked, the bullet sped its way, and the head of the nail was buried in the wood, covered by the piece of flattened lead.

"Well, Jasper, lad," continued Pathfinder, dropping the breech of his rifle to the ground, and resuming the discourse, as if he thought nothing of his own exploit, "you improve daily. A few more tramps on land, in my company, and the best marksman on the frontiers will have occasion to look keenly, when he takes his stand ag'in you. The quartermaster is respectable, but he will never get any further; whereas you, Jasper, have the gift, and may one day defy any who pull trigger."

"Hoot—hoot!" exclaimed Muir, "do you call hitting the head of the nail respectable only, when it's the perfection of the art? Any one, in the least refined and elevated in sentiment, knows that the delicate touches denote the master; whereas your sledge hammer blows come from the rude and uninstructed. If 'a miss is as good as a mile,' a hit ought to be better, Pathfinder, whether it wound or kill."

"The surest way of settling this rivalry will be to make another trial," observed Lundie, "and that will be of the potato. You're Scotch, Mr. Muir, and might fare better were it a cake or a thistle; but frontier law has declared for the American fruit, and the potato it shall be."

As Major Duncan manifested some impatience of manner, Muir had too much tact to delay the sports any longer with his discursive remarks, but judiciously prepared himself for the next appeal. To say the truth, the quartermaster had little or no faith in his own success in the trial of skill that was to follow, nor would he have been so free in presenting himself as a competitor at all, had he anticipated it would have been made. But Major Duncan, who was somewhat of a humorist, in his own quiet Scotch way, had secretly ordered it to be introduced, expressly to mortify him; for, a laird himself, Lundie did not relish the notion that one who might claim to be a gentleman, should bring discredit on his caste by forming an unequal alliance. As soon as everything was prepared, Muir was summoned to the stand, and the potato was held in readiness to be thrown. As the sort of feat we are about to offer to the reader, however, may be new to him, a word in explanation will render the matter more clear. A potato of large size was selected, and given to one, who stood at the distance of twenty yards from the stand. At the word "Heave," which was given by the marksman, the vegetable was thrown with a gentle toss into the air, and it was the business of the adventurer to cause a ball to pass through it, before it reached the ground.

The quartermaster, in a hundred experiments, had once succeeded in accomplishing this difficult feat, but he now essayed to perform it again, with a sort of blind hope, that was fated to be disappointed. The potato was thrown in the usual manner, the rifle was discharged, but the flying target was untouched.

"To the right about, and fall out, quartermaster," said Lundie, smiling at the success of his own artifice; "the honor of the silken calash will lie between Jasper Eau-douce and Pathfinder."

"And how is the trial to end, major?" inquired the latter. "Are we to have the two-potato trial, or is it to be settled by center and skin?"

"By center and skin, if there is any perceptible difference; otherwise the double shot must follow."

"This is an awful moment to me, Pathfinder," observed Jasper, as he moved toward the stand, his face actually losing its color in intensity of feeling.

Pathfinder gazed earnestly at the young man, and then begging Major Duncan to have patience for a moment, he led his friend out of the hearing of all near him, before he spoke.

"You seem to take this matter to heart, Jasper?" the hunter remarked, keeping his eyes fastened on those of the youth.

"I must own, Pathfinder, that my feelings were never before so much bound up in success."

"And do you so much crave to outdo me, an old and tried friend?—and that, as it might be, in my own way? Shooting is my gift, boy, and no common hand can equal mine!"

"I know it—I know it, Pathfinder; but—yet—"

"But what, Jasper, boy?—speak freely; you talk to a friend."

The young man compressed his lips, dashed a hand across his eye, and flushed and paled alternately, like a girl confessing her love. Then squeezing the other's hand, he said calmly, like one whose manhood has overcome all other sensations,—

"I would lose an arm, Pathfinder, to be able to make an offering of that calash to Mabel Dunham."

The hunter dropped his eyes to the ground, and as he walked slowly back toward the stand, he seemed to ponder deeply on what he had just heard.

"You never could succeed in the double trial, Jasper!" he suddenly remarked.

"Of that I am certain, and it troubles me."

"What a creature is mortal man! He pines for things which are not of his gifts, and treats the bounties of Providence lightly. No matter—no matter. Take your station, Jasper, for the major is waiting; and, harkee, lad, I must touch the skin, for I could not show my face in the garrison with less than that."

"I suppose I must submit to my fate," returned Jasper, flushing and losing his color, as before; "but I will make the effort, if I die."

"What a thing is mortal man!" repeated Pathfinder, falling back to allow his friend room to take his aim; "he overlooks his own gifts, and craves them of another!"

The potato was thrown, Jasper fired, and the shout that followed preceded the announcement of the fact, that he had driven his bullet through its center, or so nearly so as to merit that award.

"Here is a competitor worthy of you, Pathfinder," cried Major Duncan, with delight, as the former took his station, "and we may look to some fine shooting, in the double trial."

"What a thing is mortal man!" repeated the hunter, scarce seeming to notice what was passing around him, so much were his thoughts absorbed in his own reflections. "Toss!"

The potato was tossed, the rifle cracked—it was remarked just as the little black ball seemed stationary in the air, for the marksman evidently took unusual heed to his aim—and then a look of disappointment and wonder succeeded among those who caught the falling target.

"Two holes in one?" called out the major.

"The skin—the skin!" was the answer: "only the skin!"

"How's this, Pathfinder! Is Jasper Eau-douce to carry off the honors of the day!"

"The calash is his," returned the other, shaking his head, and walking quietly away from the stand. "What a creature is a mortal man! Never satisfied with his own gifts, but forever craving that which Providence denies!"

As Pathfinder had not buried his bullet in the potato, but had cut through the skin, the prize was immediately adjudged to Jasper. The calash was in the hands of the latter, when the quartermaster approached, and with a politic air of cordiality, he wished his successful rival joy of his victory.

"But now you've got the calash, lad, it's of no use to you," he added; "it will never make a sail, or even an ensign. I'm thinking, Eau-douce, you'd no be sorry to see its value in good silver of the King?"

"Money cannot buy it, lieutenant," returned Jasper, whose eye lighted up with all the fire of success and joy. "I would rather have won this calash than have obtained fifty new suits of sails for the *Scud!*"

"Hoot, hoot, lad! you are going mad like all the rest of them. I'd even venture to offer half a guinea for the trifle, rather than it should lie kicking about in the cabin of your cutter, and, in the end, become an ornament for the head of a squaw."

Although Jasper did not know that the wary quartermaster had not offered half the actual cost of the prize, he heard the proposition with indifference. Shaking his head in the negative, he advanced toward the stage, where his approach excited a little commotion, the officers' ladies, one and all, having determined to accept the present, should the gallantry of the young sailor induce him to offer it. But Jasper's diffidence, no less than admiration for another, would have prevented him from aspiring to the honor of complimenting any whom he thought so much his superiors.

"Mabel," he said, "this prize is for you, unless—"

"Unless what, Jasper?" answered the girl, losing her own bashfulness in the natural and generous wish to relieve his embarrassment, though both reddened in a way to betray strong feeling.

"Unless you may think too indifferently of it, because it is offered by one who may have no right to believe his gift will be accepted."

"I do accept it, Jasper; and it shall be a sign of the danger I have passed in your company, and of the gratitude I feel for your care of me —your care, and that of the Pathfinder."

"Never mind me, never mind me," exclaimed the latter, "this is Jasper's luck and Jasper's gift; give him full credit for both. My turn may come another day; mine and the quartermaster's, who seems to grudge the boy the calash, though what *he* can want of it, I cannot understand, for he has no wife."

"And has Jasper Eau-douce a wife? Or have you a wife yoursel', Pathfinder? I may want it to help to get a wife, or as a memorial that I have had a wife, or as proof how much I admire the sex, or because it is a female garment, or for some other equally respectable motive. It's not the unreflecting that are the most prized by the thoughtful, and there is no surer sign that a man made a good husband to his first consort, let me tell you all, than to see him speedily looking around for a competent successor. The affections are good gifts from Providence, and they that have loved one faithfully, prove how much of this bounty has been lavished upon them, by loving another as soon as possible."

"It may be so—it may be so. I am no practitioner in such things, and cannot gainsay it. But Mabel, here, the sergeant's daughter, will give you full credit for the words. Come, Jasper, although our hands are out, let us see what the other lads can do with the rifle."

Pathfinder and his companions retired, for the sports were about to proceed. The ladies, however, were not so much engrossed with rifle-shooting as to neglect the calash. It passed from hand to hand; the silk was felt, the fashion criticized, and the work examined, and divers opinions were privately ventured concerning the fitness of so handsome a thing passing into the possession of a noncommissioned officer's child.

"Perhaps you will be disposed to sell that calash, Mabel, when it has been a short time in your possession?" inquired the captain's lady. "Wear it, I should think, you never can."

"I may not wear it, madam," returned our heroine, modestly, "but I should not like to part with it, either."

"I dare say Sergeant Dunham keeps you above the necessity of selling your clothes, child; but, at the same time, it is money thrown away to keep an article of dress you can never wear."

"I should be unwilling to part with the gift of a friend."

"But the young man himself will think all the better of you, for your prudence, after the triumph of the day is forgotten. It is a pretty and a becoming calash, and ought not to be thrown away."

"I've no intention to throw it away, ma'am, and, if you please, would rather keep it."

"As you will, child; girls of your age often overlook their real advantages. Remember, however, if you do determine to dispose of the thing, that it is bespoke, and that I will not take it, if you ever even put it on your own head."

"Yes, ma'am," said Mabel, in the meekest voice imaginable, though her eyes looked like diamonds, and her cheeks reddened to the tints of two roses, as she placed the forbidden garment over her well-turned shoulders, where she kept it a minute, as if to try its fitness, and then quietly removed it again.

The remainder of the sports offered nothing of interest. The shooting was reasonably good, but the trials were all of a scale lower than those related, and the competitors were soon left to themselves. The ladies and most of the officers withdrew, and the remainder of the females soon followed their example. Mabel was returning along the low flat rocks that line the shore of the lake, dangling her pretty calash from a prettier finger, when Pathfinder met her. He carried the rifle which he had used that day, but his manner had less of the frank ease of the hunter about it than usual, while his eye seemed roving and uneasy. After a few unmeaning words concerning the noble sheet of water before them, he turned toward his companion with strong interest in his countenance, and said,—

"Jasper earned that calash for you, Mabel, without much trial of his gifts."

"It was fairly done, Pathfinder."

"No doubt, no doubt. The bullet passed neatly through the potato, and no man could have done more; though others might have done as much."

"But no one did as much!" exclaimed Mabel, with an animation that she instantly regretted, for she saw by the pained look of the guide, that he was mortified equally by the remark, and by the feeling with which it was uttered.

"It is true—it is true, Mabel, no one did as much then, but yet, there is no reason I should deny my gifts which come from Providence; yes, yes—no one did as much there, but you shall know what *can* be done here. Do you observe the gulls that are flying over our heads?"

"Certainly, Pathfinder; there are too many to escape notice."

"Here, where they cross each other, in sailing about," he added, cocking and raising his rifle; "the two—the two; now look!"

The piece was presented quick as thought, as two of the birds came in a line, though distant from each other many yards; the report followed, and the bullet passed through the bodies of both the victims. No sooner had the gulls fallen into the lake, than Pathfinder dropped the breech of the rifle, and laughed in his own perculiar manner, every shade of dissatisfaction and mortified pride having left his honest face.

"That is something, Mabel, that is something; although I've no calash to give you! But ask Jasper himself; I'll leave it all to Jasper, for a truer tongue and heart are not in America."

"Then it was not Jasper's fault that he gained the prize!"

"Not it. He did his best, and he did well. For one that has water gifts, rather than land gifts, Jasper is oncommonly expart, and a better backer no one need wish, ashore or afloat. But it was my fault, Mabel, that he got the calash; though it makes no difference—it makes no difference, for the thing has gone to the right person."

"I believe I understand you, Pathfinder," said Mabel, blushing in spite of herself, "and I look upon the calash as the joint gift of yourself and Jasper."

"That would not be doing justice to the lad, neither. He won the garment, and had a right to give it away. The most you may think, Mabel, is to believe that had I won it, it would have gone to the same person."

"I will remember that, Pathfinder, and take care that others know your skill, as it has been proved upon the poor gulls, in my presence."

"Lord bless you, Mabel, there is no more need of your talking in favor of my shooting, on this frontier, than of your talking about the water in the lake, or the sun in the heavens. Everybody knows what I can do in that way, and your words would be thrown away, as much as French would be thrown away on an American bear."

"Then you think that Jasper knew you were giving him this advantage, of which he had so unhandsomely availed himself?" said Mabel, the color which had imparted so much luster to her eyes gradually leaving her face, which became grave and thoughtful.

"I do not say that, but very far from it. We all forget things that we have known, when eager after our wishes. Jasper is satisfied that I can pass one bullet through two potatoes, as I sent my bullet through the gulls; and he knows no other man on the frontier can do the same thing. But with the calash before his eyes, and the hope of giving it to you, the lad was inclined to think better of himself, just at that moment, perhaps, than he ought. No, no; there's nothing mean or distrustful about Jasper Eau-douce, though it is a gift, nat'ral to all young men, to wish to appear well in the eyes of handsome young women."

"I'll try to forget all, but the kindness you've both shown to a poor motherless girl," said Mabel, struggling to keep down emotions that she scarcely knew how to account for herself. "Believe me, Pathfinder, I can never forget all you have already done for me—you and Jasper—and this new proof of your regard is not thrown away. Here—here is a brooch that is of silver; I offer it as a token that I owe you life or liberty."

6

AFTER the shooting match, another and more important diversion presented itself. The British post at Oswego, and the French post of Fort Frontenac (at what is now Kingston, Ontario) frowned at each other from opposite sides of Lake Ontario. Fort Frontenac was supplied by boats ascending the St. Lawrence from Montreal. The commander at Oswego had sent a party down to take a perilous station among the Thousand Islands, where they might cut off some of the supply boats. Already this party had captured two batteaux loaded with goods for trading with the Indians. It was now necessary to send a relief expedition to it. This was confided to Sergeant Dunham, with ten privates and two noncommissioned officers. The slinking quartermaster, David Muir, went along, and so did Hawkeye or Pathfinder, Cap, Jasper Western with his subordinates, one of them a boy of fourteen, and two women—Mabel Dunham and the wife of a soldier.

A cutter called the Scud *was prepared to carry the relief expedition up to the Thousand Islands. Jasper Western commanded the craft. The lake was as calm as a millpond when, just at nightfall, they embarked.*

Jasper was in readiness to receive his passengers, and, as the deck of the *Scud* was but two or three feet above the water, no difficulty was experienced in getting on board her. As soon as this was effected, the young man pointed out to Mabel and her companion the accommodations prepared for their reception, and they took possession of them.

The little vessel contained four apartments below, all between decks having been expressly constructed with a view to the transportation of officers and men, with their wives and families. First in rank was what was called the after cabin, a small apartment that contained four berths, and which enjoyed the advantage of possessing small windows, for the admission of air and light. This was uniformly devoted to females, whenever any were on board; and as Mabel and her companion were alone, they had ample space and accommodation. The main cabin was larger, and lighted from above. It was now appropriated to the uses of the quartermaster, the sergeant, Cap, and Jasper; the Pathfinder roaming through any part of the cutter he pleased, the female apartment excepted. The corporals and common soldiers occupied the space beneath the main hatch, which had a deck for such a purpose; while the crew were berthed, as usual, in the forecastle. Although the cutter did not measure quite fifty tons, the draft of officers and men was so light, that there was ample room for all on board, there being space enough to accommodate treble the number, if necessary.

As soon as Mabel had taken possession of her own really comfortable and pretty cabin, in doing which she could not abstain from indulging in the pleasant reflection that some of Jasper's favor had been especially manifested in her behalf, she went on deck again. Here all was momentarily in motion; the men were roving to and fro, in quest of their knapsacks and other effects; but method and habit soon reduced things to order, when the stillness on board became even imposing, for it was connected with the idea of future adventure, and ominous preparation.

Darkness was now beginning to render objects on shore indistinct, the whole of the land forming one shapeless black outline, of even forest summits, that was to be distinguished from the impending heavens only by the greater light of the sky. The stars, however, soon began to appear in the latter, one after another, in their usual mild, placid luster, bringing with them that sense of quiet which ordinarily accompanies night. There was something soothing as well as exciting in such a scene; and Mabel, who was seated on the quarter-deck, sensibly felt both influences. The Pathfinder was standing near her, leaning, as usual, on his long rifle, and she fancied that, through the glowing darkness of the hour, she could trace even stronger lines of thought than usual, in his rugged countenance.

"To you, Pathfinder, expeditions like this can be no great novelty," she said, "though I am surprised to find how silent and thoughtful the men appear to be."

"We l'arn this, by making war agin Injins. Your militia are great talkers, and little doers, in gin'ral; but the soger who has often met the Mingoes, l'arns to know the value of a prudent tongue. A silent army, in the woods, is doubly strong; and a noisy one, doubly weak. If tongues made sogers, the women of a camp would gin'rally carry the day."

"But we are neither an army, nor in the woods. There can be no danger of Mingoes in the *Scud*."

"Ask Jasper how he got to be master of this cutter, and you will find yourself answered as to that opinion! No one is safe from a Mingo who doesn't understand his very natur', and even then he must act up to his own knowledge, and that closely. Ask Jasper how he got command of this very cutter."

"And how *did* he get the command?" inquired Mabel, with an earnestness and interest that delighted her simple-minded and true-hearted companion, who was never better pleased than when he had an opportunity of saying aught in favor of a friend. "It is honorable to him that he has reached this station while yet so young."

"That is it; but he deserved it all, and more. A frigate wouldn't have been too much to pay for so much spirit and coolness, had there been such a thing on Ontario, as there is not, howsever, or likely to be."

"But Jasper—you have not yet told me how he got the command of the schooner?"

"It is a long story, Mabel, and one your father, the sergeant, can tell much better than I, for he was present, while I was off on a distant scoutin'. Jasper is not good at a story, I will own that; I've heard him questioned about this affair, and he never made a good tale of it, although everybody knows it was a good thing. No, no; Jasper is not good at a story, as his best friends must own. The *Scud* had near fallen into the hands of the French and the Mingoes, when Jasper saved her, in a way that none but a quick-witted mind and a bold heart would have attempted. The sergeant will tell the tale better than I can, and I wish you to question him some day, when nothing better offers. As for Jasper himself, there will be no use in worrying the lad, since he will make a bungling matter of it, for he don't know how to give a history at all."

Mabel determined to ask her father to repeat the incidents of the affair that very night, for it struck her young fancy that nothing better could well offer than to listen to the praises of one who was a bad historian of his own exploits.

"Will the *Scud* remain with us when we reach the island?" she asked, after a little hesitation about the propriety of the question, "or shall we be left to ourselves?"

"That's as may be. Jasper does not often keep the cutter idle, when anything is to be done, and we may expect activity on his part. My gifts, however, run so little toward the water, and vessels gin'rally, unless it be among rapids and falls, and in canoes, that I pretend to know nothing about it. We shall have all right, under Jasper, I make no doubt, who can find a trail on Ontario as well as a Delaware can find one on the land."

"And our own Delaware, Pathfinder—the Big Serpent—why is he not with us tonight?"

"Your question would have been more nat'ral had you said, why are *you* here, Pathfinder? The Sarpent is in his place, while I am not in mine. He is out with two or three more scouting the lake shores, and will join us down among the islands with the tidings he may gather. The sergeant is too good a soldier to forget his rear, while he is facing the enemy in front! It's a thousand pities, Mabel, your father wasn't born a gin'ral, as some of the English are who come among us, for I feel sartain he wouldn't leave a Frencher in the Canadas a week could he have his own way with them."

"Shall we have enemies to face in front?" asked Mabel, smiling, and for the first time feeling a slight apprehension about the dangers of the expedition. "Are we likely to have an engagement?"

"If we have, Mabel, there will be men enough ready and willing to stand atween you and harm. But you are a soldier's daughter, and we all know have the spirit of one. Don't let the fear of a battle keep your pretty eyes from sleeping."

"I do feel braver out here in the woods, Pathfinder, than I ever felt before, amid the weaknesses of the towns, although I have always tried to remember what I owe to my dear father."

"Ay, your mother was so before you! 'You will find Mabel like her mother, no screamer, or a fainthearted girl to trouble a man in his need, but one who would encourage her mate, and help to keep his heart up when sorest pressed by danger'—said the sergeant to me, before I ever laid eyes on that sweet countenance of yours—he did!"

"And why should my father have told you this, Pathfinder?" the girl demanded, a little earnestly. "Perhaps he fancied you would think the better of me, if you did not believe me a silly coward, as so many of my sex love to make themselves appear."

Deception, unless it were at the expense of his enemies in the field, —nay, concealment of even a thought, was so little in accordance with the Pathfinder's very nature, that he was not a little embarrassed by this simple question. To own the truth openly, he felt, by a sort of instinct, for which it would have puzzled him to account, would not be proper; and to hide it, agreed with neither his sense of right nor his habits. In such a strait he involuntarily took refuge in the middle course, not revealing that which he fancied ought not to be told, nor yet absolutely concealing it.

"You must know, Mabel," he said, "that the sergeant and I are old friends, and have stood side by side—or if not actually side by side, I a little in advance, as became a scout, and your father, with his own men, as better suited a soldier of the King—on many a hard-fought and bloody day. It's the way of us skirmishers to think little of the fight, when the rifle has done cracking; and at night, around our fires, or on our marches, we talk of the things we love, just as you young women convarse about your fancies and opinions, when you get together to laugh over your idees. Now it was natural that the sergeant, having such a daughter as you, should love her better than anything else, and that he should talk of her oftener than of anything else,—while I, having neither daughter, nor sister, nor mother, nor kith nor kin, nor anything but the Delawares to love, I naturally chimed in, as it were, and got to love you, Mabel, before I ever saw you—yes, I did—just by talking about you so much."

"And now you *have* seen me," returned the smiling girl, whose unmoved and natural manner proved how little she was thinking of anything more than parental or fraternal regard, "you are beginning to see the folly of forming friendships for people before you know anything about them, except by hearsay."

"It wasn't friendship—it isn't friendship, Mabel, that I feel for you. I am the friend of the Delawares, and have been so from boyhood; but my feelings for them, or for the best of them, are not the same as them I got from the sergeant for you; and especially now that I begin to know you better. I'm sometimes afeard it isn't wholesome for one who is much occupied in a very manly calling, like that of a guide, or a scout, or a soldier even, to form friendships for women,—young women in particular,—as they seem to me to lessen the love of enterprise, and to turn the feelings away from their gifts and natural occupations."

"You surely do not mean, Pathfinder, that a friendship for a girl like me would make you less bold, and more unwilling to meet the French, than you were before?"

"Not so—not so. With you in danger, for instance, I fear I might become foolhardy; but before we became so intimate, as I may say, I loved to think of my scoutin's, and of my marches, and outlyings, and fights, and other adventures; but now my mind cares less about them; I think more of the barracks and of evenings passed in discourse, of feelings in which there are no wranglings and bloodshed, and of young women, and of their laughs, and their cheerful soft voices, their pleasant looks, and their winning ways! I sometimes tell the sergeant, that he and his daughter will be the spoiling of one of the best and most experienced scouts on the lines!"

"Not they, Pathfinder; they will try to make that which is already so excellent, perfect. You do not know us, if you think that either wishes to see you in the least changed. Remain, as at present, the same honest, upright, conscientious, fearless, intelligent, trustworthy guide, that you are, and neither my dear father nor myself can ever think of you differently from what we now do."

It was too dark for Mabel to note the workings of the countenance of her listener, but her own sweet face was turned toward him, as she spoke with an energy equal to her frankness, in a way to show how little embarrassed were her thoughts, and how sincere were her words. Her countenance was a little flushed, it is true, but it was with earnestness and truth of feeling; though no nerve thrilled, no limb trembled, no pulsation quickened. In short, her manner and appearance were those of a sincere-minded and frank girl, making such a declaration of good will and regard for one of the other sex, as she felt that his services and good qualities merited, without any of the emotion that invariably accompanies the consciousness of an inclination which might lead to softer disclosures.

The Pathfinder was too unpracticed, however, to enter into distinctions of this kind, and his humble nature was encouraged by the directness and strength of the words he had just heard. Unwilling, if not unable to say any more, he walked away, and stood leaning on his rifle, and looking up at the stars, for quite ten minutes, in profound silence.

In the meanwhile, the interview on the bastion, to which we have already alluded, took place between Lundie and the sergeant.

"Have the men's knapsacks been examined?" demanded Major Duncan, after he had cast his eye at a written report, handed to him by the sergeant, but which it was too dark to read.

"All, your honor; and all are right."

"The ammunition—arms?"

"All in order, Major Duncan, and fit for any service."

"You have the men named in my own draft, Dunham?"

"Without an exception, sir. Better men could not be found in the regiment."

"You have need of the best of our men, sergeant. This experiment has now been tried three times; always under one of the ensigns, who have flattered me with success, but have as often failed. After so much preparation and expense, I do not like to abandon the project entirely, but this will be the last effort: and the result will mainly depend on you and on the Pathfinder."

"You may count on us both, Major Duncan. The duty you have given us is not above our habits and experience, and I think it will be well done. I know that the Pathfinder will not be wanting."

"On that, indeed, it will be safe to rely. He is a most extraordinary man, Dunham—one who long puzzled me; but who, now that I understand him, commands as much of my respect as any general in His Majesty's service."

"I was in hopes, sir, that you would come to look at the proposed marriage with Mabel, as a thing I ought to wish and forward."

"As for that, sergeant, time will show," returned Lundie, smiling, though here, too, the obscurity concealed the nicer shades of expression; "one woman is sometimes more difficult to manage than a whole regiment of men. By the way, you know that your would-be son-in-law, the quartermaster, will be of the party; and I trust you will at least give him an equal chance in the trial for your daughter's smiles."

"If respect for his rank, sir, did not cause me to do this, your honor's wish would be sufficient."

"I thank you, sergeant. We have served much together, and ought to value each other in our several stations. Understand me, however: I ask no more for Davy Muir than a clear field and no favor. In love, as in war, each man must gain his own victories. Are you certain that the rations have been properly calculated?"

"I'll answer for it, Major Duncan; but if they were not, we cannot suffer with two such hunters as Pathfinder and the Serpent in company."

"That will never do, Dunham," interrupted Lundie, sharply, "and it comes of your American birth and American training! No thorough soldier ever relies on anything but his commissary for supplies; and I beg no part of my regiment may be the first to set an example to the contrary."

"You have only to command, Major Duncan, to be obeyed; and yet, if I might presume, sir—"

"Speak freely, sergeant, you are talking with a friend."

"I was merely about to say, that I find even the Scotch soldiers like venison and birds quite as well as pork, when they are difficult to be had."

"That may be very true; but likes and dislikes have nothing to do with system. An army can rely on nothing but its commissaries. The irregularity of the provincials has played the devil with the King's service too long to be winked at any longer."

"General Braddock, your honor, might have been advised by Colonel Washington."

"Out upon your Washington! You're all provincials together, man, and uphold each other as if you were of a sworn confederacy."

"I believe his majesty has no more loyal subjects than the Americans, your honor."

"In that, Dunham, I'm thinking you're right; and I have been a little too warm, perhaps. I do not consider *you* a provincial, however, sergeant; for, though born in America, a better soldier never shouldered a musket."

"And Colonel Washington, your honor?"

"Well; and Colonel Washington may be a useful subject, too. He is the American prodigy; and I suppose I may as well give him all the credit you ask. You have no doubt of the skill of this Jasper Eau-douce?"

"The boy has been tried, sir; and found equal to all that can be required of him."

"He has a French name, and has passed much of his boyhood in the French colonies: has he French blood in his veins, sergeant?"

"Not a drop, your honor. Jasper's father was an old comrade of my own, and his mother came of an honest and loyal family, in this very province."

"How came he then so much among the French, and whence his name? He speaks the language of the Canadas, too, I find!"

"That is easily explained, Major Duncan. The boy was left under the care of one of our mariners in the old war, and he took to the water like a duck. Your honor knows that we have no ports on Ontario, that can be named as such, and he naturally passed most of his time on the other side of the lake, where the French have had a few vessels these fifty years. He learned to speak their language, as a matter of course, and got his name from the Indians and Canadians, who are fond of calling men by their qualities, as it might be."

"A French master is but a poor instructor for a British sailor, notwithstanding!"

"I beg your pardon, sir; Jasper Eau-douce was brought up under a real English seaman; one that had sailed under the King's pennant, and may be called a thoroughbred: that is to say, a subject born in the colonies, but none the worse at his trade, I hope, Major Duncan, for that."

"Perhaps not, sergeant; perhaps not; nor any better. This Jasper behaved well, too, when I gave him the command of the *Scud;* no lad could have conducted himself more loyally, or better."

"Or more bravely, Major Duncan. I am sorry to see, sir, that you have doubts as to the fidelity of Jasper."

"It is the duty of the soldier who is intrusted with the care of a distant and important post like this, Dunham, never to relax in his vigilance. We have two of the most artful enemies that the world has ever produced, in their several ways, to contend with—the Indians and the French; and nothing should be overlooked than can lead to injury."

"I hope your honor considers me fit to be intrusted with any particular reason that may exist for doubting Jasper, since you have seen fit to intrust me with this command."

"It is not that I doubt you, Dunham, that I hesitate to reveal all I may happen to know, but from a strong reluctance to circulate an evil report concerning one of whom I have hitherto thought well. You must think well of the Pathfinder, or you would not wish to give him your daughter?"

"For the Pathfinder's honesty, I will answer with my life, sir," returned the sergeant, firmly, and not without a dignity of manner that struck his superior. "Such a man doesn't know how to be false."

"I believe you are right, Dunham, and yet this last information has unsettled all my old opinions. I have received an anonymous communication, sergeant, advising me to be on my guard against Jasper Western, or Jasper Eau-douce, as he is called; who, it alleges, has been bought by the enemy, and giving me reason to expect that further and more precise information will soon be sent."

"Letters without signatures to them, sir, are scarcely to be regarded in war."

"Or in peace, Dunham. No one can entertain a lower opinion of the writer of an anonymous letter, in ordinary matters, than myself. The very act denotes cowardice, meanness, and baseness; and it usually is a token of falsehood, as well as of other vices. But, in matters of war, it is not exactly the same thing. Besides, several suspicious circumstances have been pointed out to me—"

"Such as is fit for an orderly to hear, your honor?"

"Certainly, one in whom I confide as much as in yourself, Dunham. It is said, for instance, that your daughter and her party were permitted to escape the Iroquois, when they came in, merely to give Jasper credit with me. I am told that the gentry at Frontenac will care more for the capture of the *Scud*, with Sergeant Dunham and a party of men, together with the defeat of our favorite plan, than for the capture of a girl, and the scalp of her uncle."

"I understand the hint, sir, but I do not give it credit. Jasper can hardly be true, and Pathfinder false; and as for the last, I would as soon distrust your honor, as distrust him!"

"It would seem so, sergeant; it would indeed seem so. But Jasper is not the Pathfinder after all, and I will own, Dunham, I should put more faith in the lad, if he didn't speak French!"

"It's no recommendation in my eyes, I assure your honor; but the boy learned it by compulsion, as it were, and ought not to be condemned too hastily, for the circumstance, by your honor's leave. If he does speak French, it's because he can't well help it."

"It's a d——d lingo, and never did any one good—at least, no British subject; for I suppose the French themselves must talk together in some language or other. I should have much more faith in this Jasper did he know nothing of their language. This letter has made me uneasy; and, were there another to whom I could trust the cutter, I would devise some means to detain him here."

7

THE RELIEF EXPEDITION departed for the Thousand Islands with Jasper Western in charge of the Scud, *but with suspicion of the young man firmly implanted in the breast of Sergeant Dunham. "I give you full powers," Major Duncan said on parting, "and should you detect this Jasper in any treachery, make a sacrifice at once to offended justice." The major also urged Dunham to place great confidence in Pathfinder. The* Scud *had not travelled far on Lake Ontario when it sighted a bark canoe. Chase was given; the frail craft was overhauled and seized with a boathook; and the occupants proved to be the treacherous Arrowhead and his wife. The Tuscarora gave some plausible explanations for his previous conduct. Hearing them, Sergeant Dunham became negligent, and Arrowhead and his wife, taking advantage of gathering darkness and fog, escaped in their canoe. It was plain that they would tell the French of the British expedition. Alarmed and chagrined, Sergeant Dunham (with the advice of Cap) decided to put Jasper under arrest. Cap then took charge of the* Scud, *and promptly fell into grave difficulties; for a heavy gale smote the lake, and following his deep-sea traditions, he ran westward and northward before it until he reached the wild northern shore. Here he had to call Jasper back to the command. Knowing how to manage a ship on the Great Lakes, Jasper anchored the* Scud *in the lee of a high bluff, where the undertow kept her out of the breakers.*

They had to wait until the waters grew calmer, and this wait gave Pathfinder an opportunity for which he had been looking.

It was near noon when the gale broke; and then its force abated as suddenly as its violence had arisen. In less than two hours after the wind fell, the surface of the lake, though still agitated, was no longer glittering with foam; and in double that time, the entire sheet presented the ordinary scene of disturbed water, that was unbroken by the violence of a tempest. Still, the waves came rolling incessantly toward the shore, and the lines of breakers remained, though the spray had ceased to fly; the combing of the swells was more moderate, and all that there was of violence proceeded from the impulsion of wind that had abated.

As it was impossible to make head against the sea that was still up, with the light opposing air that blew from the eastward, all thoughts of getting under way that afternoon were abandoned. Jasper, who had now quietly resumed the command of the *Scud*, busied himself, however, in heaving up to the anchors, which were lifted in succession. The kedges that backed them were weighed, and everything was got in readiness for a prompt departure, as soon as the state of the weather would allow. In the meantime, they who had no concern with those duties sought such means of amusement as their peculiar circumstances allowed.

As is common with those who are unused to the confinement of a vessel, Mabel cast wistful eyes toward the shore, nor was it long before she expressed a wish that it were possible to land. The Pathfinder was near her at the time, and he assured her that nothing would be easier, as they had a bark canoe on deck, which was the best possible mode of conveyance to go through a surf. After the usual doubts and misgivings, the sergeant was appealed to; his opinion proved to be favorable, and preparations to carry the whim into effect were immediately made.

The party that was to land consisted of Sergeant Dunham, his daughter, and the Pathfinder. Accustomed to the canoe, Mabel took her seat in the center with great steadiness, her father was placed in the bow, while the guide assumed the office of conductor, by steering in the stern. There was little need of impelling the canoe by means of the paddle, for the rollers sent it forward, at moments, with a violence that set every effort to govern its movements at defiance. More than once, ere the shore was reached, Mabel repented of her temerity, but Pathfinder encouraged her, and really manifested so much self-possession, coolness, and strength of arm himself, that even a female might have hesitated about owning all her apprehensions. Our heroine was no coward, and while she felt the novelty of her situation, she also experienced a fair proportion of its wild delight. At moments, indeed, her heart was in her mouth, as the bubble of a boat floated on the very crest of a foaming breaker, appearing to skim the water like a swallow, and then she flushed and laughed, as, left by the glancing element, they appeared to linger behind, ashamed of having been outdone in the headlong race. A few minutes sufficed for this excitement, for, though the distance between the cutter and the land considerably exceeded a quarter of a mile, the intermediate space was passed in a very few moments.

On landing, the sergeant kissed his daughter kindly, for he was so much of a soldier as always to feel more at home on *terra firma* than when afloat, and taking his gun, he announced his intention to pass an hour in quest of game.

"Pathfinder will remain near you, girl, and no doubt he will tell you some of the traditions of this part of the world, or some of his own experiences with the Mingoes."

The guide laughed, promised to have a care of Mabel, and in a few minutes the father had ascended a steep acclivity, and disappeared in the forest. The others took another direction, which, after a few minutes of sharp ascent also, brought them to a small naked point on the promontory, where the eye overlooked an extensive and very peculiar panorama. Here Mabel seated herself on a fragment of fallen rock, to recover her breath and strength, while her companion, on whose sinews no personal exertion seemed to make any impression, stood at her side, leaning in his own and not ungraceful manner on his long rifle. Several minutes passed, and neither spoke; Mabel, in particular, being lost in admiration of the view.

The position the two had attained was sufficiently elevated to command a wide reach of the lake, which stretched away toward the northeast in a boundless sheet, glittering beneath the rays of an afternoon sun, and yet betraying the remains of that agitation which it had endured while tossed by the late tempest. The land set bounds to its limits, in a huge crescent, disappearing in distance toward the southeast and the north. Far as the eye could reach, nothing but forest was visible, not even a solitary sign of civilization breaking in upon the uniform and grand magnificence of nature. The gale had driven the *Scud* beyond the line of those forts with which the French were then endeavoring to gird the English North American possessions; for, following the channels of communication between the Great Lakes, their posts were on the banks of the Niagara, while our adventurers had reached a point many leagues westward of that celebrated strait. The cutter rode at single anchor, without the breakers, resembling some well imagined and accurately executed toy, that was intended rather for a glass case than for the struggles with the elements which she had so lately gone through; while the canoe lay on the narrow beach, just out of reach of the waves that came booming upon the land, a speck upon the shingles.

"We are very far, here, from human habitations!" exclaimed Mabel, when, after a long and musing survey of the scene, its principal peculiarities forced themselves on her active and ever brilliant imagination; "this is, indeed, being on the frontier!"

"Have they more sightly scenes than this, nearer the sea, and around their large towns?" demanded Pathfinder, with an interest he was apt to discover in such a subject.

"I will not say that; there is more to remind one of his fellow-beings there than here; less, perhaps, to remind one of God."

"Ay, Mabel, that is what my own feelings say. I am but a poor hunter, I know; untaught and unl'arned; but God is as near me, in this my home, as He is near the King in his royal palace."

"Who can doubt it?" returned Mabel, looking from the view up into the hard-featured but honest face of her companion, though not without surprise at the energy of his manner; "one feels nearer to God in such a spot, I think, than when the mind is distracted by the objects of the towns."

"You say all I wish to say myself, Mabel, but in so much plainer speech that you make me ashamed of wishing to let others know what I feel on such matters. I have coasted this lake in s'arch of skins, afore the war, and have been here already; not at this very spot, for we landed yonder, where you may see the blasted oak that stands above the cluster of hemlocks—"

"How! Pathfinder, can you remember all these trifles so accurately!"

"These are our streets and houses; our churches and palaces. Remember them, indeed! I once made an appointment with the Big Sarpent, to meet at twelve o'clock at noon near the foot of a certain pine, at the end of six months, when neither of us was within three hundred miles of the spot. The tree stood, and stands still, unless the judgment of Providence has lighted on that too, in the midst of the forest, fifty miles from any settlement, but in a most extraordinary neighborhood for beaver."

"And did you meet at that very spot and hour?"

"Does the sun rise and set? When I reached the tree, I found the Sarpent leaning against its trunk, with torn leggings and muddied moccasins. The Delaware had got into a swamp, and it worried him not a little to find his way out of it; but, as the sun, which comes over the eastern hills in the morning, goes down behind the western at night, so was he true to time and place. No fear of Chingachgook when there is either a friend or an enemy in the case. He is equally sart'in with each."

"And where is the Delaware now—why is he not with us today?"

"He is scoutin' on the Mingo trail, where I ought to have been too, but for a great human infirmity."

"You seem above, beyond, superior to all infirmity, Pathfinder; I never yet met with a man who appeared to be so little liable to the weaknesses of nature."

"If you mean in the way of health and strength, Mabel, Providence has been kind to me; though I fancy the open air, long hunts, active scoutin's, forest fare, and the sleep of a good conscience, may always keep the doctors at a distance. But I am human a'ter all; yes, I find I'm very human in some of my feelin's."

Mabel looked surprised, and it would be no more than delineating the character of her sex, if we added that her sweet countenance expressed a good deal of curiosity, too, though her tongue was more discreet.

"There is something bewitching in this wild life of yours, Pathfinder," she exclaimed, a tinge of enthusiasm mantling her cheeks. "I find I'm fast getting to be a frontier girl, and am coming to love all this grand silence of the woods. The towns seem tame to me; and, as my father will probably pass the remainder of his days here, where he has already lived so long, I begin to feel that I should be happy to continue with him, and not return to the seashore."

"The woods are never silent, Mabel, to such as understand their meaning. Days at a time, have I travelled them alone, without feeling the want of company; and, as for conversation, for such as can comprehend their language, there is no want of rational and instructive discourse."

"I believe you are happier when alone, Pathfinder, than when mingling with your fellow-creatures."

"I will not say that—I will not say exactly that! I have seen the time when I have thought that God was sufficient for me in the forest, and that I craved no more than his bounty, and his care. But other feelin's have got uppermost, and I suppose natur' will have its way. All other creatur's mate, Mabel, and it was intended man should do so, too."

"And have you never bethought you of seeking a wife, Pathfinder, to share your fortunes?" inquired the girl, with the directness and simplicity that the pure of heart, and the undesigning, are the most apt to manifest, and with that feeling of affection which is inbred in her sex. "To me, it seems, you only want a home to return to, from your wanderings, to render your life completely happy. Were I a man, it would be my delight to roam through these forests at will, or to sail over this beautiful lake."

"I understand you, Mabel; and God bless you for thinking of the welfare of men as humble as we are. We have our pleasures, it is true, as well as our gifts, but we might be happier; yes, I do think we might be happier."

"Happier! in what way, Pathfinder? In this pure air, with these cool and shaded forests to wander through, this lovely lake to gaze at, and sail upon, with clear consciences, and abundance for all the real wants, men ought to be nothing less than as perfectly happy as their infirmities will allow."

"Every creatur' has its gifts, Mabel, and men have their'n," answered the guide, looking stealthily at his beautiful companion, whose cheeks had flushed and eyes brightened under the ardor of feelings excited by the novelty of her striking situation; "and all must obey them. Do you see yonder pigeon that is just alightin' on the beech,—here in a line with the fallen chestnut?"

"Certainly; it is the only thing stirring with life in it, besides ourselves, that is to be seen in this vast solitude."

"Not so, Mabel, not so; Providence makes nothing that lives, to live quite alone. Here is its mate, just rising on the wing; it has been feedin' near the other beech, but it will not long be separated from its companion."

"I understand you, Pathfinder," returned Mabel, smiling sweetly, though as calmly as if the discourse was with her father. "But a hunter may find a mate, even in this wild region. The Indian girls are affectionate and true, I know, for such was the wife of Arrowhead, to a husband who oftener frowned than smiled."

"That would never do, Mabel, and good would never come of it. Kind must cling to kind, and country to country, if one would find happiness. If, indeed, I could meet with one like you, who would consent to be a hunter's wife, and who would not scorn my ignorance and rudeness, then, indeed, would all the toil of the past appear like the sporting of the young deer, and all the future like sunshine!"

"One like me! A girl of my years and indiscretion would hardly make a fit companion for the boldest scout and surest hunter on the lines."

"Ah! Mabel, I fear me that I have been improving a redskin's gifts, with a paleface's natur'! Such a character would insure a wife, in an Injin village."

"Surely, surely, Pathfinder, you would not think of choosing one as ignorant, as frivolous, as vain, and as inexperienced as I, for your wife!" Mabel would have added, "and as young," but an instinctive feeling of delicacy repressed the words.

"And why not, Mabel? If you are ignorant of frontier usages, you know more than all of us of pleasant anecdotes and town customs; as for frivolous, I know not what it means, but if it signifies beauty, ah's me! I fear it is no fault in my eyes. Vain you are not, as is seen by the kind manner in which you listen to all my idle tales about scoutin's, and trails; and as for experience, that will come with years. Besides, Mabel, I fear men think little of these matters, when they are about to take wives, I do."

"Pathfinder! your words—your looks—surely all this is meant in trifling—you speak in pleasantry!"

"To me it is always agreeable to be near you, Mabel, and I should sleep sounder this blessed night, than I have done for a week past, could I think that you find such discourse as pleasant as I do."

We shall not say that Mabel Dunham had not believed herself a favorite with the guide. This her quick, feminine sagacity had early discovered, and perhaps she had occasionally thought there had mingled with his regard and friendship, some of that manly tenderness which the ruder sex must be coarse indeed not to show, on occasions, to the gentler; but the idea that he seriously sought her for his wife had never before crossed the mind of the spirited and ingenuous girl. Now, however, a gleam of something like the truth broke in upon her imagination, less induced by the words of her companion, perhaps, than by his manner. Looking earnestly into the rugged, honest countenance of the scout, Mabel's own features became concerned and grave, and when she spoke again, it was with a gentleness of manner that attracted him to her even more powerfully than the words themselves were calculated to repel.

"You and I should understand each other, Pathfinder," she said, with an earnest sincerity, "nor should there be any cloud between us. You are too upright and frank to meet with anything but sincerity and frankness in return. Surely, surely, all this means nothing, has no other connection with your feelings, than such a friendship as one of your wisdom and character would naturally feel for a girl like me!"

"I believe it's nat'ral, Mabel; yes, I do; the sergeant tells me he had such feelings toward your own mother, and I think I've seen something like it, in the young people I have from time to time guided through the wilderness. Yes, yes; I dare say it's all nat'ral enough, and that makes it come so easy, and is a great comfort to me."

"Pathfinder, your words make me uneasy! Speak plainer, or change the subject forever. You do not—cannot mean that—you—cannot wish me to understand"—even the tongue of the spirited Mabel faltered, and she shrank with maiden shame from adding what she wished so earnestly to say. Rallying her courage, however, and determined to know all as soon and as plainly as possible, after a moment's hesitation she continued, "I mean, Pathfinder, that you do not wish me to understand that you seriously think of me as a wife?"

"I do, Mabel; that's it—that's just it, and you have put the matter in a much better point of view than I, with my forest gifts and frontier ways, would ever be able to do. The sergeant and I have concluded on the matter, if it is agreeable to you, as he thinks is likely will be the case, though I doubt my own power to please one who deserves the best husband America can produce."

Mabel's countenance changed from uneasiness to surprise, and then by a transition still quicker, from surprise to pain.

"My father!" she exclaimed. "My dear father has thought of my becoming your wife, Pathfinder!"

"Yes, he has, Mabel; he has indeed. He has even thought such a thing might be agreeable to you, and has almost encouraged me to fancy it might be true."

"But you, yourself—you certainly can care nothing whether this singular expectation shall ever be realized or not?"

"Anan?"

"I mean, Pathfinder, that you have talked of this match more to oblige my father than anything else; that your feelings are no way concerned, let my answer be what it may?"

The scout looked earnestly into the beautiful face of Mabel, which had flushed with the ardor and novelty of her sensations, and it was impossible to mistake the intense admiration that betrayed itself in every lineament of his ingenuous countenance.

"I have often thought myself happy, Mabel, when ranging the woods, on a successful hunt, breathing the pure air of the hills, and filled with vigor and health, but I now feel that it has all been idleness and vanity compared with the delight it would give me to know that you thought better of me than you think of most others."

"Better of you! I do indeed think better of you, Pathfinder, than of most others; I am not certain that I do not think better of you than of any other; for your truth, honesty, simplicity, justice, and courage are scarcely equalled by any of earth."

"Ah! Mabel! These are sweet and encouraging words from you, and the sergeant, a'ter all, was not as near wrong as I feared."

"Nay, Pathfinder, in the name of all that is sacred and just, do not let us misunderstand each other, in a matter of so much importance. While I esteem, respect—nay, reverence you, almost as much as I reverence my own dear father, it is impossible that I should ever become your wife—that I—"

The change in her companion's countenance was so sudden and so great, that the moment the effect of what she had uttered became visible in the face of the Pathfinder, Mabel arrested her own words, notwithstanding her strong desire to be explicit, the reluctance with which she could at any time cause pain being sufficient of itself to induce the pause. Neither spoke for some time, the shade of disappointment that crossed the rugged lineaments of the hunter amounting so nearly to anguish, as to frighten his companion, while the sensation of choking became so strong in the Pathfinder, that he fairly gripped his throat, like one who sought physical relief for physical suffering. The convulsive manner in which his fingers worked actually struck the alarmed girl with a feeling of awe.

"Nay, Pathfinder," Mabel eagerly added, the instant she could command her voice, "I may have said more than I mean, for all things of this nature are possible, and women, they say, are never sure of their own minds. What I wish you to understand is, that it is not likely that you and I should ever think of each other, as man and wife ought to think of each other."

"I do not—I shall never think in that way again, Mabel," gasped forth the Pathfinder, who appeared to utter his words like one just raised above the pressure of some suffocating substance. "No, no; I shall never think of you, or any one else, again, in that way."

"Pathfinder—dear Pathfinder, understand me; do not attach more meaning to my words than I do myself; a match like that would be unwise—unnatural, perhaps."

"Yes, unnat'ral—agin natur'; and so I told the sergeant, but he *would* have it otherwise."

"Pathfinder! O! this is worse than I could have imagined; take my hand, excellent Pathfinder, and let me see that you do not hate me. For God's sake, smile upon me again!"

"Hate you, Mabel! Smile upon you! Ah's me!"

"Nay, give me your hand—your hardy, true, and manly hand; both, both, Pathfinder, for I shall not be easy until I feel certain that we are friends again, and that all this has been a mistake."

"Mabel," said the guide, looking wistfully into the face of the generous and impetuous girl, as she held his two hard and sunburnt hands in her own pretty and delicate fingers, and laughing in his own silent and peculiar manner, while anguish gleamed over lineaments which seemed incapable of deception, even while agitated with emotions so conflicting, "Mabel, the sergeant was wrong!"

The pent-up feelings could endure no more, and the tears rolled down the cheeks of the scout like rain. His fingers again worked convulsively at his throat, and his breast heaved, as if it possessed a tenant of which it would be rid, by any effort, however desperate.

"Pathfinder! Pathfinder!" Mabel almost shrieked, "anything but this—anything but this. Speak to me, Pathfinder; smile again—say one kind word—anything to prove you can forgive me."

"The sergeant was wrong!" exclaimed the guide, laughing amid his agony, in a way to terrify his companion by the unnatural mixture of anguish and lightheartedness. "I knew it—I knew it, and said it; yes, the sergeant was wrong, a'ter all."

"We can be friends, though we cannot be man and wife," continued Mabel, almost as much disturbed as her companion, scarce knowing what she said; "we can always be friends, and always will."

"I thought the sergeant was mistaken," resumed the Pathfinder, when a great effort had enabled him to command himself, "for I did not think my gifts were such as would please the fancy of a town-bred gal. It would have been better, Mabel, had he not overpersuaded me into a different notion; and it might have been better, too, had you not been so pleasant and friendly, like; yes, it would."

"If I thought any error of mine had raised false expectations in you, Pathfinder, however unintentionally on my part, I should never forgive myself; for, believe me, I would rather endure pain in my own feelings than you should suffer."

"That's just it, Mabel; that's just it. These speeches and opinions, spoken in so soft a voice, and in a way I'm so unused to in the woods, have done the mischief. But I now see plainly, and begin to understand the difference between us better, and will strive to keep down thought, and to go abroad ag'in as I used to do, looking for the game and the inimy. Ah's me! Mabel, I have indeed been on a false trail since we met!"

"But you will now travel on the true one. In a little while you will forget all this, and think of me as a friend who owes you her life."

"This may be the way in the towns, but I doubt if it's nat'ral to the woods. With us, when the eye sees a lovely sight, it is apt to keep it long in view, or when the mind takes in an upright and proper feeling, it is loath to part with it."

"But it is not a proper feeling that you should love me, nor am I a lovely sight. You will forget it all, when you come seriously to recollect that I am altogether unsuited to be your wife."

"So I told the sergeant; but he would have it otherwise. I knew you was too young and beautiful for one of middle age, like myself, and who never was comely to look at, even in youth; and then your ways have not been my ways, nor would a hunter's cabin be a fitting place for one who was edicated among chiefs, as it were. If I were younger and comelier, though, like Jasper Eau-douce—"

"Never mind Jasper Eau-douce," interrupted Mabel, impatiently; "we can talk of something else."

"Jasper is a worthy lad, Mabel; ay, and a comely," returned the guileless guide, looking earnestly at the girl, as if he distrusted her judgment in speaking slightingly of his friend. "Were I only half as comely as Jasper Western, my misgivings in this affair would not have been so great, and they might not have been so true."

"We will not talk of Jasper Western," repeated Mabel, the color mounting to her temples; "he may be good enough in a gale or on the lake, but he is not good enough to talk of here."

"I fear me, Mabel, he is better than the man who is likely to be your husband, though the sergeant says that never can take place. But the sergeant was wrong once, and he may be wrong twice."

"And who is likely to be my husband, Pathfinder? This is scarcely less strange than what has just passed between us!"

"I know it is nat'ral for like to seek like, and for them that have consorted much with officers" ladies, to wish to be officers' ladies themselves. But, Mabel, I may speak plainly to you, I know, and I hope my words will not give you pain, for, now I understand what it is to be disappointed in such feelings, I wouldn't wish to cause even a Mingo sorrow, on this head. But happiness is not always to be found in a marquee, any more than in a tent; and though the officers' quarters may look more tempting than the rest of the barracks, there is often great misery between husband and wife, inside of their doors."

"I do not doubt it in the least, Pathfinder; and did it rest with me to decide, I would sooner follow you to some cabin in the woods, and share your fortune, whether it might be better or worse, than go inside the door of any officer I know, with an intention of remaining there as its master's wife."

"Mabel, this is not what Lundie hopes, or Lundie thinks!"

"And what care I for Lundie? He is major of the 55th, and may command his men to wheel and march about as he pleases, but he cannot compel me to wed the greatest or the meanest of his mess: besides, what can you know of Lundie's wishes on such a subject?"

"From Lundie's own mouth. The sergeant had told him that he wished me for a son-in-law; and the major being an old and a true friend, conversed with me on the subject; he put it to me plainly, whether it would not be more gin'rous in me to let an officer succeed, than to strive to make you share a hunter's fortune. I owned the truth, I did; and that was, that I thought it might; but when he told me that the quartermaster would be his choice, I would not abide by the conditions. No, no, Mabel; I know Davy Muir well, and though he may make you a lady, he can never make you a happy woman, or himself a gentleman. I say this honestly, I do; for I now plainly see that the sergeant has been wrong."

"My father has been very wrong if he has said or done aught to cause you sorrow, Pathfinder; and so great is my respect for you, so sincere my friendship, that were it not for one—I mean that no person need fear Lieutenant Muir's influence with me. I would rather remain as I am to my dying day, than become a lady at the cost of being his wife."

"I do not think you would say that which you do not feel, Mabel," returned Pathfinder, earnestly.

"Not at such a moment, on such a subject, and least of all to you. No; Lieutenant Muir may find wives where he can—my name shall never be on his catalogue."

"Thank you—thank you for that, Mabel; for though there is no longer any hope for me, I could never be happy were you to take to the quartermaster. I feared the commission might count for something, I did, and I know the man. It is not jealousy that makes me speak in this manner, but truth, for I know the man. Now, were you to fancy a deserving youth, one like Jasper Western, for instance—"

"Why always mention Jasper Eau-douce, Pathfinder? he can have no concern with our friendship; let us talk of yourself, and of the manner in which you intend to pass the winter."

"Ah's me! I'm little worth at the best, Mabel, unless it may be on a trail, or with the rifle; and the less worth now that I've discovered the sergeant's mistake. There is no need, therefore, of talking of me. It has been very pleasant to me to be near you so long, and even to fancy that the sergeant was right; but that is all over now. I shall go down the lake with Jasper, and then there will be business to occupy us, and that will keep useless thoughts out of the mind."

"And you will forget this—forget me—no, not forget me either, Pathfinder; but you will resume your old pursuits, and cease to think a girl of sufficient importance to disturb your peace?"

"I never know'd it afore, Mabel, but girls, as you call them, though gals is the name I've been taught to use, are of more account in this life than I could have believed. Now, afore I know'd you, the newborn babe did not sleep more sweetly than I used to could; my head was no sooner on the root, or the stone, or mayhap on the skin, than all was lost to the senses, unless it might be to go over, in the night, the business of the day, in a dream, like; and there I lay till the moment came to be stirring, and the swallows were not more certain to be on the wing with the light, than I to be afoot at the moment I wished to be. All this seemed a gift, and might be calculated on, even in the midst of a Mingo camp; for I've been outlying, in my time, in the very villages of the vagabonds."

"And all this will return to you, Pathfinder; for one so upright and sincere will never waste his happiness on a mere fancy. You will dream again of your hunts, of the deer you have slain, and of the beaver you have taken."

"Ah's me, Mabel, I wish never to dream again! Before we met I had a sort of pleasure in following up the hounds, in fancy, as it might be; and even in striking a trail of the Iroquois, nay, I've been in scrimmages and ambushments in thought, like, and found satisfaction in it according to my gifts; but all those things have lost their charms since I've made acquaintance with you. Now, I think no longer of anything rude in my dreams, but the very last night we stayed in the garrison, I imagined I had a cabin in a grove of sugar maples, and at the root of every tree was a Mabel Dunham, while the birds that were among the branches sang ballads, instead of the notes that natur' gave, and even the deer stopped to listen. I tried to shoot a fa'an, but Killdeer missed fire, and the creatur' laughed in my face, as pleasantly as a young girl laughs in her merriment, and then it bounded away, looking back as if expecting me to follow."

"No more of this, Pathfinder—we'll talk no more of these things," said Mabel, dashing the tears from her eyes; for the simple, earnest manner in which this hardy woodsman betrayed the deep hold she had taken of his feelings, nearly proved too much for her own generous heart. "Now let us look for my father; he cannot be distant, as I heard his gun quite near."

"The sergeant was wrong—yes, he was wrong, and it's of no use to attempt to make the dove consort with the wolf."

8

WITH the lake smooth again, the Scud *sailed eastward to regain the distance lost, keeping close along the south shore. Next morning they approached Fort Niagara. "East, west, and north, nothing was visible but water, glittering in the rising sun; but southward stretched the endless belt of woods that then held Ontario in a setting of forest verdure. Suddenly an opening appeared ahead, and then the massive walls of a chateau-looking house, with outworks, bastions, blockhouses, and palisades, frowned on a headland that bordered the outlet of a broad stream. Just as the fort became visible, a little cloud rose over it, and the white ensign of France was seen fluttering from a lofty flagstaff." As they passed the mouth of the river they heard the thunder of the falls upstream. The* Scud *pushed on east. At one point it was chased by a larger French vessel, the* Montcalm, *but under Jasper Western's expert guidance kept well ahead. By nightfall it had reached the Thousand Islands, and shook off its pursuer. A little later and Jasper brought the cutter to anchor at the advanced post of the British. The garrison at Station Island, as it was called, greeted the relief party with exultation.*

On this island a small two-story blockhouse had been built of bulletproof logs. The room on the ground floor contained stores and provisions; the second story was barracks and citadel combined. Care had been taken to place the blockhouse so near an opening in the limestone rock that a bucket might be lowered from the projecting upper story for water. "The post is as well chosen as any I ever put foot into," exclaimed Pathfinder on viewing it.

It was at once decided that part of the augmented force should be left at the blockhouse, under Corporal McNab, with David Muir to advise him, while Sergeant Dunham, Pathfinder, and another force should take to the waters of the Thousand Islands to halt all shipping bound for Fort Frontenac. The sergeant bade Mabel and Cap to stay at the blockhouse. She expostulated.

"But why leave us behind, dear father? I have come thus far to be a comfort to you, and why not go farther?"

"You are a good girl, Mabel, and very like the Dunhams! But you must halt here. We shall leave the island tomorrow before the day dawns, in order not to be seen by any prying eyes coming from under cover, and we shall take the two largest boats, leaving you the other and one bark canoe. We are about to go into the channel used by the French, where we shall lie in wait perhaps a week to intercept their supply boats that are about to pass up, on their way to Frontenac, loaded in particular with a heavy amount of Indian goods."

"Have you looked well to your papers, brother?" Cap anxiously demanded. "Of course you know a capture on the high seas is piracy, unless your boat is regularly commissioned either as a public or a private armed cruiser."

"I have the honor to hold the colonel's appointment as sergeant-major of the 55th," returned the other, drawing himself up with dignity, "and that will be sufficient even for the French king. If not, I have Major Duncan's written orders."

"No papers them, for a warlike cruiser."

"They must suffice, brother, as I have no other. It is of vast importance to His Majesty's interests in this part of the world, that the boats in question should be captured and carried into Oswego. They contain the blankets, trinkets, rifles, ammunition—in short, all the stores with which the French bribe their accursed savage allies to commit their unholy acts, setting at naught our holy religion and its precepts, the laws of humanity, and all that is sacred and dear among men. By cutting off these supplies we shall derange their plans, and gain time on them; for the articles cannot be sent across the ocean again this autumn."

"But, father, does not His Majesty employ Indians also?" asked Mabel, with some curiosity.

"Certainly, girl, and he has a right to employ them—God bless him! It's a very different thing whether an Englishman or a Frenchman employs a savage, as everybody can understand."

"That is plain enough, brother Dunham; but I do not see my way so clear in the matter of the ship's papers."

"An *English* colonel's appointment ought to satisfy any *Frenchman* of my authority; and what is more, brother, it shall."

"But I do not see the difference, father, between an Englishman's and a Frenchman's employing savages in war."

"All the odds in the world, child, though you may not be able to see it. In the first place, an Englishman is naturally humane and considerate, while a Frenchman is naturally ferocious and timid."

"And you may add, brother, that he will dance from morning till night, if you'll let him."

"Very true," gravely returned the sergeant.

"But, father, I cannot see that all this alters the case. If it be wrong in a Frenchman to hire savages to fight his enemies, it would seem to be equally wrong in an Englishman. *You* will admit this, Pathfinder?"

"It's reasonable—it's reasonable, and I have never been one of them that has raised a cry agin the Frenchers for doing the very thing we do ourselves. Still, it is worse to consort with a Mingo than to consort with a Delaware. If any of that just tribe were left, I should think it no sin to send them out agin the foe."

"And yet they scalp and slay young and old—women and children!"

"They have their gifts, Mabel, and are not to be blamed for following them. Natur' is natur', though the different tribes have different ways of showing it. For my part, I am white, and endeavor to maintain white feelings."

"This is all unintelligible to me," answered Mabel. "What is right in King George, it would seem, ought to be right in King Louis."

"The King of France's real name is Caput," observed Cap, with his mouth full of venison. "I once carried a great scholar as a passenger, and he told me that these Louis thirteenth, fourteenth, and fifteenth, were all humbugs, and that the men's real name was Caput; which is French for 'head'; meaning that they ought to be put at the *foot* of the ladder, until ready to go up to be hanged."

"Well, this does look like being given to scalping, as a nat'ral gift," Pathfinder remarked, with the air of surprise with which one receives a novel idea, "and I shall have less compunction than ever in sarving agin the miscreants, though I can't say I ever yet felt any worth naming."

As all parties, Mabel excepted, seemed satisfied with the course the discussion had taken, no one appeared to think it necessary to pursue the subject. The trio of men, indeed, in this particular, so much resembled the great mass of their fellow-creatures, who usually judge of character equally without knowledge and without justice, that we might not have thought it necessary to record the discourse, had it not some bearing in its facts on the incidents of the legend, and in its opinions on the motives of the characters.

Supper was no sooner ended than the sergeant dismissed his guests, and then held a long and confidential dialogue with his daughter. He was little addicted to giving way to the gentler emotions, but the novelty of his present situation awakened feelings that he was unused to experience. The soldier, or the sailor, so long as he acts under the immediate supervision of a superior, thinks little of the risks he runs; but the moment he feels the responsibility of command, all the hazards of his undertaking begin to associate themselves in his mind with the chances of success or failure. While he dwells less on his own personal danger, perhaps, than when that is the principal consideration, he has more lively general perceptions of all the risks, and submits more to the influence of the feelings which doubt creates. Such was now the case with Sergeant Dunham, who, instead of looking forward to victory as certain, according to his usual habits, began to feel the possibility that he might be parting with his child forever.

Never before had Mabel struck him as so beautiful as she appeared that night. Possibly she never had displayed so many engaging qualities to her father; for concern on his account had begun to be active in her breast, and then her sympathies met with unusual encouragement through those which had been stirred up in the sterner bosom of the veteran. She had never been entirely at her ease with her parent, the great superiority of her education creating a sort of chasm, which had been widened by the military severity of manner he had acquired by dealing so long and intimately with beings who could only be kept in subjection by an unremitted discipline. On the present occasion, however, or after they were left alone, the conversation between the father and daughter became more confidential than usual, until Mabel rejoiced to find that it was gradually becoming endearing; a state of feeling that the warmhearted girl had silently pined for in vain, ever since her arrival.

"Then, mother was about my height?" Mabel said, as she held one of her father's hands in both her own, looking up into his face with humid eyes. "I had thought her taller."

"This is the way with most children, who get a habit of thinking of their parents with respect, until they fancy them larger and more commanding than they actually are. Your mother, Mabel, was as near your height as one woman could be to another."

"And her eyes, father?"

"Her eyes were like thine, child, too—blue and soft, and inviting like; though hardly so laughing."

"Mine will never laugh again, dearest father, if you do not take care of yourself in this expedition."

"Thank you, Mabel—hem—thank you, child; but I must do my duty. I wish I had seen you comfortably married before we left Oswego!—my mind would be easier."

"Married! to whom, father?"

"You know the man I wish you to love. You may meet with many gayer, and many dressed in finer clothes, but with none with so true a heart and just a mind."

"None, father?"

"I know of none; in these particulars Pathfinder has few equals, at least."

"But I need not marry at all. You are single, and I can remain to take care of you."

"God bless you, Mabel! I know you would, and I do not say that the feeling is not right, for I suppose it is; and yet I believe there is another that is more so."

"What can be more right than to honor one's parents?"

"It is just as right to honor one's husband, my dear child."

"But I have no husband, father."

"Then take one as soon as possible, that you may have a husband to honor. I cannot live forever, Mabel, but must drop off in the course of nature ere long, if I am not carried off in the course of war. You are young, and may yet live long; and it is proper that you should have a male protector, who can see you safe through life, and take care of you in age as you now wish to take care of me."

"And do you think, father,"—said Mabel, playing with his sinewy fingers with her own little hands, and looking down at them as if they were subjects of intense interest, though her lips curled in a slight smile as the words came from them—"and do you think, father, that Pathfinder is just the man to do this? Is he not within ten or twelve years as old as yourself?"

"What of that? His life had been one of moderation and exercise, and years are less to be counted, girl, than constitution. Do you know another more likely to be your protector?"

Mabel did not; at least another who had expressed a desire to that effect, whatever might have been her hopes and her wishes.

"Nay, father, we are not talking of another, but of the Pathfinder," she answered evasively. "If he were younger, I think it would be more natural for me to think of him for a husband."

" 'Tis all in the constitution, I tell you, child: Pathfinder is a younger man than half our subalterns."

"He is certainly younger than one, sir—Lieutenant Muir."

Mabel's laugh was joyous and lighthearted, as if just then she felt no care.

"That he is—young enough to be his grandson; he is younger in years, too. God forbid, Mabel, that you should ever become an officer's lady, at least until you are an officer's daughter."

"There will be little fear of that, father, if I marry Pathfinder!" returned the girl, looking up archly in the sergeant's face again.

"Not by the King's commission, perhaps, though the man is even now the friend and companion of generals. I think I could die happy, Mabel, if you were his wife."

"Father!"

" 'Tis a sad thing to go into battle with the weight of an unprotected daughter laid upon the heart."

"I would give the world to lighten yours of its load, my dear sir!"

"It might be done," said the sergeant, looking fondly at his child, "though I could not wish to put a burden on yours in order to do so."

The voice was deep and tremulous, and never before had Mabel witnessed such a show of affection in her parent. The habitual sternness of the man lent an interest to his emotions that they might otherwise have wanted, and the daughter's heart yearned to relieve the father's mind.

"Father, speak plainly," she cried, almost convulsively.

"Nay, Mabel, it might not be right—your wishes and mine may be very different."

"I have no wishes—know nothing of what you mean; would you speak of my future marriage?"

"If I could see you promised to Pathfinder—know that you were pledged to become his wife, let my own fate be what it might, I think I could die happy. But I will ask no pledge of you, my child—I will not force you to do what you might repent. Kiss me, Mabel, and go to your bed."

Had Sergeant Dunham exacted of Mabel the pledge that he really so much desired, he would have encountered a resistance that he might have found difficult to overcome, but, by letting nature have its course, he enlisted a powerful ally on his side, and the warmhearted, generous-minded Mabel was ready to concede to her affections, much more than she would ever have yielded to menace. At that touching moment she thought only of her parent, who was about to quit her, perhaps forever; and all of that ardent love for him, which had possibly been as much fed by the imagination as by anything else, but which had received a little check by the restrained intercourse of the last fortnight, now returned with a force that was increased by pure and intense feeling. Her father seemed all in all to her; and to render him happy, there was no proper sacrifice that she was not ready to make. One painful, rapid, almost wild gleam of thought shot across the brain of the girl, and her resolution wavered; but endeavoring to trace the foundation of the pleasing hope on which it was based, she found nothing positive to support it. Trained like a woman, to subdue her most ardent feelings, her thoughts reverted to her father, and to the blessings that awaited the child who yielded to a parent's wishes.

"Father," she said quietly, almost with a holy calm, "God blesses the dutiful daughter!"

"He will, Mabel; we have the Good Book for that."

"I will marry whomsoever you desire."

"Nay, nay, Mabel—you may have a choice of your own—"

"I have no choice—that is—none have asked me to have a choice, but Pathfinder and Mr. Muir; and between *them*, neither of us would hesitate. No, father, I will marry whomsoever you may choose."

"Thou knowest my choice, beloved girl; none other can make thee as happy as the noblehearted guide."

"Well, then, if he wish it—if he ask me again—for, father, you would not have me offer myself, or that any one should do that office for me,"—and the blood stole across the pallid cheeks of Mabel, as she spoke, for high and generous resolutions had driven back the stream of life to her heart,—"no one must speak to him of it; but if he seek me again, and, knowing all that a true girl ought to tell the man she marries, and he then wishes to make me his wife, I will be his."

"Bless you, my Mabel—God in heaven bless you, and reward you as a pious daughter deserves to be rewarded."

"Yes, father, put your mind at peace; go on this expedition with a light heart, and trust in God. For me, you will have now no care. In the spring—I must have a little time, father—but, in the spring, I will marry Pathfinder, if that noblehearted hunter shall then desire it."

"Mabel, he loves you as I loved your mother. I have seen him weep like a child, when speaking of his feelings toward you."

"Yes, I believe it; I've seen enough to satisfy me that he thinks better of me than I deserve; and certainly the man is not living for whom I have more respect than for Pathfinder; not even for you, dear father."

"That is as it should be, child, and the union will be blessed. May I not tell Pathfinder this?"

"I would rather you would not, father. Let it come of itself—come naturally; the man should seek the woman, and not the woman the man—" The smile that illuminated Mabel's handsome face was angelic, as even her parent thought, though one better practiced in detecting the passing emotions, as they betray themselves in the countenance, might have traced something wild and unnatural in it. "No, no, *we* must let things take their course; father, you have my solemn promise."

"That will do—that will do, Mabel; now kiss me; God bless and protect you, girl; you are a good daughter."

9

IT SOON became clear that the garrison left at Station Island under Corporal McNab were in greater peril than the party which Sergeant Dunham had led forth to intercept French supply boats. This garrison numbered only six men and two women. The first token of danger was the sudden appearance of Arrowhead's wife, Dew-of-June, to warn Mabel Dunham that an attack was near, and that she should keep inside the blockhouse. June brought the additional information that a white man who talked French had treacherously told the Indians the whereabouts of the well-hidden post and the easiest means of reaching it. But this dastardly white man was not Jasper Western. It was none other than the sneaking David Muir, who (as Mabel quickly found out, though she did not understand his guilt), hovered about the shore; and who fastened a bit of bunting to a tree in such fashion that it was visible from the channel.

The blow soon fell. While Mabel was making an effort to get all the soldiers into the blockhouse, Corporal McNab was shot dead by her side. She rushed inside the post, and peering out, saw that three other soldiers had been slain by enemy fire. While she gazed, the traitorous Arrowhead, with twenty horribly painted savages behind him, pushed forward, slew the wife of one of the soldiers, and took the scalps of the murdered men. A Frenchman was in charge of the attackers. Fortunately for Mabel, cowering behind some barrels in the blockhouse, he did not allow this structure to be burned, for he wished to preserve it. When some lawless savages did apply the torch, Mabel used water to quench the flames. Immediately, thereafter, June entered the scene, and Mabel admitted her to the blockhouse. The two passed an undisturbed night. Next morning Arrowhead appeared again at the head of eight or ten

Indians, escorting the wily David Muir and the unterrified Cap. While Muir urged her to unbar the door, Cap bade her to keep it tightly shut. "A round turn and two half hitches make a fast belay," he advised her.

The Indians departed. The island fell into quiet again. June went to the ground floor to prepare a meal; Mabel ascended to the roof to scan the horizon. Suddenly she descried a bark canoe, and waved eagerly to its occupant. It was Chingachgook, who waved his paddle to her in reply, but cautiously kept away from the island. When night fell, a light tap was heard at the door. It was none other than Pathfinder.

"God be praised!" Mabel exclaimed, for the idea that the block-house would be impregnable with such a garrison, at once crossed her mind. "O! Pathfinder, what has become of my father?"

"The sergeant is safe as yet, and victorious, though it is not in the gift of man to say what will be the ind of it. Is not that the wife of Arrowhead, skulking in the corner there?"

"Speak not of her reproachfully, Pathfinder; I owe her my life—my present security; tell me what has happened to my father's party, why you are here, and I will relate all the horrible events that have passed upon this island."

"Few words will do the last, Mabel; for one used to Indian deviltries needs but little explanations on such a subject. Everything turned out as we had hoped with the expedition, for the Sarpent was on the lookout, and he met us with all the information heart could desire. We ambushed three boats, druv' the Frenchers out of them, got possession and sunk them, according to orders, in the deepest part of the channel; and the savages of Upper Canada will fare badly for Indian goods this winter. Both powder and ball too, will be scarcer among them than keen hunters and actyve warriors may relish. We did not lose a man, or have even a skin barked; nor do I think the inimy suffered to speak of. In short, Mabel, it has been just such an expedition as Lundie likes; much harm to the foe, and little harm to ourselves."

"Ah! Pathfinder, I fear when Major Duncan comes to hear the whole of the sad tale, he will find reason to regret he ever undertook the affair!"

"I know what you mean—I know what you mean; but by telling my story straight you will understand it better. As soon as the sergeant found himself successful, he sent me and the Sarpent off in canoes to tell you how matters had turned out, and he is following with the two boats; which being so much heavier, cannot arrive before morning. I parted from Chingachgook this forenoon, it being agreed that he should come up one set of channels, and I another, to see that the path was clear. I've not seen the chief since."

Mabel now explained the manner in which she had discovered the Mohican, and her expectation that he would yet come to the block-house.

"Not he—not he! A regular scout will never get behind walls or logs, so long as he can keep the open air and find useful employment. I should not have come myself, Mabel, but I promised the sergeant to comfort you, and to look a'ter your safety. Ah's me! I reconnoitered the island with a heavy heart this forenoon; and there was a bitter hour when I fancied you might be among the slain."

"By what lucky accident were you prevented from paddling up boldly to the island, and from falling into the hands of the enemy?"

"By such an accident, Mabel, as Providence employs to tell the hound where to find the deer, and the deer how to throw off the hound. No, no; these artifices and deviltries with dead bodies may deceive the soldiers of the 55th, and the King's officers; but they are all lost upon men who have passed their days in the forest. I came down the channel in face of the pretended fisherman, and, though the riptyles have set up the poor wretch with art, it was not ingenious enough to take in a practysed eye. The rod was held too high; for the 55th have learned to fish at Oswego, if they never knew how before; and then the man was too quiet for one who got neither prey nor bite. But we never come in upon a post blindly; and I have lain outside a garrison a whole night, because they had changed their sentries and their mode of standing guard. Neither the Sarpent nor myself would be likely to be taken in by these contrivances, which were most probably intended for the Scotch, who are cunning enough in some particulars, though anything but witches when Indian sarcumventions are in the wind."

"Do you think my father and his men may yet be deceived?" said Mabel, quickly.

"Not if I can prevent it, Mabel. You say the Sarpent is on the look-out too; so there is a double chance of our succeeding in letting him know his danger; though it is by no means sartain by which channel the party may come."

"Pathfinder," said our heroine solemnly, for the frightful scenes she had witnessed had clothed death with unusual horrors, "Pathfinder, you have professed love for me—a wish to make me your wife!"

"I did ventur' to speak on that subject, Mabel, and the sergeant has even lately said that you are kindly disposed; but I am not a man to parsecute the thing I love."

"Hear me, Pathfinder! I respect you—honor you—revere you; save my father from this dreadful death, and I can worship you. Here is my hand as a solemn pledge for my faith, when you come to claim it."

"Bless you—bless you, Mabel; this is more than I desarve; more, I fear, than I shall know how to profit by, as I ought. It was not wanting, however, to make me sarve the sergeant. We are old comrades, and owe each other a life; though I fear me, Mabel, being a father's comrade is not always the best recommendation with the daughter!"

"You want no other recommendation than your own acts—your courage—you fidelity; all that you do and say, Pathfinder, my reason approves, and the heart will, nay, it *shall* follow."

"This is a happiness I little expected this night; but we are in God's hands, and He will protect us in His own way. These are sweet words, Mabel, but they were not wanting to make me do all that man can do, in the present sarcumstances; they will not lessen my endeavors neither."

"Now we understand each other, Pathfinder," Mabel added hoarsely, "let us not lose one of the precious moments, which may be of incalculable value. Can we not get into your canoe, and go and meet my father?"

"That is not the course I advise. I don't know by which channel the sergeant will come, and there are twenty; rely on it, the Sarpent will be winding his way through them all. No, no, my advice is to remain here. The logs of this blockhouse are still green, and it will not be easy to set them on fire; and I can make good the place, bating a burning, agin a tribe. The Iroquois nation cannot dislodge me from this fortress, so long as we can keep the flames off it. The sergeant is now 'camped on some island, and will not come in until morning. If we hold the block, we can give him timely warning, by firing rifles for instance; and should he determine to attack the savages, as a man of his temper will be very likely to do, the possession of this building will be of great account in the affair. No, no; my judgment says remain, if the object be to sarve the sergeant; though escape for our two selves will be no very difficult matter."

"Stay," murmured Mabel, "stay, for God's sake, Pathfinder. Anything—everything, to save my father!"

"Yes, that is natur'. I am glad to hear you say this, Mabel, for I own a wish to see the sergeant fairly supported. As the matter now stands, he has gained himself credit; and could he once drive off these miscreants, and make an honorable retreat, laying the huts and block in ashes, no doubt, no doubt, Lundie would remember it, and sarve him accordingly. Yes, yes, Mabel, we must not only save the sergeant's life, but we must save his ripitation."

"No blame can rest on my father, on account of the surprise of this island!"

"There's no telling—there's no telling; military glory is a most unsartain thing. I've seen the Delawares routed, when they desarved more credit than at other times when they've carried the day. A man is wrong to set his head on success of any sort, and worst of all, on success in war. I know little of the settlements, or of the notions that men hold in them; but, up here-a-way, even the Indians rate a warrior's character according to his luck. The principal thing with a soldier is, never to be whipt; nor do I think mankind stops long to consider how the day was won or lost. For my part, Mabel, I make it a rule when facing the inimy, to give him as good as I can send, and to try to be moderate as I can, when we get the better; as for feeling moderate after a defeat, little need be said on that score, as a flogging is one of the most humbling things in natur'. The parsons preach about humility, in the garrisons; but if humility would make Christians, the King's troops ought to be saints, for they've done little, as yet, this war, but take lessons from the French, beginning at Fort du Quesne, and ending at Ty!"

"My father could not have suspected that the position of the island was known to the enemy," resumed Mabel, whose thoughts were running on the probable effect of the recent events, on the sergeant.

"That is true; nor do I well see how the Frenchers found it out. The spot is well chosen, and it is not an easy matter, even for one who has travelled the road to and from it, to find it again. There has been treachery, I fear; yes, yes, there must have been treachery!"

"O! Pathfinder, can this be?"

"Nothing is easier, Mabel, for treachery comes as nat'ral to some men, as eating. Now, when I find a man all fair words, I look close to his deeds; for when the heart is right, and raally intends to do good, it is generally satisfied to let the conduct speak, instead of the tongue."

"Jasper Western is not one of these," said Mabel, impetuously. "No youth can be more sincere in his manner, or less apt to make the tongue act for the head."

"Jasper Western! tongue and heart are both right with that lad, depend on it, Mabel; and the notion taken up by Lundie, and the quartermaster, and the sergeant, and your uncle, too, is as wrong as it would be to think that the sun shone by night, and the stars shone by day. No, no; I'll answer for Eau-douce's honesty with my own scalp, or, at need, with my own rifle."

"Bless you—bless you, Pathfinder!" exclaimed Mabel, extending her own hand, and pressing the iron fingers of her companion, under a state of feeling that far surpassed her own consciousness of its strength. "You are all that is generous—all that is noble; God will reward you for it."

"Ah! Mabel, I fear me, if this be true, I should not covet such a wife as yourself, but would leave you to be sued for by some gentleman of the garrison, as your desarts require!"

"We will not talk of this any more tonight," Mabel answered, in a voice so smothered as to seem nearly choked. "We must think less of ourselves, just now, Pathfinder, and more of our friends. But I rejoice from my soul that you believe Jasper innocent. Now let us talk of other things; ought we not to release June?"

"I've been thinking about the woman, for it will not be safe to shut our eyes and leave hers open, on this side of the blockhouse door. If we put her in the upper room and take away the ladder, she'll be a prisoner at least."

"I cannot treat one thus who has saved my life. It would be better to let her depart; I think she is too much my friend to do anything to harm me."

"You do not know the race, Mabel; you do not know the race. It's true she's not a full-blooded Mingo, but she consorts with the vagabonds, and must have l'arned some of their tricks. What is that?"

"It sounds like oars—some boat is passing through the channel!"

Pathfinder closed the trap that led to the lower room, to prevent June from escaping, extinguished the candle, and went hastily to a loop, Mabel looking over his shoulder in breathless curiosity. These several movements consumed a minute or two; and by the time the eye of the scout had got a dim view of things without, two boats had swept past, and shot up to the shore, at a spot some fifty yards beyond the block, where there was a regular landing. The obscurity prevented more from being seen; and Pathfinder whispered to Mabel, that the newcomers were as likely to be foes as friends, for he did not think her father could possibly have arrived so soon. A number of men were now seen to quit the boats, and then followed three hearty English cheers, leaving no further doubts of the character of the party. Pathfinder sprang to the trap, raised it, glided down the ladder, and began to unbar the door with an earnestness that proved how critical he deemed the moment. Mabel had followed, but she rather impeded than aided his exertions, and but a single bar was turned when a heavy discharge of rifles was heard. They were still standing in breathless suspense, as the war whoop rang in all the surrounding thickets. The door now opened, and both Pathfinder and Mabel rushed into the open air. All human sounds had ceased. After listening half a minute, however, Pathfinder thought he heard a few stifled groans near the boats; but the wind blew so fresh, and the rustling of the leaves mingled so much with the murmurs of the passing air, that he was far from certain. But Mabel was borne away by her feelings, and she rushed by him, taking the way toward the boats.

"This will not do, Mabel," said the scout in an earnest but low voice, seizing her by an arm,—"this will never do. Sartain death would follow, and that without sarving any one. We must return to the block."

"Father!—my poor, dear, murdered father!" said the girl wildly, though habitual caution, even at that trying moment, induced her to speak low. "Pathfinder, if you love me, let me go to my dear father!"

"This will not do, Mabel. It is singular that no one speaks; no one from the boats returns the fire—and I have left Killdeer in the block! But of what use would a rifle be when no one is to be seen!"

At that moment the quick eye of Pathfinder, which, while he held Mabel firmly in his grasp, had never ceased to roam over the dim scene, caught an indistinct view of five or six dark, crouching forms, endeavoring to steal past him, doubtless with the intention of intercepting their retreat to the blockhouse. Catching up Mabel, and putting her under an arm as if she were an infant, the sinewy frame of the woodsman was exerted to the utmost, and he succeeded in entering the building. The tramp of his pursuers seemed immediately at his heels. Dropping his burden, he turned, closed the door, and had fastened one bar, as a rush against the solid mass threatened to force it from the hinges. To secure the other bar was the work of an instant.

Mabel now ascended to the first floor, while Pathfinder remained as a sentinel below. Our heroine was in that state in which the body exerts itself apparently without the control of the mind. She relighted the candle mechanically, as her companion had desired, and returned with it below, where he was waiting her reappearance. No sooner was Pathfinder in possession of the light than he examined the place carefully, to make certain no one was concealed in the fortress, ascending to each floor in succession, after assuring himself that he left no enemy in his rear. The result was the conviction that the blockhouse now contained no one but Mabel and himself, June having escaped. When perfectly convinced on this material point, Pathfinder rejoined our heroine in the principal apartment, setting down the light, and examining the priming of Killdeer before he seated himself.

"Our worst fears are realized," said Mabel, to whom the hurry and excitement of the last five minutes appeared to contain the emotions of a life. "My beloved father, and all his party, are slain or captured!"

"We don't know that—morning will tell us all. I do not think the affair as settled as that, or we should hear the vagabond Mingoes yelling out their triumph around the blockhouse. Of one thing we may be sartain; if the inimy has really got the better, he will not be long in calling upon us to surrender. The squaw will let him into the secret of our situation, and, as they well know the place cannot be fired by daylight so long as Killdeer continues to desarve his reputation, you may depend on it, that they will not be backward in making their attempt while darkness helps them."

"Surely, I hear a groan!"

" 'Tis fancy, Mabel,—when the mind gets to be skeary, especially a woman's mind, she often consaits things that have no reality. I've known them that imagined there was truth in dreams—"

"Nay, I am *not* deceived; there is surely one below, and in pain!"

Pathfinder was compelled to own that the quick senses of Mabel had not deceived her. He cautioned her, however, to repress her feelings; and reminded her that the savages were in the practice of resorting to every artifice to attain their ends, and that nothing was more likely than that the groans were feigned with a view to lure them from the blockhouse, or at least to induce them to open the door.

"No, no, no," said Mabel, hurriedly, "there is no artifice in those sounds, and they come from anguish of body, if not of spirit. They are fearfully natural."

"Well, we shall soon know whether a friend is there or not. Hide the light again, Mabel, and I will speak the person from a loop."

Not a little precaution was necessary, according to Pathfinder's judgment and experience, in performing even this simple act, for he had known the careless slain by their want of proper attention to what might have seemed to the ignorant, supererogatory means of safety. He did not place his mouth to the loop itself, but so near it that he could be heard without raising his voice, and the same precaution was observed as regards his ear.

"Who is below?" Pathfinder demanded, when his arrangements were made to his mind. "Is anyone in suffering? If a friend, speak boldly, and depend on our aid."

"Pathfinder!" answered a voice that both Mabel and the person addressed at once knew to be the sergeant's, "Pathfinder, in the name of God, tell me what has become of my daughter?"

"Father, I am here! unhurt—safe; and O! that I could think the same of you!"

The ejaculation of thanksgiving that followed was distinctly audible to the two, but it was clearly mingled with a groan of pain.

"My worst forebodings are realized!" said Mabel, with a sort of desperate calmness. "Pathfinder, my father must be brought within the block, though we hazard everything to do it."

"This is natur', and it is the law of God. But, Mabel, be calm, and endivor to be cool. All that can be effected for the sergeant by human invention, shall be done. I only ask you to be cool."

"I am—I am, Pathfinder. Never in my life was I more calm, more collected, than at this moment. But remember how perilous may be every instant; for Heaven's sake, what we do, let us do without delay."

Pathfinder was struck with the firmness of Mabel's tones, and perhaps he was a little deceived by the forced tranquillity and self-possession she had assumed. At all events he did not deem any further explanations necessary, but descended forthwith, and began to unbar the door. This delicate process was conducted with the usual caution, but as he warily permitted the mass of timber to swing back on the hinges, he felt a pressure against it that had nearly induced him to close it again. But catching a glimpse of the cause through the crack, the door was permitted to swing back, when the body of Sergeant Dunham, which was propped against it, fell partly within the block. To draw in the legs and secure the fastenings, occupied the Pathfinder but a moment. Then there existed no obstacle to their giving their undivided care to the wounded man.

Mabel, in this trying scene, conducted herself with the sort of unnatural energy that her sex, when aroused, is apt to manifest. She got the light, administered water to the parched lips of her father, and assisted Pathfinder in forming a bed of straw for his body, and a pillow of clothes for his head. All this was done earnestly, and almost without speaking; nor did Mabel shed a tear until she heard the blessings of her father murmured on her head, for this tenderness and care. All this time, Mabel had merely conjectured the condition of her parent. Pathfinder, however, showed greater attention to the physical danger of the sergeant. He ascertained that a rifle ball had passed through the body of the wounded man; and he was sufficiently familiar with injuries of this nature, to be certain that the chances of his surviving the hurt were very trifling, if any.

The eyes of Sergeant Dunham had not ceased to follow the form of his beautiful daughter from the moment that the light appeared. He next examined the door of the block, to ascertain its security; for he was left on the ground below, there being no available means of raising him to the upper floor. Then he sought the face of Mabel; for as life wanes fast, the affections resume their force, and we begin to value that most which we feel we are about to lose forever.

"God be praised, my child, you at least have escaped their murderous rifles!" he said; for he spoke with strength, and seemingly with no additional pain. "Give me the history of this sad business, Pathfinder."

"Ah's me, sergeant! it *has* been sad, as you say. That there has been treachery, and the position of the island has been betrayed, is now as sartain, in my judgment, as that we still hold the block. But—"

"Major Duncan was right," interrupted Dunham, laying a hand on the other's arm.

"Not in the sense you mean, sergeant—no, not in that p'int of view; never. At least, not in my opinion. I know that natur' is weak—human natur', I mean—and that we should none of us vaunt of our gifts, whether red or white; but I do not think a truer-hearted lad lives on the lines than Jasper Western."

"Bless you—bless you for that, Pathfinder!" burst forth from Mabel's very soul, while a flood of tears gave vent to emotions that were so varied, while they were so violent: "O, bless you, Pathfinder, bless you! The brave should never desert the brave—the honest should sustain the honest."

The father's eyes fastened anxiously on the face of his daughter, until the latter hid her countenance in her apron to conceal her tears; and then they turned with inquiry to the hard features of the guide. The latter merely wore their usual expression of frankness, sincerity, and uprightness; and the sergeant motioned to him to proceed.

"You know the spot where the Sarpent and I left you, sergeant," Pathfinder resumed; "and I need say nothing of all that happened afore. It is now too late to lament what is gone and passed; but I do think if I had stayed with the boats, this would not have come to pass! Other men may be as good guides; I make no doubt they are: but then natur' bestows its gifts, and some must be better than other some. I dare say poor Gilbert, who took my place, has suffered for his mistake."

"He fell at my elbow," the sergeant answered, in a low, melancholy tone. "We have, indeed, all suffered for our mistakes!"

"No, no, sergeant, I meant no condemnation on you; for men were never better commanded than your'n, in this very expedition. I never beheld a prettier flanking; and the way in which you carried your own boat up agin their howitzer might have teached Lundie himself a lesson."

The eyes of the sergeant brightened; his face even wore an expression of military triumph, though it was of a degree that suited the humble sphere in which he had been an actor.

" 'Twas not badly done, my friend," he said; "we carried their log breastwork by storm!"

" 'Twas nobly done, sergeant; though I fear when all the truth comes to be known, it will be found that these vagabonds have got their howitzer back ag'in. Well, well, put a stout heart upon it, and try to forget all that is disagreeable, and to remember only the pleasant part of the matter. That is your truest philosophy; ay, and truest religion too. If the inimy has got the howitzer ag'in, they've only got what belonged to them afore, and what we couldn't help. They haven't got the blockhouse yet, nor are they likely to get it, unless they fire it in the dark. Well, sergeant, the Sarpent and I separated about ten miles down the river; for we thought it wisest not to come upon even a friendly camp without the usual caution. What has become of Chingachgook, I cannot say; though Mabel tells me he is not far off; and I make no question the noblehearted Delaware is doing his duty, although he is not now visible to our eyes. Mark my word, sergeant; before this matter is over, we shall hear of him at some critical time, and that in a discreet and creditable manner. Ah! the Sarpent is, indeed, a wise and virtuous chief; and any white man might covet his gifts, though his rifle is not quite as sure as Killdeer, it must be owned. Well, as I came near the island, I missed the smoke, and that put me on my guard; for I knew that the men of the 55th were not cunning enough to conceal that sign, notwithstanding all that has been told them of its danger. This made me more careful, until I came in sight of this mock fisherman, as I've just told Mabel; and then the whole of their infernal arts was as plain before me, as if I saw it on a map. I need not tell you, sergeant, that my first thoughts were of Mabel; and that, finding she was in the block, I came here, in order to live or die in her company."

The father turned a gratified look upon his child, and Mabel felt a sinking of the heart that, at such a moment, she could not have thought possible, when she wished to believe all her concern centered in the situation of her parent. As the latter held out his hand she took it in her own, and kissed it. Then kneeling at his side, she wept as if her heart would break.

"Mabel," he said, steadily, "the will of God must be done. It is useless to attempt deceiving either you or myself; my time has come, and it is a consolation to me to die like a soldier. Lundie will do me justice, for our good friend Pathfinder will tell him what has been done, and how all came to pass. You do not forget our last conversation?"

"Nay, father, my time has probably come, too," exclaimed Mabel, who felt just then as if it would be a relief to die. "I cannot hope to escape; and Pathfinder would do well to leave us, and return to the garrison, with the sad news, while he can."

"Mabel Dunham," said Pathfinder, reproachfully, though he took her hand with kindness. "I have not desarved this; I know I am wild, and uncouth, and ungainly—"

"Pathfinder!"

"Well—well, we'll forget it; you did not mean it; you could not think it. It is useless, now, to talk of escaping, for the sergeant cannot be moved; and the blockhouse must be defended, cost what it will. Maybe Lundie will get the tidings of our disaster, and send a party to raise the siege."

"Pathfinder—Mabel!" said the sergeant, who had been writhing with pain, until the cold sweat stood on his forehead, "come both to my side. You understand each other, I hope?"

"Father, say nothing of that—it is all as you wish."

"Thank God! Give me your hand, Mabel—here, Pathfinder, take it. I can do no more than give you the girl in this way. I know you will make her a kind husband. Do not wait on account of my death; there will be a chaplain in the fort, before the season closes; let him marry you at once. My brother, if living, will wish to go back to his vessel, and then the child will have no protector. Mabel, your husband will have been my friend, and that will be some consolation to you, I hope."

"Trust this matter to me, sergeant," put in Pathfinder; "leave it all in my hands, as your dying request; and depend on it, all will go as it should."

"I do—I do put all confidence in you, my trusty friend, and empower you to act, as I could act myself, in every particular. Mabel, child—hand me the water—you will never repent this night. Bless you, my daughter—God bless and have you in his holy keeping!"

This tenderness was inexpressibly touching to one of Mabel's feelings; and she felt at that moment, as if her future union with Pathfinder had received a solemnization that no ceremony of the Church could render more holy. Still, a weight, as that of a mountain, lay upon her heart, and she thought it would be happiness to die. Then followed a short pause, when the sergeant, in broken sentences, briefly related what had passed since he parted with Pathfinder and the Delaware. The wind had become more favorable, and instead of encamping on an island, agreeably to the original intention, he had determined to continue, and reach the station that night. Their approach would have been unseen, and a portion of the calamity avoided, he thought, had they not grounded on the point of a neighboring island, where, no doubt, the noise made by the men, in getting off the boat, gave notice of their approach, and enabled the enemy to be in readiness to receive them. They had landed without the slightest suspicion of danger, though surprised at not finding a sentinel, and had actually left their arms in the boat, with the intention of first securing their knapsacks and provisions. The fire had been so close, that notwithstanding the obscurity, it was very deadly. Every man had fallen; two or three, however, subsequently arose, and disappeared. Four or five of the soldiers had been killed, or so nearly so as to survive but a few minutes; though, for some unknown reason, the enemy did not make the usual rush for the scalps. Sergeant Dunham fell with the others; and he had heard the voice of Mabel, as she rushed from the blockhouse. This frantic appeal aroused all his parental feelings, and had enabled him to crawl as far as the door of the building, where he had raised himself against the logs, in the manner already mentioned.

After this simple explanation was made, the sergeant was so weak as to need repose; and his companions, while they ministered to his wants, suffered some time to pass in silence. Pathfinder took the occasion to reconnoiter from the loops and the roof, and he examined the condition of the rifles, of which there were a dozen kept in the building, the soldiers having used their regimental muskets in the expedition. But Mabel never left her father's side for an instant, and when, by his breathing, she fancied he slept, she bent her knees and prayed.

The half hour that succeeded was awfully solemn and still. The moccasin of Pathfinder was barely heard overhead, and occasionally the sound of the breech of a rifle fell upon the floor, for he was busied in examining the pieces, with a view to ascertain the state of their charges, and their primings. Beyond this nothing was so loud as the breathing of the wounded man. Mabel's heart yearned to be in communication with the father she was so soon to lose, and yet she would not disturb his apparent repose. But Dunham slept not; he was in that state when the world suddenly loses its attractions, its illusions, and its power; and the unknown future fills the mind with its conjectures, its revelations, and its immensity. He had been a moral man for one of his mode of life, but he had thought little of this all important moment. Had the din of battle been ringing in his ears, his martial ardor might have endured to the end; but there, in the silence of that nearly untenanted blockhouse, with no sound to enliven him, no appeal to keep alive factitious sentiment, no hope of victory to impel, things began to appear in their true colors, and this state of being to be estimated at its just value. He would have given treasures for religious consolation, yet he knew not where to turn to seek it. He thought of Pathfinder, but he distrusted his knowledge. He thought of Mabel; for the parent to appeal to the child for such succor, appeared like reversing the order of nature. Then it was that he felt the full responsibility of the parental character, and had some clear glimpses of the manner in which he himself had discharged the trust toward an orphan child. While thoughts like these were rising in his mind, Mabel, who watched the slightest change in his breathing, heard a guarded knock at the door. Supposing it might be Chingachgook, she rose, undid two of the bars, and held the third in her hand, as she asked who was there. The answer was in her uncle's voice, and he implored her to give him immediate admission. Without an instant of hesitation, she turned the bar, and Cap entered. He had barely passed the opening, when Mabel closed the door again, and secured it as before, for practice had rendered her expert in this portion of her duties.

The sturdy seaman, when he had made sure of the state of his brother-in-law, and that Mabel as well as himself, was safe, was softened nearly to tears. His own appearance he explained by saying that he had been carelessly guarded, under the impression that he and the quartermaster were sleeping under the fumes of liquor with which they had been plied, with a view to keep them quiet in the expected engagement. Muir had been left asleep, or seeming to sleep; but Cap had run into the bushes, on the alarm of the attack, and having found Pathfinder's canoe, had only succeeded, at that moment, in getting to the blockhouse, whither he had come with the kind intent of escaping with his niece by water. It is scarcely necessary to say, that he changed his plan when he ascertained the state of the sergeant, and the apparent security of his present quarters.

"If the worst comes to the worst, Master Pathfinder," he said, "we must strike, and that will entitle us to quarter. We owe it to our manhood to hold out a reasonable time, and to ourselves to haul down the ensign in season to make saving conditions. I wished Master Muir to do the same thing, when we were captured by these chaps you call vagabonds,—and rightly are they named, for viler vagabonds do not walk the earth—"

"You've found out their characters!" interrupted Pathfinder, who was always as ready to chime in with abuse of the Mingoes, as with the praises of his friends. "Now, had you fallen into the hands of the Delawares, you would have l'arned the difference."

"Well, to me they seem much of a muchness; blackguards fore and aft, always excepting our friend the Serpent, who is a gentleman, for an Injin. But, when these savages made the assault on us, killing Corporal McNab and his men, as if they had been so many rabbits, Lieutenant Muir and myself took refuge in one of the holes of this here island, of which there are so many among the rocks,—regular geological underground burrows made by the water, as the lieutenant says,—and there we remained stowed away like two leaguers in a ship's hold, until we gave out for want of grub. A man may say that grub is the foundation of human nature. I desired the quartermaster to make terms, for we could have defended ourselves for an hour or two in the place, bad as it was; but he declined, on the ground that the knaves wouldn't keep faith if any of them were hurt, and so there was no use in asking them to. I consented to strike, on two principles; one, that we might be said to have struck already, for running below is generally thought to be giving up the ship; and the other, that we had an enemy in our stomachs that was more formidable in his attacks than the enemy on deck. Hunger is a d——ble circumstance, as any man who has lived on it eight-and-forty hours will acknowledge."

"Uncle!" said Mabel, in a mournful voice, and with an expostulatory manner, "my poor father is sadly, sadly hurt."

"True, Magnet, true; I will sit by him, and do my best at consolation. Are the bars well fastened, girl? on such an occasion, the mind should be tranquil and undisturbed."

"We are safe, I believe, from all but this heavy blow of Providence."

"Well, then, Magnet, do you go up to the deck above, and try to compose yourself, while Pathfinder runs aloft and takes a lookout from the crosstrees. Your father may wish to say something to me, in private, and it may be well to leave us alone. These are solemn scenes, and inexperienced people, like myself, do not always wish what they say to be overheard."

Although the idea of her uncle's affording religious consolation by the side of a deathbed, certainly never obtruded itself on the imagination of Mabel, she thought there might be a propriety in the request with which she was unacquainted; and she complied accordingly. Pathfinder had already ascended to the roof to make his survey, and the brothers-in-law were left alone. Cap took a seat by the side of the sergeant, and bethought him seriously of the grave duty he had before him. A silence of several minutes succeeded, during which brief space the mariner was digesting the substance of his intended discourse.

"I must say, Sergeant Dunham," Cap at length commenced, in his peculiar manner, "that there has been mismanagement somewhere in this unhappy expedition, and, the present being an occasion when truth ought to be spoken, and nothing but the truth, I feel it my duty to say as much in plain language. In short, sergeant, on this point there cannot well be two opinions; for, seaman as I am, and no soldier, I can see several errors myself, that it needs no great education to detect."

"What would you have, brother Cap!" returned the other, in a feeble voice; "what is done is done; it is now too late to remedy it."

"Very true, brother Dunham, but not to repent of it; the Good Book tells us it is never too late to repent; and I've always heard that this is the precious moment. If you've anything on your mind, sergeant, hoist it out freely, for you know you trust it to a friend. You were my own sister's husband, and poor little Magnet is my own sister's daughter; and, living or dead, I shall always look upon you as a brother. It's a thousand pities that you didn't lie off and on with the boats, and send a canoe ahead to reconnoiter; in which case your command would have been saved, and this disaster would not have befallen us all. Well, sergeant, we are *all* mortal; that is some consolation, I make no doubt; and if you go before a little, why, we must follow. Yes, that *must* give him consolation."

"I know all this, brother Cap; and hope I'm prepared to meet a soldier's fate; there is poor Mabel—"

"Ay, ay,—that's a heavy drag, I know; but you wouldn't take her with you, if you could, sergeant; and so the better way is to make as light of the separation as you can. Mabel is a good girl, and so was her mother before her, she was my sister, and it shall be my care to see that her daughter gets a good husband, if our lives and scalps are spared; for I suppose no one would care about entering into a family that has no scalps."

"Brother, my child is betrothed—she will become the wife of Pathfinder."

"Well, brother Dunham, every man has his opinions, and his

manner of viewing things; and to my notion this match will be anything but agreeable to Mabel; I have no objections to the age of the man; I'm not one of them that thinks it necessary to be a boy to make a girl happy, but on the whole I prefer a man of about fifty for a husband; still, there ought not to be any circumstance between the parties to make them unhappy. Circumstances play the devil with matrimony; and I set it down as one, that Pathfinder don't know as much as my niece. You've seen but little of the girl, sergeant, and have not got the run of her knowledge; but let her pay it out freely, as she will do when she gets to be thoroughly acquainted; and you'll fall in with but few schoolmasters that can keep their luffs in her company."

"She's a good child—a dear, good child," muttered the sergeant, his eyes filling with tears; "it is my misfortune that I have seen so little of her."

"She is, indeed, a good girl, and knows altogether too much for poor Pathfinder, who is a reasonable man, and an experienced man in his own way; but who has no more idea of the main chance than you have of spherical trigonometry, sergeant."

"Ah! brother Cap, had Pathfinder been with us in the boats, this sad affair might not have happened!"

"That is quite likely; his worst enemy will allow that the man is a good guide; but, sergeant, if the truth must be spoken you have managed this expedition in a loose way, altogether: you should have hove to off your haven and sent in a boat to reconnoiter, as I told you before. That is a matter to be repented of; and I tell it to you because truth, in such a case, ought to be spoken."

"My errors are dearly paid for, brother; and poor Mabel, I fear, will be the sufferer. I think, however, that the calamity would not have happened had there not been treason. I fear me, brother, that Jasper Eau-douce has played us false!"

"That is just my notion; this fresh-water life must, sooner or later, undermine any man's morals. Lieutenant Muir and myself talked this matter over, while we lay in a bit of a hole, out here, on this island; and we both came to the conclusion that nothing short of Jasper's treachery could have brought us all into this infernal scrape. Well, sergeant, you had better compose your mind, and think of other matters; when a vessel is about to enter a strange port, it is more prudent to think of the anchorage inside than to be underrunning all the events that have turned up during the v'y'ge; there's the logbook, expressly to note all these matters in; and what stands there must form the column of figures that's to be posted up, for or against us. How now, Pathfinder! is there anything in the wind, that you come down the ladder like an Indian in the wake of a scalp?"

The guide raised a finger for silence, then beckoned to Cap to ascend the first ladder, and to allow Mabel to take his place at the side of the sergeant.

"We must be prudent, and we must be bold, too," he said, in a low voice. "The riptyles are in earnest in their intention to fire the block, for they know there is now nothing to be gained by letting it stand. I hear the voice of that vagabond Arrowhead, among them, and he is urging them to set about their diviltry this very night. We must be stirring, Salt-water, and doing too. Luckily, there are four or five barrels of water in the block, and these are something towards a siege. My reckoning is wrong, too, or we shall yet reap some advantage from that honest fellow, the Sarpent, being at liberty."

Cap did not wait for a second invitation, but stealing away, he was soon in the upper room with Pathfinder, while Mabel took his post at the side of her father's humble bed. Pathfinder had opened a loop, having so far concealed the light that it would not expose him to a treacherous shot, and, expecting a summons, he stood with his face near the hole, ready to answer. The stillness that succeeded was at length broken by the voice of Muir.

"Master Pathfinder," called out the Scotchman, "a friend summons you to a parley. Come freely to one of the loops, for you've nothing to fear so long as you are in converse with an officer of the 55th."

"What is your will, quartermaster—what is your will? I know the 55th, and believe it to be a brave regiment, though I rather incline to the 60th, as my favorite, and to the Delawares more than to either. But what would you have, quartermaster? It must be a pressing errand that brings you under the loops of a blockhouse, at this hour of the night, with the sartainty of Killdeer's being inside of it."

"O! you'll no harm a friend, Pathfinder, I'm certain, and that's my security. You're a man of judgment, and have gained too great a name on this frontier for bravery, to feel the necessity of foolhardiness to obtain a character. You'll very well understand, my good friend, there is as much credit to be gained by submitting gracefully, when resistance becomes impossible, as by obstinately holding out contrary to the rules of war. The enemy is too strong for us, my brave comrade, and I come to counsel you to give up the block, on condition of being treated as a prisoner of war."

"I thank you for this advice, quartermaster, which is the more acceptable, as it costs nothing. But I do not think it belongs to my gifts to yield a place like this, while food and water last."

"Well, I'd be the last, Pathfinder, to recommend anything against so brave a resolution, did I see the means of maintaining it. But ye'll remember that Master Cap has fallen—"

"Not he—not he!" roared the individual in question through another loop; "so far from that, lieutenant, he has risen to the height of this here fortification, and has no mind to put his head of hair into the hands of such barbers again, so long as he can help it. I look upon this blockhouse as a circumstance, and have no mind to throw it away."

"If that is a living voice," returned Muir, "I am glad to hear it, for we all thought the man had fallen in the late fearful confusion! But, Master Pathfinder, although ye're enjoying the society of your friend Cap, and a great pleasure do I know it to be, by the experience of two days and a night passed in a hole in the earth, we've lost that of Sergeant Dunham, who has fallen, with all the brave men he led in the late expedition. Lundie would have it so, though it would have been more discreet and becoming to send a commissioned officer in command. Dunham was a brave man, notwithstanding, and shall have justice done his memory. In short, we have all acted for the best, and that is as much as could be said in favor of Prince Eugene, the Duke of Marlborough, or the great Earl of Stair himself."

"You're wrong ag'in, quartermaster—you're wrong ag'in," answered Pathfinder, resorting to a ruse to magnify his force. "The sergeant is safe in the block too, where one might say the whole family is collected."

"Well, I rejoice to hear it, for we had certainly counted the sergeant among the slain. If pretty Mabel is in the block still, let her not delay an instant, for Heaven's sake, in quitting it, for the enemy is about to put it to the trial by fire. Ye know the potency of that dread element, and will be acting more like the discreet and experienced warrior ye're universally allowed to be, in yielding a place you canna' defend, than in drawing down ruin on yourself and companions."

"I know the potency of fire, as you call it, quartermaster, and am not to be told, at this late hour, that it can be used for something else besides cooking a dinner. But I make no doubt you've heard of the potency of Killdeer, and the man who attempts to lay a pile of brush agin these logs will get a taste of his powder. As for arrows, it is not in their gift to set this building on fire, for we've no shingles on our roof, but good solid logs and green bark, and plenty of water besides. The roof is so flat, too, as you know yourself, quartermaster, that we can walk on it, and so no danger on that score while water lasts. I'm peaceable enough if let alone, but he who endivers to burn this block over my head will find the fire squinched in his own blood."

"This is idle and romantic talk, Pathfinder, and ye'll no maintain it yourself when ye come to meditate on the realities. I hope ye'll no gainsay the loyalty or the courage of the 55th, and I feel convinced that a council of war would decide on the propriety of a surrender forthwith. Na, na, Pathfinder, foolhardiness is na mair like the bravery of Wallace or Bruce, than Albany on the Hudson is like the town of Edinbro'."

"As each of us seems to have made up his mind, quartermaster, more words are useless. If the riptyles near you are disposed to set about their hellish job, let them begin at once. They can burn wood, and I'll burn powder. If I were an Injin at the stake, I suppose I could brag as well as the rest of them, but my gifts and natur' being both white, my turn is rather for doing than talking. You've said quite enough, considering you carry the King's commission; and should we all be consumed, none of us will bear *you* any malice."

"Pathfinder, you'll no be exposing Mabel, pretty Mabel Dunham, to sic' a calamity!"

"Mabel Dunham is by the side of her wounded father, and God will care for the safety of a pious child. Not a hair of her head shall fall, while my arm and sight remain true; and though *you* may trust the Mingoes, Master Muir, I put no faith in them. You've a knavish Tuscarora in your company there, who has art and malice enough to spoil the character of any tribe with which he consorts, though he found the Mingoes ready ruined to his hands, I fear. But, enough said; let each party go to the use of his means and gifts."

Throughout this dialogue Pathfinder kept his body covered, lest a treacherous shot should be aimed at the loop; and he now directed Cap to ascend to the roof in order to be in readiness to meet the first assault. Although the latter used sufficient diligence, he found no less than ten blazing arrows sticking to the bark, while the air was filled with the yells and whoops of the enemy. A rapid discharge of rifles followed, and the bullets came pattering against the logs, in a way to show that the struggle had indeed seriously commenced.

These were sounds, however, that appalled neither Pathfinder nor Cap, while Mabel was too much absorbed in her affliction to feel alarm. She had good sense enough, too, to understand the nature of the defences, and fully to appreciate their importance. As for her father, the familiar noises revived him, and it pained his child, at such a moment, to see that his glassy eye began to kindle, and that the blood returned to a cheek it had deserted, as he listened to the uproar. It was now Mabel first perceived that his reason began slightly to wander.

"Order up the light companies," he muttered, "and let the grenadiers charge! Do they dare to attack us in our fort? Why does not the artillery open on them?"

At that instant, the heavy report of a gun burst on the night; and the crashing of rending wood was heard, as a heavy shot tore the logs in the room above, and the whole block shook with the force of a shell that lodged in the work. The Pathfinder narrowly escaped the passage of this formidable missile, as it entered; but when it exploded, Mabel could not suppress a shriek; for she supposed all over her head, whether animate or inanimate, destroyed. To increase her horror, her father shouted, in a frantic voice, to "Charge!"

"Mabel," said Pathfinder, with his head at the trap, "this is true Mingo work—more noise than injury. The vagabonds have got the howitzer we took from the French, and have discharged it agin the block; but, fortunately, they have fired off the only shell we had, and there is an ind of its use, for the present. There is some confusion among the stores up in this loft, but no one is hurt. Your uncle is still on the roof; and as for myself, I've run the gauntlet of too many rifles to be skeary about such a thing as a howitzer, and that in Injin hands."

Mabel murmured her thanks, and tried to give all her attention to her father, whose efforts to rise were only counteracted by his debility. During the fearful minutes that succeeded, she was so much occupied with the care of the invalid, that she scarce heeded the clamor that reigned around her. Indeed, the uproar was so great that, had not her thoughts been otherwise employed, confusion of faculties, rather than alarm, would probably have been the consequence.

Cap preserved his coolness admirably. He had a profound and increasing respect for the power of the savages, and even for the majesty of fresh water, it is true; but his apprehensions of the former proceeded more from his dread of being scalped and tortured, than from any unmanly fear of death: and as he was now on the deck of a house, if not on the deck of a ship, and knew that there was little danger of boarders, he moved about with a fearlessness and a rash exposure of his person that Pathfinder, had he been aware of the fact, would have been the first to condemn. Instead of keeping his body covered, agreeably to the usages of Indian warfare, he was seen on every part of the roof, dashing the water right and left, with the apparent steadiness and unconcern he would have manifested had he been a sail trimmer exercising his art in a battle afloat. His appearance was one of the causes of the extraordinary clamor among the assailants, who, unused to see their enemies so reckless, opened upon him with their tongues like the pack that has the fox in view. Still he appeared to possess a charmed life; for, though the bullets whistled around him on every side, and his clothes were several times torn, nothing cut his skin. When the shell passed through the logs below, the old sailor dropped his bucket, waved his hat, and gave three cheers; in which heroic act he was employed as the dangerous missile exploded. This characteristic feat probably saved his life; for from that instant the Indians ceased to fire at him, and even to shoot their flaming arrows at the block—having taken up the notion simultaneously, and by common consent, that the "Salt-water was mad"; and it was a singular effect of their magnanimity, never to lift a hand against those whom they imagined devoid of reason.

The conduct of Pathfinder was very different. Everything he did was regulated by the most exact calculation, the result of long experience and habitual thoughtfulness. His person was kept carefully out of a line with the loops, and the spot that he selected for his lookout was one that was quite removed from danger. This celebrated guide had often been known to lead forlorn hopes; he had once stood at the stake, suffering under the cruelties and taunts of savage ingenuity and savage ferocity, without quailing; and legends of his exploits, coolness, and daring, were to be heard all along that extensive frontier, or wherever men dwelt and men contended. But on this occasion, one who did not know his history and character, might have thought his exceeding care and studied attention to self-preservation proceeded from an unworthy motive. But such a judge would not have understood his subject. The Pathfinder bethought him of Mabel, and of what might possibly be the consequences to that poor girl, should any casualty befall himself. But the recollection rather quickened his intellect than changed his customary prudence. He was, in fact, one of those who was so accustomed to fear, that he never bethought him of the constructions others might put upon his conduct. But while, in moments of danger, he acted with the wisdom of the serpent, it was also with the simplicity of a child.

For the first ten minutes of the assault, Pathfinder never raised the breech of his rifle from the floor, except when he changed his own position—for he well knew that the bullets of the enemy were thrown away upon the massive logs of the work; and, as he had been at the capture of the howitzer, he felt certain that the savages had no other shell than the one found in it when the piece was taken. There existed no reason, therefore, to dread the fire of the assailants, except as a casual bullet might find a passage through a loophole. One or two of these accidents did occur, but the balls entered at an angle that deprived them of all chance of doing any injury, so long as the Indians kept near the block; and if discharged from a distance, there was scarcely the possibility of one in a hundred's striking the apertures. But when Pathfinder heard the sound of moccasined feet, and the rustling of brush at the foot of the building, he knew that the attempt to build a fire against the logs was about to be renewed. He now summoned Cap from the roof, where indeed all the danger had ceased, and directed him to stand in readiness with his water at a hole immediately over the spot assailed.

One less trained than our hero would have been in a hurry to repel this dangerous attempt also, and might have resorted to his means prematurely; not so with Pathfinder. His aim was not only to extinguish the fire, about which he felt little apprehension, but to give the enemy a lesson that would render him wary during the remainder of the night. In order to effect the latter purpose, it became necessary to wait until the light of the intended conflagration should direct his aim, when he well knew that a very slight effort of his skill would suffice. The Iroquois were permitted to collect their heap of dried brush, to pile it against the block, to light it, and to return to their covers, without molestation. All that Pathfinder would suffer Cap to do was, to roll a barrel filled with water to the hole immediately over the spot, in readiness to be used at the proper instant. That moment, however, did not arrive, in his judgment, until the blaze illuminated the surrounding bushes, and there had been time for his quick and practiced eye to detect the forms of three or four lurking savages, who were watching the progress of the flames, with the cool indifference of men accustomed to look on human misery with apathy. Then indeed he spoke.

"Are you ready, friend Cap?" he asked. "The heat begins to strike through the crevices, and, although these green logs are not of the fiery natur' of an ill-tempered man, they may be kindled into a blaze if one provokes them too much. Are you ready with the barrel? See that it has the right cut, and that none of the water is wasted."

"All ready!" answered Cap, in the manner in which a seaman replies to such a demand.

"Then wait for the word. Never be over-impatient in a critical time, nor fool-risky in a battle. Wait for the word."

While the Pathfinder was giving these directions, he was also making his own preparations, for he saw it was time to act. Killdeer was deliberately raised, pointed, and discharged. The whole process occupied about half a minute, and, as the rifle was drawn in, the eye of the marksman was applied to the hole.

"There is one riptyle the less!" Pathfinder muttered to himself; "I've seen that vagabond afore, and know him to be a marciless devil. Well, well; the man acted according to his gifts, and he has been rewarded according to his gifts. One more of the knaves, and that will sarve the turn for tonight. When daylight appears, we may have hotter work."

All this time, another rifle was getting ready; and as Pathfinder ceased, a second savage fell. This, indeed, sufficed; for, indisposed to wait for a third visitation from the same hand, the whole band, which had been crouching in the bushes around the block, ignorant of who was and who was not exposed to view, leaped from their covers, and fled to different places for safety.

"Now, pour away, Master Cap," said Pathfinder; "I've made my mark on the blackguards, and we shall have no more fires lighted tonight."

"Scaldings!" cried Cap, upsetting the barrel with a care that at once and completely extinguished the flames.

This ended the singular conflict; and the remainder of the night passed in peace. Pathfinder and Cap watched alternately, though neither can be said to have slept. Sleep, indeed, scarcely seemed necessary to them, for both were accustomed to protracted watchings; and there were seasons and times when the former appeared to be literally insensible to the demands of hunger and thirst, and callous to the effects of fatigue.

Mabel watched by her father's pallet, and began to feel how much our happiness, in this world, depends even on things that are imaginary. Hitherto, she had virtually lived without a father, the connection with her remaining parent being ideal, rather than positive; but, now that she was about to lose him, she thought, for the moment, that the world would be a void after his death, and that she could never be acquainted with happiness again.

As the light returned, Pathfinder and Cap ascended again to the roof, with a view once more to reconnoiter the state of things on the island. This part of the blockhouse had a low battlement around it, which afforded a considerable protection to those who stood in its center; the intention having been to enable marksmen to lie behind it, and to fire over its top. By making proper use, therefore, of these slight defences—slight as to height, though abundantly ample as far as they went—the two lookouts commanded a pretty good view of the island, its covers excepted; and of most of the channels that led to the spot.

The gale was still blowing very fresh at south; and there were places in the river where its surface looked green and angry, though the wind had hardly sweep enough to raise the water into foam. The shape of the little island was generally oval, and its greatest length was from east to west. By keeping in the channels that washed it, in consequence of their several courses, and of the direction of the gale, it would have been possible for a vessel to range past the island on either of its principal sides, and always to keep the wind very nearly abeam. These were the facts first noticed by Cap, and explained to his companion; for the hopes of both now rested on the chances of relief sent from Oswego. At this instant, while they stood gazing anxiously about them, Cap cried out in his lusty, hearty manner,—

"Sail, ho!"

10

THE VESSEL which so opportunely arrived was the Scud *under Jasper; and coming abreast of the principal cove of the island, he unmasked the howitzer which was the ship's sole armament, and sent a shower of case shot hissing into the bushes. The result was the surrender of the Indians under Captain Sanglier, though they were four times as numerous as the little English force. Pathfinder, who had witnessed one or two Indian massacres, required the savages to give up their arms, even to their knives and tomahawks. The termination of the conflict had a dramatic denouement. Quartermaster Muir, arrogating to himself the post of chief command on the English side, suddenly put Jasper under arrest as a traitor. At once Pathfinder came to the rescue of the sailor. Jasper, he said, was a brave, honest, and loyal lad, who would remain free. "You may have authority over your soldiers, but you will have none over Jasper or me, Master Muir." A heated quarrel ensued. With knavish effrontery, Muir repeated his accusations. But suddenly one of the hostile Indians sprang into action.*

"Too much lie!" shouted Arrowhead, striking Muir's breast with ungovernable anger. "Where my warriors? Where Yengeese scalp? Too much lie!" And seizing a concealed knife, he stabbed Muir to death. Sanglier, as Arrowhead escaped into the bushes with Chingachgook in hot pursuit, let out an exclamation of approval. He jerked a purse from the pocket of the dying Muir,

emptied from it the French gold pieces which had bought the quartermaster, and commented, "One rascal the less!" The real traitor was exposed.

Pathfinder earnestly congratulated Jasper on his vindication, declaring that he had never for a moment believed the accusations against the young man. The sergeant, Pathfinder announced, had given Mabel to him for a wife; but now that the sergeant was dying, he felt overwhelmed by the responsibility. "Ah's me, Jasper! I sometimes feel that I am not good enough for that sweet child!" Jasper was naturally thunderstruck by this intelligence.

Shortly after, Cap appeared to tell them that Arrowhead had met with his just deserts, and to urge them to give Sergeant Dunham the news of the death of both traitors. The three men joined Mabel in the blockhouse, where Mabel was praying on her knees at the dying man's side. Jasper knelt down opposite her, while Pathfinder remained erect, watching the moving scene sorrowfully, but like one accustomed to death.

Sergeant Dunham laid his hand feebly on the head of Mabel as she ceased praying, and buried her face in his blanket.

"Bless you, my beloved child, bless you," he rather whispered than uttered aloud; "this is truly consolation; would that I, too, could pray!"

"Father, you know the Lord's prayer; you taught it to me yourself, while I was yet an infant."

The sergeant's face gleamed with a smile; for he *did* remember to have discharged that portion, at least, of the paternal duty; and the consciousness of it gave him inconceivable gratification at that solemn moment. He was then silent for several minutes, and all present believed that he was communing with God.

"Mabel, my child," he at length uttered, in a voice that seemed to be reviving, "Mabel, I'm quitting you"—the spirit, at its great and final passage, appears ever to consider the body as nothing—"I'm quitting you, my child; where is your hand?"

"Here, dearest father—here are both; O! take both."

"Pathfinder," added the sergeant, feeling on the opposite side of the bed, where Jasper still knelt, and getting one of the hands of the young man, by mistake, "take it—I leave you as her father—as you and she may please—bless you—bless you both—"

At that awful instant no one would rudely apprize the sergeant of his mistake; and he died a minute or two later, holding Jasper's and Mabel's hands covered by both his own. Our heroine was ignorant of the fact, until an exclamation of Cap's announced the death of her father; when, raising her face, she saw the eyes of Jasper riveted on her own, and felt the warm pressure of his hand. But a single feeling was predominant at that instant; and Mabel withdrew to weep, scarcely conscious of what had occurred. The Pathfinder took the arm of Eau-douce, and he left the block.

The two friends walked in silence past the fire, along the glade, and nearly reached the opposite shore of the island, in profound silence. Here they stopped, and Pathfinder spoke.

" 'Tis all over, Jasper," he said; " 'tis all over. Ah's me! Poor Sergeant Dunham has finished his march, and that, too, by the hand of a venomous Mingo. Well, we never know what is to happen, and his luck may be your'n or mine, tomorrow, or next day!"

"And Mabel? What is to become of Mabel, Pathfinder?"

"You heard the sergeant's dying words; he has left his child in my care, Jasper; and it is a most solemn trust, it is; yes, it is a most solemn trust!"

"It's a trust, Pathfinder, of which any man would be glad to relieve you," returned the youth, with a bitter smile.

"I've often thought it has fallen into wrong hands. I'm not consaited, Jasper—I'm not consaited, I do think I'm not; but if Mabel Dunham is willing to overlook all my imperfections and ignorance like, I should be wrong to gainsay it on account of any sartainty I may have myself about my own want of merit."

"No one will blame you, Pathfinder, for marrying Mabel Dunham, any more than they will blame you for wearing a precious jewel in your bosom, that a friend had freely given you."

"Do you think they'll blame Mabel, lad? I've had my misgivings about that too; for all persons may not be as disposed to look at me with the same eyes as you and the sergeant's daughter." Jasper Eau-douce started, as a man flinches at sudden bodily pain; but he otherwise maintained his self-command. "And mankind is envious and ill-natured, more particularly in and about the garrisons. I sometimes wish, Jasper, that Mabel could have taken a fancy to you, I do; and that you had taken a fancy to her; for it often seems to me that one like you, after all, might make her happier than I ever can."

"We will not talk about this, Pathfinder," interrupted Jasper, hoarsely and impatiently; "you will be Mabel's husband, and it is not right to speak of any one else in that character. As for me, I shall take Master Cap's advice, and try and make a man of myself, by seeing what is to be done on the salt water."

"You, Jasper Western! you quit the lakes, the forests, and the lines; and this, too, for the towns and wasty ways of the settlements, and a little difference in the taste of the water! Haven't we the salt licks, if salt is necessary to you? and oughtn't man to be satisfied with what contents the other creatur's of God? I counted on you, Jasper—I counted on you, I did—and thought, now that Mabel and I intend to dwell in a cabin of our own, that some day you might be tempted to choose a companion, too, and come and settle in our neighborhood. There is a beautiful spot about fifty miles west of the garrison, that I had chosen in my mind for my own place of abode; and there is an excellent harbor about ten leagues this side of it, where you could run in and out with the cutter, at any leisure minute; and I'd even fancied you and your wife in possession of the one place, and Mabel and I in possession of t'other. We should be just a healthy hunt apart; and if the Lord ever intends any of his creatures to be happy on 'arth, none could be happier than we four."

"You forget, my friend," answered Jasper, taking the guide's hand and forcing a friendly smile, "that I have no fourth person to love and cherish; and I much doubt if I ever shall love any other as I love you and Mabel."

"Thank'ee, boy—I thank you with all my heart; but what you call love for Mabel is only friendship like, and a very different thing from what I feel. Now, instead of sleeping as sound as natur' at midnight, as I used to could, I dream nightly of Mabel Dunham. The young does sport before me; and when I raise Killdeer in order to take a little venison, the animals look back, and it seems as if they all had Mabel's sweet countenance, laughing in my face, and looking as if they said, 'Shoot me if you dare!' Then I hear her soft voice calling out among the birds as they sing; and no later than the last nap I took, I bethought me in fancy of going over the Niagara, holding Mabel in my arms rather than part from her. The bitterest moments I've ever known were them in which the devil or some Mingo conjuror, perhaps, has just put into my head to fancy in dreams that Mabel is lost to me by some unaccountable calamity—either by changefulness or by violence."

"O! Pathfinder, if you think this so bitter in a dream, what must it be to one who feels its reality, and knows it all to be true—true—true! So true, as to leave no hope; to leave nothing but despair!"

These words burst from Jasper as a fluid pours from the vessel that has been suddenly broken. They were uttered involuntarily, almost unconsciously, but with a truth and feeling that carried with them the instant conviction of their deep sincerity. Pathfinder started, gazed at his friend for quite a minute like one bewildered; and then it was that in despite of all his simplicity the truth gleamed upon him. All know how corroborating proofs crowd upon the mind as soon at it catches a direct clue to any hitherto unsuspected fact; how rapidly the thoughts flow, and premises tend to their just conclusions under such circumstances. Our hero was so confiding by nature, so just, and so much disposed to imagine that all his friends wished him the same happiness as he wished them, that, until this unfortunate moment, a suspicion of Jasper's attachment for Mabel had never been awakened in his bosom. He was, however, now too experienced in the emotions that characterize the passion; and the burst of feeling in his companion was too violent and too natural to leave any further doubt on the subject. The feeling that first followed this change of opinion was one of deep humility and exquisite pain. He bethought him of Jasper's youth, his higher claims to personal appearance, and all the general probabilities that such a suitor would be more agreeable to Mabel than he could possibly be himself. Then the noble rectitude of mind for which the man was so distinguished asserted its power; it was sustained by his rebuked manner of thinking of himself, and all that habitual deference for the rights and feelings of others, which appeared to be inbred in his very nature. Taking the arm of Jasper, he led him to a log, where he compelled the young man to seat himself, by a sort of irresistible exercise of his iron muscles, and where he placed himself at his side.

The instant his feelings had found vent, Eau-douce was both alarmed at and ashamed of their violence. He would have given all he possessed on earth could the last three minutes be recalled, but he was too frank by disposition, and too much accustomed to deal ingenuously by his friend, to think a moment of attempting further concealment, or of any evasion of the explanation that he knew was about to be demanded. Even while he trembled in anticipation of what was about to follow, he never contemplated equivocation.

"Jasper," Pathfinder commenced, in a tone so solemn as to thrill on every nerve in his listener's body, "this *has* surprised me! You have kinder feelings toward Mabel than I had thought; and unless my own mistaken vanity and consait have cruelly deceived me, I pity you, boy, from my soul, I do! Yes, I think I know how to pity anyone who has set his heart on a creature like Mabel, unless he sees a prospect of her regarding him as he regards her. This matter must be cleared up, Eau-douce, as the Delawares say, until there shall not be a cloud atween us."

"What clearing up can it want, Pathfinder? I love Mabel Dunham, and Mabel Dunham does not love me; she prefers you for a husband; and the wisest thing I can do, is to go off at once to the salt water and try to forget you both."

"Forget me, Jasper!—that would be a punishment I don't desarve. But how do you know that Mabel prefars *me?* how do you know it, lad? to me it seems impossible like!"

"Is she not to marry you, and would Mabel marry a man she does not love?"

"She has been hard urged by the sergeant, she has; and a dutiful child may have found it difficult to withstand the wishes of a dying parent. Have you ever told Mabel that you prefarred her, Jasper; that you bore her these feelings?"

"Never, Pathfinder; I would not do you that wrong!"

"I believe you, lad, I do believe you; and I think you would now go to the salt water and let the scent die with you. But this must not be. Mabel shall hear all, and she shall have her own way, if my heart breaks in the trial, she shall. No words have ever passed atween you, then, Jasper?"

"Nothing of account—nothing direct. Still, I will own all my foolishness, Pathfinder, for I ought to own it to a generous friend like you, and there will be an end of it. You know how young people understand each other, or think they understand each other, without always speaking out in plain speech; and get to know each other's thoughts, or to think they know them, by means of a hundred little ways!"

"Not I, Jasper, not I," truly answered the guide; for, sooth to say, his advances had never been met with any of that sweet and precious encouragement that silently marks the course of sympathy united to passion. "Not I, Jasper; I know nothing of all this. Mabel has always treated me fairly, and said what she had to say in speech as plain as tongue could tell it."

"You have had the pleasure of hearing her say that she loved you, Pathfinder?"

"Why no, Jasper, not just that, in words. She has told me that we never could—never ought to be married; that *she* was not good enough for *me;* though she *did* say that she honored me, and respected me. But then the sergeant said it was always so with the youthful and timid,—that her mother did so, and said so, afore her; and that I ought to be satisfied if she would consent, on any terms, to marry me: and, therefore, I have concluded that all was right, I have."

In spite of all his friendship for the successful wooer—in spite of all his honest, sincere wishes for his happiness, we should be unfaithful chroniclers, did we not own that Jasper felt his heart bound with an uncontrollable feeling of delight, at this admission. It was not that he saw or felt any hope connected with the circumstance; but it was grateful to the jealous covetousness of unlimited love, thus to learn that no other ears had heard the sweet confessions that were denied its own.

"Tell me more of this manner of talking without the use of the tongue," continued Pathfinder, whose countenance was getting to be grave, and who now questioned his companion, like one that seemed to anticipate evil in the reply. "I can and have conversed with Chingachgook, and with his son Uncas, too, in that mode, afore the latter fell; but I didn't know that young girls practysed this art; and, least of all, Mabel Dunham!"

" 'Tis nothing, Pathfinder. I mean only a look, or a smile, or a glance of the eye, or the trembling of an arm, or a hand, when the young woman has had occasion to touch me; and because I have been weak enough to tremble even at Mabel's breath, or her brushing me with her clothes, my vain thoughts have misled me. I never spoke plainly to Mabel, myself; and now there is no use for it, since there is clearly no hope."

"Jasper," returned Pathfinder, simply, but with a dignity that precluded further remarks at the moment, "we will talk of the sergeant's funeral, and of our own departure from this island. After these things are disposed of, it will be time enough to say more of the sergeant's daughter. This matter must be looked into; for the father left me the care of his child."

Jasper was glad enough to change the subject, and the friends separated, each charged with the duty most peculiar to his own station and habits.

That afternoon all the dead were interred—the grave of Sergeant Dunham being dug in the center of the glade, beneath the shade of a huge elm. Mabel wept bitterly at the ceremony, and she found relief in thus disburdening her sorrow. The night passed tranquilly, as did the whole of the following day, Jasper declaring that the gale was too severe to venture on the lake. This circumstance detained Captain Sanglier, also; who did not quit the island until the morning of the third day after the death of Dunham, when the weather had moderated, and the wind had become fair. Then, indeed, he departed, after taking leave of the Pathfinder, in the manner of one who believed he was in company of a distinguished character for the last time. The two separated like those who respect one another, while each felt that the other was an enigma to himself.

The occurrences of the last few days had been too exciting, and had made too many demands on the fortitude of our heroine, to leave her in the helplessness of grief. She mourned for her father, and she occasionally shuddered, as she recalled all the horrible scenes she had witnessed; but, on the whole, she had aroused herself, and was no longer in the deep depression that usually accompanies grief. Perhaps the overwhelming, almost stupefying sorrow that crushed poor June, and left her for nearly twenty-four hours in a state of stupor, assisted Mabel in conquering her own feelings, for she had felt called on to administer consolation to the young Indian woman. This she had done, in the quiet, soothing, insinuating way, in which her sex usually exerts its influence on such occasions.

The morning of the third day was set for that on which the *Scud* was to sail. Jasper had made all his preparations; the different effects were embarked, and Mabel had taken leave of June—a painful and affectionate parting. In a word, all was ready, and every soul had left the island but the Indian woman, Pathfinder, Jasper, and our heroine. The former had gone into a thicket to weep, and the three last were approaching the spot where three canoes lay; one of which was the property of June, and the other two were in waiting to carry the others off to the *Scud*. Pathfinder led the way, but, when he drew near the shore, instead of taking the direction to the boats, he motioned to his companions to follow, and proceeded to a fallen tree that lay on the margin of the glade, and out of view of those in the cutter. Seating himself on the trunk, he signed to Mabel to take her place on one side of him, and to Jasper to occupy the other.

"Sit down here, Mabel; sit down there, Eau-douce," he commenced, as soon as he had taken his own seat; "I've something that lies heavy on my mind, and now is the time to take it off, if it's ever to be done. Sit down, Mabel, and let me lighten my heart, if not my conscience, while I've the strength to do it."

The pause that succeeded lasted two or three minutes, and both the young people wondered what was to come next,—the idea that Pathfinder could have any weight on his conscience seeming equally improbable to each.

"Mabel," our hero at length resumed, "we must talk plainly to each other afore we join your uncle in the cutter, where the Salt-water has slept every night since the last rally; for he say's it's the only place in which a man can be sure of keeping the hair on his head, he does. Ah's me! what have I to do with these follies and sayings now? I try to be pleasant, and to feel lighthearted, but the power of man can't make water run upstream. Mabel, you know that the sergeant, afore he left us, had settled it atween us two, that we were to become man and wife, and that we were to live together, and to love one another as long as the Lord was pleased to keep us both on 'arth, yes, and afterwards, too?"

Mabel's cheeks had regained a little of their ancient bloom in the fresh air of the morning; but at this unlooked-for address they blanched again, nearly to the pallid hue which grief had imprinted there. Still she looked kindly, though seriously, at Pathfinder, and even endeavored to force a smile.

"Very true, my excellent friend," she answered; "this was my poor father's wish, and I feel certain that a whole life devoted to your welfare and comforts could scarcely repay you for all you have done for us."

"I fear me, Mabel, that man and wife needs to be bound together by a stronger tie than such feelings, I do. You have done nothing for me, or nothing of any account, and yet my very heart yearns toward you, it does; and therefore it seems likely that those feelings come from something besides saving scalps and guiding through woods."

Mabel's cheek had begun to glow again; and though she struggled hard to smile, her voice trembled a little as she answered.

"Had we not better postpone this conversation, Pathfinder?" she said; "we are not alone; and nothing is so unpleasant to a listener, they say, as family matters in which he feels no interest."

"It's because we are not alone, Mabel, or rather because Jasper is with us, that I wish to talk of this matter. The sergeant believed I might make a suitable companion for you; and, though I had misgivings about it—yes, I had many misgivings—he finally persuaded me into the idee, and things came round atween us, as you know. But when you promised your father to marry me, Mabel, and gave me your hand so modestly, but so prettily, there was one circumstance, as your uncle called it, that you didn't know; and I've thought it right to tell you what it is, before matters are finally settled. I've often taken a poor deer for my dinner, when good venison was not to be found; but it's as nat'ral not to take up with the worst when the best may be had."

"You speak in a way, Pathfinder, that is difficult to be understood. If this conversation is really necessary, I trust you will be more plain."

"Well, then, Mabel, I've been thinking it was quite likely, when you gave in to the sergeant's wishes, that you did not know the natur' of Jasper Western's feelings toward you?"

"Pathfinder!" and Mabel's cheek now paled to the livid hue of death; then it flushed to the tint of crimson; and her whole frame shuddered. Pathfinder, however, was too intent on his own object to notice this agitation; and Eau-douce had hidden his face in his hands in time to shut out its view.

"I've been talking with the lad; and, on comparing his dreams with my dreams, his feelings with my feelings, and his wishes with my wishes, I fear we think too much alike concerning you, for both of us to be very happy."

"Pathfinder! you forget—you should remember that we are betrothed!" said Mabel hastily, and in a voice so low, that it required acute attention in the listeners to catch the syllables. Indeed, the last word was not quite intelligible to the guide, and he confessed his ignorance by the usual—

"Anan?"

"You forget that we are to be married; and such allusions are improper as well as painful."

"Everything is proper that is right, Mabel; and everything is right that leads to justice and fair dealing; though it *is painful* enough, as you say—as I find on trial, I do. Now, Mabel, had you known that Eau-douce thinks of you in this way, maybe you never would have consented to be married to one as old and as uncomely as I am."

"Why this cruel trial, Pathfinder? To what can all this lead? Jasper Western thinks no such thing: he says nothing—he feels nothing."

"Mabel!" burst from out of the young man's lips, in a way to betray the uncontrollable nature of his emotions, though he uttered not another syllable.

Mabel buried her face in both her hands; and the two sat like a pair of guilty beings, suddenly detected in the commission of some crime that involved the happiness of a common patron. At that instant, perhaps, Jasper himself was inclined to deny his passion, through an extreme unwillingness to grieve his friend; while Mabel, on whom this positive announcement of a fact, that she had rather unconsciously hoped than believed, came so unexpectedly, felt her mind momentarily bewildered; and she scarce knew whether to weep or to rejoice. Still she was first to speak; since Eau-douce could utter naught that would be disingenuous, or that would pain his friend.

"Pathfinder," she said. "you talk wildly. Why mention this at all?"

"Well, Mabel, if I talk wildly, I *am* half wild you know; by natur', I fear, as well as by habit." As he said this, he endeavored to laugh in his usual noiseless way, but the effect produced a strange and discordant sound; and it appeared nearly to choke him. "Yes, I *must* be wild; I'll not attempt to deny it."

"Dearest Pathfinder! my best, almost my only friend! you *cannot, do not* think I intended to say that!" interrupted Mabel, almost breathless in her haste to relieve his mortification. "If courage, truth, nobleness of soul and conduct, unyielding principles, and a hundred other excellent qualities can render any man respectable, esteemed, or beloved, your claims are inferior to those of no other human being."

"What tender and bewitching voices they have, Jasper!" resumed the guide, now laughing freely and naturally. "Yes, natur' seems to have made them on purpose to sing in our ears when the music of the woods is silent! But we must come to a right understanding, we must. I ask you again, Mabel, if you had known that Jasper Western loves you as well as I do, or better perhaps—though that is scarce possible; that in his dreams he sees your face in the water of the lake; that he talks to you and of you in his sleep; fancies all that is beautiful like Mabel Dunham, and all that is good and virtuous; believes he never knowed happiness until he knowed you; could kiss the ground on which you have trod, and forgets all the joys of his calling to think of you, and of the delight of gazing at your beauty, and in listening to your voice, would you then have consented to marry me?"

Mabel could not have answered this question if she would; but, though her face was buried in her hands, the tint of the rushing blood was visible between the openings, and the suffusion seemed to impart itself to her very fingers. Still nature asserted her power, for there was a single instant when the astonished, almost terrified girl stole a glance at Jasper, as if distrusting Pathfinder's history of his feelings, read the truth of all he said in that furtive look, and instantly concealed her face again, as if she would hide it from observation forever.

"Take time to think, Mabel," the guide continued, "for it is a solemn thing to accept one man for a husband, while the thoughts and wishes lead to another. Jasper and I have talked this matter over, freely and like old friends, and though I always knowed that we viewed most things pretty much alike, I couldn't have thought that we regarded any particular object with the very same eyes, as it might be, until we opened our minds to each other about you. Now, Jasper owns that the very first time that he beheld you, he thought you the sweetest and winningest creatur' he had ever met; that your voice sounded like murmuring water in his ears; that he fancied his sails were your garments, fluttering in the wind; that your laugh haunted him in his sleep; and that, ag'in and ag'in, has he started up affrighted, because he has fancied some one wanted to force you out of the *Scud,* where he imagined you had taken up your abode. Nay, the lad has even acknowledged that he often weeps at the thought that you are likely to spend your days with another and not with him."

"Jasper!"

"It's solemn truth, Mabel, and it's right you should know it. Now stand up, and choose atween us. I do believe Eau-douce loves you as well as I do myself; he has tried to persuade me that he loves you better, but that I will not allow, for I do not think it possible; but I will own the boy loves you, heart and soul, and he has a good right to be heard. The sergeant left me your protector, and not your tyrant. I told him that I would be a father to you, as well as a husband, and it seems to me no feeling father would deny his child this small privilege. Stand up, Mabel, therefore, and speak your thoughts as freely as if I were the sergeant himself, seeking your good, and nothing else."

Mabel dropped her hands, arose, and stood face to face with her two suitors, though the flush that was on her cheek was feverish, the evidence of excitement rather than of shame.

"What would you have, Pathfinder?" she asked. "Have I not already promised my poor father to do all you desire?"

"Then I desire this. Here I stand, a man of the forest, and of little l'arning, though I fear with an ambition beyond my desarts, and I'll do my endivors to do justice to both sides. In the first place, it is allowed that so far as feelings in your behalf are consarned we love you just the same. Jasper thinks his feelings *must* be the strongest, but this I cannot say, in honesty, for it doesn't seem to me that it *can* be true; else I would frankly and freely confess it, I would. So in this particular, Mabel, we are here before you on equal tarms. As for myself being the oldest, I'll first say what little can be produced in my favor, as well as agin it. As a hunter, I do think there is no man near the lines that can outdo me. If venison or bear's meat, or even birds and fish, should ever be scarce in our cabin, it would be more likely to be owing to natur' and Providence, than to any fault of mine. In short, it does seem to me that the woman who depended on me, would never be likely to want for food. But I'm fearful ignorant! It's true, I speak several tongues, such as they be, while I'm very far from being expart at my own. Then, my years are greater than your own, Mabel; and the circumstance that I was so long the sergeant's comrade can be no great merit in your eyes. I wish, too, I was more comely, I do; but we are all as natur' made us, and the last thing that a man ought to lament, except on very special occasions, is his looks. When all is remembered, age, looks, l'arning, and habits, Mabel, conscience tells me I ought to confess that I'm altogether unfit for you, if not downright unworthy; and I would give up the hope, this minute, I would, if I didn't feel something pulling at my heartstrings which seems hard to undo."

"Pathfinder! noble, generous Pathfinder!" cried our heroine, seizing his hand, and kissing it with a species of holy reverence, "you do yourself injustice; you forget my poor father and your promise; you do not know *me!*"

"Now, here's Jasper," continued the guide, without allowing the girl's caresses to win him from his purpose; "with *him,* the case is different. In the way of providing, as in that of loving, there's not much to choose atween us, for the lad is frugal, industrious, and careful. Then he is quite a scholar—knows the tongue of the Frenchers—reads many books, and some, I know, that you like to read yourself—can understand you at all times, which, perhaps, is more than I can say for myself."

"What of all this?" interrupted Mabel, impatiently; "why speak of it now—why speak of it at all?"

"Then the lad has a manner of letting his thoughts be known, that I fear I can never equal. If there's anything on 'arth that would make my tongue bold and persuading, Mabel, I do think it's yourself; and yet in our late conversations Jasper has outdone me, even on this point, in a way to make me ashamed of myself. He has told me how simple you were, and how truehearted; and kindhearted; and how you looked down upon vanities, for though you might be the wife of more than one officer, as he thinks, that you cling to feeling, and would rather be true to yourself, and natur' than a colonel's lady. He fairly made my blood warm, he did, when he spoke of having beauty without seeming ever to have looked upon it, and the manner in which you moved about like a young fa'an, so nat'ral and graceful-like, without knowing it; and the truth and justice of your idees, and the warmth and generosity of your heart—"

"Jasper!" interrupted Mabel, giving way to feelings that had gathered an ungovernable force by being so long pent, and falling into the young man's willing arms, weeping like a child, and almost as helpless. "Jasper!—Jasper! why have you kept this from me?"

The answer of Eau-douce was not very intelligible, nor was the murmured dialogue that followed, remarkable for coherency. But the language of affection is easily understood. The hour that succeeded passed like a very few minutes of ordinary life, so far as a computation of time was concerned; and when Mabel recollected herself, and bethought her of the existence of others, her uncle was pacing the cutter's deck in great impatience, and wondering why Jasper should be losing so much of a favorable wind. Her first thought was of him who was so likely to feel the recent betrayal of her real emotions.

"O! Jasper!" she exclaimed, like one suddenly self-convicted, "the Pathfinder!"

Eau-douce fairly trembled, not with unmanly apprehension, but with the painful conviction of the pang he had given his friend; and he looked in all directions in the expectation of seeing his person. But Pathfinder had withdrawn, with a tact and a delicacy that might have done credit to the sensibility and breeding of a courtier. For several minutes the two lovers sat silently waiting his return, uncertain what properly was required of them, under circumstances so marked and so peculiar. At length they beheld their friend advancing slowly toward them, with a thoughtful and even a pensive air.

"I now understand what you meant, Jasper, by speaking without a tongue, and hearing without an ear," he said, when close enough to the tree to be heard. "Yes, I understand it now, I do, and a very pleasant sort of discourse it is, when one can hold it with Mabel Dunham. Ah's me! I told the sergeant I wasn't fit for her; that I was too old, too ignorant, and too wildlike—but he *would* have it otherwise."

Jasper and Mabel sat, resembling Milton's picture of our first parents, when the consciousness of sin first laid its leaden weight on their souls. Neither spoke, neither even moved; though both at that moment fancied they could part with their new-found happiness, in order to restore their friend to his peace of mind. Jasper was pale as death; but, in Mabel, maiden modesty had caused the blood to mantle on her cheeks, until their bloom was heightened to a richness that was scarce equalled in her hours of lighthearted buoyancy and joy. As the feeling, which, in her sex always accompanies the security of love returned, threw its softness and tenderness over her countenance, she was singularly beautiful. Pathfinder gazed at her with an intentness he did not endeavor to conceal, and then he fairly laughed in his own way, and with a sort of wild exultation, as men that are untutored are wont to express their delight. This momentary indulgence, however, was expiated by the pang that followed the sudden consciousness that this glorious young creature was lost to him forever. It required a full minute for this simple-minded being to recover from the shock of this conviction; and then he recovered his dignity of manner, speaking with gravity, almost with solemnity.

"I have always known, Mabel Dunham, that men have their gifts," he said; "but I'd forgotten that it did not belong to mine, to please the young, and beautiful, and l'arned. I hope the mistake has been no very heavy sin; and if it was, I've been heavily punished for it, I have. Nay, Mabel, I know what you'd say, but it's unnecessary; I *feel* it all, and that is as good as if I *heard* it all. I've had a bitter hour, Mabel—I've had a very bitter hour, lad—"

"Hour!" echoed Mabel, as the other first used the word, the telltale blood which had begun to ebb toward her heart rushing again tumultuously to her very temples. "Surely not an hour, Pathfinder?"

"Hour!" exclaimed Jasper at the same instant, "no, no, my worthy friend, it is not ten minutes since you left us!"

"Well, it may be so; though to me it has seemed to be a day. I begin to think, however, that the happy count times by minutes, and the miserable count it by months. But we will talk no more of this; it is all over now, and many words about it will make you no happier, while they will only tell me what I've lost; and quite likely how much I desarved to lose her. No, no, Mabel, 'tis useless to interrupt me; I admit it all, and your gainsaying it, though it be so well meant, cannot change my mind. Well, Jasper, she is yours; and though it's hard to think it, I do believe you'll make her happier than I could, for your gifts are better suited to do so, though I would have strived hard to do as much, if I knew myself, I would. I ought to have known better than to believe the sergeant; and I ought to have put faith in what Mabel told me at the head of the lake, for reason and judgment might have shown me its truth; but it is so pleasant to think what we wish, and mankind so easily overpersuade us when we overpersuade ourselves. But what's the use in talking of it, as I said afore? It's true, Mabel seemed to be consenting, though it all came from a wish to please her father, and from being skeary about the savages—"

"Pathfinder!"

"I understand you, Mabel, and have no hard feelings, I haven't. I sometimes think I should like to live in your neighborhood that I might look at your happiness; but on the whole it is better I should quit the 55th altogether, and go back to the 60th, which is my natyve rigiment, as it might be. It would have been better, perhaps, had I never left it, though my sarvices were much wanted in this quarter, and I'd been with some of the 55th years agone—Sergeant Dunham, for instance, when he was in another corps. Still, Jasper, I do not regret that I've known you—"

"And me, Pathfinder!" impetuously interrupted Mabel, "do you regret having known *me?*—could I think so, I should never be at peace with myself!"

"You, Mabel!" returned the guide, taking the hand of our heroine, and looking up into her countenance with guileless simplicity but earnest affection—"how could I be sorry that a ray of the sun came across the gloom of a cheerless day? that light has broken in upon darkness, though it remained so short a time! I do not flatter myself with being able to march quite as lighthearted as I once used to could, or to sleep as sound for some time to come; but I shall always remember how near I was to being undesarvedly happy, I shall. So far from blaming you, Mabel, I only blame myself for being so vain as to think it possible I could please such a creatur'; for, sartainly you told me how it was when we talked it over on the mountain, and I ought to have believed you then; for I do suppose it's nat'ral that young women should know their own minds better than their fathers. Ah's me! It's settled now, and nothing remains but for me to take leave of you that you may depart; I feel that Master Cap must be impatient, and there is danger of his coming on shore to look for us all."

"To take leave!" exclaimed Mabel.

"Leave!" echoed Jasper; "you do not mean to quit us, my friend?"

" 'Tis best, Mabel—'tis altogether best, Eau-douce; and it's wisest. I could live and die in your company if I only followed feeling; but if I follow reason, I shall quit you here. You will go back to Oswego, and become man and wife as soon as you arrive; for all that is determined with Master Cap, who hankers after the sea again, and who knows what is to happen; while I shall return to the wilderness and my Maker. Come, Mabel," continued Pathfinder, rising and drawing nearer to our heroine with grave decorum, "kiss me. Jasper will not grudge me one kiss; then we'll part."

"O! Pathfinder," exclaimed Mabel, falling into the arms of the guide, and kissing his cheeks again and again, with a freedom and warmth she had been far from manifesting while held to the bosom of Jasper, "God bless you, dearest Pathfinder! You will come to us hereafter. We shall see you again. When old, you will come to our dwelling and let me be a daughter to you?"

"Yes—that's it," returned the guide, almost gasping for breath; "I'll try to think of it in that way. You're more befitting to be my daughter than to be my wife, you arc. Farewell, Jasper. Now we'll go to the canoe; it's time you were on board."

The manner in which Pathfinder led the way to the shore was solemn and calm. As soon as he reached the canoe, he again took Mabel by the hands, held her at the length of his own arms, and gazed wistfully into her face, until the unbidden tears rolled out of the fountains of feeling, and trickled down his rugged cheeks in streams.

"Bless me, Pathfinder," said Mabel, kneeling reverently at his feet. "O! at least bless me before we part."

That untutored, but noble-minded being, did as she desired; and, aiding her to enter the canoe, seemed to tear himself away as one snaps a strong and obstinate cord. Before he retired, however, he took Jasper by the arm, and led him a little aside, when he spoke as follows:—

"You're kind of heart, and gentle by natur', Jasper; but we are both rough and wild, in comparison with that dear creatur'. Be careful of her, and never show the roughness of man's natur' to her soft disposition. You'll get to understand her in time; and the Lord, who governs the lake and the forest alike—who looks upon virtue with a smile, and upon vice with a frown—keep you happy, and worthy to be so!"

Pathfinder made a sign for his friend to depart; and he stood leaning on his rifle until the canoe had reached the side of the *Scud*. Mabel wept as if her heart would break; nor did her eyes once turn from the open spot in the glade, where the form of the Pathfinder was to be seen, until the cutter had passed a point that completely shut out the island. When last in view, the sinewy frame of this extraordinary man was as motionless as if it were a statue set up in that solitary place, to commemorate the scenes of which it had so lately been the witness.

For a month, while Dew-of-June obstinately refused to abandon the grave of her husband, Pathfinder killed game and cooked food for her use. Finally, when the leaves had all fallen from the trees and the nights were growing cold, he, June, and Chingachgook returned to Oswego. The ramparts of the British fort were crowded with spectators as their canoe approached, but the tactful commander refused to let them even be hailed. They pressed on to a little bay where the Scud *lay at anchor. In a clearing on the shore stood a newly built log cabin. "There was an air of frontier comfort and of frontier abundance around the place, though it was necessarily wild and solitary." Jasper and Mabel, now married, welcomed Pathfinder to a meal, after which he said farewell. They urged him to repeat his visit. "When shall we see you again?" asked Mabel.*

"I've thought of that, too; yes, I've thought of that, I have," returned Pathfinder. "If the time should ever come when I can look upon you altogether as a sister, Mabel, or a child—it might be better to say a child, since you're young enough to be my daughter—depend on it, I'll come back; for it would lighten my very heart

to witness your gladness. But if I cannot, farewell, farewell—the sergeant was wrong—yes, the sergeant was wrong." He turned away as if the words choked him.

Jasper and his wife never saw the Pathfinder again. A year later, Cap induced the pair to join him in New York, where Jasper prospered as a merchant. Thrice, at intervals of years, Mabel received valuable but anonymous presents of furs, which she knew came from the scout. Once, too, after the Revolution, she heard of Pathfinder as the most renowned hunter in western New York, "a being of great purity of character, and of as marked peculiarities." Meanwhile, one figure in the Ontario drama, Major Duncan of Lundie, the commander at Oswego, married and retired; his family becoming famous when a younger brother rose to be Lord Duncan of Camperdown, one of the great admirals of Nelson's time.

THE PIONEERS

Being the FOURTH SERIES OF ADVENTURES *of*

LEATHERSTOCKING

THE TIME IS 1793, in Washington's Presidency; the place is again Otsego Lake or Glimmerglass, but a lake changed beyond recognition. Settlers have come in; a village has sprung up—the village of Cooperstown, here called Templeton; elegance shows itself in the mansion of a great landowner, science in the activities of a crudely educated but shrewd physician, religion in the person of an Episcopal divine, class distinctions in the marked gap between rich and poor, educated and uneducated. The abundant land still offers riches for the taking. Deer can be shot on every hand; forests await the lumberman; the spring flight of wild pigeons darkens the skies; when the black bass make their annual run from the depths of the lake to its shallow margins, they can be taken in thousands. Tokens of a different era, how-

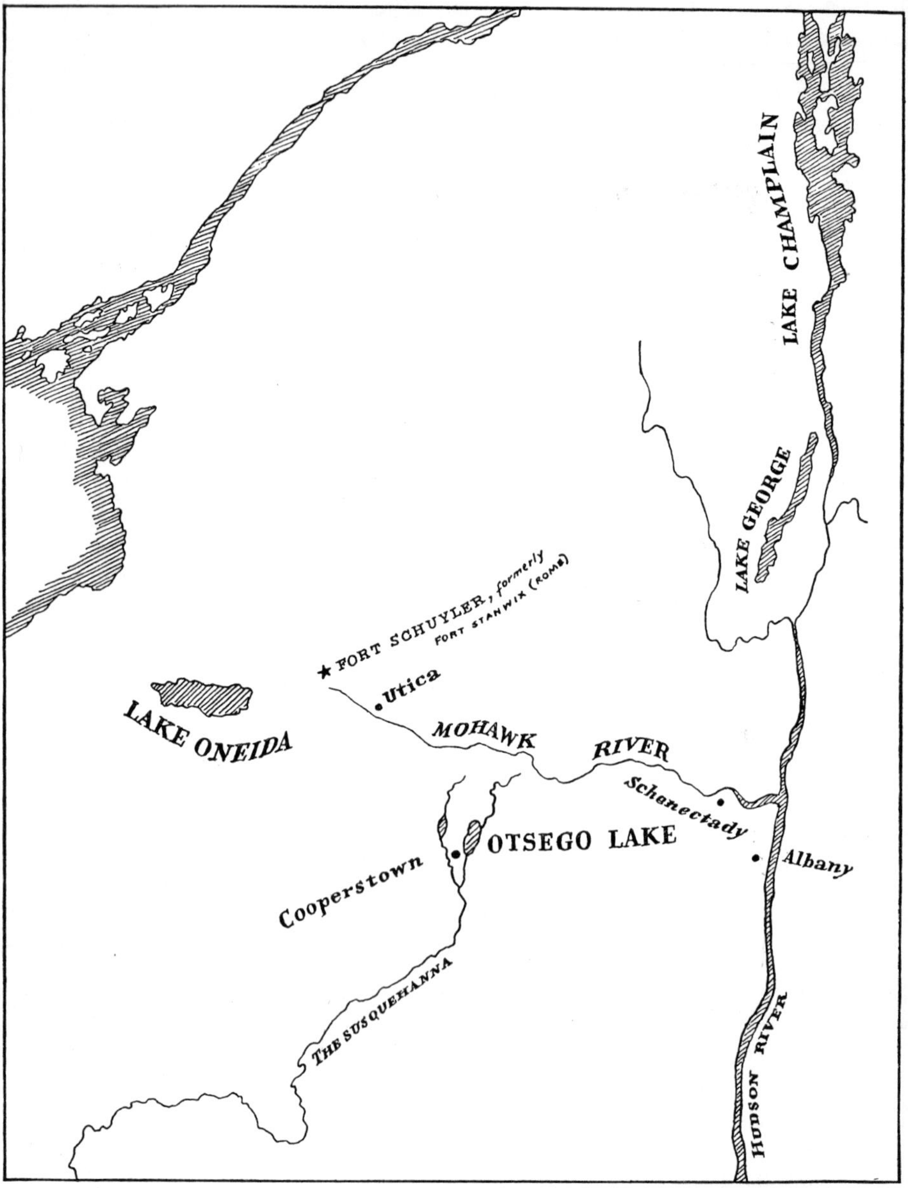

THE SCENE OF *The Pioneers*

ever, are appearing. The first game laws are being enforced; farsighted men grumble that the destruction of the woodlands is going forward too fast, and deplore the slaughter of many times as many pigeons as can be eaten; officers of the law frown upon frontier violence.

The actual history of Otsego Lake is interesting. In the days of British rule, title to the lands about it was granted to Colonel George Croghan, assistant superintendent of the Northern Indians. He mortgaged the tract to Benjamin Franklin's natural son, William Franklin, and lost it by foreclosure. In due course ownership passed to two gentlemen of Burlington, New Jersey, William Cooper and Andrew Craig; the former the father of the novelist. A sturdy, active man, William Cooper made his first visit to the lake in 1785, and three years later drew up a plan for the village. He was a resourceful leader—as resourceful as Judge Marmaduke Temple in The Pioneers. *He opened a general store, induced the settlers to make potash and maple syrup for sale, organized community effort in the building of roads and bridges, and encouraged education. In 1789 he opened a manor house and began dispensing a liberal hospitality. The district attracted many Europeans along with the Yankees—British, Germans, and even Poles. A French émigré from Martinique who kept a small shop on the principal street of Cooperstown was named Monsieur Le Quoi, an appellation which Fenimore Cooper took over for the Frenchman in the novel.*

"Occasionally," wrote Susan Fenimore Cooper (the novelist's daughter) of the years at the beginning of the nineteenth century, "a bear was seen feasting on the wild fruits. Now and then the howl of the wolf came across the icy field of the Otsego in winter. . . . One of the very last deer seen near the village was observed about the year 1805, drinking in the early morning from a brook." Nor were the first human inhabitants lacking in wildness. "The first settlement of Cooperstown," wrote William Cooper himself, "was made by the poorer class of men; they labored hard all the week, but on Sunday they either went hunting, or fishing, or else collected in taverns, and loitered away the day, careless of their dress or actions. The sons caught the manners of the fathers. . . ." But thickening population, churches, schools, and magistrates reformed the pioneer manners.

Leatherstocking appears in this rather realistic and at times even caustic picture of a pioneer settlement as a man on the verge of age, too broken physically to shoot with his old unerring aim, but with intellect unimpaired, and spiritual stature greater than ever. The scene in which, after Judge Temple has sentenced him to fine and imprisonment, he asserts his right to freedom as the only means of paying what the law requires, shows him with a fire and eloquence hardly equalled in his earlier career. Chingachgook, alas, has been sadly changed since what Leatherstocking calls "the fifty-eight war"; and religious as the scout is, he regrets that the Moravians ever Christianized the Indian. But though Leatherstocking's own worldly fortunes have sunk, his manly dignity, his heroism, moral and physical, his indomitable independence, and his delicacy of feeling, make him as attractive a hero as ever.

1

NEAR THE CENTER of the state of New York lies an extensive district of country, whose surface is a succession of hills and dales, or, to speak with greater deference to geographical definitions, of mountains and valleys. It is among these hills that the Delaware takes it rise; and flowing from the limpid lakes and thousand springs of this region, the numerous sources of the Susquehanna meander through the valleys, until, uniting their streams, they form one of the proudest rivers of the United States. The mountains are generally arable to the tops, although instances are not wanting, where the sides are jutted with rocks, that aid greatly in giving to the country that romantic and picturesque character which it so eminently possesses. The vales are narrow, rich, and cultivated; with a stream uniformly winding through each. Beautiful and thriving villages are found interspersed along the margins of the small lakes, or situated at those parts of the streams which are favorable to manufacturing; and neat and comfortable farms, with every indication of wealth about them, are scattered profusely through the vales, and even to the mountain tops. Roads diverge in every direction, from the even and graceful bottoms of the valleys, to the most rugged and intricate passes of the hills. Academies, and minor edifices of learning, meet the eye of the stranger, at every few miles, as he winds his way through this uneven territory; and places for the worship of God abound with that frequency which characterizes a moral and reflecting people, and with that variety of exterior and canonical government which flows from unfettered liberty of conscience. In short, the whole district is hourly exhibiting how much can be done, in even a rugged country, and with a severe climate, under the dominion of mild laws, and where every man feels a direct interest in the prosperity of a commonwealth, of which he knows himself to form a part. The expedients of the pioneers who first broke ground in the settlement of this country, are succeeded by the permanent improvements of the yeoman, who intends to leave his remains to moulder under the sod which he tills, or, perhaps, of the son, who, born in the land, piously wishes to linger around the grave of his father. Only forty years [1] have passed since this territory was a wilderness.

Very soon after the establishment of the independence of the States, by the peace of 1783, the enterprise of their citizens was directed to a development of the natural advantages of their widely extended dominions. Before the war of the Revolution the inhabited parts of the colony of New York were limited to less than a tenth of its possessions. A narrow belt of country, extending for a short distance on either side of the Hudson, with a similar occupation of fifty miles on the banks of the Mohawk, together with the islands of Nassau and Staten, and a few insulated settlements on chosen land along the margins of streams, composed the country, which was then inhabited by less than two hundred thousand souls. Within the short period we have mentioned, the population has spread itself over five degrees of latitude and seven of longitude, and has swelled to a million and a half of inhabitants,[2] who are maintained in abundance, and can look forward to ages before the evil day must arrive when their possessions shall become unequal to their wants.

Our tale begins in 1793, about seven years after the commencement of one of earliest of those settlements, which have conduced to effect that magical change in the power and condition of the state, to which we have alluded.

It was near the setting of the sun, on a clear, cold day in December, when a sleigh was moving slowly up one of the mountains, in the district we have described. The day had been fine for the season, and but two or three large clouds, whose color seemed brightened by the light reflected from the mass of snow that covered the earth, floated in a sky of the purest blue. The road wound along the brow of a precipice, and on one side was upheld by a foundation of logs, piled one upon the other, while a narrow excavation in the mountain, in the opposite direction, had made a passage of sufficient width for the ordinary travelling of that day. But logs, excavation, and everything that did not

---

[1] The book was written in 1823. (*Cooper's note*)
[2] The population of New York is now (1831) quite 2,000,000. (*Cooper's note*)

reach several feet above the earth, lay alike buried beneath the snow. A single track, barely wide enough to receive the sleigh,[1] denoted the route of the highway, and this was sunken near two feet below the surrounding surface. In the vale, which lay at a distance of several hundred feet lower, there was what in the language of the country was called a clearing, and all the usual improvements of a new settlement; these even extended up the hill to the point where the road turned short and ran across the level land, which lay on the summit of the mountain; but the summit itself remained in forest. There was a glittering in the atmosphere, as if it were filled with innumerable shining particles, and the noble bay horses that drew the sleigh were covered, in many parts, with a coat of hoarfrost. The vapor from their nostrils was seen to issue like smoke; and every object in the view, as well as every arrangement of the travellers, denoted the depth of a winter in the mountains. The harness, which was of a deep dull black, differing from the glossy varnishing of the present day, was ornamented with enormous plates and buckles of brass, that shone like gold in those transient beams of the sun which found their way obliquely through the tops of the trees. Huge saddles, studded with nails, and fitted with cloth that served as blankets to the shoulders of the cattle, supported four high, square-topped turrets, through which the stout reins led from the mouths of the horses to the hands of the driver, who was a Negro, of apparently twenty years of age. His face, which nature had colored with a glistening black, was now mottled with the cold, and his large shining eyes filled with tears; a tribute to its power, that the keen frosts of those regions always extracted from one of his African origin. Still there was a smiling expression of good humor in his happy countenance, that was created by the thoughts of home, and a Christmas fireside, with its Christmas frolics. The sleigh was one of those large, comfortable old-fashioned conveyances, which would admit a whole family within its bosom, but which now contained only two passengers besides the driver. The color of its outside was a modest green, and that of its inside a fiery red. The latter was intended to convey the idea of heat, in that cold climate. Large buffalo skins, trimmed around the edges with red cloth, cut into festoons, covered the back of the sleigh, and were spread over its bottom, and drawn up around the feet of the

---

[1] Sleigh is the word used in every part of the United States to denote a *traineau*. It is of local use in the west of England, whence it is most probably derived by the Americans. The latter draw a distinction between a sled or sledge, and a sleigh; the sleigh being shod with metal. Sleighs are also subdivided into two-horse and one-horse sleighs. Of the latter, there are the cutter, with thills so arranged as to permit the horse to travel in the side track; the 'pung,' or 'tow-pung,' which is driven with a pole, and the 'gumper,' a rude construction used for temporary purposes, in the new countries.

Many of the American sleighs are elegant, though the use of this mode of conveyance is much lessened with the melioration of the climate, consequent on the clearing of the forests. (*Cooper's note*)

travellers—one of whom was a man of middle age, and the other a female, just entering upon womanhood. The former was of a large stature; but the precautions he had taken to guard against the cold left but little of his person exposed to view. A greatcoat, that was abundantly ornamented by a profusion of furs, enveloped the whole of his figure, excepting the head, which was covered with a cap of marten skins, lined with morocco, the sides of which were made to fall, if necessary, and were now drawn close over the ears, and fastened beneath his chin with a black riband. The top of the cap was surmounted with the tail of the animal whose skin had furnished the rest of the materials, which fell back, not ungracefully, a few inches behind the head. From beneath this mask were to be seen part of a fine manly face, and particularly a pair of expressive, large blue eyes, that promised extraordinary intellect, covert humor, and great benevolence. The form of his companion was literally hid beneath the garments she wore. There were furs and silks peeping from under a large camlet cloak, with a thick flannel lining, that, by its cut and size, was evidently intended for a masculine wearer. A huge hood of black silk, that was quilted with down, concealed the whole of her head, except at a small opening in front for breath, through which occasionally sparkled a pair of animated jet-black eyes.

Both the father and daughter (for such was the connection between the travellers) were too much occupied with their reflections to break a stillness, that received little or no interruption from the easy gliding of the sleigh, by the sound of their voices. The former was thinking of the wife that had held this their only child to her bosom, when, four years before, she had reluctantly consented to relinquish the society of her daughter, in order that the latter might enjoy the advantages of an education, which the city of New York could only offer at that period. A few months afterward, death had deprived him of the remaining companion of his solitude; but still he had enough of real regard for his child, not to bring her into the comparative wilderness in which he dwelt, until the full period had expired, to which he had limited her juvenile labors. The reflections of the daughter were less melancholy, and mingled with a pleased astonishment, at the novel scenery she met at every turn in the road.

The mountain on which they were journeying was covered with pines, that rose without a branch some seventy or eighty feet, and which frequently doubled that height, by the addition of the tops. Through the innumerable vistas that opened beneath the lofty trees, the eye could penetrate, until it was met by a distant inequality in the ground, or was stopped by a view of the summit of the mountain, which lay on the opposite side of the valley to which they were hastening. The dark trunks of the trees rose from the pure white of the snow, in regularly formed shafts, until, at a great height, their branches shot forth horizontal limbs, that were covered with the meager foliage of an evergreen, affording a melancholy contrast to the torpor of nature below. To the travellers there seemed to be no wind; but these pines waved majestically at their topmost boughs, sending forth a dull, plaintive sound, that was quite in consonance with the rest of the melancholy scene.

The sleigh had glided for some distance along the even surface, and the gaze of the female was bent in inquisitive, and, perhaps, timid glances, into the recesses of the forest, when a loud and continued howling was heard, pealing under the long arches of the woods, like the cry of a numerous pack of hounds. The instant the sounds reached the ears of the gentleman, he cried aloud to the black—

"Hold up, Aggy; there is old Hector; I should know his bay among ten thousand! The Leatherstocking has put his hounds into the hills, this clear day, and they have started their game. There is a deer track a few rods ahead;—and now, Bess, if thou canst muster courage enough to stand fire, I will give thee a saddle for thy Christmas dinner."

The black drew up, with a cheerful grin upon his chilled features, and began thrashing his arms together, in order to restore the circulation to his fingers, while the speaker stood erect, and, throwing aside his outer covering, he stepped from the sleigh upon a bank of snow, which sustained his weight without yielding.

In a few moments the speaker succeeded in extricating a double-barreled fowling piece from among a multitude of trunks and band-boxes. After throwing aside the thick mittens which had encased his hands, that now appeared in a pair of leather gloves tipped with fur, he examined his priming, and was about to move forward, when the light bounding noise of an animal plunging through the woods was heard, and a fine buck darted into a path, a short distance ahead of him. The appearance of the animal was sudden, and his flight inconceivably rapid; but the traveller appeared to be too keen a sportsman to be disconcerted by either. As it came first into view he raised the fowling piece to his shoulder, and, with a practiced eye and steady hand, drew a trigger. The deer dashed forward undaunted, and apparently unhurt. Without lowering his piece, the traveller turned its muzzle towards his victim, and fired again. Neither discharge, however, seemed to have taken effect.

The whole scene had passed with a rapidity that confused the female, who was unconsciously rejoicing in the escape of the buck, as he rather darted like a meteor than ran across the road, when a sharp, quick sound struck her ear, quite different from the full, round reports of her father's gun, but still sufficiently distinct to be known as the concussion produced by firearms. At the same instant that she heard this unexpected report, the buck sprang from the snow, to a great height in the air, and directly a second discharge, similar in sound to the first, followed, when the animal came to the earth, falling headlong, and rolling over on the crust with its own velocity. A loud shout was given by the unseen marksman, and a couple of men instantly appeared from behind the trunks of two of the pines, where they had evidently placed themselves in expectation of the passage of the deer.

"Ha! Natty, had I known you were in ambush, I should not have fired," cried the traveller, moving toward the spot where the deer lay —near to which he was followed by the delighted black, with the sleigh; "but the sound of old Hector was too exhilarating to be quiet; though I hardly think I struck him either."

"No—no—Judge," returned the hunter, with an inward chuckle, and with that look of exultation that indicates a consciousness of superior skill; "you burnt your powder, only to warm your nose this cold evening. Did ye think to stop a full-grown buck, with Hector and the slut open upon him, within sound, with that popgun in your hand? There's plenty of pheasants among the swamps; and the snowbirds are flying round your own door, where you may feed them with crumbs, and shoot them at pleasure, any day; but if you're for a buck, or a little bear's meat, Judge, you'll have to take the long rifle, with a greased wadding, or you'll waste more powder than you'll fill stomachs, I'm thinking."

As the speaker concluded, he drew his bare hand across the bottom of his nose, and again opened his enormous mouth with a kind of inward laugh.

"The gun scatters well, Natty, and it has killed a deer before now," said the traveller, smiling good-humoredly. "One barrel was charged with buckshot; but the other was loaded for birds, only. Here are two hurts; one through the neck, and the other directly through the heart. It is by no means certain, Natty, but I gave him one of the two."

"Let who will kill him," said the hunter, rather surlily, "I suppose the creatur' is to be eaten." So saying, he drew a large knife from a leathern sheath, which was stuck through his girdle or sash, and cut the throat of the animal. "If there are two balls through the deer, I would ask if there weren't two rifles fired—besides, who ever saw such a ragged hole from a smoothbore, as this through the neck?—and you will own yourself, Judge, that the buck fell at the last shot, which was sent from a truer and a younger hand than your'n or mine either; but for my part, although I am a poor man, I can live without the venison, but I don't love to give up my lawful dues in a free country. Though, for the matter of that, might often makes right here, as well as in the old country, for what I can see."

An air of sullen dissatisfaction pervaded the manner of the hunter during the whole of this speech; yet he thought it prudent to utter the close of the sentence in such an undertone, as to leave nothing audible but the grumbling sounds of his voice.

"Nay, Natty," rejoined the traveller, with undisturbed good-humor, "it is for the honor that I contend. A few dollars will pay for the venison; but what will requite me for the lost honor of a buck's tail in my cap? Think, Natty, how I should triumph over that quizzing dog, Dick Jones, who has failed seven times already this season, and has only brought in one woodchuck and a few gray squirrels."

"Ah! the game is becoming hard to find, indeed, Judge, with your clearings and betterments," said the old hunter, with a kind of compelled resignation. "The time has been, when I have shot thirteen deer, without counting the fa'ans, standing in the door of my own hut!—and for bear's meat, if one wanted a ham or so, he had only to watch a-nights, and he could shoot one by moonlight, through the cracks of the logs; no fear of his oversleeping himself, neither, for the howling of the wolves was sartain to keep his eyes open. There's old Hector,"—patting with affection a tall hound, of black and yellow spots, with white belly and legs, that just then came in on the scent, accompanied by the slut he had mentioned; "see where the wolves bit his throat, the night I druv them from the venison that was smoking on the chimbly top;—that dog is more to be trusted than many a Christian man; for he never forgets a friend, and loves the hand that gives him bread."

There was a peculiarity in the manner of the hunter, that attracted the notice of the young female, who had been a close and interested observer of his appearance and equipments, from the moment he came into view. He was tall, and so meager as to make him seem above even the six feet that he actually stood in his stockings. On his head, which was thinly covered with lank, sandy hair, he wore a cap made of fox-skin, resembling in shape the one we have already described, although much inferior in finish and ornaments. His face was skinny and thin almost to emaciation; but yet it bore no signs of disease;—on the contrary, it had every indication of the most robust and enduring health. The cold and the exposure had, together, given it a color of uniform red. His gray eyes were glancing under a pair of shaggy brows, that overhung them in long hairs of gray mingled with their natural hue; his scraggy neck was bare, and burnt to the same tint with his face; though a small part of a shirt collar, made of the country check, was to be seen above the overdress he wore. A kind of coat, made of dressed deerskin, with the hair on, was belted close to his lank body, by a girdle of colored worsted. On his feet were deerskin moccasins, ornamented with porcupines' quills, after the manner of the Indians, and his limbs were guarded with long leggings of the same material as the moccasins, which, gartering over the knees of his tarnished buckskin breeches, had obtained for him, among the settlers, the nickname of Leatherstocking. Over his left shoulder was slung a belt of deerskin, from which depended an enormous ox horn, so thinly scraped, as to discover the powder it contained. The larger end was fitted ingeniously and securely with a wooden bottom, and the other was stopped tight by a little plug. A leathern pouch hung before him, from which, as he concluded his last speech, he took a small measure, and, filling it accurately with powder, he commenced reloading the rifle, which, as its butt rested on the snow before him, reached nearly to the top of his foxskin cap.

The traveller had been closely examining the wounds during these movements, and now, without heeding the ill-humor of the hunter's manner, he exclaimed—

"I would fain establish a right, Natty, to the honor of this death; and surely if the hit in the neck be mine, it is enough; for the shot in the heart was unnecessary—what we call an act of supererogation, Leatherstocking."

"You may call it by what larned name you please, Judge," said the hunter, throwing his rifle across his left arm, and knocking up a brass lid in the breech, from which he took a small piece of greased leather, and wrapping a ball in it, forced them down by main strength on the powder, where he continued to pound them while speaking. "It's far easier to call names, than to shoot a buck on the spring; but the creatur' came by his end from a younger hand than either your'n or mine, as I said before."

"What say you, my friend," cried the traveller, turning pleasantly to Natty's companion; "shall we toss up this dollar for the honor, and you keep the silver if you lose; what say you, friend?"

"That I killed the deer," answered the young man, with a little haughtiness, as he leaned on another long rifle, similar to that of Natty's.

"Here are two to one, indeed," replied the Judge, with a smile; "I am outvoted—overruled, as we say on the bench. There is Aggy, he can't vote, being a slave; and Bess is a minor—so I must even make the best of it. But you'll sell me the venison; and the deuce is in it, but I make a good story about its death."

"The meat is none of mine to sell," said Leatherstocking, adopting a little of his companion's hauteur; "for my part I have known animals travel days with shots in the neck, and I'm none of them who'll rob a man of his rightful dues."

"You are tenacious of your rights, this cold evening, Natty," returned the Judge, with unconquerable good nature; "but what say you, young man; will three dollars pay you for the buck?"

"First let us determine the question of right to the satisfaction of us both," said the youth, firmly but respectfully, and with a pronunciation and language vastly superior to his appearance; "with how many shot did you load your gun?"

"With five, sir," said the Judge, a little struck with the other's manner; "are they not enough to slay a buck like this?"

"One would do it; but," moving to the tree from behind which he had appeared, "you know, sir, you fired in this direction—here are four of the bullets in the tree."

The Judge examined the fresh marks in the bark of the pine, and shaking his head, said, with a laugh—

"You are making out the case against yourself, my young advocate—where is the fifth?"

"Here," said the youth, throwing aside the rough overcoat that he wore, and exhibiting a hole in his under garment, through which large drops of blood were oozing.

"Good God!" exclaimed the Judge, with horror; "have I been trifling here about an empty distinction, and a fellow-creature suffering from my hands without a murmur? But hasten—quick—get into my sleigh—it is but a mile to the village, where surgical aid can be obtained;—all shall be done at my expense, and thou shalt live with me until thy wound is healed—ay, and forever afterward."

"I thank you for your good intention, but I must decline your offer. I have a friend who would be uneasy were he to hear that I am hurt and away from him. The injury is but slight, and the bullet has missed the bones; but I believe, sir, you will now admit my title to the venison."

"Admit it!" repeated the agitated Judge; "I here give thee a right to shoot deer, or bears, or anything thou pleasest in my woods, forever. Leatherstocking is the only other man that I have granted the same privilege to; and the time is coming when it will be of value. But I buy your deer—here, this bill will pay thee, both for thy shot and my own."

The old hunter gathered his tall person up into an air of pride, during this dialogue, but he waited until the other had done speaking.

"There's them living who say that Nathaniel Bumppo's right to shoot on these hills is of older date than Marmaduke Temple's right to forbid him," he said. "But if there's a law about it at all, though who ever heard of a law that a man shouldn't kill deer where he pleased!—but if there is a law at all, it should be to keep people from the use of smoothbores. A body never knows where his lead will fly, when he pulls the trigger of one of them uncertain firearms."

Without attending to the soliloquy of Natty, the youth bowed his head silently to the offer of the bank note, and replied—

"Excuse me; I have need of the venison."

"But this will buy you many deer," said the Judge; "take it, I entreat you," and lowering his voice to a whisper, he added—"it is for a hundred dollars."

For an instant only, the youth seemed to hesitate, and then, blushing even through the high color that the cold had given to his cheeks, as if with inward shame at his own weakness, he again declined the offer.

During this scene the female arose, and, regardless of the cold air, she threw back the hood which concealed her features, and now spoke with great earnestness.

"Surely, surely,—young man,—sir—you would not pain my father so much, as to have him think that he leaves a fellow-creature in this wilderness, whom his own hand has injured. I entreat you will go with us and receive medical aid."

Whether his wound became more painful, or there was something irresistible in the voice and manner of the fair pleader for her father's feelings, we know not, but the distance of the young man's manner was sensibly softened by this appeal, and he stood in apparent doubt, as if reluctant to comply with, and yet unwilling to refuse her request. The Judge, for such being his office, must in future be his title, watched, with no little interest, the display of this singular contention in the feelings of the youth, and advancing kindly took his hand, and, as he pulled him gently toward the sleigh, urged him to enter it.

"There is no human aid nearer than Templeton," he said; "and the hut of Natty is full three miles from this;—come—come, my young friend, go with us, and let the new doctor look to this shoulder of thine. Here is Natty will take the tidings of thy welfare to thy friend; and shouldst thou require it, thou shalt return home in the morning."

The young man succeeded in extricating his hand from the warm grasp of the Judge, but he continued to gaze on the face of the female, who, regardless of the cold, was still standing with her fine features exposed, which expressed feelings that eloquently seconded the request of her father. Leatherstocking stood, in the meantime, leaning upon his long rifle with his head turned a little to one side, as if engaged in sagacious musing; when having apparently satisfied his doubts by revolving the subject in his mind, he broke silence.

"It may be best to go, lad, after all; for if the shot hangs under the skin, my hand is getting too old to be cutting into human flesh, as I once used to. Though some thirty years agone, in the old war, when I was out under Sir William, I travelled seventy miles alone in the howling wilderness with a rifle bullet in my thigh, and then cut it out with my own jackknife. Old Indian John knows the time well. I met him with a party of the Delawares on the trail of the Iroquois, who had been down and taken five scalps on the Schoharie. But I made a mark on the redskin that I'll warrant he carried to his grave! I took him on his posteerum, saving the lady's presence, as he got up from the ambushment, and rattled three buckshot into his naked hide, so close that you might have laid a broad joe upon them all"—here Natty stretched out his long neck and straightened his body as he opened his mouth, which exposed a single tusk of yellow bone, while his eyes, his face, even his whole frame seemed to laugh, although no sound was emitted except a kind of thick hissing, as he inhaled his breath in quavers. "I had lost my bullet mould in crossing the Oneida outlet, and had to make shift with the buckshot; but the rifle was true, and didn't scatter like your two-legged thing there, Judge, which don't do, I find, to hunt in company with."

Natty's apology to the delicacy of the young lady was unnecessary, for while he was speaking she was too much employed in helping her father to remove certain articles of baggage to hear him. Unable to resist the kind urgency of the travellers any longer, the youth, though still with an unaccountable reluctance, suffered himself to be persuaded to enter the sleigh. The black, with the aid of his master, threw the buck across the baggage, and entering the vehicle themselves, the Judge invited the hunter to do so likewise.

"No, no," said the old man, shaking his head; "I have work to do at home this Christmas Eve—drive on with the boy, and let your doctor look to the shoulder; though if he will only cut out the shot, I have yarbs that will heal the wound quicker than all his foreign 'intments." He turned and was about to move off, when, suddenly recollecting himself he again faced the party and added—"If you see anything of Indian John about the foot of the lake, you had better take him with you and let him lend the doctor a hand; for old as he is, he is curious at cuts and bruises, and it's likelier than not he'll be in with brooms to sweep your Christmas ha'arths."

"Stop, stop!" cried the youth, catching the arm of the black as he prepared to urge his horses forward; "Natty—you need say nothing of the shot, nor of where I am going—remember, Natty, as you love me!"

"Trust old Leatherstocking," returned the hunter significantly; "he hasn't lived fifty years in the wilderness and not l'arnt from the savages how to hold his tongue—trust to me, lad; and remember old Indian John."

"And, Natty," said the youth eagerly, still holding the black by the arm, "I will just get the shot extracted, and bring you up tonight a quarter of the buck for the Christmas dinner."

He was interrupted by the hunter, who held up his finger with an expressive gesture for silence. He then moved softly along the margin of the road keeping his eyes steadfastly fixed on the branches of a pine. When he had obtained such a position as he wished, he stopped, and cocking his rifle, threw one leg far behind him, and stretching his left arm to its utmost extent along the barrel of his piece, he began slowly to raise its muzzle in a line with the straight trunk of the tree. The eyes of the group in the sleigh naturally preceded the movement of the rifle, and they soon discovered the object of Natty's aim. On a small dead branch of the pine, which at the distance of seventy feet from the ground shot out horizontally immediately beneath the living members of the tree, sat a bird that in the vulgar language of the country was indiscriminately called a pheasant or a partridge. In size it was but little smaller than a common barnyard fowl. The baying of the dogs, and the conversation that had passed near the root of the tree on which it was perched, had alarmed the bird, which was now drawn up near the body of the pine, with a head and neck so erect as to form nearly a straight line with its legs. As soon as the rifle bore on the victim, Natty drew his trigger, and the partridge fell from its height with a force that buried it in the snow.

"Lie down, you old villain," exclaimed Leatherstocking, shaking his ramrod at Hector as he bounded toward the foot of the tree, "lie down, I say." The dog obeyed, and Natty proceeded with great rapidity, though with the nicest accuracy, to reload his piece. When this was ended he took up his game, and showing it to the party, without a head, he cried—"Here is a titbit for an old man's Christmas—never mind the venison, boy, and remember Indian John; his yarbs are better than all the foreign 'intments. Here, Judge," holding up the bird again, "do you think a smoothbore would pick game off their roost and not ruffle a feather?" The old man gave another of his remarkable laughs, which partook so largely of exultation, mirth, and irony, and shaking his head, he turned with his rifle at a trail, and moved into the forest with steps that were between a walk and a trot. At each movement he made, his body lowered several inches, his knees yielding with an inclination inward; but as the sleigh turned at a bend in the road, the youth cast his eyes in quest of his old companion, and he saw that he was already nearly concealed by the trunks of the trees, while his dogs were following quietly in his footsteps, occasionally scenting the deer track that they seemed to know instinctively was now of no further use to them. Another jerk was given to the sleigh, and Leatherstocking was hid from view.

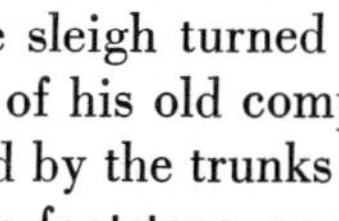

2

JUDGE MARMADUKE TEMPLE, the wealthiest and most important resident of the village of Templeton, took the young stranger to his house for medical treatment. While waiting for the doctor, the young man was introduced to several leading figures of the neighborhood. One was Judge Temple's nephew and general factotum, Squire Richard Jones, whose vocation (when he chose to work) was that of architect; another was Monsieur Le Quoi, a short, foreign-looking French refugee; a third was Major Frederick Hartman, a Revolutionary veteran of Palatinate German extraction. The young man also became acquainted with the redfaced butler or major-domo of the Judge's household, Benjamin Penguillum; with Elizabeth Temple's housekeeper, a sharp-visaged woman named Remarkable Pettibone; and with the Rev. Mr. Grant, the Episcopal clergyman of the village. All these people made up a picturesque group.

The frontier physician, Dr. Elnathan Todd, shortly arrived, made an incision, and extracted the ball from the young man's shoulder. Already Judge Temple had offered the stranger the hospitality of the Temple mansion, an imposing house richly furnished. The newcomer, however, seemed to regard the Judge with cold suspicion, and declined the invitation.

"I thank you, sir, for what you have done," he said austerely, "but here is one who will take me under his care, and spare you all, gentlemen, any further trouble on my account." The whole group turned in surprise, and saw at one of the distant doors of the hall,

the tall person of Indian John—that is, of Chingachgook, now in his later years a Christian resident of the community. His history since the time of the French wars required some explanation.

Before the Europeans, or, to use a more significant term, the Christians, dispossessed the original owners of the soil, all that section of country which contains the New England States, and those of the Middle, which lie east of the mountains, was occupied by two great nations of Indians from whom had descended numberless tribes. But, as the original distinctions between these nations were marked by a difference in language, as well as by repeated and bloody wars, they never were known to amalgamate until after the power and inroads of the whites had reduced some of the tribes to a state of dependence that rendered not only their political, but, considering the wants and habits of a savage, their animal existence also, extremely precarious.

These two great divisions consisted, on the one side, of the Five, or, as they were afterwards called, the Six Nations, and their allies; and, on the other, of the Lenni Lenape or Delawares, with the numerous and powerful tribes that owned that nation as their Grandfather. The former were generally called by the Anglo-Americans, Iroquois, or the Six Nations, and sometimes Mingoes. Their appellation among their rivals seems generally to have been the Mengwe, or Maqua. They consisted of the tribes, or, as their allies were fond of asserting in order to raise their consequence, of the several nations of the Mohawks, the Oneidas, the Onondagas, Cayugas, and Senecas; who ranked, in the confederation, in the order in which they are named. The Tuscaroras were admitted to this union near a century after its formation, and thus completed the number to six.

Of the Lenni Lenape, or as they were called by the whites, from the circumstance of their holding their great council fire on the banks of that river, the Delaware Nation, the principal tribes besides that which bore the generic name were, the Mahicanni, Mohicans or Mohegans, and the Nanticokes or Nentigoes. Of these, the latter held the country along the waters of the Chesapeake and the seashore; while the Mohegans occupied the district between the Hudson and the ocean, including much of New England. Of course, these two tribes were the first who were dispossessed of their lands by the Europeans.

The wars of a portion of the latter are celebrated among us, as the wars of King Philip; but the peaceful policy of William Penn, or Miquon, as he was termed by the natives, effected its object with less difficulty, though not with less certainty. As the natives gradually disappeared from the country of the Mohegans, some scattering families sought a refuge around the council fire of the mother tribe, or the Delawares.

This people had been induced to suffer themselves to be called *women,* by their old enemies the Mingoes, or Iroquois, after the latter, having in vain tried the effects of hostility, had recourse to artifice in order to prevail over their rivals. According to this declaration the Delawares were to cultivate the arts of peace, and to entrust their defence entirely to the *men,* or warlike tribes of the Six Nations.

This state of things continued until the war of the Revolution, when the Lenni Lenape formally asserted their independence, and fearlessly declared that they were again men. But in a government so peculiarly republican as the Indian polity it was not, at all times, an easy task to restrain its members within the rules of the nation. Several fierce and renowned warriors of the Mohegans, finding the conflict with the whites to be in vain, sought a refuge with their Grandfather, and brought with them the feelings and principles that had so long distinguished them in their own tribe. These chieftains kept alive, in some measure, the martial spirit of the Delawares; and would, at times, lead small parties against their ancient enemies, or such other foes as incurred their resentment.

Among these warriors was one race particularly famous for their prowess and for those qualities that render an Indian hero celebrated. But war, time, disease, and want had conspired to thin their number; and the sole representative of this once renowned family now stood in the hall of Marmaduke Temple. He had, for a long time, been an associate of the white men, particularly in their wars; and having been, at a season when his services were of importance, much noticed and flattered, he had turned Christian, and was baptized by the name of John. He had suffered severely in his family during the recent war, having had every soul to whom he was allied cut off by an inroad of the enemy; and when the last, lingering remnant of his nation extinguished their fires among the hills of the Delaware, he alone had remained, with a determination of laying his bones in that country where his father had so long lived and governed.

It was only, however, within a few months that he had appeared among the mountains that surrounded Templeton. To the hut of the old hunter he seemed peculiarly welcome; and, as the habits of the Leather-stocking were so nearly assimilated to those of the savages, the conjunction of their interests excited no surprise. They resided in the same cabin, ate of the same food, and were chiefly occupied in the same pursuits.

We have already mentioned the baptismal name of this ancient chief; but in his conversation with Natty, held in the language of the Delawares, he was heard uniformly to call himself Chingachgook, which, interpreted, means the Great Snake. This name he had acquired in youth by his skill and prowess in war; but when his brows began to wrinkle with time, and he stood alone, the last of his family and his particular tribe, the few Delawares who yet continued about the head-waters of their river gave him the mournful appellation of Mohegan. Perhaps there was something of deep feeling excited in the bosom of this inhabitant of the forest by the sound of a name that recalled the idea of his nation in ruins, for he seldom used it himself—never indeed, excepting on the most solemn occasions; but the settlers had united, according to the Christian custom, his baptismal with his national name, and to them he was generally known as John Mohegan, or, more familiarly, as Indian John.

From his long association with the white men the habits of Mohegan were a mixture of the civilized and savage states, though there was certainly a strong preponderance in favor of the latter. In common with all his people who dwelt within the influence of the Ango-Americans he had acquired new wants, and his dress was a mixture of his native and European fashions. Notwithstanding the intense cold without, his head was uncovered; but a profusion of long, black, coarse hair concealed his forehead, his crown, and even hung about his cheeks, so as to convey the idea, to one who knew his present and former conditions, that he encouraged its abundance as a willing veil to hide the shame of a noble soul, mourning for glory once known. His forehead, when it could be seen, appeared lofty, broad, and noble. His nose was high, and of the kind called Roman, with nostrils that expanded, in his seventieth year, with the freedom that had distinguished them in youth. His mouth was large, but compressed, and possessing a great share of expression and character, and, when opened, it discovered a perfect set of short, strong, and regular teeth. His chin was full, though not prominent; and his face bore the infallible mark of his people in its square, high cheekbones. The eyes were not large, but their black orbs glittered in the rays of the candles, as he gazed intently down the hall, like two balls of fire.

The instant that Mohegan observed himself to be noticed by the group around the young stranger, he dropped the blanket which covered the upper part of his frame from his shoulders, suffering it to fall over his leggings of untanned deerskin, where it was retained by a belt of bark that confined it to his waist.

As he walked slowly down the long hall, the dignified and deliberate tread of the Indian surprised the spectators. His shoulders, and body to his waist, were entirely bare, with the exception of a silver medallion of Washington that was suspended from his neck by a thong of buckskin, and rested on his high chest amidst many scars. His shoulders were rather broad and full; but the arms, though straight and graceful, wanted the muscular appearance that labor gives to a race of men. The medallion was the only ornament he wore, although enormous slits in the rim of either ear which suffered the cartilages to fall two inches below the members, had evidently been used for the purposes of decoration in other days. In his hand he held a small basket of the ash-wood slips, colored in divers fantastical conceits with red and black paints mingled with the white of the wood.

As this child of the forest approached them, the whole party stood aside, and allowed him to confront the object of his visit. He did not speak, however, but stood fixing his glowing eyes on the shoulder of the young hunter, and then turning them intently on the countenance of the Judge. The latter was a good deal astonished at this unusual departure from the ordinarily subdued and quiet manner of the Indian; but he extended his hand, and said—

"Thou art welcome, John. This youth entertains a high opinion of thy skill, it seems, for he prefers thee to dress his wound even to our good friend Dr. Todd."

Mohegan now spoke in tolerable English, but in a low, monotonous, guttural tone—

"The children of Miquon do not love the sight of blood; and yet, the Young Eagle has been struck by the hand that should do no evil!"

"Mohegan! old John!" exclaimed the Judge, "thinkest thou that my hand has ever drawn human blood willingly? For shame! for shame, old John! thy religion should have taught thee better."

"The Evil Spirit sometimes lives in the best heart," returned John, "but my brother speaks the truth; his hand has never taken life, when awake; no! not even when the children of the great English Father were making the waters red with the blood of his people."

"Surely, John," said Mr. Grant, with much earnestness, "you remember the divine command of our Saviour, Judge not, lest ye be judged. What motive could Judge Temple have for injuring a youth like this; one to whom he is unknown, and from whom he can receive neither injury nor favor?"

John listened respectfully to the divine, and when he had concluded, he stretched out his arm and said with energy—

"He is innocent—my brother has not done this."

Marmaduke received the offered hand of the other with a smile, that showed, however he might be astonished at his suspicion, he had ceased to resent it; while the wounded youth stood, gazing from his red friend to his host, with interest powerfully delineated in his countenance. No sooner was this act of pacification exchanged than John proceeded to discharge the duty on which he had come. Dr. Todd was far from manifesting any displeasure at this invasion of his rights, but made way for the new leech with an air that expressed a willingness to gratify the humors of his patient, now that the all-important part of the business was so successfully performed, and nothing remained to be done but what any child might effect. Indeed, he whispered as much to Monsieur Le Quoi, when he said—

"It was fortunate that the ball was extracted before this Indian came in; but any old woman can dress the wound. The young man, I hear, lives with John and Natty Bumppo, and it's always best to humor a patient when it can be done discreetly—I say, discreetly, Monsieur."

"Certainement," returned the Frenchman; "you seem ver happy, Mister Todd, in your pratique. I tink de elder lady might ver well finish vat you so skeelfully begin."

But Richard had, at the bottom, a great deal of veneration for the knowledge of Mohegan, especially in external wounds; and retaining all his desire for a participation in glory, he advanced nigh the Indian, and said—

"Sago, sago, Mohegan! sago, my good fellow! I am glad you have come; give me a regular physician, like Dr. Todd, to cut into flesh, and a native to heal the wound. Do you remember, John, the time when I and you set the bone of Natty Bumppo's little finger, after he broke it by falling from the rock, when he was trying to get the partridge that fell on the cliffs. I never could tell yet whether it was I or Natty who killed that bird: he fired first, and the bird stooped, but then it was rising again as I pulled trigger. I should have claimed it, for a certainty, but Natty said the hole was too big for shot, and he fired a single ball from his rifle; but the piece I carried then didn't scatter, and I have known it to bore a hole through a board, when I've been shooting at the mark, very much like rifle bullets. Shall I help you, John? You know I have a knack at these things."

Mohegan heard this disquisition quite patiently, and when Richard concluded, he held out the basket which contained his specifics, indicating, by a gesture, that he might hold it. Mr. Jones was quite satisfied with this commission; and, ever after, in speaking of the event, was used to say that "Doctor Todd and I cut out the bullet, and I and Indian John dressed the wound."

The patient was much more deserving of that epithet while under the hands of Mohegan, than while suffering under the practice of the physician. Indeed, the Indian gave him but little opportunity for the exercise of a forbearing temper, as he had come prepared for the occasion. His dressings were soon applied, and consisted only of some pounded bark, moistened with a fluid that he had expressed from some of the simples of the woods.

Among the native tribes of the forest, there were always two kinds of leeches to be met with. The one placed its whole dependence on the exercise of a supernatural power, and was held in greater veneration than their practice could at all justify; but the other was really endowed with great skill in the ordinary complaints of the human body, and was, more particularly, as Natty had intimated, "cur'ous in cuts and bruises."

While John and Richard were placing the dressings on the wound, Elnathan was acutely eyeing the contents of Mohegan's basket, which Mr. Jones in his physical ardor had transferred to the Doctor, in order to hold, himself, one end of the bandages. Here he was soon enabled to detect sundry fragments of wood and bark, of which he, quite coolly, took possession, very possibly without any intention of speaking at all upon the subject; but when he beheld the full blue eye of Marmaduke watching his movements, he whispered to the Judge—

"It is not to be denied, Judge Temple, but what the savages are knowing in small matters of physic. They hand these things down in their traditions. Now in cancers and hydrophoby they are quite ingenious. I will just take this bark home and analyze it; for, though it can't be worth sixpence to the young man's shoulder, it may be good for the toothache, or rheumatism, or some of them complaints. A man should never be above learning, even if it be from an Indian."

It was fortunate for Dr. Todd that his principles were so liberal, as, coupled with his practice, they were the means by which he acquired all his knowledge, and by which he was gradually qualifying himself for the duties of his profession. The process to which he subjected the specific, differed, however, greatly from the ordinary rules of chemistry; for, instead of separating, he afterwards united the component parts of Mohegan's remedy, and thus was able to discover the tree whence the Indian had taken it.

Some ten years after this event, when civilization and its refinements had crept, or rather rushed, into the settlements among these wild hills, an affair of honor occurred, and Elnathan was seen to apply a salve to the wound received by one of the parties, which had the flavor that was peculiar to the tree or root that Mohegan had used. Ten years later still, when England and the United States were again engaged in war, and the hordes of the western parts of the state of New York were rushing to the field, Elnathan, presuming on the reputation obtained by these two operations, followed in the rear of a brigade of militia as its surgeon!

When Mohegan had applied the bark, he freely relinquished to Richard the needle and thread that were used in sewing the bandages, for these were implements of which the native but little understood the use; and, stepping back with decent gravity awaited the completion of the business by the other.

"Reach me the scissors," said Mr. Jones, when he had finished, and finished for the second time, after tying the linen in every shape and form that it could be placed; "reach me the scissors, for here is a thread that must be cut off, or it might get under the dressings and inflame the wound. See, John, I have put the lint I scraped between two layers of the linen; for though the bark is certainly best for the flesh, yet the lint will serve to keep the cold air from the wound. If any lint will do it good, it is this lint; I scraped it myself, and I will not turn my back at scraping lint to any man on the Patent. I ought to know how, if anybody ought, for my grandfather was a doctor and my father had a natural turn that way."

"Here, Squire, is the scissors," said Remarkable, producing from beneath her petticoat of green moreen a pair of dull-looking shears; "well, upon my say-so, you *have* sewed on the rags as well as a woman."

"As well as a woman!" echoed Richard, with indignation; "what do women know of such matters? and you are proof of the truth of what I say. Who ever saw such a pair of shears used about a wound? Dr. Todd, I will thank you for the scissors from the case. Now, young man, I think you'll do. The shot has been very neatly taken out, although, perhaps, seeing I had a hand in it I ought not to say so; and the wound is admirably dressed. You will soon be well again; though the jerk you gave my leaders must have a tendency to inflame the shoulder, yet you will do, you will do. You were rather flurried, I suppose, and not used to horses; but I forgive the accident for the motive:—no doubt you had the best of motives;—yes, now you will do."

"Then, gentlemen," said the wounded stranger, rising and resuming his clothes, "it will be unnecessary for me to trespass longer on your time and patience. There remains but one thing more to be settled, and that is, our respective rights to the deer, Judge Temple."

"I acknowledge it to be thine," said Marmaduke; "and much more deeply am I indebted to thee, than for this piece of venison. But in the morning thou wilt call here, and we can adjust this as well as more important matters. Elizabeth,"—for the young lady being apprised that the wound was dressed had re-entered the hall,—"thou wilt order a repast for this youth before we proceed to the church; and Aggy will have a sleigh prepared to convey him to his friend."

"But, sir, I cannot go without a part of the deer," returned the youth, seemingly struggling with his own feelings; "I have already told you that I needed the venison for myself."

"Oh! we will not be particular," exclaimed Richard; "the Judge will pay you in the morning for the whole deer; and, Remarkable, give the lad all the animal excepting the saddle; so on the whole, I think you may consider yourself as a very lucky young man;—you have been shot without being disabled; have had the wound dressed in the best possible manner here in the woods, as well as it would have been done in the Philadelphia hospital, if not better; have sold your deer at a high price, and yet can keep most of the carcass with the skin in the bargain. 'Marky, tell Tom to give him the skin too; and in the morning bring the skin to me and I will give you half a dollar for it, or at least three and sixpence. I want just such a skin to cover the pillion that I am making for Cousin Bess."

"I thank you, sir, for your liberality, and I trust am also thankful for my escape," returned the stranger; "but you reserve the very part of the animal that I wished for my own use. I must have the saddle myself."

"Must!" echoed Richard; "must is harder to be swallowed than the horns of the buck."

"Yes, must," repeated the youth: when, turning his head proudly around him, as if to see who would dare to controvert his rights, he met the astonished gaze of Elizabeth and proceeded more mildly—"that is, if a man is allowed the possession of that which his hand hath killed, and the law will protect him in the enjoyment of his own."

"The law will do so," said Judge Temple, with an air of mortification mingled with surprise. "Benjamin, see that the whole deer is placed in the sleigh; and have this youth conveyed to the hut of Leatherstocking. But, young man, thou hast a name, and I shall see you again in order to compensate thee for the wrong I have done thee?"

"I am called Edwards," returned the hunter, "Oliver Edwards. I am easily to be seen, sir, for I live nigh by, and am not afraid to show my face, having never injured any man."

"It is we who have injured you, sir," said Elizabeth; "and the knowledge that you decline our assistance would give my father great pain. He would gladly see you in the morning."

The young hunter gazed at the fair speaker until his earnest look brought the blood to her temples; when, recollecting himself, he bent his head, dropping his eyes to the carpet, and replied—

"In the morning, then, will I return and see Judge Temple; and I will accept his offer of the sleigh in token of amity."

"Amity!" repeated Marmaduke; "there was no malice in the act that injured thee, young man; there should be none in the feelings which it may engender."

"Forgive our trespasses, as we forgive those who trespass against us," observed Mr. Grant, "is the language used by our Divine Master Himself, and it should be the golden rule of us, His humble followers."

The stranger stood a moment lost in thought, and then glancing his dark eyes rather wildly around the hall, he bowed low to the divine, and moved from the apartment with an air that would not admit of detention.

" 'Tis strange that one so young should harbor such feelings of resentment," said Marmaduke, when the door closed behind the stranger; "but while the pain is recent and the sense of the injury so fresh, he must feel more strongly than in cooler moments. I doubt not we shall see him in the morning more tractable."

Elizabeth, to whom this speech was addressed, did not reply, but moved slowly up the hall by herself, fixing her eyes on the little figure of the English ingrained carpet that covered the floor; while, on the other hand, Richard gave a loud crack with his whip as the stranger disappeared, and cried—

"Well, 'Duke, you are your own master, but I would have tried law for the saddle before I would have given it to the fellow. Do you not own the mountains as well as the valleys? are not the woods your own? what right has this chap or the Leatherstocking to shoot in your woods without your permission? Now, I have known a farmer in Pennsylvania order a sportsman off his farm with as little ceremony as I would order Benjamin to put a log in the stove. By the bye, Benjamin, see how the thermometer stands. Now, if a man has a right to do this on a farm of a hundred acres, what power must a landlord have who owns sixty thousand—ay! for the matter of that, including the late purchases a hundred thousand? There is Mohegan, to be sure, he may have some right, being a native; but it's little the poor fellow can do now with his rifle. How is this managed in France, Monsieur Le Quoi? do you let everybody run over your land in that country, helter-skelter as they do here, shooting the game so that a gentleman has but little or no chance with his gun?"

"Bah! diable, no, Meester Deeck," replied the Frenchman; "we give in France no liberty except to de ladi."

"Yes, yes, to the women, I know," said Richard; "that is your Salick law. I read, sir, all kinds of books; of France as well as England; of Greece as well as Rome. But if I were in 'Duke's place I would stick up advertisements tomorrow morning, forbidding all persons to shoot or trespass in any manner on my woods. I could write such an advertisement myself in an hour as would put a stop to the thing at once."

"Richart," said Major Hartmann, very coolly knocking the ashes from his pipe into the spitting-box by his side, "now listen; I have livet seventy-five years on ter Mohawk and in ter woots. You hat petter mettle as mit ter deyvel, as mit ter hunters. Tey live mit ter gun, and a rifle is petter as ter law."

"A'nt Marmaduke a judge?" said Richard indignantly. "Where is the use of being a judge or having a judge if there is no law? Damn the fellow! I have a great mind to sue him in the morning myself, before Squire Doolittle for meddling with my leaders. I am not afraid of his rifle. I can shoot too. I have hit a dollar many a time at fifty rods."

"Thou hast missed more dollars than ever thou hast hit, Dickon," exclaimed the cheerful voice of the Judge. "But we will now take our evening's repast which, I perceive by Remarkable's physiognomy, is ready. Monsieur Le Quoi, Miss Temple has a hand at your service. Will you lead the way, my child?"

"Ah! ma chère Mam'selle, comme je suis enchanté!" said the Frenchman. "Il ne manque que les dames de faire un paradis de Templeton."

Mr. Grant and Mohegan continued in the hall, while the remainder of the party withdrew to an eating parlor, if we except Benjamin, who civilly remained, to close the rear after the clergyman, and to open the front door for the exit of the Indian.

"John," said the divine, when the figure of Judge Temple disappeared, the last of the group, "tomorrow is the festival of the nativity of our blessed Redeemer, when the church has appointed prayers and thanksgivings to be offered up by her children, and when all are invited to partake of the mystical elements. As you have taken up the cross, and become a follower of good, and an eschewer of evil, I trust I shall see you before the altar with a contrite heart and a meek spirit."

"John will come," said the Indian, betraying no surprise; though he did not understand all the terms used by the other.

"Yes," continued Mr. Grant, laying his hand gently on the tawny shoulder of the aged chief, "but it is not enough to be there in the body; you must come in the spirit and in truth. The Redeemer died for all, for the poor Indian as well as for the white man. Heaven knows no difference in color; nor must earth witness a separation of the church. It is good and profitable, John, to freshen the understanding, and support the wavering, by the observance of our holy festivals; but all form is but stench in the nostrils of the Holy One, unless it be accompanied by a devout and humble spirit."

The Indian stepped back a little, and, raising his body to its utmost powers of erection, he stretched his right arm on high, and dropped his forefinger downward as if pointing from the heavens, then striking his other hand on his naked breast, he said, with energy—

"The eye of the Great Spirit can see from the clouds;—the bosom of Mohegan is bare!"

"It is well, John, and I hope you will receive profit and consolation from the performance of this duty. The Great Spirit overlooks none of His children; and the man of the woods is as much an object of His care, as he who dwells in a palace. I wish you a good night, and pray God to bless you."

The Indian bent his head, and they separated—the one to seek his hut, and the other to join the party at the supper table. While Benjamin was opening the door for the passage of the chief, he cried, in a tone that was meant to be encouraging—

"The parson says the word that is true, John. If so be that they took count of the color of a skin in heaven, why, they might refuse to muster on their books a Christian-born, like myself, just for the matter of a little tan, from cruising in warm latitudes; though, for the matter of that, this damned nor'wester is enough to whiten the skin of a blackamoor. Let the reefs out of your blanket, man, or your red hide will hardly weather the night, without a touch from the frost."

3

WE HAVE MADE our readers acquainted with some variety in character and nations, in introducing the most important personages of this legend to their notice: but, in order to establish the fidelity of our narrative, we shall briefly attempt to explain the reason why we have been obliged to present so motley a *dramatis personæ.*

Europe, at the period of our tale, was in the commencement of that commotion which afterwards shook her political institutions to the center. Louis the Sixteenth had been beheaded, and a nation, once esteemed the most refined among the civilized people of the world, was changing its character, and substituting cruelty for mercy, and subtlety and ferocity for magnanimity and courage. Thousands of Frenchmen were compelled to seek protection in distant lands. Among the crowds who fled from France and her islands, to the United States of America, was the gentleman whom we have already mentioned as Monsieur Le Quoi. He had been recommended to the favor of Judge Temple, by the head of an eminent mercantile house in New York, with whom Marmaduke was in habits of intimacy, and accustomed to exchange good offices. At his first interview with the Frenchman, our Judge had discovered him to be a man of breeding, and one who had seen much more prosperous days in his own country. From certain hints that had escaped him, Monsieur Le Quoi was suspected of having been a West India planter, great numbers of whom had fled from San Domingo and the other islands, and were now living in the Union, in a state of comparative poverty, and some in absolute want. The latter was not, however, the lot of Monsieur Le Quoi. He had but little, he acknowledged, but that little was enough to furnish, in the language of the country, an assortment for a store.

The knowledge of Marmaduke was eminently practical, and there was no part of a settler's life with which he was not familiar. Under his direction, Monsieur Le Quoi made some purchases, consisting of a few cloths; some groceries, with a good deal of gunpowder and tobacco; a quantity of ironware, among which was a large proportion of Barlow's jackknives, potash kettles, and spiders; a very formidable collection of crockery, of the coarsest quality and most uncouth forms; together with every other common article that the art of man has devised for his wants, not forgetting the luxuries of looking glasses and Jews'-harps. With this collection of valuables, Monsieur Le Quoi had stepped behind a counter, and, with a wonderful pliability of temperament, had dropped into his assumed character as gracefully as he had ever moved in any other. The gentleness and suavity of his manners rendered him extremely popular; besides this, the women soon discovered that he had a taste. His calicoes were the finest, or, in other words, the most showy, of any that were brought into the country; and it was impossible to look at the prices asked for his goods by "so pretty a spoken man." Through these conjoint means the affairs of Monsieur Le Quoi were again in a prosperous condition, and he was looked up to by the settlers as the second-best man on the Patent.

This term, "Patent," which we have already used, and for which we may have further occasion, meant the district of country that had been originally granted to old Major Effingham by the "King's letters patent," and which had now become, by purchase under the act of confiscation, the property of Marmaduke Temple. It was a term in common use throughout the *new* parts of the state; and was usually annexed to the landlord's name, as Temple's or Effingham's Patent.

Major Hartmann was the descendant of a man who, in company with a number of his countrymen, had emigrated, with their families, from the banks of the Rhine to those of the Mohawk. This migration had occurred as far back as the reign of Queen Anne; and their descendants were now living, in great peace and plenty, on the fertile borders of that beautiful stream.

The Germans, or High Dutchers, as they were called, to distinguish them from the original or Low Dutch colonists, were a very peculiar people. They possessed all the gravity of the latter, without any of their phlegm; and, like them, the High Dutchers were industrious, honest, and economical.

Fritz, or Frederick, Hartmann was an epitome of all the vices and virtues, foibles and excellences, of his race. He was passionate, though silent, obstinate, and a good deal suspicious of strangers; of immovable courage, inflexible honesty, and undeviating in his friendships. Indeed there was no change about him, unless it were from grave to gay. He was serious by months, and jolly by weeks. He had, early in their acquaintance, formed an attachment for Marmaduke Temple, who was the only man that could not speak High Dutch that ever gained his entire confidence. Four times in each year, at periods equidistant, he left his low stone dwelling on the banks of the Mohawk, and travelled thirty miles, through the hills, to the door of the mansion house in Templeton. Here he generally stayed a week; and was reputed to spend much of that time in riotous living, greatly countenanced by Mr. Richard Jones. But everyone loved him, even to Remarkable Pettibone, to whom he occasioned some additional trouble, he was so frank, so sincere, and, at times, so mirthful. He was now on his regular Christmas visit, and had not been in the village an hour when Richard summoned him to fill a seat in the sleigh, to meet the landlord and his daughter.

Before explaining the character and situation of Mr. Grant, it will be necessary to recur to times far back in the brief history of the settlement.

There seems to be a tendency in human nature to endeavor to provide for the wants of this world, before our attention is turned to the business of the other. Religion was a quality but little cultivated amid the stumps of Temple's Patent for the first few years of its settlement; but, as most of its inhabitants were from the moral states of Connecticut and Massachusetts, when the wants of nature were satisfied, they began seriously to turn their attention to the introduction of those customs and observances which had been the principal care of their forefathers. There was certainly a great variety of opinions on the subject of grace and free will among the tenantry of Marmaduke; and, when we take into consideration the variety of the religious instruction which they received, it can easily be seen that it could not well be otherwise.

Soon after the village had been formally laid out into the streets and blocks that resembled a city, a meeting of its inhabitants had been convened, to take into consideration the propriety of establishing an academy. This measure originated with Richard, who, in truth, was much disposed to have the institution designated a university, or at least a college. Meeting after meeting was held, for this purpose, year after year. The resolutions of these assemblages appeared in the most conspicuous columns of a little, blue-looking newspaper, that was already issued weekly from the garret of a dwelling house in the village, and which the traveller might as often see stuck into the fissure of a stake, erected at the point where the footpath from the log cabin of some settler entered the highway, as a post office for an individual. Sometimes the stake supported a small box, and a whole neighborhood received a weekly supply for their literary wants, at this point, where the man who "rides post" regularly deposited a bundle of the precious commodity. To these flourishing resolutions, which briefly recounted the general utility of education, the political and geographical rights of the village of Templeton to a participation in the favors of the regents of the university, the salubrity of the air, and wholesomeness of the water, together with the cheapness of food and the superior state of morals in the neighborhood, were uniformly annexed, in large Roman capitals, the names of Marmaduke Temple as chairman, and Richard Jones as secretary.

Happily for the success of this undertaking, the regents were not accustomed to resist these appeals to their generosity, whenever there was the smallest prospect of a donation to second the request. Eventually Judge Temple concluded to bestow the necessary land, and to erect the required edifice at his own expense. The skill of Mister, or, as he was now called, from the circumstance of having received the commission of a justice of the peace, Squire Doolittle, was again put in requisition; and the science of Mr. Jones was once more resorted to.

We shall not recount the different devices of the architects on the occasion; nor would it be decorous so to do, seeing that there was a convocation of the society of the ancient and honourable fraternity "of the Free and Accepted Masons," at the head of whom was Richard, in the capacity of master, doubtless to approve or reject such of the plans as, in their wisdom, they deemed to be for the best. The knotty point was, however, soon decided; and, on the appointed day, the brotherhood marched in great state, displaying sundry banners and mysterious symbols, each man with a little mimic apron before him, from a most cunningly contrived apartment in the garret of the "Bold Dragoon," an inn kept by one Captain Hollister, to the site of the intended edifice.

Here Richard laid the cornerstone, with suitable gravity, amidst an assemblage of more than half the men, and all the women, within ten miles of Templeton.

In the course of the succeeding week there was another meeting of the people, not omitting swarms of the gentler sex, when the abilities of Hiram, at the "square rule," were put to the test of experiment. The frame fitted well; and the skeleton of the fabric was reared without a single accident, if we except a few falls from horses while the laborers were returning home in the evening. From this time the work advanced with great rapidity, and in the course of the season the labor was completed; the edifice standing, in all its beauty and proportions, the boast of the village, the study of young aspirants for architectural fame, and the admiration of every settler on the Patent.

It was a long, narrow house of wood, painted white, and more than half windows; and when the observer stood at the western side of the building, the edifice offered but a small obstacle to a full view of the rising sun. It was, in truth, but a very comfortless open place, through which the daylight shone with natural facility. On its front were divers ornaments in wood, designed by Richard, and executed by Hiram; but a window in the center of the second story, immediately over the door, or grand entrance, and the "steeple," were the pride of the building. The former was, we believe, of the composite order; for it included in its composition a multitude of ornaments, and a great variety of proportions. It consisted of an arched compartment in the center, with a square and small division on either side, the whole encased in heavy frames, deeply and laboriously moulded in pine-wood, and lighted with a vast number of blurred and green-looking glass of those dimensions which are commonly called "eight by ten." Blinds, that were intended to be painted green, kept the window in a state of preservation; and probably might have contributed to the effect of the whole, had not the failure in the public funds, which seems always to be incidental to any undertaking of this kind, left them in the somber coat of lead color with which they had been originally clothed. The "steeple" was a little cupola, reared on the very center of the roof, on four tall pillars of pine, that were fluted with a gouge, and loaded with mouldings. On the tops of the columns was reared a dome or cupola, resembling in shape an inverted teacup without its bottom, from the center of which projected a spire or shaft of wood, transfixed with two iron rods, that bore on their ends the letters N. S. E. and W., in the same metal. The whole was surmounted by an imitation of one of the finny tribe, carved in wood by the hands of Richard, and painted what he called a "scale-color." This animal Mr. Jones affirmed to be an admirable resemblance of a great favorite of the epicures in that country, which bore the title of "lake fish"; and doubtless the assertion was true; for, although intended to answer the purposes of a weathercock, the fish was observed invariably to look, with a longing eye, in the direction of the beautiful sheet of water that lay embedded in the mountains of Templeton.

For a short time after the charter of the regents was received, the trustees of this institution employed a graduate of one of the eastern colleges to instruct such youth as aspired to knowledge, within the walls of the edifice which we have described. The upper part of the building was in one apartment, and was intended for gala days and exhibitions; and the lower contained two rooms, that were intended for the great divisions of education, viz. the Latin and the English scholars. The former were never very numerous; though the sounds of "nominative, *pennaa,*—gentive, *penny,*" were soon heard to issue from the windows of the room, to the great delight and manifest edification of the passenger.

Only one laborer in this temple of Minerva, however, was known to get so far as to attempt a translation of Virgil. He indeed appeared at the annual exhibition, to the prodigious exultation of all his relatives, a farmer's family in the vicinity, and repeated the whole of the first eclogue from memory, observing the intonations of the dialogue with much judgment and effect. The sounds, as they proceeded from his mouth, of

> "*Titty-ree too patty-lee ree-coo-bans sub teg-mi-nee faa-gy*
> *Syl-ves-trem ten-oo-i moo-sam med-i-taa-ris aa-ve-ny*"—

were the last that had been heard in that building, as probably they were the first that had ever been heard, in the same language, there or anywhere else. By this time the trustees discovered that they had anticipated the age, and the instructor, or principal, was superseded by a master, who went on to teach the more humble lesson of "the more haste the worse speed," in good, plain English.

From this time, until the date of our incidents, the academy was a common country school; and the great room of the building was sometimes used as a courtroom on extraordinary trials; sometimes for conferences of the religious and the morally disposed in the evening; at others for a ball, in the afternoon, given under the auspices of Richard; and on Sundays, invariably, as a place of public worship.

When an itinerant priest of the persuasion of the Methodists, Baptists, Universalists, or of the more numerous sect of the Presbyterians, was accidentally in the neighborhood, he was ordinarily invited to officiate, and was commonly rewarded for his services by a collection in a hat, before the congregation separated. When no such regular minister offered, a kind of colloquial prayer or two was made by some of the more gifted members, and a sermon was usually read, from Sterne, by Mr. Richard Jones.

The consequence of this desultory kind of priesthood was, as we have already intimated, a great diversity in opinion, on the more abstruse points of faith. Each sect had its adherents, though neither was regularly organized and disciplined. Of the religious education of Marmaduke we have already written, nor was the doubtful character of his faith completely removed by his marriage. The mother of Elizabeth was an Episcopalian, as, indeed, was the mother of the Judge himself; and the good taste of Marmaduke revolted at the familiar colloquies which the leaders of the conferences held with the Deity in their nightly meetings. In form, he was certainly an Episcopalian, though not a sectary of that denomination. On the other hand, Richard was as rigid in the observance of the canons of his church as he was inflexible in his opinions. Indeed, he had once or twice essayed to introduce the Episcopal form of service, on the Sundays that the pulpit was vacant; but Richard was a good deal addicted to carrying things to an excess, and then there was something so papal in his air that the greater part of his hearers deserted him on the second Sabbath—on the third, his only auditor was Ben Pump, who had all the obstinate and enlightened orthodoxy of a High Churchman.

Before the war of the Revolution, the English church was supported in the colonies with much interest, by some of its adherents in the mother country, and a few of the congregations were very amply endowed. But for a season, after the independence of the States was established, this sect of Christians languished for the want of the highest order of its priesthood. Pious and suitable divines were at length selected, and sent to the mother country to receive that authority, which, it is understood, can only be transmitted directly from one to the other, and thus obtain, in order to preserve, that unity in their churches, which properly belonged to a people of the same nation. But unexpected difficulties presented themselves in the oaths with which the policy of England had fettered their establishment; and much time was spent before a conscientious sense of duty would permit the prelates of Britain to delegate the authority so earnestly sought. Time, patience, and zeal, however, removed every impediment; and the venerable men, who had been set apart by the American churches, at length returned to their expecting dioceses, endowed with the most elevated functions of their earthly church. Priests and deacons were ordained; and missionaries provided to keep alive the expiring flame of devotion in such members as were deprived of the ordinary administrations, by dwelling in new and unorganized districts.

Of this number was Mr. Grant. He had been sent into the county of which Templeton was the capital, and had been kindly invited by Marmaduke, and officiously pressed by Richard to take up his abode in the village. A small and humble dwelling was prepared for his family, and the divine had made his appearance in the place but a few days previously to the time of his introduction to the reader. As his forms were entirely new to most of the inhabitants, and a clergyman of another denomination had previously occupied the field, by engaging the academy, the first Sunday after his arrival was suffered to pass in silence; but now that his rival had passed on, like a meteor, filling the air with the light of his wisdom, Richard was empowered to give notice, that "Public worship, after the forms of the Protestant Episcopal Church, would be held, on the night before Christmas, in the long room of the academy in Templeton, by the Rev. Mr. Grant."

This annunciation excited great commotion among the different sectaries. Some wondered as to the nature of the exhibition; others sneered; but a far greater part, recollecting the essays of Richard in that way, and mindful of the liberality or rather laxity of Marmaduke's notions on the subject of sectarianism, thought it most prudent to be silent.

4

DINNER at Judge Marmaduke Temple's house was a tremendous occasion; the table groaned. At one end of the damask tablecloth was an enormous roasted turkey; at the other, a turkey boiled. In the center were a fricassee of squirrels, a dish of fried fish, a platter of boiled fish, and a venison steak. Elsewhere stood a prodigious chine of roasted bear's meat, and a leg of delicious mutton. Vegetables, cakes, sweetmeats, and five kinds of pies—apple, mince, pumpkin, cranberry, and custard—filled the rest of the board; with room for brandy, rum, gin, wine, cider, beer, and flip. As the Judge, Squire Jones, Monsieur Le Quoi, and others ate, the talk fell on the young hunter whom the judge had wounded. Nobody knew his identity, but the major-domo of the household, Benjamin, reported that for three weeks "he has been backing and filling in the wake of Natty Bumppo, through the mountains after deer, like a Dutch longboat in tow of an Albany sloop." The party was soon summoned by the bell of the Episcopal Church to the Christmas Eve service which the Rev. Mr. Grant had arranged. They found a goodly congregation at the church, among them Indian John or Chingachgook and the anonymous young man of whom they had been chatting.

Immediately after the service a number of the men hurried to the taproom of the village tavern, the "Bold Dragoon," a spacious room lined on three sides by benches and on the fourth by a wide fireplace. Dr. Todd, standing before the blaze, told how he had cut the bullet from the hunter's back. Several expressed the hope that the injured man would not let the matter drop, but would bring suit for damages against the wealthy and none too popular Judge.

A subject so momentous, as that of suing Judge Temple, was not very palatable to the present company in so public a place; and a short silence ensued, that was only interrupted by the opening of the door, and the entrance of Natty himself.

The old hunter carried in his hand his never-failing companion, the rifle; and although all of the company were uncovered, excepting the lawyer, who wore his hat on one side, with a certain dam'me air, Natty moved to the front of one of the fires, without in the least altering any part of his dress or appearance. Several questions were addressed to him, on the subject of the game he had killed, which he answered readily, and with some little interest; and the landlord, between whom and Natty there existed much cordiality, on account of their both having been soldiers in youth, offered him a glass of a liquid, which, if we might judge from its reception, was no unwelcome guest. When the forester had gotten his potation also, he quietly took his seat on the end of one of the logs, that lay nigh the fires, and the slight interruption produced by his entrance seemed to be forgotten.

"The testimony of the blacks could not be taken, sir," continued the lawyer, "for they are all the property of Mr. Jones, who owns their time. But there is a way by which Judge Temple, or any other man, might be made to pay for shooting another, and for the cure in the bargain. There is a way, I say, and that without going into the 'court of errors' too."

"And a mighty big error ye would make of it, Mister Todd," cried the landlady, "should ye be putting the matter into the law at all, with

Joodge Temple, who has a purse as long as one of them pines on the hill, and who is an asy man to dale wid, if yees but mind the humor of him. He's a good man is Joodge Temple, and a kind one, and one who will be no the likelier to do the pratty thing, bekaase ye would wish to tarrify him wid the law. I know of but one objaction to the same, which is an overcarelessness about his sowl. It's neither a Methodie, nor a Papish, nor Prasbetyrian, that he is, but just nothing at all; and it's hard to think that he, 'who will not fight the good fight, under the banners of a rig'lar church, in this world, will be mustered among the chosen in heaven,' as my husband, the captain there, as you call him, says—though there is but one captain I know, who desaarves the name. I hopes, Latherstocking, ye'll no be foolish, and putting the boy up to try the law in the matter; for 'twill be an evil day to ye both, when ye first turn the skin of so paceable an animal as a sheep into a bone of contention. The lad is wilcome to his drink for nothing, until his shouther will bear the rifle ag'in."

"Well, that's gin'rous," was heard from several mouths at once, for this was a company in which a liberal offer was not thrown away; while the hunter, instead of expressing any of that indignation which he might be supposed to feel, at hearing the hurt of his young companion alluded to, opened his mouth, with the silent laugh for which he was so remarkable; and after he had indulged his humor made this reply:—

"I know'd the Judge would do nothing with his smoothbore, when he got out of his sleigh. I never saw but one smoothbore, that would carry at all, and that was a French ducking-piece, upon the Big Lakes; it had a barrel half as long ag'in as my rifle, and would throw fine shot into a goose, at a hundred yards; but it made dreadful work with the game, and you wanted a boat to carry it about in. When I went with Sir William ag'in the French, at Fort Niagara, all the rangers used the rifle; and a dreadful weapon it is, in the hands of one who knows how to charge it, and keep a steady aim. The Captain knows, for he says he was a soldier in Shirley's; and though they were nothing but baggonet-men, he must know how we cut up the French and Iroquois in the scrimmages in that war. Chingachgook, which means Big Sarpent in English, old John Mohegan, who lives up at the hut with me, was a great warrior then, and was out with us; he can tell all about it too; though he was an overhand for the tomahawk, never firing more than once or twice, before he was running in for the scalps. Ah! times is dreadfully altered since then. Why, Doctor, there was nothing but a footpath, or at the most a track for pack horses, along the Mohawk, from the Jarman Flats up to the forts. Now, they say, they talk of running one of them wide roads with gates on it along the river; first making a road, and then fencing it up! I hunted one season back of the

Kaats Kills, nigh-hand to the settlements, and the dogs often lost the scent, when they came to them highways, there was so much travel on them; though I can't say that the brutes was of a very good breed. Old Hector will wind a deer in the fall of the year, across the broadest place in the Otsego, and that is a mile and a half, for I paced it myself on the ice, when the tract was first surveyed, under the Indian grant."

"It sames to me, Natty, but a sorry compliment, to call your comrad after the evil one," said the landlady; "and it's no much like a snake that Old John is looking now. Nimrood would be a more besaming name for the lad, and a more Christian too, seeing that it comes from the Bible. The sargeant read me the chapter about him, the night before my christening, and a mighty asement it was, to listen to anything from the book."

"Old John and Chingachgook were very different men to look on," returned the hunter, shaking his head at his melancholy recollections. "In the 'fifty-eighth war,' he was in the middle of manhood, and taller than now by three inches. If you had seen him, as I did, the morning we beat Dieskau, from behind our log walls, you would have called him as comely a redskin as ye ever set eyes on. He was naked, all to his breechcloth and leggens; and you never seed a creater so handsomely painted. One side of his face was red, and the other black. His head was shaved clean, all to a few hairs on the crown, where he wore a tuft of eagle's feathers, as bright as if they had come from a peacock's tail. He had colored his sides, so that they looked like an atomy, ribs and all; for Chingachgook had a great taste in such things; so that, what with his bold, fiery countenance, his knife, and his tomahawk, I have never seen a fiercer warrior on the ground. He played his part, too, like a man; for I saw him next day, with thirteen scalps on his pole. And I will say this for the Big Snake, that he always dealt fair, and never scalped any that he didn't kill with his own hands."

"Well, well," cried the landlady; "fighting is fighting, anyway, and there is different fashions in the thing; though I can't say that I relish mangling a body after the breath is out of it; neither do I think it can be uphild by doctrine. I hope, sargeant, ye niver was helping in sich evil worrek."

"It was my duty to keep my ranks, and to stand or fall by the baggonet or lead," returned the veteran. "I was then in the fort, and, seldom leaving my place, saw but little of the savages, who kept on the flanks, or in front, scrimmaging. I remember, howsomever, to have heard mention made of the Great Snake, as he was called, for he was a chief of renown; but little did I ever expect to see him enlisted in the cause of Christianity, and civilized like old John."

"Oh! he was Christianized by the Moravians, who were always overintimate with the Delawares," said Leatherstocking. "It's my opinion, that, had they been left to themselves, there would be no such doings now, about the headwaters of the two rivers, and that these hills mought have been kept as good hunting ground by their right owner, who is not too old to carry a rifle, and whose sight is as true as a fish hawk hovering—"

He was interrupted by more stamping at the door, and presently the party from the mansion house entered, followed by the Indian himself.

Some little commotion was produced by the appearance of the new guests, during which the lawyer slunk from the room. Most of the men approached Marmaduke, and shook his offered hand, hoping "that the Judge was well"; while Major Hartmann, having laid aside his hat and wig, and substituted for the latter a warm, peaked, woollen nightcap, took his seat very quietly on one end of the settee which was relinquished by its former occupants. His tobacco box was next produced, and a clean pipe was handed him by the landlord. When he had succeeded in raising a smoke, the Major gave a long whiff, and, turning his head towards the bar, he said—

"Petty, pring in ter toddy."

In the meantime, the Judge had exchanged his salutations with most of the company, and taken a place by the side of the Major, and Richard had bustled himself into the most comfortable seat in the room. Monsieur Le Quoi was the last seated, nor did he venture to place his chair finally, until, by frequent removals, he had ascertained that he could not possibly intercept a ray of heat from any individual present. Mohegan found a place on an end of one of the benches, and somewhat approximated to the bar. When these movements had subsided, the Judge remarked, pleasantly—

"Well, Betty, I find you retain your popularity through all weathers, against all rivals, and among all religions. How liked you the sermon?"

"Is it the sarmon?" exclaimed the landlady. "I can't say but it was rasonable; but the prayers is mighty unasy. It's no so small a matter for a body, in their fifty-nint' year, to be moving so much in church. Mr. Grant sames a godly man, anyway, and his garrel is a hoomble one, and a devout.—Here, John, is a mug of cider laced with whisky. An Indian will drink cider, though he niver be athirst."

"I must say," observed Hiram, with due deliberation, "that it was a tonguey thing; and I rather guess that it gave considerable satisfaction. There was one part, though, which might have been left out, or something else put in; but then, I s'pose that, as it was a written discourse, it is not so easily altered, as where a minister preaches without notes."

"Ay! there's the rub, Joodge," cried the landlady. "How can a man stand up and be praching his word, when all that he is saying is written down, and he is as much tied to it as iver a thaving dragoon was to the pickets?"

"Well, well," cried Marmaduke, waving his hand for silence, "there is enough said; as Mr. Grant told us, there are different sentiments on such subjects, and in my opinion he spoke most sensibly.—So, Jotham, I am told you have sold your betterments to a new settler, and have moved into the village and opened a school. Was it cash or dicker?"

The man who was thus addressed occupied a seat immediately behind Marmaduke; and one who was ignorant of the extent of the Judge's observation might have thought he would have escaped notice. He was of a thin, shapeless figure, with a discontented expression of countenance, and with something extremely shiftless in his whole air. Thus spoken to, after turning and twisting a little, by way of preparation, he made a reply.

"Why, part cash, and part dicker. I sold out to a Pumfret man, who was so'thin forehanded. He was to give me ten dollars an acre for the clearin, and one dollar an acre over the first cost, on the woodland; and we agreed to leave the buildins to men. So I tuck Asa Mountagu, and he tuck Absalom Bement, and they two tuck old Squire Naphtali Green. And so they had a meetin, and made out a vardict of eighty dollars for the buildins. There was twelve acres of clearin, at ten dollars, and eighty-eight at one, and the whull came to two hundred and eighty-six dollars and a half, after paying the men."

"Hum," said Marmaduke, "what did you give for the place?"

"Why, besides what's comin to the Judge, I gi'n my brother Tim a hundred dollars for his bargain; but then there's a new house on't, that cost me sixty more, and I paid Moses a hundred dollars, for choppin, and loggin, and sowin; so that the whull stood me in about two hundred and sixty dollars. But then I had a great crop off on't, and as I got twenty-six dollars and a half more than it cost, I conclude I made a pretty good trade on't."

"Yes, but you forgot that the crop was yours without the trade, and you have turned yourself out of doors for twenty-six dollars."

"Oh! the Judge is clean out," said the man, with a look of sagacious calculation; "he turned out a span of horses, that is wuth a hundred and fifty dollars of any man's money, with a bran new waggon; fifty dollars in cash; and a good note for eighty more; and a side saddle that was valued at seven and a half—so there was jist twelve shillings betwixt us. I wanted him to turn out a set of harness, and take the cow and the sap troughs. He wouldn't—but I saw through it; he thought I should have to buy the tacklin afore I could use the wagon and horses; but I know'd a thing or two myself; I should like to know of what use is the tacklin to him! I offered him to trade back ag'in, for one hundred and fifty-five. But my woman said she wanted a churn, so I tuck a churn for the change."

"And what do you mean to do with your time this winter? You must remember that time is money."

"Why, as the master is gone down country to see his mother, who, they say, is going to make a die on't, I agreed to take the school in hand till he comes back. If times doosn't get worse in the spring, I've some notion of going into trade, or maybe I may move off to the Genessee; they say they are carryin' on a great stroke of business that-a-way. If the wust comes to the wust, I can but work at my trade, for I was brought up in a shoe manufactory."

It would seem that Marmaduke did not think his society of sufficient value, to attempt inducing him to remain where he was; for he addressed no further discourse to the man, but turned his attention to other subjects. After a short pause, Hiram ventured a question:—

"What news does the Judge bring us from the legislature? it's not likely that congress has done much this session; or maybe the French haven't fit any more battles lately?"

"The French, since they have beheaded their king, have done nothing but fight," returned the Judge. "The character of the nation seems changed. I knew many French gentlemen during our war, and they all appeared to me to be men of great humanity and goodness of heart; but these Jacobins are as bloodthirsty as bulldogs."

"There was one Roshambow wid us, down at Yorrektown," cried the landlady; "a mighty pratty man he was, too; and their horse was the very same. It was there that the sargeant got the hurt in the leg, from the English batteries, bad luck to 'em."

"Ah! mon pauvre Roi!" murmured Monsieur Le Quoi.

"The legislature have been passing laws," continued Marmaduke, "that the country much required. Among others, there is an act prohibiting the drawing of seines, at any other than proper seasons, in certain of our streams and small lakes; and another, to prohibit the killing of deer in the teeming months. These are laws that were loudly called for by judicious men; nor do I despair of getting an act to make the unlawful felling of timber a criminal offence."

The hunter listened to this detail with breathless attention, and when the Judge had ended, he laughed in open derision.

"You may make your laws, Judge," he cried, "but who will you find to watch the mountains through the long summer days, or the lakes at night? Game is game, and he who finds may kill; that has been the law in these mountains for forty years to my sartain knowledge; and I think one old law is worth two new ones. None but a green one would wish to kill a doe with a fa'an by its side, unless his moccasins was getting old, or his leggins ragged, for the flesh is lean and coarse.

But a rifle rings among the rocks along the lake shore, sometimes, as if fifty pieces were fired at once:—it would be hard to tell where the man stood who pulled the trigger."

"Armed with the dignity of the law, Mr. Bumppo," returned the Judge gravely, "a vigilant magistrate can prevent much of the evil that has hitherto prevailed, and which is already rendering the game scarce. I hope to live to see the day when a man's rights in his game shall be as much respected as his title to his farm."

"Your titles and your farms are all new together," cried Natty; "but laws should be equal, and not more for one than another. I shot a deer, last Wednesday was a fortnight, and it floundered through the snowbanks till it got over a brush fence; I catch'd the lock of my rifle in the twigs, in following, and was kept back, until finally the creater got off. Now I want to know who is to pay me for that deer; and a fine buck it was. If there hadn't been a fence I should have gotten another shot into it; and I never draw'd upon anything that hadn't wings three times running, in my born days. No, no, Judge, it's the farmers that makes the game scarce, and not the hunters."

"Ter teer is not so plenty as in ter old war, Pumppo," said the Major, who had been an attentive listener, amidst clouds of smoke; "put ter lant is not mate as for ter teer to live on, put for Christians."

"Why, Major, I believe you're a friend to justice and the right, though you go so often to the grand house; but it's a hard case to a man to have his honest calling for a livelihood stopped by laws, and that too when, if right was done, he mought hunt or fish on any day in the week, or on the best flat in the Patent, if he was so minded."

"I unterstant you, Letterstockint," returned the Major, fixing his black eyes, with a look of peculiar meaning, on the hunter; "put you tidn't use to be so prutent, as to look ahet mit so much care."

"Maybe there wasn't so much occasion," said the hunter, a little sulkily; when he sunk into a silence from which he was not roused for some time.

"The Judge was saying so'thin about the French," Hiram observed, when the pause in the conversation had continued a decent time.

"Yes, sir," returned Marmaduke, "the Jacobins of France seem rushing from one act of licentiousness to another. They continue those murders, which are dignified by the name of executions. You have heard that they have added the death of their queen to the long list of their crimes."

"Les monstres!" again murmured Monsieur Le Quoi, turning himself suddenly in his chair, with a convulsive start.

"The province of La Vendée is laid waste by the troops of the republic, and hundreds of its inhabitants, who are royalists in their sentiments, are shot at a time. La Vendée is a district in the southwest of

France, that continues yet much attached to the family of the Bourbons; doubtless Monsieur Le Quoi is acquainted with it, and can describe it more faithfully."

"Non, non, non, mon cher ami," returned the Frenchman, in a suppressed voice, but speaking rapidly, and gesticulating with his right hand, as if for mercy, while with his left he concealed his eyes.

"There have been many battles fought lately," continued Marmaduke, "and the infuriated republicans are too often victorious. I cannot say, however, that I am sorry they have captured Toulon from the English, for it is a place to which they have a just right."

"Ah—ha!" exclaimed Monsieur Le Quoi, springing on his feet, and flourishing both arms with great animation; "ces Anglais!"

The Frenchman continued to move about the room with great alacrity for a few minutes, repeating his exclamations to himself; when, overcome by the contradictory nature of his emotions, he suddenly burst out of the house, and was seen wading through the snow toward his little shop, waving his arms on high, as if to pluck down honor from the moon. His departure excited but little surprise, for the villagers were used to his manner; but Major Hartmann laughed outright, for the first time during his visit, as he lifted the mug, and observed—

"Ter Frenchman is mat—put he is goot as for notting to trink; he is trunk mit joy."

"The French are good soldiers," said Captain Hollister; "they stood us in hand a good turn, down at Yorktown; nor do I think, although I am an ignorant man about the great movements of the army, that his Excellency would have been able to march against Cornwallis, without their reinforcements."

"Ye spake the trut', sargeant," interrupted his wife, "and I would iver have ye be doing the same. It's varry pratty men is the French; and jist when I stopt the cart, the time when ye was pushing on in front it was, to kape the rig'lers in, a rigiment of the jontlemen marched by, and so I dealt them out to their liking. Was it pay I got? sure did I, and in good solid crowns: the divil a bit of continental could they muster among them all, for love nor money. Och! the Lord forgive me for swearing, and spakeing of such vanities: but this I will say for the French, that they paid in good silver; and one glass would go a great way wid 'em, for they gin'rally handed it back wid a drop in the cup; and that's a brisk trade, Joodge, where the pay is good, and the men not over partic'lar."

"A thriving trade, Mrs. Hollister," said Marmaduke. "But what has become of Richard? he jumped up as soon as seated, and has been absent so long that I am fearful he has frozen."

"No fear of that, cousin 'Duke," cried the gentleman himself;

"business will sometimes keep a man warm, the coldest night that ever snapt in the mountains. Betty, your husband told me, as we came out of church, that your hogs were getting mangy, so I have been out to take a look at them, and found it true. I stepped across, Doctor, and got your boy to weigh me out a pound of salts, and have been mixing it with their swill. I'll bet a saddle of venison against a gray squirrel that they are better in a week. And now, Mrs. Hollister, I'm ready for a hissing mug of flip."

"Sure I know'd yee'd be wanting that same," said the landlady; "it's mixt and ready to the boiling. Sargeant, dear, be handing up the iron, will ye?—no, the one in the far fire, its black, ye will see.—Ah! you've the thing now; look if it's not as red as a cherry."

The beverage was heated, and Richard took that kind of draught which men are apt to indulge in, who think that they have just executed a clever thing, especially when they like the liquor.

"Oh! you have a hand, Betty, that was formed to mix flip," cried Richard, when he paused for breath. "The very iron has a flavor in it. Here, John, drink, man, drink. I and you and Dr. Todd, have done a good thing with the shoulder of that lad this very night. 'Duke, I made a song while you were gone—one day when I had nothing to do; so I'll sing you a verse or two, though I haven't really determined on the tune yet:—

What is life but a scene of care,
Where each one must toil in his way?
Then let us be jolly, and prove that we are
A set of good fellows, who seem very rare,
And can laugh and sing all the day.
Then let us be jolly,
And cast away folly,
For grief turns a black head to gray.

There, 'Duke, what do you think of that? There is another verse of it, all but the last line. I haven't got a rhyme for the last line yet. Well, old John, what do you think of the music? as good as one of your war songs, ha?"

"Good," said Mohegan, who had been sharing deeply in the potations of the landlady besides paying a proper respect to the passing mugs of the Major and Marmaduke.

"Pravo! pravo! Richart," cried the Major, whose black eyes were beginning to swim in moisture; "pravissimo! it is a goot song; put Natty Pumppo hast a petter. Letterstockint, vilt sing? say, olt poy, vilt sing ter song, as apout ter woots?"

"No, no, Major," returned the hunter, with a melancholy shake of the head, "I have lived to see what I thought eyes could never behold in these hills, and I have no heart left for singing. If he, that has a right to be master and ruler here, is forced to squinch his thirst, when a-dry, with snow-water, it ill becomes them that have lived by his bounty to be making merry, as if there was nothing in the world but sunshine and summer."

When he had spoken, Leatherstocking again dropped his head on his knees, and concealed his hard and wrinkled features with his hands. The change from the excessive cold without to the heat of the barroom, coupled with the depth and frequency of Richard's draughts, had already levelled whatever inequality there might have existed between him and the other guests, on the score of spirits; and he now held out a pair of swimming mugs of foaming flip toward the hunter, as he cried—

"Merry! ay! merry Christmas to you, old boy! Sunshine and summer! no! you are blind, Leatherstocking, 'tis moonshine and winter;—take these spectacles and open your eyes—

So let us be jolly,
And cast away folly,
For grief turns a black head to gray.

Hear how old John turns his quavers. What damned dull music an Indian song is, after all, Major. I wonder if they ever sing by note."

While Richard was singing and talking, Mohegan was uttering dull, monotonous tones, keeping time by a gentle motion of his head and body. He made use of but few words, and such as he did utter were in his native language, and consequently only understood by himself and Natty. Without heeding Richard, he continued to sing a kind of wild, melancholy air, that rose, at times, in sudden and quite elevated notes, and then fell again into the low, quavering sounds, that seemed to compose the character of his music.

The attention of the company was now much divided, the men in the rear having formed themselves into little groups, where they were discussing various matters; among the principal of which were, the treatment of mangy hogs, and Parson Grant's preaching; while Dr. Todd was endeavoring to explain to Marmaduke the nature of the hurt received by the young hunter. Mohegan continued to sing, while his countenance was becoming vacant, though, coupled with his thick bushy hair, it was assuming an expression very much like brutal ferocity. His notes were gradually growing louder, and soon rose to a height that caused a general cessation in the discourse. The hunter now raised his head again, and addressed the old warrior, warmly, in the Delaware language, which, for the benefit of our readers, we shall render freely into English.

"Why do you sing of your battles, Chingachgook, and of the warriors you have slain, when the worst enemy of all is near you, and keeps the Young Eagle from his rights? I have fought in as many battles as any warrior in your tribe, but cannot boast of my deeds at such a time as this."

"Hawkeye," said the Indian, tottering with a doubtful step from his place, "I am the Great Snake of the Delawares; I can track the Mingoes, like an adder that is stealing on the whippoorwill's eggs, and strike them, like the rattlesnake, dead at a blow. The white man made the tomahawk of Chingachgook bright as the waters of Otsego when the last sun is shining; but it is red with the blood of the Maquas."

"And why have you slain the Mingo warriors? Was it not to keep these hunting grounds and lakes to your father's children? and were they not given in solemn council to the Fire-eater? and does not the blood of a warrior run in the veins of a young chief, who should speak aloud, where his voice is now too low to be heard?"

The appeal of the hunter seemed in some measure to recall the confused faculties of the Indian, who turned his face towards the listeners, and gazed intently on the Judge. He shook his head, throwing his hair back from his countenance, and exposed eyes that were glaring with an expression of wild resentment. But the man was not himself. His hand seemed to make a fruitless effort to release his tomahawk, which was confined by its handle to his belt, while his eyes gradually became vacant. Richard at that instant thrusting a mug before him, his features changed to the grin of idiocy, and seizing the vessel with both hands, he sank backward on the bench, and drank until satiated, when he made an effort to lay aside the mug with the helplessness of total inebriety.

"Shed not blood!" exclaimed the hunter as he watched the countenance of the Indian in its moment of ferocity; "but he is drunk, and can do no harm. This is the way with all the savages; give them liquor, and they make dogs of themselves. Well, well—the time will come when right will be done; and we must have patience."

Natty still spoke in the Delaware language, and of course was not understood. He had hardly concluded, before Richard cried—

"Well, old John is soon sowed up. Give him a berth, Captain, in the barn, and I will pay for it. I am rich tonight, ten times richer than 'Duke, with all his lands, and military lots, and funded debts, and bonds, and mortgages.

Come let us be jolly,
And cast away folly,
For grief——

Drink, King Hiram—drink, Mr. Doo-nothing—drink, sir, I say. This is a Christmas Eve, which comes, you know, but once a year."

5

POOR INDIAN JOHN, or Chingachgook, whom civilization had in some respects worsened, slept off his liquor on a bed of straw in a barn; other Christmas Eve roisterers spent the night in similar recuperation. Next day came the great shooting match for the Christmas turkey. That morning Squire Jones and his cousin Elizabeth Temple, out for a walk, saw Leatherstocking or Natty Bumppo, Chingachgook, and the young hunter, whom Natty called Mr. Oliver, in earnest consultation. Their talk was of the contest.

"The bird must be had," Elizabeth Temple heard Natty say, "by fair means or foul. Heigho! I've known the time, lad, when the wild turkeys wasn't overscarce in the country; though you must go into the Virginy gaps if you want them now. To be sure there is a different taste to a partridge, and a well-fattened turkey; though, to my eating, a beaver's tail and bear's hams makes the best of food. But then everyone has his own appetite. I gave the last farthing, all to that shilling, to the French trader this very morning as I came through the town, for powder; so, as you have nothing, we can have but one shot for it. I know that Bill Kirby is out, and means to have a pull of the trigger at that very turkey. John has a true eye for a single fire, and somehow, my hand shakes so whenever I have to do anything extrawnary that I often lose my aim."

Young Oliver held up a shilling with the exclamation that it was his last penny. He was for having Leatherstocking make the shot —"with your aim it cannot fail to be successful." Natty still insisted, however, that Chingachgook was the best marksman. To this Indian John replied that his best days were gone. "When John was young, eyesight was not straighter than his bullet," he declared. "When did he ever shoot twice?" But now he was old, and with something worse than his seventy winters. "No!—the white man brings old age with him—rum is his tomahawk."

At this point Elizabeth Temple intervened, and declaring that she wished to try her chance for a turkey, gave a dollar to Natty Bumppo with the request that he shoot once for her.

The ancient amusement of shooting the Christmas turkey is one of the few sports that the settlers of a new country seldom or never neglect to observe. It was connected with the daily practices of a people who often laid aside the ax or the scythe to seize the rifle, as the deer glided through the forests they were felling, or the bear entered their rough meadows to scent the air of a clearing, and to scan, with a look of sagacity, the progress of the invader.

On the present occasion, the usual amusement of the day had been a little hastened, in order to allow a fair opportunity to Mr. Grant, whose exhibition was not less a treat to the young sportsmen than the one which engaged their present attention. The owner of the birds was a free black, who had prepared for the occasion a collection of game that was admirably qualified to inflame the appetite of an epicure, and was well adapted to the means and skill of the different competitors, who were of all ages. He had offered to the younger and more humble marksmen divers birds of an inferior quality, and some shooting had already taken place, much to the pecuniary advantage of the sable owner of the game. The order of the sports was extremely simple, and well understood. The bird was fastened by a string to the stump of a large pine, the side of which, toward the point where the marksmen were placed, had been flattened with an ax, in order that it might serve the purpose of a target, by which the merit of each individual might be ascertained. The distance between the stump and shooting stand was one hundred measured yards: a foot more or a foot less being thought an invasion of the right of one of the parties. The Negro affixed his own price to every bird, and the terms of the chance: but when these were once established he was obliged, by the strict principles of public justice that prevailed in the country, to admit any adventurer who might offer.

The throng consisted of some twenty or thirty young men, most of whom had rifles, and a collection of all the boys in the village. The little urchins, clad in coarse but warm garments, stood gathered around the more distinguished marksmen, with their hands stuck under their waistbands, listening eagerly to the boastful stories of skill that had been exhibited on former occasions, and were already emulating in their hearts these wonderful deeds in gunnery.

The chief speaker was the man who had been mentioned by Natty, as Billy Kirby. This fellow, whose occupation, when he did labor, was that of clearing lands or chopping jobs, was of great stature, and carried, in his very air, the index of his character. He was a noisy, boisterous, reckless lad, whose good-natured eye contradicted the bluntness and bullying tenor of his speech. For weeks he would lounge around the taverns of the county, in a state of perfect idleness, or doing small jobs for his liquor and his meals, and cavilling with applicants about the prices of his labor: frequently preferring idleness to an abatement of a tittle of his independence, or a cent in his wages. But when these embarrassing points were satisfactorily arranged, he would shoulder his ax and his rifle, slip his arms through the straps of his pack, and enter the woods with the tread of a Hercules. His first object was to learn his limits, round which he would pace, occasionally freshening, with a blow of his ax, the marks on the boundary trees; and then he would proceed, with an air of great deliberation, to the center of his premises, and, throwing aside his superfluous garments, measure, with a knowing eye, one or two of the nearest trees that were towering apparently into the very clouds as he gazed upward. Commonly selecting one of the most noble, for the first trial of his power, he would approach it with a listless air, whistling a low tune; and wielding his ax, with a certain flourish, not unlike the salutes of a fencing master, he would strike a light blow into the bark, and measure his distance. The pause that followed was ominous of the fall of the forest, which had flourished there for centuries. The heavy and brisk blows that he struck were soon succeeded by the thundering report of the tree, as it came, first cracking and threatening, with the separation of its own last ligaments, then threshing and tearing with its branches the tops of its surrounding brethren, and finally meeting the ground with a shock but little inferior to an earthquake. From that moment the sounds of the ax were ceaseless, while the falling of the trees was like a distant cannonading; and the daylight broke into the depths of the woods with the suddenness of a winter morning.

For days, weeks, nay months, Billy Kirby would toil, with an ardor that evinced his native spirit, and with an effect that seemed magical, until, his chopping being ended, his stentorian lungs could be heard emitting sounds, as he called to his patient oxen, which rung through the hills like the cries of an alarm. He had been often heard, on a mild summer's evening, a long mile across the vale of Templeton; when the echoes from the mountains would take up his cries, until they died away in feeble sounds from the distant rocks that overhung the lake. His piles, or, to use the language of the country, his logging, ended, with a despatch that could only accompany his dexterity and Herculean strength, the jobber would collect together his implements of labor, like the heaps of timber, and march away, under the blaze of the prostrate forest, like the conqueror of some city, who, having first prevailed over his adversary, applies the torch as the finishing blow to his conquest. For a long time Billy Kirby would then be seen, sauntering around the taverns, the rider of scrub races, the bully of cockfights, and not unfrequently the hero of such sports as the one in hand.

Between him and the Leatherstocking there had long existed a jealous rivalry on the point of skill with the rifle. Notwithstanding the long practice of Natty, it was commonly supposed that the steady nerves and quick eye of the wood chopper rendered him his equal. The competition had, however, been confined hitherto to boastings, and comparisons made from their success in various hunting excursions; but this was the first time that they had ever come in open collision. A good deal of higgling about the price of the choicest bird had taken place between Billy Kirby and its owner before Natty and his companions rejoined the sportsmen. It had, however, been settled at one shilling [1] a shot, which was the highest sum ever exacted, the black taking care to protect himself from losses, as much as possible, by the conditions of the sport. The turkey was already fastened at the "mark," but its body was entirely hid by the surrounding snow, nothing being visible but its red swelling head and long neck. If the bird was injured by any bullet that struck below the snow, it was to continue the property of its present owner, but if a feather was touched in a visible part, the animal became the prize of the successful adventurer.

These terms were loudly proclaimed by the Negro, who was seated in the snow, in a somewhat hazardous vicinity to his favorite bird, when Elizabeth and her cousin approached the noisy sportsmen. The sounds of mirth and contention sensibly lowered at this unexpected visit; but, after a moment's pause, the curious interest exhibited in the face of the young lady, together with her smiling air, restored the freedom of the morning; though it was somewhat chastened, both in language and vehemence, by the presence of such a spectator.

"Stand out of the way there, boys!" cried the wood chopper, who was placing himself at the shooting point—"stand out of the way, you little rascals, or I will shoot through you. Now, Brom, take leave of your turkey."

"Stop!" cried the young hunter; "I am a candidate for a chance. Here is my shilling, Brom; I wish a shot, too."

"You may wish it in welcome," cried Kirby, "but if I ruffle the gobbler's feathers, how are you to get it? Is money so plenty in your deerskin pocket that you pay for a chance that you may never have?"

---

[1] Before the Revolution each province had its own money of account, though neither coined any but copper pieces. In New York the Spanish dollar was divided into eight shillings, each of the value of a fraction more than sixpence sterling. At present the Union has provided a decimal system, and coins to represent it. (*Cooper's note*)

"How know you, sir, how plenty money is in my pocket?" said the youth fiercely. "Here is my shilling, Brom, and I claim a right to shoot."

"Don't be crabbed, my boy," said the other, who was very coolly fixing his flint. "They say you have a hole in your left shoulder, yourself: so I think Brom may give you a fire for half price. It will take a keen one to hit that bird, I can tell you, my lad, even if I give you a chance, which is what I have no mind to do."

"Don't be boasting, Billy Kirby," said Natty, throwing the breech of his rifle into the snow, and leaning on its barrel; "you'll get but one shot at the creater, for if the lad misses his aim, which wouldn't be a wonder if he did, with his arm so stiff and sore, you'll find a good piece and an old eye coming a'ter you. Maybe it's true that I can't shoot as I used to could, but a hundred yards is a short distance for a long rifle."

"What, old Leatherstocking, are you out this morning?" cried the reckless opponent. "Well, fair play's a jewel. I've the lead of you, old fellow; so here goes, for a dry throat or a good dinner."

The countenance of the Negro evinced not only all the interest which his pecuniary adventure might occasion, but also the keen excitement that the sport produced in the others, though with a very different wish as to the result. While the wood chopper was slowly and steadily raising his rifle, he bawled—

"Fair play, Billy Kirby—stand back—make 'em stand back, boys—gib a nigger fair play—poss-up, gobbler; shake a head, fool; don't a see 'em taking aim?"

These cries, which were intended as much to distract the attention of the marksman, as for anything else, were fruitless. The nerves of the wood chopper were not so easily shaken, and he took his aim with the utmost deliberation. Stillness prevailed for a moment, and he fired. The head of the turkey was seen to dash on one side, and its wings were spread in momentary fluttering; but it settled itself down calmly into its bed of snow, and glanced its eyes uneasily around. For a time long enough to draw a deep breath, not a sound was heard. The silence was then broken by the noise of the Negro, who laughed and shook his body with all kinds of antics, rolling over in the snow in the excess of delight.

"Well done a gobbler," he cried, jumping up and affecting to embrace his bird; "I tell 'em to poss-up, and you see 'em dodge. Gib anoder shillin, Billy, and hab anoder shot."

"No—the shot is mine," said the young hunter; "you have my money already. Leave the mark, and let me try my luck."

"Ah! it's but money thrown away, lad," said Leatherstocking. "A turkey's head and neck is but a small mark for a new hand and a lame shoulder. You'd best let me take the fire, and maybe we can make some settlement with the lady about the bird."

"The chance is mine," said the young hunter. "Clear the ground that I may take it."

The discussions and disputes concerning the last shot were now abating, it having been determined that if the turkey's head had been anywhere but just where it was at the moment, the bird must certainly have been killed. There was not much excitement produced by the preparations of the youth, who proceeded in a hurried manner to take his aim, and was in the act of pulling the trigger, when he was stopped by Natty.

"Your hand shakes, lad," he said, "and you seem over eager. Bullet wounds are apt to weaken flesh, and, to my judgment, you'll not shoot so well as in common. If you will fire, you should shoot quick before there is time to shake off the aim."

"Fair play," again shouted the Negro; "fair play—gib a nigger fair play. What right a Nat Bumppo advise a young man? Let 'em shoot—clear a ground."

The youth fired with great rapidity, but no motion was made by the turkey; and when the examiners for the ball returned from the "mark," they declared that he had missed the stump.

Elizabeth observed the change in his countenance, and could not help feeling surprise that one so evidently superior to his companions should feel a trifling loss so sensibly. But her own champion was now preparing to enter the lists.

The mirth of Brom which had been again excited, though in a much smaller degree than before, by the failure of the second adventurer, vanished the instant Natty took his stand. His skin became mottled with large brown spots that fearfully sullied the luster of his native ebony, while his enormous lips gradually compressed around two rows of ivory, that had hitherto been shining in his visage like pearls set in jet. His nostrils, at all times the most conspicuous features of his face, dilated until they covered the greater part of the diameter of his countenance; while his brown and bony hands unconsciously grasped the snow crust near him, the excitement of the moment completely overcoming his native dread of cold.

While these indications of apprehension were exhibited in the sable owner of the turkey, the man who gave rise to this extraordinary emotion was as calm and collected as if there was not to be a single spectator of his skill.

"I was down in the Dutch settlements on the Scoharie," said Natty, carefully removing the leather guard from the lock of his rifle, "just before the breaking out of the last war, and there was a shooting match among the boys; so I took a hand. I think I opened a good many Dutch eyes that day, for I won the powder horn, three bars of lead, and a pound of as good powder as ever flashed in pan. Lord! how they did swear in Jarman! They did tell of one drunken Dutchman who said he'd have the life of me before I got back to the lake ag'in. But if he had put his rifle to his shoulder with evil intent, God would have punished him for it; and even if the Lord didn't and he had missed his aim, I know one that would have given him as good as he sent and better too, if good shooting could come into the 'count."

By this time the old hunter was ready for his business, and throwing his right leg far behind him, and stretching his left arm along the barrel of his piece he raised it toward the bird. Every eye glanced rapidly from the marksman to the mark; but at the moment when each ear was expecting the report of the rifle, they were disappointed by the ticking sound of the flint.

"A snap, a snap!" shouted the Negro, springing from his crouching posture like a madman before his bird. "A snap good as fire—Natty Bumppo gun he snap—Natty Bumppo miss a turkey!"

"Natty Bumppo hit a nigger," said the indignant old hunter, "if you don't get out of the way, Brom. It's contrary to the reason of the thing, boy, that a snap should count for a fire when one is nothing more than a firestone striking a steel pan, and the other is sudden death; so get out of my way, boy, and let me show Billy Kirby how to shoot a Christmas turkey."

"Gib a nigger fair play!" cried the black, who continued resolutely to maintain his post, and making that appeal to the justice of his auditors which the degraded condition of his caste so naturally suggested. "Ebberybody know dat snap as good as fire. Leab it to Massa Jone—leab it to lady."

"Sartain," said the wood chopper; "it's the law of the game in this part of the country, Leatherstocking. If you fire ag'in, you must pay up the other shilling. I b'lieve I'll try luck once more myself; so, Brom, here's my money and I take the next fire."

"It's likely you know the laws of the woods better than I do, Billy Kirby," returned Natty. "You come in with the settlers with an ox goad in your hand, and I come in with moccasins on my feet and with a good rifle on my shoulders, so long back as afore the old war. Which is likely to know the best? I say no man need tell me that snapping is as good as firing when I pull the trigger."

"Leab it to Massa Jone," said the alarmed Negro; "he know ebberyting."

This appeal to the knowledge of Richard was too flattering to be unheeded. He therefore advanced a little from the spot whither the delicacy of Elizabeth had induced her to withdraw, and gave the following opinion with the gravity that the subject and his own rank demanded:—

"There seems to be a difference in opinion," he said, "on the subject of Nathaniel Bumppo's right to shoot at Abraham Freeborn's turkey without the said Nathaniel paying one shilling for the privilege." This fact was too evident to be denied, and, after pausing a moment that the audience might digest his premises, Richard proceeded:—"It seems proper that I should decide this question as I am bound to preserve the peace of the county; and men with deadly weapons in their hands should not be heedlessly left to contention and their own malignant passions. It appears that there was no agreement, either in writing or in words, on the disputed point; therefore we must reason from analogy, which is, as it were, comparing one thing with another. Now, in duels where both parties shoot, it is generally the rule that a snap is a fire; and if such is the rule where the party has a right to fire back again, it seems to me unreasonable to say that a man may stand snapping at a defenceless turkey all day. I therefore am of opinion that Nathaniel Bumppo has lost his chance and must pay another shilling before he renews his right."

As this opinion came from so high a quarter and was delivered with effect, it silenced all murmurs,—for the whole of the spectators had begun to take sides with great warmth,—except from the Leatherstocking himself.

"I think Miss Elizabeth's thoughts should be taken," said Natty. "I've known the squaws give very good counsel when the Indians have been dumbfoundered. If she says that I ought to lose I agree to give it up."

"Then I adjudge you to be a loser for this time," said Miss Temple; "but pay your money and renew your chance; unless Brom will sell me the bird for a dollar. I will give him the money and save the life of the poor victim."

This proposition was evidently but little relished by any of the listeners, even the Negro feeling the evil excitement of the chances. In the meanwhile, as Billy Kirby was preparing himself for another shot, Natty left the stand with an extremely dissatisfied manner, muttering—

"There hasn't been such a thing as a good flint sold at the foot of the lake since the Indian traders used to come into the country;—and if a body should go into the flats along the streams in the hills to hunt for such a thing, it's ten to one but they will be all covered up with the plough. Heigho! it seems to me that just as the game grows scarce and a body wants the best ammunition to get a livelihood, everything that's bad falls on him like a judgment. But I'll change the stone, for Billy Kirby hasn't the eye for such a mark, I know."

The wood chopper seemed now entirely sensible that his reputation depended on his care; nor did he neglect any means to ensure success. He drew up his rifle, and renewed his aim again and again, still appearing reluctant to fire. No sound was heard from even Brom during these portentous movements, until Kirby discharged his piece with the same want of success as before. Then, indeed, the shouts of the Negro rang through the bushes, and sounded among the trees of the neighboring forest like the outcries of a tribe of Indians. He laughed, rolling his head first on one side then on the other, until nature seemed exhausted with mirth. He danced until his legs were wearied with motion in the snow; and, in short, he exhibited all that violence of joy that characterizes the mirth of a thoughtless Negro.

The wood chopper had exerted all his art, and felt a proportionate degree of disappointment at the failure. He first examined the bird with the utmost attention, and more than once suggested that he had touched its feathers; but the voice of the multitude was against him, for it felt disposed to listen to the often repeated cries of the black to "gib a nigger fair play."

Finding it impossible to make out a title to the bird, Kirby turned fiercely to the black and said—

"Shut your oven, you crow! Where is the man that can hit a turkey's head at a hundred yards? I was a fool for trying. You needn't make an uproar like a falling pine tree about it. Show me the man who can do it."

"Look this-a-way, Billy Kirby," said Leatherstocking, "and let them clear the mark, and I'll show you a man who's made better shots afore now, and that when he's been hard-pressed by the savages and wild beasts."

"Perhaps there is one whose rights come before ours, Leatherstocking," said Miss Temple; "if so, we will wave our privilege."

"If it be me that you have reference to," said the young hunter, "I shall decline another chance. My shoulder is yet weak, I find."

Elizabeth regarded his manner, and thought that she could discern a tinge on his cheek that spoke the shame of conscious poverty. She said no more, but suffered her own champion to make a trial. Although Natty Bumppo had certainly made hundreds of more momentous shots at his enemies or his game, yet he never exerted himself more to excel. He raised his piece three several times: once to get his range, once to calculate his distance, and once because the bird, alarmed by the deathlike stillness, turned its head quickly to examine its foes. But the fourth time he fired. The smoke, the report, and the momentary shock prevented most of the spectators from instantly knowing the result; but Elizabeth, when she saw her champion drop the end of his rifle in the snow and open his mouth in one of its silent laughs, and then proceed very coolly to recharge his piece, knew that he had been successful.

The boys rushed to the mark and lifted the turkey on high, lifeless, and with nothing but the remnant of a head.

"Bring in the creater," said Leatherstocking, "and put it at the feet of the lady. I was her deputy in the matter, and the bird is her property."

"And a good deputy you have proved yourself," returned Elizabeth,—"so good, Cousin Richard, that I would advise you to remember his qualities." She paused, and the gaiety that beamed on her face gave place to a more serious earnestness. She even blushed a little as she turned to the young hunter, and, with the charm of a woman's manner, added—"But it was only to see an exhibition of the far-famed skill of Leatherstocking that I tried my fortunes. Will you, sir, accept the bird, as a small peace offering, for the hurt that prevented your own success?"

The expression with which the youth received this present was indescribable. He appeared to yield to the blandishment of her air, in opposition to a strong inward impulse to the contrary. He bowed, and raised the victim silently from her feet, but continued silent.

Elizabeth handed the black a piece of silver as a remuneration for his loss, which had some effect in again unbending his muscles, and then expressed to her companion her readiness to return homeward.

6

IMMEDIATELY following the turkey-shoot, Judge Temple, who was losing the services of his kinsman Squire Richard Jones, offered a position as his business assistant to the young hunter, Oliver Edwards. The youth listened to him with a reluctance amounting almost to loathing. Chingachgook, however, exhorted the young man to close with the Judge. "Listen to your Father," he argued; "his words are old. Let the Young Eagle and the Great Land Chief eat together; let them sleep without fear, near each other." Finally Edwards took the place, and entered the Judge's household. "Who could have foreseen this a month since!" he exclaimed privately to Natty Bumppo. "I have consented to serve Marmaduke Temple—to be an inmate in the dwelling of the greatest enemy of my race." As yet he did not disclose the reason for this secret enmity, but it was plain to Chingachgook and Bumppo that he but awaited an opportunity to settle an account with the Judge. As the winter wore on, Edwards busied himself during the day with Marmaduke Temple's business, but spent many of his nights in the hut of Leatherstocking. "The intercourse between the three hunters was maintained with a certain air of mystery, it is true, but with much zeal and apparent interest to all the parties."

When spring approached it brought its characteristic outdoor occupations. One of these was the boiling-down of maple syrup and maple sugar from the sap of a sugar bush near the village. A party consisting of the Judge and his daughter, Squire Jones, Monsieur Le Quoi, young Edwards, and Louisa Grant, the minis-

ter's young daughter, rode out one day to see this and other sights. The rude plenty of the country reminded Temple of the hardships of the period just after the Revolution, when he was trying to bring emigrants and settle a great tract of land in the region of Lake Otsego.

"But, my dear father," cried the wondering Elizabeth, "was there actual suffering? where were the beautiful and fertile vales of the Mohawk? could they not furnish food for your wants?"

"It was a season of scarcity, the necessities of life commanded a high price in Europe, and were greedily sought after by the speculators. The emigrants, from the east to the west, invariably passed along the valley of the Mohawk, and swept away the means of subsistence like a swarm of locusts. Nor were the people on the flats in a much better condition. They were in want themselves, but they spared the little excess of provisions that nature did not absolutely require with the justice of the German character. There was no grinding of the poor. The word speculator was then unknown to them. I have seen many a stout man bending under the load of the bag of meal which he was carrying from the mills of the Mohawk through the rugged passes of these mountains to feed his half-famished children, with a heart so light as he approached his hut that the thirty miles he had passed seemed nothing. Remember, my child, it was in our very infancy; we had neither mills, nor grain, nor roads, nor often clearings; we had nothing of increase but the mouths that were to be fed; for even at that inauspicious moment the restless spirit of emigration was not idle; nay, the general scarcity, which extended to the east, tended to increase the number of adventurers."

"And how, dearest father, didst thou encounter this dreadful evil?" said Elizabeth, unconsciously adopting the dialect of her parent in the warmth of her sympathy. "Upon thee must have fallen the responsibility, if not the suffering."

"It did, Elizabeth," returned the Judge, pausing for a single moment as if musing on his former feelings. "I had hundreds at that dreadful time daily looking up to me for bread. The sufferings of their families and the gloomy prospect before them had paralyzed the enterprise and efforts of my settlers; hunger drove them to the woods for food, but despair sent them at night, enfeebled and wan, to a sleepless pillow. It was not a moment for inaction. I purchased cargoes of wheat from the granaries of Pennsylvania; they were landed at Albany and brought up the Mohawk in boats; from thence it was transported on pack horses into the wilderness and distributed among my people. Seines were made, and the lakes and rivers were dragged for fish. Something like a miracle was wrought in our favor, for enormous shoals of herrings were discovered to have wandered five hundred miles through the windings of the impetuous Susquehanna, and the lake was alive with their numbers. These were at length caught and dealt out to the people with proper portions of salt; and from that moment we again began to prosper." [1]

"Yes," cried Richard, "and I was the man who served out the fish and the salt. When the poor devils came to receive their rations, Benjamin, who was my deputy, was obliged to keep them off by stretching ropes around me, for they smelt so of garlic from eating nothing but the wild onion, that the fumes put me out often in my measurement. You were a child then, Bess, and knew nothing of the matter, for great care was observed to keep both you and your mother from suffering. That year put me back dreadfully, both in the breed of my hogs and of my turkeys."

"No, Bess," cried the Judge in a more cheerful tone, disregarding the interruption of his cousin, "he who hears of the settlement of a country knows but little of the toil and suffering by which it is accomplished. Unimproved and wild as this district now seems to your eyes, what was it when I first entered the hills! I left my party the morning of my arrival near the farms of the Cherry Valley, and, following a deer path, rode to the summit of the mountain that I have since called Mount Vision; for the sight that there met my eyes seemed to me as the deceptions of a dream. The fire had run over the pinnacle, and, in a great measure, laid open the view. The leaves were fallen, and I mounted a tree and sat for an hour looking on the silent wilderness. Not an opening was to be seen in the boundless forest, except where the lake lay like a mirror of glass. The water was covered by myriads of the wild fowl that migrate with the changes in the season; and, while in my situation on the branch of the beech, I saw a bear with her cubs descend to the shore to drink. I had met many deer gliding through the woods in my journey, but not the vestige of a man could I trace during my progress, nor from my elevated observatory. No clearing, no hut, none of the winding roads that are now to be seen were there; nothing but mountains rising behind mountains, and the valley with its surface of branches, enlivened here and there with the faded foliage of some tree that parted from its leaves with more than ordinary reluctance. Even the Susquehanna was then hid by the height and density of the forest."

"And were you alone?" asked Elizabeth; "passed you the night in that solitary state?"

"Not so, my child," returned her father. "After musing on the

---

[1] This harvest of herrings was actually taken at Cooperstown in the spring of 1789. Judge William Cooper, father of the novelist, described it in a historical letter which Susan Fenimore Cooper incorporates in her introduction to *The Pioneers*.—Ed.

scene for an hour with a mingled feeling of pleasure and desolation, I left my perch and descended the mountain. My horse was left to browse on the twigs that grew within his reach, while I explored the shores of the lake and the spot where Templeton stands. A pine of more than ordinary growth stood where my dwelling is now placed! a windrow had been opened through the trees from thence to the lake, and my view was but little impeded. Under the branches of that tree I made my solitary dinner; I had just finished my repast as I saw a smoke curling from under the mountain, near the eastern bank of the lake. It was the only indication of the vicinity of man that I had then seen. After much toil I made my way to the spot, and found a rough cabin of logs built against the foot of a rock, and bearing the marks of a tenant, though I found no one within it——"

"It was the hut of Leatherstocking," said Edwards, quickly.

"It was; though I, at first, supposed it to be a habitation of the Indians. But while I was lingering around the spot, Natty made his appearance, staggering under the carcass of a buck that he had slain. Our acquaintance commenced at that time; before, I had never heard that such a being tenanted the woods. He launched his bark canoe and set me across the foot of the lake to the place where I had fastened my horse, and pointed out a spot where he might get a scanty browsing until the morning; when I returned and passed the night in the cabin of the hunter."

Miss Temple was so much struck by the deep attention of young Edwards during this speech that she forgot to resume her interrogatories; but the youth himself continued the discourse by asking—

"And how did the Leatherstocking discharge the duties of a host, sir?"

"Why, simply but kindly, until late in the evening, when he discovered my name and object, and the cordiality of his manner very sensibly diminished or, I might better say, disappeared. He considered the introduction of the settlers as an innovation on his rights, I believe; for he expressed much dissatisfaction at the measure, though it was in his confused and ambiguous manner. I hardly understood his objections myself, but supposed they referred chiefly to an interruption of the hunting."

"Had you then purchased the estate, or were you examining it with an intent to buy?" asked Edwards, a little abruptly.

"It had been mine for several years. It was with a view to people the land that I visited the lake. Natty treated me hospitably, but coldly, I thought, after he learned the nature of my journey. I slept on his own bearskin, however, and in the morning joined my surveyors again."

"Said he nothing of the Indian rights, sir? The Leatherstocking is much given to impeach the justice of the tenure by which the whites hold the country."

"I remember that he spoke of them, but I did not clearly comprehend him, and may have forgotten what he said; for the Indian title was extinguished so far back as the close of the old war; and if it had not been at all, I hold under the patents of the Royal Governors, confirmed by an act of our own State Legislature, and no court in the country can affect my title."

"Doubtless, sir, your title is both legal and equitable," returned the youth coldly, reining his horse back and remaining silent till the subject was changed.

It was seldom Mr. Jones suffered any conversation to continue for a great length of time without his participation. It seems that he was of the party that Judge Temple had designated as his surveyors; and he embraced the opportunity of the pause that succeeded the retreat of young Edwards to take up the discourse, and with it a narration of their further proceedings, after his own manner. As it wanted, however, the interest that had accompanied the description of the Judge, we must decline the task of committing his sentences to paper.

They soon reached the point where the promised view was to be seen. It was one of those picturesque and peculiar scenes that belong to the Otsego, but which required the absence of the ice and the softness of a summer's landscape to be enjoyed in all its beauty. Marmaduke had early forewarned his daughter of the season, and of its effect on the prospect; and after casting a cursory glance at its capabilities, the party returned homeward, perfectly satisfied that its beauties would repay them for the toil of a second ride at a more propitious season.

"The spring is the gloomy time of the American year," said the Judge; "and it is more peculiarly the case in these mountains. The winter seems to retreat to the fastnesses of the hills as to the citadel of its dominion, and is only expelled after a tedious siege, in which either party at times would seem to be gaining the victory."

"A very just and apposite figure, Judge Temple," observed the Sheriff; "and the garrison under the command of Jack Frost made formidable sorties—you understand what I mean by sorties, Monsieur; sallies in English—and sometimes drives General Spring and his troops back again into the low countries."

"Yes, sair," returned the Frenchman, whose prominent eyes were watching the precarious footsteps of the beast he rode, as it picked its dangerous way among the roots of trees, holes, log bridges, and sloughs that formed the aggregate of the highway. "Je vous entend; de low countrie is freeze up for half de year."

The error of Monsieur Le Quoi was not noticed by the Sheriff; and the rest of the party were yielding to the influence of the changeful season, which was already teaching the equestrians that a continuance of its mildness was not to be expected for any length of time. Silence and thoughtfulness succeeded the gaiety and conversation that had prevailed during the commencement of the ride, as clouds began to gather about the heavens, apparently collecting from every quarter in quick motion, without the agency of a breath of air.

While riding over one of the cleared eminences that occurred in their route, the watchful eye of Judge Temple pointed out to his daughter the approach of a tempest. Flurries of snow already obscured the mountain that formed the northern boundary of the lake, and the genial sensation which had quickened the blood through their veins was already succeeded by the deadening influence of an approaching northwester.

All of the party were now busily engaged in making the best of their way to the village, though the badness of the roads frequently compelled them to check the impatience of their animals, which often carried them over places that would not admit of any gait faster than a walk.

Richard continued in advance, followed by Monsieur Le Quoi, next to whom rode Elizabeth, who seemed to have imbibed the distance which pervaded the manner of young Edwards since the termination of the discourse between the latter and her father. Marmaduke followed his daughter, giving her frequent and tender warnings as to the management of her horse. It was, possibly, the evident dependence that Louisa Grant placed on his assistance which induced the youth to continue by her side as they pursued their way through a dreary and dark wood, where the rays of the sun could but rarely penetrate, and where even the daylight was obscured and rendered gloomy by the deep forests that surrounded them. No wind had yet reached the spot where the equestrians were in motion, but that dead stillness that often precedes a storm contributed to render their situation more irksome than if they were already subject to the fury of the tempest. Suddenly the voice of young Edwards was heard shouting in those appalling tones that carry alarm to the very soul, and which curdle the blood of those that hear them—

"A tree! a tree! whip—spur for your lives! a tree! a tree!"

"A tree! a tree!" echoed Richard, giving his horse a blow that caused the alarmed beast to jump nearly a rod, throwing the mud and water into the air like a hurricane.

"Von tree! von tree!" shouted the Frenchman, bending his body on the neck of his charger, shutting his eyes, and playing on the ribs of his beast with his heels, at a rate that caused him to be conveyed on the crupper of the Sheriff with a marvellous speed.

Elizabeth checked her filly and looked up with an unconscious but alarmed air at the very cause of their danger, while she listened to the crackling sounds that awoke the stillness of the forest; but the next instant her bridle was seized by her father, who cried—

"God protect my child!" and she felt herself hurried onward, impelled by the vigor of his nervous arm.

Each one of the party bowed to their saddlebows as the tearing of branches was succeeded by a sound like the rushing of the winds, which was followed by a thundering report, and a shock that caused the very earth to tremble, as one of the noblest ruins of the forest fell directly across their path.

One glance was enough to assure Judge Temple that his daughter and those in front of him were safe, and he turned his eyes in dreadful anxiety to learn the fate of the others. Young Edwards was on the opposite side of the tree, his form thrown back in his saddle to its utmost distance, his left hand drawing up his bridle with its greatest force, while the right grasped that of Miss Grant, so as to draw the head of her horse under its body. Both the animals stood shaking in every joint with terror and snorting fearfully. Louisa herself had relinquished her reins, and with her hands pressed on her face sat bending forward in her saddle, in an attitude of despair, mingled strangely with resignation.

"Are you safe?" cried the Judge, first breaking the awful silence of the moment.

"By God's blessing," returned the youth; "but if there had been branches to the tree we must have been lost—"

He was interrupted by the figure of Louisa, slowly yielding in her saddle; and but for his arm she would have sunk to the earth. Terror, however, was the only injury that the clergyman's daughter had sustained, and with the aid of Elizabeth she was soon restored to her senses. After some little time was lost in recovering her strength, the young lady was replaced in her saddle, and, supported on either side by Judge Temple and Mr. Edwards, she was enabled to follow the party in their slow progress.

7

THE FURTHER ADVANCE of spring gave the inhabitants of the village an opportunity to enjoy an annual marvel, the flight of the passenger pigeons from lands farther south. Leatherstocking, who deplored the killing of more game than could be eaten, witnessed with mixed feelings the reception the hunters gave to a mass of birds that extended from mountain to mountain across the sky in a solid blue mass.

From this time to the close of April the weather continued to be a succession of great and rapid changes. One day the soft airs of spring seemed to be stealing along the valley, and, in unison with an invigorating sun, attempting covertly to rouse the dormant powers of the vegetable world; while on the next the surly blasts from the north would sweep across the lake, and erase every impression left by their gentle adversaries. The snow, however, finally disappeared, and the green wheatfields were seen in every direction spotted with the dark and charred stumps that had the preceding season supported some of the proudest trees of the forest. Ploughs were in motion, wherever those useful implements could be used, and the smokes of the sugar camps were no longer seen issuing from the woods of maple. The lake had lost the beauty of a field of ice, but still a dark and gloomy covering concealed its waters, for the absence of currents left them yet hid under a porous crust, which, saturated with the fluid, barely retained enough strength to preserve the contiguity of its parts. Large flocks of wild geese were seen passing over the country, which hovered for a time around the hidden sheet of water, apparently searching for a resting place; and then, on finding themselves excluded by the chill covering, would soar away to the north, filling the air with discordant screams, as if venting their complaints at the tardy operations of nature.

For a week the dark covering of the Otsego was left to the undisturbed possession of two eagles, who alighted on the center of its field, and sat eyeing their undisputed territory. During the presence of these monarchs of the air the flocks of migrating birds avoided crossing the plain of ice by turning into the hills, apparently seeking the protection of the forests, while the white and bald heads of the tenants of the lake were turned upward with a look of contempt. But the time had come when even these kings of birds were to be dispossessed. An opening had been gradually increasing at the lower extremity of the lake, and around the dark spot where the current of the river prevented the formation of ice during even the coldest weather; and the fresh southerly winds that now breathed freely upon the valley made an impression on the waters. Mimic waves began to curl over the margin of the frozen field, which exhibited an outline of crystallizations that slowly receded toward the north. At each step the power of the winds and the waves increased, until, after a struggle of a few hours, the turbulent little billows succeeded in setting the whole field in motion, when it was driven beyond the reach of the eye, with a rapidity that was as magical as the change produced in the scene by this expulsion of the lingering remnant of winter. Just as the last sheet of agitated ice was disappearing in the distance, the eagles rose, and soared with a wide sweep above the clouds, while the waves tossed their little caps of snow into the air, as if rioting in their release from a thraldom of five months' duration.

The following morning Elizabeth was awakened by the exhilarating sounds of the martins, who were quarrelling and chattering around the little boxes suspended above her windows, and the cries of Richard, who was calling, in tones animating as the signs of the season itself—

"Awake! awake! my fair lady! the gulls are hovering over the lake already, and the heavens are alive with pigeons. You may look an hour before you can find a hole through which to get a peep at the sun. Awake! awake! lazy ones! Benjamin is overhauling the ammunition, and we only wait for our breakfasts, and away for the mountains and pigeon-shooting."

There was no resisting this animated appeal, and in a few minutes Miss Temple and her friend descended to the parlor. The doors of the hall were thrown open, and the mild, balmy air of a clear spring morning was ventilating the apartment, where the vigilance of the ex-steward had been so long maintaining an artificial heat with such unremitted diligence. The gentlemen were impatiently waiting for their morning's repast, each equipped in the garb of a sportsman. Mr. Jones made many visits to the southern door, and would cry—

"See, cousin Bess! see, 'Duke, the pigeon roosts of the south have broken up! They are growing more thick every instant. Here is a flock that the eye cannot see the end of. There is a food enough in it to keep the army of Xerxes for a month, and feathers enough to make beds for the whole country. Xerxes, Mr. Edwards, was a Grecian king, who—no, he was a Turk, or a Persian, who wanted to conquer Greece, just the same as these rascals will overrun our wheatfields when they come back in the fall. Away! away! Bess; I long to pepper them."

In this wish both Marmaduke and young Edwards seemed equally to participate, for the sight was exhilarating to a sportsman; and the ladies soon dismissed the party, after a hasty breakfast.

If the heavens were alive with pigeons, the whole village seemed equally in motion with men, women, and children. Every species of firearms, from the French ducking-gun, with a barrel near six feet in length, to the common horseman's pistol, was to be seen in the hands of the men and boys; while bows and arrows, some made of the simple stick of a walnut sapling, and others in a rude imitation of the ancient crossbows, were carried by many of the latter.

The houses and the signs of life apparent in the village drove the alarmed birds from the direct line of their flight towards the mountains, along the sides and near the bases of which they were glancing in dense masses, equally wonderful by the rapidity of their motion and their incredible numbers.[1]

We have already said that across the inclined plane which fell from the steep ascent of the mountain to the banks of the Susquehanna ran the highway, on either side of which a clearing of many acres had been made at a very early day. Over those clearings, and up the eastern mountain, and along the dangerous path that was cut into its side, the different individuals posted themselves, and in a few moments the attack commenced.

Among the sportsmen was the tall, gaunt form of Leatherstocking, walking over the field with his rifle hanging on his arm, his dogs at his heels; the latter now scenting the dead or wounded birds that were beginning to tumble from the flocks, and then crouching under the legs of their master, as if they participated in his feelings at this wasteful and unsportsmanlike execution.

The reports of the firearms became rapid, whole volleys rising from the plain, as flocks of more than ordinary numbers darted over the

---

[1] Susan Fenimore Cooper wrote in her introduction to *The Pioneers*, dated 1876, that although the great flights of passenger pigeons had ended, small flocks of a score or two still occasionally attracted attention in the neighborhood of Cooperstown.—Ed.

opening, shadowing the field like a cloud; and then the light smoke of a single piece would issue from among the leafless bushes on the mountain, as death was hurled on the retreat of the affrighted birds, who were rising from a volley in a vain effort to escape. Arrows and missiles of every kind were in the midst of the flocks; and so numerous were the birds, and so low did they take their flight, that even long poles in the hands of those on the sides of the mountain were used to strike them to the earth.

During all this time Mr. Jones, who disdained the humble and ordinary means of destruction used by his companions, was busily occupied, aided by Benjamin, in making arrangements for an assault of a more than ordinarily fatal character. Among the relics of the old military excursions that occasionally are discovered throughout the different districts of the western part of New York, there had been found in Templeton, at its settlement, a small swivel which would carry a ball of a pound weight. It was thought to have been deserted by a war party of the whites in one of their inroads into the Indian settlements, when, perhaps, convenience or their necessity induced them to leave such an incumbrance behind them in the woods. This miniature cannon had been released from the rust, and being mounted on little wheels, was now in a state for actual service. For several years it was the sole organ for extraordinary rejoicings used in those mountains. On the mornings of the Fourths of July it would be heard ringing among the hills, and even Captain Hollister, who was the highest authority in that part of the country on all such occasions, affirmed that, considering its dimensions, it was no despicable gun for a salute. It was somewhat the worse for the service it had performed, it is true, there being but a trifling difference in size between the touchhole and the muzzle. Still, the grand conceptions of Richard had suggested the importance of such an instrument in hurling death at his nimble enemies. The swivel was dragged by a horse into a part of the open space that the Sheriff thought most eligible for planting a battery of the kind, and Mr. Pump proceeded to load it. Several handfuls of duck shot were placed on top of the powder, and the major-domo announced that his piece was ready for service.

The sight of such an implement collected all the idle spectators to the spot, who, being mostly boys, filled the air with cries of exultation and delight. The gun was pointed high, and Richard, holding a coal of fire in a pair of tongs, patiently took his seat on a stump, awaiting the appearance of a flock worthy of his notice.

So prodigious was the number of the birds, that the scattering fire of the guns, with the hurling of missiles and the cries of the boys, had no other effect than to break off small flocks from the immense masses that continued to dart along the valley, as if the whole of the feathered tribe were pouring through that one pass. None pretended to collect the game, which lay scattered over the fields in such profusion as to cover the very ground with the fluttering victims.

Leatherstocking was a silent but uneasy spectator of all these proceedings, but was able to keep his sentiments to himself until he saw the introduction of the swivel into the sports.

"This comes of settling a country!" he said; "here have I known the pigeons to fly for forty long years, and, till you made your clearings, there was nobody to skear or to hurt them. I loved to see them come into the woods, for they were company to a body; hurting nothing; being, as it was, as harmless as a garter snake. But now it gives me sore thoughts when I hear the frighty things whizzing through the air, for I know it's only a motion to bring out all the brats in the village. Well! the Lord won't see the waste of His creaters for nothing, and right will be done to the pigeons as well as others, by and by. There's Mr. Oliver, as bad as the rest of them, firing into the flocks, as if he was shooting down nothing but Mingo warriors."

Among the sportsmen was Billy Kirby, who, armed with an old musket, was loading, and without even looking into the air, was firing and shouting as his victims fell even on his own person. He heard the speech of Natty, and took upon himself to reply—

"What! old Leatherstocking," he cried, "grumbling at the loss of a few pigeons! If you had to sow your wheat twice and three times as I have done, you wouldn't be so massyfully feeling'd towards the divils. Hurrah, boys! scatter the feathers! This is better than shooting at a turkey's head and neck, old fellow."

"It's better for you, maybe, Billy Kirby," replied the indignant old hunter, "and all them that don't know how to put a ball down a rifle barrel, or how to bring it up again with a true aim; but it's wicked to be shooting into flocks in this wasty manner; and none do it who know how to knock over a single bird. If a body has a craving for pigeon's flesh, why! it's made the same as all other creaters, for man's eating; but not to kill twenty and eat one. When I want such a thing I go into the woods till I find one to my liking, and then I shoot him off the branches, without touching a feather of another, though there might be a hundred on the same tree. You couldn't do such a thing, Billy Kirby—you couldn't do it if you tried."

"What's that, old cornstalk! you sapless stub!" cried the wood chopper. "You've grown wordy, since the affair of the turkey; but if you're for a single shot, here goes at that bird which comes on by himself."

The fire from the distant part of the field had driven a single pigeon below the flock to which it belonged, and, frightened with the constant reports of the muskets, it was approaching the spot where the disputants stood, darting first from one side, and then to the other, cutting the air with the swiftness of lightning, and making a noise with its wings not unlike the rushing of a bullet. Unfortunately for the wood chopper, notwithstanding his vaunt, he did not see this bird until it was too late to fire as it approached, and he pulled his trigger at the unlucky moment when it was darting immediately over his head. The bird continued its course with the usual velocity.

Natty lowered the rifle from his arm when the challenge was made, and, waiting a moment until the terrified victim had got in a line with his eye, and had dropped near the bank of the lake, he raised it again with uncommon rapidity and fired. It might have been chance, or it might have been skill, that produced the result; it was probably a union of both; but the pigeon whirled over in the air, and fell into the lake with a broken wing. At the sound of his rifle both his dogs started from his feet, and in a few minutes the slut brought out the bird, still alive.

The wonderful exploit of Leatherstocking was noised through the field with great rapidity, and the sportsmen gathered in to learn the truth of the report.

"What!" said young Edwards, "have you really killed a pigeon on the wing, Natty, with a single ball?"

"Haven't I killed loons before now, lad, that dive at the flash?" returned the hunter. "It's much better to kill only such as you want, without wasting your powder and lead, than to be firing into God's creaters in this wicked manner. But I come out for a bird, and you know the reason why I like small game, Mr. Oliver, and now I have got one I will go home, for I don't relish to see these wasty ways that you are all practysing, as if the least thing wasn't made for use, and not to destroy."

"Thou sayest well, Leatherstocking," cried Marmaduke, "and I begin to think it time to put an end to this work of destruction."

"Put an ind, Judge, to your clearings. An't the woods His work as well as the pigeons? Use, but don't waste. Wasn't the woods made for the beasts and birds to harbor in? and when man wanted their flesh, their skins, or their feathers, there's the place to seek them. But I'll go to the hut with my own game, for I wouldn't touch one of the harmless things that cover the ground here, looking up with their eyes on me, as if they only wanted tongues to say their thoughts."

With this sentiment in his mouth, Leatherstocking threw his rifle over his arm, and followed by his dogs, stepped across the clearing with great caution, taking care not to tread on one of the wounded birds in his path. He soon entered the bushes on the margin of the lake, and was hid from view.

Whatever impression the morality of Natty made on the Judge, it was utterly lost on Richard. He availed himself of the gathering of the sportsmen to lay a plan for one "fell swoop" of destruction. The musketmen were drawn up in battle array, in a line extending on each side of his artillery, with orders to await the signal of firing from himself.

"Stand by, my lads," said Benjamin, who acted as an aide-de-camp on this occasion, "stand by, my hearties, and when Squire Dickens heaves out the signal to begin firing, d'ye see, you may open upon them in a broadside. Take care and fire low, boys, and you'll be sure to hull the flock."

"Fire low!" shouted Kirby:—"hear the old fool! If we fire low, we may hit the stumps, but not ruffle a pigeon."

"How should you know, you lubber?" cried Benjamin, with a very unbecoming heat for an officer on the eve of battle—"how should you know, you grampus? Haven't I sailed aboard of the *Boadishy* for five years? and wasn't it a standing order to fire low, and to hull your enemy? Keep silence at your guns, boys, and mind the order that is passed."

The loud laughs of the musketmen were silenced by the more authoritative voice of Richard, who called for attention and obedience to his signals.

Some millions of pigeons were supposed to have already passed that morning, over the valley of Templeton; but nothing like the flock that was now approaching had been seen before. It extended from mountain to mountain in one solid blue mass, and the eye looked in vain, over the southern hills, to find its termination. The front of this living column was distinctly marked by a line but very slightly indented, so regular and even was the flight. Even Marmaduke forgot the morality of Leatherstocking as it approached, and, in common with the rest, brought his musket to a poise.

"Fire!" cried the Sheriff, clapping a coal to the priming of the cannon. As half of Benjamin's charge escaped through the touchhole, the whole volley of the musketry preceded the report of the swivel. On receiving this united discharge of small arms, the front of the flock darted upward, while, at the same instant, myriads of those in the rear rushed with amazing rapidity into their places, so that when the column of white smoke gushed from the mouth of the little cannon, an accumulated mass of objects was gliding over its point of direction.—The roar of the gun echoed along the mountains, and died away to the north like distant thunder, while the whole flock of alarmed birds seemed, for a moment, thrown into one disorderly and agitated mass. The air was filled with their irregular flight, layer rising above layer, far above the tops of the highest pines, none daring to advance beyond the dangerous pass; when, suddenly, some of the leaders of the feathered tribe shot across the valley, taking their flight directly over the village, and hundreds of thousands in their rear followed the example, deserting the eastern side of the plain to their persecutors and the slain.

"Victory!" shouted Richard, "victory! we have driven the enemy from the field."

"No so, Dickon," said Marmaduke; "the field is covered with them; and, like the Leatherstocking, I see nothing but eyes in every direction, as the innocent sufferers turn their heads in terror. Full one-half of those that have fallen are yet alive; and I think it is time to end the sport, if sport it be."

"Sport!" cried the Sheriff; "it is princely sport! There are some thousands of the blue-coated boys on the ground, so that every old woman in the village may have a potpie for the asking."

"Well, we have happily frightened the birds from this side of the valley," said Marmaduke, "and the carnage must of necessity end for the present. Boys, I will give you sixpence a hundred for the pigeons' heads only: so go to work, and bring them into the village."

This expedient produced the desired effect, for every urchin on the ground went industriously to work to wring the necks of the wounded birds. Judge Temple retired towards his dwelling with that kind of feeling that many a man has experienced before him, who discovers, after the excitement of the moment has passed, that he has purchased pleasure at the price of misery to others. Horses were loaded with the dead; and, after this first burst of sporting, the shooting of pigeons became a business, with a few idlers, for the remainder of the season. Richard, however, boasted for many a year of his shot with the "cricket"; and Benjamin gravely asserted that he thought they killed nearly as many pigeons on that day as there were Frenchmen destroyed on the memorable occasion of Rodney's victory.

8

JUNE wore into July in the frontier village, while men still speculated on the identity and antecedents of the mysterious Oliver Edwards. His dark complexion and eyes gave rise to a theory that he was partly of Indian blood, and his intimacy with Chingachgook strengthened the supposition. He continued, however, to serve capably as business assistant to Judge Temple, and was treated as a member of the Judge's family. One mild midsummer morning the Judge and Squire Jones rode away on a business errand. Elizabeth Temple and her friend Louisa Grant, declining the company of young Edwards, undertook a walk in the woods. The youth was both offended and disturbed, for he knew that wild beasts were sometimes encountered. He was further irritated when he discovered that the village carpenter, Hiram Doolittle, who was also a petty magistrate, was prowling in the bushes near the hut occupied by Natty Bumppo and young Edwards. The fact was that Doolittle shared the general inquisitiveness respecting Edwards; and that, bearing a grudge against Bumppo, he hoped to find some evidence that the old scout had violated a recent act of the New York legislature which forbade the killing of deer between January and August.

But after padlocking the door of the hut, Oliver Edwards suppressed his vexation, took a fishing rod, walked to the shore of Otsego Lake, and pushing off in his boat, applied himself to catching a mess of fish for dinner. He little thought what stormy events lay just ahead.

There were several places in the Otsego that were celebrated fishing ground for perch. One was nearly opposite to the cabin, and another, still more famous, was near a point at the distance of a mile and a half above it, under the brow of the mountain, and on the same side of the lake with the hut. Oliver Edwards pulled his little skiff to the first, and sat for a minute, undecided whether to continue there with his eyes on the door of the cabin, or to change his ground with a view to get superior game. While gazing about him, he saw the light-colored bark canoe of his old companions riding on the water, at the point we have mentioned, and containing two figures, that he at once knew to be Mohegan and the Leatherstocking. This decided the matter, and the youth pulled, in a very few minutes, to the place where his friends were fishing, and fastened his boat to the light vessel of the Indian.

The old men received Oliver with welcoming nods, but neither drew his line from the water, nor in the least varied his occupation. When Edwards had secured his own boat, he baited his hook and threw it into the lake without speaking.

"Did you stop at the wigwam, lad, as you rowed past?" asked Natty.

"Yes, and I found all safe; but that carpenter and justice of the peace, Mister, or, as they call him, Squire Doolittle, was prowling through the woods. I made sure of the door before I left the hut, and I think he is too great a coward to approach the hounds."

"There's little to be said in favor of that man," said Natty, while he drew in a perch and baited his hook. "He craves dreadfully to come into the cabin, and has as good as asked me as much to my face; but I put him off with unsartain answers, so that he is no wiser than Solomon. This comes of having so many laws that such a man may be called on to intarpret them."

"I fear he is more knave than fool," cried Edwards: "he makes a tool of that simple man, the Sheriff; and I dread that his impertinent curiosity may yet give us much trouble."

"If he harbors too much about the cabin, lad, I'll shoot the creater," said the Leatherstocking, quite simply.

"No, no, Natty, you must remember the law," said Edwards, "or we shall have you in trouble; and that, old man, would be an evil day, and sore tidings to us all."

"Would it, boy!" exclaimed the hunter, raising his eyes with a look of friendly interest toward the youth. "You have the true blood in your veins, Mr. Oliver; and I'll support it, to the face of Judge Temple, or in any court in the country. How is it, John? Do I speak the true word? Is the lad stanch, and of the right blood?"

"He is a Delaware," said Mohegan, "and my brother. The Young Eagle is brave, and he will be a chief. No harm can come."

"Well, well," cried the youth impatiently, "say no more about it, my good friends; if I am not all that your partiality would make me, I am yours through life—in prosperity as in poverty. We will talk of other matters."

The old hunters yielded to his wish, which seemed to be their law. For a short time a profound silence prevailed, during which each man was very busy with his hook and line; but Edwards, probably feeling that it remained with him to renew the discourse, soon observed, with the air of one who knew not what he said—

"How beautifully tranquil and glassy the lake is! Saw you it ever more calm and even than at this moment, Natty?"

"I have known the Otsego water for five-and-forty years," said Leatherstocking; "and I will say that for it, which is, that a cleaner spring or better fishing is not to be found in the land. Yes, yes; I had the place to myself once, and a cheerful time I had of it. The game was plenty as heart could wish; and there was none to meddle with the ground, unless there might have been a hunting party of the Delawares crossing the hills, or, may be, a rifling scout of them thieves the Iroquois. There was one or two Frenchmen that squatted in the flats farther west, and married squaws; and some of the Scotch-Irishers from the Cherry Valley would come on to the lake and borrow my canoe to take a mess of parch, or drop a line for a salmon-trout; but, in the main, it was a cheerful place, and I had but little to disturb me in it. John would come, and John knows."

Mohegan turned his dark face at this appeal; and, moving his hand forward with a graceful motion of assent, he spoke, using the Delaware language—

"The land was owned by my people; we gave it to my brother, in council—to the Fire-eater; and what the Delawares give lasts as long as the waters run. Hawkeye smoked at that council, for we loved him."

"No, no, John," said Natty; "I was no chief, seeing that I know'd nothing of scholarship, and had a white skin. But it was a comfortable hunting ground then, lad, and would have been so to this day, but for the money of Marmaduke Temple, and the twisty ways of the law."

"It must have been a sight of melancholy pleasure indeed," said Edwards, while his eye roved along the shores and over the hills, where the clearings, groaning with the golden corn, were cheering the forests with the signs of life, "to have roamed over these mountains, and along this sheet of beautiful water, without a living soul to speak to or to thwart your humor."

"Haven't I said it was cheerful?" said Leatherstocking. "Yes, yes; when the trees began to be covered with leaves, and the ice was out of the lake, it was a second paradise. I have travelled the woods for fifty-three years, and have made them my home for more than forty; and I can say that I have met but one place that was more to my liking; and that was only to eyesight, and not for hunting or fishing."

"And where was that?" asked Edwards.

"Where! why up on the Kaats Kills. I used often to go up into the mountains after wolves' skins and bears; once they paid me to get them a stuffed painter, and so I often went. There's a place in them hills that I used to climb to, when I wanted to see the carryings on of the world, that would well pay any man for a barked shin or a torn moccasin. You know the Kaats Kills, lad; for you must have seen them on your left, as you followed the river up from York, looking as blue as a piece of clear sky, and holding the clouds on their tops as the smoke curls over the head of an Indian chief at a council fire. Well, there's the High Peak and the Round Top, which lay back, like a father and mother among their children, seeing they are far above all the other hills. But the place I mean is next to the river, where one of the ridges juts out a little from the rest, and where the rocks fall, for the best part of a thousand feet, so much up and down, that a man standing on their edges is fool enough to think he can jump from top to bottom."

"What see you when you get there?" asked Edwards.

"Creation," said Natty, dropping the end of his rod into the water, and sweeping one hand around him in a circle: "all creation, lad. I was on that hill when Vaughan burned 'Sopus, in the last war; and I saw the vessels come out of the Highlands as plain as I can see that lime-scow rowing into the Susquehanna, though one was twenty times farther from me than the other. The river was in sight for seventy miles, looking like a curled shaving, under my feet, though it was eight long miles to its banks. I saw the hills in the Hampshire grants, the highlands of the river, and all that God had done or man could do, far as eye could reach—you know that the Indians named me for my sight, lad; and from the flat on the top of that mountain I have often found the place where Albany stands. And as for 'Sopus, the day the royal troops burnt the town the smoke seemed so nigh that I thought I could hear the screeches of the women."

"It must have been worth the toil to meet with such a glorious view."

"If being the best part of a mile in the air, and having men's farms and housen at your feet, with rivers looking like ribands, and mountains bigger than the Vision, seeming to be haystacks of green grass under you, gives any satisfaction to a man, I can recommend the spot. When I first came into the woods to live, I used to have weak spells when I felt lonesome; and then I would go into the Kaats Kills, and spend a few days on that hill to look at the ways of man; but it's now many a year since I felt any such longings, and I'm getting too old for rugged rocks. But there's a place, a short two miles back of that very hill, that in late times I relished better than the mountain; for it was more covered with the trees, and nateral."

"And where was that?" inquired Edwards, whose curiosity was strongly excited by the simple description of the hunter.

"Why, there's a fall in the hills, where the water of two little ponds that lie near each other breaks out of their bounds, and runs over the rocks into the valley. The stream is, maybe, such a one as would turn a mill, if so useless a thing was wanted in the wilderness. But the Hand that made that Leap never made a mill. There the water comes crooking and winding among the rocks; first so slow that a trout could swim in it, and then starting and running like a creater that wanted to make a far spring, till it gets to where the mountain divides, like the cleft hoof of a deer, leaving a deep hollow for the brook to tumble into. The first pitch is nigh two hundred feet, and the water looks like flakes of driven snow afore it touches the bottom; and there the stream gathers itself together again for a new start, and maybe flutters over fifty feet of flat rock before it falls for another hundred, when it jumps about from shelf to shelf, first turning this-a-way and then turning that-a-way, striving to get out of the hollow, till it finally comes to the plain."

"I have never heard of this spot before: it is not mentioned in the books."

"I never read a book in my life," said Leatherstocking; "and how should a man who has lived in towns and schools know anything about the wonders of the woods? No, no, lad; there has that little stream of water been playing among the hills, since He made the world, and not a dozen white men have ever laid eyes on it. The rock sweeps like masonwork, in a half-round, on both sides of the fall, and shelves over the bottom for fifty feet; so that when I've been sitting at the foot of the first pitch, and my hounds have run into the caverns behind the sheet of water, they've looked no bigger than so many rabbits. To my judgment, lad, it's the best piece of work that I've met with in the woods; and none know how often the hand of God is seen in a wilderness but them that rove it for a man's life."

"What becomes of the water? In which direction does it run? Is it a tributary of the Delaware?"

"Anan!" said Natty.

"Does the water run into the Delaware?"

"No, no; it's a drop for the old Hudson, and a merry time it has till it gets down off the mountain. I've sat on the shelving rock many a long hour, boy, and watched the bubbles as they shot by me, and thought how long it would be before that very water, which seemed made for the wilderness, would be under the bottom of a vessel, and tossing in the salt sea. It is a spot to make a man solemnize. You can see right down into the valley that lies to the east of the High Peak, where, in the fall of the year, thousands of acres of woods are before your eyes, in the deep hollow, and along the side of the mountain, painted like ten thousand rainbows, by no hand of man, though without the ordering of God's Providence."

"You are eloquent, Leatherstocking," exclaimed the youth.

"Anan!" repeated Natty.

"The recollection of the sight has warmed your blood, old man. How many years is it since you saw the place?"

The hunter made no reply; but, bending his ear near the water, he sat holding his breath, and listening attentively as if to some distant sound. At length he raised his head, and said—

"If I hadn't fastened the hounds with my own hands, with a fresh leash of green buckskin, I'd take a Bible oath that I heard old Hector ringing his cry on the mountain."

"It is impossible," said Edwards: "it is not an hour since I saw him in his kennel."

By this time the attention of Mohegan was attracted to the sounds; but, notwithstanding the youth was both silent and attentive, he could hear nothing but the lowing of some cattle from the western hills. He looked at the old men, Natty sitting with his hand to his ear, like a trumpet, and Mohegan bending forward, with an arm raised to a level with his face, holding the forefinger elevated as a signal for attention, and laughed aloud at what he deemed to be their imaginary sounds.

"Laugh if you will, boy," said Leatherstocking, "the hounds be out, and are hunting a deer. No man can deceive me in such a matter. I wouldn't have had the thing happen for a beaver's skin. Not that I care for the law! but the venison is lean now, and the dumb things run the flesh off their own bones for no good. Now do you hear the hounds?"

Edwards started, as a full cry broke on his ear, changing from the distant sounds that were caused by some intervening hill to confused echoes that rung among the rocks that the dogs were passing, and then directly to a deep and hollow baying that pealed under the forest on the lake shore. These variations in the tones of the hounds passed with amazing rapidity; and while his eyes were glancing along the margin of the water, a tearing of the branches of the alder and dogwood caught his attention, at a spot near them, and at the next moment a noble buck sprang on the shore, and buried himself in the lake. A full-mouthed cry followed, when Hector and the slut shot through the opening in the bushes, and darted into the lake also, bearing their breasts gallantly against the water.

"I know'd it—I know'd it!" cried Natty, when both deer and hounds were in full view;—"the buck has gone by them with the wind, and it has been too much for the poor rogues; but I must break them of these tricks, or they'll give me a deal of trouble. He-ere, he-ere—

shore with you, rascals—shore with you—will ye?—Oh! off with you, old Hector, or I'll hatchel your hide with my ramrod when I get ye."

The dogs knew their master's voice, and after swimming in a circle, as if reluctant to give over the chase, and yet afraid to persevere, they finally obeyed, and returned to the land, where they filled the air with their cries.

In the meantime the deer, urged by his fears, had swam over half the distance between the shore and the boats before his terror permitted him to see the new danger. But at the sounds of Natty's voice he turned short in his course, and for a few moments seemed about to rush back again and brave the dogs. His retreat in this direction was, however, effectually cut off, and turning a second time, he urged his course obliquely for the center of the lake, with an intention of landing on the western shore. As the buck swam by the fishermen, raising his nose high into the air, curling the water before his slim neck like the beak of a galley, the Leatherstocking began to sit very uneasy in his canoe.

" 'Tis a noble creater!" he exclaimed; "what a pair of horns! a man might hang up all his garments on the branches. Let me see—July is the last month, and the flesh must be getting good." While he was talking, Natty had instinctively employed himself in fastening the inner end of the bark rope that served him for a cable to a paddle, and, rising suddenly on his legs, he cast this buoy away, and cried—"Strike out, John! let her go. The creater's a fool to tempt a man in this way."

Mohegan threw the fastening of the youth's boat from the canoe, and with one stroke of his paddle sent the light bark over the water like a meteor.

"Hold!" exclaimed Edwards. "Remember the law, my old friends. You are in plain sight of the village, and I know that Judge Temple is determined to prosecute all, indiscriminately, who kill deer out of season."

The remonstrance came too late: the canoe was already far from the skiff, and the two hunters were too much engaged in the pursuit to listen to his voice.

The buck was now within fifty yards of his pursuers, cutting the water gallantly, and snorting at each breath with terror and his exertions, while the canoe seemed to dance over the waves, as it rose and fell with the undulations made by its own motion. Leatherstocking raised his rifle and freshened the priming, but stood in suspense whether to slay his victim or not.

"Shall I, John, or no?" he said. "It seems but a poor advantage to take of the dumb thing too. I won't; it has taken to the water on its own nater, which is the reason that God has given to a deer, and I'll give it the lake play; so, John, lay out your arm, and mind the turn of the buck; it's easy to catch them, but they'll turn like a snake."

The Indian laughed at the conceit of his friend, but continued to send the canoe forward with a velocity that proceeded much more from his skill than his strength. Both of the old men now used the language of the Delawares when they spoke.

"Hugh!" exclaimed Mohegan; "the deer turns his head. Hawkeye, lift your spear."

Natty never moved abroad without taking with him every implement that might, by possibility, be of service in his pursuits. From his rifle he never parted; and although intending to fish with the line, the canoe was invariably furnished with all of its utensils, even to its grate. This precaution grew out of the habits of the hunter, who was often led, by his necessities or his sports, far beyond the limits of his original destination. A few years earlier than the date of our tale, the Leather-stocking had left his hut on the shores of the Otsego, with his rifle and his hounds, for a few days' hunting in the hills; but before he returned he had seen the waters of Ontario. One, two, or even three hundred miles had once been nothing to his sinews, which were now a little stiffened by age. The hunter did as Mohegan advised, and prepared to strike a blow with the barbed weapon into the neck of the buck.

"Lay her more to the left, John," he cried, "lay her more to the left; another stroke of the paddle and I have him."

While speaking, he raised the spear, and darted it from him like an arrow. At that instant the buck turned, the long pole glanced by him, the iron striking against his horn, and buried itself, harmlessly, in the lake.

"Back water," cried Natty, as the canoe glided over the place where the spear had fallen; "hold water, John."

The pole soon reappeared, shooting upward from the lake, and as the hunter seized it in his hand the Indian whirled the light canoe round, and renewed the chase. But this evolution gave the buck a great advantage; and it also allowed time for Edwards to approach the scene of action.

"Hold your hand, Natty!" cried the youth, "hold your hand! remember it is out of season."

This remonstrance was made as the batteau arrived close to the place where the deer was struggling with the water, his back now rising to the surface, now sinking beneath it, as the waves curled from his neck, the animal still sustaining itself nobly against the odds.

"Hurrah!" shouted Edwards, inflamed beyond prudence at the sight; "mind him as he doubles—mind him as he doubles; sheer more to the right, Mohegan, more to the right, and I'll have him by the horns; I'll throw the rope over his antlers."

The dark eye of the old warrior was dancing in his head with a wild animation, and the sluggish repose in which his aged frame had been resting in the canoe was now changed to all the rapid inflections of practiced agility. The canoe whirled with each cunning evolution of the chase, like a bubble floating in a whirlpool; and when the direction of the pursuit permitted of a straight course, the little bark skimmed the lake with a velocity that urged the deer to seek its safety in some new turn. It was the frequency of these circuitous movements that, by confining the action to so small a compass, enabled the youth to keep near his companions. More than twenty times both the pursued and the pursuers glided by him, just without the reach of his oars, until he thought the best way to view the sport was to remain stationary, and, by watching a favorable opportunity, assist as much as he could in taking the victim.

He was not required to wait long, for no sooner had he adopted this resolution, and risen in the boat, than he saw the deer coming bravely toward him, with an apparent intention of pushing for a point of land at some distance from the hounds, who were still barking and howling on the shore. Edwards caught the painter of his skiff, and, making a noose, cast it from him with all his force, and luckily succeeded in drawing its knot close around one of the antlers of the buck.

For one instant the skiff was drawn through the water, but in the next the canoe glided before it, and Natty, bending low, passed his knife across the throat of the animal, whose blood followed the wound, dyeing the waters. The short time that was passed in the last struggles of the animal was spent by the hunters in bringing their boats together, and securing them in that position, when Leatherstocking drew the deer from the water, and laid its lifeless form in the bottom of the canoe. He placed his hands on the ribs and on different parts of the body of his prize, and then, raising his head, he laughed in his peculiar manner—

"So much for Marmaduke Temple's law!" he said. "This warms a body's blood, old John; I haven't killed a buck in the lake afore this, sin' many a year. I call that good venison, lad; and I know them that will relish the creater's steaks, for all the betterments in the land."

The Indian had long been drooping with his years, and perhaps under the calamities of his race, but this invigorating and exciting sport caused a gleam of sunshine to cross his swarthy face that had long been absent from his features. It was evident the old man enjoyed the chase more as a memorial of his youthful sports and deeds than with any expectation of profiting by the success. He felt the deer, however, lightly, his hand already trembling with the reaction of his unusual exertions, and smiled with a nod of approbation as he said, in the emphatic and sententious manner of his people—

"Good."

"I am afraid, Natty," said Edwards, when the heat of the moment had passed and his blood began to cool, "that we have all been equally transgressors of the law. But keep your own counsel, and there are none here to betray us. Yet, how came those dogs at large? I left them securely fastened, I know, for I felt the thongs, and examined the knots, when I was at the hut."

"It has been too much for the poor things," said Natty, "to have such a buck take the wind of them. See, lad, the pieces of the buckskin are hanging from their necks yet. Let us paddle up, John, and I will call them in and look a little into the matter."

When the old hunter landed, and examined the thongs that were yet fast to the hounds, his countenance sensibly changed, and he shook his head doubtingly.

"Here has been a knife at work," he said; "this skin was never torn, nor is this the mark of a hound's tooth. No, no—Hector is not in fault, as I feared."

"Has the leather been cut?" cried Edwards.

"No, no—I didn't say it had been cut, lad; but this is a mark that was never made by a jump or a bite."

"Could that rascally carpenter have dared?"

"Ay! he durst to do anything when there is no danger," said Natty: "he is a curious body, and loves to be helping other people on with their consarns. But he had best not harbor so much near the wigwam!"

In the meantime, Mohegan had been examining, with an Indian's sagacity, the place where the leather thong had been separated. After scrutinizing it closely, he said in Delaware—

"It was cut with a knife—a sharp blade and a long handle—the man was afraid of the dogs."

"How is this, Mohegan?" exclaimed Edwards: "you saw it not! how can you know these facts?"

"Listen, son," said the warrior. "The knife was sharp, for the cut is smooth;—the handle was long, for a man's arm would not reach from this gash to the cut that did not go through the skin:—he was a coward, or he would have cut the thongs around the necks of the hounds."

"On my life," cried Natty, "John is on the scent! It was the carpenter; and he has got on the rock back of the kennel, and let the dogs loose by fastening his knife to a stick. It would be an easy matter to do it where a man is so minded."

"And why should he do so?" asked Edwards: "who has done him wrong, that he should trouble two old men like you?"

"It's a hard matter, lad, to know men's ways, I find, since the settlers have brought in their new fashions. But is there nothing to be found out in the place? and maybe he is troubled with his longings after other people's business, as he often is."

"Your suspicions are just. Give me the canoe: I am young and strong, and will get down there yet, perhaps, in time to interrupt his plans. Heaven forbid that we should be at the mercy of such a man!"

His proposal was accepted, the deer being placed in the skiff in order to lighten the canoe, and in less than five minutes the little vessel of bark was gliding over the glassy lake, and was soon hid by the points of land, as it shot close along the shore.

Mohegan followed slowly with the skiff, while Natty called his hounds to him, bade them keep close, and, shouldering his rifle, he ascended the mountain, with an intention of going to the hut by land.

While the chase was occurring on the lake, Miss Temple and her companion pursued their walk on the mountain. Male attendants, on such excursions, were thought to be altogether unnecessary, for none were ever known to offer an insult to a female who respected herself. After the embarrassment created by the parting discourse with Edwards had dissipated, the girls maintained a conversation that was as innocent and cheerful as themselves.

The path they took led them but a short distance above the hut of Leatherstocking, and there was a point in the road which commanded a bird's-eye view of the sequestered spot.

From a feeling that might have been natural, and must have been powerful, neither of the friends, in their frequent and confidential dialogues, had ever trusted herself to utter one syllable concerning the equivocal situation in which the young man, who was now so intimately associated with them, had been found. If Judge Temple had deemed it prudent to make any inquiries on the subject, he had also thought it proper to keep the answers to himself; though it was so common an occurrence to find the well-educated youth of the eastern states in every stage of their career to wealth, that the simple circumstance of his intelligence, connected with his poverty, would not, at that day and in that country, have excited any very powerful curiosity. With his breeding it might have been different; but the youth himself had so effectually guarded against surprise on this subject by his cold, and even, in some cases, rude deportment, that when his manners seemed to soften by time, the Judge, if he thought about it at all, would have been most likely to imagine that the improvement was the result of his late association. But women are always more alive to such subjects than men; and what the abstraction of the father had overlooked, the observation of the daughter had easily detected. In the thousand little courtesies of polished life she had early discovered that Edwards was not wanting, though his gentleness was so often crossed by marks of what she conceived to be fierce and uncontrollable passions. It may, perhaps, be unnecessary to tell the reader that Louisa Grant never reasoned so much after the fashions of the world. The gentle girl, however, had her own thoughts on the subject, and, like others, she drew her own conclusions.

"I would give all my other secrets, Louisa," exclaimed Miss Temple, laughing, and shaking back her dark locks, with a look of childish simplicity that her intelligent face seldom expressed, "to be mistress of all that those rude logs have heard and witnessed."

They were both looking at the secluded hut at the instant, and Miss Grant raised her mild eyes as she answered—

"I am sure they would tell nothing to the disadvantage of Mr. Edwards."

"Perhaps not; but they might, at least, tell who he is."

"Why, dear Miss Temple, we know all that already. I have heard it all very rationally explained by your cousin——"

"The executive chief! he can explain anything. His ingenuity will one day discover the philosopher's stone. But what did he say?"

"Say!" echoed Louisa, with a look of surprise; "why, everything that seemed to me to be satisfactory, and I have believed it to be true. He said that Natty Bumppo had lived most of his life in the woods, and among the Indians, by which means he had formed an acquaintance with old John, the Delaware chief."

"Indeed! that was quite a matter-of-fact tale for cousin Dickon. What came next?"

"I believe he accounted for their close intimacy by some story about the Leatherstocking saving the life of John in a battle."

"Nothing more likely," said Elizabeth, a little impatiently; "but what is all this to the purpose?"

"Nay, Elizabeth, you must bear with my ignorance, and I will repeat all that I remember to have overheard; for the dialogue was between my father and the Sheriff, so lately as the last time they met. He then added, that the kings of England used to keep gentlemen as agents among the different tribes of Indians, and sometimes officers in the army, who frequently passed half their lives on the edge of the wilderness."

"Told with wonderful historical accuracy! And did he end there?"

"Oh, no!—then he said that these agents seldom married; and—and—they must have been wicked men, Elizabeth! but I assure you he said so."

"Never mind," said Miss Temple, blushing and smiling, though so slightly that both were unheeded by her companion—"skip all that."

"Well, then he said that they often took great pride in the education of their children, whom they frequently sent to England, and even to the colleges; and this is the way that he accounts for the liberal manner in which Mr. Edwards has been taught; for he acknowledges that he knows almost as much as your father—or mine—or even himself!"

"Quite a climax in learning! And so he made Mohegan the granduncle or grandfather of Oliver Edwards."

"You have heard him yourself, then?" said Louisa.

"Often; but not on this subject. Mr. Richard Jones, you know, dear, has a theory for everything; but has he one which will explain the reason why that hut is the only habitation within fifty miles of us whose door is not open to every person who may choose to lift its latch?"

"I have never heard him say anything on this subject," returned the clergyman's daughter; "but I suppose that, as they are poor, they very naturally are anxious to keep the little that they honestly own. It is sometimes dangerous to be rich, Miss Temple; but you cannot know how hard it is to be very, very poor."

"Nor you, I trust, Louisa; at least I should hope, that in this land of abundance, no minister of the Church could be left to absolute suffering."

"There cannot be actual misery," returned the other, in a low and humble tone, "where there is a dependence on our Maker; but there may be such suffering as will cause the heart to ache."

"But not you—not you," said the impetuous Elizabeth—"not you, dear girl; you have never known the misery that is connected with poverty."

"Ah! Miss Temple, you little understand the troubles of this life, I believe. My father has spent many years as a missionary in the new countries, where his people were poor, and frequently we have been without bread; unable to buy, and ashamed to beg, because we would not disgrace his sacred calling. But how often have I seen him leave his home, where the sick and the hungry felt, when he left them, that they had lost their only earthly friend, to ride on a duty which could not be neglected for domestic evils. Oh! how hard it must be to preach consolation to others when your own heart is bursting with anguish!"

"But it is all over now! your father's income must now be equal to his wants—it must be—it shall be——"

"It is," replied Louisa, dropping her head on her bosom to conceal the tears which flowed in spite of her gentle Christianity,—"for there are none left to be supplied but me."

The turn the conversation had taken drove from the minds of the young maidens all other thoughts but those of holy charity; and Elizabeth folded her friend in her arms, when the latter gave vent to her momentary grief in audible sobs. When this burst of emotion had subsided, Louisa raised her mild countenance, and they continued their walk in silence.

By this time they had gained the summit of the mountain, where they left the highway, and pursued their course, under the shade of the stately trees that crowned the eminence. The day was becoming warm, and the girls plunged more deeply into the forest, as they found its invigorating coolness agreeably contrasted to the excessive heat they had experienced in the ascent. The conversation, as if by mutual consent, was entirely changed to the little incidents and scenes of their walk, and every tall pine, and every shrub or flower, called forth some simple expression of admiration.

In this manner they proceeded along the margin of the precipice, catching occasional glimpses of the placid Otsego, or pausing to listen to the rattling of wheels and the sounds of hammers, that rose from the valley, to mingle the signs of men with the scenes of nature, when Elizabeth suddenly started, and exclaimed—

"Listen! there are the cries of a child on this mountain! is there a clearing near us? or can some little one have strayed from its parents?"

"Such things frequently happen," returned Louisa. "Let us follow the sounds: it may be a wanderer starving on the hill."

Urged by this consideration, the females pursued the low, mournful sounds, that proceeded from the forest, with quick and impatient steps. More than once the ardent Elizabeth was on the point of announcing that she saw the sufferer, when Louisa caught her by the arm, and pointing behind them, cried—

"Look at the dog!"

Brave had been their companion, from the time the voice of his young mistress lured him from his kennel, to the present moment. His advanced age had long before deprived him of his activity; and when his companions stopped to view the scenery, or to add to their bouquets, the mastiff would lay his huge frame on the ground, and await their movements with his eyes closed and a listlessness in his air that ill accorded with the character of a protector. But when, aroused by this cry from Louisa, Miss Temple turned, she saw the dog with his eyes keenly set on some distant object, his head bent near the ground, and his hair actually rising on his body, through fright or anger. It was most probably the latter, for he was growling in a low key, and occasionally showing his teeth, in a manner that would have terrified his mistress had she not so well known his good qualities.

"Brave!" she said, "be quiet, Brave! what do you see, fellow?"

At the sounds of her voice the rage of the mastiff, instead of being at all diminished, was very sensibly increased. He stalked in front of the ladies, and seated himself at the feet of his mistress, growling louder than before, and occasionally giving vent to his ire by a short, surly barking.

"What does he see?" said Elizabeth: "there must be some animal in sight."

Hearing no answer from her companion, Miss Temple turned her head, and beheld Louisa, standing with her face whitened to the color of death, and her finger pointing upward, with a sort of flickering, convulsed motion. The quick eye of Elizabeth glanced in the direction indicated by her friend, where she saw the fierce front and glaring eyes of a female panther, fixed on them in horrid malignity, and threatening to leap.

"Let us fly!" exclaimed Elizabeth, grasping the arm of Louisa, whose form yielded like melting snow.

There was not a single feeling in the temperament of Elizabeth Temple that could prompt her to desert a companion in such an extremity. She fell on her knees, by the side of the inanimate Louisa, tearing from the person of her friend, with instinctive readiness, such parts of her dress as might obstruct her respiration, and encouraging their only safeguard, the dog, at the same time, by the sounds of her voice.

"Courage, Brave!" she cried, her own tones beginning to tremble, "courage, courage, good Brave!"

A quarter-grown cub, that had hitherto been unseen, now appeared, dropping from the branches of a sapling that grew under the shade of the beech which held its dam. This ignorant but vicious creature approached the dog, imitating the actions and sounds of its parent, but exhibiting a strange mixture of the playfulness of a kitten with the ferocity of its race. Standing on its hind legs, it would rend the bark of a tree with its forepaws, and play the antics of a cat; and then, by lashing itself with its tail, growling, and scratching the earth, it would attempt the manifestations of anger that rendered its parent so terrific.

All this time Brave stood firm and undaunted, his short tail erect, his body drawn backward on its haunches, and his eyes following the movements of both dam and cub. At every gambol played by the latter it approached nigher to the dog, the growling of the three becoming more horrid at each moment, until the younger beast, overleaping its intended bound, fell directly before the mastiff. There was a moment of fearful cries and struggles, but they ended almost as soon as commenced, by the cub appearing in the air, hurled from the jaws of Brave, with a violence that sent it against a tree so forcibly as to render it completely senseless.

Elizabeth witnessed the short struggle, and her blood was warming with the triumph of the dog, when she saw the form of the old panther in the air, springing twenty feet from the branch of the beech to the back of the mastiff. No words of ours can describe the fury of the conflict that followed. It was a confused struggle on the dried leaves, accompanied by loud and terrific cries. Miss Temple continued on her knees, bending over the form of Louisa, her eyes fixed on the animals, with an interest so horrid, and yet so intense, that she almost forgot her own stake in the result. So rapid and vigorous were the bounds of the inhabitant of the forest, that its active frame seemed constantly in the air, while the dog nobly faced his foe at each successive leap. When the panther lighted on the shoulders of the mastiff, which was its constant aim, old Brave, though torn with her talons and stained with his own blood, that already flowed from a dozen wounds, would shake off his furious foe like a feather, and rearing on his hind legs, rush to the fray again, with jaws distended and a dauntless eye. But age and his pampered life greatly disqualified the noble mastiff for such a struggle. In everything but courage he was only the vestige of what he had once been. A higher bound than ever raised the wary and furious beast far beyond the reach of the dog, who was making a desperate but fruitless dash at her, from which she alighted in a favorable position on the back of her aged foe. For a single moment only could the panther remain there, the great strength of the dog returning with a convulsive effort. But Elizabeth saw, as Brave fastened his teeth in the side of his enemy, that the collar of brass around his neck, which had been glittering throughout the fray, was of the color of blood, and directly, that his frame was sinking to the earth, where it soon lay prostrate and helpless. Several mighty efforts of the wildcat to extricate herself from the jaws of the dog followed, but they were fruitless until the mastiff turned on his back, his lips collapsed, and his teeth loosened, when the short convulsions and stillness that succeeded announced the death of poor Brave.

Elizabeth now lay wholly at the mercy of the beast. There is said to be something in the front of the image of the Maker that daunts the hearts of the inferior beings of His creation; and it would seem that some such power, in the present instance, suspended the threatened blow. The eyes of the monster and the kneeling maiden met for an instant when the former stooped to examine her fallen foe; next to scent her luckless cub. From the latter examination it turned, however, with its eyes apparently emitting flashes of fire, its tail lashing its sides furiously, and its claws projecting inches from her broad feet.

Miss Temple did not, or could not, move. Her hands were clasped in the attitude of prayer, but her eyes were still drawn to her terrible enemy—her cheeks were blanched to the whiteness of marble, and her lips were slightly separated with horror. The moment seemed now to have arrived for the fatal termination, and the beautiful figure of Elizabeth was bowing meekly to the stroke, when a rustling of leaves behind seemed rather to mock the organs than to meet her ears.

"Hist! hist!" said a low voice; "steep lower, gal; your bonnet hides the creater's head."

It was rather the yielding of nature than a compliance with this unexpected order that caused the head of our heroine to sink on her bosom; when she heard the report of the rifle, the whizzing of the bullet, and the enraged cries of the beast, who was rolling over on the earth, biting its own flesh, and tearing the twigs and branches within its reach. At the next instant the form of the Leatherstocking rushed by her, and he called aloud—

"Come in, Hector, come in, old fool; 'tis a hard-lived animal, and may jump ag'in."

Natty fearlessly maintained his position in front of the females, notwithstanding the violent bounds and threatening aspect of the wounded panther, which gave several indications of returning strength and ferocity, until his rifle was again loaded, when he stepped up to the enraged animal, and placing the muzzle close to its head, every spark of life was extinguished by the discharge.

The death of her terrible enemy appeared to Elizabeth like a resurrection from her own grave. There was an elasticity in the mind of our heroine that rose to meet the pressure of instant danger, and the more direct it had been the more her nature had struggled to overcome it. But still she was woman. Had she been left to herself, in her late extremity, she would probably have used her faculties to the utmost, and with discretion, in protecting her person, but encumbered with her inanimate friend, retreat was a thing not to be attempted.—Notwithstanding the fearful aspect of her foe, the eye of Elizabeth had never shrunk from its gaze, and long after the event her thoughts would recur to her passing sensations, and the sweetness of her midnight sleep would be disturbed, as her active fancy conjured, in dreams, the most trifling movements of savage fury that the beast had exhibited in its moment of power.

We shall leave the reader to imagine the restoration of Louisa's senses, and the expressions of gratitude which fell from the young women. The former was effected by a little water, that was brought from one of the thousand springs of those mountains in the cap of the Leatherstocking; and the latter were uttered with the warmth that might be expected from the character of Elizabeth. Natty received her vehement protestations of gratitude with a simple expression of good will, and with indulgence for her present excitement, but with a carelessness that showed how little he thought of the service he had rendered.

"Well, well," he said, "be it so, gal; let it be so, if you wish it—

we'll talk the thing over another time. Come, come—let us get into the road, for you've had terror enough to make you wish yourself in your father's house ag'in."

This was uttered as they were proceeding, at a pace that was adapted to the weakness of Louisa, toward the highway: on reaching which the ladies separated from their guide, declaring themselves equal to the remainder of the walk without his assistance, and feeling encouraged by the sight of the village which lay beneath their feet, like a picture, with its limpid lake in front, the winding stream along its margin, and its hundred chimneys of whitened bricks.

The reader need not be told the nature of the emotions which two youthful, ingenuous, and well-educated girls would experience at their escape from a death so horrid as the one which had impended over them while they pursued their way in silence along the track on the side of the mountain; nor how deep were their mental thanks to that Power which had given them their existence, and which had not deserted them in their extremity; neither how often they pressed each other's arms, as the assurance of their present safety came, like a healing balm, athwart their troubled spirits, when their thoughts were recurring to the recent moments of horror.

Leatherstocking remained on the hill, gazing after their retiring figures, until they were hid by a bend in the road, when he whistled in his dogs, and shouldering his rifle, he returned into the forest.

"Well, it was a skeary thing to the young creaters," said Natty, while he retrod the path towards the slain. "It might frighten an older woman to see a she painter so near her, with a dead cub by its side. I wonder if I had aimed at the varmint's eye if I shouldn't have touched the life sooner than in the forehead; but they are hard-lived animals, and it was a good shot, consid'ring that I could see nothing but the head and the peak of its tail. Hah! who goes there?"

"How goes it, Natty?" said Mr. Doolittle, stepping out of the bushes, with a motion that was a good deal accelerated by the sight of the rifle, that was already lowered in his direction. "What! shooting this warm day! mind, old man, the law don't get hold on you."

"The law, Squire! I have shook hands with the law these forty year," returned Natty; "for what has a man who lives in the wilderness to do with the ways of the law?"

"Not much, maybe," said Hiram; "but you sometimes trade in venison. I s'pose you know, Leatherstocking, that there is an Act passed to lay a fine of five pounds currency, or twelve dollars and fifty cents, by decimals, on every man who kills a deer betwixt January and August. The Judge had a great hand in getting the law through."

"I can believe it," returned the old hunter; "I can believe that or anything of a man who carries on as he does in the country."

"Yes, the law is quite positive, and the Judge is bent on putting it in force—five pounds penalty. I thought I heard your hounds out on the scent of so'thing this morning: I didn't know but they might get you in difficulty."

"They know their manners too well," said Natty carelessly. "And how much goes to the state's evidence, Squire?"

"How much!" repeated Hiram, quailing under the honest but sharp look of the hunter; "the informer gets half, I—I b'lieve;—yes, I guess it's half. But there's blood on your sleeve, man—you haven't been shooting anything this morning?"

"I have, though," said the hunter, nodding his head significantly to the other, "and a good shot I made of it."

"H-e-m!" ejaculated the magistrate; "and where is the game? I s'pose it's of a good nater, for your dogs won't hunt at anything that isn't choice."

"They'll hunt anything I tell them to, Squire," cried Natty, favoring the other with his laugh. "They'll hunt you, if I say so. He-e-e-re, he-e-e-re, Hector—he-e-e-re, slut—come this-a-way, pups—come this-a-way—come hither."

"Oh! I have always heard a good character of the dogs," returned Mr. Doolittle, quickening his pace by raising each leg in rapid succession, as the hounds scented around his person. "And where is the game, Leatherstocking?"

During this dialogue the speakers had been walking at a very fast gait, and Natty swung the end of his rifle round, pointing through the bushes, and replied—

"There lies one. How do you like such meat?"

"This!" exclaimed Hiram; "why, this is Judge Temple's dog Brave. Take care, Leatherstocking, and don't make an enemy of the Judge. I hope you haven't harmed the animal?"

"Look for yourself, Mr. Doolittle," said Natty, drawing his knife from his girdle, and wiping it, in a knowing manner, once or twice across his garment of buckskin; "does his throat look as if I had cut it with this knife?"

"It is dreadfully torn! it's an awful wound—no knife never did this deed. Who could have done it?"

"The painters behind you, Squire."

"Painters!" echoed Hiram, whirling on his heel with an agility that would have done credit to a dancing master.

"Be easy, man," said Natty; "there's two of the venomous things; but the dog finished one, and I have fastened the other's jaws for her; so don't be frightened, Squire, they won't hurt you."

"And where's the deer?" cried Hiram, staring about him with a bewildered air.

"Anan! deer!" repeated Natty.

"Sartain, an't there ven'son here, or didn't you kill a buck?"

"What! when the law forbids the thing, Squire!" said the old hunter. "I hope there's no law ag'in killing the painters."

"No; there's a bounty on the scalps—but—will your dogs hunt painters, Natty?"

"Anything; didn't I tell you they'd hunt a man? He-e-re, he-e-re, pups——"

"Yes, yes, I remember. Well, they are strange dogs, I must say—I am quite in a wonderment."

Natty had seated himself on the ground, and having laid the grim head of his late ferocious enemy in his lap, was drawing his knife with a practiced hand around the ears, which he tore from the head of the beast in such a manner as to preserve their connection, when he answered—

"What at, Squire? did you never see a painter's scalp afore? Come, you are a magistrate, I wish you'd make me out an order for the bounty."

"The bounty!" repeated Hiram, holding the ears on the end of his finger for a moment, as if uncertain how to proceed. "Well, let us go down to your hut, where you can take the oath, and I will write out the order. I suppose you have a Bible? all the law wants is the four Evangelists and the Lord's prayer."

"I keep no books," said Natty, a little coldly; "not such a Bible as the law needs."

"Oh! there's but one sort of Bible that's good in law," returned the magistrate; "and yourn will do as well as another's. Come, the carcasses are worth nothing, man; let us go down and take the oath."

"Softly, softly, Squire," said the hunter, lifting his trophies very deliberately from the ground, and shouldering his rifle; "why do you want an oath at all for a thing that your own eyes has seen? won't you believe yourself, that another man must swear to a fact that you know to be true? You have seen me scalp the creaters, and if I must swear to it, it shall be before Judge Temple, who needs an oath."

"But we have no pen or paper here, Leatherstocking; we must go to the hut for them, or how can I write the order?"

Natty turned his simple features on the cunning magistrate with another of his laughs, as he said—

"And what should I be doing with scholars' tools? I want no pens or paper, not knowing the use of either; and I keep none. No, no, I'll bring the scalps into the village, Squire, and you can make out the order on one of your law books, and it will be all the better for it. The deuce take this leather on the neck of the dog, it will strangle the old fool. Can you lend me a knife, squire?"

Hiram, who seemed particularly anxious to be on good terms with his companion, unhesitatingly complied. Natty cut the thong from the neck of the hound, and, as he returned the knife to its owner, carelessly remarked—

" 'Tis a good bit of steel, and has cut such leather as this very same before now, I daresay."

"Do you mean to charge me with letting your hounds loose?" exclaimed Hiram, with a consciousness that disarmed his caution.

"Loose!" repeated the hunter—"I let them loose myself. I always let them loose before I leave the hut."

The ungovernable amazement with which Mr. Doolittle listened to this falsehood would have betrayed his agency in the liberation of the dogs had Natty wanted any further confirmation; and the coolness and management of the old man now disappeared in open indignation.

"Look you here, Mr. Doolittle," he said, striking the breech of his rifle violently on the ground; "what there is in the wigwam of a poor man like me, that one like you can crave, I don't know; but this I tell you to your face, that you never shall put foot under the roof of my cabin with my consent, and that if you harbor round the spot as you have done lately, you may meet with treatment that you will little relish."

"And let me tell you, Mr. Bumppo," said Hiram, retreating, however, with a quick step, "that I know you've broke the law, and that I'm a magistrate, and will make you feel it too before you are a day older."

"That for you and your law too," cried Natty, snapping his fingers at the justice of the peace; "away with you, you varmint, before the devil tempts me to give you your desarts. Take care, if I ever catch your prowling face in the woods ag'in, that I don't shoot it for an owl."

There is something at all times commanding in honest indignation, and Hiram did not stay to provoke the wrath of the old hunter to extremities. When the intruder was out of sight Natty proceeded to the hut, where he found all quiet as the grave. He fastened his dogs, and tapping at the door, which was opened by Edwards, asked—

"Is all safe, lad?"

"Everything," returned the youth. "Someone attempted the lock, but it was too strong for him."

"I know the creater," said Natty, "but he'll not trust himself within reach of my rifle very soon——" What more was uttered by the Leatherstocking in his vexation was rendered inaudible by the closing of the door of the cabin.

9

THE general puzzlement concerning Oliver Edwards, as he called himself, continued to deepen; and Judge Temple himself was perplexed when Squire Jones showed him that a cave on his property had been mysteriously excavated. Jones believed that Natty Bumppo, Chingachgook, and Edwards had found a vein of silver, and were busy mining and smelting it. This was incredible to the Judge, who pointed to the evident poverty of Edwards, and his good conduct in the Temple home. "Besides, there is an elevation of character about Oliver, that proceeds from education, which would forbid so clandestine a proceeding." Nevertheless, Judge Temple became uneasy.

It was not to be expected that the spiteful Hiram Doolittle would give up his object of arresting Bumppo for killing deer out of season. He was certain that Natty had venison in his cabin. Hurrying to Judge Temple, he obtained a warrant to search the hut. As Elizabeth Temple liked Leatherstocking, she remonstrated warmly, but the Judge pacified her by saying that the offense was punishable by only a small fine, and that she could pay this out of her own purse. Hiram Doolittle pocketed the warrant, collected two kindred spirits, Billy Kirby and a wood chopper named Jotham, to aid him, and set out for Natty Bumppo's door.

As the whole party moved at a great pace, they soon reached the hut, where Hiram thought it prudent to halt on the outside of the top of the fallen pine which formed a *chevaux-de-frise* to defend the approach to the fortress on the side next to the village. The delay was but little relished by Kirby, who clapped his hands to his mouth and gave a loud halloo, that brought the dogs out of their kennel, and, almost at the same instant, the scantily covered head of Natty from the door.

"Lie down, old fool," cried the hunter; "do you think there's more painters about you?"

"Ha! Leatherstocking, I've an errand with you," cried Kirby: "here's the good people of the state have been writing you a small letter, and they've hired me to ride post."

"What would you have with me, Billy Kirby?" said Natty, stepping across his threshold, and raising his hand over his eyes to screen them from the rays of the setting sun, while he took a survey of his visitor. "I've no land to clear; and heaven knows I would set out six trees afore I would cut down one. Down, Hector, I say; into your kennel with ye."

"Would you, old boy?" roared Billy; "then so much the better for me. But I must do my errand. Here's a letter for you, Leatherstocking. If you can read it, it's all well, and if you can't, here's Squire Doolittle at hand to let you know what it means. It seems you mistook the twentieth of July for the first of August, that's all."

By this time Natty had discovered the lank person of Hiram drawn up under the cover of a high stump; and all that was complacent in his manner instantly gave way to marked distrust and dissatisfaction. He placed his head within the door of his hut, and said a few words in an undertone, when he again appeared and continued—

"I've nothing for ye; so away, afore the evil one tempts me to do you harm. I owe you no spite, Billy Kirby, and what for should you trouble an old man who has done you no harm?"

Kirby advanced through the top of the pine to within a few feet of the hunter, where he seated himself on the end of a log with great composure, and began to examine the nose of Hector, with whom he was familiar from their frequently meeting in the woods, where he sometimes fed the dog from his own basket of provisions.

"You've outshot me, and I'm not ashamed to say it," said the wood chopper; "but I don't owe you a grudge for that, Natty! though it seems that you've shot once too often, for the story goes that you've killed a buck."

"I've fired but twice today, and both times at the painters," returned the Leatherstocking: "see, here are the scalps! I was just going in with them to the Judge's to ask the bounty."

While Natty was speaking, he tossed the ears to Kirby, who continued playing with them with a careless air, holding them to the dogs, and laughing at their movements when they scented the unusual game.

But Hiram, emboldened by the advance of the deputed constable, now ventured to approach also, and took up the discourse with the air of authority that became his commission. His first measure was to read the warrant aloud, taking care to give due emphasis to the most material parts, and concluding with the name of the Judge in very audible and distinct tones.

"Did Marmaduke Temple put his name to that bit of paper?" said Natty, shaking his head;—"well, well, that man loves the new ways, and his betterments, and his lands, afore his own flesh and blood. But I won't mistrust the gal: she has an eye like a full-grown buck! Poor thing, she didn't choose her father, and can't help it. I know but little of the law, Mr. Doolittle; what is to be done, now you have read your commission?"

"Oh! it's nothing but form, Natty," said Hiram, endeavoring to assume a friendly aspect. "Let's go in, and talk the thing over in reason. I dare to say that the money can be easily found, and I partly conclude, from what passed, that Judge Temple will pay it himself."

The old hunter had kept a keen eye on the movements of his three visitors from the beginning, and had maintained his position, just without the threshold of his cabin, with a determined manner that showed he was not to be easily driven from his post. When Hiram drew nigher, as if expecting his proposition would be accepted, Natty lifted his hand and motioned for him to retreat.

"Haven't I told you more than once not to tempt me?" he said. "I trouble no man; why can't the law leave me to myself? Go back—go back, and tell your Judge that he may keep his bounty; but I won't have his wasty ways brought into my hut."

This offer, however, instead of appeasing the curiosity of Hiram, seemed to inflame it the more; while Kirby cried—

"Well, that's fair, Squire; he forgives the county his demand, and the county should forgive him the fine; it's what I call an even trade, and should be concluded on the spot. I like quick dealings, and what's fair 'twixt man and man."

"I demand entrance into this house," said Hiram, summoning all the dignity he could muster to his assistance, "in the name of the people, and by virtue of this warrant, and of my office, and with this peace officer."

"Stand back, stand back, Squire, and don't tempt me," said the Leatherstocking, motioning for him to retire, with great earnestness.

"Stop us at your peril," continued Hiram. "Billy! Jotham! close up—I want testimony."

Hiram had mistaken the mild but determined air of Natty for submission, and had already put his foot on the threshold to enter when he was seized unexpectedly by his shoulders, and hurled over the little bank toward the lake, to the distance of twenty feet. The suddenness of the movement, and the unexpected display of strength on the part of Natty, created a momentary astonishment in his invaders that silenced all noises; but at the next instant Billy Kirby gave vent to his mirth in peals of laughter, that he seemed to heave up from his very soul.

"Well done, old stub!" he shouted: "the Squire know'd you better than I did. Come, come, here's a green spot; take it out like men, while Jotham and I see fair play."

"William Kirby, I order you to do your duty," cried Hiram, from under the bank; "seize that man; I order you to seize him in the name of the people."

But the Leatherstocking now assumed a more threatening attitude; his rifle was in his hand, and its muzzle was directed toward the wood chopper.

"Stand off, I bid ye," said Natty; "you know my aim, Billy Kirby; I don't crave your blood, but mine and yourn both shall turn this green grass red, afore you put foot into the hut."

While the affair appeared trifling, the wood chopper seemed disposed to take sides with the weaker party; but when the firearms were introduced his manner very sensibly changed. He raised his large frame from the log, and, facing the hunter with an open front, he replied—

"I didn't come here as your enemy, Leatherstocking; but I don't value the hollow piece of iron in your hand so much as a broken ax helve;—so, Squire, say the word, and keep within the law, and we'll soon see who's the best man of the two."

But no magistrate was to be seen! The instant the rifle was produced Hiram and Jotham vanished; and when the wood chopper bent his eyes about him in surprise at receiving no answer, he discovered their retreating figures moving towards the village at a rate that sufficiently indicated that they had not only calculated the velocity of a rifle bullet, but also its probable range.

"You've scared the creaters off," said Kirby, with great contempt expressed on his broad features; "but you are not going to scare me; so, Mr. Bumppo, down with your gun, or there'll be trouble 'twixt us."

Natty dropped his rifle, and replied—

"I wish you no harm, Billy Kirby; but I leave it to yourself, whether an old man's hut is to be run down by such varmint. I won't deny the buck to you, Billy, and you may take the skin in, if you please, and show it as testimony. The bounty will pay the fine, and that ought to satisfy any man."

" 'Twill, old boy, 'twill," cried Kirby, every shade of displeasure vanishing from his open brow at the peace offering; "throw out the hide, and that shall satisfy the law."

Natty entered his hut and soon reappeared, bringing with him the desired testimonial; and the wood chopper departed, as thoroughly reconciled to the hunter as if nothing had happened. As he paced along the margin of the lake, he would burst into frequent fits of laughter while he recollected the summerset of Hiram; and, on the whole, he thought the affair a very capital joke.

Long before Billy reached the village, however, the news of his danger, and of Natty's disrespect of the law, and of Hiram's discomfiture, were in circulation. A good deal was said about sending for the Sheriff; some hints were given about calling out the *posse comitatus* to avenge the insulted laws; and many of the citizens were collected, deliberating how to proceed. The arrival of Billy with the skin, by removing all grounds for a search, changed the complexion of things materially. Nothing now remained but to collect the fine, and assert the dignity of the people; all of which, it was unanimously agreed, could be done as well on the succeeding Monday as on a Saturday night,—a time kept sacred by a large portion of the settlers. Accordingly, all further proceedings were suspended for six-and-thirty hours.

The commotion was just subsiding, and the inhabitants of the village had begun to disperse from the little groups they had formed, each retiring to his own home, and closing his door after him, with the grave air of a man who consulted public feeling in his exterior deportment, when Oliver Edwards, on his return from the dwelling of Mr. Grant, encountered the young lawyer who is known to the reader as Mr. Lippet. There was very little similarity in the manners or opinions of the two; but as they both belonged to the more intelligent class of a very small community, they were, of course, known to each other; and as their meeting was at a point where silence would have been rudeness, the following conversation was the result of their interview:—

"A fine evening, Mr. Edwards," commenced the lawyer, whose disinclination to the dialogue was, to say the least, very doubtful; "we want rain sadly;—that's the worst of this climate of ours, it's either a drought or a deluge. It's likely you've been used to a more equal temperature?"

"I am a native of this state," returned Edwards coldly.

"Well, I've often heard that point disputed; but it's so easy to get a man naturalized that it's of little consequence where he was born. I wonder what course the Judge means to take in this business of Natty Bumppo!"

"Of Natty Bumppo!" echoed Edwards; "to what do you allude, sir?"

"Haven't you heard!" exclaimed the other with a look of surprise, so naturally assumed as completely to deceive his auditor. "It may turn out an ugly business. It seems that the old man has been out in the hills and has shot a buck this morning, and that, you know, is a criminal matter in the eyes of Judge Temple."

"Oh, he has, has he?" said Edwards, averting his face to conceal the color that collected in his sunburnt cheek. "Well, if that be all, he must even pay the fine."

"It's five pounds currency," said the lawyer; "could Natty muster so much money at once?"

"Could he!" cried the youth. "I am not rich, Mr. Lippet; far from it—I am poor, and I have been hoarding my salary for a purpose that lies near my heart; but before that old man should lie one hour in a gaol, I would spend the last cent to prevent it. Besides, he has killed two panthers, and the bounty will discharge the fine many times over."

"Yes, yes," said the lawyer, rubbing his hands together with an expression of pleasure that had no artifice about it; "we shall make it out; I see plainly we shall make it out."

"Make what out, sir? I must beg an explanation."

"Why, killing the buck is but a small matter compared to what took place this afternoon," continued Mr. Lippet with a confidential and friendly air, that insensibly won upon the youth, little as he liked the man. "It seems that a complaint was made of the fact, and a suspicion that there was venison in the hut was sworn to, all which is provided for in the statute, when Judge Temple granted a search warrant——"

"A search warrant!" echoed Edwards in a voice of horror, and with a face that should have been again averted to conceal its paleness; "and how much did they discover? What did they see?"

"They saw old Bumppo's rifle; and that is a sight which will quiet most men's curiosity in the woods."

"Did they! did they!" shouted Edwards, bursting into a convulsive laugh; "so the old hero beat them back!—he beat them back! did he?"

The lawyer fastened his eyes in astonishment on the youth, but as his wonder gave way to the thoughts that were commonly uppermost in his mind, he replied—

"It's no laughing matter, let me tell you, sir; the forty dollars of bounty and your six months of salary will be much reduced before you can get the matter fairly settled. Assaulting a magistrate in the execution of his duty, and menacing a constable with firearms at the same time, is a pretty serious affair, and is punishable with both fine and imprisonment."

"Imprisonment!" repeated Oliver; "imprison the Leatherstocking! No, no, sir; it would bring the old man to his grave. They shall never imprison the Leatherstocking."

"Well, Mr. Edwards," said Lippet, dropping all reserve from his manner, "you are called a curious man; but if you can tell me how a jury is to be prevented from finding a verdict of guilty, if this case comes fairly before them, and the proof is clear, I shall acknowledge that you know more law than I do, who have had a license in my pocket for three years."

By this time the reason of Edwards was getting the ascendency of his feelings; and as he began to see the real difficulties of the case, he listened more readily to the conversation of the lawyer.

Oliver and Lawyer Lippet soon parted, the lawyer going to his office, the young man hurrying to the mansion house of Judge Temple. On arrival, Oliver found that the Judge had not only issued a search warrant, but was determined to let justice take its course with the stubborn Leatherstocking. The young man was indignant. "Will not the years, the habits, nay, the ignorance, of my old friend, avail him anything against this charge?" To which Judge Temple returned: "Ought they? They may extenuate, but can they acquit?" As the two continued to converse, Oliver's temper rose. Finally, when the Judge spoke of Leatherstocking's crime, Edwards grew fierce:

"Crime!" he said. "Is it a crime to drive a prying miscreant from his door? Crime! Oh, no, sir; if there be a criminal involved in this affair, it is not he."

"And who may it be, sir?" asked Judge Temple, coldly.

"Who? And this to me?" cried the agitated young man. "Ask your own conscience, Judge Temple. Walk to that door, sir, and look out upon the valley, the placid lake, and those dusky mountains, and say to your own heart, if heart you have, Whence came these riches, this vale, those hills, and why am I their owner?"

After this outburst, Oliver Edwards left the employ of the Judge. But they did not part on bad terms, and Oliver's farewell to Elizabeth had a tender character.

The law now indeed took its course with Leatherstocking. Squire Richard Jones, as sheriff of the county, gathered together two deputies and a half dozen constables. Natty Bumppo, as they soon found, had taken his predicament with tragic intensity of feeling. Sheriff Jones feared a violent reception, but hoped that his little force would overawe the old scout.

With this force Richard led the way through the village, toward the bank of the lake, undisturbed by any noise, except the barking of one or two curs, who were alarmed by the measured tread of the party, and by the low murmurs that ran through their own numbers, as a few cautious questions and answers were exchanged relative to the object of their expedition. When they had crossed the little bridge of hewn logs that was thrown over the Susquehanna, they left the highway, and struck into that field which had been the scene of the victory over the pigeons. From this they followed their leader into the low bushes of pines and chestnuts which had sprung up along the shores of the lake, where the plough had not succeeded the fall of the trees, and soon entered the forest itself. Here Richard paused, and collected his troop around him.

"I have required your assistance, my friends," he said in a low voice, "in order to arrest Nathaniel Bumppo, commonly called the Leatherstocking. He has assaulted a magistrate, and resisted the execution of a search warrant by threatening the life of a constable with his rifle. In short, my friends, he has set an example of rebellion to the laws, and has become a kind of outlaw. He is suspected of other misdemeanors and offences against private rights; and I have this night taken on myself, by the virtue of my office of Sheriff, to arrest the said Bumppo, and bring him to the county gaol, that he may be present and forthcoming to answer to these heavy charges before the court tomorrow morning. In executing this duty, friends and fellow-citizens, you are to use courage and discretion. Courage, that you may not be daunted by any lawless attempts that this man may make with his rifle and his dogs to oppose you; and discretion, which here means caution and prudence, that he may not escape from this sudden attack—and for other good reasons that I need not mention. You will form yourselves in a complete circle around his hut, and at the word 'advance,' called aloud by me, you will rush forward, and, without giving the criminal time for deliberation, enter his dwelling by force, and make him your prisoner. Spread yourselves for this purpose, while I shall descend to the shore with a deputy, to take charge of that point; and all communications must be made directly to me, under the bank in front of the hut, where I shall station myself, and remain in order to receive them."

This speech, which Richard had been studying during his walk, had the effect that all similar performances produce, of bringing the dangers of the expedition immediately before the eyes of his forces. The men divided, some plunging deeper into the forest in order to gain their stations without giving an alarm, and others continuing to advance, at a gait that would allow the whole party to get in order; but all devising the best plan to repulse the attack of a dog, or to escape a rifle bullet. It was a moment of dread expectation and interest.

When the Sheriff thought time enough had elapsed for the different divisions of his force to arrive at their stations, he raised his voice in the silence of the forest and shouted the watchword. The sounds played among the arched branches of the trees in hollow cadences; but when the last sinking tone was lost on the ear, in place of the expected howls of the dogs, no other noises were returned but the crackling of torn branches and dried sticks as they yielded before the advancing steps of the officers. Even this soon ceased as if by a common consent, when the curiosity and impatience of the Sheriff getting the complete ascendency over discretion, he rushed up the bank, and in a moment stood on the little piece of cleared ground in front of the spot where Natty had so long lived. To his amazement, in place of the hut he saw only its smouldering ruins.

The party gradually drew together about the heap of ashes and the ends of smoking logs; while a dim flame in the center of the ruin, which still found fuel to feed its lingering life, threw its pale light, flickering with the passing currents of the air, around the circle,—now showing a face with eyes fixed in astonishment, and then glancing to another countenance, leaving the former shaded in the obscurity of night. Not a voice was raised in inquiry, nor an exclamation made in astonishment. The transition from excitement to disappointment was too powerful for speech; and even Richard lost the use of an organ that was seldom known to fail him.

The whole group were yet in the fullness of their surprise, when a tall form stalked from the gloom into the circle, treading down the hot ashes and dying embers with callous feet; and, standing over the light, lifted his cap and exposed the bare head and weather-beaten features of the Leatherstocking. For a moment he gazed at the dusky figures who surrounded him, more in sorrow than in anger, before he spoke.

"What would ye have with an old and helpless man?" he said. "You've driven God's creaters from the wilderness, where His providence had put them for His own pleasure; and you've brought in the troubles and divilties of the law, where no man was ever known to disturb another. You have driven me, that have lived forty long years of my appointed time in this very spot, from my home and the shelter of my head, lest you should put your wicked feet and wasty ways in my cabin. You've driven me to burn these logs, under which I've eaten and drunk—the first of Heaven's gifts, and the other of the pure springs—for the half of a hundred years; and to mourn the ashes under my feet, as a man would weep and mourn for the children of his body. You've rankled the heart of an old man, that has never harmed you or your'n, with bitter feelings toward his kind, at a time when his thoughts should be on a better world; and you've driven him to wish that the beasts of the forest, who never feast on the blood of their own families, was his kindred and race; and now, when he has come to see the last brand of his hut before it is melted into ashes, you follow him up at midnight like hungry hounds on the track of a worn-out and dying deer. What more would ye have? for I am here—one to many. I come to mourn, not to fight; and, if it is God's pleasure, work your will on me."

When the old man ended, he stood with the light glimmering around his thinly covered head, looking earnestly at the group which receded from the pile with an involuntary movement, without the reach of the quivering rays, leaving a free passage for his retreat into the bushes, where pursuit in the dark would have been fruitless. Natty seemed not to regard this advantage; but stood facing each individual in the circle in succession, as if to see who would be the first to arrest him. After a pause of a few moments, Richard began to rally his confused faculties; and, advancing, apologized for his duty and made him his prisoner. The party now collected; and, preceded by the Sheriff, with Natty in their center, they took their way toward the village.

During the walk, divers questions were put to the prisoner concerning his reasons for burning the hut, and whither Mohegan had retreated; but to all of them he observed a profound silence, until, fatigued with their previous duties and the lateness of the hour, the Sheriff and his followers reached the village, and dispersed to their several places of rest after turning the key of a gaol on the aged and apparently friendless Leatherstocking.

The long days and early sun of July allowed time for a gathering of the interested, before the little bell of the academy announced that the appointed hour had arrived for administering right to the wronged and punishment to the guilty. Ever since the dawn of day, the highways and woodpaths that, issuing from the forests and winding along the sides of the mountains, centered in Templeton, had been thronged with equestrians and footmen bound to the haven of justice. There was to be seen a well-clad yeoman, mounted on a sleek, switch-tailed steed, ambling along the highway, with his red face elevated in a manner that said, "I have paid for my land and fear no man"; while his bosom was swelling with the pride of being one of the grand inquest for the county. At his side rode a companion, his equal in independence of feeling, perhaps, but his inferior in thrift as in property and consideration. This was a professed dealer in lawsuits,—a man whose name appeared in every calendar,—whose substance, gained in the multifarious expedients of a settler's changeable habits, was wasted in feeding the harpies of the courts. He was endeavoring to impress the mind of the grand juror with the merits of a cause now at issue. Along with these was a pedestrian, who, having thrown a rifle frock over his shirt, and placed his best wool hat above his sunburnt visage, had issued from his retreat in the woods by a footpath, and was striving to keep company with the others, on his way to hear and to decide the disputes of his neighbors, as a petit juror. Fifty similar little knots of countrymen might have been seen, on that morning, journey toward the shire town on the same errand.

By ten o'clock the streets of the village were filled with busy faces; some talking of their private concerns, some listening to a popular expounder of political creeds; and others gaping in at the open stores, admiring the finery, or examining scythes, axes, and such other manufactures as attracted their curiosity or excited their admiration. A few women were in the crowd, mostly carrying infants, and followed, at a lounging, listless gait, by their rustic lords and masters. There was one young couple, in whom connubial love was yet fresh, walking at a respectful distance from each other; while the swain directed the timid steps of his bride by a gallant offering of a thumb!

At the first stroke of the bell Richard issued from the door of the "Bold Dragoon," flourishing a sheathed sword that he was fond of saying his ancestors had carried in one of Cromwell's victories, and crying in an authoritative tone to "clear the way for the court." The order was obeyed promptly though not servilely, the members of the crowd nodding familiarly to the members of the procession as it passed. A party of constables with their staves followed the Sheriff, preceding Marmaduke, and four plain, grave-looking yeomen, who were his associates on the bench. There was nothing to distinguish these subordinate judges from the better part of the spectators except gravity, which they affected a little more than common, and that one of their number was attired in an old-fashioned military coat, with skirts that reached no lower than the middle of his thighs, and bearing two little silver epaulettes, not half so big as a modern pair of shoulder knots. This gentleman was a colonel of the militia, in attendance on a court-martial, who found leisure to steal a moment from his military to attend to his civil jurisdiction; but this incongruity excited neither notice nor comment. Three or four clean-shaved lawyers followed, as meekly as if they were lambs going to the slaughter. One or two of their number had contrived to obtain an air of scholastic gravity by wearing spectacles. The rear was brought up by another posse of constables, and the mob followed the whole into the room where the court held its sittings.

The edifice was composed of a basement of squared logs, perforated here and there with small grated windows, through which a few wistful faces were gazing at the crowd without. Among the captives were the guilty, downcast countenances of the counterfeiters, and the simple but honest features of the Leatherstocking. The dungeons were to be distinguished externally from the debtors' apartments only by the size of the apertures, the thickness of the grates, and by the heads of the spikes that were driven into the logs as a protection against the illegal use of edge-tools. The upper story was of framework, regularly covered with boards, and contained one room decently fitted up for the purposes of justice. A bench, raised on a narrow platform to the height of a man above the floor, and protected in front by a light railing, ran along one of its sides. In the center was a seat, furnished with rude arms, that was always filled by the presiding judge. In front, on a level with the floor of the room, was a large table covered with green baize and surrounded by benches; and at either of its ends were rows of seats rising one over the other for jury boxes. Each of these divisions was surrounded by a railing. The remainder of the room was an open space appropriated to the spectators.

When the judges were seated, the lawyers had taken possession of the table, and the noise of moving feet had ceased in the area, the proclamations were made in the usual form, the jurors were sworn, the charge was given, and the court proceeded to hear the business before them.

We shall not detain the reader with a description of the captious discussions that occupied the court for the first two hours. Judge Temple had impressed on the jury, in his charge, the necessity for despatch on their part, recommending to their notice, from motives of humanity, the prisoners in the gaol as the first objects of their attention. Accordingly, after the period we have mentioned had elapsed, the cry of the officer to "clear the way for the grand jury" announced the entrance of that body. The usual forms were observed, when the foreman handed up to the bench two bills, on both of which the Judge observed, at the first glance of his eye, the name of Nathaniel Bumppo. It was a leisure moment with the court; some low whispering passed between the bench and the Sheriff, who gave a signal to his officers, and in a very few minutes the silence that prevailed was interrupted by a general movement in the outer crowd, when presently the Leather-stocking made his appearance, ushered into the criminal's bar under the custody of two constables. The hum ceased, the people closed into the open space again, and the silence soon became so deep that the hard breathing of the prisoner was audible.

Natty was dressed in his buckskin garments, without his coat, in place of which he wore only a shirt of coarse linen-check, fastened at his throat by the sinew of a deer, leaving his red neck and weather-beaten face exposed and bare. It was the first time that he had ever crossed the threshold of a court of justice, and curiosity seemed to be strongly blended with his personal feelings. He raised his eyes to the bench, thence to the jury boxes, the bar, and the crowd without, meeting everywhere looks fastened on himself. After surveying his own person, as searching the cause of this unusual attraction, he once more turned his face around the assemblage, and opened his mouth in one of his silent and remarkable laughs.

"Prisoner, remove your cap," said Judge Temple.

The order was either unheard or unheeded.

"Nathaniel Bumppo, be uncovered," repeated the Judge.

Natty started at the sound of his name, and raising his face earnestly toward the bench, he said—

"Anan!"

Mr. Lippet arose from his seat at the table, and whispered in the ear of the prisoner; when Natty gave him a nod of assent, and took the deerskin covering from his head.

"Mr. District Attorney," said the Judge, "the prisoner is ready; we wait for the indictment."

The duties of public prosecutor were discharged by Dirck Van der School, who adjusted his spectacles, cast a cautious look around him at his brethren of the bar, which he ended by throwing his head aside so as to catch one glance over the glasses, when he proceeded to read the bill aloud. It was the usual charge for an assault and battery on the person of Hiram Doolittle, and was couched in the ancient language of such instruments, especial care having been taken by the scribe not to omit the name of a single offensive weapon known to the law. When he had done, Mr. Van der School removed his spectacles, which he closed and placed in his pocket, seemingly for the pleasure of again opening and replacing them on his nose. After this evolution was repeated once or twice, he handed the bill over to Mr. Lippet, with a cavalier air, that said as much as "Pick a hole in that if you can."

Natty listened to the charge with great attention, leaning forward towards the reader with an earnestness that denoted his interest; and when it was ended, he raised his tall body to the utmost, and drew a long sigh. All eyes were turned to the prisoner, whose voice was vainly expected to break the stillness of the room.

"You have heard the presentment that the grand jury have made, Nathaniel Bumppo," said the Judge; "what do you plead to the charge?"

The old man dropped his head for a moment in a reflecting attitude, and then raising it, he laughed before he answered—

"That I handled the man a little rough or so, is not to be denied; but that there was occasion to make use of all the things that the gentleman had spoken of is downright untrue. I am not much of a wrestler, seeing that I'm getting old; but I was out among the Scotch-Irishers—lets me see—it must have been as long ago as the first year of the old war——"

"Mr. Lippet, if you are retained for the prisoner," interrupted Judge Temple, "instruct your client how to plead; if not, the court will assign him counsel."

Aroused from studying the indictment by this appeal, the attorney got up, and after a short dialogue with the hunter in a low voice, he informed the court that they were ready to proceed.

"Do you plead guilty or not guilty?" said the Judge.

"I may say not guilty with a clean conscience," returned Natty;

"for there's no guilt in doing what's right; and I'd rather died on the spot than had him put foot in the hut at that moment."

Richard started at this declaration, and bent his eyes significantly on Hiram, who returned the look with a slight movement of his eyebrows.

"Proceed to open the cause, Mr. District Attorney," continued the Judge. "Mr. Clerk, enter the plea of not guilty."

After a short opening address from Mr. Van der School, Hiram was summoned to the bar to give his testimony. It was delivered to the letter, perhaps, but with all that moral coloring which can be conveyed under such expressions as, "thinking no harm," "feeling it my bounden duty as a magistrate," and "seeing that the constable was back'ard in the business." When he had done, and the District Attorney declined putting any further interrogatories, Mr. Lippet arose, with an air of keen investigation, and asked the following questions:

"Are you a constable of this county, sir?"

"No, sir," said Hiram, "I'm only a justice-peace."

"I ask you, Mr. Doolittle, in the face of this court, putting it to your conscience and your knowledge of the law, whether you had any right to enter that man's dwelling?"

"Hem!" said Hiram, undergoing a violent struggle between his desire for vengeance and his love of legal fame; "I do suppose—that in—that is—strict law—that supposing—maybe I hadn't a real—lawful right;—but as the case was—and Billy was so back'ard—I thought I might come for'ard in the business."

"I ask you again, sir," continued the lawyer, following up his success, "whether this old, this friendless old man, did or did not repeatedly forbid your entrance?"

"Why, I must say," said Hiram, "that he was considerable cross-grained; not what I call clever, seeing that it was only one neighbor wanting to go into the house of another."

"Oh! then you own it was only meant for a neighborly visit on your part, and without the sanction of law. Remember, gentlemen, the words of the witness, 'one neighbor wanting to enter the house of another.' Now, sir, I ask you if Nathaniel Bumppo did not again and again order you not to enter?"

"There was some words passed between us," said Hiram, "but I read the warrant to him aloud."

"I repeat my question: did he tell you not to enter his habitation?"

"There was a good deal passed betwixt us—but I've the warrant in my pocket; maybe the court would wish to see it?"

"Witness," said Judge Temple, "answer the question directly: did or did not the prisoner forbid your entering his hut?"

"Why, I some think——"

"Answer without equivocation," continued the Judge sternly.

"He did."

"And did you attempt to enter after this order?"

"I did; but the warrant was in my hand."

"Proceed, Mr. Lippet, with your examination."

But the attorney saw that the impression was in favor of his client, and, waving his hand with a supercilious manner, as if unwilling to insult the understanding of the jury with any further defence, he replied—

"No, sir; I leave it for your honor to charge; I rest my case here."

"Mr. District Attorney," said the Judge, "have you anything to say?"

Mr. Van der School removed his spectacles, folded them, and replacing them once more on his nose, eyed the other bill which he held in his hand, and then said, looking at the bar over the top of his glasses—

"I shall rest the prosecution here, if the court please."

Judge Temple arose and began the charge.

"Gentlemen of the jury," he said, "you have heard the testimony, and I shall detain you but a moment. If an officer meet with resistance in the execution of a process, he has an undoubted right to call any citizen to his assistance; and the acts of such assistant come within the protection of the law. I shall leave you to judge, gentlemen, from the testimony, how far the witness in this prosecution can be so considered, feeling less reluctance to submit the case thus informally to your decision, because there is yet another indictment to be tried, which involves heavier charges against the unfortunate prisoner."

The tone of Marmaduke was mild and insinuating, and as his sentiments were given with such apparent impartiality, they did not fail of carrying due weight with the jury. The grave-looking yeomen, who composed this tribunal, laid their heads together for a few minutes, without leaving the box, when the foreman arose, and, after the forms of the court were duly observed, he pronounced the prisoner to be—

"Not guilty."

"You are acquitted of this charge, Nathaniel Bumppo," said the Judge.

"Anan!" said Natty.

"You are found not guilty of striking and assaulting Mr. Doolittle."

"No, no, I'll not deny but that I took him a little roughly by the shoulders," said Natty, looking about him with great simplicity, "and that I——"

"You are acquitted," interrupted the Judge; "and there is nothing further to be said or done in the matter."

A look of joy lighted up the features of the old man, who now comprehended the case, and, placing his cap eagerly on his head again, he threw up the bar of his little prison, and said feelingly—

"I must say this for you, Judge Temple, that the law has not been so hard on me as I dreaded. I hope God will bless you for the kind things you've done to me this day."

But the staff of the constable was opposed to his egress, and Mr. Lippet whispered a few words in his ear, when the aged hunter sunk back into his place, and, removing his cap, stroked down the remnants of his gray and sandy locks, with an air of mortification mingled with submission.

"Mr. District Attorney," said Judge Temple, affecting to busy himself with his minutes, "proceed with the second indictment."

Mr. Van der School took great care that no part of the presentment, which he now read, should be lost on his auditors. It accused the prisoner of resisting the execution of a search warrant, by force of arms, and particularized, in the vague language of the law, among a variety of other weapons, the use of the rifle. This was indeed a more serious charge than an ordinary assault and battery, and a corresponding degree of interest was manifested by the spectators in its result. The prisoner was duly arraigned, and his plea again demanded. Mr. Lippet had anticipated the answers of Natty, and in a whisper advised him how to plead. But the feelings of the old hunter were awakened by some of the expressions of the indictment, and, forgetful of his caution, he exclaimed—

" 'Tis a wicked untruth; I crave no man's blood. Them thieves, the Iroquois, won't say it to my face that I ever thirsted after man's blood. I have fou't as a soldier that feared his Maker and his officer, but I never pulled trigger on any but a warrior that was up and awake. No man can say that I ever struck even a Mingo in his blanket. I believe there's some who thinks there's no God in a wilderness!"

"Attend to your plea, Bumppo," said the Judge. "You hear that you are accused of using your rifle against an officer of justice; are you guilty or not guilty?"

By this time the irritated feelings of Natty had found vent; and he rested on the bar for a moment, in a musing posture, when he lifted his face, with his silent laugh, and, pointing to where the wood chopper stood, he said—

"Would Billy Kirby be standing there, d'ye think, if I had used the rifle?"

"Then you deny it," said Mr. Lippet; "you plead not guilty?"

"Sartain," said Natty; "Billy knows that I never fired at all. Billy, do you remember the turkey last winter? Ah me! that was better than common firing; but I can't shoot as I used to could."

"Enter the plea of not guilty," said Judge Temple, strongly affected by the simplicity of the prisoner.

Hiram was again sworn, and his testimony given on the second charge. He had discovered his former error, and proceeded more cautiously than before. He related very distinctly, and, for the man, with amazing terseness, the suspicion against the hunter, the complaint, the issuing of the warrant, and the swearing in of Kirby; all of which, he affirmed, were done in due form of law. He then added the manner in which the constable had been received; and stated distinctly that Natty had pointed the rifle at Kirby, and threatened his life, if he attempted to execute his duty. All this was confirmed by Jotham, who was observed to adhere closely to the story of the magistrate. Mr. Lippet conducted an artful cross-examination of these two witnesses, but after consuming much time, was compelled to relinquish the attempt to obtain any advantage, in despair.

At length the district attorney called the wood chopper to the bar. Billy gave an extremely confused account of the whole affair, although he evidently aimed at the truth, until Mr. Van der School aided him by asking some direct questions:—

"It appears, from examining the papers, that you demanded admission into the hut legally; so you were put in bodily fear by his rifle and threats?"

"I didn't mind them that, man," said Billy, snapping his fingers; "I should be a poor stick to mind old Leatherstocking."

"But I understood you to say (referring to your previous words, as delivered here in court, in the commencement of your testimony), that you thought he meant to shoot you?"

"To be sure I did; and so would you too, Squire, if you had seen the chap dropping a muzzle that never misses, and cocking an eye that has a nateral squint by long practice. I thought there would be a dust on't, and my back was up at once; but Leatherstocking gi'n up the skin, and so the matter ended."

"Ah! Billy," said Natty, shaking his head, " 'twas a lucky thought in me to throw out the hide, or there might have been blood spilt; and I'm sure, if it had been your'n, I should have mourn'd it sorely the little while I have to stay."

"Well, Leatherstocking," returned Billy, facing the prisoner with a freedom and familiarity that utterly disregarded the presence of the court, "as you are on the subject, it may be that you've no——"

"Go on with your examination, Mr. District Attorney."

That gentleman eyed the familiarity between his witness and the prisoner with manifest disgust, and indicated to the court that he was done.

"Then you didn't feel frightened, Mr. Kirby?" said the counsel for the prisoner.

"Me! no," said Billy, casting his eyes over his own huge frame with evident self-satisfaction; "I'm not to be skeared so easy."

"You look like a hardy man; where were you born, sir?"

"Varmount State; 'tis a mountaynious place, but there's a stiff soil, and it's pretty much wooded with beach and maple."

"I have always heard so," said Mr. Lippet soothingly. "You have been used to the rifle yourself, in that country?"

"I pull the second-best trigger in this county. I knock under to Natty Bumppo there, sin' he shot the pigeon."

Leatherstocking raised his head, and laughed again, when he abruptly thrust out a wrinkled hand, and said—

"You're young yet, Billy, and haven't seen the matches that I have; but here's my hand; I bear no malice to you, I don't."

Mr. Lippet allowed this conciliatory offering to be accepted, and judiciously paused while the spirit of peace was exercising its influence over the two; but the Judge interposed his authority.

"This is an improper place for such dialogues," he said. "Proceed with your examination of this witness, Mr. Lippet, or I shall order the next."

The attorney started, as if unconscious of any impropriety, and continued—

"So you settled the matter with Natty amicably on the spot, did you?"

"He gi'n me the skin, and I didn't want to quarrel with an old man; for my part, I see no such mighty matter in shooting a buck!"

"And you parted friends? and you would never have thought of bringing the business up before a court, hadn't you been subpœnaed?"

"I don't think I should; he gi'n the skin, and I didn't feel a hard thought, though Squire Doolittle got some affronted."

"I have done, sir," said Mr. Lippet, probably relying on the charge of the Judge, as he again seated himself, with the air of a man who felt that his success was certain.

When Mr. Van der School arose to address the jury he commenced by saying—

"Gentlemen of the jury, I should have interrupted the leading questions put by the prisoner's counsel (by leading questions I mean telling him what to say), did I not feel confident that the law of the land was superior to any advantages (I mean legal advantages) which he might obtain by his art. The counsel for the prisoner, gentlemen, has endeavored to persuade you, in opposition to your own good sense, to believe that pointing a rifle at a constable (elected or deputed) is a very innocent affair, and that society (I mean the commonwealth, gentlemen,) shall not be endangered thereby. But let me claim your attention while we look over the particulars of this heinous offence." Here Mr. Van der School favored the jury with an abridgement of the testimony, recounted in such a manner as utterly to confuse the faculties of his worthy listeners. After this exhibition he closed as follows—"And now, gentlemen, having thus made plain to your senses the crime of which this unfortunate man has been guilty (unfortunate both on account of his ignorance and his guilt), I shall leave you to your own consciences; not in the least doubting that you will see the importance (notwithstanding the prisoner's counsel—doubtless relying on your former verdict—wishes to appear so confident of success) of punishing the offender, and asserting the dignity of the laws."

It was now the duty of the Judge to deliver his charge. It consisted of a short, comprehensive summary of the testimony, laying bare the artifice of the prisoner's counsel, and placing the facts in so obvious a light that they could not well be misunderstood. "Living as we do, gentlemen," he concluded, "on the skirts of society, it becomes doubly necessary to protect the ministers of the law. If you believe the witnesses, in their construction of the acts of the prisoner, it is your duty to convict him; but if you believe that the old man, who this day appears before you, meant not to harm the constable, but was acting more under the influence of habit than by the instigations of malice, it will be your duty to judge him, but to do it with lenity."

As before, the jury did not leave their box; but, after a consultation of some little time, their foreman arose, and pronounced the prisoner—

"Guilty."

There was but little surprise manifested in the courtroom at this verdict, as the testimony, the greater part of which we have omitted, was too clear and direct to be passed over. The judges seemed to have anticipated this sentiment, for a consultation was passing among them also, during the deliberation of the jury, and the preparatory movements of the "bench" announced the coming sentence.

"Nathaniel Bumppo," commenced the Judge, making the customary pause.

The old hunter, who had been musing again, with his head on the bar, raised himself, and cried, with a prompt, military tone—

"Here."

The Judge waved his hand for silence, and proceeded—

"In forming their sentence, the court have been governed as much by the consideration of your ignorance of the laws as by a strict sense of the importance of punishing such outrages as this of which you have been found guilty. They have, therefore, passed over the obvious punishment of whipping on the bare back, in mercy to your years; but as the dignity of the law requires an open exhibition of the consequences of your crime, it is ordered that you be conveyed from this room to the public stocks, where you are to be confined for one hour; that you pay a fine to the state of one hundred dollars; and that you be imprisoned in the gaol of this county for one calendar month; and furthermore, that your imprisonment do not cease until the said fine shall be paid. I feel it my duty, Nathaniel Bumppo——"

"And where should I get the money?" interrupted the Leatherstocking eagerly; "where should I get the money? You'll take away the bounty on the painters, because I cut the throat of a deer; and how is an old man to find so much gold or silver in the woods? No, no, Judge; think better of it, and don't talk of shutting me up in a gaol for the little time I have to stay."

"If you have anything to urge against the passing of the sentence, the court will yet hear you," said the Judge mildly.

"I have enough to say ag'in it," cried Natty, grasping the bar on which his fingers were working with a convulsed motion. "Where am I to get the money? Let me out into the woods and hills, where I've been used to breathe the clear air, and though I'm threescore and ten, if you've left game enough in the country, I'll travel night and day but I'll make you up the sum afore the season is over. Yes, yes—you see the reason of the thing, and the wickedness of shutting up an old man that has spent his days, as one may say, where he could always look into the windows of heaven."

"I must be governed by the law——"

"Talk not to me of law, Marmaduke Temple," interrupted the hunter. "Did the beast of the forest mind your laws when it was thirsty and hungering for the blood of your own child! She was kneeling to her God for a greater favor than I ask, and He heard her; and if you now say no to my prayers, do you think He will be deaf?"

"My private feelings must not enter into——"

"Hear me, Marmaduke Temple," interrupted the old man, with melancholy earnestness, "and hear reason. I've travelled these mountains when you was no judge, but an infant in your mother's arms; and I feel as if I had a right and a privilege to travel them ag'in afore I die. Have you forgot the time that you come on to the lake shore, when there wasn't even a gaol to lodge in; and didn't I give you my own bearskin to sleep on, and the fat of a noble buck to satisfy the cravings of your hunger? Yes, yes—you thought it no sin then to kill a deer! And this I did, though I had no reason to love you, for you had never done anything but harm to them that loved and sheltered me. And now, will you shut me up in your dungeons to pay me for my kindness? A hundred dollars! where should I get the money? No, no—there's them that says hard things of you, Marmaduke Temple, but you an't so bad as to wish to see an old man die in a prison because he stood up for the right. Come, friend, let me pass: it's long sin' I've been used to such crowds, and I crave to be in the woods ag'in. Don't fear me, Judge—I bid you not to fear me; for if there's beaver enough left on the streams, or the buckskins will sell for a shilling apiece, you shall have the last penny of the fine. Where are ye, pups! come away, dogs! come away! we have a grievous toil to do for our years, but it shall be done—yes, yes, I've promised it, and it shall be done!"

It is unnecessary to say that the movement of the Leatherstocking was again intercepted by the constable; but before he had time to speak, a bustling in the crowd, and a loud hem, drew all eyes to another part of the room.

Benjamin had succeeded in edging his way through the people, and was now seen balancing his short body, with one foot in a window and the other on the railing of the jury box. To the amazement of the whole court, the steward was evidently preparing to speak. After a good deal of difficulty, he succeeded in drawing from his pocket a small bag, and then found utterance.

"If so be," he said, "that your honor is agreeable to trust the poor fellow out on another cruise among the beasts, here's a small matter that will help to bring down the risk, seeing that there's just thirty-five of your Spaniards in it; and I wish, from the bottom of my heart, that they was raal British guineas, for the sake of the old boy. But 'tis as it is; and if Squire Dickens will just be so good as to overhaul this small bit of an account, and take enough from the bag to settle the same, he's welcome to hold on upon the rest, till such time as the Leatherstocking can grapple with them said beaver, or, for that matter, for ever, and no thanks asked."

As Benjamin concluded, he thrust out the wooden register of his arrears to the "Bold Dragoon" with one hand, while he offered his bag of dollars with the other. Astonishment at this singular interruption produced a profound stillness in the room, which was only interrupted by the Sheriff, who struck his sword on the table, and cried—

"Silence!"

"There must be an end to this," said the Judge, struggling to overcome his feelings. "Constable, lead the prisoner to the stocks. Mr. Clerk, what stands next on the calendar?"

Natty seemed to yield to his destiny, for he sunk his head on his chest, and followed the officer from the courtroom in silence. The crowd moved back for the passage of the prisoner, and when his tall form was seen descending from the outer door, a rush of the people to the scene of his disgrace followed.

The punishments of the common law were still known, at the time of our tale, to the people of New York; and the whipping post, with its companion the stocks, were not yet supplanted by the more merciful expedients of the public prisons. Immediately in front of the gaol those relics of the elder times were situated, as a lesson of precautionary justice to the evildoers of the settlement.

Natty followed the constables to this spot, bowing his head with submission to a power that he was unable to oppose, and surrounded by the crowd that formed a circle about his person, exhibiting in their countenances strong curiosity. A constable raised the upper part of the stocks, and pointed with his finger to the holes where the old man was to place his feet. Without making the least objection to the punishment the Leatherstocking quietly seated himself on the ground, and suffered his limbs to be laid in the openings without even a murmur; though he cast one glance about him in quest of that sympathy that human nature always seems to require under suffering. If he met no direct manifestations of pity, neither did he see any unfeeling exultation, or hear a single reproachful epithet. The character of the mob, if it could be called by such a name, was that of attentive subordination.

The constable was in the act of lowering the upper plank, when Benjamin, who had pressed close to the side of the prisoner, said, in his hoarse tones, as if seeking for some cause to create a quarrel—

"Where away, master constable, is the use of clapping a man in them here bilboes? it neither stops his grog nor hurts his back; what for is it that you do the thing?"

" 'Tis the sentence of the court, Mr. Penguillum, and there's law for it, I s'pose."

"Ay, ay, I know that there's law for the thing; but where away do you find the use, I say? it does no harm, and it only keeps a man by the heels for the small matter of two glasses."

"Is it no harm, Benny Pump," said Natty, raising his eyes with a piteous look to the face of the steward—"is it no harm to show off a man in his seventy-first year like a tame bear, for the settlers to look on! Is it no harm to put an old soldier that has sarved through the war of 'fifty-six, and seen the inimy in the 'seventy-six business, into a place like this, where the boys can point at him and say, I have known the time when he was a spectacle for the county! Is it no harm to bring down the pride of an honest man to be the equal of the beasts of the forest!"

Benjamin stared about him fiercely, and could he have found a single face that expressed contumely, he would have been prompt to quarrel with its owner.

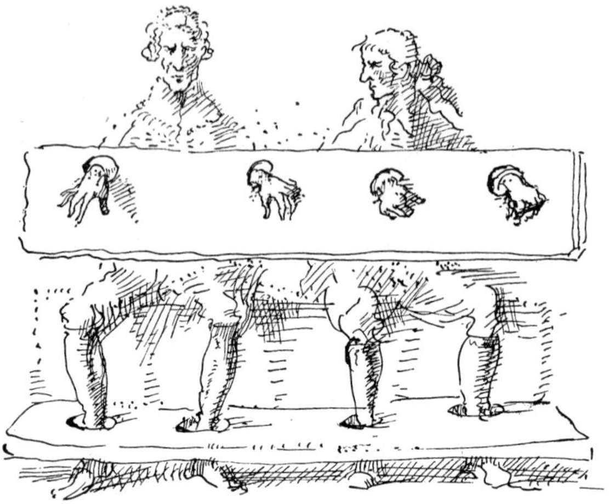

10

DEEPLY HUMILIATED, Leatherstocking was confined in the stocks all afternoon. But he had good company; Judge Temple's old steward, Benjamin Penguillum, was so outraged by the sentence passed on the scout that he had himself locked in the stocks too. Anyone who wanted to see a bear, he said, should see two of them. What was more, he seized the unwary Hiram Doolittle by the legs, threw him down, and knocked his countenance out of shape. For this he had to go to jail that night in the same cell with Natty Bumppo. The village was in an uproar over the whole affair. Not the least deeply disturbed was Elizabeth Temple, who warmly reproached her father for helping to visit so severe a punishment on the old frontiersman. The Judge half agreed. "Thou hast reason, Bess, and much of it, too," he admitted, "but thy heart lies too near thy head."

It soon became plain that Natty need not languish long behind bars. That evening, Oliver Edwards visited the jail. He talked long at the window with Leatherstocking; and after he departed, it was thought that he had communicated words of comfort to the hunter, who threw himself on his pallet, and was soon in a deep sleep. Judge Temple meanwhile gave Elizabeth two hundred dollars, and bade her to visit the jail, talk with Leatherstocking, and pay his fine. Elizabeth at once set out. On the way she passed a teamster, driving a yoke of oxen attached to a hay cart, and she was startled to recognize the driver as Oliver Edwards. "I am quite sorry, Mr. Edwards, to see you reduced to such labor," the girl exclaimed. She then pressed on to the rude jail. The jailer showed her into Natty Bumppo's room with a warning that he must close the place in twenty minutes.

Elizabeth little thought how soon the scene of action was to be transferred outdoors, and how tempestuous that action was to be.

"Leatherstocking!" said Elizabeth, when the key of the door was turned on them again, "my good friend Leatherstocking! I have come on a message of gratitude. Had you submitted to the search, worthy old man, the death of the deer would have been a trifle, and all would have been well——"

"Submit to the sarch!" interrupted Natty, raising his face from resting on his knees, without rising from the corner where he had seated himself; "d'ye think, gal, I would let such a varmint into my hut? No, no—I wouldn't have opened the door to your own sweet countenance then. But they are wilcome to sarch among the coals and ashes now; they'll find only some such heap as is to be seen at every pot-ashery in the mountains."

The old man dropped his face again on one hand, and seemed to be lost in melancholy.

"The hut can be rebuilt and made better than before," returned Miss Temple; "and it shall be my office to see it done, when your imprisonment is ended."

"Can ye raise the dead, child?" said Natty, in a sorrowful voice: "can ye go into the place where you've laid your fathers and mothers and children and gather together their ashes, and make the same men and women of them as afore? You do not know what 'tis to lay your head for more than forty years under the cover of the same logs, and to look on the same things for the better part of a man's life. You are young yet, child, but you are one of the most precious of God's creaters. I had a hope for ye that it might come to pass, but it's all over now; this put to that will drive the thing quite out of his mind for ever."

Miss Temple must have understood the meaning of the old man better than the other listeners; for, while Louisa stood innocently by her side, commiserating the griefs of the hunter, she bent her head aside so as to conceal her features. The action and the feeling that caused it lasted but a moment.

"Other logs and better, though, can be had, and shall be found for you, my old defender," she continued. "Your confinement will soon be over, and, before that time arrives, I shall have a house prepared for you, where you may spend the close of your harmless life in ease and plenty."

"Ease and plenty! house!" repeated Natty slowly. "You mean

well, you mean well, and I quite mourn that it cannot be; but he has seen me a sight and a laughingstock for——"

"Damn your stocks," said Benjamin, flourishing his bottle with one hand, from which he had been taking hasty and repeated draughts, while he made gestures of disdain with the other; "who cares for his bilboes? there's a leg that's been stuck up an end like a gib-boom for an hour, d'ye see, and what's it the worse for't, ha! canst tell me, what's it the worser, ha!"

"I believe you forget, Mr. Pump, in whose presence you are," said Elizabeth.

"Forget you, Miss Lizzy," returned the steward; "if I do, dam'me; you are not to be forgot, like Goody Prettybones, up at the big house there. I say, old sharpshooter, she may have pretty bones, but I can't say so much for her flesh, d'ye see, for she looks somewhat like an atomy with another man's jacket on. Now, for the skin of her face, it's all the same as a new topsail with a taught boltrope, being snug at the leaches, but all in a bight about the inner cloths."

"Peace—I command you to be silent, sir!" said Elizabeth.

"Ay, ay, ma'am," returned the steward. "You didn't say I shouldn't drink, though."

"We will not speak of what is to become of others," said Miss Temple, turning again to the hunter—"but of your own fortunes, Natty. It shall be my care to see that you pass the rest of your days in ease and plenty."

"Ease and plenty!" again repeated the Leatherstocking; "what ease can there be to an old man who must walk a mile across the open fields before he can find a shade to hide him from a scorching sun? or what plenty is there where you may hunt a day, and not start a buck, or see anything bigger than a mink, or maybe a stray fox? Ah! I shall have a hard time after them very beavers, for this fine. I must go low toward the Pennsylvany line in sarch of the creaters, maybe a hundred mile; for they are not to be got here-a-way. No, no—your betterments and clearings have druv the knowing things out of the country; and instead of beaver dams, which is the nater of the animal, and according to Providence, you turn back the waters over the low grounds with your milldams, as if 'twas in man to stay the drops from going where He wills them to go.—Benny, unless you stop your hand from going so often to your mouth, you won't be ready to start when the time comes."

"Hark'ee, Master Bump-ho," said the steward; "don't you fear for Ben. When the watch is called, set me on my legs and give me the bearings and distance of where you want to steer, and I'll carry sail with the best of you, I will."

"The time has come now," said the hunter, listening; "I hear the horns of the oxen rubbing ag'in the side of the gaol."

"Well, say the word, and then heave ahead, shipmate," said Benjamin.

"You won't betray us, gal?" said Natty, looking up simply into the face of Elizabeth—"you won't betray an old man who craves to breathe the clear air of heaven? I mean no harm; and if the laws says that I must pay the hundred dollars, I'll take the season through, but it shall be forthcoming; and this good man will help me."

"You catch them," said Benjamin, with a sweeping gesture of his arm, "and if they get away again, call me a slink, that's all."

"But what mean you?" cried the wondering Elizabeth. "Here you must stay for thirty days; but I have the money for your fine in this purse. Take it; pay it in the morning, and summon patience for your month. I will come often to see you with my friend; we will make up your clothes with our own hands; indeed, indeed, you shall be comfortable."

"Would ye, children?" said Natty, advancing across the floor with an air of kindness, and taking the hand of Elizabeth; "would ye be so kearful of an old man, and just for shooting the beast which cost him nothing? Such things doesn't run in the blood, I believe, for you seem not to forget a favor. Your little fingers couldn't do much on a buckskin, nor be you used to such a thread as sinews. But if he hasn't got past hearing, he shall hear it and know it, that he may see, like me, there is some who know how to remember a kindness."

"Tell him nothing," cried Elizabeth earnestly; "if you love me, if you regard my feelings, tell him nothing. It is of yourself only I would talk, and for yourself only I act. I grieve, Leatherstocking, that the law requires that you should be detained here so long; but, after all, it will be only a short month, and——"

"A month!" exclaimed Natty, opening his mouth with his usual laugh; "not a day, nor a night, nor an hour, gal. Judge Temple may sintence, but he can't keep, without a better dungeon than this. I was taken once by the French, and they put sixty-two of us in a block-house, nigh hand to old Frontinac; but 'twas easy to cut through a pine log to them that was used to timber." The hunter paused, and looked cautiously around the room, when, laughing again, he shoved the steward gently from his post, and removing the bedclothes, discovered a hole recently cut in the logs with a mallet and chisel. "It's only a kick and the outside piece is off, and then——"

"Off! ay, off!" cried Benjamin, rousing from his stupor; "well, here's off. Ay! ay! you catch 'em, and I'll hold on to them said beaver-hats."

"I fear this lad will trouble me much," said Natty; " 'twill be a hard pull for the mountain should they take the scent soon, and he is not in a state of mind to run."

"Run!" echoed the steward; "no, sheer alongside, and let's have a fight of it."

"Peace!" ordered Elizabeth.

"Ay, ay, ma'am."

"You will not leave us, surely, Leatherstocking," continued Miss Temple; "I beseech you, reflect that you will be driven to the woods entirely, and that you are fast getting old. Be patient for a little time, when you can go abroad openly and with honor."

"Is there beaver to be catched here, gal?"

"If not, here is money to discharge the fine, and in a month you are free. See, here it is in gold."

"Gold!" said Natty, with a kind of childish curiosity; "it's long sin' I've seen a gold piece. We used to get the broad joes in the old war, as plenty as the bears be now. I remember there was a man in Dieskau's army that was killed, who had a dozen of the shining things sewed up in his shirt. I didn't handle them myself, but I seen them cut out with my own eyes; they was bigger and brighter than them be."

"These are English guineas, and are yours," said Elizabeth; "an earnest of what shall be done for you."

"Me! why should you give me this treasure?" said Natty, looking earnestly at the maiden.

"Why, have you not saved my life! did you not rescue me from the jaws of the beast?" exclaimed Elizabeth, veiling her eyes, as if to hide some hideous object from her view.

The hunter took the money, and continued turning it in his hand for some time, piece by piece, talking aloud during the operation.

"There's a rifle, they say, out on the Cherry Valley, that will carry a hundred rods and kill. I've seen good guns in my day, but none quite equal to that. A hundred rods with any sartainty is great shooting! Well, well—I'm old, and the gun I have will answer my time. Here, child, take back your gold. But the hour has come; I hear him talking to the cattle, and I must be going. You won't tell of us, gal—you won't tell of us, will ye?"

"Tell of you!" echoed Elizabeth. "But take the money, old man; take the money, even if you go into the mountains."

"No, no," said Natty, shaking his head kindly; "I would not rob you so for twenty rifles. But there's one thing you can do for me, if ye will, that no other is at hand to do."

"Name it—name it."

"Why, it's only to buy a canister of powder; 'twill cost two silver dollars. Benny Pump has the money ready, but we daren't come into the town to get it. Nobody has it but the Frenchman. 'Tis of the best, and just suits a rifle. Will you get it for me, gal?—say, will you get it for me?"

"Will I! I will bring it to you, Leatherstocking, though I toil a day in quest of you through the woods. But where shall I find you, and how?"

"Where!" said Natty, musing a moment—"tomorrow, on the Vision; on the very top of the Vision, I'll meet you, child, just as the sun gets over our heads. See that it's the fine grain; you'll know it by the gloss, and the price."

"I will do it," said Elizabeth firmly.

Natty now seated himself, and, placing his feet in the hole, with a slight effort he opened a passage through into the street. The ladies heard the rustling of hay, and well understood the reason why Edwards was in the capacity of a teamster.

"Come, Benny," said the hunter; " 'twill be no darker tonight, for the moon will rise in an hour."

"Stay!" exclaimed Elizabeth; "it should not be said that you escaped in the presence of the daughter of Judge Temple. Return, Leatherstocking, and let us retire before you execute your plan."

Natty was about to reply, when the approaching footsteps of the gaoler announced the necessity of his immediate return. He had barely time to regain his feet and to conceal the hole with the bedclothes, across which Benjamin very opportunely fell, before the key was turned and the door of the apartment opened.

"Isn't Miss Temple ready to go?" said the civil gaoler; "it's the usual hour for locking up."

"I follow you, sir," returned Elizabeth. "Good-night, Leatherstocking."

"It's a fine grain, gal, and I think 'twill carry lead farther than common. I am getting old, and can't follow up the game with the step that I used to could."

Miss Temple waved her hand for silence, and preceded Louisa and the keeper from the apartment. The man turned the key once, and observed that he would return and secure his prisoners, when he had lighted the ladies to the street. Accordingly, they parted at the door of the building, when the gaoler retired to his dungeons, and the ladies walked, with throbbing hearts, towards the corner

"Now the Leatherstocking refuses the money," whispered Louisa, "it can all be given to Mr. Edwards, and that added to——"

"Listen!" said Elizabeth; "I hear the rustling of the hay; they are escaping at this moment. Oh! they will be detected instantly!"

By this time they were at the corner, where Edwards and Natty were in the act of drawing the almost helpless body of Benjamin through the aperture. The oxen had started back from their hay, and were standing with their heads down the street, leaving room for the party to act in.

"Throw the hay into the cart," said Edwards, "or they will suspect how it has been done. Quick, that they may not see it."

Natty had just returned from executing this order, when the light of the keeper's candle shone through the hole, and instantly his voice was heard in the gaol, exclaiming for his prisoners.

"What is to be done now?" said Edwards, "this drunken fellow will cause our detection, and we have not a moment to spare."

"Who's drunk, ye lubber!" muttered the steward.

"A break-gaol! a break-gaol!" shouted five or six voices from within.

"We must leave him," said Edwards.

" 'Twouldn't be kind, lad," returned Natty; "he took half the disgrace of the stocks on himself today, and the creater has feeling."

At this moment two or three men were heard issuing from the door of the "Bold Dragoon," and among them the voice of Billy Kirby.

"There's no moon yet," cried the wood chopper; "but it's a clear night. Come, who's for home? Hark! what a rumpus they're kicking up in the gaol—here's go and see what it's about."

"We shall be lost," said Edwards, "if we don't drop this man."

At that instant Elizabeth moved close to him, and said rapidly, in a low voice—

"Lay him in the cart, and start the oxen; no one will look there."

"There's a woman's quickness in the thought," said the youth.

The proposition was no sooner made than executed. The steward was seated on the hay, and enjoined to hold his peace, and apply the goad that was placed in his hand, while the oxen were urged on. So soon as this arrangement was completed, Edwards and the hunter stole along the houses for a short distance, when they disappeared through an opening that led into the rear of the buildings. The oxen were in brisk motion, and presently the cries of pursuit were heard in the street. The ladies quickened their pace, with a wish to escape the crowd of constables and idlers that were approaching, some execrating, and some laughing at the exploit of the prisoners. In the confusion, the voice of Kirby was plainly distinguishable above all the others, shouting and swearing that he would have the fugitives, threatening to bring back Natty in one pocket and Benjamin in the other.

"Spread yourselves, men," he cried, as he passed the ladies, his heavy feet sounding along the street like the tread of a dozen; "spread yourselves; to the mountains; they'll be in the mountain in a quarter of an hour, and then look out for a long rifle."

His cries were echoed from twenty mouths, for not only the gaol, but the taverns had sent forth their numbers, some earnest in the pursuit, and others joining it as in sport.

As Elizabeth turned in at her father's gate she saw the wood chopper stop at the cart, when she gave Benjamin up for lost. While they were hurrying up the walk, two figures, stealing cautiously but quickly under the shades of the trees, met the eyes of the ladies, and in a moment Edwards and the hunter crossed their path.

"Miss Temple, I may never see you again," exclaimed the youth; "let me thank you for all your kindness; you do not, cannot know, my motives."

"Fly! fly!" cried Elizabeth: "the village is alarmed. Do not be found conversing with me at such a moment, and in these grounds."

"Nay, I must speak, though detection were certain."

"Your retreat to the bridge is already cut off; before you can gain the wood your pursuers will be there. If——"

"If what?" cried the youth. "Your advice has saved me once already; I will follow it to death."

"The street is now silent and vacant," said Elizabeth, after a pause; "cross it and you will find my father's boat in the lake. It would be easy to land from it where you please in the hills."

"But Judge Temple might complain of the trespass."

"His daughter shall be accountable, sir."

The youth uttered something in a low voice that was heard only by Elizabeth, and turned to execute what she had suggested. As they were separating, Natty approached the females, and said—

"You'll remember the canister of powder, children. Them beavers must be had, and I and the pups be getting old; we want the best of ammunition."

"Come, Natty," said Edwards impatiently.

"Coming, lad, coming. God bless you, young ones, both of ye, for ye mean well and kindly to the old man."

The ladies paused until they lost sight of the retreating figures, when they immediately entered the mansion house.

While this scene was passing in the walk, Kirby had overtaken the cart, which was his own, and had been driven by Edwards without asking the owner, from the place where the patient oxen usually stood at evening, waiting the pleasure of their master.

"Woa—come hither, Golden," he cried; "why, how come you off the end of the bridge, where I left you, dummies?"

"Heave ahead," muttered Benjamin, giving a random blow with his lash, that alighted on the shoulder of the other.

"Who the devil be you?" cried Billy, turning round in surprise, but unable to distinguish in the dark the hard visage that was just peering over the cart rails.

"Who be I! why, I'm helmsman aboard of this here craft, d'ye see, and a straight wake I'm making of it. Ay, ay! I've got the bridge right ahead, and the bilboes dead-aft; I calls that good steerage, boy. Heave ahead."

"Lay your lash in the right spot, Mr. Benny Pump," said the wood chopper, "or I'll put you in the palm of my hand, and box your ears. Where be you going with my team?"

"Team!"

"Ay, my cart and oxen."

"Why, you must know, Master Kirby, that the Leatherstocking and I—that's Benny Pump—you knows Ben?—well, Benny and I—no, me and Benny; dam'me if I know how 'tis; but some of us are bound after a cargo of beaver-skins, d'ye see, and so we've pressed the cart to ship them 'ome in. I say, Master Kirby, what a lubberly oar you pull—you handle an oar, boy, pretty much as a cow would a musket, or a lady would a marlingspike."

Billy had discovered the state of the steward's mind, and he walked for some time alongside of the cart, musing with himself, when he took the goad from Benjamin (who fell back on the hay, and was soon asleep) and drove his cattle down the street, over the bridge, and up the mountain toward a clearing, in which he was to work the next day, without any other interruption than a few hasty questions from parties of the constables.

Elizabeth stood for an hour at the window of her room, and saw the torches of the pursuers gliding along the side of the mountain, and heard their shouts and alarms; but, at the end of that time, the last party returned, wearied and disappointed, and the village became as still as when she issued from the gate on her mission to the gaol.

It was yet early on the following morning, when Elizabeth and Louisa met by appointment, and proceeded to the store of Monsieur Le Quoi, in order to redeem the pledge the former had given to the Leatherstocking. The people were again assembling for the business of the day, but the hour was too soon for a crowd, and the ladies found the place in possession of its polite owner, Billy Kirby, one female customer, and the boy who did the duty of helper or clerk.

Monsieur Le Quoi was perusing a packet of letters with manifest delight, while the wood chopper, with one hand thrust in his bosom, and the other in the folds of his jacket, holding an ax under his right arm, stood sympathizing in the Frenchman's pleasure with good-natured interest. The freedom of manners that prevailed in the new settlements commonly levelled all difference in rank, and with it, frequently, all considerations of education and intelligence. At the time the ladies entered the store they were unseen by the owner, who was saying to Kirby—

"Ah! ha! Monsieur Beel, dis lettair mak me de most happi of mans. Ah! ma chère France! I vill see you aga'n."

"I rejoice, Monsieur, at anything that contributes to your happiness," said Elizabeth, "but hope we are not going to lose you entirely."

The complaisant shopkeeper changed the language to French, and recounted rapidly to Elizabeth his hopes of being permitted to return to his own country. Habit had, however, so far altered the manners of this pliable personage that he continued to serve the wood chopper who was in quest of some tobacco, while he related to his more gentle visitor the happy change that had taken place in the dispositions of his own countrymen.

The amount of it all was that Monsieur Le Quoi, who had fled from his own country more through terror than because he was offensive to the ruling powers of France, had succeeded at length in getting an assurance that his return to the West Indies would be unnoticed; and the Frenchman, who had sunk into the character of a country shopkeeper with so much grace, was about to emerge again from his obscurity into his proper level in society.

We need not repeat the civil things that passed between the parties on this occasion, nor recount the endless repetitions of sorrow that the delighted Frenchman expressed at being compelled to quit the society of Miss Temple. Elizabeth took an opportunity, during this expenditure of polite expressions, to purchase the powder privately of the boy, who bore the generic appellation of Jonathan. Before they parted, however, Monsieur Le Quoi, who seemed to think that he had not said enough, solicited the honor of a private interview with the heiress, with a gravity in his air that announced the importance of the subject. After conceding the favor and appointing a more favorable time for the meeting, Elizabeth succeeded in getting out of the store, into which the countrymen now began to enter as usual, where they met with the same attention and *bienséance* as formerly.

Elizabeth and Louisa pursued their walk as far as the bridge in profound silence; but when they reached that place, the latter stopped and appeared anxious to utter something that her diffidence suppressed.

"Are you ill, Louisa?" exclaimed Miss Temple; "had we not better return and seek another opportunity to meet the old man?"

"Not ill, but terrified. Oh! I never, never can go on that hill again with you only. I am not equal to it, indeed I am not."

This was an unexpected declaration to Elizabeth, who, although she experienced no idle apprehension of a danger that no longer existed, felt most sensitively all the delicacy of maiden modesty. She stood for some time deeply reflecting within herself; but sensible it was a time for action instead of reflection, she struggled to shake off her hesitation, and replied firmly—

"Well, then it must be done by me alone. There is no other than yourself to be trusted, or poor old Leatherstocking will be discovered. Wait for me in the edge of these woods, that at least I may not be seen strolling in the hills by myself just now. One would not wish to create remarks, Louisa—if—if— You will wait for me, dear girl?"

"A year, in sight of the village, Miss Temple," returned the agitated Louisa, "but do not, do not ask me to go on that hill."

Elizabeth found that her companion was really unable to proceed, and they completed their arrangement by posting Louisa out of the observation of the people who occasionally passed, but nigh the road and in plain view of the whole valley. Miss Temple then proceeded alone. She ascended the road which has been so often mentioned in our narrative with an elastic and firm step, fearful that the delay in the store of Monsieur Le Quoi, and the time necessary for reaching the summit, would prevent her being punctual to the appointment. Whenever she passed an opening in the bushes she would pause for breath, or, perhaps drawn from her pursuits by the picture at her feet, would linger a moment to gaze at the beauties of the valley. The long drought had, however, changed its coat of verdure to a hue of brown, and, though the same localities were there, the view wanted the lively and cheering aspect of early summer. Even the heavens seemed to share in the dried appearance of the earth, for the sun was concealed by a haziness in the atmosphere, which looked like a thin smoke without a particle of moisture, if such a thing were possible. The blue sky was scarcely to be seen, though now and then there was a faint lighting up in spots, through which masses of rolling vapor could be discerned gathering around the horizon, as if nature were struggling to collect her floods for the relief of man. The very atmosphere that Elizabeth inhaled was hot and dry, and by the time she reached the point where the course led her from the highway, she experienced a sensation like suffocation. But, disregarding her feelings, she hastened to execute her mission, dwelling on nothing but the disappointment, and even the helplessness the hunter would experience without her aid.

On the summit of the mountain which Judge Temple had named the Vision, a little spot had been cleared in order that a better view might be obtained of the village and the valley. At this point, Elizabeth understood the hunter, she was to meet him; and thither she urged her way as expeditiously as the difficulty of the ascent and the impediments of a forest in a state of nature would admit. Numberless were the fragments of rocks, trunks of fallen trees and branches, with which she had to contend; but every difficulty vanished before her resolution, and, by her own watch, she stood on the desired spot several minutes before the appointed hour.

After resting a moment on the end of a log, Miss Temple cast a glance about her in quest of her old friend, but he was evidently not in the clearing; she arose and walked around its skirts, examining every place where she thought it probable Natty might deem it prudent to conceal himself. Her search was fruitless; and, after exhausting not only herself but her conjectures, in efforts to discover or imagine his situation, she ventured to trust her voice in that solitary place.

"Natty! Leatherstocking! old man!" she called aloud in every direction; but no answer was given, excepting the reverberations of her own clear tones as they were echoed in the parched forest.

Elizabeth approached the brow of the mountain, where a faint cry like the noise produced by striking the hand against the mouth, at the same time that the breath is strongly exhaled, was heard answering to her own voice. Not doubting in the least that it was the Leatherstocking lying in wait for her, and who gave that signal to indicate the place where he was to be found, Elizabeth descended for near a hundred feet until she gained a little natural terrace thinly scattered with trees, that grew in the fissures of the rocks, which were covered by a scanty soil. She had advanced to the edge of this platform, and was gazing over the perpendicular precipice that formed its face, when a rustling among the dry leaves near her drew her eyes in another direction. Our heroine certainly was startled by the object that she then saw, but a moment restored her self-possession, and she advanced firmly and with some interest in her manner to the spot.

Mohegan was seated on the trunk of a fallen oak, with his tawny visage turned towards her, and his eyes fixed on her face with an expression of wildness and fire that would have terrified a less resolute female. His blanket had fallen from his shoulders and was lying in folds around him, leaving his breast, arms, and most of his body bare. The medallion of Washington reposed on his chest, a badge of distinction that Elizabeth well knew he only produced on great and solemn occasions. But the whole appearance of the aged chief was more studied than common, and in some particulars it was terrific. The long black hair was plaited on his head, falling away so as to expose his high forehead and piercing eyes. In the enormous incisions of his ears were entwined ornaments of silver, beads, and porcupine's quills, mingled in a rude taste and after the Indian fashions. A large drop, composed of similar materials, was suspended from the cartilage of his nose, and, falling below his lips, rested on his chin. Streaks of red paint crossed his wrinkled brow, and were traced down his cheeks with such variations in the lines as caprice or custom suggested. His body was also colored in the same manner; the whole exhibiting an Indian warrior prepared for some event of more than usual moment.

"John! how fare you, worthy John?" said Elizabeth as she approached him; "you have long been a stranger in the village. You promised me a willow basket, and I have long had a shirt of calico in readiness for you."

The Indian looked steadily at her for some time without answering, and then, shaking his head, he replied in his low, guttural tones—

"John's hand can make baskets no more—he wants no shirt."

"But if he should, he will know where to come for it," returned Miss Temple. "Indeed, old John, I feel as if you had a natural right to order what you will from us."

"Daughter," said the Indian, "listen:—Six times ten hot summers have passed since John was young; tall like a pine; straight like the bullet of Hawkeye; strong as the buffalo; spry as the cat of the mountain. He was strong, and a warrior like the Young Eagle. If his tribe wanted to track the Maquas for many suns, the eye of Chingachgook found the print of their moccasins. If the people feasted and were glad as they counted the scalps of their enemies, it was on his pole they hung. If the squaws cried because there was no meat for their children, he was the first in the chase. His bullet was swifter than the deer.—Daughter, then Chingachgook struck his tomahawk into the trees; it was to tell the lazy ones where to find him and the Mingoes—but he made no baskets."

"Those times have gone by, old warrior," returned Elizabeth; "since then your people have disappeared, and, in place of chasing your enemies, you have learned to fear God and to live at peace."

"Stand here, daughter, where you can see the great spring, the wigwams of your father, and the land on the crooked river. John was young when his tribe gave away the country, in council, from where the blue mountain stands above the water to where the Susquehanna is hid by the trees. All this, and all that grew in it, and all that walked over it, and all that fed there, they gave to the Fire-eater—for they loved him. He was strong, and they were women, and he helped them. No Delaware would kill a deer that ran in his woods, nor stop a bird that flew over his land; for it was his. Has John lived in peace? Daughter, since John was young, he has seen the white man from Frontenac come down on his white brothers at Albany and fight. Did they fear God? He has seen his English and his American fathers burying their tomahawks in each other's brains, for this very land. Did they fear God, and live in peace? He has seen the land pass away from the Fire-eater, and his children, and the child of his child, and a new chief set over the country. Did they live in peace who did this? did they fear God?"

"Such is the custom of the whites, John. Do not the Delawares fight and exchange their lands for powder, and blankets, and merchandise?"

The Indian turned his dark eyes on his companion, and kept them there, with a scrutiny that alarmed her a little.

"Where are the blankets and merchandise that bought the right of the Fire-eater?" he replied, in a more animated voice; "are they with him in his wigwam? Did they say to him, Brother, sell us your land,

and take this gold, this silver, these blankets, these rifles, or even this rum? No; they tore it from him, as a scalp is torn from an enemy; and they that did it looked not behind them, to see whether he lived or died. Do such men live in peace, and fear the Great Spirit?"

"But you hardly understand the circumstances," said Elizabeth, more embarrassed than she would own, even to herself. "If you knew our laws and customs better you would judge differently of our acts. Do not believe evil of my father, old Mohegan, for he is just and good."

"The brother of Miquon is good, and he will do right. I have said it to Hawkeye—I have said it to the Young Eagle, that the brother of Miquon would do justice."

"Whom call you the Young Eagle?" said Elizabeth, averting her face from the gaze of the Indian as she asked the question; "whence comes he, and what are his rights?"

"Has my daughter lived so long with him, to ask this question?" returned the Indian warily. "Old age freezes up the blood, as the frosts cover the great spring in winter; but youth keeps the streams of the blood open like a sun in the time of blossoms. The Young Eagle has eyes; had he no tongue?"

The loveliness to which the old warrior alluded was in no degree diminished by his allegorical speech; for the blushes of the maiden who listened covered her burning cheeks, till her dark eyes seemed to glow with their reflection; but, after struggling a moment with shame, she laughed, as if unwilling to understand him seriously, and replied in pleasantry—

"Not to make me the mistress of his secret. He is too much of a Delaware to tell his secret thoughts to a woman."

"Daughter, the Great Spirit made your father with a white skin, and He made mine with a red; but He colored both their hearts with blood. When young, it is swift and warm; but when old it is still and cold. Is there difference below the skin? No. Once John had a woman. She was the mother of so many sons"—he raised his hand with three fingers elevated—"and she had daughters that would have made the young Delawares happy. She was kind, daughter, and what I said she did. You have different fashions; but do you think John did not love the wife of his youth—the mother of his children?"

"And what has become of your family, John, your wife and your children?" asked Elizabeth, touched by the Indian's manner.

"Where is the ice that covered the great spring? It is melted, and gone with the waters. John has lived till all his people have left him for the land of spirits; his time has come, and he is ready."

Mohegan dropped his head in his blanket, and sat in silence. Miss Temple knew not what to say. She wished to draw the thoughts of the old warrior from his gloomy recollections, but there was a dignity in his sorrow and in his fortitude that repressed her efforts to speak. After a long pause, however, she renewed the discourse, by asking—

"Where is the Leatherstocking, John? I have brought this canister of powder at his request; but he is nowhere to be seen. Will you take charge of it and see it delivered?"

The Indian raised his head slowly, and looked earnestly at the gift, which she put in his hand.

"This is the great enemy of my nation. Without this, when could the white men drive the Delawares? Daughter, the Great Spirit gave your fathers to know how to make guns and powder, that they might sweep the Indians from the land. There will soon be no redskin in the country. When John has gone the last will leave these hills, and his family will be dead." The aged warrior stretched his body forward, leaning an elbow on his knee, and appeared to be taking a parting look at the objects of the vale, which were still visible through the misty atmosphere; though the air seemed to thicken at each moment around Miss Temple, who became conscious of an increased difficulty of respiration. The eye of Mohegan changed gradually from its sorrowful expression to a look of wildness that might be supposed to border on the inspiration of a prophet, as he continued—"But he will go to the country where his fathers have met. The game shall be plenty as the fish in the lakes. No woman shall cry for meat, no Mingo can ever come. The chase shall be for children, and all just red men shall live together as brothers."

"John! this is not the heaven of a Christian!" cried Miss Temple; "you deal now in the superstition of your forefathers."

"Fathers! sons!" said Mohegan with firmness—"all gone—all gone!—I have no son but the Young Eagle, and he has the blood of a white man."

"Tell me, John," said Elizabeth, willing to draw his thoughts to other subjects, and at the same time yielding to her own powerful interest in the youth; "who is this Mr. Edwards? why are you so fond of him, and whence does he come?"

The Indian started at the question, which evidently recalled his recollection to earth. Taking her hand, he drew Miss Temple to a seat beside him, and pointed to the country beneath them—

"See, daughter," he said, directing her looks toward the north; "as far as your young eyes can see, it was the land of his——"

But immense volumes of smoke at that moment rolled over their heads, and, whirling in the eddies formed by the mountains, interposed a barrier to their sight while he was speaking. Startled by this circumstance, Miss Temple sprang on her feet, and turning her eyes toward the summit of the mountain, she beheld it covered by a similar canopy, while a roaring sound was heard in the forest above her, like the rushing of winds.

"What means it, John?" she exclaimed; "we are enveloped in smoke, and I feel a heat like the glow of a furnace."

Before the Indian could reply, a voice was heard, crying in the woods—

"John! where are you, old Mohegan? the woods are on fire, and you have but a minute for escape."

The chief put his hand before his mouth, and making it play on his lips, produced the kind of noise that had attracted Elizabeth to the place, when a quick and hurried step was heard dashing through the dried underbrush and bushes, and presently Edwards rushed to his side, with horror in every feature.

"It would have been sad indeed to lose you in such a manner, my old friend," said Oliver, catching his breath for utterance. "Up and away! even now we may be too late; the flames are circling around the point of the rock below, and, unless we can pass there, our only chance must be over the precipice. Away! away! shake off your apathy, John; now is the time of need."

Mohegan pointed toward Elizabeth, who, forgetting her danger, had shrunk back to a projection of the rock, soon as she recognized the sounds of Edwards's voice, and said with something like awakened animation—

"Save her—leave John to die."

"Her! whom mean you?" cried the youth, turning quickly to the place the other indicated; but when he saw the figure of Elizabeth, bending toward him in an attitude that powerfully spoke terror, blended with reluctance to meet him in such a place, the shock deprived him of speech.

"Miss Temple!" he cried, when he found words; "you here! is such a death reserved for you?"

"No, no, no—no death, I hope, for any of us, Mr. Edwards," she replied, endeavoring to speak calmly: "there is smoke, but no fire to harm us. Let us endeavor to retire."

"Take my arm," said Edwards; "there must be an opening in some direction for your retreat. Are you equal to the effort?"

"Certainly. You surely magnify the danger, Mr. Edwards. Lead me out the way you came."

"I will—I will," cried the youth, with a kind of hysterical utterance. "No, no—there is no danger—I have alarmed you unnecessarily."

"But shall we leave the Indian—can we leave him, as he says, to die?"

An expression of painful emotion crossed the face of the young man; he stopped, and cast a longing look at Mohegan; but, dragging his companion after him, even against her will, he pursued his way, with enormous strides, toward the pass by which he had just entered the circle of flame.

"Do not regard him," he said, in those tones that denote a desperate calmness; "he is used to the woods and such scenes; and he will escape up the mountain—over the rock—or he can remain where he is in safety."

"You thought not so this moment, Edwards!—Do not leave him there to meet with such a death," cried Elizabeth, fixing a look on the countenance of her conductor that seemed to distrust his sanity.

"An Indian burn! who ever heard of an Indian dying by fire? an Indian cannot burn; the idea is ridiculous. Hasten, hasten, Miss Temple, or the smoke may incommode you."

"Edwards! your look, your eye, terrifies me! tell me the danger; is it greater than it seems? I am equal to any trial."

"If we reach the point of yon rock before that sheet of fire, we are safe, Miss Temple!" exclaimed the young man, in a voice that burst without the bounds of his forced composure. "Fly! the struggle is for life!"

The place of the interview between Miss Temple and the Indian has been already described as one of those platforms of rock which form a sort of terrace in the mountains of that country, and the face of it, we have said, was both high and perpendicular. Its shape was nearly a natural arc, the ends of which blended with the mountain, at points where its sides were less abrupt in their descent. It was round one of these terminations of the sweep of the rock that Edwards had ascended, and it was toward the same place that he urged Elizabeth to a desperate exertion of speed.

Immense clouds of white smoke had been pouring over the summit of the mountain, and had concealed the approach and ravages of the element; but a crackling sound drew the eyes of Miss Temple, as she flew over the ground, supported by the young man, toward the outline of smoke, where she already perceived the waving flames shooting forward from the vapor, now flaring high in the air, and then bending to the earth, seeming to light into combustion every stick and shrub on which they breathed. The sight aroused them to redoubled efforts; but, unfortunately, a collection of the tops of trees, old and dried, lay directly across their course; and, at the very moment when both had thought their safety insured, the warm currents of the air swept a forked tongue of flame across the pile, which lighted at the touch; and when they reached the spot, the flying pair were opposed by the surly roaring of a body of fire, as if a furnace were glowing in their path. They recoiled from the heat, and stood on a point of the rock, gazing in a stupor at the flames, which were spreading rapidly down the mountain, whose side soon became a sheet of living fire. It was dangerous for one clad in the light and airy dress of Elizabeth to approach even the vicinity of the raging element; and those flowing robes, that gave such softness and grace to her form, seemed now to be formed for the instruments of her destruction.

The villagers were accustomed to resort to that hill in quest of timber and fuel; in procuring which, it was their usage to take only the bodies of the trees, leaving the tops and branches to decay under the operations of the weather. Much of the hill was, consequently, covered with such light fuel, which, having been scorching under the sun for the last two months, was ignited with a touch. Indeed, in some cases, there did not appear to be any contact between the fire and these piles, but the flames seemed to dart from heap to heap, as the fabulous fire of the temple is represented to relumine its neglected lamp.

There was beauty as well as terror in the sight, and Edwards and Elizabeth stood viewing the progress of the desolation with a strange mixture of horror and interest. The former, however, shortly roused himself to new exertions, and drawing his companion after him, they skirted the edge of the smoke, the young man penetrating frequently into its dense volumes in search of a passage, but in every instance without success. In this manner they proceeded in a semicircle around the upper part of the terrace, until, arriving at the verge of the precipice, opposite to the point where Edwards had ascended, the horrid conviction burst on both at the same instant, that they were completely encircled by the fire. So long as a single pass up or down the mountain was unexplored, there was hope; but when retreat seemed to be absolutely impracticable, the horror of their situation broke upon Elizabeth as powerfully as if she had hitherto considered the danger light.

"This mountain is doomed to be fatal to me!" she whispered; "we shall find our graves on it!"

"Say not so, Miss Temple; there is yet hope," returned the youth, in the same tone, while the vacant expression of his eye contradicted his words: "let us return to the point of the rock; there is, there must be, some place about it where we can descend."

"Lead me there," exclaimed Elizabeth; "let us leave no effort untried." She did not wait for his compliance, but, turning, retraced her steps to the brow of the precipice, murmuring to herself, in suppressed, hysterical sobs, "My father! my poor, my distracted father!"

Edwards was by her side in an instant, and with aching eyes he examined every fissure in the crags in quest of some opening that might offer the facilities of flight. But the smooth, even surface of the rocks afforded hardly a resting place for a foot, much less those continued projections which would have been necessary for a descent of nearly a hundred feet. Edwards was not slow in feeling the conviction that this hope was also futile, and, with a kind of feverish despair that still urged him to action, he turned to some new expedient.

"There is nothing left, Miss Temple," he said, "but to lower you from this place to the rock beneath. If Natty were here, or even that Indian could be roused, their ingenuity and long practice would easily devise methods to do it; but I am a child, at this moment, in everything but daring. Where shall I find means? This dress of mine is so light, and there is so little of it—then the blanket of Mohegan.—We must try—we must try—anything is better than to see you a victim to such a death!"

"And what will become of you?" said Elizabeth. "Indeed, indeed, neither you nor John must be sacrificed to my safety."

He heard her not, for he was already by the side of Mohegan, who yielded his blanket without a question, retaining his seat with Indian dignity and composure, though his own situation was even more critical than that of the others. The blanket was cut into shreds, and the fragments fastened together; the loose linen jacket of the youth, and the light muslin shawl of Elizabeth were attached to them, and the whole thrown over the rocks with the rapidity of lightning; but the united pieces did not reach half way to the bottom.

"It will not do, it will not do!" cried Elizabeth; "for me there is no hope! The fire comes slowly, but certainly. See, it destroys the very earth before it!"

Had the flames spread on that rock with half the quickness with which they leaped from bush to tree in other parts of the mountain, our painful task would have soon ended; for they would have consumed already the captives they enclosed. But the peculiarity of their situation afforded Elizabeth and her companion the respite of which they had availed themselves to make the efforts we have recorded.

The thin covering of earth on the rock supported but a scanty and faded herbage, and most of the trees that had found root in the fissures had already died during the intense heats of preceding summers. Those which still retained the appearance of life bore a few dry and withered leaves, while the others were merely the wrecks of pines, oaks, and maples. No better materials to feed the fire could be found, had there been a communication with the flames; but the ground was destitute of the brush that led the destructive element, like a torrent, over the remainder of the hill. As auxiliary to this scarcity of fuel, one of the large springs which abound in that country gushed out of the side of the ascent above, and, after creeping sluggishly along the level land, saturating the mossy covering of the rock with moisture, it swept round the base of the little cone that formed the pinnacle of the mountain, and, entering the canopy of smoke near one of the terminations of the terrace, found its way to the lake, not by dashing from rock to rock, but by the secret channels of the earth. It would rise to the surface, here and there, in the wet seasons, but in the droughts of summer it was to be traced only by the bogs and moss that announced the proximity of water. When the fire reached this barrier it was compelled to pause, until a concentration of its heat would overcome the moisture, like an army waiting the operations of a battering train, to open its way to desolation.

That fatal moment seemed now to have arrived; for the hissing steams of the spring appeared to be nearly exhausted, and the moss of the rocks was already curling under the intense heat, while fragments of bark, that yet clung to the dead trees, began to separate from their trunks, and fall to the ground in crumbling masses. The air seemed quivering with rays of heat, which might be seen playing along the parched stems of the trees. There were moments when dark clouds of smoke would sweep along the little terrace; and, as the eye lost its power, the other senses contributed to give effect to the fearful horror of the scene. At such moments the roaring of the flames, the crackling of the furious element, with the tearing of falling branches, and, occasionally, the thundering echoes of some falling tree, united to alarm the victims. Of the three, however, the youth appeared much the most agitated. Elizabeth, having relinquished entirely the idea of escape, was fast obtaining that resigned composure with which the most delicate of her sex are sometimes known to meet unavoidable evils; while Mohegan, who was much nearer to the danger, maintained his seat with the invincible resignation of an Indian warrior. Once or twice the eye of the aged chief, which was ordinarily fixed in the direction of the distant hills, turned toward the young pair, who seemed doomed to so early a death, with a slight indication of pity crossing his composed features, but it would immediately revert again to its former gaze, as if already looking into the womb of futurity. Much of the time he was chanting a kind of low dirge in the Delaware tongue, using the deep and remarkably guttural tones of his people.

"At such a moment, Mr. Edwards, all earthly distinctions end," whispered Elizabeth; "persuade John to move nearer to us—let us die together."

"I cannot—he will not stir," returned the youth in the same horridly still tones. "He considers this as the happiest moment of his life. He is past seventy, and has been decaying rapidly for some time; he received some injury in chasing that unlucky deer, too, on the lake. Oh! Miss Temple, that was an unlucky chase indeed! it has led, I fear, to this awful scene."

The smile of Elizabeth was celestial. "Why name such a trifle now—at this moment the heart is dead to all earthly emotions!"

"If anything could reconcile a man to this death," cried the youth, "it would be to meet it in such company!"

"Talk not so, Edwards, talk not so," interrupted Miss Temple, "I am unworthy of it; and it is unjust to yourself. We must die; yes—yes—we must die—it is the will of God, and let us endeavor to submit like His own children."

"Die!" the youth rather shrieked than exclaimed, "No—no—there must yet be hope—you at least must not, shall not die."

"In what way can we escape?" asked Elizabeth, pointing, with a look of heavenly composure, toward the fire. "Observe! the flame is crossing the barrier of wet ground—it comes slowly, Edwards, but surely. Ah! see! the tree! the tree is already lighted!"

Her words were too true. The heat of the conflagration had, at length, overcome the resistance of the spring, and the fire was slowly stealing along the half-dried moss; while a dead pine kindled with the touch of a forked flame that, for a moment, wreathed around the stem of the tree, as it whirled, in one of its evolutions, under the influence of the air. The effect was instantaneous. The flames danced along the parched trunk of the pine like lightning quivering on a chain, and immediately a column of living fire was raging on the terrace. It soon spread from tree to tree; and the scene was evidently drawing to a close. The log on which Mohegan was seated lighted at its farther end, and the Indian appeared to be surrounded by fire. Still he was unmoved. As his body was unprotected, his sufferings must have been great; but his fortitude was superior to all. His voice could yet be heard, even in the midst of these horrors. Elizabeth turned her head from the sight, and faced the valley. Furious eddies of the wind were created by the heat, and just at the moment the canopy of fiery smoke that overhung the valley was cleared away, leaving a distinct view of the peaceful village beneath them.

"My father!—my father!" shrieked Elizabeth. "Oh! this—this surely might have been spared me—but I submit."

The distance was not so great but the figure of Judge Temple could be seen standing in his own grounds, and apparently contemplating, in perfect unconsciousness of the danger of his child, the mountain in flames. This sight was still more painful than the approaching danger; and Elizabeth again faced the hill.

"My intemperate warmth has done this!" cried Edwards, in the accents of despair. "If I had possessed but a moiety of your heavenly resignation, Miss Temple, all might yet have been well."

"Name it not—name it not," she said. "It is now of no avail. We must die, Edwards, we must die—let us do so as Christians. But—no—you may yet escape, perhaps. Your dress is not so fatal as mine. Fly!

leave me. An opening may yet be found for you, possibly—certainly it is worth the effort. Fly! leave me—but stay! You will see my father; my poor, my bereaved father! Say to him, then, Edwards, say to him all that can appease his anguish. Tell him that I died happy and collected; that I have gone to my beloved mother; that the hours of this life are as nothing when balanced in the scales of eternity. Say how we shall meet again. And say," she continued, dropping her voice, that had risen with her feelings, as if conscious of her worldly weaknesses, "how dear, how very dear, was my love for him; that it was near, too near, to my love for God."

The youth listened to her touching accents, but moved not. In a moment he found utterance, and replied—

"And is it me that you command to leave you! to leave you on the edge of the grave! Oh! Miss Temple, how little have you known me!" he cried, dropping on his knees at her feet, and gathering her flowing robe in his arms, as if to shield her from the flames. "I have been driven to the woods in despair; but your society has tamed the lion within me. If I have wasted my time in degradation, 'twas you that charmed me to it. If I have forgotten my name and family, your form supplied the place of memory. If I have forgotten my wrongs, 'twas you that taught me charity. No—no—dearest Elizabeth, I may die with you, but I can never leave you!"

Elizabeth moved not, nor answered. It was plain that her thoughts had been raised from the earth. The recollection of her father, and her regrets at their separation, had been mellowed by a holy sentiment that lifted her above the level of earthly things, and she was fast losing the weakness of her sex in the near view of eternity. But as she listened to these words she became once more woman. She struggled against these feelings, and smiled as she thought she was shaking off the last lingering feeling of nature, when the world, and all its seductions, rushed again to her heart with the sounds of a human voice, crying in piercing tones—

"Gal! where be ye, gal? gladden the heart of an old man, if ye yet belong to 'arth!"

"List!" said Elizabeth, " 'tis the Leatherstocking; he seeks me!"

" 'Tis Natty!" shouted Edwards, "and we may yet be saved!"

A wide and circling flame glared on their eyes for a moment, even above the fire of the woods, and a loud report followed.

" 'Tis the canister! 'tis the powder," cried the same voice, evidently approaching them. " 'Tis the canister, and the precious child is lost!"

At the next instant Natty rushed through the steams of the spring, and appeared on the terrace without his deerskin cap, his hair burnt to his head, his shirt, of country check, black and filled with holes, and his red features of a deeper color than ever, by the heat he had encountered.

For an hour after Louisa Grant was left by Miss Temple in the situation already mentioned, she continued in feverish anxiety awaiting the return of her friend. But as the time passed by without the reappearance of Elizabeth, the terror of Louisa gradually increased, until her alarmed fancy had conjured ever species of danger that appertained to the woods, excepting the one that really existed. The heavens had become obscured by degrees, and vast volumes of smoke were pouring over the valley; but the thoughts of Louisa were still recurring to beasts, without dreaming of the real cause for apprehension. She was stationed in the edge of the low pines and chestnuts that succeed the first or large growth of the forest, and directly above the angle where the highway turned from the straight course to the village, and ascended the mountain, laterally. Consequently, she commanded a view not only of the valley, but of the road beneath her. The few travellers that passed, she observed, were engaged in earnest conversation, and frequently raised their eyes to the hill, and at length she saw the people leaving the courthouse, and gazing upward also. While under the influence of the alarm excited by such unusual movements, reluctant to go, and yet fearful to remain, Louisa was startled by the low, cracking, but cautious treads of some one approaching through the bushes. She was on the eve of flight, when Natty emerged from the cover, and stood at her side. The old man laughed as he shook her kindly by a hand that was passive with fear.

"I am glad to meet you here, child," he said; "for the back of the mountain is afire, and it would be dangerous to go up it now, till it has been burnt over once, and the dead wood is gone. There's a foolish man, the comrade of that varmint who has given me all this trouble, digging for ore on the east side. I told him that the kearless fellows, who thought to catch a practys'd hunter in the woods after dark, had thrown the lighted pine knots in the brush, and that 'twould kindle like tow, and warned him to leave the hill. But he was set upon his business, and nothing short of Providence could move him. If he isn't burnt and buried in a grave of his own digging, he's made of salamanders. Why, what ails the child! you look as skeary as if you see'd more painters! I wish there were more to be found; they'd count up faster than the beaver. But where's the good child of a bad father? did she forget her promise to the old man?"

"The hill! the hill!" shrieked Louisa; "she seeks you on the hill with the powder!"

Natty recoiled several feet at this unexpected intelligence.

"The Lord of Heaven have mercy on her! She's on the Vision, and that's a sheet of fire ag'in this. Child, if ye love the dear one, and hope to find a friend when you need it most, to the village, and give the alarm. The men are used to fighting fire, and there may be a chance left. Fly! I bid ye fly! nor stop even for breath."

The Leatherstocking had no sooner uttered this injunction, than he disappeared in the bushes, and when last seen by Louisa was rushing up the mountain, with a speed that none but those who were accustomed to the toil could attain.

"Have I found ye!" the old man exclaimed, when he burst out of the smoke; "God be praised that I've found ye; but follow,—there is no time for talking."

"My dress!" said Elizabeth; "it would be fatal to trust myself nearer to the flames in it."

"I bethought me of your flimsy things," cried Natty, throwing loose the folds of a covering of buckskin that he carried on his arm, and wrapping her form in it, in such a manner as to envelop her whole person; "now follow, for it's a matter of life and death to us all."

"But John! what will become of John?" cried Edwards; "can we leave the old warrior here to perish?"

The eyes of Natty followed the direction of Edwards's finger, when he beheld the Indian, still seated as before, with the very earth under his feet consuming with fire. Without delay the hunter approached the spot, and spoke in Delaware—

"Up and away, Chingachgook! will ye stay here to burn, like a Mingo at the stake? The Moravians have teached ye better, I hope; the Lord preserve me if the powder hasn't flashed atween his legs, and the skin of his back is roasting. Will ye come, I say? will ye follow?"

"Why should Mohegan go?" returned the Indian gloomily. "He has seen the days of an eagle, and his eye grows dim. He looks on the valley; he looks on the water; he looks in the hunting grounds—but he sees no Delawares. Every one has a white skin. My fathers say, from the far-off land, Come. My women, my young warriors, my tribe, say, Come. The Great Spirit says, Come. Let Mohegan die."

"But you forget your friend," cried Edwards.

" 'Tis useless to talk to an Indian with the death fit on him, lad," interrupted Natty, who seized the strips of the blanket, and with wonderful dexterity strapped the passive chieftain to his own back; when he turned, and with a strength that seemed to bid defiance, not only to his years, but to his load, he led the way to the point whence he had issued. As they crossed the little terrace of rock, one of the dead trees, that had been tottering for several minutes, fell on the spot where they had stood, and filled the air with its cinders.

Such an event quickened the steps of the party, who followed the Leatherstocking with the urgency required by the occasion.

"Tread on the soft ground," he cried, when they were in a gloom where sight availed them but little, "and keep in the white smoke; keep the skin close on her, lad; she's a precious one, another will be hard to be found."

Obedient to the hunter's directions, they followed his steps and advice implicity; and although the narrow passage along the winding of the spring led amid burning logs and falling branches, they happily achieved it in safety. No one but a man long accustomed to the woods could have traced his route through a smoke, in which respiration was difficult, and sight nearly useless; but the experience of Natty conducted them to an opening through the rocks, where, with a little difficulty, they soon descended to another terrace, and emerged at once into a tolerably clear atmosphere.

11

CHINGACHGOOK, however, was past saving. Asking that his bow, tomahawk, pipe, and wampum be laid in his grave, he gave up his spirit. Elizabeth Temple returned home. She was accompanied part of the way by Oliver Edwards, who made her a promise: "The moment of concealment is over, Miss Temple. By this time tomorrow, I shall remove a veil that perhaps it has been weakness to keep around me and my affairs so long." He was as good as his word. Next day a large body of village volunteers proceeded to

Mount Vision to bring down Natty Bumppo and Benjamin Penguillum, as fugitives from justice. A clash of arms seemed likely to begin, when a dramatic event seized the attention of everyone. Oliver Edwards and the German veteran, Major Hartman, rushed inside the cave which had been such an object of suspicion to Squire Jones as a possible seat of silver-mining operations. They emerged bearing a rude chair, covered with deerskins, on which sat a venerable gentleman, his hair snowy white, his face grave and dignified but deeply marked with age. Behind the three came Leatherstocking, carrying his rifle.

All eyes gazed intently on the strange old man. His mind evidently wandered, for he said: "The council will open immediately. Each one who loves a good and virtuous king will wish to see these colonies continue loyal. Be seated. . . . The troops shall halt for the night." Judge Temple was thunderstruck. "Who is this man?" he inquired.

Oliver Edwards at once introduced him as the lost Major Effingham, rightful proprietor of the land on which they stood; "I am his grandson," said the young man. The whole situation was then made plain by explanations from Edwards (henceforth Oliver Effingham) and Judge Temple. The now-aged Major Effingham had been a Loyalist; on the outbreak of the Revolution he had left his estates in the hands of Marmaduke Temple as trustee; the family had fallen into poverty. Natty Bumppo, who had served with Major Effingham in various western campaigns, had taken up his residence on the major's lands "as a kind of locum tenens." *Major Effingham's son, Oliver's father, had been adopted before his death into the Delaware or Mohican tribe; hence the connection with Chingachgook. Judge Temple for his part quickly proved that he had been a faithful trustee of the Effingham estate, had tried in vain to make payments to the heirs, and had arranged to protect their legal claim to the lands. These statements cleared the air. As the aged Major Effingham was put to bed, Judge Temple gave up all his suspicions of Oliver, and Oliver Effingham apologized for his unjust suspicions of the Judge. And the Judge, declaring that half the estate would at once be conveyed to Oliver, took the young man's hand and united it with that of his blushing daughter Elizabeth.*

The events of our tale carry us through the summer; and, after making nearly the circle of the year, we must conclude our labors in the delightful month of October. Many important incidents had, however, occurred in the intervening period; a few of which it may be necessary to recount.

The two principal were, the marriage of Oliver and Elizabeth, and the death of Major Effingham. They both took place early in September; and the former preceded the latter only a few days. The old man passed away like the last glimmering of a taper; and though his death cast a melancholy over the family; grief could not follow such an end.

One of the chief concerns of Marmaduke was to reconcile the even conduct of a magistrate with the course that his feelings dictated to the criminals. The day succeeding the discovery at the cave, however, Natty and Benjamin re-entered the gaol peaceably, where they continued, well fed and comfortable, until the return of an express to Albany, who brought the Governor's pardon to the Leatherstocking. In the meantime, proper means were employed to satisfy Hiram for the assaults on his person; and on the same day, the two comrades issued together into society again, with their characters not at all affected by the imprisonment.

Mr. Doolittle began to discover that neither his architecture nor his law was quite suitable to the growing wealth and intelligence of the settlement; and, after exacting the last cent that was attainable in his compromises, to use the language of the country, he "pulled up stakes," and proceeded farther west, scattering his professional science and legal learning through the land; vestiges of both of which are to be discovered there even to the present hour.

Poor Jotham, whose life paid the forfeiture of his folly, acknowledged, before he died, that his reasons for believing in a mine were extracted from the lips of a sibyl, who, by looking in a magic glass, was enabled to discover the hidden treasures of the earth. Such superstition was frequent in the new settlements; and after the first surprise was over, the better part of the community forgot the subject. But, at the same time that it removed from the breast of Richard a lingering suspicion of the acts of the three hunters, it conveyed a mortifying lesson to him, which brought many quiet hours, in future, to his cousin Marmaduke. It may be remembered that the Sheriff confidently pronounced this to be no "visionary" scheme, and that word was enough to shut his lips at any time within the next ten years.

Monsieur Le Quoi, who has been introduced to our readers because no picture of that country would be faithful without some such character, found the island of Martinique and his "sucre-boosh" in possession of the English; but Marmaduke and his family were much gratified in soon hearing that he had returned to his bureau in Paris, where he afterward issued yearly bulletins of his happiness and of his gratitude to his friends in America.

With this brief explanation we must return to our narrative. Let the American reader imagine one of our mildest October mornings, when the sun seems a ball of silvery fire, and the elasticity of the air is felt while it is inhaled; imparting vigor and life to the whole system; the weather neither too warm, nor too cold, but of that happy temperature which stirs the blood, without bringing the lassitude of spring.

It was on such a morning, about the middle of the month, that

Oliver entered the hall where Elizabeth was issuing her usual orders for the day, and requested her to join him in a short excursion to the lake side. The tender melancholy in the manner of her husband caught the attention of Elizabeth, who instantly abandoned her concerns, threw a light shawl across her shoulders, and, concealing her raven hair under a gipsy, she took his arm and submitted herself without a question to his guidance. The crossed the bridge, and had turned from the highway along the margin of the lake, before a word was exchanged. Elizabeth well knew by the direction the object of the walk, and respected the feelings of her companion too much to indulge in untimely conversation. But when they gained the open fields, and her eye roamed over the placid lake covered with wild fowl, already journeying from the great northern waters to seek a warmer sun, but lingering to play in the limpid sheet of the Otsego, and to the sides of the mountain, which were gay with the thousand dyes of autumn, as if to grace their bridal, the swelling heart of the young wife burst out in speech.

"This is not a time for silence, Oliver!" she said, clinging more fondly to his arm; "everything in nature seems to speak the praises of the Creator; why should we, who have so much to be grateful for, be silent?"

"Speak on!" said her husband, smiling; "I love the sounds of your voice. You must anticipate our errand hither: I have told you my plans: how do you like them?"

"I must first see them," returned his wife. "But I have had my plans too; it is time I should begin to divulge them."

"You! It is something for the comfort of my old friend Natty, I know."

"Certainly of Natty; but we have other friends besides the Leather-stocking to serve. Do you forget Louisa and her father?"

"No, surely; have I not given one of the best farms in the county to the good divine. As for Louisa, I should wish you to keep her always near us."

"You do," said Elizabeth, slightly compressing her lips; "but poor Louisa may have other views for herself; she may wish to follow my example, and marry."

"I don't think it," said Effingham, musing a moment; "I really don't know any one hereabouts good enough for her."

"Perhaps not here; but there are other places besides Templeton, and other churches besides New St. Paul's."

"Churches, Elizabeth! you would not wish to lose Mr. Grant, surely! Though simple, he is an excellent man. I shall never find another who has half the veneration for my orthodoxy. You would humble me from a saint to a very common sinner."

"It must be done, sir," returned the lady, with a half-concealed smile, "though it degrades you from an angel to a man."

"But you forget the farm."

"He can lease it, as others do. Besides, would you have a clergyman toil in the fields?"

"Where can he go? You forget Louisa."

"No, I do not forget Louisa," said Elizabeth, again compressing her beautiful lips. "You know, Effingham, that my father has told you that I ruled him, and that I should rule you. I am now about to exert my power."

"Anything, anything, dear Elizabeth, but not at the expense of us all; not at the expense of your friend."

"How do you know, sir, that it will be so much at the expense of my friend?" said the lady, fixing her eyes with a searching look on his countenance, where they met only the unsuspecting expression of manly regret.

"How do I know it? why, it is natural that she should regret us."

"It is our duty to struggle with our natural feelings," returned the lady; "and there is but little cause to fear that such a spirit as Louisa's will not effect it."

"But what is your plan?"

"Listen, and you shall know. My father has procured a call for Mr. Grant, to one of the towns on the Hudson, where he can live more at his ease than in journeying through these woods; where he can spend the evening of his life in comfort and quiet; and where his daughter may meet with such society and form such a connection as may be proper for one of her years and character."

"Bless! you amaze me! I did not think you had been such a manager!"

"Oh! I manage more deeply than you imagine, sir," said the wife, archly smiling again; "but it is my will, and it is your duty to submit,—for a time at least."

Effingham laughed; but as they approached the end of their walk the subject was changed by common consent.

The place at which they arrived was the little spot of level ground where the cabin of the Leatherstocking had so long stood. Elizabeth found it entirely cleared of rubbish, and beautifully laid down in turf, by the removal of sods, which, in common with the surrounding country, had grown gay, under the influence of profuse showers, as if a second spring had passed over the land. The little place was surrounded by a circle of masonwork, and they entered by a small gate, near which, to the surprise of both, the rifle of Natty was leaning against the wall. Hector and the slut reposed on the grass by its side, as if conscious that, however altered, they were lying on ground, and were surrounded by objects with which they were familiar. The hunter himself was stretched on the earth, before a headstone of white marble, pushing aside with his fingers the long grass that had already sprung up from the luxuriant soil around its base, apparently to lay bare the inscription. By the side of this stone, which was a simple slab at the head of a grave, stood a rich monument, decorated with an urn, and ornamented with a chisel.

Oliver and Elizabeth approached the graves with a light tread unheard by the old hunter, whose sunburnt face was working, and whose eyes twinkled as if something impeded their vision. After some little time, Natty raised himself slowly from the ground, and said aloud—

"Well, well—I'm bold to say it's all right! There's something that I suppose is reading; but I can't make anything of it; though the pipe and the tomahawk, and the moccasins be pretty well—pretty well, for a man that, I dares to say, never seed 'ither of the things. Ah's me! there they lie, side by side, happy enough! Who will there be to put me in the 'arth, when my time comes?"

"When that unfortunate hour arrives, Natty, friends shall not be wanting to perform the last offices for you," said Oliver, a little touched at the hunter's soliloquy.

The old man turned, without manifesting surprise, for he had got the Indian habits in this particular, and running his hand under the bottom of his nose, seemed to wipe away his sorrow with the action.

"You've come out to see the graves, children, have ye?" he said; "well, well, they're wholesome sights to young as well as old."

"I hope they are fitted to your liking," said Effingham; "no one has a better right than yourself to be consulted in the matter."

"Why, seeing that I ain't used to fine graves," returned the old man, "it is but little matter consarning my taste. Ye laid the Major's head to the west, and Mohegan's to the east, did ye, lad?"

"At your request it was done."

"It's so best," said the hunter; "they thought they had to journey different ways, children; though there is One greater than all, who'll bring the just together, at his own time, and who'll whiten the skin of a blackmoor, and place him on a footing with princes."

"There is but little reason to doubt that," said Elizabeth, whose decided tones were changed to a soft, melancholy voice; "I trust we shall all meet again, and be happy together."

"Shall we child? shall we?" exclaimed the hunter, with unusual fervor; "there's comfort in that thought too. But before I go, I should like to know what 'tis you tell these people, that be flocking into the country like pigeons in the spring, of the old Delaware, and of the bravest white man that ever trod the hills."

Effingham and Elizabeth were surprised at the manner of the

Leatherstocking, which was unusually impressive and solemn; but attributing it to the scene the young man turned to the monument and read aloud—

" 'Sacred to the memory of Oliver Effingham, Esquire, formerly a Major in his B. Majesty's 60th Foot; a soldier of tried valor; a subject of chivalrous loyalty; and a man of honesty. To these virtues he added the graces of a Christian. The morning of his life was spent in honor, wealth, and power; but its evening was obscured by poverty, neglect, and disease, which were alleviated only by the tender care of his old, faithful, and upright friend and attendant, Nathaniel Bumppo. His descendants rear this stone to the virtues of the master, and to the enduring gratitude of the servant.' "

The Leatherstocking stared at the sound of his own name, and a smile of joy illumined his wrinkled features, as he said—

"And did ye say it, lad? have you then got the old man's name cut in the stone, by the side of his master's? God bless ye, children! 'twas a kind thought, and kindness goes to the heart as life shortens."

Elizabeth turned her back to the speakers. Effingham made a fruitless effort before he succeeded in saying—

"It is there cut in plain marble; but it should have been written in letters of gold!"

"Show me the name, boy," said Natty, with simple eagerness; "let me see my own name placed in such honor. 'Tis a gin'rous gift to a man who leaves none of his name and family behind him, in a country where he has tarried so long."

Effingham guided his finger to the spot, and Natty followed the windings of the letters to the end with deep interest, when he raised himself from the tomb, and said—

"I suppose it's all right, and it's kindly thought, and kindly done! But what have ye put over the redskin?"

"You shall hear—

" 'This stone is raised to the memory of an Indian Chief, of the Delaware tribe, who was known by the several names of John Mohegan; Mohican——' "

"Mo-hee-can, lad, they call theirselves! 'he-can."

" 'Mohican; and Chingagook——' "

" 'Gach, boy;—'gach-gook; Chingachgook, which, intarpreted, means Big Sarpent. The name should be set down right, for an Indian's name has always some meaning in it."

"I will see it altered. 'He was the last of his people who continued to inhabit this country; and it may be said of him, that his faults were those of an Indian, and his virtues those of a man.' "

"You never said truer word, Mr. Oliver; ah's me! if you had know'd him as I did, in his prime, in that very battle, where the old gentleman, who sleeps by his side, saved his life, when them thieves, the Iroquois, had him at the stake, you'd have said all that, and more too. I cut the thongs with this very hand, and gave him my own tomahawk and knife, seeing that the rifle was always my fav'rite weapon. He did lay about him like a man! I met him as I was coming home from the trail, with eleven Mingo scalps on his pole. You needn't shudder, Madam Effingham, for they was all from shaved heads and warriors. When I look about me, at these hills, where I used to could count sometimes twenty smokes, curling over the treetops, from the Delaware camps, it raises mournful thoughts to think that not a redskin is left of them all; unless it may be a drunken vagabond from the Oneidas, or them Yankee Indians, who, they say, be moving up from the seashore; and who belong to none of God's creaters, to my seeming, being, as it were, neither fish nor flesh—neither white man nor savage. Well, well! the time has come at last, and I must go——"

"Go!" echoed Edwards; "whither do you go?"

The Leatherstocking, who had imbibed, unconsciously, many of the Indian qualities, though he always thought of himself as of a civilized being, compared with even the Delawares, averted his face to conceal the workings of his muscles, as he stooped to lift a large pack from behind the tomb, which he placed deliberately on his shoulders.

"Go!" exclaimed Elizabeth, approaching him, with a hurried step; "you should not venture so far in the woods alone at your time of life, Natty; indeed, it is imprudent. He is bent, Effingham, on some distant hunting."

"What Mrs. Effingham tells you is true, Leatherstocking," said Edwards; "there can be no necessity for your submitting to such hardships now! So throw aside your pack, and confine your hunt to the mountains near us, if you will go."

"Hardship! 'tis a pleasure, children, and the greatest that is left me on this side the grave."

"No, no; you shall not go to such a distance!" cried Elizabeth, laying her white hand on his deerskin pack. "I am right! I feel his camp kettle, and a canister of powder! He must not be suffered to wander so far from us, Oliver; remember how suddenly Mohegan dropped away."

"I know'd the parting would come hard, children; I know'd it would!" said Natty, "and so I got aside to look at the graves by myself, and thought if I left ye the keepsake which the Major gave me, when we first parted in the woods, ye wouldn't take it unkind, but would know that, let the old man's body go where it might, his feelings stayed behind him."

"This means something more than common!" exclaimed the youth; "where is it, Natty, that you purpose going?"

The hunter drew nigh him with a confident, reasoning air, as if what he had to say would silence all objections, and replied—

"Why, lad, they tell me that on the Big Lakes there's the best of hunting, and a great range, without a white man on it, unless it may be one like myself. I'm weary of living in clearings, and where the hammer is sounding in my ears from sunrise to sundown. And though I'm much bound to ye both, children—I wouldn't say it if it was not true—I crave to go into the woods ag'in, I do."

"Woods!" echoed Elizabeth, trembling with her feelings; "do you not call these endless forests woods?"

"Ah! child, these be nothing to a man that's used to the wilderness. I have took but little comfort sin' your father come on with his settlers; but I wouldn't go far, while the life was in the body that lies under the sod there. But now he's gone, and Chingachgook is gone; and you be both young and happy. Yes! the big house has rung with merriment this month past! And now, I thought, was the time to try to get a little comfort in the close of my days. Woods! indeed! I doesn't call these woods, Madam Effingham, where I lose myself, every day of my life, in the clearings."

"If there be anything wanting to your comfort, name it, Leatherstocking; if it be attainable, it is yours."

"You mean all for the best, lad; I know it; and so does Madam, too: but your ways isn't my ways. 'Tis like the dead there, who thought, when the breath was in them, that one went east, and one went west, to find their heavens; but they'll meet at last; and so shall we, children. Yes, ind as you've begun, and we shall meet in the land of the just at last."

"This is so new! so unexpected!" said Elizabeth, in almost breathless excitement; "I had thought you meant to live with us, and die with us, Natty."

"Words are of no avail;" exclaimed her husband; "the habits of forty years are not to be dispossessed by the ties of a day. I know you too well to urge your further, Natty; unless you will let me build you a hut on one of the distant hills, where we can sometimes see you, and know that you are comfortable."

"Don't fear the Leatherstocking, children; God will see that his days be provided for, and his ind happy. I know you mean all for the best, but our ways doesn't agree. I love the woods, and ye relish the face of man; I eat when hungry, and drink when a-dry, and ye keep stated hours and rules; nay, nay, you even overfeed the dogs, lad, from pure kindness; and hounds should be gaunty to run well. The meanest of God's creaters be made for some use, and I'm form'd for the wilderness; if ye love me, let me go where my soul craves to be ag'in!"

The appeal was decisive; and not another word of entreaty for him to remain was then uttered; but Elizabeth bent her head to her bosom and wept, while her husband dashed away the tears from his eyes, and, with hands that almost refused to perform their office, he produced his pocketbook, and extended a parcel of bank notes to the hunter.

"Take these," he said, "at least, take these; secure them about your person, and in the hour of need they will do you good service."

The old man took the notes, and examined them with a curious eye.

"This, then, is some of the new-fashioned money that they've been making at Albany, out of paper! It can't be worth much to they that hasn't larning! No, no, lad—take back the stuff; it will do me no sarvice. I took kear to get all the Frenchman's powder, afore he broke up, and they say lead grows where I'm going. It isn't even fit for wads, seeing that I use none but leather!—Madam Effingham, let an old man kiss your hand, and wish God's choicest blessings on you and your'n."

"Once more let me beseech you, stay!" cried Elizabeth. "Do not, Leatherstocking, leave me to grieve for the man who has twice rescued me from death, and who has served those I love so faithfully. For my sake, if not for your own, stay. I shall see you in those frightful dreams that still haunt my nights, dying in poverty and age, by the side of those terrific beasts you slew. There will be no evil that sickness, want, and solitude can inflict, that my fancy will not conjure as your fate. Stay with us, old man; if not for your own sake, at least for ours."

"Such thoughts and bitter dreams, Madam Effingham," returned the hunter solemnly, "will never haunt an innocent parson long. They'll pass away with God's pleasure. And if the catamounts be yet brought to your eyes in sleep, 'tis not for my sake, but to show you the power of Him that led me there to save you. Trust in God, Madam, and your honorable husband, and the thoughts for an old man like me can never be long nor bitter. I pray that the Lord will keep you in mind—the Lord that lives in clearings as well as in the wilderness—and bless you, and all that belong to you, from this time till the great day when the whites shall meet the redskins in judgment, and justice shall be the law, and not power."

Elizabeth raised her head, and offered her colorless cheek to his salute, when he lifted his cap and touched it respectfully. His hand was grasped with convulsive fervor by the youth, who continued silent. The hunter prepared himself for his journey, drawing his belt tighter, and wasting his moments in the little reluctant movements of a sorrowful departure. Once or twice he essayed to speak, but a rising in his throat prevented it. At length he shouldered his rifle, and cried with a clear huntsman's call, that echoed through the woods—

"He-e-e-re, he-e-e-re, pups—away, dogs, away;—ye'll be footsore afore ye see the ind of the journey!"

The hounds leaped from the earth at this cry, and, scenting around the graves and the silent pair, as if conscious of their own destination, they followed humbly at the heels of their master. A short pause succeeded, during which even the youth concealed his face on his grandfather's tomb. When the pride of manhood, however, had suppressed the feelings of nature, he turned to renew his entreaties, but saw that the cemetery was occupied only by himself and his wife.

"He is gone!" cried Effingham.

Elizabeth raised her face, and saw the old hunter standing, looking back for a moment, on the verge of the wood. As he caught their glances, he drew his hard hand hastily across his eyes again, waved it on high for an adieu, and, uttering a forced cry to his dogs, who were crouching at his feet, he entered the forest.

This was the last that they ever saw of the Leatherstocking, whose rapid movements preceded the pursuit which Judge Temple both ordered and conducted. He had gone far toward the setting sun,—the foremost in that band of pioneers who are opening the way for the march of the nation across the continent.

THE PRAIRIE

Being the FIFTH SERIES OF ADVENTURES *of*

LEATHERSTOCKING

THE PRAIRIES (or the Great Prairies, as Cooper sometimes calls them) are really the Great Plains. The author brings Leatherstocking out upon the flat country that is now Nebraska, with the Platte and the Missouri behind him, in the autumn of 1804. As the scout was twenty in the early 1740's, he would now be fully eighty. But it is not well to be minutely precise about either Cooper's chronology or his geography. It is sufficient to say that as a very old man, Leatherstocking now lives by taking pelts along the streams of the Far West. This was a country which Cooper himself had never visited. But he had done more than read of it. As already noted, he had visited dele-

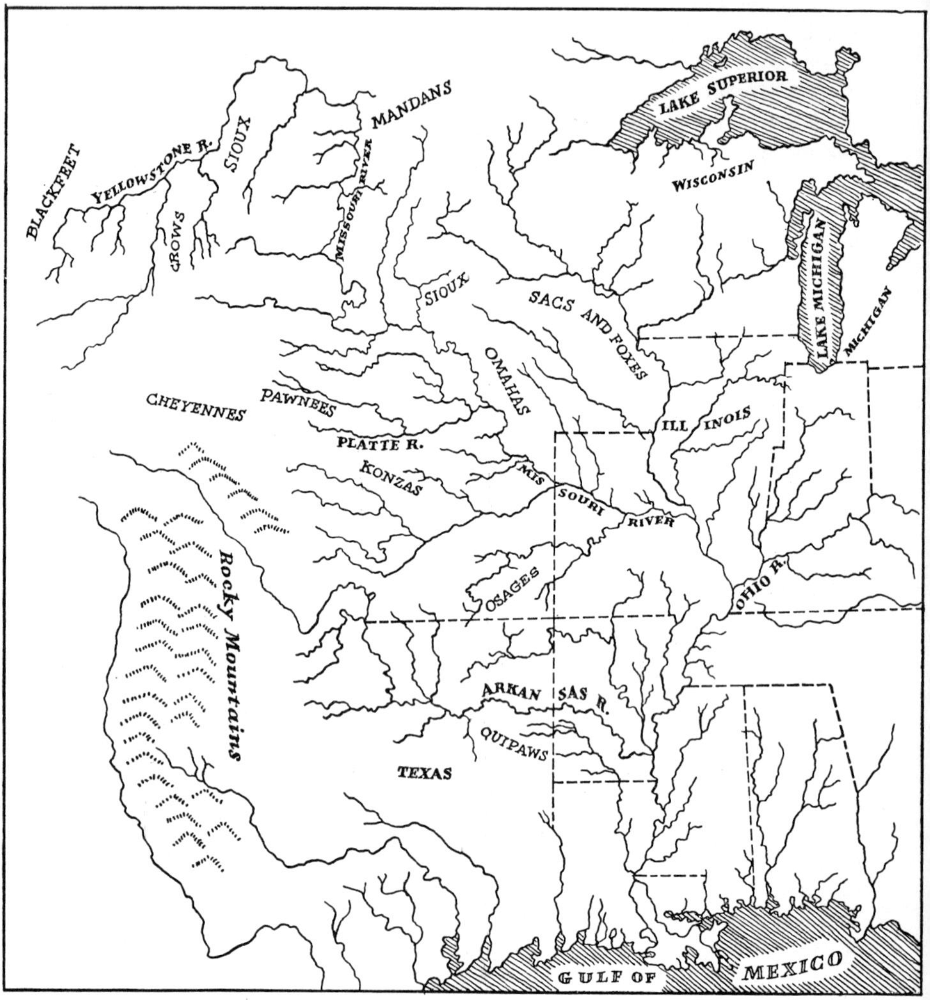

THE WESTERN COUNTRY OF *The Prairie*
as mapped by George Catlin

(From Catlin's *Manners, Customs, and Condition of the North American Indians,* 1841. The map was drawn in 1833. Cooper, though dating *The Prairie* in 1804, was actually writing of the Platte Valley about 1826.)

gations of Sioux and Pawnee Indians on their way to or from Washington. He had studied the individual types, had been impressed by their laconic eloquence and poetic phrasing, and had marked their natural dignity and their grace of manner. He had questioned them carefully through interpreters, and had talked with the army officers who accompanied them. Thus he had learned something at first hand about the buffalo hunts, the terrible prairie fires, and the implacable struggles between mounted bands of rival tribes.

"This book," writes Cooper in his introduction, "closes the career of Leatherstocking. Pressed upon by time, he has ceased to be the hunter and warrior, and has become a trapper of the great West. The sound of the ax has driven him from his beloved forests to seek a refuge, by a species of desperate resignation, on the denuded plains that stretch to the Rocky Mountains. Here he passes the few remaining years of his life, dying as he had lived, a philosopher of the wilderness, with few of the failings, none of the vices, and all of the nature and truth of his position."

This is an accurate statement of the central element of the book; for Leatherstocking even in extreme age still dominates the tale. The plot is awkward and complicated, and the canvas contains too many figures. To be sure, three of the personages depicted are wonderfully alive and picturesque. The old squatter Ishmael Bush, with his crooked dealings and brutal ways, is a fugitive from justice; but he has his own rough code, as he shows when he inexorably sentences his brother-in-law to death. His harsh-tongued wife Esther, a savage Deborah when aroused to anger, a grief-stricken Niobe when bereft of her child, has the best virtues as well as some of the worst faults of pioneer womanhood. In the hearty, resolute heroine Ellen we have almost a match for Mabel Dunham. But of other characters the less said the better. A certain repetitiousness mars the plot. Again we have a dastardly tribe of Indians, this time one of the branches of the Sioux; again we have a savage villain, this time Mahtoree; again we have a Chingachgook, this time the brave young Pawnee chief Hard-Heart; again we have the capture and the rescue of forlorn maidens. Leatherstocking, however, along with Ishmael Bush and his virago spouse, lifts the book to distinction. And it must again be said that it gains no little distinction from Cooper's imaginative rendition of the Great Plains, as vast and almost as solitary as the ocean.

Leatherstocking has undiminished impressiveness to the end. Much as he mourns the lost wilderness, and blames those who have made such haste to "strip the airth of its lawful covering," much as he repines because he is old, worn-out, and useless, on the whole he is resigned to his lot. Looking back, he sees that he has lived a good life. "If it was given me to choose my time and place again," he muses, "I would say, twenty and the wilderness." The philosophic peace of age has descended upon him, as he notes in rebuking a rashly impetuous junior; "a gray head should cover the brain of reason." He dies, seated in his chair, his rifle on his knee, his hound at his feet, his last words full of thoughtfulness for others, as Leatherstocking ought to die.

1

MUCH WAS SAID and written, at the time, concerning the policy of adding the vast regions of Louisiana to the already immense and but half-tenanted territories of the United States. As the warmth of controversy, however, subsided, and party considerations gave place to more liberal views, the wisdom of the measure began to be generally conceded. It soon became apparent to the meanest capacity, that, while nature had placed a barrier of desert to the extension of our population in the west, the measure had made us the masters of a belt of fertile country, which, in the revolutions of the day, might have become the property of a rival nation. It gave us the sole command of the great thoroughfare of the interior, and placed the countless tribes of savages, who lay along our borders, entirely within our control; it reconciled conflicting rights, and quieted national distrusts; it opened a thousand avenues to the inland trade, and to the waters of the Pacific; and, if ever time or necessity shall require a peaceful division of this vast empire, it assures us of a neighbor that will possess our language, our religion, our institutions, and it is also to be hoped, our sense of political justice.

Although the purchase was made in 1803, the spring of the succeeding year was permitted to open before the official prudence of the Spaniard, who held the province for his European master, admitted the authority, or even of the entrance of its new proprietors. But the forms of the transfer were no sooner completed, and the new government acknowledged, than swarms of that restless people, which is ever found hovering on the skirts of American society, plunged into the thickets that fringed the right bank of the Mississippi, with the same careless hardihood as had already sustained so many of them in their toilsome progress from the Atlantic States to the eastern shores of the "father of rivers." [1]

Time was necessary to blend the numerous and affluent colonists of the lower province with their new compatriots; but the thinner and more humble population above was almost immediately swallowed in the vortex which attended the tide of instant emigration. The inroad from the east was a new and sudden outbreaking of a people, who had endured a momentary restraint, after having been rendered nearly resistless by success. The toils and hazards of former undertakings were forgotten, as these endless and unexplored regions, with all their fancied as well as real advantages, were laid open to their enterprise. The consequences were such as might easily have been anticipated, from so tempting an offering, placed, as it was, before the eyes of a race long trained in adventure and nurtured in difficulties.

Thousands of the elders, of what were then called the *New* States,[2] broke up from the enjoyment of their hard-earned indulgences, and were to be seen leading long files of descendants, born and reared in the forests of Ohio and Kentucky, deeper into the land, in quest of that which might be termed, without the aid of poetry, their natural and more congenial atmosphere. The distinguished and resolute forester who first penetrated the wilds of the latter state was of the number. This adventurous and venerable patriarch was now seen making his last remove; placing the "endless river" between him and the multitude his own success had drawn around him, and seeking for the renewal of enjoyments which were rendered worthless in his eyes, when trammelled by the forms of human institutions.[3]

In the pursuit of adventures such as these, men are ordinarily governed by their habits or deluded by their wishes. A few, led by the phantoms of hope, and ambitious of sudden affluence, sought the

---

[1] The Mississippi is thus termed in several of the Indian languages. The reader will gain a more just idea of the importance of this stream, if he recalls to mind the fact, that the Missouri and the Mississippi are properly the same river. Their united lengths cannot be greatly short of four thousand miles. (*Cooper's note*)

[2] All the states admitted to the American Union, since the Revolution, are called New States, with the exception of Vermont: that had claims before the war; which were not, however, admitted until a later day. (*Cooper's note*)

[3] Colonel Boone, the patriarch of Kentucky. This venerable and hardy pioneer of civilization emigrated to an estate three hundred miles west of the Mississippi, in his ninety-second year, because he found a population of ten to the square mile inconveniently crowded! (*Cooper's note*)—Actually, Boone did not quite reach the age of 87, and removed to Missouri at 64 or 65 because he had lost his Kentucky lands through imperfect titles, and was able to obtain a grant west of the Mississippi.—Ed.

mines of the virgin territory; but by far the greater portion of the emigrants were satisfied to establish themselves along the margins of the larger watercourses, content with the rich returns that the generous, alluvial bottoms of the rivers never fail to bestow on the most desultory industry. In this manner were communities formed with magical rapidity; and most of those who witnessed the purchase of the empty empire, have lived to see already a populous and sovereign state, parcelled from its inhabitants, and received into the bosom of the national Union, on terms of political equality.

The incidents and scenes which are connected with this legend, occurred in the earliest periods of the enterprises which have led to so great and so speedy a result.

The harvest of the first year of our possession had long been passed, and the fading foliage of a few scattered trees was already beginning to exhibit the hues and tints of autumn, when a train of wagons issued from the bed of a dry rivulet, to pursue its course across the undulating surface of what, in the language of the country of which we write, is called a "rolling prairie." The vehicles, loaded with household goods and implements of husbandry, the few straggling sheep and cattle that were herded in the rear, and the rugged appearance and careless mien of the sturdy men who loitered at the sides of the lingering teams, united to announce a band of emigrants seeking for the Eldorado of the West. Contrary to the usual practice of the men of their caste, this party had left the fertile bottoms of the low country, and had found its way, by means only known to such adventurers, across glen and torrent, over deep morasses and arid wastes, to a point far beyond the usual limits of civilized habitations. In their front were stretched those broad plains, which extend, with so little diversity of character, to the bases of the Rocky Mountains; and many long and dreary miles in their rear foamed the swift and turbid waters of La Platte.

The appearance of such a train, in that bleak and solitary place, was rendered the more remarkable by the fact, that the surrounding country offered so little that was tempting to the cupidity of speculation, and, if possible, still less that was flattering to the hopes of an ordinary settler of new lands.

The meager herbage of the prairie promised nothing, in favor of a hard and unyielding soil, over which the wheels of the vehicles rattled as lightly as if they travelled on a beaten road; neither wagons nor beasts making any deeper impression, than to mark that bruised and withered grass, which the cattle plucked, from time to time, and as often rejected, as food too sour for even hunger to render palatable.

Whatever might be the final destination of these adventurers, or the secret causes of their apparent security in so remote and unprotected a situation, there was no visible sign of uneasiness, uncertainty, or alarm, among them. Including both sexes, and every age, the number of the party exceeded twenty.

At some little distance in front of the whole marched the individual, who, by his position and air, appeared to be the leader of the band. He was a tall, sunburnt man, past the middle age, of a dull countenance and listless manner. His frame appeared loose and flexible; but it was vast, and in reality of prodigious power. It was only at moments, however, as some slight impediment opposed itself to his loitering progress, that his person, which, in its ordinary gait seemed so lounging and nerveless, displayed any of those energies, which lay latent in his system, like the slumbering and unwieldy, but terrible, strength of the elephant. The inferior lineaments of his countenance were coarse, extended and vacant; while the superior, or those nobler parts which are thought to affect the intellectual being, were low, receding and mean.

The dress of this individual was a mixture of the coarsest vestments of a husbandman with the leathern garments, that fashion as well as use, had in some degree rendered necessary to one engaged in his present pursuits. There was, however, a singular and wild display of prodigal and ill-judged ornaments blended with his motley attire. In place of the usual deerskin belt, he wore around his body a tarnished silken sash of the most gaudy colors; the buck-horn haft of his knife was profusely decorated with plates of silver; the marten's fur of his cap was of a fineness and shadowing that a queen might covet; the buttons of his rude and soiled blanket-coat were of the glittering coinage of Mexico; the stock of his rifle was of beautiful mahogany, riveted and banded with the same precious metal, and the trinkets of no less than three worthless watches dangled from different parts of his person. In addition to the pack and the rifle which were slung at his back, together with the well-filled and carefully guarded pouch and horn, he had carelessly cast a keen and bright wood ax across his shoulder, sustaining the weight of the whole with as much apparent ease, as if he moved, unfettered in limb, and free from incumbrance.

A short distance in the rear of this man came a group of youths very similarly attired, and bearing sufficient resemblance to each other, and to their leader, to distinguish them as the children of one family. Though the youngest of their number could not much have passed the period that, in the nicer judgment of the law, is called the age of discretion, he had proved himself so far worthy of his progenitors as to have reared already his aspiring person to the standard height of his race. There were one or two others, of different mould, whose descriptions must, however, be referred to the regular course of the narrative.

Of the females, there were but two who had arrived at womanhood; though several white-headed, olive-skinned faces were peering out of the foremost wagon of the train, with eyes of lively curiosity and characteristic animation. The elder of the two adults was the sallow and wrinkled mother of most of the party, and the younger was a sprightly, active girl of eighteen, who in figure, dress, and mien seemed to belong to a station in society several gradations above that of any one of her visible associates. The second vehicle was covered with a top of cloth so tightly drawn, as to conceal its contents, with the nicest care. The remaining wagons were loaded with such rude furniture and other personal effects as might be supposed to belong to one, ready at any moment to change his abode, without reference to season or distance.

Perhaps there was little in this train, or in the appearance of its proprietors, that is not daily to be encountered on the highways of this changeable and moving country. But the solitary and peculiar scenery, in which it was so unexpectedly exhibited, gave to the party a marked character of wildness and adventure.

In the little valleys, which, in the regular formation of the land, occurred at every mile of their progress, the view was bounded, on two of the sides, by the gradual and low elevations, which give name to the description of prairie we have mentioned; while on the others, the meager prospect ran off in long, narrow, barren perspectives, but slightly relieved by a pitiful show of coarse, though somewhat luxuriant, vegetation. From the summits of the swells, the eye became fatigued with the sameness and chilling dreariness of the landscape. The earth was not unlike the ocean, when its restless waters are heaving heavily, after the agitation and fury of the tempest have begun to lessen. There was the same waving and regular surface, the same absence of foreign objects, and the same boundless extent to the view. Indeed, so very striking was the resemblance between the water and the land, that, however much the geologist might sneer at so simple a theory, it would have been difficult for a poet not to have felt, that the formation of the one had been produced by the subsiding dominion of the other. Here and there a tall tree rose out of the bottoms, stretching its naked branches abroad, like some solitary vessel; and, to strengthen the delusion, far in the distance, appeared two or three rounded thickets, looming in the misty horizon like islands resting on the waters. It is unnecessary to warn the practiced reader, that the sameness of the surface, and the low stands of the spectators, exaggerated the distances; but, as swell appeared after swell, and island succeeded island, there was a disheartening assurance that long, and seemingly interminable, tracts of territory must be passed, before the wishes of the humblest agriculturist could be realized.

Still, the leader of the emigrants steadily pursued his way, with no other guide than the sun, turning his back resolutely on the abodes of civilization, and plunging, at each step, more deeply if not irretrievably, into the haunts of the barbarous and savage occupants of the country. As the day drew nigher to a close, however, his mind, which was, perhaps, incapable of maturing any connected system of forethought, beyond that which related to the interests of the present moment, became, in some slight degree, troubled with the care of providing for the wants of the hours of darkness.

On reaching the crest of a swell that was a little higher than the usual elevations, he lingered a minute, and cast a half-curious eye, on either hand, in quest of those well-known signs, which might indicate a place where the three grand requisites of water, fuel and fodder were to be obtained in conjunction.

It would seem that his search was fruitless; for after a few moments of indolent and listless examination, he suffered his huge frame to descend the gentle declivity, in the same sluggish manner that an over-fatted beast would have yielded to the downward pressure.

His example was silently followed by those who succeeded him, though not until the young men had manifested much more of interest, if not of concern in the brief inquiry, which each, in his turn, made on gaining the same lookout. It was now evident, by the tardy movements both of beasts and men, that the time of necessary rest was not far distant. The matted grass of the lower land presented obstacles which fatigue began to render formidable, and the whip was becoming necessary to urge the lingering teams to their labor. At this moment, when, with the exception of the principal individual, a general lassitude was getting the mastery of the travellers, and every eye was cast, by a sort of common impulse, wistfully forward, the whole party was brought to a halt, by a spectacle, as sudden as it was unexpected.

The sun had fallen below the crest of the nearest wave of the prairie, leaving the usual rich and glowing train on its track. In the center of this flood of fiery light, a human form appeared, drawn against the gilded background, as distinctly, and, seemingly as palpable, as though it would come within the grasp of any extended hand. The figure was colossal; the attitude musing and melancholy, and the situation directly in the route of the travellers. But imbedded, as it was, in its setting of garish light, it was impossible to distinguish its just proportions or true character.

The effect of such a spectacle was instantaneous and powerful. The man in front of the emigrants came to a stand, and remained gazing at the mysterious object, with a dull interest, that soon quickened into superstitious awe. His sons, so soon as the first emotions of surprise had a little abated, drew slowly around him, and, as they who governed the teams gradually followed their example, the whole party was soon condensed in one, silent, and wondering group. Notwithstanding, the impression of a supernatural agency was very general among the travellers, the ticking of gunlocks was heard, and one or two of the bolder youths cast their rifles forward, in readiness for service.

"Send the boys off to the right," exclaimed the resolute wife and mother, in a sharp, dissonant voice; "I warrant me, Asa, or Abner will give some account of the creature!"

"It may be well enough to try the rifle," muttered a dull-looking man, whose features, both in outline and expression, bore no small resemblance to the first speaker, and who loosened the stock of his piece and brought it dexterously to the front, while delivering this opinion; "the Pawnee Loups are said to be hunting by hundreds in the plains; if so, they'll never miss a single man from their tribe."

"Stay!" exclaimed a soft-toned, but alarmed female voice, which was easily to be traced to the trembling lips of the younger of the two women; "we are not altogether; it may be a friend!"

"Who is scouting, now?" demanded the father, scanning, at the same time, the cluster of his stout sons, with a displeased and sullen eye. "Put by the piece, put by the piece"; he continued, diverting the other's aim, with the finger of a giant, and with the air of one it might be dangerous to deny. "My job is not yet ended; let us finish the little that remains, in peace."

The man, who had manifested so hostile an intention, appeared to understand the other's allusion, and suffered himself to be diverted from his object. The sons turned their inquiring looks on the girl, who had so eagerly spoken, to require an explanation; but, as if content with the respite she had obtained for the stranger, she sunk back in her seat, and chose to affect a maidenly silence.

In the meantime, the hues of the heavens had often changed. In place of the brightness, which had dazzled the eye, a gray and more sober light had succeeded, and as the setting lost its brilliancy, the proportions of the fanciful form became less exaggerated, and finally distinct. Ashamed to hesitate, now that the truth was no longer doubtful, the leader of the party resumed his journey, using the precaution, as he ascended the slight acclivity, to release his own rifle from the strap, and to cast it into a situation more convenient for sudden use.

There was little apparent necessity, however, for such watchfulness. From the moment when it had thus unaccountably appeared, as it were, between the heavens and the earth, the stranger's figure had neither moved nor given the smallest evidence of hostility. Had he harbored any such evil intention, the individual who now came plainly into view seemed but little qualified to execute them.

A frame that had endured the hardships of more than eighty seasons was not qualified to awaken apprehension in the breast of one as powerful as the emigrant. Notwithstanding his years, and his look of emaciation, if not of suffering, there was that about this solitary being, however, which said that time, and not disease, had laid his hand heavily on him. His form had withered, but it was not wasted. The sinews and muscles, which had once denoted great strength, though shrunken, were still visible; and his whole figure had attained an appearance of induration, which, if it were not for the well-known frailty of humanity, would have seemed to bid defiance to the further approaches of decay. His dress was chiefly of skins, worn with the hair to the weather; a pouch and horn were suspended from his shoulders; and he leaned on a rifle of uncommon length, but which, like its owner, exhibited the wear of long and hard service.

As the party drew nigher to this solitary being, and came within a distance to be heard, a low growl issued from the grass at his feet, and then a tall, gaunt, toothless hound arose lazily from his lair, and shaking himself, made some show of resisting the nearer approach of the travellers.

"Down, Hector, down," said his master, in a voice that was a little tremulous and hollow with age. "What have ye to do, pup, with men who journey on their lawful callings?"

"Stranger, if you ar' much acquainted in this country," said the leader of the emigrants, "can you tell a traveller where he may find necessaries for the night?"

"Is the land filled on the other side of the Big River?" demanded the old man solemnly, and without appearing to hearken to the other's question; "or why do I see a sight I had never thought to behold again?"

"Why, there is country left, it is true, for such as have money, and ar' not particular in the choice," returned the emigrant; "but to my taste, it is getting crowdy. What may a man call the distance, from this place to the nighest point on the main river?"

"A hunted deer could not cool his sides in the Mississippi, without travelling a weary five hundred miles."

"And what may you name the district, here-a-way?"

"By what name," returned the old man, pointing significantly upward, "would you call the spot where you see yonder cloud?"

The emigrant looked at the other, like one who did not comprehend his meaning, and who half suspected he was trifled with, but he contented himself by saying——

"You ar' but a new inhabitant, like myself, I reckon, stranger, otherwise you would not be backward in helping a traveller to some advice; words cost but little, and sometimes lead to friendships."

"Advice is not a gift, but a debt that the old owe to the young. What would you wish to know?"

"Where I may 'camp for the night. I'm no great difficulty maker, as to bed and board; but all old journeyers, like myself, know the virtue of sweet water, and a good browse for the cattle."

"Come then with me, and you shall be master of both; and little more is it that I can offer on this hungry prairie."

As the old man was speaking, he raised his heavy rifle to his shoulder, with a facility a little remarkable for his years and appearance, and without further words led the way over the acclivity to the adjacent bottom.

The travellers soon discovered the usual and unerring evidences that the several articles necessary to their situation were not far distant. A clear and gurgling spring burst out of the side of the declivity, and joining its waters to those of other similar little fountains, in its vicinity, their united contributions formed a run, which was easily to be traced, for miles, along the prairie, by the scattering foliage and verdure which occasionally grew within the influence of its moisture. Hither, then, the stranger held his way, eagerly followed by the willing teams, whose instinct gave them a prescience or refreshment and rest.

On reaching what he deemed a suitable spot, the old man halted, and with an inquiring look, he seemed to demand if it possessed the needed conveniences. The leader of the emigrants cast his eyes, understandingly, about him, and examined the place with the keenness of one competent to judge of so nice a question, though in that dilatory and heavy manner, which rarely permitted him to betray precipitation.

"Ay, this may do," he said, when satisfied with his scrutiny; "boys, you have seen the last of the sun; be stirring."

The young men manifested a characteristic obedience. The order, for such in tone and manner it was, in truth, was received with respect; but the utmost movement was the falling of an ax or two from the shoulder to the ground, while their owners continued to regard the place with listless and incurious eyes. In the meantime, the elder traveller, as if familiar with the nature of the impulses by which his children were governed, disencumbered himself of his pack and rifle, and, assisted by the man already mentioned as disposed to appeal so promptly to the rifle, he quietly proceeded to release the cattle from the gears.

At length the eldest of the sons stepped heavily forward, and, without any apparent effort, he buried his ax to the eye in the soft body of a cottonwood tree. He stood a moment regarding the effect of the blow, with that sort of contempt with which a giant might be supposed to contemplate the puny resistance of a dwarf, and then flourishing the implement above his head, with the grace and dexterity with which a master of the art of offence would wield his nobler though less useful weapon, he quickly severed the trunk of the tree, bringing its tall top crashing to the earth in submission to his prowess. His companions regarded the operation with indolent curiosity, until they saw the prostrate trunk stretched on the ground, when, as if a signal for a general attack had been given, they advanced in a body to the work, and in a space of time, and with a neatness of execution that would have astonished an ignorant spectator, they stripped a small but suitable spot of its burden of forest, as effectually, and almost as promptly, as if a whirlwind had passed along the place.

The stranger had been a silent but attentive observer of their progress. As tree after tree came whistling down, he cast his eyes upward, at the vacancies they left in the heavens, with a melancholy gaze, and finally turned away, muttering to himself with a bitter smile, like one who disdained giving a more audible utterance to his discontent. Pressing through the group of active and busy children, who had already lighted a cheerful fire, the attention of the old man became next fixed on the movements of the leader of the emigrants and of his savage-looking assistant.

These two had already liberated the cattle, which were eagerly browsing the grateful and nutritious extremities of the fallen trees, and were now employed about the wagon, which has been described as having its contents concealed with so much apparent care. Notwithstanding, this particular conveyance appeared to be as silent and as tenantless as the rest of the vehicles, the men applied their strength to its wheels, and rolled it apart from the others, to a dry and elevated spot, near the edge of the thicket. Here they brought certain poles, which had, seemingly, been long employed in such a service, and fastening their larger ends firmly in the ground, the smaller were attached to the hoops that supported the covering of the wagon. Large folds of cloth were next drawn out of the vehicle, and after being spread around the whole, were pegged to the earth in such a manner as to form a tolerably capacious and an exceedingly convenient tent. After surveying their work with inquisitive, and perhaps jealous eyes, arranging a fold here, and driving a peg more firmly there, the men once more applied their strength to the wagon, pulling it by its projecting tongue from the center of the canopy, until it appeared in the open air, deprived of its covering, and destitute of any other freight than a few light articles of furniture. The latter were immediately removed by the traveller into the tent with his own hands, as though to enter it were a privilege, to which even his bosom companion was not entitled.

Curiosity is a passion that is rather quickened than destroyed by seclusion, and the old inhabitant of the prairies did not view these precautionary and mysterious movements without experiencing some of its impulses. He approached the tent, and was about to sever two of its folds, with the very obvious intention of examining, more closely, into the nature of its contents, when the man who had once already placed his life in jeopardy, seized him by the arm, and with a rude exercise of his strength threw him from the spot he had selected as the one most convenient for his object.

"It's an honest regulation, friend," the fellow drily observed, though with an eye that threatened volumes, "and sometimes it is a safe one, which says, mind your own business."

"Men seldom bring anything to be concealed into these deserts," returned the old man, as if willing, and yet a little ignorant how to apologize for the liberty he had been about to take, "and I had hoped no offence, in examining your comforts."

"They seldom bring themselves, I reckon; though this has the look of an old country, to my eye it seems not to be overly peopled."

"The land is as aged as the rest of the works of the Lord, I believe; but you say true concerning its inhabitants. Many months has passed since I have laid eyes on a face of my own color, before your own. I say again, friend, I meant no harm; I did not know but there was something behind the cloth that might bring former days to my mind."

As the stranger ended his simple explanation, he walked meekly away, like one who felt the deepest sense of the right which every man has to the quiet enjoyment of his own, without any troublesome interference on the part of his neighbor; a wholesome and just principle that he had, also, most probably imbibed from the habits of his secluded life. As he passed toward the little encampment of the emigrants, for such the place had now become, he heard the voice of the leader calling aloud, in its hoarse tones, the name of——

"Ellen Wade."

The girl who has been already introduced to the reader, and who was occupied with the others of her sex around the fires, sprang willingly forward at this summons; and, passing the stranger with the activity of a young antelope, she was instantly lost behind the forbidden folds of the tent. Neither her sudden disappearance, nor any of the arrangements we have mentioned, seemed, however, to excite the smallest surprise among the remainder of the party. The young men, who had already completed their tasks with the ax, were all engaged after their lounging and listless manner; some in bestowing equitable portions of the fodder among the different animals; others in plying the heavy pestle of a moveable hominy-mortar; and one or two in wheeling the remainder of the wagons aside, and arranging them in such a manner as to form a sort of outwork for their otherwise defenseless bivouac.

These several duties were soon performed, and, as darkness now began to conceal the objects on the surrounding prairie, the shrill-toned termagant whose voice since the halt had been diligently exercised among her idle and drowsy offspring, announced, in tones that might have been heard at a dangerous distance, that the evening meal waited only for the approach of those who were to consume it. Whatever may be the other qualities of a border man, he is seldom deficient in the virtue of hospitality. The emigrant no sooner heard the sharp call of his wife, than he cast his eyes about him in quest of the stranger, in order to offer him the place of distinction, in the rude entertainment to which they were so unceremoniously summoned.

"I thank you, friend," the old man replied to the rough invitation to take a seat nigh the smoking kettle; "you have my hearty thanks; but I have eaten for the day, and am not one of them who dig their graves with their teeth. Well, as you wish it, I will take a place, for it is long sin' I have seen people of my color eating their daily bread."

"You ar' an old settler in these districts, then?" the emigrant rather remarked than inquired, with a mouth filled nearly to overflowing with the delicious hominy, prepared by his skilful, though repulsive spouse. "They told us below, we should find settlers something thinnish, here-a-way, and I must say the report was mainly true; for, unless we count the Canada traders on the Big River, you ar' the first white face I have met, in a good five hundred miles; that is calculating according to your own reckoning."

"Though I have spent some years in this quarter, I can hardly be called a settler, seeing that I have no regular abode, and seldom pass more than a month at a time on the same range."

"A hunter, I reckon?" the other continued, glancing his eyes aside, as if to examine the equipments of his new acquaintance; "your fixen seem none of the best for such a calling."

"They are old, and nearly ready to be laid aside, like their master," said the old man, regarding his rifle, with a look in which affection and regret were singularly blended; "and I may say they are but little needed, too. You are mistaken, friend, in calling me a hunter; I am nothing better than a trapper."[1]

"If you ar' much of the one, I'm bold to say you ar' something of the other; for the two callings go mainly together in these districts."

"To the shame of the man who is able to follow the first be it so said!" returned the trapper, whom in future we shall choose to designate by his pursuit; "for more than fifty years did I carry my rifle in the wilderness, without so much as setting a snare for even a bird that flies the heavens;—much less a beast that has nothing but legs for its gifts."

[1] It is scarcely necessary to say, that this American word means one who takes his game in a trap. It is of general use on the frontiers. The beaver, an animal too sagacious to be easily killed, is oftener taken in this way than in any other. (*Cooper's note*)

"I see but little difference whether a man gets his peltry by the rifle or by the trap," said the ill-looking companion of the emigrant, in his rough manner. "The 'arth was made for our comfort; and, for that matter, so ar' its creaturs."

"You seem to have but little plunder,[1] stranger, for one who is far abroad," bluntly interrupted the emigrant, as if he had a reason for wishing to change the conversation. "I hope you ar' better off for skins."

"I make but little use of either," the trapper quietly replied. "At my time of life, food and clothing be all that is needed; and I have little occasion for what you call plunder, unless it may be, now and then, to barter for a horn of powder, or a bar of lead."

"You ar' not, then, of these parts by natur, friend," the emigrant continued, having in his mind the exception which the other had taken to the very equivocal word, which he himself, according to the custom of the country, had used for "baggage," or "effects."

"I was born on the seashore, though most of my life has been passed in the woods."

The whole party now looked up at him, as men are apt to turn their eyes on some unexpected object of general interest. One or two of the young men repeated the words "seashore"; and the woman tendered him one of those civilities with which, uncouth as they were, she was little accustomed to grace her hospitality, as if in deference to the travelled dignity of her guest. After a long and, seemingly, a meditating silence, the emigrant, who had, however, seen no apparent necessity to suspend the functions of his masticating powers, resumed the discourse.

"It is a long road, as I have heard, from the waters of the west to the shores of the main sea?"

"It is a weary path, indeed, friend; and much have I seen, and something have I suffered, in journeying over it."

"A man would see a good deal of hard travel in going its length!"

"Seventy and five years have I been upon the road; and there are not half that number of leagues in the whole distance, after you leave the Hudson, on which I have not tasted venison of my own killing. But this is vain boasting. Of what use are former deeds, when time draws to an end?"

"I once met a man that had boated on the river he names," observed the eldest son, speaking in a low tone of voice, like one who distrusted his knowledge, and deemed it prudent to assume a becoming

[1] The cant word for luggage in the western states of America is "plunder." The term might easily mislead one as to the character of the people, who, notwithstanding their pleasant use of so expressive a word, are, like the inhabitants of all new settlements, hospitable and honest. Knavery of the description conveyed by "plunder," is chiefly found in regions more civilized. (*Cooper's note*)

diffidence in the presence of a man who had seen so much: "from his tell, it must be a considerable stream, and deep enough for a keelboat, from top to bottom."

"It is a wide and deep watercourse, and many sightly towns are there growing on its banks," returned the trapper; "and yet it is but a brook to the waters of the endless river!"

"I call nothing a stream that a man can travel round," exclaimed the ill-looking associate of the emigrant: "a real river must be crossed; not headed, like a bear in a county hunt."[1]

"Have you been far toward the sundown, friend?" interrupted the emigrant, as if he desired to keep his rough companion as much as possible out of the discourse. "I find it is a wide tract of clearing, this, into which I have fallen."

"You may travel weeks, and you will see it the same. I often think the Lord has placed this barren belt of prairie behind the States, to warn men to what their folly may yet bring the land! Ay, weeks, if not months, may you journey in these open fields, in which there is neither dwelling nor habitation for man or beast. Even the savage animals travel miles on miles to seek their dens; and yet the wind seldom blows from the east, but I conceit the sound of axes, and the crash of falling trees, are in my ears."

As the old man spoke with the seriousness and dignity that age seldom fails to communicate even to less striking sentiments, his auditors were deeply attentive, and as silent as the grave. Indeed, the trapper was left to renew the dialogue himself, which he soon did by asking a question, in the indirect manner so much in use by the border inhabitants.

"You found it no easy matter to ford the watercourses, and to make your way so deep into the prairies, friend, with teams of horses and herds of horned beasts?"

"I kept the left bank of the main river," the emigrant replied, "until I found the stream leading too much to the north, when we rafted ourselves across without any great suffering. The woman lost a fleece or two from the next year's shearing, and the girls have one cow less to their dairy. Since then, we have done bravely, by bridging a creek every day or two."

"It is likely you will continue west, until you come to land more suitable for a settlement?"

"Until I see reason to stop, or to turn ag'in," the emigrant bluntly answered, rising at the same time, and cutting short the dialogue by

[1] There is a practice, in the new countries, to assemble the men of a large district, sometimes of an entire county, to exterminate the beasts of prey. They form themselves into a circle of several miles in extent, and gradually draw nearer, killing all before them. The allusion is to this custom, in which the hunted beast is turned from one to another. (*Cooper's note*)

the suddenness of the movement. His example was followed by the trapper, as well as the rest of the party; and then, without much deference to the presence of their guest, the travellers proceeded to make their dispositions to pass the night. Several little bowers, or rather huts, had already been formed of the tops of trees, blankets of coarse country manufacture, and the skins of buffaloes, united without much reference to any other object than temporary comfort. Into these covers the children, with their mother, soon drew themselves, and where, it is more than possible, they were all speedily lost in the oblivion of sleep. Before the men, however, could seek their rest, they had sundry little duties to perform; such as completing their works of defence, carefully concealing the fires, replenishing the fodder of their cattle, and setting the watch that was to protect the party in the approaching hours of night.

The former was effected by dragging the trunks of a few trees into the intervals left by the wagons, and along the open space between the vehicles and the thicket, on which, in military language, the encampment would be said to have rested; thus forming a sort of *chevaux-de-frise* on three sides of the position. Within these narrow limits (with the exception of what the tent contained), both man and beast were now collected; the latter being far too happy in resting their weary limbs, to give any undue annoyance to their scarcely more intelligent associates. Two of the young men took their rifles; and, first renewing the priming, and examining the flints with the utmost care, they proceeded, the one to the extreme right, and the other to the left, of the encampment, where they posted themselves, within the shadows of the thicket; but in such positions as enabled each to overlook a portion of the prairie.

The trapper loitered about the place, declining to share the straw of the emigrant, until the whole arrangement was completed; and then, without the ceremony of an adieu, he slowly retired from the spot.

It was now in the first watch of the night; and the pale, quivering, and deceptive light from a new moon was playing over the endless waves of the prairie, tipping the swells with gleams of brightness, and leaving the interval land in deep shadow. Accustomed to scenes of solitude like the present, the old man, as he left the encampment, proceeded alone into the waste, like a bold vessel leaving its haven to enter on the trackless field of the ocean. He appeared to move for some time without object, or, indeed, without any apparent consciousness, whither his limbs were carrying him. At length, on reaching the rise of one of the undulations, he came to a stand; and, for the first time since leaving the band, who had caused such a flood of reflections and recollections to crowd upon his mind, the old man became aware of his present situation. Throwing one end of his rifle to the earth, he stood leaning on the other, again lost in deep contemplation for several minutes, during which time his hound came and crouched at his feet. A deep, menacing growl from the faithful animal first aroused him from his musing.

"What now, dog?" he said, looking down at his companion, as if he addressed a being of an intelligence equal to his own, and speaking in a voice of great affection. "What is it, pup? ha! Hector; what is it nosing now? It won't do, dog; it won't do; the very fa'ns play in open view of us, without minding so worn-out curs as you and I. Instinct is their gift, Hector; and they have found out how little we are to be feared, they have!"

The dog stretched his head upward, and responded to the words of his master by a long and plaintive whine, which he even continued after he had again buried his head in the grass, as if he held an intelligent communication with one who so well knew how to interpret dumb discourse.

"This is a manifest warning, Hector!" the trapper continued, dropping his voice to the tones of caution, and looking warily about him. "What is it, pup; speak plainer, dog; what is it?"

The hound had, however, already laid his nose to the earth, and was silent; appearing to slumber. But the keen quick glances of his master soon caught a glimpse of a distant figure, which seemed, through the deceptive light, floating along the very elevation on which he had placed himself. Presently its proportions became more distinct, and then an airy, female form appeared to hesitate, as if considering whether it would be prudent to advance. Though the eyes of the dog were now to be seen glancing in the rays of the moon, opening and shutting lazily, he gave no further signs of displeasure.

"Come nigher; we are friends," said the trapper, associating himself with his companion by long use, and, probably, through the strength of the secret tie that connected them together; "we are your friends; none will harm you."

Encouraged by the mild tones of his voice, and perhaps led on by the earnestness of her purpose, the female approached until she stood at his side; when the old man perceived his visitor to be the young woman, with whom the reader has already become acquainted by the name of Ellen Wade.

"I had thought you were gone," she said, looking timidly and anxiously around. "They said you were gone; and that we should never see you again. I did not think it was you!"

"Men are no common objects in these empty fields," returned the trapper, "and I humbly hope, though I have so long consorted with the beasts of the wilderness, that I have not yet lost the look of my kind."

"Oh! I knew you to be a man, and I thought I knew the whine of the hound, too," she answered hastily, as if willing to explain she knew not what, and then checking herself, like one fearful of having already said too much.

"I saw no dogs among the teams of your father," the trapper remarked.

"Father!" exclaimed the girl feelingly, "I have no father! I had nearly said no friend."

The old man turned toward her with a look of kindness and interest, that was even more conciliating than the ordinary, upright, and benevolent expression of his weather-beaten countenance.

"Why then do you venture in a place where none but the strong should come?" he demanded. "Did you not know that, when you crossed the Big River, you left a friend behind you that is always bound to look to the young and feeble, like yourself."

"Of whom do you speak?"

"The law—'tis bad to have it, but, I sometimes think, it is worse to be entirely without it. Age and weakness have brought me to feel such weakness, at times. Yes—yes, the law is needed, when such as have not the gifts of strength and wisdom are to be taken care of. I hope, young woman, if you have no father, you have at least a brother."

The maiden felt the tacit reproach conveyed in this covert question, and for a moment she remained in an embarrassed silence. But catching a glimpse of the mild and serious features of her companion, as he continued to gaze on her with a look of interest, she replied firmly, and in a manner that left no doubt she comprehended his meaning:

"Heaven forbid that any such as you have seen should be a brother of mine, or anything else near or dear to me! But, tell me, do you then actually live alone, in this desert district, old man; is there really none here besides yourself?"

"There are hundreds, nay, thousands of the rightful owners of the country roving about the plains; but few of our own color."

"And have you then met none who are white, but us?" interrupted the girl, like one too impatient to await the tardy explanations of age and deliberation.

"Not in many days—Hush, Hector, hush," he added in reply to a low, and nearly inaudible, growl from his hound. "The dog scents mischief in the wind! The black bears from the mountains sometimes make their way, even lower than this. The pup is not apt to complain of the harmless game. I am not so ready and true with the piece as I used-to-could-be, yet I have struck even the fiercest animals of the prairie in my time; so you have little reason for fear, young woman."

2

AS LEATHERSTOCKING well knew, the old pioneer Ishmael Bush, his seven sledgehammer-fisted sons, and the girl Ellen Wade, were in a country dangerously infested by hostile Indians. The party was shortly joined by a bee hunter named Paul Hover. The Bush tribe camped in one spot on the prairies; Leatherstocking, Ellen, and the bee hunter in another. Low growls of Leatherstocking's dog Hector gave warning that danger was near. He was right; before long a band of roving Sioux swooped down on horseback and took the three whites prisoners. The same band then succeeded in stampeding the horses of Ishmael Bush; but as they did so, Leatherstocking by quick and courageous action cut loose the steeds of the Sioux, and set them too running helter-skelter through the darkness which had settled upon the scene. The Indians raced in pursuit.

Morning therefore found the white folk free, but stranded on the open plain, with no means of transport but their own legs. Leatherstocking had a short talk with Ishmael Bush, and revealed the fact that he had fought briefly under the command of Mad Anthony Wayne in the West. "I was passing from the States on the seashore into these far regions, when I cross'd the trail of his army, and I fell in, on his rear, just as a looker-on; but when they got to blows, the crack of my rifle was heard among the rest." Soon after daybreak still another white man appeared, an eccentric figure, riding on a donkey. It was Dr. Obed Battius, a shortsighted, fumbling scientist intent on compiling a natural history of the United States that would make Buffon seem an amateur. He had left in Ishmael's safekeeping books and boxes well-stored with botanical specimens and defunct animals. It immediately struck him that the marauding Sioux would not neglect the opportunity to despoil him of his treasures.

The day had now fairly opened on the seemingly interminable waste of the prairie. The entrance of Obed at such a moment into the camp, accompanied as it was by vociferous lamentations over his anticipated loss, did not fail to rouse the drowsy family of the squatter. Ishmael and his sons, together with the forbidding-looking brother of his wife, were all speedily afoot; and then, as the sun began to shed his light on the place, they became gradually apprised of the extent of their loss.

Ishmael looked round upon the motionless and heavily loaded vehicles with his teeth firmly compressed, cast a glance at the amazed and helpless group of children, which clustered around their sullen but desponding mother, and walked out upon the open land, as if he found the air of the encampment too confined. He was followed by several of the men, who were attentive observers, watching the dark expression of his eye as the index of their own future movements. The whole proceeded in profound and moody silence to the summit of the nearest swell, whence they could command an almost boundless view of the naked plains. Here nothing was visible but a solitary buffalo, that gleaned a meager subsistence from the decaying herbage, at no great distance, and the ass of the physician, who profited by his freedom to enjoy a meal richer than common.

"Yonder is one of the creatures left by the villains to mock us," said Ishmael, glancing his eye toward the latter, "and that the meanest of the stock. This is a hard country to make a crop in, boys; and yet food must be found to fill many hungry mouths!"

"The rifle is better than the hoe, in such a place as this," returned the eldest of his sons, kicking the hard and thirsty soil on which he stood, with an air of contempt. "It is good for such as they who make their dinner better on beggars' beans than on hominy. A crow would shed tears if obliged by its errand to fly across the district."

"What say you, trapper?" returned the father, showing the slight impression his powerful heel had made on the compact earth, and laughing with frightful ferocity. "Is this the quality of land a man would choose who never troubles the county clerk with title deeds?"

"There is richer soil in the bottoms," returned the old man calmly, "and you have passed millions of acres to get to this dreary spot, where he who loves to till the 'arth might have received bushels in return for pints, and that too at the cost of no very grievous labor. If you have come in search of land, you have journeyed hundreds of miles too far, or as many leagues too little."

"There is then a better choice toward the other ocean?" demanded the squatter, pointing in the direction of the Pacific.

"There is, and I have seen it all," was the answer of the other, who dropped his rifle to the earth, and stood leaning on its barrel, like one who recalled the scenes he had witnessed with melancholy pleasure. "I have seen the waters of the two seas! On one of them was I born, and raised to be a lad like yonder tumbling boy. America has grown, my men, since the days of my youth, to be a country larger than I once had thought the world itself to be. Near seventy years I dwelt in York, province and state together:—you've been in York, 'tis like?"

"Not I—not I; I never visited the towns; but often have heard the place you speak of named. 'Tis a wide clearing there, I reckon."

"Too wide! too wide! They scourge the very 'arth with their axes. Such hills and hunting grounds as I have seen stripped of the gifts of the Lord, without remorse or shame! I tarried till the mouths of my hounds were deafened by the blows of the chopper, and then I came west in search of quiet. It was a grievous journey that I made; a grievous toil to pass through falling timber and to breathe the thick air of smoky clearings, week after week, as I did! 'Tis a far country too, that state of York from this!"

"It lies ag'in the outer edge of old Kentuck, I reckon; though what the distance may be I never knew."

"A gull would have to fan a thousand miles of air to find the eastern sea. And yet it is no mighty reach to hunt across, when shade and game are plenty! The time has been when I followed the deer in the mountains of the Delaware and Hudson, and took the beaver on the streams of the upper lakes, in the same season: but my eye was quick and certain at that day, and my limbs were like the legs of a moose! The dam of Hector," dropping his look kindly to the aged hound that crouched at his feet, "was then a pup, and apt to open on the game the moment she struck the scent. She gave me a deal of trouble, that slut, she did!"

"Your hound is old, stranger, and a rap on the head would prove a mercy to the beast."

"The dog is like his master," returned the trapper, without appearing to heed the brutal advice the other gave, "and will number his days, when his work amongst the game is over, and not before. To my eye things seem ordered to meet each other in this creation. 'Tis not the swiftest running deer that always throws off the hounds, nor the biggest arm that holds the truest rifle. Look around you, men; what will the Yankee choppers say, when they have cut their path from the eastern to the western waters, and find that a hand, which can lay the 'arth bare at a blow, has been here and swept the country, in very mockery of their wickedness. They will turn on their tracks like a fox that doubles, and then the rank smell of their own footsteps will show them the madness of their waste. Howsomever, these are thoughts that are more likely to rise in him who has seen the folly of eighty seasons, than to teach wisdom to men still bent on the pleasures of their kind! You have need, yet, of a stirring time, if you think to escape the craft and hatred of the burnt-wood Indians. They claim to be the lawful owners of this country, and seldom leave a white more than the skin he boasts of, when once they get the power, as they always have the will, to do him harm."

"Old man," said Ishmael sternly, "to which people do you belong? You have the color and speech of a Christian, while it seems that your heart is with the redskins."

"To me there is little difference in nations. The people I loved most are scattered as the sands of the dry river beds fly before the fall hurricanes, and life is too short to make use and custom with strangers, as one can do with such as he has dwelt amongst for years. Still am I a man without the cross of Indian blood; and what is due from a warrior to his nation, is owing by me to the people of the States; though little need have they, with their militia and their armed boats, of help from a single arm of fourscore."

"Since you own your kin, I may ask a simple question. Where are the Sioux who have stolen my cattle?"

"Where is the herd of buffaloes, which was chased by the panther across this plain no later than the morning of yesterday! It is as hard——"

"Friend," said Dr. Battius, who had hitherto been an attentive listener, but who now felt a sudden impulse to mingle in the discourse, "I am grieved when I find a venator or hunter, of your experience and observation, following the current of vulgar error. The animal you describe is in truth a species of the *bos ferus* (or *bos sylvestris,* as he has been happily called by the poets), but, though of close affinity, it is altogether distinct from the common *bubulus.* Bison is the better word; and I would suggest the necessity of adopting it in future, when you shall have occasion to allude to the species."

"Bison or buffalo, it makes but little matter. The creatur' is the same, call it by what name you will, and——"

"Pardon me, venerable venator; as classification is the very soul of the natural sciences, the animal or vegetable must, of necessity, be characterized by the peculiarities of its species, which is always indicated by the name——"

"Friend," said the trapper, a little positively, "would the tail of a beaver make the worse dinner for calling it a mink; or could you eat of the wolf, with relish, because some bookish man had given it the name of venison?"

As these questions were put with no little earnestness and some spirit, there was every probability that a hot discussion would have succeeded between two men, of whom one was so purely practical and the other so much given to theory, had not Ishmael seen fit to terminate the dispute, by bringing into view a subject that was much more important to his own immediate interests.

"Beavers' tails and minks' flesh may do to talk about before a maple fire and a quiet hearth," interrupted the squatter, without the smallest deference to the interested feelings of the disputants; "but something more than foreign words, or words of any sort, is now needed. Tell me, trapper, where are your Sioux skulking?"

"It would be as easy to tell you the colors of the hawk that is floating beneath yonder white cloud! When a redskin strikes his blow, he is not apt to wait until he is paid for the evil deed in lead."

"Will the beggarly savages believe they have enough, when they find themselves master of all the stock?"

"Natur' is much the same, let it be covered by what skin it may. Do you ever find your longings after riches less when you have made a good crop, than before you were master of a kernel of corn? If you do, you differ from what the experience of a long life tells me is the common cravings of man."

"Speak plainly, old stranger," said the squatter, striking the butt of his rifle heavily on the earth, his dull capacity finding no pleasure in a discourse that was conducted in so obscure allusions; "I have asked a simple question, and one I know well that you can answer."

"You are right, you are right. I can answer, for I have too often seen the disposition of my kind to mistake it when evil is stirring. When the Sioux have gathered in the beasts, and have made sure that you are not upon their heels, they will be back nibbling like hungry wolves to take the bait they have left: or it may be, they'll show the temper of the great bears, that are found at the falls of the Long River, and strike at once with the paw, without stopping to nose their prey."

"You have then seen the animals you mention!" exclaimed Dr. Battius, who had now been thrown out of the conversation quite as long as his impatience could well brook, and who approached the subject with his tablets ready-opened, as a book of reference. "Can you tell me if what you encountered was of the species *ursus horribilis*—with the *ears*, rounded—*front*, arquated—*eyes*—destitute of the remarkable supplemental lid—with six incisores, one false, and four perfect molars——"

"Trapper, go on, for we are engaged in reasonable discourse," interrupted Ishmael; "you believe we shall see more of the robbers."

"Nay—nay—I do not call them robbers, for it is the usage of their people, and what may be called the prairie law."

"I have come five hundred miles to find a place where no man can ding the words of the law in my ears," said Ishmael fiercely, "and I am not in a humor to stand quietly at a bar, while a redskin sits in judgment. I tell you, trapper, if another Sioux is seen prowling around my camp, wherever it may be, he shall feel the contents of old Kentuck," slapping his rifle, in a manner that could not be easily misconstrued, "though he wore the medal of Washington,[1] himself. I call the man a robber who takes that which is not his own."

"The Teton, and the Pawnee, and the Konza, and men of a dozen other tribes, claim to own these naked fields."

"Natur' gives them the lie in their teeth. The air, the water, and the ground, are free gifts to man, and no one has the power to portion them out in parcels. Man must drink, and breathe, and walk,—and therefore each has a right to his share of 'arth. Why do not the surveyors of the States set their compasses and run their lines over our heads as well as beneath our feet? Why do they not cover their shining sheepskins with big words, giving to the landholder, or perhaps he should be called air-holder, so many rods of heaven, with the use of such a star for a boundary mark, and such a cloud to turn a mill?"

As the squatter uttered his wild conceit, he laughed from the very bottom of his chest, in scorn. The deriding but frightful merriment passed from the mouth of one of his ponderous sons to that of the other, until it had made the circuit of the whole family.

"Come, trapper," continued Ishmael, in a tone of better humor, like a man who feels that he has triumphed, "neither of us, I reckon, has ever had much to do with title deeds, or county clerks, or blazed trees; therefore we will not waste words on fooleries. You ar' a man that has tarried long in this clearing, and now I ask your opinion, face to face, without fear or favor, if you had the lead in my business, what would you do?"

The old man hesitated, and seemed to give the required advice with deep reluctance. As every eye, however, was fastened on him, and whichever way he turned his face, he encountered a look riveted on the lineaments of his own working countenance, he answered in a low, melancholy tone—

"I have seen too much mortal blood poured out in empty quarrels, to wish ever to hear an angry rifle again. Ten weary years have I sojourned alone on these naked plains, waiting for my hour, and not a

---

[1] The American government creates chiefs among the western tribes, and decorates them with silver medals bearing the impression of the different presidents. That of Washington is the most prized. (*Cooper's note*)

blow have I struck ag'in an enemy more humanized than the grizzly bear."

"*Ursus horribilis*," muttered the Doctor.

The speaker paused at the sound of the other's voice, but perceiving it was no more than a sort of mental ejaculation, he continued in the same strain—

"More humanized than the grizzly bear, or the panther of the Rocky Mountains; unless the beaver, which is a wise and knowing animal, may be so reckoned. What would I advise? Even the female buffalo will fight for her young!"

"It never then shall be said, that Ishmael Bush has less kindness for his children than the bear for her cubs!"

"And yet this is but a naked spot for a dozen men to make head in, ag'in five hundred."

"Ay, it is so," returned the squatter, glancing his eye towards his humble camp; "but something might be done with the wagons and the cottonwood."

The trapper shook his head incredulously, and pointed across the rolling plain in the direction of the west, as he answered—

"A rifle would send a bullet from these hills into your very sleeping cabins; nay, arrows from the thicket in your rear would keep you all burrowed, like so many prairie dogs: it wouldn't do, it wouldn't do. Three long miles from this spot is a place, where, as I have often thought in passing across the desert, a stand might be made for days and weeks together, if there were hearts and hands ready to engage in the bloody work."

Another low, deriding laugh passed among the young men, announcing, in a manner sufficiently intelligible, their readiness to undertake a task even more arduous. The squatter himself eagerly seized the hint which had been so reluctantly extorted from the trapper, who by some singular process of reasoning had evidently persuaded himself that it was his duty to be strictly neutral. A few direct and pertinent inquiries served to obtain the little additional information that was necessary, in order to make the contemplated movement, and then Ishmael, who was, on emergencies, as terrifically energetic, as he was sluggish in common, set about effecting his object without delay.

Notwithstanding the industry and zeal of all engaged, the task was one of great labor and difficulty. The loaded vehicles were to be drawn by hand across a wide distance of plain without track or guide of any sort, except that which the trapper furnished by communicating his knowledge of the cardinal points of the compass. In accomplishing this object, the gigantic strength of the men was taxed to the utmost, nor were the females or the children spared a heavy proportion of the toil.

While the sons distributed themselves about the heavily loaded wagons, and drew them by main strength up the neighboring swell, their mother and Ellen, surrounded by the amazed group of little ones, followed slowly in the rear, bending under the weight of such different articles as were suited to their several strengths.

Ishmael himself superintended and directed the whole, occasionally applying his colossal shoulder to some lagging vehicle, until he saw that the chief difficulty, that of gaining the level of their intended route, was accomplished. Then he pointed out the required course, cautioning his sons to proceed in such a manner that they should not lose the advantage they had with so much labor obtained, and beckoning to the brother of his wife, they returned together to the empty camp.

Throughout the whole of this movement, which occupied an hour of time, the trapper had stood apart, leaning on his rifle, with the aged hound slumbering at his feet, a silent but attentive observer of all that passed. Occasionally, a smile lighted his hard, muscular, but wasted features, like a gleam of sunshine flitting across a ragged ruin, and betrayed the momentary pleasure he found in witnessing, from time to time, the vast power the youths discovered. Then, as the train drew slowly up the ascent, a cloud of thought and sorrow threw all into the shade again, leaving the expression of his countenance in its usual state of quiet melancholy. As vehicle after vehicle left the place of the encampment, he noted the change, with increasing attention; seldom failing to cast an inquiring look at the little neglected tent, which, with its proper wagon, still remained as before, solitary and apparently forgotten. The summons of Ishmael to his gloomy associate had, however, as it would now seem, this hitherto neglected portion of his effects for its object.

First casting a cautious and suspicious glance on every side of him, the squatter and his companion advanced to the little wagon, and caused it to enter within the folds of the cloth, much in the manner that it had been extricated the preceding evening. They both then disappeared behind the drapery, and many moments of suspense succeeded, during which the old man, secretly urged by a burning desire to know the meaning of so much mystery, insensibly drew nigh to the place, until he stood within a few yards of the proscribed spot. The agitation of the cloth betrayed the nature of the occupation of those whom it concealed, though their work was conducted in rigid silence. It would appear that long practice had made each of the two acquainted with his particular duty; for neither sign nor direction of any sort was necessary from Ishmael, in order to apprise his surly associate of the manner in which he was to proceed. In less time than has been consummated in relating it, the interior portion of the arrangement was completed, when the men reappeared without the tent.

Too busy with his occupation to heed the presence of the trapper, Ishmael began to release the folds of the cloth from the ground, and to dispose of them in such a manner around the vehicle, as to form a sweeping train to the new form the little pavilion had now assumed. The arched roof trembled with the occasional movement of the light vehicle which, it was now apparent, once more supported its secret burden. Just as the work was ended the scowling eye of Ishmael's assistant caught a glimpse of the figure of the attentive observer of their movements. Dropping the shaft, which he had already lifted from the ground preparatory to occupying the place that was usually filled by an animal less reasoning and perhaps less dangerous than himself, he bluntly exclaimed—

"I am a fool, as you often say! But look for yourself: if that man is not an enemy, I will disgrace father and mother, call myself an Indian, and go hunt with the Sioux!"

The cloud, as it is about to discharge the subtle lightning, is not more dark nor threatening than the look with which Ishmael greeted the intruder. He turned his head on every side of him, as if seeking some engine sufficiently terrible to annihilate the offending trapper at a blow; and, then, possibly recollecting the further occasion he might have for his counsel, he forced himself to say, with an appearance of moderation that nearly choked him—

"Stranger, I did believe this prying into the concerns of others was the business of women in the towns and settlements, and not the manner in which men, who are used to live where each has room for himself, deal with the secrets of their neighbors. To what lawyer or sheriff do you calculate to sell your news?"

"I hold but little discourse except with one; and then chiefly of my own affairs," returned the old man, without the least observable apprehension, and pointing imposingly upward; "a Judge; and Judge of all. Little does He need knowledge from my hands, and but little will your wish to keep anything secret from Him profit you, even in this desert."

The mounting tempers of his unnurtured listeners were rebuked by the simple, solemn manner of the trapper. Ishmael stood sullen and thoughtful; while his companion stole a furtive and involuntary glance at the placid sky, which spread so wide and blue above his head, as if he expected to see the Almighty eye itself beaming from the heavenly vault. But impressions of a serious character are seldom lasting on minds long indulged in forgetfulness. The hesitation of the squatter was consequently of short duration. The language, however, as well as the firm and collected air of the speaker, were the means of preventing much subsequent abuse, if not violence.

"It would be showing more of the kindness of a friend and comrade," Ishmael returned, in a tone sufficiently sullen to betray his humor, though it was no longer threatening, "had your shoulder been put to the wheel of one of yonder wagons, instead of edging itself in here, where none are wanted but such as are invited."

"I can put the little strength that is left me," returned the trapper, "to this, as well as to another of your loads."

"Do you take us for boys!" exclaimed Ishmael, laughing, half in ferocity and half in derision, applying his powerful strength at the same time to the little vehicle, which rolled over the grass with as much seeming facility as if it were drawn by its usual team.

The trapper paused, and followed the departing wagon with his eye, marvelling greatly as to the nature of its concealed contents, until it had also gained the summit of the eminence, and in its turn disappeared behind the swell of the land. Then he turned to gaze at the desolation of the scene around him. The absence of human forms would have scarce created a sensation in the bosom of one so long accustomed to solitude, had not the site of the deserted camp furnished such strong memorials of its recent visitors, and as the old man was quick to detect, of their waste also. He cast his eye upward, with a shake of the head, at the vacant spot in the heavens which had so lately been filled by the branches of those trees that now lay stripped of their verdure, worthless and deserted logs, at his feet.

"Ay," he muttered to himself, "I might have know'd it—I might have know'd it! Often have I seen the same before; and yet I brought them to the spot myself, and have now sent them to the only neighborhood of their kind within many long leagues of the spot where I stand. This is man's wish, and pride, and waste, and sinfulness! He tames the beasts of the field to feed his idle wants; and, having robbed the brutes of their natural food, he teaches them to strip the 'arth of its trees to quiet their hunger."

3

ISHMAEL BUSH and his large family, in well-justified fear of the Indians, made a new camp on the top of a rocky eminence, where they would be fairly safe from the arrows of the Sioux. Near at hand, Leatherstocking entertained at dinner the bee hunter and the learned clown Dr. Obed Battius; offering them a juicy buffalo hump. They were chatting comfortably when the dog Hector, by some uneasy motions, gave notice that a stranger was near. Leatherstocking and Paul Hover at once challenged the figure who was breaking his way through the thickets. "Come forward, if a friend; if an enemy, stand ready for the worst!" A voice replied: "A friend, a white man, and, I hope, a Christian."

It was no unusual thing for strangers to encounter each other in the endless wastes of the west. By signs, which an unpracticed eye would pass unobserved, these borderers knew when one of his fellows was in his vicinity, and he avoided or approached the intruder as best comported with his feelings or his interests. Generally, these interviews were pacific; for the whites had a common enemy to dread, in the ancient and perhaps more lawful occupants of the country; but instances were not rare in which jealousy and cupidity had caused them to terminate in scenes of the most violent and ruthless treachery. The meeting of two hunters on the American desert, as we find it convenient sometimes to call this region, was consequently somewhat in the suspicious and wary manner in which two vessels draw together in a sea that is known to be infested with pirates. While neither party is willing to betray its weakness by exhibiting distrust, neither is disposed to commit itself by any acts of confidence, from which it may be difficult to recede.

Such was, in some degree, the character of the present interview. The stranger drew nigh deliberately; keeping his eyes steadily fastened on the movements of the other party, while he purposely created little difficulties to impede an approach which might prove too hasty. On the other hand, Paul stood playing with the lock of his rifle, too proud to let it appear that three men could manifest any apprehension of a solitary individual, and yet too prudent to omit, entirely, the customary precautions. The principal reason of the marked difference which the two legitimate proprietors of the banquet made in the receptions of their guests, was to be explained by the entire difference which existed in their respective appearances.

While the exterior of the naturalist was decidely pacific, not to say abstracted, that of the newcomer was distinguished by an air of vigor, and a front and step which it would not have been difficult to have at once pronounced to be military.

He wore a forage cap of fine blue cloth, from which depended a soiled tassel in gold, and which was nearly buried in a mass of exuberant, curling, jet-black hair. Around his throat he had negligently fastened a stock of black silk. His body was enveloped in a hunting shirt of dark green, trimmed with the yellow fringes and ornaments that were sometimes seen among the border troops of the Confederacy. Beneath this, however, were visible the collar and lapels of a jacket, similar in color and cloth to the cap. His lower limbs were protected by buckskin leggings, and his feet by the ordinary Indian moccasins. A richly ornamented, and exceedingly dangerous straight dirk was stuck in a sash of red silk network; another girdle, or rather belt, of uncolored leather contained a pair of the smallest sized pistols, in holsters nicely made to fit, and across his shoulder was thrown a short, heavy, military rifle; its horn and pouch occupying the usual places beneath his arms. At his back he bore a knapsack, marked by the well-known initials that have since gained for the government of the United States the good-humored and quaint appellation of Uncle Sam.

"I come in amity," the stranger said, like one too much accustomed to the sight of arms to be startled at the ludicrously belligerent attitude which Dr. Battius had seen fit to assume. "I come as a friend; and am one whose pursuits and wishes will not at all interfere with your own."

"Harkee, stranger," said Paul Hover bluntly; "do you understand lining a bee from this open place into a wood, distant, perhaps, a dozen miles?"

"The bee is a bird I have never been compelled to seek," returned the other, laughing; "though I have, too, been something of a fowler in my time."

"I thought as much," exclaimed Paul, thrusting forth his hand frankly, and with the true freedom of manner that marks an American borderer. "Let us cross fingers. You and I will never quarrel about the comb, since you set so little store by the honey. And now, if your stomach has an empty corner, and you know how to relish a genuine dew-drop when it falls into your very mouth, there lies the exact morsel to put into it. Try it, stranger; and having tried it, if you don't call it as snug a fit as you have made since—— How long ar' you from the settlements, pray?"

" 'Tis many weeks, and I fear it may be as many more before I can return. I will, however, gladly profit by your invitation, for I have fasted since the rising of yesterday's sun, and I know too well the merits of a bison's hump to reject the food."

"Ah! you ar' acquainted with the dish! Well, therein you have the advantage of me, in setting out, though I think I may say we could now start on equal ground. I should be the happiest fellow between Kentucky and the Rocky Mountains, if I had a snug cabin, near some old wood that was filled with hollow trees, just such a hump every day as that for dinner, a load of fresh straw for hives, and little El——"

"Little what?" demanded the stranger, evidently amused with the communicative and frank disposition of the bee hunter.

"Something that I shall have one day, and which concerns nobody so much as myself," returned Paul, picking the flint of his rifle, and beginning very cavalierly to whistle an air well known on the waters of the Mississippi.

During this preliminary discourse the stranger had taken his seat by the side of the hump, and was already making a serious inroad on its relics. Dr. Battius, however, watched his movements with a jealousy still more striking than the cordial reception which the open-hearted Paul had just exhibited.

But the doubts, or rather apprehensions, of the naturalist were of a character altogether different from the confidence of the bee hunter. He had been struck with the stranger's using the legitimate, instead of the perverted name of the animal off which he was making his repast; and as he had been among the foremost himself to profit by the removal of the impediments which the policy of Spain had placed in the way of all explorers of her transatlantic dominions, whether bent on the purposes of commerce, or, like himself, on the more laudable pursuits of science, he had a sufficiency of everyday philosophy to feel that the same motives, which had so powerfully urged himself to his present undertaking, might produce a like result on the mind of some other student of nature. Here, then, was the prospect of an alarming rivalry, which bade fair to strip him of at least a moiety of the just rewards of all his labors, privations, and dangers. Under these views of his character, therefore, it is not at all surprising that the native meekness of the naturalist's disposition was a little disturbed, and that he watched the proceedings of the other with such a degree of vigilance as he believed best suited to detect his sinister designs.

"This is truly a delicious repast," observed the unconscious young stranger, for both young and handsome he was fairly entitled to be considered; "either hunger has given a peculiar relish to the viand, or the bison may lay claim to be the finest of the ox family!"

"Naturalists, sir, are apt, when they speak familiarly, to give the cow the credit of the genus," said Dr. Battius, swelling with secret distrust, and clearing his throat, before speaking, much in the manner that a duellist examines the point of the weapon he is about to plunge into the body of his foe. "The figure is more perfect; as the *bos*, meaning the ox, is unable to perpetuate his kind; and the *bos*, in its most extended meaning, or *vacca*, is altogether the nobler animal of the two."

The Doctor uttered this opinion with a certain air, that he intended should express his readiness to come, at once, to any of the numerous points of difference which he doubted not existed between them; and he now awaited the blow of his antagonist, intending that his next thrust should be still more vigorous. But the young stranger appeared much better disposed to partake of the good cheer, with which he had been so providentially provided, than to take up the cudgels of argument on this, or on any other of the knotty points which are so apt to furnish the lovers of science with the materials of a mental joust.

"I dare say you are very right, sir," he replied, with a most provoking indifference to the importance of the points he conceded. "I daresay you are quite right; and that *vacca* would have been the better word."

"Pardon me, sir; you are giving a very wrong construction to my language, if you suppose I include, without many and particular qualifications, the *bibulus Americanus* in the family of the *vacca*. For, as you well know, sir—or, as I presume I should say, Doctor—you have the medical diploma, no doubt?"

"You give me credit for an honor I cannot claim," interrupted the other.

"An undergraduate!—or perhaps your degrees have been taken in some other of the liberal sciences?"

"Still wrong, I do assure you."

"Surely, young man, you have not entered on this important—I may say, this awful service, without some evidence of your fitness for the task! Some commission by which you can assert an authority to proceed, or by which you may claim an affinity and a communion with your fellow-workers in the same beneficent pursuits!"

"I know not by what means, or for what purposes, you have made yourself master of my objects!" exclaimed the youth, reddening and rising with a quickness which manifested how little he regarded the grosser appetites, when a subject nearer his heart was approached. "Still, sir, your language is incomprehensible. That pursuit, which in another might perhaps be justly called beneficent, is, in me, a dear and cherished duty; though why a commission should be demanded or needed is, I confess, no less a subject of surprise."

"It is customary to be provided with such a document," returned the Doctor gravely; "and on all suitable occasions to produce it, in order that congenial and friendly minds may, at once, reject unworthy suspicions, and, stepping over what may be called the elements of discourse, come at once to those points which are desiderata to both."

"It is a strange request!" the youth muttered, turning his frowning eye from one to the other, as if examining the characters of his companions, with a view to weigh their physical powers. Then, putting his hand into his bosom, he drew forth a small box, and extending it with an air of dignity towards the Doctor, he continued—"You will find by this, sir, that I have some right to travel in a country which is now the property of the American States."

"What have we here," exclaimed the naturalist, opening the folds of a large parchment. "Why, this is the sign manual of the philosopher, Jefferson! The seal of state! Countersigned by the minister of war! Why, this is a commission creating Duncan Uncas Middleton a captain of artillery!"

"Of whom? of whom?" repeated the trapper, who had sat regarding the stranger, during the whole discourse, with eyes that seemed greedily to devour each lineament. "How is the name? did you call him Uncas?—Uncas! Was it Uncas?"

"Such is my name," returned the youth, a little haughtily. "It is the appellation of a native chief, that both my uncle and myself bear with pride; for it is the memorial of an important service done my family by a warrior in the old wars of the provinces."

"Uncas! did ye call him Uncas?" repeated the trapper, approaching the youth and parting the dark curls which clustered over his brow, without the slightest resistance on the part of their wondering owner. "Ah! my eyes are old, and not so keen as when I was a warrior myself; but I can see the look of the father in the son! I saw it when he first came nigh; but so many things have since passed before my failing sight, that I could not name the place where I had met his likeness! Tell me, lad, by what name is your father known?"

"He was an officer of the States in the war of the Revolution, of my own name of course; my mother's brother was called Duncan Uncas Heyward."

"Still Uncas! still Uncas!" echoed the other, trembling with eagerness. "And *his* father?"

"Was called the same, without the appellation of the native chief. It was to him, and to my grandmother, that the service of which I have just spoken was rendered."

"I know'd it! I know'd it!" shouted the old man, in his tremulous voice, his rigid features working powerfully, as if the names the other mentioned awakened some long dormant emotions, connected with the events of an anterior age. "I know'd it! son or grandson, it is all the same; it is the blood, and 'tis the look! Tell me, is he they call'd Duncan, without the Uncas—is he living?"

The young man shook his head sorrowfully, as he replied in the negative.

"He died full of days and of honors. Beloved, happy, and bestowing happiness!"

"Full of days!" repeated the trapper, looking down at his own meager, but still muscular hands. "Ah! he lived in the settlements, and was wise only after their fashions. But you have often seen him; and you have heard him discourse of Uncas, and of the wilderness?"

"Often! he was then an officer of the King; but when the war took place between the Crown and her colonies, my grandfather did not forget his birthplace, but threw off the empty allegiance of names, and was true to his proper country; he fought on the side of liberty."

"There was reason in it; and what is better, there was natur'! Come, sit ye down beside me, lad; sit ye down, and tell me of what your grand'ther used to speak, when his mind dwelt on the wonders of the wilderness."

The youth smiled, no less at the importunity than at the interest manifested by the old man; but as he found there was no longer the least appearance of any violence being contemplated, he unhesitatingly complied.

"Give it all to the trapper by rule, and by figures of speech," said Paul, very coolly taking his seat on the other side of the young soldier. "It is the fashion of old age to relish these ancient traditions, and, for that matter, I can say that I don't dislike to listen to them myself."

Middleton smiled again, and perhaps with a slight air of derision; but, good-naturedly turning to the trapper, he continued—

"It is a long, and might prove a painful, story. Bloodshed and all the horrors of Indian cruelty and of Indian warfare are fearfully mingled in the narrative."

"Ay, give it all to us, stranger," continued Paul; "we are used to these matters in Kentuck, and, I must say, I think a story none the worse for having a few scalps in it!"

"But he told you of Uncas, did he?" resumed the trapper, without regarding the slight interruptions of the bee hunter, which amounted to no more than a sort of byplay. "And what thought he and said he of the lad, in his parlor, with the comforts and ease of the settlements at his elbow?"

"I doubt not he used a language similar to that he would have adopted in the woods, and had he stood face to face with his friend——"

"Did he call the savage his friend; the poor, naked, painted warrior? he was not too proud then to call the Indian his friend?"

"He even boasted of the connection; and as you have already heard, bestowed a name on his first-born, which is likely to be handed down as an heirloom among the rest of his descendants."

"It was well done! like a man: ay! and like a Christian, too! He used to say the Delaware was swift of foot—did he remember that?"

"As the antelope! Indeed, he often spoke of him by the appellation of Le Cerf Agile, a name he had obtained by his activity."

"And bold, and fearless, lad!" continued the trapper, looking up into the eyes of his companion, with a wistfulness that bespoke the delight he received in listening to the praises of one whom it was so very evident he had once tenderly loved.

"Brave as a blooded hound! Without fear! He always quoted Uncas and his father, who from his wisdom was called the Great Serpent, as models of heroism and constancy."

"He did them justice! he did them justice! Truer men were not to be found in tribe or nation, be their skins of what color they might. I see your grand'ther was just, and did his duty, too, by his offspring! 'Twas a perilous time he had of it, among them hills, and nobly did he play his own part! Tell me, lad, or officer, I should say—sincc officer you be—was this all?"

"Certainly not; it was, as I have said, a fearful tale, full of moving incidents, and the memories both of my grandfather and of my grandmother——"

"Ah!" exclaimed the trapper, tossing a hand into the air as his whole countenance lighted with the recollections the name revived. "They called her Alice! Elsie or Alice; 'tis all the same. A laughing, playful child she was, when happy; and tender and weeping in her misery! Her hair was shining and yellow, as the coat of the young fawn, and her skin clearer than the purest water that drips from the rock. Well do I remember her! I remember her right well!"

The lip of the youth slightly curled, and he regarded the old man with an expression, which might easily have been construed into a declaration that such were not his own recollections of his venerable and revered ancestor, though it would seem he did not think it necessary to say as much in words. He was content to answer—

"They both retained impressions of the dangers they had passed, by far too vivid easily to lose the recollection of any of their fellow-actors."

The trapper looked aside, and seemed to struggle with some deeply innate feeling; then, turning again toward his companion, though his honest eyes no longer dwelt with the same open interest, as before, on the countenance of the other, he continued—

"Did he tell you of them *all?* Were they *all* redskins, but himself and the daughters of Munro?"

"No. There was a white man associated with the Delawares. A scout of the English army, but a native of the provinces."

"A drunken worthless vagabond, like most of his color who harbor with the savages, I warrant you!"

"Old man, your gray hairs should caution you against slander. The man I speak of was of great simplicity of mind, but of sterling worth. Unlike most of those who live a border life, he united the better, instead of the worst, qualities of the two people. He was a man endowed with the choicest and perhaps rarest gift of nature; that of distinguishing good from evil. His virtues were those of simplicity, because such were the fruits of his habits, as were indeed his very prejudices. In courage he was the equal of his red associates; in warlike skill, being better instructed, their superior. 'In short, he was a noble shoot from the stock of human nature, which never could attain its proper elevation and importance, for no other reason than because it grew in the forest;' such, old hunter, were the very words of my grandfather, when speaking of the man you imagine so worthless!"

The eyes of the trapper had sunk to the earth, as the stranger delivered this character in the ardent tones of generous youth. He played with the ears of his hound; fingered his own rustic garment, and opened and shut the pan of his rifle, with hands that trembled in a manner that would have implied their total unfitness to wield the weapon. When the other had concluded, he hoarsely added—

"Your grand'ther didn't then entirely forget the white man!"

"So far from that, there are already three among us who have also names derived from that scout."

"A name, did you say?" exclaimed the old man, starting; "what, the name of the solitary, unl'arned hunter? Do the great, and the rich, and the honored, and, what is better still, the just, do they bear his very, actual name?"

"It is borne by my brother, and by two of my cousins, whatever may be their titles to be described by the terms you have mentioned."

"Do you mean the actual name itself; spelt with the very same letters, beginning with an N and ending with an L?"

"Exactly the same," the youth smilingly replied. "No, no, we have forgotten nothing that was his. I have at this moment a dog brushing a deer, not far from this, who is come of a hound that very scout sent as a present after his friends, and which was of the stock he always used himself: a truer breed, in nose and foot, is not to be found in the wide Union."

"Hector!" said the old man, struggling to conquer an emotion that nearly suffocated him, and speaking to his hound in the sort of tones he would have used to a child, "do ye hear that, pup? your kin and blood are in the prairies! A name—it is wonderful—very wonderful!"

Nature could endure no more. Overcome by a flood of unusual and extraordinary sensations, and stimulated by tender and long dormant recollections, strangely and unexpectedly revived, the old man had just self-command enough to add, in a voice that was hollow and unnatural, through the efforts he made to command it—

"Boy, I am that scout; a warrior once, a miserable trapper now!" when the tears broke over his wasted cheeks, out of fountains that had long been dried, and, sinking his face between his knees, he covered it decently with his buckskin garment, and sobbed aloud.

The spectacle produced correspondent emotions in his companions. Paul Hover had actually swallowed each syllable of the discourse as they fell alternately from the different speakers, his feelings keeping equal pace with the increasing interest of the scene. Unused to such strange sensations, he was turning his face on every side of him, to avoid he knew not what, until he saw the tears and heard the sobs of the old man, when he sprang to his feet, and grappling his guest fiercely by the throat, he demanded by what authority he had made his aged companion weep. A flash of recollection crossing his brain at the same instant, he released his hold, and stretching forth an arm in the very wantonness of gratification, he seized the Doctor by the hair, which instantly revealed its artificial formation, by cleaving to his hand, leaving the white and shining poll of the naturalist with a covering no warmer than the skin.

"What think you of that, Mr. Bug-gatherer?" he rather shouted than cried: "is not this a strange bee to line into his hole?"

" 'Tis remarkable! wonderful! edifying!" returned the lover of nature, good-humoredly recovering his wig, with twinkling eyes and a husky voice. " 'Tis rare and commendable! Though I doubt not in the exact order of causes and effects."

With this sudden outbreaking, however, the commotion instantly subsided; the three spectators clustering around the trapper with a species of awe, at beholding the tears of one so aged.

"It must be so, or how could he be so familiar with a history that is little known beyond my own family," at length the youth observed, not ashamed to acknowledge how much he had been affected, by unequivocally drying his own eyes.

"True!" echoed Paul; "if you want any more evidence, I will swear to it! I know every word of it myself to be true as the gospel!"

"And yet we had long supposed him dead!" continued the soldier. "My grandfather had filled his days with honor, and he had believed himself the junior of the two."

"It is not often that youth has an opportunity of thus looking down on the weakness of age!" the trapper observed, raising his head, and looking around him with composure and dignity. "That I am still here, young man, is the pleasure of the Lord, who has spared me until I have seen fourscore long and laborious years, for His own secret ends. That I am the man I say, you need not doubt; for why should I go to my grave with so cheap a lie in my mouth?"

"I do not hesitate to believe; I only marvel that it should be so! But why do I find you, venerable and excellent friend of my parents, in these wastes, so far from the comforts and safety of the lower country?"

"I have come into these plains to escape the sound of the ax; for here surely the chopper can never follow! But I may put the like question to yourself. Are you of the party which the States have sent into their new purchase, to look after the natur' of the bargain they have made?"

"I am not. Lewis is making his way up the river, some hundreds of miles from this. I come on a private adventure."

"Though it is no cause of wonder that a man whose strength and eyes have failed him as a hunter should be seen nigh the haunts of the beaver, using a trap instead of a rifle, it is strange that one so young and prosperous, and bearing the commission of the Great Father, should be moving among the prairies, without even a camp colorman to do his biddings!"

"You would think my reasons sufficient did you know them, as know them you shall if you are disposed to listen to my story. I think you all honest, and men who would rather aid than betray one bent on a worthy object."

"Come, then, and tell us at your leisure," said the trapper, seating himself, and beckoning to the youth to follow his example. The latter willingly complied; and after Paul and the Doctor had disposed of themselves to their several likings, the newcomer entered into a narrative of the singular reasons which had led him so far into the deserts.

4

THE FULL HISTORY of the artillery captain, Duncan Uncas Middleton (grandnephew of the brave British officer Duncan Heyward under whom Leatherstocking had served in the old wars with the French), soon developed itself. The young man had been an officer in the first American garrison sent to Louisiana, and had there married a Spanish beauty named Inez. But the wedding had hardly been performed when she was kidnapped by a lawless border miscreant, the brother of Ishmael Bush's wife, and carried up the Mississippi and the Missouri by the Bush family. Now Captain Middleton quickly recovered his wife, who had been kept hidden in the mysterious wagon. The kidnapper fled. With Ishmael Bush the lovely Inez had no special quarrel, calling him but a beginner in wickedness. "He quarrelled frightfully in my presence with the wretch who seized me." Middleton and Inez made valuable accessions to the wandering group of whites.

This group needed all the strength it could gather, for the hostilities with the war party of the Sioux, under the bloodthirsty chief Mahtoree, continued. In fact, they reached a new pitch of intensity when the savages apparently slew the eldest of Ishmael Bush's boys, Asa, who had been driven by a quarrel with his father to separate himself from the rest of the Bush family. The wild grief of the mother, Esther, who had led the search for her son, was pitiful to behold.

Fortunately for the whites, some Pawnees, natural enemies of the Sioux under Mahtoree, appeared as a factor in the contest. One day, as Leatherstocking was advancing with his group over the prairie, he came upon a Pawnee scout hidden in a thicket. The young warrior, painted black, white, yellow, and vermilion, was of splendid stature and of features almost Roman in their dignity. His head was shaved to the crown, where he wore a long scalp lock; his chief garments were of finely dressed deerskin; his leggings of scarlet cloth were fringed from knee to foot with the hair of human scalps. For arms he carried a short hickory bow and a long ashen lance. A quiver made of cougar skins was slung at his back, and a shield of hides, quaintly emblazoned, was suspended from his neck by a thong of sinews.

"Is my brother far from his village?" asked Leatherstocking. The young brave replied that he had good reason to rove the plains. "Can the women and children of the paleface live without the meat of the bison? There was hunger in my lodge." As they talked, the bee hunter Paul came up with a shout. He had found the horse which the Pawnee had concealed behind a hill, a fine steed. It was clear that the handsome savage, while pretending to hunt buffalo, was actually on the watch for war parties of Sioux. After a little talk, he rode away from the group of whites. Hardly had he gone when the keen senses of the old trapper told them that they faced a new peril.

The old man, while he neglected not to note the smallest incident, had no opportunity of expressing his opinion concerning the stranger's motives. After the Pawnee had disappeared, however, he shook his head and muttered, while he walked slowly to the angle of the thicket that the Indian had just quitted—

"There are both scents and sounds in the air, though my miserable senses are not good enough to hear the one, or to catch the taint of the other."

"There is nothing to be seen," cried Middleton, who kept close at his side. "My eyes and my ears are good, and yet I can assure you that I neither hear nor see anything."

"Your eyes are good! and you are not deaf!" returned the other with a slight air of contempt; "no, lad, no; they may be good to see across a church, or to hear a town bell, but afore you had passed a year in these prairies you would find yourself taking a turkey for a buffalo, or conceiting, fifty times, that the roar of a buffalo bull was the thunder of the Lord! There is a deception of natur' in these naked plains, in which the air throws up the images like water, and then it is hard to tell the prairies from a sea. But yonder is a sign that a hunter never fails to know!"

The trapper pointed to a flight of vultures that were sailing over the plain at no great distance, and apparently in the direction in which the Pawnee had riveted his eye. At first Middleton could not distinguish the small dark objects that were dotting the dusky clouds, but as they came swiftly onward, first their forms, and then their heavy waving wings, became distinctly visible.

"Listen," said the trapper, when he had succeeded in making Middleton see the moving column of birds. "Now you hear the buffaloes, or bisons, as your knowing Doctor sees fit to call them, though buffaloes is their name among all the hunters of these regions. And I conclude that a hunter is a better judge of a beast and of its name," he added, winking to the young soldier, "than any man who has turned over the leaves of a book, instead of travelling over the face of the 'arth, in order to find out the natur's of its inhabitants."

"Of their habits, I will grant you," cried the naturalist, who rarely missed an opportunity to agitate any disputed point in his favorite studies. "That is, provided always deference is had to the proper use of definitions, and that they are contemplated with scientific eyes."

"Eyes of a mole! as if man's eyes were not as good for names as the eyes of any other creatur'! Who named the works of His hand? can you tell me that, with your books and college wisdom? Was it not the first man in the Garden, and is it not a plain consequence that his children inherit his gifts?"

"That is certainly the Mosaic account of the event," said the Doctor; "though your reading is by far too literal!"

"My reading! nay, if you suppose that I have wasted my time in schools, you do such a wrong to my knowledge, as one mortal should never lay to the door of another without sufficient reason. If I have ever craved the art of reading, it has been that I might better know the sayings of the book you name, for it is a book which speaks, in every line, according to human feelings, and therein according to reason."

"And do you then believe," said the Doctor, a little provoked by the dogmatism of his stubborn adversary, and perhaps, secretly, too confident in his own more liberal, though scarcely as profitable, attainments—"do you then believe that all these beasts were literally collected in a garden, to be enrolled in the nomenclature of the first man?"

"Why not? I understand your meaning; for it is not needful to live in towns to hear all the devilish devices that the conceit of man can invent to upset his own happiness. What does it prove, except indeed it may be said to prove that the garden He made was not after the miserable fashions of our times, thereby directly giving the lie to what the world calls its civilizing? No, no, the garden of the Lord was the forest then, and is the forest now, where the fruits do grow, and the birds do sing, according to His own wise ordering. Now, lady, you may see the mystery of the vultures! There come the buffaloes themselves, and a noble herd it is! I warrant me, that Pawnee has a troop of his people in some of the hollows nigh by; and as he has gone scampering after them, you are about to see a glorious chase. It will serve to keep the squatter and his brood under cover, and for ourselves there is little reason to fear. A Pawnee is not apt to be a malicious savage."

Every eye was now drawn to the striking spectacle that succeeded. Even the timid Inez hastened to the side of Middleton to gaze at the sight, and Paul summoned Ellen from her culinary labors, to become a witness of the lively scene.

Throughout the whole of those moving events, which it has been our duty to record, the prairies had lain in the majesty of perfect solitude. The heavens had been blackened with the passage of the migratory birds, it is true, but the dogs of the party and the ass of the doctor were the only quadrupeds that had enlivened the broad surface of the waste beneath. There was now a sudden exhibition of animal life, which changed the scene, as it were, by magic, to the very opposite extreme.

A few enormous bison bulls were first observed, scouring along the most distant roll of the prairie, and then succeeded long files of single beasts, which, in their turns, were followed by a dark mass of bodies, until the dun-colored herbage of the plain was entirely lost, in the deeper hue of their shaggy coats. The herd, as the column spread and thickened, was like the endless flocks of the smaller birds, whose extended flanks are so often seen to heave up out of the abyss of the heavens, until they appear as countless as the leaves in those forests over which they wing their endless flight. Clouds of dust shot up in little columns from the center of the mass, as some animal, more furious than the rest, ploughed the plain with his horns, and, from time to time, a deep hollow bellowing was borne along on the wind, as if a thousand throats vented their plaints in a discordant murmuring.

A long and musing silence reigned in the party, as they gazed on this spectacle of wild and peculiar grandeur. It was at length broken by the trapper, who, having been long accustomed to similar sights, felt less of its influence, or, rather, felt it in a less thrilling and absorbing manner than those to whom the scene was more novel.

"There go ten thousand oxen in one drove, without keeper or

master, except Him who made them, and gave them these open plains for their pasture! Ay, it is here that man may see the proofs of his wantonness and folly! Can the proudest governor in all the States go into his fields and slaughter a nobler bullock than is here offered to the meanest hand; and when he has gotten his surloin, or his steak, can he eat it with as good a relish as he who has sweetened his food with wholesome toil, and earned it according to the law of natur', by honestly mastering that which the Lord hath put before him?"

"If the prairie platter is smoking with a buffalo's hump, I answer, No," interrupted the luxurious bee hunter.

"Ay, boy, you have tasted, and you feel the genuine reasoning of the thing! But the herd is heading a little this-a-way, and it behoves us to make ready for their visit. If we hide ourselves altogether, the horned brutes will break through the place and trample us beneath their feet, like so many creeping worms; so we will just put the weak ones apart, and take post, as becomes men and hunters, in the van."

As there was but little time to make the necessary arrangements, the whole party set about them in good earnest. Inez and Ellen were placed in the edge of the thicket on the side farthest from the approaching herd. Asinus was posted in the center, in consideration of his nerves, and then the old man, with his three male companions, divided themselves in such a manner as they thought would enable them to turn the head of the rushing column, should it chance to approach too nigh their position. By the vacillating movements of some fifty or a hundred bulls that led the advance, it remained questionable, for many moments, what course they intended to pursue. But a tremendous and painful roar, which came from behind the cloud of dust that rose in the center of the herd, and which was horridly answered by the screams of the carrion birds, that were greedily sailing directly above the flying drove, appeared to give a new impulse to their flight, and at once to remove every symptom of indecision. As if glad to seek the smallest signs of the forest, the whole of the affrighted herd became steady in its direction, rushing in a straight line toward the little cover of bushes, which has already been so often named.

The appearance of danger was now, in reality, of a character to try the stoutest nerves. The flanks of the dark, moving mass were advanced in such a manner as to make a concave line of the front, and every fierce eye, that was glaring from the shaggy wilderness of hair in which the entire heads of the males were enveloped, was riveted with mad anxiety on the thicket. It seemed as if each beast strove to outstrip his neighbor in gaining this desired cover; and as thousands in the rear pressed blindly on those in front, there was the appearance of an imminent risk that the leaders of the herd would be precipitated on the concealed party, in which case the destruction of every one of them was certain. Each of our adventurers felt the danger of his situation in a manner peculiar to his individual character and circumstances.

Middleton wavered. At times he felt inclined to rush through the bushes, and, seizing Inez, attempt to fly. Then recollecting the impossibility of outstripping the furious speed of an alarmed bison, he felt for his arms, determined to make head against the countless drove. The faculties of Dr. Battius were quickly wrought up to the very summit of mental delusion. The dark forms of the herd lost their distinctness, and then the naturalist began to fancy he beheld a wild collection of all the creatures of the world, rushing upon him in a body, as if to revenge the various injuries, which in the course of a life of indefatigable labor in behalf of the natural sciences, he had inflicted on their several genera. The paralysis it occasioned in his system was like the effect of the incubus. Equally unable to fly or to advance, he stood riveted to the spot, until the infatuation became so complete that the worthy naturalist was beginning, by a desperate effort of scientific resolution, even to class the different specimens. On the other hand, Paul shouted, and called on Ellen to come and assist him in shouting, but his voice was lost in the bellowings and trampling of the herd. Furious, and yet strangely excited by the obstinacy of the brutes and the wildness of the sight, and nearly maddened by sympathy and a species of unconscious apprehension, in which the claims of nature were singularly mingled with concern for his mistress, he nearly split his throat in exhorting his aged friend to interfere.

"Come forth, old trapper," he shouted, "with your prairie inventions! or we shall be all smothered under a mountain of buffalo humps!"

The old man, who had stood all this while leaning on his rifle, and regarding the movements of the herd with a steady eye, now deemed it time to strike his blow. Levelling his piece at the foremost bull, with an agility that would have done credit to his youth, he fired. The animal received the bullet on the matted hair between his horns, and fell to his knees, but shaking his head he instantly arose, the very shock seeming to increase his exertions. There was now no longer time to hesitate. Throwing down his rifle, the trapper stretched forth his arms, and advanced from the cover with naked hands, directly toward the rushing column of the beasts.

The figure of a man, when sustained by the firmness and steadiness that intellect can only impart, rarely fails of commanding respect from all the inferior animals of the creation. The leading bulls recoiled, and for a single instant there was a sudden stop to their speed, a dense mass of bodies rolling up in front, until hundreds were seen floundering and tumbling on the plain. Then came another of those hollow bellowings from the rear, and set the herd again in motion. The head of the column, however, divided. The immovable form of the trapper, cutting it, as it were, into two gliding streams of life. Middleton and Paul instantly profited by his example, and extended the feeble barrier by a similar exhibition of their own persons.

For a few moments the new impulse given to the animals in front served to protect the thicket. But, as the body of the herd pressed more and more upon the open line of its defenders, and the dust thickened, so as to obscure their persons, there was, at each instant, a renewed danger of the beasts breaking through. It became necessary for the trapper and his companions to become still more and more alert; and they were gradually yielding before the headlong multitude, when a furious bull darted by Middleton, so near as to brush his person, and, at the next instant, swept through the thicket with the velocity of the wind.

"Close, and die for the ground," shouted the old man, "or a thousand of the devils will be at his heels!"

All their efforts would have proved fruitless, however, against the living torrent, had not Asinus, whose domains had just been so rudely entered, lifted his voice in the midst of the uproar. The most sturdy and furious of the bulls trembled at the alarming and unknown cry, and then each individual brute was seen madly pressing from that very thicket, which, the moment before, he had endeavored to reach with the eagerness with which the murderer seeks the sanctuary.

As the stream divided, the place became clear; the two dark columns moving obliquely from the copse, to unite again at the distance of a mile, on its opposite side. The instant the old man saw the sudden effect which the voice of Asinus had produced, he coolly commenced reloading his rifle, indulging at the same time in a heartfelt fit of his silent and peculiar merriment.

"There they go, like dogs with so many half-filled shot-pouches dangling at their tails, and no fear of their breaking their order; for what the brutes in the rear didn't hear with their own ears, they'll conceit they did: besides, if they change their minds, it may be no hard matter to get the Jack to sing the rest of his tune!"

5

THE BUFFALO HERD careered away over the plains. The trapper granted that they had narrowly escaped being trodden into pulp; but he remarked that the bison was a beast without any courage. "Lord, man, if you should once get fairly beset by a brood of grizzly bears, as happened to Hector and I, at the great falls of the Miss—." He broke off to point out that the herd was being followed in the distance not only by a pack of wolves, anxious to pick off any weak or ailing animal, but by some fifteen or twenty mounted men. As Leatherstocking gazed, he suddenly discovered that these were not friendly Pawnees, but a body of hostile Indians.

"It is a band of the accursed Sioux!" he exclaimed. "To cover, lads, to cover." But the Indians soon scattered over the prairie, and discovered the hill on which Ishmael Bush and his family had taken refuge. In the hour of peril, the dauntless Esther Bush proved herself as stern a fighter as any of her strong-limbed sons.

Once more, however, the Indians captured Leatherstocking, with Obed Battius, Middleton, the bee hunter, Ellen, and Inez; and once more he made good his escape with his friends. After a flight of twenty miles over the prairies, the six camped for rest.

The sleep of the fugitives lasted for several hours. The trapper was the first to shake off its influence, as he had been the last to court its refreshment. Rising, just as the gray light of day began to brighten that portion of the studded valt which rested on the eastern margin of the plain, he summoned his companions from their warm lairs, and pointed out the necessity of their being once more on the alert. While Middleton attended to the arrangements necessary to the comforts of Inez and Ellen, in the long and painful journey which lay before them, the old man and Paul prepared the meal, which the former had advised them to take before they proceeded to horse. These several dispositions were not long in making, and the little group was soon seated about a repast which, though it might want the elegancies to which the bride of Middleton had been accustomed, was not deficient in the more important requisites of savor and nutriment.

"When we get lower into the hunting grounds of the Pawnees," said the trapper, laying a morsel of delicate venison before Inez, on a little trencher neatly made of horn, and expressly for his own use, "we shall find the buffaloes fatter and sweeter, the deer in more abundance, and all the gifts of the Lord abounding to satisfy our wants. Perhaps we may even strike a beaver, and get a morsel from his tail [1] by way of a rare mouthful."

"What course do you mean to pursue, when you have once thrown these bloodhounds from the chase?" demanded Middleton.

"If I might advise," said Paul, "it would be to strike a water-course, and get upon its downward current, as soon as may be. Give me a cottonwood, and I will turn you out a canoe that shall carry us all, the jackass excepted, in perhaps the work of a day and a night. Ellen, here, is a lively girl enough, but then she is no great race rider; and it would be far more comfortable to boat six or eight hundred miles, than to go loping along like so many elks measuring the prairies; besides, water leaves no trail."

"I will not swear to that," returned the trapper; "I have often thought the eyes of a redskin would find a trail in air."

"See, Middleton," exclaimed Inez, in a sudden burst of youthful pleasure, that caused her for a moment to forget her situation, "how lovely is that sky; surely it contains a promise of happier times!"

"It is glorious!" returned her husband. "Glorious and heavenly is that streak of vivid red, and here is a still brighter crimson; rarely have I seen a richer rising of the sun."

"Rising of the sun!" slowly repeated the old man, lifting his tall person from its seat with a deliberate and abstracted air, while he kept his eye riveted on the changing, and certainly beautiful tints, that were garnishing the vault of heaven. "Rising of the sun! I like not such risings of the sun. Ah's me! the imps have circumvented us with a vengeance. The prairie is on fire!"

---

[1] The American hunters consider the tail of the beaver the most nourishing of all food. (*Cooper's note*)

"God in Heaven protect us!" cried Middleton, catching Inez to his bosom, under the instant impression of the imminence of their danger. "There is no time to lose, old man; each instant is a day; let us fly."

"Whither?" demanded the trapper, motioning him, with calmness and dignity, to arrest his steps. "In this wilderness of grass and reeds, you are like a vessel in the broad lakes without a compass. A single step on the wrong course might prove the destruction of us all. It is seldom danger is so pressing, that there is not time enough for reason to do its work, young officer; therefore let us await its biddings."

"For my own part," said Paul Hover, looking about him with no equivocal expression of concern, "I acknowledge, that should this dry bed of weeds get fairly in a flame, a bee would have to make a flight higher than common to prevent his wings from scorching. Therefore, old trapper, I agree with the captain, and say mount and run."

"Ye are wrong—ye are wrong; man is not a beast to follow the gift of instinct, and to snuff up his knowledge by a taint in the air, or a rumbling in the sound; but he must see and reason, and then conclude. So follow me a little to the left, where there is a rise in the ground, whence we may make our reconnoiterings."

The old man waved his hand with authority, and led the way without further parlance to the spot he had indicated, followed by the whole of his alarmed companions. An eye less practiced than that of the trapper might have failed in discovering the gentle elevation to which he alluded, and which looked on the surface of the meadow like a growth a little taller than common. When they reached the place, however, the stinted grass itself announced the absence of that moisture which had fed the rank weeds of most of the plain, and furnished a clue to the evidence by which he had judged of the formation of the ground hidden beneath. Here a few minutes were lost in breaking down the tops of the surrounding herbage, which, notwithstanding the advantage of their position, rose even above the heads of Middleton and Paul, and in obtaining a lookout that might command a view of the surrounding sea of fire.

The frightful prospect added nothing to the hopes of those who had so fearful a stake in the result. Although the day was beginning to dawn, the vivid colors of the sky continued to deepen, as if the fierce element were bent on an impious rivalry of the light of the sun. Bright flashes of flame shot up here and there, along the margin of the waste, like the nimble coruscations of the North, but far more angry and threatening in their color and changes. The anxiety on the rigid features of the trapper sensibly deepened, as he leisurely traced these evidences of a conflagration, which spread in a broad belt about their place of refuge, until he had encircled the whole horizon.

Shaking his head, as he again turned his face to the point where the danger seemed nighest and most rapidly approaching, the old man said—

"Now have we been cheating ourselves with the belief that we had thrown these Tetons from our trail, while here is proof enough that they not only know where we lie, but that they intend to smoke us out, like so many skulking beasts of prey. See; they have lighted the fire around the whole bottom at the same moment, and we are as completely hemmed in by the devils as an island by its waters."

"Let us mount and ride," cried Middleton; "is life not worth a struggle?"

"Whither would ye go? Is a Teton horse a salamander that can walk amid fiery flames unhurt, or do you think the Lord will show His might in your behalf, as in the days of old, and carry you harmless through such a furnace as you may see glowing beneath yonder red sky? There are Sioux, too, hemming the fire with their arrows and knives on every side of us, or I am no judge of their murderous deviltries."

"We will ride into the center of the whole tribe," returned the youth fiercely, "and put their manhood to the test."

"Ay, it's well in words, but what would it prove in deeds? Here is a dealer in bees, who can teach you wisdom in a matter like this."

"Now for that matter, old trapper," said Paul, stretching his athletic form like a mastiff conscious of his strength, "I am on the side of the captain, and am clearly for a race against the fire, though it line me into a Teton wigwam. Here is Ellen, who will—"

"Of what use, of what use are your stout hearts, when the element of the Lord is to be conquered as well as human men. Look about you, friends; the wreath of smoke that is rising from the bottoms plainly says that there is no outlet from the spot, without crossing a belt of fire. Look for yourselves, my men; look for yourselves; if you can find a single opening, I will engage to follow."

The examination which his companions so instantly and so intently made, rather served to assure them of their desperate situation than to appease their fears. Huge columns of smoke were rolling up from the plain, and thickening in gloomy masses around the horizon. The red glow, which gleamed upon their enormous folds, now lighting their volumes with the glare of the conflagration, and now flashing to another point, as the flame beneath glided ahead, leaving all behind enveloped in awful darkness, and proclaiming louder than words the character of the imminent and approaching danger.

"This is terrible!" exclaimed Middleton, folding the trembling Inez to his heart. "At such a time as this, and in such a manner!"

"The gates of heaven are open to all who truly believe," murmured the pious devotee in his bosom.

"This resignation is maddening! But we are men, and will make a struggle for our lives! How now, my brave and spirited friend, shall we yet mount and push across the flames, or shall we stand here, and see those we most love perish in this frightful manner, without an effort?"

"I am for a swarming time, and a flight before the hive is too hot to hold us," said the bee hunter, to whom it will be at once seen that Middleton addressed himself. "Come, old trapper, you must acknowledge this is but a slow way of getting out of danger. If we tarry here much longer, it will be in the fashion that the bees lie around the straw after the hive has been smoked for its honey. You may hear the fire begin to roar already, and I know by experience that when the flame once gets fairly into the prairie grass, it is no sloth that can outrun it."

"Think you," returned the old man, pointing scornfully at the mazes of the dry and matted grass which environed them, "that mortal feet can outstrip the speed of fire on such a path! If I only knew now on which side these miscreants lay!"

"What say you, friend Doctor," cried the bewildered Paul, turning to the naturalist with that sort of helplessness with which the strong are often apt to seek aid of the weak, when human power is baffled by the hand of a mightier being, "what say you; have you no advice to give away, in a case of life and death?"

The naturalist stood, tablets in hand, looking at the awful spectacle with as much composure as if the conflagration had been lighted in order to solve the difficulties of some scientific problem. Aroused by the question of his companion, he turned to his equally calm though differently occupied associate, the trapper, demanding, with the most provoking insensibility to the urgent nature of their situation—

"Venerable hunter, you have often witnessed similar prismatic experiments——"

He was rudely interrupted by Paul, who struck the tablets from his hands with a violence that betrayed the utter intellectual confusion which had overset the equanimity of his mind. Before time was allowed for remonstrance, the old man, who had continued during the whole scene like one much at a loss how to proceed, though also like one who was rather perplexed than alarmed, suddenly assumed a decided air, as if he no longer doubted on the course it was most advisable to pursue.

"It is time to be doing," he said, interrupting the controversy that was about to ensue between the naturalist and the bee hunter; "it is time to leave off books and moanings, and to be doing."

"You have come to your recollections too late, miserable old man," cried Middleton; "the flames are within a quarter of a mile of us, and the wind is bringing them down in this quarter with dreadful rapidity."

"Anan! the flames! I care but little for the flames. If I only knew how to circumvent the cunning of the Tetons, as I know how to cheat the fire of its prey, there would be nothing needed but thanks to the Lord for our deliverance. Do you call this a fire? If you had seen what I have witnessed in the eastern hills, when mighty mountains were like the furnace of a smith, you would have known what it was to fear the flames, and to be thankful that you were spared! Come, lads, come; 'tis time to be doing now, and to cease talking; for yonder curling flame is truly coming on like a trotting moose. Put hands upon this short and withered grass where we stand, and lay bare the 'arth."

"Would you think to deprive the fire of its victims in this childish manner?" exclaimed Middleton.

A faint but solemn smile passed over the features of the old man, as he answered—

"Your gran'ther would have said, that when the enemy was nigh, a soldier could do no better than to obey."

The captain felt the reproof, and instantly began to imitate the industry of Paul, who was tearing the decayed herbage from the ground in a sort of desperate compliance with the trapper's direction. Even Ellen lent her hands to the labor, nor was it long before Inez was seen similarly employed, though none amongst them knew why or wherefore. When life is thought to be the reward of labor, men are wont to be industrious. A very few moments sufficed to lay bare a spot of some twenty feet in diameter. Into one edge of this little area the trapper brought the females, directing Middleton and Paul to cover their light and inflammable dresses with the blankets of the party. So soon as this precaution was observed, the old man approached the opposite margin of the grass, which still environed them in a tall and dangerous circle, and selecting a handful of the driest of the herbage he placed it over the pan of his rifle. The light combustible kindled at the flash. Then he placed the little flame in a bed of the standing fog, and withdrawing from the spot to the center of the ring, he patiently awaited the result.

The subtle element seized with avidity upon its new fuel, and in a moment forked flames were gliding among the grass, as the tongues of ruminating animals are seen rolling among their food, apparently in quest of its sweetest portions.

"Now," said the old man, holding up a finger, and laughing in his peculiarly silent manner, "you shall see fire fight fire! Ah's me! many is the time I have burnt a smooty path, from wanton laziness to pick my way across a tangled bottom."

"But is this not fatal?" cried the amazed Middleton; "are you not bringing the enemy nigher to us instead of avoiding it?"

"Do you scorch so easily? your gran'ther had a tougher skin. But we shall live to see; we shall all live to see."

The experience of the trapper was in the right. As the fire gained strength and heat, it began to spread on three sides, dying of itself on the fourth, for want of aliment. As it increased, and the sullen roaring announced its power, it cleared everything before it, leaving the black and smoking soil far more naked than if the scythe had swept the place. The situation of the fugitives would have still been hazardous had not the area enlarged as the flame encircled them. But by advancing to the spot where the trapper had kindled the grass, they avoided the heat, and in a very few moments the flames began to recede in every quarter, leaving them enveloped in a cloud of smoke, but perfectly safe from the torrent of fire that was still furiously rolling onward.

The spectators regarded the simple expedient of the trapper with that species of wonder with which the courtiers of Ferdinand are said to have viewed the manner in which Columbus made his egg stand on its end, though with feelings that were filled with gratitude instead of envy.

"Most wonderful!" said Middleton, when he saw the complete success of the means by which they had been rescued from a danger that he had conceived to be unavoidable. "The thought was a gift from heaven, and the hand that executed it should be immortal!"

"Old trapper," cried Paul, thrusting his fingers through his shaggy locks, "I have lined many a loaded bee into his hole, and know something of the nature of the woods, but this is robbing a hornet of his sting without touching the insect!"

"It will do—it will do," returned the old man, who after the first moment of his success seemed to think no more of the exploit; "now get the horses in readiness. Let the flames do their work for a short half-hour, and then we will mount. That time is needed to cool the meadow, for these unshod Teton beasts are as tender on the hoof as a barefooted girl."

Middleton and Paul, who considered this unlooked-for escape as a species of resurrection, patiently awaited the time the trapper mentioned with renewed confidence in the infallibility of his judgment. The Doctor regained his tablets, a little worse from having fallen among the grass which had been subject to the action of the flames, and was consoling himself for this slight misfortune by recording uninterruptedly such different vacillations in light and shadow as he chose to consider phenomena.

In the meantime the veteran, on whose experience they all so implicitly relied for protection, employed himself in reconnoitering objects in the distance, through the openings which the air occasionally made in the immense bodies of smoke, that by this time lay in enormous piles on every part of the plain.

"Look you here, lads," the trapper said, after a long and anxious examination, "your eyes are young and may prove better than my worthless sight—though the time has been when a wise and brave people saw reason to think me quick on a lookout; but those times are gone, and many a true and tried friend has passed away with them. Ah's me! if I could choose a change in the orderings of Providence—which I cannot, and which it would be blasphemy to attempt, seeing that all things are governed by a wiser mind than belongs to mortal weakness—but if I were to choose a change, it would be to say, that such as they who have lived long together in friendship and kindness, and who have proved their fitness to go in company, by many acts of suffering and daring in each other's behalf, should be permitted to give up life at such times, as when the death of one leaves the other but little reason to wish to live."

"Is it an Indian that you see?" demanded the impatient Middleton.

"Redskin or white-skin it is much the same. Friendship and use can tie men as strongly together in the woods as in the towns—ay, and for that matter, stronger. Here are the young warriors of the prairies. Often do they sort themselves in pairs, and set apart their lives for deeds of friendship; and well and truly do they act up to their promises. The deathblow to one is commonly mortal to the other! I have been a solitary man much of my time, if he can be called solitary who has lived for seventy years in the very bosom of natur', and where he could, at any instant, open his heart to God, without having to strip it of the cares and wickednesses of the settlements—but making that allowance, have I been a solitary man; and yet have I always found that intercourse with my kind was pleasant, and painful to break off, provided that the companion was brave and honest. Brave, because a skeary comrade in the woods," suffering his eyes inadvertently to rest a moment on the person of the abstracted naturalist, "is apt to make a short path long; and honest, inasmuch as craftiness is rather an instinct of the brutes than a gift becoming the reason of a human man."

"But the object that you saw—was it a Sioux?"

"What the world of America is coming to, and where the machinations and inventions of its people are to have an end, the Lord, He only knows. I have seen, in my day, the chief who, in his time, had beheld the first Christian that placed his wicked foot in the regions of York! How much has the beauty of the wilderness been deformed in two short lives! My own eyes were first opened on the shores of the eastern sea, and well do I remember, that I tried the virtues of the first rifle I ever bore, after such a march, from the door of my father to the forest, as a stripling could make between sun and sun; and that without offence to the rights, or prejudices, of any man who set himself up to be the owner of the beasts of the fields. Natur' then lay in its glory along the whole coast, giving a narrow stripe, between the woods and the ocean, to the greediness of the settlers. And where am I now? Had I the wings of an eagle, they would tire before a tenth of the distance, which separates me from that sea, could be passed; and towns and villages, farms and highways, churches and schools, in short, all the inventions and deviltries of man, are spread across the region. I have known the time when a few redskins, shouting along the borders, could set the provinces in a fever; and men were to be armed; and troops were to be called to aid from a distant land; and prayers were said, and the women frighted, and few slept in quiet, because the Iroquois were on the warpath, or the accursed Mingo had the tomahawk in hand. How is it now? The country sends out her ships to foreign lands, to wage their battles; cannon are plentier than the rifle used to be, and trained soldiers are never wanting, in tens of thousands, when need calls for their services. Such is the difference atween a province and a state, my men; and I, miserable and worn out as I seem, have lived to see it all!"

"That you must have seen many a chopper skimming the cream from the face of the earth, and many a settler getting the very honey of nature, old trapper," said Paul, "no reasonable man can, or, for that matter, shall doubt. But here is Ellen getting uneasy about the Sioux, and now you have opened your mind so freely concerning these matters, if you will just put us on the line of our flight, the swarm will make another move."

"Anan!"

"I say that Ellen is getting uneasy; and as the smoke is lifting from the plain, it may be prudent to take another flight."

"The boy is reasonable. I had forgotten we were in the midst of a raging fire, and that Sioux were round about us, like hungry wolves watching a drove of buffaloes. But when memory is at work in my old brain, on times long past, it is apt to overlook the matters of the day. You say right, my children; it is time to be moving, and now comes the real nicety of our case. It is easy to outwit a furnace, for it is nothing but a raging element; and it is not always difficult to throw a grizzly bear from his scent, for the creatur' is both enlightened and blinded by his instinct; but to shut the eyes of a waking Teton is a matter of greater judgment, inasmuch as his deviltry is backed by reason."

Notwithstanding the old man appeared so conscious of the difficulty of the undertaking, he set about its achievement with great steadiness and alacrity. After completing the examination, which had been interrupted by the melancholy wanderings of his mind, he gave the signal to his companions to mount. The horses, which had continued passive and trembling amid the raging of the fire, received their burdens with a satisfaction so very evident, as to furnish a favorable augury of their future industry. The trapper invited the Doctor to take his own steed, declaring his intention to proceed on foot.

"I am but little used to journeying with the feet of others," he added, as a reason for the measure, "and my legs are a-weary of doing nothing. Besides, should we light suddenly on an ambushment, which is a thing far from impossible, the horse will be in a better condition for a hard run with one man on his back than with two. As for me, what matters it whether my time is to be a day shorter, or a day longer! Let the Tetons take my scalp, if it be God's pleasure: they will find it covered with gray hairs; and it is beyond the craft of man to cheat me of the knowledge and experience by which they have been whitened."

6

MORE HARDSHIPS, more perils, and one more perilous captivity had to be endured by Leatherstocking and his companions as they tried to flee from the toils of Mahtoree and his painted warriors. It was Middleton's wife Inez who stood in the direst position when the whole group was recaptured. Mahtoree desired her for his wife. He had found a flower on the prairie, he said, and he meant to keep it. "Her feet are very tender. She cannot walk to the door of her father; she will stay in the lodge of a valiant warrior forever." Dr.

Obed Battius was cruelly humiliated when the savages shaved all his head but the scalp lock, painted him heavily, and clad him in deerskin, to be their new medicine man. As for Leatherstocking, he and the bee hunter were about to be slain when Ishmael Bush and his sons intervened and carried them away to his own encampment.

The warfare on the prairies culminated in a grand battle between the Sioux under Mahtoree, and the Pawnees under their chief Hard-Heart. At the very crisis of the struggle, Bush and his sons came to the rescue of the hardpressed Pawnee fighters. They poured in a volley from their long western rifles. "Some five or six Sioux leaped forward in the death agony, and every arm among them was as suddenly suspended as if the lightning had flashed from the clouds to aid the cause of the Loups." This ended the campaign. The retreating Sioux were fiercely harried by the triumphant Pawnee braves. Ishmael Bush was left in control of the situation, and he prepared to execute some rough justice. As a result of a highly informal trial, it was proved that his brother-in-law Abiram—the man who had kidnapped Inez—had slain the first-born son, Asa Bush. That deed, at first attributed to the Sioux, had been committed by Abiram because Asa had hotly condemned the kidnapping. "My words are plain," said the pitiless Ishmael, "thou hast done murder, and for the same thou must die." The culprit was promptly bound and placed in such a position that the moment he tried to move, he would hang himself—a fitting fate.

With the hostile savages dispersed, and with the criminal member of the Bush clan put to death, the prairies were now safe. But Captain Middleton, the bee hunter, the nearsighted naturalist, and the two girls Ellen and Inez, were anxious to return to civilization. They floated down the river which the party had reached, leaving Leatherstocking behind to continue his trapping. "He was last seen standing on the low point, leaning on his rifle, with Hector crouched at his feet. . . ."

Middleton at once began a new career, holding government positions of importance in the West. Paul Hover the bee hunter, who married Ellen, also prospered and entered the legislature. But Middleton did not forget Leatherstocking.

In the autumn of the year that succeeded the season in which the preceding events occurred, the young man, still in the military service, found himself on the waters of the Missouri, at a point not far remote from the Pawnee towns. Released from any immediate calls of duty, and strongly urged to the measure by Paul, who was in his company, he determined to take horse and cross the country to visit the partisan, and to inquire into the fate of his friend the trapper. As his train was suited to his functions and rank, the journey was effected with the privations and hardships that are the accompaniments of all travelling in a wild, but without any of those dangers and alarms that marked his former passage through the same regions. When within a proper distance, he dispatched an Indian runner belonging to a friendly tribe to announce the approach of himself and party, continuing his route at a deliberate pace, in order that the intelligence might, as was customary, precede his arrival. To the surprise of the travellers their message was unanswered. Hour succeeded hour, and mile after mile was passed, without bringing either the signs of an honorable reception, or the more simple assurances of a friendly welcome. At length the cavalcade, at whose head rode Middleton and Paul, descended from the elevated plain on which they had long been journeying to a luxuriant bottom, that brought them to the level of the village of the Loups. The sun was beginning to fall, and a sheet of golden light was spread over the placid plain, lending to its even surface those glorious tints and hues that, the human imagination is apt to conceive, form the embellishment of still more imposing scenes. The verdure of the year yet remained, and herds of horses and mules were grazing peacefully in the vast natural pasture under the keeping of vigilant Pawnee boys. Paul pointed out among them the well-known form of Asinus, sleek, fat, and luxuriating in the fullness of content, as he stood with reclining ears and closed eyelids, seemingly musing on the exquisite nature of his present indolent enjoyment.

The route of the party led them at no great distance from one of those watchful youths, who was charged with a trust heavy as the principal wealth of his tribe. He heard the trampling of the horses, and cast his eye aside, but instead of manifesting curiosity or alarm, his look instantly returned whence it had been withdrawn to the spot where the village was known to stand.

"There is something remarkable in all this," muttered Middleton, half offended at what he conceived to be not only a slight to his rank, but offensive to himself personally; "yonder boy has heard of our approach, or he would not fail to notify his tribe; and yet he scarcely deigns to favor us with a glance. Look to your arms, men; it may be necessary to let these savages feel our strength."

"Therein, Captain, I think you're in an error," returned Paul; "if honesty is to be met on the prairies at all, you will find it in our old friend Hard-Heart; neither is an Indian to be judged of by the rules of a white. See! we are not altogether slighted, for here comes a party at last to meet us, though it is a little pitiful as to show and numbers."

Paul was right in both particulars. A group of horsemen were at length seen wheeling round a little copse, and advancing across the plain directly toward them. The advance of this party was slow and dignified. As it drew nigh, the partisan of the Loups was seen at its head, followed by a dozen younger warriors of his tribe. They were all unarmed, nor did they even wear any of those ornaments or feathers which are considered testimonials of respect to the guest an Indian receives, as well as evidence of his own importance.

The meeting was friendly, though a little restrained on both sides. Middleton, jealous of his own consideration no less than of the authority of his government, suspected some undue influence on the part of the agents of the Canadas; and, as he was determined to maintain the authority of which he was the representative, he felt himself constrained to manifest a hauteur that he was far from feeling. It was not so easy to penetrate the motives of the Pawnees. Calm, dignified, and yet far from repulsive, they set an example of courtesy, blended with reserve, that many a diplomatist of the most polished court might have strove in vain to imitate.

In this manner the two parties continued their course to the town. Middleton had time, during the remainder of the ride, to revolve in his mind all the probable reasons which his ingenuity could suggest for this strange reception. Although he was accompanied by a regular interpreter, the chiefs made their salutations in a manner that dispensed with his services. Twenty times the Captain turned his glance on his former friend, endeavoring to read the expression of his rigid features. But every effort and all conjectures proved equally futile. The eye of Hard-Heart was fixed, composed, and a little anxious; but as to every other emotion, impenetrable. He neither spoke himself, nor seemed willing to invite discourse in his visitors; it was therefore necessary for Middleton to adopt the patient manners of his companions, and to await the issue for the explanation.

When they entered the town, its inhabitants were seen collected in an open space, where they were arranged with the customary deference to age and rank. The whole formed a large circle, in the center of which were perhaps a dozen of the principal chiefs. Hard-Heart waved his hand as he approached, and, as the mass of bodies opened, he rode through, followed by his companions. Here they dismounted; and as the beasts were led apart, the strangers found themselves environed by a thousand grave, composed, but solicitous faces.

Middleton gazed about him in growing concern, for no cry, no song, no shout welcomed him among a people from whom he had so lately parted with regret. His uneasiness, not to say apprehensions, was shared by all his followers. Determination and stern resolution began to assume the place of anxiety in every eye, as each man silently felt for his arms, and assured himself that his several weapons were in a state for service. But there was no answering symptom of hostility on the part of their hosts. Hard-Heart beckoned for Middleton and Paul to follow, leading the way toward the cluster of forms that occupied the center of the circle. Here the visitors found a solution of all the movements which had given them so much reason for apprehension.

The trapper was placed on a rude seat, which had been made, with studied care, to support his frame in an upright and easy attitude. The first glance of the eye told his former friends that the old man was at length called upon to pay the last tribute of nature. His eye was glazed, and apparently as devoid of sight as of expression. His features were a little more sunken and strongly marked than formerly; but there all change, so far as exterior was concerned, might be said to have ceased. His approaching end was not to be ascribed to any positive disease, but had been a gradual and mild decay of the physical powers. Life, it is true, still lingered in his system; but it was as if at times entirely ready to depart, and then it would appear to reanimate the sinking form, reluctant to give up the possession of a tenement that had never been corrupted by vice, or undermined by disease. It would have been no violent fancy to have imagined that the spirit fluttered about the placid lips of the old woodsman, reluctant to depart from a shell that had so long given it an honest and an honorable shelter.

His body was placed so as to let the light of the setting sun fall full upon the solemn features. His head was bare, the long, thin locks of gray fluttering lightly in the evening breeze. His rifle lay upon his knee, and the other accoutrements of the chase were placed at his side, within reach of his hand. Between his feet lay the figure of a hound, with its head crouching to the earth as if it slumbered; and so perfectly easy and natural was its position, that a second glance was necessary to tell Middleton he saw only the skin of Hector, stuffed by Indian tenderness and ingenuity in a manner to represent the living animal. His own dog was playing at a distance with the child of Tachechana and Mahtoree. The mother herself stood at hand, holding in her arms a second offspring, that might boast of a parentage no less honorable than that which belonged to the son of Hard-Heart. Le Balafré was seated nigh the dying trapper, with every mark about his person that the hour of his own departure was not far distant. The rest of those immediately in the center were aged men, who had apparently drawn near, in order to observe the manner in which a just and fearless warrior would depart on the greatest of his journeys.

The old man was reaping the rewards of a life remarkable for temperance and activity in a tranquil and placid death. His vigor in a manner endured to the very last. Decay, when it did occur, was rapid, but free from pain. He had hunted with the tribe in the spring, and even throughout most of the summer, when his limbs suddenly refused to perform their customary offices. A sympathizing weakness took possession of all his faculties; and the Pawnees believed that they were going to lose, in this unexpected manner, a sage and counsellor whom they had begun both to love and respect. But as we have already said, the immortal occupant seemed unwilling to desert its tenement. The lamp of life flickered without becoming extinguished. On the morning of the day on which Middleton arrived, there was a general reviving of the powers of the whole man. His tongue was again heard in wholesome maxims, and his eye from time to time recognized the persons of his friends. It merely proved to be a brief and final intercourse with the world on the part of one who had already been considered, as to mental communion, to have taken his leave of it forever.

When he had placed his guests in front of the dying man, Hard-Heart, after a pause that proceeded as much from sorrow as decorum, leaned a little forward and demanded—

"Does my father hear the words of his son?"

"Speak," returned the trapper, in tones that issued from his chest, but which were rendered awfully distinct by the stillness that reigned in the place. "I am about to depart from the village of the Loups, and shortly shall be beyond the reach of your voice."

"Let the wise chief have no cares for his journey," continued Hard-Heart, with an earnest solicitude that led him to forget, for the moment, that others were waiting to address his adopted parent; "a hundred Loups shall clear his path from briers."

"Pawnee, I die as I have lived, a Christian man," resumed the trapper, with a force of voice that had the same startling effect on his hearers as is produced by the trumpet, when its blast rises suddenly and freely on the air after its obstructed sounds have been heard struggling in the distance; "as I came into life so will I leave it. Horses and arms are not needed to stand in the presence of the Great Spirit of my people. He knows my color, and according to my gifts will he judge my deeds."

"My father will tell my young men how many Mingoes he has struck, and what acts of valor and justice he has done, that they may know how to imitate him."

"A boastful tongue is not heard in the heaven of a white man!" solemnly returned the old man. "What I have done He has seen. His eyes are always open. That which has been well done will He remember; wherein I have been wrong will He not forget to chastise, though He will do the same in mercy. No, my son; a paleface may not sing his own praises, and hope to have them acceptable before his God!"

A little disappointed, the young partisan stepped modestly back, making way for the recent comers to approach. Middleton took one of the meager hands of the trapper, and struggling to command his voice, he succeeded in announcing his presence. The old man listened like one whose thoughts were dwelling on a very different subject, but when the other had succeeded in making him understand that he was present, an expression of joyful recognition passed over his faded features—

"I hope you have not so soon forgotten those whom you so materially served!" Middleton concluded. "It would pain me to think my hold on your memory was so light."

"Little that I have ever seen is forgotten," returned the trapper; "I am at the close of many weary days, but there is not one among them all that I could wish to overlook. I remember you with the whole of your company; ay, and your gran'ther that went before you. I am glad that you have come back upon these plains, for I had need of one who speaks the English, since little faith can be put in the traders of these regions. Will you do a favor to an old and dying man?"

"Name it," said Middleton; "it shall be done."

"It is a far journey to send such trifles," resumed the old man, who spoke at short intervals, as strength and breath permitted; "a far and weary journey is the same; but kindnesses and friendships are things not to be forgotten. There is a settlement among the Otsego hills——"

"I know the place," interrupted Middleton, observing that he spoke with increasing difficulty; "proceed to tell me what you would have done."

"Take this rifle, and pouch, and horn, and send them to the person whose name is graven on the plates of the stock—a trader cut the letters with his knife,—for it is long that I have intended to send him such a token of my love!"

"It shall be so. Is there more that you could wish?"

"Little else have I to bestow. My traps I give to my Indian son; for honestly and kindly has he kept his faith. Let him stand before me."

Middleton explained to the chief what the trapper had said, and relinquished his own place to the other.

"Pawnee," continued the old man, always changing his language to suit the person he addressed, and not unfrequently according to the ideas he expressed, "it is a custom of my people for the father to leave his blessing with the son before he shuts his eyes forever. This blessing I give to you; take it, for the prayers of a Christian man will never make the path of a just warrior to the blessed prairies either longer or more tangled. May the God of a white man look on your deeds with friendly eyes, and may you never commit an act that shall cause Him to darken His face. I know not whether we shall ever meet again. There are many traditions concerning the place of Good Spirits. It is not for one like me, old and experienced though I am, to set up my opinions against a nation's. You believe in the blessed prairies, and I have faith in the sayings of my fathers. If both are true, our parting will be final; but if it should prove that the same meaning is hid under different words, we shall yet stand together, Pawnee, before the face of your Wahcondah, who will then be no other than my God. There is much to be said in favor of both religions, for each seems suited to its own people, and no doubt it was so intended. I fear I have not altogether followed the gifts of my color, inasmuch as I find it a little painful to give up forever the use of the rifle, and the comforts of the chase. But then the fault has been my own, seeing that it could not have been His. Ay, Hector," he continued, leaning forward a little, and feeling for the ears of the hound, "our parting has come at last, dog, and it will be a long hunt. You have been an honest, and a bold, and a faithful hound. Pawnee, you cannot slay the pup on my grave, for where a Christian dog falls, there he lies forever; but you can be kind to him after I am gone, for the love you bear his master."

"The words of my father are in my ears," returned the young partisan, making a grave and respectful gesture of assent.

"Do you hear what the chief has promised, dog?" demanded the trapper, making an effort to attract the notice of the insensible effigy of his hound. Receiving no answering look, nor hearing any friendly whine, the old man felt for the mouth and endeavored to force his hand between the cold lips. The truth then flashed upon him, although he was far from perceiving the whole extent of the deception. Falling back in his seat, he hung his head like one who felt a severe and unexpected shock. Profiting by this momentary forgetfulness, two young Indians removed the skin with the same delicacy of feeling that had induced them to attempt the pious fraud.

"The dog is dead!" muttered the trapper, after a pause of many minutes; "a hound has his time as well as a man; and well has he filled his days! Captain," he added, making an effort to wave his hand for Middleton, "I am glad you have come; for though kind and well meaning according to the gifts of their color, these Indians are not the men to lay the head of a white man in his grave. I have been thinking, too, of this dog at my feet; it will not do to set forth the opinion that a Christian can expect to meet his hound again; still there can be little harm in placing what is left of so faithful a servant nigh the bones of his master."

"It shall be as you desire."

"I'm glad you think with me in this matter. In order, then, to save labor, lay the pup at my feet, or, for that matter, put him side by side. A hunter need never be ashamed to be found in company with his dog!"

"I charge myself with your wish."

The old man made a long and apparently a musing pause. At times he raised his eyes wistfully as if he would again address Middleton, but some innate feeling appeared always to suppress his words. The other, who observed his hesitation, inquired in a way most likely to encourage him to proceed, whether there was aught else that he could wish to have done.

"I am without kith or kin in the wide world!" the trapper answered; "when I am gone, there will be an end of my race. We have never been chiefs; but honest and useful in our way, I hope it cannot be denied, we have always proved ourselves. My father lies buried near the sea, and the bones of his son will whiten on the prairies——"

"Name the spot, and your remains shall be placed by the side of your father," interrupted Middleton.

"Not so, not so, Captain. Let me sleep where I have lived, beyond the din of the settlements! Still, I see no need why the grave of an honest man should be hid, like a redskin in his ambushment. I paid a man in the settlements to make and put a graven stone at the head of my father's resting place. It was of the value of twelve beaver skins, and cunningly and curiously was it carved! Then it told to all comers that the body of such a Christian lay beneath; and it spoke of his manner of life, of his years, and of his honesty. When we had done with the Frenchers in the old war, I made a journey to the spot in order to see that all was rightly performed, and glad I am to say the workman had not forgotten his faith."

"And such a stone you would have at your grave?"

"I! no, no, I have no son but Hard-Heart, and it is little that an Indian knows of white fashions and usages. Besides, I am his debtor already, seeing it is so little I have done since I have lived in his tribe. The rifle might bring the value of such a thing—but then I know it will give the boy pleasure to hang the piece in his hall, for many is the deer and the bird that he has seen it destroy. No, no, the gun must be sent to him whose name is graven on the lock!"

"But there is one who would gladly prove his affection in the way you wish; he who owes you not only his own deliverance from so many dangers, but who inherits a heavy debt of gratitude from his ancestors. The stone shall be put at the head of your grave."

The old man extended his emaciated hand and gave the other a squeeze of thanks.

"I thought you might be willing to do it, but I was backward in asking the favor," he said, "seeing that you are not of my kin. Put no boastful words on the same, but just the name, the age, and the time of the death, with something from the Holy Book; no more, no more. My name will then not be altogether lost on 'arth; I need no more."

Middleton intimated his assent, and then followed a pause that was only broken by distant and broken sentences from the dying man. He appeared now to have closed his accounts with the world, and to await merely for the final summons to quit it. Middleton and Hard-Heart placed themselves on the opposite sides of his seat, and watched with melancholy solicitude the variations of his countenance. For two hours there was no very sensible alteration. The expression of his faded and time-worn features was that of a calm and dignified repose. From time to time he spoke, uttering some brief sentence in the way of advice, or asking some simple questions concerning those in whose fortunes he still took a friendly interest. During the whole of that solemn and anxious period each individual of the tribe kept his place in the most self-restrained patience. When the old man spoke, all bent their heads to listen; and when his words were uttered, they seemed to ponder on their wisdom and usefulness.

As the flame drew nigher to the socket, his voice was hushed, and there were moments when his attendants doubted whether he still belonged to the living. Middleton, who watched each wavering expression of his weather-beaten visage with the interest of a keen observer of human nature, softened by the tenderness of personal regard, fancied he could read the workings of the old man's soul in the strong lineaments of his countenance. Perhaps what the enlightened soldier took for the delusion of mistaken opinion did actually occur, for who has returned from that unknown world to explain by what forms and in what manner he was introduced into its awful precincts? Without pretending to explain what must ever be a mystery to the quick, we shall simply relate facts as they occurred.

The trapper had remained nearly motionless for an hour. His eyes alone had occasionally opened and shut. When opened, his gaze seemed fastened on the clouds which hung around the western horizon, reflecting the bright colors and giving form and loveliness to the glorious tints of an American sunset. The hour—the calm beauty of the season—the occasion, all conspired to fill the spectators with solemn awe. Suddenly, while musing on the remarkable position in which he was placed, Middleton felt the hand which he held grasp his own with incredible power, and the old man, supported on either side by his friends, rose upright to his feet. For a moment he looked about him, as if to invite all in presence to listen (the lingering remnant of human frailty), and then, with a fine military elevation of the head, and with a voice that might be heard in every part of that numerous assembly, he pronounced the word—

"Here!"

A movement so entirely unexpected, and the air of grandeur and humility which were so remarkably united in the mien of the trapper, together with the clear and uncommon force of his utterance, produced a short period of confusion in the faculties of all present. When Middleton and Hard-Heart, each of whom had involuntarily extended a hand to support the form of the old man, turned to him again, they found that the subject of their interest was removed forever beyond the necessity of their care. They mournfully placed the body in its seat, and Le Balafré arose to announce the termination of the scene to the tribe. The voice of the old Indian seemed a sort of echo from that invisible world to which the meek spirit of the trapper had just departed.

"A valiant, a just, and a wise warrior has gone on the path which will lead him to the blessed grounds of his people!" he said. "When the voice of the Wahcondah called him, he was ready to answer. Go, my children; remember the just chief of the pale-faces, and clear your own tracks from briers!"

The grave was made beneath the shade of some noble oaks. It has been carefully watched to the present hour by the Pawnees of the Loup, and is often shown to the traveller and the trader as a spot where a just white man sleeps. In due time the stone was placed at its head, with the simple inscription which the trapper had himself requested. The only liberty taken by Middleton was to add—*"May no wanton hand ever disturb his remains!"*

BIBLIOGRAPHY

WORKS

The first comprehensive edition of Cooper's novels, containing all of them except *Ned Myers,* was issued in 1859–61 by W. A. Townsend & Company of New York in 32 volumes, with admirably graphic illustrations by F. O. C. Darley. Nearly a generation later came the Household Edition of Cooper's works, published by Houghton, Osgood & Company (later Houghton Mifflin), 1876–1884, also in 32 volumes. This was distinguished by the interesting introductions prefixed to many of the volumes by Susan Fenimore Cooper, a daughter; her essays in *The Pioneers* and *The Prairie* having special biographical value. Various later collections have been published, notably by G. P. Putnam and by Charles Scribner's Sons.

The five volumes of the Leatherstocking Tales are available in the Everyman Library (E. P. Dutton Company), and *The Last of the Mohicans* in the World's Classics (Oxford University Press). Various school editions of *The Spy* and *The Last of the Mohicans* are procurable, those in The Modern Readers' Series, with introductions by Tremaine McDowell and Fred Lewis Pattee respectively (Macmillan) being specially well edited. Two interesting volumes of Cooper's travel observations abroad, his *Gleanings in Europe: France* and *Gleanings in Europe: England,* were published by Robert E. Spiller 1928–30 (Oxford), with an illuminating thirty-page introduction. The same editor has given us in his *Representative Selections* from Cooper (American Book Company, 1936), our only good collection of the highly controversial nonfiction writings, enriched with an eighty-page introduction, a bibliography, and notes.

BIOGRAPHY

Thomas R. Lounsbury's volume in the American Men of Letters Series, *James Fenimore Cooper* (Houghton Mifflin, 1882) was hailed on its appearance as a minor biographical and critical classic, and still holds its place. Other books on the novelist have been written by William B. S. Clymer (1900), Mary E. Phillips (1913), and Henry W. Boynton (1931). The first of these three is briefly incisive, the second gossipy, and the third marked by considerable new biographical material of value. The most important work supplementary to Lounsbury, however, is Robert E. Spiller's *Fenimore Cooper: Critic of His Times* (Minton, Balch & Company, 1931), which deals with Cooper as a social observer, first in America, then in Europe for seven years, and then in America again. "His writings," states Mr. Spiller, "are at once a reflection and an interpretation of the emerging

American civilization about him." The later chapters, which treat of Cooper in his famous wars with the press and his battles with the people of Cooperstown and others, are particularly interesting.

Cooper's grandson of the same name in 1922 published in two volumes the *Correspondence of James Fenimore Cooper* (Yale University Press). It is a valuable but disappointingly dull work; Cooper's own letters are few compared with those from other pens, and he was not a good letter writer.

CRITICAL ESSAYS

Few American authors have received more critical attention than Cooper, or have attracted the attention of more eminent writers. Immediately after his death, William Cullen Bryant pronounced a commemorative "Discourse on the Life and Genius of Cooper," which, published in the *Memorial of James Fenimore Cooper* (1852) and reprinted in Bryant's Prose Works (1882), remains well worth reading. It combines exact biographical information with a discriminating estimate of Cooper's personal qualities and literary achievement, and sometimes reaches a high level of quiet eloquence. Francis Parkman published in the *North American Review* (January, 1852, Vol. CLIV) an interesting essay dealing chiefly with Cooper's treatment of the wilderness, and the Indians, but not slighting his plots and his character studies. Henry T. Tuckerman a little later also published an essay on Cooper in the *North American Review* (October, 1859, Vol. CLXXV). Thereafter criticism slept until the centenary of Cooper's birth, which brought forth a number of minor notices, and a more important if brief paper by Brander Matthews ("The Centenary of Cooper," reprinted from the *Century Magazine* in *Americanism and Briticisms,* 1892).

Mark Twain prefixed eulogistic quotations from Lounsbury, Brander Matthews, and Wilkie Collins ("Cooper is the greatest artist in the domain of romantic fiction yet produced by America") to his jeering essay on "Fenimore Cooper's Literary Offences," which attacked the novelist for bad characterization, bad plots, bad topography, bad word-sense, and bad artistry, winding up with the assertion that *The Deerslayer* is simply literary delirium tremens. This essay, first published in the *North American Review* (July, 1895, Vol. CLXI) is now available in Mark Twain's Literary Essays in his collected works. It so far overshot its mark that it made little impression. True criticism—and appreciation—reappeared in William C. Brownell's glowing study of Cooper first published in *Scribner's Magazine* in April, 1906, and later reprinted in *American Prose Masters* (1909). Equally appreciative, but less penetrating, was John Erskine's long chapter in *Leading American Novelists* (1910), a rather minute account of the man, the novels, and the social attitudes of Cooper. The *Cambridge History of American Literature* contained a balanced essay on Cooper by Carl Van Doren, which was later expanded into a longer treatment in his *The American Novel* (1921).

Among later treatments of Cooper the most distinguished are by Henry Seidel Canby in *Classic Americans* (Harcourt, Brace, 1931), which points out that the novelist excelled in the detail of movement, that he was an amateur rather than a professional writer, and that the influence of Quakerism lies deep in his books; the provocative chapter by Vernon L. Parrington in the second volume of his *Main Currents of American Thought* (1927), devoted chiefly to Cooper's "obsolete" political ideas as "the last of our eighteenth century squires"; and the fascinatingly pictorial presentation of Cooper in three phases, his early American years, his years abroad, and his later New York years, by Van Wyck Brooks in *The World of Washington Irving* (E. P. Dutton, 1924). Fred Lewis Pattee's "James Fenimore Cooper," a personal portrait, in the *American Mercury* (March, 1925, Vol. IV), and Robert E. Spiller's "Fenimore Cooper's Defense of Slave-Owning America" in the *American Historical Review* (April, 1930, Vol. XXXV) should also be noted.

The two most notable foreign estimates of Cooper are by Balzac, a paper first contributed to the *Revue Parisienne* (July 25, 1840) and republished in translation in Katherine Prescott Wormeley's *Personal Opinions of Balzac* (1899), and by D. H. Lawrence in *Studies in Classic American Literature* (1923). Both are highly favorable, though Balzac thinks little of Cooper as a painter of men and women. Lawrence strives to find psychological values in Cooper's work which no other reader has ever seen, and specially praises his Leatherstocking and Chingachgook.

BIBLIOGRAPHY

A very full "Selective Bibliography" down to 1936 is to be found in Robert E. Spiller's *Representative Selections* in the American Writers Series; and a briefer bibliography in Robert E. Spiller, Willard Thorp, Thomas H. Johnson, and Henry Seidel Canby, *Literary History of the United States*, Vol. III, pp. 450–455 (1948).